PD 5310.F6

CATHEDRAL
LIBRARY
CANTERBURY

Withdrawn from
Canterbury Cathedral
Library

D1420420

WALTER SCOTT

THE
FORTUNES OF NIGEL

Edited by
Frank Jordan

EDINBURGH
University
Press

© The University Court of the University of Edinburgh 2004
Edinburgh University Press
22 George Square, Edinburgh

Typeset in Linotronic Ehrhardt
by Speedspools, Edinburgh
and printed and bound in Great Britain
on acid-free paper at The Cromwell Press, Trowbridge, Wilts.

ISBN 0 7486 0577 0

A CIP record for this book is available from the British Library

No part of this publication may be reproduced or transmitted in any form or
by any means, electronic or mechanical, including photocopying, recording
or any information storage or retrieval system, without the prior permission
in writing from the publisher.

05/03

FOREWORD

THE PUBLICATION of *Waverley* in 1814 marked the emergence of the modern novel in the western world. It is difficult now to recapture the impact of this and the following novels of Scott on a readership accustomed to prose fiction either as picturesque romance, 'Gothic' quaintness, or presentation of contemporary manners. For Scott not only invented the historical novel, but gave it a dimension and a relevance that made it available for a great variety of new kinds of writing. Balzac in France, Manzoni in Italy, Gogol and Tolstoy in Russia, were among the many writers of fiction influenced by the man Stendhal called 'notre père, Walter Scott'.

What Scott did was to show history and society in motion: old ways of life being challenged by new; traditions being assailed by counter-statements; loyalties, habits, prejudices clashing with the needs of new social and economic developments. The attraction of tradition and its ability to arouse passionate defence, and simultaneously the challenge of progress and 'improvement', produce a pattern that Scott saw as the living fabric of history. And this history was rooted in *place*; events happened in localities still recognisable after the disappearance of the original actors and the establishment of new patterns of belief and behaviour.

Scott explored and presented all this by means of stories, entertainments, which were read and enjoyed as such. At the same time his passionate interest in history led him increasingly to see these stories as illustrations of historical truths, so that when he produced his final *Magnum Opus* edition of the novels he surrounded them with historical notes and illustrations, and in this almost suffocating guise they have been reprinted in edition after edition ever since. The time has now come to restore these novels to the form in which they were presented to their first readers, so that today's readers can once again capture their original power and freshness. At the same time, serious errors of transcription, omission, and interpretation, resulting from the haste of their transmission from manuscript to print can now be corrected.

DAVID DAICHES

EDINBURGH
University
Press

CONTENTS

ACKNOWLEDGEMENTS

The Scott Advisory Board and the editors of the Edinburgh Edition of the Waverley Novels wish to express their gratitude to The University Court of the University of Edinburgh *for its vision in initiating and supporting the preparation of the first critical edition of Walter Scott's fiction. Those Universities which employ the editors have also contributed greatly in paying the editors' salaries, and awarding research leave and grants for travel and materials. In the case of* The Fortunes of Nigel *particular thanks are due to* Miami University, Ohio, *and the* University of Aberdeen.

Although the edition is the work of scholars employed by universities, the project could not have prospered without the help of the sponsors cited below. Their generosity has met the direct costs of the initial research and of the preparation of the text of the novels appearing in this edition.

BANK OF SCOTLAND
The collapse of the great Edinburgh publisher Archibald Constable in January 1826 entailed the ruin of Sir Walter Scott who found himself responsible for his own private debts, for the debts of the printing business of James Ballantyne and Co. in which he was co-partner, and for the bank advances to Archibald Constable which had been guaranteed by the printing business. Scott's largest creditors were Sir William Forbes and Co., bankers, and the Bank of Scotland. On the advice of Sir William Forbes himself, the creditors did not sequester his property, but agreed to the creation of a trust to which Scott committed his future literary earnings, and which ultimately repaid the debts of over £120,000 for which he was legally liable.

In the same year the Government proposed to curtail the rights of the Scottish banks to issue their own notes; Scott wrote the 'Letters of Malachi Malagrowther' in their defence, arguing that the measure was neither in the interests of the banks nor of Scotland. The 'Letters' were so successful that the Government was forced to withdraw its proposal and to this day the Scottish Banks issue their own notes.

A portrait of Sir Walter appears on all current bank notes of the Bank of Scotland because Scott was a champion of Scottish banking, and because he was an illustrious and honourable customer not just of the Bank of Scotland itself, but also of three other banks now incorporated within it—the British Linen Bank which continues today as the merchant banking arm of the Bank of Scotland, Sir William Forbes and Co., and Ramsays, Bonars and Company.

Bank of Scotland's support of the EEWN continues its long and fruitful involvement with the affairs of Walter Scott.

THE BRITISH ACADEMY AND THE ARTS AND HUMANITIES RESEARCH BOARD

Between 1992 and 1998 the EEWN was greatly assisted by the British Academy through the award of a series of research grants which provided most of the support required for employing a research fellow, without whom steady progress could not have been maintained. In 2000 the AHRB awarded the EEWN with a major grant which ensured the completion of the Edition. To both of these bodies, the British Academy and the Arts and Humanities Research Board, the Advisory Board and the editors express their thanks.

OTHER BENEFACTORS

The Advisory Board and the editors also wish to acknowledge with gratitude the generous grants and gifts to the EEWN from the P. F. Charitable Trust, the main charitable trust of the Fleming family which founded the City firm which bears their name; the Edinburgh University General Council Trust, now incorporated within the Edinburgh University Development Trust; Sir Gerald Elliott; the Carnegie Trust for the Universities of Scotland; and the Robertson Trust whose help has been particularly important.

THE FORTUNES OF NIGEL

All but twelve leaves of the manuscript of The Fortunes of Nigel *are part of the Walpole Collection in The King's School, Canterbury. The editor is indebted first and foremost to the former Walpole Librarian David Goodes, who arranged for the manuscript to be microfilmed, and, subsequently, for its temporary transfer the Library of Canterbury Cathedral where it could be more conveniently read and collated. For continuing this arrangement as needed he is similarly obligated to the current Walpole Librarian Peter Henderson. The editor's second great debt, consequently, is to the former Librarian Sheila Hingley and her staff, Sarah Gray, Jean Hargreaves, and Jean Utting for their many courtesies to him while working there, and to the current Cathedral Librarian Keith O'Sullivan. Six of the remaining leaves are in the National Library of Scotland, Edinburgh, to which the editor is in general beholden and in particular to Iain Brown, and to the staff of the North Reading Room who not infrequently went far out of their way to accommodate his needs and requests. One leaf of the manuscript is in the collections of the Bibliotheca Bodmeriana of the Fondation Martin Bodmer, Cologny-Geneva, which kindly photocopied it for the edition. Edinburgh University Library, Edinburgh Public Library, and Stirling University Library were particularly helpful with later editions.*

In the United States the editor is principally obliged to the Miami University Library, most especially to William Wortman, Ralph E. Via, Martin Miller, Janet Stuckey, Ruth Miller, Janice McLaughlin and Barry Zaslow. Other libraries that have materially assisted the editor's researches are Aberdeen University Library, the Bodleian Library, the British Library,

Indiana University Library, the New York Public Library, New York University Library, and the University of South Carolina Library. Finally, the editor is grateful to Miami University and to the Department of English, most especially its former chair C. Barry Chabot and its devoted secretarial staff, for two leaves of absence and a summer research appointment which provided relief from teaching and funding for travel and research.

Without the help of colleagues at home and abroad this edition would never have materialised. For assistance with period matters the editor wishes to thank most especially James D. Clark for being so generous with both his knowledge and his library; he also thanks department colleagues Francis Dolan, Richard Erlich, Katharine Gillespie, Laura Mandell, David Mann, and Randolph Wadsworth. Other Miami colleagues Judith De Luce and John Romano were consistently helpful with Latin; Louise and Stanford Luce, Pierre Sotteau, and Annette Tomarken with French; Michael Ferreira with Spanish; and Sante Matteo with Italian. Assisting the editor with the language of mathematics were Charles Holmes, David Kullman, and Emily Murphree, and with the language of clock-making, Randolph Wadsworth. Without the technical expertise and unfailing patience of Jerome Rosenberg the editor would long since have departed his senses. From a distance scholars and friends Steven Collier, Jane Millgate, Michael Papio, Patrick Scott, Mary Ann Wimsatt, and fellow-editors Claire Lamont and Mark Weinstein provided both timely assistance and advice. In particular the late Jill Rubenstein was a ready source of information and cheer. Caroline McCracken-Fleisher, David Parlett, Sharon Ragaz, and Charles Snodgrass responded to queries about allusions and references.

In addition the editor is deeply obligated to Editor-in-chief David Hewitt, the EEWN *research fellow Alison Lumsden, and Ian Clark, Sheena Ford, and Audrey Inglis, whose collective vigilance prevented many errors from reaching the light of print. The experts nominated by the Edition to provide particular expertise have been unfailingly supportive, in particular John Cairns (Scots Law), Thomas Craik (Shakespeare), Caroline Jackson Houlston (popular song), Roy Pinkerton (Classical literature), and Mairi Robinson (Scots language).*

Finally, the editor is profoundly grateful to J. H. Alexander for his exemplary guidance and unremitting patience at every stage and in every aspect of preparing the edition for publication.

The General Editor for this volume was J. H. Alexander, who also prepared the glossary.

GENERAL INTRODUCTION

What has the Edinburgh Edition of the Waverley Novels achieved? The original version of this General Introduction said that many hundreds of readings were being recovered from the manuscripts, and commented that although the individual differences were often minor, they were 'cumulatively telling'. Such an assessment now looks tentative and tepid, for the textual strategy pursued by the editors has been justified by spectacular results.

In each novel up to 2000 readings never before printed are being recovered from the manuscripts. Some of these are major changes although they are not always verbally extensive. The restoration of the pen-portraits of the Edinburgh literati in *Guy Mannering*, the reconstruction of the way in which Amy Robsart was murdered in *Kenilworth*, the recovery of the description of Clara Mowbray's previous relationship with Tyrrel in *Saint Ronan's Well*—each of these fills out what was incomplete, or corrects what was obscure. A surprising amount of what was once thought loose or unidiomatic has turned out to be textual corruption. Many words which were changed as the holograph texts were converted into print have been recognised as dialectal, period or technical terms wholly appropriate to their literary context. The mistakes in foreign languages, in Latin, and in Gaelic found in the early printed texts are usually not in the manuscripts, and so clear is this manuscript evidence that one may safely conclude that Friar Tuck's Latin in *Ivanhoe* is deliberately full of errors. The restoration of Scott's own shaping and punctuating of speech has often enhanced the rhetorical effectiveness of dialogue. Furthermore, the detailed examination of the text and supporting documents such as notes and letters has revealed that however quickly his novels were penned they mostly evolved over long periods; that although he claimed not to plan his work yet the shape of his narratives seems to have been established before he committed his ideas to paper; and that each of the novels edited to date has a precise time-scheme which implies formidable control of his stories. The Historical and Explanatory Notes reveal an intellectual command of enormously diverse materials, and an equal imaginative capacity to synthesise them. Editing the texts has revolutionised the editors' understanding and appreciation of Scott, and will ultimately generate a much wider recognition of his quite extraordinary achievement.

The text of the novels in the Edinburgh Edition is normally based on the first editions, but incorporates all those manuscript readings which were lost through accident, error, or misunderstanding in the process of converting holograph manuscripts into printed books. The Edition is the first to investigate all Scott's manuscripts and proofs, and all the printed editions to have appeared in his lifetime, and it has adopted the textual strategy which best makes sense of the textual problems.

It is clear from the systematic investigation of all the different states of Scott's texts that the author was fully engaged only in the early stages (manuscripts and proofs, culminating in the first edition), and when preparing the last edition to be published in his lifetime, familiarly known as the Magnum Opus (1829–33). There may be authorial readings in some of the many intermediate editions, and there certainly are in the third edition of *Waverley*, but not a single intermediate edition of any of the nineteen novels so far investigated shows evidence of sustained authorial involvement. There are thus only two stages in the textual development of the Waverley Novels which might provide a sound basis for a critical edition.

Scott's holograph manuscripts constitute the only purely authorial state of the texts of his novels, for they alone proceed wholly from the author. They are for the most part remarkably coherent, although a close examination shows countless minor revisions made in the process of writing, and usually at least one layer of later revising. But the heaviest revising was usually done by Scott when correcting his proofs, and thus the manuscripts could not constitute the textual basis of a new edition; despite their coherence they are drafts. Furthermore, the holograph does not constitute a public form of the text: Scott's manuscript punctuation is light (in later novels there are only dashes, full-stops, and speech marks), and his spelling system though generally consistent is personal and idiosyncratic.

Scott's novels were, in theory, anonymous publications—no title page ever carried his name. To maintain the pretence of secrecy, the original manuscripts were copied so that his handwriting should not be seen in the printing house, a practice which prevailed until 1827, when Scott acknowledged his authorship. Until 1827 it was these copies, not Scott's original manuscripts, which were used by the printers. Not a single leaf of these copies is known to survive but the copyists probably began the tidying and regularising. As with Dickens and Thackeray in a later era, copy was sent to the printers in batches, as Scott wrote and as it was transcribed; the batches were set in type, proof-read, and ultimately printed, while later parts of the novel were still being written. When typesetting, the compositors did not just follow what was before them, but supplied punctuation, normalised spelling, and corrected minor errors. Proofs were first read in-house against the transcripts, and, in addition to the normal checking for mistakes, these proofs were used to improve the punctuation and the spelling.

When the initial corrections had been made, a new set of proofs went to James Ballantyne, Scott's friend and partner in the printing firm which bore his name. He acted as editor, not just as proof-reader. He drew Scott's attention to gaps in the text and pointed out inconsistencies in detail; he asked Scott to standardise names; he substituted nouns for pronouns when they occurred in the first sentence of a paragraph, and inserted the names of speakers in dialogue; he changed incorrect punctuation, and added punctuation he thought desirable; he corrected grammatical errors; he removed close verbal repetitions; and in a cryptic correspondence in the margins of the proofs he told Scott when he could not follow what was happening, or when he particularly enjoyed something.

These annotated proofs were sent to the author. Scott usually accepted Ballantyne's suggestions, but sometimes rejected them. He made many more changes; he cut out redundant words, and substituted the vivid for the pedestrian; he refined the punctuation; he sometimes reworked and revised passages extensively, and in so doing made the proofs a stage in the creative composition of the novels.

When Ballantyne received Scott's corrections and revisions, he transcribed all the changes on to a clean set of proofs so that the author's hand would not be seen by the compositors. Further revises were prepared. Some of these were seen and read by Scott, but he usually seems to have trusted Ballantyne to make sure that the earlier corrections and revisions had been executed. When doing this Ballantyne did not just read for typesetting errors, but continued the process of punctuating and tidying the text. A final proof allowed the corrections to be inspected and the imposition of the type to be checked prior to printing.

Scott expected his novels to be printed; he expected that the printers would correct minor errors, would remove words repeated in close proximity to each other, would normalise spelling, and would insert a printed-book style of punctuation, amplifying or replacing the marks he had provided in manuscript. There are no written instructions to the printers to this effect, but in the proofs he was sent he saw what Ballantyne and his staff had done and were doing, and by and large he accepted it. This assumption of authorial approval is better founded for Scott than for any other writer, for Scott was the dominant partner in the business which printed his work, and no doubt could have changed the practices of his printers had he so desired.

It is this history of the initial creation of Scott's novels that led the editors of the Edinburgh Edition to propose the first editions as base texts. That such a textual policy has been persuasively theorised by Jerome J. McGann in his *A Critique of Modern Textual Criticism* (1983) is a bonus: he argues that an authoritative work is usually found not in the artist's manuscript, but in the printed book, and that there is a collective responsibility in converting an author's manuscript into print, exercised by author, printer and publisher, and governed by the nature of the understanding between the author and the other parties. In Scott's case the exercise of such a collective responsibility produced the first editions of the Waverley Novels. On the whole Scott's printers fulfilled his expectations. There are normally in excess of 50,000 variants in the first edition of a three-volume novel when compared with the manuscript, and the great majority are in accordance with Scott's general wishes as described above.

But the intermediaries, as the copyist, compositors, proof-readers, and James Ballantyne are collectively described, made mistakes; from time to time they misread the manuscripts, and they did not always understand what Scott had written. This would not have mattered had there not also been procedural failures: the transcripts were not thoroughly checked against the original manuscripts; Scott himself does not seem to have read the proofs against the manuscripts and thus did not notice transcription errors which made sense in their context; Ballantyne continued his editing in post-authorial proofs. Furthermore, it has become increasingly evident that, although in theory Scott as partner in the printing firm could get what he wanted, he also succumbed to the pressure of printer and publisher. He often had to accept mistakes both in names and the spelling of names because they were enshrined in print before he realised what had happened. He was obliged to accept the movement of chapters between volumes, or the deletion or addition of material, in the interests of equalising the size of volumes. His work was subject to bowdlerisation, and to a persistent attempt to have him show a 'high example' even in the words put in the mouths of his characters; he regularly objected, but conformed nonetheless. From time to time he inserted, under protest, explanations of what was happening in the narrative because the literal-minded Ballantyne required them.

The editors of modern texts have a basic working assumption that what is written by the author is more valuable than what is generated by compositors and proof-readers. Even McGann accepts such a position, and argues that while the changes made in the course of translating the manuscript text into print are a feature of the acceptable 'socialisation' of the authorial text, they have authority only to the extent that they fulfil the author's expectations about the public form of the text. The editors of the Edinburgh Edition normally choose the first edition of a novel as base-text, for the first edition usually represents the culmination of the initial creative process, and usually seems closest to the form of his work Scott wished his public to have. But they also recognise the failings of the first editions, and thus after the careful collation of all pre-publication materials, and in the light of their investigation into the factors governing the writing and printing of the Waverley Novels, they incorporate into the base-text those manuscript readings which were lost in the production process through accident, error, misunderstanding, or a misguided attempt to 'improve'. In certain cases they also introduce into the base-texts revisions found in editions published almost immediately after the first, which they believe to be Scott's, or which complete the intermediaries' preparation of the text. In addition, the editors correct various kinds of error, such as typographical and copy-editing mistakes including the misnumbering of chapters, inconsistencies in the naming of characters, egregious errors of fact that are not part of the fiction, and failures of sense which a simple emendation can restore. In doing all this the editors follow the model for editing the Waverley Novels which was provided by Claire Lamont in her edition of *Waverley* (Oxford, 1981): her base-text is the first edition emended in the light of the manuscript. But they have also developed that model because working on the Waverley Novels as a whole has greatly increased knowledge of the practices and procedures followed by Scott, his printers and his publishers in translating holograph manuscripts into printed books. The result is an 'ideal' text, such as his first readers might have read had the production process been less pressurised and more considered.

The Magnum Opus could have provided an alternative basis for a new edition. In the Advertisement to the Magnum Scott wrote that his insolvency in 1826 and the public admission of authorship in 1827 restored to him 'a sort of parental control', which enabled him to re-issue his novels 'in a corrected and . . . an improved form'. His assertion of authority in word and deed gives the Magnum a status which no editor can ignore. His introductions are fascinating autobiographical essays which write the life of the Author of Waverley. In addition, the Magnum has a considerable significance in the history of culture. This was the first time all Scott's works of fiction had been gathered together, published in a single uniform edition, and given an official general title, in the process converting diverse narratives into a literary monument, the Waverley Novels.

There were, however, two objections to the use of the Magnum as the base-text for the new edition. Firstly, this has been the form of Scott's work which has been generally available for most of the nineteenth and twentieth centuries; a Magnum-based text is readily accessible to anyone who wishes to read it. Secondly, a proper recognition of the Magnum does not extend to approving its text. When Scott corrected his novels for the Magnum, he marked up printed books (specially prepared by the binder with interleaves, hence the title the 'Interleaved Set'), but did not perceive the extent to which these had slipped from the text of the first editions. He had no means of recognising that, for example, over 2000 differences had accumulated between the first edition of *Guy Mannering* and the text which he corrected, in the 1822 octavo edition of the *Novels and Tales of the Author of Waverley*. The printed text of *Redgauntlet* which he corrected, in the octavo *Tales and Romances of the Author of Waverley* (1827), has about 900 divergences from the first edition, none of which was authorially sanctioned. He himself made about 750 corrections to the text of *Guy Mannering* and

200 to *Redgauntlet* in the Interleaved Set, but those who assisted in the production of the Magnum were probably responsible for a further 1600 changes to *Guy Mannering*, and 1200 to *Redgauntlet*. Scott marked up a corrupt text, and his assistants generated a systematically cleaned-up version of the Waverley Novels.

The Magnum constitutes the author's final version of his novels and thus has its own value, and as the version read by the great Victorians has its own significance and influence. To produce a new edition based on the Magnum would be an entirely legitimate project, but for the reasons given above the Edinburgh editors have chosen the other valid option. What is certain, however, is that any compromise edition, that drew upon both the first and the last editions published in Scott's lifetime, would be a mistake. In the past editors, following the example of W. W. Greg and Fredson Bowers, would have incorporated into the first-edition text the introductions, notes, revisions and corrections Scott wrote for the Magnum Opus. This would no longer be considered acceptable editorial practice, as it would confound versions of the text produced at different stages of the author's career. To fuse the two would be to confuse them. Instead, Scott's own material in the Interleaved Set is so interesting and important that it will be published separately, and in full, in the two parts of Volume 25 of the Edinburgh Edition. For the first time in print the new matter written by Scott for the Magnum Opus will be wholly visible.

The Edinburgh Edition of the Waverley Novels aims to provide the first reliable text of Scott's fiction. It aims to recover the lost Scott, the Scott which was misunderstood as the printers struggled to set and print novels at high speed in often difficult circumstances. It aims in the Historical and Explanatory Notes and in the Glossaries to illuminate the extraordinary range of materials that Scott weaves together in creating his stories. All engaged in fulfilling these aims have found their enquiries fundamentally changing their appreciation of Scott. They hope that readers will continue to be equally excited and astonished, and to have their understanding of these remarkable novels transformed by reading them in their new guise.

DAVID HEWITT
January 1999

THE

FORTUNES OF NIGEL.

BY THE AUTHOR OF " WAVERLEY,

KENILWORTH," &c.

———————————

Knifegrinder. Story ? Lord bless you ! I have none to tell, sir.
POETRY OF THE ANTI-JACOBIN.

———————————

IN THREE VOLUMES.

VOL. I.

══════

EDINBURGH :

PRINTED FOR ARCHIBALD CONSTABLE AND CO. EDINBURGH ;

AND HURST, ROBINSON, AND CO.,

LONDON.

———

1822.

INTRODUCTORY EPISTLE.

CAPTAIN CLUTTERBUCK,

TO

THE REV. DR DRYASDUST

DEAR SIR,

I readily accept of, and reply to the civilities with which you have been pleased to honour me in your obliging letter, and entirely agree with your quotation of "*Quam bonum et quam jucundum.*" We may indeed esteem ourselves as come of the same family, or, according to our country proverb, as being all one man's bairns; and there needed no apology on your part, reverend and dear sir, for demanding of me any information which I may be able to supply respecting the subject of your curiosity. The interview which you allude to took place in the course of last winter, and is so deeply imprinted on my recollection, that it requires no effort to collect all its most minute details.

You are aware that the share which I had in introducing the Romance called THE MONASTERY to public notice, has given me a sort of character in the literature of our Scottish metropolis. I no longer stand in the outer shop of our bibliopolists, bargaining for the objects of my curiosity with an unrespective shop-lad, hustled among boys who come to buy Corderies and copy-books, and servant-girls cheapening a penny-worth of paper, but am cordially welcomed by the bibliopolist himself, with, "Pray, walk into the back-shop, Captain—Boy, get a chair for Captain Clutterbuck—There is the newspaper, Captain—to-day's paper—or here is the last new work—there is a folder—make free with the leaves—or put it in your pocket and carry it home—or we will make a bookseller of you, sir, you shall have it at trade price." Or, perhaps, if it is the worthy trader's own publication, his liberality may even extend itself to—"Never mind booking such a trifle to *you*, sir—it is an over-copy—pray, mention the work to your literary friends." I say nothing of the snug well-selected literary party arranged around a turbot, leg of five-year-old mutton, or some such gear, or of the circulation of a quiet bottle of Robert Cockburn's choicest black—or perhaps of his best blue, to quicken our talk about old books, or our plans for new ones. All these are comforts reserved to such as are freemen of the corporation of letters, and I have the advantage of enjoying them in perfection.

But all things change under the sun; and it is with no ordinary feelings of regret, that, in my annual visits to the metropolis, I now miss the social and warm-hearted welcome of the quick-witted and kindly friend who first introduced me to the public, who had more original wit than would have set up a dozen of professed sayers of good things, and more racy humour than would have made the fortune of as many more. To this great deprivation has been added, I trust for a time only, the loss of another bibliopolical friend, whose vigorous intellect, and liberal ideas, have not only rendered his native country the mart of her own literature, but established there a Court of Letters, which must command respect, even from those most inclined to dissent from many of its canons. The effect of these changes, operated in a great measure by the strong sense and sagacious calculation of an individual, who knew how to avail himself, to an unhoped-for extent, of the various kinds of talent which his country produced, will probably appear more clearly to the generation which shall follow the present.

I entered the shop at the Cross, to inquire after the health of my worthy friend, and learned with satisfaction that his residence in the south had abated the rigour of the symptoms of his disorder. Availing myself, then, of the privileges to which I have alluded, I strolled onwards in that labyrinth of small dark rooms, or *crypts*, to speak our own antiquarian language, which form the extensive back-settlements of that celebrated publishing house. Yet, as I proceeded from one obscure recess to another, filled, some of them with old volumes, some with such as, from the equality of their rank on the shelves, I suspected to be the less saleable modern books of the concern, I could not help feeling a holy horror creep upon me, when I thought of the risk of intruding on some ecstatic bard giving vent to his poetical fury; or, it might be, on the yet more formidable privacy of a band of critics, in the act of worrying the game which they had just run down. In such a supposed case, I felt by anticipation the horrors of the Highland seers, whom their gift of Deuteroscopy compels to witness things unmeet for mortal eye; and who, to use the expression of Collins,

——heartless, oft, like moody madness, stare,
To see the phantom train their secret work prepare.

Still, however, the irresistible impulse of an undefined curiosity drove me on through this succession of darksome chambers, till, like the jeweller of Delhi in the house of the magician Bennaskar, I at length reached a vaulted room, dedicated to secrecy and silence, and beheld, seated by a lamp, and employed in reading a blotted *revise*, the person, or perhaps I should rather say the Eidolon, or Representation, of the Author of Waverley. You will not be surprised at the filial instinct which enabled me at once to acknowledge the features borne by this venerable apparition, and that I at once bended the knee, with the classical salutation of, *Salve, magne parens!* The vision, however, cut me short, by pointing to a seat, and intimating that my presence was not unexpected, and that he had something to say to me.

I sate down with humble obedience, and endeavoured to note the features of him with whom I now found myself so unexpectedly in society. But on this point I can give your reverence no satisfaction; for, besides the obscurity of the apartment, and the fluttered state of my own nerves, I seemed to myself over-whelmed by a sense of filial awe, which prevented my noting and recording what it is probable the Personage before me might most desire to have concealed. Indeed, his figure was so closely veiled and wimpled, either with a mantle, morning-gown, or some such loose garb, that the verses of Spenser might well have been applied—

> Yet, certes, by her face and physnomy,
> Whether she man or woman inly were,
> That could not any creature well descry.

I must, however, proceed as I have begun, to apply the masculine gender; for, notwithstanding very ingenious reasons, and indeed something like positive evidence, have been offered to prove the Author of Waverley to be two ladies of talent, I abide by the general opinion, that he is of the rougher sex. There are in his writings too many things

> Quæ maribus sola tribuuntur,

to permit me to entertain any doubt on that subject. I will proceed, in the manner of dialogue, to repeat as nearly as I can what passed betwixt us, only observing, that in the course of the conversation, my timidity imperceptibly gave way under the familiarity of his address; and, latterly, I perhaps argued with fully as much confidence as was beseeming.

Author of Waverley. I was willing to see you, Captain Clutterbuck, being the person of my family whom I have most regard for, since the death of Jedidiah Cleishbotham; and I am afraid I may have done you some wrong, in assigning to you the Monastery as a portion of my effects. I have some thoughts of making it up to you, by naming you godfather to this yet unborn babe—(he indicated the proof-sheet with his finger)—But first, touching The Monastery—How says the world —you are abroad, and can learn?

Captain Clutterbuck. Hem! hem!—The—the inquiry is delicate—I have not heard any complaints from the Publishers.

Author. That is the principal matter; but yet an indifferent work is sometimes towed on by those which have left harbour before it, with the breeze in their poop. What say the Critics?

Captain. There is a general—feeling—that the White Lady is no favourite.

Author. I think she is a failure myself; but rather in execution than conception. Could I have evoked an *esprit follet*, at the same time fantastic and interesting, capricious and kind; a sort of wildfire of the elements, bound by no fixed laws, or motives of action; faithful and fond, yet teazing and uncertain——

Captain. If you will pardon the interruption, sir, I think you are describing a pretty woman.

Author. On my word, I believe I am. I must invest my elementary spirits with a little human flesh and blood—they are too fine-drawn for the present taste of the public.

Captain. They object too, that the objects of your Nixie ought to have been more uniformly noble—her ducking the priest was no naiad-like amusement.

Author. Oh! they ought to allow for the capricios of what is after all but a better sort of goblin. The bath into which Ariel, the most delicate creation of Shakespeare's imagination, seduces our jolly friend Trinculo, was not of amber or rose-water. But no one shall find me rowing against the stream. I care not who knows it—I write for the public amusement; and though I never will aim at popularity by what I think unworthy means, I will not, on the other hand, be pertinacious in the defence of my own errors against the voice of the public.

Captain. You abandon then, in the present work—(looking in my turn towards the proof-sheet)—the mystic, and the magical, and the whole system of signs, wonders, and omens? There are no dreams, or presages, or obscure allusions to future events?

Author. Not a Cock-lane scratch, my son—not one bounce on the drum of Tedworth, not so much as the poor tick of a solitary death-watch in the wainscot. All is clear and above board—a Scotch metaphysician might believe every word of it.

Captain. And the story is, I hope, natural and probable; commencing strikingly, like the source of a famed river which gushes from the mouth of some obscure and romantic grotto—then gliding on, never pausing, never precipitating, visiting, as it were by natural instinct, whatever worthy subjects of interest are presented by the country through which it passes—widening and deepening in interest as it flows on; and at length arriving at the final catastrophe as at some mighty haven, where ships of all kinds strike sail and yard——

Author. Hey! hey! what the deuce is all this? Why 'tis Ercles's vein. And it would require some one much more like Hercules than me, to produce a story which should gush, and glide, and never pause, and visit, and widen, and deepen, and all the rest on't. I should be chin-deep in my grave, man, before I was done with my task; and, in the meanwhile, all the quirks and quiddits which I might have devised for my reader's amusement, would lie rotting in my gizzard, like Sancho's suppressed witticisms when he was under his master's displeasure. There never was a novel written on this plan while the world stood.

Captain. Pardon me—Tom Jones.

Author. True, and perhaps Amelia also. Fielding had high notions of the dignity of an art which he may be considered as having founded. He challenges a comparison between the Novel and the Epic. Smollett, Le Sage, and others, emancipating themselves from the strictness of the rules he has laid down, have written rather a history of the miscellaneous adventures which befall an individual in the course of life, than the plot of a regular and connected epopeia, where every step brings us a point nearer to the final catastrophe. These great masters have been satisfied if they amused the reader upon the road, though the conclusion only arrived because the tale must have an end, just as the traveller alights at the inn because it is evening.

Captain. A very commodious mode of travelling, for the author at least. In short, sir, you are of opinion with Bayes,—"What the devil does the plot signify, except to bring in fine things?"

Author. Grant that I were so, and that I should write with sense and spirit a few scenes, unlaboured and loosely put together, but which had sufficient interest in them to amuse in one corner the pain of body; in another, to relieve anxiety of mind; in a third place, to unwrinkle a brow bent with the furrows of daily toil; in another, to fill the place of bad thoughts, or to suggest better; in yet another, to induce an idler to study the history of his country; in all, save where the perusal interrupted the discharge of serious duties, to furnish harmless amusement,—might not the author of such a work, however inartificially executed, plead for his errors and negligences the excuse of the slave who was about to be punished for having spread the false report of a victory,—"Am I to blame, O Athenians, who have given you one happy day?"

Captain. Will your goodness permit me, sir, to mention an anecdote of my excellent grandmother?

Author. I see little she can have to do with the subject, Captain Clutterbuck.

Captain. It may come into our dialogue on Bayes's plan. The sagacious old lady, rest her soul, was a good friend to the church, and could never hear a minister maligned by evil tongues, without taking his part warmly. There was one fixed point, however, at which she always abandoned the cause of her reverend *protegé*—it was so soon as she learned he had preached a regular sermon against slanderers and backbiters.

Author. And what is that to the purpose?

Captain. Only that I have heard engineers say, that one may betray the weak point to the enemy, by too much ostentation in fortifying it.

Author. And, once more I pray, what is that to the purpose?

Captain. Nay then, without farther metaphor, I am afraid this new production, in which your generosity seems willing to give me some concern, will stand much in need of apology, since you think proper to begin your defence before the case is on trial. The story is hastily huddled up, I would venture a pint of claret.

Author. A pint of port, I suppose you mean?

Captain. I say of claret—good claret of the Monastery. Ah, sir, would ye but take the advice of your friends, and try to deserve at least one-half of the public favour you have met with, we might all drink Tokay!

Author. I care not what I drink, so the liquor be wholesome.

Captain. Care for your reputation then—for your fame.

Author. *My* fame?—I will answer you as a very ingenious, able, and experienced friend, when counsel for the notorious Jem MacCoul, replied to the opposite side of the bar, when they laid weight on his client's refusing to answer certain queries, which they said every man who had a regard for his reputation would not hesitate to reply to. "My client," said he—by the way, Jem was standing behind him at the time, and a rich scene it was—"is so unfortunate as to have no regard for his reputation; and I should deal very uncandidly with the Court, should I say he had any that was worth his attention." I am, though from very different reasons, in Jem's happy state of indifference. Let fame follow those who have a substantial shape. A shadow—and an impersonal author is nothing better—can cast no shade.

Captain. You are not now, perhaps, so impersonal as heretofore. These Letters to the Member for the University of Oxford——

Author. Shew the wit, genius, and delicacy of the author, which I heartily wish to see engaged on a subject of more importance; and shew, besides, that the preservation of my character of *incognito* has engaged early talent in the discussion of a curious question of evidence. But a cause, however ingeniously pleaded, is not therefore gained. You may remember the neatly-wrought chain of circumstantial evidence, so artificially brought forward to prove Sir Philip Francis's title to the Letters of Junius, seemed at first irrefragable; yet the influence of the reasoning has passed away, and Junius, in the general opinion, is as much unknown as ever. But on this subject I will not be soothed or provoked into saying one word more—to say who I am not, would be one step towards saying who I am; and as I desire not, any more than a certain justice of peace mentioned by Shenstone, the noise or report such things make in the world, I shall continue to be silent on a subject, which, in my opinion, is very undeserving the rout that has been made about it, and still more unworthy of the serious employment of such ingenuity as has been displayed by the young letter-writer.

Captain. But allowing, my dear sir, that you care not for your personal reputation, or for that of any literary person upon whose shoulders your faults may be visited, allow me to say, that common gratitude to the public, who have received you so kindly, and to the critics, who have treated you so leniently, ought to induce you to bestow more pains on your story.

Author. I do entreat you, my son, as Dr Johnson would have said, "Free your mind from cant." For the critics, they have their business, and I mine; as the nursery proverb goes—

> The children in Holland take pleasure in making
> What the children in England take pleasure in breaking.

I am their humble jackall, too busy in providing food for them, to have time for considering whether they swallow or reject it.—To the public, I stand pretty near in the relation of the postman who leaves a packet at the door of an individual. If it contains pleasing intelligence, —a billet from a mistress, a letter from an absent son, a remittance from a correspondent supposed to be bankrupt,—the letter is acceptably welcome, and read and re-read, folded up, filed, and safely deposited in the bureau. If the contents are disagreeable, if it comes from a dun or from a bore, the correspondent is cursed, the letter is thrown on the fire, and the expence of postage is heartily regretted; while all the while the bearer of the dispatches is, in either case, as little thought on as the snow of last Christmas. The utmost extent of kindness between the author and the public which can really exist, is, that the world are disposed to be somewhat indulgent to the succeeding works of an original favourite, were it but on account of the habit which the public mind has acquired; while the author very naturally thinks well of *their* taste, who have so liberally applauded *his* productions. But I deny there is any call for gratitude, properly so called, either on one side or other.

Captain. Respect to yourself, then, ought to teach caution.

Author. Ay, if caution could augment the chance of my success. But, to confess to you the truth, the works and passages in which I have succeeded, have uniformly been written with the greatest rapidity; and when I have seen some of these placed in opposition with others, and commended as more highly finished, I could appeal to pen and standish, that the parts in which I have come feebly off, were by much the more laboured. Besides, I doubt the beneficial effect of too much delay, both on account of the author and the public. A man should strike while the iron is hot, and hoist sail while the wind is fair. If a successful author keeps not the stage, another instantly takes his ground. If a writer lies by for ten years ere he produces a second work, he is superseded by others; or, if the age is so poor of genius that this does not happen, his own reputation becomes his greatest obstacle. The public will expect the new work to be ten times better than its predecessor; the author will expect it should be ten times more popular, and 'tis a hundred to ten that both are disappointed.

Captain. This may justify a certain degree of rapidity in publication, but not that which is proverbially said to be no speed. You should take time at least to arrange your story.

Author. That is a sore point with me, my son. Believe me, I have not been fool enough to neglect ordinary precautions. I have repeatedly laid down my future work to scale, divided it into volumes and chapters, and endeavoured to construct a story which I meant should evolve itself gradually and strikingly, maintain suspense, and stimulate curiosity; and which, finally, should terminate in a striking catastrophe. But I think there is a dæmon who seats himself on the feather of my pen when I begin to write, and leads it astray from the purpose. Characters expand under my hand; incidents are multiplied; the story lingers, while the materials increase—my regular mansion turns out a Gothic anomaly, and the work is complete long before I have attained the point I proposed.

Captain. Resolution and determined forbearance might remedy that evil.

Author. Alas, my dear son, you do not know the force of fraternal affection.—When I light on such a character as Bailie Jarvie, or Dalgetty, my imagination brightens, and my conception becomes clearer at every step which I make in his company, although it leads me many a weary mile away from the regular road, and forces me to leap hedge and ditch to get back into the route again. If I resist the temptation, as you advise me, my thoughts become prosy, flat, and dull; I write painfully to myself, and under a consciousness of flagging which makes me flag still more; the sunshine with which fancy had invested the incidents, departs from them, and leaves every thing dull and gloomy. I am no more the same author, than the dog in a wheel, condemned to go round and round for hours, is like the same dog merrily chasing his own tail, and gambolling in all the frolic of unrestrained freedom. In short, on such occasions, I think I am bewitched.

Captain. Nay, sir, if you plead sorcery, there is no more to be said—
he must needs go whom the devil drives. And this, I suppose, sir, is the
reason why you do not make the theatrical attempt to which you have
been so often urged?

Author. It may pass for one good reason for not writing a play, that I
cannot frame a plot. But the truth is, that the idea adopted by the
favourable judges, of my having some aptitude for that department of
poetry, has been much founded on those scraps of old plays, which,
being taken from a source inaccessible to collectors, they have hastily
concluded the off-spring of my mother-wit. Now, the manner in
which I became possessed of these fragments is so extraordinary, that
I cannot help telling it to you.

You must know, then, that some twenty years since, I went down to
visit an old friend in Worcestershire, who had served with me in the
———— Dragoons.

Captain. Then you *have* served, sir?

Author. I have—or I have not, which signifies the same thing—
Captain is a good travelling name.—I found my friend's house unexpectedly crowded with guests, and, as usual, was condemned—the
mansion being an old one—to the *haunted apartment*. I had, as a great
Modern said, seen too many ghosts to believe in them, so betook
myself serenely to my repose, lulled by the wind rustling among the
lime-trees, the branches of which chequered the moonlight which fell
on the floor through the diamonded casement, when, behold, a darker
shadow interposed itself, and I beheld visibly on the floor of the
apartment——

Captain. The White Lady of Avenel, I suppose?—you have told the
very story before.

Author. No—I beheld a female form with round mob-cap, bib
and apron, sleeves tucked up to the elbow, a dredging-box in the
one hand, and in the other a sauce-ladle. I concluded, of course,
that it was my friend's cook-maid walking in her sleep; and as I
knew he had a value for Sally, who can toss a pancake with any girl
in the county, I got up to conduct her safely to the door. But as I
approached her, she said—"Hold, sir! I am not what you take me
for;"—words which seemed so apposite to the circumstances, that
I should not have much minded them, had it not been for the
peculiarly hollow sound in which they were uttered.—"Know then,"
she said in the same unearthly accents, "that I am the Spirit of
Betty Barnes"—"Who hanged herself for love of the stage-coach-
man," thought I; "this is a proper spot of work."—"Of that unhappy
Elizabeth or Betty Barnes, long cook-maid to Mr Warburton the
painful collector, but ah! the too careless custodier of the largest

collection of ancient plays ever known—of most of which the titles only are left to gladden the Prologomena of the Variorum Shakespeare. Yes, stranger, it was these ill-fated hands that consigned to grease and conflagration the scores of small quartos, which, did they now exist, would drive the whole Roxburghe Club out of their sense— it was these unhappy pickers and stealers that singed fat fowls and wiped dirty trenchers with the lost works of Beaumont and Fletcher, Massinger, Jonson, Webster—What shall I say?—even of Shakespeare himself."

Like every dramatic antiquary, my ardent curiosity after some play named in the Book of the Master of Revels, had often been checked by finding the object of my research numbered among the holocaust of victims which this unhappy woman had sacrificed to the God of Good Cheer. It is no wonder then, that, like the Hermit of Parnell,

> I broke the bands of fear, and madly cried,
> "You careless jade!"—But scarce the words began,
> When Betty brandish'd high her saucing-pan.

"Beware," she said, "you do not, by your ill-timed anger, cut off the opportunity I yet have to indemnify the world for the errors of my ignorance. In yonder coal-hole, not used for many a year, repose the few greasy and blackened fragments of the elder Drama which were not totally destroyed. Do thou then"—Why, what do you stare at, Captain? By my soul, it is true; as my friend Major Longbow says, "what should I tell you a lie for?"

Captain. Lie, sir!—Heaven forbid I should apply the word to a person so veracious. You are only inclined to chase your tail a little this morning, that is all. Had you not better reserve this legend to form an introduction to "Three Recovered Dramas," or so?

Author. You are quite right—habit's a strange thing, my son. I had forgot whom I was speaking to. Yes, "Plays for the closet, not for the stage"—

Captain. Right, and so you are sure to be acted; for the managers, while thousands of volunteers are desirous of serving them, are wonderfully partial to pressed men.

Author. I am a living witness, having been, like a second Laberius, made a dramatist whether I would or not. I believe my muse would be *Terrified* into treading the stage, even if I should write a sermon.

Captain. Truly, if you did, I am afraid folks might make a farce of it. And, therefore, should you change your style, I still advise a volume of dramas like Lord Byron's.

Author. No, his lordship is a cut above me—I wonot run my horse against his, if I can help myself. But there is my friend Allan has written just such a play as I might write myself, in a very sunny day, and with one of Bramah's extra patent-pens. I cannot make neat work without such appurtenances.

Captain. Do you mean Allan Ramsay?

Author. No, nor Barbara Allan either. I mean Allan Cunningham, who has just published his tragedy of Sir Marmaduke Maxwell, full of merry-making and murdering, kissing and cutting of throats, and passages which lead to nothing, and which are very pretty passages for all that. Not a glimpse of probability is there about the plot, but so much animation in particular passages, and such a vein of poetry through the whole, as I dearly wish I could infuse into my Culinary Remains, should I ever be tempted to publish them. With a popular impress, people would read and admire the beauties of Allan—as it is, they may perhaps only note his defects—or, what is worse, not note him at all. But never mind them, honest Allan; you are a credit to Caledonia for all that.—There are some lyrical effusions of his too, which you would do well to read, Captain. "It's hame, and it's hame," is equal to Burns.

Captain. I will take the hint—The club at Kennaquhair are turned fastidious since Catalani visited the Abbey. My "Poortith Cauld" has been received both poorly and coldly, and "the Banks of Bonnie Doon" have been positively coughed down—*Tempora mutantur*.

Author. They cannot stand still, they will change with all of us. What then?

A man's a man for a' that.

But the hour of parting approaches.

Captain. You are determined to proceed then in your own system. Are you aware that an unworthy motive may be assigned for this succession of publications? You will be supposed to work merely for the lucre of gain.

Author. Supposing that I did permit the great advantages which must be derived from success in literature, to join with other motives in inducing me to come more frequently before the public. That emolument is the voluntary tax which the public pays for a certain species of literary amusement—it is extorted from no one, and paid, I presume, by those only who can afford it, and who receive gratification in proportion to the expense. If the capital sum which these volumes have put into circulation be a very large one, has it contributed to my indulgences only? or can I not say to hundreds, from honest Duncan the paper manufacturer, to the most snivelling of printer's devils, "Didst thou not share? hadst thou not fifteen pence?" I profess I think our modern Athens much obliged to me for having established such an extensive manufacture; and when universal suffrage comes in fashion, I intend to stand for a seat in the House on the interest of all the unwashed artificers connected with literature.

Captain. This would be called the language of a calico-manufacturer.

Author. Cant again, my dear son—there is lime in this sack too—nothing but sophistication in this world! I do say it, in spite of Adam Smith and his followers, that a successful author is a productive labourer, and that his works constitute as effectual a part of the public wealth, as that which is created by any other manufactor. If a new commodity, having an actually intrinsic and commercial value, be the result of the operation, why are the author's bales of books to be esteemed a less profitable part of the public stock than the goods of any other manufacturer? I speak with reference to the diffusion of the wealth arising to the public, and the degree of industry which even such a trifling work as the present must stimulate and reward, before the volumes leave the publisher's shop. Without me it could not exist, and to this extent I am a benefactor to the country. As for my own emolument, it is won by my toil, and I account myself answerable to Heaven only for the mode in which I expend it. The candid may hope it is not all dedicated to selfish purposes; and, without much pretensions to merit in him who expends it, a part may "wander, heaven-directed, to the poor."

Captain. Yet it is generally held base to write, from the mere motive of gain.

Author. It would be base to do so exclusively, or even to make it a principal motive of literary exertion. Nay, I will venture to say, that no work of imagination, proceeding from the mere consideration of a certain sum of copy-money, ever did, or ever will, succeed. So the lawyer who pleads, the soldier who fights, the physician who prescribes, the clergyman—if such there be—who preaches, without any zeal for their profession, without any sense of its dignity, and merely on account of their fee, pay, or stipend, degrade themselves to the rank of sordid mechanics. Accordingly, in the case of two of the learned faculties at least, their services are considered as unappreciable, and are acknowledged not by any exact estimate of the services rendered, but by a *honorarium*, or voluntary acknowledgment. But let a client or patient make the experiment of omitting this little ceremony of the *honorarium*, which is *censé* to be a thing entirely out of consideration between them, and mark how the learned gentleman will look upon his case. Cant set apart, it is the same thing with literary emolument—no man of sense, in any rank of life, is, or ought to be, above accepting a just recompence for his time, and a reasonable share of the capital which owes its very existence to his exertions. When Czar

Peter wrought in the trenches, he took the pay of a common soldier; and nobles, statesmen, and divines, the most distinguished of their time, have not scorned to square accounts with their bookseller.

Captain. (*Sings.*)

> O if it were a mean thing,
> The gentles would not use it;
> And if it were ungodly,
> The clergy would refuse it.

Author. You say well. But no man of honour, genius, or spirit, would make the mere love of gain the chief, far less the only, purpose of his labours. For myself, I am not displeased to find the game a winning one; yet while I pleased the public, I should probably continue it merely for the pleasure of playing; for I have felt as strongly as most folks that love of composition which is perhaps the strongest of all instincts, driving the author to the pen, the painter to the pallet, often without either the chance of fame or the prospect of reward. Perhaps I have said too much of this. I might perhaps, with as much truth as most people, exculpate myself from the charge of being either of a greedy or mercenary disposition; but I am not, therefore, hypocrite enough to disclaim the ordinary motives, on account of which the whole world around me is toiling unremittingly, to the sacrifice of ease, comfort, health, and life. I do not affect the disinterestedness of that ingenious association of gentlemen mentioned by Goldsmith, who sold their magazine for sixpence a-piece, merely for their own amusement.

Captain. I have but one thing more to hint.—The world say you will run yourself out.

Author. The world say true; and what then? When they dance no longer, I will no longer pipe; and I will not want flappers enough to remind me of the apoplexy.

Captain. And what will become of us then, your poor family?—we shall fall into contempt and oblivion.

Author. Like many a poor fellow, already overwhelmed with the number of his family, I cannot help going on to increase it—"'Tis my vocation, Hal."—Such of you as deserve oblivion—perhaps the whole of you—may be consigned to it. At any rate, you have been read in your day, which is more than can be said of some of your contemporaries, of less fortune and more merit. They cannot say but what you *had* the crown. As for myself, I shall always deserve, at least, the unwilling tribute which Johnson paid to Churchill, when he said, though the fellow's genius was a tree which bore only crabs, yet it was prolific, and had plenty of fruit, such as it was. It is always something to have engaged the public attention for seven years. Had I only written

Waverley, I should have long since been, according to the established phrase, "the ingenious author of a novel much admired at the time." I believe, on my soul, that the reputation of Waverley is sustained very much by the praises of those, who may be inclined to prefer that tale to its successors.

Captain. You are willing, then, to barter future reputation for present popularity?

Author. Meliora spero. Horace himself expected not to survive in all his works—I may hope to live in some of mine;—*non omnis moriar.* It is some consolation to reflect, that the best authors in all countries have been the most voluminous; and it has often happened, that those who have been best received in their own time, have also continued to be acceptable to posterity. I do not think so ill of the present generation, as to suppose that its present favour necessarily infers future condemnation.

Captain. Were all to act on such principles, the public would be inundated.

Author. Once more, my dear son, beware of cant. You speak as if the public were obliged to read books merely because they are printed—your friends the booksellers would thank you to make the proposition good. The most serious grievance attending such inundations as you talk of is, that they make rags dear. The multiplicity of publications does the present age no harm, and may greatly advantage that which is to succeed us.

Captain. I do not see how that is to happen.

Author. The complaints in the time of Elizabeth and James, of the alarming fertility of the press, were as loud as they are at present—yet look at the shore on which the inundation of that age flowed, and it resembles now the Rich Strand of the Faery Queen—

> ——Bestrew'd all with rich aray,
> Of pearl and precious stones of great assay;
> And all the gravel mix'd with golden ore.

Believe me, that even in the most neglected works of the present age, the next may discover treasures.

Captain. Some books will defy all alchemy.

Author. They will be but few in number; since, as for writers, who are possessed of no merit at all, unless indeed they publish their works at their own expense, like Sir Richard Blackmore, their power of annoying the public will be soon limited by the difficulty of finding undertaking booksellers.

Captain. You are incorrigible. Are there no bounds to your audacity?

Author. There are the sacred and eternal boundaries of Honour and

Virtue. My course is like the enchanted chamber of Britomart—

> Where as she look'd about, she did behold
> How over that same door was likewise writ,
> *Be Bold—Be Bold*, and every where *Be Bold*.
> Whereat she mused, and could not construe it;
> At last she spied at that room's upper end
> Another iron door, on which was writ—
> BE NOT TOO BOLD.

Captain. Well, you must take the risk and act only on your own principles.

Author. Do you act on yours, and take care you do not stay idling here till the dinner hour is over.—I will add this work to your patrimony, *valeat quantum.*

Here our dialogue terminated; for a little sooty-faced Apollyon from the Canongate came to demand the proof-sheet on the part of M'Corkindale; and I heard Mr C. rebuking Mr F. in another compartment of the labyrinth I have described, for suffering any one to penetrate so far into the *penetralia* of their temple.

I leave it to you to form your own opinion concerning the import of this dialogue, and I cannot but believe I shall meet the wishes of our common parent in prefixing this letter to the work which it concerns.

I am, reverend and dear Sir,
Very sincerely and affectionately
Yours, &c. &c.
CUTHBERT CLUTTERBUCK.
Kennaquhair, 1st April, 1822.

THE FORTUNES OF NIGEL

VOLUME I

━━━━━

Chapter One

> Now Scot and English are agreed,
> And Saunders hastes to cross the Tweed,
> Where, such the splendours that attend him,
> His very mother scarce had kenn'd him.
> His metamorphosis behold,
> From Glasgow frieze to cloth of gold;
> His back-sword with the iron hilt,
> To rapier fairly hatch'd and gilt;
> Was ever seen a gallant braver!
> His very bonnet's grown a beaver.
> *The Reformation*

THE LONG-CONTINUED hostilities which had for centuries divided the south and the north divisions of the Island of Britain, had been happily terminated by the succession of the pacific James I. to the English crown. But although the united crown of England and Scotland was worn by the same individual, it required a long lapse of time, and the succession of more than one generation, ere the inveterate national prejudices which had so long existed betwixt the sister kingdoms were removed, and the subjects of either side of the Tweed brought to regard those upon the other bank as friends and as brethren.

These prejudices were, of course, most inveterate during the reign of King James. His English subjects accused him of partiality to those of his ancient kingdom; while the Scots, with equal injustice, charged him with having forgotten the land of his nativity, and with neglecting those early friends to whose allegiance he had been so much indebted.

The temper of the King, peaceable even to timidity, inclined him perpetually to interfere as mediator amongst the contending factions, whose brawls disturbed his court. But notwithstanding all his precautions, historians have recorded many instances when the mutual hatred of two nations, who, after being enemies for a thousand years, had been so very recently united, broke forth with a fury which menaced a general convulsion; and, spreading from the highest to the lowest classes, as it occasioned debates in council and parliament, factions in the court, and duels among the gentry, was no less productive of riots and brawls amongst those of the lower orders.

While these heart-burnings were at the highest, there flourished in the city of London an ingenious, but whimsical and self-opinioned mechanic, much devoted to abstract studies, David Ramsay by name, who, whether recommended by his great skill in his profession, as the courtiers alleged, or, as was murmured among his neighbours, by his birth-place, in the good town of Dalkeith, near Edinburgh, held in James's household the post of Maker of watches and horologes to his Majesty. He scorned not, however, to keep open shop within Temple-Bar, a few yards to the eastward of Saint Dunstan's Church.

The shop of a London tradesman at that time, as it may be supposed, was something very different from those we now see in the same locality. The goods were exposed to sale in cases, only defended from the weather by a covering of canvas, and the whole resembled the stalls and booths now erected for temporary accommodation of dealers at a country fair, rather than the established emporium of a respectable citizen. But most of the shopkeepers of note, and David Ramsay amongst others, had their booth connected with a small apartment which opened backwards from it, and bore the same resemblance to the front shop that Robinson Crusoe's cavern did to the tent which he erected before it. To this Master Ramsay was often accustomed to retreat to the labour of his abstruse calculations; for he aimed at improvement and discoveries in his own art, and sometimes pushed his researches, like Napier, and other mathematicians of the period, into abstract science. When thus engaged, he left the outer posts of his commercial establishment to be maintained by two stout-bodied and strong-voiced apprentices, who kept up the cry of, "What d'ye lack? What d'ye lack?" accompanied with the appropriate recommendations of the articles in which they dealt. This direct and personal application for custom to those who chanced to pass by, is now, we believe, limited to Monmouth Street, (if it still exists even in that repository of ancient garments,) under the guardianship of the scattered remnant of Israel. But, at the time we are speaking of, it was practised alike by Jew and Gentile, and served, instead of all our present newspaper puffs and advertisements, to solicit the attention of the public in general, and of friends in particular, to the unrivalled excellence of the goods, which they offered to sale upon such easy terms, that it might fairly appear that the venders had rather a view to the general service of the public, than to their own particular advantage.

The verbal proclaimers of the excellence of their commodities, had this advantage over those who, in the present day, use the public papers for the same purpose, that they could in many cases adapt their address to the peculiar appearance and apparent taste of the passengers. [This, as we have said, was also the case in Monmouth Street in our remembrance. We have ourselves been reminded of the deficiencies of our femoral habiliments, and exhorted upon that score to fit ourselves more beseemingly; but this is a digression.] This direct and personal mode of invitation to customers became, however, a dangerous temptation to the young wags who were employed in the task of solicitation during the absence of the principal person interested in the traffic; and, confiding in their numbers and civic union, the 'prentices of London were often seduced into taking liberties with the passengers, and exercising their wit at the expence of those whom they had no hopes of converting into customers by their eloquence. If this was resented by any act of violence, the inmates of each shop were ready to pour forth in succour; and, in the words of an old song which Dr Johnson was used to hum,—

> Up then rose the 'prentices all,
> Living in London, both proper and tall.

Desperate riots often arose on such occasions, especially when the Templars, or other youths connected with the aristocracy, were insulted, or conceived themselves to be so. Upon such occasions, bare steel was frequently opposed to the clubs of the citizens, and death frequently ensued on both sides. The tardy and inefficient police of the time had no other resource than by the Alderman of the ward calling out the householders, and putting a stop to the strife by overpowering numbers, as the Capulets and Montagues are separated upon the stage.

At the period when such was the universal custom of the most respectable, as well as the most inconsiderable shopkeepers in London, David Ramsay, upon the evening to which we solicit the attention of the reader, retiring to more abstruse and private labours, left the administration of his outer shop, or booth, to the aforesaid sharp, active, able-bodied, and well-voiced apprentices, namely, Jenkin Vincent and Frank Tunstall.

Vincent had been educated at the excellent foundation of Christ Church Hospital, and was bred, therefore, as well as born, a Londoner, with all the peculiar acuteness and address, and audacity, which belongs peculiarly to the youth of a metropolis. He was now about twenty years old, short in stature, but remarkably strongly made, eminent for his feats upon holidays at the foot-ball, and other gymnastic exercises; scarce rivalled in the broad-sword play, though hitherto only exercised in the form of single-stick; he knew every lane, blind alley, and sequestered court of the ward, better than his Catechism; was alike active in his master's affairs, and in his own adventures of fun and mischief; and so managed matters, that the credit he acquired by the former bore him out, or at least served for his apology, when the latter propensity led him into scrapes, of which, however, it is but fair to state, that they had hitherto inferred nothing mean or discreditable. Some aberrations there were, which David Ramsay, his master, endeavoured to reduce to regular order when he discovered them, and others which he winked at, supposing them to answer the purpose of the escapement of a watch, which disposes of a certain quantity of the extra power of that mechanical impulse which puts the whole in motion.

The physiognomy of Jin Vin, by which abbreviation he was familiarly known through the ward, corresponded with the sketch we have given of his character. His head, upon which his prentice's flat cap was generally flung in a careless and oblique fashion, was closely covered with thick hair of raven black, which curled naturally and closely, and would have grown to great length, but for the modest custom enjoined by his state of life, and strictly enforced by his master, which compelled him to keep it short-cropped,—not unreluctantly, as he looked with envy on the flowing ringlets, in which the courtiers and aristocratical students of the neighbouring Temple began to indulge themselves, as marks of superiority and of gentility. Vincent's eyes were deep set in his head, of a strong vivid black, full of fire, roguery, and intelligence, and conveying a humorous expression, even while he was uttering the usual small-talk of his trade, as if he ridiculed those who were disposed to give any weight to his common-places. He had address enough, however, to add little touches of his own, which gave a turn of drollery even to this ordinary routine of the booth; and the alacrity of his manner—his ready and obvious wish to oblige—his intelligence and civility, when he thought civility necessary, made him a universal favourite with his master's customers. His features were far from regular, for his nose was flattish, his mouth tending to the larger size, and his complexion inclining to be more dark than was then thought consistent with masculine beauty. But then, in despite of his having always breathed the air of a crowded city, his complexion had the ruddy and manly expression of redundant health; his turned-up nose gave an air of spirit and raillery to what he said, and seconded the laugh of his eyes, and his wide mouth was garnished with a pair of well-formed and well-coloured lips, which, when he laughed, disclosed a range of teeth strong and well set, and white as the very pearl. Such was the elder apprentice of David Ramsay, watch-maker, and constructor of horologes, to his Most Sacred Majesty James I.

Jenkin's companion was the younger apprentice, though, perhaps, he might be the elder of the two in years. At any rate he was of a much more staid and composed temper. Francis Tunstall was of that ancient and proud descent, who claimed the style of the "Unstained," because, amid the various chances of the long and bloody wars of the roses, they had, with undeviating faith, followed the House of Lancaster, to which they had originally attached themselves. The meanest sprig of such a tree attached importance to the root from which he derived himself; and Tunstall was supposed to nourish in secret a proportion of that family pride, which had extorted tears from his widowed and almost indigent mother, when she saw herself obliged to consign him to a line of life, inferior, as her prejudices suggested, to the course held by his progenitors. Yet, with all this aristocratic prejudice, his master found the well-born youth more docile, regular, and strictly attentive to his duty, than his far more active and alert comrade. Tunstall also gratified his master by the particular attention which he seemed disposed to bestow on the abstract principles of science connected with the trade which he was bound to study, the limits of which were daily enlarged with the increase of mathematical science. Vincent beat his companion beyond the distance-post, in every thing like the practical adaptation of theory to practice, in the dexterity of hand necessary to execute the mechanical branches of the art, and double-distanced him in all respecting the commercial affairs of the shop. Still David Ramsay was wont to say, that if Vincent knew how to do a thing the better of the two, Tunstall was much better acquainted with the principles on which it ought to be done; and he sometimes objected to the latter, that he knew critical excellence too well ever to be satisfied with practical mediocrity.

The disposition of Tunstall was shy, as well as studious; and though perfectly civil and obliging, he never seemed to feel himself in his place while he went through the duties of the shop. He was tall and handsome, with fair hair, well-formed limbs, good features, light blue eyes, well opened, a straight Grecian nose, and a countenance which expressed both good humour and intelligence, but qualified by a gravity unsuitable to his years, and which almost amounted to dejection. He lived on the best terms with his companion, and readily stood by him whenever he was engaged in any of the frequent skirmishes, which, as we have already observed, often disturbed the city of London about this period. But, though Tunstall was allowed to understand quarter-staff, (the weapon of the North country,) in a superior degree, and though he was naturally both strong and active, his interference in such affrays seemed always matter of necessity; and, as he never voluntarily joined either their brawls or their sports, he held a far lower place in the opinion of the youth of the ward than his hearty and active friend Jin Vin. Nay, had it not been for the interest made for his comrade by the intercession of Vincent, Tunstall would have stood some chance of being altogether excluded from the society of his contemporaries of the same condition, who called him, in scorn, Cavaliero Frank, and the Gentle Tunstall. On the other hand, the lad himself, deprived of the fresh air in which he had been brought up, and foregoing the exercise to which he had been formerly accustomed, while the inhabitant of his native mansion, lost gradually the freshness of his complexion, and, without exhibiting any formal symptoms of disease, grew more thin and pale as he grew older, and at length exhibited the appearance of indifferent health, without any thing of the habits or complaints of an invalid, excepting a disposition to avoid society, and to spend his leisure time in private study, rather than mingle in the sports of his companions, or even resort to the theatres, then the general rendezvous of his class; where, according to high authority, they fought for half-bitten apples, cracked nuts, and filled the upper gallery with their clamours.

Such were the two youths who called David Ramsay master, and with both of whom he used to fret from morning till night, as their peculiarities interfered with his own, or with the quiet and beneficial course of his traffic.

Upon the whole, however, the youths were attached to their master, and he, a good-natured, though an absent and whimsical man, was scarce less so to them; and, when a little warmed with wine at an occasional junketting, he used to boast, in his northern dialect, of his "twa bonnie lads, and the looks that the court ladies threw at them when visiting his shop in their caroches, when on a frolic into the city." But David Ramsay never failed at the same time to draw up his own tall, thin, lathy skeleton, extend his lean jaws into an alarming grin, and indicate, by a nod of his yard-long visage, and a twinkle of his little grey eye, that there might be more faces in Fleet-Street worth looking at than those of Frank and Jenkin. His old neighbour, Widow Simmons the sempstress, who had served in her day the very tip-top revellers of the Temple, with ruffs, cuffs, and bands, distinguished more deeply the sort of attention paid by the females of quality who so regularly visited David Ramsay's shop to its inmates. "The boy Frank," she admitted, "used to attract the attention of the young ladies, as having something gentle and downcast in his looks; but then he could not better himself, for the poor youth had not a word to throw at a dog. Now Jin Vin was so full of his jibes and his jeers, and so willing, and so ready, and so serviceable, and so mannerly all the while, with his step that sprung like a buck's in Epping Forest, and his eye that twinkled as black as a gipsey's, that no woman who knew the world would make a comparison betwixt the lads. As for poor neighbour Ramsay himself, the man," she said, "was a civil neighbour, and a learned man, doubtless, and might be a rich man, if he had common sense to back his learning; and doubtless, for a Scot, neighbour Ramsay was nothing of a bad man; but he was so constantly grimed with smoke, gilded with brass filings, and smeared with lamp-black and oil, that Dame Simmons judged it would require his whole shop-full of watches to induce any feasible woman to touch the said neighbour Ramsay with any thing save a pair of tongs."

Such were, in natural qualities and public estimation, the two youths, who, on a fine April day, having first rendered their dutiful service and attendance on the table of their master and his daughter, at their dinner at one o'clock—Such, O ye lads of London, was the severe discipline undergone by your predecessors—and having regaled themselves upon the fragments, in company with two female domestics, one a cook, and maid of all work, the other called Mistress Margaret's maid, now relieved their master on the duty of the outward shop; and, agreeable to the established custom, were soliciting, by their entreaties and recommendations of their master's manufactures, the attention and encouragement of the passengers.

In this species of service it may be easily supposed that Jenkin Vincent left his more reserved and bashful comrade far in the background. The latter could only articulate with difficulty, and as an act of duty which he was rather ashamed of discharging, the established words of form—"What d'ye lack?—What d'ye lack?—Clocks—watches—barnacles?—What d'ye lack?—Watches—clocks—barnacles?—What d'ye lack, sir? What d'ye lack, madam?—Barnacles, watches, clocks?"

But this dull and dry iteration, however varied by diversity of verbal arrangement, sounded flat when mingled with the rich and recommendatory oratory of the bold-faced, deep-mouthed, and ready-witted Jenkin Vincent. "What d'ye lack, noble sir?—What d'ye lack, beauteous madam?" he said, in a tone at once bold and soothing, which often was so applied as both to gratify the persons addressed, and to excite a smile from other hearers. "God bless your reverence," to a beneficed clergyman; "the Greek and Hebrew have blinded your reverence's eyes—Buy a pair of David Ramsay's barnacles—the King, God bless his Majesty, never reads Hebrew or Greek without them."

"Are you well avised of that?" said a fat parson from the Vale of Evesham. "Nay, if the Head of the Church wears them, God bless his Sacred Majesty, I will try what they can do for me; for I have not been able to distinguish one Hebrew letter from another, since—I cannot remember the time—when I had a bad fever. Chuse me a pair of his most Sacred Majesty's own wearing, my good youth."

"This is a pair, an it please your reverence," said Jenkin, producing a pair of spectacles which he touched as with an air of great deference and respect, "which his most blessed Majesty placed this day three weeks on his own blessed nose, and would have kept them for his own sacred use, but that the setting being, as your reverence sees, of the purest jet, was, as his Sacred Majesty was pleased to say, fitter for a bishop than for a secular prince."

"His Sacred Majesty the King," said the worthy divine, "was as ever a very Daniel in his judgment; give me the barnacles, good youth, and who can say what nose they may bestride in two years hence. Our reverend brother of Gloucester waxes in years." He then pulled out his purse, paid for the spectacles, and left the shop with even a more important step than that which had paused to enter it.

"For shame," said Tunstall to his companion; "these glasses will never suit one of his years."

"You are a fool, Frank," said Vincent in reply; "had the good doctor wished glasses to read withal, he would have tried them before buying. He does not want to look through them himself, and these will serve the purpose of being looked at by other folks as well as the best magnifiers in the shop.—What d'ye lack?" he cried, resuming his solicitations. "Mirrors for your toilette, my pretty madam; your head-gear is something awry—pity, since it is so well fancied." The woman stopped and bought a mirror.—"What d'ye lack?—A watch, Master Serjeant—a watch that will go as steady and true as your own elo-quence?"

"Hold your peace, sir," answered the Knight of the Coif, who was disturbed by Vin's address whilst in deep consultation with an eminent attorney; "hold your peace! you are the loudest-tongued varlet betwixt the Devil-tavern and Guildhall."

"A watch," reiterated the undaunted Jenkin, "that shall not lose thirteen minutes in a thirteen years' law-suit.—He's out of hearing—a watch with five wheels and a bar-movement—A watch that shall tell you, Master Poet, how long the patience of the audience will endure your next piece at the Black Bull." The bard laughed, and fumbled in the pocket of his slops till he chased into a corner, and fairly caught, a small piece of coin.

"Here is a tester to cherish thy wit, good boy," he said.

"Gramercy," said Vin; "and the next play of yours I will bring down a set of roaring boys that shall make all the critics of the pit, and the gallants on the stage, civil, or else the curtain shall smoke for it."

"Now, that I call mean," said Tunstall, "to take the poor rhymer's money, who has so little left behind."

"You are an owl, once again," said Vincent; "if he has nothing left to buy cheese and radishes, he will only dine a day the sooner with some patron or some player, for that is his fate five days out of the seven. It is unnatural that a poet should pay for his own pot of beer; I will drink his tester for him, to save him from such shame; and when his third night comes round, he shall have pennyworths for his coin, I promise you.—But here comes another-guess customer. Look at that strange fellow—See how he gapes at every shop, as if he would swallow the wares.—O! Saint Dunstan has caught his eye; pray God he swallow not the images. See how he stands astonished, as old Adam and Eve ply their ding-dong! Come, Frank, thou art a scholar; construe me that same fellow, with his blue cap with a cock's feather in it, to shew he's of gentle blood, God wot—his grey eyes, his yellow hair, his sword with a ton of iron in the handle—his grey thread-bare cloak —his step like a French-man—his look like a Spaniard—a book at his girdle, and a broad dudgeon-dagger on the other side, to shew him half-pedant, half-bully. How call you that motion*?"

"A raw Scotsman," said Tunstall; "just come up, I suppose, to help the rest of his countrymen to gnaw old England's bones; a palmer-worm, I reckon, to devour what the locust has spared."

"Even so, Frank," answered Vincent; "just as the poet sings sweetly,—

> In Scotland he was born and bred,
> And, though a beggar, must be fed."

"Hush!" said Tunstall, "remember our master."

"Pshaw!" answered his mercurial companion; "he knows on which side his bread is buttered, and I warrant you has not lived so long among Englishmen, and by Englishmen, to quarrel with us for bearing an English mind. But see, our Scot has done gazing at old Saint Dunstan's, and comes our way. By this light, a proper lad and a sturdy, in spite of freckles and sun-burning.—He comes nearer still, I will have at him."

"And if you do," said his comrade, "you may get a broken head—he looks not as if he would carry coals."

"A figo for your threat," said Vincent, and instantly addressed the stranger. "Buy a watch, most noble northern Thane—buy a watch, to count the hours of plenty since the blessed moment you left Berwick

* *Motion*—Puppet-shew.

behind you.—Buy barnacles, to see the English gold lies ready for your gripe.—Buy what you will, you shall have credit for three days; for, were your pockets as bare as Father Fergus's, you are a Scot in London, and you will be stocked in that time." The stranger looked sternly at the waggish apprentice, and seemed to grasp his cudgel in rather a menacing fashion. "Buy physic," said the undaunted Vincent, "if you will buy neither time nor light—physic for a proud stomach, sir;—there is a 'pothecary's shop on the other side of the way."

Here the probationary disciple of Galen, who stood at his master's door in his flat cap and canvas sleeves, with a large wooden pestle in his hand, took up the ball which was flung to him by Jenkin, with, "What d'ye lack, sir?—Buy a choice Caledonian salve, *Flos sulphur: cum butyro quant: suff:.*"

"To be taken after a gentle rubbing-down with an English oaken towel," said Vincent.

The bonny Scot had given full scope to the play of this small artillery of city wit, by halting his stately pace, and viewing grimly, first the one assailant, and then the other, as if menacing either repartee, or more violent revenge. But phlegm or prudence got the better of his indignation, and tossing his head as one who valued not the raillery to which he had been exposed, he walked down Fleet Street, pursued by the horse-laugh of his tormentors.

"The Scot will not fight till he sees his own blood," said Tunstall, whom his north of England extraction had made familiar with all manner of proverbs against those who lay yet farther north than himself.

"Faith, I know not," said Jenkin; "he looks dangerous that fellow— he will hit some one over the noddle before he goes far. Hark!—hark! —they are rising."

Accordingly, the well-known cry of, "'Prentices—'prentices— Clubs—clubs!" now rang along Fleet Street; and Jenkin, snatching up his weapon, which lay beneath the counter ready at the slightest notice, and calling to Tunstall to take his bat and follow him, leaped over the hatch-door which protected the outer shop, and ran as fast as he could towards the affray, echoing the cry as he ran, and elbowing, or shoving aside, whomsoever stood in his way. His comrade, first calling to his master to give an eye to the shop, followed Jenkin's example, and ran after him as fast as he could, but with more attention to the safety and convenience of others; while old David Ramsay, with hands and eyes uplifted, a green apron before him, and a glass which he had been polishing thrust into his bosom, came forth to look after the safety of his goods and chattels, knowing, by old experience, that when the cry of "Clubs" once arose, he would have little assistance on the part of his apprentices.

Chapter Two

This, sir, is one among the Signory,
Has wealth at will, and will to use his wealth,
And wit to encrease it. Marry, his worst folly
Lies in a thriftless sort of charity,
That goes a gadding sometimes after objects,
Which wise men will not see when thrust upon them.

The Old Couple

THE ANCIENT GENTLEMAN bustled about his shop in pettish displeasure, at being summoned thither so hastily, to the interruption of his more abstract studies; and, unwilling to renounce the train of calculation which he had put in progress, he mingled whimsically with the fragments of the arithmetical operation, his oratory to the passengers, and angry reflections on his idle apprentices. "What d'ye lack, sir? Madam, what d'ye lack—clocks for hall or table—night-watches —day-watches?—*Locking wheel being* 48—*the pinion of report,* 8—*the striking pins are* 13——What d'ye lack, honoured sir?—*the quotient— the multiplicand*—that the knaves should have gone out at this blessed minute!—*the acceleration being at the rate of* 5 *minutes,* 55 *seconds,* 53 *thirds,* 59 *fourths*—I will switch them both when they come back—I will, by the bones of the immortal Napier!"

Here the vexed philosopher was interrupted by the entrance of a grave citizen of a most respectable appearance, who, saluting him familiarly by the name of "Davie, my old acquaintance," demanded what had put him so much out of sorts, and gave him at the same time a cordial grasp of his hand.

The stranger's dress was, though grave, rather richer than usual. His paned hose were of black velvet, lined with purple silk, which garniture appeared at the slashes. His doublet was of purple cloth, and his short cloak of black velvet to correspond with his hose; and both were adorned with a great number of small silver buttons richly wrought in filigree. A triple chain of gold hung round his neck; and in place of a sword or dagger, he wore at his belt an ordinary knife for the purpose of the table, with a small silver case, which appeared to contain writing materials. He might have seemed some secretary or clerk engaged in the service of the public, only that his low, flat, and unadorned cap, and his well-blacked shining shoes, indicated that he belonged to the city. He was a well-made man, about the middle size, and seemed firm in health though advanced in years. His looks expressed sagacity and good humour; and the air of respectability which his dress announced was well supported by his clear eye, ruddy cheek, and grey hair. He used the Scottish idiom in his first address, but in such a manner that it could hardly be distinguished whether he was passing upon his friend a sort of jocose mockery, or whether it was his own native dialect, for his ordinary discourse had little provincialism.

In answer to the queries of his respectable friend, Ramsay groaned heavily, answering by echoing back the question, "What ails me, Master George? Why, everything ails me! I profess to you that a man may as well live in Fairyland as in the Ward of Faringdon-Without—my apprentices are turned into mere goblins—they appear and disappear like spunkies, and have no more regularity in them than a watch without a scapement. If there is a ball to be tossed up, or a bullock to be driven mad, or a quean to be ducked for scolding, or a head to be broken, Jenkin is sure to be at the one end or the other of it, and then away skips Francis Tunstall for company. I think the prize-fighters, bear-leaders, and mountebanks, are in a league against me, my dear friend, and that they pass my house ten times for any other in the city. Here's an Italian fellow come over too, that they call Punchinello"——

"Well," interrupted Master George, "but what is all this to the present case?"

"Why," replied Ramsay, "here has been a cry of thieves or murder, (I hope that will prove the least of it amongst these English pock-pudding swine!) and I have been interrupted in the deepest calculation ever mortal man plunged into, Master George."

"What, man!" replied Master George, "you must take patience—You are a man that deals in time, and can make it go fast and slow at pleasure; you, of all the world, have least reason to complain if a little of it be lost now and then. And here come your boys—and bringing a slain man between them, I think—here has been serious mischief, I am afraid."

"The more mischief the better sport," said the crabbed old watchmaker. "I am blithe, though, that it's neither of the twa loons themselves.—What are ye bringing a corpse here for, ye fause villains?" he added, addressing the two apprentices, who, at the head of a considerable mob of their own class, some of whom bore evident marks of a recent fray, were carrying the body betwixt them.

"He is not dead yet, sir," answered Tunstall.

"Carry him into the apothecary's then," replied his master. "D'ye think I can set a man's life in motion again, as if he were a clock or a time-piece?"

"For godsake, old friend," said his acquaintance, "let us have him here at the nearest—he seems only in a swoon."

"A swoon!" said Ramsay, "and what business had he to swoon in the streets? Only, if it will oblige my friend Master George, I would take in all the dead men in Saint Dunstan's parish. Call Sam Porter to look after the shop."

So saying, the stunned man, being the identical Scotsman who had passed a short time ago amidst the jeers of the apprentices, was carried into the back shop of the artist, and there placed in an armchair till the apothecary from over the way came to his assistance. This gentleman, as sometimes happens to those of the learned professions, had rather more lore than knowledge, and began to talk of the sinciput and occiput, the cerebrum and cerebellum, until he exhausted David Ramsay's brief stock of patience.

"Bell-um! Bell-ell-um!" he repeated, with great indignation; "What signifies all the bells in London, if you do not put a plaister on the chield's crown?"

Master George, with better directed zeal, asked the apothecary whether bleeding might not be useful; when, after humming and hawing for a moment, and being unable, upon the spur of the occasion, to suggest anything else, the man of pharmacy observed, that it would, at all events, relieve the brain or cerebrum, in case there was a tendency to the deposition of any extravasated blood, to operate as a pressure upon that delicate organ. Fortunately he was adequate to performing this operation; and being powerfully aided by Jenkin Vincent, (who was learned in all cases of broken head,) with plenty of cold water, and a little vinegar, applied according to the scientific method practised by the bottle-holders in a modern ring, the man began to raise himself in his chair, draw his cloak tightly around him, and look about like one who struggles to recover sense and recollection.

"He had better lie down on the bed in the little back closet," said Mr Ramsay's visitor, who seemed perfectly familiar with the accommodations which the house afforded.

"He is welcome to my share of the truckle," said Jenkin,—for in the said back closet were the two apprentices accommodated in one truckle-bed,—"I can sleep under the counter."

"So can I," said Tunstall, "and the poor fellow can have the bed all night."

"Sleep," said the apothecary, "is, in the opinion of Galen, a restorative and febrifuge, and is most naturally taken in a truckle-bed."

"Where a better cannot be come by—" said Master George; "but these are two honest lads, to give up their bed so willingly. Come, off with his cloak, and let us bear him to his couch. I will send for Dr Irving the king's chirurgeon—he does not live far off, and that shall be my share of the Samaritan's duty, neighbour Ramsay."

"Well, sir," said the apothecary, "it is at your pleasure to send for other advice, and I shall not object to consult with Dr Irving or any other medical person of skill, neither to continue to furnish such drugs as may be needful from my pharmacopeia. However, whatever Dr Irving, who, I think, hath had his degrees in Edinburgh, or Dr Any-one-beside, be he Scottish or English, may say to the contrary, sleep, taken timeously, is a febrifuge or sedative, and also a restorative."

He muttered a few more learned words, and concluded by informing Ramsay's friend in English far more intelligible than his Latin, that he would look to him as his paymaster, for medicines, care, and attendance, furnished, or to be furnished, to this party unknown.

Master George only replied by desiring him to send his bill for what he had already to charge, and to give himself no farther trouble unless he heard from him. The pharmacopolist, who, from discoveries made by the cloak falling a little aside, had no great opinion of the faculty of this chance patient to make reimbursement, had no sooner seen his case espoused by a substantial citizen, than he shewed some reluctance to quit possession of the case, and it required a short and stern hint from Master George, which, with all his good humour, he was capable of expressing when occasion served, to send to his own dwelling this Esculapius of Temple Bar.

When they were rid of Mr Raredrench, the charitable efforts of Jenkin and Francis, to divest the patient of his long grey cloak, were firmly resisted on his own part.—"My life suner—my life suner," he muttered in indistinct murmurs. In these efforts to retain his upper garment, which was too tender to undergo much handling, it gave way at length with a loud rent, which almost threw the patient into a second syncope, and he sate before them in his under garments, the looped and repaired wretchedness of which moved at once pity and laughter, and had certainly been the cause of his unwillingness to resign the mantle, which, like the virtue of charity, served to cover so many imperfections.

The man himself cast his eyes on his poverty-struck garb, and seemed so much ashamed of the disclosure, that, muttering between his teeth, that he would be too late for an appointment, he made an effort to rise and leave the shop, which was easily prevented by Jenkin Vincent and his comrade, who, at the nod of Master George, laid hold of and detained him in his chair. The patient next looked round him a moment, and then said faintly in his broad northern language —"What sort of usage ca' ye this, gentlemen, to a stranger and a sojourner in your town? Ye hae broken my head—ye hae riven my cloak, and now ye are for restraining my personal liberty! They were

wiser than me," he said, after a moment's pause, "that counselled me
to wear my warst claithing in the streets of London; and if I could have
got any things worse than these mean garments,"—("Which would
have been very difficult," said Jin Vin, in a whisper to his companion,)
"they would have been e'en ower guid for the grips o' men sae little
acquented with the laws of honest civility."

"To say the truth," said Jenkin, unable to forbear any longer,
although the discipline of the times prescribed to those in his situation
a degree of respectful distance and humility in the presence of parents, masters, or seniors, of which the present age has no idea—"To
say truth, the good gentleman's clothes look as if they would not brook
much handling."

"Hold your peace, young man," said Master George, with a tone of
authority; "never mock the stranger, or the poor—the black ox has not
trode on your foot yet—you know not what lands you may travel in, or
what clothes you may wear, before you die."

Vincent held down his head and stood rebuked, but the stranger did
not accept the apology which was made for him.

"I *am* a stranger, sir," said he, "that is certain; though methinks,
that being such, I have been somewhat familiarly treated in this town
of yours;—but as for being poor, I think I need not be obraided with
poverty, till I beg siller of somebody."

"The dear country all over," said Master George in a whisper to
David Ramsay, "pride and poverty."

But David had taken out his tablets and silver pen, and, deeply
immersed in calculations, in which he rambled over all the terms of
arithmetic, from the simple unit to millions, billions, and trillions,
neither heard nor answered the observation of his friend, who, seeing
his abstraction, turned again to the Scot.

"I fancy now, Jockey, if a stranger were to offer you a noble, you
would chuck it back at his head?"

"Not if I could do him honest service for it, sir," said the Scot; "I am
willing to do what I may to be useful, though I come of an honourable
house, and may be said to be in a sort indifferently weel provided for."

"Ay!" said the interrogator, "and what house may claim the honour
of your descent?"

"An ancient coat belongs to it, as the play says," whispered Vincent
to his companion.

"Come, Jockey, out with it," continued Master George, observing
that the Scot, as usual with his countrymen, when asked a blunt,
straight-forward question, took a little time before answering it.

"I am no more Jockey than you, sir, are John," said the stranger, as if
offended at being addressed by a name, which at that time was used, as

Sawney now is, for a general appellative of the Scottish nation. "My name, if you must know it, is Richie Moniplies; and I come of the old and honourable house of Castle Collop, weel kenn'd at the West Port of Edinburgh."

"What is that you call the West Port?" proceeded the interrogator.

"Why, an it like your honour," said Richie, who now having recovered his senses sufficiently to observe the respectable exterior of Master George, threw more civility into his manner than at first, "the West Port is a gate of our city, as yonder brick arches at Whitehall form the entrance to the King's palace here, only that the West Port is of stonern work, and mair decorated with architecture and the policy of bigging."

"Nouns, man, the Whitehall gateways were planned by the great Holbein," answered Master George, "I suspect your accident has jumbled your brains, my good friend. I suppose you will tell me next, you have at Edinburgh as fine a navigable river as the Thames, with all its shipping."

"The Thames!" exclaimed Richie, in a tone of ineffable contempt —"God bless your honour's judgment, we have at Edinburgh the Water-of-Leith and the Nor-Loch!"

"And the Pow-Burn, and the Quarry-holes, and the Gusedub, fause loun," answered Master George, speaking Scotch with a strong and natural emphasis; "it is such land-loupers as you that, with your falset and fair fashions, bring reproach on our whole country."

"God forgie me, sir," said Richie, much surprised at finding the supposed Southron converted into a native Scot, "I took your honour for an Englisher! But I hope there was naething wrang in standing up for ane's ain country's credit in a strange land, where all men cry her down."

"Do you call it for your country's credit, to shew that she has a lying puffing rascal for one of her children?" said Master George. "But come, man, never look grave on it,—as you have found a countryman, so you have found a friend if you deserve one—and specially if you answer me truly."

"I see nae gude it wad do to speak ought else but truth," said the worthy North Briton.

"Well then—to begin," said Master George, "I suspect you are a son of old Mungo Moniplies, the flesher, at the West-Port."

"Your honour is a witch, I think," said Richie, grinning.

"And how dared you, sir, to uphold him for a noble?"

"I dinna ken, sir," said Richie, scratching his head; "I hear mickle of an Earl of Warwick in these South parts,—Guy I think his name was,—and he has great reputation here for slaying dun cows, and boars, and such like; and I am sure my father has killed mair cows and boars, not to mention bulls, calves, sheep, ewes, lambs, and pigs, than the hail Baronage of England."

"Go to! you are a shrewd knave," said Master George; "charm your tongue, and take care of saucy answers. Your father was an honest burgher, and the deacon of his craft: I am sorry to see his son in so poor a coat."

"Indifferent, sir," said Richie Moniplies, looking down on his garments—"very indifferent; but it is the wonted livery of poor burghers' sons in our country—one of Luckie Want's bestowing upon us—rest us patient. The King's leaving Scotland has taken all custom frae Edinburgh; and there is hay made at the Cross, and a dainty crop of fouats in the Grass-market. There is as much grass grows where my father's stall stood, as might have been a good bite for the beasts he was used to kill."

"It is even too true," said Master George; "and while we make fortunes here, our old neighbours and their families are starving at home. This should be thought upon oftener.—And how came you by that broken head, Richie?—tell me honestly."

"Troth, sir, I'se no lee about the matter," answered Moniplies. "I was coming alang the street here, and ilk ane was at me with their jests and roguery. So I thought to mysell, ye are ower mony for me to mell with; but let me catch ye in Barford's Park, or at the fit of the Vennel, I could gar some of ye sing another sang. Sae ae auld hirpling deevil of a potter behoved just to step in my way and offer me a pig, as he said, to put my Scotch ointment in, and I gave him a push, as but natural, and the tottering deevil couped ower amang his ain pigs, and damaged a score of them. And then the reird raise, and hadna thae twa gentlemen helped me out of it, murdered I suld hae been, without remeid. And as it was, just when they got had of my arm to have me out of the fray, I got the lick that donnerit me from a left-handed lighter-man."

Master George looked to the apprentices as if to demand the truth of this story.

"It is just as he says, sir," replied Jenkin; "only I heard nothing about pigs—the people said he had broke some crockery, and that—I beg pardon, sir—nobody could thrive within the kenning of a Scot."

"Well, no matter what they said, you were honest fellows to help the weaker side—And you, sirrah," continued Master George, addressing his countryman, "will call at my house to-morrow morning, agreeable to this direction."

"I will wait upon your honour," said the Scot, bowing very low; "that is, if my honourable master will permit me."

"Thy master?" said George,—"Hast thou any other master save

Want, whose livery you say you wear?"

"Troth, in one sense, if please your honour, I serve twa masters," said Richie; "for both my master and me are slaves to that same beldame, whom we thought to shew our heels to by coming off from Scotland. So that you see, sir, I hold in a sort of black-ward tenure, as we call it in our country, being the servant of a servant."

"And what is your master's name?" said George; and observing that Richie hesitated, he added, "Nay, do not tell me, if it is a secret."

"A secret that there is little use in keeping," said Richie; "only ye ken that our northern stomachs are ower proud to call in witnesses to our distress. No that my master is in mair than present pinch, sir," he added, looking towards the two English apprentices, "having a large sum in the Royal Treasury—that is," he continued, in a whisper to Master George,—"the King is owing him a lot of siller; but it's ill getting at it it's like.—My master is the young Lord Glenvarloch."

Master George testified surprise at the name.—"You one of the young Lord Glenvarloch's followers, and in such a condition!"

"Troth, and I am all the followers he has, for the present that is; and blithe wad I be if he were muckle better aff than I am, though I were to bide as I am."

"I have seen his father with four gentlemen and ten lackeys at his heels," said Master George, "rustling in their laces and velvets—well —this is a changeful world, but there is a better beyond it.—The good old House of Glenvarloch, that stood by king and country five hundred years!"

"Your honour may say a thousand," said the follower.

"I will say what I know to be true, friend," said the citizen, "and not a word more.—You seem well recovered now—Can you walk?"

"Bravely, sir," said Richie; "it was but a bit dover. I was bred at the West Port, and my cantle will stand a clour wad bring a stot down."

"Where does your master lodge?"

"We pit up, an it like your honour," replied the Scot, "in a sma' house at the fit of ane of the wynds that ging down to the waterside, with a decent man, John Christie—his father came from Dundee— he is a ship-chandler, as they ca'd. I wotna the name of the wynd, but it's right anent the mickle kirk yonder; and your honour will mind that we pass only by our family-name of simple Mr Nigel Olifaunt, as keeping ourselves retired for the present, though in Scotland we be called the Lord Nigel."

"It is wisely done of your master," said the citizen. "I will find out your lodgings, though your direction be none of the clearest." So saying, and slipping a piece of money at the same time into Richie Moniplies's hand, he bid him hasten home, and get into no more affrays.

"I will take care of that now, sir," said Richie, with a look of import-ance, "having a charge about me. And so, wussing ye a' weel, with special thanks to these twa young gentlemen"——

"I am no gentleman," said Jenkin, flinging his cap on his head.—"I am a tight London 'prentice, and hope to be a freeman one day. Frank may write himself gentleman, if he will."

"I *was* a gentleman once," said Tunstall, "and I hope I have done nothing to lose the name of one."

"Weel, weel, as ye list," said Richie Moniplies; "but I am muckle behalden to ye baith—and I am not a hair the less like to bear it in mind that I say but little about it just now.—Gude night to you, my kind countryman." So saying, he thrust out of the sleeve of his ragged doublet a long bony hand and arm, on which the muscles rose like whip-cord.

Master George shook it heartily, while Jenkin and Frank exchanged sly looks with each other. Richie Moniplies would next have addressed his thanks to the master of the shop, but seeing him, as he afterwards said, "scribbling in his bit bookie as if he were demented," he contented his politeness with "giving him a hat," and so left the shop.

"Now there goes Scotch Jockey, with all his bad and good about him," said Master George to Master David, who suspended, though unwillingly, the calculations with which he was engaged, and, keeping his pen within an inch of the tablets, gazed on his friend with great lack-lustre eyes, which expressed any thing rather than intelligence or interest in the discourse addressed to him. "That fellow," proceeded Master George, without heeding his friend's state of abstraction, "shews, with great liveliness of colouring, how our Scotch pride and poverty makes liars and braggarts of us; and yet the knave, whose every third word to an Englishman is a boastful lie, will, I warrant you, be a true and tender friend and follower to his master, and has perhaps parted with his mantle to him in the cold blast, although he walked himself *in cuerpo*, as the Don says. Strange, that Courage and Fidelity —for I will warrant that the knave is stout—should have no better companions than this vain swaggering braggadochio humour. But you mark me not, friend Davie."

"I do—I do, most heedfully," said Davie; "for as the sun goeth round the dial-plate in twenty-four hours—add for the moon fifty minutes and a half"——

"You are in the seventh heavens, man," said his companion.

"I crave your pardon," replied Davie; "let the wheel A go round in twenty-four hours—I have it—and the wheel B in twenty-four hours, fifty minutes and a half—fifty-seven being to fifty-four—as fifty-nine to twenty-four hours fifty minutes and a half—or very nearly,—I crave your forgiveness, Master George, and heartily wish you good-even."

"Good-even?" said Master George; "why, you have not wished me good-day yet. Come, old friend, lay by these tablets, or you will crack the inner machinery of *your* skull, as our friend yonder has got the outer case of his damaged.—Good-night, quotha! I mean not to part with you so easily; I came to get my four-hour's nuncheon from you, man, besides a tune on the lute from my god-daughter, Mrs Marget."

"Good faith! I was oblivious, Master George—but you know me—When once I get amongst the wheels,"—said Mr Ramsay, "why"——

"Lucky that you deal in small ones," said his friend, as, awakened from his reveries and calculations, Ramsay led the way up a little back-stair to the first story, occupied by his daughter and his little household.

The apprentices resumed their places in the front shop, and relieved Sam Porter, when Jenkin said to Tunstall—"Didst see, Frank, how the old goldsmith cottoned in with his beggarly country-man? when would one of his having have shaken hands so courteously with a poor Englishman? Well, I'll say that for the best of the Scots, that they will go over head and ears to serve a countryman, when they will not wet a nail of their finger to save a Southron, as they call us, from drowning. And yet Master George is but half-bred Scot neither in that respect; for I have known him do many a kind thing to the English too."

"But hark ye, Jenkin," said Tunstall, "I think you are but half-bred English yourself;—how came you to strike on the Scotsman's side after all?"

"Why, you did so too," answered Vincent.

"Ay, because I saw you begin; and, besides, it is no Cumberland fashion to fall fifty upon one," replied Tunstall.

"And no Christ-Church fashion neither," said Jenkin. "Fair play and old England for ever. Besides, to tell you a secret, his voice had a tang in it—in the dialect I mean—reminded me of a little tongue which I think sweeter—sweeter—than the last toll of Dunstan's will sound, on the day that I am shot of my indentures—ha!—you guess who I mean, Frank?"

"Not I, indeed," answered Tunstall. "Scotch Janet, I suppose, the laundress."

"Off with Janet in her own bucking basket!—no, no—no!—you blind buzzard,—do you not know I mean pretty Mrs Marget!"

"Umph!" answered Tunstall, drily.

A flash of anger, not unmingled with suspicion, shot from Jenkin's keen black eyes.

"Umph!—and what signifies Umph? I am not the first 'prentice has married his master's daughter, I think."

"They kept their own secret, I fancy," said Tunstall, "at least till they were out of their time."

"I tell you what it is, Frank," answered Jenkin, sharply; "that may be the fashion of you gentle-folks that are taught from your biggen to carry two faces under the same hood, but it shall never be mine."

"There are the stairs then," said Tunstall, coolly; "go up and ask Mrs Marget of our master just now, and see what sort of a face he will wear under *his* hood."

"No, I wonnot," answered Jenkin; "I am not such a fool as that neither; but I will take my own time, and all the Counts in Cumberland shall not cut my comb, and this is that which you may depend upon."

Francis made no reply; and they resumed their usual attention to the business of the shop, and their usual solicitations to the passengers.

Chapter Three

Bobadil. I pray you possess no gallant of our
acquaintance with the knowledge of my lodging.
Master Matthew. Who, I, sir?—Lord, sir!
BEN JONSON

THE NEXT MORNING found Nigel Olifaunt, the young Lord of Glenvarloch, seated, sad and solitary, in his little apartment in the mansion of John Christie, the ship-chandler, which that honest tradesman, in gratitude perhaps to the profession from which he derived his chief support, seemed to have constructed as nearly as possible upon the plan of a ship's cabin.

It was situated near to Paul's Wharf, at the end of one of those intricate and narrow lanes, which, until that part of the city was swept away by the great fire in 1666, constituted an extraordinary labyrinth of small, dark, damp, and unwholesome streets and alleys, in one corner or other of which the plague was then as surely found lurking, as in the obscure corners of Constantinople in our own time. But John Christie's house looked out upon the river, and had the advantage, therefore, of free air,—impregnated, however, with the odoriferous fumes of the articles in which the ship-chandler dealt, with the odour of pitch, and the natural scent of the ouze and slush left by the reflux of the tide.

Upon the whole, except that his dwelling did not float with the flood-tide, and become stranded with the ebb, the young lord was nearly as comfortably accommodated as he was while on board of the little trading brig from the Long Town of Kirkcaldy, in Fife, by which he had come a passenger to London. He received, however, every attention which could be paid him by his honest landlord, John Christie; for Richie Moniplies had not thought it necessary to preserve his master's *incognito* so completely, but what the honest ship-chandler could form a guess that his guest's quality was superior to his appearance. As for Dame Nell, his wife, a round, buxom, laughter-loving dame, with black eyes, a tight well-laced boddice, a green apron, and a red petticoat edged with a slight silver lace, and judiciously shortened so as to shew that a short heel and tight clean ancle rested upon her well-burnished shoe,—she, of course, felt interest in a young man, who, besides being very handsome, good-humoured, and easily satisfied with the accommodations her house afforded, was evidently of a rank, as well as manners, highly superior to the skippers, (or Captains, as they called themselves,) of merchant vessels, who were the usual tenants of the apartment which she let to hire; and at whose departure she was sure to find her well-scrubbed floor soiled with the relics of tobacco, (which, spite of King James's Counterblast, was then forcing itself into use,) and the bed-curtains impregnated with the odour of Geneva and strong waters, to Dame Nelly's great indignation; for, as she truly said, the smell of the shop and warehouse was bad enough without these additions.

But all Mr Olifaunt's habits were regular and cleanly, and his address, though frank and simple, shewed so much of the courtier and gentleman, as formed a strong contrast with the loud halloo, coarse jests, and boisterous impatience, of her maritime inmates. Dame Nelly saw that her guest was melancholy also, notwithstanding his efforts to seem contented and cheerful; and in short she took that sort of interest in him, without being herself aware of its extent, which an unscrupulous gallant might have been tempted to improve to the prejudice of honest John, who was at least a score of years older than his helpmate. Olifaunt, however, had not only other matters to think of, but would have regarded such an intrigue, had the idea ever occurred to him, as an abominable and ungrateful encroachment upon the laws of hospitality, his religion having been by his late father formed upon the strict principles of the national faith, and his morality upon those of the nicest honour. He had not escaped the predominant weakness of his country, an overweening sense of the pride of birth, and a disposition to value the worth and consequence of others according to the number and the fame of their deceased ancestors; but this pride of family was well subdued, and in general almost entirely concealed, by his good sense and general courtesy.

Such as we have described him, Nigel Olifaunt, or rather the young Lord Glenvarloch, was, when our narrative takes him up, under great perplexity respecting the fate of his trusty and only follower. Richard Moniplies had been dispatched by his young master, early in the preceding morning, as far as the court at Westminster, but had not yet returned. His evening adventures the reader is already acquainted with, and so far knows more of Richie than did his master, who had not heard of him for twenty-four hours. Dame Nelly Christie, in the meantime, regarded her guest with some anxiety, and a great desire to comfort him if possible. She placed on the breakfast-table a noble piece of cold powdered beef, with its usual guards of turnip and carrot, recommended her mustard as coming direct from her cousin at Tewksbury, made and spiced the toast with her own hands—and with her own hands, also, drew a jug of stout and nappy ale, all of which were elements of the substantial breakfast of the period.

When she saw that her guest's anxiety prevented him from doing justice to the good cheer which she set before him, she commenced her career of verbal consolation with the usual volubility of those women in her station, who, conscious of good looks, good intentions, and good lungs, entertain no fear either of wearying themselves or of fatiguing their auditor.

"Now, what the good year, sir! are we to send you down to Scotland as thin as you came up?—I am sure it would be contrary to the course of nature. There was my good man's father, old Sandie Christie, I have heard he was an atomy when he came up from the North, and I am sure he died, Saint Barnaby was ten years, at twenty stone weight —I was a bare-headed girl at the time and lived in the neighbourhood, though I had little thought of marrying John then, who had a score of years the better of me—but he is a thriving man and a kind husband— and his father, as I was saying, died as fat as a churchwarden. Well, sir, but I hope I have not offended you for my little joke—and I hope the ale is to your honour's liking,—and the beef—and the mustard?"

"All excellent—all too good," answered Olifaunt; "you have every thing so clean and tidy, dame, that I shall not know how to live when I go back to my own country—if ever I go back there."

This was added as it seemed involuntarily, and with a deep sigh.

"I warrant your honour go back again if you like it," said the dame; "unless you think rather of taking a pretty, well-dowered English lady, as some of your country-folks have done. I assure you, some of the best of the city have married Scotsmen. There was Lady Treble-plumb, Sir Thomas Trebleplumb the great Turkey merchant's widow, married Sir Awley Macauley, whom your honour knows, doubtless; and pretty Mistress Doublefee, old Serjeant Doublefee's daughter, jumped out of window, and was married at May-fair to a Scotsman with a hard name; and old Pitchpost the timber-merchant's daughters did little better, for they married two Irishmen; and when folks jeer me about my having a Scotchman for lodger, meaning your honour, I tell them they are afraid of their daughters and their mistresses; and sure I have a right to stand for the Scotch, since John Christie is half a Scotchman, and a thriving man, and a good husband, though there is a score of years between us; and so I would have your honour cast care away, and mend your breakfast with a morsel and a draught."

"At a word, my kind hostess, I cannot," said Olifaunt; "I am anxious about this knave of mine, who has been so long absent in this dangerous town of yours."

It may be noticed in passing, that Dame Nelly's ordinary mode of consolation was to disprove the existence of any cause for distress; and she is said to have carried this so far as to comfort a neighbour, who had lost her husband, with the assurance that the dear defunct would be better to-morrow, which perhaps might not exactly have proved an appropriate, even if it had been a possible, mode of relief. On this occasion she denied stoutly that Richie had been absent altogether twenty hours; and by dint of minute calculation showed it wanted nearly half an hour of that span—then as for people being killed in the streets of London, to be sure two men had been found in Tower-ditch last week, but that was far to the east, and the other poor man that had his throat cut in the fields, had met his mishap near by Islington; and he that was stabbed by the young Templar in a drunken frolic, by Saint Clement's in the Strand, was an Irishman. All which evidence she produced to shew that none of these casualties had occurred in a case exactly parallel with that of Richie, a Scotsman and on his return from Westminster.

"My better comfort is, my good dame," answered Olifaunt, "that the lad is no brawler or quarreller, unless strongly urged, and that he has no charge about him excepting papers of some moment."

"Your honour speaks very well," retorted the inexhaustible hostess, who protracted her task of taking away, and putting to rights, in order that she might prolong her gossip. "I'll uphold Master Moniplies to be neither reveller nor brawler, for if he liked such things he might be visiting and junketting with the young folks about here in the neighbourhood, and he never dreams of it; and when I asked the young man to go as far as my gossip's, Dame Drinkwater, to taste a glass of anniseed, and a bit of the groaning cheese,—for Dame Drinkwater has had twins, as I told your honour, sir—and I meant it quite civilly to the young man, but he chose to sit and keep house with John Christie;

and I dare say there is a score of years between them, for your honour's servant looks scarce much older than I am. I wonder what they
could have to say to each other. I asked John Christie, but he bid me go
to sleep."

"If he comes not soon," said his master, "I will thank you to tell me
what magistrate I can address myself to; for, besides my anxiety for
the poor fellow's safety, he has papers of importance about him."

"O! your honour may be assured he will be back in a quarter of an
hour," said Dame Nelly; "he is not the lad to stay out twenty-four
hours at a stretch. And for the papers, I am sure your honour will
pardon him for just giving me a peep at the corner, as I was giving him
a small cup, not so large as my thimble, of distilled waters, to fortify his
stomach against the damps—And it was directed to the King's Most
Excellent Majesty; and so doubtless his Majesty has kept Richie out of
civility to consider your honour's letter, and send back a fitting reply."

Dame Nelly here hit by chance on a more available topic of consolation than those she had hitherto touched upon; for the youthful lord
had himself some vague hopes that his messenger might have been
delayed at Court until a fitting and favourable answer should be dispatched back to him. Inexperienced, however, in public affairs as he
certainly was, it required only a moment's consideration to convince
him of the improbability of an expectation so contrary to all he had
heard of the etiquette, as well as the dilatory proceeding in a court-
suit, and he answered the good-natured hostess with a sigh, that he
doubted whether the King would even look on the paper addressed to
him, far less take it into his immediate consideration.

"Now, out upon you for a faint-hearted gentleman," said the good
dame; "and why should he not do as much for us as our gracious
Queen Elizabeth? Many people say this and that about a queen and a
king, but I always think a king comes more natural to us English
folks; and this good gentleman goes as often down by water to Greenwich, and employs as many of the barge-men and water-men of all
kinds; and maintains, in his royal grace, John Taylor the water-poet,
who keeps both a sculler and a pair of oars. And he has made a
comely Court at Whitehall, just by the river; and since the King is so
good a friend to the Thames, I cannot see, if it please your honour,
why all his subjects, and your honour in specialty, should not have
satisfaction by his hands."

"True, dame, true—let us hope for the best; but I must take my
cloak and rapier, and pray your husband of courtesy to teach me the
way to a magistrate."

"Sure, sir," said the prompt dame, "I can do that as well as he, who
has been a slow man of his tongue all his life, though I will give him his

due for being a loving husband, and a man as well to pass in the world as any betwixt us and the top of the lane. And so there is the sitting alderman, that is always at the Guildhall, which is close by Paul's, and so I warrant you he puts all to rights in the city that wisdom can mend; and for the rest there is no help but patience. But I wish I were as sure of forty pounds, as I am that the young man will come back safe and sound."

Olifaunt, in great and anxious doubt of what the good dame so strongly averred, had already flung his cloak on one shoulder, and was about to belt on his rapier, when first the voice of Richie Moniplies on the stair, and then that faithful emissary's appearance in the chamber, put the matter beyond question. Dame Nelly, after congratulating Moniplies on his return, and paying several compliments to her own sagacity for having foretold it, was at length pleased to leave the apartment. The truth was, that, besides some instinctive feelings of good breeding which combated her curiosity, she saw there was no chance of Richie's proceeding in his narrative while she was in the room, and she therefore retreated, trusting that her own address would get the secret out of one or other of the young men, when she should have either by himself.

"Now, in Heaven's name, what is the matter?" said Nigel Olifaunt. —"Where have you been, or what have you been about? You look as pale as death—there is blood on your band, and your clothes are torn. What barns-breaking have you been at? You have been drunk, Richard, and fighting."

"Fighting I have been," said Richard, "in a small way; but for being drunk, that's a job ill to manage in this town, without money to come by liquor; and as for barns-breaking, the de'il a thing's broken but my head. It's no made of iron, I wot, nor my claithes of chenzie-mail; so a club smashed the tane, and a claucht damaged the tither. Some mis-leard rascals abused my country, but I think I cleared the causey of them. However, the haill hive was ower mony for me at last, and I got this cleepie on the crown, and then I was carried, beyond my kenning, to a sma' booth at the Temple Port, whare they sell the whirly-gigs and mony-go-rounds that measure out time as a man wald measure a tartan web; and then they bled me, wold I nold I, and were reasonably civil, especially an auld countryman of ours, of whom more hereafter."

"And what o'clock might this be?" said Nigel.

"The twa iron carles yonder, at the kirk beside the Port, were just banging out sax o' the clock."

"And why came ye not home so soon as you recovered?" said Nigel.

"In troth, my lord, every *why* has its *wherefore*, and this has a gude ane," answered his follower. "To come hame, I behoved to ken whare

hame was; now, I had clean tint the name of the wynd, and the mair I
asked, the mair the folk leugh, and the farther they sent me wrang; sae
I gave it up till God should send daylight to help me, and as I saw
mysell near a kirk at the lang run, I e'en crap in to take up my night's
quarters in the kirk-yard."

"In the church-yard?" said Nigel; "but I need not ask what drove
you to such a pinch."

"It wasna sae much the want o' siller, my Lord Nigel," said Richie,
with an air of mysterious importance, "for I was no sae absolute
without means, of whilk mair anon. But I thought I wad never ware a
saxpence sterling on ane of their saucy chamberlains at a hostelry, sae
lang as I could sleep fresh and fine in a fair, dry, spring night. Mony a
time whan I hae come hame ower, and fand the West Port steekit, and
the waiter ill-willy, I have garr'd the sexton of Saint Cuthbert's calf-
ward serve me for my quarters. But then there are dainty green graffs
in Saint Cuthbert's kirk-yard, whare ane may sleep as if they were in a
down-bed, till they hear the lavrock singing up in the air as high as the
Castle; whereas, and behold, these London kirk-yards are causeyed
with through-stanes, panged hard and fast thegither; and my cloak
being something thread-bare, made but a thin mattress, so I was fain
to give up my bed before every limb about me was crippled. Dead folks
may sleep yonder sound enow, but de'il haet else."

"And what became of you next?" said his master.

"I just took to a canny bulk-head, as they ca' them here; that is, the
boards on the tap of their bits of outshots of stalls and booths, and
there I sleeped as sound as if I was in a castle. Not but I was disturbed
with some of the night-walking queans and billies, but when they
found there was nothing to be got by me but a slash of my Andrew
Ferrara, they bid me good-night for a beggarly Scot; and I was e'en
weel pleased to be sae cheap rid of them. And in the morning, I cam
daikering here, but auld wark I had to find the way, for I had been east
as far as a place they ca' Mile-End, though it is mair like sax-mile-
end."

"Well, Richie," answered Nigel, "I am glad all this has ended so
well—Go get something to eat—I am sure you need it."

"In troth do I, sir," replied Moniplies; "but, with your lordship's
leave"——

"Forget the lordship for the present, Richie, as I have often told you
before."

"Faith," replied Richie, "I could weel forget that your honour was a
lord, but then I behuved to forget that I am a lord's man, and that's not
so easy. But, however," he added, assisting his description with the
thumb and the two fore-fingers of his right hand, thrust out after the

fashion of a bird's-claw, while the little finger and ring-finger were closed upon the palms, "however to the Court I went—And my friend that promised me a sight of his Majesty's most gracious presence, was as gude as his word, and carried me into the back offices, where I got the best breakfast I have had since we came here, and it did me gude for the rest of the day; for as to what I have eaten in this accursed town, it is aye sauced with the disquieting thought that it maun be paid for. After a', there was but beef-banes and fat brose; but king's cauff, your honour kens, is better than ither folk's corn; at ony rate, it was aw in free awmous. But I see," he added, stopping short, "that your honour waxes impatient."

"By no means, Richie," said the young nobleman, with an air of resignation, for he well knew his domestic would not mend his pace for goading; "you have suffered enough in the embassy to have got the right to tell the story in your own way. Only let me pray for the name of the friend who was to introduce you into the King's presence. You were very mysterious on the subject, when you undertook, through his means, to have the Supplication put into his Majesty's own hands, since those sent heretofore, I have every reason to think, went no further than his secretary's."

"Weel, my lord," said Richie, "I did not tell you his name and quality at first, because I thought you would be affronted at the like of him having to do in your lordship's affairs. But mony a man climbs up in Court by waur help. It was just Laurie Linklater, one of the yeomen of the kitchen, that was my father's apprentice lang syne."

"A yeoman of the kitchen—a scullion!" exclaimed Lord Nigel, pacing the room in displeasure.

"But consider, sir," said Richie, composedly, "that a' your great friends hung back, and shunned to own you, or to advocate your petition; and then, though I am sure I wish Laurie a higher office, for your lordship's sake and for mine, and specially for his ain sake, being a friendly lad, yet your lordship maun consider, that a scullion, if a yeoman of the King's maist royal kitchen may be called scullion, may weel rank with a master-cook elsewhere; being that king's cauff, as I said before, is better than"——

"You are right, and I was wrong," said the young nobleman. "I have no choice of means of making my case known, so that they be honest."

"Laurie is as honest a lad as ever lifted a ladle," said Richie; "not but what I dare to say he can lick his fingers like other folks, and reason good. But in fine, for I see your honour is waxing impatient, he brought me to the palace, where a' was astir for the King going out to hunt or hawk on Blackheath, I think they ca'd it. And there was a horse stood with all the quarries about it, a bonny grey as ever was foaled;

and the saddle and the stirrups, and the curb and bit, a' burning gowd,
or silver gilded at least; and down he came, with all his nobles, dressed
out in his hunting-suit of green, doubly laced, and laid down with
gowd. I minded the very face o' him, though it was lang since I saw
him. But, my certie lad, thought I, times are changed wi' you since ye
came fleeing down the back-stairs of auld Holyrood-House, in grit
fear, having your breeks in your hand without time to put them on, and
Frank Stuart, the wild Earl of Bothwell, hard at your hanches; and if
auld Lord Glenvarloch hadna cast his mantle about his arm, and taken
bluidy wounds mair than ane in your behalf, you wald not have craw'd
sae crouse the day; and so saying, I could not but think your lordship's
Sifflication could not be less than most acceptable; and so I banged in
among the crowd of lords. Laurie thought me mad, and held me by the
cloak-lap till the cloth rave in his hand; and so I banged in right before
the King just as he mounted, and cram'd the Sifflication into his hand,
and he open'd it like in amaze; and just as he saw the first line, I was
minded to make a reverence, and I had the ill luck to hit his jaud o' a
beast on the nose with my hat, and scaur the creature, and she swarved
aside, and the King, that sits na mickle better than a draff-pock on the
saddle, was like to have gotten a clean coup, and that might have cost
my craig a raxing—and he flung down the paper amang the beast's
feet, and cried, Away wi' the fause loon that brought it. And they
grippit me, and cried Treason; and I thought of the Ruthvens that
were dirked in their ain house, for it may be as small a forfeit. However, they spak only of scourging me, and had me away to the porter's
lodge to try the tawse on my back, and I was crying mercy as loud as I
could; and the King, when he had righted himsell in the saddle, and
gathered his breath, cried to do me nae harm; for, said he, he is ane of
our ain Norland stots, I ken by the rowt of him,—and they a' laughed
and rowted loud eneugh. And then he said, Gie him a copy of the
Proclamation, and let him go down to the North by the next light
collier, before waur come on't. So they let me go, and rode out aw
sniggering, laughing, and rounding in ilk ithers lugs. A sair life I had
wi' Laurie Linklater; for he said it wad be the ruin of him. And then,
when I told him it was in your matter, he said if he had known before
he would have risked a scauding for you, because he minded the brave
old Lord, your father. And then he shewed me how I suld have done,
—and that I suld have held up my hand to my brow, as if the grandeur
of the King and his horse-graith thegither had casten the glaiks in my
een, and mair jack-an-ape tricks I suld hae played, instead of offering
the Sifflication as if I was bringing guts to a bear. 'For,' said he,
'Richie, the King is a weel-natured and just man of his ain kindly
nature, but he has a whin maggots that maun be cannily guided; and

then, Richie,' says he, in a very laigh tone, 'I would tell it to nane but a wise man like yoursell, but the King has them about him wad corrupt an angel from heaven; but I could have gi'en you avisement how to have guided him, but now it's like after meat mustard.'—'Aweel, aweel, Laurie,' said I, 'it may be as you say; but since I am clear of the tawse and the porter's lodge, sifflicate wha like, de'il hae Richie Moniplies if he come sifflicating here again.'—And so away I came, and I wasna far by the Temple Port, or Bar, or whatever they ca' it, when I met with the misadventure that I tauld you of before."

"Well, my honest Richie," said Lord Nigel, "your attempt was well meant, and not so ill conducted, I think, as to have deserved so bad an issue; but go to your beef and mustard, and we'll talk of the rest afterward."

"There is nae mair to be spoken, sir," said his follower, "except it be that I met ane very honest, fair-spoken, weel put-on gentleman, or rather burgher, as I think, that was in the whigmaleery man's back-shop, and when he learned wha I was, behold he was a Scot himsell, and what is more, a town's-bairn o' the gude-town, and he behoved to compel me to take this Portugal piece, to drink, forsooth—my certie, thought I, we ken better, for we will eat it—and he spoke of paying your lordship a visit."

"You did not tell him where I lived, you knave?" said the Lord Nigel angrily. "'Sdeath, I shall have every gutter-blood from Edinburgh come to gaze on my distress, and pay a shilling for having seen the Motion of the Poor Noble."

"Tell him where you lived?" said Richie, evading the question, "How could I tell him what I kenn'd na mysell? If I had minded the name of the wynd, I need not have slept in the kirk-yard yestreen."

"See then that you give no one notice of our lodging," said the young nobleman; "those with whom I have business I can meet at Paul's, or in the Court of Requests."

"This is steeking the stable-door when the steed is stolen," thought Richie to himself; "but I must put him on another pin."

So thinking, he asked the young lord what was in the Proclamation which he still held folded in his hand; "for, having little time to spell at it," said he, "your lordship well knows I ken nought about it but the grand blazon with the lion and unicorn at the tap—the lion has gotten a claught of our auld Scottish shield now, but it was as weel upheld when it had an unicorn on ilk side of it."

Lord Nigel read the Proclamation, and he coloured deep with shame and indignation as he read; for the purport was, to his injured feelings, like the pouring of ardent spirits upon a recent wound.

"What deil's in the paper, my lord?" said Richie, unable to suppress his curiosity as he observed his master change colour, "I wadna ask such a thing, only the Proclamation is not a private thing, but is meant for a' men's hearing."

"It is indeed meant for all men's hearing," replied Lord Nigel, "and it proclaims the shame of our country, and the ingratitude of our Prince."

"Now the Lord preserve us, and to publish it in London too!" ejaculated Moniplies.

"Hark ye, Richard," said Nigel Olifaunt, "in this paper the Lords of the Council set forth, that, 'in consideration of the resort of idle persons of low condition forth from his Majesty's kingdom of Scotland to his English Court—filling the same with their suits and supplications, and dishonouring the royal presence with their base, poor, and beggarly persons, to the disgrace of their country in the estimation of the English; these are to prohibit the skippers, masters of vessels, and others, in every part of Scotland, from bringing such miserable creatures up to Court, under pain of fine and imprisonment.'"

"I marle the skipper took us on board," said Richie.

"Then you need not marvel how you are to get back again," said Lord Nigel, "for here is a clause which says, that such idle suitors are to be transported back to Scotland at his Majesty's expence, and punished for their audacity with stripes, stocking, or incarceration, according to their demerits—that is to say, I suppose, according to the degree of their poverty, for I see no other demerit qualified."

"This will scarcely," said Richie, "square with our old proverb—
> A King's face
> Should give grace;

But what says the paper further, my lord?"

"O, only a small clause which especially concerns us, making some still heavier denunciations against those suitors who shall be so bold as to approach the Court, under pretext of seeking payment of old debts due to them by the King, which, the paper states, is of all species of importunity that which is most odious to his Majesty."

"The King has neighbours in that matter," said Richie; "but it is not every one that can shift off that sort of cattle so easily as he does."

Their conversation was here interrupted by a knocking at the door. Olifaunt looked out at the window, and saw an elderly respectable person whom he knew not. Richie also peeped, and recognized, but recognizing, chose not to acknowledge, his friend of the preceding evening. Afraid that his share in the visit might be detected, he made his escape out of the apartment under pretext of going to his breakfast; and left to their landlady the task of ushering Master George into Lord Nigel's apartment, which she performed with much courtesy.

Chapter Four

Ay, sir, the clouted shoe hath oft times craft in't,
As says the rustic proverb; and your citizen,
In his grogram suit, gold chain, and well-black'd shoes,
Bears under his flat cap oft times a brain
Wiser than burns beneath the hat and feather,
Or seethes within the statesman's velvet night-cap.
Read me my Riddle

THE YOUNG SCOTTISH nobleman received the citizen with distant politeness, expressing that sort of reserve by which those of the higher ranks are sometimes willing to make a plebian sensible that he is an intruder. But Master George seemed neither displeased nor disconcerted. He assumed the chair, which, in deference to his respectable appearance, Lord Nigel offered to him, and said, after a moment's pause, during which he had looked attentively at the young man, with respect not unmingled with emotion—"You will forgive me for this rudeness, my lord; but I was endeavouring to trace in your youthful countenance the features of my good old Lord, your excellent father."

There was a moment's pause ere young Glenvarloch replied, still with a reserved manner,—"I have been reckoned like my father, sir,— and am happy to see any one that respects his memory. But the business which calls me to this city is of a hasty as well as a private nature, and——"

"I understand the hint, my lord," said Master George, "and would not be guilty of long detaining you from business, or more agreeable conversation. My errand is almost done when I have said, that my name is George Heriot, warmly befriended, and introduced into the employment of the royal family of Scotland, more than twenty years since, by your excellent father; and that, learning from a follower of yours that your lordship was in this city in prosecution of some business of importance, it is my duty—it is my pleasure—to wait on the son of my respected patron; and, as I am somewhat known both at the court and in the city, to offer him such aid in the furthering of his affairs, as my credit and experience may be able to afford."

"I have no doubt of either, Master Heriot," said Lord Nigel, "and I thank you heartily for the good-will with which you have placed them at a stranger's disposal; but my business at court is done and ended, and I intend to leave London, and, indeed, the island, for foreign travel and military service. I may add that the suddenness of my departure occasions my having little time at my disposal."

Master Heriot did not take the hint, but sat fast, with an embarrassed countenance however, like that of one who had something to say that he knew not exactly how to make effectual. At length he said, with a dubious smile, "You are fortunate, my lord, in having so soon dispatched your business at court. Your talking landlady informs me you have been but a fortnight in this city. It is usually months and years ere the Court and a suitor shake hands and part."

"My business," said Lord Nigel, with a brevity which was intended to stop further discussion, "was summarily dispatched."

Still Master Heriot remained seated, and there was a cordial good-humour added to the reverence of his appearance, which rendered it impossible for Lord Nigel to be more explicit in requesting his absence.

"Your lordship has not yet had time," said the citizen, still attempting to sustain the conversation, "to visit the places of amusement,—the play-houses, and other places to which youth resort. But I see in your lordship's hand one of the new-invented plots of the piece, which they hand about of late—May I ask what play?"

"Oh! a well-known piece," said Lord Nigel, impatiently throwing down the Proclamation, which he had hitherto been twisting to and fro in his hand,—"an excellent and well-approved piece—*A New Way to Pay Old Debts*."

Master Heriot stooped down, saying, "Ah! my old acquaintance, Philip Massinger;" but, having opened the paper and seen the purport, he looked at Lord Nigel Olifaunt with surprise, saying, "I trust your lordship does not think this prohibition can extend either to your person or your claims?"

"I should scarce have thought so myself," said the young nobleman; "but so it proves. His Majesty, to close this discourse at once, has been pleased to send me this Proclamation, in answer to a respectful Supplication for the re-payment of large loans advanced by my father for the service of the state, in the King's utmost emergencies."

"It is impossible!" said the citizen—"it is absolutely impossible!— If the King could forget what was due to your father's memory, still he would not have wished—would not, I may say, have dared—to be so unjust to the memory of such a man as your father, who, dead in the body, will long live in the memory of the Scottish people."

"I should have been of your opinion," answered Lord Nigel, in the same tone as before; "but there is no fighting with facts."

"What was the tenor of this Supplication?" said Heriot; "or by whom was it presented? Something strange there must have been in the contents, or"——

"You may see my original draught," said the young Lord, taking it out of a small travelling strong-box; "the technical part is by my lawyer in Scotland, a skilful and sensible man; the rest is my own, drawn, I hope, with due deference and modesty."

Master Heriot hastily cast his eye over the draught. "Nothing," he said, "can be more well-tempered and respectful. Is it possible the King can have treated this petition with contempt?"

"He threw it down on the pavement," said the Lord of Glenvarloch, "and sent me for answer that Proclamation, in which he classes me with the paupers and mendicants from Scotland, who disgrace his court in the eyes of the proud English—that is all. Had not my father stood by him with heart, sword, and fortune, he might never have seen the Court of England himself."

"But by whom was this Supplication presented, my lord?" said Heriot; "for the distaste taken at the messenger will sometimes extend itself to the message."

"By my servant," said the Lord Nigel; "by the man you saw, and, I think, were kind to."

"By your servant, my lord?" said the citizen; "he seems a shrewd fellow, and doubtless a faithful; but surely"——

"You would say," said Lord Nigel, "he is no fit messenger to a King's presence?—Surely he is not; but what could I do? Every attempt I had made to lay my case before the King had miscarried, and my petitions got no farther than the budgets of clerks and secretaries; this fellow pretended he had a friend in the household that would bring him to the King's presence,—and so"——

"I understand," said Heriot; "but, my lord, why should you not, in right of your rank and birth, have appeared at court, and required an audience, which could not have been denied to you?"

The young lord blushed a little, and looked at his dress, which was very plain; and, though in perfect good order, had the appearance of having seen service.

"I know not why I should be ashamed of speaking the truth," he said, after momentary hesitation,—"I had no dress suitable for appearing at court. I am determined to incur no expences which I cannot discharge; and I think you, sir, would not have advised me to stand at the palace-door in person, and deliver my petition, along with those who were in very deed pleading their necessity, and begging an alms."

"That had been, indeed, unseemly," said the citizen; "but yet, my lord, my mind runs strangely that there must be some mistake.—Can I speak with your domestic?"

"I see little good it can do," answered the young lord, "but the interest which you take in my misfortunes seems sincere, and there-fore——" He stamped on the floor, and in a few seconds afterwards Moniplies appeared, wiping from his beard and moustaches the crumbs of bread, and the froth of the ale-pot, which plainly shewed how he had been employed.—"Will your lordship grant permission," said Heriot, "that I ask your groom a few questions?"

"His lordship's page, Master George," answered Moniplies, with a nod of acknowledgment, "if you are minded to speak according to the letter."

"Hold your saucy tongue," said his master, "and reply distinctly to the questions asked at you."

"And *truly*, if it like your pageship," said the citizen, "for you may remember I have a gift to discover falset."

"Weel, weel, weel," replied the domestic, somewhat embarrassed, in spite of his effrontery—"though I think that the sort of truth that serves my master, may weel serve ony ane else."

"Pages lie to their masters by right of custom," said the citizen; "and you write yourself in that band, though I think you be among the oldest of such springalds; but to me you must speak truth, if you would not have it end in the whipping-post."

"And that's e'en a bad resting-place," said the fellow; "so come away with your questions, Master George."

"Well, then," demanded the citizen, "I am given to understand that you yesterday presented to his Majesty's hand a Supplication, or petition, from this honourable Lord, your master."

"Troth, there's nae gainsaying that, sir," replied Moniplies; "there were enow to see it besides me."

"And you pretend that his Majesty flung it from him with con-tempt," said the citizen. "Take heed, for I have means of knowing the truth; and you were better up to the neck in the Nor-Loch, which you like so well, than tell a leasing where his Majesty's name is con-cerned."

"There is nae occasion for leasing-making about the matter," answered Moniplies, firmly; "his Majesty e'en flung it frae him as if it had dirtied his fingers."

"You hear, sir," said Olifaunt, addressing Heriot.

"Hush!" said the sagacious citizen; "this fellow is not ill named— he has more plies than one in his cloak.—Stay, fellow, (for Moniplies, muttering somewhat about finishing his breakfast, was beginning to shamble towards the door,) answer me this farther question—When you gave your master's petition to his Majesty, gave you nothing with it?"

"Ou, what should I give wi' it, ye ken, Master George?"

"That is what I desire and insist to know," replied his interrogator.

"Weel then—I am not free to say, that may be, I might not just slip into the King's hand a wee bit sifflication of mine ain, along with my lord's—just to save his Majesty trouble—and that he might consider them baith at ance."

"A supplication of your own, you varlet!" said his master.

"Ou, dear ay, my lord," said Richie—"puir bodies hae their bits of sifflications as weel as their betters."

"And pray, what might your worshipful petition import?" said Mr Heriot.—"Nay, for heaven's sake, my lord, keep your patience, or we shall never learn the truth of this strange matter.—Speak out, sirrah, and I will stand your friend with my lord."

"It's a lang story to tell—But the upshot is, that it's a scrape of an auld accompt due to my father's yestate be her Majesty the King's maist gracious mother, when she lived in the Castle, and had sundry providings and furnishings forth of our booth, whilk nae doubt was an honour to my father to supply, and whilk, doubtless, it will be a credit to his Majesty to satisfy, as it will be grit convenience to me to receive the saam."

"What string of impertinence is this?" said his master.

"Every word as true as e'er John Knox spoke," said Richie; "here's the bit double of the sifflication."

Master George took a crumpled paper from the fellow's hand, and said, muttering betwixt his teeth—"'Humbly sheweth—um—um—his Majesty's maist gracious mother—um—um—justly addebted and awing—the sum of fifteen merkis—the compt whereof followeth——Twelve nowte's feet for jeillis—ane lamb, being Christmas—ane roasted capin in grease for the privy chalmer, when my Lord of Bothwell suppit with hir grace.'—I think, my lord, you can hardly be surprised that the King gave this petition a brusk reception; and I conclude, Master Page, that you took care to present your own supplication before your master's."

"Troth did I not," answered Moniplies, "I thought to have given my lord's first, as was reason gude; and besides that, it wad have red the gate for my ain little bill. But what wi' the dirdum an confusion, an the loupin here and there of the skeigh brute of a horse, I believe I crammed them baith into his hand cheek for jowl, and maybe my ain was boonmost; and say there was aught wrang, I am sure I had a' the fright and a' the risk"——

"And shall have all the beating, you rascal knave," said Nigel; "am I to be insulted and dishonoured by your pragmatical insolence, in blending your base concerns with mine?"

"Nay, nay, nay—my lord," said the good-humoured citizen, inter-
posing; "I have been the means of bringing the fellow's blunder to
light—allow me interest enough with your lordship to be bail for his
bones. You have cause to be angry—but still I think the knave mistook
more out of conceit than of purpose; and I judge you will have the
better service of him another time, if you look over this fault.—Get you
gone, sirrah—I'll make your peace."

"Na, na," said Moniplies, keeping his ground firmly, "if he likes to
strike a lad that has followed him for pure love, for I think there has
been little servant's fee between us, aw the way frae Scotland, just let
my lord be doing, and see the credit he will get by it—and I would
rather (mony thanks to you though, Maister George,) stand by a lick
of his batton, than it suld e'er be said a stranger came between us."

"Go then," said his master, "and get out of my sight."

"Aweel I wot that is sune done," said Moniplies, retiring slowly; "I
did not come without I had been ca'd for—and I wad have been away
half an hour since with my gude will, only Maister George keepit me
to answer his interrogations, forsooth, and that has made aw this
steer."

And so he made his grumbling exit, with the tone much rather of
one who has sustained an injury, than who has done wrong.

"There never was a man so plagued as I am with a malapert knave!
—The fellow is shrewd, and I have found him faithful—I believe he
loves me too, and he has given proofs of it—But then he is so uplifted
in his own conceit, so self-willed, and so self-opinioned, that he seems
to become the master and I the man; and whatever blunder he com-
mits, he is sure to make as loud complaints, as if the whole error lay
with me, and not with himself."

"Cherish him, and maintain him, nevertheless," said the citizen;
"for believe my grey hairs, that affection and fidelity are now rarer
qualities in a servitor, than when the world was younger. Yet trust him,
my good lord, with no commission above his birth or breeding, for you
see yourself how it may chance to fall."

"It is but too evident, Master Heriot," said the young nobleman;
"and I am sorry I have done injustice to my sovereign, and your
master. But I am, like a true Scotsman, wise behind the hand—the
mistake has happened—my Supplication has been refused, and my
only resource is to employ the rest of my means to carry Moniplies and
I to some counterscarp, and die in the battle-front like my ancestors."

"It were better to live and serve your country like your noble father,
my lord," replied Master George. "Nay, nay, never look down or
shake your head—the King has not refused your Supplication, for he
has not seen it—you ask but justice, and that his place obliges him to

give to his subjects—ay, my lord, and I will say that his natural temper doth in this hold bias with his duty."

"I were well pleased to think so, and yet——" said Nigel Olifaunt, —"I speak not of my own wrongs, but my country hath many that are unredressed."

"My lord," said Master Heriot, "I speak of my royal master, not only with the respect due from a subject—the *gratitude* to be paid by a favoured servant—but also with the frankness of a free and loyal Scotsman. The King is himself well disposed to hold the scales of justice even; but there are those around him who can throw without detection their own selfish wishes and base interests into the scale. You are already a sufferer by this, and without your knowing it."

"I am surprised, Master Heriot," said the young lord, "to hear you, upon so short an acquaintance, talk as if you were familiarly acquainted with my affairs."

"My lord," replied the goldsmith, "the nature of my employment affords me direct access to the interior of the palace; I am well known to be no meddler in intrigues or party affairs, so that no favourite has as yet endeavoured to shut against me the door of the royal closet; on the contrary, I have stood well with each while he was in power, and I have not shared the fall of any. But I cannot be thus connected with the Court, without hearing, even against my will, what wheels are in motion, and how they are checked or forwarded. Of course, when I chuse to seek such intelligence, I know the sources in which it is to be traced. I have told you why I was interested in your lordship's fortunes. It was last night only that I knew you were in this city, yet I have been able, in coming hither this morning, to gain for you some information respecting the impediments to your suit."

"Sir, I am obliged by your zeal, however little it may be merited," answered Nigel, still with some reserve; "yet I hardly know how I have deserved this interest."

"First let me satisfy you that it is real," said the citizen; "I blame you not for being unwilling to credit the fair professions of a stranger in my inferior class of society, when you have met so little friendship from relations, and those of your own rank, bound to have assisted you by so many ties. But mark the cause. There is a mortgage over your father's extensive estate, to the amount of 40,000 merks, due ostensibly to Peregrine Peterson, the Conservator of Scottish Privileges at Campvere."

"I know nothing of a mortgage," said the young lord; "but there is a wadset for such a sum, which, if unredeemed, will occasion the forfeiture of my whole paternal estate, for a sum not above a fourth of its value—and it is for that very reason that I press the King's government for a settlement of the debts due to my father, that I may be able to redeem my land from this rapacious creditor."

"A wadset in Scotland," said Heriot, "is the same with a mortgage on this side of the Tweed; but you are not acquainted with your real creditor. The Conservator Peterson only lends his name to shroud no less a man than the Lord Chancellor of Scotland, who hopes, under cover of this debt, to gain possession of the estate himself, or perhaps to gratify a yet more powerful third party. He will probably suffer his creature Peterson to take possession, and when the odium of the transaction shall be forgotten, the property and lordship of Glenvarloch will be conveyed to the great man by his obsequious instrument, under cover of a sale, or some similar device."

"Can this be possible?" said Lord Nigel; "the Chancellor wept when I took leave of him—called me his cousin—even his son—furnished me with letters, and, though I asked him for no pecuniary assistance, excused himself unnecessarily for not pressing it on me, alleging the expences of his rank and his large family. No, I cannot believe a nobleman would carry deceit so far."

"I am not, it is true, of noble blood," said the citizen; "but once more I bid you look on my grey hairs, and think what can be my interest in dishonouring them with falsehood in affairs in which I have no interest, save as they regard the son of my benefactor. Reflect also, have you had any advantage from the Lord Chancellor's letters?"

"None," said Nigel Olifaunt, "save cold deeds and fair words. I have thought for some time, their only object was to get rid of me—there was one who yesterday pressed money on me when I talked of going abroad, in order that I might not want the means of exiling myself."

"Right," said Heriot; "rather than you fled not, they would themselves furnish wings for you to fly withal."

"I will to him this instant," said the incensed youth, "and tell him my mind of his baseness."

"Under your favour," said Heriot, detaining him, "you shall not do so. By a quarrel you would become the ruin of me your informer; and though I would venture half my shop to do your lordship a service, I think you would hardly wish me to come by damage, when it can be of no service to you."

The word *shop* sounded harshly in the ear of the young nobleman, who replied hastily—"Damage, sir?—so far am I from wishing you to incur damage, that I would to heaven you would cease your fruitless offers of serving one whom there is no chance of ultimately assisting."

"Leave me alone for that," said the citizen; "you are now as far erring on the bow-hand. Permit me to take this Supplication—I will have it suitably engrossed, and take my own time, (and it shall be an early one,) for placing it, with more prudence I trust than that used by your follower, in the King's hand—I will almost answer for his taking up the matter as you would have him—but should he fail to do so, even then I will not give up the good cause."

"Sir," said the young nobleman, "your speech is so friendly, and my own estate so helpless, that I know not how to refuse your kind proffer, even while I blush to accept it at the hands of a stranger."

"We are, I trust, no longer such," said the goldsmith; "and for my guerdon, when my mediation proves successful, and your fortunes are re-established, you shall order your first cupboard of plate from George Heriot."

"You would have a bad paymaster, Master Heriot," said Lord Nigel.

"I do not fear that," replied the goldsmith; "and I am glad to see you smile, my lord—methinks it makes you look still more like the good old lord your father. And it emboldens me beside to bring out a small request—that you would take a homely dinner with me to-morrow. I lodge hard beside, in Lombard street. For the cheer, my lord, a mess of white broth, a fat capon well larded, a dish of beef collops for auld Scotland's sake, and it may be a cup of right old wine, that was barrelled before Scotland and England were one nation—Then for company, one or two of our own loving countrymen—and may be my house-wife may find out a bonny Scots lass or so."

"I would accept your courtesy, Master Heriot," said Nigel, "but I hear the city ladies of London love to see a man gallant—I would not like to let down a Scottish nobleman in their ideas, as doubtless you have said the best of our poor country, and I rather lack the means of bravery for the present."

"My lord, your frankness leads me a step further," said Master George. "I owed your father some monies; and—nay, if your lordship looks at me so fixedly I shall never tell my story—and—to speak plainly, for I never could carry a lie well through in my life—it is most fitting, that, to solicit this matter properly, your lordship should go to court in a manner beseeming your quality. I am a goldsmith, and live by lending money as well as by selling plate. I am ambitious to put an hundred pounds to be at interest in your hands, till your affairs are settled."

"And if they are never favourably settled?" said Nigel.

"Then, my lord," returned the citizen, "the miscarriage of such a sum will be of little consideration to me, compared with other subjects of regret."

"Master Heriot," said the Lord Nigel, "your favour is generously

offered, and shall be frankly accepted. I must presume that you see
your way through this business, though I hardly do; for I think you
would be grieved to add any fresh burthen to me, by persuading me to
incur debt which I am not likely to discharge. I will, therefore, take
your money, under the hope and trust that you will enable me to repay
you punctually."

"I will convince you, my lord," said the goldsmith, "that I mean to
deal with you as a creditor from whom I expect payment; and, therefore, you shall, with your good pleasure, sign an acknowledgment for
these monies, and an obligation to content and repay me."

He then took from his girdle his writing materials, and writing a few
lines to the purport he expressed, pulled out a small bag of gold from a
side-pouch under his cloak, and, observing that it should contain an
hundred pounds, proceeded to tell out the contents very methodically
upon the table. Nigel Olifaunt could not help intimating that this was
an unnecessary ceremonial, and that he would take the bag of gold on
the word of his obliging creditor; but this was repugnant to the old
man's forms of transacting business.

"Bear with me," he said, "my good lord,—we citizens are a wary
and thrifty generation; and I should lose my good name for ever within
the toll of Paul's, were I to grant quittance, or take acknowledgment,
without bringing the money to actual tale. I think it be now right—
And, body of me," he said, looking out at window, "yonder come my
boys with my mule—for I must Westward Hoe. Put your monies
aside, my lord; it is not well to be seen with such gold-finches chirping
about one in the lodgings of London. I think the lock of your casket be
indifferent good; if not, I can serve you at an easy rate with one that
has held thousands;—it was the good old Sir Faithful Frugal's;—his
spendthrift son sold the shell when he had eaten the kernel—And
there is the end of a city-fortune."

"I hope yours will make a better termination, Master Heriot," said
the Lord Nigel.

"I hope it will, my lord," said the old man, with a smile; "but," (—to
use honest John Bunyan's phrase—'therewithal the water stood in his
eyes,'—) "it has pleased God to try me by the loss of two children; and
for one adopted child who lives—ah! woe is me! and well-a-day!—
But I am patient and thankful; and for the wealth heaven has sent me,
it shall not want inheritors while there are orphan lads in Auld Reekie.
—I wish you good morrow, my lord."

"One orphan has cause to thank you already," said Nigel, as he
attended him to the door of his chamber, where, resisting further
escort, the old citizen made his escape.

As, in going down stairs, he passed the shop where Dame Christie stood becking, he made civil inquiries after her husband. The dame of course regretted his absence; but he was down, she said, at Deptford, to settle with a Dutch ship-master.

"Our way of business, sir," she said, "takes him much from home, and my husband must be the slave of every tarry-jacket that wants but a pound of oakum."

"All business must be minded, dame," said the goldsmith. "Make my remembrances—George Heriot of Lombard-street's remembrances, to your good man. I have dealt with him—he is just and punctual, true to time and engagements;—be kind to your noble guest, and see he want nothing. Though it be his pleasure at present to lie private and retired, there be those that care for him, and I have a charge to see him supplied; so that you may let me know by your husband, my good dame, from time to time, how my lord is, and whether he wants aught."

"And so he *is* a real lord after all?" said the good dame. "I am sure I always thought he looked like one. But why does he not go to the Parliament then?"

"He will, dame," answered Heriot, "to the Parliament of Scotland, which is his own country."

"Oh! he is but a Scots lord, then," said the good dame; "and that's the reason makes him ashamed to take the title, as they say."

"Let him not hear *you* say so, dame," replied the citizen.

"Who, I, sir?" answered she; "no such matter in my thought, sir. Scot or English, he is at any rate a likely man, and a civil man; and rather than he should want any thing, I would wait upon him myself, and come as far as Lombard-street to wait on your worship too."

"Let your husband come to me, good dame," said the goldsmith, who, with all his experience and worth, was somewhat of a formalist and disciplinarian in manners. "The proverb says, 'House goes mad when women gad;' and let his lordship's own man wait upon his master in his chamber—it is more seemly. God give ye good-morrow."

"Good-morrow to your worship," said the dame, somewhat coldly; and so soon as the adviser was out of hearing, was ungracious enough to mutter, in contempt of his counsel, "Marry guep of your advice, for an old Scots tinsmith, as you are! My husband is as wise, and very near as old, as yourself; and if I please him, it is well enough; and though he is not just so rich just now as some folks, yet I hope to see him ride upon his moyle, with a foot-cloth, and have his three blue-coats after him, as well as they do."

Chapter Five

Wherefore come ye not to court?
Certain 'tis the rarest sport;
There are silks and jewels glistening,
Prattling fools and wise men listening,
Billies among brave men justling,
Beggars amongst nobles bustling;
Low-breath'd talkers, minion lispers,
Cutting honest throats by whispers;
Wherefore come ye not to court?
Skelton swears 'tis glorious sport.
                    Skelton Skeltonizeth

IT WAS NOT ENTIRELY out of parade that the benevolent citizen
was mounted and attended in that manner, which, as the reader has
been informed, excited a gentle degree of spleen on the part of
Dame Christie, which, to do her justice, vanished in the little soliloquy which we have recorded. The good man, besides the natural
desire to maintain the exterior of a man of worship, was at present
bound to Whitehall in order to exhibit a piece of valuable workmanship to King James, which he deemed his Majesty might be pleased
to view, or even to purchase. He himself was therefore mounted
upon his caparisoned mule, that he might the better make his way
through the narrow, dirty, and crowded streets; and while one of
his attendants carried under his arm the piece of plate, wrapped up
in red baize, the other two gave an eye to its safety; for such
was the state of the police of the metropolis, that men were often
assaulted in the public street for the sake of revenge or of plunder;
and those who apprehended being beset, usually endeavoured, if
their estate admitted such expense, to secure themselves by the
attendance of armed followers. And this custom, which was at first
limited to the nobility and gentry, extended by degrees to those
citizens of consideration, who being understood to travel with a
charge, as it was called, might otherwise have been selected as safe
subjects of plunder by the street-robbers.

As Master George Heriot paced forth westward with this gallant
attendance, he paused at the shop-door of his countryman and friend,
the ancient horologer, and having caused Tunstall, who was in
attendance, to adjust his watch by the real time, he desired to speak
with his master; in consequence of which summons, the old Time-
meter came forth from his den, his face like a bronze bust, darkened
with dust, and glistening here and there with copper filings, and his
senses so immersed in the intensity of calculation, that he gazed on his

friend the goldsmith for a minute before he seemed personally to comprehend who he was, and heard him express his invitation to David Ramsay, and pretty Mistress Margaret, his daughter, to dine with him next day at noon, to meet with a noble young countryman, without returning any answer.

"I'll make thee speak—with a murrain to thee," muttered Heriot to himself; and suddenly changing his tone, he said aloud,—"I pray you, neighbour David, when are you and I to have a settlement for the bullion wherewith I supplied you to mount yonder costly hall-clock at Theobald's, and that other whirligig that you made for the Duke of Buckingham? I have had the Spanish house to satisfy for the ingots, and I must needs put you into mind that you have been eight months behind hand."

There is something so sharp and *aigre* in the demand of a peremptory dun, that no human tympanum, however inaccessible to other tones, can resist the application. David Ramsay started at once from his reverie, and answered in a pettish tone, "Wow, George, man, what needs aw this din about sax score o' pounds? Aw the warld ken I can answer aw claims on me, and you proffered yoursell fair time, till his maist gracious Majesty and the noble Duke suld make settled accompts wi' me; and ye may ken, by your ain experience, that I canna gang rowting like an unmannered Hieland stot to their doors, as ye come to mine."

Heriot laughed, and replied, "Well, David, I see a demand of money is like a bucket of water about your ears, and makes you a man of the world at once. And now, friend, will you tell me, like a Christian man, if you will dine with me to-morrow at noon, and bring pretty Mistress Margaret, my god-daughter, with you, to meet with our noble young countryman, the Lord of Glenvarloch?"

"The young Lord of Glenvarloch!" said the old mechanist; "wi' aw my heart, and blithe I will be to see him again. We have not met these forty years—he was two years before me at the Humanity classes—he is a sweet youth."

"That was his father—his father—his father, you old dotard Dot-and-carry-one that you are," answered the goldsmith; "a sweet youth he would have been by this time, had he lived, worthy nobleman. This is his son, the Lord Nigel."

"His son!" said Ramsay; "maybe he will want something of a chronometer, or watch—few gallants care to be without them now-a-days."

"He may buy half your stock-in-trade, if ever he comes to his own, for what I know," said his friend; "but Davie, remember your bond, and use me not as you did when my housewife had the sheep's-head and the cock-a-leek boiling for you as late as two of the clock, after-noon."

"She had the more credit by her cookery," answered David, now fully awake; "a sheep's head, over-boiled, were poison, according to our saying."

"Well," answered Master George, "but as there will be no sheep's-head to-morrow, it may chance you to spoil a dinner which a proverb cannot mend. It may be you forgather with our friend Sir Mungo Malagrowther, for I purpose to ask his worship—So bide tryste, Davie."

"I will be true as a chronometer," said Ramsay.

"I will not trust you though," replied Heriot.—"Hear you, Jenkin boy—Tell Scots Janet to tell pretty Mistress Margaret, my god-child, she must put her father in remembrance to put on his best doublet to-morrow, and to bring him to Lombard Street at noon. Tell her they are to meet a brave young Scots lord."

Jenkin coughed that sort of dry short cough uttered by those who are either charged with errands which they do not like, or hear opin-ions to which they must not enter a dissent.

"Umph!" repeated Master George, who, as we have already noticed, was something of a martinet in domestic discipline; "what does *umph* mean? will you do mine errand, or not, sirrah?"

"Sure, Master George Heriot," said the apprentice, touching his cap. "I only meant that Mistress Margaret was not like to forget such an invitation."

"Why, no," said Master George, "she is a dutiful girl to her god-father, though I sometimes call her a jill-flirt. And, hark ye, Jenkin, you and your comrade had best come with your clubs, to see your master and her safely home; but first shut shop, and loose the bull-dog, and let the porter stay in the fore-shop till you return. I will send two of my knaves with you, for I hear these wild youngsters of the Temple are broken out worse and lighter than ever."

"We can keep their steel in order with good handbats," said Jenkin, "and never trouble your servants for the matter."

"Or, if need be," said Tunstall, "we have swords as well as the Templars."

"Fye upon it—fye upon it, young man," said the citizen—"An apprentice with a sword!—Marry, Heaven forefend. I would as soon see him in a hat and feather."

"Well, sir," said Jenkin—"we will find arms fitting to our station, and will defend our master and his daughter, if we should tear up the very stones of the pavement."

"There spoke a London 'prentice bold," said the citizen; "and, for your comfort, my lads, you shall crush a cup of wine to the health of the fathers of the city. I have my eye on both of you—you are thriving lads, each in his own way.—God be wi' you, Davie. Forget not to-morrow, at noon." And so saying, he again turned his mule's head westward, and crossed Temple-Bar, at that slow and decent amble which at once became his rank and civic importance, and put his pedestrian followers to no inconvenience to keep up with him.

At the Temple Gate he again paused, dismounted, and sought his way into one of the small booths occupied by scriveners in the neighbourhood. A young man with lank smooth hair, combed straight to his ears, and then cropped short, rose with a cringing reverence, pulled off a slouched hat, which he would, upon no signal, replace on his head, and answered, with much demonstration of reverence, to the goldsmith's question of, "How goes business, Andrew?" "Aw the better for your worship's kind countenance and maintenance."

"Get a large sheet of paper, man, and make a new pen, with a sharp neb and fine hair-stroke—do not slit the quill up sae high—its a wastrife course in your trade, Andrew—they that do not mind corn-pickles, never come to forpits. I have known a learned man write a thousand pages with one quill."

"Ah! sir," said the lad, who listened to the goldsmith, though instructing him in his own trade, with an air of veneration and acquiescence, "how sune ony puir creature like mysell may rise in the warld, wi' the instruction of such a man as your worship!"

"My instructions are few, Andrew, soon told, and not hard to practise. Be honest—be industrious—be frugal, and you will soon win wealth and worship.—Here, copy me this Supplication in your best and most formal hand. I will wait by you till it is done."

The youth lifted not his eye from the paper, and laid not the pen from his hand, until the task was finished to his employer's satisfaction. The citizen then gave the young scrivener an angel, and bidding him, on his life, to be secret in all business entrusted to him, again mounted his mule, and rode on westward along the Strand.

It may be worth while to remind our readers, that the Temple-Bar which Heriot passed, was not the arched screen, or gateway, of the present day, but an open railing, or palisade, which at night, and in times of alarm, was closed with a barricade of posts and chains. The Strand also, alongst which he rode, was not, as now, a continued street, although it was beginning already to assume that character. It still might be considered as an open road, along the south side of which stood various houses and hotels belonging to the nobility, having gardens behind them down to the water-side, with stairs to the river for the convenience of taking boat, which mansions have bequeathed the names of their lordly owners to many of the streets leading from the Strand to the Thames. The north side of the Strand was also a long line of houses, behind which, as in Saint Martin's Lane, and other points, buildings were rapidly arising; but Covent-Garden was still a garden, in the literal sense of the word, or at least but beginning to be studded with irregular buildings. All around, however, marked the rapid increase of a capital which had long enjoyed peace, wealth, and a regular government; houses were arising in every direction, and the shrewd eye of our citizen already saw the period not distant which should convert the nearly open highway on which he travelled, into a connected and regular street, uniting the court end of the town with the city of London.

He next passed Charing Cross, which was no longer the pleasant solitary village at which the judges were wont to breakfast on their way to Westminster Hall, but was still further from resembling the artery through which, to use Johnson's expression, "pours the full tide of London population." The buildings were rapidly increasing, yet scarcely gave even a faint idea of its present appearance.

At last Whitehall received our traveller, who passed under one of the beautiful gates designed by Holbein, and composed of tesselated brick-work, being the same to which Moniplies had profanely likened the West-Port of Edinburgh, and entered the ample precincts of the palace of Whitehall, now full of all the confusion attending improvement. It was just at the time when James, little suspecting that he was employed in constructing a palace, from the window of which his only son was to pass to die upon a scaffold before it, was busied in removing the ancient and ruinous buildings of De Burgh, Henry VIII., and Queen Elizabeth, to make way for the superb architecture on which Inigo Jones exerted all his genius. The King, ignorant of futurity, was now engaged in pressing on his work, and for that purpose still maintained his royal apartments at Whitehall, amidst the rubbish of old buildings, and the various confusion attending the erection of the new pile, which formed at present a labyrinth not easily to be traversed.

The Goldsmith to the Royal Household, and who, if fame spoke true, oftentimes acted as their banker, (for these professions were not as yet separated from each other,) was a person of too much importance to receive the slightest interruption from centinel or porter; and leaving his mule and two of his followers in the outer court, he gently knocked at a postern-gate of the building, and was presently admitted, while the most trusty of his attendants followed him closely with the piece of plate under his arm. This man also he left behind him in an anti-room, where three or four pages in the royal livery, but untrussed, unbuttoned, and dressed more carelessly than their place and nearness to a King's person seemed to admit, were playing at dice and draughts, or stretched upon benches, and slumbering with half-shut eyes. A corresponding gallery, which opened from the anti-room, was occupied by two gentlemen-ushers of the chamber, who gave each a smile of recognition as the wealthy goldsmith entered. No word was spoken on either side, but one of the ushers looked first to Heriot, and then to a little door half-covered by the tapestry, which seemed to say as plain as a look could—"Lies your business that way?" The citizen nodded, and the court-attendant, moving on tiptoe and with as much precaution as if the floor had been paved with eggs, advanced to the door, opened it gently, and spoke a few words in a low tone. The broad Scottish accent of King Jamie was heard in reply—"Admit him instanter, Maxwell—have ye hairboured sae lang at the court, and not learned that gold and silver is ever welcome?"

The usher signed to Heriot to advance, and the honest citizen was presently introduced into the cabinet of his Sovereign.

The scene of confusion amid which he found the King seated, was no bad picture of the state and quality of James's own mind. There was much that was rich and costly in cabinet pictures and valuable ornaments, but they were slovenly arranged, covered with dust, and lost half their value, or at least their effect, from the manner in which they were presented to the eye. The table was loaded with huge folios, amongst which lay light books of jest and ribaldry; and notes of unmercifully long orations to Parliament, and essays on king-craft, were mingled with miserable roundels and ballats by the royal 'Prentice, as he styled himself, in the art of poetry, and schemes for the general pacification of Europe, with a list of the names of the King's hounds, and remedies against canine madness.

The King's dress was of green velvet, quilted so full as to be dagger-proof, which gave him the appearance of clumsy and ungainly protuberance; while its being buttoned awry communicated to his figure an air of distortion. Over his green doublet he wore a sad-coloured night-gown, out of the pocket of which peeped his hunting-horn. His high-crowned grey hat lay on the floor, covered with dust, but encircled by a carkanet of large balas rubies; and he wore a blue velvet night-cap, in the front of which was placed the plume of a heron, which had been struck down by a favourite hawk in some critical moment of the flight, for remembrance of which the King wore this highly honoured feather.

But such inconsistencies in dress and appointments were mere outward types of those which existed in the royal character, rendering it a subject of doubt amongst his contemporaries, and bequeathing it as a problem to future historians. He was deeply learned, without possessing useful knowledge; sagacious in many individual cases, without having real wisdom; fond of his power, and desirous to maintain and augment it, yet willing to resign the direction of that and of himself, to the most unworthy favourites; a big and bold assertor of his rights in words, yet one who tamely saw them trampled in deeds; a lover of negociations, in which he was always outwitted; and a fearer of war, where conquest might have been easy. He was fond of his dignity, which he was perpetually degrading by undue familiarity; capable of much public labour, yet often neglecting it for the meanest amusement; a wit, though a pedant; and a scholar, though fond of the conversation of the ignorant and uneducated. Even his timidity of temper was not uniform, and there were moments of his life, and those critical, in which he shewed the spirit of his ancestors. He was laborious in trifles, and a trifler where serious labour was required; devout in his sentiments, and yet too often profane in his language; just and beneficent by nature, he yet gave way to the iniquities and oppression of others. He was penurious respecting money which he had to give from his own hand, yet inconsiderately and unboundedly profuse of that which he did not see. In a word, those good qualities which displayed themselves in particular cases and occasions, were not of a nature sufficiently firm and comprehensive to regulate his general conduct; and, shewing themselves as they occasionally did, only entitled James to the character bestowed on him by Sully—that he was the wisest fool in Christendom.

That the fortunes of this monarch might be as little of a piece as his character, he, certainly the least talented of the Stuarts, succeeded peaceably to that kingdom, against the power of which his predecessors had, with so much difficulty, defended his native throne. And, lastly, although his reign appeared calculated to ensure to Great Britain that lasting tranquillity and internal peace which so much suited the King's disposition, yet, during that very reign, were sown those seeds of dissension, which, like the teeth of the fabulous dragon, had their harvest in a bloody and universal civil war.

Such was the monarch, who, saluting Heriot familiarly by the name of Jingling Geordie, (for it was his well-known custom to give nicknames to all his familiars,) inquired what new clatter-traps he had brought with him, to cheat his lawful and native Prince out of his siller.

"God forbid, my liege," said the citizen, "that I should have any such disloyal purpose. I did but bring a piece of plate to shew to your most gracious Majesty, which, both for the subject and for the workmanship, I were loth to put into the hands of any subject until I knew your Majesty's pleasure anent it."

"Body o' me, man, let's see it, Heriot; though, by my saul, Steenie's

service o' plate was sae dear a bargain, I had 'maist pawned my word as
a Royal King, to keep my ain gold and silver in future, and let you,
Geordie, keep yours."

"Respecting the Duke of Buckingham's plate," said the goldsmith,
"your Majesty was pleased to direct that no expence should be spared,
and"——

"What signifies what I desired, man? when a wise man is with fules
and bairns, he maun e'en play at the chucks. But you should have had
mair sense and consideration than to gie Babie Charles and Steenie
their ain gate; they wad hae floored the very rooms wi' silver, and I
wonder they didna."

George Heriot bowed, and said no more. He knew his master too
well to vindicate himself otherwise than by a distant allusion to his
order; and James, with whom economy was only a transient and
momentary twinge of conscience, became immediately afterwards
desirous to see the piece of plate which the goldsmith proposed to
exhibit, and dispatched Maxwell to bring it to his presence. In the
meanwhile he demanded of the citizen whence he had procured it.

"From Italy, may it please your Majesty," replied Heriot.

"It has naething in it tending to papestrie?" said the King, looking
graver than his wont.

"Surely not, please your Majesty," said Heriot; "I were not wise to
bring any thing to your presence that had the mark of the beast."

"You would be the mair beast yourself to do so," said the King; "it
is well kenn'd that I wrestled wi' Dagon in my youth, and smote him on
the groundsill of his awn temple; a gude evidence I should be
in time called, however unworthy, the Defender of the Faith.—But
here comes Maxwell, bending under his burthen, like the Golden Ass
of Apuleius."

Heriot hastened to relieve the usher, and to place the embossed
salver, for such it was, and of extraordinary dimensions, in a light
favourable for his Majesty's viewing the sculpture.

"Saul of my body, man," said the King, "it is a curious piece, and, as
I think, fit for a King's chalmer; and the subject, as you say, Master
George, vara adequate and beseeming—being, as I see, the judgment
of Solomon—a prince in whose paths it weel becomes a' leeving
monarchs to walk with emulation."

"But whose footsteps," said Maxwell, "only one of them—if a subject may say so much—hath ever overtaken."

"Haud your tongue, for a fause fleeching loun," said the King, but
with a smile on his face that shewed the flattery had done its part.
"Look at the bonnie piece of workmanship, man, and haud your
clavering tongue—and whase handy-work may it be, Geordie?"

"It was wrought, sir," replied the goldsmith, "by the famous Florentine, Benvenuto Cellini, and designed for Francis the First of France; but I hope it will find a fitter master."

"Francis of France!" said the King; "send Solomon, King of the Jews, to Francis!—Body of me, man, it would have kythed Cellini mad, had he never done ony thing else out of the gate. Francis!— Why, he was a fighting fule, man—a mere fighting fule,—got himsell ta'en at Pavia, like our ain David at Durham lang syne;—if they could hae sent him Solomon's wit, and love of peace and godliness, they wad hae dune him a better turn. But Solomon should sit in other gate company than Francis of France."

"I trust that such will be his good fortune," said Heriot.

"It is a curious and vara artificial sculpture," said the King, in continuation; "but yet, methinks, the carnifex, or executioner there, is brandishing his gulley ower near the King's face, seeing he is within reach of his weapon. I think less wisdom than Solomon's wald have taught him that there was danger in edge-tools, and that he wald have bidden the smaik either sheath his shable, or stand farther back."

George Heriot endeavoured to alleviate this objection, by assuring the King that the vicinity betwixt Solomon and the executioner was nearer in appearance than in reality, and that the perspective should be allowed for.

"Gang to the de'il wi' your prospective, man," said the King; "there canna be a waur prospective for a lawfu' king, wha wishes to reign in luve, and die in peace and honour, than to have naked swords flashing in his een. I am accounted as brave as maist folks; and yet I profess to ye I could never look on a bare blade without blinking and winking. But a' thegether it is a brave piece;—and what is the price of it, man?"

The goldsmith replied by observing, that it was not his own property, but that of a distressed countryman.

"Whilk you mean to mak your excuse for asking the double of its worth, I warrant," answered the King. "I ken the tricks of you burrows-town merchants, man."

"I have no hopes of baffling your Majesty's sagacity," said Heriot; "the piece is really what I say, and the price a hundred and fifty pounds sterling—if it pleases your Majesty to make present payment."

"A hundred and fifty fiends, man! and as mony witches and warlocks to raise them!" said the irritated Monarch. "My saul, Jingling Geordie, ye are minded that your purse shall jingle to a bonnie tune! —How am I to tell you down a hundred and fifty punds for what will not weigh as many merks? and ye ken that my very household servitors, and the officers of my mouth, are sax months in arrear!"

The goldsmith stood his ground against all this objurgation, as being what he was well accustomed to, and only answered, that, if his Majesty liked the piece, and desired to possess it, the price could be easily settled. It was true that the party could not want the money, but he, George Heriot, would advance it on his Majesty's account, if such were his pleasure, and wait his royal conveniency for payment, for that and other matters; the money, meanwhile, lying at the ordinary usage.

"By my honour," said James, "and that is speaking like an honest and reasonable tradesman. We maun get another subsidy frae the Commons, and that will make ae compting of it. Awa wi' it, Maxwell—awa wi' it, and let it be set where Steenie and Babie Charles shall see it as they return from Richmond.—And now that we are secret, my good auld servant Geordie, I do truly opine, that speaking of Solomon and ourselves, the hail wisdom in the country left Scotland, when we took our travels to the Southland here."

George Heriot was courtier enough to say, "that the wise naturally follow the wisest, as stags follow their leader."

"Troth, I think there is something in what thou sayest," said James; "for we ourselves, and those of our court and household, as thou thyself, for example, are allowed by the English, for as self-opinioned as they are, to pass for reasonable good wits; but the brains of those we have left behind us are all astir, and run clean hirdie-girdie, like sae mony warlocks and witches on the Devil's Sabbath-e'en."

"I am sorry to hear this, my liege," said Heriot. "May it please your grace to say what our countrymen have done to deserve such a character?"

"They are become frantic, man—clean brain-crazed," answered the King. "I cannot keep them out of the Court by all the proclamations that the heralds roar themselves hoarse with. Yesterday, nae farther gane, just as we were mounted, and about to ride forth, in rushes a thorough Edinburgh gutterblood—a ragged rascal, every dud upon whose back was bidding good-day to the other, with a coat and a hat that would have served a pease-bogle, and, without either havings or reverence, thrusts into our hands, like a sturdy beggar, some Supplication about debts owing by our gracious mother, and sic-like trash; whereat the horse spangs an end, and, but for our admirable sitting, wherein we have been thought to excel maist sovereign princes, as well as subjects, in Europe, I promise you we would have been laid endlang on the causeway."

"Your Majesty," said Heriot, "is their common father, and therefore they are the bolder to press into your gracious presence."

"I ken I am *pater patriæ* well enough," said James; "but one would think they had a mind to squeeze my puddings out, that they may divide the inheritance. Ud's death, Geordie, there is not a loon among them can deliver a Supplication, as it suld be done in the face of Majesty."

"I would I knew the fitting and beseeming mode to do so," said Heriot, "were it but to instruct our poor countrymen in better fashions."

"By my halidome," said the King, "ye are a ceevileezed fellow, Geordie, and I care na if I fling awa as much time as may teach ye. And, first, see you, sir—ye shall approach the presence of Majesty thus,—shadowing your eyes with your hand, to typify that you are in the presence of the Vicegerent of Heaven.—Vara weel, George, that is done in a comely manner.—Then, sir, ye sall kneel, and make as if ye would kiss the hem of our garment, the latches of our shoe, or such like.—Vara weel enacted—whilk we, as being willing to be debonair and pleasing toward our lieges, prevent thus,—and motion to you to rise;—whilk, having a boon to ask, as yet you obey not, but, gliding your hand into your pouch, bring forth your Supplication, and place it reverentially in our open palm." The goldsmith, who had complied with great accuracy with all the prescribed points of the ceremonial, here completed it, to James's no small astonishment, by placing in his hand the petition of the Lord of Glenvarloch. "What means this, ye fause loon?" said he, reddening and sputtering; "hae I been teaching you the manual exercise, that ye suld present your piece at our ain royal body?—now, by this light, I had as lief that ye had bended a real pistolet again me, and yet this hae ye done in my very cabinet, where nought suld enter but at my ain pleasure."

"I trust, your Majesty," said Heriot, as he continued to kneel, "will forgive my exercising the lesson you condescended to give me in the behalf of a friend?"

"Of a friend!" said the King; "so much the warse—so much the warse, I tell ye—if it had been something to do *yoursell* gude, there would have been sense in it, and some chance that you wald not have come back on me in a hurry; but a man may have a hundred friends, and petitions for every ane of them, ilk ane after other."

"Your Majesty, I trust," said Heriot, "will judge me by former experience, and will not suspect me of such presumption."

"I kenna," said the placable monarch; "the world goes daft, I think —*sed semel insanivimus omnes*—thou art my old and faithful servant, that is the truth; and, wer't any thing for thy own behoof, man, thou shouldst not ask twice. But, troth, Steenie loves me so dearly, that he cares not that any one should ask favours of me but himself.—Maxwell, (for the usher had re-entered after having carried off the plate,) get into the anti-chamber wi' your lang lugs.—In conscience, Geordie, I think as that thou hast been mine ain auld fiduciary, and wert my goldsmith when I might say with the Ethnic poet—*Non mea renidet in domo lacunar*—for, faith, they had pillaged my mither's auld house sae, that beechen bickers, and treen trenchers, and latten platters, were whiles the best at our board, and glad we were of something to put on them, without quarrelling with the metal of the dishes. D'ye mind, for thou wert in maist of our complots, how we were fain to send sax of the Blue-banders to harry the Lady of Loganhouse's dow-cote and poultry-yard, and what an awfu' plaint the poor dame made against Jock of Milch, and the thieves of Annandale, wha were as sackless of the deed as I am of the sin of murther?"

"It was the better for Jock," said Heriot; "for if I remember weel, it saved him from a strapping at Dumfries, which he had weel deserved for other misdeeds."

"Ay, man, mind ye that?" said the King; "but he had other virtues, for he was a tight huntsman, moreover, that Jock of Milch, and could hollow to a hound till all the woods rang again. But he came to an Annandale end at last, for Lord Torthorwald run his lance out through him.—Cocksnails, man, when I think of these wild passages, in my conscience, I am not sure but we lived merrier in auld Holyrood in these shifting days, than now when we are dwelling at heck and manger. *Cantabit vacuus*—we had but little to care for."

"And if your Majesty please to remember," said the goldsmith, "the awful task we had to gather silver-vessail and gold-wark enough to make some shew before the Spanish Ambassador."

"Vara true," said the King, now in a full tide of gossip, "and I mind not the name of the right leal lord that helped us with every unce he had in his house, that his native Prince might have some credit in the eyes of them that had the Indies at their beck."

"I think if your Majesty," said the citizen, "will cast your eye on the paper in your hand, you will recollect his name."

"Ay!" said the King, "say ye sae, man?—Lord Glenvarloch, that was his name indeed—*Justus et tenax propositi*—A just man, but as obstinate as a baited bull. He stood whiles against us, that Lord Randal Olifaunt of Glenvarloch, but he was a loving and a leal subject in the main. But this supplicator man be his son—Randal has been long gone where king and lord must go, Geordie, as well as the like of you—And what does his son want of us?"

"The settlement," answered the citizen, "of a large debt due by your Majesty's treasury, for money advanced to your Majesty in great state emergency, about the time of the Raid of Ruthven."

"I mind the thing weel," said King James—"Od's death, maun, I was just out of the clutches of the Master of Glamis and his complices, and there was never siller mair welcome to a born Prince,—the mair

the shame and pity that crowned King should need sic a petty sum.
But what need he dun us for it, man, like a baxter at the breaking? we
aught him the siller, and will pay him wi' our convenience, or mak it
otherwise up to him, whilk is enow between prince and subject—we
are not *in meditatione fugæ*, man, to be arrested thus peremptorily."

"Alas! an it please your Majesty," said the goldsmith, shaking his
head, "it is the poor young nobleman's extreme necessity, and not his
will, that makes him importunate; for he must have money, and that
briefly, to discharge a debt due to Peregrine Peterson, Conservator of
the Privileges at Campvere, or his haill hereditary barony and estate of
Glenvarloch will be evicted in virtue of an unredeemed wadset."

"How say ye, man—how say ye?" exclaimed the King impatiently;
"the carle of a Conservator, the son of a Low-Dutch skipper, evict the
auld estate and lordship of the House of Olifaunt?—God's bread,
man, that mun not be—we maun suspend the diligence by writ of
favour, or otherwise."

"I doubt that may hardly be," answered the citizen, "if it please your
Majesty; your learned counsel in the law of Scotland advise, that there
is no remeid but in paying the money."

"Uds fish," said the King, "let him keep haud by the strong hand
against the carle, until we can take some order about his affairs."

"Alas!" insisted the goldsmith, "if it like your Majesty, your own
pacific government and your doing of equal justice to all men, has
made main force a kittle line to walk by, unless in the rough bounds of
the Highlands."

"Weel—weel—weel, man," said the perplexed monarch, whose
ideas of justice, expedience, and convenience, became on such occasions strangely embroiled; "just it is we should pay our debts, that the
young man may pay his—and he must be paid, and *in verbo regis* he
shall be paid—but how to come by the siller, man, is a difficult chapter
—ye maun try the city, Geordie."

"To say the truth," answered Heriot, "please your gracious Majesty, what betwixt loans and benevolences, and subsidies, the city is at
this present"——

"Donna tell me of what the city is," said King James; "our
Exchequer is as dry as Dean Giles's discourses on the penitentiary
psalms—*Ex nihilo nihil fit*—It's ill taking the breeks aff a wild High-
landman—they that come to me for siller, should tell me how to come
by it—the city ye maun try, Heriot; and donna think to be called
Jingling Geordie for nothing—and *in verbo regis* I will pay the lad if you
get me the loan—I wonnot haggle on the terms; and between you and
me, Geordie, we will redeem the brave auld estate of Glenvarloch.—
But wherefore comes not the young lord to Court, Heriot—is he

comely—is he presentable in the presence?"

"No one can be more sae," said George Heriot; "but——"

"Ah, I understand ye," said his Majesty—"I understand ye—*Res angusta domi*—puir lad—puir lad!—and his father a right true leal Scots heart, though stiff in some opinions. Hark ye, Heriot—let the lad have twa hundred pounds to fit him out. And, here—here—(taking the carcanet of rubies from his old hat)—ye have had these in pledge before for a larger sum, ye auld Levite that ye are. Keep them in gage, till I gie ye back the siller out of the next subsidy."

"If it please your Majesty to give me such directions in writing," said the cautious citizen.

"The de'il is in your nicety, George," said the King; "ye are as preceese as a Puritan in form, and a mere Nullifidian in the marrow of the matter. May not a King's word serve you for advancing your pitiful twa hundred pounds?"

"But not for detaining the crown jewels," said George Heriot.

And the King, who from long experience was inured to dealing with suspicious creditors, wrote an order upon George Heriot, his well-beloved Goldsmith and Jeweller, for the sum of two hundred pounds, to be paid presently to Nigel Olifaunt, Lord of Glenvarloch, to be imputed as so much payment of debts due to him by the crown; and authorizing the retention of a carcanet of balas rubies, with a great diamond, as described in a Catalogue of his Majesty's Jewels, to remain in possession of the said George Heriot, advancer of the said sum, and so forth, until he was lawfully contented and paid thereof. By another rescript, his Majesty gave the same George Heriot directions to deal with some of the moneyed men, upon equitable terms, for a sum of money for his Majesty's present use, not to be under 50,000 merks, but as much more as could conveniently be procured.

"And has he ony lair, this Lord Nigel of ours?" said the King.

George Heriot "could not exactly answer this question; but believed the young lord had studied abroad."

"He shall have our own advice," said the King, "how to carry on his studies to maist advantage; and it may be we will have him come to court, and study with Steenie, and Babie Charles. And, now we think on't—away, away, George, for the bairns will be coming hame presently, and we would not as yet they kenned of this matter we have been treating anent. *Propera pedem*, O Geordie. Clap your mule between your houghs, and god-den with ye."

Thus ended the conference betwixt the gentle King Jamie and his benevolent Jeweller and Goldsmith.

Chapter Six

O I do know him—'tis the mouldy lemon
Which our court wits will wet their lips withal,
When they would sauce their honied conversation
With somewhat sharper flavour.—Marry, sir,
That virtue's well nigh left him—all the juice
That was so sharp and poignant, is squeez'd out;
While the poor rind, although as sour as ever,
Must season soon the draff we give our grunters,
For two-legg'd things are weary on't.
                        The Chamberlain—A Comedy

THE GOOD COMPANY invited by the hospitable citizen assembled
at his house in Lombard-street at the "hollow and hungry hour" of
noon, in order to partake of that meal which divides the day; being
about the time when modern persons of fashion, turning themselves
upon their pillow, begin to think, not without a great many doubts and
much hesitation, that they will by and by commence it. Thither came
the young Nigel, arrayed plainly, but in a dress, nevertheless, more
suitable to his age and quality than he had formerly worn, accompanied by his servant Moniplies, whose outside also was considerably
improved. His solemn and stern features glanced forth from under a
blue velvet bonnet, fantastically placed sideways on his head—he had
a sound and tough cloak of English blue broad-cloth, which, unlike
his former vestment, would have stood the tug of all the apprentices in
Fleet-street. The buckler and broadsword he wore as the arms of his
condition, and a neat silver badge, bearing his lord's arms, announced
that he was an appendage of aristocracy. He sat down in the good
citizen's buttery, not a little pleased to find his attendance upon the
table in the hall was like to be rewarded with his share of a meal such as
he had seldom partaken of.

Mr David Ramsay, that profound and ingenious mechanic, was
safely conducted to Lombard-street, according to promise, well
washed, brushed, and cleansed from the soot of the furnace and the
forge. His daughter came with him, a girl about twenty years old, very
pretty, very demure, yet with lively black eyes, that ever and anon
contradicted the expression of sobriety, to which silence, reserve, a
plain velvet hood, and a cambric ruff, had condemned Mistress Margaret, as the daughter of a quiet citizen.

There were also two citizens and natives of London, men ample in
cloak, and many-linked golden chain, well to pass in the world, and
experienced in their craft of merchandize, but who require no particular description. There was an elderly clergyman also, in his gown

and cassock, a decent venerable man, partaking in his manners of the plainness of the citizens amongst whom he had his cure.

These may be dismissed with brief notice; but not so Sir Mungo Malagrowther, of Girnigo Castle, who claims a little more attention, as an original character of the time in which he flourished.

That good knight knocked at Master Heriot's door just as the clock began to strike twelve, and was seated in his chair ere the last stroke had chimed. This gave the knight an excellent opportunity of making sarcastic observations on all who came later than himself, not to mention a few rubs at the expence of those who had been so superfluous as to appear earlier.

Having little or no property save his bare designation, Sir Mungo had been early attached to Court in the capacity of whipping-boy, as the office was then called, to King James the Sixth, and, with his Majesty, trained to all polite learning by his celebrated preceptor, George Buchanan. The office of whipping-boy doomed its unfortunate occupant to undergo all the corporal punishment which the Lord's Anointed, whose proper person was of course sacred, might chance to incur, in the course of travelling through his grammar and prosody. Under the stern rule, indeed, of George Buchanan, who did not approve of the vicarious mode of punishment, James bore the penance of his own faults, and Mungo Malagrowther enjoyed a sinecure; but James's other pedagogue, Master Patrick Young, went more ceremoniously to work, and appalled the very soul of the youthful king by the floggings which he bestowed on the whipping-boy, when the royal task was not suitably performed. And be it told to Sir Mungo's praise, that there were points about him in the highest respect suited to his official situation. He had even in youth a naturally irregular and grotesque set of features, which, when distorted by fear, pain, and anger, looked like one of the whimsical faces which present themselves in a Gothic cornice. His voice also was high-pitched and querulous, so that, when smarting under Master Peter Young's unsparing inflictions, the expression of his grotesque physiognomy, and the super-human yells which he uttered, were well suited to produce all the effects on the monarch who deserved the lash, that could possibly be produced by seeing another and an innocent individual suffering for his delict.

Sir Mungo Malagrowther, for such he became, thus got an early footing at court, which another would have improved and maintained. But when he grew too big to be whipped, he had no other means of rendering himself acceptable. A bitter, caustic, and backbiting humour, a malicious wit, and an envy of others more prosperous than the possessor of such amiable qualities, have not indeed always been

found obstacles to a courtier's rise; but then they must be amalgam-
ated with a degree of selfish cunning and prudence, of which Sir
Mungo had no share. His satire run riot, his envy could not conceal
itself, and it was not long after his majority till he had as many quarrels
upon his hands as would have required a cat's nine lives to answer. In
one of these rencontres he received, perhaps we should say fortunately, a wound, which served him as an excuse for answering no
invitations of the kind in future. Sir Rullion Rattray, of Ranagullion,
cut off, in mortal combat, three of the fingers of his right hand, so that
Sir Mungo never could hold sword again. At a later period, having
written some satirical verses upon the Lady Cockpen, he received so
severe a chastisement from some persons employed for the purpose,
that he was found half dead on the spot where they had thus dealt with
him, and one of his thighs having been broken, and ill set, gave him a
hitch in his gait, with which he hobbled to his grave. The lameness of
his foot and hand, besides that they added considerably to the grotesque appearance of this original, procured him in future a personal
immunity from the more dangerous consequences of his own
humour; and he gradually grew old in the service of the court, in safety
of life and limb, though without either making friends or attaining
preferment. Sometimes, indeed, the King was amused with his caustic sallies, but he had never art enough to improve the favourable
opportunity; and his enemies, (who were upon the matter the whole
court,) always found means to throw him out of favour again. The
celebrated Archie Armstrong offered Sir Mungo, in his generosity, a
skirt of his own fool's coat, proposing thereby to communicate to him
the privileges and immunities of a professed jester—"For," said the
man of motley, "Sir Mungo, as he goes on just now, gets no more for a
good jest than just the King's pardon for having made it."

Even in London, the golden shower which fell around him, did not
moisten the blighted fortunes of Sir Mungo Malagrowther. He grew
old, deaf, and peevish—lost even the spirit which had formerly animated his strictures, and was barely endured by James, who, though
himself nearly as far stricken in years, retained, to an unusual and even
an absurd degree, the desire to be surrounded by young people. Sir
Mungo, thus fallen into the yellow leaf of years and fortune, shewed
his emaciated form and faded embroidery at court as seldom as his
duty permitted; and spent his time in indulging his food for satire, in
the public walks and in the aisles of Saint Paul's, which were then the
general resort of newsmongers and characters of all descriptions,
associating himself chiefly with such of his countrymen as he
accounted of inferior birth and rank to himself. In this manner, hating
and contemning commerce and those who pursued it, he nevertheless

lived a good deal among the Scottish artists and merchants who had followed the court to London. To these he could shew his cynicism without much offence, for some submitted to his ill-humour in deference to his birth and knighthood, which in these days conferred high privileges; and others, of more sense, pitied and endured the old man, unhappy alike in his fortunes and his temper.

Amongst the latter was George Heriot, who, though his habits and education induced him to carry aristocratical feelings to a degree which would now be thought extravagant, had too much spirit and good sense to permit himself to be intruded upon to an unauthorized excess, or used with the slightest improper freedom, by such a person as Sir Mungo, to whom he was, nevertheless, not only respectfully civil, but essentially kind and even generous.

Accordingly this appeared from the manner in which Sir Mungo Malagrowther conducted himself upon entering the apartment. He paid his respects to Master Heriot, and a decent, elderly, somewhat severe-looking female, in a coif, who, by the name of Aunt Judith, did the honours of his house and table, with little or no portion of the supercilious acidity which his singular physiognomy assumed when he made his bow successively to David Ramsay and the two sober citizens. He thrust himself into the conversation of the latter, to observe, he had heard in Paul's that the bankrupt concerns of Pindivide, a great merchant, who, as he expressed it, had given the crows a pudding, (and on whom he knew, from the same authority, each of the honest citizens had some unsettled claim,) was like to prove a total loss—"stock and block, ship and cargo, keel and rigging, all lost, now and for ever."

The two citizens grinned on each other, but, too prudent to make their private affairs the subject of public discussion, drew their heads together, and evaded further conversation by speaking in a whisper. The old Scotch knight next attacked the watchmaker with the same unrespective familiarity. "Davie," he said,—"Davie, ye donnard auld ideot—have ye no gane mad yet with applying your mathematical science, as ye call it, to the Book of Apocalypse? I expected to have heard ye make out the sign of the beast as clear as a tout on a bawbee whistle."

"Why, Sir Mungo," said the mechanist, after making an effort to recal to his recollection what had been said to him, and by whom, "it may be that ye are nearer the mark than ye are yoursell aware of—for taking the ten horns o' the beast, ye may easily estimate by your digitals"——

"My digits! you daamned auld rusty good-for-nothing timepiece!" exclaimed Sir Mungo, while betwixt jest and earnest, he laid

on his hilt his hand, or rather his claw, (for Sir Rullion's broad-sword
had abridged it into that form,)—"D'ye mean to upbraid me with my
mutilation?"

Master Heriot interfered. "I cannot persuade our friend David," he
said, "that scriptural prophecies are intended to remain in obscurity,
until their unexpected accomplishment shall make, as in former days,
that fulfilled which was written. But you must not exert your knightly
valour on him for all that."

"By my saul, and it would be throwing it away," said Sir Mungo,
laughing. "I would as soon set out with hound and horn to hunt
a sturdied sheep, for he is in a doze again, and up to the chin in
numerals, quotients, and dividends.—Mistress Margaret, my pretty
hinny," for the beauty of the young citizen made even Sir Mungo
Malagrowther's grim features relax themselves a little, "Is your father
always as entertaining as he seems just now?"

Mistress Margaret simpered, bridled, looked to either side, then
straight before her, and having assumed all the airs of bashful embarrassment and timidity which were necessary, as she thought, to cover a
certain shrewd readiness which really belonged to her character, at
length replied, "that indeed la! her father was very thoughtful, but she
had heard that he took the habit of mind from her grandfather."

"Your grandfather!" said Sir Mungo, after doubting if he had
heard her aright,—"said she her grandfather! The lassie is destraught. I ken nae wench on this side of Temple Bar that is derived
from so distant a relation."

"She has got a godfather, however, Sir Mungo," said George
Heriot, again interfering; "and I hope you will allow him interest
enough with you to request you will not put his pretty godchild to so
deep a blush."

"The better—the better," said Sir Mungo. "It is a credit to her,
that, bred and born within the sound of Bow-bell, she can blush for
any thing; and, by my saul, Master George," he continued, chucking
the irritated and reluctant damsel under the chin, "she is bonny
enough to make amends for her lack of ancestry, at least in such a
region as Cheapside, where, d'ye mind me, the kettle cannot call the
porridge-pot"——

The damsel blushed, but not so angrily as before. Master George
Heriot hastened to interrupt the conclusion of Sir Mungo's homely
proverb, by introducing him personally to Lord Nigel. Sir Mungo
could not at first understand what his host said. "Bread of heaven, wha
say ye, man?"

Upon the name of Nigel Olifaunt, Lord Glenvarloch, being again
hollowed into his ear, he drew up, and, regarding his entertainer

with some austerity, rebuked him for not making persons of quality acquainted with each other, that they might exchange courtesies before they mingled with other folks. He then made as handsome and courtly a congee to his new acquaintance as a man maimed in foot and hand could do; and observing he had known my lord, his father, bid him welcome to London, and hoped he should see him at court.

Nigel in an instant comprehended, as well from Sir Mungo's manner, as from a strict compression of their entertainer's lips, which intimated the suppression of a desire to laugh, that he was dealing with an original of no ordinary description, and accordingly returned his courtesy with suitable punctiliousness. Sir Mungo, in the meanwhile, gazed on him with much earnestness; and, as the contemplation of natural advantages was as odious to him as that of wealth, or other adventitious benefits, he had no sooner completely perused the handsome form and good features of the young lord, than, like one of the comforters of the Man of Uzz, he drew close up to him to enlarge on the former grandeur of the Lords of Glenvarloch, and the regret with which he had heard that their representative was not likely to possess the domains of his ancestry. Anon, he enlarged upon the beauties of the principal mansion of Glenvarloch; the commanding site of the old castle; the noble expanse of the lake, stocked with wild-fowl for hawking; the commanding screen of forest, terminating in a mountain-ridge abounding with deer, and all the other advantages of that fair and ancient barony, till Nigel, in spite of every effort to the contrary, was unwillingly obliged to sigh.

Sir Mungo, skilful in discerning when the withers of those he conversed with were wrung, observed that his new acquaintance winced, and would willingly have pressed the discussion; but the cook's impatient knock upon the dresser with the haft of his dudgeon-knife, now gave a signal loud enough to be heard from the top of the house to the bottom, summoning, at the same time, the serving-men to place the dinner upon the table, and the guests to partake of it. Sir Mungo, who was an admirer of good cheer, (a taste which, by the way, might have some weight in reconciling his dignity to these city visits,) was tolled off by the sound, and left Nigel and the other guests in peace, until his anxiety to place himself in his due place of pre-eminence at the genial board was duly gratified. Here, seated on the left hand of Aunt Judith, he beheld Nigel occupy the station of yet higher honour on the right, dividing that matron from pretty Mistress Margaret; but he saw this with the more patience, that there stood betwixt him and the young lord a superb larded capon.

The dinner proceeded according to the form of the times: All was excellent of the kind, and besides the Scottish cheer promised, the board displayed beef and pudding, the statutory dainties of Old England. A small cupboard of plate, very choicely and beautifully wrought, did not escape the compliments of some of the company, and an oblique sneer from Sir Mungo, as intimating the owner's excellence in his own mechanical craft.

"I am not ashamed of the workmanship, Sir Mungo," said the honest citizen. "They say a good cook knows how to lick his own fingers, and methinks it were unseemly that I, who have furnished half the cupboards in broad Britain, should have my own covered with paltry pewter."

The blessing of the clergyman now set the guests at liberty to attack what was placed before them; and the meal went forward with great decorum, until Aunt Judith, in further recommendation of the capon, assured her company that it was of a celebrated breed of poultry, which she had herself brought from Scotland.

"Then, like some of its countrymen, madam," said the pitiless Sir Mungo, not without a glance towards his landlord, "it has been well larded in England."

"There are some others of his countrymen," answered Master Heriot, "to whom all the lard in England has not been able to render that good office."

Sir Mungo sneered and reddened, the rest of the company laughed; and the satirist, who had his reasons for not coming to extremity with Master George, was silent for the rest of the dinner. The dishes were exchanged for confections, and wine of the highest quality and flavour; and Nigel saw the entertainments of the wealthiest burgomasters which he had witnessed abroad, fairly outshone by the hospitality of a London citizen. Yet there was nothing ostentatious, or which seemed inconsistent with the degree of an opulent burgher.

While the collation proceeded, Nigel, according to the good breeding of the time, addressed his discourse principally to Mrs Judith, whom he found to be a woman of a strong Scottish understanding, more inclined towards the Puritans than was her brother George, (for in that relation she stood to him, though he always called her aunt,) attached to him in the strongest degree, and sedulously attentive to all his comforts. As the conversation of this good dame was neither lively nor fascinating, the young lord naturally addressed himself to the old horologer's very pretty daughter, who sate upon his left hand. From her, however, there was no extracting any reply beyond the measure of a monosyllable; and when the young gallant had said the best and most complaisant things which his courtesy supplied, the smile that mantled upon her pretty mouth was so slight and evanescent, as scarce to be discernible. Nigel was beginning to tire of his company, for the old citizens were speaking with his host of commercial matters in language to him totally unintelligible, when Sir Mungo Malagrowther suddenly summoned their attention.

That amiable personage had for some time withdrawn from the company into the recess of a projecting window, so formed and placed as to command a view of the door of the house, and of the street. This situation was probably preferred by Sir Mungo on account of the number of objects which the streets of a metropolis usually offer, of a kind congenial to the thoughts of a splenetic man. What he had hitherto seen passing there, was probably of little consequence, but now a trampling of horse was heard without, and the knight suddenly exclaimed,—"By my faith, Master George, you had better go look to shop; for here comes Knighton, the Duke of Buckingham's groom, and two fellows after him, as if he were my Lord Duke himself."

"My cash-keeper is below," said Heriot, without disturbing himself, "and he will let me know if his Grace's commands require my immediate attention."

"Umph!—cash-keeper?" muttered Sir Mungo to himself; "he would have had an easy office when I first kenn'd ye. But," said he, speaking aloud, "will you not come to the window, at least? for Knighton has trundled a piece of silver plate into your house—ha! ha! ha!—trundled it upon its edge as a callan' would drive a hoop—I cannot help laughing—ha! ha! ha!—at the fellow's impudence."

"I believe you could not help laughing, Sir Mungo," said George Heriot, rising up and leaving the room, "if your best friend lay dying."

"Bitter that, my lord—ha!" said Sir Mungo, addressing Nigel. "Our friend is not a goldsmith for nothing—he hath no leaden wit—but I will go down and see what comes on't."

Heriot, as he descended the stairs, met his cash-keeper coming up, with some concern on his face. "Why, how now, Roberts," said the goldsmith, "what means all this, man?"

"It is Knighton, Master Heriot, from the court—Knighton, the Duke's man—he brought back the salver you carried to Whitehall, flung it into the entrance as if it had been an old pewter platter, and bade me tell you the King would none of your trumpery."

"Ay!—indeed," said George Heriot—"none of my trumpery!—Come hither into the compting-room, Roberts.—Sir Mungo," he added, bowing to the knight, who had joined, and was preparing to follow them, "I pray your forgiveness for an instant."

In virtue of this prohibition, Sir Mungo, who, as well as the rest of the company, had overheard what passed betwixt George Heriot and his cash-keeper, saw himself condemned to wait in the outer busi-

ness-room, where he would have endeavoured to slake his eager
curiosity by questioning Knighton; but that emissary of greatness,
after having added to the uncivil message of his master some rudeness
of his own, had again scampered westward, with his satellites at his
heels.

In the meanwhile, the name of the Duke of Buckingham, the omnipotent favourite both of the King and the Prince of Wales, had struck
some anxiety into the party which remained in the great parlour. He
was more feared than beloved, and, if not absolutely of a tyrannical
disposition, was accounted haughty, violent, and vindictive. It pressed
on Nigel's heart, that he himself, though he could not conceive how,
nor why, might be the original cause of the resentment of the Duke
against his benefactor. The others made their comments in whispers,
until the sounds reached Ramsay, who had not heard a word of what
had previously passed, but, plunged in those studies with which he
connected every other incident and event, took up only the catchword,
and replied,—"The Duke—the Duke of Buckingham—George Villiers—ay—I have spoke with Lambe about him."

"Our Lord and our Lady! now how can you say so, father?" said his
daughter, who had shrewdness enough to see that her father was
touching upon dangerous ground.

"Why, ay, child," answered Ramsay; "the stars do but incline, they
cannot compel. But well you wot, it is commonly said of his Grace, by
those who have the skill to cast nativities, that there was a notable
conjunction of Mars and Saturn—the apparent or true time of
which, reducing the calculations of Eichstadius made for the latitude
of Oranienburgh to that of London, gives seven hours, fifty-five minutes, and forty-one seconds"——

"Hold your peace, old soothsayer," said Heriot, who at that instant
entered the room with a calm and steady countenance; "your calculations are true and undeniable when they regard brass and wire, and
mechanical force; but future events are at the pleasure of him who
bears the hearts of kings in his hand."

"Ay, but, George," answered the watchmaker, "there was a concurrence of signs at this gentleman's birth, which shewed his course
would be a strange one. Long has it been said of him, he was born at
the very meeting of night and day, and under crossing and contending
influences that may affect both us and him.

> Full moon and high sea,
> Great man shalt thou be;
> Red dawning, stormy sky,
> Bloody death shalt thou die."

"It is not good to speak of such things," said Heriot, "especially of the great; stone walls have ears, and a bird of the air shall carry the matter."

Several of the guests seemed to be of their host's opinion. The two merchants took brief leave, as if under consciousness that something was wrong. Mistress Margaret, her body-guard of 'prentices being in readiness, plucked her father by the sleeve, and rescuing him from a brown study, (whether referring to the wheels of Time, or to that of Fortune, is uncertain,) wished good-night to her friend Mrs Judith, and received her god-father's blessing, who, at the same time, put upon her slender finger a ring of much taste and some value; for he seldom suffered her to leave him without some token of his affection. Thus honourably dismissed, and accompanied by her escort, she set forth on her return to Fleet Street.

Sir Mungo had bid adieu to Master Heriot as he came out from the back compting-room, but such was the interest which he took in the affairs of his friend, that, when Master George went up stairs, he could not help walking into that sanctum sanctorum, to see how Master Roberts was employed. The knight found the honest cash-keeper busy in making extracts from those huge brass-clasped leath-ern-bound manuscript folios, which are the pride and trust of dealers, and the dread of customers whose year of grace is out. The good knight leant his elbows on the desk, and said to the functionary, in a condoling tone of voice,—"What! you have lost a good customer, I fear, Master Roberts, and are busied in making out his bill of charges?"

Now it chanced that Roberts, like Sir Mungo himself, was a little deaf, and, like Sir Mungo, knew also how to make the most of it. So he answered at cross purposes,—"I humbly crave your pardon, Sir Mungo, for not having sent in your bill of charge sooner, but my master bade me not disturb you. I will bring the items together in a moment." So saying, he began to turn over the leaves of his book of fate, murmuring, "Repairing ane silver seal—new golden clasp to his chain of office—ane over-gilt brooch to his hat, being a Saint Andrew's cross, with thistles—a copper gilt pair of spurs,—this to Daniel Driver, we not dealing in the article."

He would have proceeded; but Sir Mungo, not prepared to endure recital of the catalogue of his own petty debts, and still less willing to satisfy them on the spot, wished the book-keeper, cavalierly, good-night, and left the house without further ceremony. The clerk looked after him with a civil city sneer, and immediately resumed the more serious labours which Sir Mungo's entrance had interrupted.

Chapter Seven

Things needful we have thought on; but the thing
Of all most needful—that which Scripture terms,
As if alone it merited regard,
The ONE thing needful—that's yet unconsider'd.
                                    The Chamberlain

WHEN THE REST of the company had taken their departure from
Master Heriot's house, the young Lord of Glenvarloch also offered to
take leave; but his host detained him for a few minutes, until all were
gone excepting the clergyman.

"My lord," then said the worthy citizen, "we have had our permitted hour of honest and hospitable pastime, and now I would fain delay
you for another and graver purpose, as it is our custom, when we have
the benefit of good Mr Windsor's company, that he reads the prayers
of the church for the evening before we separate. Your excellent
father, my lord, would not have departed before family worship—I
hope the same from your lordship."

"With pleasure, sir," answered Nigel; "and you add in the invitation an additional obligation to those with which you have loaded me.
When young men forget what is their duty, they owe deep thanks to
the friend who will remind them of it."

While they talked together in this manner, the serving-men had
removed the folding-tables, brought forwards a portable reading-
desk, and placed chairs and hassocks for their master, their mistress,
and the noble stranger. Another low chair, or rather a sort of stool, was
placed close beside that of Master Heriot; and though the circumstance was trivial, Nigel was induced to notice it, because, when about
to occupy that seat, he was prevented by a sign from the old gentleman, and motioned to another of somewhat more elevation. The
clergyman took his station behind the reading-desk. The domestics, a
numerous family both of clerks and servants, including Moniplies,
attended with great gravity, and were accommodated with benches.

The household were all seated, and, externally at least, composed
to devout attention, when a low knock was heard at the door of the
apartment. Mrs Judith looked anxiously at her brother, as if desiring
to know his pleasure. He nodded his head gravely, and looked to the
door. Mrs Judith immediately crossed the chamber, opened the door,
and led into the apartment a beautiful creature, whose sudden and
singular appearance might have made her almost pass for an apparition. She was deadly pale: there was not the least shade of vital red to
enliven features, which were exquisitely formed, and might, but for

that circumstance, have been termed transcendently beautiful. Her long black hair fell down over her shoulders and down her back, combed smoothly and regularly, but without the least appearance of decoration or ornament, which looked very singular at a period when head-gear, as it was called, of one sort or other, was generally used by all ranks. Her dress was of pure white, of the simplest fashion, and hiding all her person excepting the throat, face, and hands. Her form was rather beneath than above the middle size, but so justly proportioned and elegantly made, that the spectator's attention was entirely withdrawn from her size. In contradiction of the extreme plainness of all the rest of her attire, she wore a necklace which a duchess might have envied, so large and lustrous were the brilliants of which it was composed; and around her waist a zone of rubies of scarce inferior value.

When this singular figure entered the apartment, she cast her eyes on Nigel, and paused, as if uncertain whether to advance or retreat. The glance which she took of him seemed to be one rather of uncertainty and hesitation, than of bashfulness or timidity. Aunt Judith took her by the hand, and led her slowly forward—her dark eyes, however, continued to be fixed on Nigel, with an expression of melancholy by which he felt strangely affected. Even when she was seated on the vacant stool, which was placed there probably for her accommodation, she again looked upon him more than once with the same pensive, lingering, and anxious expression, but without either shyness or embarrassment, not even so much as to call the slightest degree of complexion into her cheek.

So soon as this singular female had taken up the prayer-book which was laid upon her cushion, she seemed immersed in devotional duty; and although Nigel's attention to the service was so much disturbed by this extraordinary apparition, that he looked towards her repeatedly in the course of the service, he could never observe that her eyes or her thoughts strayed so much as a single moment from the task in which she was engaged. Nigel himself was less attentive, for the appearance of this lady seemed so extraordinary, that, strictly as he had been bred up by his father to pay the most reverential attention during performance of divine service, his thoughts in spite of himself were disturbed by her presence, and he earnestly wished the prayers were ended, that his curiosity might obtain some gratification. When the service was concluded, and each had remained, according to the decent and edifying practice of the church, concentrated in mental devotion for a short space, the mysterious visitant arose ere any other person stirred; and Nigel remarked that none of the domestics left their places, or even moved, until she had first kneeled on one knee to Heriot, who seemed to bless her with his hand laid on her head, and a melancholy solemnity of look and action. She then bended her body, but without kneeling, to Mrs Judith, and having performed these two acts of reverence, she left the room; yet just in the act of her departure, she once more turned her penetrating eyes on Nigel with a fixed look, which compelled him to turn his own eyes aside. When he looked towards her again, he saw only the skirt of the white mantle as she left the apartment.

The domestics then rose and dispersed themselves—wine, and fruit, and spices, were offered to Lord Nigel and to the clergyman, and the latter took his leave. The young lord would fain have accompanied him, in hope to get some explanation of the apparition which he had beheld, but he was stopped by his host, who requested to speak with him in his compting-room.

"I hope, my lord," said the citizen, "that your preparations for attending court are in such forwardness that you can go thither the day after to-morrow. It is perhaps the last day, for some time, that his Majesty will hold open court for all who have pretensions by birth, rank, or office, to attend upon him. On the subsequent day he goes to Theobald's, where he is so much occupied with hunting and other pleasures, that he cares not to be intruded on."

"I shall be in all outward readiness to pay my duty," said the young nobleman, "yet I have little heart to do it. The friends from whom I ought to have found encouragement and protection, have proved cold and false—I certainly will not trouble *them* for their countenance on this occasion—And yet I must confess my childish unwillingness to enter quite alone upon so new a scene."

"It is bold of a mechanic like me to make such an offer to a nobleman," said Heriot; "but I must attend at court to-morrow.—I can accompany you as far as the presence-chamber, from my privilege as being of the household. I can facilitate your entrance, should you find difficulty, and I can point out the proper manner and time of approaching the King. But I do not know," he added, smiling, "whether these little advantages will not be overbalanced by the incongruity of a nobleman receiving them from the hand of an old smith."

"From the hands rather of the only friend I have found in London," said Nigel, offering his hand.

"Nay, if you think of the matter in that way," replied the honest citizen, "there is no more to be said—I will come to you to-morrow, with a barge proper for the occasion.—But remember, my good young lord, that I do not, like some men of my degree, wish to take opportunity to step beyond it, and associate with my superiors in rank, and therefore do not fear to mortify my presumption, by suffering me to keep my distance in the presence, and where it is fitting for both of us to separate; and for what remains, most truly happy will I be in proving of service to the son of my ancient patron."

This style of conversation led so far from the point which had interested the young nobleman's curiosity, that there was no returning to it that night. He therefore exchanged thanks and greeting with George Heriot, and took his leave, promising to be equipped and in readiness to embark with him on the second successive morning at ten o'clock.

The generation of link-boys, celebrated by Count Anthony Hamilton, as peculiar to London, had already, in the reign of James I. begun their functions, and the service of one of them, with his smoky torch, had been secured to light the young Scottish lord and his follower to their own lodgings, which, though better acquainted than formerly with the city, they might in the dark have run some danger of missing. This gave the ingenious Mr Moniplies an opportunity of gathering close up to his master, after he had gone through the form of slipping his left arm into the handles of his buckler, and loosening his broad-sword in the sheath that he might be ready for whatever should befall.

"If it were not for the wine and the good cheer which we have had in yonder old man's house, my lord," said this sapient follower, "and that I ken him by report to be a just living man in many respects, and a real Edinburgh gutter-blood, I should have been well pleased to have seen how his feet were shaped, and whether he had not a cloven cloot under the braw roses and cordovan shoon of his."

"Why, you rascal," answered Nigel, "you have been too kindly treated, and now that you have filled your ravenous stomach, you are railing on the good gentleman that relieved you."

"Under favour, no, my lord," said Moniplies,—"I would only like to see something mair about him. I have eat his meat, it is true—more shame that the like of him should have meat to give, when your lordship and me could scarce have gotten, on our own accompt, brose and a bear bannock—I have drunk his wine too."

"I see you have," replied his master, "a great deal more than you should have done."

"Under your patience, my lord," said Moniplies, "you are pleased to say that, because I crushed a quart with that jolly boy Jenkin, as they call the 'prentice boy, and that was out of mere acknowledgment to his former kindness—I own that I, moreover, sung the good old song of Elsie Marley, so as they never heard it chaunted in their lives——"

And withal (as John Bunyan says,) as they went on their way, he sung—

> "O, do ye ken Elsie Marley, honey—
> The wife that sells the barley, honey?
> For Elsie Marley's grown sae fine,
> She winna get up to feed the swine.—
> O, do ye ken"——

Here in mid career was the songster interrupted by the stern gripe of his master, who threatened to batton him to death if he brought the city-watch upon them by his ill-timed melody.

"I crave pardon, my lord—I humbly crave pardon—Only when I think of that Jin Vin, as they call him, I can hardly help humming—'O do ye ken'—but I crave your honour's pardon, and will be totally dumb, if you command me so."

"No, sirrah!" said Nigel, "talk on, for I well know you would say and suffer more under pretence of holding your peace, than when you get an unbridled licence. How is it, then? What have you to say against Master Heriot?"

It seems more than probable, that in permitting this licence, the young lord hoped his attendant would stumble upon the subject of the strange young lady who had appeared at prayers in a manner so mysterious. But whether this was the case, or whether he merely desired that Moniplies should utter, in a subdued and under tone of voice, those spirits which might otherwise have vented themselves in obstreperous song, it is certain he permitted his attendant to proceed with his story in his own way.

"And therefore," said the orator, availing himself of his immunity, "I would like to ken what for a carle this Master Heriot is. He hath supplied your lordship with wealth of gold, as I can understand. And if he has, I make it for certain he hath had his ain end in it, according to the fashion of the warld. Now had your lordship your own good lands at your guiding, doubtless this person, with most of his craft—goldsmiths they call themsells—I say usurers—wald be glad to exchange so many pounds of African dust, by whilk I understand gold, against so many broad acres and hundreds of acres of a brave Scottish laird."

"But you know I have no land," said the young lord, "at least none that can be affected by any debt which I can at present become obliged for—I think you need not have reminded me of that."

"True, my lord, most true; and as your lordship says, open to the meanest capacity, without any unnecessary expositions. Now therefore, my lord, unless Master George Heriot has something mair to allege as a motive for his liberality, vara different from the possession of your estate—and moreover, as he could gain little by the capture of your body, wherefore should it not be your soul that he is in pursuit of?"

"My soul, you rascal!" said the young lord; "What good should my soul do him?"

"What do I ken about that?" said Moniplies; "they go about roaring and seeking whom they may devour—doubtless, they like the food that they rage so much about—And, my lord, they say," added Moniplies, drawing up still closer to his master's side, "that Master Heriot has one spirit in his house already."

"How, or what do you mean?" said Nigel; "I will break your head, you drunken knave, if you palter with me any longer."

"Drunken?" answered his trusty adherent, "and is this the story?—why, how could I but drink your lordship's health on my bare knee, when Master Jenkin began it to me?—hang them that would not—I would have cut the impudent knave's hams with my broad-sword, that should make scruple of it, and so have made him kneel when he should have found it difficult to rise again. But touching the spirit," he proceeded, finding that his master made no answer to his valorous tirade, "your lordship has seen her with your own eyes."

"I saw no spirit," said Glenvarloch, but yet breathing thick as one who expects some singular disclosure; "what mean you by a spirit?"

"You saw a young lady come into prayers, that spoke not a word to any one, only made becks and bows to the old gentleman and lady of the house—Ken ye wha she is?"

"No indeed," answered Nigel; "some relation of the family, I suppose."

"De'il a bit—de'il a bit," answered Moniplies, hastily, "not a blood-drop's kin to them, if she had a drap of blood in her body—I tell you but what all human beings allege to be truth, that dwell within hue and cry of Lombard-street—that lady, or quean, or whatever you chuse to call her, has been dead in the body these many a year, though she haunts them, as we have seen, even at their very devotions."

"You will allow her to be a good spirit at least," said Nigel Olifaunt, "since she chuses such a time to visit her friends."

"For that I kenna, my lord," answered the superstititous follower; "I ken no spirit that would have faced the right down hammer blow of Mess John Knox, whom my father stood by in his very warst days, bating when the court was against him, which my father supplied with butcher-meat. But yon divine has another airt from powerful Master Rollock, and Mess David Black, of North Leith, and sic like.—Alack-a-day! whae can ken, if it please your lordship, whether sic prayers as the Southron read out of their auld blethering black mess-book there, may not be as powerful to invite the fiend, as a right red-het prayer warm frae the heart, may be powerful to drive him away, even as the Evil Spirit was driven by the smell of the fish's liver from the bridal-chamber of Sara, the daughter of Raguel? As to whilk story, nevertheless, I make scruple to say whether it be truth or not, better men than I am having doubted on that matter."

"Well, well, well," said his master, impatiently, "we are now near home, and I have permitted you to speak of this matter for once, that we may have an end of your prying folly, and your ideotical superstitions, for ever. For whom do you, or your absurd authors and informers, take this lady?"

"I can say naething preceesely as to that," answered Moniplies; "certain it is her body died and was laid in the grave many a day since, notwithstanding she still wanders on earth, and chiefly amongst Master Heriot's family, though she hath been seen in other places too by them that well knew her. But who she is, I will not warrant to say, or how she becomes attached, like a Highland Brownie, to some peculiar family. They say she has a row of apartments of her own, anti-room, parlour, and bed-room; but de'il a bed she sleeps in but her own coffin, and the walls, doors, and windows are so chinked up, as to prevent the least blink of daylight from entering; and then she dwells by torch-light."

"To what purpose, if she be a spirit?" said Nigel Olifaunt.

"How can I tell your lordship?" answered his attendant. "I thank God, I know nothing of her likings, or mislikings—only her coffin is there; and I leave your lordship to guess what a live person has to do with a coffin—as little as a ghost with a lantern, I trow."

"Her coffin!" repeated Nigel. "Does a creature so young and so beautiful, already contemplate her bed of last long rest?"

"In troth, even so, my lord," answered Moniplies, "for, as they told me who have seen it, it is made of heben-wood, with silver nails, and lined all through with three-piled damask, might serve a princess to rest in."

"Singular," said Nigel, whose brain, like that of most active young spirits, was easily caught by the singular and the romantic; "does she not eat with the family?"

"Who!—She!"—exclaimed Moniplies, as if surprised at the question; "they would need a lang spoon would sup with her, I trow—always there is something put for her into the tower, as they call it, whilk is a whigmaleery of a whirling-box, that turns round and round half on the tae side o' the wa', half on the t'other."

"I have seen the contrivance in foreign nunneries," said the Lord of Glenvarloch. "And is it thus she receives her food?"

"They tell me something is put in ilka day, for fashion's sake," replied the attendant; "but it's no to be supposed she would consume it, ony mair than the images of Baal and the Dragon consumed the dainty vivers that were placed before them. There are stout yeomen and chamber-queans in the house, enow to play the part of Lick it up a', as well as the threescore and ten priests of Bel, besides their wives and children."

"And she is never seen in the family but when the hour of prayer arrives?" said the master.

"Never, that I hear of," replied the servant.

"It is singular," said Nigel Olifaunt, musing. "Were it not for the ornaments which she wears, and still more for her attendance upon the service of the Protestant Church, I would know what to think, and should believe her either a Catholic votaress, who, for some cogent reason, was allowed to make her cell here in London, or some unhappy Popish devotee who was in the course of undergoing a dreadful penance. As it is, I know not what to deem of it."

His reverie was interrupted by the link-boy knocking at the door of honest John Christie, whose wife came forth with "quips, and becks, and wreathed smiles," to welcome her honoured guest on his return to his apartments.

Chapter Eight

> Ay! mark the matron well—and laugh not, Harry,
> At her old steeple hat and velvet guard—
> I've call'd her like the ear of Dionysius;
> I mean that ear-form'd vault built o'er his dungeon,
> To catch the groans and discontented murmurs
> Of his poor bondsmen—even so doth Martha
> Drink up for her own purpose all that passes,
> Or is supposed to pass in this wide city—
> She can retail it too, if that her profit
> Shall call on her to do so; and retail it
> For your advantage, so that you can make
> Your profit jump with hers.
> *The Conspiracy*

WE MUST NOW introduce to the reader's acquaintance another character, busy and important far beyond her ostensible situation in society, in a word, Dame Ursula Suddlechop, wife of Benjamin Suddlechop, the most renowned barber in all Fleet-street. This dame had her own particular merits, the principal part of which was (if her own report could be trusted,) an infinite desire to be of service to her fellow-creatures. Leaving to her thin half-starved partner the boast of having the most dexterous snap with his fingers of any shaver in London, and the care of a shop where starved apprentices flayed the

faces of those who were boobies enough to trust them, the dame drove
a separate and more lucrative trade, which yet had so many odd turns
and windings, that it seemed in many respects to contradict itself.

Its highest and most important duties were of a very secret and
confidential nature, and Dame Ursula Suddlechop was never known
to betray any transaction intrusted to her, unless she had either been
indifferently paid for her service, or that some one found it convenient
to give her a double douceur to make her disgorge the secret; and
these contingencies happened in so few cases, that her character for
trustiness remained as unimpeached as that for honesty and benevolence.

In fact, she was a most admirable matron, and could be useful to the
impassioned and the frail in the rise, progress, and consequences of
their passion. She could contrive an interview for lovers who could
shew proper reasons for meeting privately; she could relieve the frail
fair one of the burthen of a guilty passion, and perhaps establish the
hopeful offspring of unlicensed love as the heir of some family whose
love was lawful, but where an heir had not followed the union. More
than this she could do, and had been concerned in deeper and dearer
secrets: She had been a pupil of Mrs Turner, and learned from her
the secret of making the yellow starch, and, it may be, two or three
other secrets of more consequence, though perhaps none that went to
the criminal extent of those whereof her mistress was accused. But all
that was deep and dark in her real character, was covered by the shew
of outward mirth and good-humour, the hearty laugh and buxom jest
with which the dame knew well how to conciliate the elder part of her
neighbours, and the many petty arts by which she could recommend
herself to the younger, those especially of her own sex.

Dame Ursula was, in appearance, scarce past forty, and her full, but
not overgrown form, and still comely features, although her person
was plumped out, and her face somewhat coloured by good cheer, had
a joyous expression of gaiety and good humour, which set off the
remains of beauty in the wane. Marriages, births, and christenings,
were seldom thought to be performed with sufficient ceremony, for a
considerable distance around her abode, unless Dame Ursley, as they
called her, was present. She could contrive all sorts of pastimes,
games, and jests, which might amuse the large companies whom the
hospitality of our ancestors assembled together on such occasions, so
that her presence was literally considered as indispensable in the
family of all citizens of ordinary rank, on such joyous occasions. So
much also was she supposed to know of life and its labyrinths, that she
was the willing confidante of half the loving couples in the vicinity,
most of whom used to communicate their secrets, and receive their

counsel from Dame Ursley. The rich rewarded her services with rings, owches, and gold pieces which she liked still better; and she very generously gave her assistance to the poor on the same mixed principles as young practitioners in medicine assist the poor, partly from compassion, and partly to keep her hand in use.

Dame Ursley's reputation in the city was the greater that her practice had extended beyond Temple-Bar, and that she had acquaintances, nay, patrons and patronesses, among the quality, whose rank, as their members were much fewer, and the prospect of approaching the courtly sphere much more difficult, bore a degree of consequence unknown to the present day, when the toe of the citizen presses so close on the courtier's heel. Dame Ursley maintained her intercourse with this superior rank of customers, partly by driving a small trade in perfumes, essences, pomades, head-gears from France, dishes or ornaments from China, then already beginning to become fashionable; not to mention drugs of various descriptions, chiefly for the use of the ladies, and partly by other services, more or less connected with the esoteric branches of her profession heretofore alluded to.

Possessing such and so many various modes of thriving, Dame Ursley was nevertheless so poor, that she might probably have mended her own circumstances, as well as her husband's, if she had renounced them all, and set herself quietly down to take care of her own household, and to assist Benjamin in the concerns of his trade. But Ursula was luxurious and genial in her habits, and could no more have endured the stinted economy of Benjamin's board, than she could have reconciled herself to the bald chat of his conversation.

It was on the evening of the day on which Lord Nigel Olifaunt dined with the wealthy goldsmith, that we must introduce Ursula Suddlechop upon the stage. She had that morning made a long tour to Westminster, was fatigued, and had assumed a certain large elbow-chair, smooth with frequent use, placed on one side of her chimney, in which there was lit a small but bright fire. Here she observed, betwixt sleeping and waking, the simmering of a pot of well-spiced ale, on the brown surface of which bobbed a small crab-apple, sufficiently roasted, while a little mulatto girl watched, still more attentively, the process of dressing a veal sweet-bread, in a silver stew-pan which occupied the other side of the chimney. With these viands, doubtless, Dame Ursula proposed concluding the well-spent day, of which she reckoned the labour over, and the rest at her own command. She was deceived, though; for just as the ale, or, to speak technically, the lamb's-wool, was fitted for drinking, and the little dingy maiden intimated that the sweet-bread was ready to be eaten, the thin cracked voice of Benjamin was heard from the bottom of the stairs.

"Why, Dame Ursley—why, wife, I say—Why, dame—Why, love, you are wanted more than a strop for a blunt razor—Why, dame!"——

"I would some one would draw the razor across thy wind-pipe, thou bawling ass," said the dame to herself, in the first moment of irritation, against her clamorous helpmate; and then called aloud,—"Why, what is the matter, Master Suddlechop? I am just going to slip into bed; I have been daggled to and fro the whole day."

"Nay, sweetheart, it is not me," said the patient Benjamin, "but the Scotch laundry-maid from neighbour Ramsay's, who must speak with you incontinent."

At the word, sweetheart, Dame Ursley cast a wistful look at the mess which was stewed to a second in the stew-pan, and then replied, with a sigh,—"Bid Scotch Jenny come up, Master Suddlechop. I will be very happy to hear what she has to say;" then added in a lower tone, "and I hope she will go to the devil in the flame of a tar-barrel, like many a Scotch witch before her."

The Scotch laundress entered accordingly, and having heard nothing of the last kind wish of Dame Suddlechop, made her reverence with considerable respect, and said, her young mistress was returned home unwell, and wished to see her neighbour, Dame Ursley, directly. "And why will it not do to-morrow, Jenny, my good woman?" said Dame Ursley; "for I have been as far as Whitehall to-day already, and I am well nigh worn off my feet, my good woman."

"Aweel!" answered Jenny, with great composure, "and if that sae be sae, I maun take the langer tramp mysell, and maun gae down the waterside for auld Mother Redcap, at the Hungerford Stairs, that deals in comforting young creatures, e'en as you do yoursell, hinny; for ane of ye the bairn maun see before she sleeps, and that's aw that I ken on't."

So saying, the old emissary, without further entreaty, turned on her heel, and was about to retreat, when Dame Ursley exclaimed,—"No, no—if the sweet child, your mistress, has any necessary occasion for good advice and kind tendance, you need not go to Mother Redcap, Janet. She may do very well for skippers' wives, chandlers' daughters, and such like; but nobody shall wait on pretty Mistress Margaret, the daughter of his most Sacred Majesty's horologer, excepting and saving myself. And so I will but take my chopines and my cloak, and put on my muffler, and cross the street to neighbour Ramsay's in an instant. But tell me yourself, good Jenny, are you not something tired of your young lady's frolics and change of mind twenty times a-day?"

"In troth, not I," said the patient drudge, "unless it may be when she is a wee fashious about washing her laces; but I have been her keeper since she was a bairn, neighbour Suddlechop, and that makes a difference."

"Ay," said Dame Ursley, still busied putting on additional defences against the night air; "and you know for certain that she has two hundred pounds a-year in good land, at her own free disposal?"

"Left by her grandmother, Heaven rest her soul," said the Scotchwoman; "and to a daintier lassie she could not have bequeathed it."

"Very true, very true, mistress; for, with all her little whims, I have always said Mistress Margaret Ramsay was the prettiest girl in the ward; and, Jenny, I warrant the poor child has had no supper."

Jenny could not say but it was the case, for her master being out, the twa poor 'prentice lads had gone out after shutting shop, to fetch them home—And she and the other maid had gone out to Sandy Mac-Given's, to see a friend frae Scotland.

"As was very natural, Mrs Janet," said Dame Ursley, who found her interest in assenting to all sorts of propositions from all sorts of persons.

"And so the fire went out, too—," said Jenny.

"Which was the most natural of the whole," said Dame Suddlechop; "and so, to cut the matter short, Jenny, I'll carry over the little bit of supper that I was going to eat. For dinner I have tasted none, and it may be my young pretty Mistress Marget will eat a morsel with me; for it is mere emptiness, Mistress Jenny, that often puts these fancies of illness into young folk's heads." So saying, she put the silver posset-cup with the ale into Jenny's hands, and assuming her mantle with the alacrity of one determined to sacrifice inclination to duty, she hid the stew-pan under its folds, and commanded Wiba, the little mulatto girl, to light them across the street.

"Whither away, so late?" said the barber, whom they passed seated with his starveling boys round a mess of stock-fish and parsnips, in the shop below.

"If I were to tell you, Gaffer," said the dame, with most contemptuous coolness, "I do not think you could do my errand, so I will e'en keep it to myself." Benjamin was too much accustomed to his wife's independent mode of conduct, to pursue his inquiry further; nor did the dame tarry for farther question, but marched out at door, telling the eldest of the boys "to sit up till her return, and look to the house the whilst."

The night was dark and rainy, and although the distance betwixt the two shops was short, it allowed Dame Ursley leisure enough, while she strode along with high-tucked petticoats, to embitter it by the following grumbling reflections—"I wonder what I have done, that I must need trudge at every old beldame's bidding, and every young minx's maggot! I have been marched from Temple-Bar to White-chapel, on the matter of a pin-maker's wife having pricked her finger —marry, her husband that made the weapon might have salved the wound.—And here is this fantastic ape, pretty Mistress Marget for-sooth—such a beauty as I could make of a Dutch doll, and as fant-astic, and humorous, and conceited, as if she were a duchess. I have seen her in the same day as changeful as a marmozet, and as stubborn as a mule. I should like to know whether her little conceited noddle, or her father's old crazy, calculating jolter-pate, breeds most whimsies. But then there's that two hundred pounds a-year in dirty land, and the father is held a close chuff, though a fanciful—he is our landlord beside, and she has begged a late day from him for our rent; so God help me, I must be conformable—besides, the little capricious devil is my only key to get at Master George Heriot's secret, and it concerns my character to find that out; and so, *andiamos*, as the lingua franca hath it."

Thus pondering, she moved forwards with hasty strides until she arrived at the watch-maker's habitation. The attendant admitted them by means of a pass-key. Onward glided Dame Ursula, now in glimmer and now in gloom, not like the lovely Lady Christabelle through Gothic sculpture and ancient armour, but creeping and stumbling amongst relics of old machines, and models of new inventions in various branches of mechanics, with which wrecks of useless ingenu-ity, either in a broken or half-finished shape, the apartment of the fanciful though ingenious mechanist was continually lumbered.

At length they attained, by a very narrow stair-case, pretty Mistress Margaret's apartment, where she, the cynosure of the eyes of every bold young bachelor in Fleet-street, sate in a posture which hovered between the discontented and the disconsolate. For her pretty back and shoulders were rounded into a curve, her round and dimpled chin reposed in the hollow of her little palm, while the fingers were folded over her mouth; her elbow rested on a table, and her eyes seemed fixed upon the dying charcoal, which was expiring in a small grate. She scarce turned her head when Dame Ursula entered, and when the presence of that estimable matron was more precisely announced in words by the old Scots-woman, Mistress Margaret, without changing her posture, muttered some sort of answer that was totally unintelli-gible.

"Go your ways down to the kitchen with Wiba, good Mistress Jenny," said Dame Ursula, who was used to all sorts of freaks on the part of her patients or clients, whichever they might be termed; "put the stew-pan and the porringer by the fire-side, and go down below—I must speak to my pretty love, Mistress Margaret, by myself—and there is not a bachelor betwixt this and Bow but will envy me the privilege."

The attendants retired as directed, and Dame Ursula, having availed herself of the embers of charcoal, to place her stew-pan to the best advantage, drew herself as close as she could to her patient, and began in a low, soothing, and confidential tone of voice, to inquire what ailed her pretty flower of neighbours.

"Nothing, dame," said Margaret, somewhat pettishly, and changing her posture so as rather to turn her back upon the kind inquirer.

"Nothing, lady-bird?" answered Dame Suddlechop; "and do you use to send for your friends out of bed at this hour for nothing?"

"It was not I who sent for you, dame," replied the malcontent maiden.

"And who was it, then?" said Ursula; "for if I had not been sent for, I had not been here at this time of night, I promise you!"

"It was the old Scotch fool Jenny, who did it out of her own head, I suppose," said Margaret; "for she has been stunning me these two hours about you and Mother Redcap."

"Me and Mother Redcap!" said Dame Ursula, "an old fool indeed, that couples folks up so.—But come, come, my sweet little neighbour, Jenny is no such fool after all; she knows young folks want more and better advice than her own, and she knows too where to find it for them; so you must take heart of grace, my pretty maiden, and tell me what you are moping about, and then let Dame Ursula alone for finding out a cure."

"Nay, an ye be so wise, Mother Ursula," replied the girl, "you may guess what I ail without my telling you."

"Ay, ay, child," answered the complaisant matron, "no one can play better than I at the good old game of What is my thought like? Now I'll warrant that little head of yours is running on a new head-tire, a foot higher than those our city dames wear—Or you are all for a trip to Islington or Ware, and your father is cross and will not consent—or"——

"Or you are an old fool, Dame Suddlechop," said Margaret, peevishly, "and must needs trouble yourself about matters you know nothing of."

"Fool as much as you will, mistress," said Dame Ursula, offended in her turn, "but not very many years older than yourself, mistress."

"Oh we are angry, are we?" said the beauty; "and pray, Madam Ursula, how come you, that are not so many years older than me, to talk about such nonsense to me, who am so many years younger, and who yet have too much sense to care about head-gears and Islington?"

"Well, well, young mistress," said the sage counsellor, rising, "I perceive I can be of no use here; and methinks, since you know your own matters so much better than other people do, you might dispense with disturbing folks at midnight to ask their advice."

"Why, now you are angry, mother," said Margaret, detaining her; "this comes of your coming out at even-tide without eating your supper—I never heard you utter a cross word after you had finished your little morsel.—Here Janet, a trencher and salt for Dame Ursula —And what have you in that porringer, dame?—filthy clammy ale, as I would live—Let Janet fling it out of window, or keep it for my father's morning draught; and she shall bring you the pottle of sack that was set ready for him—good man, he will never find out the difference, for ale will wash down his dusty calculations quite as well as wine."

"Truly, sweetheart, I am of your opinion," said Dame Ursula, whose temporary displeasure vanished at once before these preparations for good cheer; and so, settling herself on the great easy-chair, with a three-legged table before her, she began to dispatch, with good appetite, the little delicate dish which she had prepared for herself. She did not fail, however, in the duties of civility, and earnestly, but in vain, pressed Mistress Margaret to partake her dainties. The damsel declined the invitation.

"At least pledge me in a glass of sack," said Dame Ursula; "I have heard my grandame say, that before the gospellers came in, the old Catholic father confessors and their penitents always had a cup of sack together before confession, to loosen the tongue of the one, and to soften the rigour of the other. Now I am your confessor, and you are my penitent."

"I shall drink no sack, I am sure," said Margaret; "and I told you before, that if you cannot find out what ails me, I shall never have the heart to tell it."

So saying, she turned away from Dame Ursula once more, and resumed her musing posture, with her hand on her elbow, and her back, at least one shoulder, turned towards her confidante.

"Nay then," said Dame Ursula, "I must exert my skill in good earnest—you must give me this pretty hand, and I will tell you by palmistry, as well as any gipsey of them all, what foot it is you halt upon."

"As if I halted on any foot at all," said Margaret, something scornfully, but yielding her left hand to Ursula, and continuing at the same time her averted position.

"I see brave lines here," said Ursula, "and not ill to read neither— pleasure and wealth, and merry nights and late mornings to my Beauty, and such an equipage as shall shake Whitehall. O, have I touched you there?—and smile you now, my pretty one?—for why should not he be Lord Mayor, and go to court in his gilded caroch, as others have done before him?"

"Lord Mayor? pshaw!" replied Margaret.

"And why pshaw at my Lord Mayor, sweetheart? or perhaps you pshaw at my prophecy; but there is a cross in every one's line of life as well as in yours, darling. And what though I see a 'prentice's flat cap in this pretty palm, yet there is a sparkling black eye under it, hath not its match in the Ward of Farringdon-Without."

"Whom do you mean, dame?" said Margaret, coldly.

"Whom should I mean," said Dame Ursula, "but the prince of 'prentices, and king of good company, Jenkin Vincent?"

"Out, woman—Jenkin Vincent—a clown—a cockney!" exclaimed the indignant damsel.

"Ay, sits the wind in that corner, Beauty!" quoth the dame; "why, it has changed something since we spoke together last, for then I would have sworn it blew fairer for poor Jin Vin; and the poor lad doats on you too, and would rather see your eyes than the first glimpse of the sun on the great holiday on May-day."

"I would my eyes had the power of the sun to blind his then," said Margaret, "to teach the drudge his place."

"Nay," said Dame Ursula, "there be some who say that Frank Tunstall is as proper a lad as Jin Vin, and of surety he is third cousin to a knighthood, and come of a good house; and so mayhap you may be for Northward ho!"

"Maybe I may"—answered Margaret, "but not with my father's 'prentice—I thank you, Dame Ursula."

"Nay then, the devil may guess your thoughts for me," said Dame Ursula; "this comes of trying to shoe a filly that is eternally wincing and shifting ground!"

"Hear me then," said Margaret, "and mind what I say.—This day I dined abroad"——

"I can tell you where," answered her counsellor,—"with your god-father the rich goldsmith—ay, you see I know something—nay, I could tell you an I would, with whom too."

"Indeed!" said Margaret, turning suddenly round with an accent of strong surprise, and colouring up to the eyes.

"With old Sir Mungo Malagrowther," said the oracular dame,— "he was trimmed in my Benjamin's shop on his way to the city."

"Pshaw! the frightful old mouldy skeleton!" said the damsel.

"Indeed you say true, my dear," replied the confidante,—"it is a shame to him to be out of Saint Pancras's charnel-house, for I know no other place he is fit for, the foul-mouth old railer—he said to my husband"——

"Somewhat which signifies nothing to our purpose, I dare say," interrupted Margaret. "I *must* speak then.—There dined with us a nobleman"——

"A nobleman! the maiden's mad—" said Dame Ursula.

"There dined with us, I say," continued Margaret, without regarding the interruption, "a nobleman—a Scottish nobleman."

"Now Our Lady keep her," said the confidante, "she is quite frantic!—heard ever any one of a watchmaker's daughter falling in love with a nobleman—and a Scotch nobleman, to make the matter complete, who are all as proud as Lucifer, and as poor as Job? A Scotch nobleman, quotha? I had as lief you told me of a Jew pedlar. I would have you think how all this is to end, pretty one, before you jump in the dark."

"That is nothing to you, Ursula—it is your assistance," said Mistress Margaret, "and not your advice that I am desirous to have, and you know I can make worth your while."

"O, it is not for the sake of lucre, Mistress Margaret," answered the obliging dame; "but truly I would have you listen to some advice—bethink you of your own condition."

"My father's calling is mechanical," said Margaret, "but our blood is not so. I have heard my father say that we are descended, at a distance indeed, from the great Earls of Dalwolsey."

"Ay, ay," said Dame Ursula; "even so—I never knew a Scot of you but was *descended*, as ye call it, from some great house or other; and a piteous descent it often is—and as for the distance you speak of, it is so great as to put you out of sight of each other.—Yet do not toss your pretty head so scornfully, but tell me the name of this lordly northern gallant, and we will try what can be done in the matter."

"It is Lord Glenvarloch, whom they call Lord Nigel Olifaunt," said Margaret in a low voice, and turning away to hide her blushes.

"Marry, heaven forefend!" exclaimed Dame Suddlechop; "this is the very devil, and something worse!"

"How mean you?" said the damsel, surprised at the vivacity of her exclamation.

"Why, know ye not," said the dame, "what powerful enemies he has at court? know ye not—but my tongue blusters on, it runs too fast for my wit—enough to say, that you had better make your bridal-bed under a falling house, than think of young Glenvarloch."

"He *is* unfortunate then," said Margaret; "I knew it—I divined it—there was sorrow in his voice when he said even what was gay—there was a touch of misfortune in his melancholy smile—he had not thus clung to my thoughts had I seen him in all the mid-day glare of prosperity."

"Romances have cracked her brain!" said Dame Ursula; "she is a castaway girl—utterly distraught—loves a Scotch lord—and likes him the better for being unfortunate! Well, mistress, I am sorry this is a matter I cannot aid you in—it goes against my conscience—and it is an affair above my condition, and beyond my management;—but I will keep your secret."

"You will not be so base as to desert me, after having drawn my secret from me!" said Margaret indignantly; "if you do, I know how to have my revenge; and if you do not, I will reward you well. Remember the house your husband dwells in is my father's property."

"I remember it but too well, Mistress Margaret," said Ursula, after a moment's reflection, "and I would serve you in any thing in my condition; but to meddle with such high matters—I shall never forget poor Mistress Turner, my honoured patroness, peace be with her!— she had the ill luck to meddle in the matter of Somerset and Overbury, and so the great earl and his lady slipt their necks out of the collar, and left her and some half dozen others to suffer in their stead. I shall never forget the sight of her standing on the scaffold with the ruff round her pretty neck, all done up with the yellow starch which I had so often helped her to make, and that was so soon to give place to a rough hempen cord—such a sight, sweetheart, will make one loth to meddle with matters that are too hot or heavy for your handling."

"Out, you fool!" answered Mistress Margaret; "am I one to speak to you about such criminal practices as that wretch died for? All I desire of you, is to get me precise knowledge of what affair brings this young nobleman to Court."

"And when you have his secret," said Ursula, "what will it avail you, sweetheart?—and yet I would do your errand, if you could do as much for me."

"And what is it you would have of me?" said Mistress Margaret.

"What you have been angry with me for asking before," answered Dame Ursula. "I want to have some light about the story of your god-father's ghost, that is only seen at prayers."

"Not for the world," said Mistress Margaret, "will I be a spy on my kind god-father's secrets—no, Ursula—that I will never pry into, which he desires to keep hidden. But thou knowst that I have a fortune of my own, which must at no distant day come under my own management."

"Ay, that I well know," said the counsellor—"it is that two hundred per year, with your father's indulgence, that makes you so wilful, sweetheart."

"It may be so—" said Margaret Ramsay; "meanwhile, do you serve me truly, and here is a ring of value in pledge, that when my fortune is in my own hand, I will redeem the token with fifty broad pieces of gold."

"Fifty broad pieces of gold!" repeated the dame; "and this ring, which is a right fair one, in token you fail not of your word!—Well, sweetheart, if I must put my throat in peril, I am sure I cannot risk it for a friend more generous than you; and I would not think of more than the pleasure of serving you, only Benjamin gets more idle every day, and our family"——

"Say no more of it," said Margaret; "we understand each other. And now, tell me what you know of this young man's affairs, which made you so unwilling to meddle with them."

"Of that I can say no great matter, as yet," answered Dame Ursula; "only I know the most powerful among his own countrymen are against him, and also the most powerful at the court here. But I will learn more of it, for it will be a dim print that I will not read for your sake, pretty Mistress Margaret. Know you where this gallant dwells?"

"I—I—heard by accident," said Margaret, as if ashamed of the minute particularity of her memory upon such an occasion,—"he lodges, I think—at one Christie's—if I mistake not—at Paul's Wharf—A ship-chandler's."

"A proper lodging for a young baron!—Well, but cheer you up, Mistress Margaret—if he has come up a caterpillar, like some of his countrymen, he may cast his slough like them, and come out a butter-fly. So I drink good-night, and sweet dreams to you, in another parting cup of sack; and you shall hear tidings of me within four-and-twenty hours. And once more, I commend you to your pillow, my pearl of pearls, and Marguerite of Marguerites."

So saying, she kissed the reluctant cheek of her young friend, or patroness, and took her departure with the light and stealthy pace of one accustomed to accommodate her footsteps to the purposes of dispatch and secrecy. Margaret Ramsay looked after her for some time, in anxious silence. "I did ill," she at length murmured, "to let her wring this out of me—but she is artful, bold, and serviceable—and I think faithful—or if not, she will be true at least to her interest, and that I can command. I would I had not spoken, however—I have begun a hopeless work—for what has he said to me, to warrant my meddling in his fortunes?—nothing but words of the most ordinary import—mere table-talk and terms of course. Yet who knows—" she said, and then broke off, looking at the glass the while, which, as it reflected back a face of great beauty, probably suggested to her mind a more favourable conclusion of the sentence than she cared to trust her tongue withal.

Chapter Nine

So pitiful a thing is suitor's state!
Most miserable man, whom wicked fate
Hath brought to Court to sue, for *Had I wist*,
That few have found, and many a one hath miss'd!
Full little knowest thou, that hast not tried,
What hell it is, in sueing long to bide:
To lose good days, that might be better spent;
To waste long nights in pensive discontent;
To speed to–day, to be put back to–morrow;
To feed on hope, to pine with fear and sorrow;
To have thy Prince's grace, yet want her Peers',
To have thy asking, yet wait many years;
To fret thy soul with crosses and with cares—
To eat thy heart through comfortless despairs.
To fawn, to crouch, to wait, to ride, to run,
To spend, to give, to want, to be undone.
Mother Hubberd's Tale

ON THE MORNING of the day on which George Heriot had prepared to escort the young Lord of Glenvarloch to the court at Whitehall, it may be reasonably supposed that the young man, whose fortunes were likely to depend upon this cast, felt himself more than usually anxious. He rose early, made his toilette with unusual care, and, being enabled, by the generosity of his more plebeian country-man, to set out a very handsome person to the best advantage, he obtained a momentary approbation from himself as he glanced at the mirror, and a loud and distinct plaudit from his landlady, who declared at once that in her judgment, he would take the wind out of the sail of every gallant in the Presence; so much had she been able to enrich her discourse with the metaphors of those with whom her husband dealt.

At the appointed hour, the barge of Master George Heriot arrived, handsomely manned and appointed, having a tilt, with his own cypher, and the arms of his company painted thereupon.

The young Lord of Glenvarloch received the friend who had evinced such disinterested attachment, with the kind courtesy which well became him.

Master Heriot then made him acquainted with the bounty of his Sovereign, which he paid over to his young friend, declining what he had himself formerly advanced to him. Nigel felt all the gratitude which the citizen's disinterested friendship had deserved, and was not wanting in expressing it suitably.

Yet as the young and high-born nobleman embarked to go to the presence of his Prince, under the patronage of one whose best, or most distinguished qualification, was his being an eminent member of the Goldsmith's Incorporation, he felt a little surprised, if not abashed, at his own situation; and Richie Moniplies, as he stepped over the gang-way to take his place forward in the boat, could not help muttering,—"It was a changed day betwixt Master Heriot and his honest father in the Kræmes;—but, doubtless, there was a difference between clinking on gold and silver, and clattering upon blue pewter."

On they glided, by the assistance of the oars of four stout watermen, along the Thames, which then served for the principal high-road betwixt London and Westminster; for few ventured on horseback through the narrow and crowded streets of the city, and coaches were then a luxury reserved only for the higher nobility, and to which no citizen, whatever was his wealth, presumed to aspire. The beauty of the banks, especially on the northern side, where the gardens of the nobility descended from their hotels, in many places, down to the water's edge, was pointed out to Nigel by his kind conductor, and was pointed out in vain. The mind of the young Lord of Glenvarloch was filled with anticipations, not the most pleasant, concerning the manner in which he was likely to be received by that monarch, in whose behalf his family had been nearly reduced to ruin; and he was, with the usual anxiety of those in such a situation, framing imaginary questions from the King, and over-toiling his spirit in devising answers to them. His conductor saw the labour of Nigel's mind, and avoided increasing it by farther conversation; so that when he had explained to him briefly the ceremonies observed at court on such occasions of presentation, the rest of their voyage was performed in silence.

They landed at Whitehall-Stairs, and entered the Palace upon announcing their names, the guards paying to Lord Glenvarloch the respect and honours due to his rank. The young man's heart beat high and thick within him as he came within the royal apartments. His education abroad, conducted as it had been on a narrow and limited scale, had given him but imperfect ideas of the grandeur of a court; and the philosophical reflections which taught him to set ceremonial and exterior splendour at defiance, proved, like other maxims of mere philosophy, ineffectual at the moment they were weighed against the impression naturally made on the mind of an inexperienced youth, by the unusual magnificence of the scene. The splendid apartments through which they passed, the rich apparel of the grooms, guards, and domestics in waiting, and the unusual ceremonial attending their passage through the long suite of apartments, had something in it, trifling and common-place as it might appear to practised courtiers, embarrassing, and even alarming, to one, who, for the first time, went through these forms, and who was doubtful what sort of reception was to accompany his first appearance before his Sovereign.

Heriot, in anxious attention to save his young friend from the least momentary embarrassment, had taken care to give the necessary password to the warders, grooms of the chambers, ushers, or by whatever name they were designated; so they went onward without interruption.

In this manner they passed several anti-rooms, filled chiefly with guards, attendants of the court, and their acquaintances, male and female, who, dressed in their best apparel, and with eyes rounded by eager curiosity to make the most of their opportunity, stood, with beseeming modesty, ranked against the wall, in a manner which indicated that they were spectators, not performers, in the courtly exhibition.

Through these exterior apartments Lord Glenvarloch and his city friend went onward into a large and splendid withdrawing-room, communicating with the presence-chamber, into which anti-room were admitted those only, who, from birth, their posts in the state or household, or by the particular grant of the King, had right to attend the court, as men entitled to pay their respects to their Sovereign.

Amid this favoured and selected company, Nigel observed Sir Mungo Malagrowther, who, shaken off and discountenanced by those who knew how low he stood in court interest and favour, was but too happy in the opportunity of hooking himself upon a person of Lord Glenvarloch's rank, who was, as yet, so inexperienced as to feel it difficult to shake off an intruder.

The knight forthwith framed his grim features to a ghastly smile, and after a preliminary and patronizing nod to George Heriot, accompanied with an aristocratic wave of the hand, which intimated at once superiority and protection, he laid aside altogether the honest citizen, to whom he owed many a dinner, to attach himself exclusively to the young lord, although he suspected he might be occasionally in the predicament of needing one as much as himself. And even the notice of this original, singular and unamiable as he was, was not entirely indifferent to the Lord Glenvarloch, since the absolute and somewhat constrained silence of his good friend Heriot, which left him at liberty to retire painfully to his own agitating reflections, was now relieved; while, on the other hand, he could not help feeling interest in the sharp and sarcastic information poured upon him by an observant, though discontented courtier, to whom a patient auditor, and he a man of title and rank, was as much a prize, as his acute and communicative disposition rendered him an entertaining companion to Nigel Olifaunt. Heriot, in the mean time, neglected by Sir Mungo, and

avoiding every attempt by which the grateful politeness of Lord Glenvarloch strove to bring him into the conversation, stood by, with a kind
of half smile on his countenance; but whether excited by Sir Mungo's
wit, or arising at his expence, did not exactly appear.

In this manner, the trio occupied a nook of the anti-room, next to
the door of the presence-chamber, which was not yet thrown open,
when Maxwell, with his rod of office, came bustling into the apartment, where most men, excepting those of high rank, made way for
him. He stopped beside the party in which we are interested, looked
for a moment at the young Scotch nobleman, then made a slight
obeisance to Heriot, and, lastly, addressing Sir Mungo Malagrowther, began a hurried complaint to him of the misbehaviour of the
gentlemen pensioners and warders, who suffered all sort of citizens,
suitors, and scriveners, to sneak into the outer apartments, without
either respect or decency. "The English," he said, "were scandalized,
for such a thing durst not be attempted in the Queen's days—there
was then the court-yard for the mobility, and the apartments for
the nobility. And it reflects on your place, Sir Mungo," he added,
"belonging to the household as you do, that such things should not be
better ordered."

Here Sir Mungo, afflicted, as was frequently the case on such
occasions, with one of his usual fits of deafness, answered, "It was no
wonder the mobility used freedoms, when those whom they saw in
office were so little better in blood and havings than themselves."

"You are right, sir—quite right," said Maxwell, putting his hand on
the tarnished embroidery of the old knight's sleeve,—"when such
fellows see men in office dressed in cast-off suits like paltry stage-
players, it is no wonder the court is thronged with intruders."

"Were you lauding the taste of my embroidery, Maister Maxwell?"
answered the knight, who apparently interpreted the deputy-chamberlain's meaning rather from his action than his words;—"it is of an
ancient and liberal pattern, having been made by your mother's father,
auld James Stitchell, a master-fashioner of honest repute, in Merlin's
Wynd, whom I made a point to employ, as I am now happy to remember, seeing your father thought fit to intermarry with sic a person's
daughter."

Maxwell looked stern, but conscious there was nothing to be got of
Sir Mungo in the way of amends, and that prosecuting the quarrel
with such an adversary would only render him ridiculous, and make
public a mesalliance of which he had no reason to be proud, he
covered his resentment with a sneer; and expressing his regret that Sir
Mungo was become too deaf to understand or attend to what was said
to him, walked on, and planted himself beside the folding-doors of the

presence-chamber, at which he was to perform the duty of deputy-chamberlain, or usher, so soon as they should be opened.

"The door of the presence is about to open," said the goldsmith, in a whisper, to his young friend; "my condition permits me to go no farther with you. Fail not to present yourself boldly, according to your birth, and offer your Supplication, which the King will not refuse to accept, and, as I hope, to consider favourably."

As he spoke, the door of the presence-chamber opened accordingly, and, as is usual on such occasions, the courtiers began to advance towards it, and to enter in a slow, but continuous and uninterrupted stream. As Nigel presented himself in his turn at the entrance, and mentioned his name and title, Maxwell seemed to hesitate. "You are not known to any one," he said; "it is my duty to suffer no one to pass to the presence, my lord, whose face is unknown to me, unless upon the word of a responsible person."

"I came with Master George Heriot," said Nigel, in some embarrassment at this unexpected interruption.

"Master Heriot's name will pass current for much gold and silver, my lord," replied Maxwell, with a civil sneer, "but not for birth and rank. I am compelled by my office to be peremptory. The entrance is impeded—I am much concerned to say it—your lordship must stand back."

"What is the matter?" said an old Scottish nobleman, who had been speaking with George Heriot, after he had separated from Nigel, and who now came forward, observing the altercation betwixt the latter and Maxwell.

"It is only Master Deputy-Chamberlain Maxwell," said Sir Mungo Malagrowther, "expressing his joy to see Lord Glenvarloch at court, whose father gave him his office—at least I think he is speaking to that purport—for your lordship kens my imperfection." A subdued laugh, such as the situation permitted, passed round amongst those who heard this specimen of Sir Mungo's sarcastic temper. But the old nobleman stepped still more forwards, saying,—"What!—the son of my gallant old opponent, Ochtred Olifaunt?—I will introduce him to the presence myself."

So saying, he took Nigel by the arm, without farther ceremony, and was about to lead him forward, when Maxwell, still keeping his rod across the door, said, but with hesitation and embarrassment,—"My lord, this gentleman is not known, and I have orders to be scrupulous."

"Tutti-taiti, man," said the old lord, "I will be answerable he is his father's son, from the cut of his eye-brow—and thou, Maxwell, knewst his father well enough to have spared thy scruples—let us pass, man." So saying, he put aside the deputy-chamberlain's rod, and entered the presence-room, still holding the young man by his arm.

"Why, I must know you, man," he said; "I must know you. I knew your father well, man—I have broke a lance and crossed a blade with him, and it is to my credit that I am living to brag of it. He was king's-man, and I was queen's-man, during the Douglas wars—young fellows both, that feared neither fire nor steel; and we had some old feudal quarrels beside, that had come down from father to son, with our seal-rings, two-handed broad-swords, and plate-coats, and the crests on our burgonets."

"Too loud, my Lord of Huntinglen," whispered a gentleman of the chamber,—"The King!—the King!"

The old Earl (for such he proved,) took the hint, and was silent; and James, advancing from a side-door, received in succession the compliments of strangers, while a little group of favourite courtiers, or officers of the household, stood around him, to whom he addressed himself from time to time. Some more pains had been bestowed on his toilette than upon the occasion when we first presented the monarch to our readers; but there was a natural awkwardness about his figure which prevented his clothes from sitting handsomely, and the prudence or timidity of his disposition had made him take the custom, already noticed, of wearing a dress so thickly quilted as might withstand the stroke of a dagger, which added an ungainly stiffness to his whole appearance, contrasting oddly with the frivolous, ungraceful, and fidgetting motions with which he accompanied his conversation. And yet, though the King's deportment was very undignified, he had a manner so kind, familiar, and good-humoured, was so little apt to veil over or conceal his own foibles, and had so much indulgence and sympathy for those of others, that his address, joined to his learning, and a certain proportion of shrewd mother-wit, failed not to make a favourable impression on those who approached his person.

When the Earl of Huntinglen had presented Nigel to his Sovereign, a ceremony which the good peer took upon himself, the King received the young lord very graciously, and observed to his introducer, that he "was fain to see them twa stand side by side; for I trow, my Lord Huntinglen," continued he, "your ancestors, ay, and e'en your lordship's self and this lad's father, have stood front to front at sword's point, and that is a worse posture."

"Until your Majesty," said Lord Huntinglen, "made Lord Ochtred and me cross palms, upon the memorable day when your Majesty feasted all the nobles that were at feud together, and made them join hands in your presence"——

"I mind it weel," said the King; "I mind it weel—it was a blessed

day, being the nineteen of September, of all days in the year—and it
was a blithe sport to see how some of the carles girned as they clapped
loofs together. By my saul, I thought some of them, mair special the
Hieland chiels, wad have broken out in our own presence; but we
caused them to march hand in hand to the Cross, ourselves leading
the way, and there drink a blithe cup of kindness with ilk other, to the
staunching of feud, and perpetuation of amity. Auld John Anderson
was Provost that year—the carle grat for joy, and the Bailies and
Councillors danced bare-headed in our presence like five-year-auld
colts, for very triumph."

"It was indeed a happy day," said Lord Huntinglen, "and will not be
forgotten in the history of your Majesty's reign."

"I would not that it were, my lord," replied the Monarch—"I would
not that it were prætermitted in our annals. Ay, ay—*Beati pacifici*. My
English lieges here may weel make much of me, for I would have them
to know, they have gotten the only peaceable man that ever came of my
family. If James with the Fiery Face had come amongst you," he said,
looking round him, "or my great grandsire, of Flodden memory!"

"We should have sent them back to the north again," whispered one
English nobleman.

"At least," said another, in the same inaudible tone, "we should
have then had a *man* to our sovereign, though it were but a Scotchman."

"And now, my young springald," said the King to Lord Glenvarloch, "where have you been spending your calf-time?"

"At Leyden, of late, may it please your Majesty," answered Lord
Nigel.

"Aha! a scholar," said the King; "and, by my saul, a modest and
ingenuous youth, that hath not forgotten how to blush, like most of our
travelled Monsieurs. We will treat him conformably."

Then drawing himself up, coughing slightly, and looking around
him with the conscious importance of superior learning, while all the
courtiers who understood, or understood not Latin, pressed eagerly
forward to listen, the sapient monarch prosecuted his inquiries as
follows.—

"Hem! hem! *Salve bis, quaterque salve, Glenvarlochides noster!
Nuperumne ab Lugduno Batavorum Britanniam rediisti?*"

The young nobleman replied, bowing low—

"*Imo, Rex augustissime—biennium fere apud Lugdunenses moratus
sum.*"

James proceeded—

"*Biennium dicis? bene, bene, optume factum est—Non uno die quod
dicunt,—intelligisti, Domine Glenvarlochiensis?* Aha!"

Nigel replied by a reverent bow, and the King, turning to those behind him, said—

"*Adolescens quidem ingenui vultus ingenuique pudoris.*" Then resumed his learned queries. "*Et quid hodie Lugdunenses loquuntur—Vossius vester nihil ne novi scripsit?—nihil certe, quod doleo, typis recenter edidit.*"

"*Valet quidem Vossius, Rex benevole,*" replied Nigel, "*ast senex veneratissimus annum agit, ni fallor, septuagesimum.*"

"*Virum, mehercle, vix tam grandævum crediderim,*" replied the monarch. "*Et Vorstius iste?—Arminii improbi successor æque ac sectator—Herosne adhuc, ut cum Homero loquar,* Ζωος εστι και εσι χθονι δερκων?"

Nigel, by good fortune, remembered that Vorstius, the divine last mentioned in his Majesty's queries about the state of Dutch literature, had been engaged in a personal controversy with James, in which the King had taken so deep an interest, as at length to hint in his public correspondence with the United States, that they would do well to apply the secular arm to stop the progress of heresy by violent measures against the Professor's person—a demand which their Mighty Mightinesses' principles of universal toleration induced them to elude, though with some difficulty. Knowing all this, Lord Glenvarloch, though a courtier of five minutes standing, had address enough to reply—

"*Vivum quidem, haud diu est, hominem videbam—vigere autem quis dicat qui sub fulminibus eloquentiæ tuæ, Rex magne, jamdudum pronus jacet, et prostratus?*"*

This last tribute to his polemical powers completed James's happiness, which the triumph of exhibiting his erudition had already raised to a considerable height.

He rubbed his hands, snapped his fingers, fidgetted, chuckled, exclaimed—"*Euge! belle! optime!*" and turning to the Bishops of Exeter and Oxford, who stood behind him, he said,—"Ye see, my lords, no bad specimen of our Scottish Latinity, with which language we would all our subjects of England were as well embued as this, and other youths of honourable birth, in our auld kingdom; also, we keep the genuine and Roman pronunciation, like other learned nations on the continent, sae that we can hold communing with any scholar in the universe, who can but speak the Latin tongue; whereas ye, our learned subjects of England, have introduced into your universities, otherwise most learned, a fashion of pronouncing like unto the 'nippit

---

* Lest any lady or gentleman should suspect there is aught of mystery concealed under the sentences printed in Italics, they will be pleased to understand that they contain only a few common-place Latin phrases, relating to the state of letters in Holland, which neither deserve, nor would endure, a literal translation.

foot and clippit foot,' of the bride in the fairy tale, whilk manner of
speech, (take it not amiss that I be round with you,) can be understood
by no nation on earth saving yourselves; whereby Latin, *quoad Anglos*,
ceaseth to be *communis lingua*, the general dragoman, or interpreter,
between all the wise men of the earth."

The Bishop of Exeter bowed, as in acquiescence to the royal censure; but he of Oxford stood upright, as mindful over what subjects
his see extended, and as being equally willing to become food for
faggots in defence of the Latinity of the university, as for any article of
his religious creed.

The King, without awaiting an answer from either prelate, proceeded to question Lord Nigel, but in the vernacular tongue,—"Weel,
my likely Alumnus of the Muses, and what make you so far from the
north?"

"To pay my homage to your Majesty," said the young nobleman,
kneeling on one knee, "and to lay before you," he added, "this my
humble and dutiful Supplication."

The presenting of a pistol would certainly have startled King James
more, but could (setting apart the fright) hardly have been more
unpleasing to his indolent disposition.

"And is it even so, man?" said he; "and can no single man, were it
but for the rarity of the case, ever come up frae Scotland, excepting *ex
proposito*—on set purpose, to see what he can make of his loving
Sovereign? It is but three days syne that we had weel nigh lost our life,
and put three kingdoms into dule-weeds, from the over-haste of a
clumsy-handed peasant, to push a packet into our hand, and now we
are beset by the like impediment in our very court. To our Secretary
with that gear, my lord—to our Secretary with that gear."

"I have already offered my humble Supplication to your Majesty's
Secretary of State," said Lord Glenvarloch—"but it seems"——

"That he would not receive it, I warrant?" said the King, interrupting him; "by my saul, our Secretary kens that point of king-craft,
called refusing, better than we do, and will look at nothing but what he
likes himsell—I think I wad make a better Secretary to him than he to
me.—Weel, my lord, you are welcome to London; and, as ye seem an
acute and learned youth, I advise ye to turn your neb northward as
soon as ye like, and settle yoursell for a while at Saint Andrews, and we
will be right glad to hear that you prosper in your studies.—*Incumbite
remis fortiter*."

While the King spoke thus, he held the petition of the young lord
carelessly, like one who only delayed till the suppliant's back was
turned, to throw it away, or at least lay it aside to be no more looked at.
The petitioner, who read this in his cold and indifferent looks, and in

the manner in which he twisted and crumpled together the paper, arose with a bitter sense of anger and disappointment, made a profound obeisance, and was about to retire hastily. But Lord Hunt-inglen, who stood by him, checked his intention by an almost imperceptible touch upon the skirt of his cloak, and Nigel, taking the hint, retreated only a few steps from the royal presence, and then made a pause. In the meanwhile, Lord Huntinglen kneeled before James in his turn, and said—"May it please your Majesty to remember, that upon one certain occasion you did promise to grant me a boon every year of your sacred life."

"I mind it weel, man," answered James, "I mind it weel, and good reason why—it was when you unclasped the fause traitor Ruthven's fangs from about our royal throat, and drove your dirk into him like a true subject. We did then, as you remind us, (whilk was unnecessary,) being partly beside ourselves with joy at our liberation, promise we would grant you a free boon every year; whilk promise, on our coming to mensefull possession of our royal faculties, we did confirm, *restrictivé* always and *conditionaliter*, that your lordship's demand should be such as we, in our royal discretion, should think reasonable."

"Even so, gracious Sovereign," said the old Earl, "and may I yet farther crave to know, if I have ever exceeded the bounds of your royal benevolence?"

"By my word, man, no!" said the King; "I cannot remember you have asked much for yoursell, if it be not a dog, or a hawk, or a buck out of our park at Theobald's, or such like. But to what serves this preface?"

"To the boon which I am now to ask of your grace," said Lord Huntinglen; "which is, that your Majesty would be pleased, on the instant, to look at the placet of Lord Glenvarloch, and do upon it what your own just and royal nature shall think meet and just, without reference to your Secretary or any other of your Council."

"By my saul, my lord, this is strange," said the King; "ye are pleading for the son of your enemy!"

"Of one who *was* my enemy till your Majesty made him my friend," answered Lord Huntinglen.

"Weel spoken, my lord!" said the King; "and with a true Christian spirit. And, respecting the Supplication of this young man, I partly guess where the matter lies; and in plain troth I had promised to George Heriot to be good to the lad—But then, here the shoe pinches. Steenie and Baby Charles cannot abide him—neither can your own son, my lord; and so methinks he had better go down to Scotland before he comes to ill luck by them."

"My son, an it please your Majesty, so far as he is concerned, shall not direct my doings," said the Earl, "nor any wild-headed young man of them all."

"Why, neither shall they mine," replied the Monarch; "by my father's saul, none of them all shall play Rex with me—I will do what I will, and what I aught, like a free king."

"Your Majesty will then grant me my boon?" said the Lord Huntinglen.

"Ay, marry will I—marry will I," said the King; "but follow me this way, man, where we may be more private."

He led Lord Huntinglen with rather a hurried step through the courtiers, all of whom gazed earnestly on this unwonted scene, as is the fashion of all courts on similar occasions. The King passed into a little cabinet, and bade, in the first moment, Lord Huntinglen lock or bar the door; but countermanded his direction in the next, saying,—"No—no—no—bread o' life, man, I am a free King—will do what I will and what I should—I am *justus et tenax propositi*, man—nevertheless, keep by the door, Lord Huntinglen, in case Steenie should come in with his mad humour."

"O my poor master," groaned the Earl of Huntinglen. "When you were in your own cold country, you had warmer blood in your veins."

The King hastily glanced over the petition or memorial, ever now and then glancing his eye towards the door, and then sinking it hastily on the paper, ashamed that Lord Huntinglen, whom he respected, should suspect him of timidity.

"To grant the truth," he said, after he had finished his hasty perusal, "this is a hard case; and harder than it was represented to me, though I had some inkling of it before. And so the lad only wants payment of the siller due from us, in order to reclaim his paternal estate? But then, Huntinglen, the lad will have other debts—and for what burthen himsell with sae mony acres of barren woodland? let the land gang, man—let the land gang; Steenie has the promise of it from our Scottish Chancellor—it is the best hunting ground in Scotland—and Baby Charles and Steenie want to kill a buck there this next year—they mun hae the land—they mun hae the land—and our debt shall be paid to this young man plack and bawbee, and he may hae the spending of it at our court; or if he has such an eard hunger, oons! man, we'll stuff his stomach with English land, which is worth twice so much, ay, ten times so much, as these accursed hills and heughs, and mosses and muirs, that he is sae keen after."

All this while the poor King ambled up and down the apartment in a piteous state of uncertainty, which was made more ridiculous by his shambling circular mode of managing his legs, and his ungainly fashion of fiddling on such occasions with the bunches of ribbands which fastened the lower part of his dress.

Lord Huntinglen listened with great composure, and answered, "An it please your Majesty, there was an answer yielded by Naboth when Ahab coveted his vineyard—'The Lord forbid that I should give the inheritance of my fathers unto thee.'"

"Ey, my lord—ey, my lord!" ejaculated James, while the colour mounted both to his cheeks and nose; "I hope ye mean not to teach me divinity? Ye need not fear, my lord, that I will shun to do justice to every man—and—since your lordship will give me no help to take up this in a more peaceful manner—whilk, methinks, would be better for the young man, as I said before,—why—since it maun be so—'sdeath, I am a free king, man—and he shall have his money and redeem his land, and make a kirk and a miln of it, an he will." So saying, he hastily wrote an order on the Scottish Exchequer for the sum in question—and then added, "How they are to pay it I see not; but I warrant he will find money on the order among the goldsmiths, who can find it for every one but me.—And now you see, my Lord of Huntinglen, that I am neither an untrue man, to deny you the boon whilk I became bound for, nor an Ahab, to covet Naboth's vineyard; nor a mere nose-of-wax, to be twisted this way and that by favourites and counsellors at their pleasure. I think you will grant now that I am none of those?"

"You are my own native and noble Prince," said Huntinglen, as he knelt to kiss the royal hand—"just and generous, whenever you listen to the workings of your own heart."

"Ay, ay," said the King, laughing good-naturedly, as he raised his faithful servant from the ground, "that is what ye all say when I do any thing to please ye. There—there—take the sign-manual, and away with you and this young fellow. I wonder Steenie and Baby Charles have not broken in on us before now."

Lord Huntinglen hastened from the cabinet, foreseeing a scene at which he was unwilling to be present, but which sometimes occurred when James roused himself so far as to exert his own free will, of which he boasted so much, in spite of that of his imperious favourite Steenie, as he called the Duke of Buckingham, from a supposed resemblance betwixt his very handsome countenance, and that with which the Italian artists represented the proto-martyr Stephen. In fact, the haughty favourite, who had the unusual good fortune to stand as high in the opinion of the heir-apparent as of the existing monarch, had considerably diminished his respect towards the latter; and it was apparent, to the more shrewd courtiers, that James endured his domination rather from habit, timidity, and a dread of encountering his stormy passions, than from any heart-felt continuation of regard towards him, whose greatness had been the work of his own hands. To save himself the pain of seeing what was likely to take place on the Duke's return, and to preserve the King from the additional humiliation which the presence of such a witness must have occasioned, the Earl left the cabinet as speedily as possible, having first carefully pocketed the important sign-manual.

No sooner had he entered the presence-room, than he hastily sought Lord Glenvarloch, who had withdrawn into the embrazure of one of the windows, from the general gaze of men who seemed disposed only to afford him the notice which arises from surprise and curiosity, and taking him by the arm, without speaking, led him out of the presence-chamber into the first anti-room. Here they found the worthy goldsmith, who approached them with looks of curiosity, which were checked by the old lord, who said hastily,—"All is well—is your barge in waiting?" Heriot answered in the affirmative. "Then," said Lord Huntinglen, "you shall give me a cast in it, as the watermen say, and I, in requital, will give you both your dinner; for we must have some conversation together."

They both followed the Earl without speaking, and were in the second anti-chamber when the important annunciation of the ushers, and the hasty murmur with which all made ample way as the company repeated to each other,—"The Duke—the Duke!" made them aware of the approach of the omnipotent favourite.

He entered, that unhappy minion of court favour, sumptuously dressed in the picturesque attire which will live for ever on the canvas of Vandyke, and which marks so well the proud age, when aristocracy, though undermined and nodding to its fall, still, by external show and profuse expence, endeavoured to assert its paramount superiority over the inferior orders. The handsome and commanding countenance, stately form, and graceful action and manners of the Duke of Buckingham, made him become that picturesque dress beyond any man of his time. At present, however, his countenance seemed discomposed, his dress a little more disordered than became the place, his step hasty, and his voice imperative.

All marked the angry spot upon his brow, and bore back so suddenly to make way for him, that the Earl of Huntinglen, who affected no extraordinary haste on the occasion, with his companions, who could not, if they would, have decently left him, remained as it were by themselves in the middle of the room, and in the very path of the angry favourite. He touched his cap sternly as he looked on Huntinglen, but unbonnetted to Heriot, and sunk his beaver, with its shadowy plume, as low as the floor, with a profound air of mock respect. In returning his greeting, which he did simply and unaffectedly, the citizen only said,—"Too much courtesy, my lord duke, is often the reverse of kindness."

"I grieve you should think so, Master Heriot," answered the Duke; "I only meant, by my homage, to claim your protection, sir—your patronage. You are become, I understand, a solicitor of suits—a promoter—an undertaker—a fautor of court suitors of merit and quality, who chance to be pennyless. I trust your bags will bear you out in your new boast."

"They will bear me the further, my lord duke," answered the goldsmith, "that my boast is but small."

"O, you do yourself less than justice, my good Master Heriot," continued the Duke, in the same tone of irony; "you have a marvellous court-faction, to be the son of an Edinburgh tinker. Have the goodness to prefer me to the knowledge of the high-born nobleman who is honoured and advantaged by your patronage."

"That shall be *my* task," said Lord Huntinglen, with emphasis. "My Lord Duke, I desire you to know Nigel Olifaunt, Lord Glenvarloch, representative of one of the most ancient and powerful baronial houses in Scotland.—Lord Glenvarloch, I present you to his Grace the Duke of Buckingham, representative of Sir George Villiers, Knight, of Brookesby, in the county of Leicester."

The Duke coloured still more high as he bowed to Lord Glenvarloch scornfully, a courtesy which the other returned haughtily, and with restrained indignation. "We know each other, then," said the Duke, after a moment's pause, and as if he had seen something in the young nobleman which merited more serious notice than the bitter raillery with which he had commenced. "We know each other—and you know me, my lord, for your enemy."

"I thank you for your plainness, my lord duke," replied Nigel; "an open enemy is better than a hollow friend."

"For you, my Lord Huntinglen," said the Duke, "methinks you have but now overstepped the limits of the indulgence permitted to you, as the father of the Prince's friend, and my own."

"By my faith, my lord duke," replied the Earl, "it is easy for any one to overstep boundaries, of the existence of which he was not aware. It is neither to secure my protection nor approbation, that my son keeps such exalted company."

"O, my lord, we know you, and indulge you," said the Duke; "you are one of those who presume for a life-long upon the merit of one good action."

"In faith, my lord, and if it be so," said the old Earl, "I have at least the advantage of such as presume more than I do, without having done any action of merit whatever. But I mean not to quarrel with you, my lord—we can neither be friends nor enemies—you have your path, and I have mine."

Buckingham only replied by throwing on his bonnet, and shaking its lofty plume with a careless and scornful toss of the head. They parted thus; the Duke walking onward through the apartments, and the others leaving the palace and repairing to Whitehall stairs, where they embarked on board the barge of the citizen.

Chapter Ten

Bid not thy fortune troll upon the wheels
Of yonder dancing cubes of mottled bone;
And drown it not, like Egypt's royal harlot,
Dissolving her rich pearl in the brimm'd wine-cup.
These are the arts, Lothario, which shrink acres
Into brief yards—bring sterling pounds to farthings,
Credit to infamy; and the poor gull
Who might have lived an honour'd, easy life,
To ruin, and an unregarded grave.
                                        The Changes

WHEN THEY WERE fairly embarked on the Thames, the Earl took from his pocket the Supplication, and pointing out to George Heriot the royal warrant indorsed thereon, asked him, if it were in due and regular form? The worthy citizen hastily read it over, thrust forth his hand as if to gratulate the Lord Glenvarloch, then checked himself, pulled out his barnacles, (a present from old David Ramsay,) and again perused the warrant with the most business-like and critical attention. "It is strictly correct and formal," he said, looking to the Earl of Huntinglen; "and I sincerely rejoice at it."

"I doubt nothing of its formality," said the Earl; "the King understands business well, and if he does not practise it often, it is only because indolence obscures parts which are naturally well qualified for the discharge of affairs. But what is next to be done for our young friend, Master Heriot? You know how I am circumstanced. Scottish lords living at the English court have seldom command of money; yet, unless a sum can be presently raised on this warrant, matters standing as you hastily hinted to me, the mortgage, wadsett, or whatever it is called, will be foreclosed."

"It is true," said Heriot, in some embarrassment; "there is a large sum wanted in redemption—yet, if it is not raised, there will be an expiry of the legal, as our lawyers call it, and the estate will be evicted."

"My noble—my worthy friends, who have taken my cause up so undeservedly, so unexpectedly," said Nigel, "do not let me be a burthen on your kindness—you have already done too much where nothing was merited."

"Peace, man, peace," said Lord Huntinglen, "and let old Heriot and I puzzle this scent out—he is about to open—hark to him!"

"My lord," said the citizen, "the Duke of Buckingham sneers at our city money-bags; yet they can sometimes open, to prop a falling and a noble house."

"We know they can," said Lord Huntinglen—"mind not Buckingham, he is a Peg-a-Ramsay—and now for the remedy."

"I partly hinted to Lord Glenvarloch already," said Heriot, "that the redemption-money might be advanced upon such a warrant as the present, and I will engage my credit that it can. But then, in order to secure the lender, he must come in the shoes of the creditor to whom he advances payment."

"Come in his shoes!" replied the Earl; "Why, what have boots or shoes to do with this matter, my good friend?"

"It is a law phrase, my lord—my experience has made me pick up a few of them," said Heriot.

"Ay, and of better things alongst with them, Master George," replied Lord Huntinglen; "but what means it?"

"Simply this," resumed the citizen; "that the lender of this money will transact with the holder of the mortgage, or wadsett, over the estate of Glenvarloch, and obtain from him such a conveyance to his right as shall leave the lands pledged for the debt, in case the warrant upon the Scottish Exchequer should prove unproductive. I fear, in this uncertainty of public credit, that, without some such counter-security, it will be very difficult to find so large a sum."

"Ho la!" said the Earl of Huntinglen, "halt there! a thought strikes me.—What if the new creditor should admire the estate as a hunting-field, as much as my Lord Grace of Buckingham seems to do, and should wish to kill a buck there in the summer season? it seems to me, that on your plan, Master George, our new friend will be as well entitled to block Lord Glenvarloch out of his inheritance as the present holder of the mortgage."

The citizen laughed. "I will engage," he said, "that the keenest sportsman to whom I may apply on this occasion, shall not have a thought beyond the Lord Mayor's Easter-hunt, in Epping-Forest. But your lordship's caution is reasonable. The creditors must be bound to allow Lord Glenvarloch sufficient time to redeem his estate by means of the royal warrant—they must waive in his favour the right of instant foreclosure, which may be, I should think, the more easily managed, as the right of redemption must be exercised in his own name."

"But where shall we find a person in London fit to draw the necessary writings?" said the Earl. "If my old friend Sir John Skene of Halyards had lived, we should have had his advice; but time presses, and"——

"I know," said Heriot, "an orphan lad, a scrivener, that dwells by Temple-Bar; he can draw deeds both after the English and Scots fashion, and I have trusted him often in things of weight and of importance. I will send one of my serving-men for him, and the mutual deeds may be executed in your lordship's presence; for as things stand, there should be no delay." His lordship readily assented; and, as they now landed upon the private stairs leading down to the river from the gardens of the handsome hotel which he inhabited, the messenger was dispatched without loss of time.

Nigel, who had sate almost stupified while these zealous friends volunteered for him in arranging the measures by which his fortune was to be disembarrassed, now made another eager attempt to force upon them his broken expressions of thanks and of gratitude. But he was again silenced by Lord Huntinglen, who declared he would hear no word on that topic, and proposed instead, that they should take a turn in the pleached alley, or sit upon the stone bench which overlooked the Thames, until his son's arrival should give the signal for dinner.

"I desire to introduce Dalgarno and Lord Glenvarloch to each other," said he, "as two who must be near neighbours, and I trust will be more kind ones than their fathers were formerly. There is but three Scots miles betwixt the castles, and the turrets of the one are visible from the battlements of the other."

The good Earl was silent for a moment, and appeared to muse upon the recollections which the vicinity of the castles had summoned up.

"Does Lord Dalgarno follow the court to Newmarket next week?" said Heriot, by way of removing the conversation.

"He proposes so, I think," answered Lord Huntinglen, relapsed into his reverie for a minute or two, and then addressed Nigel somewhat abruptly—

"My young friend, when you attain possession of your inheritance, as I trust you soon will, I hope you will not add one to the idle followers of the court, but reside on your patrimonial estate, cherish your ancient tenants, relieve and assist your poor kinsmen, protect the poor against subaltern oppression, and do what our fathers used to do, with fewer lights and with less means than we have."

"And yet the advice to keep the country," said Heriot, "comes from an ancient and constant ornament of the court."

"From an old courtier indeed," said the Earl, "and the first of my family that could so write himself—my grey beard falls on a cambric ruff, and a silken doublet—my father's descended upon a buff coat and a breast-plate. I would not that these days of battle returned; but I should love well to make the oaks of my old forest of Dalgarno ring once more with halloo, and horn, and hound, and to hear the old stone-arched hall return the hearty shout of my vassals and tenants, as the bicker and the quaigh walked their rounds amongst them. I should like to see the broad Tay once more before I die—not even the Thames can match it, in my mind."

"Surely, my lord," said the citizen, "all this might be easily done—it costs but a moment's resolution, and the journey of some brief days, and you would be where you desire to be—what is there to prevent you?"

"Habits, Master George, habits," replied the Earl, "which to young men are like threads of silk, so lightly are they worn, so soon broken; but which hang on our old limbs as if time had stiffened them into gyves of iron. To go to Scotland for a brief space were but labour in vain; and when I think of abiding there, I cannot bring myself to leave my old Master, to whom I fancy myself sometimes useful, and whose weal and woe I have shared for so many years. But Dalgarno shall be a Scottish noble."

"Has he visited the North?" said Heriot.

"He was there last year, and made such a report of the country, that the Prince has expressed a longing to see it."

"Lord Dalgarno is in high grace with his Highness, and the Duke of Buckingham?" observed the goldsmith.

"He is so," answered the Earl,—"I pray it may be for the advantage of them all. The Prince is just and equitable in his sentiments, though cold and stately in his manners, and very obstinate in his most trifling purposes; and the Duke, noble and gallant, and generous and open, is fiery, ambitious, and impetuous. Dalgarno has none of these faults, and such as he may have of his own, may perchance be corrected by the society in which he moves.—See, here he comes."

Lord Dalgarno accordingly advanced from the end of the alley to the bench on which his father and his guests were seated, so that Nigel had full leisure to peruse his countenance and figure. He was dressed point-device, and almost to extremity, in the splendid fashion of the time, which suited well with his age, probably about five-and-twenty, with a noble form and fine countenance, in which last could easily be traced the manly features of his father, but softened by a more habitual air of assiduous courtesy than the stout old Earl had ever condescended to assume towards the world in general. In other respects, his address was gallant, free, and unencumbered either by pride or ceremony—far remote certainly from the charge either of haughty coldness or forward impetuosity; and so far his father had justly freed him from the marked faults which he ascribed to the manners of the Prince and his favourite Buckingham.

While the old Earl presented his young acquaintance Lord Glenvarloch to his son, as one whom he would have him love and honour, Nigel marked the countenance of Lord Dalgarno closely, to see if he could detect aught of that secret dislike which the King had, in one of his broken expostulations, seemed to intimate, as arising from a clashing of interests betwixt his new friend and the great Buckingham. But nothing of this was visible; on the contrary, Lord Dalgarno received his new acquaintance with the open frankness and courtesy which makes conquest at once, when addressed to the feelings of an ingenious young man.

It need hardly be told that his open and friendly address met equally ready and cheerful acceptation from Nigel Olifaunt. For many months, and while a youth not much above two-and-twenty, he had been restrained by circumstances from the conversation of his contemporaries. When, on his father's sudden death, he left the Low Countries for Scotland, he had found himself involved, apparently inextricably, with the details of the law, all of which threatened to end in the alienation of the patrimony which should support his hereditary rank. His term of sincere mourning, joined to injured pride and the swelling of the heart under unexpected and undeserved misfortune, together with the uncertainty attending the issue of his affairs, had induced the young Lord Glenvarloch to lead, while in Scotland, a very private and reserved course of life. How he had passed his time in London, the reader is partly acquainted. But this melancholy and secluded course of life was neither agreeable to his age nor to his temper, which was genial and sociable. He hailed, therefore, with sincere pleasure, the approaches which a young man of his own age and rank made towards him; and when he had exchanged with Lord Dalgarno some of those words and signals by which, as surely as by those of free-masonry, young people recognize a mutual wish to be agreeable to each other, it seemed as if the two noblemen had been acquainted for some time.

Just as this tacit intercourse had been established, one of Lord Huntinglen's attendants came down the alley, marshalling onwards a man dressed in black buckram, who followed him with considerable speed, considering that, according to his sense of reverence and propriety, he kept his body bent and parallel to the horizon from the moment that he came in sight of the company to which he was about to ᵉ presented.

"Who is this, you cuckoldly knave," said the old lord, who had retained the keen appetite and impatience of a Scotish Baron even during a long alienation from his native country; "and why does John Cook, with a murrain to him, keep back dinner?"

"I believe we are ourselves responsible for this person's intrusion," said George Heriot; "this is the scrivener whom we desired to see.— Look up, man, and see us in the face as an honest man should, instead of bearing thy noddle charged against us thus like a battering-ram."

The scrivener did look up accordingly, with the action of an automaton which suddenly obeys the impulse of a pressed spring. But, strange to tell, not even the haste he had made to attend his patron's mandation, a business, as Master Heriot's message expressed, of weight and importance—nay, not even the state of depression in which, out of sheer humility doubtless, he had his head stooped to the earth from the instant he had trode the demesnes of the Earl of Huntinglen, had called any colour into his countenance. The drops stood on his brow from haste and toil, but his cheek was still pale and tallow-coloured as before; nay, what seemed stranger, his very hair, when he raised his head, hung down on either cheek as straight and sleek and undisturbed as it was when we first introduced him to our readers, seated at his quiet and humble desk.

Lord Dalgarno could not forbear a stifled laugh at the ridiculous and puritanical figure which presented itself like a starved anatomy to the company, and whispered at the same time into Lord Glenvarloch's ear—

> "The devil damn thee black, thou cream-faced loun,
> Where got'st thou that goose look?"

Nigel was too little acquainted with the English stage, to understand a quotation which had already grown matter of common allusion in London. Lord Dalgarno saw that he was not understood, and continued, "That fellow, by his visage, should either be a saint, or a most hypocritical rogue—and such is my excellent opinion of human nature, that I always suspect the worst. But they seem deep in business. Will you make a turn with me in the garden, my lord, or will you remain a member of the serious conclave?"

"With you, my lord, most willingly," said Nigel; and they were turning away accordingly, when George Heriot, with the formality belonging to his station, observed, that, "as their whole business concerned Lord Glenvarloch, he had better remain, to make himself master of it, and witness to it."

"My presence is utterly needless, my good lord;—and, my best friend, Master Heriot," said the young nobleman, "I shall understand nothing the better for cumbering you with my ignorance in these

matters; and can only say at the end, as I now say at the beginning, that
I dare not take the helm out the hand of the kind pilots who have
already guided my course within sight of a fair and unhoped-for
haven. Whatever you recommend to me as fitting, I shall sign and seal;
and the import of the deeds I will better learn by a brief explanation
from Master Heriot, if he will bestow so much trouble in my behalf,
than by a thousand learned words and law terms from this person of
skill."

"He is right," said Lord Huntinglen; "our young friend is right, in
confiding these matters to you and me, Master George Heriot—he
has not misplaced his confidence."

Master George Heriot cast a long look after the two young noblemen, who had now walked down the alley arm in arm, and at length
said, "He hath not indeed misplaced his confidence, as your lordship
well and truly says—but, nevertheless, he is not in the right path; for it
behoves every man to become acquainted with his own affairs, so soon
as he hath any that are worth attending to."

When he had made this observation, they applied themselves, with
the scrivener, to look into various papers, and to direct in what manner
writings should be drawn, which might at once afford sufficient security to those who were to advance the money, and at the same time to
preserve the right of the young nobleman to redeem his family estate,
provided he should obtain the means of doing so, by the expected
reimbursement from the Scottish Exchequer, or otherwise. It is needless to enter into these details. But it is not unimportant to mention, as
an illustration of character, that Heriot entered into the most minute
legal details with a precision which shewed that experience had made
him master even of the intricacies of Scottish conveyancing; and that
the Earl of Huntinglen, though far less acquainted with technical
detail, suffered no step of the business to pass over, until he had
attained a general but distinct idea of its import and its propriety.

They seemed to be admirably seconded in their benevolent intentions towards the young Lord Glenvarloch, by the skill and eager
willing zeal of the scrivener, whom Heriot had introduced to this piece
of business, the most important which Andrew had ever transacted in
his life, and the particulars of which were moreover agitated in his
presence between an actual earl, and one whose wealth and character
might entitle him to be alderman of his ward, if not to be lord mayor, in
his turn.

While they were thus in eager conversation on business, the good
Earl, even forgetting the calls of his appetite, and the delay of dinner,
in his anxiety to see that the scrivener received proper instructions,
and that all was rightly weighed and considered, before dismissing

him to engross the necessary deeds, the two young men walked together on the terrace which overhung the river, and talked on the topics which Lord Dalgarno, the eldest, and the most experienced, thought most likely to interest his new friend.

These naturally regarded the pleasures attending a court life; and Lord Dalgarno expressed much surprise at understanding that Nigel proposed an instant return to Scotland.

"You are jesting with me," he said. "All the court rings, it is needless to mince it, with the extraordinary success of your suit—against the highest interest, it is said, now influencing the horizon at Whitehall. Men think on you—talk of you—fix their eyes on you—ask each other, who is this young Scotch lord, who has stepped so far in a single day? They augur, in whispers to each other, how high and how far you may push your fortune—and all that you design to make of it, is to return to Scotland, eat raw oatmeal cakes, baked upon a peat-fire, have your hand shaken by every loon of a blue-bonnet who chooses to dub you cousin, though your relationship comes by Noah; drink Scots twopenny ale, eat half-starved red-deer venison, when you can kill it, ride upon a galloway, and be called my right honourable and maist worthy laird."

"There is no great gaiety in the prospect before me, I confess," said Lord Glenvarloch, "even if your father and good Master Heriot should succeed in putting my affairs on some footing of plausible hope. And yet I trust to do something for my vassals, as my ancestors before me, and to teach my children, as I have myself been taught, to make some personal sacrifices, if they be necessary, in order to maintain with dignity the situation in which they are placed by Providence."

Lord Dalgarno, after having once or twice stifled his laughter during this speech, at length broke out into a fit of mirth, so hearty and so resistless, that, angry as he was, the call of sympathy swept Nigel along with him, and, despite of himself, he could not forbear to join in a burst of laughter, which he thought not only causeless, but almost impertinent.

He soon recollected himself however; and said, in a tone qualified to allay Lord Dalgarno's extreme mirth, "This is all well, my lord; but how am I to understand your merriment?" Lord Dalgarno only answered him with redoubled peals of laughter, and at length held by Lord Glenvarloch's cloak, as if to prevent his falling down on the ground, in the extremity of his convulsion.

At length, while Nigel stood half abashed, half angry, at becoming thus the subject of his new acquaintance's ridicule, and was only restrained from expressing his resentment against the son, by a sense of the obligations he owed the father, Lord Dalgarno recovered himself, and spoke in a half-broken voice, his eyes still running with tears. "I crave your pardon, my dear Lord Glenvarloch—ten thousand times do I crave your pardon. But that last picture of rural dignity, accompanied by your grave and angry surprise at my laughing at what would have made any court-bred hound laugh, that had but so much as bayed the moon once from the court-yard at Whitehall, totally overcame me. Why, my liefest and dearest lord, you, a young and handsome fellow, with high birth, a title, and the name of an estate, so well received by the King at your first starting, as makes your further progress scarce matter of doubt, if you know how to improve it—for the King has already said you are 'a braw lad, and weel studied in the more humane letters'—you, too, whom all the women, and the very marked beauties of the court, desire to see, because you came from Leyden, were born in Scotland, and have gained a hard contested suit in England—you, I say, with a person like a prince, an eye of fire, and a wit as quick, to think of throwing your cards on the table when the game is in your very hand, running back to the frozen north, marrying —let me see—a tall, stalking, blue-eyed, fair-skinned bony wench, with eighteen quarters in her scutcheon, a sort of Lot's wife, newly descended from her pedestal, and with her to shut yourself up in your tapestried chamber! Uh, gad!—Swouns, I shall never survive the idea!"

It is seldom that youth, however high-minded, is able, from mere strength of character and principle, to support itself against the force of ridicule. Half angry, half mortified, and, to say truth, half ashamed of his more manly and better purpose, Nigel was unable, and flattered himself it was unnecessary, to play the part of a rigid moral patriot, in presence of a young man whose current fluency of language, as well as his experience in the highest circles of society, gave him, in spite of Nigel's better and firmer thoughts, a temporary ascendancy over him. He sought, therefore, to compromise the matter, and avoid farther debate, by frankly owning, that if to return to his own country were not his choice, it was at least a matter of necessity. "His affairs," he said, "were unsettled—his income precarious."

"And where is he whose affairs are settled, or whose income is less than precarious, that is to be found in attendance on the court?" said Lord Dalgarno; "all are either losing or winning—those who have wealth, come hither to get rid of it, while the happy gallants who, like you and I, dear Glenvarloch, have little or none, have every chance to be sharers in their spoils."

"I have no ambition of that sort," said Nigel, "and if I had, I must tell you plainly, Lord Dalgarno, I have not the means to do so. I can scarce as yet call the suit I wear my own; I owe it, and I do not blush to say so, to the friendship of yonder good man."

"I will not laugh again, if I can help it," said Lord Dalgarno. "But, Lord! that you should have gone to a wealthy goldsmith for your habit —Why, I could have brought you to an honest confiding tailor, who should have furnished you with half a dozen, merely for love of the little word, 'lordship,' which you place before your name;—and then your goldsmith, if he be really a friendly goldsmith, should have equipped you with such a purse of fair rose-nobles as would have bought you thrice as many suits, or done better things for you."

"I do not understand these fashions, my lord," said Nigel, his displeasure mastering his shame; "were I to attend the court of my Sovereign, it should be when I could maintain, without shifting or borrowing, the dress and retinue which my rank requires."

"Which my rank requires!" said Lord Dalgarno, repeating his last words; "that, now, is as good as if my father had spoke it. I fancy you would love to move to court like him, followed by a round score of old blue-bottles, with white heads and red noses, with bucklers and broadswords, which their hands, trembling betwixt age and strong waters, can make no use of—as many huge silver badges on their arms, to shew whose fools they are, as would furnish forth a court cupboard of plate—rogues fit for nothing but to fill our anti-chambers with the flavour of onions and geneva—pah!"

"The poor knaves!" said Lord Glenvarloch; "they have served your father, it may be, in the wars—what would become of them were he to turn them off?"

"Why, let them to the hospital," said Dalgarno, "or to the bridge-end, to sell switches—the King is a better man than my father, and you see those who have served in *his* wars do so every day—or, when their blue coats were well worn out, they would make rare scare-crows. There is a fellow, now, comes down the walk; the stoutest raven dared not come within a yard of his red nose. I tell you, there is more service, as you will soon see, in my valet of the chamber, and such a lither lad as my page Lutin, than there is in a score of these old memorials of the Douglas' wars, where they cut each other's throats for the chance of finding twelve pennies Scots on the person of the slain. Marry, my lord, to make amends, they will eat mouldy victuals, and drink stale ale, as if their bellies were puncheons.—But the dinner-bell is going to sound—hark, it is clearing its rusty throat, with a preliminary towl. That is another clamorous relique of antiquity, that, were I master, should soon be at the bottom of Thames. How the foul fiend can it interest the peasants and mechanics in the Strand, to know that the Earl of Huntinglen is sitting down to dinner? But my father looks our way—we must not be late for the grace, or we shall be in *dis*-grace, if you will forgive a quibble which would have made his Majesty laugh. You will find us all of a piece, and having been accustomed to eat in *saucieres* abroad, I am ashamed you should witness our larded capons, our mountains of beef, and oceans of brewis, as large as Highland hills and lochs; but you shall see better cheer to-morrow. Where lodge you? I will call for you. I must be your guide through this peopled desert, to certain enchanted lands, which you will scarce discover without chart and pilot. Where lodge you?"

"I will meet you in Paul's," said Nigel, a good deal embarrassed, "at any hour you please to name."

"O, you would be private," said the young lord; "nay, fear not me— I will be no intruder. But we have attained this huge larder of flesh, fowl, and fish. I marvel the oaken boards groan not under it."

They had indeed arrived in the dining-parlour of the mansion, where the table was super-abundantly loaded, and where the number of attendants, to a certain extent, vindicated the sarcasm of the young nobleman. The chaplain, and Sir Mungo Malagrowther, were of the party. The latter complimented Lord Glenvarloch upon the impression he had made at court. "One would have thought ye had brought the apple of discord in your pouch, my lord, or that you were the very fire-brand of whilk Althea was delivered, and that she had laid-in in a barrel of gunpowder. For the King, and the Prince, and the Duke, have been by the lugs about ye, and so have many more, that kenned na before this blessed day that there was such a man living on the face of the earth."

"Mind your victuals, Sir Mungo," said the Earl; "they get cold while you talk."

"Troth, and that needs na, my lord," said the knight; "your lordship's dinners seldom scald one's mouth—the serving-men are turning auld, like oursells, my lord, and it is far between the kitchen and the ha'."

With this little explosion of his spleen, Sir Mungo remained satisfied until the dishes were removed, when, fixing his eyes on the brave new doublet of Lord Dalgarno, he complimented him on his economy, pretending to recognize it as the same which his father had worn in Edinburgh in the Spanish ambassador's time. Lord Dalgarno, too much a man of the world to be moved by any thing from such a quarter, proceeded to crack his nuts with great deliberation, as he replied, that the doublet was in some sort his father's, as it was likely to cost him fifty pounds some day soon. Sir Mungo forthwith proceeded in his own way to convey this agreeable intelligence to the Earl, observing, that his son was a better maker of bargains than his lordship, for he had bought a doublet as rich as that his lordship wore when the Spanish ambassador was at Holyrood, and it had cost him but fifty punds Scots. "That was no fool's bargain, my lord."

"Pounds sterling, if you please, Sir Mungo," answered the Earl, calmly, "and a fool's bargain it is, in all the tenses. Dalgarno *was* a fool when he bought, I *will* be a fool when I pay, and you, Sir Mungo, craving your pardon, *are* a fool *in præsenti*, for speaking of what concerns you not."

"So saying, the Earl addressed himself to the serious business of the table, and sent the wine around with a profusion which increased the hilarity, but rather threatened the temperance of the company, until their joviality was interrupted by the annunciation, that the scrivener had engrossed such deeds as required to be presently executed. George Heriot rose from the table, observing, that wine-cups and legal documents were unseemly neighbours. The Earl asked the scrivener if they had laid a trencher and set a cup for him in the buttery, and received the respectful answer, that Heaven forbid he should be such an ungracious beast as to eat or drink until his lordship's pleasure was performed.

"Thou shalt eat before thou goest," said Lord Huntinglen, "and I will have thee try, moreover, whether a cup of sack cannot bring some colour into these cheeks of thine—it were a shame to my household, thou shouldst glide out into the Strand after such a spectre-fashion as thou now wearest.—Look to it, Dalgarno, for the honour of our roof is concerned."

Lord Dalgarno gave directions that the man should be attended to. Lord Glenvarloch and the citizen, in the meanwhile, signed and interchanged, and thus closed a transaction, of which the principal party concerned understood little, save that it was under the management of a zealous and faithful friend, who undertook that the money should be forthcoming, and the estate released from forfeiture, by payment of the stipulated sum for which it stood pledged, and that at the term of Lambmas, and at the hour of noon, and beside the tomb of the Regent Earl of Murray, in the High Kirk of Saint Giles, at Edinburgh, being the day and place assigned for such redemption.

When this business was transacted, the old Earl would fain have renewed his carouse; but the citizen, alleging the importance of the deeds he had about him, and the business he had to transact betimes the next morning, not only refused to return to table, but carried off with him to his barge Lord Glenvarloch, who might, perhaps, have been otherwise found more tractable.

When they were seated in the boat, and fairly once more afloat on the river, George Heriot looked back seriously on the mansion they had left. "There live," he said, "the old and the new fashion. The father is like a noble old broad-sword, but harmed with rust, from neglect and inactivity—the son is your modern rapier, well mounted, fairly gilt, and fashioned to the taste of the time—And it is time must shew if the metal be as good as the show. God grant it prove so, says an old friend to the family."

Nothing of consequence passed betwixt them, until Lord Glenvarloch, landing at Paul's Wharf, took leave of his friend the citizen, and retired to his own apartment, where his attendant, Richie, not a little elevated with the events of the day, and with the hospitality of Lord Huntinglen's house-keeping, gave a most splendid account of them to the buxom dame Nelly, who rejoiced to hear that the sun at length was shining upon what Richie called the right side of the hedge.

Chapter Eleven

> You are not for the manner nor the times.
> They have their vices now most like to virtues;
> You cannot know them apart by any difference,
> They wear the same clothes, eat the same meat—
> Sleep i'the self-same beds, ride in those coaches,
> Or very like four horses in a coach,
> As the best men and women.
>
> BEN JONSON

ON THE NEXT MORNING, while Nigel, his breakfast finished, was thinking how he should employ the day, there was a little bustle upon the stairs which attracted his attention, and presently entered Dame Nelly, blushing like scarlet, and scarce able to bring out—"A young nobleman, sir—no one less," she added, drawing her hand slightly over her lips, "would be so saucy—a young nobleman, sir, to wait of you!"

And she was followed into the little cabin by Lord Dalgarno, gay, easy, disembarrassed, and apparently as much pleased to rejoin his new acquaintance as if he had found him in the apartments of a palace. Nigel, on the contrary, (for youth is slave to such circumstances,) was discountenanced and mortified at being surprised by so splendid a gallant in a chamber, which at the moment the elegant and high-dressed cavalier appeared in it, seemed yet lower, narrower, darker, and meaner to its inhabitant, than it had ever shewn before. He would have made some apology for the situation, but Lord Dalgarno cut him short—

"Not a word of it," he said, "not a single word—I know why you ride at anchor here—but I can keep counsel—so pretty a hostess would recommend worse quarters—"

"On my word—on my honour," said Lord Glenvarloch——

"Nay, nay—make no words of the matter," said Lord Dalgarno; "I am no tell-tale, nor shall I cross your walk; there is game enough in the forest, thank heaven, and I can strike a doe for myself."

All this he said in so significant a manner, and the explanation which he had adopted seemed to put Lord Glenvarloch's gallantry on so respectable a footing, that Nigel ceased to try to undeceive him; and less ashamed, perhaps, (for such is human weakness,) of supposed vice than of real poverty, changed the discourse to something else, and left poor Dame Nelly's reputation and his own at the mercy of the young courtier's misconstruction.

He offered refreshments with some hesitation. Lord Dalgarno had long since breakfasted, but had just come from playing a sett of tennis, he said, and would willingly taste a cup of the pretty hostess's single beer. This was easily procured, was drank, was commended, and, as the hostess failed not to bring the cup herself, Lord Dalgarno profited by the opportunity to take a second and more attentive view of her, and then gravely drank to her husband's health, with an almost imperceptible nod to Lord Glenvarloch. Dame Nelly was much honoured, smoothed her apron down with her hands, and said—"Her John was greatly honoured by their lordships—and truly he was a kind, painstaking man for his family, as was in the alley, or indeed as far north as Paul's Chain."

She would have proceeded probably to state the difference betwixt their ages, as the only alloy to their nuptial happiness; but her lodger, who had no mind to be farther exposed to his gay friend's raillery, gave her, contrary to his wont, a signal to leave the room.

Lord Dalgarno looked after her, then looked at Glenvarloch, shook his head, and repeated the well-known lines—

> "My lord, beware of jealousy—
> It is the green-eyed monster which doth make
> The meat it feeds on.——

But come," he said, changing his tone, "I know not why I should worry you thus—I who have so many follies of my own, when I should rather make excuse for being here at all, and tell you wherefore I came."

So saying he reached a seat, and placing another for Lord Glenvarloch, in spite of his anxious haste to anticipate this act of courtesy, he proceeded in the same tone of easy familiarity:—

"We are neighbours, my lord, and are just made known to each other. Now, I know enough of the dear North, to be well aware that Scottish neighbours must be either dear friends or deadly enemies—must either walk hand in hand, or stand sword-point to sword-point;

so I chuse the hand in hand, unless you should reject my proffer."

"How were it possible, my lord," said Lord Glenvarloch, "to refuse what is offered so frankly, even if your father had not been a second father to me?"—And as he took Lord Dalgarno's hand, he added—"I have, I think, lost no time, since, during one day's attendance at court, I have made a kind friend and a powerful enemy."

"The friend thanks you," replied Lord Dalgarno, "for your just opinion; but, my dear Glenvarloch—or rather, for titles are too formal between us of the better file, what is your christened name?"

"Nigel," replied Lord Glenvarloch.

"Then we will be Nigel and Malcolm to each other," said his visitor, "and my lord to the plebeian world around us. But I was about to ask you whom you supposed your enemy?"

"No less than the all-powerful favourite, the great Duke of Buckingham."

"You dream? what could possess you with such an opinion?" said Dalgarno.

"He told me so himself," replied Glenvarloch; "and so far dealt frankly and honourably with me."

"O, you know him not yet," said his companion; "the Duke is moulded of an hundred noble and fiery qualities, that prompt him, like a generous horse, to spring aside in impatience at the least obstacle to his forward course. But he means not what he says in such passing heats—I can do more with him, I thank heaven, than most who are around him; you shall go visit him with me, and you will see how you shall be received."

"I told you, my lord," said Glenvarloch firmly, and with some haughtiness, "the Duke of Buckingham, without the least offence, declared himself my enemy in the face of the court; and he shall retract that aggression as publicly as it was given, ere I will make the slightest advance towards him."

"You would act becomingly in every other case," said Lord Dalgarno, "but here you are wrong. In the court horizon, Buckingham is Lord of the Ascendant, and as he is adverse or favouring, so sinks or rises the fortune of a suitor. The King would bid you remember your Phædrus,

> Arripiens geminas, ripis cedentibus, ollas,

and so forth. You are the vase of earth—beware of knocking yourself against the vase of iron."

"The vase of earth," said Glenvarloch, "will avoid the encounter, by getting ashore out of the current. I mean to go no more to court."

"O, to court you necessarily must go; you will find your Scotch suit move ill without it, for there is both patronage and favour necessary to enforce the sign-manual you have obtained. Of that we will speak more hereafter; but tell me in the meanwhile, my dear Nigel, whether you did not wonder to see me here so early?"

"I am surprised that you could find me out in this obscure corner," said Lord Glenvarloch.

"My page Lutin is a very devil for that sort of discovery," replied Lord Dalgarno; "I have but to say, 'Goblin, I would know where He or She dwells,' and he guides me thither as if by art magic."

"I hope he waits not now in the street, my lord," said Nigel; "I will send my servant to seek him."

"Do not concern yourself—he is by this time," said Lord Dalgarno, "playing at hustle-cap and chuck-farthing with the most blackguard imps upon the wharf, unless he hath foregone his old customs."

"Are you not afraid," said Lord Glenvarloch, "that in such company his morals may become depraved?"

"Let his company look to their own," answered Lord Dalgarno coolly; "for it will be a company of real fiends in which Lutin cannot teach more mischief than he can learn: he is, I thank the gods, most thoroughly versed in evil for his years. I am spared the trouble of looking after his moralities, for nothing can make him either better or worse."

"I wonder you can answer this to his parents, my lord," said Nigel.

"I wonder where I should find his parents," replied his companion, "to render an account to them."

"He may be an orphan," said Lord Nigel; "but surely, being a page in your lordship's family, his parents must be of rank."

"Of as high rank as the gallows could exalt them to," replied Lord Dalgarno with the same indifference; "they were both hanged, I believe—at least the gipsies, from whom I bought him five years ago, intimated as much to me.—You are surprised at this, now. But is it not better, that instead of a lazy, conceited, whey-faced slip of gentility, to whom, in your old-world idea of the matter, I was bound to stand Sir Pedagogue, and see that he washed his hands and face, said his prayers, learned his *accidens*, spoke no naughty words, brushed his hat, and wore his best doublet only of Sunday,—that instead of such a Jacky Goodchild, I should have something like this?"

He whistled shrill and clear, and the page he spoke of darted into the room, almost with the effect of an actual apparition. From his height he seemed but fifteen, but, from his face, might be two or even three years older, very neatly made, and richly dressed; with a thin bronzed visage, which marked his gipsey descent, and a pair of piercing black eyes, which seemed to look almost through those whom he looked at.

"There he is," said Lord Dalgarno, "fit for every element—prompt to execute every command, good, bad, or indifferent—unmatched in his tribe, as rogue, thief, and liar."

"All which qualities," said the undaunted page, "have each in turn stood your lordship in stead."

"Out, you imp of Satan!" said his master; "vanish—begone—or my conjuring rod goes about your ears." The boy turned, and disappeared as suddenly as he had entered. "You see," said Lord Dalgarno, "that in choosing my household, the best regard I can pay to gentle blood, is to exclude it from my service—that very gallows-bird were enough to corrupt a whole anti-chamber of pages, though they were descended from Kings and Kesars."

"I can scarce think that a nobleman should need the offices of such an attendant as your goblin," said Nigel; "you are but jesting with my inexperience."

"Time will shew whether I jest or not, my dear Nigel," replied Dalgarno; "in the mean time, I have to propose to you to take the advantage of the flood-tide, to run up the river for pastime; and at noon I trust you will dine with me."

Nigel acquiesced in a plan which promised so much amusement; and his new friend and he, attended by Lutin and Moniplies, who greatly resembled, when thus associated, the conjunction of a bear and a monkey, took possession of Lord Dalgarno's wherry, which, with its badged watermen, bearing his lordship's crest on their arms, lay in readiness to receive them. The air was delightful upon the river; and the lively conversation of Lord Dalgarno added zest to the pleasures of the little voyage. He could not only give an account of the various public buildings and noblemen's houses which they passed in ascending the Thames, but knew how to season his information with abundance of anecdote, political inuendo, and personal scandal: if he had not very much wit, he was at least completely master of the fashionable tone, which in that time, as in ours, more than amply supplied any deficiency of the kind.

It was a style of conversation entirely new to his companion, as was the world which Lord Dalgarno opened to his observation; and it is no wonder that Nigel, notwithstanding his natural good sense and high spirit, admitted, more readily than seemed consistent with either, the tone of authoritative instruction which his new friend assumed towards him. There would, indeed, have been some difficulty in making a stand. To attempt a tone of high and stubborn morality, in answer to the light strain of Lord Dalgarno's conversation, which kept on the frontiers between jest and earnest, would have seemed pedantic and ridiculous; and every attempt which Nigel made to combat his companion's propositions, by reasoning as jocose as his own, only shewed his inferiority in that gay species of controversy. And it must be owned, besides, though internally disapproving much of what he heard, Lord Glenvarloch was less alarmed by the language and manners of his new associate, than in prudence he ought to have been.

Lord Dalgarno was unwilling to startle his proselyte, by insisting upon any topic which appeared particularly to jar with his habits or principles; and he blended his mirth and his earnest so dexterously, that it was impossible for Nigel to discover how far he was serious in his propositions, how far they flowed from a wild and extravagant spirit of raillery. And, ever and anon, those flashes of spirit and honour crossed his conversation, which seemed to intimate, that when stirred to action by some adequate motive, Lord Dalgarno would prove something very different from the court-haunting and ease-loving voluptuary, which he was pleased to represent as his chosen character.

As they returned down the river, Lord Glenvarloch remarked, that the boat passed the mansion of Lord Huntinglen, and noticed the circumstance to Lord Dalgarno, observing, that he thought they were to have dined there. "Surely no," said the young nobleman, "I have more mercy on you than to gorge you a second time on raw beef and canary wine. I propose something better for you, I promise you, than such a second Scythian festivity. And as for my father, he proposes to dine to-day with my grave, ancient Earl of Northampton, whilome that celebrated putter-down of pretended prophecies Lord Henry Howard."

"And do you not go with him?" said his companion.

"To what purpose?" said Lord Dalgarno. "To hear his wise lordship speak musty politics in false Latin, which the old fox always uses, that he may give the learned Majesty of England an opportunity of correcting his slips in grammar?—that were a rare employment!"

"Nay," said Nigel, "but out of respect, to wait on my lord your father."

"My lord my father," replied Lord Dalgarno, "has blue-bottles enough to wait on him, and can well dispense with such a butterfly as myself. He can lift the cup of sack to his head without my assistance; and should the said paternal head turn something giddy, there be men enough to guide his right honourable lordship to his lordship's right honourable couch. Now, do not stare at me, Nigel, as if my words were to sink the boat with us. I love my father—I love him dearly—and I

respect him too, though I respect not many things; a trustier old
Trojan never belted a broad-sword by a loop of leather. But what
then? He belongs to the old world, I to the new. He has his follies, I
have mine; and the less either of us sees of the other's peccadilloes,
the greater will be the honour and respect—that, I think, is the proper
phrase,—I say, the *respect* in which we shall hold each other. Being
apart, each of us is himself, such as nature and circumstance have
made him; but couple us up too closely together, you will be sure to
have in your leash either an old hypocrite or a young one, or perhaps
both the one and t'other."

As he spoke thus, the boat put in to the landing-place at Blackfriar's. Lord Dalgarno sprung ashore, and flinging his cloak and
rapier to his page, recommended to his companion to do the like.
"We are coming among press of gallants," he said; "and if we
walk thus muffled, we shall look like your tawney-visaged Don,
who wraps him close in his cloak, to conceal the defects of his
doublet."

"I have known many an honest man do that, if it please your
lordship," said Richie Moniplies, who had been watching for an
opportunity to intrude himself on the conversation, and probably
remembered what had been his own condition, in respect to cloak and
doublet, at a very recent period.

Lord Dalgarno stared at him, as if surprised at his assurance; but
immediately answered, "You may have known many things, friend;
but, in the meanwhile, you do not know what principally concerns
your master, namely, how to carry his cloak, so as to shew to advantage
the gold-laced seams, and the lining of sables—see how Lutin holds
the sword, with the cloak cast partly over it, yet so as to set off the
embossed hilt, and the silver work of the mounting.—Give your familiar your sword, Nigel," he continued, addressing Lord Glenvarloch,
"that he may practise a lesson in an art so necessary."

"Is it altogether prudent," said Nigel, unclasping his weapon, and
giving it to Richie, "to walk entirely unarmed?"

"And wherefore not?" said his companion. "You are thinking now
of Auld Reekie, as my father fondly calls your good Scotch capital,
where there is such bandying of private feuds and public factions, that
a man of any note shall not cross your High Street twice, without
endangering his life thrice. Here, sir, no brawling in the street is
permitted. Your bull-headed citizen takes up the case so soon as a
sword is drawn, and *clubs* is the word."

"And a hard word it is," said Richie, "as my brain-pan kens at this
blessed moment."

"Were I your master, sirrah," said Lord Dalgarno, "I would make your brain-pan, as you call it, boil over, were you to speak a word to me before you were spoken to."

Richie murmured some indistinct answer, but took the hint, and ranked himself behind his master along with Lutin, who failed not to expose his new companion to the ridicule of the passengers, by mimicking, as often as he could do so unobserved by Richie, his stiff and upright stalking gait and discontented physiognomy.

"And tell me now, my dear Malcolm," said Nigel, "where we are bending our course, and whether we shall dine at an apartment of yours."

"An apartment of mine—yes, surely," answered Lord Dalgarno, "you shall dine at an apartment of mine, and an apartment of yours, and of twenty gallants beside; and where the board shall present better cheer, better wine, and better attendance, than if our whole united exhibitions went to maintain it. We are going to the most noted ordinary of London."

"That is, in ordinary language, an inn or a tavern," said Nigel.

"An inn or a tavern, my most green and simple friend!" exclaimed Lord Dalgarno. "No, no—these are places where greasy citizens take pipe and pot, where the knavish pettifoggers of the law sponge on their most unhappy victims—where Templars crack jests as empty as their nuts, and where small gentry imbibe such thin potations, that they get dropsies instead of getting drunk. An ordinary is a late invented institution, sacred to Bacchus and Comus, where the first noble gallants of the time meet with the first and most ethereal wits of the age,—where the wine is the very soul of the choicest grape, refined as the genius of the poet, and ancient and generous as the blood of the nobles. And then the fare is something beyond your ordinary gross terrestrial food! Sea and land are ransacked to supply it; and the invention of six ingenious cooks kept eternally upon the rack to make their art hold pace with, and if possible enhance, the exquisite quality of the materials."

"By all which rhapsody," said Lord Glenvarloch, "I can only understand, as I did before, that we are going to a choice tavern, where we shall be handsomely entertained, on paying probably as handsome a reckoning."

"Reckoning!" exclaimed Lord Dalgarno in the same tone as before, "perish the peasantly phrase! What profanation! Monsieur le Chevalier de Beaujeu, pink of Paris and flower of Gascony—he who can tell the age of his wine by the bare smell, who distils his sauces in an alembic by the aid of Lullie's philosophy,—who carves with such exquisite precision, that he gives to noble knight and squire the portion of the pheasant which exactly accords with his rank—nay, he who shall divide a becafico into twelve parts with such scrupulous exactness, that of twelve guests not one shall have the advantage of the other in a hair's breadth, or the twentieth part of a drachm, yet you talk of him and of a reckoning in the same breath! Why, man, he is the well-known and general referee in all matters affecting the mysteries of Passage, Hazard, In and In, Penneeck and Verquire, and what not —why, Beaujeu is King of the Card-pack, and Duke of the Dice-box —*he* call a reckoning like a green-aproned, red-nosed, son of the vulgar spiggot! Oh, my dearest Nigel, what a word you have spoken, and of what a person! That you know him not, is your only apology for such blasphemy; and yet I scarce hold it adequate, for to have been a day in London and not to know Beaujeu, is a crime of its own kind. But you shall know him this blessed moment, and shall learn to hold yourself in horror for the enormities you have uttered."

"Well, but mark you," said Nigel, "this worthy chevalier keeps not all this good cheer at his own cost, does he?"

"No, no," answered Lord Dalgarno; "there is a sort of ceremony which my chevalier's friends and intimates understand, but with which you have no business at present—there is, as Majesty might say, a *symbolum* to be disbursed—in other words, a mutual exchange of courtesies takes place betwixt Beaujeu and his guests. He makes them a free present of the dinner and wine, as often as they choose to consult their own felicity by frequenting his house at the hour of noon, and they, in gratitude, make the chevalier a present of a Jacobus. Then, you must know, that besides Comus and Bacchus, that princess of sublunary affairs the Diva Fortuna is frequently worshipped at Beaujeu's, and he, as officiating high-priest, hath, as in reason he should, a considerable advantage from a share of the sacrifice."

"In other words," said Lord Glenvarloch, "this man keeps a gaming-house."

"A house in which you may certainly game," said Lord Dalgarno, "as you may in your own chamber, if you have a mind; nay, I remember old Tom Tally played a hand at putt for a wager with Quinze le Va, the Frenchman, during morning prayers in Saint Paul's; the morning was misty, and the parson drowsy, and the whole audience consisted of themselves and a blind old woman, and so they escaped detection."

"For all this, Malcolm," said the young lord, gravely, "I cannot dine with you to-day, at this same ordinary."

"And wherefore, in the name of Heaven, should you draw back from your word?" said Lord Dalgarno.

"I do not retract my word, Malcolm; but I am bound, by an early promise to my father, never to enter the doors of a gaming-house."

"I tell you this is none," said Lord Dalgarno; "it is but, in plain terms, an eating-house, arranged on civiller terms, and frequented by better company, than others in this town; and if some of them do amuse themselves with cards and hazard, they are men of honour, and who play as such, and for no more than they can well afford to lose. It was not, and could not be, such houses that your father desired you to avoid—besides, he might as well have made you swear you would never take the accommodation of an inn, tavern, eating-house, or place of public reception of any kind. For there is no such place of public resort but what your eyes may be therein contaminated by the sight of a pack of pieces of painted pasteboard, and your ears profaned by the rattle of those little spotted cubes of ivory. The difference is, that where we go, we may happen to see persons of quality amusing themselves with a civil game; and in the ordinary houses you will meet bullies and sharpers, who will strive either to cheat or to swagger you out of your money."

"I am sure you would not willingly lead me to do what is wrong," said Nigel; "but my father had a horror of games of chance, religious I believe, as well as prudential: he judged from I know not what circumstance, a fallacious one I should hope, that I had a propensity to such courses, and I have told you the promise which he exacted from me."

"Now, by my honour," said Dalgarno, "what you have said, affords the strongest reason for my insisting that you go with me. A man who would shun any danger, should first become acquainted with its real bearing and extent, and that in the company of a confidential guide and guard. Do you think I myself game?—good faith, my father's oaks grow too far from London, and stand too fast rooted in the rocks of Perthshire, for me to troll them down with a die, though I have seen whole forests go down like nine-pins. No, no—these are sports for the wealthy Southron, not for the poor Scottish noble. The place is an eating-house, and as such you and I will use it—if others use it to game in, it is their fault, but neither that of the house nor ours."

Unsatisfied with this reasoning, Nigel still insisted upon the promise he had given to his father, until his companion appeared rather displeased, and disposed to impute to him injurious and unhandsome suspicions. Lord Glenvarloch could not stand this change of tone. He recollected that much was due from him to Lord Dalgarno, on account of his father's ready and efficient friendship, and something also on account of the frank manner in which the young man himself had offered him his intimacy. He had no reason to doubt his assurances that the house where they were about to dine did not fall under the description of places to which his father's prohibition referred; and, finally, he was strong in his own resolution to resist every temptation to join in games of chance. He therefore pacified Lord Dalgarno, by intimating his willingness to go along with him; and the good humour of the young courtier instantaneously returning, he again ran on in a grotesque and rhodomontade account of the host, Monsieur de Beaujeu, which he did not conclude until they had reached the Temple of Hospitality over which that eminent professor presided.

END OF VOLUME FIRST

THE FORTUNES OF NIGEL

VOLUME II

Chapter One

—This is the very barn-yard,
Where muster daily the prime cocks o' the game,
Ruffle their pinions, crow till they are hoarse,
And spar about a barley-corn—here too chickens,
The callow, unfledged brood of forward folly,
Learn first to rear the crest, and aim the spur,
And tune their note like full-plumed Chaunticleer.
The Bear-Garden

THE ORDINARY, now an ignoble sound, was, in the days of James, a new institution, as fashionable among the youth of that age as the first-rate modern club-houses are amongst those of the present day. It differed chiefly, in being open to all whom good clothes and good assurance combined to introduce there. The company usually dined together at an hour fixed, and the manager of the establishment presided as master of the ceremonies.

Monsieur Le Chevalier, (as he qualified himself,) Saint Priest de Beaujeu, was a sharp, thin Gascon, about sixty years old, banished from his own country, as he said, on account of an affair of honour, in which he had the misfortune to kill his antagonist, though the best swordsman in the south of France. His pretensions to gentility were supported by a feathered hat, a long rapier, and a suit of embroidered taffeta, not much the worse for wear, in the extreme fashion of the Parisian court, and fluttering like a May-pole with many knots of ribband, of which it was computed he bore at least five hundred yards about his person. But, notwithstanding this profusion of decoration, there were many who thought Monsieur le Chevalier so admirably calculated for his present situation, that nature could never have meant to place him an inch above it. It was, however, part of the amusement of the place, for Lord Dalgarno and other young men of

quality to treat Monsieur de Beaujeu with a great deal of mock ceremony, which being observed by the herd of more ordinary and simple
gulls, they paid him, in imitation, much real deference. The Gascon's
natural forwardness being much enhanced by these circumstances, he
was often guilty of presuming beyond the limits of his situation, and of
course had sometimes the mortification to be disagreeably driven
back into them.

When Nigel entered the mansion of this eminent person, which had
been but of late the residence of a great Baron of Queen Elizabeth's
court, who had retired to his manors in the country on the death of that
great princess, he was surprised at the extent of the accommodation
which it afforded, and the number of guests who were already assembled. Feathers waved, spurs jingled, lace and embroidery glanced
every where; and, at first sight at least, it certainly made good Lord
Dalgarno's encomium, who represented the company as composed
almost entirely of youth of the first quality. A more close review was
not quite so favourable. Several individuals might be discovered who
were not exactly at their ease in the splendid dresses which they wore,
and who, therefore, might be supposed not habitually familiar with
such finery. Again, there were others, whose dress, though upon the
general view it did not seem inferior to that of the rest of the company,
displayed, on being observed more closely, some of those petty expedients, by which vanity endeavours to disguise poverty.

Nigel had very little time to make such observations, for the
entrance of Lord Dalgarno created an immediate bustle and sensation
among the company, as his name passed from one mouth to another.
Some stood forward to gaze, others stood back to make way—those of
his own rank hastened to welcome him—those of inferior degree
endeavoured to catch some point of his gesture, or of his dress, to be
worn and practised upon a future occasion, as the newest and most
authentic fashion.

The *Genius Loci*, the Chevalier himself, was not the last to welcome
this prime stay and ornament of his establishment. He came shiffling
forward with a hundred apish congés and *chers milors*, to express his
happiness at seeing Lord Dalgarno again.—"I hope you do bring back
the sun with you, mi lor—you did carry away the sun and the moon
from your pauvre Chevalier when you leave him for so long. Pardieu, I
believe you take them away in your pockets."

"That must have been because you left me nothing else in them,
Chevalier," answered Lord Dalgarno; "but Monsieur le Chevalier, I
pray you to know my countryman and friend Lord Glenvarloch."

"Ah, ha! tres honoré—Je m'en souviens,—oui. J'ai connu autrefois
un Milor Kenfarloque en Ecosse. Yes, I have memory of him—le pere

de mi lor apparemment—we were vera intimate when I was at Oly Root with Monsieur de la Motte—I did often play at tennis vit Milor Kenfarloque at L'Abbaie de Oly Root—il etoit même plus fort que moi—Ah le beau coup de revers qu'il avoit!—I have memory too that he was among the pretty girls—ah un vrai diable dechainé—Aha! I have memory"——

"Better have no more memory of the late Lord Glenvarloch," said Lord Dalgarno, interrupting the Chevalier without ceremony; who perceived that the encomium which he was about to pass on the deceased was likely to be as disagreeable to the son, as it was totally undeserved by the father, who, far from being either a gamester or libertine, as the Chevalier's reminiscences falsely represented him, was, on the contrary, strict and severe in his course of life, almost to the extent of rigour.

"You have the reason, milor," answered the Chevalier, "you have the right—Qu'est ce que nous avons a faire, avec le tems passé?—the time passed did belong to our fathers—our ancetres—very well—the time present is to us—they have their pretty tombs, with their memories and armorial, all in brass and marbre—we have the petits plats exquis, and the Soupe-a-Chevalier, which I will cause to mount up immediately."

So saying, he made a pirouette on his heel, and put his attendants in motion to place dinner on the table. Dalgarno laughed, and observing his young friend looked grave, said to him, in a tone of reproach—"Why, what!—you are not owl enough to be angry with such a gull as that?"

"I keep my anger, I trust, for better purpose," said Lord Glenvarloch; "but I confess I was moved to hear such a fellow mention my father's name—and you too, who told me this was no gaming-house, talked to him of having left it with emptied pockets."

"Pshaw, man!" said Lord Dalgarno, "I spoke but according to the trick of the time; besides, a man must set a piece or two sometimes, or he would be held a cullionly niggard. But here comes dinner, and we will see whether you like the Chevalier's good cheer better than his conversation."

Dinner was announced accordingly, and the two friends, being seated in the most honourable station at the board, were most ceremoniously attended to by the Chevalier, who did the honours of his table to them and to the other guests, and seasoned the whole with his agreeable conversation. The dinner was really excellent, in that piquant style of cookery which the French had already introduced, and which the home-bred young men of England, when they aspired to the rank of connoisseurs and persons of taste, were under the necessity of admiring. The wine was also of the first quality, and circulated in great variety, and no less abundance. The conversation among so many young men, was, of course, light, lively, and amusing, and Nigel, whose mind had been long depressed by anxiety and misfortune, naturally found himself at ease, and his spirits raised and animated.

Some of the company had real wit, and could use it both politely and to advantage; others were coxcombs, and were laughed at without discovering it; and, again, others were originals, who seemed to have no objection that the company should be amused with their folly instead of their wit. And almost all the rest who played any prominent part in the conversation, had either the real tone of good society which belonged to the period, or the jargon which often passes current for it.

In short, the company and conversation was so agreeable, that Nigel's rigour was softened by it, even towards the master of ceremonies, and he listened with patience to various details which the Chevalier de Beaujeu, seeing, as he said, that Milor's talent lay for the "curieux and l'utile," chose to address to him in particular, on the subject of cookery. To gratify, at the same time, the taste for antiquity, which he somehow supposed that his new guest possessed, he launched out in commendation of the great artists of former days, particularly one whom he had known in his youth, "Maitre de Cuisine to the Marechal Strozzi—tres bon gentilhomme pourtant;" who had maintained his master's table with twelve covers every day during the long and severe blockade of Le petit Leyth, although he had nothing better to place on it than the quarter of a carrion-horse now and then, and the grass and weeds that grew on the ramparts. "Des par dieux c'etoit un homme superbe! With on tistle-head, and a nettle or two, he could make a soupe for twenty guest—an haunch of a little puppy-dog made a roti des plus excellents; but his coup de maitre was when the rendition—what you call surrender, took place and appened; and then, dieu me damne, he made out of the hind quarter of one salted horse, forty-five—mais forty-five—couverts; that the English and Scottish officers and nobility, who had the honour to dine with Monseigneur upon the rendition, could not tell what the devil any one of them were made upon at all."

The good wine had by this time gone so merrily round, and had such genial effect on the guests, that those of the lower end of the table, who had hitherto been listeners, began, not greatly to their own credit, or that of the ordinary, to make innovation.

"You speak of the siege of Leith," said a tall, raw-boned man, with thick moustaches turned up with a military twist, a broad buff belt, a long rapier, and other outward symbols of the honoured profession, which lives by killing other people,—"you talk of your siege of Leith, and I have seen the place—a pretty kind of a hamlet it is, with a plain wall, or rampart, and a pigeon-house or two of a tower at every angle. Uds daggers and scabbards, if a leaguer of our days had lain twenty-four hours, not to say so many months before it, without carrying the place and all its cock-lofts, one after other, by pure storm, they would have deserved no better grace than the Provost Marshall gives when his noose is reeved."

"Saar," said the Chevalier, "Monsieur le Capitaine, I vas not at the siege of the Petit Leyth, and I know not what you say about de cock-loft; but I will say for Monseigneur de Strozzi, that he understood the grande guerre, and was grand capitain—plus grand—that is more great it may be, than some of the capitaines of Angleterre, who do speak very loud—tenez, Monsieur, car c'est a vous!"

"O Monsieur," answered the swordsman, "we know the French-man will fight well behind his barrier of stone, or when he is armed with back, breast, and pot."

"Pot!" exclaimed the Chevalier, "what do you mean by pot—do you mean to insult me among my noble guests? Saar, I have done my duty as a pauvre gentilhomme under the Grand Henri Quatre, both at Courtrai and Yvry, and, Ventre saint gris! we had neither pot nor marmite, but did always charge in our shirt."

"Which refutes another base scandal," said Lord Dalgarno, laughing, "alleging that linen was scarce among the French gentle-men-at-arms."

"Gentlemen out at arms and at elbows both, you mean, my lord," said the captain, from the bottom of the table. "Craving your lord-ship's pardon, I do know something of these same gens-d'armes."

"We will spare your knowledge at present, captain, and save your modesty at the same time the trouble of telling us how that knowledge was acquired," answered Lord Dalgarno, rather contemptuously.

"I need not speak of it, my lord," said the man of war; "the world knows it—all, perhaps, but the men of mohair—the poor sneaking citizens of London, who would see a man of valour eat his very hilts for hunger, ere they would draw a farthing from their long purses to relieve him. O, if a band of the honest fellows I have seen were once to come near that cuckoo's nest of theirs!"

"A cuckoo's nest!—and that said of the city of London," said a gallant who sate on the opposite side of the table, and who, wearing a splendid and fashionable dress, seemed yet scarce at home in it,—"I will not brook to hear that repeated."

"What!" said the soldier, bending a most terrific frown from a pair of broad black eye-brows, handling the hilt of his weapon with one hand, and twirling with the other his huge mustachoes; "will you quarrel for your city?"

"Ay, marry will I," replied the other. "I am a citizen, I care not who knows it; and he who shall speak a word in its dispraise, is an ass and a peremptory gull, and I will break his pate, to teach him sense and manners."

The company, who probably had their reasons for not valuing the captain's courage at the high rate which he put upon it, were much entertained with the manner in which the quarrel was taken up by the indignant citizen; and they exclaimed on all sides, "Well rung, Bow Bell!" "Well crowed, the Cock of Saint Paul's!" "Sound a charge there, or the soldier will mistake his signals, and retreat when he should advance."

"You mistake me, gentlemen," said the captain, looking round with an air of dignity. "I will but inquire whether this cavaliero citizen is of rank and degree fitted to measure swords with a man of action; (for, conceive me, gentlemen, it is not with every one that I can match myself without loss of reputation;) and in that case he shall hear from me honourably, by way of chartel."

"You shall feel me most dishonourably in the way of cudgel," said the citizen, starting up, and taking his sword, which he had laid in a corner. "Follow me."

"It is my right to name the place of combat, by all the rules of the sword," said the captain; "and I do nominate the Maze, in Tothill-Fields, for place—two gentlemen who shall be indifferent judges, for witnesses;—and for time—let me say—this day fortnight, at daybreak."

"And I," said the citizen, "do nominate the Bowling-alley behind the house for place, the present good company for witnesses, and for time, the present moment."

So saying, he cast on his beaver, struck the soldier smartly across the shoulders with his sheathed sword, and ran down stairs. The captain shewed no instant alacrity to follow him; yet, at last, roused by the laugh and sneer around him, he assured the company, that what he did, he would do deliberately, and, assuming his hat, which he put on with the air of Ancient Pistol, he descended the stairs to the place of combat, where his more prompt adversary was already stationed, with his sword unsheathed. Of the company, all of whom seemed highly delighted with the approaching fray, some ran to the windows which overlooked the bowling-alley, and others followed the combatants down stairs. Nigel could not help asking Dalgarno whether he would not interfere to prevent mischief.

"Heaven forbid, man!—heaven forbid!" said the young nobleman;

"there can no mischief happen between two such originals, which will not be positive benefit to society, and particularly to the Chevalier's establishment, as he calls it. I have been as sick of that captain's buff belt, and red doublet, for this month past, as e'er I was of aught; and now I hope this bold linen-draper will cudgel the ass out of that filthy lion's hide. See, Nigel, see the gallant citizen has ta'en his ground about a bowl's-cast forward, in the midst of the alley—the very model of a hog in armour. Behold how he prances with his manly foot, and brandishes his blade, much as if he were about to measure forth cambric with it.—See, they bring on the reluctant soldado, and plant him opposite to his fiery antagonist, twelve paces still dividing them.— Lo, the captain draws his tool, but, like a good general, looks over his shoulder to secure his retreat, in case the worst come on't.—Behold the valiant shopkeeper stoops his head, confident, doubtless, in the civic helmet which his spouse has forfeited—Why, this is the rarest sport! By Heaven, he will run a tilt with him like a ram."

It was even as Lord Dalgarno had anticipated; for the citizen, who seemed quite serious in his zeal for combat, perceiving that the man of war did not advance towards him, rushed onwards with as much good fortune as courage, beat down the captain's guard, and pressing on, thrust his sword, as it seemed, clear through the body of his antagonist, who, with a deep groan, measured his length on the ground. A score of voices cried to the conqueror, as he stood fixed in astonishment at his own feat, "Away, away with you—fly, fly—fly by the back door—get into Whitefriars, or cross the water to the Bankside, while we keep off the mob and the constables." And the conqueror, leaving his vanquished foeman on the ground, fled accordingly, with all speed.

"By Heaven," said Lord Dalgarno, "I could never have believed that the fellow would have stood to receive a thrust—he has certainly been arrested by positive terror, and lost the use of his limbs. See, they are raising him."

Stiff and stark seemed the corpse of the swordsman, as one or two of the guests raised him from the ground; but when they began to open his waistcoat to search for the wound which nowhere existed, the man of war collected his scattered spirits, and conscious that the ordinary was no longer a stage on which to display his valour, took to heels as fast as he could run, pursued by the laughter and shouts of the company.

"By my honour," said Lord Dalgarno, "he takes the same course with his conqueror. I trust in Heaven he will overtake him, and then the valiant citizen will suppose himself haunted by the ghost of him he has slain."

"Despardieux, mi lor," said the Chevalier, "if he had stay one moment, he should have had a *torchon*—what you call dis-clout, pinned to him for a piece of shroud, to shew he be de ghost of one grand fanfaron."

"In the mean while," said Lord Dalgarno, "you will oblige us, Monsieur le Chevalier, as well as maintain your own honoured reputation, by letting your drawers receive the man-at-arms with a cudgel, in case he should venture to come this way again."

"Ventre saint gris, my lor," said the chevalier, "leave that to me—begar, the maid shall throw the wash-sud upon the grand poltron."

When they had laughed sufficiently at this ludicrous occurrence, the party began to divide themselves into little knots—some took possession of the alley, late the scene of combat, and put the field to its proper use of a bowling-ground, and it soon resounded with all the terms of the game, as "run, run—rub, rub—hold bias, you infernal trundling timber;" thus making good the saying, that three things are thrown away in a bowling-green, namely, time, money, and oaths.

In the house, many of the gentlemen betook themselves to cards or dice, and parties were formed at Ombre, at Basset, at Gleek, at Primero, and other games then in fashion; while the dice were used at various games, both with and without the tables, as Hazard, In-and-in, Passage, and so forth. The play, however, did not appear to be extravagantly deep; it was certainly conducted with great decorum and fairness; nor did there appear any thing to lead the younger Scotsman in the least to doubt his companion's assurance, that the place was frequented by men of rank and quality, and that the recreations they adopted were conducted upon honourable principles.

Lord Dalgarno neither proposed play to his friend, nor joined in the amusement himself, but sauntered from one table to another, remarking the luck of the different players, as well as their capacity to avail themselves of it, and exchanging conversation with the highest and most respectable of the guests. At length, as if tired of what in modern phrase would have been termed lounging, he suddenly remembered that Burbage was to act Shakespeare's King Richard, at the Fortune, that afternoon, and that he could not give a stranger in London, like Lord Glenvarloch, a higher entertainment than to carry him to that exhibition; "unless, indeed," he added, in a whisper, "there is a paternal interdiction of the theatre as well as of the ordinary."

"I never heard my father speak of stage-plays," said Lord Glenvarloch, "for they are shows of a modern date, and unknown in Scotland. Yet, if what I have heard to their prejudice be true, I doubt much whether he would have approved of them."

"Approved of them!" exclaimed Lord Dalgarno—"why, George

Buchanan wrote tragedies, and his pupil, learned and wise as himself, goes to see them, so it is next door to treason to abstain; and the cleverest men in England write for the stage, and the prettiest women in London resort to the play-houses; and I have a brace of nags at the door which will carry us along the streets like wild-fire, and the ride will digest our venison and ortolans, and dissipate the fumes of the wine, and so let's to horse—Godd'en to you, gentlemen—Godd'en, Chevalier de la Fortune."

Lord Dalgarno's grooms were in attendance with two horses, and the young men mounted, the proprietor upon a favourite barb, and Nigel upon a high-dressed jennet, scarce less beautiful. As they rode towards the theatre, Lord Dalgarno endeavoured to discover his friend's opinion of the company to which he had introduced him, and to combat the exceptions which he might suppose him to have taken. "And wherefore lookst thou sad," he said, "my pensive neophyte?—sage son of the Alma Mater of Low-Dutch learning, what aileth thee? Is the leaf of the living world which we have turned over in company, less fairly written than thou hadst been taught to expect?—be comforted, and pass over one little blot or two; thou wilt be doomed to read through many a page, as black as Infamy, with her sooty pinion, can make them. Remember, most immaculate Nigel, that we are in London, not Leyden—that we are studying life, not lore. Stand buff against the reproach of thine over-tender conscience, man, and when thou summest up, like a good arithmetician, the actions of the day, before you balance the account upon your pillow, tell the accusing spirit, to his brimstone beard, that if thine ears have heard the clatter of the devil's bones, thy hand hath not trowled them—that if thine eye hath seen the brawling of two angry boys, thy blade hath not been bared in their fray."

"Now, all this may be wise and witty," replied Nigel; "yet I own I cannot think but what your lordship, and other men of good quality with whom we dined, might have chosen a place of meeting free from the intrusion of bullies, and a better master of your ceremonial than yonder foreign adventurer."

"All shall be amended, Sancte Nigelle, when thou shalt come forth a new Peter the Hermit, to preach a crusade against diceing, drabbing, and company-keeping—we will meet for dinner in Saint Sepulchre's Church; we will dine in the chancel, drink our flask in the vestry, the parson shall draw every cork, and the clerk say amen to every health. Come, man, cheer up, and get rid of this sour and unsocial humour. Credit me, that the Puritans who object to us the follies and the frailties incident to human nature, have themselves the vices of absolute devils, privy malice and backbiting hypocrisy, and spiritual pride in all its presumption. There is much, too, in life, which we must see, were it only to learn to shun it. Will Shakespeare, who lives after death, and who is presently to afford thee such pleasure as none but himself can confer, has described the gallant Falconbridge as calling that man

——a bastard to the time,
That doth not smack of observation;
Which, though I will not practise to deceive,
Yet, to avoid deceit, I mean to learn.

But here we are at the door of the Fortune, where you shall hear matchless Will speak for himself.—Goblin, and you other lout, leave the horses to the grooms, and make way for us through the press."

They dismounted, and the assiduous efforts of Lutin, elbowing, bullying, and proclaiming his master's name and title, made way through a crowd of murmuring citizens, and clamorous apprentices, to the door, where Lord Dalgarno speedily procured a brace of stools upon the stage for his companion and himself, where, seated among other gallants of the same class, they had an opportunity of displaying their fair dresses and fashionable manners, while they criticized the piece during its progress; thus forming, at the same time, a conspicuous part of the spectacle, and an important proportion of the audience.

Nigel Olifaunt was too eagerly and deeply absorbed in the interest of the scenes, to be capable of playing his part as became the place where he was seated. He felt all the magic of that sorcerer, who had displayed, within the paltry circle of a wooden booth, the long jars of York and Lancaster, compelling the heroes of either line to stalk across the scene in language and fashion as they lived, as if the grave had given up the dead for the amusement and instruction of the living. Burbage, esteemed the best Richard until Garrick arose, played the tyrant and usurper with such truth and liveliness, that when the Battle of Bosworth seemed concluded by his death, the ideas of reality and deception were strongly contending in Lord Glenvarloch's imagination, and it required him to rouse himself from his reverie, so strange did the proposal at first sound when his companion declared King Richard should sup with them at the Mermaid.

They were joined, at the same time, by a small party of the gentlemen with whom they had dined, which they recruited by inviting two or three of the most accomplished wits and poets, who seldom failed to attend the Fortune Theatre, and who were even but too ready to conclude a day of amusement with a night of pleasure. Thither the whole party adjourned, and betwixt fertile cups of sack, excited spirits, and the emulous wit of their lively companions, seemed to realize the joyous boast of one of Ben Jonson's cotemporaries, when reminding the bard of

Those lyric feasts
Where men such clusters had,
As made them nobly wild, not mad;
    While yet each verse of thine
Outdid the meat, outdid the frolic wine.

Chapter Two

Let the proud salmon gorge the feather'd hook,
Then strike, and then you have him—he will wince;
Spin out your line that it shall whistle from you
Some twenty yards or so, yet you shall have him—
Marry! you must have patience—the stout rock
Which is his trust, hath edges something sharp;
And the deep pool hath ooze and sludge enough
To mar your fishing—'less you are more careful.
                        Albion, or the Double Kings

IT IS SELDOM that a day of pleasure, upon review, seems altogether
so exquisite as the partaker of the festivity may have felt it while
passing over him. Nigel Olifaunt, at least, did not feel it so, and it
required a visit from his new acquaintance, Lord Dalgarno, to reconcile him entirely to himself. But this visit took place early after breakfast, and his friend's discourse was prefaced with a question, how he
liked the company of the preceding evening?

"Why, excellently well," said Lord Glenvarloch; "only I should
have liked the wit better had it seemed to flow more freely. Every
man's invention seemed on the stretch, and each extravagant simile
seemed to set one half of your men of wit into a brown study to
produce something which should out-herod it."

"And wherefore not?" said Lord Dalgarno; "or what are these
fellows fit for, but to play the intellectual gladiators before us?—he of
them who declares himself recreant, should, d—n him, be restricted
to muddy ale, and the patronage of the watermen's company. I promise you, that many a pretty fellow has been mortally wounded with a
quibble or a carwitchet at the Mermaid, and sent from thence in a
pitiable estate to Wit's hospital in the Vintry, where they languish to
this day amongst fools and aldermen."

"It may be so," said Lord Nigel; "yet I could swear by my honour,
that last night I seemed to be in company with more than one man,
whose genius and learning ought either to have placed him higher in
our company, or to have withdrawn him altogether from a scene,
where, sooth to speak, his part seemed unworthily subordinate."

"Now, out upon your tender conscience," said Lord Dalgarno;
"and the fico for such bran of Parnassus! Why, these are the very
leavings of that noble banquet of pickled herrings and Rhenish, which

cost London so many of her principal wit-mongers and bards of misrule. What would you have said if you had seen Nash or Greene, when you interest yourself about the poor mimes you supt with last night?—suffice it, they had their drench and their doze, and have drunk and slept as much as may save them from any necessity of eating till evening, when, if they are industrious, they will find patrons or players to feed them—for the rest of their wants, they can be at no loss for cold water while the New River head holds good; and your doublets of Parnassus are eternal in duration."

"Virgil and Horace had more efficient patronage," said Nigel.

"Ay," replied his countryman, "but these fellows are neither Virgil nor Horace; besides, we have others, spirits of another sort, to whom I will introduce you on some early occasion—our Swan of Avon hath sung his last, but we have stout old Ben, with as much learning and genius as ever prompted the treader of sock or buskin. It is not, however, him of whom I mean now to speak, but I come to pray you, of dear love, to row up with me as far as Richmond, where two or three of the gallants whom you saw yesterday, mean to give music and sylla-bubs to a set of beauties, with some curious bright eyes among them; such, I promise you, as might win an astrologer from his worship of the galaxy. My sister leads the bevy, to whom I desire to present you. She hath her admirers at court, and is regarded, though I might dispense with sounding her praise, as one of the beauties of the time."

There was no refusing an engagement, where the presence of the party invited, late so low in his own regard, was demanded by a lady of quality, one of the choice beauties of the time. Lord Glenvarloch accepted, as was inevitable, and spent a lively day among the gay and the fair. He was the gallant in attendance for the day upon his friend's sister, the beautiful Countess of Blackchester, who aimed at once at the superiority in the realms of fashion, of power, and of wit. She was indeed considerably older than her brother, and had probably completed her six lustres; but the deficiency in extreme youth was more than atoned for in the most precise and curious accuracy in attire, an early acquaintance with every foreign mode, and a peculiar gift in adapting the knowledge which she acquired, to her own particular features and complexion. At court, she knew as well as any lady in the circle, the precise tone, moral, political, learned, or jocose, in which it was proper to answer the Monarch according to his prevailing humour, and was supposed to have been very active, by her personal interest, in procuring her husband a high situation, which the gouty old viscount could never have deserved by any merit of his own common-place conduct and understanding.

It was far more easy for this lady, than for her brother, to reconcile

so young a courtier as Lord Glenvarloch to the customs and habits of a
sphere so new to him. In all civilized society, the females of distinguished rank and beauty, give the tone to manners, and through these
even to morals. Lady Blackchester had, besides, interest either in the
court or over the court, (for its source could not be well traced,) which
created friends, and overawed those who might have been disposed to
play the part of enemies.

At one time, she was understood to be closely leagued with the
Buckingham family, with whom her brother still maintained a great
intimacy. And although some coldness had taken place betwixt the
Countess and the Duchess of Buckingham, so that they were little
seen together, and the former seemed considerably to have withdrawn
herself into privacy, it was whispered that Lady Blackchester's interest
with the great favourite was not diminished in consequence of her
breach with his lady.

Our accounts of the private court intrigues of that period, and of the
persons to whom they were entrusted, are not full enough to enable us
to pronounce upon the various reports which arose out of the circumstances we have detailed. It is enough to say, that Lady Blackchester
possessed great influence on the circle around her, both from her
beauty, her abilities, and her reputed talents for court-intrigue; and
that Nigel Olifaunt was not long of experiencing its power, as he
became a slave in some degree to that species of habit which carries so
many men into a certain society at a certain hour, without expecting or
receiving any particular degree of gratification, or even amusement.

His life for several weeks may be thus described. The ordinary was
no bad introduction to the business of the day, and the young lord
quickly found, that if the society there was not always irreproachable,
still it formed the most convenient and agreeable place of meeting
with the fashionable parties, with whom he visited Hyde Park, the
theatres, and other places of public resort, or joined the gay and
glittering circle which Lady Blackchester had assembled around her.
Neither did he entertain the same scrupulous horror which led him
originally even to hesitate entering into a place where gaming was
permitted; but, on the contrary, began to indulge the idea, that
as there could be no harm in beholding such recreation when only
indulged in to a moderate degree, so, from a parity of reasoning, there
could be no objection to joining in it, always under the same restrictions. But the young lord was a Scotchman, accustomed to early
reflection, and totally unaccustomed to any habit which inferred a
careless risk or profuse waste of money. Such was not the vice of his
country, nor likely to be acquired in the course of his education;
and in all probability, while his father anticipated with noble horror

the idea of his son approaching the gaming-table, he was more startled at the idea of his becoming a gaining than a losing adventurer. The first, according to his principles, had a termination, a sad one indeed, in the loss of temporal fortune—the second quality went on increasing the evil which he dreaded, and perilled at once both body and soul.

However the old lord might ground his apprehension, it was so far verified by his son's conduct, that from an observer of the various games of chance which he witnessed, he came by degrees, by moderate hazards, and small bets or wagers, to take a certain interest in them. Nor could it be denied that his rank and expectancies entitled him to hazard a few pieces, (for his game went no deeper,) against persons, who, from the readiness with which they staked their money, might be supposed well able to afford to lose it.

It chanced, or perhaps, according to the common creed, his evil genius had so decreed, that Nigel's adventures were remarkably successful. He was temperate, cautious, cool-headed, had a strong memory, and a ready power of calculation; was, besides, of a daring and intrepid character, one upon whom no one that had looked at even slightly, or spoken to though but hastily, would readily have ventured to practise any thing approaching to trick, or which required to be supported by intimidation. While Lord Glenvarloch chose to play, men played with him regularly, or, according to the phrase, upon the square; when he found his luck change, or wished to hazard his good fortune no farther, the more professed votaries of fortune who frequented the house of Monsieur le Chevalier de Saint Priest Beaujeu, did not venture openly to express their displeasure at his rising a winner. But when this happened repeatedly, the gamesters murmured among themselves equally at the caution and the success of the young Scotsman; and he became far from being a popular character among their society.

It was no slight inducement to the continuance of this most evil habit, when it was once in some degree acquired, that it seemed to place Lord Glenvarloch, haughty as he naturally was, beyond the necessity of subjecting himself to farther pecuniary obligations, which his prolonged residence in London must otherwise have rendered necessary. He had to solicit from the ministers certain forms of office, which were to render his sign manual effectually useful; and these, though they could not be denied, were delayed in such a manner, as to lead Nigel to believe there was some secret opposition, which occasioned the demur in his business. His own impulse was to have appeared at court a second time with the King's sign manual in his pocket, and to have appealed to his Majesty himself, whether the delay of the public officers ought to render his royal generosity unavailing. But the Lord Huntinglen, that good old peer, who had so frankly interfered in his behalf on a former occasion, and whom he occasionally visited, greatly dissuaded him from a similar adventure, and exhorted him quietly to await the deliverance of the ministers, which should set him free from dancing attendance upon London. Lord Dalgarno joined his father in deterring his young friend from a second attendance at court, at least till he was reconciled with the Duke of Buckingham—"a matter in which," he said, addressing his father, "I have offered my poor assistance, without being able to prevail on Lord Nigel to make any—not even the least submission to the Duke of Buckingham."

"By my faith, and I hold the laddie to be in the right on't, Malcolm!" answered the stout old Scots lord. "What right hath Buckingham, or, to speak plainly, the son of Sir George Villiers, to expect homage and fealty from one more noble than himself by eight quarters? I heard him myself, on no reason that I could perceive, term Lord Nigel his enemy; and it will never be by my counsel that the lad speaks soft word to him, till he recalls the hard one."

"That is precisely my advice to Lord Glenvarloch," answered Lord Dalgarno; "but then you will admit, my dear father, that it would be the risk of extremity for our friend to rush into the presence, the Duke being his enemy—better to leave it with me to take off the heat of the distemperature, with which some pick-thanks have persuaded the Duke to regard our friend."

"If thou canst persuade Buckingham of his error, Malcolm," said his father, "for once I will say there hath been kindness and honesty in court service. I have oft told both your sister and yourself, that in the general I esteem it as lightly as may be."

"You need not doubt my doing my best in Nigel's case," answered Lord Dalgarno; "but you must think, my dear father, I must needs use slower and gentler means than those by which you became a favourite twenty years hence."

"By my faith, I am afraid thou wilt," answered his father.—"I tell thee, Malcolm, I would sooner wish myself in the grave, than doubt thine honesty or honour; yet somehow it hath chanced, that honest, ready service hath not the same acceptance at court which it had in my younger time—and yet you rise there."

"O, the time permits not your old-world service," said Lord Dalgarno; "we have now no daily insurrections, no nightly attempts at assassination, as were the fashion in the Scottish court. Your prompt and uncourteous sword-in-hand attendance on the Sovereign is no longer necessary, and would be as unbeseeming as your old-fashioned

serving-men, with their badges, broad-swords, and bucklers, would
be at a court-masque. Besides, father, loyal haste hath its inconveniences. I have heard, and from royal lips too, that when you struck your
dagger into the traitor Ruthven, it was with such little consideration,
that the point ran a quarter of an inch into the royal buttock. The King
never talks of it but he rubs the injured part, and quoting his '*infandum - - - renovare dolorem.*' But this comes of old fashions, and of
wearing a long Liddesdale whinger instead of a poniard of Parma. Yet
this, my dear father, you call prompt and valiant service. The King, I
am told, could not sit upright for a fortnight, though all the cushions in
Falkland were placed in his chair of state, and the provost of Dumfermline's borrowed, to the boot of all."

"It is a lie," said the old Earl, "a false lie, forge it who list!—it is true
I wore a dagger of service by my side, and not a bodkin like yours, to
pick one's teeth withal—And for prompt service—Odds nouns! it
should be prompt to be useful, when kings are crying treason and
murder with the screech of a half-throttled hen. But you young courtiers know nought of these matters, and are little better than the green
geese they bring over from the Indies, whose only merit to their
masters is to repeat their own words after them—a pack of mouthers,
and flatterers, and ear-wigs—well, I am old and unable to mend, else I
would break all off, and hear the Tay once more flinging himself over
the Campsie Linn."

"But there is your dinner-bell, father," said Lord Dalgarno,
"which, if the venison I sent you prove seasonable, is at least as sweet a
sound."

"Follow me then, youngsters, if you list," said the old Earl; and
strode on from the alcove in which this conversation was held, towards
the house, followed by the two young men.

In their private discourse, Lord Dalgarno had little trouble in dis-
suading Nigel from going immediately to court; while, on the other
hand, the offers he made him of a previous introduction to the Duke
of Buckingham, were received by Lord Glenvarloch with a positive
and contemptuous refusal. His friend shrugged his shoulders, as one
who claims the merit of having given to an obstinate friend the best
counsel, and desires to be held free of the consequences of his pertinacity.

As for the father, his table and his best liquor, of which he was more
profuse than necessary, were indeed at the command of his young
friend, as well as his best advice and assistance in the prosecution of
his affairs. But Lord Huntinglen's interest was more apparent than
real; and the credit he had acquired by his gallant defence of the
King's person, was so carelessly managed by himself, and so easily

eluded by the favourites and ministers of the Sovereign, that, except upon one or two occasions when the King was in some measure taken by surprise, as in the case of Lord Glenvarloch, the royal bounty was never efficiently extended, either to himself or to his friends.

"There never was a man," said Lord Dalgarno, whose shrewder knowledge of the English court saw where his father's deficiency lay, "that had it so perfectly in his power to have made his way to the pinnacle of fortune as my poor father. He had acquired a right to build up the stair-case, step by step, slowly and surely, letting every boon, which he begged year after year, become in its turn the resting-place for a further resting-place for the next annual grant. But your fortunes shall not shipwreck upon the same coast, Nigel," he would conclude. "If I have fewer means of influence than my father has, or rather had, till he threw them away for butts of sack, hawks, hounds, and such carrion, I can, far better than he, improve that which I possess; and that, my dear Nigel, is all engaged in your behalf. Do not be surprised or offended that you now see me less than formerly: The stag-hunting is commenced, and the Prince looks that I should attend him more frequently. I must also maintain my attendance on the Duke, that I may have an opportunity of pleading your cause when occasion shall permit."

"I have no cause to plead before the Duke," said Nigel, gravely; "I have said so repeatedly."

"Why, I mean it no otherwise, thou churlish and suspicious disputant," answered Dalgarno, "than as I am now pleading the Duke's cause with thee—surely I only mean to claim a share in our royal master's favourite benediction, *Beati pacifici*."

Upon several occasions, Lord Glenvarloch's conversations, both with the old Earl and his son, took a similar turn, and had a like conclusion. He sometimes felt as if, betwixt the one and the other, not to mention the more unseen and unboasted, but scarce less certain influence of Lady Blackchester, his affair, simple as it had become, might have been somehow accelerated. But it was equally impossible to doubt the rough honesty of the father, and the eager and officious friendship of Lord Dalgarno; nor was it easy to suppose that the countenance of the lady, by whom he was received with such distinction, would be wanting, could it be effectual in his service.

Nigel was farther sensible of the truth of what Lord Dalgarno often pointed out, that the favourite being supposed to be his enemy, every petty officer, through whose hands his affair must necessarily pass, would desire to make a merit of throwing obstacles in his way, which he could only surmount by steadiness and patience, unless he preferred closing the breach, or, as Lord Dalgarno called it, making his peace with the Duke of Buckingham.

Nigel might, and doubtless would, have had recourse to the advice of his friend George Heriot upon this occasion, having found it so advantageous formerly; but the only time he saw him after their visit to court, he found the worthy citizen engaged in hasty preparation for a journey to Paris, upon business of great importance in the way of his profession, and by an especial commission from the court and the Duke of Buckingham, which was likely to be attended with considerable profit. The good man smiled as he named the Duke of Buckingham. He had been, he said, pretty sure that his disgrace in that quarter would not be of long duration.

Lord Glenvarloch expressed himself rejoiced at their reconciliation, observing, that it had been a most painful reflection to him, that Master Heriot should, in his behalf, have incurred the dislike, and perhaps exposed himself to the ill offices, of so powerful a favourite.

"My lord," said Heriot, "for your father's son I would do much; and yet truly, if I know myself, I would do as much, and risk as much, for the sake of justice, in the case of a much more insignificant person, than I have ventured for yours. But as we shall not meet for some time, I must commit to your own wisdom the further prosecution of this matter."

And thus they took a kind and affectionate leave of each other.

There were other changes in Lord Glenvarloch's situation, which require to be noticed. His present occupations, and the habits of amusement which he had acquired, rendered his living so far in the city a considerable inconvenience. He may also have become a little ashamed of his cabin on Paul's Wharf, and desirous of being lodged somewhat more according to his quality. For this purpose, he had hired a small apartment near the Temple. He was, nevertheless, almost sorry for what he had done, when he observed that his removal appeared to give some pain to John Christie, and a great deal to his cordial and officious landlady. The former, who was grave and saturnine in every thing he did, only hoped that all had been to Lord Glenvarloch's mind, and that he had not left them on account of any unbeseeming negligence on their part. But the tear twinkled in Dame Nelly's eye, while she recounted the various improvements she had made in the apartment, of express purpose to render it more convenient to his lordship.

"There was a great sea-chest," she said, "had been taken up stairs to the shopman's garret, though it left the poor lad scarce eighteen inches of opening to creep betwixt it and his bed; and heaven knew— she did not—whether it could ever be brought down that narrow stair again. Then the turning the closet into an alcove, had cost a matter of twenty round shillings; and to be sure, to any other lodger but his lordship, the closet was more convenient. There was all the linen, too, which she had bought on purpose—but heaven's will be done—she was resigned."

Every body likes marks of personal attachment; and Nigel, whose heart really smote him, as if in his rising fortunes he were disdaining the lowly accommodations and the civilities of the humble friends which had been but lately actual favours, failed not by every assurance in his power, and by as liberal payment as they could be prevailed upon to accept, to alleviate the soreness of their feelings at his departure; and a parting kiss from the fair lips of his hostess sealed his forgiveness.

Richie Moniplies lingered behind his master, to ask whether, in case of need, John Christie could help a canny Scotsman to a passage back to his own country; and receiving assurance of John's interest to that effect, he said at parting, he would remind him of his promise soon.—"For," said he, "if my lord is not weary of this London life, I ken one that is, videlicet mysell; and I am weel determined to see Arthur's Seat again ere I am many weeks older."

Chapter Three

> Bingo, why, Bingo! hey boy—here sir, here—
> He's gone and off, but he'll be home before us;—
> 'Tis the most wayward cur e'er mumbled bone,
> Or dogg'd a master's footstep.—Bingo loves me
> Better than ever beggar loved his alms;
> Yet when he takes such humour, you may coax
> Sweet Mistress Fantasy, your worship's mistress,
> Out of her sullen moods, as soon as Bingo.
> *The Dominie and his Dog*

RICHIE MONIPLIES was as good as his word. Two or three mornings after the young lord had possessed himself of his new lodgings, he appeared before Nigel, as he was preparing to dress, having left his pillow at an hour much later than had formerly been his custom.

As Nigel looked upon his attendant, he observed there was a gathering gloom upon his solemn features which expressed either additional importance or superadded discontent, or a portion of both.

"How now," he said, "what is the matter this morning, Richie, that you have made your face so like the grotesque mask on one of the spouts yonder?" pointing to the Temple Church, of which Gothic building they had a view from the window.

Richie swivelled his head a little to the right with as little alacrity as if he had the crick in his neck, and instantly resuming his posture, replied—"Mask here, mask there—it were nae such matters that I have to speak anent."

"And what matters have you to speak anent, then?" said his master, whom circumstances had enured to tolerate a good deal of freedom from his attendant.

"My lord,"—said Richie, and then stopped to cough and hem, as if what he had to say stuck somewhat in his throat.

"I guess the mystery," said Nigel, "you want a little money, Richie—will five pieces serve the present turn?"

"My lord," said Richie, "I may, it is like, want a trifle of money; and I am glad at the same time, and sorry, that it is mair plenty with your lordship than formerly."

"Glad and sorry, man!" said Lord Nigel, "why, you are reading riddles to me, Richie."

"My riddle will be briefly read," said Richie; "I come to crave of your lordship your commands for Scotland."

"For Scotland!—why, art thou mad, man?" said Nigel; "canst thou not tarry to go down with me?"

"I could be but of little service," said Richie, "since you purpose to hire another page and groom."

"Why, thou jealous ass," said the young lord, "will not thy pact of duty be the lighter?—Go, take thy breakfast, and drink thy ale double strong, to put such absurdities out of thy head—I could be angry with thee for thy folly, man—but I remember how thou hast stuck to me in adversity."

"Adversity, my lord, should never have parted us," said Richie; "methinks, had the warst come to warst, I could have starved as gallantly as your lordship, or more so, being in some sort used to it; for, though I was bred at a flesher's stall, I have not through my life had a constant intimacy with collops."

"Now, what is the meaning of all this trash?" said Nigel; "or has it no other end than to provoke my patience? You know well enough, that had I twenty serving-men, I would hold the faithful follower that stood by me in my distress the most valued of them all. But it is totally out of reason to plague me with your solemn capricios."

"My lord," said Richie, "in declaring your trust in me, you have done what is honourable to yourself, if I may with humility say so much, and in no way undeserved on my side. Nevertheless, we must part."

"Body of me, man, why?" said Lord Nigel, "what reason can there be for it, if we are mutually satisfied?"

"My lord," said Richie Moniplies, "your lordship's occupations are such as I cannot own or countenance by my presence."

"How now, sirrah!" said his master, angrily.

"Under favour, my lord," replied the domestic, "it is unequal dealing to be equally offended by my speech and my silence. If you can hear with patience the grounds of my departure, it may be, for aught I know, the better for you here and hereafter—if not, let me have my licence of departure in silence, and no mair about it."

"Go to, sir!" said Nigel; "speak out your mind—only remember to whom you speak it."

"Weel, weel, my lord—I speak it with humility, (never did Richie look with more starched dignity than when he uttered the word;) but do you think this diceing and card-shuffling, and haunting of taverns and play-houses, suits your lordship—for I am sure it does not suit me?"

"Why, you are not turned precisian or puritan?" said Lord Glenvarloch laughing, though, betwixt resentment and shame, it cost him some trouble to do so."

"My lord," replied the follower, "I ken the purport of your query. I am, it may be, over little of a precisian, and I wish to heaven I were mair worthy of the name; but let that be a pass-over.—I have stretched the duties of a serving-man as far as my northern conscience will permit. I can give my gude word to my master, or to my native country, when I am in a foreign land, even though I should leave downright truth a wee bit behind me. Ay, and I will take or give a slash with ony lad that speaks to the derogation of either. But this chambering, diceing, and play-haunting, is not my element—I cannot draw breath in it—and when I hear of your lordship winning the siller that some puir creature may full sairly miss—by my saul, if it wad serve your necessity, rather than you gained it from him, I wad tak a jump over the hedge with your lordship, and cry 'Stand!' to the first grazier we met that was coming from Smithfield with the price of his Essex calves in his leathern pouch!"

"You are a simpleton," said Nigel, who felt, however, much conscience-struck; "I never play but for small sums."

"Ay, my lord," replied the unyielding domestic, "and—still with reverence—it is even sae much the waur; if you played with your equals, there might be like sin, but there wad be mair warldly honour in it. Your lordship kens, or may ken, by experience of your ain, whilk is not as yet mony weeks auld, that small sums can ill be missed by those that have nane larger; and I maun e'en be plain wi' you, that men notice it of your lordship, that ye play wi' nane but the misguided creatures that can but afford to lose bare stakes."

"No man dare say so!" replied Nigel, very angrily. "I play with whom I please, but I will only play for what stake I please."

"That is just what they say, my lord," said the unmerciful Richie, whose natural love of lecturing, as well as his bluntness of feeling, prevented him from having any idea of the pain which he was inflicting on his master; "these are even their own very words. It was but yesterday your lordship was pleased, at that saam ordinary, to win from yonder young hafflins gentleman with the crimson velvet doublet, and the cock's feather in his beaver—him I mean who fought with the ranting captain, a matter of five pounds, or thereby. I saw him come through the hall; and if he was not cleaned out of cross and pile, I never saw a ruined man in my life."

"Impossible!" said Lord Glenvarloch; "why, who is he? he looked like a man of substance."

"All is not gold that glistens, my lord," replied Richie; "broidery and bullion buttons make bare pouches—and as to who he is—may be I have a guess, and care not to tell."

"At least, if I have done any such fellow an injury," said the Lord Nigel, "let me know how I can repair it."

"Never fash your beard about that, my lord,—with reverence always," said Richie,—"he shall be suitably cared after—think on him but as ane wha was running post to the devil, and got a shouldering from your lordship to help him on his journey. But I will stop him an if reason can, and so your lordship needs ask nae mair about it, for there is no use in your knowing it, but much the contrair."

"Hark you, sirrah," said his master, "I have borne with you thus far, for certain reasons; but abuse my good nature no further—and since you must needs go, why, go a God's name, and here is to pay your journey." So saying, he put gold into his hand, which Richie told over, piece by piece, with the utmost accuracy. "Is it all right—or are they wanting in weight, or what the devil keeps you, when your hurry was so great five minutes since?" said the young lord, now thoroughly nettled at the presumptuous formality with which Richie dealt forth his canons of morality.

"The tale of coin is complete," said Richie, with the most imperturbable gravity; "and for the weight, though they are sae scrupulous in this town as make mouths at a piece that is a wee bit light, or that has been cracked within the ring, my sooth, they will jump at them in Edinburgh like a cock at a grossart—gold pieces are not so plenty there, the mair the pity!"

"The more is your folly, then," said Nigel, whose anger was only momentary, "that leave the land where there is enough of them."

"My lord," said Richie, "to be round with you, the grace of God is better than gowd pieces. When Goblin, as you call yonder Monsieur Lutin,—and you might as well call him Gibbet, since that is what he is like to end in,—shall recommend a page to you, ye will hear little such doctrine as you have heard from me. And if they were my last words," he said, raising his voice, "I would say you are misled, and are forsaking the paths which your honourable father trode in; and, what is more, you are going,—still under correction,—to the devil with a dish-clout, for ye are laughed at by them that lead you into these disordered bye-paths."

"Laughed at?" said Nigel, who, like others of his age, was more sensible to ridicule than to reason—"who dares laugh at me?"

"My lord, as sure as I live by bread—nay, more, as I am a true man —and I think your lordship never found Richie's tongue bearing aught but the truth—unless that your lordship's credit, my country's profit, or, it may be, some sma' occasion of my ain, made it unnecessary to promulgate the hail veritie,—I say then, as I am a true man, when I saw that puir creature come through the ha', at that ordinary, whilk is accurst (Heaven forgive me for swearing) of God and man, with his teeth set, and his hands clenched, and his bonnet drawn over his brows like a desperate, Goblin said to me, 'there goes a dunghill chicken, that your master has plucked clean enough; it will be long ere his lordship ruffle a feather with a cock of the game.' And so, my lord, to speak it out, the lackies and the gallants, and more especially your sworn brother, Lord Dalgarno, call you the Sparrow-hawk. I had some thought to have cracked Lutin's pate for the speech, but the controversy was not worth it."

"Do they use such terms of me?" said Lord Nigel. "Death and the devil!"

"And the devil's dam, my lord," answered Richie; "they are all three busy in London—And, besides, Lutin and his master laughed at you, my lord, for letting it be thought that—I shame to speak it—that ye were over well with the wife of the decent honest man whose house you but now left, as not sufficient for your new bravery, whereas they said—the licentious scoffers—that you pretended to such favour when you had not courage enough for so fair a quarrel, and that the Sparrow-hawk was too craven-crested to fly at the wife of a cheese-monger." He stopped a moment, and looked fixedly in his master's face, which was inflamed with shame and anger, and then proceeded. "My lord, I did you justice in my thought, and myself too; for, thought I, he would have been as deep in that sort of profligacy as in others, if it had na been Richie's four quarters."

"What new nonsense have you got to plague me with?" said Lord Nigel. "But go on—since it is the last time I am to be tormented with your impertinence, go on, and make the most of your time."

"In troth," said Richie, "and so will I even do; and as Heaven has bestowed on me a tongue to speak and to advise"——

"Which talent you can by no means be accused of suffering to remain idle," said Lord Glenvarloch, interrupting him.

"True, my lord,"—said Richie, again waving his hand as if to bespeak his master's silence and attention. "So I trust you will think sometime hereafter;—and as I am about to leave your service, it is proper that ye suld know the truth, that ye may consider the snares to which your youth and innocence may be exposed, when aulder and doucer heads are withdrawn from beside ye. There has been a lusty good-looking kimmer, of some forty, or bygane, making mony speerings about you, my lord."

"Well, sir, what did she want with me?" said Lord Nigel.

"At first, my lord," replied his sapient follower, "as she seemed to be a well-fashioned woman, and to take pleasure in sensible conversation, I was no way reluctant to admit her to my conversation."

"I dare say not," said Lord Nigel, "nor unwilling to tell her about my private affairs."

"Not I, truly, my lord," said the attendant; "for though she asked me mony questions about your fame, your fortune, your business here, and such like, I did not think it proper to tell her altogether the truth thereanent."

"I see no call on you whatsoever," said Lord Nigel, "to tell the woman either truth or lies upon what she had nothing to do with."

"I thought so, too, my lord," replied Richie, "and so I told her neither."

"And what *did* you tell her then, you eternal babbler," said his master, impatient of his prate, yet curious to know what it was all to end in.

"I told her," said Richie, "about your warldly fortune, and sae forth, something whilk is not truth just at this time; but which hath been truth formerly, suld be truth now, and will be truth again,—and that was, that you were in possession of your fair lands, whilk ye are but in right of as yet—pleasant communing we had on that and other topics, until she shewed the cloven foot, beginning to confer with me about some wench that she said had a good will to your lordship, and fain she would have spoken with you in particular anent it; but when I heard of such inklings, I began to suspect she was little better than—— whew!" Here he concluded his narrative with a low, but very expressive whistle.

"And what did your wisdom do in these circumstances?" said Lord Nigel, who, notwithstanding his former resentment, could now scarcely forbear laughing.

"I put on a look, my lord," replied Richie, bending his solemn

brows, "that suld give her a heart-scaud of walking on such errands. I
laid her enormities clearly before her, and I threatened her, in sae
mony words, that I would have her to the ducking-stool; and she on
the contrair part miscawed me for a froward northern tyke, and so we
parted never to meet again, as I hope and trust. And so I stood
between your lordship and that temptation, which might have been
worse than the ordinary, or the play-house either; since you wot well
what Solomon, King of the Jews, sayeth of the strange woman—for,
said I to mysell, we have taken to diceing already, and if we take to
drabbing next, the Lord kens what we may land in."

"Your impertinence deserves correction, but it is the last which, for
a time at least, I shall have to forgive—and I forgive it," said Lord
Glenvarloch; "and, since we are to part, Richie, I will say no more
respecting your precautions on my account, than that I think you
might have left me to act according to my own judgment."

"Mickle better not," answered Richie—"Mickle better not—we
are a' frail creatures, and can judge better for ilk ither than in our ain
cases. And for me, even myself, saving that case of the sifflication,
which might have happened to ony one, I have always observed myself
to be much more prudential in what I have done on your lordship's
behalf, than even in what I have been able to transact for my own
interest, whilk last, I have indeed always postponed, as in duty I
ought."

"I do believe thou hast," said Lord Nigel, "having ever found thee
true and faithful—and since London pleases you so little, I will bid
you a short farewell; and you may go down to Edinburgh until I come
thither myself, when I trust you will re-enter into my service."

"Now, Heaven bless you, my lord," said Richie Moniplies, with
uplifted eyes; "for that word sounds more like grace than ony that has
come out of your mouth this fortnight. I give you Godd'en, my lord."

So saying, he thrust forth his immense bony hand, seized upon that
of Lord Glenvarloch, raised it to his lips, then turned short on his heel,
and left the room hastily, as if afraid of shewing more emotion than
was consistent with his ideas of decorum. Lord Nigel, rather surprised at his sudden exit, called after him to know whether he was
sufficiently provided with money; but Richie, shaking his head, without making any other answer, ran hastily down stairs, shut the street-
door heavily behind him, and was presently seen striding along the
Strand.

His master almost involuntarily watched and distinguished the tall
raw-boned figure of his late follower, from the window, for some
time, until he was lost among the crowd of passengers. Nigel's reflections were not altogether those of self-approval. It was no good sign of

his course of life, (he could not help acknowledging thus much to himself,) that so faithful an adherent no longer seemed to feel the same pride in his service, or attachment to his person, which he had formerly manifested. Neither could he avoid experiencing some twinges of conscience, while he felt in some degree the charges which Richie had preferred against him, and a sense of shame and mortification, arising from the colour given by others to that, which he himself would have called his caution and moderation in play. He had only the apology, that it had never occurred to himself in this light.

Then his pride and self-love suggested, that, on the other hand, Richie, with all his good intentions, was little better than a conceited pragmatical domestic, who seemed at times disposed rather to play the tutor than the lacquey, and who, out of sheer love, as he alleged, to his master's person, assumed the privilege of interfering with, and controling his actions, besides rendering him ridiculous in the gay world, from the antiquated formality, and intrusive presumption of his manners.

Nigel's eyes were scarce turned from the window, when his new landlord entering, presented to him a slip of paper, carefully bound round with a string of flox-silk and sealed—it had been given in, he said, by a woman, who did not stop an instant. The contents harped upon the same string which Richie Moniplies had already jarred. The epistle was in the following words:

> "For the Right Honourable hands of Lord Glenvarloch,
>   "These, from a friend unknown:—

"My Lord,
"You are trusting to an unhonest friend, and diminishing an honest reputation. An unknown friend of your lordship will speak in one word what you would not learn from flatterers in so many days as should suffice for your utter ruin. He whom you think most true—I say your friend Dalgarno—is utterly false to you, and doth but seek, under pretence of friendship, to mar your fortune, and diminish your good name by which you might mend it. The kind countenance which he shews to you is more dangerous than the Prince's frown; even as to gain at Beaujeu's ordinary is more discreditable than to lose. Beware of both.—And this is all from your true, but nameless friend,
>   "Ignoto."

Lord Glenvarloch paused for an instant, and crushed the paper together—then again unfolded and read it with attention—bent his brows—mused for a moment, and then tearing it to fragments, exclaimed—"Begone for a vile calumny!—but I will watch—I will observe——"

Thought after thought rushed on him; but, upon the whole, Lord Glenvarloch was so little satisfied with the result of his own reflections, that he resolved to dissipate them by a walk in the Park, and, taking his cloak and beaver, went thither accordingly.

Chapter Four

'Twas when fleet Snowball's head was woxen grey,
A luckless lev'ret met him on his way.—
Who knows not Snowball—he, whose race renown'd
Is still victorious on each coursing ground?
Swaffham, Newmarket, and the Roman Camp
Have seen them victors o'er each meaner stamp.—
In vain the youngling sought, with doubling wile,
The hedge, the hill, the thicket, or the stile.
Experience sage the lack of speed supplied,
And in the gap he sought, the victim died.—
So was I once, in thy fair street, Saint James,
Through walking cavaliers, and car-borne dames,
Descried, pursued, turn'd o'er again, and o'er,
Coursed, coted, mouth'd by an unfeeling bore.
&c.&c.&c.

THE PARK of Saint James's, though enlarged, planted with verdant alleys, and otherwise decorated by Charles II., existed, in the days of his grandfather, as a public and pleasant promenade; and, for the sake of exercise or pastime, was much frequented by the better classes.

Lord Glenvarloch repaired thither to dispel the unpleasant reflections which had been suggested by his parting with his trusty squire, Richie Moniplies, in a manner which was neither agreeable to his pride nor to his feelings; and by the corroboration which the hints of his late attendant had received from the anonymous letter mentioned in the end of the last chapter.

There was a considerable number of company in the Park when he entered it, but his present state of mind inducing him to avoid society, he kept aloof from the more frequented walks towards Westminster and Whitehall, and drew to the north, or, as we should now say, the Piccadilly verge of the enclosure, believing he might there enjoy, or rather combat, his own thoughts unmolested.

In this, however, he was mistaken; for, as he strolled slowly along with his arms folded in his cloak, and his hat drawn over his eyes, he was suddenly pounced upon by Sir Mungo Malagrowther, who, either shunning or shunned, had retreated, or had been obliged to retire, to the same less frequented corner of the Park.

Nigel started when he heard the high, sharp, and querulous tones of the Knight's cracked voice, and was no less alarmed when he beheld his tall thin figure hobbling towards him, wrapped in a thread-bare cloak, on whose surface ten thousand varied stains eclipsed the original scarlet, and surmounted with a well-worn beaver, bearing a black velvet band for a chain, and a capon's feather for an ostrich plume.

Lord Glenvarloch would fain have made his escape, but, as our motto intimates, a leveret had as little chance to free herself of an experienced greyhound. Sir Mungo, to continue the simile, had long ago learned to *run cunning*, and make sure of mouthing his game. So Nigel found himself compelled to stand and answer the hackneyed question—"What news to-day?"

"Nothing extraordinary, I believe," answered the young nobleman, attempting to pass on.

"O—ye are ganging to the French ordinary belive," replied the Knight; "but it is early day yet—we will take a turn in the Park the meanwhile—it will sharpen your appetite."

So saying, he quietly slipped his arm under Lord Glenvarloch's, in spite of all the decent reluctance which his victim could exhibit, by keeping his elbow close to his side; and having fair grappled the chase, he proceeded to take it in tow.

Nigel was sullen and silent, in hopes to shake off his unpleasant companion; but Sir Mungo was determined, that if he did not speak he should at least hear.

"Ye are bound for the ordinary, my lord?" said the cynic;—"weel, ye canna do better—there is choice company there, and peculiarly selected, as I am tauld, being, dootless, sic as it is desirable that young noblemen should herd withal—And your noble father wald have been blithe to see you keeping such worshipful society."

"I believe," said Lord Glenvarloch, thinking himself obliged to say something, "that the society is as good as generally can be found in such places, where the door can scarcely be shut against those who come to spend their money."

"Right, my lord—vara right," said his tormentor, bursting out into a chuckling, but most discordant laugh. "These citizen chuffs and clowns will press in amongst us, when there is but an inch of a door open. And what remedy?—Just e'en this, that as their cash gi'es them confidence, we should strip them of it—flea them, my lord—singe them as the kitchen wench does the rats, and then they winna long to come back again.—Ay, ay—pluck them, plume,—and then the larded capons will not be for flying so high a wing, my lord, among goss-hawks and sparrow-hawks, and the like."

And, therewithal, Sir Mungo fixed Nigel with his quick, sharp, grey eye, watching the effect of his sarcasm as keenly as the surgeon, in a delicate operation, remarks the progress of his anatomical scalpel.

Nigel, however willing to conceal his sensations, could not avoid gratifying his tormentor by wincing under the operation. He coloured with vexation and anger; but a quarrel with Sir Mungo Malagrowther would, he felt, be unutterably ridiculous; and he only muttered to himself the words, "impertinent coxcomb!" which, on this occasion, Sir Mungo's imperfection of organ did not prevent him from hearing and replying to.

"Ay, ay—vara true," exclaimed the caustic old courtier—"Impertinent coxcombs they are, that thus intrude themselves on the society of their betters; but your lordship kens how to gar them as gude—ye have the trick on't.—They had a braw sport in the presence last Friday, how ye suld have routed a young shopkeeper, horse and foot, ta'en his *spolia opima*, and a' the specie he had about him, down to the very silver buttons of his cloak, and sent him to graze with Nebuchadnezzar, King of Babylon. Muckle honour redounded to your lordship thereby.—We were tauld the loon threw himsell into the Thames in a fit of desperation—there's enow of them behind—there was mair tint on Flodden-edge."

"You have been told a budget of lies so far as I was concerned, Sir Mungo," said Nigel, speaking loud and sternly.

"Vara likely—vara likely," said the unabashed and undismayed Sir Mungo; "naething but lies are current in the circle.—So the chield is not drowned, then?—the mair's the pity.—But I never believed that part of the story—a London dealer has mair wit in his anger. I dare swear the lad has a bonny broom-shank in his hand by this time, and is scrubbing the kennels in quest after rusty nails, to help him to something to begin his pack again—he has three bairns, they say; they will help him bravely to grope in the gutters. Ye may have the ruining of him again, my lord, if they have any luck in strand-scouring."

"This is more than intolerable," said Nigel, uncertain whether to make an angry vindication of his character, or to fling the old tormentor from his arm. But an instant's recollection convinced him, that to do either, would only give an air of truth and consistency to the scandals which he began to see were affecting his character, both in the higher and lower circles. Hastily, therefore, he formed the wiser resolution, to endure Sir Mungo's studied impertinence, to ascertain, if possible, from what source those reports arose which were so prejudicial to his reputation.

Sir Mungo, in the mean while, caught up, as usual, Nigel's last words, or rather the sound of them, and amplified and interpreted them in his own way. "Tolerable luck!" he repeated; "Yes, truly, my lord, I am told that you have tolerable luck, and that ye ken weel how to use that jilting quean, Dame Fortune, like a canny douce lad, willing to warm yourself in her smiles, without exposing yoursell to her frowns. And that is what I ca' having luck in a bag."

"Sir Mungo Malagrowther," said Lord Glenvarloch, turning towards him seriously, "have the goodness to hear me for a moment."

"As weel as I can, my lord—as weel as I can," said Sir Mungo, shaking his head, and pointing the finger of his left hand to his ear.

"I will try to speak very distinctly," said Nigel, arming himself with patience. "You take me for a noted gamester; I give you my word that you have not been rightly informed—I am none such. You owe me some explanation, at least, respecting the source from which you derived such false information."

"I never heard ye were a great gamester, and never thought or said you were such, my lord," said Sir Mungo, who found it impossible to avoid hearing what Nigel said with peculiarly deliberate and distinct pronunciation. "I repeat it—I never heard, said, or thought that you were a ruffling gamester,—such as they call those of the first head.— Look you, my lord, I call *him* a gamester, that plays with equal stakes and equal skill—and stands by the fortune of the game, good or bad— and I call *him* a ruffling gamester, or ane of the first head, who ventures frankly and deeply upon such a wager. But he, my lord, who has the patience and prudence never to venture beyond small game, such as, at most, might crack the Christmas-box of a grocer's 'prentice, who vies with those that have little to hazard, and who therefore, having the larger stock, can always rook them by waiting for his good fortune, and rising from the game when luck leaves him—such a one as he, my lord, I do not call a *great* gamester, to whatever other name he may be entitled."

"And such a mean-spirited sordid wretch you would infer that I am," replied Lord Glenvarloch; "one who fears the skilful, and preys upon the ignorant—who avoids playing with his equals, that he may make sure of pillaging his inferiors—is this what I am to understand has been reported of me?"

"Nay, my lord, you will gain nought by speaking big with me," said Sir Mungo, who, besides that his sarcastic humour was really supported by a good fund of animal courage, had also full reliance on the immunities which he had derived from the broadsword of Sir Rullion Rattray, and the batton of the satellites employed by the Lady Cockpen. "And for the truth of the matter," he continued, "your lordship best knows whether you ever lost more than five pieces at a time since you frequented Beaujeu's—whether you have not most commonly

risen a winner—and whether the brave young gallants who frequent
the ordinary—I mean those of noble rank, and means conforming—
are in use to play upon those terms."

"My father was right," said Lord Glenvarloch, in the bitterness of
his spirit; "and his curse justly followed me when I first entered that
place—there is contamination in the air, and he whose fortune avoids
ruin, shall be blighted in his honour and reputation."

Sir Mungo, who watched his victim with the delighted yet wary
eye of an experienced angler, became now aware, that if he strained
the line on him too tightly, there was every risk of his breaking
hold. In order to give him room, therefore, to play, he protested
that Lord Glenvarloch should not take his free speech *in malam
partem.* "If ye are a trifle ower sicker in your amusement, my lord, it
canna be denied that it is the safest course to prevent farther endan-
germent of your somewhat dilapidated fortunes; and if ye play with
your inferiors, ye are relieved of the pain of pouching the siller of
your friends and equals; forbye, that the Plebeian knaves have had
the advantage, *tecum certasse,* as Ajax Telamon sayeth, *apud Metamorphoseos;* and for the like of them to have played with ane Scottish
nobleman, is an honest and honourable consideration to compensate
the loss of their stake, whilk, I dare say, moreover, maist of the
churls can weel afford."

"Be that as it may, Sir Mungo," said Nigel, "I would fain
know"——

"Ay, ay," interrupted Sir Mungo; "and, as you say, who cares
whether the fat bulls of Basan can spare it or no? gentlemen are not to
limit their sport for the like of them."

"I wish to know, Sir Mungo," said Lord Glenvarloch, "in what
company you have learned these offensive particulars respecting me."

"Dootless—dootless, my lord," said Sir Mungo; "I have ever
heard, and have ever reported, that your lordship kept the best of
company in a private way—there is the fine Countess of Blackchester,
but I think she stirs not much abroad since her affair with his Grace of
Buckingham; and there is the gude auld-fashioned Scottish nobleman, Lord Huntinglen, an undeniable man of quality—it is pity but he
could keep caup and can frae his head, whilk now and then doth
minish his reputation. And there is the gay, young Lord Dalgarno,
that carries the craft of gray hairs under his curled love-locks—a fair
race they are, father, daughter, and son, all of the same honourable
family. I think we needna speak of George Heriot, honest man, when
we have nobility in question. So that is the company I have heard of
your keeping, my lord, out-taken those of the ordinary."

"My company has not, indeed, been much more extended than

amongst those you mention," said Lord Glenvarloch; "but in short"——

"To court?" said Sir Mungo, "that was just what I was going to say—Lord Dalgarno says he cannot prevail on ye to come to court, and that does ye prejudice, my lord—the King hears of you by others, when he should see you in person—I speak in serious friendship, my lord. His Majesty, when you were named in the circle short while since, was heard to say, '*Jacta est alea!*—Glenvarlochides is turned dicer and drinker.'—My Lord Dalgarno took your part, and was e'en borne down by the popular voice of the courtiers, who spoke of you as one who had betaken yourself to living a town life, and risking your baron's coronet among the flat-caps of the city."

"And this was publicly spoken of me," said Nigel, "and in the King's presence?"

"Spoken openly?" repeated Sir Mungo Malagrowther; "ay, by my sooth was it—that is to say, it was whispered privately—whilk is as open promulgation as the place permitted; for ye may think the court is not a place where men are as sib as Summie and his brother, and roar out their minds as if they were at an ordinary."

"A curse on the court and the ordinary both!" cried Nigel impatiently.

"With all my heart," said the Knight; "I have got little by a life's service in the court; and the last time I was at the ordinary, I lost four angels."

"May I pray of you, Sir Mungo, to let me know," said Nigel, "the names of those who thus make free with the character of one who can be but little known to them, and who never injured any of them?"

"Have I not told ye already," answered Sir Mungo, "that the King said something to that effect—so did the Prince too;—and such being the case, ye may take it on your corporal aith, that every man in the circle who was not silent, sung the same song as they did."

"You said but now," replied Glenvarloch, "that Lord Dalgarno interfered in my behalf."

"In good troth did he," answered Sir Mungo with a sneer; "but the young nobleman was soon borne down—mair by token, he had something of a catarrh, and spoke as hoarse as a roupit raven—poor gentleman, if he had had his full extent of voice, he would have been as well listened to dootless, as in a cause of his ain, whilk no man kens better how to plead to purpose.—And let me ask you, by the way," continued Sir Mungo, "whether Lord Dalgarno has ever introduced your lordship to the Prince or the Duke of Buckingham, either of whom might soon carry through your suit?"

"I have no claim on the favour of either the Prince or the Duke of

Buckingham," said Lord Glenvarloch.—"As you seem to have made my affairs your study, Sir Mungo, although perhaps something unnecessarily, you may have heard that I have petitioned my Sovereign for payment of a debt due to my family. I cannot doubt the King's desire to do justice, nor can I in decency employ the solicitation of his Highness the Prince, or his Grace the Duke of Buckingham, to obtain from his Majesty what either should be granted me as a right, or refused altogether."

Sir Mungo twisted his whimsical features into one of his most grotesque sneers, as he replied—

"It is a vara clear and parspicuous position of the case, my lord; and in relying thereupon, ye shew an absolute and unimproveable acquaintance with the King, court, and mankind in general.—But whom have we got here?—Stand up, my lord, and make way—by my word of honour, they are the very men we spoke of—Talk of the devil —humph!"

It must here be premised, that, during the conversation, Lord Glenvarloch, perhaps in the hope of shaking himself free of Sir Mungo, had directed their walk towards the more frequented part of the Park; while the good Knight had stuck to him, totally indifferent which way they went, providing he could keep his talons clutched upon his companion. They were still, however, at some distance from the livelier part of the scene, when Sir Mungo's experienced eye noticed the appearances which occasioned the latter part of his speech to Lord Glenvarloch.

A low respectful murmur arose among the numerous groupes of persons which occupied the lower part of the Park. They first clustered together, with their faces turned towards Whitehall, then fell back on either hand to give place to a splendid party of gallants, who, advancing from the Palace, came onward through the Park; all the other company drawing off the pathway, and standing uncovered as they passed.

Most of these courtly gallants were dressed in the garb which the pencil of Vandyke has made familiar even at the distance of nearly two centuries; and which was just at this period beginning to supersede the more fluttering and frivolous dress which had been adopted from the French court of Henri Quatre.

The whole train were uncovered excepting the Prince of Wales, afterwards the most unfortunate of British monarchs, who came onward, having his long curled auburn tresses, and his countenance, which, even in early youth, bore a shade of anticipated melancholy, shaded by the Spanish hat and the single ostrich feather which drooped from it. On his right hand was Buckingham, whose

commanding, and at the same time graceful deportment, threw almost
into shade the personal demeanour and majesty of the Prince on
whom he attended. The eye, movements, and gestures of the great
courtier were so composed, so regularly observant of all etiquettes
belonging to his situation, as to form a marked and strong contrast
with the forward gaiety and frivolity by which he recommended himself to the favour of his "dear dad and gossip," King James. A singular
fate attended this accomplished courtier, in being at once the reigning
favourite of a father and son so very opposite in manners, that, to
ingratiate himself with the youthful Prince, he was obliged to com-
press within the strictest limits of respectful observance the frolic-
some and free humour which captivated his aged father.

It is true, Buckingham well knew the different dispositions both of
James and Charles, and had no difficulty in so conducting himself as
to maintain the highest post in the favour of both. It has indeed been
supposed, that the Duke, when he had completely possessed himself
of the affections of Charles, retained his hold in those of the father
only by the tyranny of custom; and that James, could he have brought
himself to form a vigorous resolution, was, in the latter years especially
of his life, not unlikely to have discarded Buckingham from his counsels and favour. But if ever indeed he meditated such a change, he was
too timid and too much accustomed to the influence which the Duke
had long exercised over him, to summon up resolution enough for
effecting such a purpose. And at all events it is certain that Buckingham, though surviving the master by whom he was raised, had the rare
chance to experience no wane of the most splendid court-favour
during two reigns, until it was at once eclipsed in his blood by the
dagger of his assassin Felton.

To return from this digression: The Prince with his train advanced,
and were near the place where Lord Glenvarloch and Sir Mungo had
stood aside according to form, in order to give the Prince passage, and
to pay the usual marks of respect. Nigel could now remark that Lord
Dalgarno walked close behind the Duke of Buckingham, and, as he
thought, whispered something in his ear as they came onward. At any
rate, both the Prince's and Duke of Buckingham's attention seemed
to be directed by some circumstance towards Nigel, for they turned
their heads in that direction and looked at him attentively—the Prince
with a countenance, the grave, melancholy expression of which
was blended with severity; while Buckingham's looks evinced some
degree of scornful triumph. Lord Dalgarno did not seem to observe
his friend, perhaps because the sun-beams fell from the side of the
walk on which Nigel stood, obliging Malcolm to hold up his hat to
screen his eyes.

As the Prince passed, Lord Glenvarloch and Sir Mungo bowed, as respect required; and the Prince returning their obeisance with that grave ceremony which paid to every rank its due, but not a tittle beyond it, signed to Sir Mungo to come forwards. Commencing an apology for his lameness as he started, which he had just completed as his hobbling gait brought him up to the Prince, Sir Mungo lent an attentive, and, as it seemed, an intelligent ear to questions asked in a tone so low, that the Knight would certainly have been deaf to them had they been put to him by any one under the rank of Prince of Wales. After about a minute's conversation, the Prince bestowed on Nigel the embarrassing notice of another fixed look, touched his hat slightly to Sir Mungo, and walked on.

"It is even as I suspected, my lord," said Sir Mungo, with an air which he designed to be melancholy and sympathetic, but which, in fact, resembled the grin of an ape when he has mouthed a scalding chesnut—"Ye have back-friends, my lord, that is, unfriends—or, to be plain, enemies—about the person of the Prince."

"I am sorry to hear it," said Nigel; "but I would I knew what they accuse me of."

"Ye shall hear, my lord," said Sir Mungo, "the Prince's vara words —'Sir Mungo,' said he, 'I rejoice to see you, and am glad your rheumatic troubles permit you to come hither for exercise.'—I bowed, as in duty bound—ye might remark, my lord, that I did so, whilk formed the first branch of our conversation.—His Highness then demanded of me, 'if he with whom I stood, was the young Lord Glenvarloch.' I answered, 'that you were such, for his Highness's service;' whilk was the second branch.—Thirdly, his Highness, resuming the argument, said, that 'truly he had been told so, (meaning that he had been told you were that personage;) but that he could not believe, that the heir of that noble and decayed house could be leading an idle, scandalous, and precarious life in the eating-houses and taverns of London, while the King's drums were beating, and colours flying in Germany in the cause of the Palatine, his son-in-law.'—I could, your lordship is aware, do nothing but make an obeisance; and a gracious 'Give ye good day, Sir Mungo Malagrowther,' licenced me to fall back to your lordship. And now, my lord, if your business or pleasure calls you to the ordinary, or any where in the direction of the city—why, have with you; for, dootless, ye will think ye have tarried lang enough in the Park, as they will likely turn at the head of the walk, and return this way —and you have a broad hint, I think, not to cross the Prince's presence again in a hurry."

"*You* may stay or go as you please, Sir Mungo," said Nigel, with an expression of calm, but deep resentment; "but, for my own part, my

resolution is taken. I will quit this public walk for pleasure of no man
—still less will I quit it like one unworthy to be seen in places of public
resort. I trust that the Prince and his retinue will return this way as you
expect; for I will abide, Sir Mungo, and beard them."

"Beard them!" exclaimed Sir Mungo, in the extremity of surprise,
—"Beard the Prince of Wales—the heir-apparent of three kingdoms!
—by my saul, ye shall beard him yoursell then."

Accordingly, he was about to leave Nigel very hastily, when some
unwonted touch of good natured interest in his youth and inexperience, seemed suddenly to soften his habitual cynicism.

"The devil is in me, for an auld fule!" said Sir Mungo; "but I must
needs concern mysell—I that owe so little either to fortune or
my fellow-creatures, must, I say, needs concern mysell—with this
springald, whom I will warrant to be as obstinate as a pig possessed
with a devil, for it's the cast of his family; and yet I maun e'en fling
away some sound advice on him.—My dainty young Lord Glenvarloch, understand me distinctly, for this is no bairn's-play. When the
Prince said sae much to me as I have repeated to you, it was equivalent
to a command not to appear again in his presence; wherefore, take an
auld man's advice that wishes you weel, and maybe a wee thing better
than he has reason to wish ony body. Jouk, and let the jaw gae bye, like
a canny bairn—gang hame to your lodgings, keep your foot frae
taverns, and your fingers frae the dice-box; compound your affairs
quietly wi' some ane that has better favour than yours about court, and
you will get a round spell of money to carry to Germany, or elsewhere,
to push your fortune—it was a fortunate soldier that made your family
four or five hundred years syne, and, if you are brave and fortunate,
you may find the way to repair it. But, take my word for it, that in this
court you will never thrive."

When Sir Mungo had completed his exhortation, in which there
was more of sincere sympathy with another's situation, than he had
been heretofore known to express in behalf of any one, Lord Glenvarloch replied, "I am obliged to you, Sir Mungo—you have spoken, I
think, with sincerity, and I thank you. But in return for your good
advice, I heartily entreat you to leave me; I observe the Prince and his
train are returning down the walk, and you may prejudice yourself, but
cannot help me, by remaining with me."

"And that is true,"—said Sir Mungo; "yet, were I ten years
younger, I wald be tempted to stand by you, and gie them the meeting
—but at three-score and upward, men's courage turns cauldrife; and
they that canna win a living, must not endanger the small sustenance
of their age. I wish you weel through, my lord, but it is an unequal
fight." So saying, he turned and limped away; often looking back,

however, as if his natural spirit, even in its present subdued state, aided by his love of contradiction and of debate, rendered him unwilling to adopt the course necessary for his own security.

Thus abandoned by his companion, whose departure he graced with better thoughts of him than those which he bestowed on his appearance, Nigel remained with arms folded, and reclining against a solitary tree which overhung the path, making up his mind to encounter a moment which he expected to be critical of his fate. But he was mistaken in supposing that the Prince of Wales would either address him, or admit him to expostulation in such a public place as the Park. He did not remain unnoticed, however; for, when he made a respectful but haughty obeisance, intimating in look and manner that he was possessed of, and undaunted by, the unfavourable opinion which the Prince had so lately expressed, Charles returned his reverence with such a frown, as is only given by those whose frown is authority and decision. The train passed on, the Duke of Buckingham not even appearing to see Lord Glenvarloch, and Lord Dalgarno, though no longer incommoded by the sun-beams, keeping his eyes, which had perhaps been dazzled by their former splendour, bent upon the ground.

Lord Glenvarloch had difficulty to restrain an indignation, to which, in the circumstances, it would have been madness to have given vent. He started from his reclining posture, and followed the Prince's train so as to keep them distinctly in sight; which was very easy, as they walked slowly. Nigel observed them keep their road towards Whitehall, where the Prince turned at the gate and bowed to the noblemen in attendance, in token of dismissing them, and entered the Palace, accompanied only by the Duke of Buckingham, and one or two of his equerries. The rest of the train, having returned in all dutiful humility the farewell of the Prince, began to disperse themselves through the Park.

All this was carefully noticed by Lord Glenvarloch, who, as he adjusted his cloak, and drew his sword-belt round so as to bring the hilt closer to his hand, muttered—"Dalgarno shall explain all this to me, for it is evident that he is in the secret."

Chapter Five

Give way—give way—I must and will have justice.
And tell me not of privilege and place;
Where I am injured, there I'll sue redress.
Look to it every one who bars my access,
I have a heart to feel the injury,
A hand to right myself, and, by my honour,
That hand shall grasp what grey-beard Law denies me.
                                        The Chamberlain

IT WAS NOT LONG ere Nigel discovered Lord Dalgarno advancing
towards him in the company of another young man of quality of the
Prince's train; and as they directed their course towards the south-
eastern corner of the Park, he concluded they were about to go to
Lord Huntinglen's. They stopped, however, and turned up another
path leading to the north; and Lord Glenvarloch conceived that this
change of direction was owing to their having seen him, and their
desire to avoid him.

Nigel followed them without hesitation, by a path which, winding
around a thicket of shrubs and trees, once more conducted him to the
less frequented part of the Park. He observed which side of the thicket
was taken by Lord Dalgarno and his companion, and he himself,
walking hastily round the other verge, was thus enabled to meet them
face to face.

"Good morrow, my Lord Dalgarno," said Lord Glenvarloch,
sternly.

"Ha! my friend Nigel," answered Lord Dalgarno, in his usual
careless and indifferent tone, "my friend Nigel, with business on his
brow—but you must wait till we meet at Beaujeu's at noon—Sir Ewes
Haldimund and I are at present engaged in the Prince's service."

"If you were engaged in the King's, my lord," said Lord Glenvarloch, "you must stand and answer me."

"Hey-day!" said Lord Dalgarno, with an air of great astonishment,
"what passion is this? Why, Nigel, this is King Cambyses' vein!—you
have frequented the theatres too much lately—Away with this folly,
man; go, dine upon soup and sallad, drink succory-water to cool your
blood, go to bed at sun-down, and defy those foul fiends, Wrath and
Misconstruction."

"I have had misconstruction enough among you," said Glenvarloch, in the same tone of determined displeasure, "and from you, my
Lord Dalgarno, in particular, and all under the mask of friendship."

"Here is a proper business!"—said Dalgarno, turning as if to appeal to Sir Ewes Haldimund; "do you see this angry ruffler, Sir Ewes? A month since he dared not have looked one of yonder sheep in the face, but now he is a prince of roisterers, a plucker of pigeons, a controller of players and poets—and in gratitude for my having shewn him the way to the eminent character which he holds upon town, he comes hither to quarrel with his best friend, if not his only one."

"I renounce such hollow friendship, my lord," said Lord Glenvarloch; "I disclaim the character which, even to my very face, you labour to fix upon me, and ere we part I will call you to a reckoning for it."

"My lords both," interrupted Sir Ewes Haldimund, "let me remind you that the royal Park is no place to quarrel in."

"I will make my quarrel good," said Nigel, who did not know, or in his passion might not recollect, the privileges of the place, "wherever I find my enemy."

"You shall find quarrelling enough," replied Lord Dalgarno, calmly, "so soon as you assign a sufficient cause for it. Sir Ewes Haldimund knows—all the Court knows—I am not backward on such occasions. But of what is it that you now complain, after having experienced nothing save kindness from me and my family?"

"Of your family I complain not," replied Lord Glenvarloch; "they have done for me all they could,—more, far more, than I could have expected; but you, my lord, have suffered me, while you called me your friend, to be traduced, where a word of your mouth would have placed my character in its true colours—and hence the injurious message which I just now received from the Prince of Wales—to permit the misrepresentation of a friend, my lord, is to share in the slander."

"You have been misinformed, my Lord Glenvarloch," said Sir Ewes Haldimund; "I have myself often heard Lord Dalgarno defend your character, and regret your exclusive attachment to the freedoms of a London life prevented your paying your duty regularly to the King and Prince."

"While he himself," said Lord Glenvarloch, "dissuaded me from presenting myself at court."

"I will cut this matter short," said Lord Dalgarno, with haughty coldness. "You seem to have conceived, my lord, that you and I were Pylades and Orestes—a second edition of Damon and Pythias —Theseus and Pirithous at the least. You are mistaken, and have given the name of friendship to what, on my part, was mere good-nature and compassion for a raw and ignorant countryman, joined to the cumbersome charge which my father gave me respecting you. Your character, my lord, is of no one's drawing, but of your own making. I introduced you where, as in all such places, there was good and indifferent company to be met with—your habits, or taste, made you prefer the worse. Your holy horror at the sight of dice and cards degenerated into the cautious resolution to play only at those times, and with such persons, as might ensure your rising a winner—No man can long do so, and continue to be held a gentleman. Such is the reputation you have made for yourself, and you have no right to be angry that I do not contradict what yourself knows to be true. Let us pass on, my lord; and if you want further explanation, seek some other time and fitter place."

"No time can be better than the present," said Lord Glenvarloch, whose resentment was now excited to the uttermost at the cold-blooded and insulting manner in which Dalgarno vindicated himself, —"no place fitter than the place where we now stand. Those of my house have ever avenged insults, at the moment, and on the spot, where they were offered, were it at the foot of the throne.—Lord Dalgarno, you are a villain! draw and defend yourself." At the same time he unsheathed his rapier.

"Are you mad?" said Lord Dalgarno, stepping back; "we are in the precincts of the court."

"The better," answered Lord Glenvarloch; "I will cleanse them from a calumniator and a coward." He then pressed on Lord Dalgarno, and struck him with the flat of the sword.

The fray had now attracted attention, and the cry went round, "Keep the peace—keep the peace—swords drawn in the Park.— What, ho! guards!—keepers—yeomen rangers!" and a number of people came rushing to the spot from all sides.

Lord Dalgarno, who had half drawn his sword on receiving the blow, returned it to the scabbard when he observed the crowd thicken, and taking Sir Ewes Haldimund by the arm, walked hastily away, only saying to Lord Glenvarloch as they left him, with deep emphasis, "You shall dearly abye this insult—we will meet again."

A decent-looking elderly man, who observed that Lord Glenvarloch remained on the spot, taking compassion on his youthful appearance, said to him, "Are you aware this is a Star-Chamber business, young gentleman, and that it may cost you your right hand?—Shift for yourself before the keepers or constables come up—Get into White-friars or somewhere, for sanctuary and concealment, till you can make friends or quit the city."

The advice was not to be neglected. Lord Glenvarloch made hastily towards the issue from the Park by Saint James's Palace, then Saint James's Hospital. The hubbub increased behind him; and several peace-officers belonging to the Royal Household came up to appre-hend the delinquent. Fortunately for Nigel, a popular edition of the cause of the affray had gone abroad. It was said that one of the Duke of Buckingham's companions had insulted a stranger gentleman from the country, and that the stranger had cudgelled him soundly. A favourite, or the companion of a favourite, is always odious to John Bull, who has, besides, a partiality to those disputants who proceed, as lawyers term it, *par voye du fait*, and both prejudices were in Nigel's favour. The officers, therefore, who came to apprehend him, could learn from the spectators no particulars of his appearance, or information concerning the road he had taken; so that, for the moment, he escaped being arrested.

What Lord Glenvarloch heard amongst the crowd as he passed along, was sufficient to satisfy him, that in his impatient passion he had placed himself in a predicament of considerable danger. He was no stranger to the severe and arbitrary proceedings of the Court of Star-Chamber, especially in cases of breach of privilege, which made it the terror of all men; and it was not longer than the Queen's time that the punishment of mutilation had been actually awarded and executed, for some offence of the same kind which he had just committed. He had also the comfortable reflection, that by his violent quarrel with Lord Dalgarno, he must now forfeit the friendship and good offices of that nobleman's father and sister, almost the only persons of consideration in whom he could claim any interest; while all the evil reports which had been put in circulation concerning his character, were certain to weigh heavily against him, in a case where much must necessarily depend on the reputation of the accused. To a youthful imagination, the idea of such a punishment as mutilation, seems more ghastly than death itself; and every word which he overheard among the groupes whom he met, mingled with, or overtook and passed, announced this as the penalty of his offence. He dreaded to increase his pace for fear of attracting suspicion, and more than once saw the ranger's officers so near him, that his wrist tingled as if it were already under the blade of the dismembering knife. At length he got out of the Park, and had a little more leisure to consider what he was next to do.

Whitefriars, adjacent to the Temple, then well known by the cant name of Alsatia, had at this time, and for nearly a century afterwards, the privilege of a sanctuary, unless against the writ of the Lord Chief Justice, or of the Lords of the Privy-Council. Indeed, as the place abounded with desperadoes of every description,—bankrupt citizens, ruined gamesters, irreclaimable prodigals, desperate duellists, bravoes, homicides, and debauched profligates of every description, all leagued together to maintain the immunities of their asylum,—it was both difficult and unsafe for the officers of the law to execute warrants emanating even from the highest authority, amongst men whose safety was inconsistent with warrants or authority of any kind. This Lord Glenvarloch well knew; and odious as the place of refuge was, it seemed the only one where, for a space at least, he might be concealed and secure from the immediate grasp of the law, until he should have leisure to provide better for his safety, or to get this unpleasant matter in some shape accommodated.

Meanwhile, as Nigel walked hastily forwards towards the place of sanctuary, he bitterly accused himself for suffering Lord Dalgarno to lead him into the haunts of dissipation; and no less accused his intemperate heat of passion, which now had driven him for refuge into the purlieus of profane and avowed vice and debauchery.

"Dalgarno spoke but too truly in that," were his bitter reflections; "I have made myself an evil reputation by acting on his insidious counsels, and neglecting the wholesome admonitions which ought to have claimed implicit obedience from me, and which recommended abstinence even from the slightest approach to evil. But if I escape from the perilous labyrinth in which folly and inexperience, as well as violent passions, have involved me, I will find some noble way of redeeming the lustre of a name which was never sullied until I bore it."

As Lord Glenvarloch formed these prudent resolutions he entered the Temple Walks, whence a gate at that time opened into Whitefriars, by which, as by the more private passage, he proposed to betake himself to the sanctuary. As he approached the entrance to that den of infamy, from which his mind recoiled even while in the act of taking shelter there, his pace slackened, while the steep and broken stairs reminded him of the *facilis descensus Averni*, and rendered him doubtful whether it were not better to brave the worst which could befall him in the public haunts of honourable men, than to evade punishment by secluding himself in those of avowed vice and profligacy.

As Nigel hesitated, a young gentleman of the Temple advanced towards him, whom he had often seen and sometimes conversed with at the ordinary, where he was a frequent and welcome guest, being a wild young gallant, indifferently well provided with money, who spent at the theatres, and other gay places of public resort, the time his father supposed he was employing in the study of the law. But Reginald Lowestoffe, such was the young Templar's name, was of opinion that little law was necessary to enable him to spend the revenues of the paternal acres which were to devolve upon him at his father's demise, and therefore gave himself no trouble to acquire more of that science than might be imbibed alongst with the learned air of the region in which he had his chambers. In other respects, he was one of the wits of the place, read Ovid and Martial, aimed at quick repartee and pun, (often very far fetched,) danced, fenced, played at tennis, and per-

formed sundry tunes on the fiddle and French horn, to the great
annoyance of old Counsellor Barratter, who lived in the chambers
immediately below him. Such was Reginald Lowestoffe, shrewd,
alert, and well acquainted with the town in all its recesses; who now
approaching the Lord Glenvarloch, saluted him by name and title,
and asked if his lordship designed for the Chevalier's this day,
observing it was near noon, and the woodcock would be on the board
ere they could reach the ordinary.

"I do not go there to-day," answered Lord Glenvarloch.

"Which way then, my lord?" said the young Templar, who was
perhaps not undesirous to parade a part of the street at least in company with a lord, though but a Scotch one.

"I—I—" said Nigel, desiring to avail himself of this young man's
local knowledge, yet unwilling and ashamed to acknowledge his intention to take refuge in so disreputable a quarter, or to describe the
situation in which he stood—"I have some curiosity to see Whitefriars."

"What, your lordship is for a frolic into Alsatia?" said Lowestoffe—
"have with you, my lord—you cannot have a better guide to the
infernal regions than myself. I promise you there are bona-robas to be
found there—good wine too, ay, and good fellows to drink it with,
though somewhat suffering under the frowns of Fortune. But your
lordship will pardon me—you are the last of our acquaintance to
whom I would have proposed such a voyage of discovery."

"I am obliged to you, Master Lowestoffe, for the good opinion you
have expressed in the observation," said Lord Glenvarloch; "but my
present circumstances may render even a residence of a day or two in
the sanctuary a matter of necessity."

"Indeed!!" said Lowestoffe, in a tone of great surprise; "I thought
your lordship had always taken care not to risk any considerable stake
—I beg pardon, but if the bones have proved perfidious, I know just so
much law as that a peer's person is sacred from arrest; and for mere
impecuniosity, my lord, better shift can be made elsewhere than in
Whitefriars, where all are devouring each other for very poverty."

"My misfortune has no connexion with want of money," said Nigel.

"Why then, I suppose," said Lowestoffe, "you have been tilting, my
lord, and have pinked your man; in which case, and with a purse
reasonably furnished, you may lie perdu in Whitefriars for a twelvemonth—marry, but you must be entered and received as a member of
their worshipful society, my lord, and a frank burgher of Alsatia—so
far you must condescend; there will be neither peace nor safety for
you else."

"My fault is not in a degree so deadly, Master Lowestoffe,"

answered Lord Glenvarloch, "as you seem to conjecture—I have stricken a gentleman in the Park, that is all."

"By my hand, my lord, and you had better have struck your sword through him at Barns elms," said the Templar. "Strike within the verge of the Court! you will find that a weighty dependence upon your hands, especially if your party be of rank and have favour."

"I will be plain with you, Master Lowestoffe," said Nigel, "since I have gone thus far—the person whom I struck was Lord Dalgarno, whom you have seen at Beaujeu's."

"A follower and favourite of the Duke of Buckingham!—it is a most unhappy chance, my lord—but my heart was formed in England, and cannot bear to see a young nobleman borne down, as you are like to be. We converse here greatly too open for your circumstances —the Templars would suffer no bailiff to execute a writ, and no gentleman to be arrested for a duel, within their precincts; but in such a matter between Lord Dalgarno and your lordship, there might be a party on either side. You must away with me instantly to my poor chambers here, hard by, and undergo some little change of dress, ere you take sanctuary; for else you will have the whole rascal rout of the Friars about you, like crows about a falcon that strays into their rookery. We must have you arrayed something more like the natives of Alsatia, or there will be no life there for you."

While Lowestoffe spoke, he pulled Lord Glenvarloch along with him into his chambers, where he had a handsome library, filled with all the poems and play-books which were then in fashion. The Templar then dispatched a boy, who waited upon him, to procure a dish or two from the next cook's shop; "and this," he said, "must be your lordship's dinner, with a glass of old sack, of which my grandmother (the heavens requite her!) sent me a dozen of bottles, with charge to use the liquor only with clarified whey, when I felt my breast ache with over study. Marry, we will drink the good lady's health in it, if it is your lordship's pleasure, and you shall see how we poor students eke out our mutton-commons in the hall."

The outward door of the chambers was barred so soon as the boy had re-entered with the food; the page was ordered to keep close watch and admit no one; and Lowestoffe, by example and precept, pressed his noble guest to partake of his hospitality. His frank and forward manners, though much differing from the courtly ease of Lord Dalgarno, were calculated to make a favourable impression, and Lord Glenvarloch, though his experience of Dalgarno's perfidy had taught him to be cautious of reposing faith in friendly professions, could not avoid testifying his gratitude to the young Templar, who seemed so anxious for his safety and accommodation.

"You may spare your gratitude any great sense of obligation, my lord," said the Templar. "No doubt I am willing to be of use to any gentleman that has cause to sing *Fortune my foe*, and particularly proud to serve your lordship's turn. But I have also an old grudge, to speak heaven's truth, at your opposite, Lord Dalgarno."

"May I ask upon what account, Master Lowestoffe?" said Lord Glenvarloch.

"O, my lord," replied the Templar, "it was for a hap that chanced after you left the ordinary, one evening about three weeks since—at least I think you were not by, as your lordship always left us before deep play began—I mean no offence, but such was your lordship's custom—when there were words between Lord Dalgarno and me concerning a certain game at gleek, and a certain mournival of aces held by his lordship, which went for eight—Tib, which went for fifteen—twenty-three in all. Now I held king and queen, being three —a natural Towser, making fifteen—and Tiddy, nineteen. We vied the ruff, and revied, as your lordship may suppose, till the stake was equal to half my yearly exhibition, fifty as fair yellow canary birds as e'er chirped in the bottom of a green silk purse. Well, my lord, I gained the cards, and lo you! it pleases his lordship to say, that we played without Tiddy; and as the rest stood by and backed him, and especially the sharking Frenchman, why I was obliged to lose more than I shall gain all the season.—So judge if I have not a crow to pluck with his lordship. Was it ever heard there was a game at gleek at the ordinary before, without counting Tiddy?—marry gip upon his lordship!—every man who comes with his purse in his hand is as free to make new laws as he I hope, since touch pot touch penny makes every man equal."

As Master Lowestoffe ran over this jargon of the gaming-table, Lord Glenvarloch was both ashamed and mortified, and felt a severe pang of aristocratic pride, when he concluded in the sweeping clause, that the dice, like the grave, levelled those distinguishing points of society, to which Nigel's early prejudices clung perhaps but too fondly. It was impossible, however, to object any thing to the learned reasoning of the young Templar, and therefore Nigel was contented to turn the conversation, by making some inquiries concerning the present state of Whitefriars. There also his host was at home.

"You know, my lord," said Master Lowestoffe, "that we Templars are a power and a dominion within ourselves, and I am proud to say that I hold some rank in our republic—was Treasurer to the Lord of Misrule last year, and am at this present moment in nomination for that dignity myself. In such circumstances, we are under the necessity of maintaining an amicable intercourse with our neighbours of Alsatia, even as the Christian States find themselves often, in mere policy, obliged to make alliance with the Grand Turk, or the Barbary States."

"I should have imagined you gentlemen of the Temple more independent of your neighbours," said Lord Glenvarloch.

"You do us something too much honour, my lord," said the Templar; "the Alsatians and we have some common enemies, and we have, under the rose, some common friends. We are in the use of blocking all bailiffs out of our bounds, and we are powerfully aided by our neighbours, who tolerate not a rag belonging to them within theirs. Moreover the Alsatians have—I beg you to understand me—the power of protecting or distressing our friends, male or female, who may be obliged to seek sanctuary within their bounds. In short, the two communities serve each other, though the league is between states of unequal quality, and I may myself say, that I have treated of sundry weighty affairs, and have been a negociator well approved on both sides.—But hark—hark—what is that?"

The sound by which Master Lowestoffe was interrupted, was that of a distant horn, winded loud and keenly, and followed by a faint and remote huzza.

"There is something doing," said Lowestoffe, "in the Whitefriars at this moment—that is the signal when their privileges are invaded by tipstaff or bailiff; and at the blast of the horn they all swarm out to the rescue, as bees when their hive is disturbed.—Jump, Jim," he continued, calling out to his attendant, "and see what they are doing in Alsatia.—That bastard of a boy," he continued, as the lad, accustomed to the precipitate haste of his master, tumbled rather than ran out of the apartment, and so down stairs, "is worth gold in this quarter—he serves six masters—four of them in distinct Numbers, and you would think him present like a fairy at the mere wish of him that for the time most needs his attendance. No scout in Oxford, no gip in Cambridge, ever matched him in speed and intelligence. He knows the step of a dun from that of a client, when it reaches the very bottom of the staircase; can tell the trip of a pretty wench from the step of a bencher, when they are at the upper end of the court; and is, take him all in all—But I see your lordship is something anxious—May I press another cup of my kind grandmother's cordial, or will you allow me to shew you my wardrope, and act as your valet or groom of the chamber?"

Lord Glenvarloch hesitated not to acknowledge that he was painfully sensible of his present situation, and anxious to do what must needs be done for his extrication.

The good-natured and thoughtless young Templar readily acquiesced, and led the way into his little bed-room, where from band-boxes, portmantles, mail-trunks, not forgetting an old walnut-tree wardrobe-press, he began to select the articles which he thought most suited effectually to disguise his guest in venturing into the lawless and turbulent society of Alsatia.

Chapter Six

Come hither, young one—Mark me! Thou art now
'Mongst men o' the sword, that live by reputation
More than by constant income—single suited
They are, I grant you; yet each single suit
Maintains, on the rough guess, a thousand followers—
And they be men, who, hazarding their all,
Needful apparel, necessary income,
And human body, and immortal soul,
Do in the very deed but hazard nothing—
So strictly is that ALL bound in reversion;
Clothes to the broker, income to the usurer—
And body to disease, and soul to the foul fiend;
Who laughs to see Soldadoes and Fooladoes,
Play better than himself his game on earth.
                    The Mohocks

"YOUR LORDSHIP," said Reginald Lowestoffe, "must be content to exchange your decent and civil-seeming rapier, which I will retain in safe keeping, for this broad-sword, with an hundred weight of rusty iron about the hilt, and to wear these huge-paned slops, instead of your civil and moderate hose. We allow no cloak, for your ruffian always walks in cuerpo; and this tarnished doublet of bald velvet, with its discoloured embroidery, and—I grieve to speak it—a few stains from the blood of the grape, will best suit the garb of a roaring boy. I will leave you to change your suit for an instant, till I can help to truss you."

Lowestoffe retired, while slowly, and with hesitation, Nigel obeyed his instructions. He felt displeasure and disgust at the scoundrelly disguise which he was under the necessity of assuming; but when he considered the bloody consequences which law attached to his rash act of violence, the easy and indifferent temper of James, the prejudices of his son, the overbearing influence of the Duke of Buckingham sure to be thrown into the scale against him; and, above all, when he reflected that he must now look upon the active, assiduous, and insinuating Lord Dalgarno as a bitter enemy, reason told him he was in a situation of peril which authorized all honest means, even the most unseemly in outward appearance, to extricate himself from so dangerous a predicament.

While he was changing his dress, and musing on these particulars, his friendly host re-entered the sleeping apartment. "Swouns!" he said, "my lord, it was well you went not straight into that same Alsatia of ours at the time you proposed, for the hawks have stooped upon it. Here is Jim comes back with tidings, that he saw a pursuivant there with a privy-council warrant, and half a score of yeomen assistants, armed to the teeth, and the horn which we heard was sounded to call out the posse of the Friars—indeed, when old Duke Hildebrod saw that the quest was after some one of whom he knew nothing, he permitted, of courtesy, the man-catcher to search through his dominions, quite certain they would take little by their motion, for Duke Hildebrod is a most judicious potentate.—Go back, you bastard, and bring us word when all is quiet."

"And who may Duke Hildebrod be?" said Lord Glenvarloch.

"Nouns! my lord," said the Templar, "have you lived so long on the town, and never heard of the valiant as wise, and politic as valiant, Duke Hildebrod, grand protector of the liberties of Alsatia? I thought the man had never whirled a die but was familiar with his fame."

"Yet I have never heard of him, Master Lowestoffe," said Lord Glenvarloch, "or, what is the same thing, I have paid no attention to aught may have passed in conversation respecting him."

"Why, then, my lord," said Lowestoffe—"but, first, let me have the honour of trussing you—now, observe, I leave several of the points untied, of set purpose; and if it pleases you to let a small portion of your shirt be seen betwixt your doublet and the band of your upper stock, it will have so much the more rakish effect, and will attract you respect in Alsatia, where linen is something scarce. Now, I tie some of the points carefully asquint, for your ruffianly gallant never appears too accurately trussed—so——"

"Arrange it as you will, sir," said Nigel; "but let me hear at least something of the conditions of the unhappy district into which, with other wretches, I am compelled to retreat."

"Why, my lord," replied the Templar, "our neighbouring state of Alsatia, which the law calls the sanctuary of Whitefriars, has had its mutations and revolutions like greater kingdoms, and being in some sort a lawless arbitrary government, it follows, of course, that these have been more frequent than our own better regulated commonwealth of the Templars, that of Gray's-Inn, and other similar associations, have had the fortune to witness. Our traditions and records speak of twenty revolutions within the last twelve years, in which the aforesaid state has repeatedly changed from absolute despotism to republicanism, not forgetting the intermediate stages of oligarchy, limited monarchy, and even gynocracy; for I myself remember Alsatia governed for nearly nine months by an old fishwoman; then it fell under the dominion of a broken attorney, who was dethroned by a reformado captain, who proving tyrannical, was deposed by a hedge parson, who was succeeded, upon resignation of his power, by Duke Jacob Hildebrod, of that name the first, whom Heaven long preserve."

"And is this potentate's government," said Lord Glenvarloch, forcing himself to take some interest in the conversation, "of a despotic character?"

"Pardon me, my lord," said the Templar; "this sage sovereign is too wise to incur, like many of his predecessors, the odium of wielding so important an authority by his own sole will. He has established a council of state, who regularly meet for their morning's draught at seven o'clock, convene a second time at eleven for their *ante-meridiem*, or whet, and assembling in solemn conclave at the hour of two afternoon, for the purpose of consulting for the good of the commonwealth, are so prodigal of their leisure in the service of the state, that they seldom separate before midnight. Into this worthy senate, composed partly of Duke Hildebrod's predecessors in his high office, whom he has associated with him to prevent the envy attending sovereign and sole authority, I must presently introduce your lordship, that they may admit you to the immunities of the Friars, and assign you a place of residence."

"Does their authority extend to such regulation?" said Lord Glenvarloch.

"The council account it a main point of their privileges, my lord," answered Lowestoffe; "and, in fact, it is one of the most powerful means by which they support their authority. For, when Duke Hildebrod and his senate find a topping householder in the Friars becomes discontented and factious, it is but assigning him for a lodger some fat bankrupt, or new residenter, whose circumstances require refuge, and whose purse can pay for it, and the malcontent becomes as tractable as a lamb. As for the poorer refugees, they let them shift as they can; but the registration of their names in the Duke's entry-book, and the payment of garnish conforming to their circumstances, is never dispensed with; and the Friars would be a very unsafe residence for the stranger who should dispute these points of jurisdiction."

"Well, Master Lowestoffe," said Lord Glenvarloch, "I must be controlled by the circumstances which dictate to me this state of concealment; of course, I am desirous not to betray my name and rank."

"It will be highly advisable, my lord," said Lowestoffe; "and is a case thus provided for in the statutes of the republic, or monarchy, or whatsoever you call it; He who desires that no questions shall be asked

at him concerning his name, cause of refuge, and the like, may escape
the usual interrogations upon payment of double the garnish otherwise belonging to his condition—complying with this essential stipulation, your lordship may register yourself as King of Bantam, if you
will, for not a question will be asked at you.—But here comes our
scout, with news of peace and tranquillity. Now I will go with your
lordship myself, and present you to the council of Alsatia, with all the
influence which I have over them as an office-bearer in the Temple,
which is not slight; for they have come halting off upon all occasions
when we have taken part against them, and that they well know. The
time is propitious, for as the council is now met in Alsatia, so the
Temple walks are quiet. Now, my lord, throw your cloak about you, to
hide your present exterior—you shall give it to the boy at the foot of
the stairs that go down to the Sanctuary; and as the ballad says that
Queen Eleanor sunk at Charing-Cross and rose at Queenhithe, so
you shall sink a nobleman in the Temple Gardens, and rise an Alsatian at Whitefriars."

They went out accordingly, attended by the little scout, traversed
the gardens, descended the stairs, and at the bottom the young Templar exclaimed,—"And now let us sing, with Ovid,

In novas fert animus mutatas dicere formas.

Off, off, ye lendings!" he continued, in the same vein. "Via, the
curtain that shadowed Borgia! But how now, my lord?" he continued, when he observed Lord Glenvarloch was really distressed at
the degrading change in his situation, "I trust you are not offended at
my rattling folly? I would but reconcile you to your present circumstances, and give you the tone of this strange place. Come, cheer up—
I trust it will only be your residence for a very few days."

Nigel was only able to press his hand, and reply in a whisper, "I am
sensible of your kindness. I know I must drink the cup which my own
folly has filled for me—pardon me only, that at the first taste I feel its
bitterness."

Reginald Lowestoffe was bustling, officious and good-natured,
but, used to live a scrambling rakish course of life himself, he had not
the least idea of the extent of Lord Glenvarloch's mental sufferings,
and thought of his temporary concealment as if it were merely the trick
of a wanton boy, who plays at hide-and-seek with his tutor. With the
appearance of the place, too, he was familiar, but on his companion it
produced a deep sensation.

The ancient sanctuary at Whitefriars lay considerably lower than
the elevated terraces and gardens of the Temple, and was therefore
generally involved in the damps and fogs arising from the Thames.

The brick buildings by which it was occupied crowded closely on each
other, for, in a place so rarely privileged, every foot of ground was
valuable; but, erected in many cases by persons whose funds were
inadequate to their speculations, the houses were generally insuffi-
cient, and exhibited the lamentable signs of having become ruinous,
while they were yet new. The wailing of children, the scolding of their
mothers, the miserable exhibition of ragged linens hung from the
windows to dry, spoke the wants and distresses of the wretched inhabitants; while the sounds of complaint were mocked and overwhelmed
in the riotous shouts, oaths, profane songs, and boisterous laughter,
that issued from the ale-houses and taverns, which, as the signs indicated, were equal in number to all the other houses. And, that the full
character of the place might be evident, several faded, tinselled, and
painted females looked boldly at the strangers from their open lattices,
or more modestly seemed busied with the cracked flower-pots, filled
with mignionette and rosemary, which were disposed in front of the
windows, to the great risk of the passengers.

"*Semi-reducta Venus*," said the Templar, pointing to one of these
nymphs, who seemed afraid of observation, and partly concealed herself behind the casement, as she chirrup'd to a miserable black-bird,
the tenant of a wicker prison, which hung outside on the black brick
wall. "I know the face of yonder waistcoateer," continued the guide;
"and I could wager a rose-noble, from the posture she stands in, that
she has clean head-gear, and a soiled night-rail. But here come two of
the male inhabitants, smoking like moving volcanoes!—these are
roaring blades, whom Nicotia and Trinidado serve, I dare swear, in
lieu of beef and pudding; for, be it known to you, my lord, that the
King's Counter-blast against the Indian weed will no more pass current in Alsatia, than will his writ of *capias*."

As he spoke, the two smokers approached; shaggy uncombed ruffians, whose enormous mustachoes were turned back over their ears,
and mingled with the wild elf-locks of their hair, much of which was
seen under the old beavers which they wore aside upon their heads,
while some straggling portion escaped through the rents of the
hats aforesaid. Their tarnished plush jerkins, large slops, or trunk-
breeches, their broad greasy shoulder-belts, and discoloured scarfs,
and, above all, the ostentatious manner in which the one wore a
broadsword, and the other an extravagantly long rapier and poniard,
marked the true Alsatian bully, then, and for a hundred years afterwards, a well-known character.

"Tour out, tour out," said the one ruffian to the other; "tout the
bien mort twiring at the gentry cove!"*

* Look sharp. See how the girl is ogling the strange gallants.

"I smell a spy," replied the other, looking at Nigel; "chalk him across the peepers with your choury."*

"Bing avast, bing avast!" replied his companion; "yon other is rattling Reginald Lowestoffe of the Temple—I know him, he is a good boy, and free of the province."

So saying, and enveloping themselves in another thick cloud of smoke, they went on without farther greeting.

"*Crasso in aere!*"—said the Templar; "you hear what a character the impudent knaves give me—but so it serves your lordship's turn I care not. And now, let me ask your lordship what name you wish to assume, for we are near the ducal palace of Duke Hildebrod."

"I will be called Grahame," said Nigel; "it was my mother's name."

"Grime," repeated the Templar, "will suit Alsatia well enough, being both a grim and grimy place of refuge."

"I said Grahame, sir, not Grime," said Nigel, something shortly, and laying an emphasis on the vowel; for few Scotsmen understand raillery upon the subject of their names.

"I beg pardon, my lord," answered the undisconcerted punster; "but *Graam* will suit the circumstance too—it signifies tribulation in the High Dutch, and your lordship must be considered as a man under trouble."

Nigel laughed at the pertinacity of the Templar, who, proceeding to point out a sign representing, or believed to represent, a dog attacking a bull, and running at his head, in the true scientific style of onset,—"There," said he, "doth Duke Hildebrod deal forth laws, as well as ale and strong waters, to his faithful Alsatians. Being a determined champion of Paris Garden, he has chosen a sign corresponding to his habits; and he deals in giving drink to the thirsty, that he himself may drink without paying, and receive pay for what is drunken by others.—Let us enter the ever open gate of this second Axylus."

As he spoke, they entered the dilapidated tavern, which was, nevertheless, more ample in dimension, and less ruinous, than many houses in the same evil neighbourhood. Two or three hagard, ragged drawers ran to and fro, whose looks, like those of owls, seemed only adapted for midnight, when other creatures sleep, and who by day seemed bleared, stupid, and only half awake. Guided by one of these blinking Ganymedes they entered a room, where the feeble rays of the sun were almost wholly eclipsed by volumes of tobacco-smoke, rolled from the tubes of the company, while out of the cloudy sanctuary arose the old chaunt of—

---

* Slash him over the eyes with your dagger.

"Old Sir Simon the King,
And old Sir Simon the King,
With his malmsey nose,
And his ale-dropped hose,
And sing hey ding-a-ding-ding."

Duke Hildebrod, who himself condescended to chaunt this ditty to his loving subjects, was a monstrously fat old man, with only one eye; and a nose which bore evidence to the frequency, strength, and depth of his potations. He wore a murrey-coloured plush jerkin, stained with the overflowings of the tankard, much the worse for wear, and unbuttoned at bottom for the ease of his enormous paunch. Behind him lay a favourite bull-dog, whose round head and single black glancing eye, as well as the creature's great corpulence, gave it a burlesque resemblance to its master.

The well-beloved counsellors who surrounded the ducal throne, incensed it with tobacco, pledged its occupier in thick clammy ale, and echoed back his choral songs, were Satraps worthy of such a Soldan. The buff jerkin, broad belt, and long sword of one, shewed him to be a Low Country soldier, whose look of scowling importance, and drunken impudence, were designed to sustain his title to call himself a Roving Blade. It seemed to Nigel that he had seen this fellow some where or other. A hedge-parson, or buckle-beggar, as that order of priesthood has been irreverently termed, sate on the Duke's left, and was easily distinguished by his torn band, flapped hat, and the remnants of a rusty cassock. Beside the parson sat a most wretched and meagre-looking old man, with a thread-bare hood of coarse kersy upon his head, and buttoned about his neck, while his pinched features, like those of old Daniel, were illuminated by

——————an eye,
Through the last look of dotage still cunning and sly.

On his left was placed a broken attorney, who, for some malpractices, had been struck from the roll of practitioners, and who had nothing left of his profession excepting its roguery. One or two persons of less figure, amongst whom there was one face, which, like that of the soldier, seemed not unknown to Nigel, though he could not recollect where he had seen it, completed the council-board of Jacob Duke Hildebrod.

The strangers had full time to observe all this; for his grace the Duke, whether irresistibly carried on by the full tide of harmony, or whether to impress the strangers with a proper idea of his consequence, chose to sing his ditty to an end before addressing them, though, during the whole time, he closely scrutinized them with his single optic.

When Duke Hildebrod had ended his song, he informed his Peers

that a worthy officer of the Temple attended them, and commanded
the captain and parson to abandon their easy chairs in behalf of the
two strangers, whom he placed on his right and left hand. The worthy
representatives of the army and the church of Alsatia, went to place
themselves on a crazy form at the bottom of the table, which, ill
calculated to sustain men of such weight, gave way under them, and
the man of the sword and man of the gown were rolled over each other
on the floor, amidst the exulting shouts of the company. They arose in
wrath, contending which should vent his displeasure in the loudest
and deepest oaths, a strife in which the parson's superior acquaintance with theology enabled him greatly to excel the captain, and were
at length with difficulty tranquillized by the arrival of the alarmed
waiters with more stable chairs, and by a long draught of the cooling
tankard. When this commotion was appeased, and the strangers courteously accommodated with flagons, after the fashion of the others
present, the Duke drank prosperity to the Temple in the most gracious manner, together with a cup of welcome to Master Reginald
Lowestoffe; and this courtesy having been thankfully accepted, the
party honoured prayed permission to call for a gallon of Rhenish, over
which he proposed to open his business.

The mention of a liquor so superior to their usual potations had an
instant and most favourable effect upon the little senate; and its
immediate appearance might be said to secure a favourable reception
of Master Lowestoffe's proposition, which, after a round or two had
circulated, he explained to be the admission of his friend Master Nigel
Grahame to the benefit of the sanctuary and other immunities of
Alsatia, in the character of a grand compounder; for so were those
termed who paid a double fee at their matriculation, in order to avoid
laying before the senate the peculiar circumstances which compelled
them to take refuge there.

The worthy Duke heard this proposition with glee, which glittered
in his single eye; and no wonder, as it was a rare occurrence, and of
peculiar advantage to his private revenue. Accordingly, he commanded his ducal register to be brought him, a huge book secured
with brass clasps like a merchant's ledger, and whose leaves, stained
with wine and slabbered with tobacco juice, bore the names probably
of as many rogues as are to be found in the Calendar of Newgate.

Nigel was then directed to lay down two nobles as his ransom, and
to claim privilege by reciting the following doggrel verses, which were
dictated to him by the Duke:—

> "Your suppliant, by name
> Nigel Grahame,
> In fear of mishap

> From a shoulder-tap;
> And dreading a claw
> From the talons of law,
>   That are sharper than briars;
> His freedom to sue,
> And rescue by you—
> Through weapon and wit,
> From warrant and writ,
> From bailiff's hand,
> From tipstaff's wand,
>   Is come hither to Whitefriars."

As Duke Hildebrod with a tremulous hand began to make the entry, and had already, with superfluous generosity, spelled Nigel with two g's instead of one, he was interrupted by the parson.* This reverend gentleman had been whispering for a minute or two, not with the captain, but with that other individual, whose face dwelt, as we have already mentioned, imperfectly in Nigel's memory, and being, perhaps, still something malcontent on account of the late accident, he now requested to be heard before the registration took place.

"The person," he said, "who hath now had the assurance to propose himself as a candidate for the privileges and immunities of this honourable society, is, in plain terms, a beggarly Scot, and we have enough of these locusts in London already—if we admit such palmer-worms and caterpillars to the sanctuary, we shall soon have the whole nation."

"We are not entitled to inquire," said Duke Hildebrod, "whether he be Scot, or French, or English; seeing he has honourably laid down his garnish, he is entitled to our protection."

"Word of denial, most Sovereign Duke," replied the parson, "I ask him no questions—his speech bewrayeth him—he is a Galilæan—and his garnish is forfeited for his assurance in coming within this our realm; and I call on you, Sir Duke, to put the laws in force against him!"

The Templar here rose, and was about to interrupt the deliberations of the court, when the Duke gravely assured him that he should be heard in behalf of his friend, so soon as the council had finished their deliberations.

The attorney next arose, and intimating that he was to speak to the point of law, said—"It was easy to be seen that this gentleman did not come here in any civil case, and that he believed it to be the story they

* This curious register is still in existence, being in possession of that eminent antiquary Dr Dryasdust, who liberally offered the author permission to have the autograph of Duke Hildebrod engraved as an illustration of this passage. Unhappily, being rigorous as Ritson himself in adhering to the very letter of his copy, the worthy Doctor clogged his munificence with the condition that we should adopt the Duke's orthography and entitle the work "The Fortunes of Niggle," with which stipulation we did not think it necessary to comply.

had already heard of, concerning a blow given within the verge of the Park—that the sanctuary would not bear out the offender in such case —and that the queer old Chief would send down a broom which should sweep the streets of Alsatia from the Strand to the Stairs; and it was even policy to think what evil might ensue to their republic, by sheltering an alien in such circumstances."

The captain, who had sate impatiently while these opinions were expressed, now sprung on his feet with the vehemence of a cork bouncing from a bottle of brisk beer, and turning up his moustachoes with a martial air, cast a glance of contempt on the lawyer and church-man, while he thus expressed his opinion.

"Most noble Duke Hildebrod! When I hear such base, skeldering, coysterel propositions come from the counsellors of your grace, and when I remember the Huffs, the Muns, and the Tityretu's by whom your grace's ancestors and predecessors were advised on such occa-sions, I begin to think the spirit of action is as dead in Alsatia as in my old grannam; and yet who thinks so thinks a lie, since I will find as many roaring boys in the Friars as shall keep the liberties against all the scavengers of Westminster. And if we should be overborne for a turn, death and darkness! have we not time to send the gentleman off by water, either to Paris Garden or to the Bankside; and if he is a gallant of true breed, will he not make us full amends for all the trouble we have? Let other societies exist by the law, I say that we brisk boys of the Huff live in spite of it; and thrive best when we are in right opposition to sign and seal, writ and warrant, serjeant and tipstaff, catch-pole and bum-bailey."

This speech was followed by a murmur of approbation, and Lowestoffe, striking before the favourable sound had subsided, reminded the Duke and his council how much the security of their state depended on the amity of the Templars, who, by shutting their gates, could at pleasure stop against the Alsatians the commun-ication betwixt the Friars and the Temple, and that as they con-ducted on this occasion, so would they secure or lose the benefit of his interest with his own body, which they knew not to be inconsid-erable. "And, in respect of my friend being a Scotsman and alien, as has been observed by the reverend divine and learned lawyer, you are to consider," said Lowestoffe, "for what he is pursued hither —Why, for giving the bastinadoe not to an Englishman, but to one of his own countrymen—And for my own simple part," he con-tinued, touching Lord Glenvarloch at the same time, to make him understand he spoke but in jest, "if all the Scotch in London were to fight a Welch main, and kill each other to a man, the survivor would, in my humble opinion, be entitled to our gratitude, as having done a most acceptable service to poor Old England."

A shout of laughter and applause followed this ingenious apology for the client's state of alienage; and the Templar followed up his plea with the following pithy proposition:—"I know well," said he, "it is the custom of the fathers of this old and most honourable republic, ripely and well to consider all their proceedings over a proper allowance of liquor; and far be it from me to propose the breach of so laudable a custom, or to pretend that such an affair as the present can be well and constitutionally considered during the discussion of a pitiful gallon of sack. But, as it is the same thing to this honourable conclave whether they drink first and determine afterwards, or whether they determine first and drink afterwards, I propose your Grace, with the advice of your wise and potent senators, shall pass your edict, granting to mine honourable friend the immunities of the place, and assigning him a lodging according to your wise forms, to which he will presently retire, being somewhat spent with this day's action; whereupon I will presently order in a rundlet of Rhenish, with a corresponding quantity of neats' tongues and pickled herrings, to make you all as glorious as George-a-Green."

This overture was received with a general shout of applause, which altogether drowned the voice of the dissidents, if any there were amongst the Alsatian senate who could have resisted a proposal so popular. The words of, kind heart! noble gentleman! generous gallant! flew from mouth to mouth; the inscription of the petitioner's name in the great book was hastily completed, and the oath administered to him by the worthy Doge. Like the Laws of the Twelve Tables, of the ancient Cambro-Britons, and other primitive nations, it was couched in poetry, and ran as follows:—

> "By spigot and barrel,
> By bilbo and buff,
> Thou art sworn to the quarrel
> Of the blades of the huff.
> For Whitefriars and its claims
> To be champion or martyr,
> And to fight for its dames
> Like a Knight of the Garter."

Nigel felt, and indeed exhibited, some disgust at this mummery; but, the Templar reminding him that he was too far advanced to draw back, he repeated the words, or rather assented as they were repeated by Duke Hildebrod, who concluded the ceremony by allowing him the privilege of sanctuary, in the following form of prescriptive doggrel:—

> "From the touch of the tip,
> From the blight of the warrant,
> From the watchmen who skip
> On the Harman Beck's errand;

From the Bailiff's cramp speech,
    That makes man a thrall,
I charm thee from each,
    And I charm thee from all.
Thy freedom's complete
    As a Blade of the Huff.
To be cheated and cheat,
    To be cuff'd and to cuff;
To slide, swear, and swagger,
To drink till you stagger,
    To stare and to stab,
And to brandish your dagger
    In the cause of your drab;
To walk wool-ward in winter,
    Drink brandy, and smoke,
And go *fresco* in summer
    For want of a cloak;
To eke out your living
    By the wag of your elbow,
By fulham and gourd,
    And by bareing of bilbo;
To live by your shifts,
    And to swear by your honour,
Are the freedom and gifts
    Of which I am the donor."

This homily being performed, a dispute arose concerning the special residence to be assigned the new brother of the Sanctuary; for, as the Alsatians held it a maxim in their commonwealth, that asses milk fattens, there was usually a competition amongst the inhabitants which should have the managing, as it was termed, of a new member of the society.

The Hector who had spoke so warmly and critically in Nigel's behalf, stood out now chivalrously in behalf of a certain Blowselinda, or Bonstrops, who had, it seems, a room to hire, once the occasional residence of Slicing Dick of Paddington, who lately suffered at Tyburn, and whose untimely exit had been hitherto mourned by the damsel in solitary widowhood, after the fashion of the turtle-dove.

The captain's interest was, however, over-ruled, in behalf of the old gentleman in the kersey hood, who was believed, even at his extreme age, to understand the plucking of a pigeon as well, or better, than any man of Alsatia.

This venerable personage was an usurer of some notoriety, called Trapbois, and had very lately done the state considerable service in advancing a subsidy necessary to secure a fresh importation of liquors to the Duke's cellars, the wine-merchants at the Vintry being scrupulous to deal with so great a man for any thing but ready money.

When, therefore, the old gentleman arose, and with much coughing reminded the Duke that he had a poor apartment to let, the claims of all others were set aside, and Nigel was assigned to Trapbois as his guest.

No sooner was this arrangement made, than Lord Glenvarloch expressed to Lowestoffe his impatience to leave this discreditable assembly, and took his leave with a careless haste, which, but for the rundlet of Rhenish wine that entered just as he left the apartment, might have been taken in bad part. The young Templar accompanied his friend to the house of the old usurer, with the road to which he and some other youngsters about the Temple were even but too well acquainted. On the way, he assured Lord Glenvarloch that he was going to the only clean house in Whitefriars; a property which it owed solely to the exertions of the old man's only daughter, an elderly damsel, ugly enough to frighten sin, yet likely to be wealthy enough to tempt a puritan, so soon as the devil had got her old dad for his due. As Lowestoffe spoke thus, they knocked at the door of the house, and the sour, stern countenance of the female by whom it was opened, fully confirmed all which the Templar had said of the hostess. She heard, with an ungracious and discontented air, the young Templar's information, that the gentleman, his companion, was to be her father's lodger, muttered something about the trouble it was like to occasion, but ended by shewing the stranger's apartment, which was better than could have been augured from the general appearance of the place, and much larger in extent, though inferior in neatness, to that which he had occupied at Paul's Wharf.

Lowestoffe having thus seen his friend fairly installed in his new apartment, and having obtained for him a note of the rate at which he could be accommodated with victuals from a neighbouring cook's shop, now took his leave, offering, at the same time, to send the whole, or any part of Lord Glenvarloch's baggage, from his former place of residence to his new lodging. Nigel mentioned so few articles, that the Templar could not help observing, that his lordship, it would seem, did not mean to enjoy his new privileges long.

"They are too little suited to my habits and taste, that I should do so," replied Lord Glenvarloch.

"You may change your opinion to-morrow," said Lowestoffe; "and so I wish you good-even. To-morrow I will visit you betimes."

The morning came, but instead of the Templar, it brought only a letter from him. The epistle stated, that Lowestoffe's visits to Alsatia had drawn down the animadversion of some crabbed old pantaloons among the benchers, and that he judged it wise not to come thither at present, for fear of drawing too much attention to Lord Glenvar-loch's place of residence. He stated, that he had taken measures for the safety of his baggage, and would send him, by a safe hand, his

money-casket, and what articles he wanted. Then followed some sage
advices, dictated by Lowestoffe's acquaintance with Alsatia and its
manners. He advised him to keep the usurer in the most absolute
uncertainty concerning the state of his funds—never to throw a main
with the captain, who was in the habit of playing dry-fisted, and paying
his losses with three vowels; and, finally, to beware of Duke Hildebrod, who was as sharp, he said, as a needle, though he had no more
eyes than are possessed by that necessary implement of female industry.

Chapter Seben

Mother. What! dazzled by a flash from Cupid's mirror,
With which the boy, as mortal urchins wont,
Flings back the sunbeam in the eye of passengers—
Then laughs to see them stumble!
Daughter. Mother! no—
It was a lightning-flash which dazzled me,
And never shall these eyes see true again.
Beef and Pudding.—An old English Comedy

IT IS NECESSARY that we should leave for a time our hero Nigel,
although in a situation neither safe, comfortable, or creditable, in
order to detail some particulars which have immediate connexion with
his fortunes.

It was but the third day after he had been forced to take refuge in the
house of old Trapbois, the noted usurer of Whitefriars, commonly
called Golden Trapbois, when the pretty daughter of old Ramsay, the
watchmaker, after having piously seen her father eat his breakfast,
(taking care that he did not, in an abstruse fit of thought swallow the
salt-cellar instead of a crust of the brown loaf,) set forth from the
house as soon as he was again plunged into the depth of calculation,
and, accompanied only by that faithful old drudge, Janet the Scotch
laundress, to whom her whims were laws, made her way to Lombard-
Street, and disturbed, at the unusual hour of eight in the morning,
Aunt Judith, the sister of her worthy godfather.

The venerable maiden received her young visitor with no great
complacency; for, naturally enough, she had neither the same
admiration of her very pretty countenance, or complacence for her
foolish and girlish impatience of temper, which Master George
Heriot entertained. Still Mistress Margaret was a favourite of her
brother's, whose will was to Aunt Judith a supreme law; and she
contented herself with asking her untimely visitor, "what she made so
early with her pale chitty face in the streets of London?"

"I would speak with the Lady Hermione," answered the almost breathless girl, while the blood ran so fast to her face as totally to remove the objection of paleness which Aunt Judith had made to her complexion.

"With the Lady Hermione," said Aunt Judith—"with the Lady Hermione? and at this time in the morning, when she will scarce see any of the family even at seasonable hours? You are crazy, you silly wench, or you abuse the indulgence which my brother and the lady have shewn to you."

"Indeed—indeed—I have not," repeated Margaret, struggling to retain the unbidden tear which seemed longing to burst out on the slightest occasion. "Do but say to the lady that your brother's god-daughter desires earnestly to speak with her, and I know she will not refuse to see me."

Aunt Judith bent an earnest, suspicious, and inquisitive glance on her young visitor. "You might make me your secretary, my lassie," she said, "as well as the Lady Hermione. I am older, and better skilled to advise. I live more in the world than one who shuts herself up within four rooms, and I have the better means to assist you."

"O! no—no—no," said Margaret, eagerly, and with more earnest sincerity than complaisance; "there are some things in which you cannot advise me, Aunt Judith. It is a case—pardon me, my dear Aunt —a case beyond your counsel."

"I am glad on't, maiden," said Aunt Judith, somewhat angrily; "for I think the follies of the young people of this generation would drive mad an old brain like mine. Here you come on the viretot, through the whole streets of London, to talk some nonsense to a lady, who scarce sees God's sun but when he shines on a brick wall. But I will tell her you are here."

She went away, and shortly returned with a dry—"Mistress Marget, the lady will be glad to see you—and that's more, my young madam, than you had right to count upon."

Mistress Margaret hung her head in silence, too much perplexed by the train of her own embarrassed thoughts, for attempting either to conciliate Aunt Judith's kindness, or, which on other occasions would have been as congenial to her own humour, to retaliate on her cross-tempered remarks and manner. She followed Aunt Judith, therefore, in silence and dejection, to the strong oaken door which divided the Lady Hermione's apartment from the rest of George Heriot's spacious house.

At the door of this sanctuary it is necessary to pause, in order to correct the reports with which Richie Moniplies had filled his master's ear respecting the singular apparition of that lady's attendance at prayers, whom we now own to be by name the Lady Hermione. Some part of these exaggerations had been communicated to the worthy Scotsman by Jenkin Vincent, who was well experienced in the species of wit which has been long a favourite in the city, under the various names of cross-biting, giving the dor, bamboozling, cramming, hoaxing, humbugging, and quizzing; for which sport Richie Moniplies, with his solemn gravity totally unapprehensive of a joke, and his natural propensity to the marvellous, formed an admirable subject. Farther ornaments the tale had received from Richie himself, whose tongue, especially when oiled with good liquor, had a considerable tendency to amplification, and who failed not, while he retailed to his master all the wonderful circumstances narrated by Vincent, to add to them many conjectures of his own, which his imagination had over-hastily converted into facts.

Yet the life which the Lady Hermione had led for two years, during which she had been the inmate of George Heriot's house, was so singular, as almost to sanction many of the wild reports which went abroad. The house which the worthy goldsmith inhabited, had in former times belonged to a powerful and wealthy baronial family, which, during the reign of Henry VIII. terminated in a dowager lady, very wealthy, very devout, and most unalienably attached to the Catholic faith. The chosen friend of the Honourable Lady Foljambe was the Abbess of Saint Roque's Nunnery, like herself, a conscientious, rigid, and devoted Papist. When the house of Saint Roque was despotically dissolved by the *fiat* of the impetuous monarch, the Lady Foljambe received her friend into her spacious mansion, together with two vestal sisters, who, like their Abbess, were determined to follow the tenor of their vows, instead of embracing the profane liberty which the Monarch's will had thrown in their choice. For their residence, the Lady Foljambe contrived, with all secrecy—for Henry might not have relished her interference—to set apart a suite of four rooms, with a little closet fitted up as an oratory, or chapel; the whole apartment fenced by a strong oaken door to exclude strangers, and accommodated with a turning wheel to receive necessaries, according to the practice of all nunneries. In this retreat, the Abbess of Saint Roque and her attendants passed many years, communicating only with the Lady Foljambe, who, in virtue of their prayers, and of the support she afforded them, accounted herself little less than a saint on earth. The Abbess, fortunately for herself, died before her munificent patroness, who lived deep in Queen Elizabeth's time, ere she was summoned by fate.

The Lady Foljambe was succeeded in this mansion by a sour fanatic knight, a distant and collateral relation, who claimed the same merit for expelling the priestesses of Baal, which his predecessor had founded on maintaining the votaresses of heaven. Of the two unhappy nuns, driven from their ancient refuge, one went beyond sea; the other, unable from old age to undertake such a journey, died under the roof of a faithful Catholic widow of low degree. Sir Paul Crambagge, having got rid of the nuns, spoiled the chapel of its ornaments, and had thoughts of altogether destroying the apartment, until checked by the reflection that the operation would be unnecessary expence, since he only inhabited three rooms of the large mansion, and had not therefore the slightest occasion for any addition to its accommodations. His son proved a waster and a prodigal, and from him the house was bought by our friend George Heriot, who finding, like Sir Paul, the house more than sufficiently ample for his accommodation, left the Foljambe apartment, or Saint Roque's rooms, as they were called, in the state in which he found them.

About two years and a half before our history opened, when Heriot was absent upon an expedition to the Continent, he sent special orders to his sister and his cash-keeper, directing that the Foljambe apartment should be fitted up handsomely, though plainly, for the reception of a lady, who would make it her residence for some time; and who would live more or less with his own family according to her pleasure. He also directed, that the necessary repairs should be made with secrecy, and that as little should be said as possible upon the subject of his letter.

When the time of his return came nigh, Aunt Judith and the household were on the tenter-hooks of impatience. Master George came, as he had intimated, accompanied by a single lady, so eminently beautiful, that had it not been for her extreme and uniform paleness, she might have been reckoned one of the fairest creatures on earth. She had with her an attendant, or humble companion, whose business seemed only to wait upon her. This person, a reserved woman, and by her dialect a foreigner, aged about fifty, was called by the lady Monna Paula, and by Master Heriot, and others, Mademoiselle Pauline. She slept in the same room with her patroness at night, ate in her apartment, and was scarce ever separated from her during the day.

These females took possession of the nunnery of the devout Abbess, and without observing the same rigorous seclusion, according to the letter, seemed well nigh to restore the apartment to the use for which it had been originally designed. The new inmates lived and took their meals apart from the rest of the family. With the domestics Lady Hermione, for so she was termed, held no communication, and Mademoiselle Pauline only such as was indispensable, which she dispatched as briefly as possible. Frequent and liberal largesses

reconciled the servants to this conduct; and they were in use to
observe to each other, that to do a service for Mademoiselle Pauline,
was like finding a fairy treasure.

To Aunt Judith the Lady Hermione was kind and civil, but their
intercourse was rare; on which account the good lady felt some pangs
both of curiosity and injured dignity. But she knew her brother so
well, and loved him so dearly, that his will, once expressed, might be
truly said to become her own. The worthy citizen was not without a
spice of the dogmatism which grows on the best disposition, when a
word is a law to all around. Master George did not endure to be
questioned by his family, and when he had generally expressed his
will, that the Lady Hermione should live in the way most agreeable
to her, and that no inquiries should be made concerning her history,
or her motives for observing such strict seclusion, his sister well knew
that he would have been seriously displeased with any attempt to pry
into the secret.

But though Heriot's servants were bribed, and his sister awed into
silent acquiescence in these arrangements, they were not of a nature
to escape the critical observation of the neighbourhood. Some opined
that the wealthy goldsmith was about to turn papist, and re-establish
Lady Foljambe's nunnery—others that he was going mad—others
that he was either going to marry, or to do worse. Master George's
constant appearance at church, and the knowledge that the supposed
votaress always attended when the prayers of the English ritual were
read in family, liberated him from the first of these suspicions; those
who had to transact business with him upon 'Change, could not doubt
the soundness of Master Heriot's mind; and to confute the other
rumours, it was credibly reported by such as made the matter their
particular interest, that Master George Heriot never visited his guest
save in presence of Mademoiselle Pauline, who sat with her work in a
remote part of the same room in which they conversed. It was also
ascertained that these visits scarcely ever exceeded an hour in length,
and were usually only repeated once a-week, an intercourse too brief
and too long interrupted, to render it probable that love was the bond
of their union.

The inquirers were, therefore, at fault, and compelled to relinquish
the pursuit of Master Heriot's secret, while a thousand ridiculous
tales were circulated amongst the ignorant and superstitious, with
some specimens of which our friend Richie Moniplies had been
crammed, as we have seen, by the malicious apprentice of worthy
David Ramsay.

There was one person in the world who, it was thought, could (if
she would) have said more of the Lady Hermione than any one in

London, except George Heriot himself; and that was the said David Ramsay's only child, Margaret.

This girl was not much past the age of fifteen when the Lady Hermione first came to England, and was a very frequent visitor at her god-father's, who was much amused by her childish sallies, and by the wild and natural beauty of execution with which she sung the airs of her native country. Spoiled she was on all hands; by the indulgence of her god-father, the absent habits and indifference of her father, and the deference of all around her to her caprices, as a beauty and as an heiress. But though, from these circumstances, the city-beauty had become as wilful, as capricious, and as affected, as unlimited indulgence seldom fails to render those to whom it is extended; and although she exhibited upon many occasions the affectation of extreme shyness, silence, and reserve, which Misses in their teens are apt to take for an amiable modesty; and upon others, a considerable portion of that flippancy which youth sometimes confounds with wit, Mistress Margaret had much real shrewdness and judgment, which wanted only opportunities of observation to refine it—a lively, good-humoured, playful disposition, and an excellent heart. Her acquired follies were much increased by her reading plays and romances, to which she devoted a great deal of her time, and from which she adopted ideas as different as possible from those which she might have acquired from the invaluable and affectionate instructions of a mother; and the freaks of which she was sometimes guilty, rendered her not unjustly liable to the charge of affectation and coquetry. But the little lass had sense and shrewdness enough to keep her failings out of sight of her god-father, to whom she was sincerely attached; and so high she stood in his favour, that, at his recommendation, she obtained permission to visit the recluse Lady Hermione.

The singular mode of life which the lady observed; her extreme beauty, rendered even more interesting by her extreme paleness; the conscious pride of being admitted farther than the rest of the world into the society of a person who was wrapped in so much mystery, made a deep impression on the mind of Margaret Ramsay; and though their conversations were at no time either long or confidential, yet, proud of the trust reposed in her, Margaret was as secret respecting their tenor as if every word repeated had been to cost her life. No inquiry, however artfully backed by flattery and insinuation, whether on the part of Dame Ursula, or any other person equally inquisitive, could wring from the little maiden one word of what she heard or saw, after she entered these mysterious and secluded apartments. The slightest question concerning Master Heriot's ghost, was sufficient, at her gayest moment, to check the current of her communicative prattle, and render her silent.

We mention this, chiefly to illustrate the early strength of Margaret's character—a strength concealed under a hundred freakish whims and humours, as an ancient and massive buttress is disguised by its fantastic covering of ivy and wild-flowers. In truth, if the damsel had told all that she heard or saw within the Foljambe apartments, she would have said but little to gratify the curiosity of inquirers.

At the earlier period of their first acquaintance, the Lady Hermione was wont to reward the attentions of her little friend with small but elegant presents, and entertain her by a display of foreign rarities and curiosities, many of them of considerable value. Sometimes the time was passed in a way much less agreeable to Margaret, by her receiving lessons from Pauline in the use of the needle. But although her preceptress practised these arts with a dexterity then only known in foreign convents, the pupil proved so incorrigibly idle and awkward, that the task of needle-work was at length given over, and lessons of music substituted in their stead. Here also Pauline was excellently qualified as an instructress, and Margaret, more successful in a science for which Nature had gifted her, made proficiency both in vocal and instrumental music. These lessons passed in presence of the Lady Hermione, to whom they seemed to give pleasure. She sometimes added her own voice to the performance, in a pure, clear stream of liquid harmony; but this was only when the music was of a devotional cast. As Margaret became older, her communication with the recluse assumed a different character. She was allowed, if not encouraged, to tell whatever she had remarked out of doors, and the Lady Hermione, while she remarked the quick, sharp, and intuitive powers of observation possessed by her young friend, often found sufficient reason to caution her against rashness in forming opinions, and giddy petulance in expressing them.

The habitual awe with which she regarded this singular personage, induced Mistress Margaret, though by no means delighting in contradiction or reproof, to listen with patience to her admonitions, and to make full allowance for the good intentions of the patroness by whom they were bestowed; although in her heart she could not conceive how Madame Hermione, who never stirred from the Foljambe apartment, should think of teaching knowledge of the world to one who walked twice a-week between Temple-Bar and Lombard Street, besides parading in the Park every Sunday that proved to be fair weather. Indeed, pretty Mistress Margaret was so little inclined to endure such remonstrances, that her intercourse with the inhabitants of the Foljambe apartment would have probably slackened as her circle of acquaintance increased in the external world, had she not, on the one hand, entertained a habitual reverence for her monitress, of which she could not divest herself, and been flattered, on the other, by being, to a certain degree, the depositary of a secret for which others thirsted in vain. Besides, although the conversation of Hermione was uniformly serious, it was not in general either formal or severe; nor was the lady offended by the flights of levity which Mistress Margaret sometimes ventured in her presence, even when they were such as made Monna Paula cast her eyes upwards, and sigh with that compassion which a devotee extends towards the votaries of a trivial and profane world. Thus, upon the whole, the little maiden was disposed to submit, though not without some wincing, to the grave admonitions of the Lady Hermione; and the rather that the mystery annexed to the person of her monitress was in her mind early associated with a vague idea of wealth and importance, which had been rather confirmed than lessened by many accidental circumstances which she had noticed since she was more capable of observation.

It frequently happens, that the council which we reckon intrusive when offered to us unasked, becomes precious in our eyes when the pressure of difficulties renders us more diffident of our own judgment than we are apt to find ourselves in the hours of ease and indifference; and this is more especially the case if we suppose that our adviser may also possess power and inclination to back his counsel with effectual assistance. Mistress Margaret was now in this situation. She was, or believed herself to be, in a condition where both advice and assistance might be necessary; and it was therefore, after an anxious and sleepless night, that she resolved to have recourse to the Lady Hermione, who she knew would readily afford her the one, and, as she hoped, might also possess means of giving her the other. The conversation between them will best explain the purport of her visit.

Chapter Eight

By this good light, a wench of matchless mettle!
This were a leaguer-lass to love a soldier,
To bind his wounds, and kiss his bloody brow,
And sing a roundel as she help'd to arm him,
Though the rough foeman's drums were beat so nigh,
They seem'd to bear the burden.
                                        Old Play

WHEN MISTRESS MARGARET entered the Foljambe apartment, she found the inmates employed in their usual manner; the lady in reading, and her attendant in embroidering a large piece of tapestry, which had occupied her ever since Margaret had been first admitted within these secluded chambers.

Hermione nodded kindly to her visitor, but did not speak; and Margaret, accustomed to this reception, and in the present case not sorry for it, as it gave her an interval to collect her thoughts, stooped over Monna Paula's frame, and observed, in a half whisper, "You were just so far as that rose, Monna, when I first saw you—see, there is the mark where I had the bad luck to spoil the flower in trying to catch the stitch—I was little above fifteen then—these flowers make me an old woman, Monna Paula."

"I wish they could make you a wise one, my child," answered Monna Paula, in whose esteem pretty Mistress Margaret did not stand quite so high as in that of her patroness; partly owing to her natural austerity, which was something intolerant of youth and gaiety, and partly to the jealousy with which a favourite domestic regards any one whom she considers as a sort of rival in the affections of her mistress.

"What is it you say to Monna, little one?" asked the lady.

"Nothing, madam," replied Mistress Margaret, "but that I have seen the real flowers blossom three times over since I first saw Monna Paula working in her canvas garden, and her violets have not budded yet."

"True, lady-bird," replied Hermione; "but the buds that are longest in blossoming will last the longest in flower. You have seen those in the garden bloom thrice, but you have seen them fade thrice also; now, Monna Paula's will remain in blow for ever—they will fear neither frost nor tempest."

"True, madam," answered Mistress Margaret; "but neither have they life or odour."

"That, little one," replied the recluse, "is to compare a life agitated by hope and fear, and chequered with success and disappointment, and fevered by the effects of love and hatred, a life of passion and of feeling, saddened and shortened by its exhausting alternations, to a calm and tranquil existence, animated but by a sense of duties, and only employed, during its smooth and quiet course, in the unvaried discharge of them; is that the moral of your answer?"

"I do not know, madam—" answered Mistress Margaret; "but of all birds in the air, I would rather be the lark, that sings while he is drifting down the summer breeze, than the weather-cock that sticks fast yonder upon his iron perch, and just moves so much as to discharge his duty, and tell us which way the wind blows."

"Metaphors are no arguments, my pretty maiden," said the Lady Hermione, smiling.

"I am sorry for that, madam," answered Margaret; "for they are such a pretty indirect way of telling one's mind when it differs from one's betters—besides, on this subject there is no end of them, and they are so civil and so becoming withal."

"Indeed?" replied the lady; "let me hear some of them, I pray you."

"It would be, for example, very bold in me," said Margaret, "to say to your ladyship, that, rather than live a quiet life, I would like a little variety of hope and fear, and liking and disliking, and—and—and the other sort of feelings which your ladyship is pleased to speak of; but I may say freely, and without blame, that I like a butterfly better than a beetle, or a trembling aspen better than a grim Scottish fir, that never wags a leaf—or that of all the wood, brass, and wire that ever my father's fingers put together, I do hate and detest a certain huge old clock of the German fashion, that rings hours and half hours, and quarters and half quarters, as if it was of such consequence that the world should know it was wound up and going. Now, dearest lady, I wish you would only compare that clumsy, clanging, Dutch-looking piece of lumber, with the beautiful time-piece that Master Heriot caused my father make for your ladyship, which uses to play a hundred merry tunes, and turns out, when it strikes the hour, a whole band of morrice-dancers, to trip the hays to the measure."

"And which of these time-pieces goes the truest, Margaret?" said the lady.

"I must confess, the old Dutchman has the advantage in that—" said Margaret. "I fancy you are right, madam, and that comparisons are no arguments; at least mine has not brought me through."

"Upon my word, maiden Margaret," said the lady, smiling, "you have been of late thinking very much of these matters."

"Perhaps too much, madam," said Margaret, so low as only to be heard by the lady, behind the back of whose chair she had now placed herself. The words were spoken very gravely, and accompanied by a half sigh, which did not escape the attention of her to whom they were addressed. The Lady Hermione turned immediately round, and looked earnestly at Margaret, then paused for a moment, and finally commanded Monna Paula to carry her frame and embroidery into the anti-chamber. When they were left alone, she desired her young friend to come from behind the chair, on the back of which she still rested, and sit down beside her upon a stool.

"I will remain thus, madam, under your favour," answered the girl, without changing her posture; "I would rather you heard me without seeing me."

"In God's name, maiden," returned her patroness, "what is it you can have to say that may not be uttered face to face, to so true a friend as I am?"

Without making any direct answer, Margaret only replied, "You were right, dearest lady, when you said I had suffered my feelings too much to engross me of late. I have done very wrong, and you will be angry with me—so will my godfather—but I cannot help it—he must be rescued."

"*He?*" repeated the lady, with emphasis; "that brief little word does indeed so far explain your mystery; but come from behind the chair, you silly popinjay. I will wager you have suffered yonder gay young apprentice of your father to sit too near your heart. I have not heard you mention young Vincent for many a day—perhaps he has not been out of mouth and out of mind both. Have you been so foolish as to let him speak to you seriously? I am told he is a bold youth."

"Not bold enough to say any thing that could displease me, madam," said Margaret.

"Perhaps, then, you were *not* displeased,"—said the lady; "or perhaps he has not *spoken*, which would be wiser and better. Be openhearted, my love—your god-father will soon return, and we will take him into our consultations—if the young man is industrious, and come of honest parentage, his poverty may be no such insurmountable obstacle. But you are both of you very young, Margaret—I know your god-father will expect that the youth shall first serve out his apprenticeship."

Margaret had hitherto suffered the lady to proceed, under the mistaken impression which she had adopted, simply because she could not tell how to interrupt her; but pure despite at hearing her last words gave her boldness at length to say, "I crave your pardon, madam; but neither the youth you mention, nor any apprentice or master within the city of London"——

"Margaret," said the lady, in reply, "the contemptuous tone with which you mention those of your own class—many hundreds, if not thousands, of whom, are in all respects better than yourself, and would greatly honour you by thinking of you—is, methinks, no warrant for the wisdom of your choice—for a choice it seems there is. Who is it, maiden, to whom you have thus rashly attached yourself— rashly I fear it must be?"

"It is the young Scottish Lord Glenvarloch, madam," answered Margaret, in a low and modest tone, but sufficiently firm, considering the subject.

"The young Lord of Glenvarloch!" repeated the lady, in great surprise,—"Maiden, you are distracted in your wits."

"I knew you would say so, madam," answered Margaret; "it is what another person has already told me—it is perhaps what all the world would tell me—it is what I am sometimes disposed to tell myself. But look at me, madam, for I will now come before you, and tell me if there is madness or distraction in my look and word, when I repeat to you again, that I have fixed my affections on this young nobleman."

"If there is not madness in your look or word, maiden, there is infinite folly in what you say," answered the Lady Hermione, sharply. "When did you ever hear that misplaced love brought any thing but misery?—seek a match among your equals, Margaret, and escape the countless kinds of risk and misery that must attend an affection bey-ond your degree.—Why do you smile, maiden? is there aught to cause scorn in what I say?"

"Surely no, madam," answered Margaret—"I only smiled to think how it should happen, that, while rank made such a wide difference between creatures formed from the same clay, the wit of the vulgar should, nevertheless, jump so exactly the same length with that of the accomplished and the exalted. It is but the variation of the phrase which divides them. Dame Ursley told me the very same thing which your ladyship has but now uttered—only you, madam, talk of count-less misery, and Dame Ursley spoke of the gallows, and Mistress Turner who was hanged upon it."

"Indeed?" answered the Lady Hermione; "and who may Dame Ursley be, that your wise choice has associated with me in the difficult task of advising a fool?"

"The barber's wife at next door, madam," answered Margaret, with feigned simplicity, but far from being sorry at heart that she had found an indirect mode of mortifying her monitress. "She is the wisest woman that I know—next to your ladyship."

"A proper confidante," said the lady, "and chosen with the same delicate sense of what is due to yourself and others. But what ails you, maiden—where are you going?"

"Only to ask Dame Ursley's advice," said Margaret, as if about to depart; "for I see your ladyship is too angry to give me any, and the emergence is pressing."

"What emergence, thou simple one?" said the lady, in a kinder tone. "Sit down, maiden, and tell out your tale.—It is true you are a fool, and a petted fool to boot; but then you are a child—an amiable child, with all your self-willed folly, and we must help you, if we can. Sit down, I say, as you are desired, and you will find me a safer and wiser counsellor than the barber-woman. And tell me how you come to suppose that you have fixed your heart unalterably upon a man whom you have seen, as I think, but once."

"I have seen him oftener," said the damsel, looking down; "but I

have only spoken with him once. I should have been able to get that
once out of my head—though the impression was so deep that I could
even now repeat every trifling word he said—but other things have
since rivetted it in my bosom for ever."

"Maiden," replied the lady, "*for ever*, is the word which comes most
lightly on the lips in such circumstances, but which is, not the less,
almost the last that we should use—the fashion of this world, its
passions, its joys, and its sorrows, pass away like the winged breeze—
there is nought for ever but that which belongs to the world beyond
the grave."

"You have corrected me justly, madam," said Margaret, calmly; "I
ought only to have spoken of my present state of mind, as what will last
me for my life time, which unquestionably may be but short."

"And what is there in this Scottish lord that can rivet what concerns
him so strongly in your fancy?" said the lady. "I admit him a person-
able man, for I have seen him, and I will suppose him courteous and
agreeable. But what are his accomplishments besides, for these surely
are not uncommon attributes?"

"He is unfortunate, madam—most unfortunate—and surrounded
by snares of different kinds, ingeniously contrived to ruin his character, destroy his estate, and perhaps to reach even his life—these
schemes have been devised by avarice originally, but they are now
followed close by vindictive ambition, animated, I think, by the absolute and concentrated spirit of malice; for the Lord Dalgarno"——

"Here, Monna Paula—Monna Paula!" exclaimed the Lady Hermione, interrupting her young friend's narrative. "She hears me not,"
she answered, rising and going out, "I must seek her—I will return
instantly." She returned again accordingly very soon after. "You mentioned a name which I thought was familiar to me," she said; "but
Monna Paula has put me right. I know nothing of your lord—how was
it you named him?"

"Lord Dalgarno," said Margaret;—"the wickedest man who lives.
Under pretence of friendship, he introduced the Lord Glenvarloch to
a gambling-house, with the purpose of engaging him in deep play; but
he with whom the perfidious traitor had to deal, was too virtuous,
moderate, and cautious, to be caught in a snare so open. What did they
next, but turn his own moderation against him, and persuade others
that, because he would not become the prey of wolves, he herded with
them for a share of their booty! And while this base Lord Dalgarno
was thus undermining his unsuspecting countryman, he took every
measure to keep him surrounded by creatures of his own, to prevent
him from attending court, and mixing with those of his proper rank.
Since the Gunpowder Treason, there never was a conspiracy more

deeply laid, more basely and more deliberately pursued."

The lady smiled sadly at Margaret's vehemence, but sighed the next moment, while she told her young friend how little she knew the world she was about to live in, since she testified so much surprise at finding it full of villainy.

"But by what means," she added, "could you, maiden, become possessed of the secret views of a man so cautious as Lord Dalgarno—as villains in general are?"

"Permit me to be secret on that subject," said the maiden; "I could not tell you without betraying others—Let it suffice that my tidings are as certain as the means by which I acquired them are secret and sure —but I must not tell them even to you."

"You are too bold, Margaret," said the lady, "to traffic in such matters at your early age—it is not only dangerous, but even unbecoming and unmaidenly."

"I knew you would say that also," said Margaret, with more meekness and patience than she usually shewed on receiving reproof; "but God knows, my heart acquits me of every other feeling save that of the wish to assist this most innocent and betrayed man.—I contrived to send him warning of his friend's falsehood;—alas! my care has only hastened his utter ruin, unless speedy aid be found. He charged his false friend with treachery, and drew on him in the Park, and is now liable to the fatal penalty due for breach of privilege of the King's palace."

"This is indeed an extraordinary tale," said Hermione; "is Lord Glenvarloch then in prison?"

"No, madam, thank God, but in the Sanctuary at Whitefriars—it is matter of doubt whether it will protect him in such a case—they speak of a warrant from the Lord Chief Justice—a gentleman of the Temple has been arrested and is in trouble, for having assisted him in his flight.—Even his taking temporary refuge in that base place, though from extreme necessity, will be used to the further defaming him. All this I know, and yet I cannot rescue him—cannot rescue him save by your means."

"By my means, maiden?" said the lady—"you are beside yourself! —What means can I possess in this secluded situation, of assisting this unfortunate nobleman?"

"You *have* means," said Margaret eagerly; "you have those means, unless I mistake greatly, which can do any thing—can do every thing, in this city, in this world. You have wealth, and the command of a small portion of it will enable me to extricate him from his present danger. He will be enabled and directed how to make his escape—and I——" she paused.

"Will accompany him, doubtless, and reap the fruits of your sage exertions in his behalf," said the Lady Hermione, ironically.

"May heaven forgive you the unjust thought, lady," answered Margaret. "I will never see him more—but I shall have saved him, and the thought shall make me happy."

"A cold conclusion to so bold and warm a flame," said the lady with a smile, which seemed to intimate incredulity.

"It is, however, the only one which I expect, madam—I could almost say the only one which I wish—I am sure I will use no efforts to bring about any other; if I am bold in his cause, I am timorous enough in my own. During our only interview I was unable to speak a word with him. He knows not the sound of my voice—and all that I have risked, and must yet risk, I am doing for one, who, were he asked the question, would say he has long since forgotten that he ever saw, spoke with, or sat beside a creature, of so little signification as I am."

"This is a strange and unreasonable indulgence of a passion equally fanciful and dangerous," said the Lady Hermione.

"You will *not* assist me then?" said Margaret; "have good-day then, madam—my secret, I trust, is safe in such honourable keeping."

"Tarry yet a little," said the lady, "and tell me what resource you have to assist this youth, if you were supplied with money to put it in motion."

"It is superfluous to ask me the question, madam," answered Margaret, "unless you purpose to assist me; and if you do so purpose, it is still superfluous—you could not understand the means I must use, and time is too brief to explain."

"But have you in reality such means?" said the lady.

"I have, with the command of a moderate sum," answered Margaret Ramsay, "the power of baffling all his enemies—of eluding the passion of the irritated King—the colder but more determined displeasure of the Prince—the vindictive spirit of Buckingham, so hastily directed against whomsoever crosses the path of his ambition—the cold, concentrated malice of Lord Dalgarno—all, I can baffle them all!"

"But is this to be done without your own personal risk, Margaret?" replied the lady; "for be your purpose what it will, you are not to peril your own reputation or person, in the romantic attempt of serving another; and I, maiden, am answerable to your god-father,—to your benefactor, and my own,—not to aid you in any dangerous or unworthy enterprize."

"Depend upon my word,—my oath,—dearest lady," replied the suppliant, "that I will act by the agency of others, and do not myself design to mingle in any enterprize in which my appearance might be either perilous or unwomanly."

"I know not what to do," said the Lady Hermione; "it is perhaps incautious, inconsiderate in me to aid so wild a project; yet the end seems honourable, if the means be sure—what is the penalty if he fall into their hands?"

"Alas! alas! the loss of his right hand," replied Margaret, her voice almost stifled with sobs.

"Are the laws of England so cruel? then there is mercy in heaven alone," said the lady, "since, even in this free land, men are wolves to each other.—Compose yourself, Margaret, and tell me what money is necessary to secure Lord Glenvarloch's escape."

"Two hundred pieces," replied Margaret; "I would speak to you of restoring them—and I must one day have the power—only that I know —that is, I think—your ladyship is indifferent on that score."

"Not a word more of it," said the lady, "call Monna Paula hither."

Chapter Nine

Credit me, friend, it hath been ever thus,
Since the Ark rested on Mount Ararat.
False man hath sworn, and woman hath believed—
Repented and reproach'd, and then believed once more.
The New World

BY THE TIME that Margaret returned with Monna Paula, the Lady Hermione was rising from the table at which she had been engaged in writing something on a small slip of paper, which she gave to her attendant.

"Monna Paula," she said, "carry this paper to Roberts the cash-keeper; let him give you the money mentioned in the note, and bring it hither presently."

Monna Paula left the room, and her mistress proceeded:

"I do not know," she said, "Margaret, if I have done, and am doing, well in this affair. My life has been one of strange seclusion, and I am totally unacquainted with the practical ways of this world—an ignorance which I know cannot be remedied by mere reading.—I fear I am doing wrong to you, and perhaps to the laws of the country which affords me refuge, by thus indulging you—and yet there is something in my heart which cannot resist your entreaties."

"O, listen to it—listen to it—dear generous lady!" said Margaret, throwing herself on her knees and grasping those of her benefactress, and looking in that attitude like a beautiful mortal in the act of supplicating her tutelary angel; "the laws of men are but the injunctions of mortality, but what the heart prompts is the echo of the voice of heaven within us."

"Rise, rise, maiden," said Hermione; "you affect me more than I thought I could have been moved by aught that should approach me. Rise and tell me whence it comes, that, in so short a time, your thoughts, your looks, your speech, and even your slightest actions, are changed from those of a capricious and fanciful girl, to all this energy and impassioned eloquence of word and action?"

"I am sure I know not, dearest lady," said Margaret, looking down; "but I suppose that when I was a trifler, I was only thinking of trifles— what I now reflect is deep and serious, and I am thankful if my speech and manner bear reasonable proportion to my thoughts."

"It must be so," said the lady; "yet the change seems a rapid and strange one—it seems to be as if a childish girl had at once shot up into a deep-thinking and impassioned woman, ready to make exertions alike, and sacrifices, with all that vain devotion to a favoured object of affection, which is often so basely rewarded."

The Lady Hermione sighed bitterly, and Monna Paula entered ere the conversation proceeded further. She spoke to her mistress in the foreign language in which they frequently conversed, but which was unknown to Margaret.

"We must have patience for a time," said the lady to her visitor; "the cash-keeper is abroad on some business, but he is expected home in the course of half an hour."

Margaret wrung her hands in vexation and impatience.

"Minutes are precious," continued the lady, "that I am well aware of, and we will at least suffer none of them to escape us. Monna Paula shall remain below and transact our business, the very instant that Roberts returns home."

She spoke to her attendant accordingly, who again left the room.

"You are very kind, madam—very good," said the poor little Margaret, while the anxious trembling of her lip and of her hand shewed all that sickening agitation of the heart which arises from hope deferred.

"Be patient, Margaret, and collect yourself," said the lady; "you may—you must have much to do to carry through this your bold purpose—reserve your spirits, which you may need so much—be patient—it is our only remedy against the evils of life."

"Yes, madam," said Margaret, wiping her eyes, and endeavouring in vain to suppress the natural impatience of her temper.—"I have heard so—very often indeed; and I dare say I have myself—heaven forgive me—said so to people in perplexity and affliction; but it was before I had suffered perplexity and vexation myself—and I am sure I

will never preach patience to any human being again, now that I know
how much the medicine goes against the stomach."

"You will think better of it, maiden," said the Lady Hermione; "I
also, when I first felt distress, thought they did me wrong who spoke to
me of patience; but my sorrows have been repeated and continued till
I have been taught to cling to it as the best, and—religious duties
excepted, of which indeed patience forms a part,—the only alleviation
which life can afford them."

Margaret, who neither wanted sense or feeling, wiped her tears
hastily, and asked her patroness forgiveness for her petulance.

"I might have thought,—" she said, "I ought to have reflected, that
even from the manner of your life, madam, it is plain you must have
suffered sorrow; and yet, God knows, the patience which I have ever
seen you display, well entitles you to recommend your own example to
others."

The lady was silent for a moment, and then replied—

"Margaret, I am about to repose a high confidence in you. You are
no longer a child, but a thinking and a feeling woman—you have told
me as much of your secret as you dared—I will let you know as much
of mine as I may venture to tell. You will ask me, perhaps, why, at a
moment when your own mind is agitated, I should force upon you the
consideration of my sorrows? and I answer, that I cannot withstand
the impulse which now induces me to do so. Perhaps from having
witnessed, for the first time these three years, the natural effects of
human passion, my own sorrows have been awakened, and are for the
moment too big for my own bosom—perhaps I may hope that you,
who seem driving full sail on the very rock on which I was wrecked for
ever, will take warning by the tale I have to tell. Enough, if you are
willing to listen, I am willing to tell you who the melancholy inhabitant
of the Foljambe apartment really is, and why she resides here. It will
serve, at least, to while away the time until Monna Paula shall bring us
the reply from Roberts."

At any other moment of her life Margaret Ramsay would have
heard, with undivided interest, a communication so flattering in itself,
and referring to a subject upon which the general curiosity had been
so strongly excited. And even at this agitating moment, although she
ceased not to listen with an anxious ear and throbbing heart for the
sound of Monna Paula's returning footsteps, she nevertheless, as
gratitude and policy, as well as a portion of curiosity dictated, composed herself, in appearance at least, to the strictest attention to the
Lady Hermione, and thanked her with humility for the high confidence she was pleased to repose in her. The Lady Hermione, with the
same calmness which always attended her speech and actions, thus

recounted her story to her young friend:

"My father," she said, "was a merchant, but he was of a city whose merchants are princes. I am the daughter of a noble house in Genoa, whose name stood as high in honour and in antiquity, as any inscribed in the Golden Register of that famous aristocracy.

"My mother was a noble Scotswoman. She was descended—do not start—and not remotely descended, of the house of Glenvarloch—no wonder that I was easily led to take concern in the misfortunes of this young lord. He is my near relation, and my mother, who was more than sufficiently proud of her descent, early taught me to take an interest in the name. My maternal grandfather, a cadet of that house of Glenvarloch, had followed the fortunes of an unhappy fugitive, Francis Earl of Bothwell, who, after shewing his miseries in many a foreign court, at length settled in Spain upon a miserable pension, which he earned by conforming to the Catholic faith. Ralph Olifaunt, my grandfather, separated from him in disgust, and settled at Barcelona, where, by the friendship of the governor, his heresy, as it was termed, was connived at. My father, in the course of his commerce, resided more at Barcelona than in his native country, though at times he visited Genoa.

"It was at Barcelona that he became acquainted with my mother, loved her, and married her; they differed in faith, but they agreed in affection. I was their only child. In public I conformed to the doctrines and ceremonial of the church of Rome; but my mother, by whom these were regarded with horror, privately trained me up in those of the reformed religion; and my father, either indifferent in the matter, or unwilling to distress the woman whom he loved, overlooked or connived at my secretly joining in her devotions.

"But when, unhappily, my father was attacked, while yet in the prime of life, by a slow wasting disease, which he felt to be incurable, he foresaw the hazard to which his widow and orphan might be exposed, after he was no more, in a country so bigotted to Catholicism as Spain. He made it his business, during the two last years of his life, to realize and to remit to England a large part of his fortune, which, by the faith and honour of his correspondent, the excellent man under whose roof I now reside, was employed to great advantage. Had my father lived to complete his purpose, by withdrawing his whole fortune from commerce, he himself would have accompanied us to England, and would have beheld us settled in peace and honour before his death. But Heaven had ordained it otherwise. He died, leaving several sums engaged in the hands of his Spanish debtors; and, in particular, he had made a large and extensive consignment to a certain wealthy society of merchants at Madrid, who shewed no willingness after his death to account for the proceeds. Would to God we had left these covetous and wicked men in possession of their booty, for such they seemed to hold the property of their deceased correspondent and friend: we had enough for comfort, and even splendour, already secured in England; but friends exclaimed upon the folly of permitting these unprincipled men to plunder us of our rightful property. The sum itself was large, and the claim having been made, my mother thought that my father's memory was interested in its being enforced, especially as the defences set up for the mercantile society went, in some degree, to impeach the fairness of his transactions.

"We went therefore to Madrid—I was then, my Margaret, about your age—young and thoughtless, as you have hitherto been—we went, I say, to Madrid, to solicit the protection of the Court and of the King, without which we were told it would be in vain to expect justice against an opulent and powerful association.

"Our residence at the Spanish metropolis drew on from weeks to months. For my part, my natural sorrow for a kind, though not a fond father, having abated, I cared not if the law-suit had detained us at Madrid for ever. My mother permitted herself and me rather more liberty than we had been accustomed to. She found relations among the Scottish and Irish officers, many of whom held a high rank in the Spanish armies; their wives and daughters became our friends and companions, and I had perpetual occasion to exercise my mother's native language, which I had learned from my infancy. By degrees, as my mother's spirits were low, and her health indifferent, she was induced, by her partial fondness for me, to suffer me to mingle occasionally in society which she herself did not frequent, under the guardianship of such ladies as she imagined she could trust, and particularly under the care of the lady of a general officer, whose weakness or falsehood was the original cause of my misfortunes. I was as gay, Margaret, and thoughtless—I again repeat it—as you were but lately—and my attention, like yours, became suddenly rivetted to one object, and to one set of feelings.

"The person by whom they were excited was young, noble, handsome, accomplished, a soldier, and a Briton. So far our cases are nearly parallel; but, may Heaven forbid that the parallel should become complete! This man, so noble, so fairly formed, so gifted, and so brave—this *villain*, for that, Margaret, was his fittest name, spoke of love to me, and I listened—could I suspect his sincerity? If he was wealthy, noble, and long-descended, I also was a noble and an opulent heiress. It is true, that he neither knew the extent of my father's wealth, nor did I communicate to him (I do not even remember if I myself knew it at the time) the important circumstance, that the greater part of that wealth was beyond the grasp of arbitrary power, and not subject to the precarious award of arbitrary judges. My lover might think, perhaps, as my mother was desirous the world at large should believe, that almost our whole fortune depended on the precarious suit which we had come to Madrid to prosecute—a belief which she countenanced out of policy, being well aware that the knowledge of my father's having remitted such a large part of his fortune to England, would in no shape aid the recovery of further sums in the Spanish courts. Yet, with no more extensive views of my fortune than were possessed by the public, I believe that He of whom I am speaking, was at first sincere in his pretensions. He had himself interest sufficient to have obtained a decision in our favour in the courts, and my fortune, reckoning only what was in Spain, would then have been no inconsiderable sum. To be brief, whatever might be his motives or temptation for so far committing himself, he applied to my mother for my hand, with my consent and avowal.

"My mother's judgment had become weaker, but her passions had become more irritable during her increasing illness. You have heard of the bitterness of the ancient Scottish feuds, of which it may be said, in the language of Scripture, that the fathers eat sour grapes, and the teeth of the children are set on edge. Unhappily, I should say *happily*, considering what this man has now shewn himself, some such strain of bitterness had divided his house from my mother's, and she had succeeded to the inheritance of hatred. When he asked her for my hand, she was no longer able to command her passions—she raked up every injury which the rival families had inflicted upon each other during a blood-feud of two centuries—heaped him with epithets of scorn, and rejected his proposal of alliance as if it had come from the basest of mankind.

"My lover retired in passion; and I remained to weep and murmur against fortune, and—I will confess my fault—against my affectionate parent. I had been educated with different feelings, and the traditions of the feuds and quarrels of my mother's family in Scotland, which were to her monuments and chronicles, seemed to me as insignificant and unmeaning as the actions and fantasies of Don Quixote; and I blamed my mother bitterly for sacrificing my happiness to an empty dream of family dignity.

"While I was in this humour, my lover sought a renewal of our intercourse. We met repeatedly in the house of the lady whom I have mentioned, and who, in levity, or in the spirit of intrigue, countenanced our secret correspondence. At length we were secretly married —so far did my blinded passion hurry me. My lover had secured the assistance of a clergyman of the English church. Monna Paula, who had been my attendant from infancy, was one witness of our union. Let me do the faithful creature justice—She conjured me to suspend my purpose till my mother's death should permit us to celebrate our marriage openly; but the entreaties of my lover, and my own wayward passion, prevailed over her remonstrances. The lady I have spoken of was another witness, but whether she was in full possession of my bridegroom's secret, I had never the means to learn. But the shelter of her name and roof afforded us the means of frequently meeting, and the love of my husband seemed as sincere and as unbounded as my own.

"He was eager, he said, to gratify his pride, by introducing me to one or two of his noble English friends. This could not be done at Lady D——'s; but by his command, which I was now entitled to consider as my law, I contrived twice to visit him at his own hotel, accompanied only by Monna Paula. There was a very small party of two ladies and two gentlemen. There was music, mirth, and dancing. I had heard of the frankness of the English nation, but I could not help thinking it bordered on license during these entertainments, and in the course of the collation which followed; but I imputed my scruples to my inexperience, and would not doubt the propriety of what was approved by my husband.

"I was soon summoned to other scenes—which I must describe very hastily: My poor mother's disease drew to a conclusion—happy I am that it took place before she discovered what would have cut her to the soul.

"In Spain you may have heard how the Catholic priests, and particularly the monks, besiege the beds of the dying, to obtain bequests for the good of the church. I have said that my mother's temper was irritated by disease, and her judgment impaired in proportion. She gathered spirits and force from the resentment which the priests around her bed excited by their importunity, and the spirit of the stern sect of reformers, to which she had secretly adhered, seemed to animate her dying tongue. She avowed the religion she had so long concealed; renounced all hope and aid which did not come by and through its dictates; rejected with contempt the ceremonial of the Romish church; loaded the astonished priests with reproaches for their greediness and hypocrisy, and commanded them to leave her house. They went in bitterness and rage, but it was to return with the inquisitorial power, its warrants, and its officers; and they found only the cold corpse left of her, on whom they had hoped to work their vengeance. As I was soon discovered to have shared my mother's heresy, I was dragged from her dead body, imprisoned in a solitary cloister, and treated with severity, which the Abbess assured me was

due to the looseness of my life, as well as my spiritual errors.
I avowed my marriage, to justify the situation in which I found myself
—I implored the assistance of the Superior to communicate my situation to my husband. She smiled coldly at the proposal, and told me
the church had provided a better spouse for me; advised me to secure
myself of divine grace hereafter, and deserve milder treatment here,
by presently taking the veil. In order to convince that I had no other
resource, she shewed me a royal decree, by which all my estate was
hypothecated to the Convent of Saint Magdalen, and became their
complete property upon my death, or my taking the vows. As I was,
both from religious principle, and affectionate attachment to my husband, absolutely immoveable in my rejection of the veil, I believe—
may Heaven forgive me if I wrong her!—that the Abbess was desirous
to make sure of my spoils, by hastening the former event.

"It was a small and a poor convent, situated among the mountains of
Guadarrama. Some of the sisters were the daughters of neighbouring
Hidalgos, as poor as they were proud and ignorant; others were
women immured there on account of their vicious conduct. The
Superior herself was of a high family, to which she owed her situation;
but she was said to have disgraced her connections by her conduct
during youth, and now, in advanced age, covetousness and the love of
power, a spirit too of severity and cruelty, had succeeded to the thirst
after licentious pleasure. I suffered much under this woman—and still
her dark glassy eye, her tall shrouded form, and her rigid features,
haunt my slumbers.

"I was not destined to be a mother. I was very ill, and my recovery
was long and doubtful—the most violent remedies were applied
—if remedies they indeed were—my health was restored at length—
against my own expectation and that of all around me. But when I first
again beheld the reflection of my own face, I thought it was the visage
of a ghost. I was wont to be flattered by all, but particularly by my
husband, for the fineness of my complexion—it was now totally gone,
and what is more extraordinary, it has never returned. I have observed
that the few who now see me, look upon me as a bloodless phantom—
Such has been the abiding effect of the treatment to which I was
subjected. May God forgive those who were the agents of it!—I thank
heaven I can say so with as sincere a wish, as that with which I pray for
forgiveness of my own sins. They now relented somewhat towards me
—moved perhaps to compassion by my singular appearance, which
bore witness to my sufferings; or afraid that the matter might attract
attention during a visitation of the bishop, which was approaching.
One day, as I was walking in the convent-garden, to the freedom of
which I had been lately admitted, a miserable old Moorish slave, who

was kept to cultivate the little spot, muttered as I passed him, but still keeping his wrinkled face and decrepit form in the same angle with the earth—'There is Heart's Ease near the postern.'

"I knew something of the symbolical language of flowers, once carried to such perfection among the Moriscoes of Spain; but if I had been ignorant of it, the captive would soon have caught at any hint that seemed to promise liberty. With all the haste consistent with the utmost circumspection, for I might be observed by the Abbess or some of the sisters from the window, I hastened to the postern—it was closely barred as usual, but when I coughed slightly, I was answered from the other side—and O, heaven! it was my husband's voice which said, 'Lose not a minute here at present, but be on this spot when the vesper bell has tolled.'

"I retired in an ecstacy of joy. I was not entitled or permitted to assist at vespers, but was accustomed to be confined to my cell while the nuns were in the choir. Since my recovery, they had discontinued locking the door; though the utmost severity was denounced against me if I left these precincts. But let the penalty be what it would, I hastened to dare it.—No sooner had the last toll of the vesper bell ceased to sound, than I stole from my chamber, reached the garden unobserved, hurried to the postern, beheld it open with rapture, and in the next moment was in my husband's arms. He had with him another cavalier of noble mien—both were masked and armed. Their horses, with one saddled for my use, stood in a thicket hard by, with two other masked horsemen who seemed to be servants—in less than two minutes we were mounted, and rode off as fast as we could, through rough and devious roads, in which one of the domestics appeared to act as guide.

"The hurried pace at which we rode, and the anxiety of the moment, kept me silent, and prevented my expressing my surprise or my joy save in a few broken words. It also served as an apology for my husband's silence. At length we stopped at a solitary hut—the cavaliers dismounted, and I was assisted from my saddle, not by M—— M—— my husband I would say, who seemed busied about his horse, but by the stranger.

"'Go into the hut,' said my husband, 'change your dress with the speed of lightning—you will find one to assist you—we must forward instantly when you have shifted your apparel.'

"I entered the hut, and was received in the arms of the faithful Monna Paula, who had waited my arrival for many hours, half distracted with fear and anxiety. With her assistance I speedily tore off the detested garments of the convent, and exchanged them for a travelling suit, made after the English fashion. I observed that Monna

Paula was in a similar dress. I had but just huddled on my change of attire, when we were hastily summoned to mount. A horse, I found, was provided for Monna Paula, and we resumed our route. On the way, my convent-garb, which had been wrapped hastily together around a stone, was thrown into a lake, along the verge of which we were then passing. The two cavaliers rode together in front, my attendant and I followed, and the servants brought up the rear. Monna Paula, as we rode on, repeatedly entreated me to be silent upon the road, as our lives depended on it. I was easily reconciled to be passive, for, the first fever of spirits which attended the sense of liberation and of gratified affection having passed away, I felt as it were dizzy with the rapid motion; and my utmost exertion was necessary to keep my place on the saddle, until we suddenly (it was now very dark,) saw a strong light before us.

"My husband reined up his horse, and gave a signal by a low whistle twice repeated, which was answered from a distance. The whole party then halted under the boughs of a large cork-tree, and my husband, drawing himself close to my side, said, in a voice which I then thought was only embarrassed by fear for my safety,—'We must now part— those to whom I commit you are *contrabandists*, who only know you as Englishwomen, whom, for a high bribe, they have undertaken to escort through the passes of the Pyrenees as far as Saint Jean de Luz.'

"'And do not you go with us?' I exclaimed with emphasis, though in a whisper.

"'It is impossible,' he said, 'and would ruin all—See that you speak no Spanish in these people's hearing, and give not the least sign of understanding what they say—your life depends on it; for, though they live by opposition to and evasion of the laws of Spain, they would tremble at the idea of violating those of the church—I see them coming—farewell—farewell.'

"The last words were hastily uttered—I endeavoured to detain him yet a moment by my feeble grasp on his cloak.

"'You will meet me then,' I said, 'at Saint Jean de Luz?'

"'Yes—yes,' he answered hastily, 'at Saint Jean de Luz you will meet your protector.'

"He then extricated his cloak from my grasp, and was lost in the darkness. His companion approached—kissed my hand—which in the agony of the moment I was scarce sensible of—and followed my husband, attended by one of the domestics."

The tears of Hermione here flowed so fast as to threaten the interruption of her narrative.—When she resumed it, it was with a kind of apology to Margaret.

"Every circumstance," she said, "occurring in these moments when

I still enjoyed a delusive idea of happiness, is deeply imprinted in my remembrance, which, respecting all that has since happened, is waste and unvaried as an Arabian desert. But I have no right to inflict on you, Margaret, agitated as you are with your own anxieties, the unavailing details of my useless recollections."

Margaret's eyes were full of tears—it was impossible it could be otherwise, considering that the tale was told by her suffering bene- factress, and resembled, in some respects, her own situation; and yet she must not be severely blamed, if, while eagerly pressing her patron- ess to continue her narrative, her eye involuntarily sought the door, as if to chide the delay of Monna Paula.

The Lady Hermione saw and forgave these conflicting emotions. And she, too, must be pardoned, if, in her turn, the minute detail of her narrative shewed, that, in the discharge of feelings so long locked in her own bosom, she rather forgot those personal to her auditor, and by which it must be supposed Margaret's mind was principally occu- pied, if not entirely engrossed.

"I told you, I think, that one domestic followed the gentlemen," thus the lady continued her story, "the other remained with us for the purpose, as it seemed, of introducing us to two persons whom M—— I say whom my husband's signal had brought to the spot. A word or two of explanation passed between them and the servant, in a sort of *patois*, which I did not understand; and one of the strangers taking hold of my bridle, the other of Monna Paula's, they led us towards the light, which I have already said was the signal for our halting. I touched Monna Paula, and was sensible that she trembled very much, which surprised me, because I knew her character to be so strong and bold as to border upon the masculine.

"When we reached the fire, the gipsey figures of those who sur- rounded it, with their swarthy features, large Sombrero hats, girdles stuck full of pistols and poniards, and all the other apparatus of a roving and perilous life, would have terrified me at another moment. But then I only felt the agony of having parted from my husband almost in the very moment of my rescue. The females of the gang, for there were four or five women amongst these counterband traders, received us with a sort of rude courtesy. They were, in dress and manners, not extremely different from the men with whom they associated—were almost as hardy and adventurous, carried arms like them, and were, as we learned from passing circumstances, scarce less experienced in the use of them.

"It was impossible not to fear these wild people, yet they gave us no reason to complain of them; but used us on all occasions with a kind of clumsy courtesy, accommodating themselves to our wants and our weakness during the journey, even while we heard them grumbling to each other against our effeminacy,—like some rude carrier, who, in charge of a package of valuable and fragile ware, takes every precaution for its preservation, while he curses the unwonted trouble which it occasions to him. Once or twice, when they were disappointed in their contraband traffic, lost some goods in a rencontre with the Spanish officers of the revenue, and were finally pursued by a military force, their murmurs assumed a more alarming tone, in the terrified ears of my attendant and myself, when, without daring to seem to understand them, we heard them curse the insular heretics, on whose account God, Saint James, and our Lady of the Pillar, had blighted their hopes of profit. These are dreadful recollections, Margaret."

"Why, then, dearest lady," answered Margaret, "will you thus dwell on them?"

"It is only," said the Lady Hermione, "because I linger like a criminal on the scaffold, and would fain protract the time that must inevitably bring on the final catastrophe. Yes, dearest Margaret, I rest and dwell on the events of that journey, marked as it was by fatigue and danger, though the road lay through the wildest and most desolate deserts and mountains, and though our companions, both men and women, were fierce and lawless themselves, and exposed to the most merciless retaliation from those with whom they were constantly engaged—yet I would rather dwell on these hazardous events than tell that which awaited me at Saint Jean de Luz."

"You arrived there in safety?" said Margaret.

"Yes, maiden," answered the Lady Hermione; "and were guided by the chief of our outlawed band to the house which had been assigned for our reception, with the same punctilious accuracy with which he would have delivered a bale of uncustomed goods to a correspondent. I was told a gentleman had expected me for two days—I rushed into the apartment, and when I expected to embrace my husband—I found myself in the arms of his friend."

"The villain!" exclaimed Margaret, whose anxiety had, in spite of herself, been a moment suspended by the narrative of the lady.

"Yes," replied Hermione, calmly, though her voice somewhat faultered, "it is the name that best—that well befits him. He, Margaret, for whom I had sacrificed all—whose love and whose memory were dearer to me than my freedom, when I was in the convent—than my life, when I was on my perilous journey—had taken his measures to shake me off, and transfer me, as a privileged wanton, to the protection of his libertine friend. At first, the stranger laughed at my tears and my agony, as the hysterical passion of a deluded and over-reached wanton, or the wily affectation of a courtezan. My claim of marriage he laughed at, assuring me he knew it was a mere farce required by me, and submitted to by his friend, to save some reserve of delicacy; and expressed his surprise that I should consider in any other light a ceremony which could be valid neither in Spain or England, and insultingly offered to remove my scruples, by renewing such a union with me himself. My exclamations brought Monna Paula to my aid—she was not indeed far distant, for she had expected some such scene."

"Good Heaven!" said Margaret, "was she a confidante of your base husband?"

"No," answered Hermione, "do her not that injustice. It was her persevering inquiries that discovered the place of my confinement—it was she who gave the information to my husband, and who remarked even then that the news was so much more interesting to his friend than to him, that she suspected, from an early period, it was the purpose of the villain to shake me off. On the journey, her suspicions were confirmed. She had heard him remark to his companion, with a cold sarcastic sneer, the total change which my prison and my illness had made on my complexion; and she had heard the other reply, that the defect might be cured by a touch of Spanish red. This and other circumstances having prepared her for such treachery, Monna Paula now entered, completely possessed of herself, and prepared to support me. Her calm representations went farther with the stranger than the expressions of my despair—if he did not entirely believe our tale, he at least acted the part of a man of honour, who would not intrude himself on defenceless females, whatever was their character; desisted from persecuting us with his presence; and not only directed Monna Paula how we should journey to Paris, but furnished her with money for the purposes of our journey. From that capital I wrote to Master Heriot, my father's most trusted correspondent; he came instantly to Paris on receiving the letter, and——But here comes Monna Paula, with more than the sum you desired. Take it, my dearest maiden—serve this youth if you will—but, O Margaret, look for no gratitude in return!"

The Lady Hermione took the bag of gold from her attendant, and gave it to her young friend, who threw herself into her arms, kissed her on both the pale cheeks over which the sorrows so newly awakened by her narrative had drawn many tears, then sprung up, wiped her own overflowing eyes, and left the Foljambe apartment with a hasty and resolved step.

Chapter Ten

Rove not from pole to pole—the man lives here
Whose razor's only equall'd by his beer;
And where, in either sense, the cockney-put
May, if he pleases, get confounded *cut*.
On the sign of an Alehouse kept by a Barber

WE ARE UNDER the necessity of transporting our readers to the habitation of Benjamin Suddlechop, the husband of the active and efficient Dame Ursula, and who also, in his own person, discharged more offices than one. For, besides trimming locks and beards, and turning whiskers upwards into the martial and swaggering curl, or downwards into the drooping form which became mustachios of civil policy; besides also occasionally letting blood, either by cupping or by the lancet, extracting a stump, and performing other actions of petty pharmacy, very nearly as well as his neighbour Raredrench, the apothecary; he could, on occasion, draw a cup of beer as well as a tooth, tap a hogshead as well as a vein, and wash, with a draught of good ale, the whiskers which his art had just trimmed. But he carried on these trades apart from each other.

His barber's shop projected its long and mysterious pole into Fleet-Street, painted party-coloured-wise, to represent the ribbons with which, in elder times, that ensign was garnished. In the window were seen rows of teeth displayed upon strings like rosaries—cups with a red rag at the bottom, to resemble blood, an intimation that patients might be bled, cupped, or blistered, with the assistance of "sufficient advice;" while the more profitable, but less honourable operations upon the hair of the head and beard, were briefly and gravely announced. Within was the well-worn leathern chair for customers, the guitar, then called a ghittern or cittern, with which a customer might amuse himself till his predecessor was dismissed from under Benjamin's hands, and which, therefore, often flayed the ears of the patient metaphorically, while his chin sustained from the razor literal scarification. All, therefore, in this department, spoke the chirurgeon-barber, or the barber-chirurgeon.

But there was a little back room, used as a private tap-room, which had a separate entrance by a dark and crooked alley, which communicated with Fleet-Street, after a circuitous passage through several bye-lanes and courts. This retired temple of Bacchus had also a connection with Benjamin's more public shop by a long and narrow entrance, conducting to the secret premises in which a few old topers used to take their morning draught, and a few gill-sippers their mod-

icum of strong waters, in a bashful way, after having entered the
barber's shop under pretence of desiring to be shaved. Besides, this
obscure tap-room gave a separate admission to the apartments of
Dame Ursley, which she was believed to make use of in the course of
her multifarious practice, both to let herself secretly out, and to admit
clients and employers who cared not to be seen to visit her in public.
Accordingly, after the hour of noon, by which time the modest and
timid whetters, who were Benjamin's best customers, had each had
his draught, or his thimble-full, the business of the tap was in a
manner ended, and the charge of attending the back-door passed
from one of the barber's apprentices to the little mulatto girl, the dingy
Iris of Dame Suddlechop. Then came mystery thick upon mystery;
muffled gallants, and masked females, in disguises of different fashions, were seen to glide through the intricate mazes of the alley; and
even the low tap on the door, which frequently demanded the attention of the little Creole, had in it something that expressed secrecy and
fear of discovery.

It was the evening of the same day when Margaret had held her long
conference with the Lady Hermione, that Dame Suddlechop had
directed her little portress to "keep the door fast as a miser's purse-
strings; and as she valued her saffron skin, to let in none but—" the
name she added in a whisper, and accompanied it with a nod. The
little animal blinked intelligence, went to her post, and in brief time
thereafter admitted and ushered into the presence of the dame, that
very city-gallant whose clothes sate awkwardly upon him, and who had
behaved so doughtily in the fray which befel at Nigel's first visit
to Beaujeu's ordinary. The mulatto introduced him—"Missis, fine
young gentleman all over gold and velvet"—then muttered to herself
as she shut the door, "fine gentleman he!—apprentice to him makes
the tick-tick."

It was indeed—we are sorry to say it, and trust our readers will
sympathize with the interest we take in the matter—it was indeed
honest Jin Vin, who had been so far left to his own devices, and
abandoned by his better angel, as occasionally to travestie himself in
this fashion, and to visit, in the dress of a gallant of the day, those
places of pleasure and dissipation, in which it would have been ever-
lasting discredit to him to have been seen in his real character and
condition; that is, had it been possible for him in his proper shape to
have gained admission. There was now a deep gloom on his brow, his
rich habit was hastily put on and buttoned awry; his belt buckled in
most disorderly fashion, so that his sword stuck outwards from his
side, instead of hanging by it with graceful negligence; while his
poniard, though fairly hatched and gilded, stuck in his girdle, like a

butcher's steel in the fold of his blue apron. Persons of fashion had, by the way, the advantage formerly of being better distinguished from the vulgar than at present; for, what the ancient farthingale and more modern hoop were to court ladies, the sword was to the gentlemen; an article of dress, which only rendered those ridiculous who assumed it for the nonce, without being in the habit of wearing it. Vincent's rapier got between his legs, and as he stumbled over it, he exclaimed —"Zounds! 'tis the second time it has served me thus—I believe the damned trinket knows I am no true gentleman, and does it of set purpose."

"Come, come, mine honest Jin Vin—come, my good boy," said the dame in a soothing tone, "never mind these trankums—a frank and hearty London 'prentice is worth all the gallants of the inns of court."

"I *was* a frank and hearty 'prentice before I knew you, Dame Suddlechop," said Vincent; "what your advice has made me, ye may find a name for; since, fore George! I am ashamed to think about it myself."

"A well-a-day," quoth the dame, "and is it even so with thee?—nay then, I know but one cure;" and with that, going to a little corner cupboard of carved wainscoat, she opened it by the assistance of a key, which, with half a dozen besides, hung in a silver chain at her girdle, and produced a long flask of thin glass cased with wicker, bringing forth at the same time two Flemish rummer glasses, with long stalks and capacious wombs. She filled the one brimful for her guest, and the other more modestly to about two-thirds of its capacity, for her own use, repeating, as the rich cordial trickled forth in a smooth oily stream—"Right Rosa Solis, as ever washed mulligrubs out of a moody brain."

But though Jin Vin tossed off his glass without scruple, while the lady sipped her's more moderately, it did not appear to produce the expected amendment upon his humour. On the contrary, as he threw himself into the great leathern chair, in which Dame Ursley was wont to solace herself of an evening, he declared himself "the most miserable dog within the sound of Bow-bell."

"And why should you be so idle as to think yourself so, you silly boy?" said Dame Suddlechop; "but 'tis always thus—fools and children never know when they are well. Why, there is not a one who walks in Paul's, whether in flat cap, or hat and feather, that has so many kind glances from the wenches, as ye swagger along Fleet-street with your bat under your arm, and your cap set aside upon your head. Thou knowst well, that from Mrs Deputy's self down to the wastcoateers in the alley, all of them are twiring and peeping betwixt their fingers when you pass; and yet you call yourself a miserable dog! and I must tell you all this over and over again, as if I were whistling the chimes of London to a petted child, in order to bring the pretty baby into good humour!"

The flattery of Dame Ursley seemed to have the fate of her cordial —it was swallowed indeed by the party to whom she presented it, and that with some degree of relish, but it did not operate as a sedative on the disturbed state of the youth's mind. He laughed for an instant, half in scorn and half in gratified vanity, but cast a sullen look on Dame Ursley as he replied to her last words.

"You do treat me like a child indeed, when you sing over and over to me a cuckoo song that I care not a copper-filing for."

"Aha!" said Dame Ursley; "that is to say, you care not if you please all, unless you please one—You are a true lover I warrant, and care not for all the city from here to Whitechapel, so you could write yourself first in your pretty Peg-a-Ramsay's good will—well, well—take patience, man, and be guided by me, for I will be the hoop will bind you together at last."

"It's time you were so," said Jenkin, "for hitherto you have been the wedge to separate us."

Dame Suddlechop had by this time finished her cordial—it was not the first she had taken that day; and though a woman of strong brain, and cautious at least, if not quite abstemious, in her potations, it may nevertheless be supposed that her patience was not improved by the regimen which she observed.

"Why, thou ungracious and ingrate knave," said Dame Ursley, "have not I done every thing to put thee in thy mistress's good graces? She loves gentry, the proud Scotch minx, as a Welsh-man loves cheese, and has her father's descent from that Duke of Daldevil, or whatsoever she calls him, as close in her heart as gold in a miser's chest, though she as seldom shews it—and none will she think of or have but a gentleman—and a gentleman I have made of thee, Jin Vin, the devil cannot deny that."

"You have made a fool of me," said poor Jenkin, looking at the sleeve of his jacket.

"Never the worse gentleman for that," said Dame Ursley, laughing.

"And what is worse," said he, turning his back to her suddenly, and writhing in his chair, "you have made a rogue of me."

"Never the worse gentleman for that neither," said Dame Ursley in the same tone; "let a man bear his folly gaily and his knavery stoutly, and let me see if gravity or honesty will look him in the face now-a-days—tut, man, it was only in the days of King Arthur or King Lud, that a gentleman was held to blemish his scutcheon by a leap over the line of reason or honesty—it is the bold look, the ready hand, the fine clothes, the brisk oath, and the wild brain, that makes the gallant now-a-day."

"I know what they have made me," said Jin Vin; "since I have given up skittles and trap-ball for tennis and bowls, good English ale for thin Bourdeaux and sour Rhenish, roast-beef and pudding for wood-cocks and kick-shaws—my bat for a sword, my cap for a beaver, my forsooth for a modish oath, my Christmas-box for a dice-box, my religion for the devil's mattins, and mine honest name for —— Woman, I could brain thee, when I think whose advice has guided me in all this!"

"Whose advice, then? whose advice, then? speak out, thou poor petty cloak-brusher, and say who advised thee!" retorted Dame Urs-ley, flushed and indignant—"Marry come up, my paltry companion—say by whose advice you have made a gamester of yourself, and a thief beside, as your words would bear—The Lord deliver us from evil!" And here Dame Ursley devoutly crossed herself.

"Hark ye, Dame Ursley Suddlechop," said Jenkin, starting up, his dark eyes flashing with anger; "remember I am none of your husband—and if I were, you would do well not to forget *whose* threshold was swept when they last rode the Skimmington* upon such another scolding jade as yourself."

"I hope to see ye ride up Holborn next," said Dame Ursley, pro-voked out of all her holiday and sugar-plum expressions, "with a nosegay at your breast, and a priest at your elbow."

"That may well be," answered Jin Vin bitterly, "if I walk by your counsels as I have begun by them; but before that day comes, you shall know that Jin Vin has the brisk boys of Fleet-street still at his wink—Yes, you jade, you shall be carted for bawd and conjuror, double dyed in grain, and bing off to Bridewell, with every brass basin betwixt the Bar and Paul's, beating before you, as if the devil were banging them with his beef-hook."

Dame Ursley coloured like scarlet, seized upon the half-emptied flask of cordial, and seemed, by her first gesture, about to hurl it at the head of her adversary; but suddenly, and as if by a strong internal effort, she checked her outrageous resentment, and putting the bottle

---

* A species of triumphal procession in honour of female supremacy, when it rose to such a height as to attract the attention of the neighbourhood. It is described at full length in Hudibras, (*Part II. Canto II.*) As the procession passed on, those who attended it in an official capacity were wont to sweep the threshold of the houses in which Fame affirmed the mistresses to exercise paramount authority, which was given and received as a hint that their inmates might, in their turn, be made the subject of a similar ovation. The Skim-mington, which in some degree resembled the proceeding of Mumbo Jumbo in an African village, has been long discontinued in England, apparently because female rule has become either milder or less frequent than among our ancestors.

to its more legitimate use, filled, with wonderful composure, the two glasses, and taking up one of them, said with a smile, which better became her comely and jovial countenance than the fury by which it was animated the moment before—

"Here is to thee, Jin Vin, my lad, in all loving kindness, whatever spite thou bearst to me, that have always been a mother to thee."

Jenkin's English good nature could not resist this forcible appeal; he took up the other glass, and lovingly pledged the dame in her cup of reconciliation, and proceeded to make a kind of grumbling apology for his own violence—

"For you know," he said, "it was you persuaded me to get these fine things, and go to that godless ordinary, and ruffle it with the best, and bring you home all the news—and you said, I, that was the cock of the ward, would soon be cock of the ordinary, and would win ten times as much at gleek and primero, as I used to do at put and beggar-my-neighbour, and turn up doublets with the dice, as busily as I was wont to trowl down the nine-pins in the skittle-ground—and then you said I should bring you such news out of the ordinary as should make us all, when used as you knew how to use it—And now you see what is come of it all."

"'Tis all true thou sayest, lad," said the dame; "but thou must have patience. Rome was not built in a day—you cannot become used to your court-suit in a month's time, any more than when you changed your long coat for a doublet and hose; and in gaming you must expect to lose as well as gain—'tis the sitting gamester sweeps the board."

"The board has swept me, I know," replied Jin Vin, "and that pretty clean out.—I would that were the worst; but I owe for all this finery—and settling-day is coming on—and my master will find my accompt worse than it should be, by a score of pieces—my old father will be called in to make them good—and I—may save the hang-man a labour and do the job myself, or go the Virginia voyage."

"Do not speak so loud, my dear boy," said Dame Ursley; "but tell me why you borrow not from a friend to make up your arrear. You could lend him as much when his settling-day came around."

"No, no—I have had enough of that work," said Vincent. "Tunstall would lend me the money, poor fellow, an he had it; but his gentle, beggarly kindred plunder him of all, and keep him as bare as a birch at Christmas—no—my fortune may be spelt in four letters, and these read, RUIN."

"Now hush, you simple craven," said the dame; "did you never hear, that when the need is highest the help is nighest?—we may find aid for you yet, and sooner than you are aware of. I am sure I would never have advised you to such a course, but only you had set heart and eye on pretty Mistress Marget, and less would not serve you—and what could I do but advise you to cast your city-slough, and try your luck where folks find fortune?"

"Ay—ay—I remember your counsel well," said Jenkin; "I was to be introduced to her by you when I was perfect in my gallantries, and as rich as the King; and then she was to be surprised to find I was poor Jin Vin, that used to watch from mattin to curfew, for one glance of her eye; and now, instead of that, she has set her soul on this Scotch Sparrow-hawk of a lord that won my last tester, and be cursed to him; and so I am bankrupt in love, fortune, and character, before I am out of my time, and all along of you, Mother Midnight."

"Do not call me out of my own name, my dear boy, Jin Vin," answered Ursula, in a tone betwixt rage and coaxing; "do not; because I am no saint, but a poor sinful woman, with no more patience than she needs to carry her through a thousand crosses—And if I have done you wrong by evil counsel, I must mend it, and put you right by good advice—And, for the score of pieces that must be made up at settling-day, why, here is, in a good green purse, as much as will make that matter good, and we will get old Crosspatch the tailor take a long day for your clothes—and"——

"Mother, are you serious?" said Jin Vin, unable to trust either his eyes or his ears.

"In troth am I," said the dame; "and will you call me Mother Midnight now, Jin Vin?"

"Mother Midnight?" exclaimed Jenkin, hugging the dame in his transport, and bestowing on her still comely cheek a hearty and not unacceptable smack, that sounded like the report of a pistolet— "Mother Mid-day rather, that has risen to light me out of my troubles —a mother more dear than she who bore me; for she, poor soul, only brought me into a world of sin and sorrow, and your timely aid has helped me out of the one and the other." And the good-natured fellow threw himself back in his chair, and fairly drew his hand across his eyes.

"You would not have me be made to ride the Skimmington then," said the dame, "or parade me in a cart with all the brass basins of the ward beating the march to Bridewell before me?"

"I would sooner be carted to Tyburn myself," replied the penitent.

"Why, then, sit up like a man, and wipe thine eyes; and if thou art pleased with what I have done, I will shew thee how thou mayest requite me in the highest degree."

"How?" said Jenkin Vincent, sitting straight up in his chair. "You would have me, then, do you some service for this friendship of yours?"

"Ay, marry would I," said Dame Ursley; "for you are to know, that although I am right glad to stead you with it, this gold is not mine, but was placed in my hands in order to find a trusty agent, for a certain purpose; and so—but what's the matter with you?—are you fool enough to be angry because you cannot get a purse of gold for nothing? I would I knew where such were to come by. I never could find them lying in my road, I promise you."

"No, no, dame," said poor Jenkin, "it is not for that; for, look you, I would rather work these ten bones to the knuckles, and live by my labour, but——" (and there he paused.)

"But what, man?" said Dame Ursley; "you are willing to work for what you want, and yet when I offer you gold for the winning, you look on me as the Devil looks over Lincoln."

"It is ill talking of the devil, mother," said Jenkin. "I had him even now in my head—for, look you, I am at that pass when they say he will appear to wretched ruined creatures, and proffer them gold for the fee-simple of their salvation. But I have been trying these two days to bring my mind strongly up to the thought, that I will rather sit down in shame, and sin, and sorrow, as I am like to do, than hold on in ill courses to get rid of my present straits; and so take care, Dame Ursula, how you tempt me to break such a good resolution."

"I tempt you to nothing, young man," answered Ursula; "and as I perceive you are too wilful to be wise, I will e'en put my purse in my pocket, and look out for some one that will work my turn with better will and more thankfulness. And you may go your own course,—break your indenture, ruin your father, lose your character, and bid pretty Mistress Marget farewell, for ever and a day."

"Stay, stay," said Jenkin; "the woman is in as great a hurry as a brown baker when his oven is overheated. First, let me hear that which you have to propose to me."

"Why, after all, it is but to get a gentleman of rank and fortune, who is in trouble, carried in secret down the river, as far as the Isle of Dogs, or somewhere thereabout, where he may lie concealed until he can escape abroad. I know thou knowest every place by the river's side as well as the devil knows an usurer, or the beggar knows his dish."

"A plague of your similies, dame," replied the apprentice; "for the devil gave me that knowledge, and beggary may be the end on't. But what has this gentleman done, that he should need to be under hiding?—no Papist, I hope—no Catesby and Piercy business—no Gunpowder Plot"——

"Fie, fie—what do you take me for?" said Dame Ursula. "I am as good a churchwoman as the parson's wife, save that necessary business will not allow me to go there oftener than on Christmas-day,

Heaven help me. No, no—this is no Popish matter; the gentleman hath but struck another in the Park"——

"Ha!" said Vincent, interrupting her with a start.

"Ay, ay, I see you guess whom I mean—it is even he we have spoken of so often—just Lord Glenvarloch, and no one else." Vincent sprung from his seat, and traversed the room with rapid and disorderly steps. "There, there it is now," continued the dame, "you are always ice or gunpowder. You sit in the great leathern arm-chair as quiet as a rocket hangs upon the frame in a rejoicing night till the match be fired, and then whizz! you are in the third heaven, beyond the reach of human voice, eye, or brain. When you have wearied yourself with padding to and fro across the room, will you tell me your determination, for time presses? Will you aid me in this matter, or not?"

"No—no—no—A thousand times no," replied Jenkin. "Have you not confessed to me that Margaret loves him?"

"Ay," answered the dame, "that she thinks she does, but that will not last long."

"And have I not told you but this instant," replied Jenkin, "that it was this same Glenvarloch that rooked me at the ordinary of every penny I had, and made a knave of me to boot, by gaining more than was my own?—O that cursed gold, which Shortyard the mercer paid me that morning on accompt, for mending the clock of Saint Stephens! If I had not, by ill chance, had that about me, I could but have beggared my purse, without blemishing my honesty—and after I had been rooked of all the rest amongst them, I must needs risk the last five pieces with that shark amongst the minnows."

"Granted," said Dame Ursula; "all this I know; and I own, that as Lord Glenvarloch was the last you played with, you have a right to charge your ruin on his head. Moreover, I admit, as already said, that Margaret has made him your rival. Yet surely, now he is in danger to lose his hand, it is not a time to remember all this."

"By my faith, but it is though," said the young citizen. "Lose his hand, indeed? They may take his head, for what I care—head and hand have made me a miserable wretch."

"Now, were it not better, my prince of flat caps," said Dame Ursula, "that matters were squared between you, and that, through means of the same Scotch lord, who has, as you say, deprived you of your money and your mistress, you should in a short time recover both?"

"And how can your wisdom come to that conclusion, dame?" said the apprentice; "my money, indeed, I can conceive—that is, if I comply with your proposal—but my pretty Margaret—how serving this lord, whom she has set her nonsensical head upon, can do me good with her, is far beyond my conception."

"That is because, in simple phrase," said Dame Ursula, "thou knowst no more of a woman's heart than doth a Norfolk gosling—look you—were I to report to Mistress Marget that the young lord has miscarried through thy lack of courtesy in refusing to help him, why, then, thou wert odious to her for ever—she will loath thee as she will loath the very cook who is to strike off Glenvarloch's hand with his cleaver—And then she will be yet more fixed in her affection towards this lord. London will hear of nothing but him—speak of nothing but him—think of nothing but him, for three weeks at least, and all that outcry will serve to keep him uppermost in her mind; for nothing pleases a girl so much as to bear relation to any one who is the talk of the whole world around her. Then, if he suffer this sentence of the law, it is a chance if she ever forgets him. I saw that handsome proper young gentleman, Babington, suffer in the Queen's time myself, and though I was then but a girl, he was in my head for a year after he was hanged. But, above all, pardoned or punished, Glenvarloch will probably remain in London, and his presence will keep up the silly girl's nonsensical fancy about him. Whereas, if he escapes"——

"Ay, shew me how that is to avail me?" said Jenkin.

"If he escapes," said the dame, resuming her argument, "he must resign the court for years, if not for life; and you know the old saying, 'out of sight, and out of mind.'"

"True—most true," said Jenkin; "spoken like an oracle, most wise Ursula."

"Ay, ay, I knew you would hear reason at last," said the wily dame; "and then, when the same lord is off and away for once and for ever, who, I pray you, is to be pretty pet's confidential person, and who is to fill up the void in her affections?—why, who but thou, thou pearl of 'prentices! And then you will have overcome your own inclinations to comply with her's, and every woman is sensible of that—and you will have run some risk, too, in carrying her desires into effect—and what is it that woman likes better than bravery and devotion to her will? Then you have her secret, and she must treat you with favour and observance, and repose confidence in you, and hold private intercourse with you, until she weeps with one eye for the absent lover whom she is never to see again, and blinks with the other blithely upon him who is in presence; and then if you know not how to improve the relation in which you stand with her, you are not the brisk lively lad that all the world takes you for—Said I well?"

"You have spoken like an empress, most mighty Ursula," said Jenkin Vincent; "and your will shall be obeyed."

"You know Alsatia well?" continued his tutoress.

"Well enough, well enough," replied he with a nod; "I have heard the dice rattle there in my day, before I must set up for gentleman, and go among the gallants at the Shavaleer Bojo's, as they call him,—the worse rookery of the two, though the feathers are the gayest."

"And they will have a respect for thee yonder, I warrant."

"Ay, ay," replied Vin, "when I am got into my fustian doublet again, with my bit of a trunnion under my arm, I can walk Alsatia at midnight as I could do that there Fleet-street in mid-day—they will not one of them swagger with the prince of 'prentices, and the king of clubs— they know I could bring every tall boy in the ward down upon them."

"And you know all the watermen, and so forth?"

"Can converse with every sculler in his own language, from Richmond to Gravesend, and know all the water-cocks, from John Taylor the Poet to little Grigg the Grinner, who never pulls but he shews all his teeth from ear to ear, as if he were grimacing through a horse-collar."

"And you can take any dress or character upon you well, such as a waterman's, a butcher's, a foot-soldier's," continued Ursula, "or the like?"

"Not such a mummer as I am within the walls, and thou knowst that well enough, dame," replied the apprentice. "I can touch the players themselves, at the Bull and at the Fortune, for presenting any thing except a gentleman. Take but this damned skin of frippery off me, which I think the devil stuck me into, and you shall put me into nothing else that I will not become as if I were born to it."

"Well, we will talk of your transmutation by and bye," said the dame, "and find you clothes withal, and money besides; for it will take a good deal to carry the thing handsomely through."

"But where is that money to come from, dame?" said Jenkin; "there is a question I would fain have answered before I touch it."

"Why, what a fool art thou to ask such a question! Suppose I am content to advance it to please young madam, what is the harm then?"

"I will suppose no such thing," said Jenkin hastily; "I know that you, dame, have no gold to spare, and may be would not spare it if you had —so that cock will not crow. It must be from Margaret herself."

"Well, thou suspicious animal, and what if it were?" said Ursula.

"Only this," replied Jenkin, "that I will presently to her, and learn if she has come fairly by so much ready money; for sooner than connive at her getting it by any indirection, I would hang myself at once. It is enough what I have done myself, no need to engage poor Margaret in such villainy—I'll to her and tell her of the danger—I will, by heaven!"

"You are mad to think of it," said Dame Suddlechop, considerably alarmed—"hear me but a moment. I know not precisely for what she got the money; but sure I am that she obtained it at her godfather's."

"Why, Master George Heriot is not returned from France," said Jenkin.

"No," replied Ursula, "but Dame Judith is at home—and the strange lady, whom they call Master Heriot's ghost—she never goes abroad."

"It is very true, Dame Suddlechop," said Jenkin; "and I believe you have guessed right—they say that lady has coin at will, and if Marget can get a handful of fairy-gold, why, she is free to throw it away at will."

"Ah, Jin Vin," said the dame, reducing her voice almost to a whisper, "we should not want gold at will neither, could we but read the riddle of that lady!"

"They may read it that list," said Jenkin, "I'll never pry into what concerns me not—Master George Heriot is a worthy and a brave citizen, and an honour to London, and has a right to manage his own household as he likes best.—There was once a talk of rabbling him the fifth of November before the last, because they said he kept a nunnery in his house, like old Lady Foljambe; but Master George is well loved among the 'prentices, and we got so many brisk boys of us together as should have rabbled the rabble, had they had but the heart to rise."

"Well, let that pass," said Ursula: "and now tell me how you will manage to be absent from shop a day or two, for you must think this matter will not be ended sooner."

"Why, as to that, I can say nothing," said Jenkin, "I have always served duly and truly; I have no heart to play truant, and cheat my master of his time as well as his money."

"Nay, but the point is to get back his money for him," said Ursula, "which he is not like to see on other conditions. Could you not ask leave to go down to your uncle at Essex for two or three days? He may be ill, you know."

"Why, if I must—I must," said Jenkin, with a heavy sigh; "but I will not be lightly caught treading these dark and crooked paths again."

"Hush thee then," said the dame, "and get leave for this very evening; and come back hither, and I will introduce you to another implement who must be employed in the matter.—Stay—stay!—the lad is mazed—you would not go into your master's shop in that guise, surely? Your trunk is in the matted chamber with your 'prentice things—go and put them on as fast as you can."

"I think I am bewitched," said Jenkin, giving a glance towards his dress, "or that these fool's trappings have made as great an ass of me as of many I have seen wear them—but let me once be rid of the harness, and if you catch me putting it on again, I will give you leave to sell me to a gipsey, to carry pots, pans, and beggar's bantlings, all the rest of my life."

So saying, he retired to change his apparel.

Chapter Eleven

Chance will not do the work—Chance sends the breeze;
But if the pilot slumber at the helm,
The very wind that wafts us toward the port
May dash us on the shelves.—The steersman's part is vigilance,
Blow it or rough or smooth.

Old Play

WE LEFT NIGEL, whose fortunes we are bound to trace by the engagement contracted in our title-page, sad and solitary in the mansion of Trapbois the usurer, having just received a letter instead of a visit from his friend the Templar, stating reasons why he could not at that time come to see him in Alsatia. So that it appeared his intercourse with the better and more respectable class of society, was, for the present, entirely cut off. This was a melancholy, and, to a proud mind like that of Nigel, a degrading reflection.

He went to the window of his apartment, and found the street enveloped in one of those thick, dingy, yellow-coloured fogs, which often invest the lower part of London and Westminster.—Amid the darkness, dense and palpable, were seen to wander like phantoms a reveller or two, whom the morning had surprised where the evening left them; and who now, with tottering steps, and by an instinct which intoxication could not wholly overcome, were groping the way to their own homes, to convert day into night, for the purpose of sleeping off the debauch which had turned night into day. Although it was broad day in the other parts of the city, it was scarce dawn yet in Alsatia; and none of the sounds of industry or occupation were there heard, which had long since aroused the slumberers in every other quarter. The prospect was too tiresome and disagreeable to detain Lord Glenvarloch at his station, so, turning from the window, he examined with more interest the furniture and appearance of the apartment which he tenanted.

Much of it had been in its time rich and curious—there was a great huge four-posted bed, with as much carved oak about it as would have made the head of a man-of-war, and tapestry hangings ample enough to have been her sails. There was a huge mirror with a massive frame of gilt brass-work, which was of Venice manufacture, and must have been worth a considerable sum before it had received the tremendous crack, which, traversing it from one corner to the other, bore the same proportion to the surface that the Nile bears to the map of Egypt. The chairs were of different forms and shapes; some had been carved, some gilded, some covered with damasked leather, some with embroidered work, but all were damaged and worm-eaten. There was a picture of Susanna and the Elders over the chimney-piece, which might have been accounted a choice piece, had not the rats made free with the chaste fair one's nose, and with the beard of one of her reverend admirers.

In a word, all that Lord Glenvarloch saw, seemed to have been articles carried off by appraisement or distress, or bought as penny-worths at some obscure broker's, and huddled together in the apartment as in a sale-room, without regard to taste or congruity.

The place appeared to Nigel to resemble the houses near the sea-coast, which are too often furnished with the spoils of wrecked vessels, as this was probably fitted up with the relics of ruined prodigals.—"My own skiff is among the breakers," thought Lord Glenvarloch, "though my wreck will add little to the profits of the spoiler."

He was chiefly interested in the state of the grate, a huge assemblage of rusted iron bars which stood in the chimney, unequally supported by three brazen feet, moulded into the form of lion's claws, while the fourth, which had been bent by an accident, seemed proudly uplifted as if to paw the ground; or as if the whole article had nourished the ambitious purpose of pacing forth into the middle of the apartment, and had one foot ready raised for the journey. A smile passed over Nigel's face as this fantastic idea presented itself to his fancy.—"I must stop it's march, howe'er," thought he; "for this morning is chill and raw enough to demand some fire."

He called accordingly from the top of a large stair-case, with a heavy oaken balustrade, which gave access to his own and other apartments, for the house was old and of considerable size; but receiving no answer to his repeated summons, he was compelled to go in search of some one who might accommodate him with what he wanted.

Nigel had, according to the fashion of the old world in Scotland, received an education which might, in most particulars, be termed simple, hardy, and unostentatious; but he had, nevertheless, been accustomed to much personal deference, and to the constant attendance and ministry of one or more domestics. This was the universal custom in Scotland, where wages were next to nothing, and where indeed a man of title or influence might have as many attendants as he pleased, for the mere expense of food, clothes, and countenance. Nigel was therefore mortified and displeased when he found himself without notice or attendance; and the more displeased, because he was at the same time angry with himself for suffering such a trifle to trouble him at all, amongst matters of more deep concernment. "There must surely be some servants in so large a house as this," said he, as he wandered over the place, through which he was conducted by a passage which branched off from the gallery. As he went on, he tried the entrance to several apartments, some of which he found were locked and others unfurnished, all apparently unoccupied; so that at length he returned to the stair-case, and resolved to make his way down to the lower part of the house, where he supposed he must at least find the old gentleman and his ill-favoured daughter. With this purpose he first made his entrance into a little low dark parlour, containing a well-worn leathern easy chair, before which stood a pair of slippers, while on the left side rested a crutch-handled staff; an oaken table stood before it, and supported a huge desk clamped with iron, and a massive pewter ink-stand. Around the apartment were shelves, cabinets, and other places convenient for depositing papers. A sword, musketoon, and a pair of pistols, hung over the chimney in ostentatious display, as if to intimate that the proprietor would be prompt in the defence of his premises.

"This must be the usurer's den," thought Nigel; and he was about to call aloud, when the old man, awakened even by the slightest noise, for avarice seldom sleeps sound, soon was heard from the inner room, speaking in a voice of irritability, rendered more tremulous by his morning cough.

"Ugh, ugh, ugh—who is there?—I say—ugh, ugh—who is there? —Why, Martha!—ugh, ugh—Martha Trapbois—here be thieves in the house, and they will not speak to me—why, Martha!—thieves— thieves—ugh, ugh, ugh!"

Nigel endeavoured to explain, but the idea of thieves had taken possession of the old man's pineal gland, and he kept coughing and screaming, and screaming and coughing, until the gracious Martha entered the apartment; and having first out-screamed her father, in order to convince him that there was no danger, and to assure him that the intruder was their new lodger, and having as often heard her sire ejaculate—"Hold him fast—ugh, ugh—hold him fast till I come," she at length succeeded in silencing his fears and his clamour, and then coldly and drily asked Lord Glenvarloch what he wanted in her father's apartment.

Her lodger had, in the meantime, leisure to contemplate her appearance, which did not by any means improve the idea he had formed of it by candle-light on the preceding evening. She was dressed in what was called a Queen Mary's ruff and farthingale; not the falling ruff with which the unfortunate Mary of Scotland is usually painted, but that which, with more than Spanish stiffness, surrounded the throat, and set off the morose head, of her fiercer namesake of Smithfield memory. This antiquated dress assorted well with the faded complexion, grey eyes, thin lips, and austere visage of the anti-quated maiden, which was, moreover, enhanced by a black hood, worn as her head-gear, carefully disposed so as to prevent any of her hair from escaping to view, probably because the simplicity of the period knew no art of disguising the colour with which time had begun to grizzle her tresses. Her figure was tall, thin, and flat, with skinny arms and hands, and feet of the larger size, cased in huge high-heeled shoes, which added height to a stature already ungainly. Apparently some art had been used by the tailor, to conceal a slight defect of shape, occasioned by the accidental elevation of one shoulder above the other; but the praiseworthy efforts of the ingenious mechanic had only succeeded in calling the attention of the observer to his benevolent purpose, without demonstrating that he had been able to achieve it.

Such was Mrs Martha Trapbois, whose dry "What were you lack-ing here, sir?" fell again, and with reiterated sharpness, on the ear of Nigel, as he gazed upon her presence, and compared it internally to one of the faded and grim figures in the old tapestry which adorned his bedstead. It was, however, necessary to reply, and he answered that he came in search of the servants, as he desired to have a fire kindled in his apartment on account of the rawness of the morning.

"The woman who does our chare-work," answered Mistress Martha, "comes at eight o'clock—if you want fire sooner, there are faggots and a bucket of sea-coal in the stone-closet at the head of the stair—and there is a flint and steel on the upper shelf—you can light fire for yourself if you will."

"No—no—no, Martha," ejaculated her father, who, having donned his rusty tunic, with his hose all ungirt, and his feet slip-shod, hastily came out of the inner apartment, with his mind probably full of robbers, for he had a naked rapier in his hand, which still looked formidable, though rust had somewhat marred its shine.—What he had heard at entrance about lighting a fire, had changed, however, the current of his ideas. "No—no—no," he cried, and each negative was more emphatic than its predecessor—"the gentleman shall not have the trouble to put on a fire—ugh, ugh—I'll put it on myself, for a con-si-de-ra-ti-ón."

This last word was a favourite expression with the old gentleman, which he pronounced in a peculiar manner, gasping it out syllable by syllable, and laying a strong emphasis upon the last. It was indeed a sort of protecting clause, by which he guarded himself against all inconveniences attendant on the rash habit of offering service or civility of any kind, the which, when hastily snapped at by those to whom they are uttered, give the profferer sometimes room to repent his promptitude.

"For shame, father," said Martha; "that must not be. Master Grahame will kindle his own fire, or wait till the chare-woman comes to do it for him—just as likes him best."

"No, child—no, child. Child Martha, no," reiterated the old miser —"no chare-woman shall ever touch a grate in my house; they put— ugh, ugh—the faggot uppermost, and so the coal kindles not, and the flame goes up the chimney—and wood and heat are both thrown away. Now, I will lay it properly for the gentleman—for a consideration—so that it shall last—ugh, ugh—last the whole day." Here his vehemence increased his cough so violently, that Nigel could only, from a scattered word here and there, comprehend that it was a recommendation to his daughter to remove the poker and tongs from the stranger's fire-side, with an assurance that, when necessary, his landlord would be in attendance to adjust it himself, "for a consideration."

Martha paid as little attention to the old man's injunctions as a predominant dame gives to those of a hen-pecked husband. She only repeated, in a deeper and more emphatic tone of censure,—"For shame, father, for shame!" then, turning to her guest, said, with her usual ungraciousness of manner,—"Master Grahame—it is best to be plain with you at first. My father is an old—a very old man, and his wits, as you may see, are somewhat weakened—though I would not advise you to make a bargain with him, else you may find them too sharp for your own—for myself, I am a lone woman, and, to speak truth, care little to see or converse with any one. If you can be satisfied with house-room, shelter, and safety, it will be your own fault if you have them not, and they are not always to be found in this unhappy quarter—but if you seek deferential observance and attendance, I tell you at once you will not find them here."

"I am not wont either to thrust myself upon acquaintance, madam, or to give trouble," said the guest; "nevertheless, I will need the assistance of a domestic to assist me to dress—perhaps you can recommend me to such."

"Yes, to twenty," answered Mistress Martha, "who will pick your purse while they tie your points, and cut your throat while they smooth your pillow."

"I will be his servant myself," said the old man, whose intellect, for a moment distanced, had again, in some measure, got up with the conversation. "I will brush his cloak—ugh, ugh—and tie his points— ugh, ugh—and clean his shoes—ugh—and run on his errands with speed and safety—ugh, ugh, ugh, ugh—for a consideration."

"Good-morrow to you, sir," said Martha, to Nigel, in a tone of direct and positive dismissal. "It cannot be agreeable to a daughter that a stranger should hear her father speak thus—if you be really a gentleman, you will retire to your own apartment."

"I will not delay a moment," said Nigel, respectfully, for he was sensible that circumstances palliated the woman's rudeness. "I would but ask you, if seriously there can be danger in procuring the assistance of a serving-man in this place?"

"Young gentleman," said Martha, "you must know little of Whitefriars to ask the question. We live alone in this house, and seldom has a stranger entered it; nor should you—to be plain—had my will been consulted. Look at the door—see if that of a castle can be better secured; the windows of the first floor are grated on the outside, and within, look to these shutters."

She pulled one of them aside, and shewed a ponderous apparatus of bolts and chains for securing the window-shuts, while her father, pressing to her side, seized her gown with a trembling hand, and said, in a loud whisper, "Shew not the trick of locking and undoing them— shew him not the trick on't, Martha—ugh, ugh—on *no* consideration." Martha went on, without paying him any attention.

"And yet, young gentleman, we have been more than once like to find all these defences too weak to protect our lives; such an evil effect on the wicked generation around us hath been made by the unhappy report of my poor father's wealth."

"Say nothing of that, housewife," said the miser, his irritability increased by the very supposition of his being wealthy—"Say nothing of that, or I will beat thee, housewife—beat thee with my staff, for fetching and carrying lies that will procure our throats to be cut at last —ugh, ugh.—I am but a poor man," he continued, turning to Nigel— "a very poor man, that am willing to do any honest turn upon earth, for a modest consideration."

"I therefore warn you of the life you must lead, young gentleman," said Martha; "the poor woman who does the chares will assist you so far as is in her power, but the wise man is his own best servant and assistant."

"It is a lesson you have taught me, madam, and I thank you for it—I will assuredly study it at leisure."

"You will do well," said Martha; "and as you seem thankful for advice, I, though I am no professed counsellor of others, will give you more. Make no intimacy with any one in Whitefriars—borrow no money, on any score, especially from my father, for, dotard as he seems, he will make an ass of you—last, and best of all—Stay here not an instant longer than you can help it—farewell, sir."

"A gnarled tree may bear good fruit, and a harsh nature may give good counsel," thought the Lord of Glenvarloch, as he retreated to his own apartment, where the same reflection occurred to him again and again, while, unable as yet to reconcile himself to the thoughts of becoming his own fire-maker, he walked up and down his bed-room, to warm himself by exercise.

At length his meditations arranged themselves in the following soliloquy—by which expression I beg leave to observe, once for all, that I do not mean that Nigel literally said aloud, with his bodily organs, the words which follow in inverted commas, (while pacing the room by himself,) but that I myself chuse to present to my dearest reader the pictures of my hero's mind, his reflections and resolutions, in the form of a speech, rather than in that of a narrative. In other words, I have put his thoughts into language; and this I conceive to be the purpose of the soliloquy upon the stage as well as in the closet, being at once the most natural, and perhaps the only way of communicating to the spectator what is supposed to be passing in the bosom of the scenic personage. There are no such soliloquies in nature, it is true; but unless they were received as a conventional medium of communication betwixt the poet and the audience, we would reduce dramatic authors to the recipe of Master Puff, who makes Lord Burleigh intimate a long train of political reasoning to the audience, by one comprehensive shake of his noddle. In narrative, no doubt, the writer has the alternative of telling that his personages thought so and so, inferred thus and thus, and arrived at such and such a conclusion. But the soliloquy is a more concise and spirited mode of communicating the same information; and therefore thus communed, or thus might have communed, the Lord of Glenvarloch with his own mind.

"She is right, and has taught me a lesson I will profit by. I have been, through my whole life, one who leant upon others for that assistance, which it is more truly noble to derive from my own exertions. I am ashamed of feeling the paltry inconvenience which long habit has led me to annex to the want of a servant's assistance—I am ashamed of that; but far, far more am I ashamed to have suffered the same habit of throwing my own burthen on others, rendering me, since I came to this city, a mere victim of those events, which I have never even attempted to influence—a thing never acting, but perpetually acted upon—protected by one friend, deceived by another; but in the advantage which I received from the one, and the evil I have sustained from the other, as passive and helpless as a boat that drifts without oar or rudder at the mercy of the winds and waves. I became a courtier, because Heriot so advised it—a gamester, because Dalgarno so contrived it—an Alsatian, because Lowestoffe so willed it. Whatever of good or bad has befallen me, hath arisen out of the agency of others, not from my own. My father's son must no longer hold this facile and puerile course. Live or die—sink or swim—Nigel Olifaunt, from this moment, shall owe his safety, success, and honour, to his own exertions, or shall fall with the credit of having at least exerted his own free agency. I will write it down in my tablets, in her very words,—'the wise man is his own best assistant.'"

He had just put his tablets in his pocket when the old chare-woman, who, to add to her efficiency, was sorely handled by the rheumatism, hobbled into the room, to try if she could gain a small gratification by waiting on the stranger. She readily undertook to get Lord Glenvarloch's breakfast, and as there was an eating-house at the next door, she succeeded in a shorter time than Nigel had augured.

As his solitary meal was finished, one of the Temple porters, or inferior officers, was announced, as seeking Master Grahame, on the part of his friend, Master Lowestoffe; and being admitted by the old woman to his apartment, he delivered to Nigel a small mail-trunk, with the clothes he had desired should be sent to him, and then, with more mystery, put into his hands the casket, or strong box, which he had carefully concealed beneath his cloak. "I am glad to be rid on't," said the fellow, as he placed it on the table.

"Why, it is surely not so very heavy," answered Nigel, "and you are a stout young man."

"Ay, sir," replied the fellow; "but Sampson himself would not have carried such a matter safely through Alsatia, had the lads of the Huff known what it was. Please to look into it, sir, and see all is right—I am an honest fellow, and it comes safe out of my hands. How long it may remain so afterwards, will depend on your own care. I would not my good name were to suffer by any after-clap."

To satisfy the scruples of the messenger, Lord Glenvarloch opened the casket in his presence, and saw that his small stock of money, with two or three valuable papers which it contained, and particularly the original sign-manual which the King had granted in his favour, were in the same order in which he had left them. At the man's further instance, he availed himself of the writing materials which the casket contained, in order to send a line to Master Lowestoffe, declaring that his property had reached him in safety. He added some grateful acknowledgments for Lowestoffe's services, and just as he was sealing and delivering his billet to the messenger, his aged landlord entered the apartment. His thread-bare suit of black clothes was now somewhat better arranged than they had been in the dishabille of his first appearance, and his nerves and intellects seemed to be less fluttered; for, without much coughing or hesitation, he invited Nigel to partake

of a morning draught of wholesome single ale, which he brought in a
large leathern tankard, or black jack, carried in the one hand, while the
other stirred it round with a sprig of rosemary, to give it, as the old man
said, a flavour.

Nigel declined the courteous proffer, and intimated by his manner,
while he did so, that he desired no intrusion on the privacy of his
own apartment; which indeed he was the more entitled to maintain,
considering the cold reception he had that morning met with when
straying from its precincts into that of his landlord. But the open
casket contained matter, or rather metal, so attractive to old Trapbois,
that he remained fixed, like a setting-dog at a dead point, his nose
advanced, and one hand expanded like the lifted fore-paw, by which
that sagacious quadruped sometimes indicates that it is a hare which
he has in the wind. Nigel was about to break the charm which had
thus arrested old Trapbois, by shutting the lid of the casket, when
his attention was withdrawn from him by the question of the messenger, who, holding out the letter, asked whether he was to leave it at
Mr Lowestoffe's chambers in the Temple, or carry it to the Marshalsea?

"The Marshalsea?" repeated Lord Glenvarloch.

"Ay, sir," said the man, "the poor gentleman is laid up there in
lavender, because, they say, his own kind heart led him to scald his
fingers with another man's broth."

Nigel hastily snatched back the letter, broke the seal, joined to the
contents his earnest entreaty that he might be instantly acquaint with
the cause of his confinement, and added, that if it arose out of his own
unhappy affair, it would be of brief duration, since he had, even before
hearing of a reason which so peremptorily demanded that he should
surrender himself, adopted the resolution to do so, as the manliest and
most proper course which his ill fortune and imprudence had left in
his own power. He conjured therefore Mr Lowestoffe to have no
delicacy upon this score, but, since his surrender was what he had
determined upon as a sacrifice due to his own character, that he
would have the frankness to mention in what manner it could be best
arranged, so as to extricate him, Lowestoffe, from the restraint to
which the writer could not but fear his friend had been subjected, on
account of the generous interest which he had taken in his concerns.
The letter concluded, that the writer would suffer twenty-four hours
to elapse in expectation to hear from him, and at the end of that
period, was determined to put his purpose in execution—he delivered
the billet to the messenger, and enforcing his request with a piece of
money, requested him, without a moment's delay, to convey it to the
hand of Master Lowestoffe.

"I will carry it to him myself," said the old usurer, "for half the consideration."

The man, who heard this attempt to take his duty and perquisites over his head, lost no time in pocketing the money and departing on his errand as fast as he could.

"Master Trapbois," said Nigel, addressing the old man somewhat impatiently, "had you any particular commands for me?"

"I—I—came to see if you rested well," answered the old man; "and —if I could do any thing to serve you, on any consideration."

"Sir," said Lord Glenvarloch, "I thank you;" and ere he could say more, a heavy footstep was heard on the stair.

"My God!" said the old man, starting up—"Why—Dorothy, chare-woman—Why, daughter—draw bolt, I say, housewives—the door hath been left on latch."

The door of the chamber opened wide, and in strutted the portly bulk of the military hero, whom Nigel had on the preceding evening in vain endeavoured to recognize.

Chapter Twelve

Swash-Buckler. Bilbo's the word.—
    Pierrot. It hath been spoke too often,
The spell hath lost its charm—I tell thee, friend,
The meanest cur that trots the street, will turn
And snarl against your proffer'd bastinadoe.
    Swash-Buckler. 'Tis art shall do it then—I will doze the mongrels—
Or in plain terms, I'll use the private knife
'Stead of the brandish'd faulchion.
                              Old Play

THE NOBLE Captain Colepepper or Peppercole, for he was known by both these names, and some others besides, had a martial and a swashing exterior, which, on the present occasion, was rendered yet more peculiar, by a patch covering his left eye and a part of the cheek. The sleeves of his thickset velvet jerkin were polished and shone with grease—his buff gloves had huge tops, which reached almost to the elbow; his sword-belt, of the same materials, extended its breadth from his haunch-bone to his small ribs, and supported on the one side his large black-hilted back-sword, on the other a dagger of like proportions. He paid his compliments to Nigel with that air of predetermined effrontery, which announces that it will not be repelled by any coldness of reception, asked Trapbois how he did, by the familiar title of old Peter Pillory, and then seizing upon the black jack, emptied it off at a draught, to the health of the last and youngest freeman of Alsatia, the noble and loving Master Nigel Grahame.

When he had set down the empty pitcher and drawn his breath, he began to criticise the liquor which it had lately contained.—"Sufficient single beer, old Pillory—and, as I take it, brewed at the rate of a nutshell of malt to a butt of Thames—as dead as a corpse too, and yet it went hissing down my throat—bubbling, by Jove, like water upon hot iron.—You left us early, noble Master Grahame, but, good faith, we had a carouse to your honour—we heard *butt* ring hollow ere we parted—we were as loving as inkle-weavers—we fought too, to finish off the gawdy. I bear some marks of the parson about me, you see—a note of the sermon or so, which should have been addressed to my ear, but missed its mark and reached my left eye—the man of God bears my sign-manual too—but the Duke made us friends again, and it cost me more sack than I could carry, and all the Rhenish to boot, to pledge the seer in the way of love and reconciliation—But Carocco! 'tis a vile old canting slave for all that, whom I will one day beat out of his devil's livery into all the colours of the rainbow.—Basta!—Said I well, old Trapbois? Where is thy daughter, man?—what says she to my suit?—'tis an honest one—wilt have a soldier for thy son-in-law, old Pillory, to mingle the soul of martial honour with thy thieving, miching, petty-larceny blood, as men put bold brandy into muddy ale?"

"My daughter receives not company so early, noble Captain," said the usurer, and concluded his speech with a dry, emphatical "ugh, ugh."

"What, upon no con-si-de-ra-ti-ón?" said the Captain; "and wherefore not, old Truepenny? she has not much time to lose in driving her bargain, methinks."

"Captain," said Trapbois, "I was upon some little business with our noble friend here, Master Nigel Green—ugh—ugh—and"——

"And you would have me gone, I warrant you," answered the bully; "but patience, old Pillory, thine hour is not yet come, man—You see," he said, pointing to the casket, "that noble Master Grahame, whom you call Green, has got the *decuses* and the *smelts*."

"Which you would willingly rid him of, ha! ha!—ugh, ugh," answered the usurer, "if you knew how—but lack-a-day, thou art one of those that come out for wool, and are sure to go home shorn. Why now, but that I am sworn against laying of wagers, I would risk some consideration that this honest guest of mine sends thee home penniless, if thou darest venture with him—ugh, ugh—at any game which gentlemen play at."

"Marry, thou hast me on the hip there, thou old miserly coney-catcher!" answered the Captain, taking a bale of dice from the sleeve of his coat; "I must always keep company with these damnable doctors, and they have made me every baby's cully, and purged my purse into an atrophy; but never mind, it passes the time as well as aught else —How say you, Master Grahame?"

The fellow paused; but even the extremity of his impudence could hardly withstand the cold look of utter contempt with which Nigel received his proposal, returning it with a simple, "I only play where I know my company, and never in the morning."

"Cards may be more agreeable," said Captain Colepepper; "and for knowing your company, here is honest old Pillory will tell you Jack Colepepper plays as truly on the square as e'er a man that trowled a die.—Men talk of high and low dice, Fulhams and bristles, topping, knapping, slurring, stabbing, and a hundred ways of rooking besides; but broil me like a rasher of bacon, if I could ever learn the trick on 'em."

"You have got the vocabulary perfect, sir, at the least," said Nigel, in the same cold tone.

"Yes, by mine honour have I," returned the Hector; "they are phrases that a gentleman learns about town.—But perhaps you would like a set at tennis—or a game at balloon—we have an indifferent good court hard by here, and a set of as gentlemen-like blades as ever banged leather against brick and mortar."

"I beg to be excused at present," said Lord Glenvarloch; "and to be plain, among the valuable privileges your society has conferred on me, I hope I may reckon that of being private in my own apartment when I have a mind."

"Your humble servant, sir," said the Captain; "and I thank you for your civility—Jack Colepepper can have enough of company, and thrusts himself on no one.—But perhaps you would like to make a match at skittles?"

"I am by no means that way disposed," replied the young nobleman.

"Or to leap a flea—run a snail—match a wherry?"

"No—I will do none of these," answered Nigel.

Here the old man, who had been watching with his little peery eyes, pulled the bulky Hector by the skirt, and whispered, "Do not vapour him the huff—it will not pass—let the trout play—he will rise to the hook presently."

But the bully, confiding in his own strength, and probably mistaking for timidity the patient scorn with which Nigel received his proposals, incited also by the open casket, began to assume a louder and more threatening tone. He drew himself up, bent his brows, assumed a look of professional ferocity, and continued, "In Alsatia, look ye, a man must be neighbourly and companionable. Zouns! sir, we would slit any nose that was turned up at us honest fellows.—Ay, sir, we would slit it up to the gristle, though it had smelled nothing all its life but musk, ambergrease, and court-scented-water.—Rabbit me, I am a soldier, and care no more for a lord than a lamplighter."

"Are you seeking a quarrel, sir?" said Nigel, calmly, having in truth no desire to engage himself in a discreditable broil in such a place, and with such a character.

"Quarrel, sir?" said the Captain; "I am not *seeking* quarrel, though I care not how soon I find one. Only I wish you to understand you must be neighbourly—that's all. What if we should go over the water to the garden, and see a bull hanked this fine morning—'sdeath, will you do nothing?"

"Something I am strangely tempted to do at this moment," said Nigel.

"Videlicet," said Colepepper, with a swaggering air, "let us hear your temptation."

"I am tempted to throw you headlong from the window, unless you presently make the best of your way down stairs."

"Throw me from window?—hell and furies!" exclaimed the Captain; "I have confronted twenty crooked sabres at Buda with my single rapier, and shall a chitty-faced beggarly Scotch lordling speak of me and a window in the same breath?—Stand off, old Pillory, let me make Scotch collops of him—he dies the death."

"For the love of Heaven, gentlemen," exclaimed the old miser, throwing himself between, "do not break the peace, on any consideration—noble guest, forbear the captain—he is a very Hector of Troy—trusty Hector, forbear my guest, he is like to prove a very Achilles"——

Here he was interrupted by his asthma, but, nevertheless, continued to interpose his person between Colepepper, who had unsheathed his whinyard and was making vain passes at his antagonist, and Nigel, who, having stept back to take his sword, now held it undrawn in his left hand.

"Make an end of this foolery, you scoundrel!" said Nigel—"Do you come hither to vent your noisy oaths and your bottled-up valour on me?—you seem to know me, and I am half ashamed to say I have at length been able to recollect you—Remember the garden behind the ordinary, you dastardly ruffian, and the speed with which fifty men saw you run from a drawn sword.—Get you gone, sir, and do not put me to the vile labour of cudgelling such a cowardly rascal down stairs."

The bully's countenance grew as dark as night at this unexpected recognition; for he had undoubtedly thought himself secure in his change of dress, and his black patch, from being discovered by a person who had seen him but once. He set his teeth, clenched his hands, and it seemed as if he was seeking for a moment's courage to fly upon his antagonist. But his heart failed, he sheathed his sword, turned his back in gloomy silence, and spoke not until he reached the door, when, turning round, he said, with a deep oath, "If I be not avenged of you for this insolence ere many days go by, I would the gallows had my body and the devil my spirit!"

So saying, and with a look where determined spite and malice made his features savagely fierce, though they could not overcome his fear, he turned and left the house. Nigel followed him as far as the gallery at the head of the staircase, with the purpose of seeing him depart, and ere he returned was met by Mistress Martha Trapbois, whom the noise of the quarrel had summoned from her own apartment. He could not resist saying to her in his natural displeasure—"I would, madam, you could teach your father and his friends the lesson which you had the goodness to bestow on me this morning, and prevail on them to leave me the unmolested privacy of my own apartment."

"If you came hither for quiet or retirement, young man," answered she, "you have been advised to an evil retreat. You might seek mercy in the Star-Chamber, or holiness in hell, with better success than quiet in Alsatia. But my father shall trouble you no longer."

So saying, she entered the apartment, and fixing her eyes on the casket said with emphasis—"If you display such a loadstone, it will draw many a steel knife to your throat."

While Nigel hastily shut the casket, she addressed her father, upbraiding him without much reverence for keeping company with the cowardly, hectoring, murthering villain, John Colepepper.

"Ay—ay—child," said the old man, with the cunning leer which intimated perfect satisfaction with his own superior address—"I know —I know—ugh—but I'll cross-bite him—I know them all, and I can manage them—ay—ay—I have the trick on't."

"*You* manage them, father!" said the austere damsel; "you will manage to have your throat cut, and that ere long. You cannot hide from them your gains and your gold as formerly."

"My gains, wench? my gold?" said the usurer; "alack-a-day, few of these and hard got—few and hard got."

"This will not serve you, father, any longer," said she, "and had not served you thus long, but that Bully Colepepper had contrived a cheaper way of plundering your hoard, even by means of my miserable self.—But why do I speak to him of all this," she said, checking herself, and shrugging her shoulders with an expression of pity which did not fall much short of scorn—"he hears me not—he thinks not of me—is it not strange that the love of gathering gold should survive the care to preserve both property and life?"

"Your father," said Lord Glenvarloch, who could not help

respecting the strong sense and feeling shewn by this poor woman, even amidst all her rudeness and severity, "your father seems to have his faculties sufficiently alert when he is in the exercise of his ordinary pursuits and functions. I wonder he is not sensible of the weight of your arguments."

"Nature made him a man senseless of danger, and that insensibility is the best thing I have derived from him," said she; "age has left him shrewdness enough to tread his old beaten paths, but not to seek new courses—the old blind horse will long continue to go its rounds in the mill, when it would stumble in the open meadow."

"Daughter—why, wench—why, housewife," said the old man, awakening out of some dream, in which he had been sneering and chuckling in imagination, probably over a successful piece of roguery, "go to chamber, wench—go to chamber—draw bolts and chain—look sharp to door—let none in or out but worshipful Master Grahame—I must take my cloak and go to Duke Hildebrod—ay, ay—time has been, my own warrant was enough—but the lower we lie, the more are we under the wind."

And with his wonted chorus of muttering and coughing, the old man left the apartment. His daughter stood for a moment looking after him with her usual expression of discontent and sorrow.

"You ought to persuade your father," said Nigel, "to leave this evil neighbourhood, if you are in reality apprehensive for his safety."

"He would be safe in no other quarter," said the daughter; "I would rather the old man were dead than publicly dishonoured. In other quarters he would be pelted and pursued like an owl which ventures into sunshine. Here he was safe while his comrades could avail themselves of his talents—he is now squeezed and fleeced by them on every pretence—they consider him as a vessel on the strand, from which each may snatch a prey, and the very jealousy which they entertain respecting him as a common property, may perhaps induce them to guard him from more private and daring assaults."

"Still, methinks, you ought to leave this place," answered Nigel, "since you might find a safe retreat in some distant country."

"In Scotland, doubtless," said she, looking at him with a sharp and suspicious eye, "and enrich strangers with our rescued wealth—ha! young man?"

"Madam, if you knew me," said Lord Glenvarloch, "you would spare the suspicion implied in your words."

"Who shall assure me of that?" said Martha, sharply. "They say you are a brawler and a gamester, and I know how far these are to be trusted by the unhappy."

"They do me wrong, by Heaven!" said Lord Glenvarloch.

"It may be so," said Martha; "I am little interested in the degree of your vice or your folly—but it is plain that the one or the other has conducted you hither, and that your best hope of peace, safety, and happiness, is to be gone, with the least possible delay, from a place which is always a stye for swine, and often a shambles." So saying, she left the apartment.

There was something in the ungracious manner of this female, amounting almost to contempt of him she spoke to; an indignity to which Glenvarloch, notwithstanding his poverty, had not as yet been personally exposed, and which, therefore, gave him a transitory feeling of painful surprise. Neither did the dark hints which Martha threw out concerning the danger of his place of refuge, sound by any means agreeably in his ears. The bravest man, placed in a situation in which he is surrounded by suspicious persons, and removed from all counsel and assistance, except those afforded by a valiant heart and a strong arm, experiences a sinking of the heart, a consciousness of abandonment, which for a moment chills his blood, and depresses his natural gallantry of disposition.

But if sad reflections arose in Nigel's mind, he had not time to indulge them; and if he saw little prospect of finding friends in Alsatia, he was not likely, he found, to be solitary for lack of visitors.

He had scarcely paced his apartment for ten minutes, endeavouring to arrange his ideas on the course which he was to pursue on quitting Alsatia, when he was interrupted by the Sovereign of the quarter, the great Duke Hildebrod himself, before whose approach the bolts and chains of the miser's dwelling fell, or withdrew, as of their own accord; and both folding leaves of the door were opened, that he might roll himself into the house like a huge butt of liquor, a vessel to which he bore a considerable outward resemblance, both in size, shape, complexion, and contents.

"Good-morrow to your lordship," said the greasy puncheon, cocking his single eye, and rolling it upon Nigel with a singular expression of familiar impudence; whilst his grim bull-dog, which was close at his heels, made a kind of gurgling in his throat, as if saluting, in similar fashion, a starved cat, the only living thing in Trapbois' house which we have not yet enumerated, and which had flown up to the top of the tester, where she stood clutching and grinning at the mastiff, whose greeting she accepted with as much good will as Nigel bestowed on that of the dog's master.

"Peace, Belzie, d—n thee, peace," said Duke Hildebrod; "beasts and fools will be meddling, my lord."

"I thought, sir," answered Nigel, with as much haughtiness as was consistent with the cool distance which he desired to preserve, "I had told you my name at present was Nigel Grahame."

His eminence of Whitefriars on this burst out into a loud, chuckling, impudent laugh, repeating the word, till his voice was almost
inarticulate,—"Niggle Green—Niggle Green—Niggle Green!—
why, my lord, you would be queered in the drinking of a penny pot of
Malmsie, if you cry before you are touched. Why, you have told me the
secret even now, had I not had a shrewd guess of it before. Why,
Master Nigel, since that is the word, I only called you my lord, because
we made you a peer of Alsatia last night, when the sack was predominant.—How you look now!"

Nigel, indeed conscious that he had unnecessarily betrayed himself, replied hastily,—"he was much obliged to him for the honours
conferred, but did not propose to remain in the sanctuary long enough
to enjoy them."

"Why, that may be as you will, an ye will walk by wise counsel,"
answered the ducal porpoise; and although Nigel remained standing,
in hopes to accelerate his guest's departure, he threw himself into
one of the old tapestry-backed easy-chairs, which cracked under his
weight, and began to call for old Trapbois. The crone of all works
appearing instead of her master, the Duke cursed her for a careless
jade, to let a strange gentleman, and a brave guest, go without his
morning's draught.

"I never take one, sir," answered Glenvarloch.

"Time to begin—time to begin," answered the Duke.—"Here, you
old refuse of Sathan, go to our palace, and fetch Lord Greene's
morning draught—let us see—what shall it be—hey, my lord?—a
humming double pot of ale, with a roasted crab dancing in it like a
wherry above bridge?—or, hum—ay—young men are sweet-toothed
—a quart of burnt sack, with sugar and spice—good against the fogs?
—or what say you to sipping a gill of right distilled waters? Come, we
will have them all, and you shall take your choice.—Here, you Jezabel,
let Tim send the ale and the sack, and the nipperkin of double-
distilled, with a bit of diet-loaf, or some such trinket, and score it to the
new comer."

Glenvarloch, bethinking himself that it might be as well to endure
this fellow's insolence for a brief season, as to get into farther
discreditable quarrels, suffered him to take his own way, without
interruption, only observing, "You make yourself at home, sir, in my
apartment; but, for the time, you may use your pleasure. Meantime, I
would fain know what has procured me the honour of this unexpected
visit?"

"You shall know that when old Deb has brought the liquor. I never
speak of business dry-lipped. Why, how she drumbles—I warrant she

stops to take a sip on the road, and then you will think you have had
unchristian measure. In the mean while, look at that dog there—look
Belzebub in the face—and tell me if you ever saw a sweeter beast—
never flew but at head in his life."

And after this general panegyric, he was proceeding with a tale of a
dog and a bull, which threatened to be somewhat of the longest, when
he was interrupted by the return of the old crone, and two of
his own tapsters, bearing the various kinds of drinkables which he
had demanded, and which probably was the only species of interruption which he would have endured with equanimity.

When the cups and cans were duly arranged upon the table, and
when Deborah, whom the ducal generosity honoured with a penny
farthing in the way of gratuity, had withdrawn with her satellites, the
worthy potentate, having first slightly invited Lord Glenvarloch to
partake of the liquor which he was to pay for, and after having
observed, that, excepting three poached eggs, a pint of bastard, and a
cup of clary, he was fasting from every thing but sin, set himself
seriously to reinforce the radical moisture. Glenvarloch had seen
Scottish lairds and Dutch burgomasters at their potations; but their
exploits, (though each might be termed a thirsty generation,) were
nothing to those of Duke Hildebrod, who seemed an absolute sand-
bed, capable of absorbing any given quantity of liquid, without being
either vivified or overflowed. He drank off the ale to quench a thirst
which, as he said, kept him in a fever from morning to night, and night
to morning; tippled off the sack to correct the crudity of the ale; sent
the spirits after the sack to keep all quiet, and then declared that,
probably, he should not again taste liquor till *post meridiem*, unless it
was in compliment to some especial friend. Finally, he intimated that
he was ready to proceed on the business which brought him from
home so early,—a proposition which Nigel readily received, though
he could not help suspecting that the most important purpose of Duke
Hildebrod's visit was already transacted.

In this, however, Lord Glenvarloch proved to be mistaken. Hildebrod, before opening what he had to say, made an accurate survey of
the apartment, laying, from time to time, his finger on his nose, and
winking on Nigel with his single eye, while he opened and shut the
doors, lifted the tapestry, which concealed, in one or two places, the
dilapidation of time upon the wainscot and walls, peeped into closets,
and, finally, looked under the bed, to assure himself that the coast was
clear of listeners and of interlopers. He then resumed his seat, and
beckoned confidentially to Nigel to draw his chair close to him.

"I am well as I am, Master Hildebrod," replied the young lord, little
disposed to encourage the familiarity which the man endeavoured to

fix on him; but the undismayed Duke proceeded as follows:—

"You shall pardon me, my lord—and I now give you the title right seriously—if I remind you that our waters may be watched; for though old Trapbois be as deaf as Paul's, yet his daughter has sharp ears, and sharp eyes enough, and it is of them that it is my business to speak."

"Say away, then, sir," said Nigel, edging his chair somewhat closer to the Quicksand, "although I cannot conceive what business I have, or can have, either with mine host or his daughter."

"We will see that in the twinkling of a quart-pot," answered the gracious Duke; "and, first, my lord, you must not think to dance in a net before old Jack Hildebrod, that has thrice your years o'er his head, and was born like King Richard, with all his eye-teeth ready cut."

"Well, sir, go on," said Nigel.

"Why, then, my lord, I presume to say, that if you are, as I believe you, that Lord Glenvarloch whom all the world talk of—the Scots gallant that has spent all, to a thin cloak and a light purse—be not moved, my lord, it is so noised of you—Men call you the Sparrow-hawk, who will fly at all—ay, were it in the very Park—be not moved, my lord."

"I am ashamed, sirrah," replied Glenvarloch, "that you should have power to move me by your insolence—but beware—and if you indeed guess who I am, consider how long I may be able to endure your tone of insolent familiarity."

"I crave pardon, my lord," said Hildebrod, with a sullen, yet apologetic look; "I meant no harm in speaking my poor mind. I know not what honour there may be in being familiar with your lordship, but I judge there is little safety, for Lowestoffe is laid up in lavender only for having shewn you the way into Alsatia; and so, what is to come of those who maintain you when you are here, or whether they will get most honour or most trouble by doing so, I leave with your lordship's better judgment."

"I will bring no one into trouble on my account," said Lord Glenvarloch. "I will leave Whitefriars to-morrow—nay, by Heaven, I will leave it this day."

"You will have more wit in your anger, I trust," said Duke Hildebrod composedly; "listen first what I have to say to you, and if honest Jack Hildebrod puts you not in way of nicking them all, may he never cast doublets, or gull a green-horn again—And so, my lord, in plain words, you must wap and win."

"Your words must be still plainer before I can understand them," said Nigel.

"What the devil—a gamester, one who deals with the devil's bones and the doctors, and not understand pedlars' French!—nay, then, I must speak plain English, and that's the simpleton's tongue."

"Speak, then, sir," said Nigel; "and I pray you to be brief, for I have little more time to bestow on you."

"Well then, my lord, to be brief, as you and the lawyers call it—I understand you have an estate in the north, which changes masters for want of the redeeming ready—ay, you start—but you cannot dance in a net before me, as I said before; and so the King runs the frowning humour on you, and the court vapours you the go-bye; and the Prince scowls at you from under his cap; and the favourite serves you out the puckered brow and the cold shoulder; and the favourite's favourite"——

"To go no further, sir," interrupted Nigel, "suppose all this true— and what follows?"

"What follows?" returned Duke Hildebrod. "Marry, this follows, that you will owe good deed, as well as good will, to him who shall put you in the way to walk with your beaver cocked in the presence, as an ye were Earl of Kildare; bully the courtiers; meet the Prince's blighting look with a bold brow; confront the favourite; baffle his deputy, and"——

"This is all well," said Nigel; "but how is it to be accomplished?"

"By making thee a Prince of Peru, my lord of the northern latitudes; propping thine old castle with ingots,—fertilizing thy failing fortunes with fair ingots—it shall but cost thee to put thy baron's coronet for a day or so on the brows of an old Caduca here, the man's daughter of the house, and thou art master of a mass of treasure that shall do all I have said for thee, and"——

"What, you would have me marry this old gentlewoman here, the daughter of mine host?" said Nigel, surprised and angry, yet unable to suppress some desire to laugh.

"Nay, my lord, I would have you marry fifty thousand good sterling pounds; for that, and better, hath old Trapbois hoarded; and thou shalt do a deed of mercy in it to the old man, who will lose his golden smelts in some worse way—for now that he is well nigh past his day of work, his day of payment is like to follow."

"Truly, this is a most courteous offer," said Lord Glenvarloch; "but, may I pray of your candour, most noble Duke, to tell me why you dispose of a ward of so much wealth on a stranger like me, who may leave you to-morrow?"

"In sooth, my lord," said the Duke, "that question smacks more of the wit of Beaujeu's ordinary, than any word I have yet heard your lordship speak, and reason it is you should be answered. Touching my peers, it is but necessary to say, that Mistress Martha Trapbois will none of them, whether clerical or laic—the captain hath asked her, so hath the parson, but she will none of them—she looks higher than either, and is, to say truth, a woman of sense, and so forth, too profound, and of spirit something too high, to put up with greasy buff or rusty prunella. For ourselves, we need but hint that we have a consort in the land of the living, and, what is more to purpose, Mrs Martha knows it. So, as she will not lace her kersey hood save with a quality binding, you, my lord, must be the man, and must carry off fifty thousand decus's, the spoils of five thousand bullies, cutters, and spendthrifts,—always deducting from the main sum some five thousand pounds for our princely advice and countenance, without which, as matters stand in Alsatia, you would find it hard to win the plate."

"But has your wisdom considered, sir," replied Glenvarloch, "how this wedlock can serve me in my present emergence?"

"As for that, my lord," said Duke Hildebrod, "if, with forty or fifty thousand pounds in your pouch, you cannot save yourself, you will deserve to lose your head for your folly, and your hand for being close-fisted."

"But, since your goodness has taken my matters into such serious consideration," continued Nigel, who conceived there was no prudence in breaking with a man, who, in his way, meant him favour rather than offence, "perhaps you may be able to tell me how my kindred will be likely to receive such a bride as you recommend to me?"

"Touching that matter, my lord, I have always heard your country-men knew as well as other folks, on which side their bread was buttered. And truly, speaking from report, I know no place where fifty thousand pounds—fifty thousand pounds, I say—will make a woman more welcome than it is likely to do in your ancient kingdom. And, truly, saving the slight twist in her shoulder, Mrs Martha Trapbois is a person of a very awful and majestic appearance, and may, for aught I know, be come of better blood than any one wots of; for old Trapbois looks not over like to be her father, and her mother was a generous, liberal sort of woman."

"I am afraid," answered Nigel, "that chance is rather too vague to assure her a gracious reception into an honourable house."

"Why then, my lord," replied Hildebrod, "I think it like she will be even with them; for I will venture to say she has as much ill-nature as will make her a match for your whole clan."

"That may inconvenience me a little," replied Nigel.

"Not a whit—not a whit," said the Duke, fertile in expedients; "if she should become rather intolerable, which is not unlikely, your honourable house, which I presume to be a castle, hath, doubtless, both turrets and dungeons, and ye may bestow your bonny bride in either the one or the other, and then you know you will be out of hearing of her tongue, and she will be either above or below the contempt of your friends."

"It is sagely counselled, most equitable sir," replied Nigel, "and such restraint would be a fit meed for her folly that gave me any power over her."

"You entertain the project then, my lord?" said Duke Hildebrod.

"I must turn it in my mind for twenty-four hours," said Nigel; "and I will pray you so to order matters that I be not further interrupted by any visitors."

"We will utter an edict to secure your privacy," said the Duke; "and you do not think," he added, lowering his voice to a commercial whisper, "that ten thousand is too much to pay to the Sovereign, in name of wardship?"

"Ten thousand!" said Lord Glenvarloch; "why, you said five thousand but now."

"Aha!—are avised of that?" said the Duke, touching the side of his nose with his finger; "nay, if you have marked me so closely, you are thinking on the case more nearly than I believed, till you trapped me. Well, well, we will not quarrel about the consideration, as old Trapbois would call it—do you win and wear the dame; it will be no hard matter with your face and figure, and I will take care that no one interrupts you. I will have an edict from the Senate soon as they meet for their meridian."

So saying, Duke Hildebrod took his leave.

Chapter Thirteen

This is the time—Heaven's maiden centinel
Hath quitted her high watch—the lesser spangles
Are paleing one by one; give me the ladder
And the short lever—bid Anthonio
Keep with his carabine the wicket-gate;
And do thou bare thy knife and follow me,
For we will in and do it—darkness like this
Is dawning of our fortunes.
                                            Old Play

WHEN DUKE HILDEBROD had withdrawn, Nigel's first impulse was an irresistible feeling to laugh at the sage adviser, who would have thus connected him with age, ugliness, and ill-temper; but his next thought was pity for the unfortunate father and daughter, who, being the only persons possessed of wealth in this unhappy district, seemed like a wreck on the sea-shore of a barbarous country, only secured from plunder for the moment by the jealousy of the tribes among whom it had been cast. Neither could he help being conscious that his own residence here was upon conditions equally precarious, and that he was considered by the Alsatians in the same light of a godsend on the Cornish coast, or a sickly but wealthy caravan travelling through the wilds of Africa, and emphatically termed by the nations of despoilers through whose regions it passes, *Dummalafong*, which signifies a thing given to be devoured—a common prey to all men.

Nigel had already formed his own plan to extricate himself, at whatsoever risk, from his perilous and degrading situation; and in order that he might carry it into instant execution, he only awaited the return of Lowestoffe's messenger. He expected him, however, in vain, and could only amuse himself by looking through such parts of his baggage as had been sent to him from his former lodgings, in order to select a small packet of the most necessary articles to take with him, in the event of his quitting his lodgings secretly and suddenly, as speed and privacy would, he foresaw, be particularly necessary, if he meant to obtain an interview with the King, which was the course his spirit and his interest alike determined him to pursue.

While he was thus engaged, he found, greatly to his satisfaction, that Master Lowestoffe had transmitted not only his rapier and poniard, but a pair of pistols, which he had used in travelling; of a smaller and more convenient size than the large petronels, or horse pistols, which were then in common use, as being made for wearing at the girdle or in the pockets. Next to having stout and friendly comrades, a man is chiefly emboldened by finding himself well armed in case of need, and Nigel, who had thought with some anxiety on the hazard of trusting his life, if attacked, to the protection of the clumsy weapon with which Lowestoffe had equipped him, in order to complete his disguise, felt an emotion of confidence approaching to triumph, as, drawing his own good and well-tried rapier, he wiped it with his handkerchief, examined its point, bent it once or twice against the ground to prove its well-known metal, and finally replaced it in the scabbard the more hastily, that he heard a tap at the door of his chamber, and had no mind to be found vapouring in the apartment with his sword drawn.

It was his old host who entered, to tell him with many cringes that the price of his apartment was to be a crown per diem; and that, according to the custom of Whitefriars, the rent was always payable per advance, although he never scrupled to let the money lie till a week or fortnight or even a month's end, in the hands of any honourable guest like Master Grahame, always upon some reasonable consideration for the use. Nigel got rid of the old dotard's intrusion, by throwing down two pieces of gold, and requesting the accommodation of his present apartment for eight days, adding however, he did not think he should tarry so long.

The miser, with a sparkling eye and a trembling hand, clutched fast the proffered coin, and having balanced the pieces with exquisite pleasure on the extremity of his withered finger, began almost instantly to shew that not even the possession of gold can gratify for more than an instant the very heart that is most eager in the pursuit of it. Suspicions arose in Trapbois' mind to disturb the rapture of enjoyment—First, the pieces might be light—with hasty hand he drew a small pair of scales from his bosom and weighed them, first together, then separately, and smiled with glee as he saw them attain the due depression in the balance—a circumstance which might add to his profits, if it were true, as was currently reported, that little of the gold coinage was current in Alsatia in a perfect state, and that none ever left the sanctuary in that condition.

Another fear then occurred to trouble the old usurer's pleasure. He had been just able to comprehend that Nigel intended to leave the Friars sooner than the arrival of the term for which he had deposited the rent. This might imply an expectation of refunding, which, as a Scotch wag said, of all species of funding, jumped least with the old gentleman's humour. He was beginning to enter a hypothetical caveat on this subject, and to quote several reasons why no part of the money once consigned as room-rent, could be repaid back on any pretence, without great hardship to the landlord, when Nigel, growing impatient, told him that the money was his absolutely, and without any intention on his part of resuming any of it—all he asked in return was the liberty of enjoying in private the apartment he had paid for. Old Trapbois, who had still at his tongue's end much of the smooth language, by which in his time he had hastened the ruin of many a young spend-thrift, began to launch out upon the noble and generous disposition of his new guest, until Nigel, growing impatient, took the old gentleman by the hand, and gently, yet irresistibly, led him to the door of his chamber, put him out, but with such a decent and moderate exertion of his superior strength as to render the action in no shape indecorous, and fastening the door, began to do that for his pistols which he had done for his favourite sword, examining with care the flints and locks, and reviewing the state of his small provision of ammunition.

In this operation he was a second time interrupted by a knocking at his door—he called upon the person to enter, having no doubt that it was Lowestoffe's messenger at length arrived. It was, however, the ungracious daughter of old Trapbois, who, muttering something about her father's mistake, laid down on the table one of the pieces of gold which Nigel had just given to him, saying, that what she retained was the full rent for the term he had specified. Nigel replied, he had paid the money, and had no desire to receive it again.

"Do as you will with it, then," replied his hostess, "for there it lies, and shall lie for me—if you are fool enough to pay more than is reason, my father shall not be knave enough to take it."

"But your father, mistress," said Nigel; "your father told me"——

"O, my father, my father," said she, interrupting him,—"my father managed these affairs while he was able—I manage them now, and that may in the long run be as well for both of us."

She then looked on the table, and observed the weapons.

"You have arms, I see," she said; "do you know how to use them?"

"I should do so, mistress," replied Nigel, "for it has been my occupation."

"You are a soldier, then?" she demanded.

"No further as yet, than as every gentleman of my country is a soldier."

"Ay, that is your point of honour—to cut the throats of the poor—a proper gentleman-like occupation for those who should protect them!"

"I do not deal in cutting throats, mistress," replied Nigel; "but I carry arms to defend myself, and my country if she needs me."

"Ay," replied Martha, "it is fairly worded; but men say ye are as prompt as others in petty brawls, where neither your safety nor your country are in hazard; and that had it not been so, you would not have been in the sanctuary to-day."

"Mistress," returned Nigel, "I should labour in vain to make you understand that a man's honour, which is, or should be, dearer to him than his life, may often call on and compel us to hazard our own lives, and that of others, on what would otherwise seem trifling contingencies."

"God's law says nought of that," said the female; "I have only read there, that thou shalt not kill—but I have neither time nor inclination to preach to you—you will find enough of fighting here if you like it, and well if it come not to seek you when you are least prepared. Farewell for the present—the chare-woman will execute your commands for your meals."

She left the room just as Nigel, provoked at her assuming a superior tone of judgment and of censure, was about to be so superfluous as to enter into a dispute with an old pawnbroker's daughter on the subject of the point of honour. He smiled at himself for the folly into which the spirit of self-vindication had so nearly hurried him.

Lord Glenvarloch then applied to the cares of old Deborah the chare-woman, by whose intermediation he was provided with a tolerably decent dinner; and the only embarrassment which he experienced, was from the almost forcible entry of the old dotard his landlord, who insisted upon giving his assistance at laying the cloth. Nigel had some difficulty to prevent him from displacing his arms and some papers which were lying on the small table at which he had been sitting; and nothing short of a stern and positive injunction to the contrary could compel him to use another board, (though there were two in the room,) for the purpose of laying the cloth.

Having at length obliged him to relinquish his purpose, he could not help observing that the attention of the old dotard seemed still anxiously fixed upon the small table on which lay his sword and pistols; and that amidst all the little duties which he seemed officiously anxious to render to his guest, he took every opportunity of looking towards and approaching these objects of his attention. At length, when Trapbois thought he had completely avoided the observation of his guest, Nigel, through the information of one of the cracked mirrors, on which channel of communication the old man had not calculated, beheld him actually extend his hand towards the table in question. He thought it unnecessary to use farther ceremony, but telling his landlord in a stern voice, that he permitted no one to touch his arms, he commanded him to leave the apartment. The old usurer commenced a maundering sort of an apology, in which all that Nigel distinctly apprehended, was a frequent repetition of the word *consideration*, and which did not seem to him to require any other answer than a reiteration of his command to him to leave the apartment, upon pain of worse consequences.

The ancient Hebe who acted as Lord Glenvarloch's cup-bearer, took his part against the intrusion of the still more antiquated Ganymede, and insisted on old Trapbois leaving the room instantly, menacing him at the same time with her mistress's displeasure if he remained there any longer. The old man seemed more under petticoat government than any other, for the threat of the chare-woman produced greater effect upon him than the more formidable displeasure of Nigel. He withdrew grumbling and muttering, and Lord Glenvarloch heard him bar a large door at the nearer end of the gallery, which served as a division betwixt the other parts of the extensive mansion, and the apartment occupied by his guest, which, as the reader is aware, had its access from the landing-place at the head of the grand stair-case.

Nigel accepted the careful sound of the bolts and bars as they were severally drawn by the trembling hand of old Trapbois, as an omen that the senior did not mean again to revisit him in the course of the evening, and heartily rejoiced that he was at length to be left to uninterrupted solitude.

The old woman asked if there was aught else to be done for his accommodation; and indeed it had hitherto seemed as if the pleasure of serving him, or more properly the reward which she expected, had renewed her youth and activity.—Nigel desired to have candles, a fire lighted in his apartment, and a few faggots placed beside it, that he might feed it from time to time, as he began to feel the chilly effects of the damp and low situation of the house, close as it was to the Thames. But while the old woman was absent upon his errand, he began to think in what way he should pass the long and solitary evening with which he was threatened.

His own reflections promised to Nigel little amusement and less applause. He had considered his own perilous situation in every light in which it could be viewed, and foresaw as little utility as comfort in resuming the survey. To divert the current of his ideas, books were, of course, the readiest resource; and although, like most of us, Nigel had, in his time, sauntered through huge libraries, and even spent a long time there without greatly disturbing their learned contents, he was now in a situation where the possession of a volume, even of very inferior merit, becomes a real treasure. The old housewife returned shortly afterwards with faggots, and some pieces of half-burned wax-candles, the perquisites probably, real or usurped, of some experienced groom of the Chambers, two of which she placed in large brass candlesticks, of different shapes and patterns, and laid the others on the table, that Nigel might renew them from time to time as they burned to the socket. She heard with interest Lord Glenvarloch's request to have a book—any sort of book—to pass away the night withal, and returned for answer, that she knew of no other books in the house but her young mistress's (as she always denominated Mistress Martha Trapbois,) Bible, which the owner would not lend; and her master's Whetstone of Witte, being the Second Part of Arithmetic, by Robert Record, with the Cossike Practice and Rule of Equation; which promising volume Nigel declined to borrow. She offered, however, to bring him some books from Duke Hildebrod—"who sometimes, good gentleman, gave a glance at a book when the State affairs of Alsatia left him as much leisure."

Nigel embraced the proposal, and his unwearied Iris scuttled away on this second embassy. She returned in a short time with a tattered quarto volume under her arm, and a pottle of sack in her hand; for the Duke, judging that mere reading was dry work, had sent the wine by way of sauce to help it down, not forgetting to add the price to the morning's score, which he had already run up against the stranger in the sanctuary.

Nigel seized on the book, and did not refuse the wine, thinking that a glass or two, as it really proved to be of good quality, would be no bad interlude to his studies. He dismissed, with thanks and assurance of reward, the poor old drudge who had been so zealous in his service; trimmed his fire and candles, and placed the easiest of the old arm-chairs in a convenient posture betwixt the fire and the table at which he had dined, and which now supported the measure of sack and the lights; and thus accompanying his studies with such luxurious appli-ances as were in his power, he began to examine the only volume with which the ducal library of Alsatia had been able to supply him.

The contents, though of a kind generally interesting, were not well calculated to dispel the gloom by which he was surrounded. The book was entitled, "God's Revenge against Murther;" not, as the biblio-maniacal reader may easily conjecture, the work which Reynolds pub-lished under that imposing name, but one of a much earlier date, printed and sold by old Wolfe; and which, could a copy now be found, would sell for much more than its weight in gold.*

Nigel had soon enough of the doleful tales which the book contains, and attempted one or two other modes of killing the evening. He looked out at window, but the night was rainy, with gusts of wind; he tried to coax the fire, but the faggots were green and smoked without burning; and as he was naturally temperate, he felt his blood some-what heated by the canary sack which he had already drank, and had no further inclination to that pastime. He next attempted to compose a memorial, addressed to the King, in which he set forth his case and his grievances. But speedily stung with the idea that his supplication would be treated with scorn, he flung the scroll into the fire, and, in a sort of desperation, resumed the book which he had laid aside.

Nigel became more interested in the volume at the second than at the first attempt which he made to peruse it. The narratives, strange and shocking as they were to human feeling, possessed yet the interest of sorcery or of fascination, which rivets the attention by its awakening horrors. Much was told of the strange and horrible acts of blood by which men, setting nature and humanity alike at defiance, had, for the thirst of revenge, the lust of gold, or the cravings of irregular ambition, broken into the tabernacle of life. Yet more surprising and mysterious tales were recounted of the mode in which such deeds of

---

* NOTE *by Captain Clutterbuck*.—Only three copies are known to exist; one in the library at Kennaquhair, and two—one foxed and cropped, the other tall and in good condition—both in the possession of an eminent member of the Roxburgh Club, now M.P. for a great university.

blood had come to be discovered and revenged. Animals, insensible animals, had told the secret, and birds of the air had carried the matter. The elements had seemed to betray the deed which had polluted them—earth had ceased to support the murderer's steps, fire to warm his frozen limbs, water to refresh his parched lips, air to relieve his gasping lungs. All, in short, bore evidence to the homicide's guilt. In other circumstances, the criminal's own awakened conscience pursued and brought him to justice; and in some narratives the grave was said to have yawned, that the ghost of the sufferer might call for revenge.

It was now wearing late into the night, and the book was still in Nigel's hands, when the tapestry which hung behind him flapped against the wall, and the wind produced by its motion, waved the flame of the candles by which he was reading. Nigel started and turned round, in that excited and irritable state of mind which arose from the nature of his studies, especially at a period when a certain degree of superstition was inculcated as a point of religious faith. It was not without emotion that he saw the bloodless countenance, meagre form, and ghastly aspect of old Trapbois, once more in the very act of extending his withered hand towards the table which supported his arms. Convinced by this untimely apparition that something evil was meditated towards him, Nigel sprung up, seized his sword, drew it, and placing it to the old man's breast, demanded of him what he did in his apartment at so untimely an hour. Trapbois shewed neither fear nor surprise, and only answered by some imperfect expressions, intimating he would part with his life rather than with his property; and Lord Glenvarloch, strangely embarrassed, knew not what to think of the intruder's motives, and still less how to get rid of him. As he again tried the means of intimidation, he was surprised by a second apparition from behind the tapestry, in the person of the daughter of Trapbois, bearing a lamp in her hand. She also seemed to possess her father's insensibility to danger, for, coming close to Nigel, she pushed aside contemptuously his naked sword, and even attempted to take it out of his hand.

"For shame," she said, "your sword on a man of eighty years and more!—this the honour of a Scottish gentleman!—give it to me to make a spindle of."

"Stand back," said Nigel; "I mean your father no injury—but I *will* know what has caused him to prowl this whole day, and even at this late hour of night, around my arms."

"Your arms!" repeated she; "alas! young man, the whole arms in the Tower of London are of little value to him, in comparison of this miserable piece of gold which I left this morning on the table of a young spendthrift, too careless to put what belonged to him into his own purse."

So saying, she shewed the piece of gold, which, still remaining on the table where she left it, had been the bait that attracted old Trapbois so frequently to the spot; and which, even in the silence of the night, had so dwelt on his imagination, that he had made use of a private passage long disused, to enter his guest's apartment, in order to possess himself of the treasure during his slumbers. He now threw himself with impotent passion on his daughter as she held out the piece of gold to Nigel, exclaiming at the highest tones of his cracked and feeble voice—

"It is mine—it is mine!—he gave it me for a consideration—I will die ere I part with my property!"

"It is indeed his own, mistress," said Nigel, "and I do entreat you to restore it to the person on whom I have bestowed it, and let me have my apartment in quiet."

"I will account with you for it then," said the maiden, reluctantly giving to her father the morsel of Mammon, on which he darted as if his bony fingers had been the talons of a hawk seizing its prey; and then making a contented muttering and mumbling, like an old dog after he has been fed, and just when he is wheeling him thrice round for the purpose of lying down, he followed his daughter behind the tapestry, through a little sliding door, which was perceived when the hangings were drawn apart.

"This shall be properly fastened to-morrow," said the daughter to Nigel, speaking in such a tone that her father, deaf and engrossed by his acquisition, could not hear her; "to-night I will continue to watch him closely.—I wish you good repose."

These few words, pronounced in a tone of more civility than she had yet made use of towards her lodger, contained a wish which was not to be accomplished, although her guest, presently after her departure, retired to bed.

There was a slight fever on Nigel's blood, occasioned by the various events of the evening, which put him, as the phrase is, beside his rest. Perplexing and painful thoughts rolled on his mind like a troubled stream, and the more he laboured to lull himself to slumber, the further he seemed from attaining his object. He tried all the resources common in such cases, kept counting from one to a thousand, until his head was giddy—he watched the embers of the wood fire till his eyes were dazzled—he listened to the dull moaning of the wind, the swinging and creaking of signs which projected from the houses, and the baying of here and there a homeless dog, till his very ear was weary.

Suddenly, however, amid this monotony, came a sound which startled him at once. It was a female shriek. He sate up in his bed to listen, then remembered he was in Alsatia, where brawls of every sort were current among the unruly inhabitants.—But another scream, and another, and another succeeded so close, that he was certain, though the noise was remote and sounded stifled, it must be in the same house with him.

Nigel jumped up hastily, put on a part of his clothes, seized his sword and pistols, and ran to the door of his chamber. Here he plainly heard the screams redoubled, and, as he thought, the sounds came from the usurer's apartment. All access to the gallery was effectually excluded by the intermediate door, which the brave young lord shook with eager, but vain impatience. But the secret passage occurred suddenly to his recollection. He hastened back into his room, and succeeded with some difficulty in lighting a candle, dreadfully agitated by hearing the cries repeated, yet still more afraid lest they should sink into silence. He rushed along the narrow and winding entrance, guided by the noise, which now burst more wildly on his ear, and while he descended a narrow staircase which terminated the passage, he heard the stifled voices of men, encouraging, as it seemed, each other. "D—n her, strike her down—silence her—beat her brains out,"—while the voice of his hostess, though now almost exhausted, was repeating the cry of "murder," and "help." At the bottom of the stair-case was a small door which gave way before Nigel as he precipitated himself upon the scene of action, a cocked pistol in one hand, a candle in the other, and his naked sword under his arm. Two ruffians had with great difficulty overpowered, or rather were on the point of overpowering, the daughter of Trapbois, whose resistance appeared to have been most desperate, for the floor was covered with fragments of her clothes, and handfuls of her hair. It appeared her life was about to be the price of her defence, for one villain had drawn a long clasp-knife, when they were surprised by the entrance of Nigel, who, as they turned towards him, shot the fellow with the knife dead on the spot, and when the other advanced on him, hurled the candle-stick at his head, and then attacked him with his sword. It was now dark, save some pale moonlight from the window, and the ruffian, after firing a pistol without effect, and fighting a traverse or two with his sword, lost heart, made for the window, leaped over it, and escaped. Nigel fired his remaining pistol after him at a venture, and then called for light.

"There is light in the kitchen," answered Martha Trapbois, with more presence of mind than could have been expected, "Stay, you know not the way—I will fetch it myself.—Oh! my father—my poor father!—I knew it would come to this—and all along of the accursed gold! They have MURTHERED him."

END OF VOLUME SECOND

THE FORTUNES OF NIGEL

VOLUME III

Chapter One

Death finds us 'mid our play-things—snatches us
As the cross nurse might do a wayward child,
From all our toys and baubles. His rough call
Unlooses all our favourite ties on earth;
And well if they are such as may be answer'd
In yonder world, where all is judged of truly.

Old Play

IT WAS A ghastly scene which opened upon Martha Trapbois' return
with a light. Her own haggard and austere features were exaggerated
by all the desperation of grief, fear, and passion; but the latter was
predominant. On the floor lay the body of the robber, who had expired
without a groan, while his blood flowing plentifully had crimsoned all
around. Another body lay also there, on which the unfortunate woman
precipitated herself in agony, for it was that of her unhappy father. In
the next moment she started up, and exclaiming—"There may be life
yet!" strove to raise the body. Nigel went to her assistance, but not
without a glance at the open window, which Martha, as acute as if
undisturbed either by passion or terror, failed not to interpret justly.

"Fear not," she cried, "fear not; they are base cowards, to whom
courage is as much unknown as mercy—If I had had weapons, I could
have defended myself against them without assistance and protected
——Oh! my poor father!—protection comes too late for this cold and
stiff corpse—he is dead—dead!"

While she spoke, they were attempting to raise the dead body of the
old miser; but it was evident, even from the feeling of the inactive
weight and rigid joints, that life had forsaken her station. Nigel looked
for a wound, but saw none. The daughter of the deceased, with more
presence of mind than a daughter could have been supposed capable
of exerting, discovered the instrument of his murder—a sort of scarf

273

which had been drawn so tight round his throat as to stifle his cries for assistance in the first instance, and afterwards to extinguish life. She undid the fatal noose, and laying the old man's body in the arms of Lord Glenvarloch, she ran for water, for spirits, for essences, in the vain hope that life might be only suspended. That hope proved indeed vain. She chafed his temples, raised his head, opened his night-gown, (for it seemed as if he had arisen from bed upon hearing the entrance of the villains,) and, finally, opened, with difficulty, his fixed and closely-clenched hands, from one of which dropped a key, from the other the very piece of gold about which the unhappy man had been a little before so anxious, and which probably, in the impaired state of his mental faculties, he was disposed to defend with as desperate energy as if its amount had been necessary to his actual existence.

"It is in vain—it is in vain," said the daughter, desisting from her fruitless attempts to recal the spirit which had been effectually dislodged, for the neck had been twisted by the violence of the murtherers; "it is in vain—he is murthered—I always knew it would be thus; and now I witness it!"

She then snatched up the key and the piece of money, but it was only to dash them again on the floor, as she exclaimed, "Accursed be ye both, for you are the causes of this deed!"

Nigel would have spoken—would have reminded her that measures should be instantly taken for the pursuit of the murderer who had escaped, as well as for her own security against his return; but she interrupted him sharply.

"Be silent," she said, "be silent—think you the thoughts of my own heart are not enough to distract me, and with such a sight as this before me? I say be silent," she said again, and in a yet sterner tone— "Can a daughter listen, and her father's murdered corpse lying on her knees?"

Lord Glenvarloch, however overpowered by the energy of her grief, felt not the less the embarrassment of his own situation. He had discharged both his pistols—the robber might return—he had probably other assistants besides the man who had fallen, and it seemed to him indeed as if he heard a muttering beneath the windows. He explained hastily to his companion the necessity of procuring ammunition.

"You are right," she said, somewhat contemptuously, "and have ventured already more than ever I expected of man—go and shift for yourself, since that is your purpose—leave me to my fate."

Without stopping for needless expostulation, Nigel hastened to his own room through the secret passage, furnished himself with the ammunition he sought for, and returned with the same celerity; wondering himself at the accuracy with which he achieved, in the dark, all the meandering of the passage which he had traversed only once, and that in a moment of such violent agitation.

He found, on his return, the unfortunate woman standing like a statue by the body of her father, which she had laid straight on the floor, having covered the face with the skirt of his gown. She testified neither surprise nor pleasure at Nigel's return, but said to him calmly —"My moan is made—my sorrow—all the sorrow at least that man shall ever have noting of, is gone and over; but I will have justice, and the base villain who murdered this poor defenceless old man, when he had not, by the course of nature, a twelvemonth's life in him, shall not cumber the earth long after him. Stranger, whom heaven has sent to forward the revenge reserved for this action, go to Hildebrod's—there they are awake all night in their revels—bid them come hither—he is bound by his duty, and dare not, and shall not, refuse his assistance, which he well knows I can reward. Why do ye tarry?—go instantly."

"I would," said Nigel, "but I am fearful of leaving you alone; the villain may return, and"——

"True—most true—he may return; and though I care little for his murdering me, he may possess himself of what has most tempted him. Keep this key and this piece of gold—they are both of importance— defend your life if assailed, and if you kill the villain I will make you rich. I go myself to call for aid."

Nigel would have remonstrated with her, but she had departed, and in a moment he heard the house-door clang behind her. For an instant he thought of following her; but upon recollection that the distance was but short betwixt the tavern of Hildebrod and the house of Trapbois, he concluded that she incurred little danger in passing it, and that he would do well in the meanwhile to remain on the watch as she recommended.

It was no pleasant situation for one unused to such scenes to remain in the apartment with two dead bodies, recently those of living and breathing men, who had both, within the space of less than half an hour, suffered violent death; one of them by the hand of the assassin, the other, whose blood still continued to flow from the wound in his throat, and to flood all around him, by the spectator's own deed of violence, though of justice. He turned his face from those wretched relics of mortality with a feeling of disgust, mingled with superstition; and he found, when he had done so, that the consciousness of the presence of these ghastly objects, though unseen by him, rendered him more uncomfortable than even when he had his eyes fixed upon, and reflected by, the cold, staring, lifeless eye-balls of the deceased. Fancy also played her usual sport with him. He now thought he heard

the well-worn damask night-gown of the deceased usurer rustle—
anon, that he heard the slaughtered bravo draw up his leg, the boot
scratching the floor as if he was about to rise—and again he deemed
he heard the footsteps and the whisper of the returned ruffian under
the window from which he had lately escaped. To face the last and
most real danger, and to parry the terrors which the other class of
feelings were like to impress upon him, Nigel went to the window, and
was much cheered to observe the light of several torches illuminating
the street, and followed, as the murmur of voices denoted, by a number of persons, armed, it would seem, with firelocks and halberds, and
attendant on Hildebrod, who (not in his fantastic office of duke, but in
that which he really possessed of bailiff of the liberty and sanctuary of
Whitefriars,) was on his way to inquire into the crime and its circumstances.

It was a strange and melancholy contrast to see these debauchees,
disturbed in the very depth of their midnight revel, on their arrival at
such a scene as this. They stared on each other, and on the bloody
work before them, with lack-lustre eyes; staggered with uncertain
steps over boards slippery with blood; their noisy brawling voices sunk
into stammering whispers; and, with spirits quelled by what they saw,
while their brains were still stupified by the liquor which they had
drank, they seemed like men walking in their sleep.

Old Hildebrod was an exception to the general condition. That
seasoned cask, however full, was at all times capable of motion, when
there occurred a motive sufficiently strong to set him a rowling. He
seemed much shocked at what he beheld, and his proceedings, in
consequence, had more in them of regularity and propriety, than he
might have been supposed capable of exhibiting upon any occasion
whatever. The daughter was first examined, and stated, with wonderful accuracy and distinctness, the manner in which she had been
alarmed with a noise of struggling and violence in her father's apartment, and that the more readily, because she was watching him on
account of some alarm concerning his health. On her entrance, she
had seen her father sinking under the strength of two men, upon
whom she rushed with all the fury she was capable of. As their faces
were blacked, and their figures disguised, she could not pretend, in
the hurry of a moment so dreadfully agitating, to distinguish either of
them as persons whom she had seen before. She remembered little
more excepting the firing of shots, until she found herself alone with
their guest, and saw that the ruffians were escaped.

Lord Glenvarloch told his story as we have given it to the reader.
The direct evidence thus received, Hildebrod examined the premises.
He found that the villains had made their entrance by the window out

of which the survivor made his escape; yet it seemed singular that they should have done so, as it was secured with strong iron bars, which old Trapbois was in the habit of shutting with his own hand at nightfall. He minuted down, with great accuracy, the state of every thing in the apartment, and examined carefully the features and person of the slain robber. He was dressed like a seaman of the lowest order, but his face was known to none present. Hildebrod next sent for an Alsatian surgeon, whose vices, undoing what his skill might have done for him, had consigned him to the wretched practice of this place. He made him examine the dead bodies, and make a proper description of the manner in which the sufferers seemed to have come by their end. The circumstance of the sash did not escape the learned judge, and, having listened to all that could be heard or conjectured on the subject, and collected all particulars of evidence which appeared to bear on the bloody transaction, he commanded the doors of the apartment to be locked until next morning; and carrying the unfortunate daughter of the murdered man into the kitchen, where there was no one in presence but Lord Glenvarloch, asked her gravely, whether she suspected no one in particular of having committed this deed.

"Do *you* suspect no one?" answered Martha, looking fixedly on him.

"Perhaps I may, mistress; but it is my part to ask questions, yours to answer them. That's the rule of the game."

"Then I suspect him who wore yonder sash. Do not you know who I mean?"

"Why, if you call on me for honours, I must needs say, I have seen the Captain have one of such a fashion, and he was not a man to change his suits often."

"Send out, then," said Martha, "and have him apprehended."

"If it is he, he will be far by this time; but I will communicate with the higher powers," answered the judge.

"You would have him escape," resumed she, fixing her eyes on him sternly.

"By cock and pie," replied Hildebrod, "did it depend on me, the murthering cut-throat should hang as high as ever Haman did—but let me take my time—he has friends amongst us that you wot well; and all that should assist me, are as drunk as fiddlers."

"I will have revenge—I will have it," repeated she; "and take heed you trifle not with me."

"Trifle! I would sooner trifle with a she-bear the minute after they had baited her. I tell you, mistress, be but patient, and we will have him. I know all his haunts, and he cannot forbear them long; and I will have trap-doors open for him. You cannot want justice, mistress, for you have the means to get it."

"They who help me in my revenge," said Martha, "shall share those means."

"Enough said," replied Hildebrod; "and now I would have you go to my house, and get something hot—you will be but dreary here by yourself."

"I will send for the old chare-woman," replied Martha, "and we have the stranger gentleman, besides."

"Umph—umph, the stranger gentleman!" said Hildebrod to Nigel, whom he drew a little apart. "I fancy the Captain has made the stranger gentleman's fortune when he was making a bold dash for his own. I can tell your honour—I must not say lordship—that I think my having chanced to give the greasy buff-and-iron scoundrel some hint of what I recommended to you to-day, has put him on this rough game. The better for you—you will get the cash without the father-in-law.—You will keep conditions, I trust?"

"I wish you had said nothing to any one of a scheme so absurd," said Nigel.

"Absurd!—Why, think you she will not have thee?—take her with the tear in her eye, man—take her with the tear in her eye.—Let me hear from you to-morrow—good-night, good-night—a nod is as good as a wink—I must to my business of sealing and locking up. By the way, this horrid work has put all out of my head—here is a fellow from Mr Lowestoffe has been asking to see you—as he said his business was express, the Senate only made him drink a couple of flagons, and he was just coming to beat up your quarters when this breeze blew up. —Ahey, friend! this is Master Nigel Grahame."

A young man, dressed in a green plush jerkin, with a badge on the sleeve, and having the appearance of a waterman, approached and took Nigel aside, while Duke Hildebrod went from place to place to exercise his authority, and to see the windows fastened, and the doors of the apartment locked up. The news communicated by Lowestoffe's messenger were not of the most pleasant. They were intimated in a courteous whisper to Nigel, to the following effect: That Mr Lowestoffe prayed him to consult his safety by instantly leaving Whitefriars, for that a warrant from the Lord Chief-Justice had been issued out for apprehending him, and would be put in force to-morrow, by the assistance of a party of musketeers, a force which the Alsatians neither would nor dared to resist.

"And so, squire," said the aquatic emissary, "my wherry is to wait you at the Temple Stairs yonder, at five this morning, and if you would give the blood-hounds the slip, why, you may."

"Why did not Master Lowestoffe write to me?" said Nigel.

"Alas! the good gentleman lies up in lavender for it himself, and has as little to do with pen and ink as if he were a parson."

"Did he send any token to me?" said Nigel.

"Token!—ay, marry did he—token enough, an I have not forgot it," said the fellow; then giving a hoist to the waistband of his breeches, he said,—"Ay, I have it—you were to believe me, because your name was written with an O, for Grahame—ay, that was it, I think.—Well, shall we meet in two hours, when tide turns, and go down the river like a twelve-oared barge?"

"Where is the King just now, knowst thou?" answered Lord Glenvarloch.

"The King? why, he went down to Greenwich yesterday by water, like a noble sovereign as he is, who will always float where he can. He was to have hunted this week, but that purpose is broken, they say; and he, the Prince, and the Duke, and all of them at Greenwich, are as merry as minnows."

"Well," replied Nigel, "I will be ready to go at five; do thou come hither to carry my baggage."

"Ay, ay, master," replied the fellow, and left the house, mixing himself with the disorderly attendants of Duke Hildebrod, who were now retiring. That potentate entreated Nigel to make fast the doors behind him, and pointing to the female who sate by the expiring fire with her limbs outstretched, like one whom the hand of Death had already arrested, he whispered, "Mind your hits—and mind your bargain—or I will cut your bow-string for you before you can draw it."

Feeling deeply the ineffable brutality which could recommend the prosecuting such views over a wretch in such a condition, Lord Glenvarloch yet commanded his temper so far as to receive the advice in silence, and attend to the former part of it, by barring the door carefully behind Duke Hildebrod and his suite, with the tacit hope he should never again see or hear of them. He then returned to the kitchen, in which the unhappy woman remained, her hands still clenched, her eyes fixed, and her limbs extended, like those of a person in a trance. Much moved with her situation, and with the prospect which lay before her, he endeavoured to awaken her to existence by every means in his power, and at length apparently succeeded in dispelling her stupor, and attracting her attention. He then explained to her that he was in the act of leaving Whitefriars in a few hours—that his future destination was uncertain, but that he desired anxiously to know whether he could contribute to her protection by apprizing any friend of her situation, or otherwise. With some difficulty she seemed to comprehend his meaning, and thanked him with her usual short ungracious manner. "He might mean well," she said, "but he ought to know that the miserable had no friends."

Nigel said, "he would not willingly be importunate, but as he was about to leave the Friars"—— She interrupted him,

"You are about to leave the Friars? I will go with you."

"You go with me!" exclaimed Lord Glenvarloch.

"Yes," she said, "I will persuade my father to leave this murthering den." But as she spoke, the more perfect recollection of what had past crowded on her mind. She hid her face in her hands, and burst out into a dreadful fit of sobs, moans, and lamentations, which terminated in hysterics, violent in proportion to the uncommon strength of her body and mind.

Lord Glenvarloch, shocked, confused, and inexperienced, was about to leave the house in quest of medical, or at least female assistance; but the patient, when the paroxysm had somewhat spent its force, held him fast by the sleeve with one hand, covering her face with the other, while a copious flood of tears came to relieve the emotions of grief by which she had been so violently agitated.

"Do not leave me," she said—"do not leave me, and call no one. I have never been in this way before, and would not now," she said, sitting upright, and wiping her eyes with her apron,—"would not now —but that—but that he loved *me*, if he loved nothing else that was human—to die so, and by such hands!"

And again the unhappy woman gave way to a paroxysm of sorrow, mingling her tears with sobbing, wailing, and all the abandonment of female grief, when at its utmost height. At length, she gradually recovered the austerity of her natural composure, and maintained it as if by a forcible exertion of resolution, repelling, as she spoke, the repeated returns of the hysterical affection, by such an effort as that with which epileptic patients are known to suspend the recurrence of their fits. Yet her mind, however resolved, could not so absolutely overcome the affection of her nerves, but what she was agitated by strong fits of trembling, which, for a minute or two at a time, shook her whole frame in a manner frightful to witness. Nigel forgot his own situation, and indeed every thing else, in the interest inspired by the unhappy woman before him—an interest which affected a proud spirit the more deeply, that she herself, with correspondent highness of mind, seemed determined to owe as little as possible either to the humanity or the pity of others.

"I am not wont to be in this way," she said,—"but—but—Nature will have power over the frail beings it has made. Over you, sir, I have some right; for, without you, I had not survived this awful night. I wish your aid had been either earlier or later—but you *have* saved my life, and you are bound to assist in making it endurable to me."

"If you will shew me how it is possible," answered Nigel.

"You are going hence, you say, instantly—carry me with you," said the unhappy woman; "by my own efforts, I shall never escape from this wilderness of guilt and misery."

"Alas! what can I do for you?" replied Nigel. "My own way, and I must not deviate from it, leads me, in all probability, to a dungeon. I might indeed transport you from hence with me, if you could afterwards bestow yourself with any friend."

"Friend!" she exclaimed—"I have no friend—they have long since discarded us—a spectre arising from the dead were more welcome than I should be at the doors of those who have disclaimed us—And if they were willing to restore their friendship to me now, I would despise it, because they withdrew it from him—from him—(here she underwent strong but suppressed agitation, and then added firmly)—from *him* who lies yonder.—I have no friend." Here she paused, and then suddenly, as if recollecting herself, added, "I have no friend—but I have that will purchase many—I have that which will purchase both friends and avengers—it is well thought of—I must not leave it for a prey to cheats and ruffians.—Stranger, you must return to yonder room; pass through it boldly to his—that is, to the sleeping apartment; push the bed-stead aside; beneath each of the posts is a brass plate, as if to support the weight, but it is that upon the left, nearest to the wall, which must serve your turn—press the corner of the plate, and it will spring up and shew a key-hole which this key will open—you will then lift a concealed trap-door, and in a cavity of the floor you will discover a small chest—bring it hither—it shall accompany our journey, and it will be hard if the contents cannot purchase me a place of refuge."

"But the door communicating with the kitchen has been locked by these people," said Nigel.

"True, I had forgot—they had their reasons for that, doubtless," answered she. "But the secret passage from your apartment is open, and you may go that way." Lord Glenvarloch took the key, and as he lighted a lamp to shew him the way, she read in his countenance some unwillingness to the task imposed. "You fear," she said—"there is no cause—the murderer and his victim are both at rest—take courage—I will go with you myself—you cannot know the trick of the spring, and the chest will be too heavy for you."

"No fear, no fear," answered Lord Glenvarloch, ashamed of the construction she put upon a momentary hesitation, arising from a dislike to look upon what was horrible, often connected with those high-wrought minds which are the last to fear what is merely dangerous. "I will do your errand as you desire, but for you—you must not—cannot go yonder."

"I can—I will," she said. "I am composed—you shall see that I am so." She took from the dresser a piece of unfinished sewing-work, and with steadiness and composure passed a silken thread into the eye of a fine needle. "Could I have done that," she said, with a smile yet more ghastly than her previous look of fixed despair, "had not my heart and hand been both steady?"

She then led the way rapidly up stairs to Nigel's chamber, and proceeded through the secret passage with the same haste, as if she had feared her resolution might have failed her ere her purpose was executed. At the bottom of the stairs she paused a moment before entering the fatal apartment—then hurried through with a rapid step to the sleeping chamber beyond, followed closely by Lord Glenvarloch, whose reluctance to approach the scene of butchery was altogether lost in the anxiety which he felt on account of the survivor of the tragedy.

Her first action was to pull aside the curtains of her father's bed; the bed-clothes were thrown aside in confusion, doubtless in the action of his starting from sleep to oppose the entrance of the villains into the next apartment. The hard mattress scarcely shewed the slight pressure where the emaciated body of the old miser had been deposited. His daughter sank beside the bed, clasped her hands, and prayed to Heaven, in a short and affecting manner, for support in her affliction, and for vengeance on the villains who had made her fatherless. A low-muttered, and still more brief petition, recommended to Heaven the soul of the sufferer, and invoked pardon for his sins, in virtue of the great Christian atonement.

This duty of piety performed, she signed to Nigel to give her assistance, and having pushed aside the heavy bed-stead, they saw the brass plate which Martha had described. She pressed the spring, and at once the plate starting up, shewed the key-hole, and a large iron ring used in lifting the trap-door, which, when raised, displayed the strong-box, or small chest, she had mentioned, and which proved indeed so very weighty, that it might perhaps have been scarcely possible for Nigel, though a very strong man, to have raised it without assistance. Having replaced every thing as they had found it, Nigel, with such assistance as his companion was able to afford, assumed his load, and made a shift to carry it into the next apartment, where lay the miserable owner, insensible to sounds and circumstances, which, if any thing could have broken his long last slumber, would certainly have done so.

His unfortunate daughter went up to his body, and had even the courage to remove the sheet which had been decently disposed over it. She put her hand on the heart, but there was no throb—held a feather to the lips, but there was no motion—then kissed with deep reverence the starting veins of the pale forehead—and then the emaciated hand.

"I would you could hear me," she said,—"father! I would you could hear me swear, that if I now save what you most valued on earth, it is only to assist me in obtaining vengeance for your death." She replaced the covering, and, without a tear, a sigh, or an additional word of any kind, renewed her efforts, until they conveyed the strong box betwixt them into Lord Glenvarloch's sleeping apartment. "It must pass," she said, "as part of your baggage. I will be in readiness so soon as the waterman calls."

She retired; and Lord Glenvarloch, who saw the hour of their departure approach, tore down a part of the old hangings to make a covering, which he corded upon the trunk, lest the peculiarity of its shape, and the care with which it was banded and counter-banded with bars of steel, might afford suspicions respecting the treasure which it contained. Having taken this measure of precaution, he changed the rascally disguise which he had assumed on entering Whitefriars, into a suit becoming his quality, and then, unable to sleep, though exhausted with the events of the night, he threw himself on his bed to await the summons of the waterman.

Chapter Two

> Give us good voyage, gentle stream—we stun not
> Thy sober ear with sounds of revelry;
> Wake not the slumbering echoes of thy banks
> With voice of flute and horn—we do but seek
> On the broad path-way of thy swelling bosom
> To glide in silent safety.
>
> *The Double Bridal*

GREY, OR RATHER yellow light was beginning to twinkle through the fogs of Whitefriars, when a low tap at the door of the unhappy miser announced to Lord Glenvarloch the summons of the boatman. He found at the door the man whom he had seen the night before, with a companion.

"Come, come, master—let us get afloat," said one of them, in a rough imperative whisper, "time and tide wait for no man."

"They shall not wait for me," said Lord Glenvarloch; "but I have some things to carry with me."

"Ay, ay—no man will take a pair of oars now, Jack, unless he means to load the wherry like a six-horse waggon—when they don't want to shift the whole kitt, they take a sculler, and be d——d to them.——Come, come, where be your rattle traps?"

One of the men was soon sufficiently loaded, in his own estimation at least, with Lord Glenvarloch's mail and its accompaniments, with which burthen he began to trudge towards the Temple Stairs. His comrade, who seemed the principal, began to handle the trunk which contained the miser's treasure, but pitched it down again in an instant, declaring, with a great oath, that it was as reasonable to expect a man to carry Paul's on his back. The daughter of Trapbois, who had by this time joined them, wrapped up in a long dark hood and mantle, exclaimed to Lord Glenvarloch——"Let them leave it if they will——let them leave all——let us but escape from the horrible place."

We have mentioned somewhere, that Nigel was a very athletic young man, and impelled by a strong feeling of compassion and indignation, he shewed his bodily strength singularly on this occasion, for, seizing on the ponderous strong-box by means of the rope he had cast around it, he threw it on his shoulders, and marched resolutely forwards under a weight, which would have sunk to the earth three young gallants, at the least, of our degenerate day. The waterman followed him in amazement, calling out, "Why, master——master——you might as well gie me t'other end on't!" and anon offered his assistance to support it in some degree behind, which after the first minute or two Nigel was fain to accept. His strength was almost exhausted when he reached the wherry, which was lying at the Temple Stairs according to appointment; and when he pitched the trunk into it, the weight sank the bow of the boat so low in the water as well nigh to overset it.

"We shall have as hard a fare of it," said the waterman to his comrade, "as if we were ferrying over an honest bankrupt with all his secreted goods——Ho, ho! good woman, what are you stepping in for? ——our gunwale lies deep enough in the water without live lumber to boot."

"This person comes with me," said Lord Glenvarloch; "she is for the present under my protection."

"Come, come, master," rejoined the fellow, "that is out of my commission. You must not double my fare on me——She may go by land——and as for protection, her face will protect her from Berwick to the Land's End."

"You will not except at my doubling the loading, if I double the fare?" said Nigel, determined on no account to relinquish the protection of this unhappy woman, for which he had already devised some sort of plan, likely now to be baffled by the characteristic rudeness of the Thames watermen.

"Ay, by G——, but I will except though," said the fellow with the green plush jacket; "I will overload my wherry neither for love nor money—I love my boat as well as my wife, and a thought better."

"Nay, nay, comrade," said his mate, "that is speaking no true water language. For double fare we are bound to row a witch in her egg-shell, if she bid us; and so pull away, Jack, and let us have no more prating."

They got into the stream-way accordingly, and, although heavily laden, began to move down the river with reasonable speed.

The lighter vessels which passed, overtook, or crossed them in their course, failed not to assail them with the boisterous raillery, which was then called water-wit; for which the extreme plainness of Mistress Martha's features, contrasted with the youth, handsome figure, and good looks of Nigel, gave the principal topics; while the circumstance of the boat being somewhat overloaded, did not escape their notice. They were hailed successively, as a grocer's wife upon a party of pleasure with her eldest apprentice—as an old woman carrying her grandson to school—and as a young strapping Irishman, carrying an ancient maiden to Dr Rigmarole's at Redriffe, who buckles beggars for a tester and a dram of Geneva. All this abuse was retorted in a similar strain of humour by Green-jacket and his companion, who maintained the war of wit with the same alacrity with which they were assailed.

Meanwhile, Lord Glenvarloch asked his desolate companion if she had thought on any place where she could remain in safety with her property. She confessed, in more detail than formerly, that her father's character had left her no friends; and that from the time he had betaken himself to Whitefriars, to escape certain legal consequences of his eager pursuit of gain, she had lived a life of total seclusion; not associating with the society which the place afforded, and by her residence there, as well as her father's parsimony, effectually cut off from all other company. What she now wished was, in the first place, to obtain the shelter of a decent lodging, and the countenance of honest people, however low in life, until she should obtain legal advice as to the mode of obtaining justice on her father's murderer. She had no hesitation to charge the guilt upon Colepepper, (commonly called Peppercole,) who she knew to be as capable of any act of treacherous cruelty, as he was cowardly, where actual manhood was required. He had been strongly suspected of two robberies before, one of which was coupled with an atrocious murther. He had, she intimated, made pretensions to her hand as the easiest and safest way of obtaining possession of her father's wealth; and on her refusing his addresses, if they could be termed so, in the most positive terms, he had thrown out such obscure hints of vengeance, as, joined with some imperfect assaults upon the house, had kept her in frequent alarm, both on her father's account and her own.

Nigel, but that his feeling of respectful delicacy to the unfortunate woman forbade him to do so, could here have communicated a circumstance corroborative of her suspicions, which had already occurred to his own mind. He recollected the hint that old Hildebrod threw forth on the preceding night, that some communication betwixt himself and Colepepper had hastened the catastrophe. As this communication related to the plan which Hildebrod had been pleased to form, of promoting a marriage betwixt Nigel himself and the rich heiress of Trapbois, the fear of losing an opportunity not to be regained, together with the mean malignity of a low-bred ruffian, disappointed in a favourite scheme, was most likely to instigate the bravo to the deed of violence which had been committed. The reflection that his own name was in some degree implicated with the causes of this horrid tragedy, doubled Lord Glenvarloch's anxiety in behalf of the victim whom he had rescued, while at the same time he formed the tacit resolution, that so soon as his own affairs were put upon some footing, he would contribute all in his power to the investigation of this bloody affair.

After ascertaining from his companion that she could form no better plan of her own, he recommended to her to take up her lodging for the time, at the house of his old landlord, Christie the shipchandler, at Paul's Wharf, describing the decency and honesty of that worthy couple, and expressing his hopes that they would receive her into their own house, or recommend her at least to that of some person for whom they could be responsible, until she should have time to enter upon other arrangements for herself.

The poor woman received advice so grateful to her in her desolate condition, with an expression of thanks, brief indeed, but deeper than anything had yet extracted from the austerity of her natural disposition.

Lord Glenvarloch then proceeded to inform Martha, that certain reasons, connected with his personal safety, called him immediately to Greenwich, and therefore it would not be in his power to accompany her to Christie's house, which he would otherwise have done with pleasure; but tearing a leaf from his tablet, he wrote on it a few lines, addressed to his landlord, as a man of honesty and humanity, in which he described the bearer as a person who stood in singular necessity of temporary protection and good advice, for which her circumstances enabled her to make ample acknowledgment. He therefore requested John Christie, as his old and good friend, to afford her the shelter of his roof for a short time; or, if that might not be consistent with his convenience, at least to direct her to a proper lodging—And finally, he imposed on him the additional, somewhat more difficult commission, to recommend her to the counsel and services of an honest, at least a reputable and skilful attorney, for the transacting some law business of importance. This note he subscribed with his real name, and delivering it to his *protegée*, who received it with another deeply uttered "I thank you," which spoke the sterling feelings of her gratitude better than a thousand combined phrases, he commanded the watermen to pull in for Paul's Wharf, which they were now approaching.

"We have not time," said Green-jacket; "we cannot be stopping every instant."

But upon Nigel insisting upon his commands being obeyed, and adding, that it was for the purpose of putting the lady ashore, the waterman declared he would rather have her room than her company, and put the wherry alongside of the wharf accordingly. Here two of the porters, who ply in such places, were easily induced to undertake the charge of the ponderous strong-box, and at the same time to guide the owner to the well-known mansion of John Christie, with whom all who lived in that neighbourhood were perfectly acquainted.

The boat, much lightened of its load, went now down the Thames at a rate increased in proportion. But we must forbear to pursue her on her voyage for a few minutes, since we have previously to mention the issue of Lord Glenvarloch's recommendation.

Mistress Martha Trapbois reached the shop in perfect safety, and was about to enter it, when a sickening sense of the uncertainty of her situation, and of the singularly painful task of telling her story, came over her so strongly, that she paused a moment at the very threshold of her proposed place of refuge, to think in what manner she could best second the recommendation of the friend whom Providence had raised up to her. Had she possessed that knowledge of the world, from which her habits of life had completely excluded her, she might have known that the large sum of money which she brought alongst with her, would have been a passport to her into the mansions of nobles, and the palaces of princes. But, however conscious of its general power, which assumes so many forms and complexions, she was so inexperienced as to be most unnecessarily afraid that the means by which the wealth had been acquired, might exclude its inheretrix from shelter even in the house of a humble tradesman.

While she thus delayed, a more reasonable cause for hesitation arose, in a considerable noise and altercation within the house, which turned louder and louder as the disputants issued forth upon the street or lane before the door.

The first who entered upon the scene was a tall, raw-boned,

hard-favoured man, who stalked out of the shop hastily, with a gait like that of a Spaniard in a passion, who, disdaining to add speed to his loco-motion by running, only condescends, in the utmost extremity of his angry haste, to add length to his stride. He faced about, so soon as he was out of the house, upon his pursuer, a decent-looking, elderly, plain tradesman—no less than John Christie himself, the owner of the shop and tenement, by whom he seemed to be followed, and who was in a state of agitation more than is usually expressed by such a person.

"I'll hear no more on't," said the personage who first appeared on the scene.—"Sir, I will hear no more on it. Besides being a most false and impudent figment, as I can testify—it is *Scaandalum Maagnatum*, sir—*Scaandalum Maagnatum*," he reiterated with a broad accentuation of the first vowel, well known at the Colleges of Edinburgh and Glasgow, which we can only express in print by doubling the said first of letters and of vowels, and which would have cheered the cockles of the reigning monarch had he been within hearing,—a severer stickler as he was for what he deemed the genuine pronunciation of the Roman tongue, than for any of the royal prerogatives upon which he was at times disposed to insist so strenuously in his speeches to Parliament.

"I care not an ounce of rotten cheese," said John Christie in reply, "what you call it—but it is TRUE—and I am a free Englishman, and have right to speak the truth in my own concerns; and your master is little better than a villain, and you no more than a swaggering coxcomb, whose head I will presently break, as I have known it well broken before on lighter occasion."

And so saying, he flourished the paring-shovel which usually made clean the steps of his little shop, and which he had caught up as the readiest weapon of working his foeman damage, and advanced therewith upon him. The cautious Scot, (for such our reader must have already pronounced him, from his language and pedantry,) drew back as the enraged ship-chandler approached, but in a surly manner, and bearing his hand on his sword-hilt rather in the act of one who was losing habitual forbearance and caution of deportment, than as alarmed by the attack of an antagonist inferior to himself in youth, strength, and weapons.

"Bide back," he said, "Maister Christie—I say bide back, and consult your safety, man. I have evited striking you in your ain house under mickle provocation, because I am ignorant how the laws here may pronounce respecting burglary and hamesucken, and such matters; and besides, I wald not willingly hurt ye, man, e'en on the causeway, that is free to us baith, because I mind your kindness of lang syne, and partly consider ye as a poor deceived creature. But de'il damn me, sir, and I am not wont to swear, but if you touch my Scots shouther with that shule of yours, I will make six inches of my Andrew Ferrara deevilish intimate with your guts, neighbour."

And therewithal, though still retreating from the brandished shovel, he made one-third of the basket-hilted broad-sword which he wore, visible from the sheath. The wrath of John Christie was abated, either by his own natural temperance of disposition, or perhaps in part by the glimmer of cold steel, which flashed on him from his adversary's last action.

"I would do well to cry clubs on thee, and have thee ducked at the wharf," he said, grounding his shovel, however, at the same time, "for a paltry swaggerer, that would draw thy bit of iron there on an honest citizen before his own door—but get thee gone, and reckon on a salt eel for thy supper, if thou shouldst ever come near my house again. I wish it had been at bottom of Thames when it first gave the use of its roof to smooth-faced, oily-tongued, double-minded Scots thieves."

"It's an ill bird that fouls it's own nest," replied his adversary, not perhaps the less bold that he saw matters were taking the turn of a pacific debate; "and a pity it is that a kindly Scot should ever have married in foreign parts, and given life to a purse-proud, pudding-headed, fat-gutted, lean-brained Southron, e'en such as you, Maister Christie. But fare ye weel—fare ye weel, for ever and a day; and if you quarrel wi' a Scot again, man, say as mickle ill o' himsell as ye like, but say nane of his patron or of his countryman, or it will scarce be your flat cap that will keep your lang lugs from the sharp abridgement of a Highland whinger, man."

"And if you continue your insolence to me before my own door, were it but two minutes longer," retorted John Christie, "I will call the constable, and make your Scotch ankles acquainted with an English pair of stocks."

So saying, he turned to retire into his shop with some shew of victory; for his enemy, whatever might be his innate valour, manifested no desire to drive matters to extremity—conscious, perhaps, that whatever advantage he might gain in singular combat with John Christie, would be more than overbalanced by incurring an affair with the constituted authorities of Old England, not at that time apt to be particularly favourable to their new fellow-subjects, in the various successive trials which were then constantly taking place between the individuals of two proud nations, who still retained a stronger sense of their national animosity during centuries, than of their late union for a few years under the government of the same prince.

Mrs Martha Trapbois had dwelt too long in Alsatia, to be either surprised or terrified at the altercation she had witnessed. Indeed she only wondered that the debate did not end in some of those acts of violence by which they were usually terminated in the sanctuary. As they separated from each other, she, who had no idea that the cause of the quarrel was more deeply rooted than in the daily scenes of the same nature which she had heard of or witnessed, did not hesitate to stop Master Christie in his return to his shop, and present to him the letter which Lord Glenvarloch had given to her. Had she been better acquainted with life and its business, she would certainly have waited for a more temperate moment; and she had reason to repent of her precipitation, when, without saying a single word, or taking the trouble to gather more of the information contained in the letter than was expressed in the subscription, the incensed ship-chandler threw it down on the ground, trampled it in high disdain, and without address- ing a single word to the bearer, excepting indeed something much more like a hearty curse than was perfectly consistent with his own grave appearance, he retired into his shop and shut the hatch-door.

It was with the most inexpressible anguish that the desolate, friend- less, and unhappy female, thus beheld her sole hope of succour, countenance, and protection, vanish at once, without being able to conceive a reason; for, to do her justice, the idea that her friend, whom she knew by the name of Nigel Grahame, had imposed on her, a solution which might readily have occurred to many in her situation, never once entered her mind. Although it was not her temper easily to bend her mind to entreaty, she could not help exclaiming after the ireful and retreating ship-chandler,—"Good master—hear me but a moment!—for mercy's sake—for honesty's sake!"

"Mercy and honesty from him, mistress!" said the Scot, who, though he essayed not to interrupt the retreat of his antagonist, still kept stout possession of the field of action,—"ye might as weel expect brandy from bean-stalks, or milk from a craig of blue whunstane—the man is mad—horn-mad to boot."

"I must have mistaken the person to whom the letter was addressed, then;" and, as she spoke, Mistress Martha Trapbois was in the act of stooping to lift the paper which had been so uncourteously received. Her companion, with natural civility, anticipated her purpose; but, what was not quite so much in etiquette, he took a sly glance at it as he was about to hand it to her, and his eye having caught the subscription, he said, with surprise, "Glenvarloch—Nigel Olifaunt, of Glenvar- loch!—do you know the Lord Glenvarloch, dame?"

"I know not of whom you speak," said Mrs Martha, peevishly. "I had that paper from one Master Nigel Grahame."

"Nigel Grahame!—umph—O, ay—very true—I had forgot," said the Scotsman. "A tall, well-set young man, about my height—bright blue eyes like a hawk's—a pleasant speech, something leaning to the kindly north-country accentuation, but not much, in respect of his having been resident abroad?"

"All this is true—and what of it all?" said the daughter of the miser.

"Hair of my complexion?"

"Yours is red," replied she.

"I pray you, peace," said the Scotchman. "I was going to say—of my complexion, but with a deeper shade of the chesnut. Weel, dame, if I have guessed the man aright, he is one with whom I am, and have been, intimate and familiar,—nay, I may truly say I have done him much service in my time, and may live to do him more. I had indeed a sincere good will for him, and I doubt he has been much at a loss since we parted; but the fault is not mine. Wherefore, as this letter will not avail you with him to whom it is directed, you may believe that Heaven hath sent it to me, who have a special regard for the writer—have, besides, as much mercy and honesty within me as man can weel make his bread with, and am willing to aid any distressed creature, that is my friend's friend, with my counsel, and otherwise, so that I am not put to much charges, being in a strange country, like a poor lamb that has wandered from its own native hirsel, and leaves a tait of its woo' in every damned Southron bramble that comes across it." While he spoke thus, he read the contents of the letter, without waiting for permission, and then continued,—"And so this is all that you are wanting, my dove?—nothing more than safe and honourable lodging, and sustenance, upon your own charges?"

"Nothing more," said she. "If you are a man and a Christian, you will help me to what I need so much."

"A man I am," replied the formal Caledonian, "e'en sic as ye see me —and a Christian I may call myself, though unworthy, and though I have heard little pure doctrine since I came hither—a' polluted with men's devices—A-hem!—Weel, and if ye be an honest woman," (here he peeped under her muffler,) "as an honest woman ye seem likely to be—though, let me tell you, they are a kind of cattle not so rife in the streets of this city as I would desire them—I was almost strangled with my own band by twa rampallians, wha wanted yestreen—nae further gane—to harle me into a change-house— however, if ye be a decent honest woman," (here he took another peep at features certainly bearing no beauty which could infer suspicion,) "as decent and honest ye seem to be—why, I will advise you to a decent honest house, where you will get douce, quiet entertainment, on reasonable terms, and the occasional benefit of my own counsel and direction—that is, from time to time, as my other avocations may permit."

"May I venture to accept of such an offer from a stranger?" said Martha, with natural hesitation.

"Troth, I see nothing to hinder you, mistress," replied the bonny Scot; "ye can but see the place and say the place, and do after as ye think best. Besides, we are nae such strangers, neither—for I know your friend, and you, it is like, know mine, whilk knowledge, on either hand, is a medium of communication between us, even as the middle of the string connecteth its twa ends, or extremities. But I will enlarge on this farther as we pass along, gin ye list to bid your twa lazy loons of porters there lift up your little kist between them, whilk ae true Scotsman might carry under his arm. Let me tell you, mistress, ye will soon make a toom pock-end of it in Lon'on, if ye hire twa knaves to do the work of ane."

So saying, he led the way, followed by Mistress Trapbois, whose singular destiny, though it had heaped her with wealth, had left her, for the moment, no wiser counsellor, or more distinguished protector, than honest Richie Moniplies, a discarded serving-man.

Chapter Three

> This way lies safety and a sure retreat;
> Yonder lies danger, shame, and punishment.
> Most welcome, danger then—Nay, let me say,
> Though spoke with swelling heart—welcome e'en shame;
> And welcome punishment—for, call me guilty,
> I do but pay the tax that's due to justice;
> And call me guiltless, then that punishment
> Is shame to those alone who do inflict it.
> *The Tribunal*

WE LEFT LORD Glenvarloch, to whose Fortunes our story chiefly attaches itself, gliding swiftly down the Thames. He was not, as the reader may have observed, very popular in his disposition, or apt to enter into conversation with those into whose company he was casually thrown. This was indeed an error in his conduct, arising less from pride, though of that feeling we do not pretend to exculpate him, than from a sort of bashful reluctance to mix in the conversation of those with whom he was not familiar. It is a fault only to be cured by experience and knowledge of the world, which soon teaches every sensible and acute person the important lesson, that amusement, and, what is more important, that information and increase of knowledge, are to be derived from the conversation of every individual whatsoever, with whom he is thrown into a natural train of communication. For ourselves, we can assure the reader—and perhaps if we have ever been able to afford him amusement, it is owing in a great degree to this cause—that we never found ourselves in company with the stupidest of all possible companions in a post-chaise, or with the most errant cumber-corner that ever occupied a place in the mail-coach, without finding, that in the course of our conversation with him, we had some ideas suggested to us, either grave or gay, or some information communicated in the course of our journey, which we should have regretted not to have learned, and which we should be sorry to have immediately forgotten. But Nigel was somewhat immured within the Bastile of his rank, as some philosopher, (Tom Paine, we think,) has happily enough expressed that sort of shyness which men of dignified situations are apt to be beset with, rather from not exactly knowing how far, or with whom, they ought to be familiar, than from any real touch of aristocratic pride; besides, the immediate pressure of his own affairs was such as exclusively to engross his attention.

He sate, therefore, wrapt in his cloak, in the stern of the boat, with his mind entirely bent upon the probable issue of the interview with the Sovereign, which it was his purpose to seek; for which abstraction of mind he may be fully justified, although perhaps, by questioning the watermen who were transporting him down the river, he might have discovered matters of high concernment to him.

At any rate, Nigel remained silent till the wherry approached the town of Greenwich, when he commanded the men to put in for the nearest landing-place, as it was his purpose to go ashore there, and dismiss them from further attendance.

"That is not possible," said the fellow with the green jacket, who, as we have already said, seemed to take on himself the charge of pilotage. "We must go," he continued, "to Gravesend, where a Scotch vessel, which dropt down the river last tide for that very purpose, lies with her anchor a-peak, waiting to carry you to your own dear northern country —your hammock is slung, and all is ready for you, and you talk of going ashore at Greenwich, as readily as if such a thing were possible!"

"I see no impossibility," said Nigel, "in your landing me where I desire to be landed; but very little possibility of your carrying me any where I am not desirous of going."

"Why, whether do you manage the wherry, or we, master?" asked Green-jacket, in a tone betwixt jest and earnest; "I take it she will keep the course we row her upon."

"Ay," retorted Nigel, "but I take it you will row her on the course I direct you to keep, otherwise your chance of payment is but a poor one."

"Suppose we are content to risk that," said the undaunted waterman, "I wish to know how you, who do talk so big—I mean no offence, master, but you *do* talk big,—would help yourself in such a case?"

"Simply thus," answered Lord Glenvarloch—"You saw me, an hour since, bring down to the boat a trunk that neither of you could lift—if we are to contest the destination of our voyage, the same strength which tossed that chest into the wherry, will suffice to fling you out of it; wherefore, before we begin the scuffle, I pray you to remember, that, whither I would go, there I will oblige you to carry me."

"Gramercy for your kindness," said Green-jacket; "and now mark me in return. My comrade and I are two men—and you, were you as stout as George-a-Green, can pass but for one; and two, you will allow, are more than a match for one. You mistake in your reckoning, my friend."

"It is you who mistake," answered Nigel, who began to grow warm; "it is I who am three to two, sirrah—I carry two men's lives at my girdle."

So saying, he opened his cloak and shewed the two pistols which he had disposed at his girdle. Green-jacket was unmoved at the display.

"I have got," said he, "a pair of barkers that will match yours," and he shewed that he also was armed with pistols; "so you may begin as soon as you list."

"Then," said Lord Glenvarloch, drawing forth and cocking a pistol, "the sooner the better. Take notice, I hold you as a ruffian, who have declared you will put force on my person; and that I will shoot you through the head if you do not instantly put me ashore at Greenwich."

The other waterman, alarmed at his gesture, lay upon his oar; but Green-jacket replied coolly—"Look you, master, I should not care a tester to venture a life with you on this matter; but the truth is, I am employed to do you good, and not to do you harm."

"By whom are you employed?" said the Lord Glenvarloch; "or who dare concern themselves in me, or my affairs, without any authority?"

"As to that," answered the waterman, in the same tone of indifference, "I shall not shew my commission. For myself, I care not, as I said, whether you land at Greenwich to get yourself hanged, or go down to get aboard the Royal Thistle, to make your escape to your own country. You will be equally out of my reach either way. But it is fair to put the choice before you."

"My choice is made," said Nigel. "I have told you thrice already it is my pleasure to be landed at Greenwich."

"Write it on a piece of paper," said the waterman, "that such is your positive will—I must have something to shew to my employers, that the transgression of their orders lies with yourself, not with me."

"I chuse to hold this trinket in my hand for the present," said Nigel, shewing his pistol, "and will write you the acquittance when I go ashore."

"I would not go ashore with you for a hundred pieces," said the waterman. "Ill luck has ever attended you, except in small gaming; do me fair justice, and give me the testimony I desire. If you are afraid of foul play while you write it, you may hold my pistols, if you will." He offered the weapons to Nigel accordingly, who, while they were under his control, and all possibility of his being taken at advantage was excluded, no longer hesitated to give his waterman an acknowledgment, in the following terms:

"Jack in the Green, with his mate, belonging to the wherry called the Jolly Raven, have done their duty faithfully by me, landing me at Greenwich by my express command; and being themselves willing and desirous to carry me on board the Royal Thistle, presently lying at Gravesend." Having finished this acknowledgment, which he signed with the letters, N. O. G. as indicating his name and title, he again requested to know of the waterman, to whom he delivered it, the name of his employers.

"Sir," replied Jack in the Green, "I have respected your secret—do not you seek to pry into mine. It would do you no good to know for whom I am taking this present trouble; and, to be brief, you shall not know it—and if you will fight in the quarrel, as you said even now, the sooner we begin the better. Only this you may be cock-sure of, that we designed you no harm, and that if you fall into any, it will be of your own wilful seeking." As he spoke, they approached the landing-place, where Nigel instantly jumped ashore. The waterman placed his small mail-trunk on the stairs, observing there were plenty of spare hands about, to carry it where he would.

"We part friends, I hope, my lad," said the young noble, offering at the same time a piece of money more than double the usual fare, to his boatmen.

"We part as we met," answered Green-jacket; "and, for your money, I am paid sufficiently with this bit of paper. Only, if you owe me any love for the cast I have given you, I pray you not to dive so deep into the pockets of the next apprentice that you find fool enough to play the cavalier.—And you, you greedy swine," said he to his companion, who still had a longing eye fixed on the money which Nigel continued to offer, "push off, or, if I take a stretcher in hand, I break the knave's pate of thee." The fellow pushed off, as he was commanded, but still could not help muttering, "This was entirely out of waterman's rules."

Glenvarloch, though without the devotion of the "injured Thales"
of the moralist to the memory of that great princess, had now attained

> The hallow'd soil which gave Eliza birth,

whose halls were now less respectably occupied by her successor. It
was not, as has been well shewn by a late author, that James was void
either of parts or of good intentions; and his predecessor was at least
as arbitrary in effect as he was in theory. But, while Elizabeth
possessed a sternness of masculine sense and determination which
rendered even her weaknesses, some of which were in themselves
sufficiently ridiculous, in a certain degree respectable, James, on the
other hand, was so utterly devoid of "Firm Resolve," so well called by
the Scottish bard,

> The stalk of carle-hemp in man,

that even his virtues and his good meaning became laughable, from
the whimsical uncertainty of his conduct; so that the wisest things he
ever said, and the best actions he ever did, were often touched with a
strain of the ludicrous and fidgetty character of the man. And accordingly, though at different periods of his reign he contrived to acquire
with his people a certain degree of temporary popularity, it never long
outlived the occasion which produced it; so true it is, that the mass of
mankind will respect a monarch stained with actual guilt, more than
one whose foibles render him only ridiculous.

To return from this digression, Lord Glenvarloch soon received, as
Green-jacket had assured him, the offer of an idle bargeman to
transport his baggage where he listed; but that *where* was a question of
momentary doubt. At length, recollecting the necessity that his hair
and beard should be properly arranged before he attempted to enter
the royal presence, and desirous, at the same time, of obtaining some
information of the motions of the Sovereign and of the court, he
desired to be guided to the next barber's shop, which we have already
mentioned as the place where news of every kind circled and centered.
He was speedily shewn the way to such an emporium of intelligence,
and soon found he was like to hear all he desired to know, and much
more, while his head was subjected to the art of a nimble tonsor, the
glibness of whose tongue kept pace with the nimbleness of his fingers
—while he ran on, without stint or stop, in the following excursive
manner:—

"The court here, master?—yes, master—much to the advantage of
trade—good custom stirring—His Majesty loves Greenwich—hunts
every morning in the Park—all decent persons admitted that have the
entries of the Palace—no rabble—frightened the King's horse with
their hallooing, the uncombed slaves.—Yes, sir—the beard more

peaked? yes, master, so it is worn. I know the last cut—dress several of the courtiers—one valet-of-the-chamber, two pages of the body—the clerk of the kitchen, two running footmen, three dog-boys, and an honourable Scotch knight—Sir Munko Malgrowler"——

"Malagrowther, I suppose?" said Nigel, thrusting in his conjectural emendation, with infinite difficulty, betwixt two clauses of the barber's text.

"Yes, sir—Malcrowder, sir, as you say, sir—hard names the Scotch have, sir, for an English mouth—Sir Munko is a handsome person, sir —perhaps you know him—bating the loss of his fingers, and the lameness of his leg, and the length of his chin—Sir, it takes me one minute, twelve seconds, more time to trim that chin of his, than any chin that I know in the town of Greenwich, sir—but he is a very comely gentleman, for all that—and a pleasant—a very pleasant gentleman, sir—and a good-humoured, saving that he is so deaf he can never hear good of any one, and so wise, that he can never believe it—but he is a very good-natured gentleman for all that, except when one speaks too low—or when a hair turns awry—did I graze you, sir? —we shall put it to right in a moment, with one drop of styptic—my styptic—or rather my wife's, sir—she makes the water herself—one drop of the styptic, sir, and a bit of black taffety patch—just big enough to be the saddle to a flea, sir—Yes, sir—rather improves than otherwise—the Prince had a patch the other day, and so had the Duke; and, if you will believe me, there are seventeen yards three quarters of black taffeta already cut into patches for the courtiers"——

"But Sir Mungo Malagrowther?" again interjected Nigel, with difficulty.

"Ay, ay, sir—Sir Munko, as you say—a pleasant, good-humoured gentleman as ever—To be spoken with, did you say?—O ay, easily to be spoken withal—that is, as easily as his infirmity will permit—He will presently—unless some one hath asked him forth to breakfast, be taking his bone of broiled beef at my neighbour Ned Kilderkin's yonder, removed from over the way—Ned keeps an eating-house, sir —famous for pork-griskins—but Sir Munko cannot abide pork—no more can the King's most Sacred Majesty—nor my Lord Duke of Lennox—nor Lord Dalgarno—nay, I am sure, sir, if I touched you this time, it was your fault, not mine—but a single drop of the styptic —another little patch that would make a doublet for a flea—just under the left mustache—it will become you when you smile, sir, as well as a dimple; and if you'd salute your fair mistress—but I beg pardon, you are a grave gentleman—very grave to be so young—hope I have given no offence—it is my duty to entertain customers—my duty, sir, and my pleasure—Sir Munko Malcrowther?—yes, sir—I dare say he is at this moment in Ned's eating-house, for few folks ask him out, now Lord Huntinglen is gone to London—you will get touched again—yes, sir—there shall you find him with his can of single ale, stirred with a sprig of rosemary, for he never drinks strong potations, sir, unless to oblige Lord Huntinglen—take heed, sir—or any other person who asks him forth to breakfast—but single beer he always drinks at Ned's, with his broiled bone of beef or mutton—or, it may be, lamb at this season—but not pork, though Ned is famous for his griskins—but the Scotch never eat pork—strange that! some folks think they are a sort of Jews—there is a resemblance, sir—do you not think so?—then they call his most gracious Sovereign the second Solomon—and Solomon, you know, was King of the Jews—so the thing bears a face, you see—I believe, sir, you will find yourself trimmed now to your content—I will be judged by the fair mistress of your affections—crave pardon—no offence, I trust—pray, consult the glass—one touch of the crisping tongs, to reduce this straggler—Thank your munificence, sir—hope your custom while you stay in Greenwich—Would you have a tune on the ghittern, sir, to put your temper in concord for the day?—Twang —twang—twang, twang, dillo—something out of tune, sir—too many hands to touch it—we cannot keep these things like artists—Let me help you with your cloak, sir—Yes, sir—you would not play yourself, sir, would you?—way to Sir Munko's eating-house?—Yes, sir—but it is Ned's eating-house—not Sir Munko's—The knight, to be sure, eats there—and that makes it his eating-house in some sense, sir—ha, ha!—yonder it is, removed from over the way—new white-washed posts, and red lattice—fat man in his doublet at the door—Ned himself, sir—worth a thousand pounds, they say—better singeing pigs' faces than trimming courtiers—but ours is the less mechanical vocation—farewell, sir—hope your custom." So saying, he at length permitted Nigel to depart, whose ears, so long tormented with his continued babble, tingled when it had ceased, as if a bell had been rung close to them for the same space of time.

Upon his arrival at the eating-house, where he proposed to meet with Sir Mungo Malagrowther, from whom, in despair of better advice, he trusted to receive some information as to the best mode of introducing himself into the royal presence, Lord Glenvarloch found, in the host with whom he communed, the consequential taciturnity of an Englishman well to pass in the world. Ned Kilderkin spoke as a banker writes, only touching the needful. Being asked if Sir Mungo Malagrowther was there? he replied, No. Being interrogated whether he was expected? he said, Yes. And being again required to say *when* he was expected, he answered, Presently. As Lord Glenvarloch next inquired, whether he himself could have any breakfast? the landlord wasted not even a monosyllable in reply, but, ushering him into a neat room where there were several tables, he placed one of them before an arm-chair, and beckoning Lord Glenvarloch to take possession, he set before him, in a very few minutes, a substantial repast of roast-beef, together with a foaming tankard, to which refreshment the keen air of the river disposed him, notwithstanding his mental embarrass-ment, to do much honour.

While Nigel was thus engaged in discussing his commons, but raising his head at the same time whenever he heard the door of the apartment open, eagerly desiring the arrival of Sir Mungo Mala-growther, (an event which had seldom been expected with so much anxious interest,) a personage, it would seem, of at least equal import-ance with the knight, entered into the apartment, and began to hold earnest colloquy with the publican, who thought proper to carry on the conference on his side unbonnetted. This important gentle-man's occupation might be guessed from his dress. A milk-white jerkin, and hose of white kersey; a white apron twisted around his body in the manner of a sash, in which, instead of a war-like dagger, was stuck a long-bladed knife, hilted with buck's-horn; a white night-cap on his head, under which his hair was neatly tucked, sufficiently displayed him as one of those priests of Comus whom the vulgar call cooks; and the air with which he rated the publican for having neg-lected to send some provisions to the Palace, shewed that he minis-tered to royalty itself.

"This will never answer," he said, "Master Kilderkin—the King twice asked for sweet-breads, and fricassied coxcombs, which are a favourite dish of his most Sacred Majesty—and they were not to be had—because Master Kilderkin had not supplied them to the clerk of the kitchen—as by bargain bound." Here Kilderkin made some apo-logy, brief, according to his own nature, and muttered in a lowly tone, after the fashion of all who find themselves in a scrape. His superior replied, in a lofty strain of voice, "Do not tell me of the carrier and his wain, and of the hen-coops coming from Norfolk with the poultry—a loyal man would have sent an express—he would have gone upon his stumps, like Widdrington—what if the King had lost his appetite, Master Kilderkin? what if his most Sacred Majesty had lost his din-ner? O Master Kilderkin—if you had but the just sense of the dignity of our profession, which is told of by the witty African slave, for so the King's most excellent Majesty designates him, Publius Terentius, *Tanquam in speculo—in patinas inspicere jubeo*."

"You are learned, Master Linklater," replied the English publican, compelling, as it were with difficulty, his mouth to utter three or four words consecutively.

"A poor smatterer," said Mr Linklater; "but it would be a shame to us, who are his most excellent Majesty's countrymen, not in some sort to have cherished those arts wherewith he is so deeply embued—*Regis ad exemplar*, Master Kilderkin, *totus componitur orbis*—which is as much as to say, as the king quotes the cook learns. In brief, Master Kilderkin, having had the luck to be bred where humanities may be had at the matter of an English five groats by the quarter, I, like others, have acquired—a hem—hem!—" Here the speaker's eye having fallen upon Lord Glenvarloch, he suddenly stopped in his learned harangue, with such symptoms of embarrassment as induced Ned Kilderkin to stretch his taciturnity so far as not only to ask him what he ailed, but whether he would take any thing.

"Ail—nothing," replied the learned rival of the philosophical Syrus —"nothing—and yet I do feel a little giddy. I could taste a glass of your dame's *aqua mirabilis*."

"I will fetch it," said Ned, giving a nod; and his back was no sooner turned, than the cook walked near the table where Lord Glenvarloch was seated, and regarding him with a look of significance, where more was meant than met the ear, said, "You are a stranger in Greenwich, sir. I advise you to take the opportunity to step into the Park—the western wicket was ajar when I came hither—I think it will be locked presently, so you had better make the best of your way —that is, if you have any curiosity—the venison are coming into season just now, sir, and there is a pleasure in looking at a hart of grease—I always think, when they are bounding so blithely past, what a pleasure it would be to broach their plump haunches on a spit, and to embattle their breasts in a noble fortification of puff-paste, with plenty of black pepper."

He said no more, as Kilderkin re-entered with the cordial, but edged off from Nigel without waiting any reply, only repeating the same look of intelligence with which he had accosted him. Nothing makes men's wits so alert as personal danger. Nigel took the first opportunity which his host's attention to the yeoman of the royal kitchen permitted, to discharge his reckoning, and readily obtained a direction to the wicket in question. He found it upon the latch, as he had been taught to expect, and perceived that it admitted him to a narrow foot-path, which traversed a close and tangled thicket, designed for the cover of the does and young fawns. Here he conjectured it would be proper to wait; nor had he been stationary above five minutes, when the cook, scalded as much with heat of motion as ever he had been at his huge fire-place, arrived almost breathless, and with his pass-key hastily locked the wicket behind him. Ere Lord Glenvarloch had time to speculate upon this action, the man approached him with anxiety, and said, "Good lord, my Lord Glenvarloch—why will you endanger yourself thus?"

"You know me, then, my friend?" said Nigel.

"Not so much of that, my lord—but I know your honour's noble house well. My name is Laurie Linklater, my lord."

"Linklater!" repeated Nigel. "I should recollect——"

"Under your lordship's favour," he continued, "I was 'prentice, my lord, to old Mungo Moniplies, the flesher at the wanton West-Port of Edinburgh, which I wish I saw again before I died—and your honour's noble father having taken Richie Moniplies into his house to wait on your lordship—there was a sort of connection—your lordship sees."

"Ah!" said Lord Glenvarloch, "I have forgot your name, but not your kind purpose—you tried to put Richie in the way of presenting a supplication to his Majesty."

"Most true, my lord," replied the King's cook. "I had like to have come by mischief in the job, for Richie, who was always wilful, 'wad nae be guided by me,' as the sang says. But nobody amangst these brave English cooks can kittle up his Majesty's most sacred palate with our own gusty Scottish dishes. So I e'en betook myself to my craft, and concocted a mess of friar's chicken for the soup, and a savoury hachis, that made the whole cabal coup the crans; and instead of disgrace, I came by preferment. I am one of the clerks of the kitchen now—make me thankful—with a finger in the purveyor's office, and may get my whole hand in by and by."

"I am truly glad," said Nigel, "to hear that you have not suffered on my account, still more so at your good fortune."

"You bear a kind heart, my lord," said Linklater, "and do not forget poor people; and troth I see not why they should be forgotten, since the King's errand may sometimes fall in the cadger's gate. I have followed your lordship in the street, just to look at such a stately shoot of the old oak-tree, and my heart jumped into my throat when I saw you sitting openly in the eating-house yonder, and knew there was such danger to your person."

"There are warrants against me, then?" said Nigel.

"It is even too true, my lord, and there are those are willing to blacken you as much as they can. God forgive them that would sacrifice an honourable house for their own base ends!"

"Amen," said Nigel.

"For, say your lordship may have been a little wild, like other young gentlemen"——

"We have little time to talk of it, my friend," said Nigel; "the point in question is, how I am to get to speech of the King?"

"The King, my lord?" said Linklater, in astonishment; "why, will not that be rushing wilfully into danger?—scalding yourself, as I may say, with your own ladle?"

"My good friend," answered Nigel, "my experience of the court, and my knowledge of the circumstances in which I stand, tell me, that the manliest and most direct road is, in my case, the surest and the safest. The King has both a head to apprehend what is just, and a heart to do what is kind."

"It is e'en true, my lord, and so we, his old servants, know," added Linklater; "but, woes me, if you knew how many folks make it their daily and nightly purpose to set his head against his heart, and his heart against his head—to make him do hard things because they are called just, and unjust things because they are represented as kind. Woes me—it is with his Sacred Majesty, and the favourites who work upon him, even according to the homely proverb, that men twit my calling with—'God sends good meat, but the devil sends cooks.'"

"It signifies not talking of it, my good friend," said Nigel, "I must take my risk; my honour peremptorily demands it. They may maim me, or beggar me, but they shall not say I fled from my accusers—my peers shall hear my vindication."

"Your peers?" exclaimed the cook—"Alack-a-day, my lord—we are not in Scotland, where the nobles can bang it out bravely, were it even with the King himself, now and then—this mess must be cooked in the Star-Chamber, and that is an oven seven times heated, my lord; and yet, if you are determined to see the King, I will not say but you may find some favour, for he likes well any thing that is appealed directly to his own wisdom, and sometimes, in the like cases, I have known him stick stiff by his own opinion, which is always a fair one. Only mind—if you will forgive me, my lord—mind to spice high with Latin—a curn or two of Greek would not be amiss—and if you can bring in any thing about the judgment of Solomon, in the original Hebrew, and season with a merry jest or so, the dish will be the more palatable. Truly, I think, that besides my skill in art, I owe much to the stripes of the Rector of the High-School, which imprinted on my mind that cooking scene in the Heautontimorumenos."

"Leaving that aside, my friend," said Lord Glenvarloch, "can you inform me which way I will most readily get to the sight and speech of the King?"

"To the sight of him readily enough," said Linklater; "he is galloping about these alleys to see them strike the hart, to get him an appetite for a nooning, and that reminds me I should be in the kitchens—to the speech of the King you will not come so easily, unless you could either meet him alone, which rarely chances, or wait for him among the crowd that go to see him alight—and now, farewell, my lord, and God speed—if I could do more for you, I would offer it."

"You have done enough, perhaps, to endanger yourself," said Lord Glenvarloch. "I pray you to be gone, and leave me to my fate."

The honest cook lingered, but a nearer burst of the horns apprized him there was no time to lose; and acquainting Nigel that he would leave the postern-door on the latch to secure his retreat in that direction, he bade God bless him, and farewell.

In the kindness of this humble countryman, flowing partly from national partiality, partly from a sense of long-remembered benefits, which had been scarce thought on by those who had bestowed them, Lord Glenvarloch thought he saw the last touch of sympathy which he was to receive in this cold and courtly region, and felt that he must now be sufficient to himself, or be utterly lost.

He traversed more than one alley, guided by the sounds of the chace, and met several of the inferior attendants upon the King's sport, who regarded him only as one of the spectators who were sometimes permitted to enter the Park by the connivance of the officers about the court. Still there was no appearance of James, or any of his principal courtiers, and Nigel began to think whether, at the risk of incurring disgrace similar to that which had attended the rash exploit of Richie Moniplies, he should not repair to the Palace-gate, in order to address the King on his return, when Fortune presented him the opportunity of doing so, in her own way.

He was in one of those long walks by which the Park was traversed, when he heard first a distant rustling, then the rapid approach of hoofs shaking the firm earth on which he trod; then a distant halloo, warned by which he stood up by the side of the avenue, leaving free room for the passage of the chase. The stag, reeling, covered with foam, and blackened with sweat, his nostrils expanded as he gasped for breath, made a shift to come up as far as where Nigel stood, and, without turning to bay, was there pulled down by two tall greyhounds of the breed still used by the hardy deer-stalkers of the Scottish Highlands, but which has been long unknown in England. One dog struck at the buck's throat, another dashed his sharp nose and fangs, I might almost say, into the animal's bowels. It would have been natural for Lord Glenvarloch, himself persecuted as if by hunters, to have thought upon the occasion like the melancholy Jaques; but habit is a strange matter, and I fear that his feelings on the occasion were rather those of the practised huntsman than of the moralist. He had no time, however, to indulge them, for mark what followed.

A single horseman followed the chase, upon a steed so thoroughly subjected to the rein, that it obeyed the touch of the bridle as if it had been a mechanical impulse operating on the nicest piece of machinery; so that, seated deep in his demi-pique saddle, and so trussed up there as to make falling almost impossible, the rider, without either fear or hesitation, might increase or diminish the speed at which he rode, which, even on the most animating occasions of the chase, seldom exceeded three-fourths of a gallop, the horse keeping his haunches under him, and never stretching forward beyond the managed pace of the academy. The security with which he chose to prosecute even this favourite, and, in the ordinary case, something dangerous amusement, as well as the rest of his equipage, marked King James. No attendant was within sight; indeed, it was often a nice strain of flattery to permit the Sovereign to suppose he had outridden and distanced all the rest of the chase.

"Weel dune, Bash—weel dune, Battie!" he exclaimed, as he came up. "By the honour of a king, ye are a credit to the Braes of Balwhither!—Haud my horse, man," he called out to Nigel, without stopping to see to whom he addressed himself—"Haud my naig, and help me doun out o' the saddle—De'il ding your saul, sirrah, canna ye mak haste before these lazy smaiks come up?—haud the rein easy—dinna let him swerve—now, haud the stirrup—that will do, man, and now we are on terra firma." So saying, without casting an eye on his assistant, gentle King Jamie, unsheathing the short sharp hanger, (*couteau de chasse*,) which was the only thing approaching to a sword that he could willingly endure the sight of, drew the blade with great satisfaction across the throat of the buck, and put an end at once to its struggles and its agonies.

Lord Glenvarloch, who knew well the sylvan duty which the occasion demanded, hung the bridle of the King's palfrey on the branch of a tree, and kneeling duteously down, turned the slaughtered deer upon its back, and kept the *quarrée* in that position, while the King, too intent upon his sport to observe any thing else, drew his *couteau* down the breast of the animal, *secundum artem;* and having made a cross cut, so as to ascertain the depth of the fat upon the chest, exclaimed, in a sort of rapture, "Three inches of white fat on the brisket!—prime—prime, as I am a crowned sinner—and de'il ane o' the lazy loons in but mysell! Seven—aught—aught tines on the antlers—by G—d—A hart of aught tines, and the first of the season!—Bash and Battie—blessings on the heart's-root of ye!—buss me, my bairns, buss me." The dogs accordingly fawned upon him, licked him with bloody jaws—and soon put him in such a state that it might have seemed treason had been doing its fell work upon his anointed body. "Bide doun, with a mischief to ye—bide doun, with a wanion," cried the King, almost overturned by the obstreperous caresses of the large staghounds. "But ye are just like ither folks—gie ye an inch and ye take an ell.—And wha may ye be, friend?" he said, now finding leisure to take a nearer view of Nigel, and discovering what in his first emotion of sylvan delight had escaped him,—"Ye are nane of our train, man—in the name of God, what the devil are ye?"

"An unfortunate man, sire," replied Nigel.

"I dare say that," answered the King, snappishly, "or I wad have seen naething of you—my lieges keep a' their happiness to themselves, but let bowls row wrang wi' them, and I am sure to hear of it."

"And to whom else can we carry our complaints but to your Majesty, who is Heaven's vicegerent over us?" answered Nigel.

"Right, man, right—very weel spoken," said the King; "but ye should leave Heaven's vicegerent some quiet on earth, too."

"If your Majesty will look on me," (for hitherto the King had been so busy, first with the dogs, and then with the mystic operation of *breaking*, in vulgar phrase, cutting up the deer, that he had scarce given his assistant above a transient glance,) "you will see whom necessity makes bold to avail himself of an opportunity which may never again occur."

King James looked; his blood left his cheek, though it continued stained with that of the animal which lay at his feet, he dropped the knife from his hand, cast behind him a faultering eye, as if he either meditated flight or looked out for assistance, and then exclaimed,—"Glenvarlochides!—as sure as I was christened James Stuart. Here is a bonny spot of work—and me alone, and on foot too!" he added, bustling to get upon his horse.

"Forgive me that I interrupt you, my liege," said Nigel, placing himself between the King and the steed; "hear me but a moment."

"I'll hear ye best on horseback," said the King. "I canna hear a word on foot, man—not a word—and it is not seemly to stand cheek-for-chowl confronting us that gate. Bide out of our gate, sir, we charge you, on your allegiance—the de'il's in them a', what can they be doing?"

"By the crown which you wear, my liege," said Nigel, "and for which my ancestors have worthily fought, I conjure you to be composed, and to hear me but a moment!"

That which he asked was entirely out of the Monarch's power to grant. The timidity which he shewed was not the plain downright cowardice, which, like a natural impulse, compels a man to flight, and which can excite little but pity or contempt, but a much more ludicrous, as well as more mingled sensation. The poor King was frightened at once and angry, desirous of securing his safety, and at the same time ashamed to compromise his dignity; so that, without attending to what Lord Glenvarloch endeavoured to explain, he kept making at his horse, and repeating, "We are a free King—man—we are a free King—we will not be controlled by a subject.—In the name of God, what keeps Steenie? And, praised be his name, they are coming—Helloa—hello—ho—here, here—Steenie—Steenie!"

The Duke of Buckingham galloped up, followed by several courtiers and attendants of the royal chase, and commenced, with his usual familiarity,—"I see Fortune has graced our dear dad, as usual.—But what's this?"

"What is it?—it is treason, for what I ken," said the King; "and a' your wyte, Steenie. Your dear dad and gossip might have been murdered, what for you care."

"Murdered? Secure the villain!" exclaimed the Duke. "By Heaven, it is Olifaunt himself!" A dozen of the hunters dismounted at once, letting their horses run wild through the park. Some seized roughly on Lord Glenvarloch, who thought it folly to offer resistance, while others busied themselves with the King. "Are you wounded, my liege —are ye wounded?"

"Not that I ken of," said the King, in the paroxysm of his apprehension, (which, by the way, might be pardoned in one of so timorous a temper, and who, in his time, had been exposed to so many strange attempts)—"Not that I ken of—but search him—search him—I am sure I saw fire-arms under his cloak—I am sure I smelled powder—I am doom's sure of that."

Lord Glenvarloch's cloak being stripped off, and his pistols discovered, there was a shout of wonder, and execration on the supposed criminal purpose arose from the crowd, now thickening every moment. Not that celebrated pistol, which, though resting on a bosom as gallant and as loyal as Nigel's, spread such causeless alarm among knights and dames at a late high solemnity—not that very pistol caused more temporary consternation than was so groundlessly excited by the arms which were taken from Lord Glenvarloch's person. And not Mhic-Allastair-More himself, could repel with greater scorn and indignation, the insinuations that they were worn for any sinister purpose.

"Away with the wretch—the parricide—the bloody-minded villain!" was echoed on all hands; and the King, who naturally enough set the same value on his own life at which it was, or seemed to be, rated by others, cried out, louder than all the rest, "Ay—ay—away with him. I have had enough of him, and so has the country. But do him no bodily harm—and, for God's sake, sirs, if ye are sure that ye have thoroughly disarmed him, put up your swords, dirks, and skenes, for you will certainly do each other a mischief."

There was a speedy sheathing of weapons at the King's command;

for those who had hitherto been brandishing them in loyal bravado, began thereby to call to mind the extreme dislike which his Majesty nourished against naked steel—a foible which seemed to be as constitutional as his timidity, and was usually ascribed to the brutal murther of Rizio having been perpetrated in his unfortunate mother's presence before he yet saw the light.

At this moment, the Prince, who had been hunting in a different part of the then extensive Park, and had received some hasty and confused information of what was going forwards, came rapidly up, with one or two noblemen in his train, and amongst others Lord Dalgarno. He sprung from his horse, and asked eagerly if his father were wounded.

"Not that I am sensible of, Baby Charles—but a wee matter exhausted, with struggling single-handed with the assassin.— Steenie, fill us a cup of wine—the leathern bottle is hanging at our pommel.—Buss me then, Baby Charles," continued the monarch, after he had taken this cup of comfort; "O man, the Commonwealth and you have had a fair escape from the heavy and bloody loss of a dear father—for we are *pater patriæ*, as weel as *pater familias—Quis desiderio sit pudor aut modus tam cari capitis!*—Woe is me—black cloth would have been dear in England—and dry e'en scarce!"

And at the very idea of the general grief which must have attended his death, the good-natured monarch cried heartily himself.

"Is this possible?" said Charles sternly; for his pride was hurt at his father's demeanour on the one hand, while, on the other, he felt the resentment of a son and a subject, at the supposed attempt on the King's life. "Let some one speak who has seen what happened—My Lord of Buckingham."

"I cannot say, my lord," replied the Duke, "that I saw any actual violence offered to his Majesty, else I should have avenged him on the spot."

"You would have done wrong then in your zeal, George," answered the Prince; "such offenders were better left to be dealt with by the laws—but was the villain not struggling with his Majesty?"

"I cannot term it so, my lord," said the Duke, who, with many faults, would have disdained an untruth; "he seemed to desire to detain his Majesty, who, on the contrary, seemed to wish to mount his horse— but they have found pistols on his person, contrary to the proclamation, and as it proves to be Nigel Olifaunt, of whose ungoverned disposition your Royal Highness has seen some samples, we seem to be justified in apprehending the worst."

"Nigel Olifaunt!" said the Prince; "can that unhappy man so soon have engaged in a new trespass? Let me see those pistols."

"Ye are not so unwise as to meddle with such snap-haunces, Baby Charles?" said James—"Do not give him them, Steenie—I command you on your allegiance. They may go off of their own accord, whilk often befalls.—You will do it then?—Saw ever man sic wilful bairns as we are cumbered with!—Havena we guardsmen and soldiers enow, but ye must unload the weapons yoursell—you, the heir of our body and dignities, and sae mony men around that are paid for venturing life in our cause?"

But without regarding his father's exclamations, Prince Charles, with the obstinacy which characterized him in trifles, as well as matters of consequence, persisted in unloading the pistols with his own hand, of the double bullets with which each was charged. The hands of all around were held up in astonishment at the horror of the crime supposed to have been intended, and the escape which was presumed so narrow.

Nigel had not yet spoken a word—he now calmly desired to be heard.

"To what purpose?" answered the Prince coldly. "You knew yourself accused of a heavy offence, and instead of rendering up yourself to justice, in the terms of the proclamation, you are here found intruding yourself on his Majesty's presence, and armed with unlawful weapons."

"May it please you, sir," answered Nigel, "I wore these unhappy weapons for my own defence; and not very many hours since, they were necessary to protect the lives of others."

"Doubtless, my lord," answered the Prince, still calm and unmoved,—"your late mode of life, and the associates with whom you have lived, have made you familiar with scenes and weapons of violence. But it is not to me you are to plead your cause."

"Hear me—Hear me, noble Prince," said Nigel eagerly. "Hear me! —you—even you yourself—may one day ask to be heard, and in vain."

"How, sir," said the Prince, haughtily—"how am I to construe that, my lord?"

"If not on earth, sir," replied the prisoner, "yet to Heaven we must all pray for patient and favourable audience."

"True, my lord," said the Prince, bending his head with haughty acquiescence; "nor would I now refuse such audience to you, could it avail you. But you shall suffer no wrong—we will ourselves look into your case."

"Ay, ay," answered the King, "he hath made *appellatio ad Cæsarem* —we will interrogate Glenvarlochides ourselves, time and place fitting; and, in the mean while, have him and his weapons away, for I am weary of the sight of them."

In consequence of directions hastily given, Nigel was accordingly removed from the presence, where, however, his words had not altogether fallen to the ground. "This is a most strange matter, George," said the Prince to the favourite; "this gentleman hath a good countenance, a happy presence, and much calm firmness in his look and speech. I cannot think he would attempt a crime so desperate and useless."

"I profess neither love nor favour to the young man," answered Buckingham, whose high-spirited ambition bore always an open character; "but I cannot but agree with your Highness, that our dear gossip hath been something hasty in apprehending personal damage from him."

"By my saul, Steenie, ye are not blate, to say so," said the King. "Do I not ken the smell of pouther, think ye?—who else nosed out the fifth of November, save our royal selves? Cecil, and Suffolk, and all of them, were at fault, like sae mony mongrel tykes, when I puzzled it out; and trow ye that I cannot smell pouther? Why, 'sblood, man—Joannes Barclaius thought my ingine was in some measure inspiration, and terms his history of the plot, *Series patefacti divinitus parricidii;* and Spondanus, in like manner, saith of us, *Divinitus evasit.*"

"The land was happy in your Majesty's escape," said the Duke of Buckingham, "and not less so in the quick wit which tracked that labyrinth of treason by so fine and almost invisible a clew."

"Saul, man, Steenie! Ye are right—there are few youths have sic true judgment as you, respecting the wisdom of their elders; and as for this fause traiterous smaik, I doubt he is a hawk of the same nest. Saw ye not something papistical about him? Let them look that he bears not a crucifix, or some sic Roman trinket, about him."

"It would ill become me to attempt the exculpation of this unhappy man," said Lord Dalgarno, "considering the height of his present attempt, which has made all true men's blood curdle in their veins— yet I cannot avoid intimating, with all due submission to his Majesty's infallible judgment, in justice to one who shewed himself formerly only my enemy, though he now displays himself in much blacker colours, that this Olifaunt always appeared to me more as a Puritan than as a Papist."

"Ah, Dalgarno—Art thou there, man?" said the King. "And ye behoved to keep back, too, and leave us to our own natural strength and the care of Providence, when we were in grips with the villain!"

"Providence, may it please your Gracious Majesty, could not fail to aid, in such a straight, the care of three weeping kingdoms," said Lord Dalgarno.

"Surely, man—surely," replied the King—"but a sight of your father, with his lang whin-yard, would have been a blithe matter a short while syne; and in future we will aid the ends of Providence in our favour, by keeping near us two stout beef-eaters of the guard.— And so this Olifaunt is a Puritan?—not the less like to be a Papist, for all that—for extremities meet, as the scholiast proveth. There are, as I have proved in my book, Puritans of papistical principles—it is just a new tout on an auld horn."

Here the King was reminded by the Prince, who dreaded perhaps that he was going to recite the whole *Basilicon Doron*, that it would be best to move towards the Palace, and consider what was to be done for satisfying the mind of the public, in whom the morning's adventure was like to excite much speculation. As they entered the gate of the Palace, a female bowed and presented a paper, which the King received, and with a sort of groan, thrust it into his side-pocket. The Prince expressed some curiosity to know its contents. "The valet in waiting will tell you them," said the King, "when I strip off my cassock. D'ye think, Baby, that I can read all that is thrust into my hands? See to me, man,"—(he pointed to the two pockets of his great trunk breeches, which were stuffed with papers)—"We are like an ass—that we should so speak—stooping betwixt two burthens. Ay, ay, *Asinus fortis accumbens inter terminos*, as the Vulgate hath it—Ay, ay, *Vidi terram quod esset optima, et supposui humerum ad portandum, et factus sum tributis serviens*. I saw this land of England, and became an over-burthened king thereof."

"You are indeed well loaded, my dear dad and gossip," said the Duke of Buckingham, receiving the papers which King James emptied out of his pocket.

"Ay, ay," continued the monarch; "take them to ye *per aversionem*, bairns—the one pouch stuffed with petitions, the t'other with pasquinadoes—a fine time we have on it. On my conscience, I believe the tale of Cadmus was hieroglyphical, and that the dragon's teeth whilk he sowed were the letters he invented. Ye are laughing, Baby Charles?—Mind what I say—when I came here first frae our ain country, where the men are as rude as the weather, by my conscience, England was a bieldy bit—one would have thought the King had little to do but to walk by quiet waters, *per aquam refectionis*. But I kenna how or why, the place is sair changed—read that libel upon us and on our regimen. The dragon's teeth are sown, Baby Charles; I pray God they bearna their armed harvest in your day, if I suld not live to see it. God forbid I should, for there will be an awful day's kemping at the shearing of them."

"I shall know how to stifle the crop in the blade,—ha, George!" said
the Prince, turning to the favourite with a look expressive of some
contempt for his father's apprehensions, and full of confidence in the
superior firmness and decision of his own counsels.

While this discourse was passing, Nigel, in charge of a poursuivant-
at-arms, was pushed and dragged through the small town, all the
inhabitants of which had been alarmed by the report of an attack on
the King's life, and now pressed forward to see the supposed traitor.
Amid the confusion of the moment, he could descry the face of the
victualler arrested into a stare of stolid wonder, and that of the barber
grinning betwixt horror and eager curiosity. He thought that he also
had a glimpse of his waterman in the green jacket.

He had no time for remarks, being placed in a boat with the poursuivant and two yeomen of the guard, and rowed up the river as fast as
the arms of six stout watermen could pull against the tide. They
passed the groves of masts which even then astonished the stranger
with the extended commerce of London, and now approached those
low and blackened walls of curtain and bastion, which exhibit here and
there a piece of ordnance, and here and there a solitary sentinel under
arms, but have otherwise so little of the military terrors of a citadel. A
projecting low-browed arch, which had loured o'er many an innocent,
and many a guilty head, in similar circumstances, now spread its dark
frowns over that of Nigel. The boat was put close up to the broad steps
against which the tide was lapping its lazy wave. The warder on duty
looked from the wicket, and spoke with the poursuivant in whispers.
In a few minutes the Lieutenant of the Tower appeared, received, and
granted an acknowledgment for the body of Nigel, Lord Glenvarloch.

Chapter Four

Ye towers of Julius! London's lasting shame;
With many a foul and midnight murder fed!
GRAY

SUCH IS THE exclamation of Gray. Bandello, long before him, has
said something like it; and the same sentiment must in some shape or
other have frequently occurred to those, who, remembering the fate of
other captives in that memorable state-prison, may have had but too
much reason to anticipate their own. The dark and low arch, which
seemed, like the entrance to Dante's Hell, to forbid hope of regress—
the muttered sounds of the warders, and petty formalities observed in
opening and shutting the grated wicket—the cold and constrained

salutation of the Lieutenant of the fortress, who shewed his prisoner that distant and measured respect which Authority pays as a tax to Decorum, all struck upon Nigel's heart, impressing on him the cruel consciousness of captivity.

"I am a prisoner," he said, the words escaping from him almost unawares; "I am a prisoner, and in the Tower!"

The Lieutenant bowed—"And it is my duty," he said, "to shew your lordship your chamber, where, I am compelled to say, my orders are to place you under some restraint. I will make it as easy as my duty permits."

Nigel only bowed in return to this compliment, and followed the Lieutenant to the ancient buildings on the western side of the parade, and adjoining to the chapel, used in those days as a state-prison, but in ours as the mess-room of the officers of the guard upon duty at the fortress. The double doors were unlocked, the prisoner ascended a few steps, followed by the Lieutenant, and a warder of the higher class. They entered a large, but irregular, low-roofed and dark apart-ment, exhibiting a very scanty proportion of furniture. The warder had orders to make a fire, and attend to Lord Glenvarloch's com-mands in all things consistent with his duty; and the Lieutenant having made his reverence with the customary compliment, that he trusted his lordship would not long remain under his guardianship, took his leave.

Nigel would have asked some questions at the warder, who remained to put the apartment into order, but the man had caught the spirit of his office: he seemed not to hear some of the prisoner's questions, though of the most ordinary kind, did not reply to others, and when he did speak, it was in a short and sullen tone, which, though not positively disrespectful, was such as at least to encourage no farther communication.

Nigel left him, therefore, to do his work in silence, and proceeded to amuse himself with the melancholy task of decyphering the names, mottoes, verses, and hieroglyphics, with which his predecessors in captivity had covered the walls of their prison-house. There he saw the names of many a forgotten sufferer mingled with others which will continue in remembrance until English History shall perish. There were the pious effusions of the devout Catholic, poured forth on the eve of his sealing his profession at Tyburn, mingled with those of the firm Protestant, about to feed the fires of Smithfield. There the slen-der hand of the unfortunate Jane Grey, whose fate was to draw tears from future generations, might be contrasted with the bolder touch which impressed deep on the walls the Bear and Ragged Staff, the proud emblem of the proud Dudleys. It was like the roll of the prophet, a record of lamentation and mourning and woe, yet not unmixed with brief interjections of resignation, and sentences expressive of the firmest resolution.

In the sad task of examining the miseries of his predecessors in captivity, Lord Glenvarloch was interrupted by the sudden opening of the door of his prison-room. It was the warder, who came to inform him, that, by orders of the Lieutenant of the Tower, his lordship was to have the society and attendance of a fellow-prisoner in his place of confinement. Nigel replied hastily, that he wished no attendance, and would rather be left alone; but the warder gave him to understand, with a kind of grumbling civility, that the Lieutenant was the best judge how his prisoners should be accommodated, and that he would have no trouble with the boy, who was such a slip of a thing as was scarce worth turning a key upon.—"Here, Giles," he said, "bring the child in."

Another warder put the lad before him into the room, and both withdrawing, bolt crashed and chain clanged, as they replaced these ponderous obstacles to freedom.

The boy was clad in a grey suit of the finest cloth, laid down with silver lace, with a buff-coloured cloak of the same pattern. His cap, which was a Montero of black velvet, was pulled over his brows, and, with the profusion of his long ringlets, almost concealed his face. He stood on the very spot where the warder had quitted his collar, about two steps from the door of the apartment, his eyes fixed on the ground, and every joint trembling with confusion and terror. Nigel could well have dispensed with his society, but it was not in his nature to behold distress, whether of body or mind, without endeavouring to relieve it.

"Cheer up," he said, "my pretty lad; we are to be companions, it seems, for a little time—at least I trust your confinement will be short, since you are too young to have done aught to deserve long restraint. Come—come—do not be discouraged. Your hand is cold and trembles—the air is warm too—but it may be the damp of this darksome room—place you by the fire.—What! weeping-ripe, my little man? I pray you do not be a child—you have no beard yet, to be dishonoured by your tears—but yet you should not cry like a girl. Think you are only shut up for playing truant, and you can pass a day without weeping, surely."

The boy suffered himself to be led and seated by the fire, but, after retaining for a long time the very posture which he assumed in sitting down, he suddenly changed it in order to wring his hands with an air of the bitterest distress, and then spreading them before his face, wept so plentifully, that the tears found their way in floods through his slender fingers.

Nigel was in some degree rendered insensible to his own situation, by his feelings for the intense agony by which so young and beautiful a creature seemed to be utterly overwhelmed; and sitting down close beside the boy, he applied the most soothing terms which occurred, to endeavour to alleviate his distress; and with an action which the difference of their age rendered natural, drew his hand kindly along the long hair of the disconsolate child. The lad appeared so shy as even to shrink from this slight approach to familiarity—yet, when Lord Glenvarloch, perceiving and allowing for his timidity, sate down on the farther side of the fire, he appeared to be more at his ease, and to hearken with some apparent interest to the arguments which from time to time Nigel used, to induce him to moderate, at least, the violence of his grief. As the boy listened, his tears, though they continued to flow freely, seemed to escape from their source more easily, his sobs were less convulsive, and became gradually changed into low sighs, which succeeded each other, indicating as much sorrow perhaps, but less alarm, than his first transports had shewn.

"Tell me who and what you are, my pretty boy," said Nigel.— "Consider me, child, as a companion in misfortune who wishes to be kind to you, would you but teach him how he can be so."

"Sir—my lord I mean," answered the boy very timidly, and in a voice which could scarce be heard even across the brief distance which divided them, "you are very good—and I—am very unhappy—"

A second fit of tears interrupted what else he intended to say, and it required a renewal of Lord Glenvarloch's good-natured expostulations and encouragements, to bring him once more to such composure as rendered the lad capable of expressing himself intelligibly. At length, however, he was able to say—"I am sensible of your goodness, my lord—and grateful for it—but I am a poor unhappy creature, and, what is worse, have myself only to thank for my misfortunes."

"We are seldom absolutely miserable, my young acquaintance," said Nigel, "without being ourselves more or less responsible for it—I may well say so, otherwise I had not been here to-day—but you are very young, and can have but little to answer for."

"O sir! I wish I could say so—I have been self-willed and obstinate —and rash and ungovernable—and now—now, how dearly do I pay the price of it!"

"Pshaw, my boy," replied Nigel; "this must be some childish frolic —some breaking out of bounds—some truant trick—and yet how should any of these have brought you to the Tower?—there is something mysterious about you, young man, which I must inquire into."

"Indeed, indeed, my lord, there is no harm about me," said the boy,

more moved it would seem to confession by the last words, by which
he seemed considerably alarmed, than by all the kind expostulations
and arguments which Nigel had previously used. "I am innocent—
that is, I have done wrong, but nothing to deserve being in this frightful place."

"Tell me the truth, then," said Nigel, with a tone in which command mingled with encouragement; "you have nothing to fear from
me, and as little to hope, perhaps—yet, placed as I am, I would know
with whom I speak."

"With an unhappy boy, sir—and idle and truantly disposed, as your
lordship said," answered the lad, looking up and shewing a countenance in which paleness and blushes succeeded each other, as fear and
shame-facedness alternately had influence. "I left my father's house
without leave, to see the King hunt in the Park at Greenwich; there
came a cry of treason, and all the gates were shut—I was frightened
and hid myself in a thicket, and I was found by some of the rangers and
examined—and they said I gave no good account of myself—and so I
was sent hither."

"I am an unhappy—a most unhappy being," said Lord Glenvarloch, rising and walking through the apartment; "nothing approaches
me but shares my own bad fate! Death and imprisonment dog my
steps, and involve all who are found near me. Yet this boy's story
sounds something strangely.—You say you were examined, my young
friend—let me pray you to say whether you told your name, and your
means of gaining admission into the Park—if so, they surely would not
have detained you."

"O, my lord," said the boy, "I took care not to tell them the name of
the friend that let me in, and as to my father—I would not he knew
where I now am for all the wealth of London!"

"But you do not expect," said Nigel, "that they will dismiss you till
you let them know who and what you are?"

"What good will it do them to keep so useless a creature as myself?"
said the boy; "they must let me go, were it but out of shame."

"Do not trust to that—tell me your name and station—I will communicate them to the Lieutenant—he is a man of quality and honour,
and will not only be willing to procure your liberation, but also, I have
no doubt, will intercede with your father. I am partly answerable for
such poor aid as I can afford, to get you out of this embarrassment,
since I occasioned the alarm owing to which you were arrested; so tell
me your name, and your father's name."

"My name to *you?* O never, never!" answered the boy, in a tone of
deep emotion, the cause of which Nigel could not comprehend.

"Are you so much afraid of me, young man," he replied, "because I am here accused and a prisoner?—consider a man may be both, and deserve neither suspicion or restraint—why should you distrust me? —you seem friendless, and I am myself so much in the same circumstances, that I cannot but pity your situation when I reflect on my own. Be wise—I have spoken kindly to you—I mean as kindly as I speak."

"O, I doubt not—I doubt it not, my lord," said the boy, "and I could tell you all—that is, almost all."

"Tell me nothing, my young friend, excepting what may assist me in being useful to you," said Nigel.

"You are generous, my lord," said the boy; "and I am sure—O sure, I might safely trust to your honour—but yet—but yet—I am so sore bestad—I have been so rash, so unguarded—I can never tell you of my folly—Besides, I have already told too much to one—whose heart I thought I had moved—yet I find myself here."

"To whom did you make the disclosure?" said Nigel.

"I dare not tell," replied the youth.

"There is something singular about you, my young friend," said Lord Glenvarloch, withdrawing with a gentle degree of compulsion the hand with which the boy had again covered his eyes; "do not pain yourself with thinking on your situation just at present—your pulse is high, and your hand feverish—lay yourself on yonder pallet, and try to compose yourself to sleep. It is the readiest and best remedy for the fancies with which you are worrying yourself."

"I thank you for your considerate kindness, my lord," said the boy; "with your leave, I will remain for a little space quiet in this chair—I am better thus than on the couch. I can think undisturbedly on what I have done, and have still to do; and if God sends slumber to a creature so exhausted, it shall be most welcome."

So saying, the boy drew his hand from Lord Nigel's, and drawing around him and partly over his face the folds of his ample cloak, he resigned himself to sleep or meditation, while his companion, notwithstanding the exhausting scenes of this and the preceding day, continued his pensive walk up and down the apartment.

Every reader has experienced, that times occur, when, far from being lords of external circumstances, man is unable to rule even the wayward realm of his own thoughts. It was Nigel's natural wish to consider his own situation coolly, and fix on the course which it became him as a man of sense and courage to adopt; and yet, in spite of himself, and notwithstanding the deep interest of the critical state in which he was placed, it did so happen that his fellow-prisoner's situation occupied more of his thoughts than did his own. There was no accounting for this wandering of the imagination, but also there was no striving with it. The pleading tones of one of the sweetest voices he

had ever heard, still rung in his ear, though it seemed that sleep had
now fettered the tongue of the speaker. He drew near on tiptoe to
satisfy himself whether it were so. The folds of the cloak hid the lower
part of the face entirely; but the bonnet, which had fallen a little aside,
permitted him to see the forehead streaked with blue veins, the closed
eyes, and the long silken eye-lashes.

"Poor child," said Nigel to himself, as he looked on him, nestled up
as it were in the folds of his mantle, "the dew is yet on thy eye-lashes,
and thou hast fairly wept thyself asleep. Sorrow is a rough nurse to one
so young and so delicate as thou art. Peace be to thy slumbers—I will
not disturb them—my own misfortunes require my attention, and it is
to their contemplation that I must resign myself."

He attempted to do so, but was crossed at every turn by conjectures
which intruded themselves as before, and which all regarded the
sleeper rather than himself. He was angry and vexed, and expostu-
lated with himself concerning the overweening interest which he
took in the concerns of one of whom he knew nothing, saving that the
boy was forced into his company—perhaps as a spy—by those to
whose custody he was committed—but the spell could not be broken,
and the thoughts which he struggled to dismiss, continued to haunt
him.

Thus passed half an hour, or more; at the conclusion of which, the
harsh sound of the revolving bolts was again heard, and the voice of
the warder announced that a man desired to speak with Lord Glenvarloch. "A man to speak with me, under my present circumstances!
—Who can it be?" And John Christie, his landlord of Paul's Wharf,
resolved his doubts, by entering the apartment. "Welcome—most
welcome, mine honest landlord!" said Lord Glenvarloch. "How
could I have dreamed of seeing you in my present close lodgings?"
And at the same time, with the frankness of old kindness, he walked
up to Christie and offered his hand; but John started back as from the
look of a basilisk.

"Keep your courtesies to yourself, my lord," said he, gruffly; "I
have had so many of them already as may serve me for my life."

"Why, Master Christie," said Nigel, "what means this? I trust I
have not offended you."

"Ask me no questions, my lord," said Christie, bluntly. "I am a man
of peace—I came not hither to wrangle with you at this place and
season—just suppose that I am well informed of all the obligements
from your honour's nobleness, and then acquaint me, in as few words
as may be—where is the unhappy woman—what have you done with
her?"

"What have I done with her!" said Lord Glenvarloch—"Done with whom? I know not what you are speaking of."

"Oh, yes, my lord," said Christie; "play surprise as well as you will, you must have some guess that I am speaking of the poor fool that was my wife, till she became your lordship's light-o'-love."

"Your wife! Has your wife left you?—and if she has, do you come to ask her of me?"

"Yes, my lord; singular as it may seem," returned Christie, in a tone of bitter irony, and with a sort of grin widely discording from the discomposure of his features, the gleam of his eye, and the froth which stood on his lip, "I do come to make that demand of your lordship— doubtless, you are surprised I should take the trouble—but I cannot tell—great men and little men think differently. She has lain in my bosom, and drunk of my cup—and such as she is, I cannot forget that —though I will never see her again—She must not starve, my lord, or do worse, to gain bread—though I reckon your lordship may think I am robbing the public in trying to change her courses."

"By my faith as a Christian—by my honour as a gentleman," said Lord Glenvarloch, "if aught amiss has chanced with your wife, I know nothing of it. I trust in Heaven you are as much mistaken in imputing guilt to her, as in supposing me her partner in it."

"Fie! fie! my lord," said Christie, "why will you make it so tough? She is but the wife of a clod-pated old chandler, who was idiot enough to marry a wench twenty years younger than himself. Your lordship cannot have more glory by it than you have had already; and for advantage and solace, I take it Dame Nelly is now unnecessary to your lordship's gratification. I should be sorry to interrupt the course of your pleasure—an old wittol should have more consideration of his condition—but your precious lordship being mewed up here among other choice jewels of the kingdom, Dame Nelly cannot, I take it, be admitted to share the hours of dalliance which——" Here the incensed husband stammered, broke off his tone of irony, and pro-ceeded, striking his staff against the ground,—"O that these false limbs of yours, which I wish had been hamstrung when they first crossed my honest threshold, were free from the fetters they have well deserved! I would give you the odds of your youth, and your weapon, and would bequeath my soul to the foul fiend if I, with this piece of oak, did not make you such an example to all ungrateful pick-thank courtiers, that it should be a proverb to the end of time, how John Christie swaddled his wife's fine leman."

"I understand not your insolence," said Nigel, "but I forgive it, because you labour under some strange delusion. In so far as I can comprehend your vehement charge, it is entirely undeserved on my part. You seem to impute to me the seduction of your wife—I trust she is innocent. For me, at least, she is innocent as an angel in bliss. I never thought of her—never touched her hand or cheek, save in honourable courtesy."

"O, ay—Courtesy!—that is the very word. She always praised your lordship's *honourable courtesy*. Ye have cozened me between ye, with your courtesy. My lord, my lord—you came to us no very wealthy man —you know it. It was for no lucre of gain I took you and your swash-buckler—your Don Diego yonder—under my poor roof. I never cared if the little room were let or no; I could live without it. If you could not have paid for it, you should never have been asked—all the wharf knows John Christie has the means and spirit to do a kindness. When you first darkened my honest door-way, I was as happy as a man need to be, who is no youngster, and has the rheumatism. Nelly was the kindest and best-humoured wench—we might have a word now and then of a gown or a ribband—but a kinder soul on the whole—and a more careful, considering her years—till you came—and what she is now!——But I will not be a fool to cry, if I can help it. *What* she is, is not the question, but *where* she is; and that I must learn, sir, of you."

"How can you, when I tell you," replied Nigel, "that I am as ignorant as yourself, or rather much more so? Till this moment, I never heard of any disagreement betwixt your dame and you."

"That is a lie," said John Christie, bluntly.

"How, you base villain!" said Lord Glenvarloch,—"do you presume on my situation? If it were not that I hold you mad, and perhaps made so by some wrong sustained, you should find my being weaponless were no protection. I would beat your brains out against the wall."

"Ay, ay," answered Christie, "bully as ye list—ye have been at the ordinaries, and in Alsatia, and learned the ruffian's rant, I doubt not. But I repeat, you have spoken an untruth, when you said you knew not of my wife's falsehood; for, when you were twitted with it amongst your gay mates, it was a common jest amongst you, and your lordship took all the credit they would give you for your gallantry and gratitude."

There was a mixture of truth in this part of the charge which disconcerted Lord Glenvarloch exceedingly; for he could not, as a man of honour, deny that Lord Dalgarno, and others, had occasionally jested with him on the subject of Dame Nelly, and that though he had not played exactly *le fanfaron des vices qu'il n'avoit pas*, he had not at least been sufficiently anxious to clear himself of the suspicion of such a crime to men who considered it as a merit. It was therefore with some hesitation, and in a sort of qualifying tone, that he admitted that some idle jests had passed upon such a supposition, although without the least foundation in truth. John Christie would not listen to his vindication any longer. "By your own account," he said, "you permitted lies to be told of you in jest. How do I know you are speaking truth, now you are serious?—you thought it, I suppose, a fine thing to wear the reputation of having dishonoured an honest family,—who will not think that you had real grounds for your base bravado to rest upon? I will not believe otherwise for one—and therefore, my lord, mark what I have to say. You are now yourself in trouble—As you hope to come through it safely, and without loss of life and property, tell me where this unhappy woman is—tell me, if you hope for heaven—tell me, if you fear hell—tell me, as you would not have the curse of an utterly ruined woman, and a broken-hearted man, attend you through life, and bear witness against you at the Great Day, which shall come after death. You are moved, my lord, I see it. I cannot forget the wrong you have done me. I cannot even promise to forgive it—but—tell me, and you shall never see me again, or hear more of my reproaches."

"Unfortunate man," said Lord Glenvarloch, "you have said more, far more than enough, to move me deeply—were I at liberty, I would lend you my best aid to search out him who has wronged you—the rather that I do suspect my having been your lodger has been in some degree the remote cause of bringing the spoiler into the sheepfold."

"I am glad your lordship grants me so much," said John Christie, resuming the tone of embittered irony with which he had opened this singular conversation; "I will spare you further reproach and remonstrance—your mind is made up, and so is mine.—So, ho, warder!" The warder entered, and John went on,—"I want to get out, brother. Look well to your charge—it were better that half the wild beasts in their dens yonder were turned loose upon Tower-Hill, than that this same smooth-faced, civil-spoken gentleman were again returned to honest men's company."

So saying, he hastily left the apartment; and Nigel had full leisure to lament the waywardness of his fate, which seemed never to tire of persecuting him for crimes of which he was innocent, and investing him with the appearances of guilt which his mind abhorred. He could not, however, help acknowledging to himself, that all the pain which he might sustain from the present accusation of John Christie, was so far deserved, from his having suffered himself, out of vanity, or rather an unwillingness to encounter ridicule, to be supposed capable of a base inhospitable crime, merely because fools called it an affair of gallantry; and it was no balsam to the wound, when he recollected what Richie had told him of his having been ridiculed behind his back by the gallants of the ordinary, for affecting the reputation of an intrigue which he had not in reality spirit enough to have carried on.

His simulation had, in a word, placed him in the unlucky predicament of being rallied as a braggart amongst the dissipated youths with whom the reality of the amour would have given him credit; whilst, on the other hand, he was branded as an inhospitable seducer by the injured husband, who was obstinately persuaded of his guilt.

Chapter Five

How fares the man on whom good men would look
With eyes where scorn and censure combated,
But that kind Christian love hath taught the lesson—
That they who merit most contempt and hate,
Do most deserve our pity.——
Old Play

IT MIGHT HAVE seemed natural that the visit of John Christie should have entirely diverted Nigel's attention from his slumbering companion, and, for a time, such was the immediate effect of the chain of new ideas which the incident introduced; yet, soon after the injured man had departed, Lord Glenvarloch began to think it extraordinary that the boy should have slept so sound, while they talked loudly in the vicinity. Yet he certainly did not appear to have stirred. Was he well—was he only feigning sleep? He went close to him to make his observations, and perceived that he had wept, and was still weeping, though his eyes were closed. He touched him gently on the shoulder—the boy shrunk from his touch, but did not awake. He pulled him harder, and asked him if he was sleeping.

"Do they waken folks in your country to know whether they are asleep or no?" said the boy, in a peevish tone.

"No, my young sir," answered Nigel; "but when they weep in the manner you do in their sleep, they awaken them to see what ails them."

"It signifies little to any one what ails me," said the boy.

"True," replied Lord Glenvarloch; "but you knew before you went to sleep how little I could assist you in your difficulties, and you seemed disposed, notwithstanding, to put some confidence in me."

"If I did, I have changed my mind," said the lad.

"And what may have occasioned this change of mind, I trow?" said Lord Glenvarloch.—"Some men speak through their sleep—perhaps you have the gift of hearing in it?"

"No, but the patriarch Joseph never dreamt truer dreams than I do."

"Indeed!" said Lord Glenvarloch. "And, pray, what dream have you had that has deprived me of your good opinion; for that, I think, seems the moral of the matter?"

"You shall judge yourself," answered the boy. "I dreamed I was in a wild forest, where there was cry of hounds, and winding of horns, exactly as I heard in Greenwich Park."

"That was because you *were* in the Park this morning, you simple child," said Nigel.

"Stay, my lord," said the youth. "I went on in my dream, till, at the top of a broad green alley, I saw a noble stag which had fallen into the toils; and methought I knew that he was the very stag whom the whole party were hunting, and that if the chase came up, the dogs would tear him to pieces, or the hunters would cut his throat; and I had pity on the gallant stag, and though I was of a different kind from him, and though I was somewhat afraid of him, I thought I would venture something to free so stately a creature; and I pulled out my little knife, and just as I begun to cut the meshes of the net, the animal started up in my face in the likeness of a tiger, much larger and fiercer than any you may have seen in the ward of the wild beasts yonder, and was just about to tear me limb from limb, when you awaked me."

"Methinks," said Nigel, "I deserve more thanks than I have got, for rescuing you from such a danger by waking you. But, my pretty master, methinks all this tale of a tiger and a stag has little to do with your change of temper towards me."

"I know not whether it has or no," said the lad; "but I will not tell you who I am."

"You will keep your secret yourself then, peevish boy," said Nigel, turning from him, and resuming his walk through the room; then stopping suddenly, he said,—"And yet you shall not escape from me without knowing that I penetrate your mystery."

"My mystery!" said the youth, at once alarmed and irritated,— "what mean you, my lord?"

"Only that I can read your dream without the assistance of a Chaldean interpreter, and my exposition is that—my fair companion does not wear the dress of her own sex."

"And if I do not, my lord," said his companion, hastily starting up, and folding her cloak tight around her, "my dress, such as it is, covers one who will not disgrace it."

"Many would call that speech a fair challenge," said Lord Glenvarloch, looking on her fixedly; "women do not masquerade in men's clothes, to make use of men's weapons."

"I have no such purpose," said the seeming boy; "I have other means of protection, and powerful—but I would first know what is *your* purpose."

"An honourable and a most respectful one," said Lord Glenvarloch; "whatever you are—whatever motive may have brought you into this ambiguous situation, I am sensible—every look, word, and action of yours, makes me sensible, that you are no proper subject of importunity, far less of ill usage. What circumstances can have forced you into so doubtful a situation, I know not; but I feel assured there is, and can be, nothing in them of premeditated wrong, which should expose you to cold-blooded insult. From me you have nothing to dread."

"I expected nothing less from your nobleness, my lord," answered the female; "my adventure, though I feel it was both desperate and foolish, is not so very foolish, nor my safety here so utterly unprotected as at first sight—and in this strange dress, it may appear to be. I have suffered enough, and more than enough, by the degradation of having been seen in this unfeminine attire, and the comments you must necessarily have made on my conduct—but I thank God that I am so far protected, that I could not have been subjected to insult unavenged."

When this extraordinary explanation had proceeded thus far, the warder appeared to place before Lord Glenvarloch a meal, which, for his present situation, might be called comfortable, and which, if not equal to the cookery of the celebrated Chevalier Beaujeu, was much superior in neatness and cleanliness to that of Alsatia. A warder attended to do the honours of the table, and made a sign to the disguised female to rise and assist him in his attendance. But Nigel declared that he knew the youth's parents, interfered, and caused his companion to eat along with him. She consented with a sort of embarrassment, which rendered her pretty features yet more interesting. Yet she maintained with a natural grace that sort of good breeding which belongs to the table; and it seemed to Nigel, whether already prejudiced in her favour by the extraordinary circumstances of their meeting, or whether really judging from what was actually the fact, that he had seldom seen a young person comport herself with more decorous propriety, mixed with ingenuous simplicity; while the consciousness of the peculiarities of her situation threw a singular colouring over her whole demeanour, which could be neither said to be formal, nor easy, nor embarrassed, but was compounded of and shaded with an interchange of all these three characteristics. Wine was placed on the table, of which she could not be prevailed to taste a glass. Their conversation was, of course, limited by the presence of the warder to the business of the table; but Nigel had, long ere the cloth was removed, formed the resolution, if possible, of making himself master of this young person's history, the more especially as he now began to think that the tones of her voice and her features were not so strange to him as he had originally supposed. This, however, was a conviction which he adopted slowly, and only as it dawned upon him from particular circumstances during the course of the repast.

At length the prison-meal was finished, and Lord Glenvarloch began to think how he might most easily enter upon the topic he meditated, when the warder announced a visitor.

"Soh!" said Nigel, something displeased, "I find even a prison does not save one from importunate visitations."

He prepared to receive his guest however, while his alarmed companion flew to the large cradle-shaped chair, which had first served her as a place of refuge, drew her cloak around her, and disposed herself as much as she could to avoid observation. She had scarce made her arrangements for that purpose when the door opened, and the worthy citizen, George Heriot, entered the prison-chamber.

He cast around the apartment his usual sharp quick glance of observation, and advancing to Nigel, said—"My lord, I wish I could say I was happy to see you."

"The sight of those who are unhappy themselves, Master Heriot, seldom produces happiness to their friends—I, however, am glad to see you."

He extended his hand, but Heriot bowed with much formal complaisance, instead of accepting the courtesy, which in those times, when distinction of ranks was much guarded by etiquette and ceremony, was considered as a distinguished favour.

"You are displeased with me, Master Heriot," said Lord Glenvarloch reddening, for he was not deceived by the worthy citizen's affectation of extreme reverence and respect.

"By no means, my lord," replied Heriot; "but I have been in France, and have thought it as well to import, along with other more substantial articles, a small sample of that good breeding which they are so renowned for."

"It is not kind of you," said Nigel, "to bestow the first use of it on an old and obliged friend."

Heriot only answered to this observation with a short dry cough. "Hem! hem! I say, ahem! My lord, as my French politeness may not carry me far, I would willingly know whether I am to speak as a friend, since your lordship is pleased to term me such; or whether I am, as befits my condition, to confine myself to the needful business which must be treated of between us."

"Speak as a friend by all means, Master Heriot," said Nigel; "I perceive you have adopted some of the numerous prejudices against me, if not all of them. Speak out, and frankly—what I cannot deny I will at least confess."

"And I trust, my lord, redress," said Heriot.

"So far as is in my power, certainly," answered Nigel.

"Ah! my lord," continued Heriot, "that is a melancholy though a necessary restriction; for how lightly may any one do an hundred times more than the degree of evil which it may be within his power to repair to the sufferers and to society. But we are not alone here," he said, stopping, and darting his shrewd eye towards the muffled figure of the disguised maiden, whose utmost efforts had not enabled her so to adjust her position as altogether to escape observation. More anxious to prevent her being discovered than to keep his own affairs private, Nigel hastily answered—

"'Tis a page of mine; you may speak freely before him. He is of France, and knows no English."

"I am then to speak freely," said Heriot, after a second glance at the chair; "perhaps my words may be more free than welcome."

"Go on, sir," said Nigel, "I have told you I can bear reproof."

"In one word then, my lord—why do I find you in this place, and whelmed with charges which must blacken a name rendered famous by ages of virtue?"

"Simply then, you find me here," said Nigel, "because, to begin from my original error, I would be wiser than my father."

"It was a difficult task, my lord," replied Heriot; "your father was voiced generally as the wisest and one of the bravest men of Scotland."

"He commanded me," continued Nigel, "to avoid all gambling; and I took it upon me to modify this injunction into regulating my play according to my skill, means, and the course of my luck."

"Ay, self-opinion, acting on a desire of acquisition, my lord—you hoped to touch pitch and not to be defiled," answered Heriot. "Well, my lord, you need not say, for I have heard with much regret, how far this conduct diminished your reputation. Your next error I may without scruple remind you of—My lord, my lord, in whatever degree Lord Dalgarno may have failed towards you, the son of his father should have been sacred from your violence."

"You speak in cold blood, Master Heriot, and I was smarting under a thousand wrongs inflicted on me under the mask of friendship."

"That is, he gave your lordship bad advice, and you," said Heriot——

"Was fool enough to follow his counsel," answered Nigel;—"but we will pass this, Master Heriot, if you please. Old men and young men, men of the sword and men of peaceful occupation, always have thought, always will think, differently on such subjects."

"I grant," answered Heriot, "the distinction between the old goldsmith and the young nobleman—Still you should have had patience for Lord Huntinglen's sake, and prudence for your own. Supposing your quarrel just"——

"I pray you pass on to some other charge," said Lord Glenvarloch.

"I am not your accuser, my lord; but I trust in heaven, that your own heart has already accused you bitterly on the inhospitable wrong which your late landlord has sustained at your hand."

"Had I been guilty of what you allude to," said Lord Glenvarloch, —"had a moment of temptation hurried me away, I had long ere now most bitterly repented it. But whoever may have wronged the unhappy woman, it was not I—I never heard of her folly until within this hour."

"Come, my lord," said Heriot, with some severity, "this sounds too much like affectation. I know there is among our modern youth a new creed respecting adultery as well as homicide—I would rather hear you speak of a revision of the Decalogue, with mitigated penalties in favour of the privileged orders—I would rather hear you do this, than deny a fact in which you have been known to glory."

"Glory! I never did, never would have taken honour to myself from such a cause," said Lord Glenvarloch; "I could not prevent other idle tongues and idle brains from making false inferences."

"You would have known well enough how to stop their mouths, my lord," replied Heriot, "had they spoke of you what was unpleasing to your ears, and what the truth did not warrant. Come, my lord, remember your promise to confess; and indeed to confess is in this case in some slight sort to redress. I will grant you are young, the woman handsome, and, as I myself have observed, light-headed enough. Let me know where she is; her foolish husband has still some compassion for her—will save her from infamy—perhaps in time receive her back, for we are a good-natured generation we traders—Do not, my lord, emulate those who work mischief merely for the pleasure of doing so —it is the very devil's worst quality."

"Your grave remonstrances will drive me mad," said Nigel; "there is a shew of sense and reason in what you say, and yet it is positively insisting on my telling the retreat of a fugitive of whom I know nothing earthly."

"It is well, my lord," answered Heriot coldly; "you have a right, such as it is, to keep your own secrets; but since my discourse on these points seems so totally unavailing, we had better proceed to business. Yet your father's image rises before me, and seems to plead that I should go on."

"Be it as you will, sir," said Glenvarloch; "he who doubts my word, shall have no additional security for it."

"Well, my lord—in the sanctuary at Whitefriars—a place of refuge so unsuitable to a young man of quality and character—I am told a murther was committed."

"And you believe that I did the deed, I suppose?"

"God forbid, my lord!" said Heriot; "the coroner's inquest hath sate, and it appeared that your lordship, under your assumed name of Grahame, behaved with the utmost bravery."

"No compliment, I pray you," said Nigel; "I am only too happy to find that I did not murther, or am not believed to have murthered, the old man."

"True, my lord," said Heriot; "but even in this affair there lacks explanation. Your lordship embarked this morning in a wherry with a female, and it is said an immense sum of money in specie and other valuables—but the woman has not since been heard of."

"I parted with her at Paul's Wharf," said Nigel, "where she went ashore with her charge. I gave her a letter to that very man John Christie."

"Ay, that is the waterman's story; but John Christie denies that he remembers any thing of the matter."

"I am sorry to hear this," said the young nobleman; "I hope in heaven she has not been trepanned, for the treasure she had with her."

"I hope not, my lord," replied Heriot; "but men's minds are much disturbed about it—our national character suffers on all hands—men remember the fatal case of Lord Sanquhar, hanged for the murder of a fencing-master, and exclaim they will not have their wives whored, and their property stolen, by the nobility of Scotland."

"And all this is laid to my door!" said Nigel; "my exculpation is easy."

"I trust so, my lord," said Heriot—"nay, in this particular I do not doubt it—but why did you leave Whitefriars under such circum-stances?"

"Master Reginald Lowestoffe sent a boat for me, with intimation to provide for my safety."

"I am sorry to say," replied Heriot, "that he denies all knowledge of your lordship's motions, after having dispatched a messenger to you with some baggage."

"The watermen told me they were employed by him."

"Watermen?" said Heriot; "one of these proves to be an idle apprentice, an old acquaintance of mine—the other has escaped—but the fellow who is in custody persists in saying he was employed by your lordship, and you only."

"He lies," said Lord Glenvarloch hastily; "he told me Master Lowestoffe had sent him. I hope that kind-hearted gentleman is at liberty?"

"He is," answered Heriot, "and has escaped with a rebuke from the benchers for interfering in such a matter as your lordship's. The Court desire to keep well with the young Templars in these times of commotion, or he had not come off so well."

"That is the only word of comfort I have heard from you," replied Nigel. "But this poor woman—she and her trunk were committed to the charge of two porters."

"So said the pretended waterman, but none of the fellows who ply at the wharf will acknowledge the employment. I see the idea makes you uneasy, my lord; but every effort is made to discover the poor woman's place of retreat—if, indeed, she yet lives. And now, my lord, my errand is spoken, so far as it relates exclusively to your lordship; what remains, is matter of business of a more formal kind."

"Let us proceed to it without delay," said Lord Glenvarloch. "I would hear of the affairs of any one rather than of my own."

"You cannot have forgotten, my lord," said Heriot, "the transaction which took place some weeks since at Lord Huntinglen's, by which a large sum of money was advanced for the redemption of your lordship's estate?"

"I remember it perfectly," said Nigel; "and your present austerity cannot make me forget your kindness on the occasion."

Heriot bowed gravely, and went on.—"That money was advanced under the expectation and hope, that it might be replaced by the contents of a grant to your lordship under the royal sign-manual, in payment of certain monies due by the crown to your father. I trust your lordship understood the transaction at the time. I trust you now understand my resumption of its import, and hold it to be correct."

"Undeniably correct," answered Lord Glenvarloch. "If the sums contained in the warrant cannot be recovered, my lands become the property of those who paid off the original holders of the mortgage, and now stand in their right."

"Even so, my lord," said Heriot; "and your lordship's unhappy circumstances having, it would seem, alarmed these creditors, they are now, I am sorry to say, pressing for one or other of these alternatives—possession of the land, or payment of their debt."

"They have a right to one or other," answered Lord Glenvarloch; "and as I cannot do the last in my present condition, I suppose they must enter on possession."

"Stay, my lord," replied Heriot; "if you have ceased to call me a friend to your person, at least you shall see I am willing to be such to your father's house, were it but for the sake of your father's memory. If you will trust me with the warrant under the sign-manual, I believe circumstances do now so stand at court, that I may be able to recover the money for you."

"I would do so gladly," said Lord Glenvarloch; "but the casket which contains it is not in my possession—it was seized when I was arrested at Greenwich."

"It will be no longer with-held from you," said Heriot; "for I understood my Master's natural good sense, and some information which he had procured, I know not how, has induced him to contradict the whole charge of the attempt on his person—it is entirely hushed up, and you will only be proceeded against for your violence on Lord Dalgarno, committed within the verge of the Palace—and that you will find heavy enough to answer."

"I will not shrink under the weight," said Lord Glenvarloch; "but that is not the present point.—If I had that casket"——

"Your baggage stood in the little anti-room, as I passed," said the citizen, "the casket caught my eye. I think you had it of me—It was my old friend Sir Faithful Frugal's—ay—he too had a son——" Here he stopped short.

"A son who, like Lord Glenvarloch's, did no credit to his father—was it not so you would have ended the sentence, Master Heriot?" said the young lord.

"My lord, it was a word spoken rashly," answered Heriot. "God may mend all in his own good time. This however I will say, that I have sometimes envied my friends their fair and flourishing families; and yet have I seen such changes when death hath removed the head, so many rich men's sons pennyless, the heirs of so many knights and nobles acreless, that I think mine own estate and memory, as I shall order it, has a fair chance of outliving those of greater men, though God has given me no heir of my name. But this is from the purpose.—Ho! warder, bring in the Lord Glenvarloch's baggage." The officer obeyed. Seals had been placed upon the trunk and casket, but were now removed, the warder said, in consequence of the subsequent orders from Court, and the whole was placed at the prisoner's free disposal.

Desirous to bring this painful visit to a conclusion, Lord Glenvarloch opened the casket, and looked through the few papers which it contained, first hastily, and then more slowly and accurately, but it was all in vain. The Sovereign's signed warrant had disappeared.

"I thought and expected nothing better," said George Heriot, bitterly. "The beginning of evil is the letting out of water. Here is a fair heritage lost, I dare say, on a foul cast at dice, or a conjuring trick at cards!—My lord, your surprise is well played. I give you full joy of your accomplishments. I have seen many as young brawlers and

spendthrifts—but never so young and accomplished a dissembler.—
Nay, man, never bend your angry brows on me. I speak in bitterness of
heart, from what I remember of your worthy father; and if his son
hears of his degeneracy from no one else, he shall hear it from the old
goldsmith."

This new suspicion drove Nigel to the very extremity of his
patience; yet the motives and zeal of the good old man, as well as the
circumstances of suspicion which created his displeasure, were so
excellent an excuse for it, that they formed an absolute curb on the
resentment of Lord Glenvarloch, and constrained him, after one or
two hasty exclamations, to observe a proud and sullen silence. At
length, Master Heriot resumed his lecture.

"Hark you, my lord," he said, "it is scarce possible that this most
important paper can be absolutely assigned away—let me know in
what obscure corner, and for what petty sum, it lies pledged—something may yet be done."

"Your efforts in my favour are the more generous," said Lord
Glenvarloch, "as you offer them to one whom you believe you have
cause to think hardly of—but they are altogether unavailing. Fortune
has taken the field against me at every point. Even let her win the
battle."

"Zouns!" exclaimed Heriot, impatiently,—"you would make a
saint swear. Why, I tell you, if this paper, the loss of which seems to sit
so light on you, be not found, farewell to the fair lordship of Glenvarloch—firth and forest—lea and furrow—lake and stream—all that
has been in the house of Olifaunt since the days of William the Lion."

"Farewell to them, then," said Nigel,—"and that moan is soon
made."

"'Sdeath! my lord—you will make more moan for it ere you die,"
said Heriot, in the same tone of angry impatience.

"Not I, my old friend," said Nigel. "If I mourn, Master Heriot, it
will be for having lost the good opinion of a worthy man, and lost it, as I
must say, most undeservedly."

"Ay, ay, young man," said Heriot, shaking his head, "make me
believe that, if you can.—To sum the matter up," he said, rising from
his seat, and walking towards that occupied by the disguised female,
"for our matters are now drawn into small compass, you shall as soon
make me believe that this masquerading mummer, on whom I now lay
the hand of paternal authority, is a French page, who understands no
English."

So saying, he took hold of the supposed page's cloak, and, not
without some gentle degree of violence, led into the middle of the
apartment the disguised fair one, who in vain attempted to cover her

face, first with her mantle, and afterward with her hands; both which impediments Master Heriot removed, something unceremoniously, and gave to view the detected daughter of the old chronologist, his own fair god-daughter, Margaret Ramsay.

"Here is goodly gear," he said; and, as he spoke, he could not prevent himself from giving her a slight shake, for we have elsewhere noticed that he was a severe disciplinarian.—"How comes it, minion, that I find you in so shameless a dress, and so unworthy a situation?— nay, your modesty is now mistimed—it should have come sooner— speak, or I will"——

"Master Heriot," said Lord Glenvarloch, "whatever right you may have over this maiden elsewhere, while in my apartment, she is under my protection."

"Your protection, my lord!—a proper protector!—And, how long, mistress, have you been under my lord's protection?—speak out, forsooth."

"For the matter of two hours, godfather," answered the maiden, with a countenance bent to the ground, and covered with blushes, "but it was against my will."

"Two hours!" repeated Heriot,—"space enough for mischief.— My lord, this is, I suppose, another victim offered to your character of gallantry—another adventure to be boasted of at Beaujeu's ordinary? Methinks, the roof under which you first met this silly maiden, should have secured her at least from such a fate."

"On my honour, Master Heriot," said Lord Glenvarloch, "you remind me now, for the first time, that I saw this young lady in your family. Her features are not easily forgotten, and yet I was trying in vain to recollect where I had last looked on them. For your suspicions, they are as false as they are injurious both to her and me. I had but discovered her disguise as you entered. I am satisfied, from her whole behaviour, that her presence here in this dress was involuntary; and God forbid that I had been capable to take advantage of it to her prejudice."

"It is well mouthed, my lord," said Master Heriot; "but a cunning clerk can read the Apocrypha as loud as the Scripture—frankly, my lord, you are come to that pass, where your words will not pass without a warrant."

"I should not speak, perhaps," said Margaret, the natural vivacity of whose temper could never be long suppressed by any situation, how- ever disadvantageous, "but I cannot be silent. Godfather, you do me wrong—and no less wrong to this young nobleman. You say his words want a warrant—I know where to find a warrant for some of them, and the rest I deeply and devoutly believe without one."

"And I thank you, maiden," replied Nigel, "for the good opinion you have expressed. I am at that point it seems, though how I have been driven to it I know not, when every fair construction of my actions and motives is refused me. I am the more obliged to her who grants me that right which the world denies me—for you, lady, were I at liberty, I have a sword and arm should know how to guard your reputation."

"Upon my word, a perfect Amadis and Oriana!" said George Heriot. "I should soon get my throat cut betwixt the knight and the princess, I suppose, but that the beef-eaters are happily within hallo. —Come, come, Lady Light-o'-love—if you mean to make your way with me, it must be by plain facts, not by speeches from romaunts and play-books. How, in Heaven's name, came you here?"

"Sir," answered Margaret, "since I must speak—I went to Green-wich this morning with Monna Paula, to present a petition to the King on the part of the Lady Hermione."

"Mercy-a-gad!" exclaimed Heriot, "is she in the dance, too?— could she not have waited my return to stir in her affairs?—but I suppose the intelligence I sent her had rendered her restless. Ah! woman, woman—he that goes partners with you, had need of a double share of patience, for you will bring none to the common stock.— Well, but what on earth had this embassy of Monna Paula's to do with your absurd disguise?—Speak out."

"Monna Paula was frightened," answered Margaret, "and did not know how to set about her errand, for you know she scarce ever goes out doors—and so—and so—I agreed to go with her to give her courage—and, for the dress, I am sure you remember I wore it at a Christmas mumming, and you thought it not unbeseeming."

"Yes, for a Christmas parlour," said Heriot, "but not to go a mask-ing through the country in. I do remember it, minion, and I knew it even now—that and your little shoe there, linked with a hint I had in the morning from a friend, or one who called himself such, led to your detection."—Here Lord Glenvarloch could not help giving a glance at the pretty foot, which even the staid citizen thought worth recol-lection—it was but a glance, for he saw how much the least degree of observation added to Margaret's distress and confusion. "And tell me, maiden," continued Master Heriot, for what we have observed was bye-play,—"did the Lady Hermione know of this fair work?"

"I dared not have told her for the world," said Margaret—"she thought one of our apprentices went with Monna Paula."

It may be here noticed, that the words, "our apprentices," seemed to have in them something of a charm to break the fascination with which Lord Glenvarloch had hitherto listened to the broken, yet interesting details of Margaret's history.

"And wherefore went he not?—he had been a fitter companion for Monna Paula than you, I wot," said the citizen.

"He was otherwise employed," said Margaret, in a voice scarce audible.

Master George darted a hasty glance at Nigel, and when he saw his features betoken no consciousness, he muttered to himself,—"It must be better than I feared.—And so this cursed Spaniard, with her head full, as they all have, of disguises, trap-doors, rope-ladders, and masks, was jade and fool enough to take you with her on this wild-goose errand?—And how sped you, I pray?"

"Just as we reached the gate of the Park," replied Margaret, "the cry of treason was raised. I know not what became of Monna, but I ran till I fell into the arms of a very decent serving-man, called Linklater; and I was fain to tell him I was your god-daughter, and he kept the rest of them from me, and got me to speech of his Majesty, as I entreated him to do."

"It is the only sign you shewed in the whole matter that common sense had not utterly deserted your little skull," said Heriot.

"His Majesty," continued the damsel, "was so gracious as to receive me alone, though the courtiers cried out against the danger to his person, and would have searched me for arms, God help me, but the King forbade it. I fancy he had a hint from Linklater how the truth stood with me."

"Well, maiden, I ask not what passed," said Heriot; "it becomes not me to pry into my Master's secrets—had you been closeted with his grandfather, the Red Tod of Saint Andrews, as Davie Lindsay used to call him, by my faith, I should have had my own thoughts of the matter; but our Master, God bless him, is douce and temperate, and Solomon in every thing, save in the chapter of wives and concubines."

"I know not what you mean, sir," answered Margaret. "His Majesty was most kind and compassionate—but said I must be sent hither, and that the Lieutenant's lady, the Lady Mansel, would have a charge of me, and see that I sustained no wrong; and the King promised to send me in a tilted barge, and under conduct of a person well known to you; and thus I come to be in the Tower."

"But how, or why, in this apartment, nymph?" said George Heriot —"Expound that to me, for I think the riddle needs reading."

"I cannot explain it, sir, further, than that the Lady Mansel sent me here, in spite of my earnest prayers, tears, and entreaties. I was not afraid of any thing, for I knew I should be protected. But I could have died then—could die now—for very shame and confusion."

"Well, well—if your tears are genuine," said Heriot, "they may the

sooner wash out the memory of your fault.—Knows your father aught
of this escape of yours?"

"I would not for the world he did," replied she; "he believes me
with the Lady Hermione."

"Ay, honest Davie can regulate his horologes better than his family.
Come, damsel mine, I will escort you back to the Lady Mansel, and
pray her, of her kindness, that when she is again trusted with a goose,
she will not give it to the fox to keep—the warders will let us pass to my
lady's lodging, I trust."

"Stay but one moment," said Lord Glenvarloch. "Whatever hard
opinion you may have formed of me I forgive, for time will shew that
you do me wrong; and you yourself, I think, will be the first to regret
the injustice you have done me. But involve not in your suspicions this
young person, for whose purity of thought angels themselves should
be vouchers. I have marked every look, every gesture; and whilst I can
draw breath, I shall ever think of her"——

"Think not at all of her, my lord," answered George Heriot, interrupting him; "it is, I have a notion, the best favour you can do her;—or
think of her as the daughter of Davie Ramsay, the clockmaker, no
proper subject for fine speeches, romantic adventures, or high-flown
Arcadian compliments.—I give you god-den, my lord. I think not
altogether so harshly as my speech may have spoken. If I can help—
that is, if I once saw my way clearly through this labyrinth—but it
avails not talking now. I give your lordship god-den.—Here, warder!
permit us to pass to the Lady Mansel's apartment."

The warder said he must have orders from the Lieutenant; and as
he retired to procure them, the parties remained standing near each
other, but without speaking, and scarce looking at each other save by
stealth, a situation which, to two of the party at least, was sufficiently
embarrassing. The difference of rank, though in that age a consideration so serious, could not prevent Lord Glenvarloch from seeing that
Margaret Ramsay was one of the prettiest young women he had ever
beheld—from suspecting, he could scarce tell why, that he himself
was not indifferent to her—from feeling assured that he had been the
cause of much of her present distress—admiration, self-love, and
generosity acted in favour of the same object, and when the yeoman
returned with permission to his guests to withdraw, Nigel's obeisance
to the beautiful daughter of the mechanic was marked with an expression, which called up in her cheeks as much colour as any incident
of the eventful day had hitherto excited. She returned the courtesy
timidly and irresolutely, clung to her godfather's arm, and left the
apartment, which, dark as it was, had never yet appeared so obscure to
Nigel, as when the door closed behind her.

Chapter Six

Yet though thou should'st be dragg'd in scorn
To yonder ignominious tree,
Thou shalt not want one faithful friend
To share the cruel fates' decree.
Ballad of Jemmy Dawson

MASTER GEORGE HERIOT and his ward, as she might justly be termed, for his affection to Margaret imposed on him all the cares of a guardian, were ushered by the yeoman of the guard to the lodging of the Lieutenant, where they found him seated with his lady. They were received by both with that decorous civility which Master Heriot's character and supposed influence demanded, even at the hand of a punctilious old soldier and courtier like Sir Edward Mansel. Lady Mansel received Margaret with like courtesy, and informed Master George that she was now only her guest, and no longer her prisoner.

"She is at liberty," she said, "to return to her friends under your charge—such is his Majesty's pleasure."

"I am glad of it, madam," answered Heriot, "but only I could have wished her freedom had taken place before her foolish interview with that singular young man; and I marvel your ladyship permitted it."

"My good Master Heriot," said Sir Edward, "we act according to the commands of one better and wiser than ourselves—our orders from his Majesty must be strictly and literally obeyed; and I need not say that the wisdom of his Majesty doth more than ensure"——

"I know his Majesty's wisdom well," said Heriot; "yet there is an old proverb about fire and flax—well—let it pass."

"I see Sir Mungo Malagrowther stalking towards the door of the lodging," said the Lady Mansel, "with the gait of a lame crane—it is his second visit this morning."

"He brought the warrant for discharging Lord Glenvarloch of the charge of treason," said Sir Edward.

"And from him," said Heriot, "I heard much of what had befallen; for I came from France only late last evening, and somewhat unexpectedly."

As they spoke, Sir Mungo entered the apartment—saluted the Lieutenant of the Tower and his lady with ceremonious civility—honoured George Heriot with a patronizing nod of acknowledgment, and accosted Margaret with—"Hey! my young charge, you have not doffed your masculine attire yet?"

"She does not mean to lay it aside, Sir Mungo," said Heriot, speaking loud, "until she has had satisfaction from you, for betraying her disguise to me, like a false knight—And in very deed, Sir Mungo, I think when you told me she was rambling about in so strange a dress, you might have said also that she was under Lady Mansel's protection."

"That was the King's secret, Master Heriot," said Sir Mungo, throwing himself into a chair with an air of atrabilious importance; "the other was a well-meaning hint to yourself as the girl's friend."

"Yes," replied Heriot, "it was done like yourself—enough told to make me unhappy about her—not a word which could relieve my uneasiness."

"Sir Mungo will not hear that remark," said the lady; "we must change the subject.—Is there any news from court, Sir Mungo?—you have been to Greenwich?"

"You might as well ask me, madam," answered the Knight, "whether there is any news from hell."

"How, Sir Mungo, how!" said Sir Edward, "measure your words something better. You speak of the court of King James."

"Sir Edward, if I spoke of the court of the twelve Kaisars, I would say it is as confused for the present as the infernal regions—courtiers of forty years standing, and such I may write myself, are as far to seek in the matter as a minnow in the Maelstrom. Some folks say the King has frowned on the Prince—some that the Prince has looked grave on the Duke—some that Lord Glenvarloch shall be hanged for high treason—and some that there is matter against Lord Dalgarno that may cost him as much as his head's worth."

"And what do you, that are a courtier of forty years standing, think of it all?" said Sir Edward Mansel.

"Nay, nay, do not ask him, Sir Edward," said the lady, with an expressive look to her husband.

"Sir Mungo is too witty," added Master Heriot, "to remember that he who says aught that may be repeated to his own prejudice, does but load a piece for any of the company to shoot him dead with, at their pleasure and convenience."

"What!" said the bold knight, "you think I am afraid of the trepan? —why now, what if I should say that Dalgarno has more wit than honesty,—the Duke more sail than ballast,—the Prince more pride than prudence—and that the King"—— The Lady Mansel held up her finger in a warning manner—"that the King is my very good master, who has given me for forty years and more, dog's wages, videlicet, bones and beating.—Why now, all this is said, and Archie Armstrong says worse than this of the best of them, every day."

"The more fool he," said George Heriot; "and yet he is not so utterly wrong, for folly is his best wisdom. But do not you, Sir Mungo, set your wit against a fool's, though he be a court fool."

"A fool, said you?" replied Sir Mungo, not having fully heard what Master Heriot said, or not choosing to have it thought so,—"I have been a fool indeed, to hang on at a close-fisted court here, when men of understanding and men of action have been making fortunes in every other place of Europe. But here a man comes indifferently off unless he gets a great key to turn, (looking at Sir Edward,) or can beat tattoo with a hammer on a pewter plate.—Well, sirs, I must make as much haste back on mine errand as if I were a fee'd messenger.—Sir Edward and my lady, I leave my commendations with you—and my good will with you, Master Heriot—and for this breaker of bounds, if you will act by my counsel, some maceration by fasting, and a gentle use of the rod, is the best cure for her giddy fits."

"If you propose for Greenwich, Sir Mungo," said the Lieutenant, "I can spare you the labour—the King comes immediately to White-hall."

"And that must be the reason the council are summoned to meet in such hurry," said Sir Mungo. "Well—I will, with your permission, go to the poor lad Glenvarloch, and bestow some comfort on him."

The Lieutenant seemed to look up, and pause for a moment as if in doubt.

"The lad will want a pleasant companion, who can tell him the nature of the punishment which he is to suffer, and other matters of concernment. I will not leave him until I shew him how absolutely he hath ruined himself from feather to spur, how deplorable is his present state, and how small his chance of mending it."

"Well, Sir Mungo," replied the Lieutenant, "if you really think all this likely to be very consolatory to the party concerned, I will send a warder to conduct you."

"And I," said George Heriot, "will humbly pray of Lady Mansel, that she will lend some of her hand-maiden's apparel to this giddy-brained girl; for I shall forfeit my reputation if I walk up Tower-hill with her in that mad guise—And yet the silly lassie looks not so ill in it neither."

"I will send my coach with you instead," said the obliging lady.

"'Faith, madam, and if you will honour us by such courtesy, I will gladly accept it at your hands," said the citizen, "for business presses hard on me, and the forenoon is already lost, to little purpose."

The coach being ordered accordingly, transported the worthy citizen and his charge to his mansion in Lombard-street. There he found his presence was anxiously expected by the Lady Hermione, who had just received an order to be in readiness to attend upon the Royal Privy Council in the course of an hour; and upon whom, in her inexperience of business, and long retirement from society and the world, the intimation had made as deep an impression as if it had not been the necessary consequence of the petition which she had presented to the King by Monna Paula. George Heriot gently blamed her for taking any steps in an affair so important until his return from France, especially as he had requested her to remain quiet, in a letter which accompanied the evidence he had transmitted to her from Paris. She could only plead in answer the influence which her immediately stirring in the matter was likely to have on the affair of her kinsman Lord Glenvarloch, for she was ashamed to acknowledge how much she had been gained on by the eager importunity of her youthful companion. The motive of Margaret's eagerness was, of course, the safety of Nigel; but we must leave it to time, to shew in what particulars that came to be connected with the petition of the Lady Hermione. Meanwhile, we return to the visit with which Sir Mungo Malagrowther favoured the afflicted young nobleman in his place of captivity.

The Knight, after the usual salutations, and having prefaced his discourse with a great deal of professed regret for Nigel's situation, sat down beside him, and composing his grotesque features into the most lugubrious despondence, began his raven-song as follows:—

"I bless God, my lord, that I was the person who had the pleasure to bring his Majesty's mild message to the Lieutenant, discharging the higher prosecution against ye, for any thing meditated against his Majesty's sacred person; for, admit you be prosecuted on the lesser offence, or breach of privilege of the palace and its precincts, *usque ad mutilationem*, even to dismemberment, as it is most likely you will, yet the loss of a member is nothing to being hanged and drawn quick, after the fashion of a traitor."

"I should feel the shame of having deserved such a punishment," answered Nigel, "more than the pain of undergoing it."

"Doubtless, my lord, the having, as you say, deserved it, must be an excruciation to your own mind," replied his tormentor; "a kind of mental and metaphysical hanging, drawing, and quartering, which may be in some measure equipollent with the external application of hemp, iron, fire, and the like, to the outer man."

"I say, Sir Mungo," repeated Nigel, "and beg you to understand my words, that I am unconscious of any error, save that of having arms on my person when I chanced to approach that of my Sovereign."

"Ye are right, my lord, to acknowledge nothing," said Sir Mungo. "We have an old proverb,—Confess, and—so forth—and indeed, as to the weapons, his Majesty has a special ill will at all arms whatsoever, and more especially pistols—but, as I said, there is an end of that matter. I wish you as well through the next, which is altogether unlikely."

"Surely, Sir Mungo," answered Nigel, "you yourself might say something in my favour concerning the affair in the Park. None knows better than you that I was at that moment urged by wrongs of the most heinous nature, offered to me by Lord Dalgarno, many of which were reported to me by yourself, much to the inflammation of my passion."

"Alack-a-day!—Alack-a-day!" replied Sir Mungo, "I remember but too well how much your choler was inflamed, in spite of the various remonstrances which I made to you respecting the sacred nature of the place. Alas! alas! you cannot say you leaped into the mire for lack of warning."

"I see, Sir Mungo, you are determined to remember nothing which can do me service," said Nigel.

"Blithely would I do ye service," said the Knight; "and the best whilk I can think of is, to tell you the process of the punishment to the whilk you will be indubitably subjected—I having had the good fortune to behold it performed in the Queen's time, on a chield that had written a pasquinadoe. I was then in my Lord Gray's train, who lay leaguer here, and being always covetous of pleasing and profitable sights, I could not dispense with being present on the occasion."

"I should be surprised indeed," said Lord Glenvarloch, "if you had so far put restraint upon your benevolence, as to stay away from such an exhibition."

"Hey! was your lordship praying me to be present at your own execution?" answered the Knight. "Troth, my lord, it will be a painful sight to a friend, but I will rather punish myself than baulk you. It is a pretty pageant, in the main—a very pretty pageant. The fallow came on with such a bold face, it was a pleasure to look on him. He was dressed all in white, to signify harmlessness and innocence. The thing was done on a scaffold at Paul's Cross, but most likely yours will be at Charing. There were the Sheriff's and the Marshal's men, and what not—the executioner, with his cleaver and mallet, and his man, with a pan of hot charcoal, and the irons for cautery. He was a dexterous fallow that Derrick—this man Gregory is not fit to jibber a joint with him—it might be worth your lordship's while to have the loon sent to a barber-surgeon's, to learn some needful scantling of anatomy—it may be for the benefit of yourself and other unhappy sufferers, and also a kindness to Gregory."

"I will not take the trouble," said Nigel.—"If the laws will demand my hand, the executioner may get it off as he best can—if the King leaves it where it is, it may chance to do him better service."

"Vara noble—vara grand, indeed, my lord," said Sir Mungo; "it is pleasant to see a brave man suffer. This fallow whom I spoke of—this Tubbs, or Stubbes, or whatever the plebeian was called, came forward as bold as an emperor, and said to the people, 'Good friends, I come to leave here the hand of a true Englishman,' and clapped it on the dressing-block with as much ease as if he had laid it on his sweetheart's shoulder, whereupon Derrick the hangman, adjusting, d'ye mind me, the edge of his cleaver on the very joint, hit it with the mallet with such force, that the hand flew as far from the owner as a gauntlet which the challenger casts down in the tilt-yard. Well, sir, Stubbes, or Tubbs, lost no whit of countenance, until the fallow clapped the hissing-hot iron on his raw stump. My lord, it fizzed like a rasher of bacon, and the fallow set up an elritch screech, which made some think his courage was abated; but not a whit, for he plucked off his hat with his left hand, and waved it, crying, 'God save the Queen, and confound all evil counsellors!' The people gave him three cheers, which he deserved for his stout heart; and, truly, I hope to see your lordship suffer with the same magnanimity."

"I thank you, Sir Mungo," said Nigel, who had not been able to forbear some natural feelings of an unpleasant nature during this lively detail,—"I have no doubt the exhibition will be a very engaging one to you and the other spectators, whatsoever it may prove to the party principally concerned."

"Vara engaging," answered Sir Mungo, "vara interesting indeed, though not altogether so much so as an execution for high-treason. I saw Digby, the Winters, Fawkes, and the rest of the gunpowder gang, suffer for that treason, whilk was a vara grand spectacle, as well in regard to their sufferings, as to their constancy in enduring."

"I am the more obliged to your goodness, Sir Mungo," replied Nigel, "that has induced you, although you have lost the sight, to congratulate me on my escape from the hazard of making the same edifying appearance."

"As you say, my lord," answered Sir Mungo, "the loss is chiefly in appearance. Nature has been vara bountiful to us, and has given duplicates of some organs, that we may endure the loss of one of them, should some such circumstance chance in our pilgrimage. See my poor dexter, abridged to one thumb, one finger, and a stump,—by the blow of my athversary's weapon, however, and not by any carnificial knife. Weel, sir, this poor maimed hand doth me, in some sort, as much service as ever; and, admit yours be taken off by the wrist, you have still your left hand for your service, and are better off than the little Dutch dwarf here about town, who threads a needle, limns, writes, and tosses a pike, merely by means of his feet, without ever a hand to help him."

"Well, Sir Mungo," said Lord Glenvarloch, "this is all no doubt very consolatory; but I hope the King will spare my hand to fight for him in battle, where, notwithstanding all your kind encouragement, I could spend my blood much more cheerfully than on a scaffold."

"It is even a sad truth," replied Sir Mungo, "that your lordship was but too like to have died on a scaffold—not a soul to speak for you but that deluded lassie, Maggie Ramsay."

"Whom mean you?" said Nigel, with more interest than he had hitherto shewn in the Knight's communications.

"Nay, who should I mean, but that travestied lassie whom we dined with when we honoured Heriot the goldsmith?—ye ken best how you have made interest with her, but I saw her on her knees to the King for you. She was committed to my charge, to bring her up hither in honour and safety—had I had my own will, I would have had her to Bridewell, to flog the wild blood out of her—a cutty quean, to think of wearing the breeches, and not so much as married yet!"

"Hark ye, Sir Mungo Malagrowther," answered Nigel, "I would have you talk of that young person with fitting respect."

"With all the respect that befits your lordship's paramour, and Davie Ramsay's daughter, I shall certainly speak of her, my lord," said Sir Mungo, assuming a dry tone of irony.

Nigel was greatly disposed to have made a serious quarrel of it, but with Sir Mungo such an affair would have been ridiculous; he smothered his resentment, therefore, and conjured him to tell what he had heard and seen respecting this young person.

"Simply, that I was in the anti-room when she had her audience, and heard the King say, to my great perplexity, '*Pulchra sane puella;*' and Maxwell, who hath but indifferent Latin ears, thought that his Majesty called on him by his own name of Sawney, and thrust into the presence, and there I saw him, with his own hand, raising up the lassie, who, as I said heretofore, was travestied in man's attire. I should have had my own thoughts of it, but our gracious Master is auld, and was nae great gillravager amang the queans even in his youth; and he was comforting her in his own way, and saying,—'Ye needna greet about it, my bonnie woman, Glenvarlochides shall have fair play; and, indeed, when the hurry was off our spirits, we could not believe that he had any design on our person—and touching his other offences, we will look wisely and closely into the matter.' So I got charge to take the young fence-louper to the Tower here, and deliver her to the charge of Lady Mansel; and his Majesty charged me to say not a word to her about your offences, for, said he, the poor thing is breaking her heart for him."

"And on this you charitably have founded the opinion to the

prejudice of this young lady, which you have now thought proper to express?" said Lord Glenvarloch.

"In honest troth, my lord," replied Sir Mungo, "what opinion would ye have me form of a wench who gets into male habiliments, and goes on her knees to the King for a wild young nobleman? I wot not what the fashionable word may be, for the phrase changes, though the custom abides. But truly I must needs think this young leddy—if you call Watchie Ramsay's daughter a young leddy—demeans herself more like a leddy of pleasure than a leddy of honour."

"You do her egregious wrong, Sir Mungo," said Nigel; "or rather you have been misled by appearances."

"So will all the world be misled, my lord, unless you were doing that to disabuse them which your father's son will hardly judge it fit to do."

"And what may that be, I pray you?"

"E'en marry the lass, make her Leddy Glenvarloch—ay, ay—ye may start—but it's the course you are driving on—rather marry than do worse—if the worst be not done already."

"Sir Mungo," said Nigel, "I pray you to forbear this subject, and rather return to that of the mutilation, upon which you enlarged a short while since."

"I have not time at present," said Sir Mungo, hearing the clock strike four; "but so soon as you shall have received sentence, my lord, you may rely on my giving you the fullest detail of the whole solemnity —and I give you my word, as a knight and gentleman, that I will myself attend you on the scaffold, whoever may cast sour looks on me for doing so. I bear a heart to stand by my friend in the worst of times." So saying, he wished Lord Glenvarloch farewell, who felt as heartily rejoiced at his departure, though it may be a bold word, as any person who had ever undergone his society.

But when left to his own reflections, Nigel could not help feeling solitude nearly as irksome as the company of Sir Mungo Mala-growther. The total wreck of his fortune, which seemed now to be rendered unavoidable by the loss of the royal warrant that had afforded him the prospect of redeeming his paternal estate, was an unexpected and additional blow. When he had last seen the warrant he could not precisely remember, but was inclined to think it was in the casket when he took out money to pay the miser for his lodgings at Whitefriars. Since that time, the casket had been almost constantly under his own eye, excepting during the short time he was separated from his baggage by the arrest in Greenwich Park. It might indeed have been abstracted at that time, for he had no reason to think either his person or his property was in the hands of those who wished him well; but, on the other hand, the locks of the strong-box had sustained no violence that he could observe, and being of a particular and complicated construction, he thought they could scarce be opened without an instrument made on purpose, adapted to their peculiarities, and for this there had been no time. But, speculate as he would on the matter, it was clear that this important document was gone, and probable that it had passed into no friendly hands. "Let it so be," said Nigel to himself; "I am scarcely worse off respecting my prospects of fortune than when I first reached this accursed city—but to be hampered with cruel accusations, and stained with foul suspicions—to be the object of pity of the most degrading kind to yonder honest citizen, and of the malignity of that envious and atrabilious courtier, who can endure the good fortune and good qualities of another no more than the mole can brook sunshine—this is indeed a deplorable reflexion, and the consequences must stick to my future life, and impede whatever my head or my hand, if it is left me, might be able to execute in my favour."

The feeling that he is the object of general dislike and dereliction, seems to be one of the most unendurably painful to which a human being can be subjected. The most atrocious criminals, whose nerves have not shrunk from the most horrid cruelty, suffer more from the consciousness that no man will sympathize with their sufferings, than from apprehension of the personal agony of their impending punishment; and are known often to attempt to palliate their enormities, and sometimes altogether to deny what is established by the clearest proof, rather than to leave life under the general ban of humanity. It was no wonder that Nigel, labouring under the sense of general, though unjust suspicion, should, while pondering on so painful a theme, recollect that one, at least, had not only believed him innocent, but hazarded herself, with all her feeble power, to interpose in his behalf.

"Poor girl," he repeated, "poor, rash, but generous maiden! Your fate is that of her in Scottish story, who thrust her arm into the staple of the door, to oppose it as a bar against the assassins who threatened the murder of her sovereign. The deed of devotion was useless, save to give an immortal name to her by whom it was done, and whose blood flows, it is said, in the veins of my house."

I cannot explain to the reader whether the recollection of this historical deed of heroism, and the lively effect which the comparison, a little overstrained perhaps, was like to produce in favour of Margaret Ramsay, was not qualified by the concomitant ideas of ancestry and ancient descent with which that recollection was mingled. But the contending feelings suggested a new train of ideas.—"Ancestry," he thought, "and ancient descent—what are they to me—my patrimony alienated—my title become a reproach, for what can be so absurd as titled beggary—my character subjected to suspicion? I will not remain in this country; and should I, at leaving it, procure the society of one so lovely, so brave, and so faithful, who should say that I derogated from the rank which I am virtually renouncing?"

There was something romantic and pleasing as he pursued this picture of an attached and faithful pair, becoming all the world to each other, and stemming the tide of fate arm in arm; and to be linked thus with a creature so beautiful, and who had taken such devoted and disinterested concern in his fortunes, formed itself into such a vision as romantic youth loves best to dwell upon.

Suddenly his dream was painfully dispelled by the recollection, that its very basis rested upon the most selfish ingratitude on his own part. Lord of his castle and his towers, his forests and fields, his fair patrimony and noble name, his mind would have rejected as a sort of impossibility the idea of elevating to his rank the daughter of a mechanic; but when degraded from his nobility, and plunged into poverty and difficulties, he was ashamed to feel himself not unwilling that this poor girl, in the blindness of her affection, should abandon all the better prospects of her own settled condition, to embrace the precarious and doubtful course which he himself was condemned to. The generosity of Nigel's mind recoiled from the selfishness of the plan of happiness which he projected; and he made a strong effort to expel from his thoughts for the rest of the evening this fascinating female, or at least not to permit them to dwell upon the perilous circumstance, that she was at present the only creature living who seemed to consider him as an object of kindness.

He could not, however, succeed in banishing her from his slumbers, when, after having spent a weary day, he betook himself to a perturbed couch. The form of Margaret mingled with the wild mass of dreams which his late adventures had suggested; and even when, copying the lively narration of Sir Mungo, fancy presented to him the blood bubbling and hissing on the heated iron, Margaret stood behind him like a spirit of light, to breathe healing on the wound. At length nature was exhausted by these fantastic creations, and Nigel at length slept, and slept soundly, until awakened in the morning by the sound of a well-known voice, which had often broken his slumbers about the same hour.

Chapter Seven

Marry come up, sir, with your gentle blood!
There's a red stream beneath this coarse blue doublet,
That warms the heart as kindly as if drawn
From the far source of old Assyrian kings,
Who first made mankind subject to their sway.
                                                        Old Play

THE SOUNDS to which we alluded in our last, were no other than the grumbling tones of Richie Moniplies's voice. This worthy, like some other persons who rank high in their own opinion, was very apt, when he could have no other auditor, to hold conversation with one who was sure to be a willing listener—I mean with himself. He was now brushing and arranging Lord Glenvarloch's clothes, with as much composure and quiet assiduity as if he had never been out of his service, and grumbling betwixt whiles to the following purpose:—"Humph—ay—time cloak and jerkin were through my hands—I question if horsehair has been passed over them since they and I last parted—the embroidery finely frayed too—and the gold buttons of the cloak—by my conscience, and as I am an honest man, there is a round dozen of them gane!—this comes of Alsatian frolics—God keep us with his grace, and not give us over to our ain devices!—I see no sword—but that will be in respect of present circumstances."

Nigel for some time could not help believing that he was still in a dream, so improbable did it seem that his domestic should have found him out, and obtained access to him in his present circumstances. Looking through the curtains, however, he became well assured of the fact, when he beheld the stiff and bony length of Richie, with a visage charged with nearly double its ordinary degree of importance, employed sedulously in brushing his master's cloak, and refreshing himself with whistling or humming, from interval to interval, some snatch of an old melancholy Scottish ballad-tune. Although sufficiently convinced of the identity of the party, Lord Glenvarloch could not help expressing his surprise in the superfluous question—"In the name of heaven, Richie—is this you?"

"And wha else suld it be, my lord?" answered Richie; "I dreamna that your lordship's levee in this place is like to be attended by ony that are not bounden thereto by duty."

"I am rather surprised," answered Nigel, "that it should be attended by any one at all—especially by you, Richie; for you know that we parted, and I thought you had reached Scotland long since."

"I crave your lordship's pardon, but we have not parted yet, nor are soon like to do; for there gang twa folk's votes to the unmaking of a bargain, as to the making of ane, and though it was your lordship's pleasure so to conduct yourself that we were like to have parted, yet it was not, on reflection, my will to be gone. To be plain, if your lordship does not ken when you have a good servant, I ken when I have a kind master; and to say truth, you will be easier served now than ever, for there is not much chance of your getting out of bounds."

"I am indeed bound over to good behaviour," said Lord Glenvarloch, with a smile; "but I hope you will not take the advantage of my situation to be too severe on my follies, Richie?"

"God forbid, my lord—God forbid," replied Richie, with an expression betwixt a conceited consciousness of superior wisdom and real feeling—"especially in consideration of your lordship's having a due sense of them. I did indeed remonstrate, as was my humble duty —but I scorn to cast that up to your lordship now—na, na—I am myself an erring creature—very conscious of some small weaknesses —there is no perfection in man."

"But, Richie," said Lord Glenvarloch, "although I am much obliged to you for your proffered service, it can be of little use to me here, and may be of prejudice to yourself."

"Your lordship shall pardon me again," said Richie, whom the relative situation of the parties had invested with ten times his ordinary dogmatism; "but as I will so manage the matter, your lordship shall be greatly benefitted by my service, and I myself no whit prejudiced."

"I see not how that can be, my friend," said Lord Glenvarloch, "since even as to your pecuniary affairs"——

"Touching my pecuniars, my lord," replied Richie, "I am indifferently weel provided; and as it chances, my living here will be no burthen to your lordship, or distress to myself. Only I crave permission to annex certain conditions to my servitude with your lordship."

"Annex what you will," said Lord Glenvarloch, "for you are pretty sure to take your own way, whether you make any conditions or not— since you will not leave, which were, I think, your wisest course, you must, and I suppose will, serve me only on such terms as you like yourself."

"All that I ask, my lord," said Richie, gravely, and with a tone of great moderation, "is to have the uninterrupted command of my own motions, for certain important purposes which I have now in hand, always giving your lordship the solace of my company and attendance at such times as may be at once convenient for me, and necessary for your service."

"Of which, I suppose, you constitute yourself the sole judge," replied Nigel, smiling.

"Unquestionably, my lord," answered Richie, gravely; "for your lordship can only know what yourself want; whereas I, who see both sides of the picture, ken both what is the best for your affairs, and what is the most needful for my own."

"Richie, my good friend," said Nigel, "I fear this arrangement, which places the master much under the disposal of the servant, would scarce suit us if we were both at large; but a prisoner as I am, I may be as well at your disposal as I am at that of so many other persons. And so you may come and go as you list, for I suppose you will not take my advice, to return to our own country and leave me to my fate."

"The de'il be in my feet if I do," said Moniplies,—"I am not the lad to leave your lordship in foul weather, when I followed you and fed upon you through the whole summer day. And besides, there may be brave days behind, for a' that has come and gane yet; for

> It's hame, and it's hame, and it's hame we fain would be,
> Though the cloud is in the lift, and the wind is on the lea;
> For the sun through the mirk blinks blithe on mine e'e,
> Says,—'I'll shine on ye yet in your ain country.'"

Having sung this stanza in the manner of a ballad-singer, whose voice has been cracked by matching his wind-pipe against the bugle of the north-blast, Richie Moniplies aided Lord Glenvarloch to rise, attended his toilette with every possible mark of the most solemn and deferential respect, then waited upon him at his breakfast, and finally withdrew, pleading that he had business of importance, which would detain him for some hours.

Although Lord Glenvarloch necessarily expected to be occasionally annoyed by the self-conceit and dogmatism of Richie Moniplies's character, yet he could not but feel the greatest pleasure from the firm and devoted attachment which this faithful follower had displayed in the present instance, and indeed promised himself an alleviation of the ennui of his imprisonment, in having the advantage of his services. It was therefore with pleasure that he learned from the warder, that his servant's attendance would be allowed at all times when the general rules of the fortress permitted the entrance of strangers.

In the meanwhile, the magnanimous Richie Moniplies had already reached Tower Wharf. Here, after looking with contempt on several scullers by whom he was plied, and whose services he rejected with a wave of his hand, he called with dignity, "First oars!" and stirred into activity several lounging Tritons of the higher order, who had not, on his first appearance, thought it worth while to accost him with proffers of service. He now took possession of a wherry, folded his arms within his ample cloak, and sitting down in the stern with an air of importance, commanded them to row to Whitehall stairs. Having reached the palace in safety, he demanded to see Master Linklater, the under-clerk of his Majesty's kitchen. The reply was, that he was not to be spoken withal, being then employed in cooking a mess of cock-a-leekie for the King's own mouth.

"Tell him," said Moniplies, "that it is a dear countryman of his, who seeks to converse with him on matter of high import."

"A dear countryman?" said Linklater, when this pressing message was delivered to him. "Well, let him come in and be damned—that I should say sae! This now is some red-headed, long-legged, gillie-white-foot frae the West Port, that, hearing of my promotion, is come up to be a turn-broche, or deputy scullion, through my interest. It is a great hinderance to ony man who would rise in the world, to have such friends to hang by his skirts, in hope of being towed up alongst with him.—Ha! Richie Moniplies, man—is it thou? and what has brought ye here?—if they should ken thee for the loon that scared the horse the other day"——

"No more o' that, neighbour," said Richie—"I am just here on the auld errand—I maun speak with the King."

"The King? ye are red wud," said Linklater; then shouted to his assistants in the kitchen, "Look to the broches, ye knaves—*pisces purga—Salsamenta fac macerentur pulchre*—I will make you under-stand Latin, ye knaves, as becomes the scullions of King James." Then in a cautious tone to Richie's private ear, he continued, "Know ye not how ill your master came off the other day?—I can tell you that job made some folks shake for their office."

"Weel, but Laurie, ye maun befriend me this time, and get this wee bit sifflication slipped into his Majesty's ain maist gracious hand. I promise you the contents will be maist grateful to him."

"Richie," answered Linklater, "you have certainly sworn to say your prayers in the porter's lodge, with your back bare; and twa grooms, with dog-whips, to cry amen to you."

"Na, na, Laurie, lad," said Richie, "I ken better what belangs to sifflications than I did yon day—but ye will say that yoursell, if ye will but get that wee bit note to the King's hand."

"I will have neither hand nor foot in the matter," said the cautious Clerk of the Kitchen; "but there is his Majesty's mess of cock-a-leekie just going to be served to him in his closet—I cannot prevent you from putting the letter between the gilt bowl and the platter—his sacred Majesty will see it when he lifts the bowl, for he aye drinks out the broth."

"Enough said," replied Richie, and deposited the paper accord-ingly, just before a page entered to carry the mess to his Majesty.

"Aweel, aweel, neighbour," said Lawrence, when the mess was

taken away, "if ye have done ony thing to bring yoursell to the withy, or the scourging post, it is your ain wilful deed."

"I will blame no other for it," said Richie; and with the undismayed pertinacity of conceit, which made a fundamental part of his character, he abode the issue, which was not long of arriving.

In a few minutes Maxwell himself arrived in the apartment, and demanded hastily who had placed a writing on the King's trencher. Linklater denied all knowledge of it; but Richie Moniplies, stepping boldy forth, pronounced the emphatical confession, "I am the man."

"Follow me, then," said Maxwell, after regarding him with a look of great curiosity.

They went up a private staircase,—even that private staircase, the privilege of which at court is accounted a nearer road to power than the *grandes entrées* themselves. Arriving in what Richie described as an "ill redd-up" anti-room, the usher made a sign to him to stop, while he went into the King's closet. Their conference was short, and as Maxwell opened the door to retire, Richie heard the conclusion of it.

"Ye are sure he is not dangerous?—I was caught once.—Bide within call, but not nearer the door than within three geometrical cubits—if I speak loud, start to me like a falcon—if I speak lownd, keep your lang lugs out of ear-shot—And now let him come in."

Richie passed forward at Maxwell's mute signal, and in a moment found himself in the presence of the King. Most men of Richie's birth and breeding, and many others, would have been abashed at finding themselves alone with their Sovereign. But Richie Moniplies had an opinion of himself too high to be controuled by any such ideas; and having made his stiff reverence, he arose once more into his perpendicular height, and stood before James as stiff as a hedge-stake.

"Have ye gotten them, man? have ye gotten them?" said the King, in a fluttering state, betwixt hope and eagerness, and some touch of suspicious fear. "Gie me them—gie me them—before ye speak a word, I charge you, on your allegiance."

Richie took a box from his bosom, and stooping on one knee, presented it to his Majesty, who hastily opened it, and having ascertained that it contained a certain carcanet of rubies, with which the reader was formerly made acquainted, he could not resist falling into a sort of rapture, kissing the gems, as if they had been capable of feeling, and repeating again and again with childish delight, "*Onyx cum prole, silexque—Onyx cum prole!*—ah, my bright and bonnie sparklers, my heart loups light to see you again." He then turned to Richie, upon whose stoical countenance his Majesty's demeanour had excited something like a grim smile, which James interrupted his rejoicing to reprehend, saying, "Take heed, sir, you are not to laugh at us—we are your anointed Sovereign."

"God forbid that I should laugh!" said Richie, composing his countenance into its natural rigidity. "I did but smile, to bring my visage
into coincidence and conformity with your Majesty's physiognomy."

"Ye speak as a dutiful subject, and an honest man," said the King;
"but what de'il's your name, man?"

"Even Richie Moniplies, the son of auld Mungo Moniplies, at the
Wast Port of Edinburgh, who had the honour to supply your Majesty's
mother's royal table, as weel as your Majesty's, with flesh, and other
vivers, when time was."

"Aha!" said the King, laughing,—for he possessed, as an useful
attribute of his situation, a tenacious memory, which recollected every
one with whom he was brought into casual contact,—"Ye are the self-
same traitor who had weel nigh coupit us endlang on the causey of our
ain court-yard—But we stuck by our mare—*Equam memento rebus in
arduis servare*. Weel, be not dismayed, Richie; for, as many honest
men have turned traitors, it is but fair that a traitor, now and then, suld
prove to be, *contra expectanda*, a true man. How cam ye by our jewels,
man?—cam ye on the part of George Heriot?"

"In no sort," said Richie. "May it please your Majesty, I come as
Harry Wynd fought, utterly for my own hand, and on no man's
errand; as, indeed, I call no one master, save Him that made me, your
most gracious Majesty who governs me, and the noble Nigel Olifaunt,
Lord of Glenvarloch, who maintained me as lang as he could maintain
himself, poor nobleman!"

"Glenvarlochides again!" exclaimed the King; "by my honour he
lies in ambush for us at every corner.—Maxwell knocks at the door—
it is George Heriot come to tell us he cannot find these jewels.—Get
thee behind the arras, Richie—stand close, man—sneeze not—cough
not—breathe not!—Jingling Geordie is so damnably ready with his
gold-ends of wisdom, and sae accursedly backward with his gold-
ends of siller, that, by our royal saul, we are glad to get a hair in his
neck."

Richie got behind the arras, in obedience to the commands of the
good-natured King, while the Monarch, who never allowed his dignity to stand in the way of a frolic, having adjusted, with his own hand,
the tapestry, so as to conceal the ambush, commanded Maxwell to tell
him what was the matter without. Maxwell's reply was so low as to be
lost by Richie Moniplies, the peculiarity of whose situation by no
means abated his curiosity and desire to gratify it to the uttermost.

"Let Geordie Heriot come in," said the King; and, as Richie could
observe through a slit in the tapestry, the honest citizen, if not actually
agitated, was at least discomposed. The King, whose talent for wit, or

humour, was precisely of a kind to be gratified by such a scene as
ensued, received his homage with coldness, and began to talk to him
with an air of serious dignity, very different from the usual indecorous
levity of his behaviour. "Master Heriot," he said, "if we aright remember—we opignorated in your hands certain jewels of the Crown, for a
certain sum of money—did we, or did we not?"

"My most gracious Sovereign," said Heriot, "indisputably your
Majesty was pleased to do so."

"The property of which jewels and *cimelia* remained with us," continued the King, in the same solemn tone, "subject only to your claim
of advance thereupon—which advance being repaid, gives us right to
repossession of the thing opignorated, or pledged, or laid in wad.
Voetius, Vinnius, Groenwigeneus, Pagenstecherus,—all who have
treated *de Contractu Opignerationis, consentiunt in eundem*,—gree in the
same point. The Roman law, the English common law, and the municipal law of our ain ancient hereditary kingdom of Scotland, though
they split in mair particulars than I could desire, unite as strictly in this
as the three strands of a twisted rope."

"May it please your Majesty," replied Heriot, "it requires not so
many learned authorities to prove to any honest man, that his interest
in a pledge is determined when the money lent is restored."

"Weel, sir, I proffer restoration of the sum lent, and I demand to be
repossessed of the jewels pledged with you. I gave ye a hint, brief while
since, that this would be essential to my service, for, as approaching
events are like to call us into public, it would seem strange if we did not
appear with those ornaments, which are heir-looms of the Crown, and
the absence whereof is like to place us in contempt and suspicion with
our loyal subjects."

Master George Heriot seemed much moved by this address of his
Sovereign, and replied with emotion, "I call Heaven to witness, that I
am totally harmless in this matter, and that I would willingly lose the
sum advanced, so that I could restore those jewels, the absence of
which your Majesty so justly laments. Had the jewels remained with
me, the accompt of them would be easily rendered; but your Majesty
will do me the justice to remember, that by your express order, I
transferred them to another person, who advanced a large sum, just
about the time of my departure for Paris. The money was pressingly
wanted, and no other means to come by it occurred to me. I told your
Majesty, when I brought the needful supply, that the man from whom
the monies were obtained, was of no good repute; and your most
princely answer was—smelling to the gold—*Non olet*, it smells not of
the means that have gotten it."

"Weel, man," said the King, "but what needs a' this din?—if ye gave my jewels in pledge to such a one, suld ye not, as a liege subject, have taken care that the redemption was in our power?—and are we to suffer the loss of our *cimelia*—by your neglect, besides being exposed to the scorn and censure of our lieges, and of the foreign ambassadors?"

"My Lord and liege King," said Heriot, "God knows, if my bearing blame or shame in this matter would keep it from your Majesty, it were my duty to endure both, as a servant grateful for many benefits; but when your Majesty considers the violent death of the man himself, the disappearance of his daughter, and of his wealth, I trust you will remember that I warned your Majesty, in humble duty, of the possibility of such casualities, and prayed you not to urge me to deal with him on your behalf."

"But you brought me nae better means," said the King—"Geordie, ye brought me nae better means. I was like a deserted man—what could I do but grip to the first siller that offered, as a drowning man grasps to the willow-wand that comes readiest?—And now, man, what for have ye not brought back the jewels?—they are surely above ground, if ye wald make strict search."

"All strict search hath been made, may it please your Majesty," replied the citizen; "hue and cry has been sent out everywhere, and it has been found impossible to recover them."

"Difficult, ye mean, Geordie, not impossible," replied the King; "for that whilk is impossible, is either naturally so, *exempli gratia*, to make two into three; or morally so, as to make what is truth, falsehood —but what is only difficult may come to pass, with assistance of wisdom and patience—as, for example, Jingling Geordie—look here!" And he displayed the recovered treasure to the eyes of the astonished jeweller—exclaiming, with great triumph, "What say ye to that, Jingler? By my sceptre and crown, the man stares as if he took his native prince for a warlock!—us, that are the very *malleus maleficarum*, the contunding and contriturating hammer of all witches, sorcerers, magicians, and the like—he thinks we are taking a touch of the black art oursells! But gang thy way, honest Geordie—thou art a good plain man—but nane of the seven sages of Greece—gang thy way, and mind the soothfast word which you spoke, small time syne, that there is one in this land that comes near to Solomon, King of Israel, in all his gifts, except in his love to strange women, forbye the daughter of Pharoah."

If Heriot was surprised at seeing the jewels so unexpectedly produced at the moment the King was upbraiding him for the loss of them, this allusion to the reflection which had escaped him while conversing with Lord Glenvarloch, altogether completed his aston-

ishment; and the King was so delighted with the superiority which it
gave him at the moment, that he rubbed his hands, chuckled, and,
finally, his sense of dignity giving way to the full feeling of triumph, he
threw himself into his easy-chair, and laughed with unconstrained
violence till he lost his breath, and the tears ran plentifully down his
cheeks as he strove to recover it. Meanwhile, the royal cachination was
echoed back by a discordant and portentous laugh from behind the
arras, like that of one who, little accustomed to give way to such
emotions, feels himself at some particular impulse unable either to
control or to modify his obstreperous mirth. Heriot turned his head
with new surprise towards the place, from which sounds so unfitting
the presence of a monarch seemed to burst with such emphatic clamour.

The King too, somewhat sensible of the indecorum, rose up, wiped
his eyes, and calling,—"Tod-lowrie, come out of your den," he produced from behind the arras the length of Richie Moniplies, still
laughing with as unrestrained mirth as ever did gossip at a country
christening. "Whisht, man, whisht, man," said the King; "ye needna
nigher that gait, like a courser at a caup o' corn, e'en though it was a
pleasing jest, and our ain framing. And yet to see Jingling Geordie,
that hauds himself so much wiser than other folk—to see him, ha! ha!
ha!—in the vein of Euclio apud Plautum, distressing himself to
recover what was lying at his elbow—

> Perii, interii, occidi—quo curram? quo non curram?—
> Tene, tene,—quem? quis? nescio—nihil video.

Ah! Geordie, your een are sharp enough to look after gowd and silver,
gems, rubies, and the like of that, and yet ye kenna how to come by
them when they are lost. Ay, ay—look at them, man—look at them—
they are a' right and tight, sound and round, not a doublet crept in
amongst them."

George Heriot, when his first surprise was over, was too old a
courtier to interrupt the King's imaginary triumph, although he
darted a look of some displeasure at honest Richie, who still continued
on what is usually termed the broad grin. He quietly examined the
stones, and finding them all perfect, he honestly and sincerely con-
gratulated his Majesty on the recovery of a treasure which could not
have been lost without some dishonour to the crown; and asked
to whom he himself was to pay the sums for which they had been
pledged, observing, that he had the money by him in readiness.

"Ye are in a deevil of a hurry, when there is paying in the case,
Geordie," said the King.—"What's a' the haste, man?—the jewels
were restored by an honest, kindly countryman of ours—there he
stands—and wha kens if he wants the money on the nail, or if he

might not be as weel pleased wi' a bit rescript on our treasury some six months hence?—ye ken that our Exchequer is even at a low ebb just now, and ye cry pay, pay, as if we had all the mines of Ophir."

"Please your Majesty," said Heriot, "if this man has the real right to these monies, it is doubtless at his will to grant forbearance, if he will —but when I remember the guise in which I first saw him, with a tattered cloak and a broken head, I can hardly conceive it.—Are not you Richie Moniplies—with the King's favour?"

"Even sae, Master Heriot—of the ancient and honourable house of Castle Collop, near to the West Port of Edinburgh," answered Richie.

"Why, please your Majesty—he is a poor serving-man," said Heriot. "This money can never be honestly at his disposal."

"What for no?" said the King. "Wad ye have naebody sprackle up the brae but yoursell, Geordie?—your ain cloak was thin enough when ye came here, though ye have lined it gay and weel—and for serving-men, there has mony a red-shank come over the Tweed wi' his master's wallet on his shoulders, that now rustles it wi' his six followers behind him. There stands the man himsell; speer at him, Geordie."

"His may not be the best authority in the case," answered the cautious citizen.

"Tut, tut, man," said the King, "ye are over scrupulous. The knave deer-stealers have an apt phrase, *Non est inquirendum unde venit* VENISON. He that brings the gudes hath surely a right to dispose of the gear.—Hark ye, friend—speak the truth and shame the de'il. Have ye plenary powers to dispose on the redemption-money, as to delay of payment, or the like, aye or no?"

"Full power, an it like your gracious Majesty," answered Richie Moniplies; "and I am maist willing to subscrive to whatsoever may in ony wise accommodate your Majesty anent the redemption-money, trusting your Majesty's grace will be kind to me in one sma' favour."

"Ey, man," said the King, "come ye to me there? I thought ye wad e'en be like the rest of them.—One wald think our subjects' lives and goods were all our ain, and holden of us at our free will; but when we stand in need of ony matter of siller from them, whilk chances more frequently than we would it did, de'il a boddle is to be had, save on the auld terms of giff-gaff—it is just niffer for niffer, grippie for grippie.— Aweel, neighbour, what is it that ye want—some monopoly, I reckon? —or it may be a grant of kirk-lands and teinds, or a knighthood, or the like?—ye maun be reasonable, unless ye propose to advance more money for our present occasions."

"My liege," answered Richie Moniplies, "the owner of these monies places them at your Majesty's command, free of all pledge or usage, as long as it is your royal pleasure, providing your Majesty will condescend to shew some favour to the noble Lord Glenvarloch, presently prisoner in your royal Tower of London."

"How—mon—how, man—how, man!" exclaimed the King, reddening and stammering, but with emotions more noble than those by which he was sometimes agitated,—"What is that you dare to say to us?—sell our justice!—sell our mercy!—and we a crowned King, sworn to do justice to our subjects in the gate, and responsible for our stewardship to Him that is over all kings?" Here he reverently looked up, touched his bonnet, and continued, with some sharpness, —"We dare not traffic in such commodities, sir; and but that ye are a poor ignorant creature, that have done us this day some not unpleasant service, we wad have a red iron driven through your tongue, *in terrorem* of others.—Awa' with him, Geordie,—pay him, plack and bawbee, out of our monies in your hands, and let them care that come ahint."

Richie, who had counted with the utmost certainty upon the success of this master-stroke of policy, was like an architect whose whole scaffolding at once gives way under him. He caught, however, at what he thought might break his fall. "Not only the sum for which the jewels were pledged," he said, "but the double of it, if required, should be placed at his Majesty's command, and even without hope or condition of repayment, if only"——

But the King did not allow him to complete the sentence, crying out, with greater vehemence than before, as if he dreaded the stability of his own good resolution, "Awa wi' him—swith, awa wi' him!—it is time he were gaen, if he doubles his bode that gate—and, for your life, let na Steenie, or ony of them, hear a word from his mouth; for whae kens what trouble that might bring me into. *Ne inducas in tentationem— Vade retro Sathanas.—Amen.*"

In obedience to the royal mandate, George Heriot hurried the abashed petitioner out of the presence, and out of the Palace; and when they were in the Palace-yard, the citizen remembering, with some resentment, the airs of equality which Richie had assumed towards him in the commencement of the scene which had just taken place, could not forbear to retaliate, by congratulating him, with an ironical smile, on his favour at court, and his improved grace in presenting a supplication.

"Never fash your beard about that, Master George Heriot," said Richie, totally undismayed; "but tell me when and where I am to sifflicate you for eight hundred pounds sterling, for which these jewels stood engaged?"

"The instant that you bring with you the real owner of the money," replied Heriot, "whom it is important that I should see, on more accounts than one."

"Then will I back to his Majesty," said Richie Moniplies, stoutly, "and get either the money or the pledge back again. I am fully commissionate to act in that matter."

"It may be so, Richie," said the citizen, "and perchance it may *not* be so neither, for your tales are not all gospel; and therefore be assured I will see that it *is* so, ere I pay you that large sum of money. I shall give you an acknowledgment for it, and I will keep it prestable at a moment's warning. But, my good Master Richard Moniplies, of Castle Collop, near the West Port of Edinburgh, in the mean time I am bound to return to his Majesty on matters of weight." So speaking, and mounting the stair to re-enter the Palace, he added, by way of summing up the whole, "George Heriot is over old a cock to be caught with chaff."

Richie stood petrified when he beheld him re-enter the Palace, and found himself, as he supposed, left in the lurch. "Now, plague on ye," he muttered, "for a cunning auld skin-flint, that because ye are an honest man yoursell, forsooth, must needs deal with all the world as if they were knaves. But de'il be in me if ye beat me yet!—Yonder comes Laurie Linklater next, and he will be on me about the sifflication—I winna stand him, by Saint Andrew."

So saying, and changing the haughty stride with which he had that morning entered the precincts of the Palace, into a skulking shamble, he retreated for his wherry, which was in attendance, with speed which, to use the approved phrase on such occasions, greatly resembled a flight.

Chapter Eight

Benedict. This looks not like a nuptial.
Much Ado about Nothing

MASTER GEORGE HERIOT had no sooner returned to the King's apartment, than James enquired at Maxwell if the Earl of Huntinglen was in attendance, and receiving an answer in the affirmative, desired that he should be admitted. The old Scotch lord having made his reverence in the usual manner, the King extended his hand to be kissed, and then began to address him in a tone of grave sympathy.

"We told your lordship in our secret epistle of this morning, written with our ain hand, in testimony we have neither prætermitted nor forgotten your faithful service, that we had that to communicate to you that would require both patience and fortitude to endure, and therefore exhorted you to peruse some of the most pithy passages of Seneca, and of Boethius *de Consolatione*, that the back might be, as we say, fitted for the burthen—this we commended to you from our ain experience.

Non ignara mali miseris succurrere disco,

sayeth Dido, and I might say in my own person, *non ignarus;* but to change the gender would affect the prosody, whereof our southern subjects are tenacious. So, my Lord of Huntinglen, I trust you have acted by our advice, and studied patience before ye need it—*venienti occurrite morbo*—mix the medicament when the disease is coming on."

"May it please your Majesty," answered Lord Huntinglen, "I am more of an old soldier than a scholar—and my own rough nature will not bear me out in any calamity, I hope I shall have grace to try a text of Scripture to boot."

"Ay, man, are you there with your bears?" said the King; "the Bible, man, (touching his cap) is indeed *principium et fons*—but it is pity your lordship cannot peruse it in the original. For although we did ourselves promote that work of translation,—since ye may read, at the beginning of every Bible, that when some palpable clouds of darkness were thought like to have overshadowed the land, after the setting of that bright occidental star, Queen Elizabeth; yet our appearance, like that of the sun in his strength, instantly dispelled these surmised mists,—I say, that although, as therein mentioned, we countenanced the preaching of the gospel, and especially the translation of the Scriptures out of the original sacred tongues; yet natheless, we ourselves confess to have found a comfort in consulting them in the original Hebrew, whilk we do not perceive even in the Latin version of the Septuagint, much less in the English traduction."

"Please your Majesty," said Lord Huntinglen, "if your Majesty delays communicating the bad news with which your honoured letter threatens me, until I am capable to read Hebrew like your Majesty, I fear I shall die in ignorance of the misfortune which hath befallen, or is about to befall, my house."

"You will learn it but too soon, my lord," replied the King; "I grieve to say it, but your son Dalgarno, whom I thought a very saint, as he was so much with Steenie and Baby Charles, hath turned out a very villain."

"Villain!" repeated Lord Huntinglen; and though he instantly checked himself and added, "but it is your Majesty speaks the word," the effect of his first tone made the King step back as if he had received a blow. He also recovered himself again, and said, in the pettish way which usually indicated his displeasure—"Yes, my lord, it

was we that said it—and as *non surdo canes*—we are not deaf—we pray
you not to raise your voice in speech with us—there is the bonnie
memorial—read, and judge for yourself."

The King then thrust into the old nobleman's hand a paper, containing the story of the Lady Hermione, with the evidence by which it
was supported, detailed so briefly and clearly, that the infamy of Lord
Dalgarno, the lover by whom she had been so shamefully deceived,
seemed undeniable. But a father yields not up so easily the cause of his
son.

"May it please your Majesty," he said, "why was this tale not sooner
told?—this woman hath been here for years—wherefore was the
claim on my son not made the instant she touched English ground?"

"Tell him how that came about, Geordie," said the King, addressing Heriot.

"I grieve to distress my Lord Huntinglen," said Heriot; "but I must
speak the truth. For a long time the Lady Hermione could not brook
the idea of making her situation public; and when her mind became
changed in that particular, it was necessary to recover the evidence of
the false marriage, and letters and papers concerning it, which, when
she came to Paris, and just before I saw her, she had deposited with a
correspondent of her father in that city. He became afterwards bankrupt, and in consequence of that misfortune the lady's papers passed
into other hands, and it was only a few days since I traced and recovered them. Without these documents of evidence, it would have been
imprudent for her to have preferred her complaint, favoured as Lord
Dalgarno is by powerful friends."

"Ye are saucy to say sae," said the King; "I ken what ye mean weel
enough—ye think Steenie wald hae putten the weight of his foot into
the scales of justice, and gard them whomle the bucket—ye forget,
Geordie, wha it is whose hand uphaulds them. And ye do puir Steenie
the mair wrang, for he confessed at anes before us and our privy
council, that Dalgarno would have put her aff on him, puir simple
bairn, making him trow that she was a light o' love; in whilk mind he
remained assured even when he parted from her, albeit Steenie might
hae weel thought ane of thae cattle wadnae have resisted the like of
him."

"The Lady Hermione," said George Heriot, "has always done the
utmost justice to the conduct of the Duke, who, although strongly
possessed with prejudice against her character, yet scorned to avail
himself of her distress, and on the contrary supplied her with the
means of extricating herself from her difficulties."

"It was e'en like himsell—blessings on his bonnie face!" said the
King; "and I believed this lady's tale the mair readily, my Lord Hunt-

inglen, that she spake nae ill of Steenie. And to make a lang tale short, my lord, it is the opinion of our council and ourself, as weel as of Baby Charles and Steenie, that your son maun amend his wrong by wedding this lady, or undergo such disgrace and discountenance as we can bestow."

The person to whom he spoke was incapable of answering him. He stood before the King motionless, and glaring with eyes of which even the lids seemed immoveable, as if suddenly converted into an ancient statue of the times of chivalry, so instantly had his hard features and strong limbs been arrested into rigidity by the blow he had received— And in a second afterwards, like the same statue when the lightning breaks upon it, he sank at once to the ground with a heavy groan. The King was in the utmost alarm, called upon Heriot and Maxwell for help, and, presence of mind not being his *forte*, ran to and fro in his cabinet, exclaiming—"My ancient and beloved servant—who saved our anointed self!—*Vae atque dolor!*—My Lord of Huntinglen—look up, look up, man, and your son may marry the Queen of Sheba if he will."

By this time Maxwell and Heriot had raised the old nobleman and placed him in a chair, while the King, observing that he began to recover himself, continued his consolations more methodically.

"Haud up your head—haud up your head, and listen to your ain kind native Prince. If there is shame, man, it comes na empty-handed —there is siller to gild it—siller to gild it—a gude tocher, and no that bad a pedigree;—if she has been a loon, it was your son made her sae, and he can make her an honest woman again."

These suggestions, however reasonable in the common case, gave no comfort to Lord Huntinglen, if indeed he fully comprehended them; but the blubbering of his good-natured old master, which began to accompany and interrupt his royal speech, produced more rapid effect. The large tear gushed reluctantly from his eye as he kissed the withered hands, which the King, weeping with less dignity and restraint, abandoned to him, first alternately and then both together, until the feelings of the man getting entirely the better of the Sovereign's sense of dignity, he grasped and shook Lord Huntinglen's hands with the sympathy of an equal and a familiar friend.

"*Compone lachrymas;* be patient, man, be patient," said James,— "the council, and Baby Charles, and Steenie, may a' gang to the deevil —he shall not marry her since it moves you so deeply."

"He shall marry her, by God!" answered the Earl, drawing himself up, dashing the tear from his eyes, and endeavouring to recover his composure. "I pray your Majesty's pardon, but he shall marry her, with her dishonour for her dowry, were she the veriest courtezan in all

Spain—If he gave his word, he shall make his word good, were it to
the meanest creature that haunts the streets—he shall do it, or my own
dagger shall take the life that I gave him. If he could stoop to use so
base a fraud, though to deceive infamy, let him wed infamy."

"No, no!" the Monarch continued to insinuate, "things are not so
bad as that—Steenie himself never thought of her being a street-
walker—even when he thought the worst of her."

"If it can at all console my Lord of Huntinglen," said the citizen, "I
can assure him of this lady's good birth, and most fair and unspotted
fame."

"I am sorry for it," said Lord Huntinglen—then interrupting himself, he said—"Heaven forgive me for being ungrateful for such comfort!—but I am well nigh sorry she should be as you represent her, so
much better than the villain deserves. To be condemned to wed
beauty and innocence and honest birth"——

"Ay, and wealth, my lord—wealth," insinuated the King, "is a
better sentence than his perfidy has deserved."

"It is long," said the embittered father, "since I saw he was selfish
and hard-hearted—but to be a perjured liar—I never dreaded that
such a blot should have fallen on my race—I will never look on him
again."

"Hoot ay, my lord, hoot ay," said the King; "ye maun tak him to task
roundly. I grant you should speak more in the vein of Demea than
Mitio, *vi nempe et via pervulgata patrum*, but as for not seeing him again,
and he your only son, that is altogether out of reason. I tell ye, man,
(but I would not for a boddle that Baby Charles heard me,) that he
might gie the glaiks to half the lasses of Lonnun, ere I could find in my
heart to speak such harsh words as you have said of this de'il of a
Dalgarno of yours."

"May it please your Majesty to permit me to retire," said Lord
Huntinglen, "and dispose of the case according to your own royal
sense of justice, for I desire no favour for him."

"Aweel, my lord, so be it—and if your lordship can think," added
the Monarch, "of any thing in our power which might comfort
you——"

"Your Majesty's gracious sympathy," said Lord Huntinglen, "has
already comforted me as far as earth can—the rest must be from the
King of Kings."

"To Him I commend you, my auld and faithful servant," said James
with emotion, as the Earl withdrew from his presence. The King
remained fixed in thought for some time, and then said to Heriot,
"Jingling Geordie—ye ken all the privy doings of our Court, and have
dune so these thirty years, though, like a wise man, ye hear, and see,

and say nothing. Now, there is a thing I fain wad ken, in the way of philosophical inquiry—Did you ever hear of the umquhile Lady Huntinglen—the departed Countess of this noble Earl—ganging a wee bit gleed in her walk through the world—I mean in the way of slipping a foot, casting a leglen-girth, or the like—ye understand me?"

"On my word as an honest man," said George Heriot, somewhat surprised at the question, "I never heard her wronged by the slightest breath of suspicion. She was a worthy lady, very circumspect in her walk, and lived in great concord with her husband, save that the good Countess was something of a puritan, and kept more company with ministers than was altogether agreeable to Lord Huntinglen, who is, as your Majesty well knows, a man of the old rough world, that will drink and swear."

"O, Geordie, Geordie," exclaimed the King, "these are auld-warld frailties, of whilk we dare not pronounce even ourselves absolutely free. But the warld grows worse from day to day, Geordie. The juveniles of this age may weel say with the poet—

Ætas parentum pejor avis tulit,
Nos nequiores—

This Dalgarno does not drink so much, or swear so much, as his father; but he wenches, Geordie, and he breaks his word and oath baith. As to what you say of the leddy and the ministers, we are a' fallible creatures, Geordie, priests and kings, as weel as others; and wha kens but what that may account for the difference between this Dalgarno and his father? The Earl is the vera soul of honour, and cares nae mair for warld's gear than a noble hound for the quest of a foulmart; but as for his son, he was like to brazen us a' out—ourselves, Steenie, Baby Charles, and our council—till he heard of the tocher, and then, by my kingly crown, he lap like a cock at a grossart! These are discrepancies betwixt parent and son not to be accounted for naturally, according to Baptista Porta, Michael Scott *de secretis*, and others.—Ah, Jingling Geordie, if your clouting the cauldron, and jingling on pots, pans, and veshels of all manner of metal, hadna jingled a' your grammar out of your head, I could have touched on that matter to ye at mair length."

Heriot was too plain-spoken to express much concern for the loss of his grammar learning on this occasion; but after modestly intimating that he had seen many men who could not fill their father's bonnet, though no one had been suspected of wearing their father's night-cap, he inquired "whether Lord Dalgarno had consented to do the Lady Hermione justice."

"Troth, man, I have small doubt that he will," quoth the King; "I gave him the schedule of her worldly substance, which you delivered to us in the council, and we allowed him half an hour to chew the cud upon that. It is rare reading for bringing him to reason. I left Baby Charles and Steenie laying his duty before him; and if he can resist doing what they desire him, why I wish he would teach me the gate of it. O, Geordie, Jingling Geordie, it was grand to hear Baby Charles laying down the guilt of dissimulation, and Steenie lecturing on the turpitude of incontinence!"

"I am afraid," said George Heriot, more hastily than prudently, "I might have thought of the old proverb of Satan reproving sin."

"De'il hae our saul, neighbour," said the King, reddening, "but ye are not blate. I gie ye license to speak freely, and, by our saul, ye do not let the privilege become lost *non utendo*—it will suffer no negative prescription in your hands. Is it fit, think ye, that Baby Charles should let his thoughts be publicly seen?—no—no—princes' thoughts are *arcana imperii*—*Qui nescit dissimulare nescit regnare*. Every liege subject is bound to speak the whole truth to the King, but there is nae reciprocity of obligation—and for Steenie having been whiles a dike-louper at a time, is it for you, who are his goldsmith, and to whom, I doubt, he awes an uncomatable sum, to cast that up to him?"

Heriot did not feel himself called on to play the part of Zeno, and sacrifice himself to upholding the cause of moral truth; he did not desert it, however, by disavowing his words, but simply expressed sorrow for having offended his Majesty, with which the placable King was sufficiently satisfied.

"And now, Geordie, man," quoth he, "we will to this culprit, and hear what he has to say for himself, for I will see the job chased this blessed day. Ye maun come wi' me, man, for your evidence may be wanted."

The King led the way, accordingly, into a larger apartment, where the Prince, the Duke of Buckingham, and one or two privy councillors, were seated at a table, before which stood Lord Dalgarno, in an attitude of as much elegant ease and indifference as could be expressed, considering the stiff dress and manners of the times.

All rose and bowed reverently, while the King, to use a north country word, expressive of his rolling mode of locomotion, *toddled* to his chair or throne, making a sign to Heriot to stand behind him.

"We hope," said his Majesty, "that Lord Dalgarno stands prepared to do justice to this unfortunate lady, and to his own character and honour?"

"May I humbly inquire the penalty," said Lord Dalgarno, "in case I should unhappily find compliance with your Majesty's commands impossible?"

"Banishment frae our court, my lord," said the King; "frae our court and our countenance."

"Unhappy exile that I may be!" said Lord Dalgarno, in a tone of subdued irony—"I will at least carry your Majesty's picture with me, for I shall never see such another king."

"And banishment, my lord," said the Prince, sternly, "from these our dominions."

"That must be by form of law, please your Royal Highness," said Dalgarno, with an affectation of deep respect; "and I have not heard that there is a statute, compelling us, under such penalty, to marry every woman we may play the fool with. Perhaps his Grace of Buckingham can tell me?"

"You are a villain, Dalgarno," said the haughty and vehement favourite.

"Fie, my lord, fie!—to a prisoner, and in presence of your royal and paternal gossip!" said Lord Dalgarno. "But I will cut this deliberation short. I have looked over this schedule of the goods and effects of Erminia Pauletti, daughter of the late noble—yes, he is called the noble, or I read wrong, Giovanni Pauletti, of the House of Sansovino, in Genoa, and of the no less noble Lady Maud Olifaunt, of the House of Glenvarloch—well, I declare that I was pre-contracted in Spain to this noble lady, and there has passed betwixt us some certain *prælib-atio matrimonii;* and now, what more does this grave assembly require of me?"

"That you should repair the gross and infamous wrong you have done the lady, by marrying her within this hour," said the Prince.

"O, may it please your Royal Highness," answered Dalgarno, "I have a trifling relationship with an old Earl, who calls himself my father, who may claim some vote in the matter. Alas! every son is not blessed with an obedient parent." He hazarded a slight glance towards the throne, to give meaning to his last words.

"We have spoken ourselves with Lord Huntinglen," said the King, "and are authorised to consent in his name."

"I could never have expected this intervention of a *proxenata*, which the vulgar translate black-foot, of such eminent dignity," said Dalgarno, scarce concealing a sneer. "And my father hath consented! He was wont to say, ere he left Scotland, that the blood of Huntinglen and of Glenvarloch would not mingle, were they poured into the same basin. Perhaps he has a mind to try the experiment?"

"My lord," said James, "we will not be longer trifled with—will you instantly, and *sine mora*, take this lady to your wife, in our chapel?"

"*Statim atque instanter*," answered Lord Dalgarno; "for, I perceive, by doing so I shall obtain power to render great services to the commonwealth—I shall have acquired wealth to supply the wants of your Majesty, and a fair wife to be at the command of his Grace of Buckingham."

The Duke rose, passed to the end of the table where Lord Dalgarno was standing, and whispered in his ear, "You have placed a fair sister at my command ere now."

This taunt cut deep through Lord Dalgarno's assumed composure. He started as if an adder had stung him, but instantly composed himself, and fixing on the Duke's still smiling countenance an eye which spoke unutterable hatred, he pointed the fore-finger of his left hand to the hilt of his sword, but in a manner which could scarce be observed by any one save Buckingham. The Duke gave him another smile of bitter scorn, and returned to his seat, in obedience to the commands of the King, who continued calling out, "Sit down, Steenie, sit down, I command ye—we will hae nae barns-breaking here."

"Your Majesty need not fear my patience," said Lord Dalgarno; "and that I may keep it the better, I will not utter another word in this presence, save those enjoined to me in that happy portion of the Prayer-Book, which begins with *Dearly Beloved*, and ends with *amazement*."

"You are a hardened villain, Dalgarno," said the King; "and were I the lass, by my father's saul, I would rather brook the stain of having been your concubine, than run the risk of becoming your wife. But she shall be under our special protection.—Come, my lords, we will ourselves see this blithesome bridal." He gave the signal by rising, and moved towards the door, followed by the train. Lord Dalgarno attended, speaking to none, and spoken to by no one, yet seeming as easy and disembarrassed in his gait and manner as if in reality a happy bridegroom.

They reached the Chapel by a private entrance which communicated from the royal apartment. The Bishop of Winchester, in his pontifical dress, stood beside the altar; on the other side, supported by Monna Paula, the colourless, faded, half-lifeless form of the Lady Hermione, or Erminia, Pauletti. Lord Dalgarno bowed profoundly to her, and the Prince, observing the horror with which she regarded him, walked up, and said to her, with much dignity,—"Madam, ere you put yourself under the authority of this man, let me inform you, he hath in the fullest degree vindicated your honour, so far as concerns your former intercourse. It is for you to consider whether you will put your fortune and happiness into the hands of one, who has shewn himself unworthy of all trust."

The lady, with much difficulty, found words to make reply. "I owe to his Majesty's goodness," she said, "the care of providing me some reservation out of my own fortune, for my decent sustenance. The rest cannot be better disposed than in buying back the fair fame of which I am deprived, and the liberty of ending my life in peace and seclusion."

"The contract has been drawn up," said the King, "under our own eye, specially discharging the *potestas maritalis*, and agreeing they shall live separate. So buckle them, my Lord Bishop, as fast as ye can, that they may sunder again the sooner."

The Bishop accordingly opened his book and commenced the marriage, under circumstances so novel and so inauspicious. The responses of the bride were only expressed by inclinations of head and body; while those of the bridegroom were spoken boldly and distinctly, with a tone resembling levity, if not scorn. When it was concluded, Lord Dalgarno advanced as if to salute the bride, but seeing that she drew back in fear and abhorrence, he contented himself with making her a low bow. He then drew up his form to its height, and stretched himself as if examining the power of his limbs, but elegantly, and without any forcible change of attitude. "I could caper yet," he said, "though I am in fetters—but they are of gold, and lightly worn.— Well—I see all eyes look cold on me, and it is time I should withdraw —the sun shines elsewhere than in England—but first I must ask how this fair Lady Dalgarno is to be bestowed—methinks it is but decent I should know—is she to be sent to the haram of my Lord Duke?—or is this worthy citizen, as before"——

"Hold thy base ribald tongue," said his father, Lord Huntinglen, who had kept in the back-ground during the ceremony, and now stepping suddenly forward, caught the lady by the arm, and confronted her unworthy husband.—"The Lady Dalgarno," he continued, "shall remain as a widow in my house—a widow I esteem her, as much as if the grave had closed over her dishonoured husband."

Lord Dalgarno exhibited momentary symptoms of extreme confusion, and said, in a submissive tone, "If you, my lord, can wish me dead, I cannot, though your heir, return the compliment. Few of the first-born of Israel," he added, recovering himself from the single touch of emotion he had displayed, "can say so much with truth. But I will convince even you ere I go, that I am a true descendant of a house famed for its memory of injuries."

"I marvel your Majesty will listen to him longer," said Prince Charles. "Methinks we have heard enough of his daring insolence."

But James, who took the interest of a true gossip in such a scene as was now passing, could not bear to cut a controversy short, but imposed silence on his son, with "Whisht, Baby Charles—there is a good bairn, whisht!—I want to hear what the frontless loon can say."

"Only, sire," said Dalgarno, "that but for one single line in this schedule, all else that it contained could not have bribed me to take that woman's hand into mine."

"That line mun hae been the *summa totalis*," said the King.

"Not so, sire," replied Dalgarno. "The sum total might indeed have been an object for consideration even to a Scottish king, at no very distant period; but it would have had little charms for me, save that I see here an entry which gives me the power of vengeance over the family of Glenvarloch; and learn from it that yonder pale bride, when she put the wedding-torch into my hand, gave the power of burning her mother's house to ashes."

"How is that?" said the King. "What is he speaking about, Jingling Geordie?"

"This friendly citizen, my lord," said Lord Dalgarno, "hath expended a sum belonging to my lady, and now, I thank Heaven, to me, in acquiring a certain mortgage, or wadset, over the estate of Glenvarloch, which, if it be not redeemed before to-morrow at noon, will put me in possession of the fair demesne of those who once called themselves our house's rivals."

"Can this be true?" said the King.

"It is even but too true, please your Majesty," answered the citizen. "The Lady Hermione having advanced the money for the original creditor, I was obliged, in honour and honesty, to take the rights to her; and, doubtless, they pass to her husband."

"But the warrant, man," said the King—"the warrant on Exchequer? couldna that supply the lad wi' the means of redemption?"

"Unhappily, my liege, he has lost it, or disposed of it—it is not to be found. He is the most unlucky youth!"

"This is a proper spot of work," said the King, beginning to amble about and fiddle with the points of his doublet and hose, in expression of dismay. "We cannot aid him without paying our debts twice over, and we have, in the present state of Exchequer, scarce the means of paying them once."

"You have told me news," said Lord Dalgarno, "but I will take no advantage."

"Do not," said his father; "be a bold villain, since thou must be one, and seek revenge with arms, and not with the usurer's weapons."

"Pardon me, my lord," said Lord Dalgarno. "Pen and ink are now your surest means of vengeance; and more land is won by the lawyer with his ram-skin, than by the Andrea Ferrara with his sheeps-head. But, as I said before, I will take no advantages. I will await in town to-morrow; if any one will pay the redemption-money to my scrivener,

with whom the deeds lie, the better for Lord Glenvarloch; if not, I will
go forward on the next day, and travel with all dispatch to the north, to
take possession."

"Take a father's malison with you, unhappy wretch!" said Lord
Huntinglen.

"And a king's, who is *pater patriæ*," said James.

"I trust to bear both lightly," said Lord Dalgarno; and bowing
around him, he withdrew; while all present, oppressed, and, as it
were, overawed by his determined effrontery, found they could draw
breath more freely, when he at length relieved them of his society.
Lord Huntinglen, applying himself to comfort his new daughter-in-
law, withdrew with her also; and the King, with his privy-council,
whom he had not dismissed, again returned to his council-chamber,
though the hour was unusually late. Heriot's attendance was still
commanded, but for what reason was not explained to him.

Chapter Nine

————I'll play the eaves-dropper.
            Richard III. Act V. Scene 3

JAMES HAD NO sooner resumed his seat at the council-board than
he began to hitch in his chair, cough, use his handkerchief, and make
other intimations that he meditated a long speech. The council composed themselves to the beseeming degree of attention. Charles, as
strict in his notions of decorum, as his father was indifferent to it, fixed
himself in an attitude of rigid and respectful attention, while the
haughty favourite, conscious of his power over both father and son,
stretched himself more easily on his seat, and in assuming an appearance of listening, seemed to pay a debt to ceremonial rather than to
duty.

"I doubt not, my lords," said the monarch, "that some of you may be
thinking the hour of refection is past, and that it is time to ask with the
slave in the comedy—*Quid de symbolo?*—Nevertheless, to do justice
and exercise judgment is our meat and drink; and now we are to pray
your wisdom to consider the case of this unhappy youth Lord Glenvarloch, and see, whether, consistently with our honour, anything can
be done in his favour."

"I am surprised at your Majesty's wisdom making the inquiry," said
the Duke; "it is plain this Dalgarno hath proved one of the most
insolent villains on earth, and it must therefore be clear, that if Lord
Glenvarloch had run him through the body, there would but have
been out of the world a knave who had lived in it too long. I think Lord

Glenvarloch hath had much wrong; and I regret that, by the persuasions of this false fellow, I have myself had some hand in it."

"Ye speak like a child, Steenie—I mean my Lord of Buckingham," answered the King, "and as one that does not understand the logic of the schools; for an action may be inconsequential or even meritorious, *quoad hominem*, that is, as touching him upon *whom* it is acted; and yet most criminal, *quoad locum*, or considering the place *wherein* it is done, as a man may lawfully dance Chrighty Beardie or any other dance in a tavern, but not *inter parietes ecclesiæ*. So that, though it might have been a good deed to have sticked Dalgarno, being such as he has shewn himself, any where else, it yet fell under the plain statute, when violence was offered within the verge of the Court. For, let me tell you, my lords, the statute against striking would be of small use in our court, if it could be elided by justifying the person stricken to be a knave. It is to be much lamented, but I ken nae court in Christendom where knaves are not to be found; and if men are to break the peace under pretence of beating them, why, it will rain Jeddart staves in our very anti-chamber."

"What your Majesty says," replied Prince Charles, "is marked with your usual wisdom—the precincts of palaces must be sacred as well as the persons of kings, which are respected even in the most barbarous nations, as being one step only beneath their divinities. But your Majesty's will can controul the severity of this and every other law, and it is in your power, on consideration of his case, to grant this rash young man a free pardon."

"*Rem acu tetigisti, Carole, mi puerule*," answered the King; "and know, my lords, that we have, by a shrewd device and gift of our own, already sounded the very depth of this Lord Glenvarloch's disposition. I trow there be among you some that remember my handling in the curious case of my Lady Lake, and how I trimmed them about the story of hearkening behind the arras. Now this put me to cogitation, and I remembered me of having read that Dionysius, King of Syracuse, whom historians call Τύραννος, which signifieth not in the Greek tongue, as in ours, a truculent usurper, but a royal king who governs, it may be, something more strictly than we and other lawful monarchs, whom the ancients termed Βασιλεῖς. Now this Dionysius of Syracuse caused cunning workmen to build for himself a *lugg*—d'ye ken what that is, my Lord Bishop?"

"A cathedral, I presume to guess," answered the Bishop.

"What the de'il, man—I crave your lordship's pardon for swearing —but it was no cathedral—only a lurking-place called the king's *lugg* or *ear*, where he could sit undescried, and hear the converse of his prisoners. Now, sirs, in imitation of this Dionysius, whom I took for my pattern, the rather that he was a great linguist and grammarian, and taught a school with good applause after his abdication, (either he or his successor of the same name, it matters not whilk)—I have caused them to make a *lugg* up at the state-prison of the Tower yonder—mair like a pulpit than a cathedral, my Lord Bishop, and communicating with the arras behind the Lieutenant's chamber, where we may sit and privily hear the discourse of such prisoners as are put up there for state offences, and so creep into the very secrets of our enemies."

The Prince cast a glance towards the Duke, expressive of great vexation and disgust. Buckingham shrugged his shoulders, but the motion was so slight as to be almost imperceptible.

"Weel, my lords, ye ken the fray at the hunting this morning—I shall not get out of the trembling exies until I have a sound night's sleep—just after that, they bring ye in a pretty page that had been found in the Park. We were warned against examining him ourselves by the anxious care of those around us—nevertheless, holding our life ever at the service of these kingdoms, we commanded all to avoid the room—the rather that we suspected this boy to be a girl. What think ye, my lords?—few of you would have thought we had a hawk's eye left for sic gear; but we thank God, that though we are old, we know so much of such toys as may beseem a man of decent gravity. Weel, my lords, we questioned this maiden in male attire ourselves, and I profess it was a very pretty interrogatory, and well followed. For, though she at first professed that she assumed this disguise in order to countenance the woman who should present us with the Lady Hermione's petition, for whom she professed entire affection; yet when we, suspecting *anguis in herba*, did put her to the very question, she was compelled to own a virtuous attachment for Glenvarlochides, in such a pretty passion of shame and fear, that we had much ado to keep our own eyes from keeping company with her's in weeping. Also she laid before us the false practices of this Dalgarno towards Glenvarlochides, inveigling him into houses of ill resort, and giving him evil counsel under pretext of sincere friendship, whereby the inexperienced lad was led to do what was prejudicial to himself and offensive to us. But, however prettily she told her tale, we determined not altogether to trust to her narration, but rather to try the experiment whilk we had devised for such occasions. And having ourselves speedily passed from Greenwich to the Tower, we constituted ourselves eaves-dropper as it is called, to observe what should pass between Glenvarlochides and this page, whom we caused to be admitted to his apartment, well judging that if they were of counsel together to deceive us, it could not be but something of it would spunk out—And what think ye we saw, my lords?—Naething for you to sniggle and laugh at, Steenie—for I question if you could have played the temperate and Christian-like part of this poor lad Glenvarloch. He might be a Father of the Church in comparison of you, man.—And then to try his patience yet farther, we loosed on him a courtier and a citizen, that is Sir Mungo Malagrowther and our servant George Heriot here, wha dang the poor lad about, and did na greatly spare our royal selves.— You mind, Geordie, what ye said about the wives and concubines? but I forgie ye, man—nae need of kneeling, I forgie ye—the readier that it regards ane particular, whilk, as it added not much to Solomon's credit, the lack of it cannot be said to impinge on ours. Aweel, my lords, for all temptation of sore distress and evil ensample, this poor lad never loosed his tongue on us to say one unbecoming word— Which inclines us the rather, acting always by your wise advice, to treat this affair of the Park as a thing done in the heat of blood, and under strong provocation, and therefore to confer our free pardon on Lord Glenvarloch."

"I am happy your gracious Majesty," said the Duke of Buckingham, "has arrived at that conclusion, though I could never have guessed at the road by which you attained it."

"I trust," said Prince Charles, "that it is not a path which your Majesty will think it consistent with your high dignity to tread frequently."

"Never while I live again, Baby Charles, that I give you my royal word on. They say that hearkeners hear ill tales of themselves—by my saul, my very ears are tingling wi' that auld sorrow Sir Mungo's sarcasms. He called us close-fisted, Steenie—I am sure you can contradict that—but it is mere envy in the auld mutilated sinner, because he himself has neither a noble to hold in his loof, or fingers to close on it if he had." Here the King lost recollection of Sir Mungo's irreverence in chuckling over his own wit, and only further alluded to it by saying—"We must give the old maunderer *bos in linguam*—something to stop his mouth, or he will rail at us from Dan to Beersheba.— And now, my lords, let our warrant of mercy to Lord Glenvarloch be presently expeded, and he put to his freedom; and as his estate is likely to go so sleaveless a gate, we will consider what means of favour we can shew him.—My lords, I wish you an appetite to an early supper—for our labours have approached that term.—Baby Charles and Steenie, you will remain till our couchee.—My Lord Bishop, you will be pleased to stay to bless our meat.—Geordie Heriot, a word with you apart."

His Majesty then drew the citizen into a corner, while the councillors, those excepted who had been commanded to remain, made their obeisance, and withdrew. "Geordie," said the King, "my good and trusty servant"—Here he busied his fingers much with the points and ribbands of his dress,—"Ye see that we have granted, from our own natural sense of right and justice, that which yon lang-backed fallow, Moniplies I think they ca' him, proffered to purchase from us with a mighty bribe; whilk we refused, as being a crowned King, who wad neither sell our justice nor our mercy for pecuniar consideration. Now, what think ye should be the upshot of this?"

"My Lord Glenvarloch's freedom, and his restoration to your Majesty's favour," said Heriot.

"I ken that—I ken that," said the King, peevishly. "Ye are very dull to-day. I mean what do ye think this fallow Moniplies should think about the matter?"

"Surely that your Majesty is a most good and gracious sovereign," answered Heriot.

"We had need to be gude and gracious baith," said the King, still more pettishly, "that have ideots about us that cannot understand what we mint at, unless we speak it out in braid Lowlands. See this chield Moniplies, and tell him what we have done for Lord Glenvarloch, in whom he takes such part, out of our ain gracious motion, though we refused to do it on ony proffer of private advantage. Now, you may put it till him as if of your own mind, whether it will be a gracious or a dutiful part in him, to press us for present payment of the two three hundred miserable pounds for whilk we were obliged to opignorate our jewels? Indeed, mony men may think ye wald do the part of a gude citizen, if you took it on yoursell to refuse him payment, seeing he hath had what he professed to esteem full satisfaction, and considering, moreover, that it is evident he hath no pressing need of money, whereof we have much necessity."

George Heriot sighed internally. "O my Master," thought he—"my dear Master, is it then fated you are never to indulge any kingly or noble sentiment, without its being sullied by some after-thought of interested selfishness?"

The King troubled himself not about what he thought, but taking him by the collar, said,—"Ye ken my meaning now, Jingler—awa' wi' ye—you are a wise man—manage it your gate—but forget not our present straits." The citizen made his obeisance, and withdrew.

"And now, bairns," said the King, "what do you look upon each other for—and what have you got to ask at your dear dad and gossip?"

"Only," said the Prince, "that it would please your Majesty to command the lurking-place at the prison to be presently built up— the groans of a captive should not be brought in evidence against him."

"What! build up my lugg, Baby Charles?—and yet better deaf than hear ill tales of one's self. So let them build it up, hard and fast, without delay, the rather that my back is sair with sitting in it for a whole hour.—And now let us see what the cooks have done for us, hinny bairns."

Chapter Ten

To this brave man the knight repairs
For counsel in his law affairs;
And found him mounted in his pew,
With books and money placed for shew,
Like nest-eggs to make clients lay,
And for his false opinion pay.
Hudibras

OUR READER may recollect a certain smooth-tongued, lank-haired, buckram-suited Scotch scrivener, who, in the first volume of this history, appeared in the character of a protegé of George Heriot. It is to his house we are about to remove, but times have changed with him. The petty booth hath become a chamber of importance—the buckram suit is changed into black velvet; and although the wearer retains his puritanical humility and politeness to clients of consequence, he can now look others broad in the face, and treat them with a full allowance of superior opulence, and the insolence arising from it. It was but a short period that had achieved these alterations, nor was the party himself as yet entirely accustomed to them, but the change was becoming less embarrassing to him with every day's practice. Among other acquisitions of wealth, you may see one of Davie Ramsay's best time-pieces on the table, and his eye is frequently observing its revolutions, while a boy, whom he employs as a scribe, is occasionally sent out to compare its progress with the clock of Saint Dunstan.

The scrivener himself seemed considerably agitated. He took from a strong box a bundle of parchments, and read passages of them with great attention; then began to soliloquize—"There is no outlet which law can suggest—no back-door of evasion—none—if the lands of Glenvarloch are not redeemed before it rings noon—Lord Dalgarno has them a cheap pennyworth. Strange, that he should have been at last able to set his patron at defiance, and achieve for himself the fair estate, with the prospect of which he so long flattered the powerful Buckingham.—Might not Andrew Skurliewhitter nick him as neatly? He hath been my patron—true—not more than Buckingham was his —and he can be so no more, for he departs presently for Scotland. I am glad of it—I hate him—and I fear him—he knows too many of my secrets, I know too many of his—but no—no—no—I need never attempt it—there are no means of over-reaching him.—Well, Willie, what's o'clock?"

"Ele'en hours just chappit, sir."

"Go to your desk without, child," said the scrivener. "What to do next—I shall lose the old Earl's fair business, and, what is worse, his son's foul practice. Old Heriot looks too close into business to permit me more than the paltry and ordinary dues. The Whitefriars business was profitable—but it has become unsafe ever since—pah!—What brought that in my head just now? I can hardly hold my pen—if men should see me this way! Willie, (calling aloud to the boy,) a cup of distilled waters—Soh!—now I could face the devil."

He spoke the last words aloud, and close by the door of the apartment, which was suddenly opened by Richie Moniplies, followed by two gentlemen, and attended by two porters bearing money-bags. "If ye can face the deevil, Maister Skurliewhitter," said Richie, "ye will be the less likely to turn your back on a sack or twa o' siller, which I have ta'en the freedom to bring you. Sathanas and Mammon are near a-kin." The porters, at the same time, ranged their load on the floor.

"I—I—" stammered the surprised scrivener—"I cannot guess what you mean, sir."

"Only that I have brought you the redemption-money on the part of Lord Glenvarloch, in discharge of a certain mortgage over his family inheritance. And here, in good time, comes Master Reginald Lowestoffe, and another honourable gentleman of the Temple, to be witnesses to the transaction."

"I—I—incline to think," said the scrivener, "that the term is expired."

"You will pardon us, Master Scrivener," said Lowestoffe. "You will not baffle us—It wants three-quarters of noon by every clock in the city."

"I must have time, gentlemen," said Andrew, "to examine the gold by tale and weight."

"Do so at your leisure, Master Scrivener," replied Lowestoffe again. "We have already seen the contents of each sack told and weighed, and we have put our seals on them—there they stand arow—twenty in number, each containing three hundred yellow-hammers—we are witnesses to the lawful tender."

"Gentlemen," said the scrivener, "this security now belongs to a mighty lord. I pray you, abate your haste, and let me send for Lord Dalgarno,—or rather, I will run for him myself."

So saying, he took up his hat; but Lowestoffe called out,—"Friend

Moniplies, keep the door fast, an thou be'st a man!—he seeks but to put off the time.—In plain terms, Andrew, you may send for the devil, if you will, who is the mightiest lord of my acquaintance, but from hence you stir not till you have answered our proposition, by rejecting or accepting the redemption-money fairly tendered—there it lies— take it, or leave it, as you will. I have skill enough to know that the law is mightier than any lord in Britain—I have learned so much at the Temple, if I have learned nothing else—and see that you trifle not with it, lest it make your long ears an inch shorter, Master Skurlie-whitter."

"Nay, gentlemen, if you threaten me," said the scrivener, "I cannot resist compulsion."

"No threats, no threats at all, my little Andrew," said Lowestoffe; "a little friendly advice only—forget not, I have seen you in Alsatia."

Without answering a single word, the scrivener sate down, and drew in proper form a full receipt for the money proffered.

"I take it on your report, Master Lowestoffe," he said; "I hope you will remember I have neither insisted upon weight or tale—I have been civil—if there is deficiency I shall come to loss."

"Fillip his nose with a gold piece, Richie," quoth the Templar. "Take up the papers, and now wend we merrily to dine thou wot'st where."

"If I might chuse," said Richie, "it should not be at yonder roguish ordinary—but as it is your pleasure, gentlemen, the treat shall be given wheresoever you will to have it."

"At the ordinary," said the one Templar.

"At Beaujeu's," said the other; "it is the only house in London for neat wines, nimble drawers, choice dishes, and"——

"And high charges," quoth Richie Moniplies. "But, as I said before, gentlemen, ye have a right to command me in this matter, having so frankly rendered me your service in this small matter of business, without other stipulation than that of a slight banquet."

The latter part of this discourse passed in the street, where, immediately afterwards, they met Lord Dalgarno. He appeared in haste, touched his hat slightly to Master Lowestoffe, who returned his reverence with the same negligence, and walked slowly on with his companion, while Lord Dalgarno stopped Richie Moniplies with a commanding sign, which the instinct of education compelled Moniplies, though indignant, to obey.

"Whom do you now follow, sirrah?" demanded the noble.

"Whomsoever goeth before me, my lord," answered Moniplies.

"No sauciness, you knave—I desire to know if you still serve Nigel Olifaunt?" said Dalgarno.

"I am friend to the noble Lord Glenvarloch," answered Moniplies, with dignity.

"True," replied Lord Dalgarno, "that noble lord has sunk to seek friends among lacqueys—Nevertheless,—hark thee hither,—nevertheless, if he be of the same mind as when we last met, thou mayst shew him, that on to-morrow at four afternoon, I shall pass northward by Enfield Chace—I will be slenderly attended, as I design to send my train through Barnet. It is my purpose to ride an easy pace through the forest, and to linger a while by Camlet Moat—he knows the place; and if he be aught but an Alsatian bully, will think it fitter for some purposes than the Park. He is, I understand, at liberty—or shortly to be so—if he fail me at the place nominated, he must seek me in Scotland, where he will find me possessed of his father's estate and lands."

"Humph!" muttered Richie; "there go twa words to that bargain."

He even meditated a joke on the means which he was conscious he possessed of baffling Lord Dalgarno's expectations, but there was something of keen and dangerous excitement in the eye of the young nobleman, that his discretion for once ruled his wit, and he only answered—

"God grant your lordship may well brook your new conquest—when you get it. I shall do your errand to my lord—whilk is to say," he added internally, "he shall never hear a word of it from Richie. I am not the lad to put him in such hazard."

Lord Dalgarno looked at him sharply for a moment, as if to penetrate the meaning of the dry ironical tone, which, in spite of Richie's awe, mingled with his answer, and then waved his hand, in signal he should pass on. He himself walked slowly till the trio were out of sight, then turned back with hasty steps to the door of the scrivener, which he had passed in his progress, knocked, and was admitted.

Lord Dalgarno found the man of law with the money-bags still standing before him; and it escaped not his penetrating glance, that Skurliewhitter was disconcerted and alarmed at his approach.

"How now, man," he said; "what, alamort—hast thou not a word of oily compliment to me on my happy marriage?—not a word of most philosophical consolation on my disgrace at court? or has my mien, as a wittol and a discarded favourite, the properties of the Gorgon head, the *turbatæ Palladis arma*, as Majesty might say?"

"My lord—I am glad—My lord, I am sorry,"—answered the trembling scrivener, who, aware of the vivacity of Lord Dalgarno's temper, dreaded the consequence of the communication he had to make to him.

"Glad and sorry!" answered Lord Dalgarno. "That is blowing hot

and cold, with a witness. Hark ye, you picture of petty-larceny personified—if you are sorry I am a cuckold, remember I am only mine
own, you knave—there is too little blood in her cheeks to have sent her
astray elsewhere—well, I will bear mine antler'd honours as I may—
gold shall gild them; and for my disgrace, revenge shall sweeten it—
ay, revenge—and there strikes the happy hour!"

The hour of noon was accordingly heard to peal from Saint Dunstan's. "Well banged, brave hammers," said Lord Dalgarno, in triumph.—"The estate and lands of Glenvarloch are crushed beneath
these clanging blows. If my steel to-morrow prove but as true as your
iron maces to-day, the poor landless lord will little miss what your peal
hath cut him out from.—The papers—the papers—thou varlet! I am
to-morrow Northward Ho!—at four, afternoon, I am bound to be at
Camlet Moat, in the Enfield Chace. To-night most of my retinue set
forward. The papers!—come, dispatch."

"My lord, the papers of the Glenvarloch mortgage—I—I have them
not."

"Have them not? hast thou sent them," echoed Lord Dalgarno,
"to my lodging, thou varlet?—did I not say I was coming hither?—
What mean you by pointing to that money? What villainy have you
done for it? It is too large to be honestly come by."

"Your lordship knows best," answered the scrivener, in great perturbation. "The gold is your own. It is—it is——"

"Not the redemption-money of the Glenvarloch estate!" said
Dalgarno. "Dare not to say it is, or I upon the spot divorce your
pettifogging soul from your carrion carcase!" So saying, he seized the
scrivener by the collar, and shook him so vehemently, that he tore it
from the cassock.

"My lord—I must call for help," said the trembling caitiff, who felt
at that moment all the bitterness of the mortal agony—"It was the
law's act, not mine—what could I do?"

"Doest ask?—Why, thou sniveling dribblet of damnation, were all
thy oaths, tricks, and lies spent? or do you hold yourself too good to
utter them in my service? Thou shouldst have lied, cozened, out-
sworn truth itself, rather than stood betwixt me and my revenge! But
mark me," he continued; "I know more of your pranks than would
hang thee—a line from me to the Attorney-General, and thou art
sped."

"What would you have me do, my lord?" said the scrivener. "All
that art and law can accomplish, I will try."

"Do so, or pity of your life!" said the lord; "and remember I never
fail my word. Then keep that accursed gold," he continued. "Or,
stay—I will not trust you—send me this gold home presently to my

lodging. I will still forward to Scotland, and it shall go hard but that I hold out Glenvarloch Castle against the owner, by means of his own ammunition. Thou art ready to serve me?" The scrivener professed the most implicit obedience.

"Then remember, the hour was passed ere payment was tendered —and see thou have witnesses of trusty memory to prove that point."

"Tush, my lord, I will do more," said Andrew, reviving—"I will prove that Lord Glenvarloch's friends threatened, swaggered, and drew swords on me—did your lordship think I was ungrateful enough to have suffered them to prejudice your lordship, save that they had bare swords at my throat?"

"Enough said," replied Dalgarno; "you are perfect. Mind that you continue so, as you would avoid my fury. I leave my page below—get porters, and let him instantly follow me with the gold."

So saying, Lord Dalgarno left the scrivener's habitation.

Skurliewhitter having dispatched his boy to get porters of trust for transporting the money, remained alone and in dismay, meditating by what means he could shake himself free of the vindictive and ferocious nobleman, who possessed at once a dangerous knowledge of his character, and the power of exposing him, where exposure would be ruin. He had indeed acquiesced in the plan, rapidly sketched, for obtaining possession of the ransomed estate, but his experience foresaw that this would be impossible; while, on the other hand, he could not anticipate various consequences of Lord Dalgarno's resentment, without fears, from which his sordid soul recoiled. To be in the power, and subject both to the humours and the extortions of a spendthrift young lord, just when his industry had shaped out the means of fortune,— it was the most cruel trick which fate could have played the incipient usurer.

While the scrivener was in this fit of anxious anticipation, one knocked at the door of the apartment; and, being desired to enter, appeared in the coarse riding-cloak of uncut Wiltshire cloth, fastened by a broad leather belt and brass buckle, which was then generally worn by graziers and countrymen. Skurliewhitter believing he saw in his visitor a country client who might prove profitable, had opened his mouth to request him to be seated, when the stranger, throwing back the frieze hood which he had drawn over his face, shewed the scrivener features well imprinted in his recollection, but which he never saw without a disposition to faint.

"Is it you?" he said faintly, as the stranger replaced the hood which concealed his features.

"Who else should it be?" said his visitor.

"Thou son of parchment, got betwixt the ink-horn
And the stuff'd process-bag—thou that mayst call
The pen thy father, and the ink thy mother,
The wax thy brother, and the sand thy sister,
And the good pillory thy cousin allied—
Rise, and do reverence unto me, thy better."

"Not yet down to the country," said the scrivener, "after every warning? do not think your grazier's cloak will bear you out, captain— no, nor your scraps of stage-plays."

"Why, what would you have me to do?" said the captain—"Would you have me starve? If I am to fly, you must eke my wings with a few feathers—you can spare them, I think."

"You had means already—you have had ten pieces—What is become of them?"

"Gone," answered Captain Colepepper—"Gone, no matter where —I had a mind to bite, and I was bitten—that's all—I think my hand shook at the thought of last night's work, for I trowled the doctors like a very babie."

"And you have lost all, then?—well, take this and be gone," said the scrivener.

"What, two poor smelts! marry, plague of your bounty!—but remember, you are as deep in as I."

"Not so, by Heaven!" answered the scrivener; "I only thought of easing the old man of some papers and a trifle of his gold, and you took his life."

"Were he living," answered Colepepper, "he would rather have lost it than his money—but there is not the question, Master Skurlie-whitter—you undid the private bolts of the window when you visited him about some affairs on the day ere he died—So satisfy yourself, that if I am taken, I will not swing alone.—Pity Jack Hempsfield is dead; it spoils the old catch,

'And three merry men, and three merry men,
    And three merry men are we,
As ever did sing three parts in a string,
    All under the triple tree.'"

"For God's sake speak lower," said the scrivener; "is this a place or time to make your midnight catches heard?—how much will serve your turn? I tell you I am but ill provided."

"You tell me a lie, then," said the bully—"a most palpable and gross lie.—How much, d'ye say, will serve my turn? Why, one of these bags will do—for the present."

"I swear to you that these bags of money are not at my disposal."

"Not honestly, perhaps," said the captain, "but that makes little difference betwixt us."

"I swear to you," continued the scrivener, "they are in no way at my disposal—they have been delivered to me by tale—I am to pay them over to Lord Dalgarno, whose boy waits for them, and I could not skelder one piece out of them, without risk of a hue and cry."

"Can you not put off the delivery," said the bravoe, his huge hand still fumbling with one of the bags, as if his fingers longed to close on it.

"Impossible," said the scrivener, "he sets forward to Scotland to-morrow."

"Ay!" said the bully, after a moment's thought—"Travels he the north road with such a charge?"

"He is well accompanied," added the scrivener; "but yet——"

"But yet—but what?" said the bravo.

"Nay, I meant nothing," said the scrivener.

"Thou didst—thou hadst the wind of some good thing," replied Colepepper; "I saw thee pause like a setting-dog—thou wilt say as little, and make as sure a sign, as a well-bred spaniel."

"All I meant to say, captain, was that his servants go by Barnet, and he himself, with his page, go through Enfield Chase; and he spoke to me yesterday of riding a soft pace."

"Aha! comest thou to me there, my boy?"

"And of resting—" continued the scrivener,—"resting a space at Camlet-Moat."

"Why, this is better than cock-fighting!" said the captain.

"I see not how it can advantage you, captain," said the scrivener. "They cannot ride fast, for his page rides the sumpter-horse, which carries all that weight," pointing to the money on the table. "Lord Dalgarno looks sharp to the world's gear."

"That horse will be obliged to those who may ease him of his burthen," said the bravoe; "for egad, he may be met with—he hath still that page—that same Lutin—that goblin?—well—the boy hath set game for me ere now. I will be revenged too, for I owe him a grudge for an old score at the ordinary. Let me see—Black Feltham, and Dick Shakebag—we shall want a fourth—I love to make sure—and the booty will stand parting, besides what I can bucket them out of—Well —scrivener, lend me two pieces—bravely done—nobly imparted. Give ye god-den." And wrapping his disguise closer around him, away he went.

When he had left the room, the scrivener wrung his hands, and exclaimed, "More blood—more blood! I thought to have had done with it—but this time there was no fault with me—none—and then I shall have all the advantage. If this ruffian falls, there is truce with his tugs at my purse-strings; and if Lord Dalgarno dies—as is most likely, for though as much afraid of cold steel as a debtor of a dun, this fellow is a deadly shot from behind a bush,—then am I in a thousand ways safe—safe—safe."

We willingly drop the curtain over him and his reflections.

Chapter Eleben

We are not worst at once—the course of evil
Begins so slowly, and from such slight source,
An infant's hand might stem its breach with clay;
But let the stream get deeper, and philosophy—
Ay, and religion too,—shall strive in vain
To turn the headlong torrent.
Old Play

THE TEMPLARS had been regaled by our friend Richie Moniplies in a private chamber at Beaujeu's, where he might be considered as good company; for he had exchanged his serving-man's cloak and jerkin for a grave yet handsome suit of clothes, in the fashion of the times, but such as might have suited an older man than himself. He had positively declined presenting himself at the ordinary, a point to which his companions were very desirous to have brought him, for it will be easily believed that such wags as Lowestoffe and his companion were not indisposed to a little merriment, at the expence of the raw and pedantic Scotsman; besides the chance of easing him of a few pieces, of which he seemed to have acquired considerable command. But not even a succession of measures of sparkling sack, in which the little brilliant atoms circulated like motes in the sun's rays, had the least effect on Richie's sense of decorum. He retained the gravity of a judge, even while he drank like a fish, partly from his own natural inclination to good liquor, partly in the way of good fellowship towards his guests. When the wine began to make some innovation on their heads, Master Lowestoffe, tired perhaps of the humours of Richie, who began to become yet more stoically contradictory and dogmatical than even in the earlier part of the entertainment, proposed to his friend to break up their debauch and join the gamesters.

The drawer was called accordingly, and Richie discharged the reckoning of the party, with a generous remuneration to the attendants, which was received with cap and knee, and many assurances of —"Kindly welcome, gentlemen."

"I grieve we should part so soon, gentlemen," said Richie to his companions,—"and I would you had cracked another quart ere you went, or staid to take some slight matter of supper, and a glass of Rhenish. I thank you, however, for having graced my poor collation thus far; and I commend you to fortune, in your own courses, for the ordinary neither was, is, nor shall be, an element of mine."

"Fare thee well, then," said Lowestoffe, "most sapient and sententious Master Moniplies—may you soon have another mortgage to redeem, and may I be there to witness it; and may you play the good fellow as heartily as you have done this day."

"Nay, gentlemen, it is merely of your grace to say so—but, if you would but hear me speak a few words of admonition respecting this wicked ordinary"——

"Reserve the lesson, most honourable Richie," said Lowestoffe, "until I have lost all my money," shewing, at the same time, a purse indifferently well provided, "and then the lecture is like to have some weight."

"And keep my share of it, Richie," said the other Templar, shewing an almost empty purse, in his turn, "till this be full again, and then I will promise to hear you with some patience."

"Ay, ay, gallants," said Richie, "the full and the empty gang a' ae gate, and that is a gray one—but the time will come"——

"Nay, it is come already," said Lowestoffe; "they have set out the hazard table. Since you will peremptorily not go with us—why, farewell, Richie."

"And farewell, gentlemen," said Richie, and left the house, into which they returned.

Moniplies was not many steps from the door, when a person, whom, lost in his reflections on gaming, ordinaries, and the manners of the age, he had not observed, and who had been as negligent on his part, ran full against him; and when Richie desired to know whether he meant "ony incivility," replied by a curse on Scotland, and all that belonged to it. A less round reflection on his country would, at any time, have provoked Richie, but more especially when he had a double quart of Canary and better in his pate. He was about to give a very rough answer, and to second his word by action, when a closer view of his antagonist changed his purpose.

"You are the vera lad in the warld," said Richie, "whom I most wished to meet."

"And you," answered the stranger, "or any of your beggarly countrymen, are the last sight I should ever wish to see—you Scots are ever fair and false, and an honest man cannot thrive within eye-shot of you."

"As to our poverty, friend," replied Richie, "that is as Heaven pleases—but touching our falset, I'll prove to you that a Scotsman bears as leal and true a heart to his friend as ever beat under English doublet."

"I care not whether he does or not," said the gallant. "Let me go—why keep you hold of my cloak? let me go, or I will thrust you into the kennel."

"I believe I could forgi'e ye, for you did me a good turn once, in plucking me out of it," said the Scot.

"Beshrew my fingers, then, if they did so," replied the stranger. "I would your whole country lay there, along with you; and Heaven's curse blight the hand that helped to raise them! Why do you stop my way?" he added, fiercely.

"Because it is a bad one, Master Jenkin," said Richie. "Nay, never stare about it, man—you see you are known. Alack-a-day! that an honest man's son should live to start at hearing himself called by his own name." Jenkin struck his brow violently with his clenched fist.

"Come, come," said Richie, "this passion availeth nothing—tell me what gate go you?"

"To the devil," answered Jin Vin.

"That is a black gate, if you speak according to the letter," answered Richie; "but if metaphorically, there are worse places in this great city than the Devil Tavern; and I care not if I go thither with you, and bestow a pottle of burned sack on you—it will correct the crudities of my stomach, and form a gentle preparative for the leg of a cold pullet."

"I pray you, in good fashion, to let me go," said Jenkin. "You may mean me kindly, and I wish you to have no wrong at my hand; but I am in the humour to be dangerous to myself, or any one."

"I will abide the risk," said the Scot, "if you will but come with me; and here is a place convenient, a howff nearer than the Devil, whilk is but an ill-omened drouthy name for a tavern—this other of the Saint Andrews is a quiet place, where I have ta'en my whitter now and then when I lodged in the neighbourhood of the Temple with Lord Glenvarloch.—What the deil's the matter wi' the man, gar'd him gie sic a spang as that, and almaist brought himself and me on the causeway?"

"Do not name that false Scot's name to me," said Jin Vin, "if you would not have me go mad!—I was happy before I saw him—he has been the cause of all the ill that befell me—he has made a knave and a madman of me!"

"If you are a knave," said Richie, "you have met an officer—if you are daft, you have met a keeper; but a gentle officer and a kind keeper. Look you, my gude friend, there has been twenty things said about this same lord, in which there is no more truth than in the leasings of Mahound. The warst they can say of him is, that he is not always so amenable to good advice as I would pray him, you, and every young man to be—come wi' me, and if a little spell of siller and a great deal of excellent counsel can relieve your occasions, all I can say is, you have

had the luck to meet one capable of giving you both, and maist willing
to bestow them."

The pertinacity of the Scot prevailed over the sullenness of Vincent, who was indeed in a state of agitation and incapacity to think for
himself, which led him to yield the more readily to the suggestions of
any other. He suffered himself to be dragged into the small tavern
which Richie recommended, and where they soon found themselves
seated in a snug niche, with a reeking pottle of burned sack, and a
paper of sugar betwixt them. Pipes and tobacco were also provided,
but were only used by Richie, who had adopted the custom of late, as
adding considerably to the gravity and importance of his manner, and
affording, as it were, a bland and pleasant accompaniment to the
words of wisdom which flowed from his tongue. After they had filled
their glasses and drank them in silence, Richie repeated the question,
whither his guest was going when they met so fortunately.

"I told you," said Jenkin, "I was going to destruction—I mean to the
gaming-house. I am resolved to hazard these two or three pieces, to
get as much as will pay for a passage with Captain Sharker, whose ship
lies at Gravesend, bound for America—and so Eastward Hoe.—I met
one devil in the way already, who would have tempted me from my
purpose, but I spurned him from me—you may be another for what I
know.—What degree of damnation do you propose for me, (he added
wildly,) and what is the price of it?"

"I would have you to know," answered Richie, "that I deal in no
such commodities, whether as buyer or seller. But if you will tell me
honestly the cause of your distress, I will do what is in my power to
help you out of it,—not being, however, prodigal of promises, until I
know the case; as a learned physician only gives advice when he has
observed the diagnostics."

"No one has any thing to do with my affairs," said the poor lad; and
folding his arms on the table he laid his head down on them, with the
sullen dejection of the over-burthened *lama* when it throws itself
down to die in desperation.

Richie Moniplies, like most folks who have a good opinion of
themselves, was fond of the task of consolation, which at once displayed his superiority, (for the consoler is always, for the time at
least, superior to the afflicted person,) and indulged his love of
talking. He inflicted on the poor penitent a harangue of pitiless
length, stuffed full of the usual topics of the mutability of human
affairs—the eminent advantages of patience under affliction—the
folly of grieving for what hath no remedy—the necessity of taking
more care for the future, and some gentle rebukes on account of
the past, which acid he threw in to assist in subduing the patient's

obstinacy, as Hannibal used vinegar in cutting his way through rocks. It was not in human nature to endure this flood of common-place eloquence in silence; and Jin Vin, whether desirous of stopping the flow of words crammed thus into his ear "against the stomach of his sense," or whether confiding in Richie's protestations of friendship, which the wretched, says Fielding, are ever so ready to believe, or whether merely to give his sorrows vent in words, raised his head, and, turning his red and swollen eyes to Richie, said: "Cock's-bones, man, only hold thy tongue, and thou shalt know all about it, and then all I ask of thee is to shake hands and part.—This here girl—my master's daughter—this Margaret Ramsay,—you have seen her, man?"

"Once," said Richie, "once—at Master George Heriot's in Lombard-street—I was in the room when they dined."

"Ay, you helped to shift their trenchers I remember," said Jin Vin. "Well, that same pretty girl—and I will uphold her the prettiest betwixt Paul's and the Bar—she is to be wedded to your Lord Glenvarloch, with a pestilence on him!"

"That is impossible," said Richie; "it is raving nonsense, man—they make April gouks of you Cockneys every month in the year—the Lord Glenvarloch marry the daughter of a Lonnon mechanick! I would as soon believe the great Prester John would marry the daughter of a Jew packman."

"Hark ye, brother," said Jin Vin, "I will allow no one to speak disregardfully of the city, for all I am in trouble."

"I crave your pardon, man—I meant no offence," said Richie; "but as to the marriage—it is a thing simply impossible."

"It is a thing that will take place though, for the Duke and the Prince, and all of them, have a finger in it; and especially the old fool of a King, that makes her out to be some great woman in her own country, as all the Scots pretend to be, you know."

"Master Vincent, but that you are under affliction," said the consoler, offended in his turn, "I would hear no national reflections."

The afflicted youth apologized in his turn, but asserted, "it was true that the King said Peg-a-Ramsay was some far-off sort of noblewoman; and that he had taken a great interest in the match, and had run about like an old gander, cackling about Peggie ever since he had seen her in hose and doublet—and no wonder," added poor Vin, with a deep sigh.

"This may be all true," said Richie, "though it sound strange in my ears; but, man, you should not speak evil of dignities—Curse not the King, Jenkin; not in thy bed-chamber—stone-walls have ears—no one knows that better than I."

"I do not curse the foolish old man," said Jenkin; "but I would have them carry things a peg lower.—If they were to see on a plain field thirty thousand such pikes as I have seen in the artillery gardens, it would not be their long-haired courtiers would help them, I trow."

"Hout tout, man," said Richie, "mind where the Stuarts come frae, and never think they would want spears or claymores either; but leaving sic matters, whilk are perilous to speak on, I say once more, what is your concern in all this matter?"

"What is it!" said Jenkin; "why, have I not fixed on Peg-a-Ramsay to be my true-love from the day I came to her old father's shop? and have I not carried her pattens and her chopines for three years, and borne her prayer-book to church, and brushed the cushion for her to kneel down upon, and did she ever say me nay?"

"I see no cause she had," said Richie, "if the like of such small services were all that ye proffered. Ah, man! there are few—very few, either of fools or of wise men, ken how to guide a woman."

"Why, did I not serve her at the risk of my freedom, and very nigh at the risk of my neck? Did she not—no, it was not her neither, but that accursed beldame whom she caused work upon me, persuade me like a fool to turn myself into a waterman to help my lord, and a plague to him, down to Scotland; and instead of going peaceably down to the ship at Gravesend, did not he rant and bully, and shew his pistols, and make me land him at Greenwich, where he played some swaggering pranks, that helped both him and me into the Tower?"

"Aha!" said Richie, throwing more than his usual wisdom into his looks; "so you were the green-jacketted waterman that rowed Lord Glenvarloch down the river?"

"The more fool I, that did not souse him in the Thames," said Jenkin; "and I was the lad that would not confess one word of who or what I was, though they threatened to make me hug the Duke of Exeter's daughter."

"Wha is she, man?" said Richie; "she must be an ill-fashioned piece, if you're so much afraid of her, and she come of such high kin."

"I mean the rack—the rack, man—Where were you bred that never heard of the Duke of Exeter's daughter?" said Jenkin; "but all the dukes and duchesses in England could have got nothing out of me— so the truth came out some other way, and I was set free—home I ran, thinking myself the cleverest and happiest fellow in the ward. And she —she—she wanted to pay me with money for all my true service— and she spoke so sweetly and so coldly at the same time—I wished myself in the deepest dungeon of the Tower—I wish they had racked me to death before I heard this Scotchman was to chouse me of my sweetheart!"

"But are ye sure ye have lost her?" said Richie; "it sounds strange in my ears that my Lord Glenvarloch should marry the daughter of a dealer, though there are uncouth marriages made in London, I'll allow that."

"Why, I tell you this lord was no sooner clear of the Tower, than he and Master George Heriot comes to make proposals for her, with the King's assent and what not; and fine fair-day prospects of court-favour for this lord, for he hath not an acre of land."

"Well, and what said the auld watch-maker?" said Richie; "was he not, as might weel beseem him, ready to loup out of his skin-case for very joy?"

"He multiplied six figures progressively, and reported the product —then gave his consent."

"And what did you do?"

"I took the streets," said the poor lad, "with a burning heart and a blood-shot eye—and where did I first find myself, but with that beldame Mother Suddlechop—and what did she propose to me, but to take the road?"

"Take the road, man? in what sense?" said Richie.

"Even as a clerk to Saint Nicholas—as a highwayman, like Poins and Peto, and the good fellows in the play—and who think you was to be my captain, for she had the whole out ere I could speak to her? I fancy she took silence for consent, and thought me damned too unutterably to have one thought left that savoured of redemption— who was to be my captain, but the knave that you saw me cudgel at the ordinary, when you waited on Lord Glenvarloch, a cowardly, shark-ing, thievish bully about town here, whom they call Colepepper."

"Colepepper—umph—I know somewhat of that smaik," said Richie; "ken ye by ony chance where he may be heard of, Master Jenkin?—ye wad do me a sincere service to tell me."

"Why, he lives something obscurely, on account of suspicion of some villainy—I believe that horrid murther in Whitefriars, or some such matter. But I might have heard all about him from Dame Suddlechop, for she spoke of my meeting him at Enfield Chase, with some other good fellows, to do a robbery on some one that goes northward with a store of treasure."

"And you did not agree to this fine project?" said Moniplies.

"I cursed her for a hag, and came away about my business," answered Jenkin.

"Ay, and what said she to that, man? That would startle her," said Richie.

"Not a whit. She laughed, and said she was in jest," answered Jenkin; "but I know the she-devil's jest from her earnest, as well as any lad in England. But she knows I would never betray her."

"Betray her! No," replied Richie, "but are ye in any shape bound to this birkie Peppercole, or Colepepper, or whatever they call him, that ye suld let him do a robbery on the honest gentleman that is travelling to the north, and may be a kindly Scot, for what we know?"

"Ay—going home with a load of English money," said Jenkin. "But be he who he will, they may rob the whole world an they list, for I am robbed and ruined."

Richie filled up his friend's cup to the brim, and insisted he should drink what he called "clean caup out." "This love," he said, "is but a bairnly matter for a brisk young fellow like yourself, Master Jenkin. And if ye must needs have a whimsey, though I think it would be safer to venture on a staid womanly body, why, here be as bonnie lasses in London as this Peg-a-Ramsay. Ye need not sigh sae deeply, for it is very true—there are as gude fish in the sea as ever came out of it. Now wherefore should you, who are as brisk and trig a young fellow of your inches, as the sun needs to shine on—wherefore need you sit moping this way, and not try some bold way to better your fortune?"

"I tell you, Master Moniplies," said Jenkin, "I am as poor as any Scot among you—I have broke my indenture, and I think of running my country."

"A-well-a-day!" said Richie; "but that maunna be, man—I ken weel, by sad experience, that poortith takes away pith, and the man sits full still that has a rent in his breeks. But courage, man; you have served me heretofore, and I will serve you now. If you will but bring me to speech of this same Captain, it shall be the best day's work you ever did."

"I guess where you are, Master Richard—you would save your countryman's long purse," said Jenkin. "I cannot see how that should advantage me, but I reck not if I should bear a hand. I hate that braggart, that bloody-minded cowardly bully. If you can get me mounted, I care not if I shew you where the dame told me I should meet him—but you must stand to the risk, for though he is a coward himself, I know he will have more than one stout fellow with him."

"We'll have a warrant, man," said Richie, "and the hue and cry, to boot."

"We will have no such thing," said Jenkin, "if I am to go with you. I am not the lad to betray any one to the harman-beck. You must do it by manhood if I am to go with you. I am sworn to cutter's law, and will sell no man's blood."

"Aweel," said Richie, "a wilful man must have his way; ye must think that I was born and bred where cracked crowns were plentier than whole ones. Besides, I have two noble friends here, Master

Lowestoffe of the Temple, and his cousin Master Ringwood, that will blithely be of so gallant a party."

"Lowestoffe and Ringwood!" said Jenkin; "they are both brave gallants—they will be sure company. Know you where they are to be found?"

"Ay, marry do I," replied Richie. "They are fast at the cards and dice, till the sma' hours, I warrant them."

"They are gentlemen of trust and honour," said Jenkin, "and, if they advise it, I will try the adventure. Go, try if you can bring them hither, since you have so much to say with them. We must not be seen abroad together.—I know not how it is, Master Moniplies," continued he, as his countenance brightened up, and while, in his turn, he filled the cups, "but I feel my heart something lighter since I have thought of this matter."

"This it is to have counsellors, Master Jenkin; and truly I hope to hear you say that your heart is as light as a lavrock's, and that before you are many days aulder. Never smile and shake your head, but mind what I tell you—and bide here in the meanwhile, till I go to seek these gallants. I warrant you, cart-ropes would not hold them back from such a ploy as I shall propose to them."

Chapter Twelve

"The thieves have bound the true men—Now, could thou and I rob the thieves, and go merrily to London."

Henry IV. Part I

THE SUN WAS HIGH upon the glades of Enfield Chase, and the deer, with which it then abounded, were seen sporting in picturesque groupes amongst the ancient oaks with which the forest abounded, when a cavalier, and a lady on foot, although in riding apparel, sauntered slowly up one of the long alleys which were cut through the park for the convenience of the hunters. Their only attendant was a page, who, riding a Spanish jennet, which seemed to bear a heavy cloak-bag, followed them at a respectful distance. The female, attired in all the fantastic finery of the period, with more than the usual quantity of bugles, flounces, and trimmings, and holding her fan of ostrich feathers in one hand, and her riding-mask of black velvet in the other, seemed anxious, by all the little coquetry practised on such occasions, to secure the notice of her companion, who sometimes heard her prattle without seeming to attend to it, and at other times interrupted his train of graver reflections, to reply to her.

"Nay, but my lord—my lord, you walk so fast, you will leave me

behind you.—Nay, I will have hold of your arm, but how to manage
with my mask and my fan! Why would you not let me bring my waiting
gentlewoman to follow us, and hold my things? But see, I will put my
fan in my girdle, soh!—and now that I have a hand to hold you with,
you shall not run away from me."

"Come on, then," answered the gallant, "and let us walk apace,
since you would not be persuaded to stay with your gentlewoman, as
you call her, and with the rest of the baggage.—You may perhaps see
that you will not like to see."

She took hold of his arm accordingly; but as he continued to walk at
the same pace, she shortly let go her hold, exclaiming that he had hurt
her hand. The cavalier stopped and looked at the pretty hand and arm
which she shewed him, with exclamations against his cruelty. "I dare
say," she said, baring her wrist and a part of her arm, "it is all black and
blue to the very elbow."

"I dare say you are a little fool," said the cavalier, carelessly kissing
the aggrieved arm; "it is only a pretty incarnate which sets off the blue
veins."

"Nay, my lord, now it is you are silly," answered the dame; "but I
am glad I can make you speak and laugh on any terms this morning. I
am sure, if I did insist on following you into the forest, it was all for the
sake of diverting you. I am better company than your page, I trow.—
And now, tell me, these pretty things with horns, be they not deer?"

"Even such they be, Nelly," answered her neglectful attendant.

"And what can the great folks do with so many of them, forsooth?"

"They send them to the city, Nell, where wise men make venison
pasties of their flesh, and wear their horns for trophies," answered
Lord Dalgarno, whom our reader has already recognized.

"Nay, now you laugh at me, my lord," answered his companion;
"but I know all about venison, whatsoever you may think. I always
tasted it once a-year when we dined with Mr Deputy," she continued,
sadly, as a sense of her degradation stole across a mind bewildered
with vanity and folly, "though he would not speak to me now, if we met
together in the narrowest lane in the Ward."

"I warrant he would not," said Lord Dalgarno, "because thou, Nell,
wouldst dash him with a single look; for I trust thou hast more spirit
than to throw away words on such a fellow as he."

"Who, I?" said Dame Nelly. "Nay, I scorn the proud princox too
much for that. Do you know he made all the folks in the ward stand
cap in hand to him, my poor old John Christie and all?" Here her
recollection began to overflow at her eyes.

"A plague on your whimpering," said Dalgarno, somewhat harshly.
—"Nay, never look pale for the matter, Nell. I am not angry with you,

you simple fool. But what would you have me think, when you are eternally looking back upon your dungeon yonder by the river, which smelt of pitch and old cheese worse than a Welchman does of onions, and all this when I am taking you down to a castle as fine as is in Fairy Land!"

"Shall we be there to-night, my lord?" said Nelly, drying her tears.

"To-night, Nelly?—no, nor this night fortnight."

"Now, the Lord be with us, and keep us!—But shall we not go by sea, my lord?—I thought every body came from Scotland by sea? I am sure Lord Glenvarloch and Richie Moniplies came up by sea."

"There is a wide difference betwixt coming up and going down, Nelly," answered Lord Dalgarno.

"And so there is, for certain," said his simple companion. "But yet I think I heard people speaking of going down to Scotland by sea, as well as coming up. Are you well avised of the way?—Do you think it possible we can go by land, my sweet lord?"

"It is but trying, my sweet lady," said Lord Dalgarno. "Men say England and Scotland are in the same island, so one would hope there may be some road betwixt them by land."

"I shall never be able to ride so far," said the lady.

"We will have your saddle stuffed softer," said the lord. "I tell you that you shall mew your city slough, and change from the catterpillar of a paltry lane into the butterfly of a prince's garden. You shall have as many tires as there are hours in the day—as many handmaidens as there are days in the week—as many menials as there are weeks in the year—and you shall ride a hunting and hawking with a lord, instead of waiting upon an old ship-chandler, who could do nothing but hawk and spit."

"Ay, but will you make me your lady?" said Dame Nelly.

"Ay, surely—what else," replied the lord—"My lady-love."

"Ay, but I mean your lady-wife," said Nelly.

"Truly, Nell, in that I cannot promise to oblige you. A lady-wife," continued Dalgarno, "is a very different thing from a lady-love."

"I heard from Mrs Suddlechop, whom you lodged me with since I left poor old John Christie, that Lord Glenvarloch is to marry David Ramsay the clockmaker's daughter."

"There is much betwixt the cup and the lip, Nelly. I wear something about me may break the bans of that hopeful alliance, before the day is much older," answered Lord Dalgarno.

"Well, but my father was as good a man as old Davie Ramsay, and as well to pass in the world, my lord; and, therefore, why should you not marry me? You have done me harm enough, I trow—wherefore should you not do me this justice?"

"For two good reasons, Nelly. Fate put a husband on you, and the King passed a wife upon me," answered Lord Dalgarno.

"Ay, my lord," said Nelly, "but they remain in England, and we go to Scotland."

"Thy argument is better than thou art aware of," said Lord Dalgarno. "I have heard Scottish lawyers say the matrimonial tie may be unclasped in our country by the gentle hand of the ordinary course of law, whereas in England it can only be burst by an act of Parliament. Well, Nelly, we will look into that matter; and whether we get married again or no, we will at least do our best to get unmarried."

"Shall we indeed, my honey-sweet lord? and then I will think less about John Christie, for he will marry again, I warrant you, for he is well to pass; and I would be glad to think he had somebody to take care of him, as I used to do, poor loving old man! He was a kind man, though he was a score of years older than I; and I hope and pray he will never let a young lord cross his honest threshold again."

Here the dame was once more much inclined to give way to a passion of tears; but Lord Dalgarno conjured down the emotion, by saying, with some asperity—"I am weary of these April passions, my pretty mistress, and I think you will do well to preserve your tears for some more pressing occasion. Who knows what turn of fortune may in a few minutes call for more of them than you can render?"

"Goodness, my lord! what mean you by such expressions? John Christie, (the kind heart!) used to keep no secrets from me, and I hope your lordship will not hide your counsel from me?"

"Sit down beside me on this bank," said the nobleman; "I am bound to remain here for a short space, and if you can be but silent, I should like to spend a part of it in considering how far I can, on the present occasion, follow the respectable example which you recommend to me."

The place at which he stopped, was at that time little more than a mound, partly surrounded by a ditch, from which it derived the name of Camlet Moat. A few hewn stones there were, which had escaped the fate of many others which had been used in building different lodges in the forest for the royal keepers. These vestiges, just sufficient to shew that "here in former times, the hand of man had been," marked the ruins of the abode of a once illustrious but long-forgotten family, the Mandevilles, Earls of Essex, to whom Enfield Chase and the extensive domains adjacent had belonged in elder days. A wild woodland prospect led the eye at various points through broad and seemingly interminable alleys, which, meeting at this point as at a common centre, diverged from each other as they receded, and had, therefore, been selected by Lord Dalgarno as the rendezvous for the combat, which, through the medium of Richie Moniplies, he had offered to his injured friend Lord Glenvarloch.

"He will surely come," he said to himself; "cowardice was not wont to be his fault—at least he was bold enough in the Park.—Perhaps yonder churl may not have carried my message? But no—he is a sturdy knave—one of those would prize his master's honour above their life.—Look to the palfrey, Lutin, and see thou let him not loose, and cast thy falcon glance down every avenue to mark if any one comes.—Buckingham has undergone my challenge, but the proud minion pleads the King's paltry commands for refusing to answer me. If I can baffle this Glenvarloch, or slay him—if I can spoil him of his honour or his life, I shall go down to Scotland with credit sufficient to gild over past mischances. I know my dear countrymen—they never quarrel with any one who brings them home either gold or martial glory."

As he thus reflected, and called to mind the disgrace which he had suffered, as well as the causes he imagined for hating Lord Glenvarloch, his countenance altered under the influence of his contending emotions, to the terror of Nelly, who, sitting unnoticed at his feet, and looking anxiously in his face, beheld the cheek kindle, the mouth become compressed, the eye dilated, and the whole countenance express the desperate and deadly resolution of one who awaits an instant and decisive encounter with a mortal enemy. The loneliness of the place, the scenery so different from that to which alone she had been accustomed, the dark and sombre air which crept so suddenly over the countenance of her seducer, his command imposing silence upon her, and the apparent strangeness of his conduct in idling away so much time without any obvious cause, when a journey of such length lay before them, brought strange thoughts into her weak brain. She had read of women, seduced from their matrimonial duties by sorcerers allied to the hellish powers, nay, by the Father of Evil himself, who, after conveying his victim into some desert remote from human kind, exchanged the pleasing shape in which he gained her affections, for all his natural horrors. She chased this wild idea away as it crowded itself upon her weak and bewildered imagination; but she might have lived to see it realized allegorically, if not literally, but for the accident which presently followed.

The page, whose eyes were remarkably acute, at length called out to his master, pointing with his finger at the same time down one of the alleys, that horsemen were advancing in that direction. Lord Dalgarno started up, and shading his eyes with his hand, gazed eagerly down the alley; when, at the same instant, he received a shot, which, grazing his hand, passed right through his brain, and laid him a lifeless corpse at the feet, or rather across the lap, of the unfortunate victim of his profligacy. The countenance, whose varied expression she had been watching for the last five minutes, was convulsed for an instant, and then stiffened into rigidity for ever. Three ruffians rushed from the brake from which the shot had been fired, ere the smoke was dispersed. One, with many imprecations, seized on the page; another on the female, upon whose cries he strove by the most violent threats to impose silence; whilst the third began to undo the burthen of the page's horse. But an instant rescue prevented their availing themselves of the advantage they had obtained.

It may easily be supposed that Richie Moniplies, having secured the assistance of the two Templars, ready enough to join in any thing which promised a fray, with Jin Vin to act as their guide, had set off, gallantly mounted and well-armed, under the belief that they would reach Camlet Moat before the robbers, and apprehend them in the fact. They had not calculated that, according to the custom of robbers in other countries, but contrary to that of the English highwaymen of these days, they meant to insure robbery by previous murther. An accident also happened to delay them a little while on the road. In riding through one of the glades of the forest, they found a man dismounted and sitting under a tree, groaning with such bitterness of spirit, that Lowestoffe could not forbear asking if he was hurt. In answer, he said he was an unhappy man in pursuit of his wife, who had been carried off by a villain; and as he raised his countenance, the eyes of Richie, to his great astonishment, encountered the visage of John Christie.

"For the Almighty's sake, help me, Master Moniplies!" he said; "I have learned my wife is but a short mile before, with that black villain Lord Dalgarno."

"Have him forward by all means," said Lowestoffe; "a second Orpheus seeking his Eurydice!—have him forward—we will save Lord Dalgarno's purse, and ease him of his mistress—have him with us, were it but for the rarity of the adventure. I owe his lordship a grudge for rooking me. We have ten minutes good."

But it is dangerous to calculate closely in matters of life and death. In all probability the minute or two which was lost in mounting John Christie behind one of their party, might have saved Lord Dalgarno from his fate. Thus his criminal amour became the indirect cause of his losing his life; and thus "our pleasant vices are made the whips to scourge us."

The riders arrived on the field at full gallop the moment after the shot was fired; and Richie, who had his own reasons for attaching himself to Colepepper, who was bustling to untie the portmanteau from the page's saddle, pushed against him with such violence as to overthrow him, his own horse at the same time stumbling and dismounting his rider, who was none of the first equestrians. The undaunted Richie grappled with the ruffian with such good will, that though a strong fellow, and though a coward now rendered desperate, he got him under, wrenched a long knife from his hand, dealt him a desperate stab with his own weapon, then leaped on his feet; and, as the wounded man struggled to follow his example, he struck him upon the head with the butt-end of a musketoon, which last blow proved fatal.

"Brave Richie!" cried Lowestoffe, who had himself engaged at sword-point with one of the ruffians, and soon put him to flight,— "Bravo! why, man, there lies Sin, struck down like an ox, and Iniquity's throat cut like a calf."

"I know not why you should upbraid me with my up-bringing, Master Lowstoffe," answered Richie, with great composure; "but I can tell you, the shambles is not a bad place for training one to this work."

The other Templar now shouted loudly to them,—"If ye be men, come hither—here lies Lord Dalgarno, murdered!"

Lowestoffe and Richard ran to the spot, and the page took the opportunity, finding himself now neglected on all hands, to ride off in a different direction; and neither he, nor the considerable sum with which his horse was burthened, were ever heard of from that moment.

The third ruffian had not waited the attack of the Templar and Jin Vin, the latter of whom had put down old Christie from behind him that he might ride the lighter; and the whole five now stood gazing with horror on the bloody corpse of the young nobleman, and the wild sorrow of the female, who tore her hair and shrieked in the most disconsolate manner, until her agony was at once checked, or rather received a new direction, by the sudden and unexpected appearance of her husband, who, fixing on her a cold and severe look, said, in a tone suited to his manner—"Ay, woman! thou takest on sadly for the loss of thy paramour."—Then, looking on the bloody corpse of him from whom he had received so deep an injury, he repeated the solemn words of Scripture,—"'Vengeance is mine, saith the Lord, and I will repay it.'—I, whom thou hast injured, will be first to render thee the decent offices due to the dead."

So saying, he covered the dead body with his cloak, and then looking on it for a moment, seemed to reflect on what he had next to perform. As the eye of the injured man slowly passed from the body of the seducer to the partner and victim of his crime, who had sunk down to his feet, which she clasped, without venturing to look up, his features, naturally coarse and saturnine, assumed a dignity of expression which overawed the young Templars, and repulsed the officious forwardness of Richie Moniplies, who was at first eager to have thrust in his advice and opinion. "Kneel not to me, woman," he said, "but kneel to the God thou hast offended, more than thou couldst offend such another worm as thyself. How often have I told thee, when thou wert at the gayest and the lightest, that pride goeth before destruction, and a haughty spirit before a fall? Vanity brought folly, and folly brought sin, and sin hath brought death, his original companion. Thou must needs leave duty, and decency, and domestic love, to revel it gaily with the wild and with the wicked; and there thou liest, like a crushed worm, writhing beside the lifeless body of thy paramour. Thou hast done me much wrong—dishonoured me among friends—driven credit from my house, and peace from my fire-side—But thou wert my first and only love, and I will not see thee an utter castaway, if it lies with me to prevent it.—Gentlemen, I render ye such thanks as a broken-hearted man can give.—Richard, commend me to your honourable master.—I added gall to the bitterness of his affliction, but I was deluded.—Rise up, woman, and follow me."

He raised her up by the arm, while, with streaming eyes, and bitter sobs, she endeavoured to express her penitence. She kept her hands spread over her face, yet suffered him to lead her away; and it was only as they turned around a brake which concealed the scene they had left, that she turned back, and casting one wild and hurried glance towards the corpse of Dalgarno, uttered a shriek, and clinging to her husband's arm, exclaimed wildly,—"Save me—save me! They have murdered him!"

Lowestoffe was much moved by what he had witnessed; but he was ashamed, as a town-gallant, of his own unfashionable emotion, and did a force to his feelings when he exclaimed,—"Ay, let them go—the kind-hearted, believing, forgiving husband—the liberal, accommodating spouse. O what a generous creature is your true London husband!—Horns hath he, but, tame as a fatted ox, he goreth not. I should like to see her when she has exchanged her mask and riding-beaver for her peaked hat and muffler. We will visit them at Paul's Wharf, coz—it will be a convenient acquaintance."

"You had better think of catching the gipsey thief, Lutin," said Richie Moniplies; "for, by my faith, he is off with his master's baggage and the siller."

A keeper, with his assistants, and several other persons, had now come to the spot, and made hue and cry after Lutin, but in vain. To their custody the Templars surrendered the dead bodies, and after going through some formal investigation, they returned, with Richard and Vincent, to London, where they received great applause for their gallantry. Vincent's errors were easily expiated, in consideration of his having been the means of breaking up this band of villains; and there is some reason to think, that what would have diminished the credit of the action in other instances, rather added to it in the actual circumstances, namely, that they came too late to save Lord Dalgarno.

George Heriot, who suspected how matters stood with Vincent, requested and obtained permission from his master to send the poor young fellow on an important piece of business to Paris. We are unable to trace his fate farther, but believe it was prosperous, and that he entered into an advantageous partnership with his fellow-apprentice, upon old Davie Ramsay retiring from business, in consequence of his daughter's marriage. That eminent antiquary, Dr Dryasdust, is possessed of an antique watch, with a silver dial-plate, and a piece of catgut instead of a chain, which bears the names of Vincent and Tunstall.

Master Lowestoffe failed not to vindicate his character as a man of gaiety, by inquiring after John Christie and Dame Nelly; but greatly to his surprise, (indeed to his loss, for he had wagered ten pieces that he would domesticate himself in the family,) he found the good-will, as it was called, of the shop, was sold, the stock auctioned, and the late proprietor and his wife gone, no one knew whither. The prevailing belief was, that they had emigrated to one of the new settlements in America.

Lady Dalgarno received the news of her unworthy husband's death with a variety of emotions, among which, horror that he should have been cut off in the middle career of his profligacy, was the most prominent. The incident greatly deepened her melancholy and injured her health, already shaken by previous circumstances. Repossessed of her own fortune by her husband's death, she was anxious to do justice to Lord Glenvarloch, by treating for the recovery of the mortgage. But the scrivener, having taken fright at the late events, had left the city and absconded, so that it was impossible to discover into whose hands the papers had now passed. Richard Moniplies was silent, for his own reasons; the Templars, who had witnessed the transaction, kept the secret at his request, and it was universally believed that the scrivener had carried off the writings alongst with him. We may here observe, that fears similar to those of the scrivener freed London for ever from the presence of Dame Suddlechop, who ended her career in the *Rasp-haus*, (viz. Bridewell,) of Amsterdam.

The stout old Lord Huntinglen, with a haughty carriage and unmoistened eye, accompanied the funeral procession of his only son to its last abode; and perhaps the only tear which fell at length upon the coffin, was given less to the fate of the individual, than to the extinction of the last male of his ancient race.

Chapter Thirteen

Jaques. There is sure another flood towards, and all these couples are coming to the ark.—Here comes a pair of very strange beasts.

As You Like It

THE FASHION of such narratives as the present, changes like other earthly things. Time was that the tale-teller was obliged to wind up his story by a circumstantial description of the wedding, bedding, and throwing the stocking, as the grand catastrophe to which, through so many circumstances of doubt and difficulty, he had at length happily conducted his hero and heroine. Not a circumstance was then omitted, from the manly ardour of the bridegroom, and the modest blushes of the bride, to the parson's new surplice, and the silk tabinet manteau of the bride's-maid. But such descriptions are now discarded, for the same reason, I suppose, that public marriages are no longer fashionable, and that, instead of calling together their friends to a feast and a dance, the happy couple elope in a solitary post-chaise, as secretly as if they meant to go to Gretna-Green, or to do worse. I am not ungrateful for a change which saves an author the trouble of attempting in vain to give a new colour to the common-place description of such matters; but, notwithstanding, I find myself forced upon it in the present instance, as circumstances sometimes compel a stranger to make use of an old road which has been for some time shut up. The experienced reader may have already remarked, that the last chapter was employed in sweeping out of the way all the unnecessary and less interesting characters, that I might clear the floor for a blithe bridal.

In truth, it would be unpardonable to pass over slightly what so deeply interested our principal personage, King James. That learned and good-humoured monarch made no great figure in the politics of Europe; but then, to make amends, he was prodigiously busy, when he could find a fair opportunity, of intermeddling with the private affairs of his loving subjects, and the approaching marriage of Lord Glenvarloch was matter of great interest to him. He had been much struck (that is, for him, who was not very accessible to such emotions,) with the beauty and embarrassment of the pretty Peg-a-Ramsay, as he called her, when he first saw her, and he glorified himself greatly on the acuteness which he had displayed in detecting her disguise, and in carrying through the whole inquiry which took place in consequence of it.

He laboured for several weeks, while the courtship was in progress, with his own royal eyes, so as well nigh to wear out, he declared, a pair of her father's best barnacles, in searching through old books and documents, for the purpose of establishing the bride's pretension to a noble, though remote descent, and thereby remove the only objection which envy might conceive against the match. In his own opinion, at least, he was eminently successful; for when Sir Mungo Malagrowther one day, in the presence-chamber, took upon him to grieve bitterly for the bride's lack of pedigree, the monarch cut him short with, "Ye may save your grief for your ain next occasions, Sir Mungo; for, by our royal saul, we will uphauld her father, Davie Ramsay, to be a gentleman of nine descents, whase great gude-sire came of the auld martial stock of the House of Dalwolsey, than whom better men never did, and better never will, draw sword for King and country. Heard ye never of Sir William Ramsay of Dalwolsey, man? of whom John Fordoun saith,—'He was *bellicosissimus, nobilissimus.*'— His castle stands to witness for itsel, not three miles from Dalkeith, man, and within a mile of Bannock-rigg. Davie Ramsay came of that auld and honoured stock, and I trust he hath not derogated from his ancestors by his present craft. They all wrought wi' steel, man; only the auld Knights drilled holes wi' their swords in their enemies' corslets, and he saws nicks in his brass wheels. And I hope it is as honourable to give eyes to the blind as to slash them out of the head of those that see, and to shew us how to value our time as it passes, as to fling it away in drinking, brawling, spear-splintering, and suchlike unchristian doings. And you maun understand, that Davie Ramsay is no mechanic, but follows a liberal art, which approacheth almost to the act of creating a living being, seeing it may be said of a watch, as Claudian saith of the sphere of Archimedes, the Syracusian—

> Inclusus variis famulatur spiritus astris,
> Et vivum certis motibus urget opus."

"Your Majesty had best give auld Davie a coat-of-arms, as well as a pedigree," said Sir Mungo.

"It's done, or ye bade, Sir Mungo," said the King; "and I trust we, who are the fountain of all earthly honour, are free to spirt a few drops of it on one so near our person, without offence to the Knight of Castle Girnigo. We have already spoken with the learned men of the Herald's College, and we propose to grant him an augmented coat-of-arms, being his paternal coat, charged with the crown-wheel of a watch in chief, for a difference; and we purpose to add Time and Eternity, for supporters, so soon as the Garter King-at-Arms shall be able to devise how Eternity is to be presented."

"I would make him twice as muckle as Time,"* said Archie Armstrong, the court fool, who chanced to be present when the King stated this dilemma.

"Peace, man—ye shall be whippet," said the King, in return for this hint; "and you, my liege subjects of England, may weel take a hint from what we have said, and not be in such a hurry to laugh at our Scottish pedigrees, though they be somewhat long derived, and difficult to be deduced. Ye see that a man of right gentle blood may, for a season, lay by his gentry, and yet ken whare to find it, when he has occasion for it. It would be as unseemly for a packman, or pedlar, as ye call a travelling-merchant, whilk is a trade to which our native subjects of Scotland are specially addicted, to be blazing his genealogy in the faces of those to whom he sells a bawbie's worth of ribband, as it would be to him to have a beaver on his head, and a rapier by his side, when the pack was on his shoulders. Na, na—he hings his sword on the cleek, lays his beaver on the shelf, puts his pedigree into his pocket, and gangs as doucely and cannily about his pedling craft as if his blood was nae better than ditch-water; but let our pedlar be transformed, as I have kenned it happen mair than ance, into a bein thriving merchant, then ye shall have a transformation, my lords,

In novas fert animus mutatas dicere formas.

Out he pulls his pedigree, on he buckles his sword, gives his beaver a brush, and cocks it in the face of all creation. We mention these things at the mair length, because we would have you all to know, that it is not without due consideration of the circumstances of all parties, that we design, in a small and private way, to honour with our own royal presence the marriage of Lord Glenvarloch with Margaret Ramsay, daughter and heiress of David Ramsay, our horologer, and a cadet only thrice removed from the ancient house of Dalwolsey. We are grieved we cannot have the presence of the noble Chief of that House at the ceremony; but where there is honour to be won abroad, the Lord Dalwolsey is seldom to be found at home. *Sic fuit, est, et erit.*— Jingling Geordie, as ye stand to the cost of the marriage-feast, we look for good cheer."

Heriot bowed, as in duty bound. In fact, the King, who was a great politician about trifles, had manoeuvred greatly on this occasion, and had contrived to get the Prince and Buckingham dispatched on an expedition to Newmarket, in order that he might find an opportunity in their absence of indulging himself in his own gossiping *coshering* habits, which were distasteful to Charles, whose temper inclined to formality, and with which even the favourite, of late, had not thought it

* Chaucer says, there is nothing new but what it has been old. The reader has here the original of an anecdote which has since been fathered on a Scottish Chief of our own time.

worth while to seem to sympathize. When the levee was dismissed, Sir Mungo Malagrowther seized upon the worthy citizen in the court-yard of the Palace, and detained him, in spite of all his efforts, for the purpose of subjecting him to the following scrutiny:—

"This is a sair job on you, Master George—the King must have had little consideration—this will cost you a bonnie penny, this wedding-dinner."

"It will not break me, Sir Mungo," answered Heriot; "the King hath a right to see the table which his bounty hath supplied for years well covered for a single day."

"Vara true—vara true—we'll have a' to pay, I doubt, less or mair—a sort of penny-wedding it will prove, where all maun contribute to the young folk's maintenance, that they may not have just four bare legs in a bed thegether. What do ye purpose to give, Master George?—we begin with the city when money is in question."

"Only a trifle, Sir Mungo—I give my god-daughter the marriage-ring; I bought it in Italy—it belonged to Cosmo de Medici. The bride will not need my help—she has an estate which belonged to her maternal grandfather."

"The auld soap-boiler," said Sir Mungo; "it will need some of his suds to scour the blot out of the Glenvarloch shield—I have heard that estate was no great things."

"It is as good as some posts at court, Sir Mungo, which are coveted by persons of high quality," replied George Heriot.

"Court favour, said ye? court favour, Master Heriot?" replied Sir Mungo, chusing then to use his malady of misapprehension; "Moon-shine in water, poor thing—if that is all she is to be tochered with—I am truly solicitous about them."

"I will let you into a secret which will relieve your tender anxiety. The dowager Lady Dalgarno gives a competent fortune to the bride, and settles the rest of her estate upon her nephew the bridegroom."

"Ay, say ye sae!" said Sir Mungo, "just to shew her regard to her husband that is in the tomb—lucky that her nephew did not send him there; it was a strange story that death of poor Lord Dalgarno—some folks think the poor gentleman had much wrong. Little good comes of marrying the daughter of the house you are at feud with; indeed, it was less poor Dalgarno's fault, than theirs that forced the match on him; but I am glad the young folks are to have something to live on, come how it like, whether by charity or inheritance. But if the Lady Dal-garno were to sell all she has, to her very wylie-coat—she canna gie them back the fair Castle of Glenvarloch—that is lost and gane—lost and gane."

"It is but too true," said George Heriot; "we cannot discover what

has become of the villain Andrew Skurliewhitter, or what Lord Dalgarno has done with the mortgage."

"Assigned it away to some one, that his wife might not get it after he
was gane—it would have disturbed him in his grave, to think Glenvarloch should get that land back again," said Sir Mungo; "depend on it,
he will have ta'en sure measures to keep that noble lordship out of her
grips or her nevoy's either."

"Indeed it is but too probable, Sir Mungo," said Master Heriot;
"but as I am obliged to go and look after many things in consequence
of this ceremony, I must leave you to comfort yourself with the reflection."

"The bride-day, you say, is to be on the thirtieth of the instant
month?" said Sir Mungo, holloing after the citizen; "I will be with you
in the hour of cause."

"The King invites the guests," said George Heriot, without turning
back.

"The base-born, ill-bred mechanic!" soliloquized Sir Mungo, "if it
were not the odd score of pounds he lent me last week, I would teach
him how to bear himself to a man of quality. But I will be at the bridal
banquet in spite of him."

Sir Mungo contrived to get invited, or commanded, to attend on
the bridal accordingly, at which there were but few persons present;
for James, on such occasions, preferred a snug privacy, which gave
him liberty to lay aside the incumbrance, as he felt it to be, of his
regal dignity. The company was therefore very small, and indeed
there were at least two persons absent whose presence might have
been expected. The first of these was the Lady Dalgarno, the state of
whose health, as well as the recent death of her husband, precluded
her attendance on the ceremony. The other absentee was Richie
Moniplies, whose conduct for some time past had been extremely
mysterious. Regulating his attendance on Lord Glenvarloch entirely
according to his own will and pleasure, he had, ever since the rencounter in Enfield Chace, appeared regularly at his bed-side in the
morning, to assist him to dress, and at his wardrobe in the evening.
The rest of the day he disposed of at his own pleasure, without
control from his lord, who had now a complete establishment of
attendants. Yet he was somewhat curious to know how the fellow
disposed of so much of his time; but on this subject Richie shewed
no desire to be communicative.

On the morning of the bridal-day, Richie was particularly attentive
in doing all a valet-de-chambre could, so as to set off to advantage the
very handsome figure of his master; and when he had arranged his
dress with the utmost exactness, and put to his long curled locks

what he called the finishing touch of "the redding kaim," he gravely kneeled down, kissed his hand, and bade him farewell, saying that he humbly craved leave to discharge himself of his lordship's service.

"Why, what humour is this?" said Lord Glenvarloch; "if you mean to discharge yourself of my service, Richie, I suppose you intend to enter my wife's?"

"I wish her good ladyship that shall soon be, and your good lordship, the blessing of as good a servant as myself, in heaven's good time," said Richie; "but fate hath so ordained it, that I can henceforth only be your servant in the way of friendly courtesy."

"Well, Richie," said the young lord, "if you are tired of service, we will seek some better provision for you—but you will wait on me to the church, and partake of the bridal dinner?"

"Under favour, my lord," answered Richie, "I must remind you of our covenants, having presently some pressing business of mine own, whilk will detain me during the ceremony; but I will not fail to prie Master George's good cheer, in respect he has made very costly fare, whilk it would be unthankful not to partake of."

"Do as you list," answered Lord Glenvarloch; and having bestowed a passing thought on the whimsical and pragmatical disposition of his follower, he dismissed the subject for others better suited to the day.

The reader must suppose the scattered flowers which strewed the path of the happy couple to church—the loud music which accompanied their procession—the marriage service performed by a Bishop —the King, who met them at Saint Paul's, giving away the bride,—to the great relief of her father, who had thus time, during the ceremony, to calculate the just quotient to be laid on the pinion of report in a time-piece which he was then putting together.

When the ceremony was finished, the company were transported in the royal carriages to George Heriot's, where a splendid collation was provided for the marriage-guests in the Foljambe apartments. The King no sooner found himself in this snug retreat, than, casting from him his sword and belt with such haste as if it burned his fingers, and flinging his plumed hat on the table, as who should say, Lie there, authority! he swallowed a hearty cup of wine to the happiness of the married couple, and began to amble about the room, mumping, laughing, and cracking jests, neither the wittiest nor the most delicate, but accompanied and applauded by shouts of his own mirth, in order to encourage that of the company. Whilst his Majesty was in the midst of this gay humour, and a call to the banquet was anxiously expected, a servant whispered Master Heriot forth of the apartment. When he re-entered, he walked up to the King, and, in his turn, whispered something, at which James started.

"He is not wanting his siller?" said the King, shortly and sharply.

"By no means, my liege—it is a subject he is quite indifferent upon, so long as it can pleasure your Majesty."

"Body of us, man!" said the King; "it is the speech of a true man and a loving subject, and we will grace him accordingly. Swith, man! have him—*pandite fores*. Moniplies?—they should have called the chield Monypennies—though I sall warrant you English think we have not such a name in Scotland."

"It is an ancient and honourable stock, the Monypennies," said Sir Mungo Malagrowther; "the only loss is, there are sae few of the name."

"The family seems to increase among your countrymen, Sir Mungo," said Master Lowestoffe, whom Lord Glenvarloch had invited to be present, "since his Majesty's happy accession brought so many of you here."

"Right, sir—right," said Sir Mungo, nodding and looking at George Heriot; "there have some of us been the better of that great blessing to the English nation."

As he spoke, the door flew open, and in entered, to the astonishment of Lord Glenvarloch, his late serving-man, Richie Moniplies, now sumptuously, nay gorgeously, attired in a superb brocaded suit, and leading in his hand the tall, thin, withered form of Martha Trapbois, arrayed in a complete dress of black velvet, which suited so strangely with the pallid and severe melancholy of her countenance, that the King himself exclaimed, in some perturbation, "What the de'il has the fallow brought us here? Body of us! it is a corpse that has run off with the mort-cloth!"

"May I sifflicate your Majesty to be gracious unto her?" said Richie, "being that she is, in respect of this morning's wark, my ain wedded wife, Mrs Martha Moniplies by name."

"Saul of our body, man! but she looks wondrous grim," answered King James. "Art thou sure she has not been in her time maid of honour to Queen Mary, our cousin, of red-hot memory?"

"I am sure, an it like your Majesty, that she has brought me fifty thousand pounds of gude siller, and better; and that has enabled me to pleasure your Majesty, and other folks."

"Ye need have said naething about that, man," said the King; "we ken our obligations in that sma' matter, and we are glad this rudas spouse of thine hath bestowed her treasure on ane wha kens to put it to the profit of his King and country. But whare the de'il did ye come by her, man?"

"In the auld Scottish fashion, my liege—she is the captive of my bow and my spear," answered Moniplies. "There was a convention that she should wed me when I avenged her father's death—so I slew, and took possession."

"It is the daughter of old Trapbois, who has been missed so long," said Lowestoffe.—"Where the devil could you mew her up so closely, Richie?"

"Master Richard, if it be your will," answered Richie; "or Master Richard Moniplies, if you like it better. For mewing of her up, I found her a shelter, in all honour and safety, under the roof of an honest countryman of my own—and for secrecy, it was a point of prudence, when wanters like you were abroad, Master Lowestoffe."

There was a laugh at Richie's magnanimous reply, on the part of every one but his bride, who made to him a signal of impatience, and said, with her usual brevity and sternness,—"Peace—Peace—I pray you, peace. Let us do that which we came for." So saying, she took out a bundle of parchments, and delivering them to Lord Glenvarloch, she said aloud,—"I take this royal presence, and all here to witness, that I restore the ransomed lordship of Glenvarloch to the right owner, as free as ever it was held by any of his ancestors."

"I witnessed the redemption of the mortgage," said Lowestoffe; "but I little dreamt by whom it had been redeemed."

"No need ye should," said Richie; "there would have been small wisdom in crying roast-meat."

"Peace," said his bride once more.—"This paper," she continued, delivering another to Lord Glenvarloch, "is also your property—take it—but spare me the question how it came into my custody."

The King had bustled forward beside Lord Glenvarloch, and fixing an eager eye on the writing, exclaimed—"Body of ourselves—it is our royal sign-manual for the money which was so long out of sight!—How came ye by it, Mistress Bride?"

"It is a secret," said Martha, drily.

"A secret which my tongue shall never utter," said Richie, resolutely, "unless the King commands me on my allegiance."

"I do—I do command you," said James, trembling and stammering with the impatient curiosity of a gossip; while Sir Mungo, with more malicious anxiety to get at the bottom of the mystery, stooped his long thin form forward like a bent fishing-rod, raised his thin grey locks from his ear, and curved his hand behind it to collect every vibration of the expected intelligence.—Martha in the meantime frowned most ominously on Richie, who went on undauntedly to inform the King, "that his deceased father-in-law, a good, careful man in the main, had a touch of worldly wisdom about him, that at times marred the uprightness of his walk—he liked to dabble amang his neighbour's gear, and some of it would at times stick to his fingers in the handling."

"For shame, man, for shame," said Martha; "since the infamy of the deed must be told, be it at least briefly.—Yes, my lord," she added, addressing Glenvarloch, "the piece of gold was not the sole bait which brought the miserable old man to your chamber that dreadful night—his object, and he accomplished it, was to purloin this paper—the wretched scrivener was with him that morning, and, I doubt not, urged the doting old man to this villainy, to prevent the ransom of your estate—if there was a yet more powerful agent at the bottom of the conspiracy, God forgive it to him at this moment, for he is now where the crime must be answered!"

"Amen!" said Lord Glenvarloch, and it was echoed by all present.

"For my father," continued she, with her stern features twitched by an involuntary and convulsive movement, "his guilt and folly cost him his life; for my belief is constant, that the wretch who counselled him that morning to purloin the paper, left open the window for the entrance of the murderers."

Every body was silent for an instant—the King was first to speak, commanding search instantly to be made for the guilty scrivener. "*I lictor*," he concluded, "*colliga manus—caput obnubito—infelici suspendite arbori*."

Lowestoffe answered with due respect, that the scrivener had absconded at the time of Lord Dalgarno's murder, and had not been heard of since.

"Let him be sought for," said the King. "And now let us change the discourse—these stories make one's very blood grew, and are altogether unfit for bridal festivity. Hymen—O Hymenee!" added he, snapping his fingers, "Lord Glenvarloch, what say you to Mistress Moniplies, this bonny bride, that has brought you back your father's estate on your bridal day?"

"Let him say nothing, my liege," said Martha, "it will best suit his feelings and mine."

"There is redemption-money, at the least, to be repaid," said Lord Glenvarloch; "in that I cannot remain debtor."

"We will speak of it hereafter," said Martha; "*my* debtor *you* cannot be." And she shut her mouth as if determined to say nothing more on the subject.

Sir Mungo, however, resolved not to part with the topic, and availing himself of the freedom of the moment, said to Richie—"A queer story that of your father-in-law, honest man—methinks your bride thanked you little for ripping it up."

"I make it a rule, Sir Mungo," replied Richie, "always to speak any evil I know about my family myself, having observed that if I do not, it is sure to be told by ither folks."

"But Richie," said Sir Mungo, "it seems to me that this bride of yours is like to be master and mair in the conjugal state."

"If she abides by words, Sir Mungo, I thank heaven I can be as deaf as any one; and if she come to dunts, I have a hand to paik her with."

"Weel said, Richie, again," said the King; "you have gotten it on baith haffits, Sir Mungo.—Troth, Mistress Bride, for a fule, your gudeman has a pretty turn of wit."

"There are fools, sire," replied she, "who have wit, and fools who have courage, and are great fools notwithstanding.—I chose this man because he was my protector when I was desolate, and neither for his wit nor his wisdom. He is truly honest, and has a heart and hand that make amends for some folly. Since I was condemned to seek a protector through the world, which is to me a wilderness, I may thank God that I have come by no worse."

"And that is sae sensibly said," replied the King, "that by my saul I'll try whether I canna make him better. Kneel down, Richie—somebody lend me a rapier—your's, Mr Langstaff; (that's a brave name for a lawyer,)—ye need not flash it out that gate, Templar fashion, as if ye were about to pink a bailiff!"

He took the drawn sword, and with averted eyes, for it was a sight he loved not to look on, endeavoured to lay it on Richie's shoulder, but nearly stuck it into his eye. Richie, starting back, attempted to rise, but was held down by Lowestoffe, while, Sir Mungo guiding the royal weapon, the honour-bestowing blow was given and received: "*Surge, carnifex*—Rise up, Sir Richard Moniplies, of Castle-Collop!—And, my lords and lieges, let us all to our dinner, for the cock-a-leekie is cooling."

THE END

ESSAY ON THE TEXT

1. THE GENESIS OF *THE FORTUNES OF NIGEL* 2. THE COM-
POSITION OF *THE FORTUNES OF NIGEL*: the Chronology; the
Manuscript; the Proofs 3. THE LATER EDITIONS: Second and
Third Editions; *Novels and Romances*; the Interleaved Set and the
Magnum 4. THE PRESENT TEXT: emendation of pre-proof changes;
treatment of author's-proof corrections; emendation of post-proof
changes.

The following conventions are used in transcriptions from Scott's
manuscript: deletions are enclosed ⟨thus⟩, deletions within deletions
⟨⟨thus⟩⟩, and insertions ↑thus↓; an insertion within an insertion is
indicated by double arrows ↑↑thus↓↓. Editorial comments within
quotations are designated by square brackets [thus]. The same conventions are used as appropriate for indicating variants between the printed
editions.

Full details of works referred to by authors or short titles in this essay
can be found at the head of the Explanatory Notes, 540–41.

1. THE GENESIS OF *THE FORTUNES OF NIGEL*

The idea for a novel with James VI and I as the principal historical
character may date to 1819, when the Englishman Abel Moysey dedicated to Scott his novel *Forman*, a tale (with a nominal hero, Hugh
Mondomer, on the pattern of Scott's Edward Waverley) about the
complicity of the notorious Lambeth physician/necromancer Simon
Forman (1552–1611) in the murder of Sir Thomas Overbury, a complicity revealed at the trial of the infamous Mrs Turner in 1615 (see
note to 102.14–19). As yet Scott had not publicly extended his range of
fiction to English history, though at the time he was writing *Ivanhoe*. He
graciously acknowledged Moysey's dedication, but he was candidly
critical of his representation of 'Jas. vi (your Jas. i)' as 'a drunken
driveller', because it undervalued the monarch's complex character and
missed its comic potential: 'I have sometimes thought his wit, his
shrewdness, his pedantry, his self-importance & vanity, his greed & his
prodigality, his love of minions & his pretensions to wisdom made him
one of the richest characters for comedy who ever existed in real
history.'[1] Only the year before, in fact, Scott had noted this potential in a
passing reference to 'the gentle King Jamie' when, in the fourth chapter
of *The Heart of Mid-Lothian*, he had pointed to Bartoline Saddletree's
greater fondness for 'talking of authority than really exercising it'.[2]

But as long ago as 1811 Scott had written the notes and introduction
for a two-volume collection of tracts, *Secret History of the Court of James*

the First, a by-product of his ongoing work on *Somers' Tracts*, of which Volumes 2 and 3, published in 1809 and 1810, were devoted to James's reign. Writing in January 1818 to Lady Louisa Stuart, Scott remarked that editing the tracts 'some years ago made me wonderfully well acquainted with the little traits which mark'd parties & characters in the 17th Century'.[3] Other projects at this time which would prove fruitful for *Nigel* centred on the drama of the period. Drawing upon old reading notes, he assisted his German protégé Henry Weber with an edition of Beaumont and Fletcher, published in 1812, while urging his brother Thomas to edit Shadwell.[4] Weber also benefited from the expertise Scott acquired in selecting and annotating eight volumes of British plays ancient and modern for the London publisher William Miller. They appeared anonymously in 1810–11.[5] The notes reveal an intimate knowledge of the culture of Jacobean theatre and often resonate with the representation of that culture in *Nigel*. Not for nothing, then, does the Eidolon of the Author of Waverley in the Introductory Epistle to Scott's novel refer to himself as a 'dramatic antiquary' (12.10). Lockhart recognised this taproot of the novel when he called it 'the best commentary on the old English drama', adding: 'hardly a single picturesque point of manners touched by Ben Jonson and his contemporaries but has been dovetailed into this story'.[6] Demonstrably, then, Scott's interest in the monarch and his times, if quickened by Moysey's novel, was of long standing; his knowledge of both was extensive.

In the early months of 1821 the possibility of a novel based on James I came up in correspondence with Isaac D'Israeli, author in 1816 of *An Inquiry into the Literary and Political Character of James the First*,[7] and with longtime literary acquaintance Mary Ann Hughes.[8] Neither knew that Scott was at work on a little volume of fiction originally entitled 'Extracts from Family Papers of a Nobleman', but now generally known as 'Private Letters of the Seventeenth Century',[9] which was bringing him closer, if not to the complex monarch himself, to his court. Although the prefatory 'Advertisement' to the letters is dated 20 March 1821, it was still under way in mid-June, when Scott invited J. B. S. Morritt, and proposed inviting Lady Louisa Stuart, to collaborate with him on 'our pirated letters'.[10] The incomplete set of letters was printed but not published, for reasons best described by Lockhart: 'When the printing had reached the 72d page . . . he was told candidly by [William] Erskine, by James Ballantyne, and also by myself, that, however clever his imitation of the epistolary style of the period in question, he was throwing away in these letters the materials of as good a romance as he had ever penned; and a few days afterwards he said to me . . . "You were all quite right: if the letters had passed for genuine they would have found favour only with a few musty antiquaries, and if the joke were detected, there was not story enough to carry it off. I shall burn the sheets, and give you Bonny King Jamie and all his tail in the old shape"'.[11]

Scott's first mention of *Nigel* is in a letter of 30 September [1821] to his publisher Archibald Constable. As was his wont when coming to the end of one novel (in this case *The Pirate* which was to be completed not later than 1 November, the date of its Advertisement[12]) Scott was beginning to project its sequel: 'The next will be a tale I think of the days of *Gentle King Jemmy* our Scottish Solomon—it is a pity that rare mixture of sense and nonsense pedantry and childishness wit and folly should remain uncelebrated.'[13] The unsatisfactory portrait of James 'attempted' in *Forman* 'but not with a strong hand' is explicitly cited as reason for turning to this period. The pseudo private letters are not mentioned. Though their role in the origins of *Nigel* has been disputed,[14] there can be no doubt that, like the earlier projects, they share period detail with the novel. However, the letters are different from the editorial projects in that they afforded Scott the opportunity to exercise his imagination in fashioning a period language for the denizens of James's realm, most especially of his court and capital city, that registers the sex and class of the speaker.

An alternative genesis was proposed in 1873 by Thomas Constable, Archibald's son, who, in a note referring to a letter of 13 November 1820 to his father from the publisher's partner Robert Cadell, suggests that Cadell's phrase 'the case of *Gowrie*' alludes to the 'embryo' of *Nigel*.[15] Cadell is, it seems, arguing against James Ballantyne's being allowed credit against printing a future novel, here called 'Gowrie', while *Kenilworth* is still in progress. His letter suggests that *Nigel* was germinating in Scott's mind, and that the Gowrie conspiracy was in some way central to its conception in late 1820. Certainly, of the several historical as opposed to 'constitutional' explanations for James's timidity,[16] the Gowrie episode has pride of place in the novel itself. The character Lord Huntinglen is based on John Ramsay, the man who came to the monarch's rescue, for which act of valour he was granted an annual boon. Huntinglen's similar privilege commemorates that time 'when you unclasped the fause traitor Ruthven's fangs from about our royal throat, and drove your dirk into him like a true subject' (113.12–14). An account of the episode, published by James's authority, was edited by Scott in *Somers' Tracts*. It is a story in two parts—or rather two locations: the buck-hunt at Falkland Palace and the attack in the tower, or turret room, of Gowrie House, the town house of the Ruthvens in Perth.[17] In the manuscript, shortly after introducing this explanation for Huntinglen's favour with the king, Scott began to miswrite the name as 'Huntingtower', bringing together in a single name the two sites of the story, and he continued to do so throughout the remainder of the chapter, failing to correct himself. Furthermore, Huntingtower is an alternative name for Ruthven Castle, 5 kilometres west of Perth, where James was captured during the Ruthven Raid (for the Gowrie Conspiracy and the Ruthven Raid see Historical Note,

524–25). *Nigel* is not a story of the Gowrie Conspiracy, but this weird affair has some claim to be the embryo of the novel.

2. THE COMPOSITION OF *THE FORTUNES OF NIGEL*

The Chronology. According to Lockhart it was 'about the middle of October' 1821 that Scott abandoned the *Private Letters* and began to compose *Nigel*: 'I well remember the morning that he began The Fortunes of Nigel. The day being destined for Newark Hill, I went over to Abbotsford before breakfast, and found Mr Terry . . . walking about with his friend's master-mason . . . . While Terry and I were chatting, Scott came out, bare-headed, with a bunch of MS. in his hand, and said, "Well, lads, I've laid the keel of a new lugger this morning—here it is— be off to the water-side, and let me hear how you like it" '.[18] By 26 December, Scott was informing Robert Cadell that the novel would be 'out of my hands by end of february', the first volume 'being finishd', and requesting two books—William Derham's *The Artificial Clock-Maker* and James Peller Malcolm's *Londinium Redivivum*—to assist him with detail. Scott's cautious enthusiasm is noteworthy: he thinks *Nigel* is 'better' than *The Pirate*, but he is 'perhaps no good judge'.[19] When returning proofs to James Ballantyne on 21 December he had insisted on more care by the transcribers: 'It will be particularly necessary in Nigel that the transcribers do not attempt to substitute their sense for what they may think my nonsense—a word that is absolute nonsense cannot escape both you & me but imperfect & flat sense sometimes may—I have observed more than once that my emendations in such cases have escaped attention altogether. There are two in this sheet where *hat* is put for *bat* & *bull* for *ball* pray lecture them tightly on this score',[20] and on 12 January 1822 he returned two further sheets to the printers, noting 'a considerable transposition' at one point and directing that 'a revise may be sent me unless the printers make it out accurately'.[21] Cadell reported on 14 January that he was unable to turn up the Derham,[22] but on 28 January he noted that the new novel was 'nearly half done'[23] and on 22 February that it was 'getting on fast, it will be out towards the end of next month'.[24] Meanwhile the ailing Archibald Constable was being helpful by sharing with Scott his extensive fund of pertinent 'bibliographical and antiquarian information', some of it to be found in his personal library.[25]

By 23 March Scott was reassuring Constable and Ballantyne, if not himself, that he was well along in the third volume. To the former he wrote that he was 'nearly finishd—i.e. within half a volume but your 12000 are heavy at press'.[26] The same day he wrote Ballantyne to say that he had 'more than one fourth of the volume done indeed towards 1/3d. but I do not send it because I forget names & petty incidents when I have nothing to refer to. . . . Nigel must be out as early in May as possible.'[27] But he did send it around the 25th, writing to Ballantyne:

'You have already received two parcels of Niggle. I send a third which willmake more than a 4th of Vol. III so you may push on without fear of stop. But I must not write longer as I have to make King Jamie step forth on the scene once more.'[28] Though Scott kept his correspondence short in order to get on with completing the novel, he experienced delays, for which he blamed the Court of Session.[29] The projected publication date was no longer late March or even early April, but early May. In fact, the delay was caused in large part by Scott's work on the introduction—published as the 'Introductory Epistle'—which had, for whateverreason, become increasingly important to him. Cadell referred to 'large alterations' in the Introductory Epistle when, on 28 April, he reported to Constable that Volume 3 is said to be 'excellent'.[30] Two days later Scott wrote James Ballantyne that 'after all I must see the 2d Revise of Introduction—it should be as well considerd as possible'.[31] Scott had persevered, it would seem, in the effort to take care with his text. In the event, he finished the introduction before the third volume, though not before an American firm had begun to print the novel.[32] If competition between front and back end of the novel slowed the pace of completion, it is also the case that Volume 3, containing 'as much matter as make [sic] several Novels', had proved difficult to close.[33] But on 5 May it was 'all but done', and by 8 May it was finished.[34] The printed volume was sent off by Cadell to Constable on 15 May.[35] Constable expressed his admiration for it in a letter of 23 May 1822 to Cadell;[36] he was less im-pressed with the Introductory Epistle, which he judged to be in ques-tionable taste,[37] yet before the year was out he was invoking it to argue for the importance of publishers' 'sagacity or good management' to authors' success in the marketplace.[38]

The Fortunes of Nigel was advertised to appear in both Edinburgh and London on Wednesday 29 May, and this is the received publication date.[39] But in a letter to Constable of 24 May Cadell envisaged a 28 May date for Edinburgh publication[40] and, at least in theory, the actual date for London publication could have been 27 May—the copies, shipped on Tuesday the 21st,[41] having arrived, been unloaded, bound in boards, and dispatched to booksellers by 10.30 on Monday the 27th: 'The Ocean [the ship] by which the book was shipped arrived in the Thames on Sunday—the bales were got out on Monday Morning at one o'clock and by half past ten they were all despatched from 90 Cheapside [Hurst, Robinson's address]'.[42] It appears from Scott's letter to Constable of 23 March quoted above that 12,000 copies were printed. Scott would seem to be referring to the printing of *Nigel*, since *The Pirate* had been published in December. Of this print-run of 12,000, 7500 copies were shipped to London, with more to follow;[43] Hurst, Robinson ultimately received 8500 (4000 + 4500) of these.[44] The price was 31s. 6d.[45] Reception was positive. On 30 May Cadell reported to Constable from Edinburgh that this latest Waverley 'Gives universal satisfaction and moves off fast';[46] four days later he noted that it had appeared to 'unmixed applause from all and sundry'.[47] Writing to Cadell on 29 May Constable had accurately predicted a similar reaction in London: 'The Fortunes of Nigel arrived in good time as you will have heard, I sent Joseph Fell to 90 Cheapside to witness the activity with which Books are dispatched in London—the number circulated was I learn quite to the extent expected, there is no fear of its success'.[48] On 30 May Constable went himself to London 'on purpose to see Robinson and to learn the progress of the sale of the Fortunes of Nigel more than Seven thousand are gone and Longman & Co have not got half their usual number of the Book'.[49] The next day he described for Scott the reception by Londoners, in terms calculated to gratify even the most modest of authors: 'I was in town yesterday and so keenly were the people devouring my friend Jingling Geordie that I actually saw them reading it in the Streets as they passed along. I assure you there is no exaggeration in this—A new novel from the Author of Waverley puts aside in other words puts down for the time every other literary performance'.[50]

During the spring Cadell had been busy negotiating with the booksellers, especially Hurst, Robinson, who were proving difficult.[51] More so even than Constable, Robinson wanted the Author of Waverley to slacken the speed of composition, if not stop altogether for the near future. As early as 28 January 1822, he had written: 'Nothing is so clear as that the author of Waverley should stand for a year or two but this I fancy cant be attempted *without great danger* however it is a Fact that the *1st Vol* is actually printed of the new novel at all events James B. asserts this to be the case':[52] thus replying to Constable, who had himself recently written to Cadell that it would be 'a matter of immense importance if the author of Waverley would not publish another novel or even be understood to be writing one for a year to come or even two'.[53] The previous November, Robinson had been told that 'the foundation is laid for another new work from the great author'.[54] To his consternation, it proved only too true. But Constable's reservations were likely to be qualified, as when the next year he was writing to Cadell about the delay of *Saint Ronan's Well*: 'I need not say to you how long and how anxiously it has been my wish—that the Great Unknown Should not come before the public quite so rapidly—there is however little harm done yet.'[55] The difference between the two men turned on the perception of degree of danger, measure of harm. Scott had bolted before and might, if thwarted, just do so again, as Cadell had reminded Constable in the summer of 1821 'when Longman and Co got Guy Mannering and the Monastery & the Abbot and Blackwood the first Tales'.[56] Robinson had glossed 'without great danger' in just this way: 'I meant that the Author might be induced to offer some new work to Murray or Longman were he in any degree requested to hold his hand.'[57] A somewhat comical version of this theme surfaces in an exchange of Scott,

Ballantyne, Cadell, and Constable, in the summer of 1823. Scott's quoting 'The mouse who only trusts to one poor hole, / Can never be a mouse of any soul' (from Pope's translation of the Wife of Bath's Prologue) required Cadell to reassure Constable: 'In case you should think Sir Walters mouse rhyme alludes to changing his hole— rely on it there is no fear of that.'[58]

In part Constable's lesser anxiety on this score had to do with the multiplied visions for repackaging both the Author of Waverley and Walter Scott that, free from responsibility for the daily operation of the firm, he 'engineered' with ever greater enthusiasm—'all these projects of mine':[59] gatherings of the novels in uniform sets of different types and styles to match pocketbooks of different sizes, a collection of poetry from the novels,[60] and a British novelist's library selected and introduced by Scott,[61] to name but three of many. It was against the background of such pressures to protract the composition of the novels and, in Cadell's words, 'diversify the scene' by those who had formerly encouraged him to proceed at full speed, relishing his unrivalled capacity for 'systematic labour'[62] and sure instinct for the novel market, that Scott drafted, elaborated, and twice revised the ironic self-critique that forms the Introductory Epistle, where he not only recognised, to Constable's satisfaction, the importance of publishers to authors but also engaged with and disposed of these same publishers' argument that prolixity tarnishes fame and depresses sales, using the self-interested, not to say selfish, Captain Clutterbuck as their stand-in. Even as he wrote the Epistle and struggled to conclude the third volume, Scott had conceived and settled on the title of *Peveril of the Peak*, that 'brother' novel.[63] On 11 May, Cadell wrote to Constable: 'I think next week will close another new Book the Great is to be in—and I see the Wind setting in that way—the Keel is laid down of the follower of Nigel.'[64] By the 15th he could indeed announce that he had closed with Scott for *Peveril*.[65]

On 6 April, in a letter to Constable, Cadell had mentioned with great but furtive pleasure a deal with Black, Young & Young for a German translation of *Nigel* and the prospect of more such deals to come; not even Scott, let alone Robinson, was to know of this coup.[66] Arrangements with booksellers in the provincial cities of the British Isles (for example Glasgow, Carlisle, Newcastle, York, Manchester, Liverpool, and Dublin) had been secured, in some instances not without considerable hard-selling by Cadell.[67] A case in point is that of the Dublin merchant Milliken, to whom Cadell wrote on 22 April: 'As you appear to be credulous about the Fortunes of Nigel, at any rate we think so as there is no order from you for the book—it is right to put you on your guard by stating that *it is nearly done*—& we think will be ready in little more than a fortnight or thereby after this warning do not blame us for any disappointment.'[68] A total of 400 copies went to Dublin.[69]

In the event the high expectations of Constables for the sale of *Nigel*

proved unjustified. It seems that the demand had dropped sharply not
long after publication. Cadell professed to be baffled by this state of
affairs, given that *Nigel* 'is one of the best of the Authors works'.[70] Scott
was no less puzzled than Cadell, but, perhaps because of the special care
he had taken with the novel and the special affection he had for it, he
saw it as temporary, telling James Ballantyne that, unlike *Peveril*, 'Nigel
deserves a better reception from the public & like the Antiquary will one
day get it'.[71] But the day when Scott's prophecy would be fulfilled, if
ever, was not to be soon. Lists of remaindered books in this shop or that
typically show the figures suddenly to balloon with *Nigel*, which would
seem to represent some sort of divide in sales of the Waverley Novels, at
least in their original editions.[72]

The Manuscript. The manuscript of *Nigel* runs to 230 folio leaves.
The bulk of it—the first 217 leaves and leaf 223—is in the Hugh
Walpole Collection at The King's School, Canterbury. Leaf 218 is the
property of the Bibliotheca Bodmeriana of the Fondation Martin Bodmer, Cologny-Geneva, Switzerland. Leaves 219–22 and 224 are missing altogether. The final six leaves (225–30) belong to the National
Library of Scotland, where they are among the Blackwood papers.[73]

The manuscript appears at first glance to be a very orderly affair—leaf
after leaf of neatly written text on the rectos to the right, revisions on the
versos to the left. Even when changing pens Scott rarely missed a beat.
With few exceptions he wrote from top edge to bottom (with the catchword in the bottom right corner), and to the extreme right margin,
crowding or hyphenating words if need be rather than waste paper. A
typical leaf will have over 800 words. But a close look at almost any leaf
of folio reveals considerable revision—mostly, to judge from the inks
and pens, either at the time of writing, just after, or before resuming. Immediate revisions appear as overwrites or cancellations that enabled
Scott to re-phrase or restructure in mid-sentence. Small insertions are
commonly made directly above—or, in rare cases, below—the line of
text; slightly more extensive changes are typically made in the left margin or on the verso (or both) and often signalled by a caret; major
revisions running from longer phrases to single or multiple sentences
are made on the verso. These longer marginal and verso insertions are
sometimes written at a right angle to the normal horizontal. Occasionally
verso insertions are keyed to identical marginal insertions by number.
From time to time batches of the manuscript were gathered for transport
to the printers. Some of these packets can be readily identified from the
heavy creases and relatively dirty paper of the versos of pages that, when
folded, formed their outsides. The intervals of the packets are irregular,
having something to do perhaps with the progress of the writing and,
even more, with the ability of the printers to keep pace with Scott.

One might expect the need to choose a motto for each chapter, a habit

Scott had initiated with *Waverley*, to have impeded the flow of composition. But such was certainly not the case in *Nigel*. More often than not Scott proceeded from new chapter heading to motto to narrative, a process made all the easier by his practice—admitted to Constable (and indirectly to his readers) while composing *Nigel* (see note 60)—of not taking time out to hunt for a suitable motto. If his memory did not instantly produce something suitable he was likely simply to create one appropriate to the scene, featured character, or episode to follow. The majority of mottoes in *Nigel* (19) were produced *currente calamo*. When Scott departed from this norm, he introduced the motto later on the verso (on 14 occasions). Twice, for Chapters 5 and 8 of the second volume, he replaced the original recto motto with another on the verso; subsequently he used the original motto for Chapter 5 in Chapter 7 and that for Chapter 8 in Chapter 9 rather than waste them. And twice, for the seventh and ninth chapters of the third volume, Scott allowed chapters to leave his hands without mottoes. The copyist George Huntly Gordon provided a motto from Shakespeare for the first of these, which Scott rejected in favour of one of his own devising from 'Old Play'.[74] (Perhaps the Shakespeare motto for Chapter 9 was also supplied by Gordon and let stand.) For Chapter 12 the manuscript is missing; for Chapter 13, a caret on the recto indicates a verso motto but the verso is missing. Four of the last five mottoes are from Shakespeare, suggesting that as Scott strove to tie up the loose ends of *Nigel* the master playwright was forefront in his mind. Jonson is credited with two mottoes, though one is bogus; Spenser, Butler, Shenstone, and Gray are each legitimately credited with one. Of the 37 chapters, 27 have mottoes by Scott or are untraceable, at least, to the titles assigned them. Support for Scott's confidence to Constable that, in the heat of composition, he could not be bothered to stop for a motto may be observed in the pattern of the second volume alone, where the mottoes for ten of the thirteen chapters (including two later replaced) can be found on the rectos and all thirteen would appear to be by Scott himself.[75]

The only other blanks or lacunae in the manuscript that Scott allowed to stand for later attention—his own or an intermediary's—are, with rare exceptions, for names that he could not recall, especially when taking up characters who had been off-stage for some length of time. In particular, the long interpolated narrative of the Lady Hermione's tragic life seems to have driven the names of incidental and prominent characters alike from his mind, a problem sufficiently vexing to delay Scott in getting manuscript to Ballantyne (see 410 above). Occasionally, it was the name of a place or of an office that he lacked. Occasionally, too, it was a Latin phrase or specific citation for a quotation for which he could not stop.

To this pattern of virtually uninterrupted flow there are three exceptions. In Volume 3, Scott changed his mind about closing Chapter 3 in which Nigel is arrested at Greenwich and delivered to the Tower of London, deciding to recount in greater detail the hero's arrival at this most dreaded of prisons—an opportunity for indulging both his own and his readers' gothic tastes not to be passed up even though the third volume already threatened to run overlong. Nigel's fortunes had reached their nadir, and Scott was inspired to strengthen the impression of impending doom that awaited him. Similarly, but before actually starting a new chapter, Scott altered the ending of the fourth chapter of Volume 2 to strengthen the emotional implications of Nigel's exchange with the court party in St James's Park. The third exception, and the most substantial, comes much earlier in the manuscript, in the passage corresponding to 64.8–65.18 in the present text. Scott had originally written a paragraph to prepare for George Heriot making his journey from the City to Westminster without stopping at Temple Gate to have a scrivener make a fresh copy of Nigel's badly crumpled supplication to the king—something he had stated his intention of doing in the preceding interview with Nigel and Richie (Chapter 4):

> It was long passd the period when the space betwixt Westminster and the walls of London was cultivated country & when the Judges in their procession to hold the courts at Westminster hall used to breakfast at "the pleasant valley of Charing" a spot which now exhibits the full tide of population but was then only a rustic hamlet distinct both from London and Westminster.

On first thought, the omission seems minor: readers might be expected to take for granted that this scrupulous, meticulous businessman would act on his words. But on second thought, Scott would have a lot to lose: he would be passing up the chance to introduce a character—the scrivener—whose role in the novel would prove to be instrumental to the plot and not merely ornamental. That Scott would choose to revise is not surprising: not to do so now would cause serious trouble down the road. But in revising Scott did more than introduce the scene with the scrivener—about 60 per cent of the new material. He picked up the reference to Temple Bar (64.5) in the last sentence before the paragraph intended to prepare for the continuation of Heriot's journey, which he decided to cancel. He elaborated on the difference between the open railing or palisade that he imagined (wrongly: see note to 64.34–37) was Temple Bar in Heriot's day and the arched gateway that the name would bring before his readers' eyes. He also took the opportunity to insert a matching account of the changes in the Strand between the seventeenth and nineteenth centuries. These protracted descriptions would resemble a mini-essay, a bonus for the reader. This additional new material accounts for the rest—about 40 per cent—of the total revision.

So numerous are the revisions in the manuscript of *Nigel* that an accurate count is, to say the least, problematic. The kinds of revisions, however, can be summarised and illustrated. Probably the largest category of change results from a false start—a mis-spelling, a wrong word ('vane' for 'vein': 353.22), an unidiomatic preposition, an omitted article, a slip Freudian ('lover' for 'lodger': 42.4) or grammatical, and so forth. Another category of change may be attributed to the desire to substitute a noun or noun phrase for a pronoun or to replace a possessive pronoun with 'the'. Somewhat like the false start is the change to avoid tautology, Scott foreseeing that he will need the word he has just written, or begun to write, later in the sentence—or, similarly, to rescue a sentence, recognising that to continue on the present syntactic course will be disastrous. At one point, for example, he writes the word 'letters' only to realise that he will need it later; at the point 'later' he sees he will need it later still. He thus cancels the first 'letters' for 'packet' and the second 'letter' for 'billet' (9.23–25). Another time, Scott substitutes 'frankness' for 'freedom' so he can finish the sentence with 'the frankness of a free and loyal Scotsman' (56.8–9). Or consider this example from the first page of the first chapter: 'The ⟨peaceab⟩ temper of the King peaceable even to timidity ⟨was⟩ inclined him . . .' (19.31). And here are two examples of syntax altered in the progress of being formed: 'and began in a ⟨tone of voice as low and ⟨⟨comfor⟩⟩ soothing⟩ low soothing and confidential tone of voice' (98.5–6); 'Weel my Lord we questiond this maiden in male attire ourselves and I profess it was a very pretty interrogatory ⟨and finally we did indeed put her to the very question and did find that though⟩ ↑and well followed. For though at first professd that ↓ she assumed this disguise . . .' (369.22–25).

The more interesting incidental changes in diction and syntax reflect Scott's desire to use a more precise word, to sharpen or abandon an analogy, to enhance a prose rhythm (if only by transposing two words), or to maximise attractive sound patterns and minimise unattractive ones. There follow some examples. For diction: 'the ⟨praise⟩ unwilling tribute which Jonson paid to Churchill' (15.39–40); 'a book at his girdle and a ⟨ponio⟩ broad ⟨knif⟩ dudgeon dagger on the other side' (27.20–21); 'His dress was of green velvet quilted so full as to be ⟨proof against the stab of a⟩ dagger proof' (66.29–30); 'so much was she supposed to know of life and of its ⟨shifts that⟩ labyrinths that . . .' (93.40–41); 'with such symptoms of embarrassment as induced Ned Kilderkin to stretch his ⟨inquiries⟩ taciturnity so far as not only to ask . . .' (300.10–11). For analogy: 'an indifferent work is sometimes ⟨floated⟩ ↑towed on↓ by those which have left harbour before it' (5.43–6.1); 'Even in London the golden shower which fell around him did not ⟨wet⟩ ↑moisten↓ the blighted fortunes of Sir Mungo Malagrowther' (77.30–31); 'He stood before the King ⟨with all⟩ ↑as if suddenly converted into ⟨stone⟩ an ancient statue of the times of chivalry . . . ↓' (359.6–9); 'for though as much afraid of cold steel as a ⟨dun⟩ ↑debtor↓ of a ⟨drum⟩ ↑dun↓' (380.1). For rhythm: 'an extraordinary labyrinth of narrow dark damp and unwholesome streets and allies in one corner or other of which the plague was as surely found lurking ⟨as at⟩ ↑ as surely as in the obscure corners of↓ Constantinople in our own time' (39.31–34); and 'We will spare your knowlege at present Captain and ↑save↓ your modesty at the same time' (145.29–30). And for sound: 'beechen bickers and treen ⟨platte⟩ trenchers' (72.3).

By far the most thoroughgoing revision is prompted by the perceived need to develop character, strengthen dialogue, adjust plot, flesh out narrative, and augment description. Characteristic is Scott's sense that he needs to round off a character sketch, conclude a conversation, or end an episode with another sentence or so in order to bring a feeling of closure or to form a bridge to the next movement of the story. A good example allows King James to polish off a folksy reminiscence of the old days in Edinburgh with a Latin summing up: ' ↑ *cantabit vacuus*—we had little to care for ↓ ' (72.21). Scott rarely misses an opportunity to expose the 'antithetical mix', or so Byron might have called it, that was this monarch's nature. But characteristic, as well, is his sense while introducing a character that he needs to supply more exemplary detail. Hence the verso insertion that precedes George Heriot's first speech in the novel: ' ↑ He used the Scottish idiom in his first address but ⟨this⟩ in such a manner that it could hardly be distinguishd whether he was ⟨drolling⟩ ↑↑passing↓↓ upon his freind a sort of jocose mockery or whether it was his ↑↑own↓↓ native dialect for his ordinary discourse had little provincialism ↓ ' (30.1–5). Perhaps the best example concerns the King himself, for it goes to the raison d'être of the novel as Scott explained it to himself and others—the oxymoronic character of the monarch and Moysey's failure to communicate it. Scott's plan was to top off his sketch by quoting the memoirist Sully's remark that James I was the 'wisest fool in Christendom' (see note to 67.23–24). Accordingly he interpolated these sentences, in the haste of rhetorical flourish miswriting the Frenchman's name:

> ↑ ↑↑He was laborious in trifles and a trifler where serious labour
> was requird devout in his sentiments and yet too often profane in
> his language—↓↓ ⟨He was⟩ just and beneficent by nature
> ↑↑the↓↓ yet gave way to the iniquities & oppression of others.
> He was penurious respecting money which he had to give from his
> own hand yet inconsiderately & unboundedly profuse of that which
> he did not see. In a word those good qualities which displayd
> themselves in particular cases & occasions were not of a quality
> sufficiently firm and comprehensive to regulate his general con-
> duct and shewing themselves as they occasionally did only entitled
> ⟨him⟩ James to the Character bestowd on him by Southey—that He
> was the Wisest Fool in Christendom ↓ (67.13–24)

Time and time again, Scott decides he needs to loosen or stretch dialogue, if the speakers are to talk like real people. A friendly disagreement about the behaviour of poets between the two London apprentices supplies an early example: '"You are an owl once again" said Vincent— "⟨he will only dine⟩ ↑ if he has nothing left to buy cheese and radishes he will only dine a day ↓ the sooner"' (27.6–7). It is not uncommon, either, to see Scott in mid-flight, as it were, hitting upon an effective tag expression and running with it to give the speaker's rhetoric greater vitality— for example, Richie's 'as I am a true man', which comes in as part of a verso insertion (163.10). Word for word, Richie Moniplies is the character who probably benefits most from Scott's revisionary largesse. If there is a longer or more pedantic way of saying something, the garrulous Scot is sure to take it, and like his master Nigel, the author indulges him as, indeed, he indulges King Jamie, who shares Richie's predilection for pedantic verbosity. In addition, Scott revises to help readers hear the sounds and stresses of the speakers' words. Trapbois's eternal 'for a consideration' becomes 'for a con–si–de–ra–ti–ón' (243.36–37), and Jin Vin's bitter reference to the Chevalier Beaujeu's ordinary is rendered, in revision, as 'Shavaleer Bojo's' (238.2). Revision does much to highlight the linguistic variety as well as to intensify the rhetorical vigour of this novel conceived with a particularly rich cast of effective talkers.

Slight adjustments to the plot produce some of the most conspicuous changes. George Heriot cannot, in fact, leave Court just yet, his business with the King being unfinished (356.11–14). The clergyman departing Heriot's dinner in company with the two tradesmen needs to stay behind, come to think of it, to conduct family prayers: '. . . something was wrong; ⟨the clergyman followd him though not till he had consulted the eye of his landlord to know whether he desired his stay⟩' (84.4–5). For whatever reason, Scott initially omitted the bailiff's interrogation of principal witness Martha Trapbois on the circumstances of her father's murder; his technical knowledge of how such examinations are conducted enabled Scott to remedy the oversight forthwith (276.29–42). As for fleshing out the narrative, the interpolated story of the Lady Hermione may be the single largest source of such revisions. Typical is the long insert in which Scott helps readers to understand how her naïvety led to the social indiscretion that left her a recluse at the time of the story:

> But the shelter of her name and roof afforded us the means of frequently meeting and the love of my husband seemd as sincere and as unbounded as my own ↑ He was eager he said to gratify his pride by introducing me to one or two his noble English friends— This could not be done at Lady D——s but by his command which he was now entitled to consider as my law I contrived twice to visit him at his own hotel accompanied only by Monna Paula. There was a very small party of two ladies and two gentlemen There was music mirth and dancing I had heard of the frankness of the English nation but I could not help thinking it borderd on license

during these entertainments and the collation which followd But I
set this down to my inexperience & could not doubt the propriety
of what was approved by my husband ↓ (221.7–21)

Augmented description clarifies what might otherwise be obscure, as in
the case of Davy Ramsay's lack of physical appeal to women: 'Ramsay
was nothing of a bad man but ↑ he was so constantly grimed with smoke
gilded with brass filings & smeard with lamp-black & oil that Dame
Simmons judged ↓ it would require his whole shop-full of watches to
induce any feasible woman ⟨t⟩ to touch the said neighbour Ramsay with
any thing save a pair of tongs' (25.8–13). Similarly with a potential
historical obscurity: Scott could not expect his readers to be familiar
with a 17th-century waterman's dress, and so he revised his original
sentence thus: 'A young man ⟨in the⟩ dress ⟨of⟩ ↑ dressd in a green
plush jerkin with a badge on the sleeve and having the appearance of ↓ a
waterman' (278.28–29). The new version also allows for the possibility, important to Scott's plot, that not all men dressed as watermen are,
in fact, watermen. Much revision serves the purpose of filling in
gaps of information that the average reader needs for comprehension
and, better still, ease of reading—who is speaking, where, when. Somewhat curious but altogether appropriate in a novel so resonant with
clocks and the sounds of clocks, most especially that of St Dunstan's, is
the number of insertions to indicate time when or time of—for instance
'the King . . . again returnd to his council chamber ↑ though the hour
was unusually late ↓' (367.12–14). King James's strategy of justifying
the commoner Margaret Ramsay's marriage to Lord Glenvarloch by
concocting an aristocratic genealogy for her and then signifying it by
creating a new coat of arms turning on the contrast between time and
eternity, in fact, inspired one of Scott's most fanciful, albeit botched,
manuscript revisions. He had tried to indicate the relative difficulty in
coming up with heraldic emblems of Time and Eternity by revising
thus: 'we propose to add [to the coat-of arms] ⟨T⟩ Chronos that is Time
and Eternity for supporters [of the wheel representing Davy's craft] so
soon as the Garter King at arms shall be able to devise how Eternity is to
be presented—'. But neither the Garter King at Arms nor Scott, it
seems, could produce the figure for Eternity, and so in proof he dropped
the one emblem he could imagine (398.38–42).

Finally, the prodigality of Scott's imagination in this novel is exempli-
fied by his supplementing a catalogue intended to be illustrative of some
general idea or situation, doubling or tripling its size as other instances
leap to mind. The denizens of Whitefriars multiply even as Scott proceeds to enumerate them: 'brankrupt citizens ruind gamesters, irreclaimable prodigals ↑ desperate duellists bravoes & homicides ↓ and
debauched profligates of every description' (181.38–40). Similarly the
names for the species of wit that thrives in the City and luxuriates in the
nimble mind and on the tongue of the London apprentice Jin Vin:

'⟨biting⟩ ↑cross-biting, giving the dor ↓ bambouzling, cramming hoaxing humbugging and quizzing' (202.5–6).

The Proofs. The National Library of Scotland possesses one full albeit mixed set of proofs for the novel proper.[76] For the Introductory Epistle there are three extant sets of proofs.[77] The first set is the so-called author's-proof, the one corrected by Ballantyne and sent to Scott for his corrections. The second set or 'revise' (the author-corrected proof returned to Scott) testifies to Scott's strong views, *pace* Adam Smith, on the value of literary production in general and his own work in particular to the economic welfare of Britain: he proceeded to expand by a third the manuscript version of the letter, the principal additions being: 8.20–29, 10.3–16, 12.32–40, 13.27–14.4, 14.17–14.42, 15.9–13, 15.16–22, 15.26–16.9, 16.16–36, and 16.41–17.9. No wonder he requested a second revise from Ballantyne: such 'large alterations', as Cadell referred to them, more than justified the request for a third proof-set or second revise (itself to be, in turn, amplified and corrected but not so extensively as the first, the principal additions being: 14.4–17, 14.42–15.9, 15.13–16, and 15.22–25). In the letter to Ballantyne of 12 January 1822, cited at 410 above, Scott had offered to read a revise if a transposed passage proved troublesome to the printers. His behaviour with the proofs of the Introductory Epistle, thus, was not unique to this late stage of composition. Two sets of proofs for pages 239–40 of Volume 1 (EEWN 110.42–111.27, 111.40–43) witness to Scott's concern that the Latin dialogue of King James and Nigel pass scrutiny, even though, in a note, he would assure readers that this talk was too trivial to merit translation. That Scott may have had help in writing this dialogue is suggested by an unaddressed request among the Abbotsford papers that begins with the words 'Make for me half a dozen tight latin ⟨qu⟩ sentences supposd to pass between K. Jamie & Nigel a student from Leyden—' and continues with a sketch of the subject these sentences are to traverse: 'The King asks after the ⟨Heresiarch Vor⟩ state of Letters there—after the heresiarch Vorstius (against whom he wrote a book) Nigel replies he lives but cannot be said to flourish since he has been prostrated by the thunders of his Majestys eloquence &c'.[78] As well, we have two sets of proofs for pages 81–82 of Volume 2 (EEWN 172.7–42), part of a conversation between Nigel and Sir Mungo Malagrowther not problematic in any obvious way.

The proof-sheets of *Nigel* acquire a special interest from the Introductory Epistle, where the Eidolon of the Author of Waverley is 'employed in reading a blotted *revise*' (4.42) when Captain Clutterbuck first enters into his presence. While reading proof, Scott added two references to this same revise, once by having the Eidolon indicate 'the proof-sheet with his finger' (5.38–39) and once by having Clutterbuck look 'in my turn towards the proof-sheet' (6.26–27). As he warmed to the subject of the epistle, Scott must have decided to make the proof-sheet, especially the revise, not only the frame of the scene but also its visual centre, for the interview that begins with a proof-sheet and continues to call attention to it is abruptly ended by the arrival of 'a little sooty-faced Apollyon from the Canongate [come] to demand the proof-sheet on the part of' the printer (17.14–15), and the epistle comes quickly to a close. Such self-reflexive 'play' is nothing new in Scott's meta-narratives, of course, but he rarely, if ever, used it to greater advantage.

The proofs are otherwise interesting for some of the memorable exchanges between Scott and James Ballantyne that, in the Waverley story, have come to characterise their working relationship. The printer was linguistically and stylistically the more conservative of the two men, not to mention the more literal-minded. Ballantyne, in fact, bears no little responsibility for the deadening of Scott's prose, even although Scott did not always follow the printer's suggestions. To Ballantyne's outburst objecting to the word 'talented'—'this detestable American fungus!'—Scott responded mildly that he thought it a good word before substituting 'able' (67.26). Any triumph Ballantyne might have felt would surely have been tempered by the suspicion that Scott was toying with him. To a question based on a misreading of the text at 189.27–31 (Ballantyne read 'malcontent' to mean that the householder was unhappy with pay-as-you-go lodgers), Scott first answered and then remarked: 'Cousin you were not wont to be so dull'—a mock-insult employing a line from *Richard III* (4.2.17) that Scott later echoed in part when Ballantyne complained that an allusion to the sheeps-head (the handle) of an Andrea Ferrara was obscure (366.41). More acerbic, to Ballantyne's question about why King James did not simply issue another warrant to replace the one Nigel had lost (366.32–33), Scott replied: 'Would you like to *pay* two bills when only one was due—James was as poor as a rat'; but even so he supplemented the text at this point converting the gist of his reply to narrative. Here (and elsewhere) Scott sounds impatient, even irritated, as well he might be since James's perpetually empty purse was a major motif. But the exchanges are best viewed as marginal conversation, typically good-humoured, between partners who fully appreciated each other's role in the business. About the literary limitations of transcriber Huntly Gordon, moreover, the author and printer were agreed. At one point Ballantyne complained that 'Gordon must be wonderfully shallow in his Shakespeare. He left this word blank in MS!' (the word—Ballantyne supplied it—is 'lend-ings': 190.22). Scott did not demur. Another time Ballantyne credited Gordon with supplying a motto only to disparage his choice: 'It is applicable, but surely reads common-place.' From Scott came the response that 'I wish Gordon would not trouble himself with more than transcription', and he substituted one of his own devising (345: see 415 above). Not that Scott always concurred with Ballantyne, but even when disagreeing, more often than not, he acquiesced and revised.

These exchanges aside, Ballantyne's correcting and querying of the author's proof performed much good service made necessary by lapses in Scott's original prose or oversights in his narration (often his mind outran his pen), by mistakes or gaps in Gordon's transcription, and by printer's accidents, errors, or misunderstandings. (A striking example of this last is to be found in Ballantyne's comment on some lines of verse (378.1–6) misprinted as prose: 'Some unutterable ass has printed this prose; but I shall see it carefully made verse.') A note late in the third volume indicates that, at times, Ballantyne resorted to the manuscript when stumped by the transcription and proof, but this was not his normal practice. His mark—an 'X' often glossed as 'not clear', 'incomplete', 'imperfect', 'illegible', 'inaccurate', 'incorrect', 'irregular', 'laxness'—or his courteous editor's formula 'please to read this' (with or without a suggested change) attests by sheer frequency to his considerable influence on the transformation of the text, for good or ill, from manuscript to first printed edition.

Many of the 250 or so verbal changes Ballantyne made were in the interest of correcting or improving the diction, style, rhetoric, or syntax of Scott's prose. They might take the form of substituting a more exact word ('advanced' for 'came onward': 174.29) or supplying a missing one, eliminating repetitious language or echoing sound, elaborating a description or speech, completing a sentence, filling in a lacuna, making a name or spelling consistent, and so on. The majority of them, however, were made in the interest of clarifying Scott's narrative. They might take the form of identifying a speaker, introducing a 'stage direction' ('Willie, ↑(calling aloud to the boy)↓ a cup of distilled waters—': 373.11–12), pointing out an obscurity or inconsistency or contradiction in the story, calling attention to a loose end to be tied up, and so on. In numerical terms, Ballantyne corrected misspellings or garbled words 88 times; he filled lacunae 15 times; he added words or phrases 36 times; he made 65 alterations; and he deleted material on 42 occasions. By today's standards some of Ballantyne's 'clarifying' interventions seem overdone, even pedantic—a complaint that a sentence was 'more irregular than it is meant to be' because of a missing noun brought from Scott the reply 'supposed to be interrupted'—but, in period, perhaps less so. (Scott supplied the noun 'wench' to reduce the irregularity: 319.14.) Illustrative of the way he kept Scott in touch with his own narrative is Ballantyne's objection to the claim that Nigel had dismissed his faithful servant Richie Moniplies: 'Nay—but most certainly and undoubtedly Lord G. *did not* discharge Richie; but quite and clear Richie discharged himself, most agt his master's remonstrances and almost requests' (Scott rewrote the sentence at 346.3 in response). Ballantyne is not always so emphatic. In the main his questions are respectfully put and, on occasion, framed by a compliment: thus a passage about Margaret's rapid maturing from child to woman (216.5–8) prompted Ballantyne to write: 'Why, I confess this rather needs explanation. But it is a truly admirable scene.'—or , as with the query about the odd word 'impecuniosity', coupled with a tactful suggestion: 'impecuniosity? should it be italic?' (183.33). (Scott's answer was 'no', and the odd word was let stand.)

These interventions intended to improve Scott's text can be problematic to assess. But there can be little argument that, with some few exceptions where repetition is rhetorically effective, reducing the clumsiness in Scott's diction resulting from the speed with which he composed—a continuing process of revision right through the Magnum—made the prose more attractive to eye and ear alike. Representative of the benefits of Ballantyne's editing is a passsage in the opening paragraph of Chapter 34, where he corrected for number a pronoun reference ('them' to 'him'), changed a wrong word ('birth' to 'booth'), and substituted 'consequence' for the second 'importance' within four lines of the same sentence (372.17–20). One of his earliest improvements—just eleven pages into the story, in fact—was to suggest the substitution of 'booth' for 'trade' in the phrase 'this ordinary routine of the trade', thereby simultaneously creating a more precise image and eliminating the echo of a nearby 'trade' (22.29, 32). The timely query 'What became of Mother Suddlechop?' (apropos of 397.25–28) that enabled Scott deftly to account for the future life of this character so central to the working of his plot (at 396.38–40) before writing '*finis*' is hard to fault. Quite possibly Ballantyne spared Scott the embarrassment of the same question put by a snippy reader or irritable reviewer.

Not so helpful was Ballantyne's overhasty reaction to 'This recognition of Margaret, *in boy's clothes*, as a female, [as] much too sudden & unexplained' (330.35–331.4). He did have the grace to add just below it: 'Beg pardon.' And when Ballantyne commented on Scott's statement that, as a town-gallant, Lowestoffe was ashamed of being moved by the simple eloquence of old Christie's charity to his strayed wife (395.28–29), with 'I wish the feeling had stifled [sic] the shame here, rather than the shame the feeling', one sees, at a glance, the editor's limitations. More telling still, perhaps, is Ballantyne's prudish comment on the Author of Waverley's note invoking the august authority of Dr Dryasdust on the spelling of the name 'Niggle' (195.41–46): 'I am scarcely sure that I would be disposed to help idiots to this misnomer; Nigel being at the best a word of doubtful utterance'. Scott's reply was a tempered, witty, but firm 'phaw good house had never bad name'.[79] Possibly, the greater subtlety and sophistication of Scott's intellect is again exposed by a query Ballantyne made concerning the Lady Hermione's surprise that 'even in this free land [England]' men and their laws can be exceedingly cruel (215.9–11). Ballantyne wrote, 'even here?', and Scott replied, 'yes, even *in England*'. If we read him literally, then

Ballantyne's debility as editor is far more serious than prudery. But the underscored 'in England' of Scott's reply should give us pause: maybe the two Scotsmen are having a bit of fun at England's expense, and Ballantyne initiated it. One might be tempted to dismiss Ballantyne's criticism of Scott's effort to draw a distinction between the character of the two London apprentices—'This distinction is nearly invisible. To "know how to do a thing," is very like being "acquainted with the way in which it ought to be done."' (23.28–30)—as quibbling, if not imperceptive; but it might be more to the point to blame Gordon for garbling the manuscript distinction between the theoretical man and the practical by misreading 'theory to practice' as 'thorough practice' at 23.24, and, still more pertinent, to reprove Scott for not spotting Gordon's mistake and fixing it.

With *Nigel* as with other novels for which proofs are extant the attribution of revisions—differentiating between Ballantyne's and Scott's— is not an exact science. Differences in ink and handwriting are often telling, but for long stretches of *Nigel* the inks are indistinguishable. Though more difficult to determine than the verbal changes, the non-verbal changes for which Ballantyne is likely to be responsible might conservatively be put at 178. Modifications of punctuation account for 145 of these: besides the expected changes with the dash, the comma, the semi-colon, and the period (94), he introduced 12 exclamation and 17 question marks, not to mention 8 parentheses—this last character almost a signature of his work, so seldom does it appear in the novel. Capitalisation or the reverse resulted in 22 changes; italicisation, 6; and new or run-on paragraphing, 5. Whatever their precise number the range of non-verbal corrections is broad: Ballantyne can be detected editing for every element of Scott's text.

Scott's own work on the proofs did, of course, include recovering lost manuscript material, especially where sense was wanting, if he could: he did not usually have access to the manuscript and, if memory failed, had to improvise. He filled in lacunae and corrected conspicuous mistakes, including printer's errors. Throughout the proofs he joined or separated paragraphs, italicised or romanised words, tagged speeches, transposed phrases or larger elements, and in general continued the compositors' work of extracting the novel from the manuscript and making it readable. Many a pronoun was converted to a noun, and not infrequently a 'here' realised as a specific place. Scott's verbal corrections ultimately number over 2000; his non-verbal corrections, some 1000. Of the latter, in rounded figures, Scott revised for punctuation some 650 times, for spelling 140, for capitalisation and the reverse 60, for italics and the reverse 50, for transpositions 20, and for paragraphing 70 (all but a few of these for new paragraphs). In almost every category the first volume was more heavily revised than the second, and the second more so than the third, perhaps a sign of the pressure to finish up from Constable and Co.

For all Scott's expressed intent to be more careful with the text of *Nigel* than with those of its immediate predecessors, it would be hard to demonstrate that, in the final analysis, he was more attentive to these proofs than to others, or even that he was more consistently attentive to the task of revising than before—always excepting the Introductory Epistle, with which he took extraordinary pains. Nor would it be easy to argue that, in all cases, the revision he did was for the best. But taken together, the changes show him to be involved at one time or another with almost every aspect of his craft. He both cut and added language to sharpen his prose; he both cut and added material to strengthen his narration.

Scott made a promising start in the novel proper, revising number and verb in the second sentence of Chapter 1—from 'crowns' to 'crown' and 'were' to 'was' (19.19–20)—and inserting 'united' ahead of 'crown' to match sense and expression more exactly. In correspondence with Ballantyne he chastised the printers for mistaking the word 'bat' for 'hat' (28.32). In the proofs he reiterated this sentiment, with some wit: 'Look that they make it Bat ↑ not *hat* ↓ they are in such cases partial'. Here Scott's judgment in following the manuscript would seem unassailable. Shortly before, in the same scene, Scott himself altered the description of Richie Moniplies from 'a proper lad and a handsome, in spite of freckles and sun-burning' to 'a proper lad and a sturdy, in spite of freckles and sun-burning' (27.35–36). Here Scott's judgment would seem, on the contrary, very much open to question, for the substitution negates the qualifying purpose of the next phrase. Sometimes a single sentence reflects the mixed result of Scott's work in the proofs—for example, the sentence about one of the apprentices who wields a bat, not a hat. When first mentioned, he is described as 'sharp, active, able-bodied' (21.36–37). His traits of mind and body are then generalised to identify him as 'a Londoner, with all the peculiar sharpness and address, and audacity, which belong peculiarly to the youth of the metropolis'. To avoid repetition Scott substituted 'acuteness' for 'sharpness', in the process strengthening the alliterative pattern of the nouns. He ignored, however, the close proximity of 'peculiar' and 'peculiarly' (21.41–42).

But if the proofs are often characterised by such alternation of authorial attention and inattention, and by such textual gains and losses, a specific feature of the text consistently preoccupied Scott—namely, the Latin and Greek throughout the novel, and especially in the conversation that ensues upon Nigel's introduction at court to King James (110.36–111.25), and the French-inflected speech of the Chevalier Beaujeu when welcoming Nigel to the ordinary (142.35–145.22, 148.1–10). Scott worked hard on these passages. Confirmation of his passion for accuracy with foreign languages, if any is needed, comes with Ballantyne's request that he examine 'this Latin very attentively', referring to a quotation late in the third volume (398.30–31). On occasion Scott added a translation of the King's Latin if he judged it problematic for the reader (e.g. 72.21).

By comparison, much of Scott's revision was routine: nonsense needed to be made sense, obscure sense needed to be clear sense, and so on. A sample correction for verbal sense from nonsense (in context) is 'violent tirade' to 'valorous tirade' (90.18–19); for more precise sense, 'drums and colours were flying' to 'drums were beating and colours flying' (175.32), or, the better to indicate Aunt Judith's habitual displeasure with Margaret, 'and at this time in the morning, when she will scarce see any of the family' to 'and at this time in the morning, when she will scarce see any of the family even at seasonable hours?' (201.6–7). Scott diligently converted the monarch's personal 'I' to the royal 'we' wherever in the manuscript he had neglected to do so (e.g. 74.34 and, again, 74.35). Similarly, he revised here and there for more accurate or specific sense of character. Monna Paula, 'humble companion' to Lady Hermione, is a case in point. Her natural proclivity and social conditioning notwithstanding, she could hardly be 'abhorrent of youth and gaiety' (manuscript), just 'something intolerant' (proof revision) of them (208.14). A sentence giving her address could be improved by both adding and subtracting. Accordingly, the manuscript 'Here' was replaced in proof with 'At the door of this sanctuary' (201.41), referring to the lady's quarters in the house of George Heriot, in pre-Reformation days the Saint Roque Nunnery. A phrase midway in the sentence explaining when and where Nigel had acquired gossip about her—'on their return from dining in Lombard-street, and which' (201.43, between 'ear' and 'respecting')—was discarded as extraneous. Such revision is nothing extraordinary. But it did not stop there: once begun Scott was inspired and for the next several pages he revised to strengthen the history of the former nunnery—interesting in its own right and for the light it throws on the Catholic-Protestant division among James's subjects, many of them, like the monarch, still haunted by the Gunpowder Plot but, unlike him, fearful of an alliance with Spain through a royal marriage. Perhaps, too, he realised that this weak subplot needed his best effort if it were to pass muster. The lady's interesting history could be made to compensate for her stereotypical gothic-heroine characterisation.

The changes Scott made in the speech of his more expressive talkers were no less random but perhaps had greater cumulative effect. Sir Mungo's 'to have him sent to a barber-surgeon's, to learn some needful branch of anatomy' became 'to have the loon sent . . . some needful scantling of anatomy' (339.37). The King's Scottish cook Laurie Linklater's 'in hope of rising with him' became 'in hope of being towed up alongst with him' (348.13–14). The Templar Reginald Lowestoffe's claim to 'some rank in our republic' was left unspecified in manuscript. Scott filled in two blanks in the proofs (suggesting the need for research) so as to make the town-gallant and bon-vivant as honest as he was charming: Reggie was 'Treasurer to the Lord of Misrule last year' and 'at this present moment in nomination for that dignity' (185.41–43). It is not surprising that, in filling the blanks, Scott introduced a form of entertainment popular at the Christmas season among the law students of Jacobean London.[80] Great patrons of the commercial theatre, they created their own private theatre on occasion. In other ways, too, from the Epistle on, Scott revised to underscore the unique social role of the drama—stage-play, court-masque, Christmas-revel, street-theatre, ceremonial-pageant, and so on—in the period. Within the first chapter he introduced an analogy to *Romeo and Juliet* to explain how street-fights were quelled with the assistance of householders (21.27–31), and he elaborated on the behaviour of theatre audiences: besides fighting 'for half-bitten apples', they also 'cracked nuts, and filled the upper gallery with their clamours' (24.20–21).

Except for the changes in the Introductory Epistle, nothing in the proofs quite rivals the most extensive manuscript revisions noted earlier in this essay. A new paragraph in the first volume established Heriot's generosity to Nigel and the latter's gratitude for it (104.38–42). A four-line motto became fourteen as Scott waxed thoughtful about the implications of the confrontation between Nigel and Dalgarno in St James's Park (167.8–21). The expanded motto also reflects earlier changes in the second volume—the most protracted in the novel proper—concerning the love-struck Margaret Ramsay's intervention in Nigel's deteriorating affairs, which conduct in turn stems from Scott's efforts, through a series of insertions, to develop the theme of Nigel's self-betrayal through gambling (154.13–14, 154.28–31, and 155.3–4). A 'page apart' was required to detail the delivery of Margaret's warning note, the contents of the note, and Nigel's Hamlet-like soliloquy in reaction to it: 'Begone for a vile calumny!—but I will watch—I will observe—' (167.1–2). In this same context of Nigel's gambling is to be found a first-rate example of Scott's ability to excise material. The sentence 'that from an observer of the various games of chance which he witnessed, and began to take an interest in, he came by degrees, by moderate hazards, and small betts or wagers, to take a certain interest in them' lost, in revision, the phrase 'and began to take an interest in' (154.8–11). In much the same incremental way that he developed the gambling motif, Scott revised the Alsatian plot to insinuate the idea that among the ruffians who keep Duke Hildebrod company is someone vaguely familiar to Nigel. Three times Scott interwove a new phrase with an old one to forward this little mystery (193.21–22, 193.34–36, 195.15–16). In the third volume the scenes in the Tower of London between Nigel and Margaret disguised as a boy in mummer's costume prompted occasional revisions of a sentence or more as Scott worked to realise the theatrical potential—i.e. the sexual frisson—of the scene (e.g. the addition at 316.13–16). But perhaps the most felicitous re-writing in the later material of the novel is the interpolated explanation of why Laurie Linklater is not available to Richie Moniplies, he, as always, it seems, 'being then employed in cooking a mess of cock-a-leekie for the King's own mouth' (348.3–4), for it harkens back to the original meeting of these two canny Scotsmen—both come to be indis-pensable to the King, one filling his stomach, one his purse—and, simultaneously, looks ahead to the final sentence of the book: 'And now, my lords and lieges, let us all to our dinner, for the cock-a-leekie is cooling' (406.25–27).

Before either Ballantyne or Scott worked on the proofs, of course, the compositors set the text of the novel from Gordon's transcription and, subsequently, introduced the changes from the revised proofs as they received them. The role of these men in the extraction of the novel from the manuscript is not to be minimised, as the account in the General Introduction to this edition makes clear, though since we have not a single page of a copyist's transcript for this or any novel we are unable to specifiy his part. Put bluntly, the celebrated wizardry of the Author of Waverley, invaluable to Scott's continuing success in the marketplace, would never have come to pass, had they not performed with dispatch the multiple tasks entrusted to them by Scott, for the simple reason that he could never have written with the speed he did had he not been able to count on Ballantyne's employees to make actual the potential novel in the manuscript—to give it the form that identified a novel to nineteenth-century readers. Their principal job was to convert Scott's ubiquitous dashes to the full-stops and commas of English sentences. They sometimes overdid it, eliminating the spontaneity of speech, obscuring the linguistic variety among speakers, and flattening the hills and valleys of Scott's prose, but they were in general following the printing conventions of the period and house rules. Besides normalising spelling, adopting current public practice with capitals and italics, supplying hyphens, expanding ampersands, distinguishing narration from dia-logue by their layout on the page, tagging speeches, making sentences of fragments, dividing sentences at appropriate intervals into paragraphs, eliminating inconsistencies of usage, substituting nouns or names for pronouns, eliminating conspicuous repetition of diction, filling blanks left by the transcriber, supplying missing articles, relatives, prepositions, conjunctions, and in other ways compensating for Scott's short-cuts while composing, where appropriate they converted English to Scots (and occasionally did the reverse); also, they fixed minor errors that came to their attention. Stated in quantitative terms, these changes, in rounded figures, number over 36,000; of these, some 32,000 are non-verbal in nature. Punctuation alone accounts for 22,700 changes; capitalisation or the reverse, 3000; and paragraphing, 2300. Supplying the 'e' before the 'd' to form the past participle accounts for 2500 changes; converting '&' to 'and' accounts for another 525; and non-phonological spelling corrections, for 770. Italicising or romanising words and phrases happens 60 times; interrupted speech is repunctu-ated to indicate incomplete speech 50 times. Verbal changes number some 4000. New words or phrases account for 450 of these; subtracted words or phrases, 390; and substitutions, 700. Corrections in general, including phonological spelling errors, account for 1000 changes; corrections involving the possessive case or contractions in particular account for another 900 changes. The inability to read the manuscript at 60 points resulted in lacunae. Misreadings and mistakes, about 400, supply the remaining figure. By the time of *Nigel* this arrangement, so useful to Scott and Ballantyne alike, was thoroughly familiar to all concerned. That it was imperfect is indicated by that complaint of Scott about the transgressions of some 'transcribers'. The great majority of emendations that differentiate the text of this new edition from that of earlier editions derive, not surprisingly, from this aspect of production. Their individual effect is usually negligible; their cumulative effect—as in, for example, the speech of the Greenwich barber—is consequential.

The post-Scott or post-proof changes to the text of *Nigel* number approximately 3500. Of these, roughly 3000 are non-verbal. Scott was responsible for these only in the sense that his corrections or additions in proof necessitated punctuation to various degrees—e.g. an inserted speech attribution might require multiple punctuation fore and aft. The first edition contains something over 1000 new commas, close to 300 new semi-colons (typically converted commas or dashes), and together nearly 300 new question and exclamation marks, replacing dashes and periods (173 periods added, 137 cancelled). Although 180 or so dashes are lost, mostly when sentences are divided—a process that accounts for nearly twice as many new capitals (192) as the reverse (103), new dashes numbering about 125 are gained. Changes in hyphens, italics, paren-theses, and even paragraphing account for roughly 100 more differences. Scott's changes in the author's proof also required the compositors to insert the 'e' before the final 'd' in the past participle over 100 times; as well as these changes, they had 28 new ampersands to convert. Along this line, 20 abbreviations of 'Master' and 'Mistress' remained to be spelled out. In contrary fashion, with each appearance the word 'damned' was gutted to read 'd——d': a small but telling correction. The regularising of spelling—for common nouns, e.g. 'bravo' for 'bravoe', and proper nouns (especially characters' names), e.g. 'Vin' for 'Win', alike—continued, as did the work of sorting out real or perceived mistakes in grammar: e.g. 'majesties' becomes 'majesty's' or 'are' replaces 'is'.

Post-Scott verbal changes number approximately 500. Over 90 of these are additions to the text—a word, a phrase, a sentence, some of dubious merit (see 455 below). One of the more ambitious changes both supplements and rearranges the text: 'To Aunt Judith the Lady Hermione was as civil as their rare intercourse permitted, on which . . .' becomes 'To Aunt Judith the Lady Hermione was kind and civil, but their intercourse was rare; on which . . .' (204.4–5). Subtractions number only about half the additions (45), most of them for the sake of economy. Such is the case at 82.21 where the attribution 'said he, raising his voice' that in the proof followed 'at least' was cut, coming as it did close on the heels of 'said he, speaking aloud' at 82.20–21, which in turn succeeded closely 'muttered Sir Mungo to himself' at 82.19. There are 250 substitutions, including changes in the form of a word (e.g. a singular made plural, a present participle made past, or a present-tense verb changed to a past-tense). Typically, the speech of Scots speakers is made more consistent—e.g. not going back and forth between 'weel' and 'well' or 'mair'and 'more'; and 'ye' is increasingly preferred to 'you'. Most of the substitutions are unremarkable—i.e. one demonstrative or relative pronoun for another ('these' for 'those'; 'which' for 'that'); the definite article for the possessive pronoun ('the' for 'her'); an 'a' for 'an'. But some continue the compositors' efforts to eliminate ugly repetitions of nouns, verbs, or adjectives in the manuscript that escaped their notice on first try. Characteristic is the substitution at 275.25 of 'an instant' for 'a moment' repeated from the previous line.

That Scott did not always accept Ballantyne's recommendations or that some of them did not reach print is, on balance, probably fortunate; but that some of Scott's own proof changes failed to reach print, coupled with a number of post-Scott changes and, for the most part, neglect of the manuscript at every stage of production, is not. Together author and editor, with the assistance of the other intermediaries, produced a text that is demonstrably different in many particulars great and small from the manuscript text. Not that returning to the manuscript would, in all cases, have improved the printed text. It would not, for example, have revealed the mistake of misnumbered chapters in the third volume, for the mistake originated in the manuscript. But resorting to the manuscript might well have solved the problem of Ballantyne's inability to see the careful distinction between the two London apprentices Scott had originally drawn but allowed to stand as corrupted almost beyond recognition in proof. This example can be replicated many times. As such, it might serve to remind us that, if the proofs—or the process of producing the Waverley Novels—provided Scott with the chance to perfect the novel he drafted, they also allowed him to do it damage. Where possible, this new edition seeks to undo that damage, as the final part of this essay, on 'The Present Text', will show.

3. THE LATER EDITIONS

Second and Third Editions. By 1822 editions of Waverley Novels subsequent to the first were less likely to be true editions than unsold copies of the first edition fitted out with a new title-page. Such was the case with *Nigel*. For all their high hopes built on the reception of the first edition, the publishers saw the demand drop sharply. By July Cadell was ordering Ballantyne to reduce the printing of *Peveril* from 12,000 to 10,500 copies because 'we have a letter from London this morning stating that *no success* has attended the subscription of the 3d Edition of Nigel—which we ordered to be subscribed & announced accordingly —that 1000 Copies are in the hands of the Trade in the Row & 1300 with HR & Co themselves, when I add to this that we have 1440 Copies you will at once say I am doing what is proper'.[81] Even the sales of the German translation had disappointed Black, Young & Young, who sought to renegotiate their agreement on *Peveril* accordingly.[82] The booksellers were balking at purchasing books by subscription—i.e. prior to publication at a reduced rate. With the lagging sales of *The Pirate*, in fact, Robinson had written to Constable on 31 January 1822— only a month after publication—that 'the Trade are waiting for our Spring Sale they dont like Bks at Subsn and I dont see how we could pretend to subscribe the Book unless as a *new editn* say *the third*—Do you think we should do wrong to print new Titles—Third editn and give the Work a good drive into the hand of the Trade . . . as 12,000 Copies have been printed I can see no harm in calling the last 3000 the *third* editn'.[83]

Detrimental to the sale of original editions was Constables' practice, since 1819, of gathering up several novels in fine sets—in effect, cannibalising its own product. As Cadell himself admitted to Constable in a letter of 6 September 1823: 'Robinson thinks the anxiety of the public for these books is as high as ever—but there are so many *thousand* readers who have them in *sets* that the sale of the first editions are diminished by those who wait—or get a reading till a connected series appears'.[84] If so, the problem was of Constables' own making, the sets victimising the original editions but especially the second and third editions. On at least one occasion Constable acknowledged to Scott that *Novels and Tales* 'has interfered somewhat with the original or coarser editions, & purchasers hang back'—before going ahead to propose the next such set, to be called 'Historical Romances by the Author of Waverley'.[85]

The 'second' edition (published in Edinburgh on 12 October 1822)[86] and 'third' edition are irrelevant to the main development of the printed text of *Nigel* (as shown in the stemma below), which proceeded, rather, from the first edition in a corrected version to the octavo (8vo) of *Novels and Romances*, the text provided for Scott in the Interleaved Set from which the Magnum Opus was to be prepared. Also irrelevant, therefore, were the duodecimo (12mo) and so-called 'miniature edition' (18mo) of *Novels and Tales*.

Novels and Romances. *Novels and Romances*, comprising *The Pirate*,

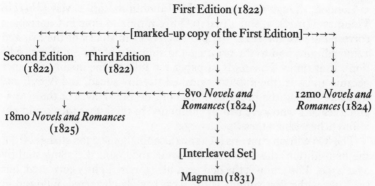

First Edition (1822)
↓
←←←←←←←←←←←[marked-up copy of the First Edition]→→→→→
↓   ↓   ↓   ↓
Second Edition Third Edition   ↓
(1822)   (1822)   ↓   ↓
                                ↓   ↓
    ←←←←←←←←←←←←←←←8vo *Novels and*   12mo *Novels and*
    ↓   *Romances* (1824)   *Romances* (1824)
18mo *Novels and Romances*   ↓
    (1825)   ↓
                                ↓
                         [Interleaved Set]
                                ↓
                         Magnum (1831)

The Fortunes of Nigel, Peveril of the Peak, and *Quentin Durward,* was the third such collection, establishing the pattern of republishing the novels in groups begun with *Novels and Tales* (1819) and continued in *Historical Romances* (1822)—the latter also a group of four. The groundwork for it was laid in April 1823, when Constable and Co. offered to buy the copyrights to the four novels for £5250, and Scott readily accepted.[87] *Quentin Durward* was drawing to a close and would be finished by the end of the month. The title for the series was not yet decided, Constable referring to it as either 'Historical Novels' or 'Romances and Tales'. On 19 May 1823, James Ballantyne was ordered to 'go on with the Novels & Romances both sizes [8vo and 12mo] with all speed'.[88] On 18 August, Cadell wrote to Scott: 'As our friend Quentin Durward is I may say done allow me to say that Five thousand pounds for him and his three precursors may be put under arrangement whenever you choose—I mean for the Pirate Fortunes of Nigel Peveril of the Peak and Quentin —we have not finished up our numbers of some of these, but that we shall not notice.'[89] A formal agreement was prepared on 10 September.[90] The next day Cadell wrote Constable that, in the agreement, he had taken the latter's 'counsil and included the miniature size of this series [the 18mo]—which makes these editions a steady dropping goose—'.[91] Cadell's metaphor speaks volumes about the role of these collected editions in the Waverley enterprise. Little wonder that Constables withstood Hurst, Robinson's argument that they interfered with sales of the originals.

In the end, the working title for the series became the official one. It may be that the credit goes to Robinson, or so Constable's letter to Cadell of 27 October 1823 suggests: 'the title . . . I expect to be Novels & Romances—as Robinson's letter terms it'.[92] The 8vo edition, in 7 volumes, appeared in Edinburgh on 10 December 1823, and in London on 3 January 1824 (*Nigel* in Volumes 2 (part), 3, and 4 (part)); the foolscap octavo (12mo), in 9 Volumes, on 3 and 22 January 1824 (*Nigel* in Volumes 3–5 (part)); and the 18mo, in 7 volumes, on 8 January 1825 in London, though not announced in Edinburgh until 2 May (*Nigel* in Volumes 2 (part), 3, and 4 (part)).[93] From time to time in Constable's correspondence for 1824, we find references to stocks of the 8vo and 12mo editions and to the printing and shipping of the 'miniature edition'. If at times the supply of paper ran low, or the quality of paper became an issue, the publisher pushed steadily ahead, and *Novels and Romances* joined the previous collections on the shelves of those imagined readers who were being conditioned to think that they could not afford to be without these 'golden eggs'.

The 8vo edition contains (at a rough count) some 2300 changes from the first edition; the 12mo edition some 1600; and the 18mo slightly over 2700. The 12mo is the odd text, being more lightly corrected, but in all three the first volume is the most heavily corrected, followed in order by the second and the third. Verbal changes number some 120 for the 8vo, 155 for the 12mo, and 180 for the 18mo. Only 3 verbal changes are unique to the 8vo, whereas 77 are unique to the 12mo and 55 to the 18mo. The three editions concur on 66 changes, suggesting the involvement of a marked-up copy of the first edition. The 12mo and the 18mo share 10 verbal changes not found in the 8vo; the 8vo and the 12mo, none. By contrast, the 8vo and the 18mo are typically identical, sharing 50 verbal changes. With few exceptions they adopt the same changes in paragraphing (27, to be precise); this is rarely the case with the 12mo. The striking similarities between the 8vo and 18mo readings, together with those of the paragraphing and of the non-verbal changes (see below), would seem to suggest that the 18mo was set from the earlier 8vo rather than from the marked-up first edition used for the 8vo and 12mo. The ten verbal changes shared by the 12mo and the 18mo editions raise the possibility that the former may have played a role, albeit a minor one, in the latter, but not enough is known about the detailed procedures in the printing house to cast light on this possibility. There is nothing in the changes to suggest that Scott himself was directly involved in any of the *Novels and Romances* texts.

Not surprisingly, the great majority of changes in each of the three editions are non-verbal. Of these, the overwhelming majority involve punctuation, preeminently the comma, with spelling accounting for most of the others. In the 8vo edition commas added, subtracted, or replaced number nearly 860 in rounded figures; all other punctuation changes number 580. Capitalisation or the reverse accounts for another 235 changes. The joining or separating of words, 85. Spelling changes not affecting sense come to about 260. Transpositions number 4. There are 36 new paragraphs. All but a few of these non-verbal changes reappear in the 18mo. Moreover, the 600-odd additional non-verbal changes in this edition are, with a few exceptions, in the same proportion —i.e. punctuation changes predominating (596), the comma leading the pack (203). Capitalisation changes come to 70. The most apparent difference between the two texts is the least significant: the 18mo does not abbreviate the word 'Chapter'. The second most noticeable difference is the absence of quotation marks for poetry set apart from prose and, along the same line, the loss of the inverted comma that signifies the elided first syllable in ''prentice', an oft-recurring word. Together these features account for the relatively greater activity with the quotation mark and the apostrophe than in the 8vo. Changes in spelling and capitalisation are in the interest of regularising and standardising the text—that is, they continue the job of refining the mechanical features of Scott's text that began with the first proof. The 5 transpositions include one unique to this edition. The striking resemblance in the non-verbal readings of the 8vo and the 18mo editions makes all the more conspicuous the departures of the 12mo edition. Although more lightly corrected, 555 non-verbal changes, including 2 of 5 transpositions, are unique to it. Moreover, some 26 times it does not observe the paragraphing of the other two editions—almost as many times as the other two concur. Colons and parentheses become part, albeit not a large part, of the punctuation scheme. The proportions of change are, however, not dissimilar: 552 comma changes, 365 all other punctuation changes, 280 spelling changes, 91 capitalisation changes, and 78 joinings or separatings of words. Put simply it is the case that, repeatedly, on a given page of text the 12mo bears no resemblance to the 8vo and the 18mo.

Many of the verbal changes in the 8vo (62) concern grammar. The most frequent single correction is the inserting of an apostrophe—23 times—to indicate the possessive case. Changes in verb forms, sometimes for agreement with subject, sometimes for tense, but also for contemporary usage, are next in number. A recurring example concerns the present and past perfect of the verb 'drink': 'drunk' is usually substituted for 'drank' (see e.g. 267.25). There are as well changes with conjunctions, prepositions, articles, relative pronouns, number—many of them 'tinkering' but bringing Scott's text in line with current practices: e.g. the adjective 'agreeable' becomes the adverb 'agreeably' (25.22). The distinguishing of homophones is another significant feature of the 8vo's verbal corrections. In particular the words 'ingenious' and 'ingenuous' (see e.g. 122.13–14) and 'councillor' and 'counsellor' (and related forms thereof: see e.g. 115.21 and 337.17) are repeatedly separated. The word 'further' typically becomes 'farther', in this instance reversing the modern distinction (see e.g. 51.11). Even the difference between 'sty' and 'stye' (255.5) and that between 'straight' and 'strait' (310.1) are recognised. Changes back and forth between Scots and English, particularly in the speech of Richie Moniplies, constitute another form of verbal change in the 8vo, which also attends to the difference between 'Scots' and 'Scotch'. Of the more interesting changes—words and phrases added, omitted, or altered—about half (20) are minor, functioning, say, to strengthen syntax as when adding

the second 'to' in 'most of whom used to communicate their secrets
↑ to ↓, and receive their counsel from Dame Ursley' (93.43–94.94);
or to improve diction as in 'that he [Duke Hildebrod] might roll himself
into the house like a huge butt of liquor, a vessel to which he bore a
considerable outward ⟨appearance⟩ resemblance' (255.29); or to address a character by name instead of title, e.g. 'Sir Mungo' rather than
'my lord' (129.3). Lengthening an interrupted speech from 'why' to
'why, 'tis' (38.10), by contrast, seems merely fussy. The most sensitive
of these changes affect meaning, for better or worse. In the sentence
'her [Margaret's] dark eyes, however, continued to be fixed on Nigel,
with an expression of melancholy by which he felt strangely affected' the
8vo alters 'he' to 'she' (86.19–21); in the phrase 'the unusual ceremonial attending their passage through the long suite of apartments' the
8vo changes 'unusual' to 'usual' (105.40–41); and in the speech expressing the waterman's displeasure with his unexpected and unwelcome extra passenger Martha Trapbois, 'You must not double my fare
on me—she may go by land' (284.35–36) the word 'fare' is exchanged
for 'freight', a demeaning term, appropriately, for the woman the
waterman proceeds to insult still further. Perhaps the happiest change
introduces the word 'out' into Jin Vin's anguished 'I wish they had
racked me to death before I heard this Scotchman was to chouse me out
of my sweetheart!' (385.40–42); it completes the apprentice's idiom. A
pair of similar corrections points to the mixed quality of these gratuitous
alterations. On the one hand a change from 'young man' to 'young
nobleman' (109.2) is purely descriptive and, as such, redundant,
Nigel's social being status long since established. On the other hand the
change from 'fine gentleman' to 'fine young gentleman' (229.29) in a
short speech by Dame Suddlechop's mulatto servant Wiba repeats, in
muttered tones, the words by which she has just announced the ill-
disguised London apprentice Jin Vin to her mistress. If read as a sarcastic echo, the exact repetition can be justified, though on balance the
missing 'young' the second time round would seem better.

Many of the verbal changes in the 18mo also involve grammar;
most of them are identical to those in the 8vo, e.g. the changes to
effect the possessive case. The slightly higher number of grammatical
changes (76) points to the greater number of changes in verbs, some
of them eccentric perhaps (see e.g. 203.34 where 18mo changes 'ate'
to 'eat'). The 18mo, with only slight variation in count, distinguishes
the same homophones: it surpasses the 8vo in changing 'further' to
'farther' by 3. Too, the 18mo is demonstrably interested in the distinctions between Scots and English and, for that matter, between 'Scots'
and 'Scotch', twice as much so in fact. All the changes in wording
and phrasing in the 8vo cited above as illustrative occur in the 18mo.
Distinctive to the miniature edition is the omission of three phrases.
One of them eliminates repetition of the word 'case': 'he shewed some

reluctance to quit possession of ⟨the case⟩ ↑it↓, and it required . . .'
(32.18–19). One of them prunes the sentence 'The twa iron carles
yonder, at the kirk beside the Port, were just ganging out sax o' the
clock' (44.39–40) by chopping off the last three words. And the
third excises some unfortunate tushery inserted at proof stage by James
Ballantyne to fill a lacuna: in 'Nevertheless,—hark thee hither,—nev-
theless, if he be of the same mind as when we last met', the 'hark thee
hither,—nevertheless' (375.4–5) is struck out. All the more disappointing, therefore, is the inserted 'ay' in 'This Dalgarno does not drink so
much, ay or swear so much' (361.21). The insertion of two more 'by' s
in 'by M——— ↑by↓ M——— ↑by↓ my husband' (223.33–34) may,
however, express more forcefully Lady Hermione's confusion and embarrassment when speaking of this most painful detail of her history.
One category of verbal change is characteristic only of the 18mo: the
occasional effort to differentiate between 'ye' and 'you' on three occasions, twice in the interest of characterisation presumably (292.12,
319.5, 360.23). The question of whether the 12mo played any role in the
18mo arises in part because of several verbal changes common to them
and not shared with the 8vo. The most impressive of these is the change
of the word 'crucifix' to 'carnifex' (69.14) in reference to the figure of an
executioner depicted on a silver charger, restoring the manuscript reading misread by the transcriber. Elsewhere both editions eliminate the
repeated word 'trust', the 18mo by substituting for it 'hope', the 12mo
by substituting 'hope' for the initial 'trust' (120.36). Both editions are
unhappy with the word 'Southron' (291.21) but come to different
solutions: the 18mo changes it to 'southern' whereas the 12mo drops it
altogether.

Verbal changes of a grammatical nature in the 12mo number 72.
Variations within this category are not significantly different from
those in the 8vo and the 18mo, though one feature peculiar to this
edition is the converting of singular nouns to plural whether called
for by sense or not (consider the pluralising of 'depth' at 193.8).
The 12mo also insists on 'spoken' rather than 'spoke' for the present
and past perfect of the verb 'speak' (see e.g. 198.32). The same
interest in distinguishing the same homophones found in the 8vo and
the 18mo is present in the 12mo, as is the attention to sorting
out the Scots and English, and in similar numbers. Several of the
verbal changes unique to the 12mo are, however, striking, beginning
with the excision of a long phrase and an adjective—8 words in total—
in the Introductory Epistle: 'but I am not, therefore, hypocrite enough
to disclaim ⟨the ordinary motives, on account of which⟩ the ⟨whole⟩
world around me is toiling unremittingly' (15.19–21). Like 'world',
other nouns are deprived of their accompanying adjectives—e.g.
'⟨auld⟩ Holyrood-House' (47.6), '⟨royal⟩ conveniency' (70.5), '⟨young⟩
nobleman' (211.5). Three of the oddest changes occur in the mottoes:

in the third line of the motto for Chapter 17 the phrase 'Single suited' is reduced to 'Single' and in the next line 'single' again loses its sequel 'suit' (187.9–10). The last line of the motto to Chapter 22 loses the first 'or' (240.9). That these may be mistakes is suggested by several changes that clearly are—i.e. 'Master' is cancelled before 'George' (58.25), creating a jarring lapse in tone; 'motioned' is changed to 'mentioned' (85.29), resulting in nearly total loss of sense, much as when 'they take a sculler' becomes 'they like a sculler' (284.1); and 'twenty-four hours' is made to read 'twenty-four fours' (145.4–5). On one page of Latin dialogue where the 8vo is silent and the 18mo speaks only once, the 12mo makes six changes. Only one is verbal but it blunders badly in rewriting 'agit' as 'ggit' (111.7). Other changes do little if any damage but do little obvious good, either. For example, 'she could best second ⟨the⟩ her recommendation of the friend whom Providence had raised up to her' (287.28–30); or 'without saying a single word, or taking the trouble ⟨to gather⟩ of gathering more of the information contained in the letter' (290.11); or 'instead of bearing thy noddle charged against us ⟨thus⟩ like a battering-ram' (123.8). An exception perhaps is the more effective contrast gained by adding 'new' to balance 'old' in the phrase 'but creeping and stumbling amongst relics of old machines, and models of new inventions in various branches of new mechanics' (97.21–23). And replacing 'in' with 'to' in the phrase 'what brought that in my mind' secures the idiom (373.9–10).

The Interleaved Set and the Magnum. The Magnum Opus edition of the Waverley Novels, the last during Scott's lifetime and, until the present edition, the standard one, is the subject of Jane Millgate's *Scott's Last Edition* (Edinburgh, 1987). The Interleaved Set of the Waverley Novels prepared to accommodate Scott's textual revisions and annotations for the Magnum Opus is described in *Scott's Interleaved Waverley Novels*, ed. Iain G. Brown (Aberdeen, 1987). For *Nigel* Scott was given an interleaved copy of the octavo edition. Robert Cadell transcribed Scott's changes into another copy of the *Novels and Romances*, making changes as he did so, and read the proof. His diaries for 1830 show that he 'revised'—his word—*Nigel* in late summer and early autumn. The eleven references to this task begin on 13 August, and continue through 6 October, when he writes: 'concluded revisal of Fortunes of Nigel to bed at 10'.[94] *Nigel* occupies Volumes 26 and 27 in the Magnum. It was published on 1 July and 1 August 1831 at a price of 5s. for each volume.

Scott's creative energies in the Interleaved Set of *Nigel* were principally invested in writing the preface and notes. Lists of names on the endpapers refer to subjects or sources, often with page numbers, for notes and research. By contrast with the proof corrections, so revealing of Scott's humour, only three or four times do we glimpse the man behind the revisions. One of these occasions comes in the Introductory Epistle, in connection with drafting a note to the already italicised word 'revise' (4.42): 'The unintiated [sic] must be informd that a second proof sheet is so calld.' Scott's desire to stress this symbol of the Epistle's theme had not diminished with time, it would seem.[95] Another is when Scott, replacing the word 'crucifix' with 'carnifex' (69.14)—a change already made in the 12mo and 18mo editions—remarks parenthetically: 'the printer will take the trouble to mind this wor[d]'. Scott introduces the same sententious perspective on two occasions: at 23.2 'David Ramsay, ↑ Memory's Monitor ↓ watchmaker', and at 396.16 'Vincent and Tunstall ↑ Memory-Monitors ↓'. The fourth also comes in connection with a note, but in this case an existing note, credited to Captain Clutterbuck, explaining that, of the three known extant copies of the scary old book Nigel attempts to read on the evening of Trapbois's murder, two belong to 'an eminent member of the Roxburgh Club, now M. P. for a great university' (267.42–43). In striking out the last phrase Scott registered the sexual scandal to which this old friend and great bibliophile, Richard Heber, had fallen prey in 1826—the same friend to whom Scott had turned in 1822 for assistance in getting his younger son Charles a place at Oxford. Otherwise, the corrections are without personal inflection. Verbal changes run to 130; all other changes concern punctuation and number 20 (several new or restored dashes but mostly changes required by verbal alterations). Three times Scott made and then cancelled changes. Few verbal changes involve more than a word or phrase. The conspicuous exceptions are three new passages intended as notes but not so marked and one passage cut from the Introductory Epistle— Scott must have had second thoughts about appropriating Johnson's 'unwilling tribute' to Churchill for the Author of Waverley (15.39–42). Since the corrections tend to come in clusters of two or three, it is no exaggeration to say that well over half the pages of text are unmarked by Scott's pen. It would be wrong, however, to appraise the quality of the revisions that are made from their quantity. If Scott was not consistently engaged with the narrative, as opposed to the apparatus, when he was attentive to it the novel benefited.

At the level of diction Scott continued to eradicate offensive verbal repetitions, resulting in some dozen or more changes in all. Beaujeu's 'ordinary' and 'ordinary language' (137.16–17), though two different senses of the word, were much too close, and Scott changed the second (with a slip of the pen): 'in ⟨ordinary⟩ ↑ common to ↓ language'. But he could also introduce repetition for rhetorical effect. In a single sentence, in fact, he did both: 'I must, however, ⟨proceed⟩ ↑ go on ↓ as I have begun, to apply the masculine gender; for, notwithstanding very ingenious reasons, and indeed something like positive evidence, have been offered to prove the Author of Waverley to be two ladies of talent ⟨—⟩ ↑ I must ↓ abide by the general opinion' (5.20–24). 'Proceed' led to an unwanted echo at 27; the second 'I must' shored up the sentence, not to mention underscoring the sense that Clutterbuck needed to get back to firmer ground. More often still, Scott substituted for a wrong word or a poor one. The old Earl Huntinglen is a 'stubborn' not 'stout' old man (121.41); Aunt Judith, relative to Lady Hermione, is the 'elder' not the 'good' lady (204.5); Duke Hildebrod, in his capacity as bailiff of White-friars, requires the surgeon to make proper 'declaration' not 'description' of the way in which the robbers' victims met their ends (277.10). And it is not 'cock-a-leek' but 'cock-a-leeky' (63.1), in the first reference to this favourite dish of King James and one of the recurring marks of Scottish identity in the novel. Though not so numerous, changes at the level of syntax are equally effective. At several points Scott fills in what seem to him to be gaps in the existing text. For example: 'I am no more the same author ↑ I was ⟨at⟩ in my better mood ↓, than the dog in a wheel . . . is like the same dog' (10.40–41). Or: 'the excuse of the slave, who ⟨was⟩ about to be punished for having spread the false report of a victory ↑ saved himself by exclaiming ↓,—"Am I . . ."' (7.32–34).

To be sure, some of the changes are simply narrative business. Scott tagged speeches: 'replied the satirist' (342.12, following 'lord,'), referring to Sir Mungo; nudged the reader's memory: 'as we before ⟨hinde⟩ hinted' (174.16, following 'supposed,'); threw in a word to avoid a possible ambiguity or misreading: 'put ↑ the quean ↓ aff on him ↑, ↓ the puir simple bairn' (358.32–33); and explained more fully a character's thinking or behaviour: 'so improbable did it seem that his domestic ↑ whom he supposed to be in Scotland ↓ should have found him out' (345.24–25). But he continued to operate as he had both in the manuscript and the proofs to strengthen the rhetorical force of the writing, in particular by ending paragraphs with a flourish. It is Dalgarno's cynical wisdom, for example, that, however black his reputation with the English, the Scots will welcome him, for 'they never quarrel with any one who brings them home either gold or martial glory ↑ much more if he has both gold and laurels ↓' (392.13–15). Scott also elaborated on motifs such as Nigel's social inexperience and Richie's exaggerated self-importance, in one speech, simply by having the latter speak an heretofore understood 'I' (291.15, before 'have'). Nigel, we are told, '⟨was⟩ ↑ young as he was in society became gradually ↓ less alarmed by the language and manners of his new associate, than in prudence he ought to have been' (135.6–8). Later, Dalgarno's claim to be Nigel's 'best friend, if not his only one', is further qualified by the phrase 'of decent station' (179.6). Shortly thereafter, Dalgarno's speech is emended to underline this same social naïvety: 'Such is the reputation you have made for yourself, and you have no right to be angry that I do not contradict ↑ in society ↓ what yourself knows to be true' (180.5–7). Particularly nice is a small addition to Margaret Ramsay's anonymous letter to Nigel warning him of Dalgarno's false friendship. Having inscribed at the top 'These, from a friend unknown:——' (166.25), in the body of the letter she repeats herself—'An unknown friend'. But as emended in the Interleaved Set, the repetition comes with a variation reflecting the conflict between heart and head: 'An unknown ↑ but real ↓ friend' (166.28). Jin Vin's masterful merchandising of Ramsay's time-pieces is enhanced by the stroke of a new analogy: 'What d'ye lack? —a watch Master Serjeant—a watch that will go ↑ as long as a lawsuit ↓ as steady and true as your own eloquence?' (26.29–31). James's own turn for apt analogy is exhibited when, gratified that Richie has not come to dun him, he orders that the Scot be admitted to his presence: 'we will grace him accordingly. ↑ What though he be but a carle—a twopenny cat may look at a King— ↓ ' (403.5). Surely one of Scott's best inspirations is the expanded speech he awards to Martha Moniplies, née Trapbois, in the final moments, where in response to the King's offensive compliment—'Troth, Mistress Bride, for a fule, your gudeman has a pretty turn of wit'—she spunkily replies: 'There are fools, sire . . . who have wit, and fools who have courage, ↑—aye and fools who have learning ↓ and are great fools notwithstanding' (406.6–9). Cleverly, Scott reminds us, here at the end, of his own view of James as a paradoxical figure and of the celebrated expression of it, quoted earlier—'the wisest fool in Christendom'—which he liked. The knighting of Richie that follows immediately perfectly illustrates Martha's point.

Less frequent sorts of change—for native language (the English 'Gaffer', as in the manuscript, not the Scots 'Gaffie' for the English barber: 96.32); for rhythm ('night-walking queans and ↑ sw[a]ggering ↓ billies': 45.27)—also attest to Scott's intermittent inspiration. One category of these is change for historical accuracy. The Earl of Northampton should join the list of those whose lack of vigilance allowed the Gunpowder Plot to flourish (though it also allowed James to boast of his superior wisdom in thwarting the conspiracy), after Suffolk (309.17); Stubbs lost his hand, not at Paul's Cross, but at Westminster (339.31); Queen Mary was James's 'kinswoman' rather than his 'cousin' (except in the general sense) (403.33). The inaccurate reference to Theobalds, James's favourite country retreat, as a castle—resulting from a misreading of the manuscript word 'costly'—is now corrected (62.9: 'yonder ⟨castle's⟩ hall-clock at Theobald's'). The most curious such change is a form of self-correction. Nigel has likened Richie's contorted features to 'the grotesque mask on one of the spouts' of the Temple Church seen through the window. Richie has turned to look 'with as little alacrity as if he had the crick in his neck'. He replies: 'Creak here, creak there—it were nae such matters that I have to speak anent' (159.38–160.2). In the Interleaved Set, Scott exchanged the 'creak's for 'mask's. Several other changes are probably unfortunate. Scott rejected the 8vo efforts to effect syntactical precision in 'as well ⟨as⟩, or better than' (198.40). He undercut Richie's speech deploring the state of Nigel's clothes when deprived of the valet's attention by altering 'buttons off' to 'buttons of' (345.18), repeating the correction he had made in the author's proof, but which had not been adopted. This time he prevailed. And he might better have left alone Jin Vin's anguished answer to Richie's question of what he did when learning that Ramsay had consented to Margaret's marrying Nigel: 'I ⟨took⟩ ↑rushd into ↓ the streets' (386.14). Two examples vividly illustrate the way that authors can lose touch with their earlier work: Scott's change at 6.36–37, 'then gliding on, never pausing, never precipitating ↑its course↓, visiting . . .' shows that he has forgotten that 'precipitating' can be intransitive, and his substitution of 'perfectly' for 'personally' at 62.1 that he thought his manuscript had been misread, forgetting that 'personally' can mean 'in relation to the person specified'. On the whole, however, Scott's work in the Interleaved Set was thoughtful.

Readers coming to the Magnum *Nigel* from the 8vo (or 18mo) edition would, of course, already have encountered many of the approximately 3300 changes that distance the Magnum from the First Edition. Nearly 2300 of these concern punctuation; another 1000 are verbal in nature, many of them variant spellings of frequently occurring words and proper names; the remaining 40 or so changes involve paragraphing and transpositions of words or phrases. New to these readers would be the 150 changes in diction or phrasing (and related punctuation) that Scott made in the Interleaved Set and approximately 1000 post-Scott corrections. No sets of Magnum proofs are known to have survived. It is likely that most, if not all, of the changes made after the Interleaved Set can be attributed to Robert Cadell's exacting editorial activity. Editorial processes at work in the first-edition proofs, in the collected editions, and in the Interleaved Set were continued in preparing the text for the Magnum: paragraphs and sentences were further divided (or, in some few cases, combined) and, occasionally, sentence elements were transposed; hyphenated words were written as one (and, to a lesser extent, the reverse procedure occurred); additional commas were supplied and existing punctuation varied by making greater use of the semi-colon and colon, especially, but also by substituting more exclamation marks for full-stops and introducing new dashes; distinctions between actual and implied speech were more closely observed, as were those between interrupted and incomplete speech, thus restoring something of the subtlety of Scott's use of the dash in the manuscript; the current fashion in diacritical marks for Greek and French was followed; spelling was still further regularised and modernised; the spelling of Scots words was made more consistent; grammatical slips not heretofore noticed were corrected; and, of course, undesirable verbal repetition—that nemesis of Scott's style—received steady attention. Perhaps an extreme case, but one nevertheless suggestive of the level of formal accuracy to which Cadell aspired in the Magnum, is the change of 'his toilette' to 'his toilet' in order to complement the gender of the character, Nigel, to whom the word refers (104.23).

More typical of the apparently post-Scott changes in the Magnum are such alterations in diction and syntax as these: (1) to eliminate seeming repetition, 'being the servant' replaced 'being the servant of a servant' (36.6), Richie's precisely accurate definition of blackward tenure; (2) to substitute standard English and, at the same time, avoid cacophony, 'when would one of his wealth have shaken hands so courteously with a poor Englishman?' replaced 'when would one of his having have shaken hands so courteously with a poor Englishman?' (38.18–19), Frank Tunstall's way of expressing Master Heriot's civility to his beggarly compatriot Richie Monoplies; (3) to make structurally parallel, 'they [the pictures and other ornaments of King James's cabinet] were arranged in a slovenly manner, covered with dust' replaced 'they were slovenly arranged, covered in dust' (66.20); (4) to achieve a more formal style, 'those with whom he was in terms of familiarity' replaced the homely 'his familiars' (67.36), the people on whom James, behaving unkingly, bestowed affectionate nicknames while for the same reason, 'the party required the money' replaced the colloquial 'the party could not want the money' (70.3); (5) for better euphony, 'to all appearances inextricably' replaced 'apparently inextricably' (122.20–21); (6) for more modern, standard English, 'it was no farther back than the Queen's time' replaced 'it was not longer than the Queen's time' (181.16), Scott's imitation of a 17th-century speech habit occurring in the old drama; (7) for more accurate diction and stronger syntax, 'having piously seen her father finish his breakfast, (from the fear that he might . . . swallow the salt-cellar . . .)' replaced 'having piously seen her father eat his breakfast, (taking care that he did not . . . swallow the salt-cellar . . .)' (200.26–28); (8) for standard English, 'they were in the habit of observing' replaced 'they were in use to observe' (204.1–2), said of servants in Heriot's house (presumably for the same reason, 'what this man has shown himself to be' replaced 'what this man has shewn himself') (220.22); and—to finish on a more 'creative' note—(9) to supplement a speech, 'I give my god-daughter the marriage-ring; it is a curious jewel—I bought it in Italy' expanded upon 'I give my god-daughter the marriage-ring; I bought it in Italy' (400.16–17), Heriot's terse answer to Sir Mungo's prying question about his wedding gift to his god-daughter Margaret. Together with the changes in language and punctuation already indicated, these and similar little alterations in diction and syntax often moved Scott's prose away from the speech usages and rhythms of Elizabethan and Jacobean drama that had inspired him during composition. In the case of every example above, most especially the last, one can easily argue that the changes were unfortunate. The Magnum was truly a new edition, even if relatively little of its

distinctive text, as opposed to the notes, was—so far as we know—
Scott's doing.

4. THE PRESENT TEXT

The Greenwich barber who trims Nigel's hair and beard entertains his
customers with a fast patter that rarely pauses, much as Scott composed his fictions at a pace calculated to keep his readers continuously
amused: as they put down the last one, a new one waited to be picked up.
In the heat of gossiping or story-telling, neither the barber nor Scott
can be bothered to stop to get a character's name correct—in the barber's
case, that of Sir Mungo Malagrowther (mangled in several ways at
several points); in Scott's, the names of most of his characters both
major and minor. It is only 'with infinite difficulty' that Nigel thrusts
'in his conjectural emendation . . . betwixt two clauses of the barber's
text' (297.5–7). In this respect Scott's titular hero is no bad emblem
of the intermediaries, whose formidable task of turning Scott's transcribed manuscript and corrected proofs into print had to be completed at comparable speed if the Author of Waverley's reputation for
wizardry was not to be compromised. The conclusion of the Introductory Epistle—where the printer's devil interrupts the conversation between the Eidolon of the Author of Waverley and Captain Clutterbuck
to 'demand' on behalf of the printer M'Corkindale the revise from
which the author has been distracted, and where other employees of the
Ballantyne firm are rebuked for allowing the captain to interfere with
business in the first place—captures beautifully the corporate sense of
urgency unique to producing the Waverley Novels. Few would deny
that, following standing orders for what they were expected to do and
not to do with Scott's text, the intermediaries did their job admirably.

But the scene with the barber may serve as well to illustrate the
pros and cons of these arrangements (see 429 above for an elaborated
list). By executing their orders the team turned Scott's manuscript
into a readable novel, but they also made it, at many points, different
from the novel *in* the manuscript, sometimes unfortunately so. Many
of the dashes that create the barber's wonderful flow of words seemingly propelled by their own momentum became full-stops in the
hands of the intermediaries, with the result that the distinctive character of his speech is lost—or, to put it another way, form and function
clash. Because *Nigel* is particularly rich in colourful characters—
Scots-speaking, English-speaking, French-speaking, Latin-speaking,
mulatto-speaking and these inflected for dialect and social class—whose
individuality is created through their rhetoric, standing orders and
house rules for punctuation, inevitably, had the effect of homogenising
Scott's gallery of characters, somewhat as the royal portraits in Holyrood Palace were homogenised by the use of the same model for
different subjects. For this reason, the single largest class of emenda-

tions in the present text involves punctuation, and within that class the restoration of dashes to Scott's prose, especially to his dialogue, bulks largest. It was not only the language and idiom of Jacobean drama that he heard in his mind as he composed but also the phrasing or speech rhythms and idiosyncratic sounds and accent patterns of actors speaking the words. Even the relatively bland characters, in moments of musing aloud, muttering, stammering, hesitancy, or upset (Nigel himself, Margaret Ramsay, Martha Trapbois, Andrew Skurliewhitter, Colepepper, and George Heriot), were well served by the flexibility of Scott's dash. A prominent sub-category of emendation is the restoration of the dash to distinguish between orderly or sequential speech and disjointed speech, as well as to point (by whether closing quotation mark precedes or follows the dash) the finer distinction between interrupted speech and incomplete speech, two ways in which Scott sought to inject verisimilitude into his dialogue by varying its pattern.

The exchange between the Greenwich barber and Nigel can also cast light on the difficulty of the intermediaries' task with words. Conspicuous among the verbal emendations in the present text are those pertaining to characters' names. Scott's habitual problem with naming his fictional characters and, once named, remembering them was no less troublesome to the intermediaries for being confessed—not to mention his penchant for using nicknames (e.g. Jin Vin for Jenkin Vincent, who started out as Edmund Vincent) or for alternating between two or more forms of names (e.g. Dame Ursula and Dame Ursley; King James and King Jamie). Thus, determining that a character's mistake with a name is deliberate on Scott's part was rarely so easy as with the barber. Elsewhere even in the barber's speech it is hard to know whether the crabby old Scot Sir Mungo Malagrowther's garbled name—'Sir Munko Malgrowler' or 'Malcrowder' (297.4, 8)—is Scott's misspelling or the barber's mispronunciation. Similarly, it is difficult to know whether the misspelling of Nigel's assumed name while hiding out in Alsatia—Nigel Grahame or Graeme (192.12–21), when pronounced by Duke Hildebrod as Niggle Green (256.4)—is Scott's way of telling us how the name would have been heard, a subtle interjecting of an indelicate joke befitting the place to be spotted by his more streetwise readers, or a casualty of his haste in writing.[96] One may compare, in Richie Moniplies' effort to interest Nigel in unflattering gossip about their late host George Heriot, the odd 'Jen Win' for the usual 'Jin Vin' (89.12). The 'precisian' Scot is typically as punctilious in speech as in ethics, so it is not likely that he mis-speaks, particularly since shortly before he has correctly named the London apprentice. In the manuscript, moreover, Scott sometimes wrote 'Win'. At the same time one does not want to rule out the possibility that here, as elsewhere in the novel, Scott is using mispronunciation to build the comic character of the speaker—or that, in time-honoured authorial tradition, he wishes to show that Richie is tipsy, by his own admission, having not only eaten Heriot's meat but also 'drunk his wine' (88.35). That the other errors with Vincent's name surviving into the first edition were gradually purged in subsequent editions, leaving only this one, might suggest that such was perceived to be Scott's intention. It is more likely, however, that the unusual spelling here was an oversight. Hence the present edition corrects it. By comparison, the problem with Wiba, the name of Dame Suddlechop's mulatto servant, seems straightforward enough. Probably unknown to the intermediaries, it emerged first as 'Wilsa' and then as 'Wilia'. The present text restores the original name. It is remarkable that, with names as with the myriad other difficulties they faced, the intermediaries did as well as they did. They had their work cut out for them!

Emendation of pre-proof changes. Of the nearly 2400 emendations in the present text, some 2000 correct errors introduced by intermediaries between the manuscript and the uncorrected author's proof. The emendations derived from pre-proof changes are divided roughly equally between the verbal and non-verbal categories, and for the restoration of Scott's text the non-verbal emendations can be seen as at least as important as the verbal ones.

1] *Capitals, italics, and punctuation.* Personified abstractions capitalised in the manuscript, though relatively rare, are returned to capitals. A good example is to be seen in the phrase 'that . . . respect which Authority pays as a tax to Decorum' (312.2–3). A little farther along, the manuscript capital is restored to the institution of history in the phrase 'until English History shall perish' (312.36). Scott's play on the novel's title in the opening of the third chapter of Volume 3—'We left Lord Glenvarloch, to whose Fortunes our story chiefly attaches itself' (292.28–29)—is recovered by returning to the manuscript capital. What may seem quaint to modern readers is the initial capital for an ordinary word in mid-sentence, a practice common to Scott's manuscript and, thus, to this edition. Most of the emendations in the present edition, in fact, are of this sort. In fashioning sentences from Scott's run-on manuscript, the intermediaries dropped quite a lot of these, as they were authorised to do and, indeed, as their job compelled them to do. But on occasion their work proved deleterious to the movement of Scott's prose. Where this would appear to be the case, the internal capital has been restored, sometimes with an accompanying restoration of the lower case for another word. Thus it is in the passage 'be not moved, my lord, it is so noised of you—Men call you the Sparrow-hawk, who will fly at all—ay, were it in the very Park—be not moved, my lord' (258.17–20). At the same time that first-edition 'men' becomes 'Men', first-edition 'Be' in the reiterated phrase 'Be not moved' becomes 'be'. But the intermediaries' decision to capitalise 'Park'—the short name for 'Park of St James'—stands. Such a composite reading is the norm in this edition. John Christie's moving plea to Nigel for the whereabouts of his strayed wife presents a still more compelling case for restoring the manuscript internal capital. Accordingly, the sentence now reads: 'She has lain in my bosom, and drunk of my cup—and such as she is, I cannot forget that—though I will never see her again—She must not starve, my lord, or do worse, to gain bread' (318.12–15). Some 130 capitals are restored in the present text, 25 or so in connection with restored dashes. At the same time some 360 capitals are changed to lower case, 290 or so in connection with restored dashes.

From time to time, Scott relied on italics as well as capital letters to provide emphasis. He called for italics when one speaker repeated another speaker's word, usually for the purpose of mocking or belittling the latter. A particularly telling example occurs in the proofs where Scott italicised 'descended' in Dame Ursula's reply to Margaret Ramsay's boast that she is 'descended ... from the great Earls of Dalwolsey': 'Ay, ay ... I never knew a Scot of you but was *descended*, as ye call it, from some great house or other' (101.21–24). The evidence of Scott's fondness for this rhetorical marker has prompted the restoration of the omitted 'do' in another passage: 'I wish to know how you, who ↑ do ↓ talk so big—I mean no offence, master, but you *do* talk big,—would help yourself in such a case?' (293.43–294.1). Perhaps because they saw the first 'do' as repetition, the intermediaries dropped it, but the italics, to be effective, need the physical presence of the word being singled out. As with capital and lower-case letters, however, the intermediaries, especially James Ballantyne, sometimes supplied italics where none existed in the manuscript. Where seemingly unjustified, they have been replaced by roman type. Some 16 emendations involve italics.

Two examples of restored dashes must suffice to exemplify the nearly 700 changes to the dash in the present text (315 of which have already been included in the discussion of capitals above), only a handful of which substitute for the dash. From the Greenwich barber's patter—the greatest concentration of them—any selection must be arbitrary, but this one is characteristic: 'Ay, ay, sir—Sir Munko, as you say—a pleasant, good-humoured gentleman as ever—To be spoken with, did you say?—O ay, easily to be spoken withal—that is, as easily as his infirmity will permit—He will presently—unless some one hath asked him forth to breakfast' (297.28–31). In the first edition, five of the seven dashes (the 2nd, 4th, 5th, 6th, and 7th) were replaced by a semi-colon, a question mark, a period, and two commas. A second example is from a passage in which the punctuation of Scott's manuscript reflects Martha Trapbois's struggle to speak in her usual firm, measured, somewhat harsh, manner—to act for her own preservation—while still grieving deeply for her murdered father. The absence of full-stops indicates that she has not yet regained her usual control. Accordingly, the present text replaces the intermediaries' punctuation with manuscript dashes at

four points (after 'cause', 'rest', 'courage', and 'spring'): '"You fear,"
she said—"there is no cause—the murderer and his victim are both at
rest—take courage—I will go with you myself—you cannot know the
trick of the spring—and the chest will be too heavy for you"'
(281.36–39).

Related to the restored dashes are the emendations to distinguish
interrupted from incomplete speech. There are 60 of these, many of
them adopted in the Magnum.

The omnipresent dashes in Scott's manuscript imply the relative
absence of other punctuation. Consequently, the present text regards
his occasional full-stop, semi-colon, colon, question mark, or exclamation mark as intentional, and restores them. There are some 120 of
these. Surely the most memorable example of Scott's resorting to conventional punctuation is when he employs a double exclamation mark to
indicate that even the worldly Reggie Lowestoffe, though never speech-
less, can be overtaken by surprise, at least when a man so circumspect as
Nigel has appeared to be, reveals that he must take up residence in
Alsatia for a while: 'Indeed!!' is the astonished Templar's immediate
response to this shocking news (183.29).

The intermediaries' commas, though excessive and even misleading
by modern writing practices and printers' conventions, are 'in period'
and, accordingly, are removed only with the sanction of the manuscript
and, then, only when seriously detrimental to sense. Some 75 emendations involve the comma.

To illustrate in general the effort of the present edition to preserve the
movement of the manuscript, we might cite the following passage. In
manuscript Scott wrote: 'Dalgarno *was* a fool when he bought I *will* be a
fool when I pay and you Sir Mungo craving your pardon are a fool . . .'.
The first edition reads: 'Dalgarno *was* a fool when he bought—I *will* be
a fool when I pay. And you, Sir Mungo, craving your pardon, *are* a fool
. . .'. The present text appears as: 'Dalgarno *was* a fool when he bought,
I *will* be a fool when I pay, and you, Sir Mungo, craving your pardon, *are*
a fool . . .' (129.4–6). (The intermediaries' decision to italicise the
third verb, in keeping with the first two, was good work.) For another
example, we might note a passage in the last scene of the novel; the
former Miss Trapbois, now Mrs Moniplies, is speaking. Scott wrote:
'"Peace" said his bride once more "This paper . . ."'. The first edition
reads: '"Peace," said his bride, "once more—This paper . . ."'
(3.344.6–7). The present text, restoring the sense of Scott's manuscript (it is the request for, not the condition of, peace that is being
repeated), returns the third quotation mark to its original position
(404.23). Trapbois's habit of dwelling on each syllable of the word
'consideration' before accenting the final syllable all but makes audible his inveterate greed, but the intermediaries do not always follow
fully Scott's manuscript directions for conveying to readers' eyes and

ears through punctuation this oral signature of the old man's character. The present text does, thereby repairing serious damage to the rhythm of Scott's prose at those points (see 243.37 and 250.24). So, too, the restoration of Scott's manuscript intention at 36.34–35. In their worthy effort to avoid repeating the manuscript's 'a ship-chandler' but making the wrong choice, intermediaries inverted the parenthetical material 'his father came from Dundee' and the principal material 'he is a ship chandler as they ca'd', sacrificing Scott's dashes in the process. Gone was the accelerating movement of Richie's speech.

2] *Substitutions.* At their smallest, these verbal emendations consist of deleting the 's' added to nouns: one or more of Scott's intermediaries seems either to have been partial to plurals or to have seen them where none existed (and none was necessary). He assigns Ramsay's apprentices two beds, for example, though the text has established that they share one (31.32–34). More hefty are the categories of single-word changes and multiple-word changes. The need for the former is occasioned by the transcriber's or another intermediary's substituting a similar or look-alike word for the original (e.g. 'hand' for 'band', 'concurrence' for 'connivance'); by his adding or subtracting articles, function words (e.g. the sign of the infinitive), and pet intensifiers (e.g. 'own', 'now', 'so', 'even') or qualifiers (e.g. 'somewhat' or 'sometime'); or by his rejecting Scott's favoured forms of words (e.g. 'amongst' rather than 'among', 'burthen' rather than 'burden'). The need for the latter results from his omitting or adding phrases, for which the rationale, either way, is obscure at best. Even the slightest single-word change has the capacity to alter meaning significantly, as when, for example, in the counsel Lady Hermione offers Margaret Ramsay, the first edition substituted 'the' for 'our' in the phrase 'be patient—it is our only remedy' (216.37–38), thereby inscribing the very hierarchy the older woman seeks to minimise. The change of 'hat' to 'cap' in the motto to Chapter 4 (50.8) vitiates Scott's concerted effort in the novel to signify class distinctions through head-gear—here between the citizen's flat cap, as worn by Vincent or Heriot, and the courtier's (even the king's) beaver hat and feather. At another point the force of Scott's imagery is spoiled by the first edition's substitution of 'have' for 'hear' in the passage: 'I should love well to make the oaks of my old forest of Dalgarno ring once more with halloo, and horn, and hound, and to hear the old stone-arched hall return the hearty shout of my vassals and tenants, as the bicker and the quaigh walked their rounds amongst them' (121.3–7). Often, of course, the change of one word sets up a domino effect, causing Scott grief in the proofs, where the solution is not always felicitous. Such is the case, to take a simple example, where he wrote 'general' but the transcriber or other intermediary produced 'genial'; Scott's unsatisfactory solution in the proofs was to write 'congenial' (257.5). Similarly, the mistake of changing 'Representation, of' to

'Representative of' led Scott to insert the noun 'Vision' in proof, making 'apparition' in the subsequent sentence redundant (4.43–5.3). A more elaborate case resulted from the misreading of 'Her coffin' as 'Wherefore' (91.27). Not in touch with his manuscript when reading proof, Scott substituted 'What reason', which required him in turn to introduce the phrase 'but there is the coffin' in the next paragraph and in other ways to make adjustments over two paragraphs of dialogue.

If the intermediaries can be characterised by their quirks, in addition to the superfluous plurals, they tended to alter or reverse numbers. Where Scott wrote 'five', it became 'four'; where Scott wrote 'two running footmen three dogboys', it became 'three . . . two'; and where Scott thought 'one or two hasty exclamations' adequate, it was upped to 'two or three'. There was nothing quirky, however, about an intermediary's substituting one word for another in order to avoid undesirable repetition. This standing order was executed conscientiously and, for the most part, successfully. Unfortunately, in some cases, effective— and quite possibly purposeful—repetition on the author's part for the sake of rhythm and emphasis was sacrificed. Moreover, on rare occasions, the intermediaries themselves created repetition where none existed in the manuscript, as when, for example, someone changed Scott's 'hope' to 'trust', causing an echo with 'trust' only five words away (120.36). Only a sample passage where arguably intentional repetition was lost through substitution is offered here, for the process starts in the Introductory Epistle and continues right through the novel. The verb phrase in Captain Clutterbuck's bold advice to the Eidolon of the Author of Waverley —'Well, you must take the risk and act only on your own principles'—became 'must take the risk of proceeding on your own principles' in the first edition, apparently because of the Eidolon's response: 'Do you act on yours' (17.9–11). The change tends to nullify the testy tone that, by this point, the interview has assumed.

More to be deplored than such losses as these, however, are those resulting from the intermediaries' unfamiliarity with the idioms of seventeenth-century English or, in some cases, English of their own day. Other losses to the vitality and authenticity of Scott's text can be attributed to their lack of ear for speech. Scott's superior knowledge of period language does not alone account for his linguistic versatility; he seems to heard his characters speaking the lines even as he was drafting them. Scott knew that the Alsatian 'nymph' hoping to elicit song from her caged blackbird stood a better chance of success if she 'chirrup'd' (191.20), not 'chirped', to it; an intermediary did not. Repeatedly in such cases the *Oxford English Dictionary* validates the manuscript, word or phrase; the early drama, both in print and in manuscript, so extensively represented in Scott's library at Abbotsford, contextualises it. People in the seventeenth century, if not in Scott's time, did omit the article in 'out at door' (96.36) and 'at window' (267.22) or the conjunction in 'two three' (371.24); Londoners, at least when speaking to each other, did drop the 'Saint' before 'Paul's' (230.38) and shorten 'window-shutters' to 'window-shuts' (245.16); and they might well say 'tell out' (211.36) where they would expect to read 'tell me'. A dinner bell can indeed sound with a 'towl' (127.38)—changed to 'jowl' by an intermediary; a human voice has a 'tang' in it (38.33)—changed to 'twang'. A seventeenth-century ruffian, when properly initiated, was licensed to 'slide, swear, and swagger' (198.9)—or so says John O'Keefe's play *Fontainbleau* (2.1.121), one of the sources for Scott's conception of Alsatia and its rituals of citizenship: this was changed to 'stride, swear, and swagger'.

There were nearly 700 wrong substitutions in the first edition of *Nigel*. Adding or (occasionally) subtracting a final 's' alone accounted for over 60 of these changes; modified verbs and auxiliaries accounted for a similar figure; and changes in spelling made up some 80 more of them. While many others were minor—'nor' for 'or', 'the' for 'an', 'meanwhile' for 'meantime'—still others, as demonstrated above, had serious implications for meaning, tone, and narrative rhythm.

3] *Omissions and Insertions.* A dropped phrase like 'from time to time' (60.14) may be no great loss to the text. And one can see why the intermediaries might have cut the middle word in 'eager willing zeal' (124.33–34). If Scott's excess language here expresses his character's excess emotion, still the reader is not seriously deprived without the full phrase. But in reducing 'to the freedom of which' to, simply, 'to which' (222.42–43), they may well have subverted Scott's intent to contrast Hermione's confining convent cell, where she was a prisoner of the Spanish Inquisition, with the relative freedom of the convent garden from which she eventually escaped to the far greater freedom of Protestant London. And in altering the manuscript sentence 'It was like the roll of the prophet a record of lamentation & mourning and woe yet . . .' to read 'It was . . . a record of lamentation and mourning, and yet . . .' (313.1) the intermediaries lightened considerably the impression of Nigel's despondency upon being imprisoned in the Tower by restricting the rhythm of the sentence and, as well perhaps, forfeited the rich literary resonance of 'woe'. Effects are not, of course, to be confused with causes. It is well to remember that few if any of the adverse consequences of these and other changes were anything but the result of following standing orders or of accident—e.g. a slip of the eye, a missing or displaced caret, an above-the-line insertion overlooked, a verso correction separated from the recto text.

Sometimes the intermediaries' response to unwanted repetition was not to substitute but to omit. In this way, too, arguably intentional or effective repetition was lost. The Chevalier Beaujeu's boasting of his culinary hero's ingenuity in preparing a victory dinner of 'forty-five couverts' for the Marechal Strozzi from nothing more than a little thistle, nettle, and puppy dog is undercut when the repeated 'mais forty-five' is ignored (144.33). A straightforward example of effective repetition lost in transcription is the second 'honest' in Richie Moniplies' appraisal of Martha Trapbois upon first meeting—'as decent and honest ye seem to be—why, I will advise you to a decent honest house' (291.39–40)—possibly because 'honest' is one of those overused epithets which the intermediaries were expected to prune. Deliberate or not, it seems unfortunate that in transcribing the phrase '[Lady Hermione] once more turned her penetrating eyes on Nigel with a fixed look which compelled him to turn his own eyes aside' (87.4–6) the second 'eyes' was lost. A case where Scott's superior linguistic experience may have worked to his disadvantage is in the cutting of the second phrase from the manuscript 'ye can but see the place and say the place' (292.4). Viewing and assessing a place are not the same thing. Repetition intended to serve the reader by maintaining continuity in a speech broken by lengthy description of gesture, tone of voice, or situation, might also be excised. This happened to one of Richie Moniplies' more dramatic performances, where Scott broke a sentence of dialogue at 'however' and resumed it with the same word. The reiteration did not survive the intermediaries.

Only one entire sentence was struck from the printed edition. It is restored except for the needless repetition of the adverb 'instantly', possibly connected in some way with its being dropped (see 263.9–10). The sentence makes a contribution, albeit a minor one perhaps, to the movement of Scott's story. One major loss, on the other hand, was clearly occasioned by eye-slip or oversight or both. In the first edition Dame Ursula tells Margaret, by way of encouraging her to share a glass of sack, that 'before the gospellers came in, the old Catholic father confessors and their penitents always had a cup of sack together before confession; and you are my penitent'. In the manuscript Scott, realising that what followed 'before confession' was a non-sequitur, inserted above the line of text the explanation 'to loosen the tongue of the one and to soften the rigour of the other', together with the missing part of the analogy Dame Ursula seeks to draw: 'Now I am your confessor' (99.21–26). Perhaps the copyist's difficulty with Scott's handwriting occasioned a bad transcription bordering on nonsense. Scott wrote: 'like the practical adaptation of theory to practice'; the copyist transcribed: 'like the practical adaptation of thorough practice' (23.24–25). Granted the second 'practice' is redundant, the original makes far more sense than the first edition. For an example of another kind: the self-consciousness of Hermione as a narrator is diminished when the manuscript parenthesis '—which I must describe very hastily—' disappears (221.22–23). We lose, too, the reminder that at least one of Scott's characters is herself a teller of story.

The approximately 150 omissions were matched by roughly 160 insertions. Slightly more in number, they probably did considerably less damage. When not made for the purpose of clarity, they seem to have been intended to embellish Scott's prose, much as were, for the most part, the post-proof changes discussed below. Hence 'so unjust' became 'so flagrantly unjust' (51.38–39); 'doth Duke' became 'doth faithful Duke' (192.25); 'Ye may' became 'Your good lordship may' (169.31); 'vara interesting indeed' became 'vara interesting—vara interesting indeed' (340.23); and 'puritan?' became 'puritan, fool?' (161.14).

There is little to fault in the intermediaries' correction for grammar whether in the form of substitutions, omissions, or insertions. Those errors that escaped their attention, if indeed they would have been errors in the early nineteenth century (narrative) or the early seventeenth century (dialogue), are corrected in the present text, sometimes from the manuscript. The second word in 'The creditor . . . they' of the first edition is corrected, on the authority of the manuscript, to 'creditors' in the new text (119.38–40), for example. However, as when performing other prescribed tasks, the intermediaries, in this area too, could inflict damage on Scott's text. They might better have preferred the manuscript verb form 'as if he heard' to 'as if he had heard' (274.35): it allows for the possibility that Nigel continues to hear 'a muttering beneath the windows'. And they would have done well not to tamper with the present tense verbs conveying the impression that Lowestoffe's chatter as he trusses Nigel for his incognito in Alsatia mimics his movements. Scott wrote: 'now observe I leave . . . and if it pleases you . . . Now I tie'; instead, they changed 'I leave' to 'I have left' (188.23). Transpositions of sentence elements in the transcription of *Nigel* follow the same pattern—mostly improvements or unobjectionable, but not always. An example of the former is the first edition's switch to 'am I' from the manuscript 'I am' in Nigel's statement: 'the point in question is, how I am to get to speech of the King' (301.41–42). An example of the latter might be the movement of 'tone of' from before 'high' to before 'morality' in the phrase 'a tone of high and stubborn morality' (134.42). Textual manipulation of Scott's grammar and syntax as of his diction often points, both in the transcription and the proofs, toward a fussy refinement of style rather than to lapses in Scott's prose —the same process so greatly accelerated several years later in editing the novels for the Magnum. It is perfectly clear from an earlier reference to France, for example, that the 'they' which follows shortly refers to the French people (324.30), even if the reference is slightly askew. But an intermediary substituted the noun for the pronoun, as standing orders permitted—and perhaps as grammatical accuracy dictated.

Treatment of author's-proof corrections. Like Scott's second thoughts in the manuscript, his self-revisions in the proofs are honoured in this edition, except in those few cases where he was demonstrably out of touch with his text, and regardless of whether they may be felt to have improved or damaged the text (filling in blanks, especially, produced mixed results). An example of one such exception concerns a word of one syllable. The proof read: 'there was a shout of wonder and execration on the supposed criminal purpose [assassinating the King], arose from the crowd'. Complicating the damage from the inserted comma, Scott introduced an 'of' ahead of 'execration', thereby completing the disaster of this unfortunate sentence (306.25–26). A second example —inserting the relative pronoun 'who' between 'him' and 'makes' in the phrase 'fine gentleman he!—apprentice to him makes the tick-tick'— suggests that Scott forgot his plan to distinguish the exotic character Wiba, servant to Dame Suddlechop, by a form of mulatto-speak (229.29–30). Perhaps Scott's greatest lapse in the proofs involves Dame Suddlechop herself. At 25.14 he inserted a one-sentence paragraph invoking her as simply a second choral voice, making narrative nonsense of the formal introduction of her character in Chapter 8 (92.36 ff.). The paragraph is omitted in the present text. Similarly, when filling a proof lacuna with the word *pageant* (27.22) Scott would seem to have forgotten that the manuscript word was *motion* and that a little later (48.25) not only had he used 'motion' in this sense but also footnoted it as meaning 'Puppet-shew'. The present text retains the original word but moves the footnote forward to explain it. Almost comical is the sequence of proof changes with the sentence 'Neither could he avoid feeling some twinges of conscience, acknowledging, in part at least, the charges which Richie had preferred against him, and a sense of shame . . .'. Scott substituted for the second clause 'while he ⟨coul⟩ felt in some degree' and inserted 'experienced' before 'a sense of shame'. He thus avoided repeating 'acknowledging' from the previous sentence but failed to note 'feel' in that sentence, not to mention 'feeling' in this one. An intermediary seeking to remedy this oversight replaced 'feeling' with 'experiencing', creating a repetition in the first edition not present either in the manuscript or in the author's-proof. The present text resolves the issue equitably: 'experiencing' is retained, 'experienced' is dropped (166.4–6).

For whatever reason some of Scott's proof corrections or parts thereof failed to appear in the first edition. A case in point is the failure to drop the phrase 'near Covent-Garden' while picking up the other changes Scott wanted at 366.18. A more difficult case to explain is the failure to catch up the adjective 'blue' which Scott introduced, presumably to add colour and strengthen rhythm as well as to reinforce sense, in the phrase 'there was a difference between clinking on gold and silver, and clattering upon blue pewter' (105.8). A problem resulting from a gap in the manuscript survived into the first edition because the proof correction was ignored. Scott wanted: 'Her John was greatly honoured by their lordships—and truly he was a kind, pains-taking man'. But what he got was: 'Her John was greatly and truly honoured by their lordships—he was a kind, pains-taking man' (131.20–22). These corrections are recognised in the present edition, in which over 70 emendations are derived from proof corrections, mostly by Scott, but some few by Ballantyne.

Emendation of post-proof changes. The approximately 250 verbal changes made after Scott's involvement with the proofs had ended are usually rejected. Several of these would appear to have been added to dress up Scott's narrative. The damage they do can be far out of proportion to the physical space they occupy, for they move the prose away from the dramatic vitality of the manuscript and toward the staginess of nineteenth-century melodrama. A characteristic touch is to throw in an exclamatory 'What!' or even a phrase such as 'What of the Marshalsea?' (248.20). The latter violates the logic of dramatic conversation, by giving the impression that Nigel is speaking to an audience rather than responding naturally to the character who has delivered the bad news. A somewhat similar effect emerges when Richie is made to repeat himself: 'Come wi' me—just come ye wi' me; and . . .' (382.42). By disposition or inclination the Scotsman is garrulous beyond belief, but he is not typically repetitive. Besides, the repeated phrase is artfully varied, making it phoney. Lowestoffe's epithet for the scrivener 'my little Andrew' (374.13) is in character; a second epithet 'my honest Andrew' inserted post-Scott between 'not' and 'I' within the same short sentence makes for self-parody.

Occasionally, changes in punctuation indicate much the same intention and result in much the same effect. The disguised Margaret Ramsay originally identifies herself as an 'unhappy boy' (315.10); this is changed to 'unhappy—boy', the slight hesitation introduced to underscore her embarrassment. The scrivener's reference to 'the papers' (376.16) is changed to 'the—the papers' on the principle of the more stammering, the greater fear. Those changes that do not extend Scott's corrected text with words or with punctuation alter the diction: 'that red' nose (127.31) becomes 'that copper' one, for example, in Dalgarno's phrase mocking a family servant.

For all their care the intermediaries could not prevent printer's errors —a mangled phrase, a missing full-stop or quotation mark or hyphen, a dropped letter, two words joined because of a tight line, and so on. Twenty-eight of these have been corrected, wherever possible using the earliest edition to have corrected the mistake as a model for how to do it, or on the authority of the manuscript. Taken singly, they are the least consequential changes, but together with the other emendations they have the ability to make the experience of reading *Nigel* something quite different from what it has been in the past.

NOTES

All manuscripts referred to, unless otherwise indicated, are in the National Library of Scotland. For the shortened forms of reference employed see 540–44.

1   *Letters*, 5.398: 15 June 1819. Corson (163) queries the date of this letter, but it is the preceding letter that is dated a day late.

2   *The Heart of Mid-Lothian*, ed. David Hewitt and Alison Lumsden, EEWN 6, 38.21.

3   *Letters*, 5.56: 16 January 1818.

4   *Letters*, 2.75: [October 1808] (see Corson, 42).

5   *The Ancient British Drama*, 3 vols (London, 1810); *The Modern British Drama*, 5 vols (London, 1811). See *Letters*, 2.113, 177, and 541, for Scott's involvement in this project.

6   Lockhart, 5.174.

7   D'Israeli's letter dated 27 February (MS 3892, ff. 59r–60v) is cited by Douglas Grant (see notes 14 and 16 below).

8   MS 3892, f. 76r: 15 March 1821.

9   For the original title see W. M. Parker, 'The Origin of Scott's "Nigel"', *Modern Language Review*, 34 (1939), 535.

10 *Letters*, 6.479–80: 16 June [1821].

11 Lockhart, 5.138.

12 *The Pirate*, ed. Mark Weinstein and Alison Lumsden, EEWN 12, 396.

13 *Letters*, 7.16.

14 In 'The Origin of Scott's "Nigel"', *Modern Language Review*, 34 (1939), 535–40, W. M. Parker follows Lockhart (5.138–43) in viewing the private letters as the beginning of the novel. He also recounts the later effort of Scott, in the winter and spring of 1832, to revive the plan for publishing them. It did not succeed, and they were first published (but without Nos 4, 6, and 8) by Andrew Lang in 'An Unpublished Work of Scott: Private Letters of King James's Reign', *Scribner's Magazine*, 14 (1893), 733–48. Douglas Grant, in the introduction to his edition *Private Letters of the Seventeenth Century by Sir Walter Scott, Bart.* (Oxford, 1947), gives the fullest account of the letters, but will not allow that the novel originated in them. To do so is to diminish the letters, one of the 'magnificent fragments' that we find in Scott's oeuvre; only parts of the novels, not excluding *Nigel*, can be so described. Grant does allow for similarities, some of the most striking of which can be readily seen in the sample letter printed by Lockhart (5.138–42), written by one J. H. or Jenkin Harman about a brawl at a fashionable London ordinary that raised the cry of 'Prentices, prentices, Clubs, clubs'.

15 Thomas Constable, *Archibald Constable and his Literary Correspondents* (Edinburgh, 1873), 3.142n. The original letter can be found in MS 323, f. 157r.

16 D'Israeli's letter to Scott on the subject of James I, partly quoted in Douglas Grant's introduction to the *Private Letters* (33–35), took up the idea of James's timidity as possibly constitutional, which Scott echoed in the novel. The seed of that constitution was popularly believed to have been sown

when Rizzio was murdered in the pregnant Mary's presence (see 307.3–6).

17 *Somers' Tracts*, 1.508–32. This authorised account of James's confinement, near murder, and escape may also be the source of his characteristic utterances echoing through Scott's novel at moments of perceived threat to his person and office: 'treason, treason' and 'I'm a free king' ('hee was born a free king, and should die a free king'; '[he] cried, that they were murthering him there in that treasonable forme': 517). The deer hunt at Greenwich best catches the terror of James when discovering that he is alone with someone—historically, Alexander Ruthven; fictionally, Nigel Oliphaunt—who may do him violence. David Mathew argues that fear was aroused in James 'in a greater or a lesser degree by all the members of the house of Gowrie': *James I* (London, 1967), p. 5.

18 Lockhart, 5.142–43. Lockhart's story brings together three literary 'events': the abandonment of the 'Private Letters', finishing *The Pirate*, and beginning *The Fortunes of Nigel*. In their Essay on the Text of *The Pirate*, Mark Weinstein and Alison Lumsden suggest that Lockhart's story is 'embellished', basically because they claim that the 'Private Letters' were printed in March, and that the first chapter of *The Fortunes of Nigel* was 'probably completed after Christmas' 1821 (EEWN, 12.396). However, the date of Scott's advertisement to the 'Private Letters', 20 March 1821, does not necessarily imply that the letters were put into print on 20 March, and Douglas Grant is plausible in suggesting that the date indicates the day on which Scott, Lady Louisa, and Morritt laid their plans (*Private Letters of the Seventeenth Century by Sir Walter Scott, Bart.* (Oxford, 1947), 37). A letter to J. B. S. Morritt of 16 June asks for Morritt's contribution as 'we are about to go to press in good earnest' (*Letters*, 6.480), which seems to imply that Scott's letters were in type and that he wished to proceed to printing. On 30 September he told Constable that the next novel would be about James VI and I (*Letters*, 7.16), and so if Lockhart did indeed advise that Scott use his King James material on a novel he gave that advice before 30 September. Secondly, it was the first volume of *Nigel*, not the first chapter, which was finished by 26 December (*Letters*, 7.40). In spite of these mistakes, Mark Weinstein and Alison Lumsden may still be right to claim that Lockhart's story is embellished. The 'Private Letters' project was abandoned sometime after June and before the end of September. The idea that Scott finished *The Pirate* and began *Nigel* on the same day is implausible because it does not accord with what is known about Scott's habits of composition, although it is not impossible. If Lockhart's story were right, it is more likely that Scott showed Terry the printed sheets of the penultimate chapter of *The Pirate* one morning, and the first hand-written section of *Nigel* on the next, which would suggest a gap of two weeks or so between finishing one novel and beginning the next.

19 *Letters*, 7.40.
20 MS 21059, ff. 137r–38v.
21 MS 1750, f. 317r.
22 MS 791, p. 471. That Scott did have access to the Derham, however, can be demonstrated from the manuscript, where a long insertion introduces technical terms and figures into the merchant's street-call that are taken

directly from that publication: see note to 29.16–17. Clearly this bit of revision at the beginning of Chapter 2 was executed considerably after the time of initial writing.

23   MS 791, p. 481: Cadell to Richard Milliken.

24   MS 791, p. 502: Cadell to Richard Milliken.

25   MS 677, ff. 43v–45v: Constable to Scott, 14 February 1822. Constable reminded Scott that at the end of the third volume of John Nichols's *The Progresses, and public Processions, of Queen Elizabeth*, 3 vols (London, 1788, 1805), which he had lent the novelist to assist with *Kenilworth*, there appeared a 'Specimen of King James's Progresses'. In fact, Scott does not appear to have drawn anything specific from these limited documents (Nichols's much more extensive *The Progresses, Processions, and Magnificent Festivities, of King James The First, His Royal Consort, Family, and Court* did not appear until 1828), nor is there evidence of his having consulted any of the 17th-century collections of James's sayings mentioned in Constable's letter.

26   *Letters*, 7.104. Corson (198–99) suggests that this letter should have been dated 13 March, but his arguments are not convincing.

27   *Letters*, 7.103. The excuse is borne out by the manuscript. Throughout composition Scott was plagued with forgetting or mistaking names. Towards the end of the second volume and for some time in the third, he gave up completely trying to remember the given name of Martha Trapbois and simply left the manuscript blank when referring to her.

28   *Letters*, 7.89. For the date of this letter see Corson, 197–98.

29   As Scott wrote to Joanna Baillie, he found 'no inspiration in . . . the Court of Session' (*Letters*, 7.59: 10 February [1822]). Specifically, he complained to Constable: 'I should have been long since finishd with what we are now doing but the removal of David Hume with a sharp fit of the gout on the part of Sir Robt. Dundas have for the time thrown some fagg on me as one brother of the Clerks table is absent & the other a novice' (*Letters*, 7.82: 25 February 1822; see also *Letters*, 7.56: 7 February 1822).

30   MS 323, f. 240r.

31   *Letters*, 7.124: [30 April 1822] (see Corson, 199). To judge by a letter of Cadell to one M. Bain about corrections for the *Index of the Edinburgh Medical Journal*, in approving a second revise especially, Ballantyne was deferring to Scott: 'you [Bain] were in the practice of getting proofs of almost every sheet a thing almost unheard of in any work going through the press a second revise is scarcely ever expected' (MS 792, pp. 296–98 (297): 21 June 1824).

32   MS 323, f. 234r: Cadell to Constable, 24 April, 1822. In order not to lose its competitive advantage over publishers in New York and Boston, the Philadelphia firm of Carey & Lea printed the first volume of its two-volume edition of *Nigel* from early sheets (but not, in the case of this novel, from proof sheets) of the British first-edition print-run and bound it before receiving the belated Introductory Epistle. As a result, it had to bind the introduction with the second volume (see William B. Todd and Ann Bowden, *Sir Walter Scott: A Bibliographical History 1796–1832* (New Castle, Delaware, 1998), 564–65, for Carey's explanation of how this came about). There were five other American editions in 1822—two in New

York, one in Albany, one in Boston, and another in Philadelphia. The Philadelphia (Edwin T. Scott) and the Albany (Webster) editions derive from the Carey & Lea, though the Introductory Epistle is in its proper place. The editions published at Boston (Samuel H. Parker) and New York (T. Longworth, and an edition 'Printed for the Booksellers') have a text closer to that of the Edinburgh first edition, with minimally accented French for instance.

33 MS 323, f. 260r: Cadell to Constable, 15 May 1822.
34 MS 323, ff. 249r, 251v: Cadell to Constable.
35 MS 323, f. 260r.
36 MS 320, f. 9r.
37 See *Letters*, 7.178, n1, and MS 677, f. 69r.
38 MS 320, f. 63v: Constable to Cadell, 24 December 1822.
39 William B. Todd and Ann Bowden, *Sir Walter Scott: A Bibliographical History 1796–1832* (New Castle, Delaware, 1998), 561.
40 MS 323, f. 263r.
41 MS 791, pp. 551, 553: Cadell to Robert Leslie on 21 May and to Richard Milliken on 22 May.
42 MS 677, f. 69r–v: Constable to Scott, 31 May 1822. See *The Pirate*, EEWN 12, 416, for Robinson's account of just how expeditiously upon arrival in London the novels were readied for the booksellers' distribution.
43 MS 323, f. 263r: Cadell to Constable, 24 May 1822.
44 MS 323, f. 230v: Cadell to Constable, 10 April 1822.
45 Jane Millgate, *Scott's Last Edition* (Edinburgh, 1987), 90.
46 MS 323, ff. 268r–68v.
47 MS 323, f. 275v: 2 June 1822.
48 MS 320, f. 10v.
49 MS 320, f. 14r: Constable to Cadell.
50 MS 677, f. 69r.
51 See MS 323, ff. 222r–27v: 6 April; ff. 230r–32r: 10 April; ff. 234r–33v: 24 April; ff. 240r–44r: 28 April; f. 265r: 29 May; ff. 276r–77r: 7 June; ff. 283r–88r: 9 June.
52 MS 326, f. 119r.
53 MS 326, f. 116v: 25 January 1822.
54 MS 326, f. 76r: 6 November 1821.
55 MS 320, f. 149r: 21 June 1823.
56 MS 323, f. 207v: 29 June 1821.
57 MS 326, f. 120r: 31 January 1822.
58 MS 323, f. 432r: 12 June 1823.
59 MS 677, f. 61v: 9 March 1822.
60 This project produced the acknowledgement from Scott to Constable that 'The author of Waverley finding it inconvenient to toss over books for a motto generally made one without much scrupling whether it was positively & absolutely his own or botchd up out of pieces & fragments of poetry floating in his memory' (*Letters*, 7.104: 23 March 1822). See the discussion of mottoes at 414–15 below.
61 This is not a continuation of John Ballantyne's 'Novelist's Library', to which Scott was already committed and which he would stick with for the widow's sake, but a similar project that would avoid what Constable regarded as marketing flaws in the late printer's scheme.

62 MS 323, f. 401r: Cadell to Constable, 19 May 1823.

63 MS 320, f. 9r: Constable to Cadell, 23 May 1822.

64 MS 323, f. 254v: 11 May. See above for Scott's use of this metaphor for the start of *Nigel*.

65 MS 323, f. 256v: Cadell to Constable.

66 MS 323, f. 227r; f. 262r: Cadell to Constable, 24 May 1822.

67 For Carlisle see MS 791, p. 524 (Constables to C. H. Thurnam: 27 March 1822); for Newcastle see MS 791, p. 637 (Constables to E. Charnley: 10 November 1822); for the other cities mentioned see MS 323, f. 277r (Cadell to Constable [7 June 1822]).

68 MS 791, p. 536.

69 MS 323, f. 277r: Cadell to Constable, 7 June 1822.

70 MS 791, p. 589: Cadell to Ballantyne, 22 July 1822.

71 MS 21059, f. 135r: 8 November 1822.

72 On 13 January 1823 Robinson notified Constable that he had 1286 copies of *Nigel* in stock, second only to 1336 copies of *Ivanhoe* (MS 326, f. 109r); Constable characterised this supply to Cadell as 'heavy' (MS 323, f. 359v: 16 January 1823). By 22 May 1823 the operative language was 'an immense stock "to use their own words" of the Pirate Nigel & Peveril' (MS 320, f. 112r). A year later little was changed: 'the Amt [of stock at Hurst, Robinson] is Very great certainly' (MS 320, f. 177v: 7 August 1824). Hurst, Robinson was not unique in being badly overstocked. At the end of 1824 Constable was advising Milliken, in Dublin, on how to disencumber his shelves. Perhaps significantly, it is with *Nigel* that the supply breaks into triple digits—117 (MS 792, pp. 375–76: 15 December 1824).

73 MS 4940, ff. 14–19. The quarto-type leaves on which most of the novel was written measure approximately 26.5 by 20 cm and were mostly formed by the folding in two and probably cutting of two sets of folio-type leaves derived from demy sheets. The main batch of paper used has a horn device as watermark (compare Heawood 2760) with the date 1817 below it, and 'VALLEYFIELD' with the same date below it as countermark (Valleyfield was the paper mill run by D. & A. Cowan at Penicuik, 20 km S of Edinburgh). The chain lines are 2.4 cm apart. Leaves 11–14 (the first four of the narrative) are on a different paper with the countermark 'D. & A. COWAN' with the date 1817 below. A schematic breakdown by folio leaf shows some of the more salient features of the whole manuscript:

Scott	Consecutive	Features
Volume 1		
None	1	start Introductory Epistle
2–6	2–6	Introductory Epistle ctd
6	7	Introductory Epistle ctd
7–8	8–9	end of Introductory Epistle
None	10	motto Ch. 1 and insert for leaf 10 on recto, and title ('The Fortunes of ⟨Olifaunt⟩ Nigel') on verso (leaf reversed)
None	11	start Ch. 1
2–19	12–29	end Ch. 3 (29)
*19	30	start Ch. 4
20	31	Ch. 4 ctd
21–24	32–35	Ch. 4 ctd

25	36	start Ch. 5 (Scott's 26 renumbered 25, perhaps by transcriber Huntly Gordon)
26	37	Ch. 5 ctd
*27	38	insertion expanding on the text (short sheet)
27	39	long sheet with Scott's regular writing
28–31	40–43	Ch. 5 ctd
32*	44	recto blank but insert for 45 on verso
32–42	45–55	end Ch. 5–end Ch. 7: last leaf ends with 'Chapter. VIII'
*42	56	repeat 'Chapter. VIII'
43–54	57–68	Ch. 8 ctd–Ch. 9
56	69	Scott mistakenly changed 55 to 56; end Ch. 9 and start Ch. 10
57–66	70–79	Ch. 10 ctd–Ch. 11
67	80	Scott corrected 68 to 67; bottom 'End of Vol 1.'

Volume 2

None	81	'The fortunes of Nigel Vol. II.'; near the bottom 'an obstinate friend' excised
None	82	start Ch. 1
2–64	83–145	Ch. 1 ctd–Ch. 12
63–72	146–55	Scott misnumbered 65 as 63 (Ch. 12 ctd) but numbered consecutively to end of volume: (the misnumbering had begun with his 52 (as 50), but he corrected the sequence to 64 (as 62)

Volume 3

None	156	'The Fortunes of Nigel Vol. III.'
None	157	start Ch. 1
2–21	158–77	Ch. 1 ctd–Ch. 3 ctd
22	178	start Ch. 4 cancelled; Ch. 3 then ends, with an additional paragraph, and Ch. 4 begins
23–44	179–200	Ch. 4 ctd–Ch. 7
45*	201	recto blank; inserts on verso for 202
45–60	202–217	Ch. 7 ctd–Ch. 11
61	218	unbound leaf (Bodmer) 383.27–385.13 'however prodigal . . . of the like of such'; insert for 219: 385.34–41 'but all the Dukes . . . chouze me of'
[62–65]	219–22	[missing leaves]
66	223	unbound leaf; Ch. 12 ctd (392.40–394.32 'direction . . . look said')
[67]	224	[missing leaf; inserts for it on verso of 223: 374.37–41 'I whom . . . perform', 396.42 'partner and victim', and 396.1 'and Vincent to']
68–73	[225–30]	(National Library of Scotland) end of Ch. 12 (396.23 'in —America'—end of novel)

74   This marginal dialogue in the proofs occurred on the bottom of the recto of MS 3403, f. 190, where James Ballantyne objected that the motto 'reads commonplace', prompting Scott's tart 'I wish Gordon would not trouble himself with more than transcription'. Gordon's most interesting intrusion into the manuscript occurred when on the verso of f. 162 he noted that the text was self-contradictory. Scott had speculated that Colepepper might have attempted to rob Trapbois because he got wind of the idea that Nigel

intended to marry Martha and acquire her fortune for himself. Accordingly, Scott had written: 'If this was indeed mentiond to the Captain who probably would have no idea of any scruple of delicacy on the part of the proposed bridegroom preventing such a profitable match . . .'. In a note keyed to Scott's word 'indeed' Gordon wrote: 'In the last chapter ↑ (Page 3) ↓ the hint which Hildebrod had given the Captain of Nigel's projected marriage was *expressly assigned by Hildebrod himself* (in his last conversation with Nigel) as the cause of the murder having been hastened—'. In other words, Scott had forgotten a detail of his plot. The solution was simply to strike out the misleading phrase—in the present text it came at 286.11 between 'Trapbois' and 'the fear of losing'—and thus eliminate the ambiguity of Colepepper's motives.

75   In Volume 1, mottoes for Chapters 4, 5, 7, and 8 are on the recto; those for Chapters 1, 2, 3, 6, 9, 10, and 11 are on the verso. In Volume 2, mottoes for Chapters 1, 2, 3, 4, 5, 8, 9, 10, 11, and 12 are on the recto; those for Chapters 5 (replacement), 6, 7, 8 (replacement), and 13 are on the verso. In Volume 3, mottoes for 1, 3, 4, 5, 10, and 11 are on the recto; those for Chapters 2, 6, and 8 (and probably 13) are on the verso. Only the mottoes taken from Gray and Butler appear on the recto; those from Shakespeare, Jonson, Shenstone, and Gray were added on the verso.

76   MSS 3402 and 3403. In Volume 1 there are two sets of proof for pages 239 and 240, no doubt because Scott and Ballantyne were concerned for the accuracy of the Latin conversation therein. In Volume 2, because of a 'page apart' there are two pages numbered 66 and, for the same reason, two pages numbered 67. As well, there are two proofs for pages 79 through 82. Page 81 of the second set is labelled 'Last Proof'. Since the pages number consecutively from this point, it may be that they too are 'last proof', though some repeated words on page 145 may indicate yet another mixing of sets. So, too, the overlapping words on page 160 of Volume 3, unless they are simply a sign of two compositors. Between pages 190 and 191 is a 'page apart' to provide a new motto but it does not alter the numbering.

77   In the binding of the proofs the three sets, though complete, were mixed. Page xvi of the first set is followed by pages xvii through xxxiv of the second set. Page xvi of the second set is followed by pages xvii–xxxv of the first. The third set is intact, except for a 'page apart', which is bound between pages xxxii and xxxiii. It belongs instead between pages xxxii and xxxiii of the second set.

78   MS 1583, f. 71r. For the Vorstius controversy see note to 111.8–11.

79   For the obscene connotations of 'niggle' see note to 195.45–46.

80   See note to 185.41–42.

81   MS 791, pp. 589–90: 22 July 1822.

82   MS 791, p. 565: Constable to Black, Young & Young, 14 June 1822.

83   MS 326, f. 121v–22r.

84   MS 323, f. 465r–v.

85   MS 677, f. 38v–39r: 15 August 1821.

86   William B. Todd and Ann Bowden, *Sir Walter Scott: A Bibliographical History 1796–1832* (New Castle, Delaware, 1998), 562.

87   *Letters*, 7.378–79: 19 April 1823.

88   MS 323, f. 400v: Cadell to Constable.

89 MS 323, f. 453r–v.

90 MS 323, f. 466v: Cadell to Constable.

91 MS 323, f. 470v.

92 MS 320, f. 164r.

93 For publication dates see *Quentin Durward*, EEWN 15, 422–24.

94 MS 21020, ff. 35r–42v. Whatever Cadell may have meant in the diaries by the term 'revised', he was scrupulous about incorporating Scott's corrections. The few exceptions—four, to be exact—may perhaps be explained by later-written notes on the overleaf that crowded or obscured earlier-written notes. Jane Millgate illustrates this problem with an example from *Nigel* (*Scott's Last Edition* (Edinburgh, 1987), 61–62 and 135, n. 27).

95 Iain Gordon Brown cites the note, with comment, as evidence that the Magnum Opus edition was aimed at the less well-educated reader (*Scott's Interleaved Waverley Novels*, ed. Iain Gordon Brown (Aberdeen, 1987), 104), for which subject see also Jane Millgate, *Scott's Last Edition* (Edinburgh, 1987), 90–93.

96 In his fourth note to *The Vision of Don Roderick* (1811) Scott explains that he spelled the hero's name 'Graeme' so as to inform the English that in Scotland the name 'Grahame' is pronounced as one syllable.

EMENDATION LIST

The base-text for this edition of *The Fortunes of Nigel* is a specific copy of the first edition, owned by the Edinburgh Edition of the Waverley Novels. All emendations to this base-text, whether verbal, orthographic, or punctuational, are listed below, with the exception of certain general categories of emendation described in the next paragraph, and of those errors which result from accidents of printing such as a letter dropping out, provided always that evidence for the 'correct' reading has been found in at least one other copy of the first edition.

Inverted commas are sometimes found in the first edition for displayed verse quotations, sometimes not; the present text has standardised the inconsistent practices of the base-text by eliminating such inverted commas, except when they occur at the beginnings or ends of speeches. The typographic presentation of mottoes, volume and chapter headings, and the opening words of volumes and chapters, has been standardised. James Ballantyne and Co. had only one italic ligature for both 'œ' and 'æ'; the two are differentiated in this edition. Ambiguous end-of-line hyphens in the base-text have been interpreted in accordance with the following authorities (in descending order of priority): predominant first-edition usage; 8vo; 12mo; 18mo; Magnum; manuscript.

Each entry in the list below is keyed to the text by page and line number; the reference is followed by the new, EEWN reading, then in brackets the reason for the emendation, and after the slash the base-text reading that has been replaced.

The great majority of emendations are derived from the manuscript, or from the proofs corrected by Scott. Most merely involve the replacement of one reading by another, and these are listed with the simple explanation '(MS)', '(proofs)', or '(proof correction)'. The spelling and punctuation of some emendations from the manuscript have been normalised in accordance with the prevailing conventions of the base-text. And although as far as possible emendations have been fitted into the existing base-text punctuation, at times it has been necessary to provide emendations with a base-text style of punctuation. Where the manuscript reading adopted by the EEWN has required editorial intervention to normalise spelling or punctuation, the exact manuscript reading is given in the form: '(MS actual reading)'. Where the new reading has required significant editorial interpretation of the manuscript, not anticipated by the first edition, the explanation is given in the form '(MS derived: actual reading)'. Occasionally, some explanation of the editorial thinking behind an emendation is required, and this is provided in a brief note. In transcriptions from Scott's manuscript and the proofs deletions are enclosed ⟨thus⟩ and insertions ↑ thus ↓.

In spite of the care taken by the intermediaries, some local confusions in the manuscript persisted into the first edition. When straightening these, the editor has studied the manuscript context so as to determine Scott's original intention, and where the original intention is discernible it is of course restored. But from time to time such confusions cannot be rectified in this way. In these circumstances, the reading from the earliest edition to offer a satisfactory solution is adopted as the neatest means of rectifying a fault. Readings from the later editions are indicated by '(Magnum)', '(8vo)', or '(12mo)'. Emendations which have not been anticipated by a contemporaneous edition are indicated by '(Editorial)'.

3.8	quotation of (MS) / quotation, of
3.17	Romance called (MS Romance calld) / Romance, called
3.17	MONASTERY to (MS Monastery to) / MONASTERY, to
3.23	Captain—Boy (MS Captain—boy) / Captain. Boy
3.24	Clutterbuck—There (MS Clutterbuck—there) / Clutterbuck. There
3.26	folder—make (MS) / folder, make
3.26	leaves—or (MS) / leaves, or
3.27	home—or (MS) / home; or
3.30	over-copy—pray (MS over copy—pray) / over-copy. Pray
4.14	calculation (MS) / calculations
4.43	Representation, of (MS Representation of) / Representative Vision, of The proofs' misreading, 'Representative, of', prompted Scott to insert 'Vision'.
5.1	Waverley. (MS) / Waverley!
5.13	Personage (MS) / personage
5.18	inly (MS) / only
5.23	talent, I (MS derived: talent I) / talent—I
5.35	Jedidiah (Editorial) / Jedediah For this spelling see *The Black Dwarf*, EEWN 4a, 174.
5.41	Hem! hem!—The—the inquiry (MS Hem! hem—The—the En-quiry) / Hem! hem! The inquiry
6.15	objects (MS) / object
6.18	Oh! (MS Oh) / Ah!
6.31	Tedworth, not (MS) / Tedworth—not
6.35	strikingly, like the source (MS strikingly like the ⟨burst⟩ ↑ source ↓) / strikingly, proceeding naturally, ending happily, like the course
6.41	yard—— (MS) / yard.
6.42	Ercles's vein. And (MS derived: Ercles's vein [end of line] And) / Ercles' vein, and
7.3	my grave (MS) / the grave
7.36	me, sir, to (MS me Sir to) / me to
8.6	in fortifying (MS) / of fortifying
8.12	would (MS wuld) / will
8.15	ye (MS) / you
8.20	*My* fame? (MS) / My fame?
8.23	every (proof correction) / any
8.39	remember the (MS) / remember, the
9.1	more—to (MS) / more. To
9.16	Free (MS) / free
9.22	near (MS) / nearly
9.23	intelligence,—a (proof correction) / intelligence, a (MS as Ed1)
9.29	on (MS) / into
9.38	side or other (MS) / side or the other

10.25 increase—my (MS) / increase; my
10.30 son (MS Son) / sir
10.30 fraternal (MS ⟨p⟩ ↑ fr ↓ aternal) / paternal
10.43 short, on such occasions, I (proof correction) / short, sir, on such occasions, I (MS short I)
11.6 frame (MS) / form
11.6 the favourable (proof correction) / too favourable
11.10 concluded (proof correction) / considered
11.13 know, then, that (MS know then that) / know, that
11.14 the——————Dragoons (MS) / the——Dragoons
11.20 had (MS) / have
11.21 Modern (MS) / modern
11.22 serenely (MS) / seriously
11.27 you (MS) / You
11.29 bib and apron (MS bib & apron) / bib, and apron
11.33 can (MS) / could
11.39 Spirit of Betty Barnes"— (MS) / spirit of Betty Barnes."—
12.5 sense (MS) / senses
12.8 What (MS) / what
12.10 curiosity after (MS curiosity ↑ after ... ↓) / curiosity, after
12.12 among (MS) / amongst
12.16 "You careless jade!"— (MS derived: "You careless jade—) / 'You careless jade!'—
12.25 sir!—Heaven (MS Sir—Heaven) / sir! Nay, heaven
12.27 that is all (MS) / that's all
12.28 "Three Recovered Dramas," (Magnum) / "Three recovered Dramas," (MS three recoverd dramas)
      Scott capitalised 'Three' and 'Dramas' in the proofs, but not 'recovered'.
12.30 "Plays ... stage"— (proof correction derived: "Plays ... stage—) / Plays ... stage— (MS plays ... stage—)
12.37 *Terrified* (proof correction) / *Terry*fied
      In a third-proofs insertion Scott wrote 'terrified'. This was changed in fourth proofs, perhaps by Ballantyne but probably seen by Scott, from '*terrified*' to '*Terrified*'. The first-edition reading was apparently introduced by an intermediary at final proof stage.
12.38 it. And (proof correction) / it; and
12.41 wonot (MS) / won't
13.18 hint—The (MS) / hint. The
13.26 system. (proofs) / system? (MS system [end of line])
13.27 this succession (proof correction: this ⟨rapided ↑ rapid ↓ pa⟩ succession) / this rapid succession
13.28 publications (proof correction) / publication
13.32 public. That (proof correction: publick. That) / public,—that
13.39 of printer's (proof correction: of Printer's) / of the printer's
13.40 hadst (proof correction) / Hadst
14.9 manufactor (proof correction) / manufacture
14.31 profession, without (proof correction: profession without) / profession, or without
14.40 emolument—no (proof correction) / emolument. No
15.14 composition which (proof correction) / composition, which
15.29 will not (MS) / shall not
15.31 family?—we (MS family—we) / family? We
16.28 on (proof correction) / over
16.43 Honour and Virtue (proof correction) / honour and virtue

17.9 and act only on (MS) / of proceeding on
17.15 of M'Corkindale (MS of ⟨MacCoki⟩ M'Corkindale) / of Mr
M'Corkindale
17.17 the labyrinth (MS) / the same labyrinth
19.27 His (MS his) / The
19.33 his court (MS) / the court
19.34 when (MS) / where
20.13 Maker (MS) / maker
20.20 for temporary (MS) / for the temporary
20.24 backwards (MS) / backward
20.33 lack? What (MS lack, What) / lack? what
21.39 Christ Church Hospital (MS Christ Church hospital) / Christ's
Church Hospital
21.42 belongs (MS) / belong
21.43 strongly (MS) / strong
23.1 and white (MS) / and as white
23.8 "Unstained," (MS "Unstaind,") / "unstained;"
23.9 wars of the roses (MS) / wars of the Roses
23.24 of theory to practice (MS) / of thorough practice
23.35 hair, well-formed (MS hair well formd) / hair, and well-formed
24.6 comrade by (MS comerade by) / comrade, by
24.9 scorn, Cavaliero (MS scorn ⟨the gentle⟩ ↑ cavaliero ↓) / scorn, the
Cavaliero
24.9 Frank (Editorial) / Cuddy (MS as Ed1)
24.16 or (MS) / and
25.11 shop-full (MS) / shop full
25.13 tongs." [new paragraph] Such (MS tongs. NL. Such) / tongs." [new
paragraph] A still higher authority, Dame Ursula, wife to Benjamin
Suddlechops the barber, was of exactly the same opinion. [new para-
graph] Such
Scott added this paragraph in proof, but it makes nonsense of his
introduction of Ursula at 92.35.
25.15 who, on (MS who on) / who, in
25.21 master on (MS master ⟨from⟩ ↑ on ↓) / master in
25.23 manufactures (MS) / manufacture
25.31 Barnacles (MS) / barnacles
25.41 barnacles—the (MS derived: barnacles the) / barnacles? The
25.42 his Majesty (MS) / his Sacred Majesty
26.7 an it (MS) / and
26.7 Jenkin (Magnum) / Jenkins (MS Edmund)
26.8 touched as with (MS) / touched with
26.14 was as ever (MS) / was ever
26.15 barnacles, good (MS barnacles good) / barnacles, my good
26.23 withal (MS) / with
26.25 folks as (MS) / folks, as
26.29 lack?—A (MS lack—A) / lack?—a
26.34 peace! you (MS peace you) / peace! You
26.35 Devil-tavern (MS) / Devil's Tavern
26.38 a watch (MS) / A watch
26.38 five (MS) / four
26.38 movement—A watch (MS) / movement—a watch
27.1 and the (MS) / at the
27.2 critics of (MS) / critics in
27.12 another-guess customer (18mo) / another guess-customer (MS another guess customer)

27.13 See (MS) / see
27.22 motion*?" (MS Motion.") / pageant, Frank?"
27.34 at old Saint (MS) / at Saint
The proofs read 'at that old Saint', prompting Scott to excise 'that old'.
27.40 figo (MS) / fig
27.43 [footnote] (Editorial) / [no footnote] (MS as Ed 1)
See Essay on the Text, 453.
28.12 *sulphur: cum butyro quant: suff:.*" (MS sulphur: cum butyro quant: suff⟨icum⟩↑ : ↓") / *sulphvr.cum butyro quant. suff.*"
28.32 and follow him, leaped (MS and follow him leapd) / and follow, leaped
28.42 assistance (MS) / aid
29.2 Signory (MS) / Seignory
29.10 thither (MS) / hither
29.16 *the pinion of report*, 8—*the striking pins are* 13——What (MS derived: the pinion of retort 8 the striking pins are 16——. What) / *the power of retort* 8—*the striking pins are* 48—What
Scott misreads Derham, and an intermediary misreads Scott.
29.17 *the quotient* (MS the Quotient) / *The quotient*
29.18 that (MS) / That
30.9 Faringdon-Without—my (MS Fleetstreet—my) / Faringdon-Without. My
30.18 Punchinello"—— (MS Punchinello.) / Punchinello; and, all together——"
30.29 And (MS) / But
30.29 boys—and bringing a (MS derived: boys—and bringin a) / boys, and bringing in a
30.30 between (MS) / betwixt
31.1 swoon! (MS) / swoon?
31.3 Saint (MS) / St
31.6 ago (MS) / before
31.7 armchair (MS) / armed chair
31.11 the cerebrum (MS the ⟨celer⟩ ⟨cel⟩ cerebrum) / and cerebrum
31.13 Bell-um! Bell-ell-um! (MS Bellum Bellellum!) / Bell-um! bell-ell-um!
Scott inserted the hyphens in the proofs.
31.14 signifies (MS) / signify
The change was made in the proofs either by Ballantyne or by Scott out of touch with his manuscript rhetoric.
31.27 in his (MS) / on his
31.40 their bed (MS) / their beds
31.41 couch. I (MS) / couch—I
32.4 Irving (MS) / Irvine
32.27 undergo (MS) / resist
32.39 him a (MS) / him for a
33.21 for being (MS) / for my being
33.21 obraided (MS) / charged
33.22 beg (MS) / seek
33.42 Jockey than you, sir, are (MS Jockey than you Sir are) / Jockey, sir, than you are
34.10 entrance to (MS) / entrance of
34.26 Southron (MS) / southern
34.35 do to (MS) / do me to
34.42 South (MS) / southern

35.1	mair (MS) / more
35.25	said, to put (MS said to put) / said, just to put
35.28	thae (MS) / these
35.30	had (MS) / haud
35.35	pigs—the (MS) / pigs.—The
35.37	were honest fellows (MS were ⟨an⟩ honest fellow ↑ s ↓) / were an honest fellow
36.2	if please (MS) / if it please
36.5	black-ward (MS) / black ward
36.22	velvets—well—this (MS velvets—well—⟨there⟩ this) / velvets. Well, this
36.24	House (MS) / house
36.28	now—Can (MS derived: now [end of line] Can) / now, can
36.33	ging (MS) / gang
36.34	Christie . . . ca'd. I (MS Christie a ship chandler his father came from Dundee—he is a ship chandler as they ca'd⟨—but⟩ I) / Christie, a ship-chandler, as they ca't. His father came from Dundee. I See Essay on the Text, 449.
37.3	gentlemen"——— (MS) / gentlemen——"
37.10	behalden (MS) / beholden
37.18	in (MS) / on
37.33	Courage and Fidelity (MS) / courage and fidelity
37.35	this vain swaggering (MS) / this swaggering
37.38	hours—add (MS) / hours, add
37.39	half"—— (Magnum) / half——" (MS as Ed1)
37.43	fifty-four—as (MS fifty four—as) / fifty-four as
38.1	half—or (MS) / half, or
38.9	oblivious (MS) / abstracted
38.10	When once (MS) / whenever
38.10	Ramsay, "why"—— [new paragraph] "Lucky (Magnum Ramsay, "why, 'tis"—— [new paragraph] "Lucky) / Ramsay, "why——" [new paragraph] "Lucky (MS Ramsay [end of line] Lucky)
38.33	tang (MS) / twang
38.34	sweeter—than (MS) / sweeter than
38.34	of Dunstan's (MS of Dunstans) / of St Dunstan's
38.39	no, no—no!—you (MS derived: no no—no—you) / no, no, no!—You
39.1	signifies Umph (MS) / signifies umph
39.2	think." (proof) / think?" (MS think")
39.5	sharply; "that (Editorial) / sharply, "that (MS sharply "that)
39.19	our (MS) / your
39.20	the knowledge (MS the knowlege) / a knowledge
39.38	slush (MS derived: ⟨sludge⟩ ↑ sluch ↓) / sludge
40.1	board of the (MS) / board the
40.2	Long Town (MS derived: Longtown) / long town
40.6	what (MS What) / that
40.11	a short heel and tight clean ancle rested (MS a ↑ short heel & ↓ tight clean ancle rested) / a short heel, and a tight clean ancle, rested
40.16	they called (MS they calld) / they call
40.17	apartment (MS) / apartments
40.20	and the bed-curtains (MS and ⟨her⟩ ↑ the ↓ bed-curtains) / and her best curtains
41.13	Tewksbury, made and (MS Tewksbury made and) / Tewksbury, and
41.21	auditor (MS) / auditors
41.22	year, sir! are (MS year Sir are) / year! are
41.26	years, at twenty stone weight—I (proof correction: years— ↑ at twenty

	stone weight ↓ I) / years, at twenty stone weight. I (MS years—I)
42.4	about my having (MS) / about having
42.4	Scotchman (MS) / Scotsman
42.18	not exactly have (MS) / not have
42.21	and by dint . . . people (MS & by dint of minute calculation shewd it wanted nearly half an hour of that span—then as to people) / and as for people
43.13	damps—And (MS derived: damps [end of line] And) / damps, and
43.15	consider your (MS) / consider of your
43.23	of the etiquette (MS) / of etiquette
43.30	I always think (MS) / I think
43.39	dame, true—let (MS derived: Dame true—let) / dame—true,—let
43.40	of courtesy (MS) / in courtesy
44.9	averred, had already flung (MS averd had already flung) / averred, flung
44.23	death—there (MS) / death. There
44.23	band (MS) / hand
44.29	It's no (MS) / It's not
	The change was made in the proofs, by Ballantyne or by Scott, but in either case mechanically.
44.33	cleepie (MS) / eclipse
44.35	wald (MS) / wad
44.38	And what (MS) / And at what
44.41	ye (MS) / you
45.10	anon. But (MS) / anon; but
45.13	ower, and (MS ower and) / ower late, and
45.13	fand (MS) / faund
45.31	auld (MS) / sad
45.32	as a place (MS) / as the place
45.35	well—Go (MS) / well—go
45.35	eat—I (MS derived: eat I) / eat. I
45.37	leave"—— (MS) / leave——"
45.41	behuved (MS) / behoved
46.2	"however to (MS) / "to
46.2	went—And (MS derived: went And) / went, and
46.8	beef-banes (MS beef-bones) / beef banes
46.20	further (MS) / farther
46.32	maun (MS) / must
46.33	maist (MS) / most
46.35	than"—— (MS) / than——"
47.1	a' (MS) / o'
47.2	down he came, with (MS down he came with) / down, sir, came the King, with
47.5	changed wi' you since (MS changed wi you since) / changed since
47.6	back-stairs (MS Back-stairs) / back stairs
	Ed1 has space at end of line for hyphen.
47.11	the day (MS) / this day
47.27	in (MS) / on
47.30	said, Gie (MS said Gie) / said, gie
47.32	on't (MS ont) / o't
47.37	shewed me how (MS shewd me how) / shewed how
47.41	was bringing (MS) / had been bringing
48.13	afterward (MS) / afterwards
48.14	except it be that (MS) / except that
48.18	gude-town (MS good-town) / gude town

48.23 gutter-blood (MS) / clownish burgher
Scott first used and then cancelled the word in line 17 in favour of
'Scot'. When he substituted 'clownish burger' here in the proofs,
presumably thinking it too difficult for his readers, he forgot it had
appeared in *The Heart of Mid-Lothian*.

48.25 Motion [no footnote] (Editorial) / Motion* [footnote] (MS as Ed1)
See Essay on the Text, 454.

48.37 blazon ... tap—the (MS derived: blazon at the tap with the lion and
unicorn at the tap—the) / blazon at the tap—the

49.6 Prince." (MS prince"——) / Prince.

49.43 left to their landlady the (MS left ↑ to their landlady ↓ the) / left their
landlady the

50.6 In his (MS) / In's

50.8 hat (MS) / cap

51.28 your person (MS) / *your* person

51.38 so unjust (MS) / so flagrantly unjust

52.2 or"—— (MS) / or——"

52.22 surely"—— (MS) / surely——"

52.28 so"—— (Magnum) / so——" (MS as Ed1)

52.36 after momentary (MS) / after a momentary

52.38 not have advised (MS) / not advise

52.40 were (MS) / are

53.2 interest which you (MS) / interest you

53.12 questions asked at you (MS questions askd at you) / questions you are
to be asked

53.22 fellow (MS) / well-grown page

53.39 fellow, (for Moniplies ... door,) answer (MS fellow (for Moniplies ...
door) answer) / fellow," for Moniplies ... door, "answer

53.41 farther (MS) / further

54.14 But (MS) / but

54.15 be her (MS) / by her

54.27 awing—the (MS) / owing the

54.27 merkis (MS) / merks

54.28 jeillis (MS) / jillies

54.30 hir (MS) / her

54.31 brusk (MS) / brisk

54.38 cheek for jowl (MS) / cheek by jowl

54.40 risk"—— (Magnum) / risk——" (MS risque——")

55.1 nay—my (MS) / nay, my

55.4 angry—but (MS) / angry, but

55.6 lookover (MS) / overlook

55.12 Maister (MS) / Master

55.18 interrogations (MS) / interrogation

55.19 steer (MS) / stir

55.24 But (MS) / but

55.28 and not with (MS) / and in no degree with

55.36 behind the hand (MS) / behind hand

55.39 I (MS) / myself

56.7 *gratitude* (MS) / gratitude

56.8 servant—but (MS) / servant, but

57.42 you are now as far erring on (MS you are now as far ↑ erring ↓ on) /
you have now erred as far

58.8 stranger." (MS) / stranger".

58.17 father. And (MS Father. And) / father; and

58.26 love (MS) / like

58.30 further (MS) / farther
58.31 "I owed (MS) / "I—I owed
58.32 and—to (MS) / and, to
58.41 consideration (MS) / consequence
59.4 debt (MS) / debts
59.9 your good (MS) / your own good
59.22 now right—And (MS) / right now—and
59.23 at window (MS) / at the window
59.24 mule—for (MS) / mule; for
59.29 kernel—And (MS) / kernel—and
59.33 "but," (—to . . . eyes,'—) "it (12mo) / eyes,'—) "it . . . eyes,' "it
59.35 by (MS) / with
59.37 heaven (MS) / God
60.5 tarry-jacket (MS) / tarry jacket
60.10 punctual, true (MS derived: punctual [end of line] true) / punctual—
true
60.11 want (MS) / wants
60.14 dame, from time to time, how (MS dame from time to time how) /
dame, how
60.17 to the Parliament (MS to ⟨p⟩ the parliament) / to Parliament
60.22 reason (MS) / thing
60.27 on (MS) / upon
60.30 disciplinarian in manners. "The (MS disciplinarian in manners "the) /
disciplinarian. "The
60.36 guep (MS) / quep
60.37 Scots (MS) / Scotch
60.40 three blue-coats (MS derived: two ⟨blue-⟩ ↑ three ↓ coats) / two
blue-coats
In MS Scott wrote 'two blue-coats', then deleted 'blue' and inserted
'three'. No doubt he meant to write 'two' rather than 'blue', since in
the proofs he inserted 'blue' in the space left by an intermediary who
could not read the MS 'three'.
61.6 Billies (MS) / Bullies
61.33 street-robbers (MS) / street-robber
61.41 immersed (MS) / bemused
62.6 speak—with (MS) / speak, with
62.9 costly (proof correction) / castle's
62.18 warld ken (MS) / world kens
62.22 Hieland (MS hieland) / Highland
62.32 Humanity (MS) / humanity
62.34 father, you (MS derived: father you) / father—you
62.35 goldsmith; "a (MS derived: goldsmith "a) / goldsmith. "A
63.8 you forgather (MS) / you may forgather
63.8 our friend (MS) / your friend
63.9 worship—So bide (MS) / worship; so, be sure and bide
63.11 "I will be (MS) / "That will I—I will be
63.13 boy—Tell (MS) / boy, tell
63.22 will (MS) / Will
63.24 like (MS) / likely
63.30 you return (MS) / your return
63.33 Jenkin, "and (Magnum) / Jenkin; "and (MS Jenkin and)
64.17 high—its (MS) / high, its
64.18 Andrew—they (MS) / Andrew; they
64.23 warld (MS) / world
64.30 to his (MS) / to the

64.38 alongst (MS) / along
65.6 All around (MS) / All that was passing around
65.8 government; houses (MS derived: government houses) / government. Houses
65.12 end of the (MS) / and the
65.15 Hall, but was still further from resembling the (MS Hall but was still further from resembling ⟨its⟩ the) / Hall; and began to resemble the Scott, out of touch with his MS, changed the MS reading in the proofs to 'and still resembled', which was further changed post-proofs.
65.34 Goldsmith (MS) / goldsmith
65.43 their (MS the ↑ ir ↓) / the
66.10 precaution (MS) / caution
66.12 Jamie (MS) / James
66.13 Maxwell—have (MS) / Maxwell. Have
66.16 his (MS) / the
66.23 jest and ribaldry; and notes (MS jest and ribaldry and notes) / jest, and ribaldry; and amongst notes
66.24 long orations to Parliament, and (MS long orations to parliament and) / long orations, and
66.25 mingled with miserable (MS) / mingled miserable
In the proofs Scott inserted 'amongst' in 'and ↑ amongst ↓ notes' in line 4, inadvertently repeating that word from the preceding phrase. He then changed 'lay mingled with miserable' to 'were mingled miserable'. The restoration of MS 'with' provides a fair resolution of the problem.
66.25 ballats (MS) / ballads
66.38 for (MS) / in
67.5 trampled in (MS) / trampled on in
67.8 which he was perpetually degrading by (MS) / while he was perpetually degrading it by
67.26 talented (MS) / able
See Essay on the Text, 422.
68.6 and"——(MS) / and——"
68.18 meanwhile (MS) / meantime
68.26 awn (MS) / own
68.26 evidence I (MS) / evidence that I
68.35 vara (MS) / vera
68.42 workmanship, man, and (MS workmanship man and) / workmanship, and
68.43 tongue—and (MS) / tongue.—And
69.5 Francis!—Body (MS Francis—Body) / Francis of France!—Body
The addition was made after Scott's proof corrections.
69.7 Why (MS) / why
69.13 vara (MS) / vera
69.14 carnifex (MS) / crucifix
69.36 sterling—if (MS derived: Sterling If) / sterling, if
69.37 fiends (MS) / punds
70.12 servant (MS) / friend
70.21 behind us are (MS) / behind are
70.30 rushes (MS) / rushed
70.32 and a hat (MS) / and hat
70.32 without either havings (MS) / without havings
70.35 an (MS) / on
71.2 Majesty (MS) / majesty
71.3 the fitting (MS) / the most fitting

71.8   Majesty (MS) / majesty
71.10   typify (MS) / testify
71.12   latches (MS) / latch
71.14   toward (MS) / towards
71.23   now (MS) / Now
71.24   again (MS) / against
71.29   warse . . . warse (MS derived: worse . . . warse) / waur . . . waur
71.30   ye—if (MS) / you. If
71.30   gude (MS) / good
71.31   been sense (MS) / been some sense
71.39   shouldst (MS) / shouldest
71.40   himsell (MS) / himself
72.12   strapping at (MS) / strapping up at
72.17   at last (MS) / at the last
72.23   gold–wark (MS goldwark) / gold–work
72.25   Vara (MS) / Vera
72.35   man (proof correction) / maun
72.37   And (MS) / and
72.37   of us (MS) / with us
72.41   maun (MS) / man
73.2   breaking? we (MS breaking we) / breaking? We
73.4   subject—we (MS) / subject—We
73.14   House (MS) / house
73.15   mun (MS) / maun
73.24   unless in the rough bounds (MS) / unless just within the bounds
        The proofs read 'unless in the bounds', prompting Scott's change to
        the Ed1 reading.
73.29   his—and (MS) / his; and
73.34   present"—— (MS) / present——"
74.2   sae (MS derived: say) / so
74.3   Ah (MS) / Ay
74.5   Heriot—let (MS Herriot—let) / Heriot, let
74.19   Goldsmith and Jeweller (proof correction: Goldsmith & Jeweller) /
        goldsmith and jeweller
74.21   much payment of debts (MS) / much debts
74.26   same (MS derived: sam) / said
74.31   "could (MS) / could
74.32   believed the (MS) / believed "the
74.36   on't—away, away, George, for (MS derived: on't—away away George
        for) / on't, away—away, George—for
74.39   ye (MS) / you
74.41   Jeweller and Goldsmith (MS) / jeweller and goldsmith
75.14   noon, in order to (MS noon in order to) / noon, to
75.21   glanced (MS glancd) / glared
75.23   cloak (MS) / coat
75.33   cleansed from (MS) / cleaned, from
75.37   and a cambric (proof correction: and ↑a cambric↓) / and cambric
75.39   natives (MS) / merchants
76.17   corporal (MS) / corporeal
77.16   foot (MS) / leg
78.3   his ill–humour (MS his ⟨jeers⟩ illhumour) / his jeers and ill–humour
78.4   these (MS) / those
78.33   ideot—have (MS) / ideot, have
78.41   digitals"—— (Magnum) / digitals——"
        The placing of the dash in MS is ambiguous.

78.42 daamned (MS daamnd) / d—d
79.13 hinny (MS) / honey
79.20 indeed la! her (proof correction: indeed ↑ la! ↓ her) / indeed her
 (MS indeed now her)
79.36 pot"——— (MS) / pot———"
80.23 fair (MS) / fine
81.16 its (MS) / his
81.38 himself to (MS) / himself next to
82.21 will (MS) / Will
82.23 hoop—I (MS) / hoop. I
82.25 laughing, Sir Mungo," said (MS laughing Sir Mungo said) /
 laughing," said
82.31 on his (MS) / in his
82.33 court—Knighton, the Duke's man—he (MS court—Knighton the
 Dukes man—he) / court; Knighton, the Duke's man. He
82.36 would none (MS) / would have none
83.19 now (MS) / Now
83.28 seconds"——— (MS seconds"—) / seconds———"
83.32 him who (MS) / Him who
83.33 hand (MS) / hands
83.37 under crossing (MS) / undercrossing
84.18 the honest cash-keeper (MS) / the cash-keeper
84.28 it. So he (MS) / it; so that he
 The proofs read 'it; so he', prompting Scott to insert 'that'.
84.32 new golden clasp (MS) / new clasp
84.36 endure recital (MS indure recital) / endure the recital
84.41 entrance (MS) / intrusion
85.23 forwards (MS) / forward
85.35 apartment. (MS) / apartment;
85.40 pale: there (MS) / pale—there
86.23 upon (MS) / on
86.27 prayer-book which (MS prayerbook which) / prayer-book, which
87.6 own eyes aside (MS) / own aside
87.7 the white (MS) / her white
87.26 And (MS) / and
87.40 to you (MS) / for you
87.41 for the (MS) / to the
88.5 This (MS) / The
88.34 accompt (MS) / account
88.35 drunk (MS) / drank
89.7 ken"——— (Magnum) / ken———." (MS ken———)
89.11 Only (MS) / only
89.12 Jin Vin (Editorial) / Jen Win (MS as Ed1)
89.13 ken'—but (MS ken"—but) / ken.'—But
89.20 the strange young (MS) / the young
 The proofs read 'stranger', prompting Scott's excision.
89.29 understand. And (MS understand." "And) / understand; and
89.31 warld (MS) / world
89.34 themsells (MS) / themselves
89.36 broad (MS) / fair
 Scott changes in the proofs to avoid repetition: but see next entry.
89.36 of a brave Scottish laird (MS) / of broad Scottish land
89.43 vara (MS) / vera
90.7 And (MS) / and
90.8 side, "that (MS side "that) / side, "they say that

90.13   knee (MS) / knees
90.21   disclosure; "what (MS derived: dis⟨pleasu⟩↑ closure↓ [end of line]
         What) / disclosure, "what
90.24   Ken (MS) / ken
90.28   drap (MS) / drop
90.35   kenna (MS ken na) / ken nae
90.41   whae (MS) / wha
90.43   invite the fiend (MS) / invite fiends
91.1   him (MS) / them
         The proofs read 'invite fiend', prompting Scott to add the 's' and
         change 'him' to 'them' below.
91.9   authors and (MS authors &) / authors or
91.14   places too by (MS) / places by
91.21   torch-light." (MS torchlight.") / torchlight—"
91.26   coffin—as (MS) / coffin. As
91.27   "Her coffin!" repeated Nigel. "Does (MS Her coffin"—repeated
         Nigel "Does) / "What reason," repeated Nigel, "can
         For this and the following emendations see Essay on the Text, 450.
91.28   beautiful, already contemplate (MS beautiful already contemplate) /
         beautiful, have already habitually to contemplate
91.29   even so (MS) / I kenna
91.29   Moniplies, "for, as (MS Moniplies "for as) / Moniplies; "but there is
         the coffin, as
91.30   it, it (MS) / it: It
91.36   She (MS) / she
91.37   trow—always (MS) / trow. Always
91.38   tower (MS) / Tower
91.39   round and round half (MS round & round half) / round half
92.20   apartments (MS) / apartment
92.28   bondsmen—even (MS) / bondsmen.—Even
92.31   it (Magnum) / it too (MS as Ed 1)
93.35   around (MS) / round
93.42   confidante (MS) / confidant
94.2   owches, and gold pieces which (MS owches and gold pieces which) /
         owches, or gold pieces, which
94.4   assist the poor (proof correction) / assist them
94.22   take (MS) / the
94.30   elbow-chair, smooth with frequent (MS elbow chair smooth with fre-
         quent) / elbow-chair, rendered smooth by frequent
94.40   though (MS) / however
95.1   say—Why, dame—Why, love (MS say—Why Dame—Why love) / say
         —why, dame—why, love
95.2   razor—Why (MS) / razor—why
95.3   dame!"—— (MS dame"——) / dame!"——"
95.29   aw (MS) / a'
96.12   twa poor 'prentice (MS twa poor prentice) / twa 'prentice
96.13   home—And (MS) / home, and
96.27   Wiba (MS) / Wilsa
96.32   Gaffer (MS) / Gaffie
96.35   further (MS) / farther
96.36   at door (MS) / at the door
96.43   need (MS) / needs
97.17   forwards (MS) / forward
97.20   Christabelle (MS) / Cristabelle
97.36   Scots-woman (MS Scots [end of line] -woman) / Scotch-woman

97.37   totally (MS) / wholly
97.39   Wiba (MS Wi- [end of line] ba) / Wilia
98.10   "Nothing, lady-bird?" (MS derived: "Nothing? lady-bird") / "Noth-
         ing, lady-bird!"
98.20   folks (MS) / folk
98.31   wear—Or (MS) / wear—or
98.33   or"—— (MS) / or——"
99.7   Ursula—And (MS) / Ursula; —and
99.8   filthy (MS) / Filthy
99.9   of window (MS) / of the window
99.18   not fail, however, in (MS not fail however in) / not, however, fail in
99.24   confession . . . and you (MS confession to loosen the tongue of the one
         and to soften the rigour of the other Now I am your confessor and
         you) / confession; and you
99.34   earnest—you (proof correction) / earnest.—You (MS earnest and
         you)
100.14   corner (MS) / quarter
100.24   Northward (MS) / northward
100.31   abroad"—— (MS) / abroad——"
100.38   on (MS) / in
100.42   foul-mouth (MS foulmouth) / foul-mouthed
100.42   railer—he (MS) / railer. He
100.43   husband"—— (Magnum) / husband——" (MS as Ed1)
101.3   nobleman"—— (MS Nobleman"——) / nobleman——"
101.4   mad—" (MS) / mad!"
         Scott reinstated this dash in the proofs.
101.16   make worth (MS) / make it worth
101.24   *descended* (proof correction) / descended (MS as Ed1)
102.4   conscience—and (MS) / conscience, and
102.21   cord—such (MS) / cord. Such
102.35   no (MS) / No
102.36   knowst (MS) / knowest
102.37   management." (MS management—") / management—think of some
         other recompence."
         Scott's proof insertion makes the next speech nonsense as a reply.
102.42   so—" said (proof correction derived: so, ↑—↓" said) / so,"—said
         Although Scott does not delete the comma, nearby examples suggest
         that the caret was meant to indicate that the dash should replace the
         comma rather than supplement it.
103.8   family"—— (MS) / family——"
103.11   them." (MS derived: them"—) / them?"
103.17   "I—I—heard (MS) / "I heard
103.19   Wharf—A (MS) / Wharf, a
103.33   me—but (MS) / me; but
103.36   work—for (MS) / work. For
104.22   upon (MS) / on
104.29   Presence (proof correction) / presence (MS as Ed 1)
105.8   upon blue pewter (proof correction: upon ↑blue↓ pewter) / upon
         pewter (MS as Ed1)
105.19   anticipations, not (MS) / anticipations not
105.22   usual anxiety (MS) / usual mental anxiety
105.28   upon (MS) / after
107.5   this manner (MS) / the mean time,
107.16   days—there (MS) / days. In her time there
107.18   nobility. And (MS) / nobility; and

107.26 of the (MS) / on the
107.40 mesalliance (MS mes [end of line] -alliance) / mis-alliance
108.33 forwards (MS) / forward
108.43 knewst (MS) / knew
108.43 scruples—let (MS) / scruples. Let
109.2 his arm (MS) / the arm
109.4 man—I (MS derived: man [end of line] I) / man, and I
109.5 him, and (MS derived: him and) / him; and
109.37 at sword's (MS at swords) / at the sword's
109.42 presence"——— (MS) / presence———"
110.19 them (MS) / him
110.22 have then had (MS) / have had
110.22 it were (MS) / he were
111.19 Mightinesses' (proof correction) / Mightiness's
112.23 make of (MS) / make out of
112.26 push (MS) / thrust
112.30 seems"——— (MS) / seems———"
112.41 suppliant's (MS suppliants) / supplicant's
113.7 In the meanwhile (MS In the mean [end of line] While) / In the
        meantime
113.25 yoursell (MS) / yourself
114.16 No—no—no (MS) / No, no, no
114.22 ever (MS) / every
114.32 man—let (MS) / man, let
114.35 mun ... mun (MS) / maun ... maun
114.35 land—and (MS) / land; and
114.36 this (MS) / the
114.36 hae (MS) / have
114.37 oons (MS) / wouns
114.38 twice so (MS) / twice as
114.39 ten times so (proof correction: ⟨thrice⟩ ↑ ten times ↓ so) / ten times
        as (MS thrice so)
115.7 while the (MS) / while all the
115.8 cheeks (proof correction) / cheek (MS as Ed1)
115.10 man—and—since (MS) / man; and, since
115.13 man—and he (MS) / man, and he
115.15 question—and (MS) / question, and
115.21 that by (MS) / that, by
115.21 counsellors (MS) / councillors
115.28 there—take (MS) / there, take
116.14 well—is (MS) / well.—Is
116.20 anti-chamber (MS) / anti-room
117.9 further (MS) / farther
117.20 Villiers, Knight, of (Editorial) / Villiers Knight, of (MS Villeirs knight
        of)
        The proofs have 'Villiers, Knight of'. Ed1 follows Scott's re-punctu-
        ation which inadvertently makes 'Knight' read as a proper name.
117.35 overstep (MS) / outstep
118.5 onward (MS) / onwards
118.23 gratulate (MS) / congratulate
118.42 burthen (MS) / burden
119.1 kindness—you (MS) / kindness. You
119.4 out—he (MS) / out. He
119.17 lord—my (MS Lord—my) / lord. My
119.31 season? it (MS season it) / season? It

119.38 creditors (MS) / creditor
Scott erroneously deleted the 's' in the proofs.
120.4 and"——(MS) / and——"
120.6 Scots (MS) / Scotch
120.17 and of gratitude (MS) / and gratitude
120.24 said he (MS) / he said
120.24 must (MS) / will
120.28 good (MS) / old
120.36 hope (MS) / trust
121.5 hear (MS) / have
121.34 the end (MS) / the farther end
Scott inserted 'farther' in the proofs but failed to notice the jingle with 'father'.
122.28 is partly acquainted (MS) / is acquainted
123.1 cuckoldly (MS) / cuckoldy
123.15 instant (MS) / moment
123.38 their whole business (MS) / their business
124.2 out the (MS) / out of the
124.22 his family (MS ⟨the⟩ ↑his↓ family) / the family
124.33 eager willing zeal (MS) / eager zeal
125.8 rings, it . . . mince it, with (MS) / rings—it . . . mince it—with
125.11 think on (MS) / think of
125.20 laird (proof correction derived: l⟨o⟩↑a↓rd) / lord (MS Lord)
126.11 weel (MS) / well
126.17 north, marrying (MS) / north, and marrying
126.18 bony (MS derived: boney) / bonny
126.34 unsettled—his (MS) / unsettled, his
126.37 winning—those (MS) / winning. Those
127.4 Why (MS) / why
127.22 geneva (MS) / genievre
127.24 wars—what (MS) / wars. What
127.26 them to (MS) / them go to
127.27 switches—the (MS) / switches. The
127.28 day—or (MS) / day; or
127.30 There (MS) / Here
127.31 his red (MS) / that copper
127.34 other's (8vo) / others (MS others)
127.38 towl (MS) / jowl
127.40 of Thames (MS) / of the Thames
128.3 saucieres (MS sauciere's) / saucers
128.6 this (MS) / the
128.16 sarcasm (MS) / sarcasms
128.18 party. (MS) / party
128.21 laid-in (MS laidin) / lain-in
128.22 gunpowder. For (MS) / gunpowder; for
129.2 Scots. "That (MS derived: Scots. ⟨"⟩That) / Scots; that
129.3 please, Sir Mungo (MS please Sir Mungo) / please, my lord
129.5 bought, I . . . pay, and (MS derived: bought I . . . pay and) / bought—I . . . pay. And
129.21 thine—it (MS derived: thine it) / thine. It
129.22 shouldst (MS) / should
129.38 carried off with (MS) / carried with
129.41 afloat on (MS) / afloat in
129.43 the old and the new fashion (MS the old and the ⟨new⟩ new fashion) / the old fashion and the new

130.2 inactivity—the (MS) / inactivity;—the
130.3 time—And (MS) / time, and
130.27 of (MS) / on
130.41 quarters—" (MS) / quarters."
Scott restores the MS dash (as a short dash) in the proofs.
131.2 nay—make (MS) / nay, make
131.21 greatly . . . truly he (proof correction: greatly ↑ honourd by their Lordships— ↓ and truly he) / greatly and truly honoured by their lordships—he (MS greatly and truly he)
132.9 file, what (MS) / file—what
132.9 christened (MS christend) / Christian
132.16 dream? what (MS) / dream! What
132.18 and so far dealt (MS derived: and far dealt) / and, in so doing, dealt
132.38 earth—beware (MS) / earth; beware
132.41 current. I (MS) / current—I
133.8 He or She (MS) / he or she
133.21 him (proof correction) / them
134.1 piercing (MS peircing) / sparkling
134.1 to look almost through (MS) / to pierce through
Correcting the proofs, Scott failed to recognise his rhetorical repetition and created another repetition with 'piercing', which an intermediary later replaced with the inappropriate 'sparkling'.
134.35 supplied (Editorial) / supplies (MS as Ed1)
134.42 a tone of high and stubborn morality (MS) / a high and stubborn tone of morality
135.13 propositions, how (MS propositions how) / propositions, or how
135.24 on raw (MS) with raw
135.28 prophecies Lord (MS and proof correction) / prophecies, Lord
135.34 grammar?—that (MS grammar—that) / grammar? That
135.35 said Nigel (MS) / said Lord Nigel
136.7 circumstance (MS) / circumstances
136.10 t'other." (MS the other.") / t'other.
136.11 in to (MS) / into
136.21 cloak and (MS) / cloth and
136.27 sables—see (MS) / sables. See
136.39 a sword (MS) / the sword
137.5 passengers (MS) / passers- [end of line] by
138.13 shall (MS) / *shall*
138.19 present—there (MS) / present. There
138.19 Majesty (MS) / majesty
138.26 affairs the Diva Fortuna (MS) / affairs, the Diva Fortuna,
139.6 avoid—besides (MS) / avoid. Besides
139.8 kind. For (MS) / kind; for
139.13 a civil game (MS derived: a civi [end of line] game) / a game
139.18 prudential: he (MS) / prudential. He
139.25 game?—good (MS game—good) / game? Good
139.30 it—if (MS) / it. If
139.35 tone. He (MS) / tone: He
141.8 corn—here (MS) / corn. Here
141.8 too (MS) / two
141.11 Chaunticleer (MS) / Chanticleer
141.24 gentility (MS) / quality
142.33 shiffling (MS shifling) / shuffling
142.34 congés (MS) / *congès*
142.36 mi lor—you (MS derived: mi Lord—you) / me lord—You

143.4   beau coup (proof correction) / beaucoup (MS beau corps)
143.6   memory"—— (MS) / memory——"
143.20   Soupe-a-Chevalier (MS Soupe a Chevalier) / soupe-a-Chevalier
143.25   owl (MS) / gull
143.25   a gull (MS) / an ass
143.27   purpose (MS) / purposes
143.37   were most ceremoniously (MS) / were ceremoniously
144.17   talent (MS) / taste
144.29   guest (MS) / guests
144.31   call surrender (MS) / call the surrender
144.32   damne (MS) / damme
144.33   forty-five—mais forty-five—couverts (MS forty five—mais forty five—
         couverts) / forty-five couverts
144.40   innovation (MS) / innovations
145.1   killing other (MS) / killing of other
145.1   your siege (MS) / the siege
145.4   lain (MS) / been
145.6   other (MS) / another
145.10   de (MS) / the
145.12   grande (MS) / grand
145.12   grand capitain (MS) / grand capitaine
145.21   Ventre (MS) / ventre
145.26   and at elbows (MS) / and elbows
145.36   him (MS) / them
146.1   mustachoes (MS) / mustachios
146.9   with (MS) / at
146.10   Bow Bell (MS) / Bow-bell
146.11   Cock (MS) / cock
146.18   shall hear (MS) / shall soon hear
146.19   chartel (proof correction) / chastel (MS as Ed1)
146.25   gentlemen who (MS) / gentlemen, who
146.26   say—this (proof correction: ↑ ... say—↓ this) / say this
146.31   soldier smartly across (MS) / soldier across
146.43   "Heaven forbid, man!—heaven forbid!" said the young nobleman;
         "there (MS "Heaven forbid man—heaven forbid—" said the young
         nobleman "there) / "It would be a crime against the public interest,"
         answered his friend: "there
         The MS '"Heaven ... nobleman' was missed out in the proofs,
         prompting Scott to invent a new phrase and speech-designator.
147.15   helmet ... Why (MS helmet which his spouse has forfeited—Why) /
         helmet with which his spouse has fortified his skull—Why
         The proofs read 'helmet with which his spouse has fortified—why',
         leading Scott to insert 'his scull'.
147.15   rarest sport (MS) / rarest of sport
147.21   thrust ... clear (MS thrust his sword as it seemd clear) / thrust, as it
         seemed, his sword clear
         The proofs read 'as it seemed, thrust his sword', prompting Scott to
         produce the Ed1 reading.
147.25   into Whitefriars (MS into White friars) / into the Whitefriars
147.37   to heels (MS) / to his heels
148.1   stay (MS) / stayed
148.2   call dis-clout (MS) / call a dish-clout
148.9   saint (MS) / Saint
148.9   me—begar (MS) / me.—Begar
149.15   lookst (MS) / lookest

149.15 neophyte?—sage (MS Neophyte—sage) / neophyte? Sage
149.18 expect?—be (MS expect—be) / expect? Be
149.37 company-keeping—we (MS company keeping—we) / company-keeping. We
149.39 amen (8vo) / ameu (MS ament)
150.9 you shall hear matchless Will speak (MS) / we shall have matchless
Will speaking
150.22 scenes (MS) / scene
150.24 jars (MS) / wars
150.38 and who were (proof correction: and ↑ who ↓ were) / and were (MS
as Ed1)
150.42 cotemporaries (MS) / contemporaries
151.8 him—he (MS) / him—He
151.19 so (MS) / s[inverted c]
151.29 us?—he (MS us—he) / us? He
151.42 bran (MS) / outcasts
152.1 cost (MS) / lost
152.2 if you had (MS) / had you
152.2 Greene (MS) / Green
152.4 night?—suffice (MS night—suffice) / night? Suffice
152.4 have drunk (MS) / they drunk
152.7 them—for (MS) / them. For
152.12 others, spirits (MS) / other spirits
152.13 occasion—our (MS) / occasion. Our
152.15 sock or buskin (MS sock or buskine) / sock and buskin
152.16 however, him of whom I (MS however him of whom I) / however, of
him I
152.29 at the superiority (MS) / at superiority
153.39 Scotchman (MS) / Scotsman
153.40 accustomed (MS accustomd) / habituated
153.41 Such . . . likely (MS derived: such was not the vice of his country nor
likely) / Profusion was not his natural vice, or one likely
154.3 first . . . second (MS) / second . . . first
154.11 expectancies (MS) / expectations
154.24 when he (MS) / and, as he
155.6 upon (MS) / in
155.22 rush (MS) / return
155.28 told both your (MS) / told your
155.33 hence (MS) / ago
156.6 *infandum - - - renovare* (MS) / *infandum - - - - renovare*
156.11 Dumfermline (MS) / Dunfermline
156.13 it is true (MS) / It is true
156.15 And (MS) / and
156.21 ear-wigs—well (MS earwigs—well) / ear-wigs.—Well
156.38 table and (Editorial) / table indeed, and (MS table indeed and)
156.39 were indeed at (MS) / were at
After Scott's involvement with the proofs was over, an intermediary
spotted the repeated 'indeed', but deleted the wrong one. (EEWN
follows Scott's second thoughts in the MS.)
157.10 resting-place . . . next (MS resting place for a further restingplace for
the next) / resting-place for the next
157.24 mean it no (MS) / meant the phrase no
The proofs have 'meant no', prompting Scott to insert 'the phrase'.
157.26 thee—surely (MS) / thee. Surely
158.19 than (MS) / as

158.20 further (MS) / farther
160.1   Mask here, mask (ISet) / Creak here, creak (MS Creak here Creak)
160.8   Richie—will (MS) / Richie; will
160.19 be but of (MS) / be of
160.21 pact (MS) / load
161.2   the domestic (MS) / his domestic
161.3   and my (MS) / and by my
161.6   and no mair (MS) / and so no more
161.14 puritan?" (MS puritan") / puritan, fool?"
161.18 over (MS) / a
161.19 were (MS) / was
161.24 lad (MS) / man
161.27 puir (MS) / poor
161.35 waur; if (MS derived: waur—if) / waur. If
161.39 wi' you (MS wi you) / with you
162.5   saam (MS) / same
162.9   pile (MS) / pell
162.13 "broidery (MS) / "'broidery
162.14 pouches—and as to (MS) / pouches. And if you ask
        The proofs have 'and ask', prompting Scott to insert 'if you'.
162.21 him an if (MS) / him if
162.25 further (MS) / farther
162.29 weight, or (MS derived: weight or) / weight—or
162.31 formality (MS) / precision
162.37 grossart—gold (MS) / grossart. Gold
162.42 gowd (MS) / gold
163.8   at? (MS) / at!
163.18 desperate, Goblin (MS desperate Goblin) / desperate man, Goblin
163.22 Sparrow-hawk (MS) / sparrow-hawk
163.23 but the (MS) / but, after a', the
163.28 London—And (MS) / London—and
163.34 Sparrow-hawk (MS) / sparrow-hawk
163.41 on—since (MS) / on, since
164.1   advise"—— (MS) / advise——"
164.9   ye (MS) / you
165.1   heart-scaud (MS heart [end of line] scaud) / heart-scald
165.16 not—we (MS) / not; we
165.20 on (MS) / in
165.25 faithful—and (MS) / faithful. And
165.29 ony that has (MS) / ony has
165.31 upon (MS up ↑ on ↓) / on
166.6   and a (MS) / and experienced a
        See Essay on the Text, 454.
166.12 seemed at times disposed (MS seemd at times disposed) / seemed
        disposed
166.29 days as (proof correction) / days, as
166.31 friend Dalgarno (proof correction) / friend Lord Dalgarno
166.32 your good (proof correction) / the good
167.1   calumny!—but (proof correction: calumny—but) / calumny! But
167.30 nor to his (MS) / nor his
167.39 however, he was (MS however he was) / however, Lord Glenvarloch
        was
167.42 retire (MS) / retreat
168.5   and surmounted with a (proof correction: and ↑ surmounted with ↓
        a) / and having his head surmounted with a (MS and a)

168.16   O—ye (MS) / O, ye
168.17   Park the (MS Park⟨s⟩ the) / Park in the
168.21   fair (MS) / fairly
168.21   chase (MS) / prize
168.22   tow. (MS) / tow
168.29   withal—And (MS withal And) / withal—and
168.29   wald (MS) / wad
168.39   it—flea (MS) / it. Flea
168.41   plume,—and (MS plume and) / plume them,—and
168.42   among goss-hawks (MS among goss hawks) / among the goss-hawks
169.1   fixed Nigel with his (MS fixd Nigel with his) / fixed on Nigel his
169.20   desperation—there's (MS desperation—theres) / desperation.
         There's
169.22   was (MS) / am
169.29   help him to something to begin (MS help him to some thing to begin)
         / help him to begin
169.30   again—he (MS) / again.—He
169.31   Ye may (MS) / Your good lordship may
169.39   impertinence, to ascertain, if (MS derived: impertinence under to
         ascertain if) / impertinence, under the hope of ascertaining, if
170.2   have (MS) / *have*
170.13   you derived (MS) / you have derived
170.15   great (MS) / *great*
170.21   skill—and . . . bad—and (MS skill— ↑ and stands by the fortune of the
         game good or bad— ↓ and) / skill, and stands by the fortune of the
         game, good or bad
170.28   and rising (MS) / and by rising
170.34   inferiors—is (MS) / inferiors?—Is
171.3   terms." (MS derived: terms" —) / terms?"
171.6   place—there (MS) / place. There
171.12   should (MS) / "should
171.13   "If (MS) / If
171.13   ye are a (MS) / you were a
171.24   know"—— (MS) / know——"
171.32   way—there (MS) / way.—There
172.2   short"—— (Magnum) / short——" (MS as Ed1)
172.12   among (MS) / amongst
172.16   sooth (MS) / troth
172.17   the place (MS) / the thing
172.18   not a (MS) / not like a
172.18   Summie (MS) / Simmie
172.22   life's (MS lifes) / knight's
172.30   aith (MS) / oath
172.35   down—mair by (MS down mair by) / down—by
172.36   raven—poor (MS) / raven. Poor
173.12   ye (MS) / you
173.15   Talk (MS) / talk
173.15   devil—humph!" (MS devil—humph—") / devil, and—humph!"
173.20   him, totally (proof correction: ↑ . . . him ↓ totally) / him, being
         totally
173.21   providing (MS) / provided
174.4   etiquettes (MS) / etiquette
174.19   years especially of his life (MS) / years of his life especially
174.21   indeed he (MS) / he indeed
174.24   purpose. And (MS) / purpose; and

174.24 certain that Buckingham (MS cer [end of line] that Buckingham) /
certain, Buckingham
175.4 forwards (MS) / forward
175.7 questions asked (MS questions askd) / questions, asked
175.34 Give (MS) / give
175.40 presence again in (MS) / presence in
176.5 three (MS) / the
176.6 by (MS) / By
176.6 ye (MS) / you
176.25 carry to (MS) / carry you to
176.26 fortune—it (MS) / fortune. It
176.39 meeting—but (MS derived: meeting but) / meeting. But
176.40 cauldrife (MS) / caldrife
177.6 with arms (MS with ⟨har⟩ arms) / with his arms
The deleted letters may be 'hur'.
177.17 Glenvarloch, and (MS Glenvarloch and) / Glenvarloch; while
177.18 keeping (MS) / kept
177.26 Whitehall (proof correction) / the Palace (MS the palace)
177.35 secret." (MS) / secret!"
178.28 brow—but (MS) / brow?—but
178.33 vein!—you (MS vein—you) / vein!—You
179.3 but (MS) / and
179.13 not recollect (MS) / not have recollected
179.17 Haldimund knows—all the Court knows—I (MS Haldimund
↑knows↓—all ⟨London⟩ ↑the Court↓ knows I) / Haldimund,
who knows the court, will warrant you that I
The proofs read: 'Haldimund, who knows all the court, knows I',
prompting Scott's further change.
179.25 Wales—to (MS) / Wales. To
179.30 regret your (MS) / regret that your
179.30 freedoms (MS) / pleasures
180.4 No (MS) / no
180.11 at (MS) / by
180.14 insults . . . they were (MS) / insult . . . it was
180.28 the scabbard (MS) / his scabbard
180.30 left him, with deep emphasis, "You (MS left him with deep emphasis" You) / left him, "You
180.42 peace-officers belonging to the (MS) / peace-officers of the
181.11 amongst (MS) / among
182.7 forwards (MS) / forward
182.34 the time his (MS ⟨what⟩ ↑the time↓ his) / the time which his
182.40 alongst (MS) / along
183.11 part of the street at least (MS) / part at least of the street
183.13 "I—I—" said (MS) / "I—I"—said
183.20 bona-robas (MS bonarobas) / bonas-roba
183.29 "Indeed!!" (MS) / "Indeed!"
183.38 twelvemonth—marry (MS) / twelvemonth—Marry
184.5 you will (MS) / You will
184.8 far—the (MS) / far. The
184.10 it (MS) / It
184.11 lord—but (MS Lord—but) / lord; but
184.13 circumstances—the (MS) / circumstances. The
184.20 crows about (MS) / crows upon
184.29 dozen of bottles (MS) / dozen bottles
185.4 turn. But (MS) / turn; but

185.25   gip (MS) / quep
185.26   comes with (MS) / comes there with
185.37   concerning (MS) / respecting
185.41   Treasurer (proof correction) / treasurer
186.4   independent (MS) / independant
186.22   moment—that (MS) / moment. That
186.25   his attendant (MS) / the attendant
186.35   when they are at (MS derived: when [end of line] are at) / when at
186.36   is something anxious (MS) / is anxious
186.38   wardrope (MS) wardrobe
187.2   portmantles (MS port-mantles) / portmanteaus
187.3   wardrobe-press (MS) / wardrobe
187.9   income—single (MS) / income—Single
187.23   civil-seeming (MS ⟨civil⟩ ↑ civil ↓ -seeming) / court-beseeming
187.27   in cuerpo; and this (MS in cuerpo—and this) / in *cuerpo;* and the
187.40   Dalgarno as a bitter enemy, reason (MS Dalgarno reason) / Dalgarno, as a bitter enemy, reason
188.2   Swouns (MS) / Zounds
188.5   comes (MS) / come
188.8   Friars—indeed (MS) / friars. Indeed
188.10   permitted, of (MS permitted of) / permitted, out of
188.11   certain they (MS) / certain that they
188.11   motion (MS) / motions
188.16   valiant as wise, and (MS valiant as wise and) / valiant, and as wise and
188.21   aught may (MS) / aught that may
188.22   then, my lord," said (MS then my Lord" said) / then," said
188.23   you—now (MS) / you. Now
188.23   I leave (MS) / I have left
188.24   pleases (MS) / please
189.9   sage (MS) / said
189.16   leisure (MS) / labour
189.31   malcontent (MS) / malcontents
189.43   it; He (MS) / it.—He
190.3   condition—complying (MS) / condition. Complying
190.13   exterior—you (MS derived: exterior you) / exterior. You
190.21   animus mutatas (MS) / animas mutatus
190.27   up—I (MS derived: up I) / up; I
190.31   folly has filled for me—pardon me only, that (MS folly has pardon me only that) / folly has filled for me. Pardon me, that
190.33   bustling, officious (MS bustling officious) / bustlingly officious
190.40   sanctuary (MS) / Sanctuary
191.1   occupied crowded (MS) / occupied, crowded
191.20   chirrup'd (MS) / chirped
191.25   volcanoes!—these (MS volcanoes—these) / volcanoes! These
191.41   "Tour out, tour out," said (MS "Tour our, tour out" said) / "Tour out," said
191.43   ogling (proof correction) / coquetting with (MS as Ed1)
192.2   choury (proof correction) / cheery (MS Cheery)
192.10   you wish to assume (MS derived: you wiss assume) / you will assume
192.13   enough, being both (MS enough being ↑ both . . . ↓) / enough; both
192.25   doth Duke (MS) / doth faithful Duke
192.32   As he spoke (MS) / As they spoke
192.33   dimension (MS) / dimensions
192.34   ragged drawers (MS) / ragged, drawers
193.10   tankard, much (MS tankard ⟨and⟩ much) / tankard, and much

194.31 heard this (MS) / heard the
195.16 individual . . . imperfectly in (MS individual whose face dwelt as we
have already mentiond imperfectly in) / individual, who dwelt imperfectly, as we have already mentioned, in
195.38 arose (MS) / rose
196.5 ensue (MS) / come
196.24 Huff (MS Huffe) / Fleet
196.28 striking before (MS) / striking in before
196.30 shutting (MS) / closing
196.31 stop (MS) / shut
196.32 conducted on (MS) / conducted themselves on
196.38 Why (MS) / why
196.39 countrymen—And (MS) / countrymen. And
197.5 and most honourable (MS & most honourable) / and honourable
197.17 in (MS) / you
197.38 but, the Templar reminding (MS derived: but the Templar reminding) / but the Templar, reminding
198.9 slide (MS) / stride
198.45 wine-merchants (MS winemerchants) / wine-merchant
199.32 mean (MS) / intend
199.39 animadversion (MS) / animadversions
199.40 come thither (proof correction) / come hither
200.11 from (MS) / of
200.20 or (MS) / nor
201.7 family even at seasonable hours? You (proof correction: family ↑ even
at seasonable hours ↓ . You) / family, even at seasonable hours? You
201.10 Indeed—indeed—I (MS) / Indeed, indeed I
201.21 in (MS) / to
201.28 sun but (MS) / sun, but
201.31 you—and (MS) / you; and
201.39 apartment (MS) / apartments
201.43 apparition (MS appartion) / appearance
202.7 gravity totally (MS) / gravity, totally
203.27 a single lady (MS) / a lady
203.29 fairest (MS) / loveliest
203.39 for (MS) / to
204.25 in family (MS) / in the family
205.6 beauty of execution with (MS) / beauty with
205.7 Spoiled (MS Spoild) / Spoilt
205.13 the affectation (MS) / that affectation
205.24 a mother (proof correction) / an excellent mother (MS her mother)
206.7 all that she (MS) / all she
206.24 harmony (MS) / melody
206.25 communication (MS) / communications
206.28 intuitive (MS) / retentive
206.36 not conceive (MS) / hardly conceive
206.37 apartment (MS) / apartments
206.43 apartment (MS) / apartments
207.4 secret (MS) / confidence
207.8 ventured in her (MS derived: ventured on her) / ventured on in her
207.9 Paula (MS) / Paulina
207.24 this (MS) / that
207.30 her visit (MS) / the visit
208.9 then—these (MS) / then. These
208.24 those (MS) / them

208.35 unvaried (MS) / unwearied
208.36 them; is (MS) / them. Is
208.37 madam—" (proof correction: madam ⟨,⟩ ↑—↓) / madam," (MS madam")
209.4 and so becoming (MS) / and becoming
209.9 disliking, and (MS derived: disliking and) / disliking—and
209.12 Scottish (MS Scotish) / Scoh
210.6 godfather—but (MS Godfather—but) / godfather, but
210.10 gay . . . father to (MS gay young appre ↑ n ↓ tice of your father to) / gay young apprentice to
210.20 consultations—if (MS) / consultations. If
210.30 London"—— (Magnum) / London—" (MS London")
211.9 seek (MS) / Seek
211.11 is (MS) / Is
211.19 uttered—only (MS utterd—only) / uttered; only
211.28 know—next (MS) / know, next
211.34 emergence (MS) / emergency
211.35 emergence (MS) / emergency
211.36 out (MS) / me
212.2 head—though (MS) / head, though
212.3 said—but (MS) / said; but
212.6 which is, not the less, almost (proof correction: which ↑ is ↓ not the less ⟨be⟩ almost) / which, not the less, is almost (MS which should not the less be almost)
212.7 use—the (MS) / use. The
212.15 strongly (MS) / closely
212.21 life—these (MS) / life. These
212.24 Dalgarno"—— (MS) / Dalgarno——"
212.28 returned again accordingly (MS returnd again accordingly) / returned accordingly
213.10 others—Let (MS derived: otherwise Let⟨t⟩) / others—let
213.11 sure—but (MS certain—but) / sure. But
213.27 Sanctuary (MS) / sanctuary
213.29 Justice—a (MS) / Justice—A
213.40 world. You (MS derived: world—You) / world—you
214.26 superfluous—you (MS) / superfluous. You
215.7 Alas! alas! (MS derived: Alas? alas!) / Alas, alas!
215.36 you—and (MS you ⟨"⟩—⟨"Does⟩ and) / your and
215.38 it—dear (MS) / it, dear
216.1 of heaven (MS) / from heaven
216.8 action? (MS action?) / action.
216.10 trifles—what (MS) / trifles. What
216.14 one—it (MS) / one. It
216.19 further (MS) / farther
216.38 our (MS) / the
216.41 myself—heaven forgive me—said (MS) / myself, heaven forgive me, said
216.43 myself—and (MS) / myself, and
217.9 or (MS) / nor
217.10 patroness (MS) / patroness's
217.33 Ramsay (MS) / amsay
218.6 Scotswoman (MS) / Scotchwoman
219.4 friend: we (MS) / friend. We
219.11 Madrid—I (MS) / Madrid. I
219.12 age—young (MS) / age, young

219.12 been—we (MS) / been—We
219.32 lately—and (MS) / lately, and
219.39 could (MS) / Could
220.6   she countenanced (MS) / she had countenanced
220.10 He (MS) / he
220.16 avowal. [new paragraph] "My (proof correction) / avowal. My
220.18 illness. You (proof correction) / illness. [new paragraph] "You
220.27 blood-feud (MS) / bloody feud
220.43 the English (Magnum) / this English (MS as Ed1)
221.22 scenes—which . . . hastily: My (MS scenes—which I must describe
        very hastily—My) / scenes: My
221.23 happy (MS) / Happy
222.7   convince that (MS) / convince me that
222.15 convent, situated (MS convent situated) / convent, and situated
222.27 doubtful—the (MS) / doubtful. The
222.27 applied—if (MS) / applied, if
222.28 were—my (MS) / were. My
222.28 length—against (MS) / length, against
222.42 to the freedom of which (MS to ↑ the freedom of ↓ which) / to
        which
223.3   postern.' (MS postern.") / postern'
223.9   postern—it (MS) / postern. It
223.25 servants—in (MS derived: ↑ . . . servants ↓ in) / servants. In
224.19 part—those (MS) / part. Those
224.21 Englishwomen, whom, for a high bribe, they have (MS English women
        whom for a high bribe they have) / English- [end of line] women, but
        who, for a high bribe, have
224.22 escort through (MS) / escort you through
224.23 do not you (MS) / do *you* not
224.26 no Spanish (MS) / in English
224.27 say—your (MS) / say in Spanish–your
224.33 then,' I said, 'at (MS then I said at) / then, I trust, at
224.34 Yes—yes (MS) / Yes, yes
224.37 hand—which . . . sensible of—and (MS) / hand, which . . . sensible of,
        and
224.43 moments when (MS) / moments, when
225.1   is deeply (12mo) / are deeply (MS are as deeply)
225.12 emotions. And (MS) / emotions; and
225.15 those personal (MS derived: those by ⟨which⟩ personal) / those which
        were personal
225.25 for (MS) / of
225.35 counterband (MS) / contraband
226.23 yet I would (MS) / yet would I
226.24 Saint (MS) / St
226.25 You (MS) / But you
226.26 answered (MS answerd) / replied
227.4   or (MS) / nor
227.24 despair—if (MS) / despair. If
227.29 that (MS) / the
227.31 letter, and (MS derived: letter and) / letter; and
227.33 will—but (MS) / will. But
228.18 whiskers (MS) / mustachoes
228.26 less honourable (MS) / less-honourable
229.18 her long (MS) / the long
229.29 him makes (MS) / him who makes

In the proofs Scott forgot this 'mulatto-speak' for Wiba and inserted 'who'.

229.40 in most (MS ↑ . . . in ↓ most) / in a most
229.43 girdle, (proof correction) / girdle
230.4 gentlemen (MS) / gentleman
230.14 hearty 'prentice (MS hearty prencice) / hearty London 'prentice
230.15 ye (MS) / you
230.33 declared himself "the (MS) / declared "himself the
230.35 so, you silly boy (MS so you silly boy) / so, silly boy
230.37 one who walks (MS) / one that walks
230.38 in Paul's (MS in Pauls) / in Saint Paul's
230.41 knowst (MS) / knowest
231.15 will—well, well—take (MS will—well well—take) / will. Well, well, take
231.18 Jenkin (Magnum) / Jenkins (MS as Ed1)
231.18 have been (MS) / have rather been
231.22 not quite abstemious (MS not ⟨temperate⟩ quite abstemious) / not abstemious
231.30 none will she (MS) / none she will
231.40 now-a-days—tut (MS) / now-a-days. Tut
231.43 it (MS) / It
232.1 now-a-day (MS) / now-a-days
232.3 they (MS) / you
232.4 skittles (MS) / skittle
232.11 speak (MS) / Speak
232.19 whose (MS) / whose
232.22 ye (MS) / you
233.6 bearst (MS) / bearest
233.13 news—and (MS) / news; and
233.14 be cock (MS) / be the cock
233.15 beggar-my-neighbour, and (MS derived: ombre and) / beggar-my-neighbour—and
233.19 it—And (MS) / it—and
233.19 is come (MS) / is to come
233.27 finery—and (MS) / finery, and
233.28 on—and (MS) / on, and
233.29 pieces—my (MS) / pieces. My
233.30 good—and (MS) / good; and
233.38 Christmas—no (MS) / Christmas. No
233.41 nighest?—we (MS ↑ . . . nighest— ↓ "we) / nighest? We
234.4 Ay—Ay (MS Aye—Aye) / Ay, ay
234.8 Scotch (MS) / Scottish
234.9 Sparrow-hawk (MS) / sparrow-hawk
234.15 crosses—And (MS) / crosses; and
234.17 advice—And (MS) / advice—and
234.19 tailor take (MS) / tailor to take
234.20 and"—— (MS) / and——"
234.27 pistolet (MS) / pistol
235.2 although (MS) / though
235.10 there (MS) / here
235.13 Devil (MS) / devil
235.25 thankfulness. (MS) / thankfulness
235.37 on't. But (MS ont. But) / on't.—But
235.38 hiding?—no (MS hiding—no) / hiding? No
235.39 Gunpowder Plot"—— (MS gunpowder-plot"——) / Gunpowder Plot?"

236.2 Park"——(MS) / Park."
236.3 "Ha!" said Vincent (MS "Ha! said Vincent) / "Ha! what?" said Vincent
236.4 mean—it (MS) / mean.—It
236.7 now," continued the dame, "you (MS now continued the Dame "you) / now—you
236.10 of human (MS of ⟨wo⟩ human) / of the human
236.14 no—A (MS) / no—a
236.16 does, but (MS derived: does but) / does; but
236.24 honesty—and (MS) / honesty; and
236.26 amongst (MS) / among
236.33 care—head (MS derived: care for head) / care. Head
236.41 but (MS) / But
237.2 knowst (MS) / knowest
237.2 gosling—look you—were (MS Gosling—look you—were) / gosling. Look you, man. Were
237.5 for ever—she (MS forever—she) / for ever. She
237.7 And (MS) / and
237.18 escapes"——(MS) / escapes——"
237.26 when the (MS) / when this
237.35 until (MS untill) / till
238.19 knowst (MS) / knowest
238.21 Bull (MS) / Ball
238.22 damned (MS damnd) / d—d
238.37 than connive (MS) / than I connive
238.38 would hang (MS) / would sooner hang
238.42 precisely for what she (MS precisely ⟨where⟩ ↑ for what ↓ she) / precisely from whom she
239.14 and a brave (MS) / and brave
239.23 think this (MS) / think that this
239.29 like (MS) / likely
239.30 at Essex (MS) / in Essex
239.32 must—I (MS) / must, I
239.36 Stay—stay (MS) / Stay, stay
239.42 them—but (MS) / them; but
240.30 since (MS) / before
240.35 a great huge (MS) / a huge
240.38 massive (MS) / massy
240.39 Venice (MS) / Venetian
240.40 it had received (MS) / it received
241.2 shapes; some (8vo) / shapes, some (MS shapes ⟨for⟩ some)
241.15 prodigals (MS) / profligates
241.26 howe'er (MS howere) / however
241.42 more displeased (MS) / more dissatisfied
242.24 there?—I (MS there—I) / there? I
242.24 there?—Why (MS there—Why) / there? Why
242.25 ugh—Martha (MS) / ugh, Martha
242.26 thieves—thieves (MS) / thieves, thieves
243.1 fiercer (MS) / fierce
243.26 light (Magnum) / lit (MS as Ed1)
243.35 the gentleman (MS) / The gentleman
243.36 ugh—ugh—I'll (MS derived: ugh [end of line] ugh—Ill) / ugh—ugh. I'll
243.37 con-si-de-ra-ti-ón (MS ⟨consideration⟩ ↑ con-si-de-ra-ti-ón . . . ↓)) / con-si-de-ra-ti-on

244.5   him—just (MS) / him, just
244.9   chimney—and (MS) / chimney, and
244.10   gentleman—for (MS) / gentleman, for
244.10   consideration—so (MS) / consideration, so
244.21   father, for (MS derived: father for) / father—for
244.23   old—a (MS) / old, a
244.26   own—for (MS) / own. For
244.26   speak (MS) / say
244.30   quarter—but (MS) / quarter. But
245.3   thus—if (MS) / thus. If
245.11   you—to (MS) / you, to
245.11   plain—had (MS) / plain, had
245.16   window-shuts (MS) / window-shutters
245.18   loud (MS) / low
245.18   them—shew (MS) / them. Shew
245.33   chares (MS) / chare-work
245.42   you—last (MS) / you. Last
245.42   all—Stay (MS) / all, stay
245.43   it—farewell (MS) / it. Farewell
246.12   pictures (MS) / picture
246.20   would (MS) / should
246.25   conclusion. But (MS) / conclusion; but
246.35   others, rendering (MS derived: others render) / others, to render
247.3   die—sink or swim—Nigel (MS) / die, sink or swim, Nigel
247.8   chare-woman (MS) / char-woman
247.19   hands the (MS) / hand a
248.9   that (MS) / those
248.10   metal (MS) / meta
248.20   Glenvarloch. [new paragraph] "Ay, sir (MS Glenvarloch "Aye Sir) /
         Glenvarloch; "what of the Marshalsea?" [new paragraph] "Why, sir
248.25   acquaint (MS acquaint⟨ed⟩) / acquainted
248.31   conjured therefore (MS) / therefore conjured
248.39   expectation to hear (MS) / expectation of hearing
248.40   execution—he (MS) / execution. He
249.1   "I will (MS) / "I—I—I—will
249.4   money and departing (MS) / money, and departed
249.10   "Sir," said Lord Glenvarloch, "I (MS "Sir said Lord Glenvarloch I) /
         "Sir, I thank you," said Lord Glenvarloch—"I
249.12   "Why—Dorothy, chare-woman—Why, daughter (MS "Why—Doro-
         thy ↑ Chare woman ↓ —Why daughter) / "Why, Dorothy—chare-
         woman—why, daughter
249.14   left on latch (MS) / left a-latch
249.28   Peppercole (Editorial) / Peppercull (MS as Ed1)
250.8   parted—we (MS) / parted; we
250.11   eye—the (MS) / eye. The
250.12   too—but (MS) / too, but
250.24   con-si-de-ra-ti-ón (MS consi-de-ra-ti-ón) / con-si-de-ra-ti-on
250.28   ugh—ugh—and"―― (MS ugh—ugh—and"――) / ugh, ugh,
         ugh—"
251.2   Grahame (MS) / Graham
251.18   tennis—or (MS) / tennis, or
251.19   gentlemen-like (MS) / gentleman-like
251.27   would (MS) / will
251.34   huff—it (MS) / huff, it
251.34   play—he (MS) / play, he

251.43 smelled (MS smelld) / smelt
252.1   court-scented-water (MS) / court-scented water
252.6   *seeking* quarrel (proof correction) / seeking a quarrel (MS seeking
        quarrel)
252.8   neighbourly—that's (MS neighbourly—thats) / neighbourly, that's
252.13 hear your temptation (MS hear your ⟨somewhat⟩ ↑ temptation ↓) /
        hear the temptation
252.17 from window (MS) / from the window
252.23 between, "do (MS between do) / between them, "do
252.23 consideration—noble (MS) / consideration. Noble
252.25 Achilles"——— (MS) / Achilles———"
252.28 Colepepper, who (MS derived: Culpepper who) / Colepepper,
        (who
252.29 whinyard and (MS) / whinyard, and
252.29 antagonist, and Nigel, who, having (MS antagonist and Nigel who
        having) / antagonist,) and Nigel, who had
252.30 sword, now (MS sword now) / sword, and now
252.34 me?—you (MS me—you) / me? You
252.35 Remember (MS) / remember
253.21 casket said (MS) / casket, she said
253.24 without much (MS) / with small
253.26 Ay—Ay—child (MS Aye—Aye—child) / Ay, ay, child
253.29 ay—ay (MS aye—aye) / ay, ay
253.37 hoard (MS) / house
253.40 scorn—"he (MS scorn—he) / scorn. "He
253.41 me—is (MS) / me.—Is
254.9   courses—the (MS) / courses. The
254.17 enough—but (MS) / enough; but
254.29 pretence—they (MS) / pretence. They
254.30 prey, and (MS derived: prey and) / prey; and
254.37 young (MS) / yonng
254.37 man?" (MS man?.") / man?
255.2   folly—but (MS) / folly, but
255.13 agreeably in (MS) / agreeably to
255.20 Alsatia . . . to be (MS Alsatia he was not likely he found to be) /
        Alsatia, he found that he was not likely to be
255.27 both folding (MS) / both the folding
255.29 resemblance (MS) / appearance
255.40 Belzie, d—n (MS Belzie d—n) / Belzie!—D—n
256.10 now!" (MS) / now!—Ha! ha! ha!"
256.15 ye (MS) / you
256.26 be—hey, my (MS be—hey my) / be, my
256.26 lord?—a (MS Lord—a) / lord? a
256.28 bridge?—or (MS bridge—or) / bridge? or
256.29 fogs?—or what (MS fogs—or what) / fogs? Or, what
257.2   there—look (MS) / there. Look
257.3   face—and (MS) / face, and
257.5   general (MS) / congenial
257.27 not again taste (MS) / not taste
257.38 wainscot and walls (MS wainscoat & walls) / wainscoted walls
257.40 and of interlopers (MS) / and interlopers
258.4   as Paul's (MS as Pauls) / as Saint Paul's
258.8   have, or can have, either (MS have or can have either) / have either
258.16 you, that (MS you that) / you are, that
258.16 Scots (MS) / Scotch

258.18 Men (MS) / men
258.19 Park—be (MS park—be) / Park—Be
258.34 to-morrow—nay (MS tomorrow—nay) / to-morrow. Nay
258.36 Hildebrod composedly; "listen (MS Hildebrod composedly ⟨and l⟩
        ↑ "L ↓ isten) / Hildebrod; "listen
258.37 first what (MS) / first to what
258.39 again—And (MS) / again. And
259.1   French!—nay (MS french—nay) / French! Nay
259.3   you to be (MS) / you be
259.7   ready—ay, you start—but (MS ready—aye you start—but) / ready.—
        Ay, you start, but
259.11 favourite"——— (MS) / favourite———"
259.20 and"——— (MS) / and———"
259.24 fair ingots (MS) / gold dust
259.27 and"——— (Magnum) / and———" (MS and.")
259.41 Beaujeu's (proof correction) / Beaujeau's
260.1   laic—the (MS) / laic. The
260.31 of a very (MS) / of very
261.18 Aha!—are (MS Aha—are) / Aha! art
261.24 Senate soon (MS) / Senate as soon
261.25 meridian (MS) / meridiem
261.31 Anthonio (MS) / Anthony
262.41 fortnight or even a month's end, in (MS fortnight or even a months
        end in) / fortnight, or even a month, in
263.9   it. Suspicions . . . First (MS derived: it. Suspicions instantly ⟨came⟩
        arose in Trapbois mind to disturb the rapture of enjoyment—First) /
        it. First
263.17 usurer's (MS usurers) / miser's
263.33 led (MS) / leading
264.1   on the (MS) / upon the
264.6   me—if (MS) / me. If
264.8   me"——— (Magnum) / me———" (MS me———)
264.17 further (MS) / farther
264.24 ye (MS) / you
264.31 and that (MS & that) / or that
264.34 kill—but (MS) / kill. But
265.17 observation (MS) / notice
265.18 information (MS) / observation
265.24 of an apology (MS) / of apology
266.23 half-burned (MS half ⟨per⟩ burned) / half-burnt
266.28 burned (MS burnd) / burnt
266.31 house but (MS) / house except
266.33 master's (Magnum) / Master's (MS Masters)
267.22 at window (MS) / at the window
267.26 further (MS) / farther
267.28 grievances. But (MS) / grievances; but
268.15 irritable (MS) / irritated
268.23 to (MS) / at
268.33 contemptuously (MS) / impetuously
269.8   He now . . . exclaiming at (MS He now threw himself with impotent
        passion on his daughter as ↑ s ↓ he held out the piece of gold to Nigel
        exclaiming ↑ at . . . ↓) / He now exclaimed, at
269.12 it me (MS) / it to me
269.17 then," said (MS then" said) / then,"—said
269.21 him thrice (MS) / himself thrice

269.37 further (MS) / farther
270.7 him (MS) / himself
270.14 into (MS) / to
270.31 appeared her (MS appeard her) / appeared that her
270.36 was now dark (MS) / was dark
273.6 As the cross (MS) / As a cross
273.13 haggard (MS) / hagard
273.25 and protected——Oh! my (MS and protected——Oh my) / or protection. Oh! my
274.16 murtherers . . . murthered (MS murtherers . . . murtherd) / murderers
. . . murdered
274.22 spoken—would (MS) / spoken, would
274.26 silent—think (MS) / silent. Think
274.34 besides (MS) / beside
274.35 he heard (MS) / he had heard
274.39 man—go and (MS) / man. Go, and
275.2 meandering (MS) / meanderings
275.14 them (MS) / him
275.18 villain (MS) / villains
275.18 and"—— (MS) / and——"
275.19 "True—most true—he (MS) / "True, most true—he
275.21 gold—they (MS) / gold; they
275.25 clang (MS) / clank
276.1 rustle—anon (MS) / rustle; anon
276.3 rise—and (MS) / rise; and
276.36 blacked (MS blackd) / blackened
276.40 their guest (MS) / her guest
276.40 were escaped (MS) / had escaped
277.1 survivor made (MS) / survivor had made
277.5 features and person of (MS features ↑ & person ↓ of) / features of
277.15 doors (MS) / door
277.18 Glenvarloch, asked (MS Glenvarloch askd) / Glenvarloch, he asked
277.19 this deed (MS) / the deed
277.35 murthering (MS) / murdering
277.36 time—he (MS) / time. He
277.36 amongst us that (MS amongst that) / among us, *that*
277.38 will (MS) / *will*
278.9 Umph—umph, the (MS derived: Umph—umph the) / Umph, umph
—the
278.19 thee?—take (MS thee—take) / thee? Take
278.20 eye.—Let (MS) / eye. Let
278.21 to-morrow—good-night (MS tomorrow—goodnight) / to-morrow.
Good-night
278.22 wink—I (MS) / wink. I
278.23 here (MS) / Here
278.24 you—as (MS) / you. As
278.27 this is (MS) / there is
278.27 Grahame (8vo) / Græme (MS Greene)
278.33 not of the (MS) / not the
279.7 Grahame—ay (8vo Grahame. Ay) / Græme. Ay (MS Græme—
aye)
279.10 knowst (MS) / knowest
279.13 and he, the (MS And he the) / and the
279.24 hits—and (MS) / hits, and
279.25 bargain—or (MS) / bargain, or

279.31 hope he (MS) / hope that he
280.4   Friars"——— (MS) / Friars———"
280.7   murthering (MS) / murdering
280.23 human—to (MS) / human.—To
280.29 with which (MS) / by which
280.39 others (MS) / thers
281.12 And (MS) / and
281.17 friend—but (MS freind—but) / friend, but
281.19 avengers—it (MS) / avengers.—It
281.19 of—I (MS) / of; I
281.25 open—you (MS) / open. You
281.27 chest—bring it hither—it (MS) / chest. Bring it hither, it
281.32 forgot—they (MS) / forgot; they
281.37 cause—the (MS) / cause. The
281.37 rest—take courage—I . . . spring—and (MS rest—⟨stay⟩ ⟨↑ so ↓⟩ ↑ take
        courage— ↓ —I . . . spring—and) / rest. Take courage, I . . . spring, and
        The deleted inserted word is unclear: it might be an attempt at 'soft'.
281.42 was horrible (MS) / is horrible
282.1   desire, but for you—you (MS derived: desire but for you—you) /
        desire—but for you, you
282.3   composed—you (MS) / composed. You
282.4   dresser (MS) / table
282.13 apartment—then (MS) / apartment, then
282.29 her assistance (MS) / her his assistance
283.4   forehead—and (MS forhead—and) / forehead, and
283.14 hangings (MS) / hanging
283.36 master—let (MS Master—let) / master, let
283.37 imperative (MS) / impressive
283.41 waggon—when (MS) waggon. When
284.5   burthen (MS) / burden
284.10 wrapped (MS wrapd) / muffled
284.12 leave all—let (MS) / leave it all; let
284.12 the horrible (MS) / this horrible
284.15 for, seizing (MS for seizing) / by seizing
284.16 strong-box by (MS strong-box ↑ by . . . ↓) / strong-box, and, by
284.17 it, he threw it on his shoulders, and marched (MS ↑ . . . it ↓ he threw
        it on his shoulders and marchd) / it, throwing it on his shoulders, and
        marching
284.17 forwards (MS) / forward
284.20 master—master—you (MS Master—Master—you) / master, master,
        you
284.21 t'other (MS t other) / 'tother
284.28 comrade (MS comerade) / companion
284.35 She (MS) / she
285.17 carrying (MS) / conveying
285.39 murther (MS) / murder
286.27 could (MS) / would
287.1   And (MS) / and
287.2   additional, somewhat (MS additional some what) / additional, and
        somewhat
287.20 went now down (MS) / went down
287.21 on (MS) / in
287.32 alongst (MS) / along
287.41 turned (MS turnd) / grew
288.11 *Scaandalum Maagnatum*, sir—*Scaandalum Maagnatum* (Editorial) /

Scaandalum Maagnatum, sir—*Scaandalum Magnaatum* (MS *Scaandalum Maagnatum* Sir *Scandaalum Magnaatum*)

288.12 accentuation (MS) / accentation
288.13 at (MS) / in
288.18 prerogatives upon which (MS prerogatives ⟨whic⟩ upon which) / prerogatives, for which
288.22 TRUE—and (MS) / TRUE; and
288.30 reader (MS) / readers
288.38 mickle (MS mickle) / muckle
288.40 wald (MS) / would
289.1 damn (MS) / d—n
289.1 Scots (MS) / Scotch
289.7 his own natural (MS) / his natural
289.13 door—but (MS) / door; but
289.15 at bottom (MS) / at the bottom
289.16 Scots (MS) / Scotch
289.24 countryman (MS) / countrymen
289.34 singular combat (MS) / single combat
290.25 master—hear (MS Master—⟨for⟩ hear) / master, hear
290.26 moment!—for mercy's sake—for (MS moment—for mercys sake—for) / moment! for mercy's sake, for
290.30 craig (MS) / crag
290.30 whunstane—the man is mad—horn-mad to (MS whinstane—the man is mad—horn-mad to) / whunstane. The man is mad, horn mad, to
290.38 Glenvarloch!—do (MS Glenvarloch—do) / Glenvarloch! Do
290.39 dame (MS Dame) / mistress
290.41 Grahame (Editorial) / Gram (MS Gram [end of line])
290.42 umph—O, ay—very (MS umph—O aye—very) / umph.—O, ay, very
290.43 height—bright (MS) / height; bright
291.1 hawk's—a (MS hawks—a) / hawk's; a
291.7 Scotchman (MS) / Scotsman
291.8 dame (MS Dame) / mistress
291.21 damned (MS damnd) / d—d
291.24 dove?—nothing (MS Dove—nothing) / dove? nothing
291.28 me—and (MS) / me; and
291.31 A-hem!—Weel (MS A-hem—Weel) / a hem! Weel
291.36 yestreen—nae further gane—to (MS yestreen—no further gane—to) / yestreen, nae farther gane, to
291.39 be—why (MS) / be, why
291.40 decent honest house (MS) / decent house
292.4 place and say the place, and (MS place and say the place and) / place, and
292.5 neither—for (MS) / neither; for
292.6 it is (MS) / it's
292.12 ye (MS Ye) / you
292.14 Mistress Trapbois (MS) / Mistress Martha Trapbois
292.20 lies (MS) / lie
292.28 Fortunes (MS) / fortunes
292.39 are (12mo) / is (MS as Ed1)
293.2 errant (MS) / arrant
293.17 the Sovereign (MS) / his Sovereign
293.26 pilotage. (8vo) / pilotage (MS pilotage—)
293.28 that (MS) / the
293.29 country—your (MS) / country. Your
293.37 will keep the course we row her upon." (MS will ⟨go the way we⟩

↑ keep the course we ↓ row her upon") / will go the way we row her."

293.40   you to keep, otherwise (MS you to keep otherwise) / you, otherwise

293.43   who do talk (MS) / who talk

294.4   lift—if (MS) / lift. If

294.32   any (MS) / my

294.38   country. You (MS) / country; you

294.43   will—I (MS) / will; I

295.11   his waterman (MS) / the waterman

295.21   secret—do (MS) / secret, do

295.29   observing there (MS) / observing that there

295.31   lad (MS) / lads

295.31   noble (MS) / nobleman

295.32   his boatmen (MS derived: his boat men) / the boatmen

295.40   I break (MS) / I'll break

295.43   waterman's (MS watermans) / watermen's

296.11   "Firm Resolve," (MS "Firm Resolve") / "firm resolve,"

296.17   And accordingly, though (MS And accordingly though) / Accordingly, though

296.35   fingers—while (MS) / fingers, while

296.39   stirring—His (MS) / stirring. His

296.42   sir—the (MS Sir—the) / sir, the

297.1   peaked? yes (MS) / peaked? Yes

297.2   body—the (MS) / body, the

297.3   two running footmen, three dog-boys (MS two running footmen three dog-boys) / three running footmen, two dog-boys

297.4   knight—Sir (MS) / knight, Sir

297.4   Malgrowler"—— (Editorial) / Malgrowler." (MS Malg ↑ r ↓ owler—⟨Malagrow⟩)

297.9   mouth—Sir (MS) / mouth. Sir

297.11   chin—Sir (MS) / chin. Sir

297.13   sir—but (MS Sir—but) / sir. But

297.14   that—and (MS) / that; and

297.17   it—but (MS) / it; but

297.18   low—or (MS) / low, or

297.18   awry—did (MS) / awry.—Did

297.18   sir?—we (MS Sir—we) / sir? We

297.19   my styptic—or (MS) / my styptic, or

297.20   she (MS) / She

297.20   herself—one (MS) / herself. One

297.21   taffety (MS) / taffeta

297.21   patch—just (MS) / patch, just

297.22   sir—rather (MS Sir—rather) / sir, rather

297.23   otherwise—the (MS) / otherwise. The

297.25   courtiers"—— (MS) / courtiers."

297.28   say—a (MS) / say; a

297.29   say?—O (MS say—O) / say? O

297.30   withal—that (MS) / withal, that

297.30   permit—He (MS) / permit. He

297.31   presently—unless (MS) / presently, unless

297.33   way—Ned (MS) / way. Ned

297.33   sir—famous (MS Sir—famous) / sir, famous

297.34   pork-griskins—but (MS) / pork-griskins; but

297.34   pork—no more can (MS) / pork, no more than

297.35   Majesty—nor (MS) / Majesty, nor

297.36   Lennox—nor (MS) / Lennox, nor

297.36 Dalgarno—nay (MS) / Dalgarno,—nay
297.37 mine—but (MS min—but) mine.—But
297.37 styptic—another (MS) / styptic, another
297.38 flea—just (MS) / flea, just
297.39 mustache—it (MS) / mustache; it
297.40 you'd (MS yould) / you would
297.41 gentleman—very (MS) / gentleman, very
297.41 young—hope (MS) / young.—Hope
297.42 offence—it (MS) / offence; it
297.43 sir—I (MS Sir—I) / sir, I
298.2 London—you (MS) / London. You
298.7 this (MS) / the
298.8 griskins—but (MS) / griskins. But
298.10 Jews—there (MS) / Jews. There
298.10 do (MS) / Do
298.10 so?—then (MS so—then) / so? Then
298.11 his (MS) / our
298.11 Solomon—and (MS) / Solomon, and
298.12 Jews—so (MS Jews—⟨though⟩ so) / Jews; so
298.12 see—I (MS) / see. I
298.13 content—I (MS) / content. I
298.14 affections—crave (MS derived: affectionss⟨o⟩ ⟨g⟩ crave) / affections.
        Crave
298.15 trust—pray (MS) / trust. Pray
298.16 straggler—Thank (MS) / straggler.—Thank
298.17 Greenwich—Would (MS) / Greenwich. Would
298.18 the ghittern, sir, to (MS the ghittern Sir to) / that ghittern, to
298.18 Twang—twang (MS) / Twang, twang
298.19 dillo—something (MS) / dillo. Something
298.20 artists—Let (MS) / artists. Let
298.21 sir—Yes, sir—you (MS Sir—Yes Sir—you) / sir—yes, sir—You
298.22 you?—way (MS you—way) / you?—Way
298.22 Yes, sir—but (MS Yes Sir—but) / yes, sir; but
298.23 eating-house—not (MS eating house—not) / eating-house, not
298.23 Munko's—The (MS Mungo's—he) / Munko's.—The
298.24 there—and (MS) / there, and
298.24 sir—ha, ha!—yonder (proof correction; MS) / ha! Yonder
        MS has 'Sir—yonder'; Scott's proof correction is: 'sir. ↑⟨Ha⟩ ha ha!—↓
        Yonder'.
298.25 way—new (MS) / way, new
298.29 vocation—farewell (MS) / vocation.—Farewell
298.29 sir—hope (MS derived: Sir hope) / sir; hope
298.40 interrogated whether (MS) / interrogated, whether
299.1 monosyllable (MS) / syllable
299.6 embarrassment (MS embarassment) / embarrassments
299.12 it would seem (MS) / as it seemed
299.27 Majesty—and (MS) / Majesty, and
299.28 had—because (MS) / had, because
299.29 kitchen—as (MS Kitchen—as) / kitchen, as
299.33 poultry—a (MS) / poultry; a
299.35 Widdrington—what (MS) / Widdrington. What
299.36 Kilderkin? what (MS Kilderkin what) / Kilderkin? What
299.37 Kilderkin—if (MS) / Kilderkin, if
300.13 "Ail—nothing (MS) / "Ail nothing
300.14 nothing—and (MS) / Nothing, and

300.21 hither—I (MS) / hither; I
300.23 curiosity—the (MS) / curiosity. The
300.25 grease—I (MS) / grease. I
300.32 men's (8vo) / mens' (MS mens)
300.38 and young (MS) / and the young
301.1 lord, my (MS Lord, my) / lord—my
301.9 died—and (MS) / died. And
301.11 lordship—there . . . connection—your (MS Lordship—there . . . con-
        nection—your) / lordship, there . . . connection, your
301.13 purpose—you (MS) / purpose. You
301.17 amangst (MS) / amongst
301.19 Scottish (MS) / Scotch
301.34 "There are (MS) / "What! There are
301.35 even too true (MS) / even true
301.40 gentlemen"——— (MS) / gentlemen———"
301.41 friend," (MS friend") / friend,
301.42 how I am (MS) / how am I
301.42 to get to speech (MS) / to get speech
302.1 danger?—scalding (MS danger—scalding) / danger? scalding
302.13 me—it (MS) / me, it
302.14 twit (MS) / taunt
302.18 accusers—my (MS) / accusers. My
302.20 lord—we (MS Lord—we) / lord, we
302.22 then—this (MS) / then. This
302.28 mind—if (MS) / mind, if
302.29 Latin—a (MS latin—a) / Latin; a
302.29 amiss—and (MS) / amiss, and
302.33 which (MS) / who
302.40 kitchens—to (MS) / kitchen. To
302.43 alight—and (MS) / alight. And
303.1 speed—if (MS) / speed; if
303.5 him there (MS) / him that there
303.17 connivance (MS) / concurrence
303.22 presented him (MS) / presented to him
303.26 trod (MS) / stood
304.2 something (MS) / somewhat
304.17 De'il (MS Deil) / de'il
304.35 tines on the antlers—by G—d—A hart (MS tines—by G—d—A hart)
        / tines on the antlers. By G—d, a hart
304.36 season!—Bash and Battie—blessings (MS season—Bash and Battie—
        blessings) / season! Bash and Battie, blessings
304.37 ye!—buss (MS ye—buss) / ye! Buss
304.39 jaws—and (MS) / jaws, and
304.40 fell work (MS) / full work
304.43 folks—gie (MS) / folks, gie
305.2 discovering (MS) / observing
305.3 man—in (MS) / man. In
305.7 you—my (MS) / you. My
305.23 Glenvarlochides!—as (MS Glenvarlochides—as) / Glenvarlochides!
        as
305.24 work—and (MS work—⟨"⟩ and) / work, and
305.29 man—not a word—and (MS) / man, not a word; and
305.31 allegiance—the (MS) / allegiance.—The
306.1 King—man (MS) / King, man
306.4 Helloa—hello—ho (MS) / Hillo, ho

The first vowels of the first two words are unclear:
'He/i/alloa', 'he/illo'.

306.4   Steenie—Steenie (MS) / Steenie, Steenie
306.9   it?—it (MS) / it? It
306.17   ye (MS) / you
306.21   him—I (MS) / him. I
306.22   cloak—I (MS) / cloak. I
306.25   wonder, and execration (MS wonder ↑ & ↓ execration) / wonder and
        of execration
        Scott's added 'of' in the proofs makes the sentence unworkable.
306.26   purpose arose (MS) / purpose, arose
306.31   person. And (MS) / person; and
306.34   purpose (MS) / purposes
306.38   Ay—ay (MS Aye—aye) / Ay, ay
307.2   steel—a (MS) / steel, a
307.4   murther (MS) / murder
307.9   forwards (MS) / forward
307.19   father—for (MS) / father; for
307.20   me—black (MS) / me, black
307.21   England—and (MS) / England, and
307.28   Buckingham." (MS derived: Buckingham—") / Buckingham!"
307.34   laws—but (MS) / laws. But
307.38   horse—but (MS) / horse; but
308.20   rendering up yourself (MS) / rendering yourself up
308.21   in the terms (MS) / in terms
308.31   me—Hear (MS me—⟨my⟩ ↑ Hear ↓) / me—hear
308.31   me!—you (MS me—you) / me! You
308.40   wrong—we (MS) / wrong. We
309.13   damage (MS) / danger
309.16   ye?—who (MS ye—who) / ye? Who
309.20   man—Joannes (MS) / man, Joannes
309.25   less so in (MS) / less in
309.27   Steenie! Ye are right—there (MS Steenie Ye are right—there) /
        Steenie, ye are right! There
309.30   them (Magnum) / him (MS as Ed1)
309.34   veins—yet (MS) / veins. Yet
309.40   Dalgarno—Art (MS) / Dalgarno, art
309.43   your Gracious (MS) / your most Gracious
309.43   could (MS) / would
310.4   lang (MS) / long
310.14   the mind of the public (MS) / the public mind
310.21   the two pockets (MS) / the pockets
310.23   burthens (MS) / burdens
310.24   *accumbens* (12mo) / *accumbans* (MS accumbans)
310.30   pocket (MS) / pockets
310.31   ye (MS) / you
310.32   petitions, the t'other (MS petitions the tother) / petitions, t'other
310.32   pasquinadoes—a fine time we have on it (MS) / pasquinadoes; a fine
        time we have on't
310.36   say—when (MS) / say.—When
310.38   bit—one (MS) / bit; one
311.8   which had (MS) / which, having
311.9   life, and now (MS life and now) / life, now
311.11   victualler arrested (MS victualler ⟨arrested⟩ arrested) / victualler,
        arrested

312.2 Authority...Decorum (MS) / authority...decorum
312.26 office: he (proof correction) / office. He (MS office &)
312.36 History (MS) / history
312.40 Grey (MS) / Gray
313.1 lamentation and mourning and woe, yet (MS lamentation & mourning and woe yet) / lamentation and mourning, and yet
313.7 orders (MS) / order
313.14 Here (MS) / There
313.16 lad before him (MS) / 'lad before him'
313.18 freedom. [new paragraph] The (MS) / freedom. The
313.28 lad; we (MS derived: lad we) / lad. We
313.31 Come—come (MS) / Come, come
313.32 trembles—the (MS) / trembles? the
313.33 room—place (MS) / room. Place
313.34 child—you (MS) / child. You
313.35 tears—but (MS) / tears; but
314.19 companion in misfortune who (MS) / companion, who
314.25 he intended (MS) / he had intended
314.40 trick—and (MS) / trick—And
314.41 Tower?—there (MS Tower—there) / Tower?—There
315.6 with a tone (MS) / in a tone
315.10 unhappy boy (MS) / unhappy—boy
315.19 unhappy—a (MS) / unhappy, a
315.23 sounds something strangely (MS) / sounds strangely
315.24 friend—let (MS freind let) / friend—Let
315.26 you." (MS derived: me"—) / you?"
315.29 of London (MS) / in London
316.1 prisoner?—consider (MS prisoner—consider) / prisoner? Consider
316.2 or restraint—why (MS) / nor restraint. Why
316.2 me?—you (MS me—you) / me? You
316.5 wise—I (MS) / wise; I
316.6 I doubt not—I doubt it not, my (MS I doubt it not [end of leaf] doubt not—I doubt it not my) / I doubt it not, my
316.11 but (MS) / But
316.12 bestad (MS) / beset
316.13 folly—Besides (proof correction: folly ↑—Besides ↓) / folly. Besides
316.13 one—whose (proof correction) / one whose
316.15 the disclosure (proof correction) / this disclosure
317.4 the face (MS) / his face
317.10 and so delicate (MS) / and delicate
317.10 slumbers—I (MS) / slumbers, I
317.11 them—my (MS) / them. My
317.18 company—perhaps as a spy—by (proof correction: company ↑—perhaps as a spy—↓ by) / company, perhaps as a spy, by
317.29 dreamed (MS dreamd) / dreamt
317.34 so (MS) / as
317.39 season—just (MS) / season. Just
317.41 be—where...woman—what (MS) / be, where...woman—What
318.5 you?—and (MS you—and) / you? and
318.10 lordship—doubtless (MS Lordship—doubtless) / lordship. Doubtless
318.11 trouble—but (MS) / trouble; but
318.12 tell—great (MS) / tell, great
318.13 cup—and (MS) / cup; and
318.14 She (MS) / she
318.15 bread—though (MS) / bread, though

318.17 Christian—by (MS) / Christian, by
318.24 and for (MS and ⟨of⟩ for) / and as for
318.25 your lordship's gratification (MS your Lordships gratification) / your gratification
318.27 pleasure—an (MS) / pleasure; an
318.28 condition—but (MS considition—but) / condition. But
319.1   is innocent (MS) / is as innocent
319.4   Courtesy (MS) / courtesy
319.6   My lord, my lord—you (MS derived: My lord my lord—you) / My lord—my lord, you
319.8   swash-buckler ... under (MS swash-buckler—your Don Diego yonder—under) / swash-buckler, your Don Diego yonder, under
319.10 asked—all (MS askd—all) / asked. All
319.15 ribband—but (MS) / ribband, but
319.16 whole—and (MS whole— ↑ and ... ↓) / whole, and
319.16 years—till (MS ↑ ... years— ↓ till) / years, till
319.28 list—ye (MS) / list. Ye
319.31 amongst your (MS) / among your
319.32 amongst you (MS) / among you
320.4   serious?—you (MS serious—you) / serious? You
320.7   one—and (MS) / one, and
320.10 is—tell (MS) / is. Tell
320.18 deeply—were (MS) / deeply. Were
320.19 you—the rather (MS) / you, the rather
320.24 further (MS) / farther
321.18 sound (MS) / soundly
321.18 the vicinity (MS) / his vicinity
321.28 their (MS) / your
322.4   was cry (MS) / was a cry
322.6   *were* (MS) / were
322.15 my little knife (MS) / my knife
322.16 as I begun (MS derived: as was begun) / as I was beginning
322.33 is that—my (MS) / is—that my
322.34 her own sex (MS) / her sex
323.34 peculiarities (MS) / peculiarity
323.38 prevailed to (MS prevaild to) / prevailed on to
324.23 when distinction (MS) / when the distinction
324.30 they (MS) / the French
324.34 cough. "Hem! (MS cough—"Hem!) / cough, and then proceeded.[new paragraph] "Hem!
325.25 took it upon (MS) / took upon
325.43 —Still (MS —⟨and s⟩ ↑ S ↓ till) / —still
326.2   just"——— (MS) / just—"
326.3   you pass (MS) / you to pass
326.43 lord—in (MS Lord—in) / lord. In
327.2   murther (MS) / murder
327.8   murther ... murthered (MS murther ... murtherd) / murder ... murdered
327.22 it—our (MS) / it; our
327.22 hands—men (MS derived: hands men) / hands. Men
327.29 it—but (MS) / it. But
327.38 escaped—but (MS) / escaped; but
327.42 him. I (MS) / him—I
328.6   woman—she (MS) / woman,—she
328.29 "Undeniably (MS) / 'Undeniably

329.4   possession—it (MS) / possession. It
329.9   person—it (MS) / person. It
329.11   Palace—and (MS palace—and) / Palace; and
329.14   casket"——(MS) / casket——"
329.17   Frugal's—ay—he (MS Frugal's—aye—he) / Frugal's. Ay, he
329.19   father—was (MS) / father. Was
329.25   hath (MS) / has
329.30   in the Lord (MS) / in Lord
329.31   obeyed. (MS obeyd.) / obeyed,
329.36   the few papers (MS) / the papers
330.1   spendthrifts—but (MS) / spendthrifts, but
330.10   one or two (MS) / two or three
330.14   away—let (MS) / away. Let
330.29   lord—you (MS Lord—you) / lord, you
331.1   afterward (MS) / afterwards
331.8   situation?—nay (MS situation—nay) / situation? Nay
331.9   sooner—speak (MS) / sooner. Speak
331.10   will"——(MS) / will——"
331.15   protection?—speak (MS protection—speak) / protection? Speak
331.22   Beaujeu's (8vo) / Beaujeau's (MS Beaujeaus)
331.32   capable to take (MS) / capable of taking
331.35   Scripture—frankly (MS scripture—frankly) / Scripture. Frankly
331.42   warrant—I (MS) / warrant. I
332.3   when (MS) / where
332.5   me—for (MS me⟨"⟩—for) / me. For
332.10   hallo (MS) / halloo
332.14   speak—I (MS) / speak, I
332.17   too?—could (MS too—could) / too? Could
332.18   affairs?—but (MS affairs—but) / affairs? But
332.20   partners (MS) / partner
332.21   none to (MS) / none into
332.23   disguise?—Speak (MS disguize—Speak) / disguise? Speak
332.25   her errand (MS) / the errand
332.26   out doors (MS out ⟨active⟩ doors) / out of doors
         The deleted word is unclear.
332.27   courage—and (MS) / courage; and
332.31   now—that (MS) / now; that
333.15   and he (MS) / and so he
333.26   secrets—had (MS secrets—⟨but⟩had) / secrets. Had
333.32   compassionate—but (MS) / compassionate, but
333.43   well—if (MS) / well, if
334.6   damsel mine, I (MS damsel mine I) / damsel, now I
334.8   keep—the (MS keep⟨"⟩—the) / keep.—The
334.9   lodging (MS) / lodgings
334.11   me I forgive, for (MS me I forgive for) / me, I forgive you, for
334.16   her"——(MS) / her with——"
334.19   Davie (Editorial) / Davy (MS as Ed1)
334.23   I once saw (MS) / I saw
334.25   permit (MS) / Permit
334.29   to two (MS) / in two
334.36   generosity acted (MS) / generosity, acting
334.36   object, and (MS derived: object and) / object; and
334.41   irresolutely, clung (MS derived: irresolutely clung) / irresolutely—
         clung
335.9   yeoman (MS) / yeomen

335.24 ensure"—— (MS) / ensure——"
335.26 well—let (MS) / well, let
336.1 And (MS) / and
336.12 Mungo?—you (MS) / Mungo? you
336.17 better. You (MS derived: better. you) / better—You
336.19 regions—courtiers (MS) / regions. Courtiers
336.34 trepan?—why (MS trepan—why) / trepan? Why
336.37 King" —— (MS) / King"——
336.42 "and yet (MS ⟨said⟩ ↑ and ↓ yet) / "yet
337.17 council (MS) / counsel
337.33 And (MS) / and
337.35 instead (MS) / instantly
338.41 forth—and (MS) / forth. And
338.43 pistols—but (MS) / pistols; but
339.17 subjected—I (MS) / subjected, I
339.31 Cross, but most (MS cross but most) / Cross—most
339.35 Derrick—this (MS) / Derrick. This
339.35 jibber (MS ⟨gipp⟩ jibber) / jipper
339.36 him—it (MS) / him; it
339.41 can—if (MS) / can. If
340.8 flew as (MS) / flew off as
340.23 "vara interesting indeed (MS) / "vara interesting—vara interesting indeed
340.33 vara bountiful (MS) / very bountiful
340.37 athversary's (MS athversarys) / adversary's
340.39 yours be (MS) / yours to be
341.11 goldsmith?—ye (MS goldsmith—ye) / goldsmith? Ye
341.14 safety—had (MS) / safety. Had
341.16 wearing (MS) / wearin
341.20 Davie (Editorial) / Davy (MS as Ed1)
341.26 had her audience (MS) / had audience
341.37 person—and (MS) / person. And
342.3 troth (MS) / truth
342.4 ye (MS) / you
342.15 lass, make her Leddy Glenvarloch—ay, ay—ye (MS lass make her Leddy Glenvarloch—aye aye—ye) / lass—make her Leddy Glenvarloch.—Ay, ay, ye
342.16 on—rather (MS) / on. Rather
342.17 worse—if (MS) / worse, if
342.19 upon which you enlarged (MS) / upon which it pleased you to enlarge
342.23 solemnity—and (MS) / solemnity; and
342.26 my friend (MS) / a friend
342.34 prospect (proof correction) / means (MS as Ed1)
343.6 so be (MS) / be so
343.8 city—but (MS) / city. But
343.30 Your (MS) / your
343.37 heroism (MS) / devotion
343.42 descent—what (MS) / descent, what
343.43 reproach, for (MS derived: reproach for) / reproach—for
344.31 narration (MS) / narrative
345.3 There's (proof correction) / Here's
345.15 ay—time (MS aye—time) / ay, time
345.17 parted—the (MS) / parted. The
345.18 buttons of (MS) / buttons off
345.20 gane!—this (MS gane—this) / gane! This

345.21 ain (MS) / own
345.34 Richie—is (MS) / Richie, is
346.1 twa folk's (8vo) / twa folks
346.2 ane, and though (MS ↑ . . . ane & ↓ though) / ane. Though
346.9 take the advantage (MS) / take advantage
346.14 duty—but (MS) / duty, but
346.15 now—na, na—I (MS now—na na—I) / now—Na, na, I
346.23 will so manage (MS) / will manage
346.26 affairs"——— (Magnum) / affairs———" (MS affairs.")
346.32 not—since . . . leave, which (MS not—since . . . leave which) / not.
        Since . . . leave me, which
346.42 yourself the sole (MS) / yourself sole
347.8 persons. And (MS) / persons; and
347.10 our (MS) / your
347.39 several (MS) / see ral
348.8 damned—that (proof correction: damnd—that) / d——d, that
348.12 ony (MS) / any
348.14 man—is (MS) / man, is
348.14 thou? and . . . here?—if (MS thou? and . . . here—if) / thou? And . . .
        here? If
348.16 day"——— (MS) / day———"
348.19 King? ye (MS) / King? Ye
348.27 maist gracious (MS) / most gracious
348.28 maist grateful (MS) / most grateful
348.33 day—but (MS) / day; and
348.34 that wee bit (MS) / that bit
348.38 platter—his (MS) / platter; his
348.42 carry the (MS) / carry away the
349.3 with the (MS) / with that
349.20 cubits—if (MS cubits of the door—if) / cubits. If
349.20 falcon—if (MS) / falcon—If
349.20 lownd (MS) / loun
349.21 And (MS) / and
349.23 King. (MS) / King
349.30 fluttering (MS) / fluttered
349.39 *prole!*—ah (MS prole—ah) / *prole!* Ah
350.8 Wast (MS wast) / West
350.15 court-yard—But (MS court yard—But) / court-[end of line] yard?
        but
350.15 mare—*Equam* (MS) / mare. *Equam*
350.16 many honest men (MS) / many men
350.27 door—it (MS derived: door it) / door. It
351.4 remember—we (MS) / remember, we
351.6 money—did (MS) / money—Did
351.11 thereupon—which (MS) / thereupon; which
351.14 gree in (MS) / gree on
351.16 ancient hereditary kingdom (MS) / ancient kingdom
351.28 loyal (MS) / liege
351.34 accompt (MS) / account
351.41 was—smelling (MS) / was, smelling
351.43 din?—if (MS din—if) / din? If
352.2 power?—and (MS power—and) / power? And
352.3 *cimelia*—by (MS cimelia—by) / *cimelia* by
352.12 casualities (MS casual⟨l⟩ities) / casualties
352.15 man—what (MS) / man; what

352.18 jewels?—they (MS jewels—they) / jewels? they
352.20 hath (MS) / has
352.25 truth, falsehood—but (MS) / truth falsehood; but
352.27 patience—as (MS) / patience; as
352.27 Geordie—look (MS) / Geordie, look
352.29 jeweller—exclaiming (MS) / jeweller, exclaiming
352.31 warlock!—us (MS warlock—us) / warlock! us
352.33 like—he (MS) / like; he
352.34 Geordie—thou (MS) / Geordie; thou
352.35 man—but (MS) / man, but
352.35 Greece—gang (MS) / Greece; gang
353.7   back (MS) / out
353.21 much wiser (MS) / much the wiser
353.21 folk (MS) / folks
353.24 quo curram? quo non curram?— (Magnum) / quo curram quo non
        curram— (MS quo curram quo non curram)
353.25 Tene, tene,—quem? (MS) / Tene, tene, quem?
353.41 man?—the (MS man—the) / man? The
353.42 ours—there (MS) / ours. There
353.43 stands—and (MS) / stands, and
354.2   hence?—ye (MS hence—ye) / hence? Ye
354.3   cry pay, pay, as (MS cry pay pay as) / cry pay, pay, pay, as
354.5   will—but (MS) / will. But
354.8   Moniplies—with (MS) / Moniplies, with
354.11 Majesty—he (MS) / Majesty, he
354.13 sprackle (MS) / spraickle
354.14 Geordie?—your (MS Geordie—you) / Geordie? Your
354.15 came (MS) / cam
354.15 weel—and (MS) / weel. And
354.25 friend—speak (MS freind—speak) / friend, speak
354.27 payment (MS) / payments
354.33 wald (MS) / would
354.35 whilk (MS) / which
354.37 giff-gaff—it (MS) / giff-gaff It
354.37 niffer, grippie for grippie.—Aweel (proof correction derived: niffer
        ↑ grippie for grippie ↓ .—Aweel) / niffer.—Aweel (MS niffer—
        Aweel)
354.38 reckon?—or (MS reckon—or) / reckon? Or
354.40 like?—ye (MS like—ye) / like? Ye
355.4   "How—mon—how (MS) / "How, man—how
355.7   us?—sell our justice!—sell (MS us—sell our justice—sell) / us?—
        Sell our justice!—Sell
355.23 only"—— (MS) / only——"
355.26 him!—it (MS him—it) / him! It
355.27 gate—and (MS) / gate. And
355.28 whae (MS) / wha
356.10 good Master Richard (MS) / good Richard
356.11 Castle Collop (Magnum) / Castle Collops (MS Castle-collops)
356.20 yet!—Yonder (MS yet—Yonder) / yet!—Gude guide us! Yonder
356.21 sifflication—I (MS siflication—I) / sifflication. I
357.2   might be (MS) / may be
357.3   this (MS) / This
357.3   commended (MS comended) / commend
357.12 and my (MS) / and if my
357.25 natheless (MS) / nevertheless

358.1 it—and as *non* (MS it—and as ⟨we⟩ *non*) / it—*non*

358.11 told?—this (MS told—this) / told? This

358.28 wald (MS) / wad

358.30 puir (MS) / poor

358.31 at anes (MS) / it ance

358.32 put her aff on him, puir (MS put her aff on him poor) / put aff on him the puir

359.1 Steenie. And (MS Steenie. ↑And . . . ↓) / Steenie—and

359.12 sank (MS) / sunk

359.16 self!—*Vae atque dolor!*—My (MS self—Vae atque dolor!—My) / self! *Vae atque dolor!* My

359.16 Huntinglen—look up, look (MS derived: Huntinglen—look up [end of line] look) / Huntinglen, look up—look

359.20 in (MS) / on

359.24 it—siller to gild it—a gude (MS) / it—a gude

359.25 loon (MS) / loun

360.6 street-walker—even (MS street walker—even) / street-walker, even

360.19 hard-hearted—but (MS hard hearted—but) / hard-hearted; but

360.20 should have (MS) / would have

360.20 race—I (MS) / race; I

360.33 it—and (MS) / it; and

360.35 you——" (8vo you—") / you"—(MS you"——)

360.37 can—the (MS) / can; the

360.42 Geordie—ye (MS) / Geordie, ye

361.3 Huntinglen—the (MS) / Huntinglen, the

361.3 Earl—ganging (MS) / Earl, ganging

361.4 world—I (MS) / world; I

361.5 like—ye (MS like—you) / like, ye

361.15 O, Geordie, Geordie (MS O Geor⟨g⟩↑d↓ie Geor⟨g⟩↑d↓ie) / O, Geordie

361.35 a' (MS) / a

361.36 ye (MS) / you

361.38 intimating (MS) / hinting

362.5 they (MS) / *they*

362.5 me (MS) / *me*

362.15 seen?—no (MS seen—no) / seen?—No

362.22 himself to (MS) / himself for

362.27 chased (MS) / cleared

362.28 me, man, for (MS me man for) / me, for

362.36 his rolling mode (MS) / his mode

362.42 commands (MS) / demands

363.21 well (MS) / Well

363.36 consented! (MS) consented?

363.37 he left (MS) / we left

365.7 ye (MS) / you

365.9 marriage (MS) / marriage-ceremony

365.11 of head (MS) / of the head

365.20 Well—I (MS) / Well, I

365.20 withdraw—the (MS) / withdraw. The

365.21 England—but (MS) / England. But

365.22 bestowed—methinks (MS bestowd—methinks) / bestowed. Methinks

365.23 know—is (MS) / know. Is

365.23 Duke?—or (MS Duke—or) / Duke? Or

365.24 before"—— (MS) / before——"

365.29 house—a (MS House—a) / house. A

365.36 convince even you (MS) / convince you
365.41 a controversy (MS) / the controversy
366.1 sire (MS Sire) / sir
366.2 contained (MS containd) / contains
366.4 hae (MS) / have
366.10 gave the (MS) / gave me the
366.18 demesne (MS) / demesnes
366.25 on Exchequer? couldna (MS on Exchequer could na) / on our Exchequer? Couldna
366.28 it—it (MS) / it—It
366.31 fiddle (MS) / play
366.33 of Exchequer (proof correction) / of our Exchequer
366.40 your (MS) / my
366.41 his ram-skin (MS ↑ ... his ↓ ram-skin) / the ram-skin
366.41 sheeps-head. But (MS) / sheeps-head handle. But
366.42 await in town to-morrow; if (proof correction: await ⟨at my lodgings⟩
  ↑ in town tomorrow ↓, ⟨near Covent-Garden⟩; if / await in town to-
  morrow, near Covent-Garden; if
368.9 might (MS) / may
368.10 sticked Dalgarno (MS) / sticked Lord Dalgarno
368.11 it yet (MS) / yet it
368.14 elided (MS) / eluded
368.14 is to be much lamented, but (MS is to be much lamented but) / is
  much to be lamented that
369.5 yonder—mair (MS) / yonder, more
369.5 Bishop, and (MS derived: Bishop ↑ and ... ↓) / Bishop—and
369.8 put (MS) / pent
369.17 around us—nevertheless (MS around ↑ us ↓—nevertheless) /
  around us; nevertheless
369.19 room—the (MS) / room, the
369.20 thought we had (MS thought ⟨I⟩ ↑ We ↓ had) / thought I had
369.20 eye left for (MS) / eye for
369.23 lords, we (Magnum) / lord, we (MS Lord we)
369.27 entire (MS) / en- [end of line] ire
370.6 ye said (MS) / you said
370.14 Which (MS) / which
370.28 that—but (MS) / that. But
370.35 expeded (MS) / expedited
370.37 for our (MS) / forour
371.4 lang-backed (MS lang⟨fallow⟩ backed) / long-backed
371.11 that—I ken that," (MS that—I ken that") / that,"
371.12 ye think (MS) / you think
371.17 ideots (MS) / idiots
371.19 Moniplies, and (MS Moniplies and) / Moniplies, sir, and
371.24 two three (MS) / two or three
371.25 wald (MS) / wad
371.26 yoursell (MS) / yourself
371.32 after-thought (MS) / after thought
371.36 ye—you (MS) / ye. You
371.36 your gate (MS) / your ain gate
372.1 Charles?—and (MS Charles—and) / Charles? And
372.4 have done (MS) / have been doing
372.5 hinny (MS) / bonnie
372.12 his (MS) / this
372.15 Scotch (MS) / Scottish

372.34 noon—Lord (MS) / noon, Lord
372.39 his—and (MS) / his; and
372.41 him—and...him—he (MS) / him, and...him. He
373.1 secrets, I (MS derived: secrets I) / secrets—I
373.1 his—but no (MS) / him. But, no
373.2 it—there (MS) / it, there
373.3 what's (MS whats) / what
373.9 profitable—but (MS) / profitable, but
373.9 What (MS) / what
373.11 me this (MS) / me in this
373.21 "I—I—" stammered (MS "I—I—" stammerd) / "I—I,"—stammered
373.28 "I—I—incline (MS) / "I—I incline
373.31 It (MS) / it
373.37 them—there (MS) / them. There
373.37 stand arow—twenty (MS) / stand in a row, twenty
374.1 man!—he (MS man—he) / man! he
374.8 else—and (MS else—⟨"⟩ and) / else. And
374.13 threats, no (MS derived: threats no) / threats—no
374.14 not, I (MS not I) / not, honest Andrew, I
374.18 neither insisted (MS) / insisted neither
374.18 or (MS) / nor
374.24 ordinary—but (MS Ordinary—but) / ordinary; but
374.25 will to have (MS) / will have
374.28 and"—— (MS) / and——"
375.5 mayst (MS) / mayest
375.11 liberty—or (MS) / liberty, or
375.12 so—if (MS) / so. If
375.18 eye (MS) / eyes
375.34 what, alamort—hast (MS) / what, hast
375.36 court? or (MS court or) / court?—Or
375.37 Gorgon (MS) / gorgon's
375.39 lord—I am glad—My lord, I (MS Lord—I am glad—My Lord I) / lord, I am glad—my lord, I
376.4 elsewhere—well (MS else where—well) / elsewhere. Well
376.5 it—ay (MS it—aye) / it. Ay
376.12 papers—thou (MS papers—⟨though⟩ thou) / papers, thou
376.13 Northward Ho!—at (MS) / Northward, ho! At
376.15 papers!—come (MS papers—come) / papers!—Come
376.16 the papers (MS) / the—the papers
376.18 not? hast (MS) / not!—Hast
376.19 varlet?—did (MS varlet—did) / varlet? Did
376.21 honestly come (MS) / come honestly
376.25 not to say (MS) / not say
376.25 I upon the spot divorce (MS I ⟨will⟩ upon the spot divorce) / I will, upon the spot, divorce
376.29 lord—I (MS Lord—I) / lord, I
376.31 mine—what (MS) / mine. What
376.32 Why (MS) / why
376.37 thee—a (MS derived: thee a) / thee. A
376.39 me do (MS) / me to do
376.41 "Do (MS) / "Ah, do
376.43 stay—I (MS) / stay, I
377.6 have (MS) / hast
377.10 me—did (MS) / me.—Did
377.13 perfect. Mind (MS) / perfect—mind

377.15 instantly follow me (MS) / follow me instantly
377.24 anticipate various (MS anticipate ⟨the⟩ various) / anticipate the various
378.2 thou that mayst (MS derived: thou who mayst) / that mayst
378.8 warning? do (MS warning "do) / warning? Do
378.12 feathers—you (MS) / feathers. You
378.16 bitten—that's (MS bitten—thats) / bitten, that's
378.19 well (MS) / Well
378.21 marry (MS) / Marry
378.21 bounty!—but (MS bounty—but) / bounty!—But
378.27 money—but there (MS) / money.—But that
378.29 So (MS) / so
378.37 heard?—how (MS heard⟨"⟩—how) / heard? —But how
378.41 do—for (MS) / do for
379.4 of a hue (MS) / of hue
379.16 setting-dog—thou (MS setting dog—thou) / setting-dog. Thou
379.21 Aha! comest (MS) / Aha!—Comest
379.26 "They (MS "they) / "But, however, they
379.30 with—he (MS with—he) / with.—He
379.31 goblin?—well—the boy (MS goblin—well—he) / goblin? Well, the boy
379.34 sure—and (MS) / sure, and
379.35 of—Well—scrivener (MS of—Well—Scrivener) / of. Well, scrivener
379.36 pieces—bravely (MS) / pieces. Bravely
379.41 it—but (MS) / it, but
380.23 seemed (MS seemd) / appeared
381.4 Moniplies—may (MS) / Moniplies. May
381.9 ordinary"——(Magnum) / ordinary—" (MS Ordinary")
381.18 come"——(MS) / come."
381.20 us—why (MS) / us, why
381.37 see—you Scots are (MS see—ye are) / see. You Scots are
381.41 pleases—but (MS) / pleases; but
381.42 under (MS) / in
382.2 let (MS) / Let
382.11 stare (MS) / start
382.14 nothing—tell (MS) / nothing. Tell
382.27 tavern—this (MS Tavern—this) / tavern. This
382.28 whitter (MS) / whetter
382.34 that befell (MS) / that has befallen
382.42 be—come (MS) / be. Come
382.42 wi' me, and (MS with me and) / wi' me—just come ye wi' me; and
383.8 burned (MS burnd) / burnt
383.30 affairs," (MS affairs") / affairs,'
384.7 whether (MS) / whether,
384.7 and, turning his red and swollen eyes to Richie, said: "Cock's-bones (MS derived: and turned his red and swollen eyes to Richie—said "Cock's-bones) / and turning his red and swollen eyes to Richie— [new paragraph] "Cock's-bones
384.9 it, and (MS derived: it and) / it,—and
384.10 This here girl—my master's daughter—this Margaret Ramsay,—you (MS This here girl—my masters daughter—this Margaret Ramsay—you) / This Margaret Ramsay,—you
384.12 once—at (MS) / once, at
384.26 marriage—it (MS) / marriage, it
384.39 sound (MS) / sounds
384.41 not in (MS) / not even in

384.41 stone-walls (MS ⟨the bri⟩ stone-walls) / stone walls
384.42 knows (MS) / has a right to know
385.31 man?" (12mo) / man," (MS missing)
385.36 free—home (MS) / free.—Home
385.37 myself the cleverest and happiest fellow (MS) / myself one of the cleverest and happiest fellows
385.38 money (MS) / *money*
385.38 service—and (MS) / service! and
385.39 time—I (MS) / time, I
386.42 earnest, as well as any lad in England. (proofs) / earnest too well to be taken in that way. (MS missing)
387.2 Peppercole (Editorial) / Peppercull (MS missing)
388.28 amongst (proofs) / among (MS missing)
389.9 that you (proof correction) / that, though, you (MS missing)
390.40 Davie (Editorial) / Davy (MS missing)
392.6 master's (proofs) / masters' (MS missing)
393.18 these (MS) / those
393.18 murther (MS) / murder
393.31 Eurydice!—have (MS Eurydice—have) / Eurydice!—Have
393.33 rarity (MS) / variety
394.4 Richie grappled (MS) / Richie immediately arose, however, and grappled
394.7 then leaped (MS) / and leaped
394.11 Brave Richie (MS) / Bravo, Richie
394.36 "'Vengeance (8vo) / ' Vengeance (MS missing)
396.6 Dalgarno. (proofs) / Dalgarno (MS missing)
396.12 Davie (Editorial) / Davy (MS missing)
396.37 alongst (MS) / along
397.15 manteau (MS) / mantua
397.26 chapter (MS) / Chapter
398.4 pretension (MS) / pretensions
398.11 Davie (Editorial) / Davy (MS as Ed1)
398.18 Davie (Editorial) / Davy (MS Davey)
398.21 enemies' (8vo) / enemies (MS as Ed1)
398.26 Davie (Editorial) / Davy (MS as Ed1)
398.29 Claudian (MS) / Claudius
398.41 so soon (MS) / as soon
400.7 dinner." (proofs) / dinner?" (MS dinner—")
400.11 true—vara (MS) / true, vara
400.12 maun (MS) / men
400.14 ye (MS) / you
400.14 George?—we (MS George—we) / George? we
400.27 thing—if (MS) / thing, if
400.40 has, to (MS has to) / has, even to
400.40 wylie-coat—she (MS) / wylie-coat, she
401.4 gane—it (MS) / gane; it
401.25 was therefore very (MS) / was very
402.1 called the finishing touch of "the (MS calld the finishing touch of "the) / called "the finishing touch of the
402.12 you—but (MS) / you; but
402.15 covenants (MS) / covenant
402.22 suppose (MS) / fancy
402.24 their (MS) / the
402.29 were transported (MS) / was transported
402.33 burned (MS burnd) / burnt

403.2   liege—it (MS derived: Lord it) / liege. It
403.6   they (MS) / They
403.7   Monypennies—though (MS) / Monypennies, though
403.26   us! it (MS us it) / us! It
403.35   gude (MS) / good
403.42   liege—she (MS) / liege. She
404.4   closely, Richie (MS closely ⟨Ma⟩ Richie) / closely, friend Richie
404.10   wanters (MS) / wantons
404.13   Peace—Peace—I (MS) / Peace—peace. I
404.23   bride once more.—"This (MS bride once more "This) / bride, "once
         more.—This
404.25   it—but (MS) / it, but
404.27   ourselves—it (MS) / ourselves, it
404.42   walk—he (MS) / walk; he
404.42   amang (MS) / among
405.5   paper—the (MS) / paper. The
405.8   estate—if (MS) / estate. If
405.17   instant—the (MS) / instant; the
405.26   Hymen—O (MS) / Hymen, O
405.39   man—methinks (MS) / man; methinks
406.4   come (MS) / comes
406.23   while, Sir Mungo guiding (Editorial) / while Sir Mungo, guiding (MS
         while Sir Mungo guiding)

END-OF-LINE HYPHENS

All end-of-line hyphens in the present text are soft unless included in the list below. The hyphens listed are hard and should be retained when quoting.

6.31	death-watch	96.24	posset-cup
7.2	chin-deep	100.32	god-father
14.21	heaven-directed	102.32	god-father's
20.14	Temple-Bar	106.4	pass-word
20.31	stout-bodied	107.27	stage-players
22.40	turned-up	108.1	deputy-chamberlain
25.26	back-ground	109.5	king's-man
25.35	ready-witted	115.20	nose-of-wax
26.27	head-gear	119.26	counter-security
27.24	palmer-worm	127.26	bridge-end
30.23	pock-pudding	130.34	high-dressed
30.32	watch-maker	131.21	pains-taking
38.12	back-stair	141.14	first-rate
43.23	court-suit	144.29	puppy-dog
45.14	calf-ward	145.4	twenty-four
45.32	sax-mile-end	145.10	cock-loft
48.16	back-shop	146.24	Tothill-Fields
51.12	good-humour	146.26	day-break
61.38	Time-meter	148.21	In-and-in
62.34	Dot-and-carry-one	163.34	cheese-monger
62.39	now-a-days	165.37	street-door
63.6	sheep's-head	168.3	thread-bare
63.14	to-morrow	168.42	goss-hawk
63.26	god-father	178.12	south-eastern
63.29	bull-dog	179.39	good-nature
64.3	to-morrow	180.11	cold-blooded
64.18	corn-pickle	181.14	Star-Chamber
65.4	Covent-Garden	187.1	band-boxes
66.2	half-shut	191.35	trunk-breeches
66.32	sad-coloured	193.31	mal-practices
66.33	hunting-horn	195.23	palmer-worms
67.35	nick-names	200.31	Lombard-Street
74.18	well-beloved	201.12	god-daughter
78.42	time-piece	201.36	cross-tempered
80.22	mountain-ridge	202.13	over-hastily
80.29	dudgeon-knife	210.18	open-hearted
80.36	pre-eminence	215.27	cash-keeper
84.18	cash-keeper	228.20	Fleet-Street
84.38	good-night	228.33	chirurgeon-barber
85.23	reading-desk	229.20	purse-strings
90.27	blood-drop's	231.40	now-a-days
90.40	Alack-a-day	232.1	now-a-day
91.2	bridal-chamber	232.5	wood-cocks
94.30	elbow-chair	233.15	beggar-my-neighbour

238.14	horse-collar	337.31	giddy-brained
241.13	sea-coast	345.16	horse-hair
250.19	petty-larceny	348.1	under-clerk
250.40	coney-catcher	348.3	cock-a-leekie
256.32	double-distilled	348.9	gillie-white-foot
257.21	sand-bed	348.36	cock-a-leekie
258.18	Sparrow-hawk	350.13	self-same
260.17	close-fisted	350.31	gold-ends
266.23	wax-candles	360.6	street-walker
267.7	arm-chairs	366.42	to-morrow
278.15	father-in-law	367.11	daughter-in-law
282.25	low-muttered	376.34	out-sworn
285.4	egg-shell	379.8	to-morrow
286.23	ship-chandler	386.6	court-favour
289.20	pudding-headed	395.34	riding-beaver
299.4	roast-beef	398.38	coat-of-arms
300.27	puff-paste	400.2	court-yard
305.29	cheek-for-chowl	400.6	wedding-dinner
310.26	over-burthened	400.16	marriage-ring
311.6	poursuivant-at-arms	402.41	re-entered
333.10	wild-goose		

HISTORICAL NOTE

Full details of works referred to by short titles in this Note can be found at the head of the Explanatory Notes, 540–41.

Historical Sketch. When he assumed the English crown on the death of Elizabeth in 1603 James hoped to unite his two kingdoms of Scotland and England. He has been credited by some with coining the term 'Great Britain' to express this goal, and continued to use it in self-flattery long after it had become hollow.[1] In a note critical of Francis Osborne's account of this effort Scott remarks that the proposal to unite Scotland and England 'was one of the few marks of attention to public utility which dignified the reign of James' (Osborne, 1.243n). But when the Hampton Court Conference of 1604, which he organised to bring the clergy of Scotland and England to agree on the form of church government, failed of its purpose (though it authorised the so-called 'King James Bible'), and the Gunpowder Plot of the next year exposed the virulence of the papists, he was reduced for most of his reign, at home, to keeping peace between the two volatile parts of his realm, while quelling papist conspiracies, and, abroad, to avoiding war with the Dutch, the French, and especially the Spanish.[2] The first off-stage marriage—that of Nigel and Margaret with which the story ends—can be read to represent the diminished achievement that was James's legacy. Although Margaret is young enough to have been born in London, and hence is English, she is the daughter of a transplanted Scot. Thus the union is one of Scot with Scot and, at that, a 'penny-wedding' (see note to 400.12). The couple are dependent upon the good will, generosity, and power of others, Nigel having no fortune beyond his Scottish lands and Margaret only a modest legacy from her grandmother. James's keen interest and personal involvement in, not to say obsession with, the wedding represents one of the several ways—hunting, racing, progresses, theological disputation were others—in which the monarch occupied himself at the expense of governing his kingdom. That he would seek to arrange a marriage for the Princess Elizabeth and, later, for the Prince of Wales with a Spanish infanta or French princess was his duty as king and father, but that as the 'father of his country'—*pater patriæ*—he would meddle in the marriages of his courtiers was less defensible, the more so that at times it bordered on the prurient.[3] In Scott's depiction of his behaviour here the king is little more than a marriage-broker—and a childish one at that[4]—of two people who have no political significance. James is, in effect, hiding from himself or from his role and duty as king or both, behaviour that brought complaints over and over again, beginning early in his reign.[5]

The second off-stage wedding—that of Richie Moniplies and Martha Trapbois—is, by contrast, clearly a union of Scotland and England. But it is also a symbol of Scotland's prospering at the expense of England—the very situation that so infuriated the English and sparked quarrels and brawls intermittently throughout James's reign, lending a heavy irony to his vaunted motto of 'peacemaker' (see notes to 68.35–36 and 110.14). In regaling Nigel with a (humorous) catalogue of such marriages (41.37–42.10) Dame Nelly establishes the pattern for Richie's conduct. By contrast with Richie, George Heriot, citizen par excellence, has earned his fortune and respect over the career of a lifetime; his legacy of a school for orphan children in Edinburgh (329.23–29) is in the tradition of Dick Whittington, the newcomer who becomes honoured citizen and, like wealthy aristocrats, establishes foundations that perpetuate his concern for the welfare of the needy long after his demise (see note to 100.1). Richie has acquired his fortune through marriage to the daughter of an immensely wealthy usurer, fufilling the narrator's prediction that she is 'likely to be wealthy enough to tempt a puritan, so soon as the devil had got her old dad for his due' (199.13–14). In a matter of weeks he has become a banker to the monarch, for which he is rewarded with a knighthood or baronetcy (Scott does not specify and his title 'Sir' can indicate either), the latter being the new honour that James created to raise money and so abused that historians trace the downfall of the English nobility to it.[6] As Scott elsewhere remarked, 'The drama of the times is full of allusions to this traffick.'[7] The clumsy motion by which James knights Nigel's erstwhile 'page' is, thus, at once an example of how James financed his court and a judgment of it. At the start of the story Richie is a servant, albeit a conceited, independent-minded one; at the close he is a knight or baronet who can trace his descent one generation to the meatmarket of Edinburgh and his father's butcher-shop there. Nigel, by contrast, can trace his ancestry for 500 years (36.23–25).

The traditional Scottish dish of cock-a-leekie, a motif carefully developed in the novel (see 63.1, 348.3–4, 406.25–27), contrasts sharply with the traditional English dish of beef which the anglicised Earl of Huntingdon serves in mountainous quantity (128.4), and the two together contrast strikingly with the modish French fare of the Chevalier Beaujeu's ordinary (137.26–32). The last is new, fashionable, foreign, and symptomatic of the generation gap that James himself puzzles over in a conversation with Heriot (361.15–33).[8] The old and new as father and son is the most consistent, most thoroughly thematised form of this binary in Scott's text. (Even Buckingham's father is mentioned in order to expose the son's arrogance and abuse of power: see 117.20–21). Scott initiates the idea with Jin Vin's saucy response to Heriot and the latter's sharp reprimand (33.7–16) on the duty of youth to their elders. It is Heriot, too, who elaborates the contrast between the old and the new, specifically father and son, as the broadsword versus the rapier (129.43–130.4), which contrast Dalgarno echoes and extends (136.2–10). He has shortly before rejected the towling dinner-bell as an irritating 'relique of antiquity' (127.37–40), and a little later dismisses 'old-world service' in a catalogue of the obsolete that characterises the Scottish court of James VI itself as irrelevant to the English one of James I, the implication being that the monarch is an irrelevance in his own court (155.39–156.2). And it is Dalgarno who lectures his father on the replacement of the sword by pen-and-ink (the legal document) as the modern means of revenge (366.39–41). Though examples of the old/new contrast are everywhere to be found in 'the old drama', it is Massinger's play *A New Way to Pay Old Debts*, strategically introduced at Nigel and Heriot's first meeting (51.18–26), that signals this theme in Scott's text. As for the simple then/now contrast, it is initiated at the beginning of the opening scene, with the description of Davy Ramsay's tradesman's booth (20.16–22), and continues randomly apace: see, for example, the national Scottish nickname 'Jockey' versus 'Sawney' (33.43–34.1); London versus Constantinople as the source of the plague (39.32–34); Temple-Bar in the early 1620s and in 1822 (64.34–65.12); and so on through the book. By far the most significant such distinction is the one Scott makes (discussed more fully below) when introducing formally the subject of James's character, the inconsistencies of which render 'it a subject of doubt amongst his contemporaries, and [bequeath] it as a problem to future historians' (66.40–44). Extra-textual explanations Scott made about his choice of subject for *Nigel* (see Essay on the Text, 407–09) are herewith introduced into the text of the novel, and Scott becomes thereby one of those 'future historians' fascinated by the problem of James's elusive character. For this formal, abstract 'character' of the monarch Scott had models in the memoirs and histories of Sir Anthony Weldon and William Sanderson which he had edited for the *Secret History of the Court of James the First* in 1811 (2.[1]–12 and 2.293–98).

Both weddings transpire at a time proximate to James's unsuccessful effort to effect a settlement with Spain through the marriage of Charles, the Prince of Wales, and the Infanta Maria. Had the journey of the Prince and Buckingham to the Spanish Court in 1623 to forward the suit with personal diplomacy succeeded, the ageing monarch's claim to peacemaker would have been finally substantiated, if not entirely justified, and his motto *Beati pacifici* impervious to irony.[9] Moreover, the incessant efforts of the papists to counter the Reformation in Britain during the reigns of Elizabeth and James would have received the ultimate check, the threat of another Spanish armada thereby abrogated. Hermione's story reminds us of this past history, not only in her life before arriving in England but since, for her residence in the Foljambe mansion-cum-nunnery allows Scott to introduce a name connected with the Babington Conspiracy, a typical papist plot of Elizabeth's reign.[10] For Margaret Ramsay, Hermione's is a cautionary tale; but so it is or can be interpreted for Britain at large. James seems eventually to have realised that in the failure of Charles's suit he and the nation had had a narrow escape: the British people had opposed such an alliance for years, the 'match having been long in treaty' (Osborne, 1.453), and resented his relative lack of interest in the marriage of the Princess Elizabeth and the unfortunate consequences thereof because of his fixation on a Spanish match for Charles.[11]

Time and Place in the Novel. Scott mentions the month but not the year in which the story begins: it is 'on a fine April day' (25.15) that the two London apprentices assume their positions in the horologer's booth just within Temple-Bar and commence to harangue the passers-by. Two other references to April late in the novel—'April gouks', i.e. fools (384.19) and 'April passions', i.e. showers of tears (391.19)—if metaphorical, may also remind us of the season of the year. With one exception —that of Nigel's wedding to Margaret—Scott never mentions a date or names a day of the week. But that the time is late in James's reign there is no question. For several reasons the year would appear to be either 1623 or 1624. The case for the latter is that, since Buckingham and Prince Charles departed England for Spain on 18 February 1623 and did not return home until 5 October of that year, they were out of the country for the spring, indeed, for the better part of the year. Moreover, it was in May 1623, while the favourite was in Spain, that he received the duke's patent, presumably to enhance his stature in the eyes of the Spanish court at a critical time in the negotiations for the Prince's marriage with the Infanta.[12] The absence of any reference to the Spanish expedition might suggest that it was some time ago. If one chooses to read Hermione's gothic story as an allegory of the ill-fated venture or as a cautionary tale of the disastrous consequences of a British/Protestant–Spanish/Catholic alliance, then this impression of a past event is strengthened. Besides, James's euphoria at the safe return of his heir and favourite seems to have been succeeded by a resentful apprehension of the powerful alliance of the two young men, stronger than ever since their homecoming.[13] Some of the early histories speak of a growing weariness of the favourite in James's last year or so (see note to 115.39–40). The case for 1623, alternatively, is that George Heriot —all but the titular hero of the novel—died on 10 February 1624, and Scott was thoroughly familiar with Heriot's biography. Moreover, in Scott's story the King's worthy jeweller seems robust, the only sign of approaching death being the occasional melancholy reference to the loss of his legitimate children and wife, leaving him with no heir (59.35; 329.23–29). It seems likely, then, that Scott deliberately omitted the date or left it vague so as to enjoy maximum flexibility for narrating the story he wanted to tell. He may also have deliberately prolonged the life of Henry Howard, the Earl of Northampton (1540–1614), by years in order to show that James's appetite for flattery did not diminish with age, for Northampton was, by most accounts, the supreme flatterer of his reign (see note to 135.27–32).[14] As with Heriot's dates, Northampton's were well known to the editor of the *Secret History*.

The events of Volume 1 occupy the space of one April evening and the five days succeeding. Volume 2 continues with days six and seven, followed by a description of Nigel's life 'for several weeks' (153.26), after which Scott resumes a daily account—five days—before bringing the second volume to an end. Volume 3 continues without break, the events between the murder of Trapbois and the death of Dalgarno on Enfield Chace transpiring on six consecutive days. (A slip at 369.13 would make it five days, James's reference to 'the hunting this morning' clashing with Richie's return to Nigel's service on the morning after the hunt at 344.35–37. The third volume in general but the hunting day in particular is, as Wilde's Lady Bracknell might put it, 'crowded with incident'.) For the second time Scott's narrative skips several weeks, the period required for the obligatory courtship of Nigel and Margaret, for James to fabricate a noble pedigree for the bride, and for other interested parties, especially George Heriot, Lady Hermione, and Richie Moniplies, to prepare their substantial contributions to the 'penny-wedding'. Perhaps the end of the story coincides with the end of the month, if that month is June, the traditional month for weddings, for as Sir Mungo is at pains to ascertain, the wedding takes place 'on the thirtieth of the instant month' (401.12–13).

The novel is something of a tale of two cities, or as James Anderson has variously put it (77, 79), *Nigel* is a 'semi-Scotch' or 'semi-English' novel, for Edinburgh shadows London throughout, most especially in Richie Moniplies' vivid, nostalgic memories of that city (e.g. 45.10–21), much as James VI of Scotland shadows James I of England throughout. But Scott's concern to represent the English capital with as much specificity as he does the Scottish one in, say, *Waverley* or *The Heart of Mid-Lothian*, is evident in many ways, among them the request for a copy of James Peller Malcolm's *Londinium Redivivum* from Cadell while composing and expanding the picture of Temple-Bar and the Strand in Chapter 5 (see Essay on the Text, 416). London's component parts— the City, the Court at Whitehall, the Inns of Court, the sanctuary of Alsatia, Greenwich, the Tower of London, St Paul's, the Thames itself —receive Scott's lavish attention. It was not Malcolm's volumes, however, but the contemporary chronicler John Stow's *A Survey of the Cities of London and Westminster* covering the period 1598–1603 and organised by wards and suburbs which was the single most important source of information about Jacobean London for Scott, as the Explanatory Notes testify. It also included abundant information about antiquities, rivers and streams, civic structures, orders and customs of citizens, their work (companies and guilds) and their play (theatre and sports), city government and governance, and institutions such as hospitals and the inns of court. Scott owned the edition of 1720 updated by John Strype. The people that populate London and their activities— merchants and their wares and apprentices; barbers and their multiple services; law-students and their quarters and festivities; proprietors of eating establishments and their menus; watermen and their fees and customers; dramatic poets and the actors who performed their plays in the theatres—are no less richly detailed than the environs they inhabit. Noteworthy, in this regard, is the London under- or night-world—in dramatic terms its 'anti-masque'—that Scott creates at the core of his fiction. Collectively the drama—the old plays—were the greatest single source of this material: Scott had anonymously collected and edited many of them some dozen years before (see Essay on the Text, 408). In effect, Scott's London is a great theatrical spectacle, the plays or masques to which the readers are continuously treated deriving from the dramatic literature of the Elizabethan and Jacobean stage. His detailed familiarity with the London of his own day from personal observation is casually revealed in the reference to Monmouth Street (20.35–38). And it was current: only two or three months before commencing to write *Nigel* he had attended the coronation of King George IV.[15]

General Sources. James Anderson has remarked (80): 'Although it has several historical characters, the plot of *Nigel* contains less historical incident than *Kenilworth*—in fact, it has none at all, so that the dramatists have it all their own way.' There are, of course, other sources, in particular the contemporary memoirs, histories, and tracts that Scott himself edited (see below and Essay on the Text, 407–09). But time and again when annotating these items Scott himself offered the dramatists as evidence or illustration or source. As one would expect, Shakespeare heads the list, and it is an allusion to *Romeo and Juliet* that is among the first really substantial proof-corrections Scott made in the narrative, inserting 'as the Capulets and Montagues are separated upon the stage' (21.30–31). But Shakespeare is simply the most prominent of a large cadre, some of them anonymous.[16] Second only to Shakespeare is Ben Jonson, in part because of his role as poet laureate to the court and chief supplier of the masques that Queen Anne, especially, enjoyed.[17] The extent of Scott's knowledge of the dramatic literature of Elizabethan and Jacobean England can be surmised from a random perusal of the Explanatory Notes to the text and of his revision in 1810 of Robert Dodsley's *Select Collection of Old Plays* as *The Ancient British Drama*. But as these notes also show, Caroline drama was an indispensable source of materials as well. Shadwell's plays in particular were critical to the creation of Alsatia or Whitefriars, but behind Shadwell are the Elizabethans and Jacobeans, and, as Scott indicates in the Magnum Introduction (26.xiv–xv), the comedies of Terence.

To focus narrowly on the dramatic literature is, however, reductive, not to say misleading. For if *Nigel* is Scott's ultimate tribute to the genre that had fascinated him since boyhood when on a visit to Bath he saw his first Shakespeare play,[18] it shares the stage, nevertheless, with lyric and narrative poetry. Again, the Explanatory Notes offer abundant evidence of Scott's phenomenal memory for lines of Chaucer, Spenser, Milton, Dryden, Pope and of the anonymous or attributed ballad poets so dear to his heart. The text itself signals the role of non-dramatic poetry in the period by foregrounding John Taylor, the Water Poet, whose long-term connection with the court and, in particular, with the wedding festivities of the Princess Elizabeth led him to visit her in the Palatinate. The Explatory Notes show the importance of Taylor's writings to Scott's portrait of London and Londoners, of the Thames and its traffic in particular. But, finally, Scott took phrases, lines, stanzas or paraphrases from both ancients and moderns of the English tradition—from both Samuel Butler's sprawling satire *Hudibras* (apparently a favourite) and William Wordsworth's simple lyrical ballad 'The Two Thieves'—and from poets who have largely disappeared from the tradition or failed to make it altogether, their forgotten books still on the shelves of Scott's library at Abbotsford. Again to cite James Anderson (79–80): 'It is almost impossible to exaggerate the depth of Scott's familiarity with' the imaginative literature of the Elizabethan, Restoration, and Augustan periods. With little exaggeration we might say the same of his familiarity with Latin literature, reflected in the Latin speech created for King James. He did request assistance for the Latin in the extended dialogue between James and Nigel (see Essay on the Text, 421), but the incidental Latin speech scattered through the novel is of Scott's devising and it is at least as highly allusive as the English or Scots speech.

If pride of place among Scott's sources belongs to imaginative literature in general and the drama in particular, next to it must be placed the *Secret History* in which two volumes Scott collected contemporaneous or early memoirs and histories by Francis Osborne, Sir Anthony Weldon, William Sanderson,[19] and Sir Edward Peyton. Together these constitute a rich repository of detail on James's appearance, character, manners, habits, behaviour, and actions. They also offer circumstantial accounts of key episodes (e.g. the Gowrie Conspiracy, the Hampton Court Conference, Prince Henry's death, Princess Elizabeth's marriage, the Overbury Affair, the trial of Sir Walter Raleigh, the Lady Lake case, the Spanish expedition of Charles and Buckingham, the several plagues) and of ongoing disputes and discontents (e.g. feuds between the Scots and the English; the selling of honours and the creation of a new one, the baronet; the extravagance of the court; the monarch's homosexuality) that marked his reign. Most pertinent to *Nigel* is the obsessive discourse on James's favourites, the tendency being to chronicle his reign as a succession of favourites culminating in George Villiers, Duke of Buckingham. In short, it would not be excessive exaggeration to claim that little would be lost from *Nigel* (always excepting the speech of the characters) if the four writers were Scott's sole source. And not just for their information, either: these memoirs or histories also comprise a rich storehouse of opinion. In the case of Sanderson and Weldon, for example, the former is expressly written in defence of James's character and conduct against the 'satire' of the latter—or as Scott puts it in a note: Sanderson 'regularly black-balls the few characters which Weldon, contrary to his usual practice, seems disposed to white-wash' (1.332n). As editor, Scott was prompted by the historians' disputes with each other to engage in dispute with them, his notes often challenging an opinion and citing authority for it. Thus, the notes to the *Secret History* require us to supplement the four authors, foundational though they would appear to be, with other sources. Not that all the notes are argumentative. Scott introduced as frontispiece to the first volume an illustration of 'James I. about to take assay of the deer'. In a note to Osborne's anonymous account of James's odd dress he identifies the source as George Turbervile's *The Noble Art of Venerie, or Hunting* (1611), which he had drawn on for *The Bride of Lammermoor* (1819), and offers the copy as 'an excellent commentary on Osborne's text' (1.196n). Nor is this the only supplementary note. But the corrective mode predominates. Scott calls Sanderson's summary of James's character 'charitable' (2.299). His first note to Weldon dismisses two of that author's five propositions enumerated in the Preface as 'false', labels the second 'dubious', and judges the third and fifth as 'partly true, partly exaggerated' (1.311n). So critical is he of Sanderson and Peyton for their careless blunders that he becomes ironical at points (e.g. 2.310n) and exasperated at others (e.g. 2.328n). At times Scott even invites the reader to join in the disputation, e.g. to compare Weldon with Osborne and Sanderson on James's early favourite James Hay, Earl of Carlisle, so as 'to consider where the truth may be' (1.332n).

These supplementary sources cited in the *Secret History* number some twenty-five.[20] But it is Scott's own edited collection known as *Somers' Tracts* (see Essay on the Text, 408–09) that best enabled him to qualify or refute weak points in the historians' arguments. Probably most important to *Nigel* was the anonymous tract entitled *Truth Brought to light and discouered by Time or A Discourse and Historicall Narration of the first XIII yeares of King Iames Reigne* (2.262–408: Scott's editorial title is *Narrative History of King James for the first fourteen years, 1651*). Herein is useful information about the continually feuding Scots and English, the Roaring Boys' anti-social behaviour, the ruin of Old England and its thrifty ways, the role of the Earl of Northampton—that 'fortuning flatter[er]' (2.267)—in the Overbury Affair, the status of Mrs Turner's claim to have invented the yellow starch for stiffening ruffs, and the fashion of wearing black patches, and so on. And Scott's use in a note of Thomas Gray's apostrophe to the 'Towers of Julius' (Tower of London) in connection with Overbury's murder there (2.349n) anticipates his choice of the same lines for the motto to Volume 3, Chapter 3 of *Nigel*, which ends with Nigel's incarceration in the dreaded prison (see 311.30–32). But the *Narrative History*, if the most important tract for *Nigel*, is not the only one to focus on James's character. For the 'obloquy and contempt' he received from English Protestants for refusing to support the Prince Palatine and Princess Elizabeth in their struggle against Spain, together with the reasons for this unpaternal behaviour (the King's pacific habits and his eagerness for the Spanish marriage of Charles), the tract entitled *Tom Tell-Troath: or, a free Discourse touching the Manners of the Time* (1621 or 1622; 2.469–92) is invaluable. Scott's note there on James's fondness for issuing proclamations (2.474n) anticipates this very point in *Nigel* (see 49.2–28). Noteworthy, too, is the series of notes that Scott, drawing upon Sir John Graham Dalyell's *Fragments of Scotish History* (Edinburgh, 1798), Roger Coke's *A Detection of the Court and State of England During the last Four Reigns* (London, 1697), Osborne, and Weldon, wrote in reply to the author's 'bitter allusions to James's private life' (2.487–89).

For all this wealth of material at Scott's disposal, he did not always feel fully informed on subjects upon which his narrative touched and had the grace to say so: 'Our accounts of the private court intrigues of that period, and of the persons to whom they were entrusted, are not full enough to enable us to pronounce upon the various reports which arose out of the circumstances we have detailed' (153.16–19).

Principal Characters. The principal historical character is, of course,

the monarch King James I. His dominant role in the novel is reflected in
his appearance in several sections of the present Note besides this one,
which is properly his. Scott took as the key to James's characterisation
the epithet 'the wisest fool in Christendom', attributed to Sully,[21] the
French diplomat whose memoirs are a rich source of information on the
early years of James's reign. In the novel the oxymoron tops-off a lengthy
catalogue of strengths and weaknesses (66.40–67.24). In this abstract
way Scott sought to achieve the balance lacking in Isaac D'Israeli's study
of the monarch who, had he been stronger, might have brought about
the union of Scotland and England a hundred years earlier than it, in
fact, happened. At the same time Scott prepared the ground for the
comic potential in a study of James's character missing in Abel Moysey's
novel *Forman* (see Essay on the Text, 407). In the text of *Nigel*
(296.4–6) Scott signals that the novel was written, at least in part,
against the grain of D'Israeli's study.[22] Scott actually introduces James
himself through his writings (66.22–28), a haphazard assortment indic-
ative of a learned but disorderly mind. It goes without saying that the
writings are significant for Scott's characterisation.[23] He turns next to
James's eccentric, slovenly dress that expresses the contradiction of his
obsession with hunting, a dangerous sport, and his fear of assassination
(66.29–39). Scott's source here—and, indeed, his principal source for
the portrait—is the *Secret History*. Appearance aside, in the first court
scene James is impressive for his skill in Latin conversation and keen
enthusiasm for learning, if a little immodest about his own erudition
(see note to 110.26 for the source of this scene). But for the most part
the court scenes reveal a weak king, insistent on his power but fearful to
cross the Duke and the Prince: his claim to being 'a free king' answerable only to God is true in theory, not in practice (see Essay on the Text,
457 (note 17)). In effect the monarch is a prisoner in his own palace.
The signal exception is in the scene where Richie overreaches and, for
it, is wrathfully expelled from court. Earlier in the same scene, however,
James is as playful as a child, revelling in the game—a version of hide-
and-seek (see note to 353.15)—of humbling the sober-sided adult
George Heriot. Both Huntinglen and Heriot are critical of James's lack
of backbone. It is his own son and the favourite, however, who judge him
most severely, expressing none of the pity that mingles with Heriot and
Huntinglen's criticism. Spying on Nigel and Margaret in the Tower
brings on James the strictest censure in the story, for in building the
'lugg' that enables him to eavesdrop on the distressed couple he has
arranged to be confined to the same quarters, he forfeits all respect due
a parent or 'gossip' (godfather), let alone a monarch.

The many references to the Gowrie Conspiracy in the text point to
that traumatic episode, together with the prior Ruthven Raid in which
this Scottish family was also complicit, as deeply formative of James's
character and, hence, the character of his reign. The Essay on the Text
explains the connection of this past history with the novel that Scott
ultimately wrote, about a time in James's life far distant from either
event (see 409–10). The Ruthvens, a noble Perthshire family prominent
in the politics of Scotland, were thorns in James's flesh for three

generations. Patrick Ruthven (1520?–66), who succeeded as third Baron Ruthven in 1552, was Protestant privy councillor to Mary Queen of Scots, approved of her marriage to Henry Stuart (1545–67), Lord Darnley, and took part in the murder of her chief adviser David Rizzio in 1566. His second son William (1541?–84), fourth Baron Ruthven, created first Earl of Gowrie in 1581, joined his father in murdering Rizzio, became the custodian of Mary Queen of Scots at Lochleven Castle, and was chief conspirator in the plot to capture the young James VI and keep him prisoner—hence the 'Raid of Ruthven'—in 1582. His sons John (1578?–1600), third Earl of Gowrie, and Alexander (1580?–1600) continued the family tradition of leading the opposition to James. They were killed in the attack on James in their own house in Perth that came to be called the 'Gowrie Conspiracy'. So sensational, if not hysterical, is the account of this event authorised by James, which Scott included entire in *Somers' Tracts* (1.508–32), and so conflicting the reports of witnesses, that its truth was much debated in the immediate aftermath and for some years thereafter. Scott, in commenting on Osborne's dismissal of the conspiracy as a laughable fiction, asserted that 'its reality is now unanimously admitted by historians', and went on to argue that the authorised account is consistent with James's character (Osborne, 1.276–77n).[24]

James's principal courtier, the Earl of Huntinglen, is imaginary. But he is based on John Ramsay, the hero of the Gowrie Conspiracy, who followed James to London where he prospered. It is principally through Huntinglen that Scott brings into the novel the traumatic effect of the Ruthvens on James. For large sections of the manuscript, in fact, Scott refers to the Earl by the name of the Ruthvens' seat near Perth and scene of the attempted assassination, 'Huntingtower' (see Essay on the Text, 409). For rescuing James, Ramsay was amply rewarded by titles and money, becoming one of James's principal favourites, with whose wedding the monarch was every bit as preoccupied as he is with Nigel's.[25] In the novel these tokens of gratitude take the form of the annual boon by which Huntinglen secures the monarch's attention to Nigel's supplication. Lord Dalgarno, the Earl of Huntinglen's only son, is entirely imaginary, Ramsay's marriage being childless. He is no chip off the old block. Rather he is the villain of the story, representing all that is wrong with the new fashion, all that is lost with the passing of his father's generation. Characters such as Dalgarno, according to Scott's Magnum Introduction (26.x–xi), are to be found in the writings of Puritan authors and of the satirists, and 'all the comedies of the age' supply 'the principal character for gaiety and wit'.

Yet the ending of *Nigel* is not dark. James's feckless, if good-natured, character comes across as comic, for this king so exalted by and defensive of his claim to rule Great Britain by divine right (see note to 71.10) is, in truth, an old man fully himself only in a domestic setting with his fellow Scots for company and a dish of cock-a-leekie for dinner. Moreover, his image of peacemaker is seen to be based on an irrational fear of weapons and fighting, rather than on spiritual principle, philosophical conviction, or diplomatic skill. His role as match-maker begs comparison with that of the nefarious Dame Ursula, and thus hints at the touchy subject of his sexuality. Scott chose not to use some of the more explicit signs of his homosexuality available to him in the old histories, but to the extent that he focuses on how Buckingham used his power rather than on how he (and by extension the earlier favourites) acquired it, this omission is not so conspicuous as it might be.[26] Still, Scott exposes James's lack of traditional masculine habits and tastes through his refusal to look at a sword, let alone carry one. More important, he does so by making women the principal movers-and-shakers in this world. Dame Ursula, based on the notorious Mrs Turner, Margaret Ramsay, Lady Hermione, and Martha Trapbois act, albeit furtively or indirectly, to bring about the changes that separate beginning from ending of the story. And, for her part, Margaret Ramsay resorts to cross-dressing to do it.[27] At a time when Britain verges on a consumer economy and jewellers double as bankers,[28] it may be significant that the four women have money at their disposal, whereas James is 'as poor as a rat', to quote Scott in the proofs.[29] Little if any of James's boasted wisdom leading to the grossly flattering analogy with Solomon is evident in the last scene of the novel (see 298.11–12 and 302.30, and notes to 309.16–19 and 368.30–31). Despite the phrase of spoken Latin—ever the sign of the King's learning—the word-play on 'fool' in the final paragraphs reminds us of the epithet to which Scott had keyed his portrait. In a nice touch he has allowed Martha Trapbois, the woman whom James had just insulted, to be the voice of wisdom and wit both, and in his royal response to her speech allowed James a modicum of grace and sense before displaying one last time unkingly behaviour, his glee at the prospect of cock-a-leekie for dinner.

Second only to James, if then, is the historical, albeit idealised, figure George Heriot, who was clearly for the publisher Constable the main character and a great favourite.[30] In the novel Heriot is the antithesis of the monarch he serves, in that his several virtues, including wisdom, are not compromised by vices, his character not complicated by parodoxes. The pair of dinner parties at his home in Lombard Street that bracket the story would suggest that Heriot has substituted the Scots in London for his missing family, of which he, not James, is, for all practical purposes, *pater familias*. His hospitality comprehends all classes of the expatriate Scottish family; his fluid movement between the City and Whitehall—between commerce and court—is assured. In life, however, Heriot was not a man of unblemished character, according to emergent Victorian moral codes. For example, he was not bereft of children altogether, only of legitimate ones, having sired two illegitimate daughters. In light of this information it might appear that Richie's suspicions of Heriot's domestic arrangements (see 90.30–31), informed by 'the wild reports that went abroad' (see 202.17–18), are not altogether wide of the mark. One suspects as well that Scott sanitised his business dealings. At the time of her death Queen Anne owed the jeweller the shocking sum of £63,000, according to the correspondence of the Reverend Thomas Lorkin and Sir Thomas Puckering, Bart, 28 May 1619;[31] Heriot's care in preserving models of the jewels cleared him of complicity in the scandal that ensued when the jewels turned out to be missing (2.167). No doubt the details of Heriot's life and career were common knowledge in the Edinburgh of Scott's time, being imparted in school to every child educated in the city, whether in the Hospital the benefactor endowed or elsewhere.[32]

Heriot's reclusive tenant Lady Hermione, by contrast, is entirely imaginary, as her affinity with Coleridge's allegorical figure might suggest, in name only connected with an actual person (see note 11 below). Douglas Grant thinks that a 'fair Venetian courtesan' mentioned three times in Scott's *Private Letters* (see Essay on the Text, 408) may be the source of Hermione, of her exotic appearance and the curiosity she provokes.[33] Such a woman was at one time the subject of much gossip among the Jacobeans of London.

Unquestionably historical are James's second son Charles and his godson Buckingham—'Babie' and 'Steenie'; both are characterised with a view toward their ultimate fate: death by execution and by assassination.[34] We visualise them as the elegant figures in Van Dyke's paintings (see note to 116.24–26), but neither is presented sympathetically. The death of Prince Henry in 1612 deprived the British people of their hope for a more respectable monarch in the successor to James, a ruler in the tradition of the Tudor Queen Elizabeth and a fully chivalric knight. A persistent contrast of James and Henry, favourable to the latter, in the old histories centres on Henry's disapproval of swearing,[35] and, in general, his keeping an orderly, dignified court, in which the feuds between the Scots and the English were absent and the privileging of favourites lacking. As his biographer Roy Strong has put it, after his untimely death Henry was long regarded as 'an ideal monarch England never had'.[36] Charles succeeded his elder brother as heir to the throne but did not succeed him in the affection of his future subjects. His bond with Buckingham—the bond of a second son, albeit a prince, and the son of a mere knight—may explain his rigidity, pride, and humourless disposition, but it condemns him at the same time. Not until the two, disappointed in the outcome of their Spanish enterprise, denounced James's long-term dream of a royal alliance between England and Spain in a rousing speech to Parliament did the British people warm to the prince.[37] Buckingham in the novel embodies the string of favourites that marked every step of James's career from his teens to his old age. He is, at once, the last and the greatest, having provided titles and wealth for his entire family—Howell (116) called them 'the Tribe of Fortune'—in every sense but bloodline joining James's family which had been gradually reduced by the deaths of five children (four in infancy), the death of Queen Anne, and the removal through marriage of his remaining daughter to the Continent. None of the other favourites had received a duke's patent. Buckingham's unique accomplishment is to 'own' both the monarch and the prince, ensuring that the latest—and, as it turned out—last favourite of the father will become, in time, the first favourite of the son. Scott's Magnum note (26.194–95) suggests that it is Weldon's account of Buckingham that is the key to his portrait and cites in illustration a passage dramatising the Duke's uncompromising ambition. In that the prince and favourite represent the future just over the horizon Charles at least may have been in Scott's mind when, in the Magnum Introduction (26.xi), he wrote that, in contrast to Dalgarno and his kind, 'another and very different sort of men were gradually forming the staid and resolved characters' we associate with the civil wars of the next two reigns.

Sir Mungo Malagrowther of Girnego Castle—the other courtier of note—is largely fictitious. His name is probably derived from *mala-grugrous* or *malagrugorous* ('dismal', 'gloomy').[38] In a Magnum note (26.130) Scott says that Sir Mungo 'borrowed some of his attributes' from an unnamed baronet formerly to be met in Edinburgh, but his portrait of his friend Charles Kirkpatrick Sharpe in his *Journal*[39] rather suggests Sharpe as a 'type of Sir Mungo', while William Gifford, the acerbic editor of the *Quarterly Review*, was proposed by Allan Cunningham.[40] However, Girnego Castle (now ruined) was a real place and in 1597 was the seat of the Earl of Caithness.[41] Through Sir Mungo, Scott is able to introduce the education of James at the hands of his two tutors, George Buchanan and Peter Young. The former supposedly made use of a surrogate whipping boy; the latter applied his lashes directly to the offending pupil. If James in fact had a whipping boy, his name has not survived. But that of Charles's whipping boy William Murray has (see note to 76.13). James Anderson (77) speculates that Malagrowther is a direct transfer from the biography of the son to the father. In following James to England and living on his patronage Sir Mungo stands for the poor Scottish nobleman among the 'beggerly rable' of Scots (Osborne 1.143), inclined to violence, who brought the contempt of the English upon James's court. But his is an extreme case, for even James's Scottish usher James Maxwell is insulting about Malagrowther's shabby attire. Maxwell is a historical character whose insolent behaviour with courtiers, in particular with one Edward Hawly of Gray's Inn, would have ended in a duel had not James intervened to make peace between them (Osborne 1.228–29). Osborne's parenthetical remark that Maxwell was 'more famous for this [the episode] and wealth, than civility or education, not being ever able to read or write' may be the source of Sir Mungo's sneer at the usher's learning (341.28). For his long service Maxwell was decorated with the Garter.

The very first Scot introduced in the novel is the celebrated horologer and watch-maker to the King, David Ramsay (d.1653?). He was equally well-known, if less respected, for his belief in astrology and magic, which for his part in attempting to locate treasure beneath the floor of Westminster Abbey by means of a divining rod brought him ridicule. (In a note to Osborne (1.264–65), Scott gives in full William Lilly the astrologer's account of the story.) This story is not used in *Nigel*, but it is Davy's preoccupation with astrology at inopportune times that marks him as one of the comical Scots and, as such, foil to George Heriot, a better because more attentive father to Margaret Ramsay than her own father.

Richard Moniplies, the second Scot to enter Scott's fiction and the most fully realised, is entirely imaginary. As a 'beggarly' Scot, Richie is representative of the abuse his countrymen, whatever their rank, sustained at the hands of the English jealous of the favouritism James showed them, while at the same time revealing James's motives in urging them, in a series of proclamations, to return home or not to come up to London at all. He is also illustrative of the general point made in Scott's note to Osborne (1.144n) that some Scottish supplicants to James's court used as pretext that the monarch owed them money for services contracted in Scotland. There are several references to his Spanish complexion and gait, which given the widespread and intense hostility to Spain in England at this time were an equally serious liability. He is evidently in the tradition of Cervantes's Sancho Panza. As 'precisian' (161.18), Richie can suggest why James, for all his antipathy to papists, also despised puritans. Economics connect this role with another: through Richie, Scott introduces the history of King James's relationship with his Catholic mother Mary Queen of Scots. Always problematic, it was exacerbated by her intimacy with the 4th Earl of Bothwell, who was one of the conspirators who murdered James's father Darnley. It is also Richie who brings in the 5th Earl of Bothwell (no relation to the 4th Earl) and who reminds us of an incident in which Bothwell, in one of his many attempts to seize the throne from James, sent the hapless king fleeing his own palace with his breeches in his hand (see note to 47.5–8). The puritan criticism of James, his court, and his reign was not limited to the Scots, but it is appropriate to voice it through a Scottish 'precisian', especially one so dogmatic as Richie, for it reminds us of the Reformation/Counter-Reformation in Scotland and, as well perhaps, of John Knox's attacks on Mary Queen of Scots, which the Bothwell affair brought to their harshest pitch—e.g. of the religious divide that separated mother and son, resulting in her execution and his ascent to the throne of England.[42] Richie's fellow Scot, the genial and accommodating Laurie Linklater, is also entirely imaginary. Together the heir to Castle Collop and the learned cook whose signature dish is cock-a-leekie establish a culinary contrast between Scots and English, initiated in the story by the Scots' distaste for pork (see note to 30.23–24). That other young Scot on the make, the scrivener patronised by Heriot, Andrew Skurliewhitter, is like Richie and Laurie in being imaginary, if in nothing else. Richie's nemesis, Dalgarno's page Lutin, is also fictitious.

Nigel Oliphant is entirely imaginary, though bearing the surname of an old Scottish family. Joseph Anderson's edition of papers tracing the history of this family records no member bearing the name of Nigel nor that of his father, variously given as Randal or Ochtred.[43] But Scott may have drawn on actual Oliphants for the sketchy political background that emerges here and there in the text.[44] Laurence, Master of Oliphant (d. 1585?), son of the fourth Baron Oliphant (who was another Laurence: c. 1527–93), was involved in an attack on Lord Ruthven in 1580 and participated in the Raid of Ruthven in 1582 (see above); his son, yet another Laurence (1583–1630?), the fifth Baron, is said to have been one of James's retinue when he travelled to London in 1603.[45] Like other imaginary characters, Nigel enables Scott to make

important points about the character of King James, who in the relationship with Nigel is revealed himself to be the most 'beggarly' Scot of
all. But through Nigel, himself 'a beggarly Scot' (195.22), Scott is also
able to show James's positive traits—i.e. his love of learning and his
genuine skill with Latin, his knowledge of right conduct in a monarch
despite his own lack of will to act on it at times, and his sincerity in
wanting to be a peacemaker instead of a war-monger. If the penalty of
losing one's hand for violating the injunction against fighting within
the precincts of the court, as precedent for which Scott invokes the
famous case of Stubbs and Page who suffered this fate for offending
Elizabeth I (see note to 181.16–17),[46] seems cruel, such punishment
only indicates just how difficult an ideal James embraced and how long-
persevering he was in sticking to it. The romantic heroine who becomes Nigel's wife, Margaret Ramsay, is equally imaginary, no mention of a female offspring of the clockmaker Davy Ramsay occurring in
accounts of the father. Given her cross-dressing, one might question
James's attraction to her, but his sympathy for her plight points to a
capacity for kindness not found in the old satires, except perhaps in
Sanderson's rebuttal of Weldon. On the other hand, his detection of
her disguise enables Scott to demonstrate, in fictional form, James's
reiterative boasting of his acuity in exposing conspiracies and frauds,
most memorably in the Gunpowder Conspiracy, the Lady Lake case to
which he refers late in the novel (368.29–31), and the claim of a Richard Haddock of New College, Oxford, to preach in his sleep.[47] The
Lieutenant of the Tower, Sir Edward Mansel and his wife, though
imaginary, bear the surname of one of James's most trusted officials,
Sir Robert Mansel, 'the only valiant man [it was said] he ever loved'
(Weldon, 2.6).
    One off-stage Scot, Dr John Irving, the Edinburgh-trained alterna-
tive to the sham doctor Raredrench (31.41–32.5), appears to be
imaginary, though he bears the name of several distinguished Scottish
physicians.[48] Another mostly off-stage Scot, James and Charles's
celebrated court fool, Archie Armstrong (d. 1672), makes only cameo
appearances (77.24–29, 336.40–337.1, 399.1–3). In a lengthy note
to Weldon's reference to Armstrong (1.400–02n) Scott cites
Osborne, Howell, and John Rushworth's *Historical Collections* as
his sources.[49]
    Priority of characterisation belongs, however, to the English, namely,
the two London apprentices, who with their flat caps and ready bats
precipitate the action of Scott's story. They are both imaginary characters, as the signature cry by which they are introduced—'What d'ye
lack?', found everywhere in the old drama—attests. Those other
decent citizens of London, the Scottish James Christie and his English
wife Nelly, are no less imaginary. But the naïve Dame Nelly's seduction
by a callous courtier voices a widespread complaint of the period
against James's court and the Inns of Court both.[50]
    Dame Ursula Suddlechop is also an imaginary Londoner, but mod-
elled upon Mrs Anne Turner, a major player in the Thomas Overbury
Affair, the pre-eminent court scandal of James's reign. Serial in devel-

opment, sensational in character and plot, it has good claim to be the precedent for the present-day soap-opera.[51] Scott drew heavily on the *Narrative History* for the details of his portrait, supplementing it with particulars from Howell (see note to 102.14–19). Abel Moisey's recent novel *Forman*, dedicated to Scott (see Essay on the Text, 407), wherein the historical woman takes centre stage, gave him the chance to see how one of his own contemporaries viewed Turner. By making Dame Ursley—Scott varies the name from time to time—the pupil and confidante of Mrs Turner, whose daylight reputation was based on the secret for inventing the yellow starch for stiffening ruffs, Scott shows his hand. The demi-world of Dame Ursula's nocturnal, secretive operations is directly indicated by the back-door entrance to her private quarters but indirectly suggested by her given name Ursula, a name synonymous with prostitute at this time, for example in Ben Jonson's *Bartholomew Fair*.[52] That she finished her days in Amsterdam's equivalent to London's Bridewell—a proof-addition prompted by a query from James Ballantyne about her fate[53]—resolves any ambiguity about her character, but saves her from Mrs Turner's end on the scaffold. Ursula's canny mulatto servant Wiba is imaginary.

Reginald Lowestoffe, one of 'these wild youngsters of the Temple' (63.31–32), is an affectionate, if imaginary, portrait of the law student in this period and thus, presumably, a figure of professional interest to Scott. From the country, he is perhaps named after the coastal village Lowestoft south of Yarmouth. His near neighbours the denizens of Alsatia are also imaginary, their counterparts everywhere in the plays. The 'noted usurer . . . Golden Trapbois' (200.24–25), like his daughter Martha, is no exception, but in his case Scott may have been influenced by Isaac D'Israeli's note on usury wherein is mentioned 'a famous usurer of that day [Hugh Audley], who died worth £400,000, an amazing sum at that period'.[54] To introduce into *Nigel* the underbelly of James's kingdom is not gratuitous, however, for one of James's early acts was to renew the privileges of this medieval sanctuary in perpetuity (see note to 181.35).

In the Magnum Introduction, with its near-exclusive focus on the characters and dismissive reference to the 'simple plot' by which they are brought together in a fiction, *The Fortunes of Nigel*, Scott suggested, 'may be perhaps one of those [novels] that are more amusing on a second perusal, than when read a first time for the sake of the story, the incidents of which are few and meagre' (26.vi, xvi). Perhaps he was rationalising in response to disappointing sales for a work of which he, his partners, and some critics thought highly and had high hopes (see Essay on the Text, 413–14). But the motto Scott chose for the original title page had made much the same point. For to an unusual degree in the Waverley series, the historical characters in *Nigel* are major players, their characters (and not the historical events that reveal them) front and centre in this novel.[55]

NOTES

All manuscripts referred to are in the National Library of Scotland. For standard abbreviations see 540–41.

1   Maximilien de Bethune, Duke of Sully, wrote in his *Mémoires* (1638), for
     the year 1603, that James 'had lately given the name of Great Britain to his
     united kingdoms' (trans. Charlotte Lennox as *The Memoirs of the Duke of
     Sully*, 5 vols (London, 1810), 3.324). After his maiden speech to Parliament
     in 1603 he was 'Proclaim'd King of *Great Britain: England* must be no more
     a Name . . .' (Wilson, 2.673). (The term had in fact been in existence since
     the 1540s when Henry VIII and Edward VI wished to unite England and
     Scotland: Adam Nicolson, *Power and Glory: Jacobean England and the
     Making of the King James Bible* (London, 2003), 13.) Four years on James
     still pursued the substance of the phrase in 'His Majesties Speech to both
     the Houses of Parliament' (*Somers' Tracts*, 2.117–32) on the last day of
     March 1607: 'I desire a perfect union of lawes and persons, and such a
     naturalizing as may make one body of both kingdomes under mee your king'
     (2.120). But the realisation of this desire proved elusive. Parliament again
     denied him the union, so that 1607 is usually seen as 'the death knell to
     James's hopes for a united Great Britain' (Andrew D. Nicholls, *The
     Jacobean Union: A Reconsideration of British Civil Policies Under the Early
     Stuarts* (Westport, Connecticut, 1999), 24). By 1619 the Venetian
     ambassador would dismiss James's self-representation as 'the chief of a great
     union in Europe' as a pose (quoted by Roger Lockyer, *James VI and I*
     (London, 1998), 149). And in 1621 or 1622 the author of the tract *Tom Tell-
     Troath* would initiate his specific attack on James for his failure to support
     the Protestant cause in general and the Princess Elizabeth and Prince
     Frederick in particular by generalising the British people's disaffection for
     their sovereign, with the words: 'They make a mock of your word, Great
     Brittaine, and offer to prove, that it is a great deal lesse, then Little England
     was wont to be' (*Somers' Tracts*, 2.471). Maurice Lee, Jr, *Government by Pen:
     Scotland under James VI and I* (Urbana, Illinois, 1980), 27–60, provides an
     excellent account of this 'abortive union'.

2   Not all contemporaneous memorialists or historians devalued James's claim
     to be a peacemaker: even the satirical Anthony Weldon allowed some truth
     to the claim (Weldon, 2.11–12). In Scott's time Isaac D'Israeli made the
     question of why peaceful kings are judged to be weak monarchs the rationale
     for his *An Inquiry into the Literary and Political Character of James the First*
     (London, 1816), using James's motto *Beati Pacifici* on the title page (*CLA*,
     9). And the recent biographer Roger Lockyer, in *James VI and I* (London,
     1998), specifically in the chapter entitled 'Blessed are the Peacemakers',
     justifies peacemaking as the cornerstone of James's domestic and foreign
     policy.

3   For James as father of his country see note to 70.41. For his pleasure in
     his favourites' weddings see Lee, 248. He and the Queen were the hosts
     for John Ramsay's wedding in 1608; in 1613 he had, besides the pleasure
     of planning his daughter the Princess Elizabeth's wedding, that of
     sponsoring the wedding of the reigning favourite Robert Carr, Earl of
     Somerset; and in 1614, of sponsoring the wedding of Lord Roxburghe

(Chamberlain, 1.487; David M. Bergeron, *Royal Family, Royal Lovers: King James of England and Scotland* (Columbia, Missouri, and London 1991), 127–28). After the wedding of Sir Philip Herbert and Lady Susan Vere in December 1604, James visited the couple's bedchamber where 'the king, in his shirt and night-gown, gave them a *reveillée matin* before they were up, and spent a good time in or upon the bed, chuse which you will believe' (Peyton, 2.349n).

4   Annotating Sir Robert Naunton's *Fragmenta Regalia* for *Somers' Tracts* (1.251–83), Scott used the adjective 'childish' for James's manner with Robert Cecil: 'King James, in his childish jargon, used to call him his little beagle, from the acuteness with which he could run the scent of policy' (1.280n).

5   Sully reported that James 'was indolent in his actions, except in hunting' (*Memoirs of the Duke of Sully*, trans. Charlotte Lennox, 5 vols (London, 1810), 3.57). This is the point as well of the story about the King's missing dog Jowler returning home in 1604 with a note attached to his neck, complaining that the King hears Jowler every day but not his people (Lodge, 3.245). In the same year the Earl of Worcester complained that hunting came first in the day, all work put off until later when people were weary (Lodge, 3.247), and on 26 January 1605 Chamberlain (1.201) wrote to Winwood that, because hunting was 'the only meanes to maintain his health', James had ordered the Privy Council 'to undertake the charge and burden of affaires, and foresee that he be not interrupted nor troubled with too much busines' (this letter is included in *Memorials of Affairs of State in the Reigns of Q. Elizabeth and K. James I. Collected (chiefly) from the Original Papers Of ... Sir Ralph Winwood*, ed. Edmund Sawyer, 3 vols (London, 1725), 2.46: *CLA*, 233).

6   Representative is the modern historian Lawrence Stone, *The Crisis of the Aristocracy, 1558–1641* (Oxford, 1965): see especially 74–128 for both the numbers of honours conferred and the (fluctuating) prices paid for them.

7   Note to the tract *Four Patents Concerning the Honourable degree and dignitie of Baronets*: *Somers' Tracts*, 2.252.

8   In the final analysis the best reason for Scott's decision to date the novel late in James's career and close to Heriot's death is his concern for the same gap in his own time, in his own life, when preoccupied with the future of his sons, merging the old/new with the then/now binary. Anxious for the welfare of Walter and Charles in the post-Waterloo world where, he feared, self-gratification was the ruling passion, Scott wrote on 27 March 1822 to Lord Montagu whose young kinsman Walter had succeeded to the Dukedom of Buccleuch: 'Selfish feelings are so much the fashion among fashionable men—it is counted so completely absurd to do any thing which is not to contribute more or less directly to the immediate personal eclat or personal enjoyment of the party that young men lose sight of real power and real importance ...' (*Letters*, 7.110). It is no accident that in the Introductory Epistle, seemingly so important to Scott, to judge from the revisions (see Essay on the Text, 411), the Eidolon of the Author of Waverley identifies himself, mimicking King James, as *pater familias* to Captain Clutterbuck, one of his by-now numerous progeny,

though here it is the son who stands for the old ways and values and the father who champions the new, establishing an ironic relationship between preface and novel.

9   For a concise analysis of this expedition and its consequences see Roger Lockyer, *James VI and I* (London, 1998), 149–57.

10   For the Babington Plot see note to 237.14; for such plots against Elizabeth in general, see Robert James Stove, *The Unsleeping Eye: Secret Police and Their Victims* (San Francisco, 2003). For similar plots against James I in England (the Main Plot, the Bye Plot, the Gunpowder Plot, etc.) see note to 155.40–41.

11   See Roger Lockyer, *James VI and I* (London, 1998), 146–49. Scott's headnote to the tract *Tom Tell-Troath* (*Somers' Tracts*, 2.469–70) makes precisely this point. The gothic conventions marking the genre of Hermione's romance may entertain, but the theme is one of unrelenting death —her father, her mother, her baby, her husband. She herself is a spectral figure that Scott's original readers may have associated with Coleridge's allegorical 'Nightmare Life-in-Death' from 'The Ancient Mariner' (see lines 190–94). Hermione, as it happens, was the name of the recently deceased John Ballantyne's wife. She appreciated the compliments to her husband in the Introductory Epistle and chided Constable for not telling her about them, but if Scott borrowed her name for his gothic lady, it did not endear the novel to her, for she told Constable that she liked the novel itself 'less than any of them!' (MS 23230, f. 216r: Hermione Ballantyne to Archibald Constable, 20 June [1822]).

12   Akrigg (351) suggests that Buckingham was elevated to Duke while in Spain in order to strengthen his position to negotiate the marriage contract of Charles and the Infanta. Roger Lockyer, *Buckingham: The Life and Political Career of George Villiers, First Duke of Buckingham 1592–1628* (London, 1981), 154–56, agrees with Akrigg but adds that the patent would quell the opposition to Buckingham at home: he could not be raised higher and the only other non-royal duke of the realm was the Scottish Duke of Lennox, who was simultaneously created Duke of Richmond and given precedence over Villiers. Buckingham was the first English commoner to be made a duke since Sir John Dudley in 1551 and the first new English duke created since the Duke of Norfolk, Thomas Howard, was executed in 1572.

13   Akrigg says that, after their appearance before Parliament upon their return from Spain, where in bellicose terms they denounced Spain and renounced the stalled marriage treaty, the Prince and the Duke were the 'idols of Parliament' (381) and, with the rumours of James's abdication (385), were his happily anticipated successors. See also Willson (441–44) for James's isolation from his people and his government by the son and the favourite.

14   For a modern assessment of James's court and of Northampton's dual role of courtier and councillor see Linda Levy Peck, *Northampton: Patronage and Policy at the Court of James I* (London, 1982).

15   For Scott's journey to London of 16–26 July 1821 see Edgar Johnson, *Sir Walter Scott: The Great Unknown*, 2 vols (London, 1970), 2.767–69.

16   *CLA* shows that Press V in the Principal Library contains 10 shelves of

plays. Listing them takes up sixteen pages (207–23) of the catalogue.

17 See Lee, 150, for Queen Anne's enthusiasm for masques. See also Leeds
Barroll, *Anna of Denmark, Queen of England* (Philadelphia, 2001),
74–116, and Clare McManus, *Women on the Renaissance Stage: Anna of
Denmark and Female Masquing in the Stuart Court (1590–1619)* (Manchester, 2002), *passim*.

18 See Scott's 'Memoirs': *Scott on Himself*, ed. David Hewitt (Edinburgh,
1981), 16. The play was *As You Like It*.

19 Scott attributes *Aulicus Coquinariae* to William Sanderson, who used
materials compiled by Bishop Godfrey Goodman (2.91–92). But elsewhere he credits Peter Heylin with the authorship, e.g. in a note to the
Narrative History (*Somers' Tracts*, 2.298–99n). The British Library
Catalogue lists it under both names with a question mark for each.

20 Those that recur three times or more in Scott's critique of the four historians are: *Biographia Britannica*, 6 vols (London, 1747–66); Howell; William Lilly, *Mr. W. Lilly's History of His Life and Times* (London, 1715);
David Lloyd, *The Statesmen and Favourites of England, since the Reformation*
(London, 1665); Wilson; and *Memorials of Affairs of State in the Reigns
of Q. Elizabeth and K. James I. Collected (chiefly) from the Original Papers
Of . . . Sir Ralph Winwood*, ed. Edmund Sawyer, 3 vols (London, 1725).

21 See note to 67.23–24 for the problem of this attribution.

22 In a letter to Scott dated 27 February 1821 (MS 3892, ff. 59r–60v)
D'Israeli had noted aspects of James's character insufficiently treated in
his own study, as if to encourage him to take up the subject. Douglas
Grant, in his edition of *Private Letters of the Seventeenth Century* (Oxford,
1947), cites parts of D'Israeli's letter and suggests the points that Scott
adopted or rejected for the portrait of James in *Nigel* (34–36). The former include the monarch's 'bon-hommie', his hunting alone in the forests, and his son's friendship with Buckingham as telling against the
rumours of a homosexual relationship between James and his favourite;
the latter, the monarch's wit and courage, for which even Grant says
D'Israeli makes extravagant claims.

23 For James's writings as means of articulating power see Jonathan Gold-
berg, *James I and the Politics of Literature* (Baltimore and London,
1983).

24 In his correspondence Scott gives much the same reason for thinking
James the victim and the Ruthvens the conspirators in this murky affair
that he gave in the note to Osborne (*Letters*, 8.457 and 11.52–54). But he
makes reference to his contemporaries James Scott and James Cant who
take the opposite view (see 8.457n). At the beginning of the twentieth
century Andrew Lang, in *James VI and the Gowrie Mystery* (London,
1902), was sceptical of the authorised account. Twentieth-century biographers have been cautious: e.g. Willson's 'Whatever the truth may be'
(129); Akrigg's 'some shadow of doubt . . . However, the official account
is probably true in the main' (10); Lee's 'Whatever the truth of' (76);
David Mathew's 'It seems very likely that we shall never know what happened in the turret room in Gowrie House'—this, after undertaking a
lengthy analysis of several theories and offering a theory of his own (*James
I* (London, 1967), 94); and Roger Lockyer's 'This extraordinary episode

is so clouded with obscurity that it still defies explanation' (*James VI and I* (London, 1998), 24).

25 To mention only the main honours and gifts: in 1603 Ramsay (1580?–1626) was granted a pension of £200 for life; in 1605 he was given lands worth £1000 a year, and the following year he was created Viscount Haddington (Scottish nobility); in 1609 he was granted the lands and baronies once the property of the dissolved Melrose Abbey and the accompanying title Lord of Melrose; in 1615 he was created Lord Ramsay of Melrose; his English peerage came in 1621, when after being lured back to England from France by a gift of £7000, he was created Baron of Kingston-upon-Thames and Earl of Holderness (*Dictionary of National Biography*, 16.700–01). His wedding in 1608, for which Ben Jonson wrote a masque that made reference to the Gowrie Conspiracy, was celebrated at court (Lodge, 3.331; Ben Jonson, *The Haddington Masque* (1608), line 226 and note). The royal gifts were lavish and in-cluded a pension of £600 a year; with the gifts came a message from the King wishing 'them as much comfort all theyre life, as he receved that day he delivered him from the daunger of Gowry' (Chamberlain, 1.255–56).

26 Anderson (90–91) has written that Scott was not deceived by James's sexual deviance but that, in not representing James's fondling and kissing of Buckingham in the text, he respected the taste of his age. Osborne's graphic evidence of James's dubious masculinity is typical of what Scott chose not to make use of (1.274–76); Peyton says that James 'would tumble and kiss [Buckingham] as a mistress' (2.348). Late twentieth-century biographers, especially David M. Bergeron, have not shied away from the subject. In *Royal Family, Royal Lovers: King James of England and Scotland* (Columbia, Missouri, and London, 1991) Bergeron reviews the question of a homosexual angle to the Gowrie Conspiracy (31). More re-cently he has devoted a book to *King James and Letters of Homoerotic Desire* (Iowa City, 1999) in which he examines the epistolary exchange between James and three of his favourites—Esmé Stuart, Duke of Lennox; Robert Carr, Earl of Somerset; and George Villiers, Duke of Buckingham. The latest and most thorough study of the subject is Michael B. Young's *James VI and I and the History of Homosexuality* (Basingstoke and London, 2000).

27 Lee, 152, notes both the fad of female transvestism in the London of James's day and the monarch's fondness for pretty young men. Margaret's situation may owe something to Allan Cunningham's *Sir Marmaduke Maxwell, A Dramatic Poem* (London, 1822), which Scott had recently read and critiqued in manuscript (see *Letters*, 6.318–19). His heroine Mary Douglas, who disguises herself as a page, shakes and sobs when interrog-ated by Sir John Gourlay, causing the knight to suspect the page's sex: 'My pretty one, you are not what you seem' (4.4.22).

28 Scott's sources led him to equate goldsmith and banker: '*but of late years the title of Goldsmith has been generally taken to signify one who banks or re-ceives, and pays running cash for others*, as well as deals in plate' (Malcolm, quoting a 1747 statement). A seventeenth-century pamphlet bears the title *The mystery of the new fashioned goldsmiths or bankers . . .* (London, 1676). But Bruce P. Lenman has recently argued that Heriot and other goldsmiths were money-lenders or 'credit-creators' rather than bankers

because people did not deposit money with them: 'Jacobean Goldsmith-Jewellers as Credit-Creators: The Cases of James Mossman, James Cockie, and George Heriot', *Scottish Historical Review*, 74 (1995), 159–77.

29 See Essay on the Text, 422 for the exchange between Scott and James Ballantyne on James's poverty.

30 Francis Espinasse thinks Scott's portrait 'idealised, it might be called ... imaginary': *Dictionary of National Biography*, 9.696. Writing to Cadell on 25 April 1822, Constable notes that *Nigel* 'will excite much new Interest about George Heriot, about whom I have planned and mean to execute a small publication to be entitled "Memorials of George Heriot Jeweller to King James ⟨and foun⟩ with an historical account of the Hospital founded by him at Edinburgh"' (MS 319, f. 315r). He continues to refer to this project in subsequent correspondence, e.g. on 8 May 1822: 'I trust you [Cadell] are inserting the Title of the Volume of Poetry from the Novels and also George Heriot in all our adverts, I shall make I think an Interesting enough little volume of Heriot' (MS 319, f. 334r).

31 *The Court and Times of James the First*, 2 vols (London, 1848), 2.167.

32 When Heriot's estate was settled, the legacy for the hospital came to £23,625. The ground for the hospital was purchased and the building begun in 1628, and the first students matriculated in 1659: Walter Scott, *Provincial Antiquities and Picturesque Scenery of Scotland*, 2 vols (London, 1826), 2.97–100.

33 *Private Letters of the Seventeenth Century by Sir Walter Scott, Bart.*, ed. Douglas Grant (Oxford, 1947), 52.

34 For the allusion to Charles's execution at Whitehall in 1649, see 65.25–26; for that to Buckingham's assassination by Felton in 1628, see 116.24.

35 Roger Coke, in *A Detection of the Court and State of England During the last Four Reigns* (London, 1697), wrote that Prince Henry, when told that his father, in a trying situation, '*would have sworn so as no Man could have endured it*', replied: '*Away ... all the Pleasure in the World is not worth an Oath*' (66). E. S. Turner, *The Court of St. James's* (London, 1959), says that the court of Prince Henry 'was sober and well-behaved, and had swear-boxes the proceeds of which were given to the poor' (134).

36 *Henry, Prince of Wales and England's Lost Renaissance* (London, 1986), 7.

37 See note 13 above.

38 *Letters*, 5.392n. (Corson notes)

39 *The Journal of Sir Walter Scott*, ed. W. E. K. Anderson (Oxford, 1972), 2–3.

40 Allan Cunningham, 'Some Account of the Life and Works of Sir Walter Scott, Bart.', *Athenaeum*, 6 October 1832, 642.

41 *Certain Matters concerning the Realme of Scotland composed together*, known from its author's name as *Monipenny's Chronicle* (London, 1603; collected in *Somers' Tracts*, 3.344–403 (356)).

42 James was *in utero* when in 1566 Scottish nobles invaded his mother Mary Queen of Scots's dining chamber and stabbed to death her secretary and confidant David Rizzio in her presence (see note to 307.4–6). At thirteen months of age he succeeded to the throne of Scotland, when in

1567 his mother abdicated and fled to England, where she was imprisoned by Queen Elizabeth for the rest of her life. James never saw her again, the relationship of mother and son depending on letters and intermediaries. Her proposal in 1581 and for several years thereafter to share the throne of Scotland with James—known by the term 'Association'—gave James pause, especially when he realised that she would be the senior monarch in such a double reign. When James allowed the proposal to languish, she intimated to England's enemies, the Catholic monarchs of Europe, that she intended to disinherit him. Her reckless involvement in Catholic plots and conspiracies to secure the throne of England for herself—e.g., the Ridolfi plot of 1570–71; the Throckmorton plot of 1582; the Babington plot of 1586—jeopardised James's own claim to the English throne, so that when an exasperated Elizabeth deliberated whether to execute Mary, James argued against it only on the political basis of setting a bad precedent and on the philosophical ground of usurping the authority of the deity. As a result he was judged acquiescent in her death and accused of sacrificing his mother's life in order to receive Elizabeth's recognition of his right to succeed her. David Bergeron's analysis of the relationship in *Royal Family, Royal Lovers: King James of England and Scotland* (Columbia, Missouri, and London, 1991), and especially of its psychological effects for the son, is acute (35–47, 73–74).

43 *The Oliphants in Scotland* (Edinburgh, 1879). For the variant names in the text see 72.34–37, 108.34, and 109.39.

44 See 47.8–10, 50.29–31, 52.13–15, 72.31–40, 108.32–109.10, 109.32–110.18, 113.33–36, and 120.23–27.

45 G. E. C[okayne], *The Complete Peerage*, 12 vols (London, 1910–59), 10.55. For a list of some of the Scots nobles who accompanied James south, see G. B. Harrison, *A Jacobean Journal* (London, 1941), 11.

46 The story of Stubbs's punishment was available to Scott in Howell, 463.

47 For the story of how James exposed Haddock's preaching in his sleep as a counterfeit see Lodge, 3.283–88, and Wilson, 2.711. The documents pertaining to this episode are conveniently collected by G. B. Harrison in *A Jacobean Journal* (London, 1941), 195–96 and 198–200.

48 If imaginary, Scott may have chosen the name for the association with Dr Christopher Irvine (*c.* 1638–85) who practised medicine in both Edinburgh and London. In the next century two eminent Scottish physicians had this name, William Irvine (1743–87) and his son William (1776–1811), the one based in Glasgow, the other in Edinburgh.

49 Rushworth's work appeared in 8 vols at London in 1659–1701. Enid Welsford, *The Fool: His Social and Literary History* (London, 1935), 171–81, provides a thorough account of Armstrong.

50 The abuse of city wives by courtiers and templars was nothing new to judge from Shakespeare's version of the Jane Shore story in *Richard III*, 3.7.7–8. Weldon comments on the subject at 2.369, to which Scott adds a note of confirmation, citing Ben Jonson.

51 Lee uses the term 'soap opera' (153).

52 For Ursula as prostitute see *London in the Age of Shakespeare: An Anthology*, ed. Lawrence Manley (London and Sydney, 1986), 274.

53 See Essay on the Text, 424.

54 *An Inquiry into the Literary and Political Character of James the First. By the author of Curiosities of Literature* (London, 1816), 177–78. In the earlier work to which the title refers, first published in 1791, D'Israeli devoted an entire essay 'Usurers of the Seventeenth Century' to the topic for which Audley was central (6th edn, 3 vols (London, 1817), 70–92): *CLA*, 201.

55 As such, the novel may remind us of the preoccupation with character in seventeenth-century Britain, beginning in James's reign and marked by the books of 'characters' or character-types produced by Joseph Hall, Thomas Overbury, John Earle, among others. According to Benjamin Boyce, *The Theophrastan Character in England to 1642* (Cambridge, Massachusetts, 1947), vii, the literary form known as the Character 'had its full growth' between 1592–1642. He notes that Joseph Hall's *Characters of Vertues and Vices* appeared in 1608 (122); Sir Thomas Overbury attached 22 characters to the poem *A Wife* in 1614 (136); and John Earle's 54 characters appeared in *Micro-cosmographie* in 1628 (235–37).

EXPLANATORY NOTES

In these notes a comprehensive attempt is made to identify Scott's sources, and all quotations, references, historical events, and historical personages, to explain proverbs, and to translate difficult or obscure language. (Phrases are explained in the notes while single words are normally treated in the glossary.) The notes are brief; they offer information rather than critical comment or exposition. When a quotation has not been recognised this is stated: any new information from readers will be welcomed. References are to standard editions, or to the editions Scott himself used. Books in the Abbotsford Library are identified by reference to the appropriate page of the *Catalogue of the Library at Abbotsford*. When quotations reproduce their sources accurately, the reference is given without comment. Verbal differences in the source are indicated by a prefatory 'see', while a general rather than a verbal indebtedness is indicated by 'compare'. Biblical references are to the Authorised Version, unless otherwise stated. Plays by Shakespeare are cited without authorial ascription, and references are to *William Shakespeare: The Complete Works*, edited by Peter Alexander (London and Glasgow, 1951, frequently reprinted).

The following publications are distinguished by abbreviations, or are given without the names of their authors, in the notes and essays:

ABD The Ancient British Drama, [ed. Robert Dodsley, rev. Walter Scott,] 3 vols (London, 1810): *CLA*, 43.

Akrigg   G. P. V. Akrigg, *Jacobean Pageant, or The Court of King James I* (London, 1962).

Anderson   James Anderson, *Sir Walter Scott and History* (Edinburgh, 1981).

Boswell   *Boswell's Life of Johnson*, ed. George Birkbeck Hill, rev. L. F. Powell, 6 vols (Oxford, 1934–50).

Chamberlain   *The Letters of John Chamberlain*, ed. Norman Egbert McClure, 2 vols (Philadelphia, 1939).

CLA   [J. G. Cochrane], *Catalogue of the Library at Abbotsford* (Edinburgh, 1838).

Corson   James C. Corson, *Notes and Index to Sir Herbert Grierson's Edition of the Letters of Sir Walter Scott* (Oxford, 1979).

Craigie   *Minor Prose Works of King James VI and I*, ed. James Craigie (Edinburgh, 1982).

Derham   W[illiam] D[erham], *The Artificial Clock-Maker, A Treatise of Watch, and Clock-work* (London, 1696).

The Faerie Queene   Edmund Spenser, *The Faerie Queene* (written 1579–96), ed. J. C. Smith, 2 vols (Oxford, 1909): *CLA* has various editions.

Friedman   *Collected Works of Oliver Goldsmith*, ed. Arthur Friedman, 5 vols (Oxford, 1966).

Howell   James Howell, *Epistolæ Ho-Elianæ: Familiar Letters*, 9th edn (London, 1726: originally published 1645): *CLA*, 181.

Hudibras   Samuel Butler, *Hudibras* (originally published 1663–78), ed. John Wilders (Oxford, 1967): compare *CLA*, 42, 182, 242.

Kelly   James Kelly, *A Compleat Collection of Scotish Proverbs Explained and made Intelligible to the English Reader* (London, 1721): *CLA*, 169.

Lee   Maurice Lee, Jr, *Great Britain's Solomon: James VI and I in His Three Kingdoms* (Urbana, Illinois, and Chicago, 1990).

Letters   *The Letters of Sir Walter Scott*, ed. H. J. C. Grierson and others, 12 vols (London, 1932–37).

Lockhart   J. G. Lockhart, *Memoirs of the Life of Sir Walter Scott, Bart.*, 7 vols (Edinburgh, 1837–38).

Lodge   Edmund Lodge, *Illustrations of British History, Biography, and Manners*, 3 vols (London, 1791): *CLA*, 240.

Malcolm   James Peller Malcolm, *Londinium Redivivum, or, an Ancient History and Modern Description of London*, 4 vols (London, 1802–07).

ODEP   *The Oxford Dictionary of English Proverbs*, 3rd edn, rev. F. P. Wilson (Oxford, 1970).

OED   *The Oxford English Dictionary*, 2nd edn, ed. J. A. Simpson and E. S. C. Weiner, 20 vols (Oxford, 1989).

Osborne   Francis Osborne, *Historical Memoirs on the Reigns of Elizabeth and King James* in *Secret History*, 1.i–297.

Peyton   Sir Edward Peyton, *The Divine Catastrophe . . . of the House of Stuart* in *Secret History*, 2.301–466.

Prose Works   *The Prose Works of Sir Walter Scott, Bart.*, 28 vols (Edinburgh, 1834–36).

Ray   J[ohn] Ray, *A Compleat Collection of English Proverbs*, 3rd edn (London, 1737): *CLA*, 169.

Secret History   [Walter Scott, ed.], *Secret History of the Court of James the First*, 2 vols (Edinburgh, 1811).

Somers' Tracts   *A Collection of Scarce and Valuable Tracts . . .*, 2nd edn, ed. Walter Scott, 13 vols (London, 1809–15).

Stow   John Stow, *A Survey of the Cities of London and Westminster*, rev. John Strype and others, 6 books (London, 1720): *CLA*, 248.

Strutt   Joseph Strutt, *Sports and Pastimes of the People of England* (London, 1801): *CLA*, 154.

Taylor   *All the Workes of Iohn Taylor the Water-Poet* (London, 1630): *CLA*, 208.

Tilley   Maurice Palmer Tilley, *A Dictionary of the Proverbs in England in the Sixteenth and Seventeenth Centuries* (Ann Arbor, Michigan, 1950).

Weldon   Anthony Weldon, *The Court and Character of King James* in *Secret History*, 1.299–2.300.

Willson   David Harris Willson, *King James VI and I* (London, 1956).

Wilson   Arthur Wilson, *The History of Great Britain, Being the Life and Reign of King James the First* (London, 1653), as reprinted in [White Kennet,] *A Complete History of England*, 3 vols (London, 1706): *CLA*, 249.

All manuscripts referred to are in the National Library of Scotland, unless otherwise stated. Information derived from the notes of the late Dr J. C. Corson is indicated by '(Corson notes)'. The following editions of *The Fortunes of Nigel* have proved helpful: the Dryburgh Edition, 25 vols (London, 1892–94), Vol. 14; The Border Edition, ed. Andrew Lang, 24 vols (London, 1898–99), Vol. 14; ed. Ernest S. Davies (London, 1902); an anonymous edition published by Macmillan (London, 1904); ed. S. V. Makower (Oxford, 1911). For legal matters the notes by D. E. C. Yale (MS 23082) have been useful.

title-page motto   see 'The Friend of Humanity and the Knife Grinder' (line 21) by George Canning, J. H. Frere, and W. Maginn, in *Poetry of the Anti-Jacobin* (London, 1799), 11: compare *CLA*, 118.

3.1   Introductory Epistle   a mode of introduction that Scott first used in *Ivanhoe* (1819), continued in *The Monastery* and *The Abbot* (both 1820), and resumed for *Nigel*.

3.2   Captain Clutterbuck   the imaginary source of *The Monastery* and resident, in retirement, of Kennaquhair (see note to 13.18).

3.4 Dr Dryasdust fictitious antiquarian first mentioned in *The Antiquary* (1816) as Mr Oldbuck's 'literary friend at York' (EEWN 3, 281.41–282.2). He joins the company of Scott's imaginary tribe of authors, editors, and collaborators in the Dedicatory Epistle to *Ivanhoe* (1819) addressed to him by Lawrence Templeton, the equally fictitious author of that novel.

3.8 Quam bonum et quam jucundum *Latin* how good and how pleasant. The phrase is part of the Vulgate version of what in the Authorised Version is Psalm 133, which begins: 'Behold, how good and how pleasant it is for brethren to dwell together in unity!'

3.9–10 according to our country proverb ... bairns Scots variant of the proverb 'We are all Adam's children' (*ODEP*, 3).

3.18 our Scottish metropolis Edinburgh.

3.20 unrespective shop-lad see *Richard III*, 4.2.28–29: 'I will converse with iron-witted fools/ And unrespective boys'.

3.21 Corderies Latin grammar books, called after Mathurin Cordier (1478–1564), a French schoolmaster whose *Colloquia Scholastica* (1564) was an influential textbook. Alexander Bower notes that, in the period 1584–1628, 'the colloquies of Corderius were to be read daily' in the second year of instruction at the High School (*The History of the University of Edinburgh*, 2 vols (Edinburgh, 1817), 1.66).

3.22 cheapening a penny-worth of paper seeing how much paper they can get for a penny (0.4p).

3.23 back-shop private quarters of the business, off limits to customers.

3.26 make free with the leaves help yourself to the unfolded and unbound sheets of a new book.

3.28 trade price wholesale price.

3.29 booking charging to the customer's account.

3.30 over-copy copies produced in excess of the number ordered, and which do not figure in the company's calculation of costs and profits.

3.32–33 some such gear something of that sort.

3.33 Robert Cockburn (1781–1844) founder of the Edinburgh firm of Cockburn & Co., which supplied Scott with wine: 'choicest black' is port and 'best blue' is wine (the colour alludes to the stopper).

3.36 freemen of the corporation of letters those entitled to the privileges of the (notional) guild of authors.

4.2 all things change under the sun the sentiment is commonplace, with variants dating back at least to Ovid (43 BC–AD 17), *Metamorphoses*, 15.165. For a close parallel compare '*all things change below*' from Sir William Alexander, *The Tragedy of Jvlivs Cæsar*, 5.2.386, in his *Recreations With the Muses* (London, 1637), 253. The expression 'under the sun' is found several times in the Old Testament.

4.4–5 the quick-witted and kindly friend ... public John Ballantyne, Scott's friend from Kelso and his literary agent, had died in 1821, depriving Scott of both his valued friendship and his professional expertise.

4.9 another bibliopical friend Archibald Constable (1774–1827), Scott's principal publisher, who was living in the south of England because of poor health during the composition of *Nigel*. He was instrumental, Scott suggests, in making Scottish publishers independent of London, and Scottish writers competitive with their English counterparts.

4.11–13 a Court of Letters ... canons principally *The Edinburgh Review*, founded in 1802 and presided over by Francis Jeffrey (1773–1850), who judged literature by the canons of conservative neo-classical poetics and liberal Whig politics.

4.19   the Cross   the market cross, E of the High Kirk (St Giles' Cathedral) in the High Street, Edinburgh, where Constable's shop was situated.

4.32   run down   hunted down.

4.33–37   Highland seers . . . prepare   the gift of second sight is attributed to 'the gifted wizard seer' on the Isle of Skye or Uist in William Collins's ode 'On the Popular Superstitions of the Highlands of Scotland' (published posthumously in 1788), from which lines 68–69 are quoted.

4.40   the jeweller of Delhi . . . Bennaskar   in 'The History of Mahoud' from *Tales of the Genii*, in Henry Weber, *Tales of the East*, 3 vols (Edinburgh, 1812), 3.479–86: *CLA*, 43. It is actually the deceased jeweller's son Mahoud whom the magician Bennaskar 'led . . . through a long variety of apartments' until they 'arrived at a small vaulted room, from the centre of which hung a lamp' (481).

5.1   the Author of Waverley   the phrase that had appeared (sometimes augmented), in lieu of the author's name, on the title-page of every Scott novel since *Waverley*, except for the three series of *Tales of my Landlord*.

5.4   Salve, magne parens   *Latin* hail, great parent: Virgil (70–19 BC), *Georgics*, 2.173.

5.14–19   veiled and wimpled . . . descry   see the description of Nature in *The Faerie Queene*, 7.7.5.5–7. See also lines 8–9: 'For, with a veile that wimpled euery where, / Her head and face was hid, that mote to none appeare'. Whereas the veil and wimple may suggest the habit of a nun, the mantle was worn by both sexes.

5.21–24   reasons . . . rougher sex   one of the two ladies is probably Mrs Anne Grant of Laggan, who according to a letter in *Blackwood's Edinburgh Magazine* and a response by the editor (3, May 1818, 187–88), was so identified by *The Glasgow Chronicle*, which as evidence printed excerpts from her acknowledged writing and from Scott's novels in parallel columns. The other lady is probably Scott's sister-in-law Mrs Thomas Scott. *The Kaleidoscope; or, Literary and Scientific Mirror*, New Series, no. 16 (17 October 1820), 121 copied from [Gold's] *London Magazine* of the same month an article making this attribution and stating that the novels 'were severally sent to him by that relative in an unfinished state, for revision, correction, and methodizing'. On 20 March 1824 Lady Abercorn wrote to Scott: 'You cannot think how often those Novels are given to Mrs. Scott' (*Letters*, 8.261n). Two months later, the same correspondent observed that, in some quarters, even Scott's wife was rumoured to be the author (*Letters*, 8.291n: 15 June 1824).

5.26   Quæ maribus sola tribuuntur   *Latin* which may be attributed only to males.

5.35   Jedidiah Cleishbotham   the fictitious literary executor of Peter Pattieson, imaginary author of the *Tales of my Landlord*. A schoolmaster, he represents, to judge by his name ('flog bottom'), the corporal-punishment theory of pedagogy.

6.3   the White Lady   the White Lady of Avenel, a supernatural character in *The Monastery* (1820) who found little favour with the reviewers.

6.6   esprit follet   *French* an imp attached to a person or house, more sly than malevolent.

6.15–17   Nixie . . . naiad-like   nixies and naiads are female water sprites, who traditionally entertain themselves at the expense of hapless human beings, as the White Lady does with Father Philip in *The Monastery*, ed. Penny Fielding, EEWN 9, 64–67.

6.19–21   The bath . . . amber or rose-water   in *The Tempest*, 4.1.181–84, Ariel is the airy spirit who serves the magician Prospero and abuses the other servants, leading the drunken jester Trinculo into a stinking pool quite unlike the sweet scent of ambergris or rose-water. Compare 'You savour'd not of amber': Philip Massinger, *A New Way to Pay Old Debts* (performed *c*. 1625, published 1633), 2.3.27.

6.21–22   no one ... stream   proverbial: see Ray, 160; *ODEP*, 782.

6.30   Cock-lane scratch   a name for such a tale as described by the Captain, derived from stories about supernatural events in Cock Lane, Smithfield, credited to the ghost of a local woman which announced its presence by a scratching sound. See (1) Oliver Goldsmith, *The Indigent Philosopher*, essay 4 (*Lloyd's Evening Post*, 8–10 February 1762): 'If a Magaziner be dull upon the Spanish War, he soon has us up again with the Ghost in Cock-lane' (Friedman, 3.191–92). See (2) Oliver Goldsmith, *The Mystery Revealed; Containing a Series of Transactions and Authentic Testimonials, Respecting the supposed Cock-Lane Ghost* (1762: Friedman, 4.419–41). See (3) [Horace and James Smith], 'Ode XII. *To Emanuel Swedenborg*', lines 58–62, in *Horace in London* (London, 1813), which couples Cock-lane with 'Old Scratch', i.e. the devil: 'She gave to life the COCK LANE GHOST,/ A nation's eyes and ears engross'd,/ E'en JOHNSON's skill deriding./ *Old Scratch* (if parsons tell us true,)/ With her found board and lodging too'. There are also several references in Boswell.

6.31   drum of Tedworth   in his *Saducismus Triumphatus: Or, full and plain Evidence Concerning Witches and Apparitions*, 3rd edn (London, 1700: originally published 1681), Part 2, 49–62, Joseph Glanvil tells how a drummer haunts John Mompesson of Tedworth with mysterious drumming and scratching noises, because Mompesson has confiscated his instrument. Scott's library includes an anonymous pamphlet on this subject, *The Drummer of Tedworth* (London, 1716; the ascription in the catalogue to J. Sacheverell derives from a misreading of the title-page): *CLA*, 143.

6.31–32   tick of a solitary death-watch in the wainscoat   compare Oliver Goldsmith, *A Citizen of the World*, no. 90: 'I listened for death-watches in the wainscot' (*Public Ledger* for 17 December 1760: Friedman, 2.367).

6.32–33   a Scotch metaphysician   i.e. a sceptic indebted to the Scottish philosopher David Hume (1711–1776) or 'Humism', the view that human knowledge is limited to the experience of ideas and impressions which cannot be verified.

6.35–36   a famed river ... grotto   possibly alluding to 'Alph, the sacred river' that 'ran/ Through caverns measureless to man' (lines 3–4), as well as to the 'deep romantic chasm' (line 12), in Coleridge's 'Kubla Khan' (written 1798; published 1816).

6.42   Ercles's vein   *A Midsummer Night's Dream*, 1.2.34. The allusion is to the ranting acting style of the Hercules or tyrant character from the old drama.

6.43   Hercules   the strong-man of Classical mythology.

7.4   quirks and quiddits   fine-points or quibbles, here digressions from his plot. Compare the description of Grimes's daughter Bettris in [Robert Greene], *George a Greene, the Pinner of Wakefield* (performed 1587, published 1599), lines 199–200: 'she, in quirks and quiddities of love,/ Sets me to school, she is so overwise' (*ABD*, 1.444).

7.5–6   lie rotting ... displeasure   see Sancho Panza's statement: 'since you have laid that bitter command [not again to make jokes of his master's doings] upon me, to hold my tongue, I have had four or five quaint conceits that have rotted in my gizzard, and now I have another at my tongue's end that I would not for any thing should miscarry'. The utterance occurs in Part 1, Ch. 21 of *The History of the Renowned Don Quixote De La Mancha. Written in Spanish by Miguel de Cervantes Saavedra. Translated by several hands: and published by the late Mr. Motteux. Revised ... By Mr. Ozell*, 4 vols (Edinburgh, 1766; originally published 1605–15), 1.236–37: *CLA*, 317.

7.8–9   Tom Jones ... Amelia   the second (1749) and third (1751) major novels of Henry Fielding.

7.11 He challenges ... Epic in the preface to Fielding's first novel *Joseph Andrews* (1742).

7.11–12 Smollett, Le Sage Tobias Smollett (1721–71) and Alain René Le Sage (1668–1747), whose novels follow Cervantes' picaresque model of plotting rather than resembling Fielding's epic-derived form.

7.16–19 great masters ... alights at the inn imitating Cervantes, Fielding, both in *Joseph Andrews* and *Tom Jones*, imaged reading as a journey by stage-coach, the narrator as either driver or fellow-passenger. Scott followed their example in *Waverley* (1814).

7.21 you are of opinion with Bayes ... things *Bayes* is a generic name for drama critics derived from a character so named in George Villiers, Duke of Buckingham's play *The Rehearsal* (1671) and intended as a satiric portrait of John Dryden (1631–1700). The original reads: 'Plot stand still! why, what a Devil is the Plot good for, but to bring in fine things?' (3.1.72–73).

7.32–35 the excuse of the slave ... happy day the source of the anecdote has not been located.

8.11–12 hastily huddled up with the loose ends wrapped up in a disorderly way.

8.12–17 a pint of claret ... Tokay the quality of the wine an author drinks is proportionate to the sale of books, the prized Hungarian red wine Tokay representing still greater success than the Bordeaux red, and that wine higher acclaim than the fortified red from Portugal. For centuries, monasteries have made wine for personal and commercial consumption: here the suggestion is that part of the author's proceeds from *The Monastery* (1820) have been devoted to enhancing his cellar.

8.21 Jem MacCoul an example of the legal folklore familiar to and enjoyed by Scott in his role of Clerk to the Court of Session. MacCoul was convicted in 1820 of robbing a Glasgow bank.

8.30–31 A shadow ... impersonal author an anonymous or incognito author.

8.33 Letters ... Oxford in his *Letters to Richard Heber, Esq. containing Critical Remarks on the Series of Novels beginning with "Waverley," and an Attempt to Ascertain their Author* (London, 1821), published anonymously, John Leycester Adolphus makes a shrewd case based on textual evidence for the writer Walter Scott as the Author of Waverley. Heber (1773–1833) was a long-time friend of Scott, and Member of Parliament for the University of Oxford 1821–26 (until the abolition of university seats in 1948 Oxford and Cambridge universities elected two MPs apiece).

8.40 artificially brought forward artfully or skilfully adduced.

8.40–43 Sir Philip Francis's title ... unknown as ever Francis (1740–1818) was reputed to be the author of a series of letters on politics, published anonymously in the *Public Advertiser* from 1768 to 1772, resulting in one of the great unsolved mysteries of the age. The title pages of the collected edition (*Junius*, 2 vols (London, 1772)), bear the Latin motto 'STET NOMINIS UMBRA' (a shadow stands for the name): compare lines 30–31 above. John Cannon, editor of *The Letters of Junius* (Oxford, 1978), writes that in the early years of the 19th century 'the list of candidates lengthened until it was fifty or more' (540).

9.3 justice of peace mentioned by Shenstone William Shenstone (1714–63), in 'INSCRIPTION. To the Memory of *A. L.* Esquire, Justice of the Peace for this County', creates an idealised portrait of the country gentleman whose charity, by design, does not occasion 'The *Noise*, or *Report* such Things generally cause/ In the World' (lines 15–16): *Poems upon Various Occasions* (Oxford, 1737: published anonymously), 48.

9.15–16 as Dr Johnson ... cant see Boswell (15 May 1783), where the phrase is 'clear your *mind* of cant'. The context, in Scott as in Boswell, points to Johnson's third definition of the word, in his *Dictionary of the English Language* (1755), as a 'whining pretension to goodness, in formal and affected terms'.

9.17–19 the nursery proverb ... breaking this is the only occurrence of the proverb cited in *ODEP*, 120.

9.20–21 I am their humble jackall ... reject it the jackal was proverbially known as 'the lion's provider' because it was supposed to go before the lion and hunt its prey for it (*ODEP*, 467).

9.22–29 the postman ... regretted before 1840 postage was paid by the recipient, not the sender, of a letter.

10.5 strike while the iron is hot proverbial: Ray, 125; *ODEP*, 781.

10.5 hoist sail while the wind is fair proverbial: *ODEP*, 376.

10.7 lies by remains inactive; rests.

10.14 proverbially said to be no speed alluding to the proverb 'The more haste, the less speed': *ODEP*, 356; compare *ODEP*, 543 and Ray, 117, 286, 305.

10.25–26 my regular mansion turns out a Gothic anomaly the architectural analogy contrasts the classical or neo-classical building (*regular*, built according to fixed rules) with the gothic *anomaly* (irregular structure) to differentiate between premeditated and spontaneous composition.

10.31–32 Bailie Jarvie, or Dalgetty characters in *Rob Roy* (1818) and *A Legend of the Wars of Montrose* (1819), respectively.

10.40 dog in a wheel dogs have been used to power spits and other small machines.

11.2 he must needs go whom the devil drives proverbial: Ray, 97; *ODEP*, 560.

11.3–4 the theatrical attempt ... urged Scott's friends frequently urged him to write plays. One of them, Daniel Terry (1780?–1829), the London actor and producer, was visiting Abbotsford when Scott began to write *Nigel* and, according to Lockhart (5.143), at the novelist's urging Terry read aloud to Lockhart the opening pages of the new novel the day they were drafted, expressing 'great delight with the animated opening'.

11.6–10 the idea ... mother-wit Scott refers to the mottoes attributed to 'Old Play' by which he frequently introduced chapters of his novels—94 by Tom B. Haber's count ('The Chapter-Tags in the Waverley Novels', *PMLA*, 45 (1930), 1140–49 (1140)). Not able to trace them, readers assumed them to be by the Author of Waverley (which they often were) and took them as evidence of a talent for writing plays.

11.14 old friend in Worcestershire fictitious character in the tall-tale that follows.

11.15 Dragoons Scott was a founding member and quartermaster of the Royal Edinburgh Volunteer Light Dragoons, formed in 1797 to guard against the anticipated invasion from France.

11.20–21 great Modern Coleridge. In his periodical *The Friend* (1809–10), he writes: 'A lady once asked me if I believed in ghosts and apparitions. I answered with truth and simplicity: *No, Madam! I have seen far too many myself*' (ed. Barbara E. Rooke, 2 vols (London and Princeton, 1969), 1.146). See *CLA*, 340.

11.33 had a value for held in high regard.

11.33 Sally generic name for a cook.

11.41—12.1 that unhappy Elizabeth ... ever known John Warburton (1682–1759) collected manuscript plays, of which all but three and a half of some fifty or sixty by Shakespeare, Massinger, Marlowe, Ford, Dekker, and other early dramatists were supposedly destroyed by his servant, who set hot pies on them or otherwise burned them. (Scott calls her Betty Barnes; she is Elizabeth Baker in the *Dictionary of National Biography*'s account of Warburton.) After sifting the evidence, W. W. Greg in 'The Bakings of Betsy' (*The Library*, 3rd series, 2:7 (July 1911), 225–59) concluded that 'we have undoubtedly to lament the loss of a few pieces, perhaps of considerable interest, but not by any means the dramatic holocaust' Warburton claimed (259).

12.1–3 of most of which ... Shakespeare refers probably to the much amplified prologomena (the subtitle of the first three volumes which brought together all information to date on Shakespeare, his milieu, and his plays) to *The Plays and Poems of William Shakspeare*, 21 vols (London, 1821), initiated by Edmond Malone (1741–1812) almost 30 years earlier and completed by James Boswell the younger (1778–1822). 'Boswell's Malone', also known as 'the third variorum' (a *variorum* being an edition including selected notes by previous commentators or editors), reprints (2.632–46) George Steevens, 'Extracts of Entries on the Books of the Stationers' Company' from 1562 to 1630, which includes the titles of works that have not survived.

12.4 small quartos popular form of publishing individual plays, referring to the four leaves produced by folding the small sheets of paper into quarters.

12.5 Roxburghe Club a select group of British collectors of antiquarian books. It was named after John Ker (1740–1804), a celebrated bibliophile, who succeeded as 3rd Duke of Roxburghe in 1755. It reprinted rare old works in limited editions. Scott was invited to become a member in 1823, and in 1831, while reviewing Pitcairn's *Criminal Trials* for the *Quarterly Review*, he gave a history of the club: see *Prose Works*, 21.213–19.

12.6 these unhappy pickers and stealers see Hamlet's unflattering reference to his hands in *Hamlet*, 3.2.320.

12.7–8 Beaumont and Fletcher ... Webster younger contemporaries of Shakespeare: Francis Beaumont (1584–1616), John Fletcher (1579–1625), Philip Massinger (1583–1640), Ben Jonson (1572–1637), and John Webster (*c.* 1580–*c.* 1638).

12.11 the Book of the Master of Revels the account books in which the Master (an officer of the royal household, formally created by Henry VIII in 1545, who in the 1590s acquired control of all aspects of the drama) entered the names of plays licensed for performance and, from 1606, for printing as well.

12.14–17 the Hermit of Parnell ... saucing-pan Scott echoes and adapts lines 171–73 of 'The Hermit' by Thomas Parnell: 'He bursts the Bands of Fear, and madly cries,/ Detested Wretch—But scarce his Speech began,/ When the strange Partner seem'd no longer Man' (published in Alexander Pope's edition of Parnell, entitled *Poems on Several Occasions* (London, 1722), 175).

12.23–24 as my friend ... lie for referring to the catch-phrase ('what will you lay it's a lie?') of the character Major Longbow, referred to as 'The Modern Munchausen', in Charles Mathews' popular entertainment *Travels in Air, on Earth and Water* (1821).

12.30–31 for the closet, not for the stage to be read in the privacy of one's home rather than to be performed in public. Scott's phrasing echoes that of Joanna Baillie in the 'Introductory Discourse' to *A Series of Plays: In Which It Is Attempted To Delineate The Stronger Passions Of The Mind. Each Passion Being The Subject Of A Tragedy And A Comedy* (London, 1798: published anonymously), where she rejects the assumption that she has 'written them for the closet rather than the stage' (65). In the Romantic period closet drama had something of a vogue, to which several of the major poets contributed, most notably Byron who insisted that his dramas not be staged.

12.35–36 a second Laberius ... would or not Decimus Laberius (*c*.105–43 BC), a knight who wrote mimes for pleasure, was humiliated by having to perform in one of them on the orders of Julius Caesar, whom he had criticised.

12.37 Terrified ... sermon Scott puns on the name of Daniel Terry (see note to 11.3–4) who since 1816 had been converting Waverley Novels into stage plays.

12.39–40 a volume of dramas like Lord Byron's Byron published a book of three plays in December 1821. One of them, 'Cain', was dedicated to Scott.

12.42 my friend Allan the Scottish writer Allan Cunningham (1784–1842).

13.1 Bramah's extra patent pens the new metal pen that replaced the quill, one of the numerous inventions of Joseph Bramah (1748–1814).

13.3–4 Allan Ramsay ... Barbara Allan alluding to the ballad heroine in 'Bonny Barbara Allan' first published in Allan Ramsay's *Tea-Table Miscellany* (1724).

13.5 his tragedy of Sir Marmaduke Maxwell Scott received the published play while writing the Introductory Epistle; he had read it in manuscript in 1820, judging it 'more fit for the closet' than the stage: *Letters*, 7.145–48, 6.298.

13.15 Caledonia a poetic name for Scotland.

13.15 lyrical effusions a popular term for lyric poetry in the Romantic period.

13.16 It's hame, and it's hame song appearing (anonymously, and with 'Hame, hame, hame' as the opening phrase) in *Remains of Nithsdale and Galloway Song*, ed. R. H. Cromek (London, 1810), 169–70: *CLA*, 199. With the first words essentially as quoted here, it reappears, again anonymously, in Cunningham's own collection, *The Songs of Scotland, Ancient and Modern*, 4 vols (London, 1825), 3.246–47 (*CLA*, 165), where he notes that it is an 'alteration' of a Jacobite song (compare Scott, *Journal*, 14 November 1826). Both the Jacobite song and Cunningham's alteration can be found in *Poems and Songs of Allan Cunningham*, ed. Peter Cunningham (London, 1847), xvi–xvii, 25–26.

13.18 Kennaquhair Clutterbuck's home town in the Introductory Epistle to *The Monastery* (1820), identified as Melrose in a Magnum note to that novel (18.xlvii).

13.19 Catalani Angelica Catalani (1780–1849), a super-star Italian soprano. She sang in Britain from 1806–1813 and again in 1824 and 1828.

13.19 "Poortith Cauld" Robert Burns, 'O poortith cauld' (O cold poverty) (1793).

13.20–21 "the Banks of Bonnie Doon" Robert Burns, 'The Banks o' Doon' (1791). It exists in two versions, beginning respectively 'Ye flowery banks o' bonie Doon' (published posthumously in 1808), and 'Ye banks and braes o' bonie Doon' (published 1792).

13.21 Tempora mutantur Latin proverbial expression ('times change'); see *ODEP*, 825.

13.24 A man's a man for a' that Robert Burns, 'Is there, for honest Poverty' (1795), line 12.

13.35–37 the capital sum ... circulation Scott uses here the language of political economy as he criticises Adam Smith in *An Inquiry into the Nature and Causes of the Wealth of Nations* (1776) for not acknowledging that an author is a 'productive' labourer, rather than an 'unproductive' one, by virtue of adding commercial value to the goods manufactured and thus contributing to the wealth of the nation.

13.38–39 from honest Duncan ... printer's devils i.e. the range of Scottish labourers who produce the novels and thereby earn their livelihoods.

Duncan is Duncan Cowan, who with his brother Alexander, ran a paper manufactory at Penicuik: see Essay on the Text, note 73 (460) (Corson notes). A *printer's devil* is the errand-boy in a printing office.

13.40 Didst thou ... pence? *The Merry Wives of Windsor*, 2.2.12–13. Pistol reminds Falstaff that he shared in the proceeds from the theft of the handle from Mistress Bridget's fan.

13.41 our modern Athens popular name for Edinburgh in Scott's day.

13.42 universal suffrage Scott refers to the political agitation that would eventually lead, with the passage of the Great Reform Bill of 1832, to extended but not universal suffrage.

14.2 unwashed artificers see *King John*, 4.2.201.

14.5 Cant again Scott mimics Dr Johnson's habit of repeating the term *cant* (see 9.15–16 for the first use in the Epistle) when exposing misleading opinion.

14.5–6 there is lime in this sack ... world see *1 Henry IV*, 2.4.116–17: 'here's lime in this sack too! There is nothing but roguery to be found in villanous man'. Falstaff complains that his wine has been adulterated; the Author of Waverley draws a parallel with the cant he has been elaborating.

14.11 bales of books before being folded and bound, the printed sheets of copies of a book would be kept in bales for transportation and storage.

14.16 the publisher's shop i.e. the printing establishment.

14.21–22 wander, heaven-directed, to the poor see Alexander Pope, 'Epistle II. To a Lady' (1735), line 150: the heirless Atossa must leave her fortune to either an unknown heir or the undifferentiated poor.

14.33–34 two of the learned faculties the lawyers and physicians referred to above.

14.36 a honorarium Scott describes the custom of giving gratuitous payments to lawyers in a letter of 10 March [1820] to Lord Montagu: *Letters*, 6.146–47. (Corson notes)

14.43—15.1 When Czar Peter ... soldier Peter the Great, Emperor of Russia from 1682 to 1725, learned the art of war, among other professions and occupations, by living and working with soldiers and sailors.

15.5–8 O if it were a mean thing ... refuse it Scott provides a variant of lines from the fourth and seventh stanzas of a mildly obscene song, 'The Fryer and the Nun' in [Thomas D'Urfey], *Wit and Mirth: or Pills to Purge Melancholy*, 6 vols (London, 1719–20), 4.176–78: *CLA*, 159.

15.23–25 that ingenious association ... amusement see Oliver Goldsmith, *The Indigent Philosopher*, no. 4, 'A modest Address to the Publick in Behalf of the Infernal Magazine' (*Lloyd's Evening Post* for 8–10 February 1762: Friedman, 3.192).

15.28–29 when they dance ... pipe see Matthew 11.17 and Luke 7.32.

15.29 flappers in Jonathan Swift, *Gulliver's Travels* (1726), Part 3, Ch. 2, the Laputians who inhabit a floating island and spend all their time in reveries of speculation wear flappers by which those wishing to converse with them can attract their attention.

15.34–35 'Tis my vocation, Hal *1 Henry IV*, 1.2.101 (Falstaff's justification for his 'purse-taking' or theft).

15.39 had the crown had great success or won the victory (signified by the laurel crown or something approximating it). Scott used the proverbial phrase again in the *Journal* entry for 12 December 1827 when contemplating the likely downfall of his literary reputation as a result of his apparently declining creative powers.

15.39–42 the unwilling tribute ... such as it was Scott adapts Dr Johnson's comment about the poet Charles Churchill: 'he is a tree that cannot produce good fruit: he only bears crabs. But, Sir, a tree that produces a great many crabs is better than a tree which produces only a few' (Boswell: 1 July 1763).

15.43—16.1 seven years ... Waverley Scott's first novel *Waverley* was published in 1814, a little over seven years before he started *Nigel*.

16.8 Meliora spero *Latin* I hope for better things.

16.9 non omnis moriar *Latin* I shall not altogether die. Horace (65–8 BC), *Odes*, 3.30.6.

16.22 make rags dear rags were used in the making of paper; the more of them that were required for paper, the fewer would be available for making rugs or cleaning floors, driving up the cost.

16.26–27 The complaints ... fertility of the press the period referred to is 1558–1625, when Queen Elizabeth I and King James VI and I reigned. Spenser's allegory in *The Faerie Queene* of such fertility in the figure of Error's disgorging of books and papers (1.1.20.6) may have been in the back of Scott's mind, given the proximate reference to that poem, or he may have been thinking of the later pamphlet wars, one strain of which, even while promoting the struggle between Crown and Parliament, blamed the press for exacerbating it by proliferating pamphlets (see *Pamphlet Wars: Prose in the English Revolution*, ed. James Holstun (London, 1992), 20–21).

16.29–32 the Rich Strand ... golden ore see *The Faerie Queene*, 3.4.18.4–6.

16.38 Sir Richard Blackmore heroic and epic poet (d. 1729), whose prolixity was not impeded by either acerbic critics or apathetic readers.

17.1–8 enchanted ... too bold see *The Faerie Queene*, 3.11.54.1–4, 6–8: Britomart is the Knight of Chastity.

17.13 valeant quantum *Latin* whatever it is worth (part of the proverb 'valeant quantum valere potest': let it have weight, so far as it may).

17.14–15 sooty-faced Apollyon from the Canongate messenger or printer's devil from Paul's Work, the Ballantyne printing house, located in the Canongate section of old Edinburgh. His face is black from ink and ink-dust. In Revelation 9.11 Apollyon is the 'angel of the bottomless pit'.

17.15 on the part of on behalf of.

17.16 M'Corkindale Daniel M'Corkindale was for many years the foreman at the Ballantyne printing house.

17.26 1st April i.e. April Fools' Day.

19.5–15 motto not identified: probably by Scott. Some of the details suggest that Scott drew upon an old song, 'The bonny Scot made a Gentleman', published by Joseph Ritson in his anonymous *The North-Country Chorister* (Durham, 1802), 13–14. Scott quotes the song in part in his note to Weldon's remarks on this subject (1.369–70), singling out those lines which refer to changes in apparel from head to foot, including the weapon. *Saunders* is the English nickname for a (young and naïve) Scot. *Glasgow frieze* is a coarse cloth associated with Glasgow (and Ireland). The *beaver* was the English hat of beaver skin, larger than the Scottish bonnet.

19.34–20.6 historians ... lower orders the authorities would include those contemporary or near-contemporary historians whom Scott edited in the *Secret History* (see Historical Note, 522–23), and in *Somers' Tracts* (especially the author of *The Narrative History of King James, for the first fourteen Years*: 2.262–304), as well as later historians such as David Hume and Isaac D'Israeli (see Historical Note, 524), who echoed them. In a letter of 13 January 1610 Chamberlain noted the political dimension of a quarrel: 'there grew a question between the earles of Argile and Pembroke, about place, which the Scot maintaines to be his by senioritie, as beeing now become all Brittaines'. On 2 May the same year he recorded 'three or fowre great quarrels' in a single week at court. And on 11 March 1612 he observed: 'On Monday there was a great race or running at Croidon where by occasion of fowle play or fowle wordes, one Ramsey a Scottishman strooke the earle of Mongomerie with his riding rod, wherupon the whole companie was redy to go together by the eares, and like enough to have made yt a nationall quarrell' (Chamberlain, 1.294, 297, 340: the first two letters appear in *Memorials of Affairs of State in the Reigns of Q. Elizabeth and K. James I. Collected (chiefly) from the Original Papers Of... Sir Ralph Winwood*, ed. Edmund Sawyer, 3 vols (London, 1725), 3.117, 154: *CLA*, 233). The author of the *Narrative History* writes of daily quarrels and brawls at all ranks and of rebellion both in London and in the country, identifying jealousy between the 'two nations' as the principal cause and stating that 'in outward shew there appeared no certain obedience, no certain government amongst us' (2.266–67). For the peasants in the country, it was not social place but physical space including the ever-accelerating enclosure of common lands (e.g. James's enclosing part of Enfield Chase to make Theobalds Park his private hunting preserve) that led to agitation in 1607 and the use of cavalry to quell the self-described 'levelers' (Lodge, 3.320–21).

20.9 David Ramsay for Ramsay see Historical Note, 528.

20.12 Dalkeith, near Edinburgh Dalkeith is 11 km SE of Edinburgh.

20.14–15 Temple-Bar ... Saint Dunstan's Church for Temple Bar see note to 64.34–37. For St Dunstan's Church see note to 27.15–16.

20.25–26 Robinson Crusoe's cavern ... before it the eponymous hero of Daniel Defoe's novel (1719) could not decide whether a cave or tent would best protect him from danger and so determined upon both.

20.29–30 Napier ... abstract science John Napier (1550–1617) was the Scotsman who discovered logarithms and invented the notation of decimal fractions. Other contemporary theoretical mathematicians Scott may have had in mind are Henry Briggs (1561–1630) and Edward Wright (1558?–1615), both Napier's admirers, and the German astronomer Johannes Kepler (1571–1630), who extended Napier's work.

20.32–33 What d'ye lack? What d'ye lack? a typical streetvendor's cry of the time: Tilley, L20.

20.36–38 Monmouth Street ... Israel Monmouth Street, in the London parish of St Giles in the Fields, was in Scott's time the centre of the second-hand clothes trade, in which Jews were especially prominent.

21.9 femoral habiliments clothes for the thigh, i.e. trousers. A jocular expression.

21.9–10 fit ourselves get suited; get fitted out.

21.14 their ... civic union like their masters the apprentices were organised, but by their common interests and civic pride rather than by their craft.

21.19–22 an old song ... tall Scott adapts lines 63–64 from the ballad of 'Queen Elizabeth's Champion: or, Great Britain's Glory. The Young Earl of Essex's Victory Over the Emperor of Germany' ('O then bespoke the prentices all, / Living in London, both proper and tall'), sung by Dr Johnson (Boswell: 22 September 1773). See *The English and Scottish Popular Ballads*, ed. Francis James Child, 5 vols (Boston and New York, 1882–98), 5.145–47.

21.24 Templars barristers or law-students who derived their name from the Knights Templars, a medieval order whose monastery and chapel, between Fleet Street and the Strand, after its abolition in 1312, became the site for the training of lawyers and the residential quarters for barristers and others affiliated with the law.

21.28 the Alderman of the ward the chief officer of an administrative district of the City, holding office for life, and responsible for maintaining order through the Watch. Since there was no police force in the modern sense until

1829 and constables were unreliable, if Shakespeare's Dogberry is in any way typical (see *Much Ado About Nothing*), the alderman relied on residents to quell disturbances of the peace, as well as to extinguish fires. Martin Holmes indicates that arrangements for keeping the watch were local to each ward: *Elizabethan London* (New York, 1969), 100.

21.30–31   as the Capulets and Montagues . . . stage   referring to the feuding families who oppose the marriage of Romeo and Juliet in Shakespeare's play named after the two lovers.

21.39–40   Christ Church Hospital   Christ's Hospital was founded in 1553 by Edward VI, for the housing and education of orphans and other needy boys, on the site in Newgate Street of the house of the Grey Friars, abolished by Henry VIII.

22.2–3   broad-sword play . . . single-stick   mock battles using a sword with a broad blade and a stick with a guard requiring only one hand to wield.

22.4   his Catechism   a set of questions and answers covering fundamental Christian doctrine which the Church of England required 'to be learned of every person before he be brought to be confirmed by the bishop'.

22.12   winked at   ignored; overlooked.

22.37–38   complexion inclining to be more dark . . . beauty   i.e. not the fair complexion which in the old romances and their successors separates the nobleman from the peasant or yeoman.

22.38   in despite of   despite.

23.8–9   the . . . wars of the roses   the struggle (1455–85) between the families of York, their badge the white rose, and Lancaster, their badge the red rose, for the throne of England.

23.23–26   distance-post . . . double-distanced   the post or flag at a fixed distance from the winning-post which in a heat a horse must pass before the winner passes the winning-post in order not to be disqualified for subsequent heats. To be so disqualified is to be *distanced*; presumably a 'double-distanced' horse would be two distances behind the winner.

23.43   quarter-staff   long pole tipped with iron used by peasants in fighting.

24.6   interest made for   personal influence brought to bear on behalf of.

24.19–20   according to high authority . . . clamours   the high authority is Shakespeare: see *Henry VIII*, 5.4.56–57 ('These are the youths that thunder at a playhouse and fight for bitten apples').

24.38   ruffs, cuffs, and bands   separable parts of men's clothing for the neck or wrist that, when dirty, could be changed to effect a clean appearance.

24.43–25.1   had not a word to throw at a dog   proverbial: *ODEP*, 915.

25.3   Epping Forest   Epping Forest, NE of London, where James and his courtiers liked to hunt deer.

25.22   agreeable to   in accordance with.

26.1   well avised of that   well informed on that subject, i.e. quite sure of that.

26.1–2   the Vale of Evesham   in Worcestershire, the fertile valley of the River Avon.

26.2   Head of the Church   the Act of Supremacy (1534) conferred on Henry VIII and his successors the title of 'supreme head in earth of the Church of England'. In 1559 Elizabeth I's new Act of Supremacy restored the legislation in a revised form (referring to 'supreme governor') after its repeal by Queen Mary.

26.15   a very Daniel in his judgment   in The History of Susanna in the Apocrypha two lustful elders observe Susanna bathing and offer her the choice of lying with them or being accused of adultery with an invented young man. Susanna defies them, and it is Daniel who through shrewd interrogation proves their accusation to be false. See also *The Merchant of Venice*, 4.1.218: 'A Daniel come to judgment!'.

26.16–17 Our reverend brother of Gloucester the Bishop of Gloucester. From 1612 to 1624 this was Miles Smith.

26.32 Knight of the Coif a sergeant at the law, i.e. a member of a superior order of barristers, abolished in 1880. Scott's mock-heroic term refers to the tight-fitting cap the sergeant wore at this time: 'The coif was a white silk head-covering which sat on the hair like a bonnet and was secured underneath the chin. By the late 16th century it was usually worn under a black skull-cap': Anthony Arlidge, *Shakespeare and the Prince of Love: The Feast of Misrule in the Middle Temple* (London, 2000), 34.

26.35 the Devil-tavern located in Fleet Street close to Temple Bar, the Devil Tavern was patronised by poets centred upon Ben Jonson whose club of wits assembled in a room dedicated to Apollo.

26.35 Guildhall the town-hall of London, in the centre of the City, built *c.* 1411–*c.* 1440.

26.38 a watch with five wheels and a bar-movement a watch movement with the conventional number of wheels in its mechanism, and with upper pivots supported by bars rather than carried in a single plate.

26.40 the Black Bull perhaps imaginary. There was a Red Bull Theatre in Clerkenwell, built *c.* 1604–06, and in use till 1663. The Bull Inn, Blackfriars, had been one of the leading Elizabethan playhouses, and there was also an inn called the Black Bull in Gray's Inn Lane.

27.2 a set of roaring boys one of a gang of rowdy young men, here apprentices, who by vocal and sometimes physical violence intimidated other citizens. Towards the end of the 17th century they were called the 'Muns', and Scott seems to have been thinking of them while composing, for in the manuscript he originally wrote 'Mun' for 'Jin' and for 'Jenkin' in passages nearby.

27.2–3 pit … smoke for it the most expensive seats were on the stage itself, the cheapest in the upper gallery, where the apprentices congregated. The cheapest option of all was paying for standing room in the pit (the modern stalls area). Since the main stage of the Elizabethan-Jacobean theatre was not curtained, Vin refers to either the curtain concealing the inner stage (the 're-cess'), or that concealing the second-level 'chamber'. The latter would be closer to the apprentices. Setting fire to the curtain would appear to be another form of gratuitous violence, like breaking windows and beating up citizens, perpetrated by the roaring boys with whom Vin proposes to swell the poet's audience.

27.6 an owl here an insult, meaning blind or imperceptive.

27.10–11 when his third night comes round … coin the proceeds from the third-night performance of a play went to the author; *pennyworths* refers to whatever can be bought for a penny, in this case, probably drinks.

27.15–16 images … ding-dong two Herculean figures (clearly masculine) ornamented the famous clock of St Dunstan in the West, in Fleet Street a few metres E of Temple Bar, striking two bells at the quarters with clubs. The clock was not installed, however, until 1671. The existing building of 1831–33 replaced the medieval church, and the clock was restored to it in 1936.

27.17–18 blue cap … gentle blood Richard Moniplies, through his dress, tries to suggest that he is a gentleman, rather than a yeoman, or a working-man who would wear a flat cap.

27.24–25 a palmer-worm … locust has spared see Joel 1.4: 'That which the palmerworm hath left hath the locust eaten'. The *locust* is the opportunistic Scot who, to better his fortune, came to London with King James at the time of his accession (Osborne uses the term in this way: 1.150, 254); the *palmer-worm* ('caterpillar') is his successor.

27.26–29 **as the poet sings sweetly . . . must be fed** the couplet is quoted by Osborne (1.174), from memory, from one of the 'libels and songes' prompted by anti-Scottish feeling following the influx from the north after 1603.

27.31–32 **he knows on which side his bread is buttered** proverbial: Ray, 179; *ODEP*, 438.

27.33 **bearing** having.

27.35 **By this light** an asseverative phrase: 'I say'.

27.39 **carry coals** submit to humiliation or insult. See *Romeo and Juliet*, 1.1.1.

27.42 **Berwick** the English border town on the NE coast.

28.3 **were your pockets as bare as Father Fergus's** the reference is probably to a legend telling how a 5th-century Irish king, Murtagh, lent the sacred coronation stone from Tara to his brother Fergus Mac Erc when he became the first King of Scots. Some believe that the stone was never returned, and that it is the Stone of Destiny, stolen from Scone by Edward I of England in 1296, repatriated to Scotland from Westminster Abbey in 1996 and now in the Crown Room in Edinburgh Castle. For one of the versions of the story known to Scott see *Hary's 'Wallace'*, ed. Matthew P. McDiarmid, 2 vols (Edinburgh and London, 1978–69), 1.5 and notes at 2.134–35: Book 1, lines 121–27.

28.6 **Buy physic** possibly a variation on 'Take physic' in *King Lear*, 3.4.33.

28.9 **Galen** famous Greek physician of the 2nd century, a principal authority on medicine at this time, as Falstaff attests: see *2 Henry IV*, 1.2.109–10.

28.12–13 **Flos sulphur: cum butyro quant: suff:** *Latin* flower of sulphur, with the proper admixture of butter (an ointment to relieve itching).

28.14–15 **oaken towel** Vincent refers to his apprentice's cudgel or club used for fighting in lieu of a formal weapon. Since 1582 apprentices had been forbidden by law to carry any weapon of offence or defence.

28.23 **The Scot will not fight till he sees his own blood** proverbial: see *ODEP*, 705 which cites only this example.

28.30 **Clubs—clubs** the call to arms that rallied citizens for fighting. See Thomas Dekker and Thomas Middleton, *The Honest Whore Part 1* (1604), 1.2.141: 'Sfoot clubs, clubs, prentices'.

28.36 **give an eye to** keep an eye on; watch.

29.2–8 **motto** not identified: probably by Scott.

29.15–16 **night-watches—day-watches** *night-watches* are 'repeating watches' (actually invented *c.* 1676), which, when a button was pressed, struck the last hour, or hour and quarter, useful at night; *day-watches* are without this facility.

29.16–17 **Locking wheel . . . are 13** Scott took this language for the mechanics of the striking mechanism of clocks fairly directly from an example cited by Derham (34). He uses only part of Derham's description, omitting some of the mechanism. In every 12 hours, a total of 78 strokes are required to sound the hours (1, 2, 3 . . . 12). The *striking wheel* has 13 pins, and thus must revolve 6 times every 12 hours. The *pinion of report*, a small wheel with 8 teeth, must also revolve 6 times, causing the *locking wheel* with its 48 teeth to revolve once: the locking wheel has 11 notches unequally spaced which make the clock strike 1, 2, 3 etc.

29.17–18 **the quotient—the multiplicand** more of the clockmaker's jargon: *quotient* is the mathematical term for the number of times one quantity is contained in another, and the clockmaker uses it in calculating the number of turns which a wheel must make to produce a desired effect (see Derham, 10); *multiplicand* is the mathematical term for a quantity to be multiplied.

29.19–20 the acceleration ... 59 fourths although these words are part of the verso insertion covering 29.10–22 they are not derived from Derham. They appear to refer to the adjustment of a clock that is gaining time. Derham has a discussion of the adjustment of pendulums (79–82), but not in these terms, which may be Scott's invention.

29.21 the bones of the immortal Napier Napier (see note to 20.29–30) 'invented a calculating device of movable rods of wood or ivory, from which they are known as *Napier's Bones*, an ancestor of the slide rule' (*Classics of Mathematics*, ed. Ronald Calinger (Oak Park, Illinois, 1982), 254).

29.36–38 low, flat, and unadorned cap ... the city the cap is to be distinguished from the high-crowned hat of beaver or velvet, with jewelled band and bright feather, worn by the inhabitants of Westminster, i.e. the courtiers at Whitehall; the shoes, from the courtier's elegant footwear crafted of 'a rare Spanish leather, / And decked with roses altogether', as the old song 'The bonny Scot made a Gentleman' quoted by Weldon (1.369) puts it: see note to 19.5–15. The rampant consumerism that preoccupied Barnabe Rich in *The Honestie of This Age* (London, 1615) could be observed in 'a hat-band, a scarfe, a paire of garters, and in Roses for ... shoo-strings' (48). It had been fuelled by the people with new Honours, who 'with their greatnesse brought in excesse of riot, both in clothes and dyet' (Sir Foulk Grevill [but probably by Arthur Wilson], *The Five Years of King Iames* (London, 1643), 3). Rich's objections were largely moral; those of Parliament, which in 1616 considered regulating excess in apparel, were rather social: it had become difficult to distinguish the prince from the subject (Wilson (in Kennet), 2.704).

30.9 the Ward of Faringdon-Without that part of Farringdon ward (N of the Thames and W of Walbrooke stream) which spilled over the city wall and, in 1394, became a large separate ward with its own alderman. In the N it takes in Holborn and Smithfield; it is bounded on the S by the Thames; in the E it takes in Old Bailey; and it runs W roughly to Chancery Lane.

30.12–13 a bullock to be driven mad referring to the popular entertainment of bull baiting. In James's reign the bull-ring was located in Paris Garden on the S bank of the Thames (see note to 192.27).

30.13 a quean to be ducked for scolding referring to the sport of publicly rebuking a scold by dunking her head in water, or tying her to a stool attached to an oscillating plank and plunging her right in—at this period in London, often in the stagnant pond at Smithfield.

30.14 sure to be ... of it echoing the proverb 'Better come at the latter end of a feast than the beginning of a fray' (Ray, 106; *ODEP*, 52).

30.18–19 Punchinello a variation of *Pulcinello*, the character in the Commedia dell' Arte who arrived in England *c.* 1650, where he became Punch, the clown of the Punch and Judy duo in the popular puppet show. The name was given, as here, to the puppet-showman.

30.23–24 English pock-pudding swine a Scot's abuse of the English which ridiculed their fondness for savoury pudding, especially *poke-pudding* (pudding made in a bag), and pork. This is the first of several references in *Nigel* to the Scots' disdain for pork. A similar reference occurs in *Waverley*, where the absence of pork from Fergus's otherwise lavish banquet table is observed for English readers. Scott's note in the Magnum edition of the earlier novel (1.219) mentions that James 'carried this prejudice to England, and is known to have abhorred pork almost as much as he did tobacco'. Both here and in the Magnum note to *Nigel* (27.176) Scott alludes to Ben Jonson's reference to James in *The Gypsies Metamorphos'd* (performed 1621, published 1640), lines 279–80: 'you should by this line / Loue a horse and a hound, but no part of a swine'.

30.26 you must take patience common variation on 'you must have patience': it is to be found in the old poetry and drama, including Ben Jonson's.

30.32 The more mischief the better sport proverbial: *ODEP*, 534.

30.43 at the nearest i.e. close at hand.

31.21 deposition of any extravasated blood deposit of blood outside the blood vessel.

31.26 the bottle-holders the seconds or supporters who wait on the pugilists at prize fights.

31.37–38 Sleep ... febrifuge Galen (see note to 28.9) has very many references to the benefits of sleep: see 'somnus' in the index to *Clavdii Galieni Opera Omnia*, ed. C. G. Kühn, 19 vols (Leipzig, 1821–30: the index was published 1965 at Hildesheim as Vol. 20).

31.41–42 Dr Irving for Irving, see Historical Note, 530.

31.43 the Samaritan's duty the duty of charity to a stranger as modelled in the parable of the Good Samaritan: Luke 10.30–37.

32.1 it is at your pleasure to you may if you wish.

32.22 Esculapius the Classical god of medicine.

32.23 Mr Raredrench Scott finishes off his satiric portrait with a name that mocks the ignorant apothecary's skill in preparing medicinal potions or 'drenches'.

32.27 too tender to undergo much handling compare: 'The tenderness of it [my coat], I do confess,/ Somewhat denies a grappling': William Cartwright, *The Ordinary* (performed 1634–35, published 1651), 3.5.88–89 (*ABD*, 3.163).

32.32–33 like the virtue of charity ... imperfections see 1 Peter 4.8: 'charity shall cover the multitude of sins'.

32.41–42 a stranger and a sojourner see Psalm 39.12.

33.14–15 the black ox ... foot yet *proverbial* misfortune has not yet come to you: Ray, 205; *ODEP*, 64.

33.24 pride and poverty compare 'this barbarous *Caledonian* breed;/ Whose Pride and Poverty has made each Slave/ Grow bold and desperate': Thomas Brown, 'The Highlander, a Satire', lines 76–78, in *The Works of Mr. Thomas Brown*, 4 vols (London, 1715), 1.128.

33.25 tablets hinged notebooks for memoranda, small enough to be kept in the pocket.

33.30 Jockey see note to 33.42.

33.34 in a sort in a way.

33.36 An ancient coat ... play says the *ancient coat* is a coat of arms; the play is *The Merry Wives of Windsor*, 1.1.16–30. Like Shakespeare, Scott plays with the literal and figurative sense of 'old/ ancient coat', Richie's old cloak having fallen apart when roughly handled by the apprentices.

33.42 Jockey ... John *Jockey* is, as the text explains, a popular term for disparaging a Scotsman; *John* is a similar term for an Englishman, as in 'John Bull'.

34.1 Sawney a variation of 'Saunders', from Alexander, an English nickname for a Scotsman, especially a young one.

34.2 Richie Moniplies for Moniplies, see Historical Note, 528–29. The most pertinent meaning of the Scots surname is 'the third stomach of a ruminant'.

34.3 Castle Collop ... the West Port Castle Collop was 'an old ruined tenement near the West Port', the Port being the west gate of Edinburgh opening directly onto the Grassmarket, where Richie's father slaughtered and sold meat: John Parker Lawson, *Scotland: Picturesque; Historical; Descriptive* (London, [1860]), 390n (Corson notes). A *collop* is a slice of meat for frying or broiling.

34.9–13 yonder brick arches at Whitehall ... Holbein gateway of alternating light and dark brick designed by the painter Hans Holbein (1497–1543) for Henry VIII after the latter appropriated Whitehall, palace of the archbishops of York (see note to 65.27–29). The arches were demolished in 1749–50 when the road was widened.

34.20 Water-of-Leith small river which in the period was N of Edinburgh and ran NW into the Firth of Forth at Leith.

34.20 the Nor-loch area of stagnant water immediately below Edinburgh Castle to the N. It was drained 1759–1816, and the area is now within Princes St Gardens.

34.21 Pow-burn ... Gusedub *respectively* a stream in the Morningside and Grange areas; a flooded depression NE of the Calton Hill (although in the 16th century there were also flooded Quarry-holes where the extension to the Royal Museum of Scotland in Chambers St now stands); and a pond near the Meadows drained in 1715.

34.28–29 cry her down disparage her.

34.36 North Briton a native of Scotland.

34.40 uphold him for maintain him to be.

34.42—35.1 an Earl of Warwick ... boars Guy of Warwick was the eponymous hero of a popular medieval romance, who according to 'The Legend of Sir Guy' in *Reliques of Ancient English Poetry*, [ed. Thomas Percy,] 3 vols (London, 1765), 3.103–11, slew both 'A bore' and 'the Dun-cow of Dunsmore heath' (lines 90, 99): see *CLA*, 172.

35.4 Go to! *exclamation* come, come; you don't say.

35.5 take care of be careful of.

35.6 deacon of his craft in Scotland, the president of an incorporated trade, or (more generally) the master of a craft.

35.10 Luckie Want i.e. Dame Want, a personification of poverty.

35.10–11 rest us patient compare 'In this poor Coate to rest me patient' from the anonymous Elizabethan verse play *The Weakest Goeth to the Wall* (1600), line 1617.

35.12–13 hay ... Grass-market because of the decline in commerce since James's removal to London, grass grows round the market cross on the High Street, and leeks in the Grassmarket.

35.23 Barford's Park Bearford's or Barefoots Parks, an area between the old North Loch and the present Rose Street (on which the New Town was begun in 1767).

35.23 the fit of the Vennel the foot of the steep street of this name on the S side of the Grassmarket.

35.25 behoved ... to *ironic* had to.

35.39–40 agreeable to this direction i.e. in accord with the address Heriot provides.

35.41 wait upon pay a respectful visit to.

36.2 two masters Richie echoes the injunction against serving two masters in Matthew 6.24 and Luke 16.13.

36.4 coming off from coming away from; leaving.

36.5 black-ward tenure *Scots law* the condition of being a subtenant of a feudal tenant or vassal.

36.11 present pinch a temporary financial need.

36.15–16 it's ill getting at it it is difficult to get access to.

36.29 a bit dover a bit of a swoon; a short swoon.

36.32 pit up lodge.

36.35–36 the wynd ... right anent the mickle kirk the narrow street or alley, very near the great church (i.e. St Paul's Cathedral), that leads to the river, accessed by Paul's Wharf (see note to 39.29).

37.10   a hair the less   at all the less.

37.18   his bit bookie   his little tablet or small book.

37.19   contented his politeness . . . hat   satisfied the requirements of good manners by doffing his hat to him.

37.33   in cuerpo, as the Don says   the Spanish expression means 'naked' or 'in breeches and doublet without a cloak'. It was popular with the Jacobean dramatists: see e.g. multiple uses in Ben Jonson's *The New Inne* (performed 1629, published 1631) and John Fletcher's *Loves Pilgrimage* (performed 1616?, published 1647). A *don* is a Spanish lord or gentleman.

37.37–38.1   as the sun . . . or very nearly   the clock referred to has figures of the sun and moon, which travel around a 'dial plate'. The moon wheel takes 50 minutes and 30 seconds longer than the sun wheel because the moon is late by that amount of time each night. The wheel that drives both the moon wheel and the sun wheel has 54 teeth; the sun wheel has 57 teeth and the moon wheel 59. The gear ratios are to each other as 1: 1.035071, while the ratio of 1440 minutes (a solar day) to 1490.5 (a lunar day) is 1: 1.035069, 'very nearly' the same as Heriot observes. The 'seventh heaven' is ecstasy or paradise, being both in Judaism and in Islam the highest heaven of all, the abode of God and of the highest class of angels.

38.7   four-hour's nuncheon   a light repast taken around 4 p.m. Compare 'Syne on my Four-hours Luntion chew'd my Cude': 'Epistle from Mr. William Starrat [to Ramsay]', line 9 (*The Works of Allan Ramsay*, Vol. 2, ed. Burns Martin and John W. Oliver (Edinburgh and London, 1953), [70]).

38.17   cottoned in with   fraternised with.

38.22   but half-bred Scot neither   only a half-bred Scot.

38.31   Christ-Church   Christ's Hospital: see note to 21.39–40.

38.32–33   his voice . . . a little tongue   compare 'For she had a tongue with a tang': *The Tempest*, 2.2.48.

38.34   the last toll of Dunstan's   see note to 27.15–16.

38.35   shot of my indentures   free of the bonds that tie me as an apprentice to my master for a fixed period of service (usually 7 years).

38.39   Off . . . bucking basket   i.e. carry the laundress off in her own dirty-clothes basket. So in *The Merry Wives of Windsor*, 3.3.134–61, Falstaff is carried off in a buck- or wash-basket by Mrs Ford's servants even as Mr Ford searches the room for him.

38.40   blind buzzard   as opposed to the sharp-eyed eagle: *buzzard* is slang for an ignorant or stupid person.

39.3–4   till they were out of their time   till after their apprenticeship was terminated.

39.7   carry two faces under the same hood   be two-faced or duplicitous.

39.12–13   all the Counts . . . cut my comb   Jenkin proclaims that he will not be bested in the cock-fight for Margaret's hand by men of higher class, including the aristocrats of Tunstall's region with whom the apprentice boasts a connection. The phrase 'cut my comb' is proverbial (see *ODEP*, 164), and is associated with gelding: see Thomas Middleton and Thomas Dekker, *The Roaring Girl* (performed 1608, published 1611), 1.2.214; ed. Andor Gomme (London, 1976), 24n.

39.19–22   motto   see Ben Jonson, *Every Man In His Humour* (performed 1598, published 1601, revised 1616), 1.5.32–35.

39.29   Paul's Wharf   a free landing place with stairs allowing entrance through a gate to the City for those travelling by barge with business in the vicinity of St Paul's Cathedral.

39.31   the great fire in 1666   the fire of 2–6 September that destroyed four-fifths of London, 89 churches including the old gothic St Paul's, and 13,000 dwellings.

39.33–34 the plague... Constantinople outbreaks of bubonic plague during James's reign were particularly virulent in 1603 and 1609, and again in 1624–25. Scott's idea of plague lurking in Constantinople 'in our own time' may have derived from Charles McLean, M. D., whose *Results of an Investigation, respecting Epidemic and Pestilential Diseases; including Researches in the Levant, concerning the Plague*, 2 vols (London, 1817–18), studied the outbreak of plague there in 1815 (2.56–236).

40.2 the Long Town nickname of Kirkcaldy that, until 1930 when it became even longer with the incorporation of Dysart, stretched 6 km along the N side of the Firth of Forth.

40.19–20 tobacco... into use according to popular belief, tobacco had been introduced to the English by Sir Walter Raleigh from his Virginia colony. King James's pamphlet *A Counterblaste to Tobacco* (1604) attempted, unsuccessfully, to check its growing popularity in his reign. According to Barnabe Rich (*The Honestie of This Age* (London, 1615), 26), over 7000 houses 'in London and neere about' depended on tobacco for their profits—£319,375 'a yeare, *Summa totalis*, All spent in smoake' (not counting that spent in taverns, inns, and alehouses). The three most lucrative businesses to be recommended to a young entrepreneur were, in fact, the alehouse, the tobacco shop, and the brothel (28).

40.20–21 Geneva and strong waters gin, made from distilled grain and flavoured with the juice of juniper berries; and other alcoholic spirits.

41.2 takes him up turns its attention to him again.

41.5 the court at Westminster the old medieval palace in the royal borough of Westminster was the scene of official and legal business of the kingdom, and James spent much of his time when in London at Whitehall Palace nearby.

41.11–12 cold powdered beef... carrot compare lines 53–54 of the ballad 'Old Tom of Bedlam': 'The man in the moone drinkes clarret,/ Eates powder'd beef, turnip, and carret' (*Reliques of Ancient English Poetry*, [ed. Thomas Percy], 2nd edn, 3 vols (London, 1767), 2.351): see *CLA*, 172.

41.12–13 mustard... Tewkesbury mustard made in this Gloucestershire town was noted for its thickness. See *2 Henry IV*, 2.4.224–25: 'his wit's as thick as Tewksbury mustard'.

41.22 what the good year *exclamation* what the deuce.

41.22–25 down to Scotland... up from the North just as to leave London for any other part of Great Britain was a descent, so to come there was an ascent.

41.26 Saint Barnaby was ten years i.e. on St Barnaby's Day, 11 June, ten years ago.

41.27 a bare-headed girl i.e. she was unmarried. Wearing a cap indicated that a woman was married.

41.37 I warrant your honour... like it Dame Nelly strongly believes that Nigel will return to Scotland if he wishes to do so.

41.41–42 the great Turkey merchant's widow i.e. the widow of a very wealthy merchant, whose trade was with Turkey, at this time a symbol of the riches of the orient. Chamberlain (2.271) notes the arrival in 1619 of 'a ship out of Turkie valued at more then any we have had yet out of the Indies'.

41.42 Sir Awley Macauley the name is that of a miscellaneous writer of Scott's time, the Rev. Aulay Macaulay (1758–1819). (Corson notes)

42.1–2 married at May-fair... hard name in the 18th century, a chapel in Curzon Street, Mayfair, run by a Scottish Episcopal clergyman Dr George Keith, was notorious for the celebration of clandestine marriages, leading in 1753 to an Act of Parliament forbidding them. Over a period of 20 years Keith and other clergy performed some 7000 weddings, and 61 marriages were performed the day before the act became effective: see Walter Thornbury, *Old and New London*, 6 vols (London, [n. d.]), 4.347–49. Behind Dame Nelly's good-natured jibe at Scots names may be John Milton's harsh way with them in the sonnets 'On the New Forcers of Conscience Under the Long Parliament' and 'A Book was writ of late called Tetrachordon'.

42.6   stand for   defend; take the part of.

42.11   At a word   in a word; in short.

42.24–27   Tower-ditch ... Islington ... Saint Clement's in the Strand Dame Nelly moves in a sweeping arc from E to W as she argues for the safety of Richie in London: Tower-ditch is the moat built *c.* 1190 to further fortify the Tower of London (it could be filled with water from the Thames at high tide); Islington is the suburban area to the N, at the time largely fields; and the Strand is the road running W along the Thames that carried traffic to and from the City and the Court at Westminster. The medieval church of St Clement Danes was destroyed in the Fire of London (1666) and rebuilt by Christopher Wren.

42.41   the groaning cheese   in a Magnum note to *Guy Mannering* (3.29), Scott refers to the 'groaning malt', ale brewed to be drunk after the pains of labour were over, and an accompanying 'large and rich cheese' for the refreshment of the women in attendance at the birth.

43.27   out upon you   an expression of horror, abhorrence, dismay, etc.

43.31–32   this good gentleman ... Greenwich   i.e. James travels as often to Greenwich as did Elizabeth, who was born in the palace there and is said to have preferred it to her other residences.

43.33   maintains ... John Taylor the water-poet   a waterman by profession who maintained a barge for hire, the ever self-promoting Taylor (1580–1653) was popular with the Court. He was commissioned by the King to arrange the water pageant for the wedding in 1613 of the Princess Elizabeth.

43.34   a sculler and a pair of oars   *respectively* a boat propelled by a single oar over the stern, and a boat with two oarsmen.

43.34–35   a comely Court at Whitehall   see note to 41.5.

43.37   in specialty   in particular.

43.40   of courtesy   kindly.

44.1   well to pass in the world   well off; well to do.

44.2–3   the sitting alderman   the alderman on duty.

44.28   the deil a thing's   *emphatic* not a thing is.

44.34   Temple Port   Ramsay's Scots term for Temple Bar.

44.36   wold I nold I   willy-nilly; whether I would or no.

44.39–40   The twa iron carles ... sax o' the clock   see note to 27.15–16.

44.42   every why has its wherefore   proverbial: Ray, 272; *ODEP*, 886.

45.2   sent me wrang   misdirected me.

45.4   at the lang run   at the end.

45.16   Saint Cuthbert's kirk-yard   St Cuthbert's church and churchyard are situated below Edinburgh Castle, on the NW.

45.22   de'il haet else   *emphatic* nothing else; nobody else.

45.27   night-walking queans and billies   prostitutes and their clients or associates.

45.28–29   Andrew Ferrara   also 'Andrea Ferrara': high-quality Scottish broad-sword named after the late 16th-century N Italian swordsmith. 'His name became a mark of quality for Scotsmen in the seventeenth and eighteenth centuries, and many Scots swords bear his name, but it is doubted whether any of them are in fact his work' (*Waverley*, ed. Claire Lamont (Oxford, 1981), 452).

45.32   Mile-End   the victim of a practical joke, Richie had left the City by Aldgate and walked E along Whitechapel Road to Mile End, each step taking him farther from his destination, Paul's Wharf.

45.41 behuved to would have to.

46.8–9 king's cauff... ither folk's corn proverbial: Ray, 298; *ODEP*, 427. The Scots word *cauff* means 'chaff'.

46.13 mend his pace walk faster.

46.23 having to do taking a role; intervening.

46.39–40 reason good with good reason.

46.42 Blackheath an open area S of Greenwich.

46.43 quarries the intestines cut from slain animals, especially deer, and wrapped in skin, to be fed to the hounds or hawks: see note to 304.29.

47.2 silver gilded Scott may have derived the episode of Richie's blunder with the supplication from Sir John Harington's *Nugæ Antiquæ*: he owned the 1804 version of this work, whose title means 'Old Trifles' (2 vols, London), ed. Thomas Park (*CLA*, 190). Harington (1561–1612) records Sir Arthur Brett's similar mishap in Waltham forest: in explanation of why he had denied the petition, King James replied, 'Shall a King give heed to a dirty paper, when a beggar noteth not his gilt stirrops?' (1.393).

47.3 his hunting-suit of green in Osborne's description of James at the next progress after his inauguration he was dressed in colours 'as greene as the grasse he trod on, with a fether in his cap, and a horne instead of a sword by his side' (1.195–96). That the green refers to a hunting suit derives from a print in [George Turbervile,] *The Noble Art of Venerie or Hunting* (London, 1611), which Scott included in the *Secret History* (the frontispiece to the first volume) and to which his note to Osborne's description refers.

47.5–8 But, my certie... hanches Scott tells this story in the *Minstrelsy of the Scottish Border* (1802–03: ed. T. F. Henderson, 4 vols (Edinburgh, 1902), 1.106n), where he gives the source as *The Diarey of Robert Birrel*, in *Fragments of Scotish History*, ed. [Sir John Graham Dalyell] (Edinburgh, 1798), 30–31: *CLA*, 4. Francis Stewart Hepburn (1563–1612), 5th Earl of Bothwell from 1576, was James's cousin. He acquired the epithet 'wild' from his several unsuccessful attempts to capture and dethrone James. The episode alluded to here occurred in 1593 at Holyrood House, in Edinburgh. The phrase *my certie* means 'goodness me!'.

47.12 Sifflication Richie's pronunciation of 'supplication'.

47.19–20 that sits... saddle for all his love of hunting, James was a poor rider, his seat on horseback said here to be no better than that of a sack of refuse from malt after distilling. In the catalogue of blessings on James and his senses in Ben Jonson's *The Gypsies Metamorphos'd* (performed 1621, published 1640), lines 1383–85, he is to be protected 'from all offences/ In his sporte', including 'From a fall'. Despite a special saddle intended to prevent spills, references to his falling from his horse are common. Roger Coke, citing his father as witness, credits James's spills as much to his drinking as to a poor seat: he was accompanied while hunting by an officer whose duty was to keep the King's cup filled (*A Detection of the Court and State of England During the Last Four Reigns and the Inter-Regnum* (London, 1697), 71).

47.23–24 cried Treason... forfeit for the so-called Gowrie Conspiracy, see Historical Note, 524–25. Richie's 'as small a forfeit' (i.e. as small a transgression) puts him in the camp of those who were sceptical of the conspiracy theory. Even years afterward, James cried 'Treason!' when viewing the Culross coal works, thinking the sudden flooding of the mines by the full tide a plot to kill him: Robert Forsyth, *The Beauties of Scotland*, 5 vols (Edinburgh, 1805–08), 4.293.

47.25–26 to the porter's lodge... my back in great houses menials were punished in the porter's lodge, which functioned as a kind of prison.

47.31 Proclamation James was given to proclamations intended to regulate the behaviour of his subjects, including his fellow Scots who through-out his reign continued to come up to London (proclamations forbidding them to do so and threatening to fine those who transported them notwithstanding) with their importunate suits to the crown. Nigel subsequently echoes some of the harsh language of these documents, in particular the 'Proclamatioun anent the Repairing of Persons to Courte', in answer to Richie's query about the contents of the copy he brings from Whitehall: see Osborne, 1.143–44. In editing *Somers' Tracts* Scott noted that 'King James was particularly fond of issuing proclamations, to which he in vain laboured to attach the sanctity of laws' (2.474n).

47.31–32 go down to the North by the next light collier i.e. return to Scotland by the next coal boat. A light collier would be one returning to Newcastle, having unloaded its cargo.

47.35 in your matter about your business.

47.41 bringing guts to a bear alluding to the proverbial 'Not worthy to carry guts to a bear' (Ray, 217; *ODEP*, 104).

47.43 a whin a few; several.

48.4 after meat mustard proverbial: Ray, 300; *ODEP*, 6.

48.6 sifflicate wha like supplicate who please; let those supplicate who wish to do so.

48.18 behoved to *ironic* had to.

48.19 Portugal piece *either* a silver coin worth 8 reals and sometimes called a piece of eight: the equivalent of some 4s. 6d. (22.5p), *or* a gold moidore worth some £1 7s. (£1.35).

48.19 my certie goodness me!

48.30–31 meet at Paul's the old cathedral, and its central aisle in particular, known as 'Paul's Walk', was at this period the principal rendezvous for the courtiers and gallants of Westminster, who gathered there in late morning and again after dinner to gossip, talk politics, and conduct such personal business as Nigel mentions: see Osborne, 1.209.

48.31 the Court of Requests the (location of the) Court of Equity, which had been formally set up in the reign of Henry VIII for relief of persons addressing the King by supplication. It met in the White Hall on the second floor of Westminster Hall, a larger space than either house of parliament. Later it met in a smaller adjoining room, and, after it had vacated the premises (by 1669), that room was used as a public social meeting place: 'One Theatre there is of vast resort,/ Which whilome of Requests was call'd the Court' (John Dryden, 'Prologue to [Nathaniel Lee's] *Caesar Borgia*' (1679), lines 22–23).

48.32 steeking the stable door ... stolen proverbial: Ray 159, 302; *ODEP*, 730 (*steek* is Scots for 'shut').

48.33 put him on another pin divert his mind to another train of thought.

48.35 spell at study.

48.36–39 the grand blazon ... side of it the coat of arms at the top of the paper reflects the union of the two crowns on James's accession to the throne, the red dragon of Henry VIII which supported Elizabeth's coat of arms on the left or sinister side being replaced by the Scottish unicorn, but her English lion supporting the right or dexter side being retained, much to Richie's evident displeasure.

48.42 the pouring of ardent spirits upon a recent wound i.e. the intense stinging caused by pouring alcohol on a raw wound to sterilise it.

48.43 What deil's what the devil's.

49.9–10 the Lords of the Council the members of the Privy Council, the chief advisory body to the monarch.

49.25–27 old proverb ... grace proverbial: see *The Heart of Mid-*

Lothian, ed. David Hewitt and Alison Lumsden, EEWN 6, 225.16; *ODEP*, 427. There are variants in Allan Ramsay, *A Collection of Scots Proverbs* (1737), in *The Works of Allan Ramsay*, 6 vols, Vol. 5, ed. Alexander M. Kinghorn and Alexander Law (Edinburgh and London: Scottish Text Society, 1972), 127, and Scott's *Minstrelsy of the Scottish Border*, 4 vols, ed. T. F. Henderson (Edinburgh, 1902), 1.356.

49.34 has neighbours is not alone.

49.35–36 shift off ... does compare Rosalind's account in *As You Like It*, 3.2.374–86, of the one suitor she succeeded in discouraging through capriciousness: 'boys and women are for the most part cattle of this colour'. *Shift off* means 'get rid of'.

50.6–10 motto not traced: probably by Scott. For the 'rustic proverb' see *ODEP*, 153. For the significance of the headgear see note to 29.36–38.

51.19–20 new-invented plots ... of late a broadsheet dating from 1602 including a plot summary of *England's Joy*, functioning as a playbill, is described in E. K. Chambers, *The Elizabethan Stage*, 4 vols (Oxford, 1923), 3.500–03.

51.23–24 A New Way to Pay Old Debts play by Philip Massinger (1583–1640): performed *c*. 1625, published 1633.

52.13–15 Had not my father ... himself see Historical Note, 529.

52.29–30 in right of by virtue of.

52.40 in very deed in fact; in reality.

52.42 my mind runs strangely ... mistake i.e. unaccountably, his mind detects a flaw in the information given him.

53.19 you write yourself in that band you acknowledge yourself a member of that company.

53.22–23 come away with get on with.

53.31 Nor-Loch see note to 34.20.

53.39 more plies than one more folds (i.e. tricks) than one. A play on Richie's surname.

54.4 wee bit small.

54.13 stand your friend act the part of a friend.

54.15–16 her Majesty the King's maist gracious mother ... Castle Mary Queen of Scots when she resided in Edinburgh Castle: see Historical Note, note 42 (537–38).

54.17 forth of at the expense of.

54.22 John Knox (1505–72), the Scottish reformer and inveterate critic of Mary, Queen of Scots 1542–67. His name was a by-word for fearless speech or 'truth' in the cause of establishing Protestantism in Scotland and organising the Presbyterian Church there.

54.28 nowte's feet calves' feet, used as a source of gelatine.

54.29–30 for the privy chalmer ... hir grace Richie's reference to an intimate supper hints at adultery and conspiracy, for Bothwell murdered Mary's husband Henry Darnley on 9/10 February 1567. The Queen's opponents were quick to accuse her of complicity.

55.3–4 be bail for his bones be security for his body, i.e. spare Richie the beating Nigel threatens him with.

55.11 be doing go ahead and do it.

55.12 stand by afford; become liable to.

55.36 wise behind the hand *proverbial* wise after the event; wise too late: Ray, 282 (a '*Scottish* man is ay wise behind the hand'); compare *ODEP*, 899.

56.2 hold bias with incline towards, a metaphor derived from the game of bowls.

56.18 favourite as used here a person regarded with peculiar favour by a monarch and thus arousing strong feelings on the part of others less privileged. In the 16th and 17th centuries 'the favourite impinged on the consciousness of

Europeans forcefully enough to create its own terminology' (*The World of the Favourite*, ed. J. H. Elliott and L. W. B. Brockliss (New Haven and London, 1999), 2). For a full list of James's favourites, see Peyton, 2.352–64.

56.38–39 Peregrine Peterson ... Campvere Peterson is fictitious, but the conservator was an officer appointed to protect the rights and settle the disputes of Scottish merchants in foreign ports, here the Dutch seaport Campvere on the island of Walcheren. Sir Robert Denniston held the office from 1589 until 1625 when Patrick Drummond succeeded him. Under Scots law Campvere, or Veere, was a staple, i.e. a seaport through which all Scottish exports were directed, from 1506 to 1799.

57.10 lordship not the peerage, but lands erected into a 'Lordship of Regality', involving extensive legal powers for the grantee.

57.24 cold deeds and fair words compare the proverb 'Fair words and foul deeds cheat wise men as well as fools': *ODEP*, 240.

57.33 Under your favour pardon me.

57.42 Leave me alone for that i.e. I'll take care of it. The expression is much used in the old drama.

57.42–43 on the bow-hand on the side of the hand that holds the bow as opposed to the side of the hand that holds the arrow—i.e. on the opposite side.

58.17 bring out express.

58.19 Lombard street named after the Italian merchants of Lombardy, the chief bankers of the Middle Ages, Lombard Street, in an area replete with 'banking-houses of the greatest eminence, insurance-offices, and other equally-respectable mercantile houses', became 'perhaps one of the richest in Europe' (Malcolm, 4.429).

58.20 white broth a rich soup of white chicken and ground almond, among other ingredients, prepared over several days.

58.37 to be at interest to be repaid with interest.

59.20–21 within the toll of Paul's within the sound of the bell of St Paul's Cathedral.

59.21–23 were I to grant quittance ... actual tale i.e. were he to release the money to Nigel or to accept the acknowledgement of the loan Nigel has agreed to sign without first counting out the cash.

59.23 body of me *oath* my body.

59.24 Westward Hoe the cry of London watermen soliciting passengers travelling to the west.

59.25–26 such gold-finches chirping about one *goldfinch* was slang for a gold coin.

59.28 Sir Faithful Frugal's an imaginary person.

59.34–35 honest John Bunyan's phrase—'therewithal ... eyes' see *The Pilgrim's Progress* (1678–84), ed. James Blanton Wharey, rev. Roger Sharrock (Oxford, 1960), 143.

59.35–38 the loss of two children ... in Auld Reekie for Heriot's biography see Historical Note, 526–27. *Auld Reekie*, meaning 'Old Smoky', was a popular nickname for Edinburgh.

60.2 Deptford W of Greenwich, Deptford was the site of the Royal Naval Dockyard 1573–1869.

60.7–8 Make my remembrances convey my kind regards.

60.19 the Parliament of Scotland the parliaments of England and Scotland, despite James's efforts, were not united until 1707.

60.30–31 The proverb says, 'House ... gad' proverbial, but *ODEP*, 389, cites only this occurrence.

60.32 God give ye good-morrow goodbye to you.

60.36 Marry guep of your advice marry [by Mary] go up: an expression of contempt for Heriot's advice. Compare 'marry go up', which occurs frequently in Shakespeare. 'Marry guep' is found in *Hudibras*, 1.3.202.

60.40   three blue-coats   three servants, so identified from the colour of their coat (blue being a cheap and stable dye): 'At the commencement of the seventeenth century, and probably long before that period, *blue coats* were common badges of servitude; and they are frequently alluded to as such in the early plays' (Joseph Strutt, *A Complete View of the Dress and Habits of the People of England*, 2 vols (London, 1796–99), 2.302): *CLA*, 154.

61.2–12   motto   not identified: probably by Scott. The first line approximates the title of the poem by John Skelton (1460?–1529) 'Why Come Ye Nat To Courte?'

61.18   a man of worship   a person of repute and standing.

61.24   gave an eye to   looked after.

61.25   the state of the police of the metropolis   at this period the constables were either unable or unwilling to protect the people of London from such crime as Scott describes, though from his experience in Paris Howell appreciated the relative safety of London (39–40).

62.10   Theobald's   the Hertfordshire estate, 19 km N of central London, with a palace built by Queen Elizabeth's minister William Cecil, Lord Burleigh (1520–98), which James first visited on his journey from Scotland to London to ascend the throne. James so coveted it that in 1607 he traded the nearby royal residence of Hatfield for it. He died there on 27 March 1625. Theobalds was mostly destroyed by order of Parliament in 1651; every vestige of it was removed in 1765.

62.10–11   the Duke of Buckingham   see Historical Note, 527–28.

62.11   the Spanish house to satisfy for the ingots   i.e. Heriot purchased the gold which Ramsay required for the clocks from a Spanish gold merchant.

62.32   Humanity classes   in the Scottish universities, classes in the study of Latin language and literature.

62.34–35   Dot-and-carry-one   teacher of elementary arithmetic. Derived from the schoolchild's expression for how to proceed in certain arithmetic processes, e.g. long division.

62.41   comes to his own   comes into his inheritance.

63.4–5   a sheep's head … our saying   the saying has not been located elsewhere.

63.8–9   Sir Mungo Malagrowther   see Historical Note, 528.

63.9   bide tryste   keep your appointment.

63.13   Scots Janet   Janet is a generic name for a female servant in Scotland.

63.31–32   these wild youngsters … ever   law students were repeatedly involved in disturbances which injured people and damaged property, particularly on holidays. Such behaviour was traditional, according to Walter Thornbury, who mentions prolonged frays between the law students and the citizens of Fleet Street in the mid-15th century (*Old and New London*, 6 vols (London, [n. d.]), 1.32).

63.41–42   tear up the very stones of the pavement   similar behaviour is attributed to apprentices in *Henry VIII*, 5.4.52–53: 'suddenly a file of boys behind 'em [apprentices wielding clubs], loose shot, deliver'd such a show'r of pebbles'.

63.43   There spoke a London 'prentice bold   compare Moses Mendez, 'Spring', in *The Seasons. In Imitation of Spenser* (Dublin, 1753), page 8 (lines 60–61): 'And if, to honour *Britain* he be led, / He sings a 'Prentice bold, in Londs profane'.

64.1   crush a cup of wine   *Romeo and Juliet*, 1.2.80 (*crush* means 'drink').

64.8   Temple Gate   Middle Temple Gate, on Fleet Street a few metres E of Temple Bar, was rebuilt in the reign of Henry VIII (and again in 1684).

Inner Temple Gate, erected in the 5th year of the reign of James I, is a little further on.

64.12 slouched hat hat with a broad brim hanging down over the face.

64.19–20 a learned man ... one quill according to Scott's Magnum note (26.91), the 'learned man' was 'Gill'. He was probably Alexander Gill (1565–1635), the high-master of St Paul's School 1608–35, who claimed to have written a biblical commentary of several hundred printed quarto pages with a single pen and still had some quill left.

64.34–37 the Temple-Bar ... chains '*Temple Bar*, is the Place where the Freedom of the City of *London*, and the Liberty of the City of *Westminster* doth part: Which Separation was antiently only Posts, Rails, and a Chain ... Afterwards [by the mid-14th century] there was a House of Timber erected cross the Street, with a narrow Gate-way, and an Entry on the South side of it, under the House' (Stow, 3.278). The timber edifice would have been present at the time of the novel. In 1670–72 it was replaced by a majestic gateway designed by Sir Christopher Wren. This in turn was removed in 1878, re-erected at Theobalds (see note to 62.10) in 1888, and moved from there to Paternoster Square, beside St Paul's Cathedral, in 2004.

65.3–4 Saint Martin's Lane running northward from the extreme W end of the Strand, at the beginning of James's reign this was a green country lane except for the church and a few surrounding houses at the southern end.

65.4–5 Covent-Garden was still a garden Covent Garden, London's first building estate in the form of a square, was developed in 1630–33 by the Earl of Bedford on land that had been the garden of Westminster Abbey's convent.

65.13 Charing Cross the junction of the Strand and Whitehall, where there was a cross built by King Edward I to mark the last of the resting places for the body of Queen Eleanor as it was transported from Harby, Nottinghamshire, to Westminster for burial in 1290. The cross erected in 1291–94 was destroyed in 1647.

65.14–15 the judges ... Westminster Hall residents of the Temple, the judges for the chief law court of England performed their duties, from 1224 to 1882, in the Hall of the medieval Old Palace of Westminster built by William Rufus in 1097.

65.16–17 Johnson's expression ... population Johnson's words were: 'Why, Sir, Fleet-street has a very animated appearance; but I think the full tide of human existence is at Charing-cross' (Boswell: 2 April 1775).

65.23–24 the confusion attending improvement the new Banqueting House was built 1619–22. It replaced a hall erected in 1607 which had burned down.

65.25–26 from the window ... a scaffold before it Charles I, the second son of James and Anne, was executed in Whitehall in 1649. (Prince Henry, the heir to the throne, had died in 1612.)

65.27–29 the ancient and ruinous buildings ... genius the original mansion was built in the 13th century by Hubert De Burgh, Lord Chief Justice under King John and Henry III, from whom it passed to the Dominicans in Holborn, who maintained possession until the Dissolution of the Monasteries, when it was sold to the Archbishop of York and became known as York House. When Henry VIII appropriated it after the fall of Wolsey, he renamed it Whitehall (see *Henry VIII*, 4.1.94–97). Inigo Jones (1573–1652), architect par excellence at this time, was retained for this improvement, but only the Banqueting House was constructed, and the rest of the Palace was almost entirely destroyed by fire in 1698.

66.9–10 with as much precaution ... paved with eggs proverbial: *ODEP*, 218.

66.13 Maxwell James's Scottish usher: see Historical Note, 528.

66.19 cabinet pictures pictures of a size and subject appropriate for this private, intimate room as opposed to large-scale canvases that might ornament the rooms of state.

66.22–27 huge folios, amongst which lay ... of Europe Scott summarises the varied forms and subjects of James's writing as well as implying the disorder that characterised his statecraft. The notes on long orations might include those given to Parliament in 1604 and 1607 on the union of the Scottish and English crowns; chief among the essays on king-craft would be the *Basilicon Doron* (Greek for 'Royal Gift'), the guide on kingship which he wrote in 1599 for his elder son Prince Henry (1594–1612). James published two volumes of poems: *The Essayes of A Prentise, in the Divine Art of Poesie* (1584) and *His Maiesties Poeticall Exercises at Vacant Houres* [1591]. Several of these poems are included under the general and very flexible term 'ballatis', and one of the metrical forms advocated by James is known as 'Ballat Royal' (*The Poems of King James VI. of Scotland*, ed. James Craigie, 2 vols (Edinburgh and London, 1955, 1958), 1.83 and 80); but none of the poems is a 'roundel', which here probably means a short lyric with refrain.

66.27–28 a list of the names of the King's hounds such a list might read: 'Ringwood, Royster, Bowman, Jowler', as in line 51 of 'Old Tom of Bedlam' (in *Reliques of Ancient English Poetry*, [ed. Thomas Percy], 2nd edn, 3 vols (London, 1767), 2.351: see *CLA*, 172), for Jowler was the name of one of James's favourite hounds (Lodge, 3.245). A similar list, naming 'Roman and Joller, Ringwood and his mate', occurred in some doggerel verses 'found in the hand of Queen Elizabeth's effigy on her tomb in the Abbey' (Akrigg, 160).

66.29–30 quilted ... dagger-proof James's fear of assassination, stemming from his childhood and, especially, the Gowrie Conspiracy, bordered on obsession, which the murder of the French king Henri IV in 1610 only exacerbated.

66.35 carkanet of large balas rubies see note to 74.22–23.

67.23–24 the character bestowed on him by Sully ... Christendom Maximilien de Bethune, duc de Sully (1560–1641), chief minister for finance of Henri IV, was the first ambassador from France to James's Court. The saying is sometimes attributed to him by modern writers, sometimes to Henri. Scott's authority for the attribution to Sully has not been located. Weldon (2.10) says simply: 'a very wise man was wont to say, he beleeved him the wisest foole in Christendome, meaning him wise in small things, but a foole in weighty affaires'. Lee suggests (xi) that Weldon may himself have been the author.

67.31–33 sown those seeds ... civil war Scott alludes to the story of Cadmus, who slew a dragon and sowed its teeth in the earth, from which sprang up armed men who threatened him. He threw a stone in their midst, and they turned on each other, all except five being killed.

67.35–36 Jingling Geordie ... nick-names Heriot's nickname alludes to his profession or wealth and to his northern origin. Both the Duke of Buckingham and Prince Charles were also given nicknames: see notes to 67.43–68.1 and 68.9.

67.43—68.1 Steenie's service o' plate in a note to Peyton (2.452n), Scott explained James's nickname for the Duke of Buckingham (the Scots diminutive of Stephen) as deriving from his perceived resemblance to the beautiful young martyr Stephen the Apostle as described in Acts 6.15: 'And all that sat in the council, looking stedfastly on him, saw his face as it had been the face of an angel.' The service of plate is only one of many such splendid tokens of James's affection lavished on his favourite and his family.

68.8 the chucks 'A game, used by girls, in tossing up, and catching pebbles as they fall, is called the *Chuckie-stanes*' (John Jamieson, *An Etymological Dictionary of the Scottish Language*, 2 vols (Edinburgh, 1808): *CLA*, 266).

68.9 Babie Charles if appropriate to the third and last child of James and Anne to survive birth or infancy, this nickname (see *Secret History*, 1.459n) ill fits the stern and sombre young man Scott depicts in the novel.

68.23 the mark of the beast according to Protestant reading of Revelation 13.16–17, this would be the Pope and, by extension, the Roman Catholic Church.

68.25–27 I wrestled wi' Dagon ... Defender of the Faith Dagon, the god of the Philistines (see 1 Samuel 5.1–7), was appropriated by the Puritans for designating Roman Catholics. James alludes to his successful campaign in 1594–95 to rid Scotland of the Catholic party by vanquishing its leaders Huntly and Errol. Ironically, it was Henry VIII who, for defending Roman Catholicism, first bore the title 'Defender of the Faith', bestowed on him in 1521 by Pope Leo X: the designation has been adopted by all subsequent English and British sovereigns.

68.28–29 the Golden Ass of Apuleius in the 2nd-century Latin satirist's story, the ass is actually a metamorphosed young man named Lucian who, because he retains his human consciousness, suffers greatly from overburdening by his owners.

68.33 Saul of my body *oath* soul of my body.

68.35–36 the judgment of Solomon the story of King Solomon's judgment, his ingenious resolution of a maternity dispute, is told in 1 Kings Ch. 3. Called the British Solomon by flatterers such as Maxwell here, James, far from being modest about the comparison, sought to keep it current by frequent instancing, e.g. his timely sagacity in uncovering the Gunpowder Plot (see note to 212.43), and his shrewd detection of forgery in the Lady Lake Affair (see note to 368.30–31). In *Basilicon Doron* (see note to 66.22–27) James calls Solomon 'that great paterne of wisdome' (ed. James Craigie, 2 vols (Edinburgh, 1944), 1.35).

69.1–3 the famous Florentine ... France Cellini (1500–71), the most celebrated of the Italian renaissance artists in metals, numbered among his eminent patrons Francis I, King of France 1515–47, whose court he visited twice between 1537 and 1545.

69.6 out of the gate extraordinary.

69.7 a fighting fule see Francis Beaumont and John Fletcher, *The Maid's Tragedy* (performed 1611, published 1619), 3.2.323.

69.8 ta'en at Pavia ... Durham lang syne Francis I was defeated and imprisoned at Pavia in 1525; David II (1324–71), crowned King of Scots in 1331, was defeated at Neville's Cross near Durham in 1346 and imprisoned for 11 years.

69.10–11 other gate company another sort of company.

69.23–26 Gang to the de'il ... his een James's congenital fear of weapons in his vicinity distracts him from Heriot's aesthetic argument. When pocket pistols were imported from Spain in 1612, 'intended by the Papists to have made a Massacre' (Sir Foulk Grevill [but probably by Arthur Wilson], *The Five Years of King Iames* (London, 1643), 25), James forthwith issued a proclamation against them (*Somers' Tracts*, 2.279).

69.32–33 burrows-town (belonging to a) town which is a borough.

69.40 tell you down count out for you.

69.42 officers of my mouth catering officers: i.e. cook, butler, etc.

70.6 lying at the ordinary usage earning the usual interest.

70.8–9 another subsidy frae the Commons for James's dependence on subsidies from the House of Commons see note to 73.33. For his poverty, see Essay on the Text, 422.

70.11 Richmond Richmond upon Thames, 13 km W of Westminster, is the site of a royal palace built by Henry VII in 1499–1503. It was mostly demolished in 1649. Before Prince Henry's death in 1612, Richmond was associated with his circle and the youthful nobility of the realm.

70.14 the Southland England.

70.15 the wise naturally follow the wisest the sentiment is proverbial: Burton Stevenson, *The Macmillan Book of Proverbs, Maxims, and Famous Phrases* (New York, 1948), 2534:2.

70.22 the Devil's Sabbath-e'en the eve of an annual midnight orgy of demons, sorcerers, and witches, presided over by the Devil.

70.28–29 nae farther gane no longer ago.

70.41 pater patriæ *Latin* father of my country. James was fond of proclaiming this role. In *Somers' Tracts* Scott includes a tract extracted from *Basilicon Doron* (see note to 66.22–27) in justification of this paternal role: 'Kings are also compared to fathers of families: for a king is truely *parens patriæ*, the politique father of his people' (3.260). The paternal language and the specific phrase *Pater Patriæ* also occur in James's *The True Lawe of Free Monarchies* (1598): Craigie, 74.10.

70.43 Ud's death God's (i.e. Christ's) death! An example of James's predilection for swearing. In editing the *Secret History* Scott noted (2.382) that with his swearing James set the tone for the Cavaliers, who swore in order to distinguish themselves from the Puritans.

71.6 By my halidome *oath* by my holiness or sanctity.

71.10 the Vicegerent of Heaven James, by virtue of the Stewart claim of Divine Right, is the sole agent of God on earth and is responsible to God alone.

71.22 manual exercise musket drill.

71.23 had as lief that would have been as pleased if.

71.32 come back on returned to.

71.37 sed semel insanivimus omnes *Latin* but we have all been mad once. See Johannes Baptista Spagnolo (1448–1516, known as Mantuanus or Mantuan), *Eclogues*, 1.118.

72.1–2 the Ethnic poet...lacunar *Latin* 'there is no [ivory or gilded] panelled ceiling gleaming in my house': see *Odes*, 2.18.1–2 by the *Ethnic* ('pagan') Roman poet Horace (65–8 BC).

72.7 the Blue-banders retainers of James VI.

72.9 Jock of Milch...Annandale Jock of Milch or Milk is a ballad character supposedly active in Annandale (the valley of the river Annan, which empties into the Solway Firth) in the 14th century. Scott considered this 'wretched Duke of Milk' exemplary of 'an impudent forgery' (*Letters*, 1.160: 17 October 1802, to C. K. Sharpe; see also 1.140–44: 2 April and 4 June 1802, to R. Cleator). John Taylor testifies to the reputation of the area for crime, including thievery, in the poem about his 1618 travels in Scotland 'The Pennyles Pilgrimage' (1618), lines 563–64: 'This County *(Anandale)* in former times,/ Was the curst climate of rebellious crimes'. He credits the lapse of such activity to James's uniting the two kingdoms: Taylor, first section, 127.

72.19 auld Holyrood see note to 47.6.

72.20 these shifting days those uncertain times.

72.20–21 at heck and manger *proverbial* in comfortable circumstances: see Ray, 207; *ODEP*, 661. A *heck* is a portable rack for holding fodder, while a *manger* is stationary.

72.21 Cantabit vacuus *Latin*. The full saying is 'cantabit vacuus coram latrone viator' (the empty-handed traveller will sing in the robber's face): Juvenal (writing *c.* 98–128), Satire 10, line 22.

72.24 the Spanish ambassador the context suggests a pre-1603 allusion. In the early 1580s Mary Queen of Scots negotiated with the French and the

Spanish to have the Spanish invade Scotland and to send her son James to Spain, where he would be raised as a Catholic and marry a Spanish princess. The Scottish ambassador to Paris, the Archbishop of Glasgow, laid the groundwork for the plan in 1580, but the Spanish ambassador to London, Mendoza, was deeply involved. For the vast expense involved in entertaining Spanish and other ambassadors post-1603 see Akrigg, Ch. 6.

72.28 the Indies at their beck alluding to Spain's colonies in the Western Hemisphere and the riches in gold and silver acquired therefrom.

72.32 Justus et tenax propositi *Latin* [a man] upright and steadfast in purpose: see Horace (65–8 BC), *Odes*, 3.3.1.

72.40–42 the Raid of Ruthven ... the Master of Glamis for the Ruthven Raid see Historical Note, 524–25. Sir Thomas Lyon (d. 1608), one of the Scottish lords who staged the Raid, taunted the young king when he tried to escape Ruthven Castle.

72.41 Od's death *oath* God's death (i.e. the death of Christ on the cross).

73.2 a baxter at the breaking this probably means 'a baker on the verge of bankruptcy'.

73.5 in meditatione fugæ *Scots legal Latin* meditating flight (from Scotland).

73.9–10 Peregrine Peterson ... Campvere see note to 56.38–39.

73.14 God's bread *oath* the bread of the Eucharist: *Romeo and Juliet*, 3.5.176.

73.15–19 suspend the diligence ... paying the money Heriot is correct in his interpretation of Scots Law here, and James is mistaken. *Diligence* is the procedure whereby a creditor can gain satisfaction of his debt from acquiring his debtor's property. The most common form at this time would have been by letters of horning followed by adjudication of property to the creditor. This procedure ran in the name of the king (making the defaulting debtor technically an outlaw). This is the kind of diligence that the king obviously has in mind, and which he could well have used his prerogative powers to suspend or stop in some way. What is at issue here, however, is something quite different. There is a wadset (mortgage) over Glenvarloch. This is a procedure whereby a debtor formally conveys ownership of his land to a creditor in return for money. The wadsetter is apparent owner of the property. There is a separate reversion, under which the debtor, known as the reverser, could have the property returned to him. Such a reversion could (but need not) have what is known as a clause of irritancy, whereby if the repayment of the money borrowed was not made by a certain date the right of reversion expired and the wadsetter became absolute owner of the property. There had been some controversy over the validity of such clauses, but by the time of the novel, it was quite clear that they were enforceable. The nature of the process here makes it impossible for the king to interfere, unlike in diligence.

73.20 Uds fish *oath* God's flesh! Body of Christ!

73.20 keep haud by the strong hand keep hold by the use of force.

73.21 take some order make some arrangements.

73.24–25 unless in the rough bounds of the Highlands in Scott's time *rough bounds* was an accepted term for the Scottish Highlands.

73.29 in verbo regis *Latin* on the word of a king.

73.33 benevolences, and subsidies contributions called *benevolences* were first requested by Edward IV in 1473 as a token of goodwill towards his rule; but by James's reign they had come to be perceived as coerced funds, as when in 1614 after dissolving Parliament he forthwith 'extorted a Benevolence from the Subject, and those who would not contribute, were to have their Names returned to the Council' (Roger Coke, *A Detection of the Court and State of England During the Last Four Reigns and the Inter-Regnum* (London, 1697),

72: compare *CLA*, 237). *Subsidies* were fixed sums of varying amounts granted to the monarch by parliament, e.g. when James received £453,000 in November 1605 in gratitude for his role in exposing the Gunpowder Plot (William Sanderson, *A Compleat History of The Lives and Reigns of Mary Queen of Scotland, And of Her Son and Successor, James the Sixth, King of Scotland...*, 2 parts (London, 1656–55), 329); in later years, James had to bargain for his subsidies.

73.36–37 Dean Giles's discourses on the penitentiary psalms the 'penitential psalms' are those numbered 6, 32, 38, 51, 102, 130, and 143 in the Authorised Version. The Book of Common Prayer prescribes them for use on Ash Wednesday. Dean Giles, if historical, has not been identified.

73.37 Ex nihilo nihil fit *Latin* nothing can come from nothing. Proverbial: see *ODEP*, 579. The idea may come from Lucretius (*c*. 99–*c*. 55 BC), *De Rerum Natura* (On the Nature of Things): 'nihil posse creari/ de nihilo' (1.155–56: nothing can be created from nothing). It appears in the form 'nihil ex nihilo exsistere uera sententia est' (that nothing can come from nothing is a true idea), in Boethius (*c*. 475–525), *De Consolatione Philosophiae* (On the Consolation of Philosophy), Bk 5, Prosa 1.9, thus implying that it was accepted wisdom by the 6th century.

74.3–4 Res angusta domi *Latin*. The full quotation from Juvenal (writing *c*. 98–128), Satire 3, lines 164–65, reads: 'Haut facile emergunt quorum virtutibus opstat/ res augusta domi' (it is not easy for men to rise when straitened circumstances at home stand in the way of their merits).

74.7 the carcanet of rubies see note to 74.22–23.

74.22–23 a carcanet of balas rubies... Catalogue of his Majesty's Jewels the itemised catalogue of crown jewels made in March 1606 includes 'a Coller of gould, containing thirteene great ballaces,and thirteene peeces of gould with thirteen cinques [clusters of 5] pearle between them' (Thomas Rymer and Robert Sanderson, *Foedera*, 10 vols (The Hague, 1745), 7:2.148 (compare 7:4.74): *CLA*, 23). A balas ruby is a delicate rose-red variety of spinel showing a blue tint when looked through, found in northern Afghanistan.

74.38 Propera pedem *Latin* hasten your steps.

74.39 god-den with good evening to.

75.2–11 motto not identified: probably by Scott.

75.13 hollow and hungry hour the source of the phrase has not been identified.

75.35 ever and anon every now and then; continually at intervals.

75.40 well to pass in the world well off; well to do.

75.42–76.1 gown and cassock the traditional dress of the Anglican clergyman.

76.4 Girnigo Castle see Historical Note, 528. The first syllable may suggest Scots *girn* ('grumble', 'whine').

76.5 an original character a personality neither derivative nor duplicated.

76.13 whipping-boy a boy educated with a young prince and flogged in his place to atone for royal misdemeanours. James's surrogate body, if such existed, has not been identified, but Gilbert Burnet twice mentions that William Murray (1600?–51), created 1st Earl of Dysart 1643, 'had been page and whipping boy to king Charles I' and that he possessed a revengeful temper: see *Burnet's History of My Own Time*, ed. Osmund Airy, 2 vols (London, 1900), 106, 436: compare *CLA*, 2. Scott may have derived this element of Sir Mungo's psycho–biography from Murray.

76.15–16 his celebrated preceptor, George Buchanan Scotland's great scholar of the period, Buchanan (1506–82) was Classical tutor to Mary

Queen of Scots before undertaking, 1570–78, the education of her son. It was Buchanan who was responsible for James's skill in reading, translating, writing, and speaking Latin. By all accounts, James admired Buchanan but was intimidated by his stern pedagogy.

76.17–18 the Lord's Anointed for James's anointings, see note to 304.40. The expression 'the Lord's anointed' is found several times in 1 and 2 Samuel.

76.23 James's other pedagogue, Master Patrick Young James's junior tutor, Young (1544–1628) came to the post in 1570 after studying in Geneva with John Calvin's protégé Theodore Beza.

76.32 Peter 'Peter' and 'Patrick' are often interchanged in Scottish usage.

77.8 Sir Rullion Rattray, of Ranagullion an imaginary character. His name is probably derived from *rullion* ('a coarse, rough person') and Rattray Head, a promontory in Aberdeenshire. 'Ranagullion' suggests *rannigant* ('a wild loose-living person, a good-for-nothing') and *gullion* ('a mean wretch' or 'a dirty quagmire, a swamp').

77.11 the Lady Cockpen an imaginary character. Her name suggests (1) the laird of Carolina Oliphant, Lady Nairne's song 'The laird o' Cockpen he's proud and he's great', first published in 1821 in *The Scotish Minstrel*, ed. R. A. Smith, 6 vols (1821–24), 3.37, and (2) *cockapenty* (high-falutin or a person whose pride makes them act and live above their income). Cockpen is a parish S of Edinburgh.

77.24–25 The celebrated Archie Armstrong see Historical Note, 530.

77.30 the golden shower which fell around him possibly an allusion to the myth of Danaë who when imprisoned was visited by Zeus in the form of a golden shower.

77.36 fallen into the yellow leaf of years and fortune compare *Macbeth* 5.3.23.

77.38 indulging his food for satire this strange phrase persists in all editions. Perhaps Scott intended to write 'taste' or 'fondness'.

77.39–40 the aisles of Saint Paul's ... descriptions see note to 48.30–31.

78.22–23 Pindivide, a great merchant fictitious character suggestive of the gossip to be gleaned at 'Paul's'. His fate suggests that the name carries the meaning of the Latin verb *divido*, i.e. to divide, to destroy, to distribute.

78.23–24 given the crows a pudding *proverbial* became carrion; died: Ray, 184; *ODEP*, 502; see also *Henry V*, 2.1.82.

78.26 stock and block everything; one's whole possessions. A set phrase expressing total loss.

78.34–40 the Book of Apocalypse ... ten horns o' the beast Revelation (also known as the Apocalypse) is full of significant numbers, which have been subjected to various numerological theories. The 'ten horns' occur in 13.1: 'And I ... saw a beast rise up out of the sea, having seven heads and ten horns, and upon his horns ten crowns, and upon his heads the name of blasphemy'.

79.31–35 bred and born within the sound of Bow-bell proverbial: *ODEP*, 76. Margaret is a (streetwise) cockney, born within the sound of the great bell of St Mary-le-Bow, a church in Cheapside, the uncommonly wide street between Lombard Street to the E and Newgate Street to the W which served medieval London, specifically, as central marketplace, and, generally, as town centre. The bell functioning in the 17th century was given in 1520 to continue a custom of sounding the curfew at 9 pm; it was destroyed in 1941.

79.35–36 the kettle ... porridge-pot proverbial: Ray, 126; *ODEP*, 421. The missing word is most commonly 'black-arse' or 'burnt-arse'.

79.40 Bread of heaven in Psalm 105.40 the expression alludes to manna, the miraculous food received by the Children of Israel in the wilderness. It is used more generally to signify the bread of the Eucharist, and functions here as an oath.

80.15–16 the comforters of the Man of Uzz the three friends who come 'to mourn with . . . and to comfort' Job, 'a man in the land of Uz': Job 2.11, 1.1.

80.26–27 when the withers . . . were wrung the *withers* are the muscles which connect the neck, back, and shoulders of a horse, i.e. that part of the animal's anatomy the most likely to be galled by a saddle or collar: compare *Hamlet*, 3.2.231–32. A proverbial concept: Tilley, H700.

80.35 tolled off enticed away.

80.37 the genial board the festive dining table. The phrase is frequently found in 18th and early 19th-century literature.

81.1–2 beef and pudding, the statutory dainties of Old England see note to 30.23–24 and motto to Vol. 2, Ch. 7 (200.11–18). That beef and pudding were the staple menu for festive meals in old England is not a matter of statute but of custom and folklore perpetuated by historical novelists such as Scott.

81.7–8 a good cook knows how to lick his own fingers proverbial: Ray, 90, 289; *ODEP*, 143.

81.23–24 coming to extremity with i.e. pushing his satire to the point of alienating.

83.18 Lambe the astrologer John Lambe, widely known as 'the Duke's wizard' because Buckingham frequently consulted him, was killed by a London mob in the summer of 1628. In a note to the *Secret History*, 2.44–45, Scott links him with other pretended astrologers, including Dr Forman (see Essay on the Text, 407).

83.24 cast nativities predict the course of a human life according to the astrological signs present at the time and place of birth.

83.25 conjunction of Mars and Saturn in astrology, two planets are in conjunction when in the same sign of the zodiac or in adjacent signs.

83.26 Eichstadius Laurenz Eichstad (d. 1600) from Stettin, formerly in Germany but now in Poland, famous as both a doctor of medicine and an astrologer.

83.27 Oranienburgh the observatory Uraniborg, built in 1576 by the Danish astrologer Tycho Brahe (1546–1601) on the island of Hven, off the SW coast of Sweden.

83.32–33 him who bears the hearts of kings in his hand God. Compare John Taylor: 'He at his pleasure worketh wond'rous things / And in his hand doth hold the hearts of kings' (*The Fearefull Summer: or Londons Calamitie* (1625), lines 401–02: Taylor, first section, 62). Compare also Sir John Beaumont: 'O gracious Maker . . . / Whose hand not onely holds the hearts of Kings' ('A thanksgiuing for the deliuerance of our Soueraigne, King Iames, from a dangerous accident, Ianuary 8', lines 1–3, in his *Bosworth-field* (London, 1629), 105); Beaumont's title refers to James's near drowning in the New River from a hunting accident on this date, 1622: see note to 47.19–20.

83.39–42 Full moon . . . die resembling but not identical with any number of sayings that predict human destiny, especially that of the traveller by sea, in terms of the stars and the weather.

84.1 stone walls have ears proverbial: G. L. Apperson, *English Proverbs and Proverbial Phrases* (London, 1929), 665. Compare *ODEP*, 864.

84.1–2 a bird of the air shall carry the matter see Ecclesiastes 10.20: 'Curse not the king, no not in thy thought; and curse not the rich in thy bedchamber: for a bird of the air shall carry the voice, and that which hath wings shall tell the matter'. Proverbial: Apperson (see previous note), 48.

84.5 her body-guard of 'prentices compare Strutt quoting Edmond Howes's continuation of John Stow, *Annales, or, A General Chronicle of England*, revised edn (London, 1631), 1040: 'When the apprentices, or the journeymen, attended upon their masters and mistresses at night, they went before them holding a lanthorn with a candle in their hands, and carried a great long club upon their shoulders; and many well-grown apprentices used to wear long daggers, in the day-time, at their backs or sides' (*A Complete View of the Dress and Habits of the People of England*, 2 vols (London, 1796–99), 2.316: *CLA*, 154).

84.6–7 a brown study a state of mental abstraction.

84.7–8 that of Fortune the goddess Fortune is often represented with a wheel in her hand, indicating her inconstancy.

84.17 sanctum sanctorum *Latin* holy of holies: Exodus 26.34 in the Vulgate. The phrase refers to the innermost chamber of the Jewish Tabernacle, where the Ark of the Covenant was kept, and hence to an 'inner sanctum' generally.

84.33–34 a Saint Andrew's cross, with thistles a white cross shaped like the letter X on an azure background. Known as the 'saltire', it is the emblem of Scotland, sign of its patron saint, and here ornamented with the national flower.

85.2–6 motto not identified: probably by Scott. See Luke 10.38–42 for the story of Martha's complaint that her sister Mary sat at the feet of Jesus listening to his words instead of helping to serve the guests and of Jesus's reply: 'But one thing is needful: and Mary hath chosen that good part, which shall not be taken away from her'.

85.14–15 the prayers of the church for the evening the service of Evening Prayer from the Church of England's Book of Common Prayer.

87.20 Theobald's . . . hunting see notes to 19.34 and 62.10.

88.9 the second successive morning the second morning after.

88.11–12 link-boys . . . London *links* were torches formed of pitch and tow, dating from the early 16th century. Often carried by boys, they were used to light pedestrians and, later, carriages, until gaslights were introduced. Anthony Hamilton (1646?–1720), an Irishman who fought for James II at the battle of the Boyne in 1690 and attended him in exile, wrote about the generation of link-boys in the early years of the Restoration (1662–64) in *Mémoires de la Vie du Comte de Grammont* (Cologne, 1713); in 1810 Scott revised and annotated the 1714 English translation by Abel Boyer for the London publisher William Miller (*Letters*, 12.400–01), and it appeared in 1811. Grammont, explaining 'the nation of link-boys' to the queen dowager, pronounces it 'charming' and claims to have once arrived at Whitehall with 'at least two hundred about my chair: The sight was new; for those who had seen me pass with this illumination, asked whose funeral it was': *Memoirs of Count Grammont, by Anthony Hamilton*, 2 vols (London, 1811), 1.209.

88.24 just living living in a faithful, honourable way.

88.26–27 a cloven cloot . . . shoon see John Webster, *The White Devil* (1612), 5.3.107–09: 'Why, 'tis the devil;/ I know him by a great rose he wears on's shoe,/ To hide his cloven foot'; see also Ben Jonson, *The Devil Is An Ass* (performed 1616, published 1631), 1.3.7–32, for a more elaborate discourse on this motif. A cloven or cleft *cloot* ('hoof') hidden by a shoe is the mark of Satan in popular belief deriving from Mosaic law on diet in Leviticus 11.1–8. For 'the braw roses and cordovan shoon' (fine leather produced in the Spanish town of Córdoba) with which it is disguised, see note to 29.36–38.

88.31 Under favour with all submission; subject to correction.

88.38 Under your patience with your patience or sufferance.

89.1–2 And withal . . . he sung in John Bunyan's *The Pilgrim's Progress*

(1678–84) variations on the phrase 'went on his/their way' are common, and the pilgrims often burst into song.

89.3–7 O, do ye ken…do ye ken 'the good old song of Elsie Marley', a Northumbrian ballad about the popular wife of the mid-18th-century inn-keeper at the Barley Mow Inn, Pictree, is included by Joseph Ritson in his anonymous *The Bishopric Garland: or, Durham Minstrell* (Stockton, 1784), 21–22. For the identification of Elsie see *Northumbrian Minstrelsy. A Collection of the Ballads, Melodies, and Small-Pipe Tunes of Northumbria*, ed. J. Collingwood Bruce and John Stokoe (Newcastle upon Tyne, 1882), 112–14.

89.28 what for what sort of.

89.30 make it for consider it as.

89.30 his ain end his own purpose.

89.32 at your guiding at your command; under your control.

90.5–6 they go about…devour see 1 Peter 5.8–9: 'Be sober, be vigilant; because your adversary the devil, as a roaring lion, walketh about, seeking whom he may devour: Whom resist stedfast in the faith'.

90.14 began it to me pledged me in a toast.

90.16 make scruple of it hesitate to do it.

90.23 made becks and bows Scott may be anticipating the lines from John Milton's 'L'Allegro' which he quotes in the last paragraph of this chapter: see note to 92.18–19. A *beck* is a nod or slight curtsy.

90.27 De'il a bit not a bit of it!

90.29–30 within hue and cry of within hearing distance of.

90.31 these many a year for many years now.

90.36 right down downright; very forceful. See the anonymous *Arden of Feversham* (1592), lines 173–74: 'Who would not venture vpon house and land?/When he may haue it for a right downe blowe.'

90.37–38 Mess John Knox…court was against him *Mess* is a term of address for clergymen: for John Knox and Mary Queen of Scots see note to 54.22.

90.39–40 Master Rollock, and Mess David Black, of North Leith in 1596 Black used his pulpit in St Andrews (not North Leith) to attack both James (all kings are '*the Devil's Barns*') and the English queen ('an *Atheist*') for being soft on Catholics. To pacify the English ambassador, James proceeded with charges of slander and treasonable calumny. The Kirk of Scotland came to Black's defence, viewing James's action as the attempt to divert the clergy from continuing to agitate against the return to Scotland of the excommunicated popish earls Huntly and Errol without the King's permission but also without his interference. Its delegation to the King included Robert Rollock (1555–99), a Scottish theologian, the first Principal of Edinburgh University and noted as a powerful preacher. Although Black did not appear before the council to submit his doctrine to trial, he was sentenced to be 'confined beyond the North water [the Firth of Forth], and enter to his Ward [his jail or the keeper thereof] within six days' (John Spottiswood, *History of the Church and State of Scotland*, 4th edn (London, 1677), 420–27): *CLA*, 13.

90.42 black mess-book especially in the 17th century, a derogatory term for the Book of Common Prayer used in the Church of England, implying a black mass or service for the worship of Satan.

91.1–3 the Evil Spirit…Raguel see Tobit Chs 6–8, in the Apocrypha, for the story of how Tobit's son Tobias, by means of smoke made from the heart and liver of a fish covered with the ashes of perfume, exorcised from the chamber of Sara, the woman he wished to marry, the demon which had killed her previous seven husbands on their wedding night.

91.4 make scruple hesitate.

91.16 Highland Brownie benevolent spirit believed to haunt old Scottish houses.

91.18 de'il a bed not a bed.

91.19 are so chinked up have their chinks filled up in such a way.

91.31 damask a richly figured woven material, originally of silk and made at Damascus.

91.31 might serve which might serve.

91.37 they would need a lang spoon would sup with her proverbial, of supping with the Devil: see Ray, 97; *ODEP*, 480.

91.38–40 the tower ... the t'other generally known as a 'turn', this device comes in various sizes and is still found in some convents.

92.2–6 the images of Baal ... wives and children see Bel and the Dragon in the Apocrypha, for the story of how Daniel convinced King Cyrus that the Babylonian idol Bel was not a living god but a mere statue of clay and brass. The fine flour, sheep, and wine supposedly devoured nightly by Bel were, in fact, consumed in secret by the 70 priests and their families, whose duplicity was exposed by Daniel's strategem of covering the floor of Bel's temple with wood-ashes, revealing their footprints.

92.18–19 quips, and becks, and wreathed smiles see John Milton, 'L'Allegro' (written 1631?, published 1645), lines 27–28: 'Quips and Cranks, and wanton Wiles,/ Nods, and becks, and wreathed smiles'.

92.22–35 motto not identified: probably by Scott.

92.24 steeple hat and velvet guard a hat in the shape of a spire or steeple such as witches are often pictured as wearing, but fashionable for both men and women at various times in the 15th, 16th, and 17th centuries (see Joseph Strutt, *A Complete View of the Dress and Habits of the People of England*, 2 vols (London, 1796–99), 2, plates CXXI, CXXII, CXXIII, and CXXXVII: *CLA*, 154): it is mocked, however, in Thomas Dekker, *The Honest Whore, Part 2* (performed 1604–05?, published 1630), 1.442ff, as an oddity amidst flat caps (see note to 27.17–18); and a garment trimmed with a velvet border (see John Marston, *Histrio-mastix* (performed 1598–99, published 1610), 3.1.247–48: 'Out on these veluet gards, and black lac'd sleeues,/ These simpering fashions simply followed', a sentiment shared by Hotspur who, in *1 Henry IV*, 3.1.257, expresses his contempt for bourgeois citizens by the epithet 'velvet-guards').

92.25–28 the ear of Dionysius ... bondsmen a reference to 'Dionysius' ear', the cave cut in rock as a listening chamber by Dionysius the elder, Tyrant of Syracuse (431–367 BC). The structure of the prison and the story of his spying, exemplary of his suspicious nature and cruelty, are elaborated in similar language in the tragedy by Arthur Murphy, *The Grecian Daughter* (London, 1772), 1.97–113 and 4.228–54.

92.33 so that providing that; if.

92.38 Suddlechop the form of the name probably derives from the Scots verb *suddle* ('soil', 'dirty'), but also suggests the soap suds a barber applies to the jaws (chops).

93.16–17 the hopeful offspring of unlicensed love the illegitimate child who hopes to achieve something.

93.20–21 Mrs Turner ... yellow starch see note to 102.14–19.

93.32 set off counterbalanced.

94.11–12 the toe of the citizen ... courtier's heel see *Hamlet*, 5.1.132–33.

95.16–17 go to the devil ... Scotch witch James himself recommended death by fire as punishment for Scots found guilty of witchcraft, in his 1597 pamphlet *Daemonologie* (Craigie, 53–54). Several Scots were burned to death in the first wave of persecutions, 1590–92, that precipitated James's little treatise (Craigie, 152).

95.25–26 if that sae be sae if that be the case.

95.27 auld Mother Redcap the name of a notorious shrew of Kentish Town, also known as 'Mother Damnable'. She is referred to in George Colman the elder's 1776 play *The Spleen*, 2.45, as well as in Peter Pindar's (John Wolcot's) poem 'One Thousand Seven Hundred and Ninety-Six; A Satire; In Two Dialogues': *The Works of Peter Pindar*, 4 vols (Boston, Massachusetts, 1811), 3.107 (line 45).

95.27 the Hungerford Stairs stairs between Hungerford Market and the Thames at the spot where now the Charing Cross railway bridge crosses the river.

95.43 a wee fashious about washing her laces a little troublesome about washing the cords or ties that draw together her bodice.

96.29 Whither away where are you off to?

96.37–38 the whilst in the meantime.

97.7 as changeful as a marmozet the *marmozet* is a small monkey from South and Central America with a playful disposition.

97.7–8 as stubborn as a mule proverbial: *ODEP*, 550.

97.11 held a close chuff considered a niggardly miser.

97.15–16 andiamos . . . hath it the Spanish word for 'let's to work' is readily accessible to non-Spanish speakers.

97.19–21 now in glimmer . . . armour Scott borrows the language of the picturesque from Coleridge's unfinished romance 'Christabel' (1816), lines 168–69: 'They steal their way from stair to stair,/ Now in glimmer, and now in gloom'. The verb 'glided' suggests that Scott may have conflated Coleridge's romance with Keats's 'The Eve of St. Agnes' (1820), lines 361–62, where Madeline and Porphyro 'glide, like phantoms, into the wide hall;/ Like phantoms, to the iron porch, they glide'.

97.27 the cynosure of the eyes see John Milton, 'L'Allegro' (written 1631?, published 1645), line 80: *cynosure* means 'centre of attraction and admiration'.

97.39 Go your ways take yourself.

98.1 Bow the church of St Mary-le-Bow, located in Cheapside near the centre of the City and, thus, a conventional reference for indicating distances. See note to 79.31–35.

98.23 take heart of grace pluck up courage.

98.27 what I ail what is wrong with me.

98.29 the good old game . . . thought like? the game of guessing what someone is thinking.

98.30–31 head-tire . . . wear the taste for elaborate headgear among city women is caught in Richard Niccols's 1614 epigram: 'To the new walks she is gone to take the air,/ But at that little gate how gets she out,/ Her head with such a compass arched about?/ With much ado; therefore these dames desire/ Great London will build little Moregate higher': see *London in the Age of Shakespeare*, ed. Lawrence Manley (London and Sydney, 1986), 245–46.

98.32 Islington or Ware Islington, now an inner suburb in N London, was at this period a village to which citizens resorted for recreation and sport. Ware, a village 40 km N of London, had a reputation for secret assignations.

99.8–9 as I would live i.e. she is as certain of her guess as she is that she will live. Compare Falstaff's 'Will I live?': *2 Henry IV*, 2.1.152.

99.22 the gospellers came in *gospellers* is a term derisive of the Protestants, who had *come in* or acquired power at the Reformation.

99.35–36 what foot it is you halt upon *proverbial* what your weak point is: see *ODEP*, 279.

100.1 gilded caroch the elaborate town-carriage, as opposed to the country *coach*, used by London's mayors on ceremonial occasions, though the journeys to Whitehall or Westminster were traditionally made by barge. In a note for his edition of Anthony Hamilton's *Memoirs of Count Grammont* (London, 1811) Scott writes that carriages were first introduced into England in 1564 (1.261: compare Stow, 1.243). By the turn of the century they had become fashionable, references to gilded caroches occurring in several plays. Ursula's vision of Jin Vin's rise in station and wealth may be informed by the story of Dick Whittington (*c.* 1358–1423), first narrated and dramatised in the early years of James's reign, wherein an apprentice to a mercer (in some versions) rose to fame and fortune, serving as London's mayor three times and in his will bequeathing great endowments and benefactions to the city.

100.5 there is a cross ... line of life a *cross* refers to a pair of crossed lines in the palm of the hand usually read by palmists as a sign of trouble, danger, or some adverse change in life.

100.7 hath not i.e. which hath not.

100.12 a clown—a cockney *clown* is a derisive term for a rustic or peasant; *cockney* is a derisive term for the clown's city counterpart, especially such a person born within the sound of Bow Bell (see note to 79.31–35).

100.14 sits the wind in that corner see *Much Ado About Nothing*, 2.3.91.

100.17–18 the first glimpse ... May-day on 1 May young men and women rose a little after midnight when, to musical accompaniment, they walked to nearby woods where they gathered greens and flowers; at sunrise they returned to decorate their houses with their spoils, commencing a day of dancing, feasting, and general merry-making. Dame Ursula alludes to the sexual implications (including many pregnancies) of this ancient spring festival.

100.22 of surety certainly.

100.24 Northward ho travelling north: compare the Thames waterman's cry of 'eastward ho' or 'westward ho'.

100.34 an I would if I wanted to.

100.41 Saint Pancras's charnel-house by 1593 Old St Pancras Church was not visited except 'when there is a corpse to be interred, they are forced to leave the same within this forsaken church or churchyard': typographer John Norden, quoted in *Survey of London*, 45 vols (London, 1900–[in progress]), 19 (1938), 75.

101.10 as proud as Lucifer, and as poor as Job Dame Ursula combines two proverbs: *ODEP*, 651, 638 (Ray 225).

101.11 had as lief would have been as pleased if.

101.19 bethink you of consider.

101.22 Earls of Dalwolsey the Ramsays, since the 13th century a Scottish noble family who received lands in Midlothian from David I, King of Scots, and the lands of Dalwolsie, Midlothian, from King Edward I of England in return for feudal obligations.

101.37–38 better make your bridal-bed under a falling house probably proverbial, but no other occurrence has been found.

102.14–19 Mistress Turner ... starch Anne Turner (1576–1615), described in *The Narrative History of King James* as 'that fomenter of lust ... whose sentence was, to be hanged at Tiburn in her yellow tiffany ruff and cuffs, being she was the first inventer and wearer of that horrid garb' (*Somers' Tracts*, 2.264). But Scott in a Magnum note (26.167) suggests that credit for the invention of yellow starch belongs to the French. Turner's crime was to assist Lady Frances Howard, the Countess of Essex, to be rid of her husband the Earl, so that she could marry the King's current favourite Sir Robert Carr (d. 1645: created Viscount Rochester 1611; Earl of Somerset 1613). In the beginning this aid took the form of conspiring with a Dr Forman of Lambeth, reputed to be skilled in witchcraft, to dampen her husband's ardours and quicken the Viscount's; but in time it led to some part in poisoning the close friend who had tried hardest to influence Carr against the Countess, Sir Thomas Overbury (1581–1613), whose name came to memorialise this the most sensational of the soap operas that epitomised James's reign: 'the Overbury affair'. Along with the other players, Turner was eventually implicated in the affair, and in 1615 she was hanged. Howell's review of her execution in the letter to his father of 1 March 1618 (19–20), which, like Ursula's, puts emphasis on the ruff and yellow starch, is typical of contemporary accounts, but there is no record of any order for the wearing of a yellow ruff: rather, the hangman mockingly wore yellow paper cuffs and bands (Miriam Allen deFord, *The Overbury Affair* (Philadelphia and New York, 1960), 71–72).

102.22   too hot or heavy   compare 'I spare nat to taken, God it woot,/ But if it be to hevy or to hoot': Geoffrey Chaucer, *The Canterbury Tales*, 'The Friar's Tale', III 1(D) 1435–36.

103.1   broad pieces   a term used after the guinea was introduced in 1663 to indicate the thinner and broader 20 shilling-piece coined in the reigns of James VI and I and Charles I.

103.12   can say no great matter   have nothing much to say.

103.22   come up a caterpillar   see note to 27.24–25.

103.26–27   my pearl of pearls ... Marguerites   until the early 17th century *margarite* was used to mean 'pearl'.

103.38   mere table-talk and terms of course   perfunctory speech, and words used without force as a mere matter of form.

104.2–18   motto   see Edmund Spenser, *Prosopopoia: or Mother Hubberds Tale* (1591), lines 891–906. To be *put back* is to be rejected.

104.23   made his toilette   washed, dressed, arranged his hair, etc.

104.28–29   take the wind out of the sail of   *proverbial* arrest the forward progress of; put at a disadvantage: *ODEP*, 801 (which gives this as the first recorded occurrence).

105.3   the Goldsmith's Incorporation   a guild dating back to Norman times, chartered and incorporated by Edward III in 1327 and re-incorporated by charter with extended powers by Richard II in 1393.

105.7   the Kræmes   shops erected against the walls of the High Kirk of St Giles, Edinburgh.

105.40   in waiting   in attendance.

107.16   in the Queen's days   i.e. in Elizabeth's reign.

107.27–28   like paltry stage-players   at this period acting was often held in low esteem as a disreputable or worthless profession.

107.33–34   Merlin's Wynd   a lane in Edinburgh associated with tailors.

108.18   pass current   be generally accepted.

108.34   Ochtred   see Historical Note, 529.

109.5–6   king's-man ... Douglas wars   a partisan of James VI rather than of his mother Queen Mary in the civil wars (named after James Douglas (d. 1581), Earl of Morton from 1553) that dominated Scotland during James's minority (1566–87).

109.25   fidgetting motions   according to Weldon (2.2), James's 'walke was ever circular, his fingers ever in that walke fidling about his cod-piece'.

110.1–5   the nineteen of September ... the Cross   it was actually on 19 June 1587 (his 21st birthday) that King James sought to end the feuds which divided Scotland by inviting the nobles to Holyrood Palace for entertainment in exchange for a promise to forgo their grievances. Afterwards he led them in pairs joined by hands to the Mercat Cross outside the High Kirk of St Giles, Edinburgh, where they feasted on sweetmeats and drank wine to each other's health. The phrase 'of all the days in the year' is simply an intensive.

110.6   a blithe cup of kindness   compare 'a cup o' kindness' in the refrain of Robert Burns, 'Auld lang syne' (published 1796).

110.7–8   Auld John Anderson . . . that year   no such name appears in the list of the Lord Provosts of Edinburgh provided by John Anderson, *A History of Edinburgh: From the Earliest Period to the Completion of the Half Century 1850* (Edinburgh and London, 1856), 608–09. There the provost for the year 1587 is identified as one John Arnot.

110.14   Beati pacifici   *Latin* blessed are the peacemakers: Matthew 5.9 in the Vulgate. Weldon (2.12: compare 1.412) says that it was James's 'owne motto'.

110.17   James with the Fiery Face   James II, King of Scots 1437–60, who assumed the throne at age six. An aggressive monarch, with a red blemish on the side of his face, he was killed by the explosion of a gun in the siege of Roxburgh Castle in 1460, the same year in which he had attempted to invade England in support of Henry VI.

110.18   my great grandsire, of Flodden memory   James IV, King of Scots 1488–1513, who, while invading England, was killed in battle at Flodden in Northumberland, along with nearly 10,000 Scots and the flower of Scottish nobility.

110.26   Leyden   the Dutch city and university Leiden (founded in 1575), famous as a centre of learning and source of religious controversy (see note to 111.8–11). The scene in which King James tests Nigel's erudition and displays his own may be modelled on a similar scene recounted by Sir John Harington in a letter of 1606–07 to his cousin Sir Amias Pawlett: 'Then he [James] enquyrede muche of lernynge, and showede me his owne in suche sorte, as made me remember my examiner at Cambridge aforetyme' (*Nugæ Antiquæ* (see note to 47.2), 1.367).

110.36–37   Salve bis . . . rediisti?   *Latin* twice hail, four times hail, our Glenvarloch! Have you not lately returned to Britain from Leiden?

110.39–40   Imo . . . moratus sum   *Latin* yes, your most august Majesty, I stayed almost two years among the people of Leiden.

110.42–43   Biennium dicis? . . . Glenvarlochiensis?   *Latin* two years, do you say? well, well, it was very well done. Not in a day, as they say—do you understand, Lord of Glenvarloch? James alludes to the proverb: 'Rome was not built in a day': Ray, 152; *ODEP*, 683.

111.3   Adolescens . . . pudoris   *Latin* a youth of a comely countenance and beautiful modesty.

111.4–5   Et quid . . . edidit   *Latin* and what is spoken of in Leiden today —your Vossius, has he written nothing new?—nothing certainly, I regret, which has appeared recently in type. Gerhard Johannes Vossius (1577–1649), the Classical scholar and philologist, was director of the theological college at Leiden 1615–19.

111.6–7   Valet . . . septuagesimum   *Latin* Vossius is indeed well, gracious king . . . but is a most venerable old man, if I am not mistaken, in his seventieth year.

111.8–11   Virum, mehercle . . . δερκων?   *Latin and Greek* so help me, Hercules, I had scarcely thought him so old a man . . . And that Vorstius, the successor to, as well as adherent of, the reprobate Arminius—is that hero, as I may say with Homer, still alive and living [*literally* seeing] upon the earth? Conrad Vorstius (1569–1622) was a Dutch theologian who espoused the anti-Calvinistic theology of Jacobus Arminius (1560–1609), succeeding him at Leiden in 1610. Vorstius's assertion that his views coincided with the doctrine of the Church of England so infuriated James that, in a tract composed of commentary on correspondence with the Dutch published in 1612, he called for the scholar's dismissal from his academic post and even for burning him at the stake (Willson, 240). The Homeric allusion is probably to *The Odyssey*, 16.439, though variants of the expression are found elsewhere in that poem (εωι is an old typographic form of επι).

111.16–19 the United States ... universal toleration 'their Mighty Mightinesses' was the title of dignity for the members of the States-General (legislative assembly) of the United Provinces of the Netherlands. The Union of Utrecht in 1579, specifically Article 13, established toleration as a founding principle of the Netherlands and consequently made this new nation the major refuge for Europeans who sought freedom from religious persecution.

111.23–25 Vivum ... prostratus? *Latin* it is not long since I saw the man, alive, indeed; but who can say he flourishes who has long lain prone and prostrate under the bolts of your eloquence, great king?

111.30 Euge! belle! optime! *Latin* well done! excellent! first-rate!

111.30–31 the Bishops of Exeter and Oxford Valentine Cary (d. 1626) was Bishop of Exeter 1621–26; Buckingham influenced his appointment. John Howson (1557?–1632) was Bishop of Oxford 1619–28; he also served as chaplain to King James who was pleased by his attacks on popery.

111.35–36 the genuine and Roman pronunciation ... continent in the 16th century Erasmus sought to return the pronunciation of Latin and Greek vowels to their Classical sounds, but his adherents in England, at Cambridge in particular, were thwarted both by the opposition of the Chancellor of the University and by the transition from the Middle English to Modern English vowel system then in process. James's views on the subject were first expressed in a speech he made at Stirling in 1617, where he is reported to have replied to compliments on his Latin: 'All the world ... knowes that my maister, Mr George Buchanan, was a great maister in that faculty. I follow his pronunciation both of the Latin and Greek, and am sorrie that my people of England doe not the like: For certainly their pronounciation utterly spoils the grace of these two learned languages; but ye see all the University and learned men of Scotland, express the true and native pronounciation of both' (Thomas Craufurd, *History of the University of Edinburgh, from 1580 to 1646* (Edinburgh, 1808), 86–87). See also David Harris Willson, *King James VI and I* (London, 1956), 21, and W. Sidney Allen, *Vox Latina*, 2nd edn (Cambridge, 1978), 103–05.

111.39—112.1 'nippit foot and clippit foot,' ... fairy tale referring to the Scottish fairy story of Rashiecoat (Coat of Rushes), in which a girl's efforts to win a prince's hand by forcing her foot into a shoe too small for her is exposed by birds which sing these words as she rides behind him. For this version of the Cinderella tale see Robert Chambers, *The Popular Rhymes of Scotland*, 4th edn (Edinburgh, 1870), 66–68.

112.3–4 quoad Anglos ... communis lingua *Latin* as far as the English people are concerned ... a common language.

112.8–9 to become food for faggots to be burned at the stake.

112.9 in defence of the Latinity of the university Oxford followed Cambridge when, in 1543, that university was plunged into controversy over the pronunciation of Greek (and Latin) by the young Cambridge scholars Thomas Smith and John Cheke, who, inspired by Erasmus, proposed reforms that would effect a break with the lazy practice of the Continent. So energetically did Oxford engage the battle that in the end 'Oxford scholars ... convinced themselves that the improvement had begun with them' (Edward Charles Mallet, *A History of the University of Oxford*, 3 vols (London, 1924–28), 2.78–80).

112.21–22 were it but for the rarity of the case if only for the sake of the rare exception.

112.22–23 ex proposito *Latin* on purpose.

112.37 Saint Andrews the first Scottish university, founded in 1412.

112.38–39 **Incumbite remis fortiter** *Latin* fall bravely to the oars. See Virgil (70–19 BC), *Aeneid*, 10.294.

113.7–16 **Lord Huntinglen ... every year** see Historical Note, 525, and Essay on the Text, 409.

113.18 **restrictivé ... conditionaliter** *Latin* under certain restrictions ... conditionally.

113.40–41 **here the shoe pinches** alluding to the proverb 'The wearer knows best where the shoe pinches': Ray, 156; *ODEP*, 725.

114.5 **play Rex** James is probably punning: *play rex* can mean 'play pranks [*reaks*]' or 'act as lord and master', 'domineer', *literally* 'play King'.

114.16 **bread o' life** an oath: Christ is the bread of life (John 6.35).

114.16 **I am a free King** from James's childhood onward, this was more the case in theory than in fact, as at times such as this he seems to be only too aware. He first put forward the concept of the free monarch in the pamphlet *The True Lawe of Free Monarchies* (Edinburgh, 1598). In the official account of the Gowrie conspiracy James is represented at the moment of greatest peril as declaiming that 'hee was born a free king, and should die a free king': see Essay on the Text, note 17 (457).

114.17 **justus et tenax propositi** *Latin* a just man and firm of purpose.

114.22 **ever now and then** every now and then.

114.30–31 **for what** why.

114.33 **Scottish Chancellor** the first officer of state in Scotland. In 1604 Alexander Seton (1555?–1622), 1st Earl of Dunfermline from 1608, assumed the post; in 1622 George Hay (1572–1634), 1st Earl of Kinnoull from 1633, succeeded him.

114.36 **plack and bawbee** every penny; in full. A *plack* was a small copper coin worth 4 pence Scots (0.14p); a *bawbee* was worth 6 pence Scots (0.2p).

114.37 **an eard hunger** James is punning on *eard hunger* ('hunger for land') and *yird-hunger* ('abnormal craving for food').

114.41 **the poor King ambled up and down** compare Henry's contemptuous recollection of Richard II in *1 Henry IV*, 3.2.60–62: 'The skipping King, he ambled up and down/ With shallow jesters and rash bavin [brushwood] wits/ Soon kindled and soon burnt'.

114.43 **shambling circular mode of managing his legs** according to Weldon (2.2), this circular walk resulted from very weak legs, James 'having had (as was thought) some foul play in his youth, or rather before he was born, that he was not able to stand at seven years of age, that weaknesse made him ever leaning on other mens shoulders'.

114.43–115.2 **his ungainly fashion ... dress** see note to 109.25.

115.4–6 **an answer yielded by Naboth ... thee** see 1 Kings 21.3.

115.14 **make a kirk and a miln of it** *proverbial* make a church and a mill (i.e. make the best) of it: Kelly 1, 252; *ODEP*, 428.

115.15 **the Scottish Exchequer** the Scottish Treasury.

115.16–17 **find money on** be able to cash.

115.20–21 **nose-of-wax** person who can be easily manipulated; a weak character. The term occurs frequently in 17th-century poetry.

115.37 **the proto-martyr Stephen** the first Christian martyr, and so the model for others: see Acts Ch. 7.

115.39–40 **had considerably diminished his respect ... latter** Gilbert Burnet is one source of this idea: *Burnet's History of My Own Time*, ed. Osmund Airy, 2 vols (London, 1900), 1.22–23: compare *CLA*, 2. Weldon's account (1.458–68) of the deteriorating relationship between Buckingham and the King emphasises James's 'wearinesse' with the favourite and their mutual 'hatred'.

116.15 **in waiting** in attendance; waiting for you.

116.16–17   a cast in it, as the watermen say   *a cast* is a 'lift', as in John Taylor, 'I o'r the Water will give thee *A Cast*', in *A Cast Over the Water* (London, 1630), line 328 (Taylor, second section, 162).

116.24   that unhappy minion   'unhappy' probably alludes to Buckingham's untimely death by assassination in 1628 at the hands of John Felton, a disgruntled soldier.

116.24–26   sumptuously dressed ... Vandyke   Anthony Vandyke (1599–1641), the Flemish painter, first visited England in 1620. By his death he had painted portraits of almost every important courtier.

116.27   nodding to its fall   i.e. swaying from the perpendicular: compare John Dryden's 'If ancient Fabricks nod, and threat to fall' (*Absalom and Achitophel* (1681), line 801), and Alexander Pope's 'Or some old temple, nodding to its fall' (*An Essay on Man* (1733–34), 4.129).

117.20–21   Duke of Buckingham ... Leicester   Buckingham was the *representative* (heir) of Sir George Villiers (d. 1606), of Brooksby Hall, near Melton Mowbray, Leicestershire, only in a general sense: he had two older half-brothers and an older brother.

117.28   you know me ... enemy   during his visit to Madrid in 1623 Buckingham addressed similar words of warning to the Duke of Olivarez: '*With regard to you, Sir, in particular, you must not consider me as your friend, but must ever expect from me all possible enmity and opposition*'. See David Hume, *The History of England*, 8 vols (London, 1812), 6.136–37 (noted by Anderson, 80; compare *CLA*, 28).

117.29–30   an open enemy ... friend   a conflation of the proverb 'Better an open enemy than a false friend' (*ODEP*, 50) and the line 'I rather wish you foes than hollow friends' from *3 Henry VI*, 4.1.139. See also the 1595 quarto *The True Tragedie of Richard Duke of Yorke, and the death of good King Henrie the Sixt*, in *The True Tragedy*, ed. Thomas Tyler (London, 1891), 57: 'Speake truelie, for I had rather haue you open/ Enemies, then hollow friends'.

118.9–18   motto   not identified: probably by Scott.

118.9–10   the wheels ... mottled bone   referring to the spinning of dice (made of bone) used in gambling. References to dice being made of bone are frequent in the old plays.

118.11–12   Egypt's royal harlot ... wine cup   Queen Cleopatra VII of Egypt (69–30 BC) possessed two enormous pearl earrings, the largest ever known. In order to win a bet with her lover, the Roman soldier and politician Mark Antony, that she could spend 10,000,000 sesterces (Roman coins worth 0.25 of a denarius or a little less than 1p) on a single banquet she trumped a lavish feast by dissolving one of the earrings in a bowl of vinegar and drinking off the liquid. Scott could find the anecdote in both Pliny the Elder (AD 23 or 24–79), *Natural History*, 9.119–22, and Macrobius (active *c.* AD 400), *Saturnalia*, 3.17.14–18. However, the mention of a 'wine-cup' suggests that he remembered one of the many allusions in the old drama, e.g. 'I giue vnto thy hand an Orient Pearle/ Of more esteeme, than that, which at a health/ Great *Cleopatra* did carouse in wine/ To Romane *Anthony*': R. A., *The Valiant Welshman* (1615), 4.1.31–34.

118.13   Lothario   the type of the libertine, derived from the character by this name in the play by Nicholas Rowe, *The Fair Penitent* (1703).

118.39   an expiry of the legal   an expiration of the legal period in which the estate may be redeemed. Huntinglen fears that there will not be time to get the money from the Scottish Exchequer to redeem the estate under the warrant of the sign manual, and that if the property is to be saved money must be borrowed on the sign manual to settle the debt in London.

119.4   puzzle this scent out ... open   terms drawn from hunting, referring to dogs as they search for and then find the scent of their prey, where-upon they commence to *open* ('bark').

119.9   Peg-a-Ramsay   a derisive name derived from a popular old song, and famously applied to Malvolio by Sir Toby Belch in *Twelfth Night*, 2.3.74.

119.13   in the shoes of   in the place of.

119.23–24   a conveyance to his right   a legal document transferring to him the title to the estate.

119.37   the Lord Mayor's Easter-hunt, in Epping-Forest   this ancient hunt, held annually on Easter Monday, possibly originating with the Forest Charter of Henry III in 1226 and continuing officially until 1858 (unofficially until 1882), was patronised by the Lord Mayor of London, who with a party of aldermen initiated the proceedings by releasing a stag, beribboned and gar-landed, brought by cart to the starting point of the hunt.

120.1–2   draw the necessary writings   draw up the necessary legal docu-ments.

120.2–3   Sir John Skene of Halyards   Sir John Skene (1543?–1617), who became Lord Curriehill on his appointment as a lord of session in 1594, was a leading authority on Scots law. The Skenes of Halyards derive from his second son John (d. 1644).

120.20   pleached alley   walk bordered by small trees and overarched by their entwined boughs: compare 'a thick-pleached alley' in *Much Ado About Nothing*, 1.2.8.

120.25–26   three Scots miles   the Scots mile (1.8 km) was one-eighth longer than the English.

120.30   follow the court to Newmarket   after James's first visit to New-market, Cambridgeshire, in 1605, the town became an important venue for horse-racing, together with hare-coursing. James had a residence there, which he rebuilt and expanded several times up to 1620 (it was later rebuilt by Charles II), and it was one of the main locations for the royal court.

120.40   with fewer lights and with less means   i.e. lacking the present-day natural or acquired capacities and information, and the financial resources.

120.41   keep the country   remain in the country.

121.1   write himself   style himself.

121.8   the broad Tay   the river flowing E through central Scotland into the Firth of Tay.

121.25   high grace   great favour.

122.33–35   words and signals ... each other   code words and gestures, e.g. handshakes, resembling those that are meaningful only to the initiates of secret organisations, of which freemasonry is one of the oldest and most wide-spread.

123.26–27   The devil ... goose look?   *Macbeth*, 5.3.11–12. The play was probably written and first produced in 1606.

125.10   influencing the horizon   see note to 132.34.

125.16   blue-bonnet   Scotsman. The blue *bonnet*, a man's brimless cap, was the standard national headgear.

125.17   though your relationship comes by Noah   this is the most dis-tant of kinships, since all people descend from Noah, according to the logic of the story of the Flood (Genesis Chs 6–10). 'Nay, they will be kin to us, or they will fetch it from Japhet [Noah's son from whom the white races are supposedly descended]' (*2 Henry IV*, 2.2.112–13).

125.17–18   Scots twopenny ale   weak beer sold at twopence (0.8p, but see note to 127.35) a Scots pint, the equivalent of 3 imperial pints.

125.31   despite of   despite.

125.37   held by   caught hold of.

126.6   bayed the moon   see *Julius Cæsar*, 4.3.27.

126.11–12 **the more humane letters** a literal translation of the Latin 'litteræ humaniores'. Nigel is learned in Classical literature, ancient history, philosophy, i.e. the humanities as opposed to divinity.

126.19 **with eighteen quarters in her scutcheon** her coat of arms is divided and subdivided into heraldic *quarters*, each division representing a union of two noble houses through marriage: eighteen quarters implies an illustrious family tree.

126.19–20 **Lot's wife ... pedestal** see Genesis 19.24–26 for the story of Lot's wife who was turned into a pillar of salt for violating God's command not to look behind her when fleeing the destruction of Sodom and Gomorrah.

127.8 **rose-nobles** gold coins stamped with a rose: a noble was worth 6*s.* 8*d.* (33.3p).

127.17 **blue-bottles** servants and retainers, identified by their blue coats.

127.18–19 **trembling ... strong waters** the trembling is caused by old age combined with indulgence in alcoholic spirits.

127.20–21 **court cupboard** sideboard for displaying plate, etc.

127.25 **turn them off** dismiss them.

127.26–27 **the hospital ... switches** compare Jasper Mayne, *The City Match* (1639), 3.4.25–35: 'Yes,/ And as for me, my destiny will be ... to move/ Compassion in my father, who in pitty/ To so much ruine may be brought to buy/ Some place for me in an Hospitall, to keep me/ From Bridges, Hill-tops, & from selling switches'. Among the many hospitals mentioned in Stow (1.174–225) for the relief of the sick, infirm, blind, poor, orphaned, etc. was Bethlehem (or 'Bedlam'), established for 'the Cure of Lunaticks: But not without Charges at so much the Week, for these brought in, if they or their Relations were of Ability; and if not, then at the Parish Charge, in which they were Inhabitants' (1.192).

127.29 **blue coats** see note to 60.40.

127.32 **lither lad** lazy and maybe rascally boy. Compare 'a very loyteringe lither ladd,/ as euer did on two feete go', from the anonymous medieval play *The Pageant of Naaman*, lines 765–66.

127.33 **Lutin** French for 'imp', 'sprite', 'goblin'.

127.33–34 **old memorials ... wars** veterans of these wars, for which see note to 109.5–6.

127.35 **twelve pennies Scots** in the 17th century the Scots penny was worth one-twelfth of an English penny (itself 0.4p).

127.40 **the foul fiend** the Devil.

128.2–3 **to eat in saucieres abroad** apparently meant to denote a continental practice construed as a sign of sophistication, but the French *saucière* means 'sauceboat' rather than 'small dish'.

128.20 **the apple of discord** referring to the apple which the Trojan warrior Paris was given to bestow on the most beautiful of three goddesses, Venus, Pallas, and Juno. His choice of Venus because she promised him Helen, the most beautiful of all women, as his wife led to war between the Trojans and the Greeks.

128.20–22 **the very firebrand ... gunpowder** in Latin mythology Althea gave birth, not to a firebrand, but to a son named Meleager. The Fates, present at the birth, decreed that the child should die when a brand then burning on the fire was consumed. Althea extinguished it and kept it in a chest for many years until, in a fit of anger against Meleager, she rekindled it, causing his death. Scott follows Shakespeare's Page (who confuses Althea with Hecuba, mother of Paris) in substituting the firebrand for the infant: see *2 Henry IV*, 2.2.85–87.

128.23 **have been by the lugs about ye** have been in close contact with you.

128.28 **that needs na** that had better not happen.

128.36 **in the Spanish ambassador's time** see note to 72.24.

128.39 **in some sort** in a way or manner.

129.2 **fifty punds Scots** a pound Scots was worth 20 English pennies or 8.3p.

129.6 **in præsenti** *Latin* in the present tense.

129.31–32 **at the term of Lambmas ... redemption** *Lambmas* or *Lammas*, 1 August, marks the third quarter of the Scottish legal calendar. The prominent tomb of James Stewart (1531?–70: created Earl of Moray 1562) in the S aisle of the High Kirk of St Giles was often made the place of assignation for legal business at this time.

130.11–12 **the sun ... the right side of the hedge** compare the proverbial sayings 'To be on the right side of the hedge' and 'The sun does not shine on both sides of the hedge at once' (*ODEP*, 732, 786).

130.14–21 **motto** see Ben Jonson, *The Devil Is An Ass* (performed 1616, published 1631), 1.1.120–26. In this period the coach drawn by four horses (the norm being two) was a measure of wealth and station and is much remarked in the drama of the period.

130.27 **wait of** pay a respectful visit to.

130.32 **youth ... circumstances** compare 'I am the very slave of circumstance' from Byron's *Sardanapalus* (1821), 4.1.330, and 'Men are the sport of circumstances' from his *Don Juan*, Canto 5 (1821), 17.7.

130.40 **keep counsel** observe secrecy.

131.23 **Paul's Chain** lane on the S side of St Paul's Churchyard, so called from a chain drawn across the carriageway to curtail traffic so as to maintain quiet during divine service.

131.30–33 **My lord ... feeds on** see *Othello*, 3.3.169–71: 'make' is an emendation by Lewis Theobald of 'mock'.

132.9 **the better file** those above the common herd.

132.16 **possess you with** give you.

132.34 **Lord of the Ascendant** *astrology* a planet rising above the horizon and exercising the predominating influence at a particular moment.

132.36–39 **Phædrus ... iron** Phædrus was a 1st century AD Roman versifier of fables by Aesop. It was not he, however, but the slightly later Babrius (also 1st century AD) who transmitted the fable of two pots, which, floating in water, are in danger of colliding, to the consternation of the clay vessel, which urges the bronze one to keep its distance: *Babrius and Phaedrus*, ed. Ben Edwin Perry (Cambridge, Massachusetts, and London, 1965), 488.

133.9 **art magic** magic art. The expression is standard from the 14th–19th centuries.

133.13 **hustle-cap and chuck-farthing** games. *Hustle-cap* is a version of pitch-and-toss, coins being shaken in a cap before tossing; in *chuck-farthing* coins are pitched at a mark, and then chucked at a hole by the player who came nearest the mark, who wins all that alight in the hole.

133.37 **a Jacky Goodchild** compare Susan Ferrier, *Marriage*, 3 vols (Edinburgh and London, 1818), 3.74: 'a Tommy Goodchild'.

134.7 **in stead** in good stead.

134.14 **Kings and Kesars** in a note for *ABD*, 1.455, Scott associates the phrase with Spenser: see *The Faerie Queene*, 2.7.5.9, 3.11.29.9, and 5.9.29.9.

135.14 **ever and anon** every now and then; continually at intervals.

135.26 **Scythian festivity** such wild festivity as was practised by the 'barbaric' nomadic tribes of N Europe and of Asia beyond the Black Sea.

135.27–32 **Earl of Northampton ... always uses** in 1583 Howard (1540–1614) attacked sham prophets and soothsayers in *A Defensative against the Poyson of Supposed Prophesies*, earning the favour of Queen Elizabeth. For his ardent labour on behalf of James's succession he was made Earl of North-ampton (1604) and Lord Privy Seal (1608). According to Weldon (1.327), he was 'the grossest flatterer of the world'. The author of *The Narrative History of King James* elucidated his 'intolerable' flattery by instancing the 'many pleasant letters' written in Latin the better to ingratiate himself with Cambridge scholars who were divided on his selection as Chancellor (*Somers' Tracts*, 2.273).

136.8   couple us up   i.e. like a pair of hunting dogs on a leash.

136.11–12   the landing-place at Blackfriar's   the next free landing place on the Thames W of Paul's Wharf (Stow, 1.21).

136.15   tawney-visaged Don   Spaniard with a yellow-brown skin.

136.35   Auld Reekie   see note to 59.35–38.

136.36–38   such bandying...thrice   Scott's Magnum note (26.239) in-dicates that in this period Edinburgh was one of the most disorderly towns in Europe.

136.40   clubs is the word   see note to 28.30.

137.22   thin potations   drinks without body or weak in alcoholic strength, of which Dalgarno takes Falstaff's view: 'If I had a thousand sons, the first humane principle I would teach them should be to forswear thin potations, and to addict themselves to sack' (*2 Henry IV*, 4.3.115–17).

137.23   An ordinary   restaurant or tavern where a meal was provided at a fixed time (noon) and price. It was at its height of fashion with Londoners in this period when, in its more expensive form, it was synonymous with 'gambling house'. Scott had used the ordinary as setting in *Private Letters of the Seven-teenth Century* (see Essay on the Text, 408) and had included William Cart-wright's play *The Ordinary* (performed 1634–35; first published 1651) in *ABD* (3.142–78).

137.24   Bacchus and Comus   in Classical mythology Bacchus is the god of wine. Comus appears as a god of revelry in Ben Jonson, *Pleasure Reconciled to Virtue* (1618), which gave Milton the idea for his masque *Comus* (produced 1634, published 1637).

137.30   upon the rack   at full stretch.

137.37–38   Monsieur le Chevalier de Beaujeu...Gascony   the name Beaujeu is a favourite with Scott for the Frenchman in England who speaks fractured English; he had used it in *Waverley* (1814) for the French officer whose attempts to discipline the Young Pretender's Scottish cavalry prove so comical. Scott may have associated the name with Gascony because in Ann Radcliffe's novel *The Mysteries of Udolpho* (1794), Ch. 4, Beaujeu is a town in the south of that province, in the Pyrenees, where Emily St Aubert and her father pause to rest. In Dalgarno's encomium Scott captures the essence of the Gascon's character: his reputation for boasting—his 'gasconade'.

137.41   Lullie's philosophy   from his strange but fascinating writings which proffered a mechanical system for acquiring knowledge and for solving all problems, Raymond Lully (Ramon Lull: *c*. 1235–*c*. 1315) acquired a large following whose arts bordering on the occult included both religious mysticism and alchemy.

138.5–7   the mysteries of Passage...Dice-box   *Passage* is a game for two people with two or three dice, thrown continually until the caster throws doublets under 10 and is out or throws doublets over 10 and wins or 'passes'. *Hazard* is played with two dice by as many as can stand around the table. *In-and-In* or *In-and-Out* is played with four dice by two or three, 'in' or 'out' being determined by the success in throwing doublets. *Penneeck* (*Penneech*, first re-corded in 1680) involves a seven-card hand and constantly changing trumps. *Verquire* (*Verquere*, Dutch in origin, and first recorded in England in 1700) is a form of backgammon but where all the table-men, not just two, are set at ace-point.

138.24 Jacobus gold coin of James I's reign, worth between £1.00 and £1.20.

138.26 the Diva Fortuna the goddess fortune.

138.33 putt ... Quinze le Va *putt* is a card game, first recorded in 1680; *Quinze le Va*, like *Tally*, is a scoring term (used in the card game of faro).

138.37 For all this notwithstanding this.

139.7 take the accommodation of use the services or creature comforts of.

139.27 troll them down with a die lose them through rolling a dice.

141.5–12 motto not identified: probably by Scott. For the bear-garden see notes to 147.25 and 192.27. A 'cock of the game' is one bred for cock-fighting, fitted with spurs. 'Chaunticleer' is the gorgeous cock with peerless voice in Geoffrey Chaucer's beast fable 'The Nun's Priest's Tale', in *The Canterbury Tales*.

141.14–15 the first-rate modern club-houses in Scott's day these would be the buildings that housed such private gentlemen's clubs as White's, Boodle's, and Brooks's, all in the elegant St James's Street.

141.21 Gascon see note to 137.37–38.

141.26 taffeta a lustrous silk or linen fabric used in fashioning elegant clothes, frequently mentioned in the literature of the period.

142.32 Genius Loci *Latin* presiding spirit of the place; in the case of an ordinary, the master of ceremonies.

142.34 a hundred apish congés and chers milors the excessively affected bows and effusively deferential speech by which Beaujeu would ingratiate himself with his patrons: *chers milors* is French for 'my dear lords'. Compare Gloucester's disclaimer, in *Richard III*, 1.3.47–49, that he 'cannot ... Duck with French nods and apish courtesy'.

142.42—143.5 tres honoré ... dechainé Beaujeu's French-speak, a mixture of French and, often, unidiomatic English, goes thus (with modern forms of apparently misspelt words in parentheses): 'very ('très') honoured —I remember—yes. I knew once a Lord Glenvarloch in Scotland. Yes, I have memory of him—the father ('père') of my lord apparently—we were very intimate when I was at Holyrood with Monsieur de la Motte—I did often play at tennis with Lord Glenvarloch at the Abbey of Holyrood—he was even better than I—Ah the fine backhand stroke he had—I have memory too that he was among the pretty girls—a regular devil unloosed ('déchaîné')'. M. de la Motte was the Marquis de La Mothe-Fénelon, sometime French ambassador at the English Court. James VI received him at the Scottish Court in 1582. Holyrood (see note to 47.5–8) was originally an Augustinian abbey founded in 1128.

143.16 Qu'est ce ... passé? *French* what have we to do ('à faire') with the past?

143.17 our ancetres our ancestors (*French* 'ancêtres').

143.19–20 petits plats exquis and the Soupe-a-Chevalier *French* exquisite little dishes and soup according to Beaujeu's recipe ('Soupe-à-Chevalier'), i.e. soup of the day.

143.20 cause to mount up have served. The French expression is 'faire monter'.

143.31–32 according to the trick of the time using the current way of saying it.

143.32 set a piece or two make a wager. The term *piece* refers to the current English gold coin, the Jacobus: see note to 138.24.

144.13 passes current for it is generally accepted for it.

144.18 the "curieux and l'utile" *French* the curious and the useful.

144.22–23 Maitre de Cuisine ... pourtant *French* chief cook to

Marshal Strozzi—a very fine gentleman all the same. Member of a noble Florentine family, Piero Strozzi (1500–58) was made a marshal of France in 1556. However, Strozzi died before the siege of Leith (1560) but his son Filippo was there. The anecdote was inspired by the *Memoires de Messire Pierre du Bourdeille, Seigneur de Brantome* (Leiden, 1665): see Scott's Magnum note (26.258).

144.24   twelve covers   complete place settings, dishes, utensils, and serviettes, for twelve people.

144.24–25   the long and severe blockade of Le petit Leyth   Leith (where the Roman Catholic and French party headed by the regent Mary of Guise had taken refuge) was besieged by the Scottish Protestants and blockaded by an English fleet from April to July 1560. Leith, the port of Edinburgh, *was* small (*French*, petit) in the 16th century.

144.27–28   Des par dieux ... superbe!   *French* by the gods he was a splendid man!

144.28   on tistle-head   one thistle-head.

144.30   a roti des plus excellents   *French* an excellent joint of roast ('rôti') meat.

144.30   coup de maitre   *French* masterpiece ('maître').

144.32   dieu me damne   *French* God damn me.

144.33   couverts   *French* covers; portions: see note to 144.24.

144.37–40   The good wine ... innovation   compare *Othello*, 2.3.34–37: *innovation* means 'revolution'.

145.4   Uds daggers and scabbards   meaningless oath (God's daggers and scabbards). See John Webster and Thomas Dekker, *Westward Hoe* (1607), 5.3.23.

145.7   the Provost Marshall ... reeved   a *provost-marshall* was a head of a military police unit; a *reeved* noose is the hangman's, passed through a block, looped and ready for an execution.

145.11–12   the grande guerre   *French* the great war. Given Strozzi's death in 1558, Beaujeu refers to the series of wars between France and Spain for control of Italy begun in 1494 and ending in 1559 with the Peace of Cateau-Cambrésis.

145.12   grand capitain—plus grand   *French* great captain—greater.

145.14   Angleterre   *French* England, although Beaujeu may intend a reference to Britain.

145.14   tenez ... vous   *French* there you are, Sir, it is you I mean ('c'est à vous').

145.17   back, breast, and pot   a standard phrase meaning 'back-plate, breast-plate, and round, pot-shaped helmet'.

145.20   pauvre gentilhomme   *French* poor gentleman.

145.20–22   the Grand Henri Quatre ... marmite   Henry of Navarre (1553–1610), who became King Henry IV of France in 1589, won key military victories at Courtras (1587) and Ivry (1590). Beaujeu mimics a nonsense oath the monarch is reputed to have used—By the belly of Holy Christ! (see Howell, 207)—but takes the soldier's word *pot* literally, associating it with the earthenware cooking pot or stock-pot known as 'marmite'.

145.24   linen was scarce   Scott alludes to the motif popular in the literature of the period that soldiers other than officers were poorly dressed, wearing little more than beggars' rags: compare Falstaff's 'There's not a shirt and a half in all my company; and the half shirt is two napkins tack'd together ... and the shirt, to say the truth, stol'n from my host at Saint Albans ... But that's all one; they'll find linen enough on every hedge' (*1 Henry IV*, 4.2.39–44).

145.26   Gentlemen out at arms and at elbows both   i.e. the French were poorly equipped with weapons and uniforms. The Captain's insult plays on the French term for soldier 'gen d'arme' and the English term 'out at elbow', meaning having a badly worn coat, being a poor, ragged man.

145.28   gens d'armes   *French* men-at-arms; mounted soldiers.

145.33   the men of mohair   i.e. civilians, so called by contemptuous soldiers for their buttons of mohair, a soft, feathery cloth made of yarn from the fleece of Angora goats; soldiers' buttons, by contrast, were of metal.

145.34   eat his very hilts   eat the leather of his sword hilt. Compare 'I had suck'd the hilts long before': Ben Jonson, *Every Man In His Humour* (performed 1598, published 1601 and revised 1616), 2.5.91.

145.38   cuckoo's nest ... city of London   Scott's Magnum note (26.258–59) cites as the source of this dispute the burlesque poem *A New Droll; or, The Counter-Scuffle* (1663), by Thomas Jordan, where a soldier insults a London lawyer with the phrase 'the Cuckowes nest,/ *Your City*' (lines 259–60), provoking a hot-headed, patriotic citizen to come boldly to the defence of London. The cuckoo is thought to be a lazy, irresponsible bird, because it lays its eggs in the nests of other birds which then hatch them.

145.41   brook to hear   put up with hearing.

146.4–5   a peremptory gull   an unquestionable fool. See Ben Jonson, *Every Man In His Humour* (performed 1598, published 1601 and revised 1616), 1.2.30.

146.10–11   Bow Bell ... the Cock of St Paul's   for Bow Bell see note to 79.31–35. The weathercock of St Paul's Cathedral, set up in 1553 and destroyed by lightning in 1561, had apparently become proverbial: see E. K. Chambers, *The Elizabethan Stage*, 4 vols (Oxford, 1923), 3.466, 4.31.

146.23–24   It is my right ... sword   according to the code of duelling, 'the rules of the sword', it is the man challenged who chooses the site of combat.

146.24–25   the Maze, in Tothill-Fields   Tothill Fields, an open area on the N bank of the Thames between Millbank and Westminster Abbey, was a popular venue for duelling, and at this period the Maze there, a labyrinth constructed of hedge and designed to pleasure both the eye and the mind, was much frequented for recreation.

146.36   the air of Ancient Pistol   a swaggering air. Ensign Pistol is the braggart soldier who serves as Falstaff's lieutenant: e.g. see *2 Henry IV*, 2.4.

147.5–6   cudgel the ass ... lion's hide   Dalgarno images the ensuing fight as a contrast between clothing material, assuming the citizen to be a tradesman in cloth; made of animal skin, the soldier's buff coat when dirty takes on the appearance of a lion's coat. The allusion is to one of Aesop's fables, where an ass wraps itself in a lionskin but betrays itself by braying: the fable has become proverbial (*ODEP*, 21).

147.8   a hog in armour   said proverbially of a person wearing clothes or equipment to which they are totally unaccustomed and hence appearing ludicrous to onlookers: *ODEP*, 147.8.

147.14–15   the civic helmet ... forfeited   i.e. his wife's cooking-pot.

147.15–16   the rarest sport   exceedingly fine sport or comedy. A frequent phrase in the old drama.

147.16   run a tilt   an image from jousting or tilting: to charge one's opponent with the lance directed toward him. Tilting was a favourite game of courtiers, usually played during Christmas or to entertain a distinguished foreign visitor.

147.25   Whitefriars ... the Bankside   areas of sanctuary, official and unofficial respectively, for fugitives from the law on either side of the Thames. For Whitefriars on the N bank see note to 181.35. On Bankside, the S bank of the river, were concentrated the disreputable and unlicensed pastimes of cock-fighting, bull and bear-baiting, and play-acting, among others.

148.4 one grand fanfaron a great braggart.

148.14–16 all the terms ... trundling timber Scott represents here the jargon of someone who has 'cast' a bowl and attempts to influence its course by exhortation: *rub* means 'slow down'; *hold bias* means 'move in a curve'; and *timber* refers to the wood of which a bowl is made.

148.16–17 the saying ... oaths proverbial: *ODEP*, 817.

148.19–22 Ombre ... Passage *Ombre* is a three-handed card game of Spanish origin played with nine cards, first recorded in England in 1660; *Basset* is a courtly card game requiring a banker, imported from Italy and first recorded in England in 1705; for *Gleek* see note to 185.13–25; *Primero*, the popular Elizabethan card game enjoyed by the Queen herself and said to be among the oldest in England, is played with a four-card hand, several cards having more than their usual values: see Strutt, 247. *Hazard*, *In-and-in*, and *Passage* (see note to 138.5–7) are described by Strutt (247–48) as 'games without the tables', that is, games of pure chance, skill being irrelevant.

148.32–33 what in modern phrase ... lounging the term *lounging* in this sense is first recorded in 1793.

148.34 Burbage ... the Fortune Scott's Magnum note (26.259) indicates that the actor Richard Burbage (1567?–1619) may have created the role of Richard III and identified with it. The Fortune Theatre was in Golden Lane, Cripplegate: opened in 1601, burned in 1621, and immediately rebuilt, it was finally destroyed in 1649.

148.40 shows of a modern date ... Scotland the English theatre was relatively recent, evolving through the second half of the preceding century; the puritanical hostility to theatre that impeded its progress in England thwarted a parallel development in Scotland.

148.43—149.2 George Buchanan ... to see them Buchanan, King James's senior tutor when a boy (see note to 76.15–16), wrote several sacred tragedies. His royal pupil attended plays performed at Whitehall especially during the Christmas revels and, in his honour, at the universities of Cambridge and Oxford and at the seats of courtiers visited on his progresses.

149.8 Chevalier de la Fortune this new epithet for Beaujeu (*French* 'Knight of Fortune') alludes to the Goddess of Fortune and the Wheel of Fortune (see notes to 84.7–8 and 138.26).

149.9–11 Lord Dalgarno's grooms ... jennet compare the opening and closing paragraphs of Ch. 5 of Thomas Dekker, *The Gull's Hornbook* (1549, revised 1552), ed. R. B. McKerrow (London, 1904), 41, 47: 'Ride thither [to the ordinary] upon your Galloway nag, or your Spanish jennet ... the French lackey and Irish footboy shrugging at the doors, with their masters' hobbyhorses [ponies], to ride to the new play: that's the rendezvous: thither they are galloped in post'.

149.16 sage son ... Low-Dutch learning Nigel's alma mater is Leiden University, in the Netherlands (see note to 110.26).

149.20–21 as black as Infamy ... can make them *black* and *infamy* are frequently linked in the old plays; the poets assign sooty pinions to human and non-human creatures alike (though not to infamy), but probably most memorable are those given the dark spirit Umbriel in Alexander Pope, *The Rape of the Lock* (1714), 4.17.

149.22 Stand buff stand firm.

149.25–26 tell the accusing spirit, to his brimstone beard the brimstone beard suggests that the accusing spirit which will not allow Nigel to fall asleep and ultimately threatens his salvation takes the form of the devil. 'Old Brimstone-Beard' is used as a term of abuse in Thomas Otway, *The Atheist* (1684), 4.46.

149.27 the devil's bones a standard phrase for dice.

149.35 Sancte Nigelle ... preach a crusade for his scruples Nigel is mocked as *Latin* 'Saint Nigel' and linked with the French hermit and monk Peter, who in 1095 preached the First Crusade.

149.37–38 Saint Sepulchre's Church the parish church W of Newgate in the ward of Farringdon Without.

149.39 the clerk say amen in the Church of England the clerk might read the lessons and would lead the responses to the priest, including saying 'Amen' at the end of each prayer.

150.2 who lives after death Shakespeare died in 1616.

150.4–8 the gallant Falconbridge ... mean to learn *King John*, 1.1.207–08, 214–15. The man is no true son of the age because he is not given to obsequiousness: in the omitted lines Falconbridge identifies with this man.

150.15–16 a brace of stools upon the stage see note to 27.2–3.

150.23–27 that sorcerer ... the living see the allusion in the Prologue to *Henry V* (lines 11–14) to either the roughly circular Curtain Theatre in Shoreditch or the octagonal Globe Theatre on Bankside, at both of which this play and others devoted to the Wars of the Roses were performed: 'Can this cockpit hold/ The vasty fields of France? Or may we cram/ Within this wooden O the very casques/ That did affright the air at Agincourt?'. The phrase 'in language and fashion as they lived' echoes *Hamlet*, 3.4.135.

150.28–32 Burbage ... imagination in support of this claim Scott's Magnum note (26.259) quotes from the poem 'Iter Boreale' (1647) by Richard Corbet (1582–1635), 'son' of Ben Jonson, an anecdote in which the speaker so identified Burbage with the role of Richard that he 'mistooke a Player for a King' (350), saying 'Burbage' died when he meant 'Richard'. Corbet's poem is included in *The Works of the English Poets*, ed. Alexander Chalmers, 21 vols (London, 1810), 5.577–81: *CLA*, 41–42. In 1741 David Garrick (1717–79) was so successful in the role of Richard III that audiences deserted the more fashionable West End theatres of Covent Garden and Drury Lane for the East End playhouse of Goodman's Fields where he was performing. *Richard III* ends with the Battle of Bosworth in Leicestershire, where in 1485 Richard was defeated and killed by Henry Tudor, afterwards Henry VII. Nigel's imaginative involvement and depth of reverie are responsive to Shakespeare's appeal in the Prologue to *Henry V* to the audience's 'imaginary forces' (line 18). He models, in fact, the imagination of the Shakespearean audience Scott had described, citing this same passage, in his 1819 *Essay on the Drama* (*Prose Works*, 6.345). That 'ideas of reality and deception were strongly contending in Lord Glenvarloch's imagination' reflects the discussion of dramatic illusion, heavily indebted to Dr Johnson, earlier in the same essay (308–12).

150.34 the Mermaid the tavern in Cheapside where Ben Jonson and his circle gathered for witty conversation.

150.42–151.5 one of Ben Jonson's cotemporaries ... frolic wine see Robert Herrick (1591–1674), 'An Ode For Him' [Ben Jonson], lines 4, 7–10 (in his *Hesperides*, 1648). The word *clusters* means grapes but, in context, the wine therefrom.

151.7–15 motto not identified: probably by Scott.

151.25 seemed on the stretch seemed to be strained or forced.

151.26 brown study a state of mental abstraction: *ODEP*, 930.

151.27 out-herod it alluding to the noisy, violent role of Herod in the medieval mystery plays. Nigel echoes Hamlet's warning to the players against such overdone acting: 'it out-Herods Herod. Pray you avoid it' (*Hamlet*, 3.2.13).

151.29 to play the intellectual gladiators a *gladiator* was (literally) a professional swordsman or fencer. That this was not considered a high calling is confirmed by a reference to the 'pitiful Trade of Gladiator, Ballad-singer, and Morrice-dancer' in Henry Baker and James Miller, *The Cit Turn'd Gentleman* (1739), 2.4.42–43, an English version of Molière's *Le Bourgeois Gentilhomme*

151.30   declares himself recreant   confesses himself a coward.

151.31   the watermen's company   established in 1555 by Act of Parliament, the Waterman's Company organised the men who transported people on the River Thames. The trade of waterman was relatively lowly, and its members were known for their rowdy, drunken behaviour; the company's patronage would not likely enhance, and might even sully, a poet's reputation.

151.33   the Mermaid   the Mermaid Tavern, Cheapside, most notably patronised by Ben Jonson.

151.34   Wit's hospital in the Vintry   the Vintry was a portion of the N bank of the Thames equidistant between London Bridge and Blackfriars where wine from Bordeaux was unloaded and sold. 'Wit's hospital' is the tavern called the Three Cranes of the Vintry, after three machines used for unloading wine: in 1577 a book by N[icholas] B[reton] entitled *The Workes of a young wyt, trust vp with a Fardell of pretie fancies*... was published 'nigh vnto the three Cranes in the Vintree', the area also being a favourite location for booksellers.

151.40   out upon   an expression of abhorrence or dismay; fie upon.

151.42   the fico for such bran of Parnassus   the *fico* is the fig, a small object of little value. With this standard expression Dalgarno expresses his contempt for the Mermaid poets, deprived as they are in his view of the inspiration of the muses who in Classical mythology were said to inhabit the Greek mountain of Parnassus. Similarly without value is the *bran* or the husk of the grain.

151.43—152.2   banquet ... Nash or Greene   according to Gabriel Harvey, *Fovre Letters, and Certeine Sonnets, Especially Touching Robert Greene*... (London, 1592), Greene died from overindulging in just such a banquet (13, 21). Thomas Nash (1567–1601) and Robert Greene (1560?–92) were important progenitors of the Elizabethan theatre in particular and of the new poetry in general, Greene being, in Harvey's view, one of the 'very ringleaders of the riming, and scribbling crew' (15). For 'bards of misrule' see Harvey on poets' claims to 'an absolute Licence' (15, 49) and note to 185.41–42.

152.6–7   patrons or players to feed them   Thomas Dekker informs his gallant that it is 'knightly' behaviour to pay for the playwright's dinner following the play: *The Gull's Hornbook* (1549, revised 1552), ed. R. B. McKerrow (London, 1904), 51. Ben Jonson's besotted playgoer Fitz-Dottrell expects to buy the playwright's dinner unless he should be so misguided as to laugh at the squire's foppish costume: 'Then he shall pay for his dinner himselfe' (*The Devil Is An Ass* (performed 1616, published 1631), 3.5.42–48).

152.8   the New River head   the reservoir now recalled by the name of Amwell Street, Islington, N London, into which the 62 km canal known as the New River, built 1609–13, discharged water principally from springs at Amwell, Hertfordshire.

152.8   holds good   i.e. continues to supply water.

152.8–9   doublets of Parnassus ... duration   i.e. cloaks worn by indigent poets last, or by necessity can be made to last, indefinitely.

152.10   Virgil and Horace ... patronage   in the 1st century BC the Roman poets Virgil and Horace were both befriended by the Roman statesman and patron of literature Gaius Maecenas, who presented Horace with his Sabine farm and encouraged Virgil to write the *Georgics*.

152.12   spirits of another sort   in *A Midsummer Night's Dream*, 3.2.388, Oberon says to Puck: 'we are spirits of another sort' than those who shun the light.

152.13 Swan of Avon Ben Jonson's epithet for Shakespeare ('Sweet swan of Avon') occurs in 'To the Memory of My Beloved, the Author Mr William Shakespeare: And What He Hath Left Us' (1618), line 71.

152.14–15 stout old Ben . . . sock and buskin by the time of the story Jonson was a seasoned writer: his collected works appeared in 1616, he was principal poet to the Court, and his masques were much in demand by Queen Anne. His learning was displayed in his Classically modelled comedies, symbolised by the *sock* or flat-soled shoe of the Classical comic actor, and tragedies, symbolised by the *buskin* or high-heeled boot of the tragic actor. The adjective *stout* may refer in particular to Jonson's courage in enduring imprisonment and risking mutilation for criticising the Court in some of his early writings.

152.16–17 of dear love out of kind affection for you.

152.17 Richmond see note to 70.11.

152.18–19 syllabubs a *syllabub* was a drink or dish made of milk or cream, curdled with wine or cider, etc. and often sweetened and flavoured.

152.29 Countess of Blackchester a fictitious figure presented as a portrait or 'character' of the female courtier.

153.22 was not long of experiencing soon experienced.

153.30–31 Hyde Park . . . public resort at this time Hyde Park was in fact not 'a place of public resort' but a royal deer park. It was first opened to the public by Charles I in 1635.

154.23–24 upon the square without cheating. The expression 'to play upon the square' was especially popular with the Restoration dramatists, but the context suggests that Scott remembered it from Thomas D'Urfey, *Love for Money* (1691), 1.1.407–08: 'besides a Wit plays cautiously, and upon the square, when a Fool sets deep without consideration, and therefore to me is the more meritorious by half'.

154.37 forms of office bureaucratic procedures to be followed if James's 'sign manual' (his signature, or the warrant signed by him) is to be effective.

155.13 in the right on't correct on the disputed point.

155.16 more noble than himself by eight quarters see note to 126.19.

155.22 the risk of extremity extremely risky.

155.23–24 take off the heat of the distemperature calm the mind overheated with emotion.

155.40–41 no daily insurrections . . . Scottish court referring, among others, to: the murder of Queen Mary's Italian secretary Rizzio at Holyrood House in 1566 (see note to 307.4–6); the assassination of James's father Darnley in 1567 at Kirk of Field in Edinburgh (see note to 54.29–30); the raid on Stirling town in 1571 that left his grandfather the Earl of Lennox dead; the sudden intrusion on Stirling Castle in 1578 by the Earls of Atholl and Argyll for the purpose of having James dismiss the Regent Morton, followed by the counter effort of the Earl of Mar to return Morton to influence; the Raid of Ruthven in 1582 whereby James became captive to a band of Protestant lords (see Historical Note, 524–25); the 5th Earl of Bothwell's repeated attempts to seize the King in 1591–93; the riot in Edinburgh against his financial officials in 1596; and the Gowrie conspiracy in 1600 (see Historical Note, 524–25). By contrast the purlieus of the English court were relatively safe. The conspiracy of Raleigh on behalf of Lady Arabella Stuart's claim to the throne (known as the Main Plot or Cobham's Plot) and that of William Watson to capture the King and make himself Lord Chancellor (known as the Bye Plot) at the start of James's reign culminated in state trials, as did the Gunpowder Plot of 1605 (see note to 212.43). From 1606 on James had no real cause to fear physical assault or deposition, though the habitual nervousness attributed to his Scottish experience never left him (see notes to 66.29–30 and 69.23–26).

155.43–156.1 your old-fashioned serving men ... bucklers see note to 249.19.

156.2 a court-masque the masque, the mixed-media spectacle which Ben Jonson and Inigo Jones complicated and perfected, was the preferred form of entertainment at the Jacobean Court, the courtiers themselves and sometimes the Queen taking the speaking parts as well as performing the dances.

156.6–7 infandum .. dolorem *Latin* '[O, Queen, you are ordering me] to relive an unutterable sorrow' (Virgil (70–19 BC), *Aeneid*, 2.3): the reply of Aeneas to Dido's request that he tell her the story of the fall of Troy.

156.8 a long Liddesdale whinger ... Parma a heavy short-sword or hanger associated with Liddesdale in the Scottish Borders as compared with the light dagger associated with the N Italian town of Parma.

156.11 Falkland the royal palace dating from the early 16th century in N Fife.

156.11–12 Dumfermline Dunfermline: a town in S Fife, the traditional royal seat, with a palace rebuilt in 1500.

156.12 to the boot of all in addition.

156.14 a dagger of service i.e. a useful, practical weapon.

156.15 Odds nouns *oath*: God's wounds (i.e. Christ's wounds).

156.16–17 when kings ... hen see note to 47.23–24.

156.18–19 the green geese ... the Indies i.e. parrots.

156.22 break all off i.e. withdraw abruptly from the court.

156.23 Campsie Linn a cataract on the River Tay in Perthshire.

157.11–12 your fortunes ... upon the same coast Scott's version of a familiar image in the old plays. Compare 'And Love lies shipwreck'd on the stormy Coast': George Granville, *The British Enchanters* (1736), 3.1.40.

157.27 favourite benediction, Beati pacifici see note to 110.14.

157.39 petty officer minion; inferior official.

158.33–34 to Lord Glenvarloch's mind i.e. to his liking.

159.1 twenty round shillings i.e. a full pound sterling.

159.19 Arthur's Seat the striking peak (250 m) S of Holyrood House, Edinburgh.

159.21–29 motto not traced: probably by Scott. Bingo is the name of the dog ('And Bingo was his name-o') in the familiar children's song 'There was a farmer who had a dog', first published in 1780 (*The Reader's Digest Children's Songbook*, ed. William Simon (New York, 1985), 124). The phrase 'takes such humour' means 'gets into such a mood'.

159.38–40 the grotesque mask ... Gothic building in gothic architecture, the gargoyle is a distorted, fantastic human or animal figure with open mouth that allows rain water in the gutters to be projected away from the structure. The Temple Church, S of Fleet Street near Temple Bar, was built by the Knights Templars in the 12th century.

160.11–12 mair plenty ... than formerly more plentiful ... than before.

160.16 your commands for Scotland your orders or permission to depart for Scotland.

160.21–22 pact of duty terms of employment.

160.28 in some sort to a certain extent.

160.40 Body of me *oath* my body.

161.2 Under favour with all submission; subject to correction.

161.2–3 unequal dealing unfair behaviour; contradictory behaviour.

161.4 the grounds of the justifying reasons for.

161.7 Go to come on.

161.7 speak out your mind i.e. speak freely, candidly.

161.19 let that be a pass-over let us pass over that matter.

161.20 my northern conscience i.e. his Scottish conscience, with the related sense of morally strict or puritanical conscience.

161.28–31 tak a jump over the hedge ... pouch i.e. Richie would become highwayman with Nigel and prey upon the cattleman from Essex returning home with the profits from selling his calves at the flesh market in Smithfield. *Stand* is the conventional robber's command to submit to the robbery as in 'This is the most omnipotent villain that ever cried "Stand" to a true man' (*1 Henry IV*, 1.2.105–06).

161.41 bare stakes minimum bets; small sums.

162.9 cross and pile head and tail of a coin; money.

162.13 All is not gold that glistens proverbial: Ray, 114; *ODEP*, 316.

162.14 bullion buttons buttons of solid silver or gold.

162.18 Never fash your beard never trouble your beard; i.e. don't worry. A proverbial expression: 'Howe'er I get them, never fash your Beard' (Allan Ramsay, *The Gentle Shepherd* (1725), 3.2.132: *The Works of Allan Ramsay*, Vol. 2, ed. Burns Martin and John W. Oliver (Edinburgh and London, 1953), 243). Compare *ODEP*, 246.

162.20 running post to the devil going with all speed to the devil. Compare 'So, now is he going to take Horse and Ride Post to the Devill': Joseph Harris and William Mountfort, *The Mistakes* (1691), 1.1.24.

162.21 an if if.

162.35–36 make mouths ... ring make mocking faces or grimace at a coin that is a little short of the gold it should contain or that gives off a faulty ring when tested.

162.36 my sooth truly; indeed.

162.36–37 jump ... like a cock at a grossart proverbial: *ODEP*, 415; compare Ray, 223. *Grossart* is Scots for 'gooseberry'.

163.5–6 going ... a dish-clout proverbial: see Kelly, 264; *ODEP*, 562. Kelly's gloss reads: 'If you will be a Knave, be not in a Trifle, but in something of Value'. The phrase *under correction* means 'subject to correction', i.e. 'if you will pardon the expression'.

163.10 as I live by bread ... a true man as I am a human being and as I am a trustworthy one.

163.18–19 dunghill chicken *literally* chicken that feeds on refuse on the dunghill. There is also a suggestion of Chauntecleer, the farmyard cock in Chaucer's mock-heroic 'Nun's Priest's Tale', in *The Canterbury Tales*, who misconceives himself and his status in the world.

163.20 ruffle a feather with a cock of the game compete with a worthy opponent in a cockfight.

163.22 the Sparrow-hawk a species of hawk that preys on small birds and other defenceless creatures.

163.25 Death and the devil vehement oath expressing the ultimate bad fate: 'next there's Poverty, next/ Repentance, next Despair, then Death and the Devil' (William Philips, *The Revengeful Queen* (1698), 5.96–97).

163.27 the devil's dam the devil's mother, thought to be a worse affliction than the devil himself: 'Why she's a Devil; a Devil! the Devil's Dam' (David Garrick, *Catharine and Petruchio* (1756), 2.148).

163.30 over well with sexually intimate with.

163.39 Richie's four quarters i.e. his arms and legs.

164.7–8 the snares .... exposed compare 'Deeming thy youth and innocence exposed/ To countless snares': J. H. Craig of Douglas [i.e. James Hogg], *The Hunting of Badlewe* (London, 1814), 120 (5.1.120–21).

164.32–33 but in right of only justifiably, legally entitled to (not in actual possession of).

164.34 the cloven foot the sign of the devil: see note to 88.26–27.

164.35   had a good will to   was favourably (possibly romantically) disposed to.

164.36   in particular   privately.

165.3   the ducking-stool   see note to 30.13.

165.8–10   what Solomon … drabbing   in Proverbs 2.16–19, 5.3–20, and 7.4–27 the nominal author Solomon repeatedly warns against consorting with 'the strange woman', that is, the prostitute—in Jacobean slang, against *drabbing*.

166.21–22   harped upon the same string   proverbial: Ray, 195; *ODEP*, 355.

166.37   Ignoto   *Italian* unknown or anonymous person.

167.7–22   motto   not identified: probably by Scott. Swaffham, in Norfolk, is the site of the oldest regular hare-coursing club, founded in 1776 by Lord Orford; but as early as the reign of Elizabeth I, the popularity of coursing induced the Duke of Norfolk to draw up the first set of rules for the sport. For Newmarket see note to 120.30: the coursing club there was founded in 1805. The 'Roman Camp' alludes to the coursing club at Beacon Hill, Burghclere, Hampshire, founded in 1812: Beacon Hill was the site of a Roman fort. 'Saint James' is the street running from Piccadilly to St James's Palace. In coursing, the term *cote* refers to one dog passing another at an angle so as to cause the hare to alter course: Scott makes the dog cote the hare.

167.23   The Park of Saint James's   the royal park situated W of Whitehall and S of St James's Palace, developed from a swampy meadow by Henry VIII, but not opened to the public until the reign of Charles II.

168.11   run cunning   sporting term, meaning 'run cleverly'.

168.17   early day   early in the day.

168.21–22   having fair grappled … in tow   the image derives from a naval ship securing another vessel by means of grappling irons and (after subduing the crew) taking it in tow with the prospect of receiving prize money for the capture.

168.41   pluck them, plume   in falconry, the falcon is said to *plume* when it plucks the feathers from its prey.

169.13   gar them as gude   pay them back; retaliate.

169.14   the trick on't   the knack of doing it skilfully. The expression is much used in the old drama.

169.15   horse and foot   *either* completely *or* with all your might.

169.16   spolia opima   *Latin* spoils won in single combat.

169.17–18   to graze with Nebuchadnezzar, King of Babylon   see Daniel Ch. 4: in a dream, correctly interpreted by Daniel, the king loses his reason, lives among beasts, and eats grass with oxen.

169.20–21   mair tint on Flodden-edge   *proverbial* more lost at the battle of Flodden (see note to 110.18), i.e. it could have been worse: *ODEP*, 500.

169.27   mair wit in his anger   probably proverbial: compare 258.36.

169.28–30   the lad has a bonny broom-shank … pack again   the youth will sell the nails salvaged from the gutters and so recover his gambling losses to Nigel. Compare Jonathan Swift, 'A Description of the Morning' (1709), lines 9–10: 'The Youth with Broomy Stumps began to trace/ The Kennel-Edge, where Wheels had worn the Place.' The phrase 'to help him to something' means 'to take something for himself', and a *pack* is a 'stock of cash'.

170.5   having luck in a bag   having an unexpected stroke of good luck; a standard expression.

170.19   ruffling gamester   sportsman making a great display or stir, with an allusion to the ruffling of the game cock (see 163.20 and note).

170.22   the first head   the first importance.

170.24   small game   game played for low stakes.

170.25   Christmas-box   earthenware box containing contributions collected from their master's customers by apprentices at Christmas; when full it was broken and the contents shared among them.

170.36   speaking big   boastful speech.

170.39–41   broadsword . . . Cockpen   see 77.8–11.

171.3   in use   accustomed.

171.10–11   breaking hold   angler's term for the fish's letting go the bait or hook.

171.12–13   in malam partem   *Latin* in bad part.

171.18–19   tecum . . . Metamorphoseos   the Latin phrases mean 'to have contended with you' and 'in the *Metamorphoses*'. The story of the battle of Ajax with Ulysses for the arms of Achilles is found in Ovid (43 BC–AD 8), *Metamorphoses*, 13.

171.26   the fat bulls of Basan   Scott conflates the threatening 'bulls of Bashan' in Psalm 22.12, with the 'fatlings of Bashan' which are to be consumed in a feast witnessing to the providence and power of God in Ezekiel 39.18.

171.40–41   I think . . . nobility in question   i.e. Heriot, though an admirable man, is not a member of the nobility.

172.8   Jacta est alea   *Latin* the die is cast.

172.15–16   by my sooth   truly; indeed.

172.18   as sib as Summie and his brother   as close as the two begging friars whose exploits are the subject of an old ballad, 'Symmie and his Bruther', collected by David Laing in *Select Remains of the Ancient Popular and Romance Poetry of Scotland* (Edinburgh, 1822: unpaginated; published anonymously): *CLA*, 6.

172.30   take it on your corporal aith   solemnly swear. A *corporal oath* was one strengthened by touching a material object such as a sacred book.

172.35   mair by token   the more so [because].

172.39   to purpose   effectively.

173.33–37   the pencil of Vandyke . . . Henri Quatre   the English began to adopt the French taste for fine fabrics, bright colours, and ornate decoration in the third decade of the 16th century. From then clothing became more extravagant, until by the end of Elizabeth's reign, and well into that of James, it was nothing short of fantastical. Towards the end of the second decade of the 17th century some courtiers adopted the more sombre dress of the Spanish Court, but most, none more so than Buckingham, continued to dress with conspicuous opulence for another decade. The first visit to England by Vandyke (see note to 116.24–26), in 1620, coincided with the general change to less ostentatious, more dignified dress.

173.38–39   the Prince of Wales . . . monarchs   this is Prince Charles, who upon his brother Prince Henry's death in 1612 became heir to the throne. He succeeded as Charles I in 1625, and was beheaded in 1649.

173.41–43   a shade . . . drooped from it   sustaining the overtones of painting, Scott reflects the visual image of Charles preserved in portraits. He also draws on the characterisation of Charles in contemporary accounts as a serious, even stern man from his youth, with none of his father's disposition for jests and silly behaviour—the 'great imbecility in his amusements' (I[saac] D'Israeli, *Curiosities of Literature*, 6th edn, 3 vols (London, 1817), 2.300): *CLA*, 9. Here, as elsewhere in the novel, Scott indicates change of fashion by reference to headgear. The Spanish hat, with drooping ostrich feather, relatively low crown and, after 1620, a very broad brim, contrasts with the tall-crowned hat with its narrow brim and short upright plume worn by King James and the senior courtiers. Its vogue was well under way in the last years of James's reign and distinguished Charles's court from his father's.

174.7   dear dad and gossip   father and chum. For Buckingham's familiar way of addressing James see Kennet's note to Wilson (2.697n): James addressed 'Steenie' as '*His Dear Child and Gossip*'.

174.15–16 It has indeed been supposed e.g. by Anthony Weldon and Gilbert Burnet: see note to 115.39–40.

174.25–28 the rare chance...Felton see note to 116.24 for the untimely end of Buckingham's extraordinary career as favourite.

175.15–16 the grin of an ape...chestnut alluding to the proverbial ape who uses a cat's or dog's paw to extract a roasted chestnut from the fire: see *ODEP*, 118.

175.32–33 the King's drums...his son-in-law in 1613 Princess Elizabeth had married Prince Frederick V, the Elector Palatine (1596–1632). The Palatinate was on the Rhine, but extended (discontinuously) to the border of Bohemia. In 1619 the Bohemians set aside the Roman Catholic Ferdinand II (1578–1637), Archduke of Austria, as heir to their throne and selected the Protestant Frederick as king; with the help of Spain, Ferdinand shortly captured Bohemia and invaded the Palatinate, a sequence of events that initiated the Thirty Years' War. Resentful of Spain, the English people were eager to to help the popular princess and her husband, but James preferred to negotiate a marriage between Prince Charles and the Spanish Infanta as a diplomatic compromise. While he dallied, English troops on the continent died in large numbers for lack of money and provision. See Historical Note, 518.

175.37–38 have with you go and deal with it.

176.4 beard them openly challenge or provoke them, as one would provoke a lion by pulling its beard.

176.5 three kingdoms England (and Wales), Scotland, and Ireland.

176.14–15 as obstinate as a pig possessed with a devil alluding to the Biblical story (Matthew 8.28–34) of Jesus casting out the devils of two possessed men and allowing them to possess, in turn, a herd of swine grazing nearby.

176.20 a wee thing a little; somewhat.

176.21 Jouk, and let the jaw gae bye *proverbial* stoop and let the wave go by: see Kelly, 189; *ODEP*, 414. Kelly's gloss reads: 'That is, prudently yield to a present Torrent'.

176.39 stand by you...meeting i.e. back Nigel up in a confrontation: *gie them the meeting* means 'arrange to meet them (in an armed encounter)'.

177.8 critical of determining; decisive of.

178.2–9 motto not identified: probably by Scott.

178.28–29 Sir Ewes Haldimund an imaginary character whose first name may denote his unquestioning subservience to Dalgarno: with a lightly comic touch Scott links the name with actual sheep at 179.1–2.

178.33 King Cambyses' vein the style of absurd (and much ridiculed) ranting associated with the title character in Thomas Preston, *A Lamentable Tragedy, Mixed Ful of Pleasant Mirth, Conteyning the Life of Cambises, King of Percia* (1570?). Dalgarno alludes here to Falstaff's adopting this style when preparing to act the part of King Henry IV (*1 Henry IV*, 2.4.376). Cambyses was the tyrannical king of Persia from 529–522 BC.

178.36 defy those foul fiends see *King Lear*, 3.4.96. Dalgarno echoes Edgar, who in his feigned madman's speech to Lear and the Fool, appears obsessed with the foul fiend (the Devil).

179.3 plucker of pigeons someone who swindles the gullible, especially in gambling.

179.5 upon town with the denizens of high society.

179.13 privileges of the place exemptions from, or exceptions to, law for the inhabitants of the place. Here the phrase refers to the ban on the use of weapons in a royal residence and environs; e.g. in *1 Henry VI*, the impassioned

Duke of Gloucester wilfully transgresses the ban in the Tower of London: 'Draw, men, for all this privileged place—Blue-coats to tawny-coats' (1.3.46–47).

179.37–38 Pylades... Pirithous three celebrated friendships in Classical literature and legend.

180.34 a Star-Chamber business an offence not covered by common law and thus to be taken to the King's Court of Star Chamber instead of a Court of Justice. Located within the Palace of Westminster, the court was probably named from the star-painted ceiling of the room in which it convened. First used by Henry VII, it acquired its reputation as an instrument of tyranny under Elizabeth. The Stewart monarchs continued to use the Star Chamber to punish offences to the Crown. The Puritans compelled Charles I to do away with it in 1641.

180.35–36 Shift for yourself depend on your own efforts.

180.40–41 Saint James's Palace... Hospital Stow says (6.4) that the Hospital of St James was 'founded by the Citizens of *London*, before the Time of any Man's Memory, for fourteen Sisters, Maidens, that were leperous, living chastly and honestly in Divine Service'. In 1531 Henry VIII suppressed the hospital in order to build the park and palace of the same name.

181.4–5 John Bull the name of a character representing the English nation from the Tory viewpoint in John Arbuthnot, *The History of John Bull* (1712). Hence, the archteypal Englishman.

181.6 par voye du fait *French* by way of (violent) action; i.e. by taking the law into one's own hands.

181.16–17 it was not longer... executed Scott refers here to the loss of the right hand inflicted by Elizabeth I in 1579 on the Puritan author John Stubbs, or Stubb (1543?–1591) and his publisher William Page.

181.35 Alsatia cant term for Whitefriars, originally the site of a Carmelite monastery founded *c*. 1241 and dissolved in 1538. The area acquired its new name, in reference to Alsace, the territory W of the middle Rhine perennially disputed by France and Germany, during the reign of James I, who confirmed its ancient right of sanctuary and other 'liberties' including exemption from most taxes. But its character as an asylum for criminals and hence as a foreign settlement in the midst of London was fixed in the imaginations of the English by Thomas Shadwell's popular play *The Squire of Alsatia* (1688). William III abolished its privileged status in 1697.

182.21 the Temple Walks the lanes that connect the buildings in the legal quarters of London were popular with strollers as a pastoral alternative to the noisy, crowded streets of the adjacent city, e.g. with Belfond Senior, who in the first scene of Thomas Shadwell's *The Squire of Alsatia* (1688) explains: 'I am a little hot-headed this morning: And come to take the fresh Air here in the Temple-walks' (1.1.5–7).

182.26 facilis descensus Averni see Virgil (70–19 BC), *Aeneid*, 6.126, 128–29: 'facilis descensus Averni:/ ... sed revocare gradum superasque evadere ad auras,/ hoc opus, hic labor est' (the descent to Avernis [the underworld] is easy ... but to recall your step and issue to the upper air—that is the toil, that is the task).

182.33–35 spent at the theatres... the law Anthony Arlidge notes that in general 'students of the Inns were theatre mad', and in particular some of them were playwrights (*Shakespeare and the Prince of Love: The Feast of Misrule in the Middle Temple* (London, 2000), 4, 6, 31). In the 1616 Preface Ben Jonson dedicated *Every Man Out of His Humour* (performed 1599) to the law students.

182.42 Ovid and Martial Roman poets instructive to would-be wits in their bold writing as well as perhaps in their loose living: Ovid (43 BC–AD 17) is best known for his narrative poem *Metamorphoses*, Martial (AD 43–104) for his books of epigrams. One alumnus of the Temple who invokes Ovid's poem is Belfond Junior in Thomas Shadwell, *The Squire of Alsatia* (1688), 3.1.308–09.

183.2 Counsellor Barratter ... chambers this gentleman is a counsellor-at-law (synonymous with the terms barrister and advocate), one whose profession is to give legal advice to clients and conduct their cases in court. His surname means 'one who vexatiously raises, or incites to, litigation; a mover or maintainer of law-suits; one who from maliciousness, or for the sake of gain, raises discord between neighbours' (*OED*).

183.6 designed for intended to go to.

183.19 have with you go and deal with it.

183.19–20 you cannot have ... than myself Lowestoffe's role as guide echoes that of Virgil in the *Inferno* of Dante Alighieri (1265–1321).

183.33 better shift better arrangements or accommodation.

183.40 frank burgher freeholder.

184.3 By my hand common oath in the drama of the period.

184.4 Barns elms a hamlet in Surrey, later known as 'The Elms, Barnes', close to London.

184.4–5 within the verge of the Court within an area of 12 miles (19 km) round the Court, subject to the jurisdiction of the Lord High Steward.

184.12 borne down overthrown; crushed.

184.13 greatly too open much too openly. (They can be easily overheard.)

184.19 rascal rout disorderly and disreputable crowd of people: 'To swear he would the rascal rout o'erthrow' (James Thomson, *The Castle of Indolence* (1748), 2.134).

184.27 the next cook's shop the nearest shop where one could buy dressed meat.

184.30 clarified whey *whey* is the watery part of milk left when the curds are extracted. If its impurities are then removed, it is *clarified whey*.

184.32–33 eke out ... in the hall supplement the food, typically mutton, dispensed from the buttery to the law students in the refectory or dining hall.

185.3 Fortune my foe the opening of a popular song frequently referred to or quoted, e.g. *The Merry Wives of Windsor*, 3.3.55–56: 'I see what thou wert, if Fortune thy foe were, not Nature, thy friend'. The anonymous play *The Maydes Metamorphosis* (1600) gives a quatrain: 'Fortune my foe, why doest thou frowne on mee? / And will my fortune neuer better bee: / Wilt thou I say, for euer breed my paine? / And wilt thou not restore my Ioyes againe?' (2.255–58). For an exhaustive account of the song see *The Three Parnassus Plays (1598–1601)*, ed. J. B. Leishman (London, 1949), 141n.

185.13–25 gleek ... counting Tiddy this 'jargon of the gaming-table' is probably not meant to be intelligible to the reader any more than to Nigel, but although it contains errors it does make sense up to a point. Gleek is a card game for three players, probably introduced to England in the reign of Henry VII (1485–1509), though perhaps not in the 17th-century form. Scott would have found a somewhat confusing description of it in J[ohn] C[otgrave]'s *Wit's Interpreter*, of which he owned the third edition published at London in 1671 (*CLA*, 111). He seems also to have known the updated version of Cotgrave's account in Charles Cotton's *Compleat Gamester* (London, 1674: published anonymously). In this complex game the twos and threes are discarded before play begins, leaving 44 cards. In the first of the 4 stages of the game each player is dealt 12 cards. They then bid for 7 of the remaining 8. The highest bidder acquires the 7 cards from the stock, discarding 7 of his original 12, and his stake is divided between the other 2 players. The eighth card of the stock is turned up to determine trumps. In the second stage, the players 'vie the ruff'. They may place stakes (*vie*) which the last in turn may decide to raise further (*revie*), thus inaugurating a new round of bids. The player with the most of a suit in his hand wins the ruff and takes the stakes. At the third stage, the players declare their mournivals (4 of a kind) and gleeks (3 of a kind) and are paid by each opponent for each one held. Dalgarno had a 'mournival of aces', which would entitle him to 8 points from each of his opponents in calculating the payments made at this stage. Finally, 12 tricks are played out and a final score is arrived at by an elaborate calculation. As part of this calculation the *tib* (ace of trumps) would count as 15. In Lowestoffe's hand, the king and queen of trumps would actually count for 3 each; according to Cotton the *towser* (5 of trumps) would count as 10 if turned up (otherwise 5), and the *tumbler* (6 of trumps, which is probably intended here) as 12 or 6. (The force of the term *natural* here is unclear: it would usually mean 'having only its normal face value'.) The *tiddy*, the four of trumps, counts as 4 if that has been agreed before the game begins: otherwise it is not reckoned as one of the 'Honours' and counts as one like the other ordinary cards. To the scores of 23 and 19 for Dalgarno and Lowestoffe would have to be added 3 points for each trick they had won. Lowestoffe 'gained the cards', an accepted expression for 'won most of the tricks'. There is not sufficient information to determine the final scores of the disputants, but presumably they were very close, so that the 3–point difference between the ordinary and Honours tiddler would determine the winner: however, since the payout for the tricks stage is based on the players' individual point scores and not on the winner-takes-all principle, that difference would not actually be of great financial consequence.

185.18 **yellow canary birds** *slang* gold coins.

185.23 **a crow to pluck** *proverbial* a fault to find: Ray, 184; *ODEP*, 157.

185.25 **gip upon** fie upon.

185.27 **touch pot touch penny** *proverbial* you must pay for what you have: Ray, 274; *ODEP*, 833.

185.41–42 **Lord of Misrule** 'In the Feast of *Christmas* there was in the King's House, wheresoever he was lodged, a Lord of Misrule, or Master of merry Disports; and the like had ye in the House of every Nobleman of Honour, or good Worship, were he Spiritual or Temporal. Among the which, the Maior of *London*, and either of the Sheriffs, had their several Lords of Misrule ... These Lords beginning their Rule at *Allhallond* Eve [31 October], continued the same till the Morrow after the Feast of the *Purification*, commonly called *Candlemas* Day [i.e. until 3 February]' (Stow, 1.252).

186.3 **the Grand Turk, or the Barbary States** the Sultan of Turkey or the Moorish countries along the N coast of Africa.

186.8 **under the rose** in confidence.

186.8 **in the use of** in the habit of.

186.29 **six masters ... distinct Numbers** four of the students occupy separate quarters, thereby compounding the already arduous work of the servant.

186.34–35 **a bencher** senior member of one of the Inns of Court, above the utter barrister who is in turn above the barrister. The benchers constitute a self-elective body that manages the affairs of its Inn and has the privilege of calling to the bar.

187.7–21 **motto** *The Mohocks* (1712) is a farce in three scenes by John Gay, but the motto is apparently by Scott. The Mohocks were to the London streets of Queen Anne's time what the Huffs, Muns, Hectors, Blades, etc. were to the times of Queen Elizabeth, King James, and King Charles I: see notes to 193.19, 196.14, and 198.32. The name was a reference to the Mohawk Indians of N America, who because of Queen Anne's War (1702–13) were the topic of many stories that underscored their ferocities. In *The Spectator*, 335 (25 March 1712) Sir Roger de Coverley tells Mr Spectator, apropos of attending the theatre and fearing danger from the Mohocks on the way home, that the night before he had 'observed two or three lusty black Men that followed me half way up *Fleetstreet*' (ed. Donald F. Bond, 6 vols (Oxford, 1965), 3.240). The black skin, whether for disguise or for representation of the Mohawk Indian, may have come from burnt cork used by masquers and mummers to blacken their faces.

187.9 single suited referring to the requirement that a man who joins a gang of ruffians such as the Mohocks dispose of all his worldly goods except for the garments covering his skin, the income therefrom to be used for the better rioting of the brotherhood.

187.16 bound in reversion legal term meaning 'conditional upon the expiry of a grant or upon the death of a person'.

187.18 the foul fiend the Devil.

187.19 Soldadoes and Fooladoes Ben Jonson, *Every Man In His Humour* (performed 1598, published 1601 and revised 1616), 4.2.116–18: 'You must haue your Poets, and your potlings [tipplers], your *soldado's*, and *foolado's*, to follow you vp and downe the citie'; 'Foolado's' is a nonce word.

187.25 huge-paned slops large, puffy, broadly-striped breeches.

187.27 in cuerpo in breeches and doublet only. See note to 37.33.

188.8 Duke Hildebrod the name may have been suggested by 'Epitaph on Old John Hildibrod' in *A Calvinistic Purge for the Conscience* (Edinburgh, 1811), 32: *CLA*, 69. (Corson notes)

188.10 of courtesy motivated by courtesy.

188.15 on the town with the denizens of high society.

188.16 the valiant ... as valiant Lowestoffe's boasting of Hildebrod's valour is reminiscent in diction and syntax of Falstaff's shameless self-promotion in *1 Henry IV*, 2.4.454–59.

188.17 the liberties of Alsatia Alsatia, like London and like Westminster, is a discrete civil society with its own system of government: in Saxon times *liberties* referred to districts given the privilege of self-government.

188.35–36 in some sort in a way; to a certain extent.

188.38 Gray's-Inn originating in the 14th century, Gray's Inn is one of the four Inns of Court; it is bounded by High Holborn on the S and Theobald's Road on the N.

189.2–3 a reformado captain *OED* defines *reformado* as 'An officer left without a command (owing to the "reforming" or disbanding of his company) but retaining his rank and seniority, and receiving full or half pay'.

189.21 the immunities of the Friars see note to 181.35.

189.34 garnish slang for the fee paid by a novice prisoner to his fellow prisoners or to the prison officers when entering a prison, typically in return for preferential treatment.

190.4 King of Bantam Bantam was the village in NW Java from which the diminutive chicken derived its name. An English trading post was established there in 1603, its officers exercising severe government over the native inhabitants.

190.9 come halting off retired from the field of battle limping.

190.14–15 the ballad ... Queenhithe for Queen Eleanor and Charing Cross see note to 65.13. Queenhithe or 'queen's bank' is beside the N bank of the Thames above the point where Southwark Bridge now stands. In lines 141–44 the ballad, 'The Lamentable Fall of Queen El[li]nor', tells that, because of a false oath, the Queen sank alive into the ground at Charing Cross and rose again alive at Queenhithe (*The Roxburgh Ballads*, ed. William Chappell and J. Woodfall Ebsworth, 9 vols (Hertford, 1871–97), 2.69–73).

190.21 In novas ... formas *Latin* my mind leads me again to speak of changed forms. See the first line of Ovid (43 BC–AD 8), *Metamorphoses*.

190.22 Off, off, ye lendings see *King Lear*, 3.4.105–06.

190.22–23 Via, the curtain that shadowed Borgia! George Chapman, Ben Jonson, and John Marston, *Eastward Hoe* (1605), 2.2.34. Cesare Borgia (*c.* 1476–1507) was an unscrupulous churchman, diplomat, ruler, and warrior who terrorised much of Italy. R. W. Van Fossen, editor of the Revels edition (Manchester, 1979), speculates that 'the curtain' may refer to the disguise of stable-boy which in 1495 Borgia used to escape from Charles VIII of France.

190.30–31 drink the cup ... bitterness the 'bitter cup' or 'cup of bitterness' is ubiquitous in the drama of the period. The phrase may be a distant echo of the biblical story of the passion of Christ.

191.18 Semi-reducta Venus *Latin* half-stooping Venus. Lowestoffe alludes to the seductive pose of Venus disrobing in Ovid (43 BC–AD 8), *Ars Amatoria*, 2.613–15.

191.26 Nicotia and Trinidado *slang* terms for, respectively, pipe tobacco and cigars from the West Indies. The terms are linked in Ben Jonson, *Every Man In His Humour* (performed 1598, published 1601 and revised 1616), 3.5.88.

191.27–28 the King's Counter-blast ... weed see note to 40.19–20.

191.28–29 pass current have currency.

191.29 writ of capias writ empowering an officer to arrest (*capias* is Latin for 'you may take') the person named in the writ. Such a writ would impinge on the liberties of Whitefriars and so have no practical effect.

191.41–42 Tour out ... tout the bien mort as a place apart from the city that surrounds it, Alsatia is distinguished by its own language, the cant or broken language derived from several tongues spoken by beggars, criminals, gypsies, and other such outcasts for purposes of mutual recognition and concealment from regular society. Though not specific borrowings, the phrases used here and below are typical and occur in the plays in *ABD*. A *gentry cove* is a 'gentleman'.

192.8 Crasso in aere! *Latin* what a dense atmosphere! See Horace (65–8 BC), *Epistles*, 2.1.244: 'Boeotum in crasso iurares aere natum' (you would swear he had been born in Boetia's heavy air).

192.19–21 Graam ... trouble *High Dutch* means German, in which language the word for grief, sorrow, or affliction is 'Gram'.

192.26 strong waters alcoholic spirits used as a beverage.

192.27 Paris Garden located at Bankside, Southwark, Paris Garden was a popular place of entertainment, especially for bull- and bear-baiting in a purpose-built circus. It was probably named after a Robert de Paris who had a house there in the reign of Richard II. At the time of the story it was owned by King James, who attended the shows.

192.30–31 this second Axylus in Homer's *Iliad* Axylus is a 'hospitable, rich and good' character (trans. Alexander Pope (London, 1715–20), 6.16).

192.38 Ganymedes ironic reference to Ganymede, the beautiful Trojan youth of Classical mythology whom Jupiter raised to the home of the gods and made his cup-bearer there.

192.41–193.5 the old chaunt ... ding-a-ding-ding the song 'Old Sir Simon the King' is sung, or its tune danced to, in several works for the stage, including the comic opera *Tom Jones* (1769) by Joseph Reed (1.200). In Henry Fielding's novel with the same title (1749) the tune is a favourite of Squire Western, especially when played on the harpsichord by his daughter (Bk 4, Ch. 5). The original of Old Simon is said to have been Simon Wadloe (d. 1627), landlord of the Devil Tavern (see note to 26.35) at the period of the novel (*London Past and Present*, ed. Henry B. Wheatley, 3 vols (London, 1891), 1.497). For 'malmsey nose' (nose red from excessive drinking) see *2 Henry IV*,

2.1.36–37: 'Yonder he comes; and that arrant malmsey-nose knave, Bardolph, with him'. *Malmsey* is a strong sweet wine from S Europe.

193.19–21 a Low Country soldier ... a Roving Blade i.e. a professional soldier or mercenary who fights for the Dutch in their on-going wars against the Spanish. The title of Roving Blade is the self-glamourising version of such a soldier-adventurer, 'blade' being the most enduring epithet for the type of the roaring boy.

193.28–30 old Daniel ... cunning and sly see William Wordsworth, 'The Two Thieves, or The last Stage of Avarice' (1800), lines 21–22.

194.37 the Calendar of Newgate the several compilations of biographies of notorious criminals by various hands between 1719 and 1841, collectively known as *The Complete Newgate Calendar* (ed. J. L. Rayner and G. T. Crook, 5 vols (London, 1926)), played no small part in giving Newgate Prison a notoriety second only to that of the Tower of London itself. By the 18th century Newgate, of medieval origin, had become the principal prison for metropolitan London; in 1902–07 it was demolished and replaced by the Central Criminal Court, the Old Bailey.

194.39–195.11 the following doggrel verses ... Whitefriars the verses are by Scott.

195.23–24 locusts ... caterpillars see note to 27.24–25.

195.30 he is a Galilæan Luke 22.59. Peter, denying any acquaintance with Jesus, is identified as one of his followers by his Galilean speech: compare Mark 14.70.

195.41–42 This curious register ... Dr Dryasdust the register is fictitious, as is Dr Dryasdust (see note to 3.4).

195.43 rigorous as Ritson the English critic and antiquary Joseph Ritson (1752–1803) evidenced his rigour by, among other things, frowning on improvements and other forms of emendation in the old ballads and romances.

195.45–46 the Duke's orthography ... Niggle David MacRitchie argued that Hildebrod's orthography reflects the way Scott himself probably sounded it (*Notes & Queries*, 8th series, 6 (13 October 1894), 281). But, given the context of Whitefriars and the cant meaning of *niggle* as 'sexual coupling' (see note to 256.4), Scott was probably anticipating the later scene in which the Duke's pronunciation follows his spelling, much to Nigel's irritation, for it strengthens the general assumption that he has seduced the chandler's wife Nelly.

196.2 bear out back up.

196.3–4 the queer old Chief ... Stairs i.e. the odd Scottish monarch, King James, will have Whitefriars searched from its northern border of the Strand to its southern, the Stairs leading to the River Thames. But it is Fleet Street, not the Strand, which actually forms the northern border of Alsatia.

196.14 the Huffs, the Muns, and the Tityretu's names for the 'roaring boys' or street gangs who amused themselves by bullying 17th-century Londoners and destroying their property. Compare 'why I knew the Hectors, and before them the *Muns* and the *Titire Tu's*, they were brave fellows indeed; in those days a man could not go from the *Rose Tavern* to the *Piazza* once, but he must venture his life twice' (Thomas Shadwell, *The Scowrers* (1691), 1.1.106–09). For *Huff* see note to 251.33–34. For *Mun* see note to 27.2. *Tityretu* (recorded from 1623) comes from Virgil (70–19 BC), first Ecologue, line 1: 'Tityre, tu patulae recubans sub tegmine fagi' (You, Tityrus, lie under your spreading beech's covert).

196.20 for a turn for a change in circumstances, here from victory to defeat.

196.20–21 send the gentleman ... Bankside for Paris Garden and Bankside see notes to 192.27 and 147.25.

196.39 for my own simple part i.e. his motives are not complex.

196.42   a Welch main   a particularly vicious form of cock-fighting in which, say, 16 pairs of cocks fight; the winners then fight again leaving 8; and so on, until only one survives.

197.17–19   a rundlet of Rhenish ... George-a-Green   Scott here associates the fabled banquet which killed the poet-playwright Robert Greene (see note to 7.4) and Greene's legendary hero who single-handedly defeats the efforts of Robin Hood, Will Scarlett, and Little John to commit a trespass on the pound he is guarding. Scott included Greene's play *George a Greene, the Pinner of Wakefield* (performed 1587, published 1599), saying its authorship was unknown, in *ABD*, 1.440–58. A *rundlet* is a 'cask'.

197.26   Doge   the chief magistrate of the Venetian Republic, another fiercely independent state with a unique form of government.

197.26–27   the Laws of the Twelve Tables ... Cambro-Britons   the earliest code of Roman law, compiled probably in 451–50 BC and serving as the basis for Roman jurisprudence, was traditionally supposed to have been incised on twelve bronze tablets. What are generally known as the Laws of Hywel Dda, are a collection of Welsh law traditionally ascribed to one King Hwyel, though in reality a compilation of traditional material: they were first printed as the *Leges Wallicae* in 1730. Neither the Twelve Tables nor the Laws of Hwyel Dda are in verse.

197.32   blades of the huff   blustering riotous fellows. See notes to 193.19–21 and 251.33–34.

197.36   Knight of the Garter   the Most Noble Order of the Garter is the highest order of English knighthood; it was instituted by King Edward III c. 1348.

197.37   this mummery   the doggerel in parody of a solemn chivalric initiation is Scott's invention, but he had models of such initiation rites in Thomas Dekker, *The Belman of London* (1608), signature C (unpaginated); in John Tatham, *The Scots Figgaries* (1652), the first act; and in John Gay, *The Mohocks* (1712), the first scene. Compare Moll in Thomas Middleton and Thomas Dekker, *The Roaring Girl* (performed 1608, published 1611), 5.1.304–06: 'I know they have their orders, offices,/ Circuits and circles, unto which they are bound,/ To raise their own damnation in'.

197.42–198.25   the tip ... fulham and gourd   among the more obscure terms in this cant homily are: *tip* (sheriff's officer whose staff is tipped with a bull horn); *Harman Beck's errand* (constable's errand); *Bailiff's cramp speech* (curt speech or jargon of a policeman); *slide* (move with an affected gait); *stare* (with an affected mannerism intended to intimidate); *walk wool-ward* (with wool next to the skin, presumably for want of a shirt); *the wag of your elbow* (body language used in throwing the dice); *fulham and gourd* (loaded and hollow dice, respectively—i.e. false dice). For a similar conjunction of terms, compare the words of an air in John O'Keefe's comic opera *Fontainebleau* (1785), 2.1.193–94: 'I lounge in the lobby [of the playhouse], laugh, swear, slide and swagger,/ Talk loud, take my money, and out again stagger'. In Tatham's play (see preceding note) the initiate is made to pawn his cloak, the last of his valuables since he is already without shirt and stockings, before he can be installed. *To live by your shifts* means 'to live by your wits, by strategems to sustain life': compare 'I see a man here needs not live by shifts' (*The Comedy of Errors*, 3.2.180).

198.28–29   a maxim ... asses milk fattens   so say the Scottish version of the Alsatians or Huffs, the figgaries or pick-pockets, in Tatham's play referred to in the two preceding notes, 2.35: ''Tis said the Milk of Asses, makes men fat'.

198.32   Hector   son of Priam and most valiant of the Trojan warriors. To *hector* is to bully with words, as here, so that *hector* is another epithet in this period for the roaring boy. According to Thornton Shirley Graves, the hectors originated in the mid-17th century and were 'the most famous of all the numerous brotherhoods' ('Some Pre-Mohock Clansmen', *Studies in Philology*, 20 (1923), 395–421 (409–10)). Graves cites (411–12) the anonymous play *The Hectors* (1656) in which the Hectors are said to 'have usurped the name of that famous Trojane Prince' (1.3.239–40). Two such characters, Ramble and Scuffle, are so identified in the cast of characters for Philip Massinger's *The City Madam* (performed 1632, published 1658).

198.33–36 a certain Blowselinda ... Tyburn Blowselinda or Blouze-linda is the hoyden with whom the country bumpkin Lobbin Clout is smitten in 'Monday; or, the Squabble', the first poem in John Gay's *The Shepherd's Week* (1714). Bonstrops and Slicing Dick of Paddington seem to be Scott's own humorously named matching pair, the latter in the mode of colourful nick-names for members of criminal gangs. Tyburn is the old place of public execution close to the site now occupied by Marble Arch.

198.37 the fashion of the turtle-dove the turtle dove is a venerable symbol of the constancy of love during and after the life of the beloved: Shake-speare's 'The Phoenix and the Turtle' (1601) is a memorable expression of this idea.

198.40 plucking of a pigeon swindling of a gullible person.

198.42–43 an usurer ... Trapbois the usurer is a stock character in the drama of the period and rarely, if ever, an admirable one, whether from the prejudice against usury instilled by Christianity or from envy of the usurer's wealth. Trapbois is an unusually visionary and skilful practitioner.

198.43 had lately done ... service a familiar boast in the drama of the period: see, most notably, *Othello*, 5.2.342.

198.44 a subsidy see note to 73.33.

198.45 the wine-merchants at the Vintry see note to 151.34.

199.13 ugly enough to frighten sin proverbial: see *ODEP*, 853.

200.4–6 to throw a main ... three vowels to make the first throw of the dice in the game of hazard is 'to throw a main'. Because the captain plays without funds or *dry-fisted*, he pays his debts with IOUs.

200.7 as sharp ... as a needle proverbial: *ODEP*, 720.

200.11–18 motto not identified: probably by Scott. The most celebrated depiction of Cupid's mirror is 'The Rokeby Venus' by Diego Velasquez (1599–1660), formerly displayed in the house of Scott's friend J. B. S. Morritt at Rokeby in Yorkshire, and now in the National Gallery in London: Venus is shown (from behind) regarding herself in a mirror held by Cupid. For 'beef and pudding' see note to 81.1–2.

200.40 what she made what she was doing.

201.26 on the viretot in a whirl. See Geoffrey Chaucer, *The Canterbury Tales*, 'The Miller's Tale', I (A) 3769–70: 'Some gay gerl, God it woot,/ Hath broght yow thus upon the viritoot.'

202.1 the Lady Hermione see Historical Note, 527.

202.7 unapprehensive of not understanding; unable to grasp.

202.20 the reign of Henry VIII. 1509–47.

202.22 the Honourable Lady Foljambe a friend of Anthony Babington (see note to 237.14), Lady Foljambe of Walton, Derbyshire, belonged to the secret society which promoted a Catholic insurrection that sought to put Mary Queen of Scots on the throne of England: see note to 237.14.

202.23–29 Saint Roque's Nunnery ... choice the imaginary house of St Rocque (or Roch, the patron saint of those afflicted with plague) would be one of those abolished by Henry VIII in 1536 through the Act for the Dissolution of Smaller Monasteries. Monks and nuns displaced by the dissolution of their houses were allowed the choice of being transferred to a surviving house of their order or accepting a dispensation from their monastic vows so as to pursue a career in the secular world.

202.34–35 a turning wheel ... all nunneries see note to 91.38–40.

203.1 the priestesses of Baal originally those women who served one of the several Canaanite deities with this name frequently mentioned in the Old Testament.

203.32–33 Monna Paula ... Mademoiselle Pauline the first version of the title and name is Italian; the second, French.

204.1 in use accustomed.

204.9 grows on gains ground on.

204.26 upon 'Change at the Exchange.

204.36 at fault puzzled. The image is of hunting dogs losing the scent.

206.40 the Park St James's Park: see note to 167.23.

207.32–37 motto not identified: probably by Scott. 'By this good light' is an asseverative phrase much used in the old drama. A *roundel* is a simple song with a refrain. By appearing *to bear the burden* the drums, incongruously, seem to provide the base or accompaniment for the melody of the girl's song.

208.26 in blow in blossom.

209.15–19 clock of the German fashion ... Dutch-looking piece of lumber compare Ben Jonson, *Epicene; or, The Silent Woman* (performed 1609, published 1616), 4.2.98–101 (Otter on his wife): 'about next day noone [she] is put together againe, like a great *Germane* clocke: and so comes forth and rings a tedious larum to the whole house, and then is quiet againe for an houre, but for her quarters'. The clock is *Dutch-looking* because *High Dutch* means 'German'.

209.21–22 a whole band of morrice-dancers some ten male dancers, adorned with bells, one of them in the role of Robin Hood, together with a hobby-horse and a woman in the role of Maid Marion.

209.22 trip the hays to the measure perform a country dance with a serpentine movement, or resembling a reel, to the rhythm of the music.

209.27 brought me through resulted in success for me.

209.40 under your favour with all submission; subject to correction.

210.13 out of mouth not mentioned.

211.16 jump so exactly the same length an image from the sport of long-jumping.

211.37 a petted fool to boot an indulged fool, besides.

212.43 the Gunpowder Treason 'the Gunpowder Plot', as it is more commonly called, was a conspiracy on the part of certain Catholic gentry to assassinate King James on the occasion of his impending visit to Parliament by setting fire to a cache of gunpowder and blowing king, princes, lords, and commons to bits. To this end 36 barrels of gunpowder were stored in a cellar beneath Parliament House rented for the purpose and guarded by the soldier Guy Fawkes. But the plot was discovered—James took the credit for exposing it—and Fawkes arrested on 5 November 1605.

213.28 matter of doubt doubtful.

214.19 have good-day good bye.

215.18–22 motto not identified: probably by Scott. In Genesis 8.4 Noah's ark lands on Mount Ararat (in E Turkey).

216.33–34 that sickening agitation ... hope deferred see Proverbs 13.12: 'Hope deferred maketh the heart sick.'

218.5 Golden Register Genoa had been since the 11th century the capital of a flourishing commercial republic that generated a wealthy aristocracy whose names, in all their branches, were inscribed in a 'book of gold', which was burned in 1796 during the revolutionary fervour inspired by the Napoleonic invasion.

218.8   take concern in   take an interest in.

218.13–15   Francis Earl of Bothwell ... Catholic faith   Bothwell (see note to 47.8) fled from Scotland in 1595 after fomenting rebellion. He took refuge first in France, then in Spain, and finally in Italy, where he died impoverished in Naples.

219.9   set up   *law* put forward.

219.16   drew on   extended in time.

219.29   general officer   army officer above the rank of colonel, i.e. an officer of superior rank and extended command.

220.20–2   the fathers ... set on edge   see Ezekiel 18.2.

220.34–35   as insignificant ... Don Quixote   the Spanish knight's adventures in Cervantes' famous satirical romance (see note to 7.5–6) are proverbial for just such irrelevance to actual human affairs.

221.38–39   the inquisitorial power   the Spanish Inquisition was established in 1479 to detect and suppress heresy. Fabled for its harsh measures, it was finally suppressed only in 1820.

222.5   the church ... a better spouse   since at least the early 5th century, a nun taking her vows has been conceived of as participating in a marriage ceremony with Christ as bridegroom.

222.16   Guadarrama   a mountain range N of Madrid.

223.3   Heart's Ease near the postern   *Heart's Ease* is the wild pansy widespread in Europe. The *postern* is the back entrance, door or gate, to an enclosure. One of the many names of the flower is 'Kiss me at the garden gate'.

223.4–5   the symbolical language ... the Moriscoes of Spain   *Morisco* is Spanish for Moor or 'little Moor', one of the mixed Berber and Arab people who in the 8th century invaded Spain from N Africa. Though Muslim at the time, they converted to Christianity. Just a few years before the time of the story (1609), the Moriscoes had been expelled from Spain. The use of flowers as elaborate emblems of human feelings and qualities, and to convey simple messages, was highly developed in the Islamic tradition.

224.1   huddled on   put on hurriedly and 'all of a heap'.

224.22   Saint Jean de Luz   in the department of the Pyrénées Atlantiques, Saint Jean de Luz is the port town in the Basque country located just a little N of the Spanish border: here in France the two women would be beyond the authority of the Inquisition.

226.11   Saint James   the patron saint of Spain.

226.11   our Lady of the Pillar   Nuestra Señora del Pilar, a church in Saragossa said to have been founded by Saint James at the request of the Virgin Mary who appeared to him in a dream accompanied by a wooden image of herself and by a column of jasper.

227.20   Spanish red   a shade of ochre closer to the reddish-yellow end of the spectrum than to the pale-yellow end but slightly more yellow than the Venetian red. The reference here is to a rouge that reproduces this colour.

227.22   possessed of herself   steady, calm, self-possessed.

228.2–6   motto   see the couplet attributed to Jonathan Swift, written 'for a barber, who also ran a public-house': 'Rove not from Pole to Pole, but step in here,/ Where nought excels the Shaving——but the Beer' (*The Poems of Jonathan Swift*, ed. Harold Williams (Oxford, 1958), 1145). The word *cut* plays on the hairdressing meaning and the slang term for 'drunk'.

228.12–13   mustachios of civil policy   the fashion in moustaches for politicians—those men who determine the course of affairs by policy or word rather than by sword.

228.13–14   letting blood ... lancet   blood could be drawn by the cupping-glass, a device which by creating a vacuum drew the blood to the surface, or by the lancet, a sharp two-edged surgical instrument. Bleeding was long a standard procedure for ridding the body of illness, whether serious or trivial.

228.15   Raredrench   see note to 32.23.

228.20–22   barber's shop ... garnished   the pole represented the staff which a barber-surgeon's patient grasped during blood-letting (see note to 228.13–14) in order to remain conscious or to control pain; its white and red spiral stripes represented respectively the bandages used to bind the patient's arm before the operation and to bandage it afterwards.

228.23   rows of teeth ... like rosaries   an advertisement for the barber as dental surgeon. In Ben Jonson, *Epicene; or, The Silent Woman* (performed 1609, published 1616), 3.5.92–93, cursing the barber Cutberd takes the form at one point of having the man 'draw his owne teeth, and adde them to the lute-string'.

228.25   blistered   have a blister or blisters raised on the skin. The aim was to draw fluids (including blood) from the body by means of applying a hot plaster of (typically) mustard to the skin so as to extract a disease or its cause.

228.25–26   sufficient advice   probably an advertising cliché.

228.29   ghittern or cittern   a wire-strung, flat-backed musical instrument resembling the lute. A note in *ABD* (3.282) indicates that it was standard furniture in barber shops, where customers would play it while waiting their turn for the barber's attention.

228.38   temple of Bacchus   in Classical mythology Bacchus is the god of wine and patron of festivities in which it figures prominently.

229.12   Iris   a messenger of the gods in Classical mythology, Iris is the bright multi-hued goddess of the rainbow.

229.34   his better angel   alluding to the concept of each person being offered contradictory advice by a good and evil angel as in Christopher Marlowe's *Doctor Faustus* (*c*. 1590).

230.3–4   ancient farthingale   circular frame of cane or (later) whalebone used to extend a woman's skirt from her body. Its vogue was in the reigns of Elizabeth I and James VI and I. It was succeeded in the 18th century by the hoopskirt.

230.16   fore George   an earlier form of 'by [St] George' often found in the old drama.

230.23   rummer glasses   large drinking glasses.

230.27   Rosa Solis   *Latin* rose of the sun: the name of the herb sundew and, as here, of a cordial flavoured with its juice.

230.34   within the sound of Bow-bell   see note to 79.31–35.

230.37–38   walks in Paul's   see note to 48.30–31.

231.11   a cuckoo song   the cuckoo sounds its call with monotonous repetition and is often viewed, besides, as a foolish bird.

231.15   Peg-a-Ramsay   see note to 119.9.

231.27–28   a Welsh-man loves cheese   'I do loue cawse boby [roasted cheese], good rosted chese', says the Welshman in *The Fyrst Boke of the Introduction of Knowledge made by Andrewe Borde of Physycke Doctor* (1547), ed. F. J. Furnivall (London, 1870), 126, introducing a stereotype propagated by the old dramatists and perpetuated in the dish consisting of cheese on toast known as 'Welsh rarebit' (or 'Welsh rabbit').

231.41   the days of King Arthur or King Lud   Arthur and Lud were legendary kings of Britain, the former (who had a shadowy historical existence *c*. 500) commemorated in chivalric romance by Malory among others, the latter (entirely mythological) in early histories and in the name 'Ludgate'.

232.4   trap-ball   game in which a ball, placed upon the slightly hollowed end of a pivoted wooden instrument called a *trap*, is thrown into the air by the batsman striking the other end with the bat, with which he then hits the ball away.

232.7 Christmas-box see note to 170.25.

232.8 the devil's mattins a service of Satanic worship attributed to witches. In Philip Massinger, *A New Way to Pay Old Debts* (performed *c.* 1625, published 1633), 4.1.162–63, Sir Giles Overreach is reported to have 'read this morning such a diuellish Matins,/ That I should thinke it a sinne next to his,/ But to repeat it'.

232.13 Marry come up an asseverative phrase expressing indignant or amused surprise or contempt.

232.15 as your words would bear i.e. as they would testify to or corroborate.

232.15 The Lord . . . evil see the Lord's Prayer: Matthew 6.13; Luke 11.4.

232.18 none of your husband not at all (not in the least) your husband.

232.22 ride up Holborn i.e. travel by cart up Holborn to your execution at Tyburn: see note to 198.33–36.

232.23 holiday and sugar-plum expressions the pleasant, calculatedly inoffensive language used in polite social intercourse. Compare the 'many holiday and lady terms' of the royal envoy which, in Hotspur's view, are irritatingly inappropriate on the scene of bloody battle (*1 Henry IV*, 1.3.46).

232.27 the brisk boys of Fleet-street compare 'Fall on my brisk boys of the blade': Thomas Shadwell, *The Amorous Bigotte* (1690), 4.1.43.

232.28 be carted for bawd and conjuror be transported in a cart through the streets to prison as a bawd and witch, thereby becoming a spectacle for the public.

232.28–29 double dyed in grain *literally* dyed so that the colour is fast by engraining the dye in the strands of the fabric and the procedure repeated; i.e. through and through.

232.29 bing off to Bridewell *cant* go off to the prison and house of correction near Whitefriars.

232.29 brass basin compare 'Let there be no baud carted that yeare, to employ a bason of his [barber Cutberd's]': Ben Jonson, *Epicene; or, The Silent Woman* (performed 1609, published 1616), 3.5.87–88.

232.29–30 betwixt the Bar and Paul's between Temple Bar to the W and St Paul's Cathedral to the E.

232.37–38 described at full length in Hudibras in Samuel Butler's poem the skimmington occupies some 70 lines (2.2.585–664), more if the sounds announcing its approach are included.

232.42–43 Mumbo Jumbo in an African village according to Mungo Park, *Travels in the Interior Districts of Africa*, new edn, 2 vols (London, 1816), 1.38–39 (entry for 7 December 1795: compare *CLA*, 236), *Mumbo Jumbo* is a form of pantomime in which the husband (or someone instructed by him) of a woman who resists subjection to his authority, masquerading in a costume made of tree bark whereby he becomes Mumbo, enters the village at dark, from which point a ceremony of song and dance builds in intensity to midnight when the offending woman is identified, humiliated, and abused by Mumbo and the other villagers until daylight brings an end to her ordeal. In England the skimmington became an offence against the Highways Act in 1882, but an occurrence is recorded in Dorset in 1884.

233.5 loving kindness affectionate tenderness.

233.22 Rome was not built in a day proverbial: Ray, 152; *ODEP*, 683.

233.25 the sitting gamester with a proverb apparently of her own Dame Ursula inverts proverbs that commend rising from the table and quitting the game while winning: *ODEP*, 295.

233.31 go the Virginia voyage emigrate to the colony established in Virginia, after several abortive efforts by Sir Walter Raleigh who named it after

Queen Elizabeth, the Virgin Queen, in 1607.

233.37–38 as bare as a birch at Christmas proverbial: Ray, 293; *ODEP*, 29.

233.41 when the need . . . nighest proverbial: Ray, 75; *ODEP*, 28.

234.2 cast your city-slough cast off your apprentice clothes, as a snake casts off its *slough* ('skin').

234.7 curfew the bell rung in every town at 8 pm or 9 pm as a signal that lights and fires should be extinguished, a custom initiated by William the Conqueror to guard against conflagration and civil disorder.

234.10–11 am out of my time have completed my apprenticeship.

234.11 along of owing to.

234.11 Mother Midnight during the 17th and early 18th centuries *Mother Midnight* was a term designating a woman who runs a lying-in hospital for whores and unwed mothers, who sells their babies if so desired, is herself a bawd, maybe a whore, an expert on sex, a gossip, a fortune-teller, and with it all something of a wise woman whose reputation as a keeper of secrets is her most valuable attribute.

234.12 out of other than by.

234.19–20 take a long day agree to an extended period for payment.

235.6 come by be acquired.

235.13 as the Devil looks over Lincoln proverbial: Ray, 224; *ODEP*, 183. The reference may be to a stone figure on Lincoln Cathedral, or to the Devil himself looking at the Cathedral with envy. Alternatively, it may refer to another stone figure on a gable at Lincoln College, Oxford, which was taken down in 1731 after being damaged in a storm; a replacement was provided in 2003.

235.14 It is ill talking of the devil alluding to the proverb 'Talk of the devil, and he is sure to appear': Ray, 97; *ODEP*, 804.

235.18 bring my mind strongly up to the thought face up to the idea, acknowledge it, and behave in accordance with it.

235.19–20 hold on in ill courses continue in bad behaviour.

235.24 work my turn work as my agent.

235.26–27 bid pretty Mistress . . . a day see *The Taming of the Shrew*, 4.4.93: 'But bid Bianca farewell for ever and a day.'

235.28–29 brown baker baker of brown bread.

235.32 the Isle of Dogs a peninsula on the N of the Thames opposite Greenwich.

235.34–35 as well as . . . his dish only the second term is recorded as proverbial: Ray, 199; *ODEP*, 41.

235.36 A plague of your similies like any number of comic characters in the drama of the period and later, Dame Suddlechop threatens to rattle off a chain of analogies tiresome to her audience. Compare 'Plague of that *Simile*': George Chapman, *The Gentleman Usher* (performed 1602–03, published 1606), 1.1.386.

235.39 no Catesby and Piercy business Robert Catesby (1573–1605) and Thomas Percy (1560–1605) were prominent among the Gunpowder Plot conspirators: see note to 212.43.

236.8–9 as quiet as a rocket . . . match be fired an analogy based upon the ignition of fireworks at a nocturnal celebration or 'rejoicing night' of, say, a great victory in battle or an end to war.

236.22–24 Shortyard the mercer . . . Saint Stephens his name suggests that the merchant in fabrics and threads provides short measure. The church of St Stephen Walbrook dated from the early 15th century: after the Great Fire of 1666 it was replaced by Sir Christopher Wren's edifice.

237.1–2 thou knowest . . . Norfolk gosling no similar expression has been located, but at the period of the novel Norfolk was famous for its poultry, especially its geese.

237.11 **bear relation to** have connection with.

237.13 **it is a chance ... him** i.e. it would be unlikely that she should ever forget him.

237.14 **Babington ... the Queen's time** Anthony Babington (1561–86) led a Catholic conspiracy to murder Queen Elizabeth I and free the imprisoned Mary Queen of Scots whom he had served as page, for which treason he was barbarously executed upon a scaffold in a field at the upper end of Holborn.

237.22 **out of sight, and out of mind** proverbial: Ray, 72; *ODEP*, 602.

238.2 **Shavaleer Bojo's** the apprentice's rough rendering of 'Chevalier Beaujeu's'.

238.3 **rookery** probably a triple pun: (1) an area where rooks build their nests and congregate; (2) a cluster of mean tenements densely populated by people of the lowest class; and (3) *rook*, 'to cheat, especially in gambling'.

238.6 **bit of a** little.

238.12–13 **John Taylor ... Grigg the Grinner** for Taylor see note to 43.33. 'Grigg the Grinner' would have been noted for his success in funny face contests.

238.18 **within the walls** inside the city walls of London.

238.21 **at the Bull and at the Fortune** see notes to 26.40 and 148.34.

238.34 **that cock will not crow** that won't do. Compare 'That cock won't fight': *ODEP*, 131.

238.38 **by any indirection** dishonestly. Jin Vin adopts the moral high ground of Julius Caesar and echoes his language in Shakespeare's play of that name (4.3.75).

239.7 **has coin at will** has money at her own volition or wish.

239.8 **fairy-gold** money given by fairies was said to crumble away rapidly to leaves or dust.

239.17 **the fifth of November** 5 November is the anniversary of the Gunpowder Plot and thus an occasion for rabble-rousing.

239.26 **duly and truly** a legal phrase.

239.38 **matted chamber** room laid with matting or mats.

240.5–10 **motto** not identified: probably by Scott.

241.5 **Susanna and the Elders** for the story of Susanna and the Elders see note to 26.15. It was a popular subject with artists.

242.29 **pineal gland** a small pine-shaped, hence 'pineal', gland of unknown function situated at the base of the brain in veterbrates. According to René Descartes's *Treatise of Man* (written 1637, published posthumously 1662) the pineal gland functions physically as a valve that directs the flow of animal spirits, those particles derived from the blood which travel through nerves, muscles, and brain conveying sensation and motion: in short it is the link between mind/ soul and body: see Lawrence I. Conrad, Michael Never, Vivian Nutton, Roy Porter, and Andrew Wear, *The Western Medical Tradition* (Cambridge, 1995), 345. Trapbois's gland, possessed by the fear of thieves, has produced in his body the symptoms of hysteria.

242.41–243.2 **a Queen Mary's ruff ... Smithfield memory** for *farthingale* see note to 230.3–4. Martha's ruff (a *falling ruff* or gathered band, not 'set' into open pleats but allowed to 'fall' down onto the shoulders from a high neckband) is named after the style worn, not by James's mother Mary Queen of Scots, but by the English Queen Mary Tudor (reigned 1553–58), who in 1554 became the wife of the Spanish King Philip II: hence perhaps the Spanish style ruff, which in her portraits resembles a stiff high collar trimmed with a small ruff, flared at the top and open at the throat. Both her father Henry

VIII before her and her sister Elizabeth I after her executed Roman Catholics, at Smithfield, formerly an open space just outside the walls of the City of London, and at Tyburn (see note to 198.33–36), but Mary, a zealous Catholic determined to reverse the Reformation, burned some 300 Protestants at the stake in Smithfield in just over three years, earning her the enduring epithet of 'Bloody Mary'.

243.26   flint and steel   apparatus of stone and steel used to start a fire from tinder.

244.40   got up with   caught up with.

245.19–20   on no consideration   on no account.

246.1   A gnarled tree may bear good fruit   this proverb inverts the familiar biblical proverb to the effect of 'like tree, like fruit': see Matthew 7.16–20 and 12.33.

246.15   the closet   see notes to 12.30–31 and 13.5.

246.21–23   Master Puff... noddle   Puff is a character in Richard Brinsley Sheridan's play *The Critic* (1781) who advises authors on how to avoid unnecessary verbiage. In 3.1.119–33 he exemplifies his method: William Cecil, Lord Burleigh, Queen Elizabeth's chief minister for 40 years and, presumably, a man of many words uttered in the line of duty, enters and exits the stage without speaking a word or being spoken to in the interval, his only communication a shake of the head, of his *noddle*, upon leaving.

246.37–38   a thing never acting, but perpetually acted upon   Nigel's negative self-appraisal echoes that of Shakespeare's Hamlet, especially as expressed in his unique series of soliloquies: see next note. See also Scott's self-criticism in his review of *Tales of My Landlord*, first series (1816), where he says that the author's 'chief characters are never actors, but always acted upon' (*Prose Works*, 19.4–5).

247.6   write it down in my tablets   compare *Hamlet*, 1.5.107–08: 'My tables—meet it is I set it down/ That one may smile, and smile, and be a villain'.

247.9   sorely handled   severely treated.

247.15–16   on the part of   on behalf of.

247.24   Sampson   Samson, whose story is told in Judges Chs 13–16, has long been proverbial for strength: see Tilley, S85.

247.25   lads of the Huff   see note to 251.33–34.

248.2   black jack   leather jug coated with tar used for carrying beer.

248.10   metal, so attractive   see *Hamlet*, 3.2.106.

248.11   like a setting-dog at a dead point   the analogy is from hunting: a *setting-dog* or *setter* was, in the 17th century, a kind of spaniel that, by pointing, signals the location of the bird it has scented ('sets' game), and holds this position unmoving until the hunter can come within shooting range.

248.14   has in the wind   has wind of; has scented on the air.

248.18–19   the Marshalsea   a prison in Southwark dating from the 14th century, and in use till 1813.

248.21–22   laid up there in lavender   cant expression for being in prison, on analogy with laying linen away in lavender so as to keep it safe from moths.

248.22–23   scald his fingers... broth   proverbial: compare Ray, 74 and *ODEP*, 703.

249.9   on any consideration   for any recompense.

249.19–27   motto   not identified: probably by Scott.

249.19   Swash-Buckler   once modish, this social type, the English version of the Classical gladiator, had become old-fashioned by the time of the story and, in general, a laughing-stock, the 'Sword and Buckler Trade being now out of date' (Wilson, 2.674). Scott observes that it was the roaring boys of James's reign who succeeded the 'sword-and-buckler-men of Queen Elizabeth's time', their more deadly rapiers and daggers replacing the heavier, less accurate swords of their predecessors (*Somers' Tracts*, 2.266n). Henry Porter's play *The Two Angry Women of Abington* (1599) waxes nostalgic on the subject: 'Sword and buckler fight begins to grow out of use; I am sorry for it; I shall never see good manhood again; if it be once gone, this poking fight of rapier and dagger will come up; then a tall man, *that is, a courageous man*, and a good sword and buckler man, will be spitted like a cat or a rabbit' (lines 1333–37: quoted in Strutt, 196n).

249.19 Bilbo's the word William Congreve, *The Old Batchelour* (1693), 3.1.200: 'Bilbo's the Word, and Slaughter will ensue'. *Bilbo* is a sword named after Bilboa, the Spanish town where fine sword blades were made; by the time of the story it was, in particular, the swashbuckler's sword of choice.

249.20 Pierrot typical French pantomime character, recognised by his whitened face and loose white clothes.

249.25 private knife concealed knife; i.e. dagger or stiletto.

249.28 Captain Colepepper or Peppercole *Cole* can mean 'kill' or 'cheat'; *pepper* means 'beat severely'. There may be suggestions of 'cabbage pepper' or 'pepper cabbage'.

249.29–30 a martial and a swashing exterior see *As You Like It*, 1.3.116–18: 'We'll have a swashing and a martial outside,/ As many other mannish cowards have/ That do outface it with their semblances'.

249.40 Peter Pillory as well as *pillory* the name suggests *pillery* ('pillaging', 'robbery').

250.8 as loving as inkle-weavers proverbial, as explained by William Cowper: 'When people are intimate, we say—They are as great as two Inkle-weavers [weavers of linen tape, on narrow looms packed tightly]' (*The Letters and Prose Writings of William Cowper*, ed. James King and Charles Ryskamp, 5 vols (Oxford, 1979–86), 3.156).

250.14–16 Carocco...Basta *Carocco* is probably derived from the Spanish oath *carajo* ('damn it all!'). *Basta* ('enough!') is still current in both Italian and Spanish.

250.15–16 devil's livery...rainbow the monochromatic black colour of the clerk's garments will become parti-coloured like that of a servant's uniform.

250.25 old Truepenny you honest old fellow. See *Hamlet*, 1.5.150: 'Ha, ha, boy! say'st thou so? Art thou there, truepenny?' (Hamlet to his father's ghost).

250.34–35 one of those...shorn proverbial: Ray, 170; *ODEP*, 913.

250.40 on the hip *wrestling* at a disadvantage. In *The Merchant of Venice*, 4.1.329, Gratiano says to Shylock: 'Now, infidel, I have you on the hip'.

250.42 doctors a pun on the usual meaning, and on that of false dice or dice which have been doctored.

251.9 on the square without cheating: see note to 154.23–24.

251.10–11 high and low dice...stabbing a catalogue of ways to cheat at gambling: dice doctored to produce high or low numbers; *Fulhams* are loaded dice; *bristles* are dice deliberately biased by bristles which have been fixed for this purpose; *topping* is dropping only one dice in the box while concealing the other behind the fingers at the top; *knapping* is striking one dice dead; *slurring* is sliding the dice so as to turn up a particular number; and *stabbing* is using a box so narrow at the bottom that the dice, which have been put in downward, fall out with the faces uppermost.

251.18 balloon game in which a man, his arm braced by wood, strikes a large leather ball inflated with air.

251.30 leap a flea...a wherry in his edition of the novel (Oxford, 1911), Stanley V. Makower notes (589) that these contests involve betting on fleas jumping (highest or farthest), on snails running (fastest), and on drinking a liquor made from the pulp of crab apples (fastest).

251.33–34 Hector . . . him the huff the Classical epithet is ironic for Colepepper and the other swashbucklers of the period known in the second half of the 17th century as Hectors, Huffs, and so forth from their verbal harassing or *huffing* of (assuming a bullying tone towards) London citizens. The expression 'vapour the huff' has not been found, but the combination of vapouring (blustering) and huffing occurs in *Hudibras* at 1.3.252 and 3.1.425.

252.1 court-scented-water compare 'court holy water' (flattery): *King Lear*, 3.2.10.

252.2 lamplighter the lighter of street lights. *OED* first records the word in 1750.

252.8–9 go over the water to the garden cross the Thames to Paris Garden: see note to 192.27.

252.13 Videlicet *Latin* that is to say; namely.

252.18 crooked sabres at Buda the curved swords or scimitars of the Turks who captured Buda, the old part of the Hungarian capital Budapest, in 1541 and held it until 1686.

252.18–19 my single rapier a word play: 'only my own rapier' and 'my rapier only (without dagger)'.

252.21 Scotch collops a savoury dish of meats and other ingredients.

252.23 on any consideration on any account.

252.24–26 Hector of Troy . . . Achilles respectively the champion of the Trojans and the champion of the Greeks in the Battle of Troy. Achilles slew Hector in revenge for Hector's slaying of his friend Patroclus, but was himself killed later.

253.18 Star-Chamber see note to 180.34.

253.29 I have the trick on't see note to 169.14.

254.9–10 the old blind horse . . . open meadow probably a combination of two proverbs: 'To go round like a horse in a mill' (Tilley, H697), and 'It is a good horse that never stumbles' (Tilley, H670).

255.27 folding leaves twin leaves.

255.40 Belzie short for Beelzebub, a name for the Devil: see e.g. Matthew 12.24–27.

255.40–41 beasts and fools will be meddling proverbial: see Ray, 108 and *ODEP*, 279.

256.4 Niggle Green *niggle*, beggars' cant for 'copulate', occurs in the demonstration of 'pedlar's French' that Trapdoor and Moll give the eager student Jack Dapper in Thomas Middleton and Thomas Dekker, *The Roaring Girl* (performed 1608, published 1611), 5.1.175.

256.25 Sathan variant spelling of Satan current until the late 17th century.

256.26–27 a humming double pot of ale . . . crab a large pot of strong ale into which a crab-apple has been dropped. Compare *Love's Labour's Lost*, 5.2.912: 'When roasted crabs hiss in the bowl'.

256.27–28 a wherry above bridge a boat upstream from London Bridge, the only bridge across the Thames at this time.

256.29 burnt sack mulled white wine, especially popular at this time with students, to judge from references in the dramatic literature, e.g. in the anonymous university play *The Pilgrimage to Parnassus* (performed 1598–99, published 1886) where it is mentioned twice (lines 208, 270), sweet wine being thought to inspire sweet verses.

256.31 Jezabel Jezebel, the infamous wife of Ahab, King of Israel (see 2 Kings Ch. 9); *hence* a wicked, shameful, or impudent woman.

256.35 bethinking himself considering; recollecting.

256.39 use your pleasure do as you like; amuse yourself. The phrase is commonplace in the drama of the period.

257.2 **unchristian measure** old Deb's sipping the liquor as she carries it will result in an ungenerous quantity by the time it reaches its destination.

257.4 **never flew but at head** attacked only the head; i.e. is a trained attack-dog.

257.12–13 **a penny farthing** one-and-a-quarter old pence (0.5p).

257.17 **fasting from every thing but sin** see Part 2, Ch. 73, of *The History of the Renowned Don Quixote De La Mancha. Written in Spanish by Miguel de Cervantes Saavedra. Translated by several hands: and published by the late Mr. Motteux. Revised ... by Mr Ozell*, 4 vols (Edinburgh, 1766; originally published 1605–15), 4.418, where the housekeeper says to Don Quixote: 'I am neither drunk nor mad, but fresh and fasting from every thing but sin': *CLA*, 317.

257.18 **radical moisture** in medieval philosophy, the humour or moisture naturally inherent in all plants and animals, its presence being a necessary condition of their vitality.

257.27 **post meridiem** *Latin* after midday.

258.3 **our waters may be watched** our territory, e.g. ports and rivers, may be under surveillance by an enemy. The Duke speaks metaphorically but very much in character as head of state in the duchy of Alsatia.

258.4 **as deaf as Paul's** compare the proverbial 'as old as Paul's' (Ray, 253; *ODEP*, 588) and 'as high as Paul's' (R. W. Dent, *Proverbial Language in English Drama Exclusive of Shakespeare: 1495–1616: An Index* (Berkeley, Los Angeles, and London, 1984), P118.11). The reference in each case is to Old St Paul's, the gothic cathedral consumed in the Great Fire of 1666, and in particular to its steeple destroyed by lightning in 1561 and never rebuilt.

258.10 **in the twinkling of a quart-pot** compare 'in the twinkling of a Bumper': Peter Anthony Motteux, *Love's a Jest* (1696), 2.14.

258.11–12 **dance in a net** *proverbial* act or behave with no guile or disguise yet with no expectation of attracting attention: Ray, 5; *ODEP*, 166.

258.13 **born like King Richard ... ready cut** 'Marry, they say my uncle [Richard III] grew so fast/ That he could gnaw a crust at two hours old': *Richard III*, 2.4.27–28.

258.28 **laid up in lavender** see note to 248.21–22.

258.36 **have more wit in your anger** probably proverbial: compare 169.27.

258.39 **cast doublets** throw the dice so as to turn up the same number on both.

258.40 **wap and win** the literal meaning of this beggars' cant is made clear in B. E., *A New Dictionary of the Terms Ancient and Modern of the Canting Crew* (London, [1720?]: unpaginated): '*If she won't wap for a Winne, let her trine for a Make*', which is glossed as: 'If she won't Lie with a Man for a Penny, let her Hang for a Half-penny'.

258.43–259.1 **the devil's bones and the doctors** the dice in general, and the false or doctored specimens.

259.1 **pedlars' French** see note to 256.4.

259.5 **to be brief, as you and the lawyers call it** Hildebrod puns on the legal term *brief* by which lawyers refer to the memorandum of points of fact or of law for use in conducting a case.

259.8–9 **the King runs the frowning humour on you** the monarch assumes the humour of being displeased with you, expressed in a frown. Compare *Henry V*, 2.1.116: 'The King hath run bad humours on the knight [i.e. he has treated the knight badly]'.

259.9 **vapours you the go-bye** ostentatiously slights or 'cuts' you.

259.10 **serves you out** metes out to you.

259.18 **Earl of Kildare** Gerald Fitzgerald (d. 1513), 8th Earl of Kildare from 1477, was called 'the great earl' by contemporary chroniclers, who report that he was 'somewhat headlong and unruly towards the nobles whom he fancied not' (*Dictionary of National Biography*).

259.22   a Prince of Peru   i.e. a nobleman in a country fabled for its gold.

259.25   Caduca   a name based on the Latin word *caducus* which denotes the legal situation of property for which there is no heir or claimant. As such, it fits the unmarried Martha.

260.6   in the land of the living   common Old Testament phrase: e.g. Job 28.13.

260.6   more to purpose   more to the purpose.

260.12   win the plate   i.e. gain Martha Trapbois's fortune; with a wordplay on a horse winning a gold or silver plate by coming first in a race.

260.21   breaking with   abruptly severing a connection or relationship with.

260.26–27   on which side their bread was buttered   proverbial: see Ray, 179; *ODEP*, 438.

260.41   Not a whit   not at all.

261.14–15   in name of wardship   in respect of his exercising the responsibility of guardian.

261.18   are avised of that?   are you informed of that? See *Measure for Measure*, 2.2.132.

261.20   thinking on the case more nearly   considering the case with closer attention.

261.22   win and wear the dame   *proverbial* win the hand of the lady and possess her as your wife: *ODEP*, 892.

261.24   soon as   as soon as.

261.28–36   motto   not identified: probably by Scott. 'Heaven's maiden centinel' is the moon, in Classical mythology sacred to Diana the goddess of chastity.

262.4–5   a godsend on the Cornish coast   a shipwreck to be plundered.

262.7   Dummalafong   the term has not been found elsewhere.

262.37   per diem   *Latin* per day.

262.39   per advance   in advance.

263.15   in a perfect state   coins were often depleted of metal, their weight and hence their value diminishing in the process.

263.20–22   an expectation of refunding . . . humour   the 'Scotch wag' has not been identified. In a letter to John Richardson, 23 March 1814 (*Letters*, 3.423), Scott attributes this *bon mot* to the comedian Joe Miller (1684–1738), whose jokes were published in 1739 by John Mottley as *Joe Miller's Jests*, but this observation is not there. (from Corson notes)

263.31   launch out   expand in speech without restraint (as a ship sets forth on water).

264.6   for me   as far as I'm concerned.

264.33–34   God's law . . . thou shalt not kill   the sixth of the ten commandments: Exodus 20.13.

265.29   Hebe   in Greek mythology, the goddess of youth and spring and cup-bearer to the gods.

265.30–31   Ganymede   see note to 192.38.

265.33–34   petticoat government   government by a woman or women.

266.33–34   Whetstone of Witte . . . Equation   a treatise on algebra by Robert Record, published in 1557 as the second part of *The Ground of Artes teachyng the worke and practise of Arithmetike* (London, [1543]). Its full title is *The Whetstone of Witte, whiche is the seconde parte of Arithmetike: containyng thextraction of Rootes: The* Cossike [algebraic] *practise, with the rule of* Equation: *and the woorkes of* Surde Nombers.

266.39   Iris   see note to 229.12.

267.15–18 God's Revenge ... Wolfe John Reynolds, *The Triumphs of Gods Revenge against the crying and execrable Sinne of (Wilfull and Premeditated) Murther*, published in six parts between 1621 and 1635; the 2nd edition (1640) is in Scott's library (*CLA*, 154). No record has been found of an earlier publication with the same title: it is probably imaginary, but the printer is not. Old (Reyner or Reginald) Wolfe (d. 1573) had a press in St Paul's Churchyard and held the position of royal printer to Edward VI, from whom he had a patent to print in Latin, Greek, and Hebrew. He printed *The Ground of Artes* (see note to 266.33–34).

267.25 canary sack a strong sweet white wine from the Canary Islands.

267.38 the tabernacle of life in the New Testament the human body is imaged as a *tabernacle* or temporary shelter (e.g. 2 Corinthians 5.1–4), with overtones of the elaborate tented shrine of the Old Testament, containing precious and sacred objects (Exodus Chs 25–30).

267.40–44 Note ... university Scott returns to the fiction of the Introductory Epistle, reminding the reader of the fictional Clutterbuck and of the actual Richard Heber (see note to 8.33). Heber's splendid library of rare books and manuscripts was a great resource for Scott. The 1635 and 1657 editions of Reynolds's work are included in the catalogue for the auction of his collection after his death: *Bibliotheca Heberiana. Catalogue of the Library of the Late Richard Heber, Esq.*, 13 parts ([London], 1834–37), 5.240 (Lot 5401) and 173 (Lot 3961). For the Roxburghe Club see note to 12.5.

268.8–10 in some narratives ... revenge such a narrative is *Hamlet*, where the restless ghost of King Hamlet seeks revenge for the crimes of murder, incest, and adultery against him (1.5.1–91). For graves 'yawning' see *Hamlet*, 3.2.379 (and compare 1.3.48–52).

269.18 Mammon in Matthew 6.24 God and *mammon* (an Aramaic word for 'riches') are put in opposition. In medieval times the hinted personification was formalised into a devil of covetousness.

269.33 a slight fever on Nigel's blood a variation of the more common phrase 'fever in the blood': compare the familiar phrase 'fever on the brain'.

269.34–35 beside his rest from or off his rest.

270.40 at a venture at adventure; at random; on chance: 1 Kings 22.34.

273.5–11 motto not identified: probably by Scott.

274.39–40 shift for yourself look after yourself; exert yourself for your own benefit.

275.9 have noting of have knowledge or evidence of; perceive.

276.23–24 That seasoned cask Scott may have remembered Prince Hal's description of Falstaff as 'a tun [cask] of man ... that huge bombard [leather bottle] of sack': *1 Henry IV*, 2.4.429–32.

276.25 a rowling a-rolling.

277.17–18 in presence present.

277.34 By cock and pie an oath of uncertain derivation, used in *The Merry Wives of Windsor*, 1.1.276: *cock* is a perversion of the word *God*; *pie* refers to the pre-Reformation ordinal, the table by which the Roman Catholic Church determined the calendar of services.

277.35 hang ... Haman did in Esther 7.10 King Ahasuerus hangs his favourite Haman on the very gallows of 50 cubits (21 to 24 metres) that Haman had had built for executing the Jew Mordecai who had refused to acknowledge his exalted status by bowing down to him.

277.37 as drunk as fiddlers proverbial: *ODEP*, 206.

278.14 put him on set him on.

278.16 keep conditions honour the conditions agreed upon.

278.21–22 a nod is as good as a wink proverbial (often extended by 'to a blind horse'): *ODEP*, 575.

278.26 **beat up your quarters** arouse you; visit you unceremoniously.

279.1 **lies up in lavender** see note to 248.21–22.

279.7 **with an O, for Graham** the 'O' signifies Nigel's actual surname of Oliphant.

279.12 **Greenwich** the royal palace down the Thames from London.

279.24–26 **Mind your hits ... draw it** i.e. look to your chances and honour our agreement, or be prevented from hitting your target before you have the chance even to take aim.

279.28 **prosecuting such views over** carrying out such plans in respect of.

280.32 **but what** but that.

282.27–28 **the great Christian atonement** the doctrine that through his crucifixion and resurrection Christ compensated for the sins of human beings the world over that would otherwise doom them at death to eternal separation from God.

282.39 **made a shift** managed with difficulty.

283.24–30 **motto** not identified: probably by Scott.

283.37 **time and tide wait for no man** proverbial: Ray, 162; *ODEP*, 822.

284.2 **rattle traps** worthless articles.

284.9 **Paul's** St Paul's Cathedral.

284.24–25 **according to appointment** as arranged or agreed upon.

284.34–35 **out of my commission** beyond my orders.

284.36–37 **from Berwick to the Land's End** from Berwick-upon-Tweed, a town on the NE coast of Northumberland and England's extreme NE point, to its extreme SW point of land in Cornwall.

284.38 **except at** take exception to.

284.41–42 **characteristic rudeness of the Thames watermen** in *The Trve Cavse of the Water-mens Suit concerning Players* John Taylor confesses 'that there are many rude vnciuill Fellowes in our company', a sentiment he also expresses in *An Apologie for Water-men*, lines 46–48: 'How they in plying are vnmannerly,/ And one from tother, hale, and pull, and teare,/ And raile, and brawle, and curse, and ban, & sweare' (Taylor, second section, 173, 267).

285.1 **green plush jacket** not as it might appear a livery since the Watermen's Company had none, but rather a way of identifying this character, subsequently referred to as 'Greenjacket'.

285.2 **a thought** a very small amount.

285.4–5 **a witch in her egg-shell** witches and other supernatural beings were sometimes depicted as travelling in an egg-shell: compare 'a Brace of as errant Enchantresses as e're bestrod Broomstick, or sail'd in an Eggshell', in John Durant Breval, *The Rape of Helen* (London, 1737), 34.

285.15–16 **a party of pleasure** an outing or occasion for the pursuit of (sensual) pleasure, sometimes with the innuendo of an assignation, as here.

285.18 **Dr. Rigmarole's ... buckles beggars** the clergyman buckles beggars together in marriage for a modest recompense. *Redriffe* is a corruption of Rotherhithe, at the time of the story a village on the S bank of the Thames E of London, spelled here as it came to be pronounced and sometimes written, as e.g. in Samuel Pepys's diary.

287.30 **raised up to** provided for.

288.11–18 **Scaandalum Maagnatum ... Roman tongue** the Latin legal term *scandalum magnatum* ('a great scandal', 'a false report') denotes an offence against those in authority who through a writ of scandalum magnatum can bring proceedings against the scandalmongers. For James's view on the correct pronunciation of Latin see note to 111.35–36. Here he lengthens the first (or antepenultimate) vowel in accordance with the Scottish preference for Classical pronunciation: the English practice was to shorten this vowel. The Latin term occurs in several of the old plays, notably in Christopher Bullock, *Woman Is A Riddle* (London, 1717: *CLA*, 220), where it is used twice by Mr Vulture, 'an Old Rich Litigious *Stock-Jobber*', 19 (2.150), 24 (2.346–47).

288.15   cockles   the heart or some element thereof: a term of uncertain origin but familiar from the saying 'It warms the cockles of my heart'.

288.42–43   kindness of lang syne   kindness of long ago. Richie echoes the refrain of Robert Burns's 'Auld Lang Syne' (written 1788; published 1796): 'We'll take a cup o' kindness yet/ For auld lang syne'.

289.3–4   Andrew Ferrara   see note to 45.29.

289.10   cry clubs   see note to 28.29–30.

289.13–14   salt eel   i.e. a whipping with a rope end made from the cured skin of an eel. In his diary entry for 24 April 1663, Samuel Pepys punishes a serving boy by whipping him with 'my salt Eele': *The Diary of Samuel Pepys*, ed. Robert Latham and William Matthews, 11 vols (London, 1970–83), 4.109.

289.17   It's an ill bird . . . own nest   proverbial: Ray, 79; *ODEP*, 397.

289.22   for ever and a day   a set phrase, emphasising 'for ever'.

291.2   in respect of   as a result of; owing to.

291.25   upon your own charges   at your own expense.

291.30–31   pure doctrine . . . a' polluted with men's devices   the former is doctrine believed to be strictly and directly derived from Scripture; the latter is doctrine wherein Scripture has been mediated, and in the process 'polluted', by priests, liturgy, and tradition. Richie contrasts the Reformed faith of his native Scotland with the Anglicanism of England.

292.19–27   motto   not identified: probably by Scott.

293.8–13   the Bastile . . . aristocratic pride   the Bastille was a 14th-century Parisian fortress, subsequently a state-prison whose destruction by a mob in 1789 initiated the French Revolution. Tom Paine (1737–1809) championed the French Revolution and called for an English revolution in *The Rights of Man* (1791), which includes the sentences: 'Titles are like circles drawn by the magician's wand, to contract the sphere of man's felicity. He lives immured within the Bastille of a word, and surveys at a distance the envied life of man' (*The Complete Writings of Thomas Paine*, ed. Philip S. Foner, 2 vols (New York, 1945), 1.287).

293.27   Gravesend   town on the S bank of the Thames, 35 km E of London. The broadened Thames here offered good anchorage for sea-going vessels.

294.11   George-a-Green   see note to 197.17–19.

294.25   put force   exert force.

294.29   venture a life   risk or gamble a life.

294.37   the Royal Thistle   Scott has underscored the Scottish identity of the ship awaiting Nigel by naming it after the national emblem of Scotland.

295.6   small gaming   gambling for small stakes.

295.10   at advantage   at a disadvantage.

295.36–38   dive so deep . . . play the cavalier   this enigmatic remark is eventually explained at 385.23–26 (see also 229.22–39).

295.41   the knave's pate of thee   your head.

295.42   out of   contrary to.

296.1–3   the "injured Thales" . . . birth   in Samuel Johnson's poem *London* (1738), lines 18–23, Thales, wishing to escape 'Vice and London', resolves on a country existence: 'While Thales waits the Wherry that contains/ Of dissipated Wealth the small Remains,/ On *Thames*'s Banks, in silent Thought we stood,/ Where Greenwich smiles upon the silver Flood:/ Struck with the Seat that gave Eliza birth,/ We kneel, and kiss the consecrated Earth'.

296.4   halls . . . her successor   Elizabeth was born in the palace of

Placentia at Greenwich, dating from the mid-15th century. In 1605 James settled the Palace and Park on his queen Anne of Denmark (d. 1619), and it was extensively altered, eventually being entirely rebuilt under Charles II.

296.4–6 It was not ... intentions the 'late author' is Isaac D'Israeli whose *An Inquiry into the Literary and Political Character of James the First* (London, 1816) was defensive: *CLA*, 9. For the connection with *Nigel* see Essay on the Text, 408.

296.11–13 "Firm Resolve" ... in man see Robert Burns, 'To Dr. Blacklock' (1789), lines 43–46: 'Come, *Firm Resolve* take thou the van,/ Thou stalk o' carle-hemp in man!'.

296.38–39 much to the advantage ... stirring the Court's removal from Whitehall to Greenwich, from one royal residence to another, was good for local business, by contrast with the Court's visits to the nobility in 'progresses' which were typically ruinous to both the hosts and those merchants and farmers unlucky enough to be along the route of the journey.

296.40–41 all decent persons ... the entries of the Palace the right to enter the park is reserved for those who would be allowed to enter the palace within it.

297.1 the last cut the latest fashion in beards, by analogy with the latest way of cutting material for fashionable garments.

297.2 pages of the body boys or young men who serve on the immediate person of the monarch as valets.

297.3 running footmen servants who run ahead of a coach to light the way with torches, to announce its approach, or on either side to help keep it from overturning.

297.21 black taffety patch though useful to cover barber's nicks and scabs, such patches were often purely decorative: 'your black Patches you wear variously, some cut like Stars, some in Half-moons, some Lozenges' (John Fletcher, *The Elder Brother* (performed 1625?, published 1637), 3.5.195–96).

297.32 Kilderkin the name means 'small barrel'. (Corson notes)

297.33 removed from over the way at a distance from just across the road; almost opposite.

297.35–36 Duke of Lennox James's cousin Ludovick Stuart (1574–1624), who succeeded as 2nd Duke in 1583 and was created Duke of Richmond in 1623 (the English peerage assured him equality with the new Duke of Buckingham). He accompanied James to England in 1603 and there served him in various capacities for many years.

298.3–4 ale, stirred with a sprig of rosemary rosemary, a member of the mint family, gives the ale a pungent taste and pleasing aroma.

298.9 the Scotch never eat pork see note to 30.23–24.

298.9–10 a sort of Jews Jewish dietary laws forbid the eating of pork as unclean or 'not kosher' meat.

298.11 the second Solomon see note to 68.35–36.

298.12 bears a face is credible.

298.15–16 crisping tongs implements for curling the hair.

298.16 Thank your munificence short for 'I thank you for your munificence'.

298.16–17 hope your custom short for 'I hope for your business'.

298.18 put your temper in concord put your temperament or physical constitution in harmony. The barber waxes witty on the popular idea that the harmony of music can be replicated in people, who by analogy with a musical instrument can be tuned so that their constituent parts co-exist in concord, not discord.

298.19 twang, dillo the refrain of a popular song and the name of the tune to which it is sung. The song specifying this tune appears e.g. as Air XIV in Henry Brooke's *Little John and the Giants: A Dramatic Opera*, 2.3.65ff.: 'Twang dillo dee' (*A Collection of the Pieces formerly published by Henry Brooke, Esq. to which are added several plays and poems now first printed*, 4 vols (London, 1778), 4.36–37).

298.27–28 singeing pigs' faces burning the bristles off the faces of pigs destined for the festive board.

298.38 well to pass in the world well off; well to do.

299.21 Comus see note to 137.24.

299.33 coming from Norfolk with the poultry see note to 237.1–2.

299.34–35 gone upon his stumps, like Widdrington in the broadside version of the popular English ballad *Chevy Chase* 'when his [Widdrington's] leggs were smitten of,/ He fought vpon his stumpes' (stanza 50, lines 197–200): *The English and Scottish Popular Ballads*, ed. Francis James Child, 5 vols (Boston and New York, 1882–98), 3.313 (Child, 162B).

299.38–40 the witty African slave ... jubeo the Roman comic poet, Terence, Publius Terentius Afer (195 or 185–159 BC). In his comedy *Adelphoe* ('The Brothers') it is the fictitious slave Syrus who compares the training of his cooks with the task of parenting. His advice echoes that which another character, the Athenian Demea, gives his son but substitutes 'to look in their pans' for 'to look into other people's lives', thus: 'I tell them to look in their pans like a mirror' ('postremo tamquam in speculum in patinas, Demea,/ inspicere iubeo et moneo quid facto usus sit' (lines 428–29)).

300.2 in some sort in some way; to some extent.

300.3–4 Regis ad exemplar ... totus componitur orbis *Latin* the whole world is modelled on the example of the king. See Claudian (active *c.* 400), *The Fourth Consulship of Honorius*, lines 299–300: 'componitur orbis/ regis ad exemplum'.

300.5 as the king quotes the cook learns in the second book of *Basilicon Doron* (see note to 66.22–27) James quotes the same Latin passage from Claudian that Linklater has just cited, noting that Claudian is, in turn, expressing in poetry 'the notable saying of *Plato*' (ed. James Craigie, 2 vols (Edinburgh and London, 1955–50), 1.53). He liked the idea enough to anticipate it (1.35) and to repeat it (1.105). Here he has translated it by adapting the proverb 'As the old cock crows the young cock learns': Ray, 280; *ODEP*, 588. Scott substituted 'quotes' for his MS 'crows' in the proofs.

300.6–7 where humanities may be had ... by the quarter for *humanities* see note to 126.11–12. In the early days of the University of Edinburgh (founded 1583) students attended classes the year round, except for the month of August (gradually extended), and the week between Christmas and New Year. Those who could afford it paid 40s. per annum (not quarterly) in fees for tutorials and, if they shared a bed, the same in chamber rent.

300.12 what he ailed what ailed him.

300.13 the philosophical Syrus see note to 299.38–40.

300.15 aqua mirabilis *Latin, literally* marvellous water, an alcoholic cordial prepared with several spices.

300.24–25 hart of grease fat stag, with the implication that the flesh when cooked will be succulent.

300.27–28 a noble fortification of puff-paste Laurie echoes the similarly creative cook Furnace in Philip Massinger, *A New Way to Pay Old Debts* (performed *c.* 1625; published 1633), 1.2.24–26: 'I cracke my braines to find out tempting sawces,/ And raise fortifications in the pastrie,/ Such as might serue for modells in the Low-Countries'.

301.8–9 West-Port of Edinburgh see note to 34.3.

301.16–17 wad nae ... as the sang says the song is a traditional one, beginning 'My wife's a wanton, wee thing ... She winna be guided by me'. In

Robert Burns's version of 1790 the first two traditional verses are supplemented by two probably of his own composition. Compare the song 'He winna
be guidit by me' in *The Jacobite Relics of Scotland... Second Series*, ed. James
Hogg (Edinburgh, 1821), 25–26, where the allusion is said (260) to be to
James Carnegy of Phinaven who defected to the Whig cause: *CLA*, 19.

301.18   kittle up   stimulate; please.

301.20   friar's chicken   chicken broth boiled with beaten eggs.

301.21   made the whole cabal coup the crans   overturned or upset the
whole plan.

301.22–23   make me thankful   God make me thankful; for which I
should be thankful.

301.29   the King's errand ... cadger's gate   proverbial: *ODEP*, 427.

301.42   get to speech of the King   gain access to the King so as to speak
directly to him.

302.15   God sends good meat ... cooks   proverbial: Ray, 90; *ODEP*,
312.

302.23   the Star-Chamber ... an oven seven times heated   for the Star
Chamber see note to 180.34. The analogy is with the fiery furnace with which
King Nebuchadnezzar threatened Shadrach, Meschach, and Abed-nego if
they refused to worship a golden image: when the men persisted in their rebellion the King became so enraged that he ordered the furnace be fired 'seven
times more than it was wont to be heated' (Daniel 3.19).

302.30   the judgment of Solomon   see note to 68.35–36.

302.32–33   the stripes of the Rector of the High-School   the marks of
a whip or rod inflicted by the head of this ancient school in Edinburgh, which
claims medieval origins.

302.34   that cooking scene in the Heautontimorumenos   there is no
cooking scene in this play ('The Self-Tormentors'), by Terence. Probably the
reference is to a scene in his *Adelphoe* (see note to 299.38–40) where the slave
Syrus carries on a conversation outside the house with the Athenean Demea
while calling out instructions on cooking a fish to the slaves Dromo and Stephanio inside (lines 365–81).

302.36–37   get to the sight and speech of the King   gain access to the
King's eye and ear.

303.30   made a shift   managed.

303.31–32   two tall greyhounds ... Scottish Highlands   the breed is
the Scottish deerhound, with rough and often grey coat standing 71–81 cm at
the shoulder.

303.37   the melancholy Jacques   in *As You Like It*, 2.1.25–43, Jacques
grieves over the sight of a deer wounded in a hunt.

304.1   demi-pique saddle   saddle with a low pommel.

304.6–7   the managed pace of the academy   the controlled motion of
the legs learned in an academy for training horses, especially cavalry horses.

304.13   Bash ... Battie   pet names (apparently fictitious) for James's dogs:
compare note to 66.27–28. In Scots *Battie* is a generic name for a dog.

304.14–15   the Braes of Balwhither   the hills of Balquhidder, which rise
above the N shore of Loch Voil, SW of Loch Tay, Perthshire.

304.17   De'il ding your saul   Devil strike your soul.

304.20   terra firma   *Latin* firm ground.

304.22   couteau de chasse   *French* hunting knife.

304.29   quarrée   in a note for *Somers' Tracts* (1.512) Scott derives this term
from '*Curee*, the opening and fleaing the deer ... Hence our word *quarry*'.

304.31   secundum artem   *Latin* in accord with established usage.

304.34   de'il ane o' the lazy loons in   not one of the lazy fellows present.

304.37   blessings on ... ye   compare James's epistolary addressing of

Buckingham: '*Blessing, Blessing, Blessing, on thy Heart's Roots*': Kennet's note to Wilson (2.697n). 'The heart's-root' is the very foundation of the affections, in particular the source of love.

304.40 his anointed body James was crowned and anointed with holy oil in Scotland (29 July 1567, at the church in Stirling, by the Bishop of Orkney, Adam Bothwell) and again in England (25 July 1603). That the anointing of a monarch was important to James can be documented from his insistence, against considerable opposition from Protestant factions, that Queen Anne be anointed at her coronation in 1590 (John Spottiswood, *History of the Church and State of Scotland*, 4th edn (London, 1677), 381–82: *CLA*, 13).

304.41 with a mischief to ye ... with a wanion may mischief come upon you ... may a plague visit you. Compare 'Mary hang you; Westward with a wanion te'yee': George Chapman, Ben Jonson, and John Marston, *Eastward Hoe* (1605), 3.2.87–88.

304.43–305.1 gie ye an inch and ye take an ell *proverbial* give you an inch and you take an ell (37 inches (94 cm) in Scotland; 45 inches (115 cm) in England): see Ray, 198; *ODEP*, 303.

305.8 let bowls row wrang wi' them let bowls roll wrong with them (i.e. let things go wrong for them), a negative form of the Scots proverbial saying 'the bows row richt' (see *The Antiquary*, ed. David Hewitt, EEWN 3, 167.18).

305.30 that gate in that way.

306.1 making at approaching in order to seize.

306.10 dear dad and gossip see note to 174.7.

306.20–21 who, in his time, had ... attempts see note to 155.40–41.

306.23 doom's sure very sure.

306.27–32 Not that celebrated pistol ... Mhic-Allastair-More the pistol belonged to Alexander Ranaldson Macdonnell of Glengarry (1771–1828) and was worn as part of his Highland dress at the coronation of George IV on 19 July 1821, where it frightened one of the ladies: see Scott's Magnum note (27.202). *Mhic-Allastair-More* is Glengarry's patronymic: 'great son of Alasdair' (properly *Mac Mhic* 'son of son of').

307.4–6 the brutal murther of Rizio ... the light secretary to Mary Queen of Scots, and keeper of the privy purse, David Rizzio was murdered on 9 March 1566 by her husband Darnley and others either before the pregnant Mary or nearby (accounts vary). James was born the following June.

307.13 a wee matter a little; somewhat.

307.15 the leathern bottle in a Magnum note (27.202–03) Scott says that he owns what claimed to be the King's hunting bottle. He quotes Roger Coke (*A Detection of the Court and State of England During the Last Four Reigns and the Inter-Regnum* (London, 1697), 70: compare *CLA*, 237) on James's habit of drinking strong wine while hunting. He also quotes Weldon (2.3) for an opposed view that the King was not generally intemperate.

307.19–20 pater patriæ ... cari capitis *Latin* we are father of the country as well as father of the family—what shame can there be in grief for the loss of a head so dear, or what limit to it? See note to 70.41.

307.20–21 black cloth ... England so widely would the dead king be mourned that the black cloth required for making mourning clothes would be in short supply and, as a result, costly.

307.39–40 pistols on his person ... proclamation for this proclamation see note to 69.23–26.

308.13 double bullets the pistols would fire two shots before needing to be reloaded.

308.42 appellatio ad Cæsarem *Latin* appeal to Caesar. It was the right of every Roman citizen to be tried at the judgment seat of Caesar, as Paul once reminded his persecutors in a ringing speech which concluded with 'I appeal unto Caesar': see Acts 25.10–11.

309.16–19 who else nosed out … puzzled it out a reference to the Gunpowder Plot (see note to 212.43) and James's reiterative boast to have been the one to detect it. A tract of 1678 records his decoding of an anonymous letter of warning and thus establishing his reputation in some quarters, and certainly in his own eyes, as a modern-day Solomon (*Somers' Tracts*, 2.103–04). Robert Cecil (1563?–1612) succeeded his father Lord Burghley as Elizabeth's chief minister and held the same post under James, who created him Earl of Salisbury in 1605; Thomas Howard (1561–1626) served Elizabeth as Vice-admiral of the Fleet, and James (who created him Earl of Suffolk in 1603) as Lord Chamberlain and, later, as Lord High Treasurer. Both deserved more credit for exposing the Gunpowder Plot than James was willing to admit.

309.20–22 Joannes Barclaius … parricidii John Barclay (1582–1621), the son of a Scottish professor of law in Lorraine, came to England in 1603, where he wrote satires against the Jesuits and was patronised by James. In 1605 he published at London a pamphlet of 17 pages entitled *Series Patefacti nuper Parricidi, in ter Maximum Regem Regnumque Brittaniæ cogitati & instructi*. The Latin phrase based on this title means 'the series of murders providentially revealed' (in the original *nuper* means 'lately'). Barclay's pamphlet is mentioned in the anonymous 1678 tract *The History of the Gunpowder Treason* in *Somers' Tracts*, 2.104.

309.22–23 Spondanus … Divinitus evasit Henri de Sponde (1568–1643) was Bishop of Pamiers, France, from 1626, and a church historian. James would know of the bishop's view from his appendix to Cardinal Caesar Baronius (1538–1607), *Annales Ecclesiastici* (1588–1608), but de Sponde says only 'Rex periculum euasit', the King escaped the danger (*Annales Ecclesiastici* (Cologne, 1623), 58). The Latin phrase used in the text, meaning 'he escaped by divine intervention', comes from *The History of the Gunpowder Treason* (see previous note), 2.104.

309.25–26 tracked that labyrinth … clew Buckingham's compliment is couched in allusion to the Classical story of the maze built by Daedalus to confine the Minotaur. The fine clew in this story was the thread made by Vulcan and presented by Ariadne to Theseus so that by unrolling the thread behind him as he searched for the Minotaur Theseus would be able to retrace his steps and not himself be trapped in the labyrinth; in the Gunpowder Plot the clew was an obscure warning of an explosion in an unsigned note.

309.29 a hawk of the same nest proverbial: see *ODEP*, 60.

309.30 look that see to it that.

309.40–41 ye behoved to *ironic* you had to.

310.1 three weeping kingdoms England (and Wales), Scotland, and Ireland.

310.6 beef-eaters of the guard popular epithet for the Yeomen of the Guard, instituted at the accession of Henry VII in 1485, and for the Warders of the Tower of London, who were named Yeomen Extraordinary of the Guard in the reign of Edward VI (1547–53).

310.8–9 for extremities … papistical principles James alludes to the proverbial 'extremes meet' (*ODEP*, 235) in his *Basilicon Doron* (see note to 66.22–27): 'the tua extremities thaim selfis, althoch thay seeme dyuers, yett grouing to the heicht, rinnis euer baith in ane' (ed. James Craigie, 2 vols (Edinburgh and London, 1955–50), 1.141).

310.9–10 a new tout on an auld horn proverbial: Ray, 282; *ODEP*, 564.

310.18–19 in waiting in attendance.

310.20–21 See to me look at me.

310.22–27 **We are like an ass ... tributis serviens** James alludes to Jacob's prophecy for his son Issachar in Genesis 49.14–15: 'Issachar is a strong ass couching down between two burdens: And he saw that rest was good, and the land that it was pleasant; and bowed his shoulder to bear, and became a servant unto tribute'. James quotes from the Vulgate, changing the third to the first person to refer to himself (and with 'accumbens' for 'accubens').

310.31 **per aversionem** *Latin* without looking at them.

310.34 **the tale of Cadmus** see note to 67.31–33.

310.39 **per acquam refectionis** *Latin* beside the restoring waters: see Psalm 23.2 in the Vulgate.

311.19 **walls of curtain and bastion** the *curtain* is the part of a fortification or rampart that connects the projecting parts or towers at the angles of the structure, called *bastions*.

311.22 **low-browed arch** this is the so-called Traitors' Gate through which prisoners of rank approaching by boat entered the Tower from the Thames.

311.30–32 **motto** Thomas Gray, *The Bard* (1757), lines 87–88. The oldest part of the Tower of London, the White Tower, was built by William the Conqueror in 1076, but according to tradition Julius Caesar was the original builder: see *Richard II*, 5.1.2, and *Richard III*, 3.1.69–71.

311.33 **Bandello** Matteo Bandello (1485–1561) was a prolific Italian writer. Scott alludes to his Novella 34 from the second part of his *Novelle*: 'Or avvenne che, desiderando egli far morire il vescovo di Vincestre (non so per qual cagione) che essendo nel conseglio privato del re, gli disse che si devesse andar a render prigione per parte del re nella torre: luogo, ove mai nessuno entrò, che non fosse ucciso, per quello che dicono i paesani' (*Le Quattro Parti de le Novelle del Bandello*, ed. Gustavo Balsamo-Crivelli, 4 vols (Turin, 1911), 3.57: Now it happened that, desiring the death of the Bishop of Winchester, for I know not what reason, while in the king's private council, he told him that, upon the king's bidding, he should betake himself as prisoner to the Tower, a place where no one ever entered without being killed according to what the people say).

311.39 **the entrance ... regress** the last line of the inscription above the lintel of the gate to hell in the *Inferno* of Dante Alighieri (1265–1321), 3.9, reads (translated from the original Italian): 'Abandon all hope, you who enter here'.

312.13–14 **state-prison ... mess-room** the principal state prison at the period of the story and for many years before was located in the Beauchamp or Cobham Tower, where inscriptions of the sort alluded to later in this passage were uncovered in 1796 when the tower was converted to a mess hall.

312.37–39 **pious effusions ... Smithfield** for Tyburn and Smithfield see notes to 198.33–36 and 242.41–243.2.

312.40–43 **Jane Grey ... Dudleys** Jane Grey (1537–1554), granddaughter of Henry VIII's sister Mary, Duchess of Suffolk, was appointed by Edward VI to succeed him on the throne of England; she was proclaimed Queen 10 July 1553, and reigned for ten days, before being deposed in favour of Mary Tudor and, after imprisonment in the Tower, executed along with her husband Guildford Dudley on 12 February 1554. Tradition has it that the deposed monarch inscribed her own name on the wall of the Beauchamp Tower, but more likely it was the work of her husband whose eldest brother John Dudley was responsible for an elaborate carving, in the form of a rampant bear and lion supporting a ragged staff encircled by four wreaths of acorns, roses, geraniums, and honeysuckle, as a memorial to the four brothers, all of whom for a time resided there with him. The 'Bear and Ragged Staff' was the emblem of

Richard Neville (1428–71), who by marrying into the Dudley family became Earl of Warwick in 1449; the double-tailed lion represents the Dudleys.

312.43–313.1 the roll of the prophet . . . woe see Ezekiel 2.9–10 where in a vision the prophet sees a hand holding 'a roll of a book', which when opened 'was written within and without: and there was written therein lamentations, and mourning, and woe'.

313.19 laid down trimmed or embroidered.

318.12–13 lain . . . cup see 2 Samuel 12.3.

318.21 make it so tough make such difficulties.

318.35 give you the odds . . . weapon i.e. accept that, in a physical contest, the ratio of probability would favour your youth and doubtless superior weapon over my age and weapon.

318.36 the foul fiend the devil.

319.8 Don Diego this may refer, in a continuation of Christie's heavy irony, to the knight-errant and bravo whose adventures are the subject of a picaresque novel *Don Diego de noche* (1623), by Alonso Jerónimo de Salas Barbadillo. More likely it alludes to the servant of that name implicated in the Lady Lake case (see note to 368.30–31). In the earlier scene of Christie's confrontation with Richie, the Scot is described walking 'with a gait like that of a Spaniard in a passion' (288.1–2), and *Diego* was a general term for Spaniard, sometimes with overtones of 'bully'.

319.39 le fanfaron des vices qu'il n'avoit pas *French* the boaster of vices which he did not have. The first four words are a stock phrase.

320.13 the Great Day a recurring phrase in biblical literature, particularly in reference to Judgment Day, e.g. in Revelation 6.17: 'For the great day of his wrath is come; and who shall be able to stand?'

320.27–28 the wild beasts in their dens the menagerie of wild beasts first installed in the Tower by Henry III. On his first visit to the Tower as the new king of England James 'took pleasure in baiting Lions' (Wilson, 2.667) and thereafter he attended such spectacles and arranged for a lion's walk to be built (Stow, 1.118–19).

321.7–12 motto not identified: probably by Scott.

321.39–40 the patriarch Joseph . . . I do the story of Joseph's prophetic dreams begins at Genesis 37.5.

322.32–33 a Chaldean interpreter in Daniel Ch. 2 King Nebuchadnezzar, requiring interpreters for his dreams, summons the experts—i.e. the Chaldeans, in the Old Testament an alternative name, in general, for the Babylonians and, in particular, for the class of magi famous for their writings on astrology and divination.

325.28 to touch pitch and not to be defiled see the Apocrypha, Ecclesiasticus 13.1: 'He that toucheth pitch shall be defiled therewith.' The expression is also proverbial: Ray, 172; *ODEP*, 834.

326.8 hurried me away carried me away.

326.15–16 a revision of the Decalogue . . . privileged orders a revision of the Ten Commandments so as to link punishment to social rank, with the most noble sinner receiving the smallest punishment and so forth.

326.24–25 in some slight sort to a little extent.

327.12 in specie in coin.

327.23–24 the fatal case of Lord Sanquhar . . . fencing-master in 1604 an English fencing master John Turner accidentally put out the eye of a Scottish nobleman Robert Crichton, 8th Lord Crichton of Sanquhar from 1569. Some years later Sanquhar hired assassins to bring about an opportunity for revenge and, when they failed, had one of his own servants do the job. On 11 May 1612 the servant shot Turner at his home in Whitefriars and was subsequently hanged. Because he was a Scot Sanquhar was not tried as a lord before his peers but as a commoner in the Court of the King's Bench where, though ably defended by Sir Francis Bacon, he was found guilty and hanged as a common felon. The case is exemplary of the aggrieved national feelings that disturbed much of James's reign.

328.3 keep well with stay on good terms with; maintain cordial relations with.

328.32 stand in their right *law* stand in their place.

329.22–23 God may mend all in his own good time 'God mend all!' was a common pious wish: e.g. *Henry VIII*, 1.2.201.

329.29 God has given me no heir of my name see Historical Note, 526.

329.29 from the purpose beside the point; irrelevant.

329.40 The beginning of evil is the letting out of water see Proverbs 17.14.

330.2 never bend your angry brows on me compare *Macbeth*, 3.4.50–51: 'never shake/ Thy gory locks at me' (Macbeth to Banquo's ghost).

330.14 assigned away *law* transferred for the benefit of creditors.

330.22–23 you would make a saint swear proverbial: *ODEP*, 696.

330.26 the days of William the Lion William the Lion (1143–1214) became King of Scots in 1165, though as Earl of Huntingdon he was vassal to the English king Henry II; in 1189 he purchased the claim to homage from Richard II and became an independent Scottish king.

331.34–35 a cunning clerk ... Scripture see note to 149.39.

332.8 Amadis and Oriana the knight-errant and his wife are central figures in a series of medieval Spanish romances that plot the obstacles to their marriage.

333.16 got me to speech of got me an audience with.

333.26–28 his grandfather ... call him 'the Red Tod' (red fox) was the nickname for King James V (1512–42; reigned 1513–42), who had a red beard and was notorious for his philandering, assisted by the use of disguise (beggar, tinker, and so forth); Scott so represented the monarch in *The Lady of the Lake* (1810), Note 74. The popular Scottish poet David Lindsay (1490–1555) was affectionately known as 'Davie'. Lindsay was on friendly terms with James V, but he does not refer to him as 'the Red Tod', and the King had no particular connection with St Andrews.

333.30 Solomon ... concubines an example of the indirect reference to James's 'femininity' found in the early histories. Solomon 'loved many strange women ... And he had seven hundred wives, princesses, and three hundred concubines': 1 Kings 11.1–3.

334.3–4 believes me with thinks I am with.

334.7 of her kindness out of kindness.

334.20–21 high-flown Arcadian compliments exaggerated, idealised language of the sort most famously found in Sir Philip Sidney's pastoral romance *Arcadia* (1590; 1593), named after a mountainous district in Greece imagined to be the perfection of rural life.

335.2–6 motto see William Shenstone, 'Jemmy Dawson, A Ballad; written about the Time of his Execution, in the Year 1745', lines 41–44: *The Works in Verse and Prose of William Shenstone, Esq.*, ed. R. Dodsley, 2 vols (London, 1764), 1.187. Dawson's crime was treason, for which he was hanged, drawn, and quartered on 30 July 1746. The site of the 'ignominious tree' was Kennington Common, Surrey.

335.13 Sir Edward Mansel an Edward Mansel (d. 1595) was knighted by Queen Elizabeth in 1572 and fathered the Robert Mansel (1573–1656) who served James as Treasurer of the Navy, 'the only valiant [military] man he [James] ever loved' (Weldon, 2.6).

335.25–26 an old proverb about fire and flax the proverb runs 'Keep flax from fire and youth from gaming': *ODEP*, 267.

336.1 in very deed in fact; in reality; in truth.

336.18 the twelve Kaisars the first twelve caesars or emperors of Rome, the subject of the chief work by Suetonius (*c*. AD 70–*c*. 160), *Lives of the Twelve Caesars*, which Scott owned both in Latin and in English translation: *CLA*, 227–28.

336.20 write myself designate myself in documents; call myself.

336.20 far to seek hard to discover.

336.21 the Maelstrom the famous whirlpool near the Lofoten Islands off NW Norway.

336.40–41 Archie Armstrong . . . every day as court jester, Armstrong (see Historical Note, 530) was permitted liberties of speech that would not be tolerated in others.

337.6 comes indifferently off leaves the field with an undistinguished or even poor outcome.

337.14 propose for intend making for.

338.11 gained on swayed; influenced.

338.25–27 usque ad mutilationem the Latin phrase is translated immediately.

338.34 hanging, drawing, and quartering convicted traitors were half-hanged, then castrated, disembowelled (*drawn*), beheaded, and their bodies cut into four quarters.

338.35–36 external application . . . outer man hempen twine would be used as a tourniquet before amputation by knife and cauterising with fire.

338.41 old proverb . . . so forth the proverb runs 'Confess and be hanged': *ODEP*, 139.

338.42 has a special ill will at particularly objects to.

339.19 my Lord Gray's train Arthur Grey (1536–93), 14th Baron Grey de Wilton from 1562, was one of Queen Elizabeth's leading military commanders.

339.19–20 lay leaguer camped.

339.28–29 came on arrived on stage.

339.31–32 Paul's Cross . . . Charing a cross (destroyed 1643) N of St Paul's Cathedral, with an open-air pulpit for the preaching of sermons; and the commemorative cross at Charing (see note to 65.13). In the Interleaved Set Scott changed 'Charing' to 'Westminster', but presumably because the sense of the sentence required the original phrasing the change was not adopted.

339.32 the Sheriff's and the Marshal's men i.e. both the civilian and the military police were in attendance.

339.35 jibber a joint the expression occurs as 'ieopard a ioint' or 'jea-bard a joynt' in Thomas Dekker, *Old Fortunatus* (1600), 1.2.181, and John Fletcher, *Women Pleased* (performed *c*. 1620, published 1647), 3.2.74. In Dekker it means 'risk the loss of a finger', and in Fletcher it is used of visiting a whore: here it seems to mean 'amputate a joint'.

339.36–37 a barber-surgeon's see notes to 228.20–22 and 23.

340.2 Tubbs, or Stubbes see note to 181.16–17.

340.6 Derrick the hangman the executioner throughout Elizabeth's reign. He is much alluded to in the literature of the period.

340.6–7 d'ye mind me are you listening, attending to me.

340.8–9 a gauntlet . . . the tilt-yard in chivalry, a glove thrown upon the ground by which act one knight challenges another to fight or tilt with lances in the arena set aside for jousting. For tilting see note to 147.16.

340.10–13 no whit . . . not a whit none at all . . . not at all.

340.25 Digby...gunpowder gang Sir Everard Digby (b. 1578), Thomas Winter (b. 1572) and his brother Robert, and Guy Fawkes (b. 1570) were among those conspirators tried and executed in the winter of 1606 for their role in the Gunpowder Plot: see note to 212.43.

340.40–43 the little Dutch dwarf...help him compare John Stow, *A Svmmarie of the Chronicles of England, from the arriuing of Brute in this Island, vnto this present yeere of Christ, 1590* (London, 1580), 704: 'This yere [1581] were to be seene in London, two Dutch men of strange statures, the one in height seuen foot & seuen inches... The other was in height but three foot, had neuer a good foote, nor any knee at all, and yet could dance a galliard, he had no arme, but a stumpe to the elbow, or a little more on the right side, on the which, singing, he would dance a cuppe, and after tosse it about three or foure times, and euery time receiue the same on the said stumpe, he would shoote an arrow neere the marke, florish with a rapior, throw a bowle, beat with a hammer, hew with an axe, sound a trumpet, and drinke euery day tenne quarts of the best beare, if hee coulde get it.'

341.12 made interest with brought personal influence to bear on.

341.15 Bridewell a prison and house of correction near Whitefriars.

341.27 Pulchra sane puella *Latin* an exceedingly beautiful girl.

341.29 Sawney see note to 34.1.

341.36 when the hurry was off our spirits when our agitation and perturbation had subsided.

342.26 bear a heart am disposed in spirit.

343.31–33 her in Scottish story...her sovereign Catherine Douglas, a lady in waiting, in this heroic manner attempted but failed to prevent the murder of King James I at Perth in 1437.

345.2–7 motto not identified: probably by Scott. For *Marry come up* see note to 60.36. For the 'old Assyrian kings' who first subjugated mankind see 2 Kings 15.19, 29 and 17.3–6. The story of one such king would have been familiar to Scott's readers from Byron's popular 1815 lyric 'The Destruction of Sennacherib'.

345.15 betwixt whiles at intervals.

345.21 not give us over to our ain devices Richie's petition echoes the biblical language, especially that nominally of Solomon, used in chastising those Israelites who prefer their ignorance or pseudo-wisdom and self-counsel to the wisdom and instruction of God, e.g. Proverbs 1.31: 'Therefore shall they eat of the fruit of their own way, and be filled with their own devices'. It may also echo the General Confession from the Order for Daily Morning Prayer in The Book of Common Prayer (1552): 'We have followed too much the devices and desires of our own hearts'.

345.22 in respect of by reason of; because of.

346.15 cast that up to bring that up so as to reproach.

346.24 no whit not at all.

347.11 The de'il be in my feet if I do an oath suggesting that Richie would return to Scotland only if his feet were possessed by the devil and so beyond his control.

347.12–13 fed upon you lived at your expense.

347.15–18 It's hame...ain country for Cunningham's song see note to 13.16.

347.38 First oars! the traditional call for summoning the Thames waterman next in line to transport a customer.

347.39 Tritons mock-heroic term for the watermen: in Greek mythology Triton, a creature half man and half fish, was the son of Poseidon, god of the sea.

348.19 red wud raving mad.

348.20–21 pisces purga ... pulchre *Latin* clean the fish—see that the salt fish is well cooked. Linklater again echoes the slave Syrus in Terence's play *Adelphoe* (see note to 299.38–40), lines 376, 380–81: 'piscis ceteros purga ... salsamenta haec, Stephanio, fac macerentur pulchre'.

348.24 came off fared.

348.26–27 wee bit small.

348.34 wee bit little.

348.35 neither hand nor foot no involvement at all.

348.39–40 drinks out the broth i.e. turns up the bowl and empties it of the liquid that remains.

349.14 the grandes entrées *French* the hours when gentlemen are accorded the privilege of entering a monarch's chamber, as distinguished from *petites entrées* or such private opportunities as Richie is accorded here.

349.19–20 three geometrical cubits the geometrical cubit is six times greater than the common cubit, a measure of length derived from the distance between the elbow and the end of the middle finger and varying slightly from country to country. Using the English figure of 18 inches (45.72 centimetres) for the common cubit, we can calculate that Maxwell is asked to come not nearer than 9 feet (some 2.75 metres) of the door.

349.38–39 Onyx cum prole, silexque—Onyx cum prole *Latin* the onyx with its offspring, and flint—the onyx with its offspring. The phrase 'cum prole' is fairly common in Classical literature. In the Bible the onyx stone is a recurring symbol of high value: see e.g. Job 28.16.

350.6 what de'il's what the devil is.

350.10 when time was in a time that is past; formerly. The expression is found in *The Tempest*, 2.2.129.

350.15 stuck by stayed on.

350.15–16 Equam memento rebus in arduis servare *Latin* remember to stick to your mare in difficulty. The King humorously adapts lines from Horace (65–8 BC), Ode, 2.3.1–2: 'Aequam memento rebus in arduis/ servare mentem' (remember in difficult circumstances to keep a steady mind).

350.18 contra expectanda *Latin* contrary to expectation.

350.19 on the part of on behalf of; as the agent of.

350.20 In no sort in no way.

350.21 Henry Wynd ... own hand Wynd was a smith who for the sum of a gold crown supplied the place of a missing clansman in the 1396 battle between Clan Chattan and Clan Quhele on the North Inch of Perth. When asked afterwards if he had not fought for Clan Chattan, he answered that he fought 'for my own hand' (i.e. on my own behalf), which answer according to Scott in *The Fair Maid of Perth* (1828), where he tells the story in full, was 'still proverbial in Scotland' (ed. Andrew Hood and Donald Mackenzie, EEWN 21, 377.30 and note). See also *ODEP*, 256.

350.29 stand close stand nearby. This phrase is much used in the old drama.

350.32–33 get a hair in his neck *proverbial* cause him irritating discomfort: *ODEP*, 342.

351.12 laid in wad left as security.

351.13 Voetius, Vinnius, Groenwigeneus, Pagenstrecherus eminent 17th-century Dutch jurists: Johannes Voet (1647–1713), Arnold Vinnen (1588–1657), Simon van Groenewegen van der Made (1613–52), and Alexander Arnold Pagenstecher (1659–1716).

351.14 de Contractu Opignerationis, consentiunt in eundem *Latin* on contract of pledge, all agree on this point.

351.15–16 The Roman law ... Scotland Roman law refers to the codifying legislation, *Corpus iuris civilis*, of the Emperor Justinian and is the basis for the legal codes of most European countries, including Scotland, and many of their former colonies; English *common* law as distinct from Roman *civil* law refers to a native law general to the country evolved over centuries through precedent, debate, and commentary in English, not Latin, rather than promulgated through legislative code (i.e. 'case law' as distinct from 'statute law'); Scottish *municipal* law is the body of law governing internal as distinct from international matters.

351.23–24 brief while since a short time ago.

351.25 into public into the public eye. In James's case beyond the verge of the court wherever it might be at any given time: from the day of his entrance into London to claim the throne James exhibited a decided distaste for going into public, especially into large crowds.

351.41 smelling to the gold smelling the gold.

351.41 Non olet alluding to the Latin adage 'pecunia non olet' (money carries no taint). Money when it reaches the hands of an innocent party cannot affect them with any irregularity by which it had been acquired before they received it.

352.16 grip to seize; take a firm hold of.

352.17 grasps to grasps at.

352.18 what for for what reason; why.

352.23–26 Difficult ... come to pass James's characteristic pedantry or hair-splitting replete with Latin (*exempli gratia* 'for example') is traceable to his education by schoolmen.

352.31 malleus maleficarum *Latin* the witch hammer. James alludes to a work with this title by Jakob Sprenger and Heinrich Kramer, published at Speyer *c*. 1486, which deals with the disciplining of witches.

352.33–34 taking a touch of the black art dabbling lightly in, or taking a brief turn at, black magic.

352.35 the seven sages of Greece the most commonly accepted list of noteworthy figures from the 7th and 6th centuries BC is: Solon of Athens, author of laws; Chilo of Sparta, source of common wisdom; Thales of Miletus, astronomer; Bias of Priene, moralist; Cleobulos of Lindos, source of common wisdom; Pittacos of Mitylene, statesman; and Periander of Corinth, statesman and patron of letters.

352.36 small time syne a short time ago.

352.37–39 Solomon ... daughter of Pharoah see 1 Kings 11.1: 'But King Solomon loved many strange women, together with the daughter of Pharoah, women of the Moabites, Ammonites, Edomites, Zidonians, and Hittites' —i.e. women of tribes with whom God had forbidden the Israelites to associate. See note to 333.30.

353.15 Tod-lowrie, come out of your den part of a child's rhyme: see Anderson, 189. 'Tod-lowrie' is a familiar name for the fox in the north of England and in Scotland.

353.19 that gait in that way.

353.22–25 in the vein of Euclio apud Plautum ... video Euclio the miser is a character in the play *Aulularia* ('The Pot of Gold') by Plautus (*c*. 254–184 BC) from which James proceeds to quote lines 713–14. The Latin means: 'I am killed, ruined, murdered—where can I run? where not run? Hold, hold,—whom do I hold? I do not know—I see nothing.'

353.27 and the like of that and such like things.

353.27–28 come by them find them.

353.29 right and tight, sound and round two set phrases meaning 'in good order, condition, etc.'

353.29 doublet 'a counterfeit jewel composed of two pieces of crystal or glass cemented together with a layer of colour between them, or of a thin slice of a gem cemented on a piece of glass or inferior stone' (*OED*).

353.33–34 continued on maintained.

353.40 where there is paying in the case i.e. when collecting payment is involved.

353.43 money on the nail money down.

354.3 the mines of Ophir the gold from these mines, most probably located on the Arabian shore of the Persian Gulf, greatly impressed the Queen of Sheba when she visited Solomon to verify the reports of his wisdom and wealth (see 1 Kings 10.11): in biblical literature this gold, used by Solomon for the walls of the temple (see 1 Chronicles 29.4), is the rarest, most precious gold (see Isaiah 13.12) and as such the measure of ultimate value to which things and people are compared. The 1606 state visit of Queen Anne's brother, King Christian IV of Denmark, was apparently conceived as analogous, with James in the role of the dazzling Solomon, the Dane in the role of the dazzled Queen. A letter of Sir John Harington (*Nugæ Antiquæ* (see note to 47.2), 1. 349–50) mentions that for his entertainment a 'representation of Solomon his Temple and the coming of the Queen of Sheba was made, or (as I may better say) was meant to have been made, before their Majesties' (the lavish spectacle miscarried because of intoxicated nobles).

354.5 at his will in his power.

354.8 with the King's favour with the king's permission (to interrogate Richie).

354.13 What for no? why not?

354.15 lined it gay and weel the well-dressed of this period lined their garments with bright and expensive material such as velvet which could be exposed to view by slashes in the outer material or by a calculated motion of the hand or leg.

354.17 rustles it goes about dressed in clothes of fine material that rustles, e.g. silk.

354.23 Non est inquirendum unde venit venison *Latin* no one is to enquire where the venison comes from.

354.24–25 He that brings ... gear compare the expression 'goods and gear' (worldly possessions; money and property).

354.25 speak the truth and shame the de'il proverbial: Ray, 163; *ODEP*, 807.

354.26 dispose on make arrangements concerning; settle (so as to finish the business).

354.32 come ye to me there? do you get at me (by exploiting my vulnerability)?

354.34 at our free will at our disposal.

354.35 ony matter of silver anything in the way of money.

354.36 de'il a boddle not a bit. A *boddle* is a small copper coin.

354.37 niffer for niffer, grippie for grippie mutual bargaining, mutual grasping.

354.38–39 some monopoly ... knighthood James enumerates three ways in which he could and did bargain for ready money: (1) he could confer a *monopoly* by which the recipient acquired exclusive trading rights for a given item, a practice he so abused that in 1621 he was forced to give it up altogether, and similarly he could confer patents or assign licensing rights, both highly lucrative; (2) he could sell land that Henry VIII had seized for the crown when dissolving the monasteries which, along with the attached *teinds* (tithes), would bring the recipient a handsome revenue; (3) and he would charge fees for elevating commoners; apparently knighthoods cost £40, baronetcies (i.e. hereditary knighthoods, an honour invented by James in 1611) £1095, and earldoms £20,000. In all he created about 2300 knights and 40 peers.

355.8 in the gate James alludes to Psalms 69.12 and 127.5, where the phrase means at the gate of the city as a place of judicial assembly.

355.13 a red iron driven through your tongue one of the possible punishments for 'leasing-making', i.e. making untrue and slanderous statements such as are likely to prejudice relations between the king and his subjects, as defined by the Scottish laws of 1584, c. 134, and 1585, c. 10.

355.13–14 in terrorem of *Latin* as a warning to; a set phrase.

355.14–15 plack and bawbee see note to 114.36.

355.15–16 let them care that come ahint *proverbial* let those who come after do the worrying (they won't get what's owed them): Alan Ramsay, *A Collection of Scots Proverbs* (1737), in *The Works of Allan Ramsay*, Vol. 5, ed. Alexander M. Kinghorn and Alexander Law (Edinburgh and London, 1972), 97.

355.27 doubles his bode that gate doubles his bid in that way.

355.29–30 Ne inducas ... Amen *Latin* lead us not into temptation— Get thee behind me, Satan—Amen. James couples a line from the Lord's Prayer with one from Matthew 16.23.

355.39 Never fash your beard see note to 162.18.

356.14–15 over old a cock ... chaff proverbial: see Ray, 141 and *ODEP*, 110.

356.21 will be on me will be upon me; will accost me.

356.25 was in attendance awaited him.

356.29–30 motto *Much Ado About Nothing*, 4.1.67.

357.2 Seneca the Roman tragedian and philosopher Lucius Annaeus Seneca (*c.* 4 BC–AD 65) commended such Stoic virtues as those mentioned here.

357.2 Boethius de Consolatione the Roman philosopher Anicius Manlius Severinus Boethius (*c.* 470–524) wrote his widely influential *De Consolatione Philosophiae* on the comfort that philosophy or natural theology combining neo-platonism and stoicism provides to those in spiritual and mental distress.

357.2–3 the back might be ... fitted for the burthen see Robert Fergusson, 'Mutual Complaint of Plainstanes and Causey, in their Mothertongue' (1773), line 64: 'Your back's best fitted for the burden'. Compare the proverb 'His back is broad enough to bear jests': Ray, 176; *ODEP*, 25.

357.5–6 Non ignara ... disco *Latin* no stranger to misfortune, I learn to succour the unhappy. With these words Dido comforts Aeneas whom a storm has driven to Carthage during his wanderings after the fall of his native Troy: Virgil (70–19 BC), *Aeneid*, 1.630.

357.6–8 I might say ... tenacious James refers to the difference in the quantity of the vowel sounds when the feminine termination 'a' is changed to the masculine 'us'. The Latin dactylic hexameter, the metre in which Virgil wrote, combines heavy and light syllables according to a set of clearly established rules. The final syllable of 'ignara' (feminine), which ends in a vowel, is light, as is required in this position in the line, but if it is replaced by the masculine 'ignarus', ending in a consonant, the final syllable is now heavy and the line no longer scans. Unlike James's earlier references to the controversy between Scottish and English Latinists, this example does not involve a preference of one pronunciation over another: it is a matter of right and wrong prosody. He may here simply be alluding to the interest of English Latinists in metrical matters, rather than to any international disagreement.

357.9–10 venienti occurrite morbo *Latin* the translation follows directly in the text—i.e. attack the disease in its early phase. James quotes the Roman satirist Persius (Aulus Persius Flaccus: AD 34–62): *Satires*, 3.64.

357.13 bear me out sustain me.

357.15 are you there with your bears proverbial for repeating the same story, idea, or question: Ray, 177; *ODEP*, 18. Tradition has it that the phrase originated in the disgust of a man who on three consecutive Sundays in three different churches heard a sermon on the text of Elisha and the bears (2 Kings 2.23–25).

357.16 principium et fons *Latin* basis and source. James quotes from Horace (65–8 BC), *De Arte Poetica*, line 309: 'Scribendi recte sapere est et principium et fons' (knowledge is the basis and source of clever writing).

357.17–28 the original . . . the English traduction the Authorised Version of the Bible of 1611 (the so-called King James translation, from the original Hebrew (Old Testament) and Greek (New Testament) but heavily indebted to earlier translations) was arranged for and superintended by James, who here paraphrases the language of the opening paragraph of the Dedication: 'For whereas it was the expectation of many . . . that upon the setting of that bright *Occidental Star*, Queen *Elizabeth* of most happy memory, some thick and palpable clouds of darkness would so have overshadowed this Land, that men should have been in doubt which way they were to walk . . .'; the Dedication, in turn, echoes the language of Exodus 10.21–22. James's encouragement of preaching and of the new translation is praised in the rest of the Dedication. The 'Latin version of the Septuagint' is a translation of the Greek version of the Old Testament made by Jewish scholars (traditionally 72 of them) at Alexandria over a period up to *c.* 130 BC. It was superseded by the Vulgate version, Jerome's 4th-century translation directly from the Hebrew.

357.31 read Hebrew like your Majesty accounts of James's education in modern biographies make much of his fluency in Greek, Latin, and French, but they do not mention Hebrew.

358.1 non surdo canes *Latin* you do not sing to one who is deaf. See Virgil (70–19 BC), *Eclogues* (37 BC), 10.8.

358.32 put her aff on foisted her upon.

359.12 breaks upon it strikes and penetrates it, causing it to collapse.

359.16 our anointed self in the course of the coronation service the new monarch is anointed with holy oil on head, hands, and breast.

359.16 Vae atque dolor *Latin* woe and pain.

359.17 the Queen of Sheba see 1 Kings 10.1–13 and note to 354.3 for the story of the wealthy Queen's visit to King Solomon.

359.27 in the common case in general; in the abstract.

359.37 Compone lachrymas *Latin* dry your tears.

360.23–25 the vein . . . patrum the Latin phrase means 'doubtless by force, the method customary with parents'. In Terence's play *Adelphoe* (see note to 299.38–40) Demea, the authoritarian parent, and Micio, the indulgent one, argue about whose is the better method for raising a son, though not in these exact words (see lines 26–154).

360.27 gie the glaiks to jilt.

360.37–38 the King of Kings the epithet is applied in the New Testament to Christ: 1 Timothy 6.15; Revelation 17.14, 19.16.

360.43–361.1 like a wise man . . . say nothing proverbial: *ODEP*, 362.

361.3–4 ganging a wee bit gleed in her walk going a little astray in her walk.

361.5 casting a leglen-girth *literally* losing the lowest hoop on a milk pail; *metaphorically* bearing an illegitimate child. In his Magnum note (27.301) Scott gives the literal meaning and cites the same metaphorical use of the phrase in Allan Ramsay's poem *Christ's Kirk on the Green* (1718), 3.65, but Ramsay has 'Legen-girth' (the lowest hoop on a cask): *The Works of Allan Ramsay*, Vol. 1, ed. Burns Martin and John W. Oliver (Edinburgh and London, [1951]), 77.

361.9–10 very circumspect in her walk conducted herself wisely, in accordance with God's laws: see Ephesians 5.15.

361.15–17 auld-warld frailties ... absolutely free for James's drinking and swearing see notes to 307.15 and 70.43.

361.19–20 Ætas ... Nos nequiores *Latin* the age of our parents, worse than that of our ancestors, has brought forth us who are worse still: Horace (65–8 BC), *Odes*, 3.6.46–47.

361.27 warld's gear material possessions.

361.28 brazen us a' out defy us all impudently, as with a face of brass.

361.30 lap at it like a cock at a grossart see note to 162.36–37.

361.30–32 These are discrepancies ... de secretis Giambattista della Porta (1538?–1615) and Michael Scot (1175?–1232) were famous throughout Europe for their knowledge of and skill in magic. Scott owned the 1644 Leiden edition of Porta's *Magiae Naturalis Libri XX*, originally published in 1589 (*CLA*, 108). The Latin phrase *de secretis* ('concerning mysteries') is part of an alternative title (*Liber de Secretis Naturæ*) for Michael Scot's treatise *Liber Phisiognomiæ*. Scott owned a copy of the first printed edition, published in 1477 (*CLA*, 148). The first part of Scot's work is not about physiognomy but about generation. According to Scot, astrology—the course of the stars and the disposition of the couple at the moment of conception—determines the nature of the human being conceived; hence it is the supernatural which accounts for the possibility of discrepancies between father and son.

361.33 clouting the cauldron mending the metal vessel for holding hot water, like a tinker. 'Clout the Caudron' is a Scottish folk tune often used with tinker songs: e.g. see Robert Burns, 'My bonie lass I work in brass', in 'Love and Liberty' (1786), lines 165–81.

361.39–40 father's bonnet ... father's night-cap compare the proverb 'Your head will never fill your father's bonnet': *ODEP*, 361, citing Kelly, 372, who glosses it 'you will never be so wise a Man as your Father'. Heriot implies there is no reason to suspect that a man who does not match his father's endowments was begotten by an intruder into the parental bed.

362.10 the old proverb of Satan reproving sin see Ray, 97; *ODEP*, 699.

362.11 De'il hae our saul *oath* the Devil take my soul.

362.13 non utendo *Latin* by not using it.

362.13–14 negative prescription in law, the loss of a right by neglecting to use it during the legally specified period.

362.16 arcana ... regnare *Latin* imperial secrets—the king knows not how to reign, who knows not how to dissemble. Compare Louis XI's use of this maxim in the first chapter of *Quentin Durward*, ed. J. H. Alexander and G. A. M. Wood, EEWN 15, 25.4–5. Weldon (1.412) notes that it was James's motto (along with 'beati pacifici': see note to 110.14).

362.18–19 whiles ... at a time formerly ... from time to time.

362.20 cast that up to him bring that up so as to reproach him.

362.21 Zeno the 5th-century BC Greek philosopher risked his life to rid his country of a tyrant and died in the attempt.

363.8 by form of law in accord with legal precedent or statute.

363.22–23 prælibatio matrimonii *Latin* foretaste of marriage.

363.41 sine mora *Latin* without delay.

363.42 Statim atque instanter *Latin* instantly and at once.

364.20–21 Prayer-Book ... amazement *Dearly Beloved* are the opening words of the marriage ceremony in the Book of Common Prayer; *amazement* is not, of course, the closing word but rather Dalgano's witty term for the state of mind of the newly joined couple when they realize that they are indeed married.

364.32 The Bishop of Winchester Lancelot Andrewes (1555–1626), probably the favourite of the clergy with whom James surrounded himself throughout his reign, was translated from the bishopric of Ely to that of Winchester in 1619 and died in the post.

365.1–4 some reservation ... seclusion the law allowed that some part of a bride's real property could be vested with trustees and reserved for her exclusive use. Dalgarno will accept the bulk of her fortune as in effect a payment for their separation.

365.6 potestas maritalis *Latin* rights of a husband acquired through marriage.

365.33–34 the first-born of Israel in biblical literature, beginning with Abraham and Isaac (Genesis Ch. 22), the first-born is the ultimate sacrifice exacted of a father by the God of Israel. Compare the questioning of this notion in Micah 6.7: 'shall I give my firstborn for my transgression, the fruit of my body for the sin of my soul?'

366.4 summa totalis *Latin* sum total.

366.10 the wedding-torch an attribute of the wedding ceremony mentioned in the old drama: e.g. *1 Henry VI*, 3.2.26–27: 'Behold, this is the happy wedding torch/ That joineth Rouen unto her countrymen.'

366.23–24 take the rights to her i.e. transfer them to her. In law, the lender acquires the rights to the property in cases of default on the loan.

366.30 a proper spot of work *ironical* a fine piece of work.

366.30–31 beginning to amble about ... hose for James's fiddling mannerism see note to 109.25.

366.46 his ram-skin i.e. his parchment or legal document.

366.46 Andrea Ferrara see note to 45.28–29.

367.6 pater patriæ *Latin* father of the country. See note to 70.41.

367.17–18 motto *Richard III*, 5.3.221.

367.20 hitch in draw in jerkily.

367.30–31 the slave in the comedy—Quid de symbolo? in *Eunuchus* by Terence (see note to 299.38–40) it is the young Athenian Antipho (not a slave) who speaks the words 'sed interim de symbolis quid actum est' ('meanwhile what's been done about dinner?': line 607). James means 'What about dinner?'

368.4–9 the logic of the schools ... inter parietes ecclesiæ in the schools or universities of the middle ages logic (one of the seven liberal arts) was a third part of the *trivium* or basic curriculum. The system of logic which students strove to master was that of Aristotle, the source of both the problems they were set and the solutions they were to find. The method with which they pursued this skill was disputation, often focused on a fine difference of detail. The end, generally speaking, was to reconcile logic and theology, or reason and faith. James was trained in this logic by his tutor Peter Young, who studied Calvin's logical system at Geneva with the great theologian's disciple Theodore Beza (see note to 76.23), and he was himself 'inclined to syllogisms and to disputation in the manner of the medieval schoolmen' (David Harris Willson, *King James VI and I* (London, 1956), 24), as is here suggested by his overfine distinction of *quoad hominem* (*Latin* 'as far as the man') from *quoad locum* ('as far as the place'). 'Chrighty Beardie' is Scott's version of a dance song popular in the early 17th century, 'Kette Bairdie' or 'Katie Beardie'. That James thinks it inappropriately danced *inter parietes ecclesiæ* (*Latin* 'within the walls of a church') would seem to reflect his Calvinist upbringing, for Psalm 150.4 explicitly commends dance as a means of praising God.

368.17 rain Jeddart staves the Jeddart (Jedburgh) staff is a kind of battle-axe: 'it rains Jeddart staves' was proverbial for 'it is raining cats and dogs'.

368.26 Rem acu tetigisti, Carole, mi puerule *proverbial Latin, literally* you have touched the thing with a needle, Charles, my little boy; i.e. you have hit the nail on the head, Baby Charles.

368.30–31 the curious case of Lady Lake . . . the arras James never tired of citing this case as evidence of his Solomonic perspicacity. In 1617 Lady Lake, the wife of Sir Thomas Lake (1567?–1630), who was made Secretary of State in 1616, accused the Countess of Exeter of proposing to kill her and her own daughter the Lady Ross, alleging that the Countess had confessed this in a letter written in the presence of Diego, a confidential servant, and that the scene had been witnessed from behind an arras by a waiting-maid. James smelled a rat, and one day while hunting at Wimbledon, the scene of the crime, he suddenly determined to investigate the story for himself. A reenactment on site confirmed his suspicion that the letter was a forgery. Sir Thomas was implicated, the Lakes were fined and imprisoned by the Star Chamber, and the servants punished (in 1619). For detailed accounts see Weldon, 1.365–69, and William Sanderson, *A Compleat History of The Lives and Reigns of Mary Queen of Scotland, And of Her Son and Successor, James the Sixth, King of Scotland* . . ., 2 parts (London, 1656–55), 446–49.

368.32–37 Dionysius . . . this Dionysius of Syracuse see note to 92.25–28.

369.1–3 he was a great linguist . . . matters not whilk it was Dionysius the Younger who is said to have kept a school at Corinth after he was driven from Syracuse for the second time.

369.8 put up accommodated; housed.

369.14 trembling exies hysterics.

369.24 well followed well conducted; effectively pursued.

369.28 anguis in herba *proverbial Latin* a snake in the grass.

369.28 put her to compel her to answer.

369.40 eaves-dropper as it is called an English legal term for one who listens secretly to conversation.

369.42 were of counsel together conspired.

370.3–4 a Father of the Church a bishop.

370.10–11 ane particular . . . on ours see note to 333.30.

370.25 They say . . . themselves proverbial: see Ray, 272 and *ODEP*, 468.

370.32 bos in linguam *Latin* ox on the tongue; i.e. a bribe weighty enough to buy silence. An ancient Athenian coin bore the figure of an ox on one side.

370.33 from Dan to Beersheba from the northern to the southern extremity of Palestine; i.e. throughout the land. See 2 Samuel 24.2: 'Go now through all the tribes of Israel, from Dan even to Beer-sheba'.

370.35 put to his freedom released from custody.

371.20 in whom he takes such part in whose cause he takes such interest.

371.20 out of our ain gracious motion of my own gracious accord.

371.22 as if of your own mind as if it is your idea.

371.36 your gate in your own way.

372.7–13 motto Samuel Butler, *Hudibras* (1663–78), 3.3.621–25.

372.38 Skurliewhitter the name, a compound of Scots words, means 'shrill chatterer'.

373.3 what's o'clock? what time is it?

373.8 The Whitefriars business this is explained at 378.23–25.

373.12 distilled waters distilled alcoholic liquor.

373.18 Sathanas and Mammon see notes to 256.25 and 269.18.

373.31 wants three-quarters of noon is not yet 11.45 a.m.

374.9 make your long ears an inch shorter if Skirliewhitter tangles with the Law it may punish him by having his long ears cropped. The ears are prominent because his hair is cut short (64.10–11); there is also probably a suggestion that he is an ass.

375.6   on to-morrow at four afternoon   tomorrow at four o'clock in the afternoon.

375.7   Enfield Chace   see note to 19.34.

375.7   I will be slenderly attended   I will travel with few servants.

375.8   Barnet   just within the S boundary of Hertfordshire, Barnet was on the Great North Road, the principal route for travelling to Scotland by land.

375.9   Camlet Moat   see note to 391.37–38.

375.11   the Park   St James's Park.

375.15   there go twa words to that bargain   *proverbial*   it takes two words (i.e. two parties) to make that bargain: see Ray, 76 and *ODEP*, 852.

375.19   his discretion for once ruled his wit   derived from the proverb 'an ounce of discretion is worth a pound of wit': Ray, 96; *ODEP*, 601.

375.37–38   the Gorgon head, the turbatæ Palladis arma   the head of Medusa, one of the three monstrous Gorgons, whose hair consisted of snakes and whose look turned all in their purview to stone. Medusa alone was mortal, and when she had been killed by Perseus, her head was affixed to 'the armour [i.e. the shield] of angry Pallas [Athene]' (Virgil (70–19 BC), *Aeneid*, 8.435).

375.43–376.1   blowing hot and cold, with a witness   being inconsistent, and no mistake. See Revelation 3.15–16, and *ODEP*, 70.

376.4   mine antler'd honours   the honours of the cuckold, a figure of endless jest in the literature of the period, whose humiliation is represented by a pair of invisible horns or antlers signifying to the knowing his bestial naïvety or stupidity.

376.12   cut him out from   deprived him of.

376.37   the Attorney-General   the king's law officer.

376.41   pity of   a pity about.

377.1–3   it shall go hard but ... ammunition   i.e. Dalgarno will do this unless thwarted by overwhelming difficulties.

377.17   porters of trust   trustworthy porters.

377.28   shaped out the means of fortune   formed the plan by which he might attain fortune.

377.33   uncut Wiltshire cloth   perhaps the light wool cloth made from the short, light wool of the Wiltshire horned sheep, here unshaped.

378.1–6   Thou son of parchment ... thy better   a free version of William Cartwright, *The Ordinary* (performed 1634–35, published 1651), 3.5.105–10 (*ABD*, 3.163).

378.8   bear you out   support you; i.e. be of any help to you.

378.11   eke my wings with a few feathers   the wings of falcons in particular were often supplemented with feathers grafted from other birds, so as either to repair damage or to add strength.

378.21   plague of   a plague upon.

378.27   there is not   that is not.

378.30   Jack Hempsfield   Hempsfield is the man from whose knife Nigel saved Martha Trapbois at the time of the attempted robbery (270).

378.31–35   the old catch ... triple tree   version of the refrain to a popular song in John Fletcher and Philip Massinger, *The Bloody Brother; or, Rollo. A Tragedy* (performed 1617, published 1639), 3.2.61–62 etc., sung by three men about to be hanged.

378.36–37   is this a place ... mid-night catches heard   compare Malvolio's rebuke to Sir Toby and Sir Andrew in *Twelfth Night*, 2.3.83–90.

378.39–40   You tell me a lie ... a most palpable and gross lie   a merging of lines from *Othello*, 5.2.183–84 ('You told a lie—an odious, damned lie./ Upon my soul, a lie—a wicked lie'), and *1 Henry IV* (2.4.216–17: 'These lies are like their father that begets them—gross as a mountain, open, palpable').

379.2 by tale by count or tally (as opposed to by weight).

379.8 sets forward to sets out for; goes forward to; starts for.

379.15–17 hadst the wind ... spaniel see note to 248.11.

379.21 comest thou to me there see note to 354.32.

379.28 looks sharp to the world's gear keeps his eye on the material world, in particular on money.

379.35 will stand parting is sufficiently large to be divided up.

379.42 truce with an end to.

380.6–12 motto not identified: probably by Scott.

380.29 the wine ... innovation see note to 144.37–40.

380.36 with cap and knee with a doffing of the cap and a bending of the knee.

381.7 merely of your grace solely attributable to your favour and good will (i.e. not obligatory in social superiors).

381.17–18 gang a' ae gate, and that is a gray one to 'gang a gray gate' is to come to a bad end; to 'gang the gate' is to die.

381.27 ran full against him bumped right into him.

381.37–38 ever fair and false compare the proverbs 'False as a Scot' (Ray, 221; *ODEP*, 243), 'Fair without, false within' (*ODEP*, 240), and 'There is many a fair thing full false' (Ray, 305; *ODEP*, 240).

382.17 according to the letter literally.

382.19 the Devil Tavern see note to 26.35.

382.20 burned sack see note to 256.29.

382.22 in good fashion in the proper way.

382.27–28 the Saint Andrews the tavern is imaginary. A Scotsman might understandably prefer a tavern bearing the name of the patron saint of Scotland.

382.39–40 the leasings of Mahound the falsehoods of *either* Mahomet (for whom 'Mahound' is a contemptuous name) *or* the Devil (in Scotland, 'Mahound' is a name for Satan).

383.18 Captain Sharker the captain is a swindler: the implication is that sea captains exploited those passengers desperate to flee London. Compare Thomas Nashe, *The Terrors of the Night* (1594): 'Next a côpanie of lusty sailors (euerie one a sharker or a swaggerer at the least)' (*The Works of Thomas Nashe*, ed. Ronald B. McKerrow, 5 vols (Oxford, 1966): 1.378–79).

383.19 Gravesend see note to 293.27.

383.19 Eastward Hoe see note to 100.24. Though America is W of London, Jenkin would initially travel E down the Thames by wherry to the docks where he would board an ocean-going vessel.

384.1 as Hannibal used vinegar ... rocks the Roman historian Livy (59 BC–AD 17) wrote that the Carthaginian general Hannibal (247–182 BC) employed this method for softening rocks where they impeded the building of roads: 21.37.

384.4–5 against the stomach of his sense see *The Tempest*, 2.1.100–01.

384.6 says Fielding Fielding's exact words are: 'Every Profession of Friendship easily gains Credit with the Miserable': *The History of Tom Jones, A Foundling* (1749), ed. Fredson Bowers and Martin C. Battestin, 2 vols (Oxford, 1974), 1.419.

384.16 betwixt Paul's and the Bar between St Paul's Cathedral and Temple Bar.

384.21 the great Prester John Prester John was, according to medieval tradition, a fabulous Christian priest and king of great wealth originally supposed to reign in the Far East, but from the 15th century identified with the king of Ethiopia.

384.41 stone-walls have ears proverbial: see *ODEP*, 864.

385.1 carry things a peg lower i.e. lower the bar of social class a step or degree—in effect, to make Jenkin eligible for the hand of Margaret.

385.2 the artillery gardens according to Stow, gunners from the Tower exercised arms every Thursday at the Artillery Yard in Bishopsgate Ward (2.96); but he also indicates that at other locations every Friday of Lent, at Easter, on summer holydays, and even in winter on the ice that formed at Moorfields, young men of London practised their skill with various weapons much to the entertainment of bystanders (1.247).

385.4 Hout tout tut tut.

385.12 say me nay i.e. forbid me to perform these courtesies.

385.29–30 the Duke of Exeter's daughter this is the rack, so named because it was the brainchild of John Holland (1395–1447), created Duke of Exeter 1443, who was in 1420 made Constable of the Tower, for whose prisoners he introduced this instrument of torture in 1447.

386.6 fine fair-day prospects such prospects as fine weather for a day at the fair promises.

386.12 multiplied six figures progressively ... product the *product* here is the final quantity that results from multiplying the first figure by the second, the resulting quantity by the third, the result of that by the fourth, the result of that by the fifth, and the result of that by the sixth.

386.14 took the streets took to walking the streets.

386.17 take the road i.e. become a highwayman.

386.19–20 as a clerk to Saint Nicholas ... fellows in the play 'St Nicholas' clerks' is an old slang term for thieves and highwaymen such as the characters mentioned from *1 Henry IV* and *2 Henry IV*. They are so called either because St Nicholas came to be regarded as the patron saint of thieves or, as Scott believed (see his footnote in *Ivanhoe*, ed. Graham Tulloch, EEWN 8, 357), with reference to 'Old Nick', the devil, jocularly canonised.

386.41 Not a whit not in the least.

387.9 clean caup out to the bottom of the vessel.

387.23 poortith takes away pith poverty takes away vigour.

387.23–25 the man sits ... breeks Richie quotes a speech made by Archibald Douglas (1369?–1424; succeeded as 4th Earl of Douglas 1400?) after being wounded and made a prisoner at the battle of Shrewsbury, 1403. See David Hume of Godscroft, *The History of the Houses of Douglas and Angus* (Edinburgh, 1644), 120: 'They tell also that being hurt in his privie members, when after the battell every man was reckoning his wounds, and complaining; hee said at last when hee had hard them all, *They sit full still that have a riven breike*. The speech continueth still in Scotland, and is past into a Proverb which is used, to designe such as have some hidde and secret cause to complaine, and say but little.' Compare *CLA*, 3, 20. See Kelly, 149 and *ODEP*, 738.

387.25–26 bring me to speech of get me access to.

387.28 I guess where you are i.e. I discern your unspoken intentions.

387.29 long purse wealth. This is a common expression in the old drama.

387.30 I reck not ... bear a hand I don't mind lending a hand.

387.33 stand to the risk face up to the danger; encounter the danger bravely.

387.39 cutter's law rogue's or highwayman's law. The suggestion is that professional colleagues will share and share alike.

387.41 a wilful man must have his way proverbial: *ODEP*, 890.

387.41–42 ye must think you need to understand.

388.10 say with them talk about with them.

388.16 your heart . . . lavrock's compare the proverbial 'merry/ gay/ happy as a lark': *ODEP*, 527.

388.22–25 motto see *1 Henry IV*, 2.2.86–88.

389.27 wear their horns for trophies see note to 376.4.

389.31 Mr Deputy a *deputy* is a member of the London Common Council appointed by the alderman of a ward to act for him in his absence.

389.43 for the matter on account of the matter.

390.3 a Welchman does of onions compare Thomas Middleton and William Rowley, *The Spanish Gypsey* (performed 1623?, published 1653), 2.6–9: 'Gipsies . . . lie in ambuscado for a rope of Onions, as if they were Welsh Free-booters'. Traditionally the Welsh wore leeks in their caps on St David's Day (1 March) to commemorate a victory over the Saxons fought in a leek garden; hence Pistol's threat to Fluellen that he'll 'knock his leek about his pate/ Upon Saint Davy's day' (*Henry V*, 4.1.54–55).

390.37 There is much . . . lip proverbial: 'there's many a slip between the cup and the lip' (Ray, 94; *ODEP*, 160).

390.38 break the bans destroy the impending marriage of Nigel and Margaret as announced in the *banns*, the legal term for the sequence of three announcements in the parish church of a couple's intention to marry.

390.41 well to pass in the world well off; well to do.

391.6–8 Scottish lawyers say . . . act of Parliament in Scotland after 1573 divorce could be granted for adultery by husband or wife and for desertion after four years by the Commissary Court of Edinburgh; in England divorce on these grounds could not be obtained before the Divorce Reform Act of 1857. Dalgarno is justified in thinking divorce in Scotland both easier and cheaper than in England but mistaken or anachronistic in thinking parliament the only source of divorce: parliament first granted divorce in the 1690s and gained control over it from the ecclesiastical courts, for centuries the sole recourse of people of any rank or fortune, only in 1753 when clandestine marriages were regulated.

391.18 conjured down the emotion caused, as by magic, the swelling emotion to subside.

391.19 April passions frequent, sudden showers of tears reminiscent of April rain showers.

391.36 here . . . had been see Wordsworth, 'Hart-Leap Well' (1800), line 112.

391.37–38 a once illustrious . . . Essex the first Mandeville was a companion of William the Conqueror. His grandson Geoffrey, like his father Constable of the Tower, was created 1st Earl of Essex before 1141 and was surpassed in power only by King Stephen. By 1143, however, he had been charged with treason for seeking to undermine the King by supporting the Empress Maud's bid for the throne and stripped of his constableship, castles, and estates. In the resulting civil war he retreated to the fens of Cambridgeshire and retaliated by sacking the towns and ravaging the churches of his former possessions. In 1144 he died from a wound received in attacking the king's castle at Burwell. His eldest son and heir Ernulf, who joined him in rebellion, was exiled for a time and disinherited so that his second son Geoffrey (d. 1166) became 2nd Earl of Essex. Dying childless, he was succeeded as Earl of Essex by the third and last son William, a knight loyal to Henry II, whose gallantry renewed the chivalric lustre so badly tarnished by his father. But when in 1189 he too died without heir the earldom came to an end. Camlet Moat, on the N edge of Trent Park, Enfield, is the site of a former moated residence believed to have belonged to the Mandeville family: the place is said to be haunted by the ghost of the 2nd Earl.

392.4 the Park St James's Park.

392.6 those would those who would.

392.31 the Father of Evil himself i.e. Satan.

393.15–16 in the fact in the act of committing the crime.

393.30–33 Have him forward ... have him with us bring him forward.

393.30–31 a second Orpheus seeking his Eurydice in Classical mythology, the Thracian poet Orpheus entered the infernal regions to seek his dead wife and so charmed Pluto and Persephone with his music that they restored her to him; but he broke a condition by looking back at her on the way to the upper regions and she was taken from him for ever.

393.39–40 our pleasant vices ... scourge us see *King Lear*, 5.3.170–71: 'The gods are just, and of our pleasant vices/ Make instruments to plague us'.

393.41 on the field on the field of battle (as it were).

394.13–14 there lies Sin, struck down ... calf see *2 Henry VI*, 4.2.25–26.

394.33 takes ton carry on; make much ado.

394.36–37 Vengeance is mine ... repay it see Romans 12.19, and compare Hebrews 10.30.

395.7–8 pride goeth before destruction ... a fall Proverbs 16.18.

395.8–9 Vanity brought folly ... original companion a similar sequence concludes the first canto of Scott's *The Bridal of Triermain* (1813): 'Where lives the man that has not tried/ How mirth can into folly glide,/ And folly into sin?' The third element of the sequence, 'and sin hath brought death', echoes Romans 5.12 and James 1.15.

395.30 did a force to his feelings i.e. exerted force to disguise his true feelings by speaking in mocking irony.

395.33 Horns hath he i.e. he wears the imaginary horns of the husband whose wife is unfaithful with just such a young man-about-town as Lowestoffe: see note to 376.4.

396.13 Dr Dryasdust see note to 3.4.

396.23–24 the new settlements in America the Virginia colony at Jamestown (1610, 1611) and the Plymouth colony in New England (1620).

396.40 the Rasp-haus, (viz. Bridewell,) of Amsterdam the Amsterdam *rasphuis* (Dutch for 'house of correction', the German form being *Raspelhaus*) was a prison for confining the lazy and the vagrant, with a reputation for severe punishment. Bridewell, its London counterpart, was near Whitefriars.

397.4–7 motto see *As You Like It*, 5.4.35–37.

397.9–16 Time was ... discarded the old fashion that Scott eschews is perfectly illustrated in Henry Fielding's *Joseph Andrews* (1742), where we follow the bride and groom from their rising in the morning to their procession to the church for the wedding ceremony to their removal to Mr Booby's for 'a most magnificent Entertainment' to their retiring in the evening for consummation of the union (ed. Martin C. Battestin (Oxford, 1967), 342–43). Scott had from *The Lay of the Last Minstrel* (1805) declined to indulge his readers with such endings—'Nought of the bridal will I tell' (6.28.1)—and in *The Tale of Old Mortality* (1816) he had written a conclusion mocking the narrative convention he here declines to observe. His motive was, at least in part, to distinguish his novels from those of the women novelists of the period, or some of them; in part, too, it was to differentiate the historical novel as type from the domestic romance and other forms of popular fiction, a project he announced in the Chapter Introductory to *Waverley* (1814). Scott's practice notwithstanding, the representative details of weddings, e.g. ardent groom, blushing bride, survived in popular literature and song, though the throwing of the bride's bouquet generally replaced the throwing of her stocking, and the materials and cut of the bridesmaids' dresses changed with fashion. The former, an ancient folk custom (e.g. 'The Bride was now laid in her Bed,/ Her left Leg Ho [single stocking] was flung': Allan Ramsay, *Christ's Kirk on the Green* (1718), 2.161–62), signified the consummation of the marriage in a time when the bedding of the married couple was a public event: *The Works of Allan Ramsay*, Vol. 1, ed. Burns Martin and John W. Oliver (Edinburgh and London, [1951]), 72). In Christopher Bullock, *Woman Is A Riddle* (London, 1717), 92 (*CLA*, 220) much is made of this convention in the context of a couple who try in vain to keep their marriage secret: 'Did you think to steal a Wedding? Come, come, we're all come to wish you Joy, to have one Dance with you, and then throw the Stocking' (5.434–36).

397.17–18 public marriages are now no longer fashionable in the final chapter of *Quentin Durward* (1823) Scott makes the identical point but helps to date the shift in fashion, in life as in fiction, by indicating that he himself can remember a time when 'the bridal minstrelsy still continued, as in the "Ancient Mariner," to "nod their heads" till morning shone on them' and links it to the new fashion of the honeymoon in its modern sense of a holiday trip (ed. J. H. Alexander and G. A. M. Wood, EEWN 15, 400.15–31).

397.20 Gretna-Green village in southern Scotland just over the border with England, NW of Carlisle. Because in Scots law marriage by mutual declaration before witnesses was binding (banns, clergyman, and wedding service not being required), English couples eager to be quickly or secretly united, or to evade the need for parents' consent (if below the age of 21), travelled to Gretna Green where between 1754 (the year following the reform of English marriage law) and 1856 (when residence in Scotland of at least 21 days by one of the parties became essential) many of them were married by the blacksmith or other local official.

397.38 he glorified himself he boasted.

398.12 nine descents i.e. nine successive stages, or generations, of gentlemen.

398.12 great gude-sire great-grandfather.

398.13 the House of Dalwolsey see note to 101.22.

398.16 John Fordoun . . . nobilissimus a canon of Aberdeen, Fordoun (d. 1384?) wrote a chronicle of Scotland down to 1153 and in notes extended it to the time of his death. His work was revised and further extended by Walter Bower (d. 1449) as *Scotichronicon*. The Latin words mean 'most warlike and most noble'. *Scotichronicon* describes a mid-14th-century William Ramsay of Dalhousie as 'strenuu[s] armis probatu[s]' (a vigorous and proven fighting man): Walter Bower, *Scotichronicon*, ed. D. E. R. Watt and others, 9 vols (Aberdeen, 1993–98), 7.278. The supporting anecdote, however, uses similarly paired epithets to James's for two other knights-errant ('fortissimus et bellicosus', 'fortis et famosus') and calls a third 'miles nobilis' (7.280).

398.18 Bannock-rigg Bonnyrigg, a village 10 km SE of Edinburgh. Dalhousie Castle, dating from the 12th century, stands 1 km further S.

398.29–31 Claudian . . . urget opus the celebrated mathematician Archimedes (287–212 BC), born in Syracuse, was especially noted for discovering relations between a sphere and a cylinder. The Latin quotation from Claudian (active *c*. AD 400), *Carminum Minorum Corpusculum* (Shorter Poems), 51.7–8, reads in translation: 'Some hidden spirit within the sphere attends the various stars, and urges on the living work with ordered motion'.

398.37–42 the learned men of the Herald's College . . . to be presented experts in the knowledge of arms and in genealogy, the 13 members of the College of Heralds under the control of the Earl Marshal had since its foundation in 1484 been responsible for assigning new coats of arms. Of the 3 kings-at-arms in the College, the chief was the Garter King-at-Arms, officer of arms for the Order of the Garter (see note to 197.36). The practice of *differencing* (modifying a coat of arms to distinguish a particular member or branch of a family) is achieved here by the *augmented* design James proposes (*augmented* signifying an additional 'charge' or 'bearing' which occupies the field). Representing Davie's profession, this new 'bearing' will occupy the upper third or *chief* of the shield which in this case is not marked off in any way from the lower two thirds; hence, it is said to be *in chief*. The *supporters* are the figures standing on either side of the shield and sometimes appearing to support it. A *crown-wheel* is a wheel with the cogs or teeth set at right angles to its plane.

399.7 long derived going far into the past or far distant from the main line of descent to establish the genealogical link.

399.21 In novas fert … formas see note to 190.21.

399.28–29 a cadet only thrice removed a member of the younger branch of the family going back only three generations (to Davie's great-grand-father).

399.32 Sic fuit, est, et erit *Latin* thus it was, is, and will be.

399.33 stand to undertake to pay for.

399.38 expedition to Newmarket for the horse-racing there: see note to 167.7–22.

399.42–43 Chaucer says … our own time see *The Knight's Tale* from *The Canterbury Tales*, 'The Knight's Tale', I (A) 2125: 'Ther is no newe gyse that it nas old'. The Scottish Chief has not been identified.

400.5 a sair job on you a sore job for you; i.e. an unwelcome one, and thus distressing or irritating.

400.12 penny-wedding a wedding at which each of the guests contributes money to the expenses of the entertainment and to the setting-up of the newly-married couple.

400.13 just four bare legs … thegether alluding to the proverb 'More belongs to marriage than four bare legs in a bed' (Ray, 44; *ODEP*, 513).

400.17 Cosmo de Medici a member of the powerful Florentine family, either the first Cosmo or Cosimo (1389–1464) or the second (1519–74): it was the former who did so much to make Florence the centre of learning and art.

400.18–19 to her maternal grandfather but see 96.6 where the legacy is credited to her grandmother: similarly the goldsmith Touchstone's daughter in George Chapman, Ben Jonson, and John Marston, *Eastward Hoe* (1605) has inherited property from her grandmother (1.1.89–90; 1.2.89–91).

400.26–27 Moonshine in water proverbial: *ODEP*, 542.

400.33 lucky that it was lucky that.

400.38–39 come how it like i.e. whatever the source of the income.

401.14 the hour of cause *Scots law* the hour when trial proceedings begin.

401.18 the odd score of pounds twenty pounds or so.

401.19 bear himself behave properly (by deferring to rank).

402.1 redding kaim comb for disentangling hair.

402.14 Under favour with all submission; subject to correction.

402.27 the just quotient to be laid on the pinion of report the *just quotient* is the exact, as opposed to the approximate, number resulting from the mathematical operation of division. See note to 29.17–18, and for 'pinion of report' see note to 29.16.

402.41 whispered Master Heriot forth of the apartment i.e. quietly, inconspicuously led him from the room.

403.4 Body of us our body. A mild oath.

403.6 pandite fores *Latin* open the doors wide.

403.7 Monypennies the new name that James proposes fits Richie's nou-veau riche condition. That the English would think this name foreign to Scotland refers to the notion popular in this period that all Scots, not excluding the monarch, were beggars.

403.32–33 Queen Mary ... of red-hot memory Mary Tudor: see note to 242.41–243.2.

404.16 this royal presence Martha follows protocol in not referring to the monarch by his name.

404.22 crying roast-meat proverbial for (foolishly) proclaiming publicly one's good fortune: Ray, 105; *ODEP*, 158.

405.18–20 I lictor ... infelici suspendite arbori *Latin* go, lictor, bind his hands, cover his head, hang him on the accursed tree. Attendant to the magistrate in Roman law, the lictor executed the sentence of judgment.

405.26 Hymen—O Hymenee *Hymen* is the Latin version of the Greek name for the god of marriage traditionally chanted in invocation during the wedding procession, e.g. in Edmund Spenser, *Epithalamion* (1595), lines 140–47: 'Hymen io Hymen, Hymen they do shout ... And euermore they Hymen Hymen sing'. The extended word of three syllables occurs also in James Mason's poem *The Birth of Fashion: An Epistolary Tale* (written 1746, published 1811), line 97, but for reasons (of number and rhyme) that do not apply here: there it means 'marriage song'.

405.37 part with relinquish.

405.40 ripping it up bringing it up; mentioning it (like re-opening a wound).

406.3 abides by is ruled by.

406.5–6 gotten it on baith haffits i.e. taken blows (of wit) on both sides of the head.

406.13 the world, which is to me a wilderness a traditional form of philosophical pessimism: compare e.g. 'Not lost? why, all the worlds a wilder-nesse' (John Fletcher and William Rowley, *The Maid in the Mill* (performed 1623, published 1647), 2.2.2).

406.18 flash it out that gate draw it quickly so as to make it flash like that.

406.22 nearly stuck it into his eye Sir Kenelm Digby, son of one of the Gunpowder conspirators, experienced a similar mishap when knighted in 1623 for his service in Spain: see R. T. Petersson, *Sir Kenelm Digby: The Ornament of England, 1603–1665* (London, 1956), 66.

406.24–25 Surge, carnifex *Latin* rise, butcher.

GLOSSARY

This selective glossary defines single words; phrases are treated in the Explanatory Notes. It covers archaic and Scots terms, and occurrences of familiar words in senses that are likely to be strange to the modern reader. For each word (or clearly distinguishable sense) glossed, up to four occurrences are noted; when a word occurs more than four times in the novel, only the first instance is given, followed by 'etc.'. Orthographical variants of single words are listed together, usually with the most common use first. Often the most economical and effective way of defining a word is to refer the reader to the appropriate explanatory note.

a' *Scots* all 13.24 etc.
a in 162.26
abide suffer, endure 113.41, 297.34, 382.25; remain, wait 176.4, 342.7; for 406.3 see note
abroad out of one's house 5.40 etc.
absolute absolutely, completely 45.9
abye pay the penalty for 180.31
acceptably so as to give satisfaction 9.25
accidens *Latin* rudiments of grammar 133.35
accident incident, occurrence 392.37, 393.19
accommodated settled 182.6
accommodation (something) supplying a want or ministering to a comfort 31.30 etc.
accompt account 54.15 etc.
account reckon for money given or received 269.17
acquaint acquainted 248.25
acquented *Scots* acquainted 33.6
addebted *Scots* owed, due 54.26
address courteous approach, manner in conversation 5.30 etc.; general preparedness, skill, dexterity 21.41 etc.
adequate fitting 68.35
adventure (gambling) venture, speculation 154.16
adventurer gambler 154.2
ae *Scots* a certain 35.24; one 70.9, 292.10, 381.17
aff *Scots* off 36.19, 73.37, 358.32

affection mental or bodily state, malady 280.29, 280.32
after-clap surprise after a matter is supposed concluded 247.29
again *Scots* against, at 71.24
agitate discuss 124.36
agreeable for 25.22 and 35.9 see note to 25.22
ahint *Scots* behind 355.16
aigre *French* sharp 62.14
ail for 98.27 and 300.12 see notes
ain *Scots* own 34.28 etc.
airt *Scots* art 90.39
aith *Scots* oath 172.30
alack-a-day alas 90.40 etc.
alamort dispirited 375.34
alang *Scots* along 35.21
alderman for 21.28, 44.3, and 124.38 see note to 21.28
ale-dropped marked with drops of beer 193.4
ale-pot beer glass 53.5
alembic still 137.41
alienage foreign condition 197.3
alienation absence 123.3
alley walk 120.20 etc.
alloy mixture of something lowering in value 131.25
almaist *Scots* almost 382.31
alongst along 64.38 etc.
alumnus pupil 112.13
amang *Scots* among 35.27, 47.21, 341.33, 404.42
amangst *Scots* among 301.17
amaze amazement 47.16

amber resinous gum 6.21

ambergrease odiferous substance deriving from sperm whale 252.1

ambitious strongly desirous 58.36

amity friendship 110.7, 196.30

amusement musing 171.13

an if 26.7 etc.; and 54.36; on 70.35

anatomy emaciated being 123.23

ance *Scots* once 54.6, 399.19

andiamos *Spanish* let us go 97.15

ane *Scots* one 34.28 etc.; a, an 48.15 etc.

anent *Scots* concerning, about 67.42 etc.; opposite 36.36

anes *Scots* once 358.31

angel gold coin worth 10 s. (£0.50) 64.31, 172.24

animadversion censure, censorious comment 199.39

anomaly irregular object 10.26

anon at once, instantly, shortly afterwards 80.19, 276.2, 284.21; for 75.35 and 135.14 see notes

another-guess of another sort or kind 27.12

answer justify, account for 133.23

ante-meridiem pre-noon drink 189.13

a-peak with the ship directly over it 293.29

apoplexy *medical* stroke 15.30

apothecary chemist 30.39 etc.

appeal submit a matter for decision 302.25

appease settle, calm 194.14

appraisement official valuation (of a debtor's property) 241.10

architecture architectural style 34.11; architectural work, building 65.28

ardent corrosive, fiery 48.42

arms coat of arms 75.26, 104.34

arow in a row 373.37

arras tapestry screen hung around walls of room 350.29 etc.

artificer craftsman 14.2

artificial skilfully made or contrived 69.13

artificially artfully 8.40

ascendancy dominant control 126.30

assay quality, standard of purity 16.31

assign transfer or make over formally 5.36, 330.14, 401.3; bring forward as a reason 179.16

assort match 243.2

assurance self-confidence, presumption 141.17, 195.20, 195.31

atrabilious acrimonious, splenetic 336.6, 343.11

atrophy emaciation 251.1

attend direct one's attention to 123.11; guard 229.10

attendance retinue 61.35; people present 137.14; for 356.25 see note

aught *adjective Scots* eight 304.35, 304.35, 304.36

aught *verb Scots* owe 73.3

augmented see note to 398.38

auld *Scots* old 35.24 etc.; very troublesome or difficult 45.31

auld-fashioned *Scots* old-fashioned 171.34

auld-warld *Scots* old-world, characteristic of a past era 361.15

austerity sternness of manner, severity of judgment 80.1, 208.14, 328.20

available potentially productive 43.16

avast hence 192.3, 192.3

avised for 26.1, 261.18, and 390.15 see note to 26.1

avisement *Scots* advice 48.3

avoid leave, quit 369.18

aw *Scots* all 46.9 etc.

awa, awa' *Scots* away 70.9 etc.

awe *Scots* owe 362.20

aweel *Scots* well 48.4 etc.

a-well-a-day, a well-a-day alas 230.18, 387.22

awful commanding respect 260.31

awing *Scots* owing, due 54.27

awmous *Scots* alms, food or money given to the poor 46.10

awn *Scots* own 68.26

ay yes 9.40 etc.

back back-plate 145.17

back support, back up 25.8, 185.21, 205.39, 207.23

back-friend pretended friend 175.16

back-settlements remote settlements, backwoods 4.24

back-shop, back shop for 3.23, 31.7, and 48.16 see note to 3.23

back-sword sword with only one cutting edge 19.11, 249.36

baffle hoodwink 69.34, 373.31; confound, foil 214.30 etc.; treat with scorn 259.19

bag money-bag 117.7

bailie *Scots* town magistrate 10.31, 110.8

bailiff officer with local public administrative authority 184.14 etc.

bairn *Scots* child 3.10 etc.

bairnly *Scots* childish 387.10

bairn's-play *Scots* child's-play 176.17

bait attack by dogs for sport 72.33, 277.41

baith *Scots* both 37.10 etc.

balas for 66.35 and 74.22 see note to 74.22

bald dull 94.26; threadbare 187.27

bale set of dice 250.41

ballat *Scots* ballad 66.25

balloon see note to 251.18

balsam aromatic ointment used for healing and soothing 320.40

ban curse, outlawry pronounced by public opinion 343.25

band bond, shackle 12.15; neckband, collar 24.38, 44.23, 188.25, 291.35; clerical collar with falling bands 193.24

band-box lightweight box for millinery 187.1

bandy band together to fight 136.36

bang rush 47.12, 47.14; fight 302.21

bannock *Scots* flat round cake made of meal cooked on a griddle 88.35

bantling young child, brat 240.1

barb breed of horse from Barbary (N Africa) 149.10

bare see note to 161.41

barker pistol 294.20

bar-movement see note to 26.38

barnacles spectacles 25.30 etc.

barns-breaking skull-breaking, head-bashing 44.24, 44.28, 364.15

basilisk fabulous reptile with a fatal gaze 317.32

basket-hilted with a hilt resembling basket-work 289.5

basset see note to 148.19

basta *Italian* enough! no matter! 250.16

bastard fellow 186.26, 188.12; sweet Spanish wine 257.16

bastinadoe beating 196.38, 249.23

bat club 28.32, 230.40, 232.6

bating except 90.38, 297.10

batton *noun* (walking) stick, cudgel

55.13, 170.40

batton *verb* beat with a walking stick 89.9

baulk disappoint 339.27

bawbee *adjective Scots* costing a halfpenny sterling (0.2p), cheap 78.35

bawbee, bawbie *noun Scots* for 114.36 and 355.15 see note to 114.36; coin worth a halfpenny sterling (0.2p) 399.13

baxter *Scots* baker 73.2

bear *Scots* barley 88.35

bearing effect 139.24

bear-leader owner of performing bear 30.16

bearna *Scots* don't bear 310.42

beaver hat of beaver skin 19.14 etc.

becafico small bird esteemed a delicacy 138.1

beck nod, curtsy 60.1, 90.23, 92.18

beef-banes *Scots* beef-bones 46.8

begar *oath* by God! 148.10

beggarly poverty-stricken 38.17 etc.

begin see note to 90.14

behalden *Scots* obliged 37.10

behind remaining, left, still to come 27.5, 169.20, 347.14

behoof benefit, advantage 71.38

behove, behuve require, need 44.43; for 35.25, 45.41, 48.18, and 309.41 see notes

bein *Scots* well-to-do 399.19

belang *Scots* belong 348.32

beldame old woman, hag, virago 36.4, 96.43, 385.18, 386.16

belive *Scots* quickly, soon 168.16

bencher senior member of Inn of Court 186.35, 199.40, 328.2

bend aim 71.23

beneficed invested with a living as vicar or rector 25.40

benevolence see note to 73.33

beseem fit, be appropriate to 58.35

beseeming fitting, appropriate 5.32 etc.

beseemingly fittingly, creditably 21.10

beset attack 61.27, 112.27, 293.11

beshrew curse 382.6

bespeak request 164.5

bestad circumstanced 316.12

bestow stow away, lodge 261.1, 281.9, 365.22

bethink see notes to 101.19 and 256.35

betimes early in the morning 129.37, 199.36

bewray betray 195.30

bias see notes to 56.2 and 148.15

bib top front part of apron 11.29

bibliomaniacal passionate about collecting books 267.15

bibliopolist bookseller 3.19, 3.23

bibliopolical dealing in books 4.9

bicker *Scots* wooden beaker 72.3, 121.7

bide stay, remain 36.20 etc.; for 63.9 see note

bieldy *Scots* affording shelter 310.38

bien good 191.42

biggen child's cap, infancy 39.6

bigging *Scots* building 34.12

bilbo slender sword 197.30, 198.21, 249.19

bill petition 54.36

billet letter, note 9.24, 247.39, 248.41

billie, billy *Scots* fellow 45.27, 61.6

bing go 192.3, 192.3, 232.29

birkie *Scots* blustering fellow 387.2

bit *Scots* indicates smallness, trivialness, endearment, contempt 36.29 etc. (see notes to 36.29 etc.); spot 310.38

black-foot go-between, matchmaker 363.35

black-ward see note to 36.5

blade dashing pleasure-seeking fellow 191.26 etc.

blate *Scots* diffident, bashful 309.15, 362.12

blaze blow as with a trumpet, proclaim 399.12

blazon coat of arms 48.37

blink *noun* glimmer 91.20

blink *verb* glance, wink 229.23, 237.36; glimmer 347.17

blithe *adjective* glad, happy, joyous, merry 30.33 etc.

blithe *adverb* merrily 347.17

blithely merrily, happily 237.36, 300.25, 339.15, 388.2

blithesome happy, merry 364.26

blood juice 187.29

bloody-minded cruel, bloodthirsty 306.35, 387.31

blotted spotted or stained with ink 4.42

Blue-banders see note to 72.7

blue-bonnet Scotsman 125.16 (see note)

blue-bottle for 127.17 and 135.37 see note to 127.17

blue-coat, blue coat for 60.40 and 127.29 see note to 60.40

bluidy *Scots* bloody 47.10

board table 72.4 etc.

boddle *Scots* smallest coin 354.36, 360.26

bode *Scots* bid 355.27

bodkin stiletto 156.14

bold strong 250.20

bona-roba wench, prostitute 183.20

bondsman serf, slave 92.28

bones dice 149.27, 183.31, 258.43

bonnet man's soft brimless headdress 19.14 etc.

booby stupid person 93.1

book see note to 3.29

bookie *Scots* small book 37.18

bookseller publisher 3.27, 15.3, 16.20, 16.40

boon favour 71.15 etc.

boonmost *Scots* uppermost 54.39

bottle-holder second 31.26

bounce thump 6.30

bounden obliged 345.37

bow-hand see note to 57.43

brae *Scots* hillside, slope 304.14, 354.14

braggadochio empty boasting, bluster 37.35

braid *Scots* plain 371.18

brake thicket 393.5, 395.23

bran husks of grain 151.42

branch division of a discussion 175.24, 175.27

brave splendid, handsome, fine 19.13 etc.

bravely admirably 36.29, 169.31, 379.36

bravery finery 58.29; splendour 163.31

bravo hired ruffian, reckless or desperate man 181.39 etc.

braw *Scots* fine 88.27, 126.11, 169.14

break change 279.14; *hunting* cut up dead quarry 305.15; for 156.22, 171.10, and 359.12 see notes

breaking see note to 73.2

breast breast-plate 145.17

breeks *Scots* breeches, trousers 47.7, 73.37, 387.24

brewis *Scots* broth 128.4

bride-day wedding day 401.12

briefly soon 73.9

brig two-masted square rigged vessel with additional lower sail 40.2

brilliant finely-cut and brilliant diamond 86.12

brimm'd brimming 118.12

brisk effervescent 196.9; smart, lively 196.23 etc.

brisket breast 304.33

bristle see note to 251.10

broad with a stare 372.21

broad-cloth fine woollen cloth 75.23

broad-sword, broadsword sword with a broad blade 22.2 etc.

broche roasting-spit 348.20

broidery embroidery 162.13

broil quarrel 252.4

broker dealer in second-hand clothing, pawnbroker 187.17, 241.11

brook endure 33.11 etc.; enjoy the use of, profit by 375.21

brose *Scots* dish of oatmeal with boiling water or milked poured on it 46.8, 88.34

brownie see note to 91.16

brusk *Scots* brisk 54.31

buck male deer 25.3 etc.

bucket *noun* scale-pan 358.29

bucket *verb* cheat 379.35

bucking see note to 38.39

buckle *Scots* marry 285.18 (see note), 365.7

buckle-beggar *Scots* clergyman performing irregular marriages 193.22

buck's-horn horn of male deer 299.19

buckler small round shield usually with handle(s) 75.25, 88.19, 127.17, 156.1

buckram (made of) coarse linen or cloth stiffened with gum or paste 122.39, 372.15, 372.18

budget bag 52.26; collection, pack 169.22

buff¹ (made of) dressed ox-leather with dull-yellow colour and velvety surface 121.2 etc.; military garment of buff 197.30, 260.4

buff² see note to 149.22

buff-and-iron wearing buff military coat and iron armour 278.13

buff-coloured dull yellow 313.20

bugle tube-shaped bead 388.35

bulk-head roof of a projecting stall 45.24

bully *noun* blustering swash-buckler 27.22 etc.

bully *verb* bluster, use violent threats 150.13, 319.28, 385.21

bum-bailey bailiff employed in arrests 196.26

burden see note to 207.37

burgonet visored helmet attachable to the neck-piece 109.10

burn for 256.29, 382.20 and 383.8 see note to 256.29

burrows-town *Scots* town with municipal corporation 69.32

burthen burden, load 68.28 etc.

buskin see note to 152.15

buss kiss 304.37, 304.37, 307.16

butt barrel 157.14, 250.4, 250.7, 255.28

butt-end thicker end 394.9

buttery store-room where provisions are served 75.28, 129.16

buxom full of health, vigour and good temper, plump and comely 40.8, 130.11; lively, gay 93.25

buzzard see note to 38.40

by beyond 48.8; in the neighbourhood 185.10

bygane *Scots* more than that 164.10

ca' *Scots* call 32.41 etc.

cabin small room 130.29, 158.27

cabinet private room 66.16 etc.; for 66.19 see note

cachination loud or immoderate laughter 353.6

ca'd *Scots* call it 36.35

cadet younger son or brother 218.11, 399.28

cadger pedlar, beggar 301.29

caitiff wretch 376.29

cake oatcake 125.15

calf-time period of youth 110.25

calf-ward *Scots* enclosure for calves 45.14

callan' *Scots* youth 82.23

cam *Scots* came 45.30, 350.18, 350.19

cambric thin linen fabric 75.37, 121.1, 147.10

can drinking-vessel 171.36, 257.11, 298.3

candid free from malice, kindly, favourably disposed 14.19

canna *Scots* can't 62.21 etc.

canny *Scots* comfortable, convenient 45.24

cant slang 181.34; for 9.16, 14.5,

14.40, and 16.18 see note to 9.16

canting whining 250.15

cantle *Scots* crown of the head 36.30

caparisoned decked with trappings 61.21

capin, capon castrated cock fattened for eating 54.29 etc.

capricio trick, prank, caper 6.18, 160.35

carabine carbine, short rifle 261.32

car-borne transported in fine carriages 167.19

carcanet, carkanet ornamental collar 66.35, 74.7, 74.22, 349.35

carle sturdy or strong fellow 44.39; mean person, low-born person 73.13, 73.21; man, fellow 89.28, 110.2, 110.8

carle-hemp robust variety of hemp plant 296.13

carnifex executioner 69.14; for 406.24 see note

carnificial of an executioner or butcher 340.37

carocco see note to 250.14

caroch, caroche stately or luxurious carriage 24.31, 100.1

carouse drinking-bout 129.36; toast 250.7

carrion garbage 157.15

carrion-horse horse fit for slaughter 144.26

carry conduct, escort 46.4 etc.; convey 55.38; capture 145.5; for 385.1 see note

carwitchet pun 151.33

cash-keeper cashier 82.16 etc.

cassock clergyman's long close-fitting tunic worn under gown 76.1, 193.25; riding-cloak 310.19; loose coat or gown 376.28

cast *noun* throw of the dice 104.22, 329.41; fate, disposition 176.15; lift in a boat or vehicle 116.16, 295.36

cast *verb* see notes to 83.24, 346.15, 361.5, and 362.20

castaway reprobate 102.2, 395.15

casten *Scots* flung 47.39

catastrophe dénouement, final resolution 6.40 etc.

catch-pole sheriff's officer arresting for debt 196.26

catchword word drawing attention 83.16

catechism see note to 22.4

cattle people 49.35, 291.33, 358.35

cauff *Scots* chaff 46.8, 46.34

cauld *Scots* cold 13.19

cauldrife *Scots* indifferent, lacking in intensity 176.40

caup *Scots* cup 171.36, 387.9 (see note); wooden bowl 353.19

cause see note to 401.14

causeway roadway 70.38, 288.42, 382.31

causey *noun Scots* cobbled street 44.31; paved or cobbled area 350.14

causeyed *verb Scots* paved with small stones 45.18

cautery the action of cauterising 339.34

cavalier fashionable gentleman, horseman 130.35 etc.

cavaliero gentleman trained to arms, courtly gentleman 24.9, 146.15

celerity rapidity 274.43

censé *French* judged 14.38

cerebellum larger part of the back of the brain 31.11

cerebrum front part of the brain 31.11, 31.20

ceremoniously in accordance with prescribed formalities 76.24, 143.37

certes assuredly, I assure you 5.17

certie see notes to 47.5 and 48.19

chalk slash 192.1

chalmer *Scots* chamber 54.29, 68.34

chambering lewd or wanton behaviour 161.24

chamberlain attendant in charge of inn bedchambers 45.11

chamber-quean *Scots* chambermaid 92.4

chambers set of rooms in Inns of Court 182.41 etc.

chance casual circumstance 23.8; for 237.13 see note

chandler retailer of provisions and equipment 95.35, 318.22

change-house *Scots* small inn or pub 291.36

chap strike 373.4

chapter subject 73.30, 333.30

character status 3.18 etc.

chares charwork, housework 245.33

chare-woman charwoman 244.4 etc.

chare-work housework 243.23

charge something entrusted to one's care 37.2, 42.33; load 61.32

chartel written challenge 146.19

chase *noun* object of pursuit 168.21, 303.41; those who hunt 322.11

chase *verb* prosecute 362.27

cheap cheaply 45.30

cheapen see note to 3.22

cheek-for-chowl cheek by jowl 305.29

cheer food, provisions 12.15 etc.

chenzie-mail *Scots* chain-mail 44.29

cherish encourage, cultivate 26.43, 300.3; protect 120.37

chevalier French title of distinction, man of fashion and pleasure, fine gentleman 137.39 etc.

chief see note to 398.40

chiel, chield *Scots* man, fellow 31.15 etc.

chimney fireplace, hearth 94.31, 94.37, 241.19, 242.16

chink see note to 91.19

chirurgeon surgeon 31.42, 228.33, 228.34

chitty pinched, baby 200.41

chitty-faced baby-faced, with a pinched face 252.19

chopine shoe raised by a cork sole or similar 95.38, 385.10

choury dagger 192.2

chouse cheat 385.41

Christmas-box see note to 170.25

christened Christian, first [name] 132.9

chronologist *usually* chronicler, *here apparently* watchmaker 331.3

chuck touch playfully under the chin 79.32

chuck-farthing see note to 133.13

chucks see note to 68.8

chuff miser 97.11, 168.36

churchwarden lay representative of an Anglican congregation 41.30

churl person of low birth 171.22, 392.5

cimelia treasures 351.9, 352.3

cittern instrument akin to the lute 228.29

civic civilian 147.15

civil refined 84.40, 108.19; refined, decent 187.26

civil-seeming decent in appearance, befitting a citizen 187.23

claithes *Scots* clothes 44.29

claithing *Scots* clothing 33.2

clammy glutinous, gluey 99.8, 193.16

clarified made transparent, purified 184.30 (see note)

clary sweet drink of wine, clarified honey, pepper, ginger, and other spices 257.17

clatter-traps *Scots* odds and ends 67.36

claucht, claught *Scots* clutch, grasp, grab 44.30, 48.38

clavering *Scots* talking nonsense 68.43

clean shapely, neatly made 40.11

cleek *Scots* hook 399.16

cleepie *Scots* severe blow and resulting bruise 44.33

clerk for 149.39 and 331.35 see note to 149.39; for 386.19 see note

clew see note to 309.26

cloak-bag portmanteau 388.32

cloak-lap overlapping collar of cloak 47.14

clod-pated blockheaded 318.22

clog encumber 195.44

cloot *Scots* hoof 88.26

close niggardly 97.11

closet study 12.30, 246.15; small room 31.29, 31.33, 202.32; monarch's private apartment 56.19, 348.37, 349.16

clour *Scots* blow 36.30

clout mend 50.4, 361.33

clown boor, ill-bred person 100.12, 168.37

cluster see note to 151.2

clutch claw 255.37

coat coat of arms 33.37, 398.39

cock-a-leek, cock-a-leekie *Scots* soup made with chicken and leeks 63.1, 348.3, 348.36, 406.26

cocked worn provocatively at a jaunty angle 259.17

cock-loft small upper loft 145.6, 145.10

cockney for 100.12 and 384.19 see note to 100.12

cockney-put Cockney blockhead 228.4

cock's-bones *oath* God's bones 384.8

cocksnails *oath* God's nails (the nails of Christ's cross) 72.18

cock-sure absolutely certain 295.25

coif white cap worn by a sergeant-at-law 26.32; close-fitting cap covering top, back, and sides of head 78.17

collop slice of meat for frying or broiling 34.3, 354.10, 356.11, 406.25

collops minced or chopped meat 58.20, 160.30; for 252.21 see note

colour complexion 166.7

comfort strengthening, refreshment 307.17

comfortable tolerable, fairly good 323.20

commanding dominating by elevated or strategic position 80.20, 80.22

commissionate commissioned, empowered 356.4

commodious convenient, useful 7.20

commons share of common provisions 299.8

communing communication 111.36, 164.33

company corporation historically representing medieval trade guild 104.34

company-keeping revelling (in bad company) 149.37

complacence satisfaction 200.36

complacency tranquil pleasure 200.35

complaisance politeness, deference 201.21, 324.21

complaisant courteous, disposed to please, obliging 81.42, 98.28

complexion colour 86.26, 291.5, 291.8

complice accomplice 72.42

compliment(s) formal greeting 109.15, 249.37, 312.11; respectful expression 312.21

complot plot, intrigue 72.6

compound settle 176.23

compounder someone who agrees to pay a fee 194.27

compromise settle 126.31

compt reckoning, account 54.27

compting reckoning 70.9

compting-room cash-office 82.38, 84.15, 87.14

concern share 8.10; interest 344.9; for 218.8 see note

concernment concern, interest, importance 242.1, 293.20, 337.24

conciliate procure 201.35

condition social position 24.8 etc.

conduct comport oneself 196.32

coney-catcher swindler 250.40

confection dessert dish 81.25

conference conversation, consultation 74.40, 229.19, 299.15, 349.16

confiding trustworthy 127.4

conformable compliant 97.13

conformably fittingly 110.30

congee, congé bow 80.4, 142.34

conjunction see note to 83.25

conjure beseech, implore 221.2, 248.31, 305.34, 341.24; for 391.18 see note

conjuring (for) invoking devils 134.9

conjuror sorcerer 232.28

conscience innermost thought, mind, heart 72.19

consequential self-important 298.37

conservator for 56.38, 57.5, 73.9, and 73.13 see note to 56.38

consideration importance, (social) consequence 61.31, 181.21

consign hand over 263.24

consort partner 260.5

construe understand 17.5; translate orally, interpret 27.16

consult consider, have consideration for 138.23, 278.35, 288.37

contemn despise 77.43

content reimburse 59.10, 74.25

continued continuous 64.38, 298.31

contrabandist smuggler 224.20

contrair Scots contrary, reverse 162.23, 165.4

contriturate pulverise 352.32

contund bruise, beat, thrash 352.32

conveniency convenience 70.5

convenient befitting, appropriate 395.36

convention agreement 403.43

conversation company 50.29 etc.

converse conversation 368.42

copy-book book containing handwriting specimens for learners to copy 3.21

copy-money money paid to author for manuscript or copyright 14.28

Cordery see note to 3.21

cordovan see note to 88.27

corn-pickle grain of corn 64.18

corporal see note to 172.30

corporation see note to 3.36

corslet armour covering the upper body 398.21

cosher take part in a feast, live at the expense of a dependant 399.39

cossike cossic, algebraic 266.34

cote see note to 167.21

cotemporary contemporary 150.42

cotton see note to 38.17

couchee evening reception 370.39

couldna *Scots* couldn't 366.26

council counsel, advice 207.18

counsel body of legal advisers 73.18; plan, intention 311.5, 391.25; for 130.40 and 369.42 see notes

countenance *noun* patronage, moral support 64.15 etc.; composure 340.10

countenance *verb* favour, encourage 220.6, 220.40, 357.23, 369.25

counterband contraband 225.35

counterscarp outer wall or slope of ditch surrounding a fortification 55.39

coup *verb Scots* tumble 35.27; upset 301.21 (see note), 350.14

coup *noun Scots* tumble 47.20

course regular manner of procedure 41.23, 275.11, 391.7; custom, (reprehensible) practice 64.18 etc.; for 103.38 see note

court courtyard, quadrangle 22.4, 65.38, 186.35, 228.38

courtesy bow, curtsy 80.11, 117.23, 334.40; courteous act 58.25; for 43.40 see note

court-masque see note to 156.2

court-scented-water see note to 252.1

cousin collateral relative 57.14

couteau *French* knife 304.22 (see note), 304.30

couvert *French* cover, place setting 144.33

cove see note to 191.42

cover place setting 144.24

coysterel knavish, base 196.13

coz form of familiar address 395.36

cozen cheat, deceive 319.5, 376.34

crab crab-apple 15.41, 256.27

crabbed irritable, cantankerous 30.32, 199.39

crack break open 170.25; open and drink (a bottle of liquor) 380.39

craig[1] *Scots* neck 47.21

craig[2] *Scots* rock 290.30

cram make a person believe false or exaggerated statements 202.5, 204.40

cramp difficult to make out 198.1

cran see note to 301.21

crap *Scots* crept 45.4

craven coward 233.40

craven-crested *cock-fighting* not up to a fight 163.34

craw *Scots* crow 47.10

cream-faced having a yellowish-white face 123.26

creature person owing fortune to another and remaining subservient to them 57.9, 212.41

cringe fawning bow or curtsy 262.37

cringing obsequious 64.11

crisping see note to 298.15

critical exact, precise, accurate 23.30

cropped with the pages trimmed 267.41

cross disappointment 104.14, 234.15; for 100.5 and 162.9 see notes

cross-bite cheat in return 253.28

cross-biting bitter censure 202.5

crouch behave submissively, bow or kneel in a cringing way 104.16

crouse boldly, confidently, vivaciously 47.11

crown-wheel see note to 398.39

crudity sourness 257.25; undigested matter 382.20

crush drink, quaff 64.1, 88.39

cubit see note to 349.20

cuckoldly term of abuse 123.1

cuckoo foolish 231.11

cullionly base 143.33

cully dupe 250.43

cumber bother, hamper, encumber 123.43, 275.12, 308.6

cumber-corner someone who inconveniently occupies a corner 293.3

cumbersome causing trouble or annoyance 179.41

cup for 228.13 and 228.25 see note to 228.13

cup-bearer person serving wine 265.29

cure pastoral charge 76.2

curious *adjective* exquisite, finely wrought 68.33, 69.13, 240.35;

meticulous, careful 152.33

curious *adverb* exquisitely 152.19

curn grain 302.29

current smoothly flowing 126.28

custodier custodian 11.43

cut see note to 228.5

cutter hired ruffian, cut-throat, highway-robber 260.9, 387.39 (see note)

cutty *Scots* naughty 341.15

cynosure centre of attraction and admiration 97.27

cypher monogram 104.33

daft mad 71.36, 382.37

daggle drag, trail about 95.8

daiker *Scots* walk slowly 45.31

dainty *adjective* choice, handsome 35.12, 92.3, 176.16; pleasant, delightful 45.15

dainty *noun* delicacy 81.1, 99.19

dam mother 163.27

damask for 91.31 and 276.1 see note to 91.31

damasked ornamented with an intricate pattern 241.3

damp fog, noxious exhalation 43.13, 190.42

darksome somewhat gloomy 313.32

day-watch see note to 29.16

deacon see note to 35.6

dealer person dealing in merchandise 20.21, 169.27, 386.2

death-watch death-watch beetle 6.31

debonair courteous 71.13

decus crown-piece (5s., 50p) 250.32, 260.9

deem judge, think, consider 61.19, 92.16, 276.3, 288.17

deep *adjective* involving heavy liability 148.23, 154.12, 185.11, 212.34; solemn 253.3

deep *adverb* far on 202.40

deeply seriously 170.23

deep-mouthed having a deep or sonorous voice 25.35

deevil *Scots* devil, troublesome or luckless person 35.24, 35.27; devil 353.40, 359.38, 373.16

deevilish devilishly, extremely 289.3

defunct departed one 42.17

degrade descend to a lower grade 344.16

degree rank, station 81.29 etc.

de'il, deil *Scots* devil 44.28 etc. (see

notes for most occurrences)

delict offence 76.37

deliverance judicial or administrative order 155.5

demean conduct (oneself) 342.8

demesne(s) landed property 123.15, 366.18

demi-pique see note to 304.1

demur delay 154.41

dependence quarrel or affair of honour awaiting settlement 184.5

deposition depositing 31.21

derogate impair by taking something away 344.3, 398.19

derogation disparagement 161.24

descent see note to 398.12

descry find out, perceive 5.19, 167.20, 311.10

design intend 69.2 etc.

despardieux, des par dieux *French oath* ye gods! 144.27, 148.1

desperado desperate or reckless person, especially a criminal 181.38

desperate person in despair 163.18

despite indignation 210.27; for 22.38 and 125.31 see notes

destraught distracted 79.23

determination decision 236.12

determine reach a decision 197.11, 197.12; conclude, terminate 351.21

deuteroscopy second sight, clairvoyance 4.34

devil errand-boy or junior assistant in a printing-shop 13.39

devotee person characterised by extreme religious devotion 92.15, 207.10

dexter right (hand) 340.36

diagnostic symptom 383.29

diamonded with diamond-shaped panes 11.24

didna *Scots* didn't 68.11

diet-loaf loaf prepared for an invalid or person with special dietary requirements 256.33

difference see note to 398.40

digit finger 78.42

digital *jocular* finger 78.41

dike-louper wild incorrigible person 362.18

dilatory slow, characterised by delays 43.23

diligence see note to 73.15

ding *Scots* hammer, thrash 304.17;

knock 370.7

dingy dark-coloured 94.41, 229.11; dirty 240.20

dinna *Scots* don't 34.41, 304.19

dirdum uproar 54.36

direction address, instruction where to go 35.40, 36.41

dirk *noun* short dagger 113.13, 306.41

dirk *verb* stab with a short dagger 47.24

dirty muddy, low-quality 97.10

discharge remove, abolish 365.6

dis-clout, dish-clout dishcloth 148.2, 163.6

discord be different 318.8

discountenance *verb* discourage by cold looks 106.22

discountenance *noun* disfavour or disapprobation shown 359.4

discuss consume 299.8

discussion consumption 197.9

disembarrassed unconstrained, unhampered 130.30, 364.29

dishabille state of being casually or partially dressed 247.41

dismembration cutting off of a limb 338.27

disordered irregular 163.7

dispatch *noun* speed 103.31, 367.2

dispatch *verb* make haste 376.15

disregardfully in a slighting way 384.24

distance leave behind 244.40, 304.12

distance-post see note to 23.23

distinguish characterise, define 24.38

distraught distracted, deranged 102.2

distress *noun* legal seizure of a debtor's property 241.10

distress *verb* strain, exert 353.22

distressed financially embarrassed 69.30

diva *Latin* goddess 138.26

dividend *mathematics* quantity to be divided by another 79.12

divine *noun* clergyman 15.2, 26.14, 90.39, 196.36; person skilled in divinity (theology) 111.12

divine *verb* guess 101.39

doctor a false or loaded dice 250.42 (see note), 259.1, 378.17

domains lands, heritable estate

80.19, 391.39

donna *Scots* don't 73.35, 73.39

donnard dull, stupid 78.32

donnerit dazed, stunned 35.31

doom see note to 306.23

dootless *Scots* doubtless 168.28 etc.

dor mockery 202.5

dot-and-carry-one teacher of elementary arithmetic 62.34

dotard *noun* senile or stupid person 245.41, 262.43, 265.4, 265.12

dotard *adjective* senile, stupid 62.34

double *noun* copy 54.23

double *verb* turn suddenly and sharply, pursue a winding course 167.14

double *adjective* for 308.13 see note

double-distance see note to 23.26

double-minded having an overt and concealed meaning, deceptive 289.16

doublet close-fitting body garment 29.29 etc.; same number on two dice thrown at once 233.16, 258.39; counterfeit jewel 353.29 (see note)

doubt fear, suspect 73.17 etc.

douce(ly) sober(ly) 164.9 etc.

douceur gratuity 93.8

doun *Scots* down 304.17, 304.41, 304.41

dover *Scots* swoon 36.29

dowager widow holding rank or property derived from husband 202.20, 400.30

dow-cote *Scots* dovecot 72.7

doze bewilder 249.24

drab slut, prostitute 198.13

drabbing whoring 149.36, 165.10

drachm one-eighth of an ounce (3.5 gm) 138.3

draff grains of malt left after brewing 75.9

draff-pock sack of draff 47.19

dragoman interpreter 112.4

drap *Scots* drop 90.28

draught draft 52.3, 52.7

draw draw up 120.1, 120.6, 124.20, 374.16; make one's way 167.36; disembowel a criminal after hanging 338.28, 338.34; for 219.16 see note

drawer tapster, bar-person 148.7, 192.34, 374.28, 380.34

dreamna *Scots* don't imagine 345.35

dredging-box container with perforated lid for sprinkling sugar or flour 11.30

drench drink 152.4

dress *noun* apparel 29.41 etc.; suit of clothes 66.29 etc.

dress *verb* arrange the hair and beard for someone 297.1

dressing-block cook's chopping-block 340.5

drive carry on 93.1, 94.13; proceed, hasten 342.16

drouthy *Scots* thirsty 382.27

drumble move sluggishly 256.43

dry-fisted in a niggardly way 200.5

dud *Scots* rag 70.31

dudgeon-dagger dagger with wooden hilt 27.21

dudgeon-knife knife with wooden handle 80.29

dule-weeds *Scots* mourning clothes 112.25

dun *noun* importunate creditor, debt-collector 9.28, 62.15, 186.33, 380.1

dun *adjective* dingy brown 34.43

dun *verb* importune for debt 73.2

dune *Scots* done 69.10, 304.13, 304.13, 360.43

dunt blow 406.4

eard see note to 114.37

earthly at all 326.35

ear-wig flatterer, insincere follower 156.21

ease relieve 380.22

easy careless 187.36

economy management of household resources 94.25

edge-tool cutting weapon or tool 69.17

edition version 179.37, 180.43

e'e (*plural* **een, ee'n**) *Scots* eye 47.40 etc.

effects property 5.37, 363.17

effectual effective, actual 14.8, 51.5

efficient effective 139.37, 152.10

egad expression of amazement or emphasis 379.30

eidolon spectre, phantom 4.43

eke lengthen 378.11

elder ancient 12.21; earlier 228.22, 391.39

elementary elemental, associated with one or more of the natural elements 6.12

elf-lock tangled mass of hair 191.32

elide weaken or destroy 368.14

ell measure of length: in England 45 inches (114 cm), in Scotland 37.2 inches (94.5 cm) 305.1

elritch weird, frightful 340.12

embassy ambassadorial mission 46.14, 266.40, 332.22

embattle fortify 300.27

embrazure recess with slanting walls 116.8

embroiled confused 73.28

emergence emergency 211.34, 211.35, 260.14

emolument profit, reward 13.33, 14.18, 14.40

emporium shop 20.21

emulous characterised by a spirit of rivalry 150.41

endlang *Scots* endlong, at full length 70.38, 350.14

eneugh *Scots* enough 47.30

enforce reinforce 248.41

engaged pledged 355.42

engross make a fair copy of a document, write out in legal form 58.1, 125.1, 129.12

enjoin prescribe 22.21, 364.19

enow enough 45.22 etc.

ensample *Scots* example 370.12

entertainer host 79.43, 80.8

entertainment banquet 81.26; hospitable provision 291.40

epopeia epic, epic poem 7.15

equality evenness 4.27

equipage retinue 99.42; equipment 304.9

equipollent identical in effect 338.35

errant arrant 293.2

escapement mechanism between motive power and regulator 22.13

esoteric not openly stated or admitted, secret 94.18

essence (alcoholic) perfume 94.14; alcoholic distilled medical solution 274.4

estate state, condition, degree of prosperity 58.7, 61.28, 151.34

esteem consider 3.9 etc.

ethnic pagan 72.1

ever always 66.14 etc.; for 75.35, 114.22, and 135.14 see notes

evict recover by legal process 73.11, 73.13, 118.40

evite avoid 288.38

excruciation state of torment 338.33

exhibition allowance of money, salary 137.15, 185.18; display, spectacle 106.13 etc.

exies see note to 369.14

expede *Scots* issue (a document) 370.35

express *adjective* urgent 278.25

express *noun* express messenger 299.34

extended extensive 171.43, 311.18

extravasated escaped 31.21

faculty profession 14.34; capacity 32.16; *plural* property, resources 113.17

fain *adjective* happy, well-pleased 72.6, 109.35, 284.23; eager 45.20; obliged 333.15

fain *adverb* gladly, willingly 85.12 etc.

fair-day see note to 386.6

fairly handsomely, beautifully 19.12; actually 20.43; totally, fully, 'clean' 26.41, 81.27, 118.19, 129.41

fairy-gold see note to 239.8

faith, 'faith fidelity, loyalty 23.9; in good faith, truly 28.26, 45.40, 72.2, 337.36; fulfilment of a trust 218.35

fallow *Scots* fellow 339.28 etc.

falset falsehood, deceit 34.24, 53.14, 381.41

familiar demon or spirit which attends its master or mistress upon call 136.29

fancied designed 26.28

fand *Scots* found 45.13

fanfaron braggart 148.4, 319.39

fang claw, talon 113.13

fantastic fanciful, existing only in the imagination 6.7, 241.25, 276.11, 344.34; capricious 97.4, 97.5; quaint, grotesque 206.6, 388.34

fantastically capriciously, eccentrically 75.22

fare passage, voyage 284.27; passengers, load 284.35

farthingale hooped petticoat 230.3, 242.41

fash *Scots* trouble, bother 162.18, 355.39 (see note to 162.18)

fashion form 91.43; for 382.22 see note

fashious tiresome, troublesome 95.43

fat greasy 12.6 (possibly), 46.8

fat-gutted big-bellied 289.21

faulchion broad curved sword 249.26

fault for 204.36 and 309.18 see note to 204.36

fause *Scots* false 30.34 etc.

fautor supporter 117.6

fealty allegiance 155.16

febrifuge medicine to reduce fever 31.38, 32.7

fee-simple perpetual tenure of a heritable estate 235.17

fell cruel, ruthless, destructive 304.40

femoral pertaining to the thigh 21.9

fence-louper wild incorrigible person 341.39

fertile abundant 150.40

fiat decree 202.25

fico, figo fig 27.40, 151.42

fiduciary trusted person, trustee 71.43

fiend devil 69.37 etc.

figo see **fico**

figure importance, standing 193.34

file see note to 132.9

fillip flip, tap 374.20

fine-drawn extremely subtle or thin 6.13

firelock musket in which sparks produced by friction or percussion ignite the priming 276.10

first leading, foremost 137.24, 137.25, 394.3

fish see note to 73.20.

fit *noun Scots* foot 35.23, 36.33

fit *verb* see note to 21.9

flagon large liquor bottle 194.15, 278.25

flapper see note to 15.29

flash see note to 406.18

flask bottle 149.38, 230.22, 232.33

flea flay 168.39

fleeching *Scots* fawning 68.40

fleet swift 167.8

flesher *Scots* butcher 34.38, 160.29, 301.8

flounce ornamental strip sewn up its upper edge 388.35

flox-silk rough silk 166.20

folding-doors door divided vertically into two flaps 107.43

fond affectionate 6.9, 219.17

fool jester 77.26, 127.20, 337.1

foolado see note to 187.19

foot-cloth richly ornamented cloth laid over back of horse 60.40

forbear have patience with 252.24, 252.25; keep away from, leave alone 277.42, 342.18

forbearance abstinence from enforcing payment of debt 354.5

forbye *Scots* besides, not to mention 171.17, 352.38

fore before 230.16

forefend forbid 63.38, 101.31

forenoon morning 337.38

fore-shop front part of a shop 63.30

forfeit crime, offence 47.24

forgie, forgi'e *Scots* forgive 34.25, 370.9, 370.9, 382.4

form protocol, formal or customary procedure 25.29 etc.

formal recognisable, unmistakable 24.13

formalist stickler for etiquette 60.29

formality accordance with legal form 118.28

forpit a dry measure (one-fourth of a peck) 64.19

forth see notes to 54.17 and 402.41

forward *adjective* presumptuous 122.2, 141.9, 174.6; eager, spirited 184.38

forward *verb* urge on 56.23

forwardness an advanced state 87.16; eagerness, spirit, presumptuousness 142.4, 395.2

fouat *Scots* house-leek 35.13

foul not according to the rules 329.41

foulmart *Scots* polecat 361.28

four-hour's see note to 38.7

foxed stained by damp affecting impurities in the paper 267.41

frae *Scots* from 35.11 etc.

frank see note to 183.40

frankly without constraint or restriction 59.1; generously, liberally 155.2, 170.23, 374.31

frankness lack of constraint or restriction 221.17, 317.30

frantic mad 70.26, 101.7

freak whim, caprice, capricious trick 97.40, 205.24

freakish whimsical 206.4

free *adjective* noble, confident 121.43

free *verb* exempt 122.2

freeman one entitled to share in the privileges of a company or

trade, or of citizenship 3.36, 37.5, 249.41

fresco *Italian* cool 198.16

frieze (made of) coarse cloth 19.10, 377.38

frolic *noun* outburst of gaiety 10.42; spree 24.31, 42.27, 183.18, 345.20; whim 95.41; prank 314.39, 350.36

frolic *adjective* mirthful 151.5

frontless shameless, audacious, brazen 365.43

froward perverse, hard to please 165.4

fule *Scots* fool 68.7 etc.

fulham loaded dice 198.20, 251.10

furnishings supplies 54.17

fury inspiration, inspired frenzy 4.30; avenging or tormenting infernal spirit 252.17

fustian (made of) coarse cloth of linen and cotton or wool 238.5

futurity future events 65.29

gad *noun* God 126.21

gad *verb* go astray, rove about 29.6, 60.31

gae *Scots* go 78.33 etc.; for 70.29 see note

gaffer sir, old fellow 96.32

gage surety 74.9

gait, gate way, path 54.36 etc.; for 69.6 etc. see notes

gallant *noun* gentleman, man of fashion 19.13 etc.

gallant *adjective* finely dressed 58.26; splendid, noble 61.34; courtly, polished 121.43

gallantly finely, splendidly 393.14

gallantry sexual flirtation or intrigue, courteous accomplishment 131.6 etc.

galloway small strong horse originally from Galloway 125.19

gallows-bird person deserving to be hanged 134.12

game gamble 138.31, 139.25, 139.31

gamester gambler 143.11 etc.

gaming gambling 153.34, 233.24, 295.6 (see note), 381.25

gaming-house gambling den 138.29, 138.42, 143.29, 383.17

gaming-table gambling table 154.1, 185.29

gang *Scots* go 62.22 etc.

gar *Scots* make 35.24, 45.14, 358.29, 382.30; for 169.13 see note

garnish for 189.34, 190.2, 195.28, and 195.31 see note to 189.34

garniture ornament, embellishment 29.29

gate see **gait**

gawdy merrymaking 250.9

gay *adjective* addicted to social pleasures and dissipations 152.27, 153.31, 166.15, 319.32

gay *adverb* see note to 354.15

gear matter, business 112.28 etc.; for 3.33, 354.25, 361.27, and 379.28 see notes

generation class or kind of people 59.20 etc.

geneva for 40.21, 127.22, and 285.19 see note to 40.21

genial festive 80.37; generously sociable 94.24; pleasantly warm 144.38

genius natural ability or capacity 8.34 etc.; demon, spirit 154.16

gentility nobility 22.26, 133.33, 141.24

gentle *adjective* well-born or of good social position, noble, distinguished 24.9 etc.

gentle *noun* person well-born or of good social position 15.6

gentle-folks people well-born or of good social position 39.6

gentry gentility 399.9; for 191.42 see note

geometrical see note to 349.19

get beget 378.1

ghittern early form of guitar 228.29, 298.18

giddy frivolous, thoughtlessly excited 206.30; mentally intoxicated, flighty 337.13

giddy-brained frivolous, inconstant 337.31

gie, gi'e *Scots* give 47.30 etc.

giff-gaff *Scots* mutual help, give and take 354.37

gild cover with a specified metal 47.2, 359.24, 359.24

gillie-white-foot *Scots* servant of Highland chieftain, worthless fellow 348.9

gillravager one who gads about 341.33

gin *Scots* if 292.9

ging *Scots* go 36.33

gip *interjection* see note to 185.25

gip *noun* gyp, college servant at Cambridge 186.31

girn grimace 110.2

give wish 329.42; expose 331.3; for 28.36 and 61.24 see notes

gizzard stomach 7.5

gladiator see note to 151.29

glaik *Scots* gleam of light 47.39; for 360.27 see note

glance shine 142.13

glass mirror 103.39, 298.15

gleed awry 361.4

gleek for 148.19, 185.13, 185.24, and 233.15 see note to 185.13

glorious happily drunk 197.19

go-bye see note to 259.9

god-den, godd'en, Godd'en good evening 74.39 (see note) etc.

gold-end broken piece of gold, scrap of precious metal 350.31, 350.31

gold-wark *Scots* objects made of gold 72.23

good-even good evening 38.2, 38.3, 199.36

good-morrow goodbye (said in the morning) 60.32 (see note), 60.34, 245.1; good morning 255.31

gorge devour greedily 151.7

gospeller see note to 99.22

goss-hawk large short-winged hawk 168.42

gossip *noun* female friend 42.40; godparent 174.7 etc.

gossip *verb* act as a familiar acquaintance, take part in a feast, make oneself at home 399.39

gouk *Scots* fool 384.19

gourd a kind of false dice 198.20

gowd *Scots* gold 47.1, 47.4, 162.42, 353.26

grace favour 43.33 etc.; permission, leave 357.13; for 98.23 and 381.7 see notes

graff *Scots* grave 45.15

gramercy thank you kindly 27.1, 294.9

grammar *Scots* learning 361.35, 361.38

grannam grandmother 196.17

grant permission 106.19

grat *Scots* wept 110.8

gratification tip 247.10

gratitude *Scots* payment to a monarch 56.7

gratulate congratulate 118.23

gray dismal, gloomy 381.18

grazier person who grazes cattle for the market 161.29, 377.35, 378.8

gree *Scots* agree 351.14

greet weep 341.34

grew *Scots* feel horror 405.25

grin *noun* grimace 175.15

grin *verb* grimace, display the teeth 238.13 (see note), 255.37, 311.12

gripe grasping, grip 28.2, 89.8

grippie see note to 354.37

grippit *Scots* gripped 47.23

griskin lean part of loin of pork 298.8

grit *Scots* great 47.6, 54.19

groaning see note to 42.41

groat coin worth 4*d.* (0.8p) 300.7

grogram (made of) a coarse fabric of silk, or mohair and wool, or of these mixed with silk 50.6

grossart *Scots* gooseberry 162.37, 361.30

groundsill threshold 68.26

grunter pig 75.9

guard border 92.23

gude, guid *Scots* good 33.5 etc.

gudeman husband 406.7

gudes *Scots* goods 354.24

gude-town *Scots* good town, Edinburgh 48.18

guep see note to 60.36

guerdon reward 58.10

guide *Scots* manage, control 47.43 etc.

guise costume 239.37, 337.33; external appearance, state 354.6

gull dupe, fool 118.15 etc.

gulley *Scots* large knife 69.15

gusty *Scots* tasty 301.19

gutter-blood, gutterblood *Scots* person of low birth or poor breeding 48.23, 70.30; native of a particular town 88.25

gynocracy government by women 188.43

gyves fetters 121.17

ha' *Scots* hall 128.31, 163.15

habiliments garments 21.9, 342.4

habit suit of clothes 127.3, 229.40

hachis hash 301.20

had *Scots* hold 35.30

hadna *Scots* had not, hadn't 35.28, 47.9, 361.34

hae *Scots* have 32.42 etc.

haet see note to 45.22

haffit *Scots* cheek 406.6

hafflins *Scots* half-grown 162.6

haft handle 80.29

hail, haill *Scots* whole 35.3 etc.

hairbour *Scots* lodge 66.13

halberd weapon combining spear and battle-axe 276.10

halidome holiness, sanctity 71.6 (see note)

hallo call 332.10

halt limp 190.9 (see note)

ham hollow of the knee 90.15

hame *Scots* home 13.16 etc.

hamesucken *Scots Law* assault on a person in their own house 288.40

handbat stick, staff, club 63.33

hanger short sword hung from the belt, hunting knife 304.21

hank bait 252.9

hap happening, unfortunate occurrence 185.8

hard-favoured ugly 288.1

hardly harshly, severely 330.19

harle *Scots* drag 291.36

harman-beck parish constable 387.38

harness equipment for horse or similar animal 239.42

harry raid 72.7

hart male deer 300.24, 302.39, 304.36

hatch-door door with upper and lower leaves 28.33, 290.16

hatched, hatch'd etched with parallel lines 19.12, 229.43

haud *Scots* hold 68.40 etc.

haven harbour 124.4

havena *Scots* haven't 308.6

having, havings wealth, property 38.18, 107.24; (good) manners 70.33

hawk bring up phlegm from the throat with an effort 390.27

hays see note to 209.22

hazard *noun* venture, stake 154.10; for 138.6, 139.3, 148.21, and 381.20 see note to 138.6

hazard *verb* stake, bet 154.12, 170.26, 383.17

head bows, figurehead 240.37

heart-burning rankling hatred, bitterness 20.7

heart-scaud *Scots* feeling of repulsion 165.1

heart's-root see note to 304.37

heat moment of passion, angry dispute 132.24, 370.15

heben-wood ebony 91.30

heck see note to 72.20

hedge-parson, hedge parson an illiterate clergyman of low status 189.3, 193.22

hedge-stake stake cut from a hedge 349.28

hence since, ago 155.33

herd *noun*common mass 142.2

herd *verb* go in company 168.29, 212.38

heugh *Scots* crag, cliff, ravine 114.39

hey-day expression of surprise 178.32

hidalgo member of the lower Spanish nobility 222.17

Hieland *Scots* Highland 62.22, 110.4

hieroglyphical symbolical, emblematic 310.34

high loudly 105.30; for 251.10 see note

high-dressed richly dressed 130.34; well-groomed 149.11

himsell *Scots* himself 47.27 etc.

hing *Scots* hang 399.15

hinny *Scots* term of endearment 79.13, 95.28, 372.5

hirdie-girdie in disorder or confusion 70.21

hirpling *Scots* hobbling 35.24

hirsel *Scots* (ground occupied by) a flock of sheep 291.20

hit chance 279.24 (see note)

hive swarm of people 44.32

hoax banter, ridicule 202.5

hogshead large cask 228.17

holiday sportive 232.23

hollo, hollow *verb* shout 72.16, 79.43, 401.13

hollow *adjective* insincere, false 117.30

honour adornment 277.26, 376.4

hoot *Scots* interjection contradicting or dismissing a statement 360.22, 360.22

horn-mad mad with rage 290.31

horologe clock 20.13, 23.3, 334.5

horologer clockmaker 61.36, 81.39, 95.37, 399.28

horse-graith *Scots* trappings of a horse 47.39

hotel large town house 64.41, 105.16, 120.12, 221.14

hough *Scots* thigh 74.39

house-keeping hospitality 130.10

howff *Scots* favourite meeting-place 382.26

huddle see notes to 8.12 and 224.1

hue for 90.29 etc. see note to 90.29

huff for 196.14 etc. see note to 251.34

huge-paned made of large strips of different-coloured cloth 187.25

humane see note to 126.12

humanity for 62.32 and 300.6 see note to 62.32

humbug deceive, cheat 202.6

humming strong 256.27

humorous capricious, whimsical 97.6

humour mood, whim, inclination, mental disposition, state of public feeling 77.19 etc.

hustle-cap see note to 133.13

hypothecate pledge 222.9

ilk *Scots* every 35.21; each 47.33 etc.

ilka *Scots* every, each 91.43

ill *adjective* hard, difficult 36.14, 44.27, 73.37, 99.40; hostile, unkind 158.15; bad, unsatisfactory 337.33, 372.2; for 338.42 see note

ill *adverb* badly 348.24; unsatisfactorily 349.15

ill-fashioned badly made 385.31

ill-favoured ugly 242.9

ill-willy *Scots* disobliging 45.14

immunity privilege 89.27 etc.

imp scamp, urchin 133.14; child, offspring 134.8

import *verb* involve, state 54.10

import *noun* importance 348.6

impress publisher's name on title-page 13.12

improve avail oneself of profitably, take advantage of 40.31 etc.

in-and-in, in and in for 138.6 and 148.21 see note to 138.6

inartifically artlessly, naturally 7.3

incarnate rosy (colour) 389.17

incline influence towards a course of action 83.22

incognito anonymous person, fictitious character 8.36

inconsiderable unimportant, insignificant 21.33

inconsiderate thoughtless, rash 215.4

incontinence promiscuity 362.8

incontinent at once, without delay

95.11
incorporation guild 105.3
indemnify compensate 12.19
indifferent *adjective* not very good
35.8, 35.9, 341.28; impartial
146.25; careless 187.36
indifferent *adverb* moderately
59.27, 251.18
indifferently moderately 33.34,
182.33, 346.27, 381.12; poorly,
badly 93.7, 337.6 (see note)
indigent destitute 23.14
indulge foster, give oneself up to
77.38 etc.
inefficient ineffective 21.27
infer imply, involve as a consequence
16.14 etc.
ingenious ingenuous, candid, frank
122.13
ingine *Scots* ingenuity, cunning
309.20
ingrate ungrateful 231.25
ink-horn small portable vessel for
holding ink 378.1
inkle-weaver weaver of linen tape
250.8
inkling hint, suggestion 164.37
inmate occupant, lodger 21.18 etc.
innovation revolution 144.40,
380.29
insensible lacking reason 268.1
instanter immediately 66.13, 363.42
intelligence understanding 37.25,
229.23, 300.31
intelligent comprehending 175.7
interest concern 152.3; for 24.6 see
note
interrogate ask 298.40
interrogation question 55.18, 190.2
interrogatory interrogation 369.24
irrefragable incontrovertible 8.41
issue outcome, result 48.12 etc.; exit
180.40
iteration repetition 25.33
i'the in the 130.18
ither *Scots* other 46.9 etc.
itsel *Scots* itself 398.17
jack-an-ape (characteristic of) a
tame ape or monkey 47.40
jacobus see note to 138.24
jade hussy, headstrong woman 12.16
etc.
jar *noun* quarrel, conflict 150.24
jar *verb* cause to sound discordantly
166.22

jaud *Scots contemptuous* horse 47.17
jaw *Scots* rushing water 176.21
jeillis *Scots* jellies 54.28
jennet small Spanish horse 149.11,
388.32
jet hard black lignite 26.12
jibber see note to 339.35
jill-flirt wanton 63.27
jilting cheating, faithless 170.3
jocose playful, jocular 30.3, 135.3,
152.37
jolter-pate stupid head 97.9
jouk *Scots* stoop 176.21
jump coincide 92.33, 263.21
junket join in a feast or festive gathering 42.38
junketting feast, festive gathering
24.29
justle jostle 61.6
kaim *Scots* comb 402.1
keeper nurse 95.43
keepit *Scots* kept 55.17
kemping contesting between reapers
311.1
ken *Scots* know, recognise 19.8 etc.
kenna *Scots* don't know 71.36, 90.35,
310.40, 353.27
kennel gutter 169.29, 382.3
kenning scope of one's knowledge
35.36, 44.33
kersey, kersy (made of) coarse cloth
of short-stapled wool 193.26,
198.39, 260.7, 299.17
kick-shaw fancy (French) cooked
dish 232.6
kimmer *Scots* married woman 164.1
kindly *adjective* natural, in keeping
with one's own nature, native,
pleasant 47.42 etc.
kindly *adverb* naturally, pleasantly
345.4; heartily 380.37
kindness friendship 110.6, 317.30;
goodwill 117.2; for 233.5 and 334.7
see notes
kirk *Scots* church 36.36 etc.
kirk-lands *Scots* church lands 354.39
(see note)
kirk-yard *Scots* churchyard 45.5,
45.16, 45.18, 48.28
kist *Scots* chest 292.10
kittle *adjective* ticklish, difficult 73.24
kittle *verb* see note to 301.18
knap see note to 251.11
knave *noun* male servant, fellow 42.12
etc.

knave *adjective* rascally 354.22
knavish rascally 137.20
kythe *Scots* prove 69.5
la *interjection* calling attention to emphatic statement 79.20, 119.28
lack want 20.33 etc.
lack-a-day alas 250.34
lackey, lacquey liveried servant, footman 36.21, 163.21, 166.13, 375.4
lady-bird darling 98.10, 208.23
laic lay 260.1
laigh *Scots* low 48.1
lair *Scots* education 74.30
laird *Scots* lord 89.36, 125.20, 257.19
lamb's-wool hot ale mixed with pulp of roasted apple sugared and spiced 94.41
lamplighter see note to 252.2
land-louper vagabond 34.23
lang *Scots* long 45.4 etc.
lap *Scots* leapt 361.30
largesse gift of money 203.43
last latest 3.25, 249.41, 297.1
latch latchet, thong used to fasten shoe 71.12
lathy long and very thin, like a lath 24.33
latten brass 72.3
laud praise 107.29
lavrock *Scots* lark 45.17, 388.16
lawfu' *Scots* lawful 69.24
lea tract of open grassland 330.25, 347.16
leagued joined 153.8, 181.41
leaguer military camp engaged in a siege 145.4; for 339.20 see note
leaguer-lass woman attached to a military camp 207.33
leal *Scots* faithful, true 72.26, 72.34, 74.4, 381.42
leasing *Scots* lie 53.32, 382.39
leasing-making *Scots* lying 53.34
leddy *Scots* lady 342.7 etc.
lee *Scots* tell a lie 35.20
leeving *Scots* living 68.36
left-handed malicious 35.31
legend story, account 12.27
leglen-girth *Scots* see note to 361.5
leman lover 318.39
letters literature, learning 3.36, 4.11, 111.42, 126.12 (see note)
leugh *Scots* laughed 45.2
levee reception of visitors on rising from bed 345.36, 400.1

Levite *loosely contemptuous* Jew, grasping moneylender 74.8
lev'ret, leveret young hare 167.9, 168.9
liberal suitable for a gentleman *or* ample 107.32
liberty, liberties privilege, district within which a privilege operates 188.17 (see note), 196.18, 276.12
lick smart blow 35.31, 55.12
lief dear 126.7; for 71.23 and 101.11 see notes
liege *noun* lord 67.38 etc.; loyal subject 71.14 etc.
liege *adjective* loyal 352.1, 362.16, 399.5; entitled to feudal allegiance 352.6
life-long lifetime 117.39
lift sky 347.16
light *adjective* unthinking 63.32
light *adverb* in a light manner 349.40
lighter-man bargeman 35.31
light-headed frivolous 326.26
light-o'-love, light o' love prostitute 318.4, 332.11, 358.33
like *verb* please 34.6 etc.
like *adjective* likely, probable 36.15 etc.
like *adverb* as if 47.16
likely good-looking 60.25
lime lime-juice 14.5
limn draw 340.41
linger proceed slowly 10.25
link-boy for 88.11 and 92.17 see note to 88.11
list please 37.9 etc.
lither lazy, rascally 127.32
livery distinctive outfit worn by a servant 35.9, 36.1, 65.42, 250.16
loading load, cargo 284.38
lock firing mechanism 263.38
locking see note to 29.16
locomotion, loco-motion progressive motion 288.3, 362.36
loof palm of the hand 110.3, 370.29
lookover overlook 55.6
loon, loun *Scots* lad, fellow 30.33 etc.
looped with loop-holes, full of holes 32.29
lor lord 142.36, 143.1, 148.1, 148.9
lordship for 57.10, 73.14, 330.24, and 404.7 see note to 57.10
lore body of traditional beliefs 31.10; learning 149.22
loup *Scots* leap, jump 54.37, 349.40,

386.9

love-lock curl or lock of hair worn on the temple or forehead 171.38

low-breath'd whispering 61.8

low-browed having a low entrance, gloomy 311.22

Low-Dutch Dutch 149.16

Lowlands Lowland Scots language, Lallans 371.18

lownd *Scots* quietly, softly 349.20

Luckie Dame, old Mrs 35.10

lucre greed, profit 13.29, 319.7; money 101.17

lug, lugg *Scots* ear 47.33 etc.

lumber useless or cumbrous material 284.30

lustre period of 5 years 152.32

lusty attractive 164.9

luve *Scots* love 69.25

luxurious fond of luxury 94.24

maceration mortification of the flesh 337.12

maggot whimsical or capricious person 47.43; whimsical fancy 97.1

magnanimity great courage, fortitude 340.17

mail-trunk travelling case 187.2, 247.17, 295.29

main see notes to 196.42 and 200.4

maintenance support, help 64.15

mair *Scots* more 34.11 etc.

mais *French* but truly 144.33

'maist *Scots* almost 68.1

maist *Scots* most 46.33 etc.

maister *Scots* master 55.12 etc.

majority attaining the age of 21 years 77.4

mak *Scots* make 69.31, 73.3, 304.18

malapert impudent, saucy, presumptuous 55.22

malison curse 367.4

malmsey, malmsie for 193.3 and 256.6 see note to 193.3

man *Scots* must 72.35

mandation command 123.12

manhood courage 285.37, 387.39

man-of-war warship 240.37

manteau loose gown worn by women 397.15

mantle spread a blush 81.43

manufactor manufacturer 14.9

manufacture manufacturing business 13.43

marbre *French* marble 143.19

marle *Scots* marvel 49.18

marmite earthenware cooking-pot 145.22

marmozet see note to 97.7

marrow pith, essential core 74.13

marry name of the Virgin Mary, used as expression of surprise, indignation, etc. 29.4 etc.

marshal, marshall *noun* see notes to 145.7 and 339.32

marshal *verb* usher, guide 122.38

mart market-place 4.11

mask participate in a masquerade 332.29

master-fashioner master tailor 107.33

match wick (the equivalent of the modern touchpaper) 236.9

maun *verb Scots* must 46.7 etc.

maun *noun Scots* man 72.41

maunna *Scots* mustn't 387.22

mayhap perhaps 100.23

mazed dazed, delirious 239.37

measure see note to 209.22

meat food 130.17 etc.

mechanic, mechanick manual worker, artisan 14.33 etc.

mechanical belonging to the artisan class 101.20, 298.28

mechanist person skilled in constructing machinery 62.30, 78.37, 97.25

meed reward, recompense 261.6

mell meddle, interfere 35.22

member limb 338.28

memorial statement of facts as petition, record, chronicle 114.22, 127.33, 267.27, 358.3

menace threaten as a danger 20.2

mend improve, supplement 42.9, 94.21, 166.33; reform 156.21; for 46.13 see note

mendicant beggar 52.12

mensefull *Scots* mature 113.17

mercer dealer in textile fabrics 236.21

mercurial lively, ready-witted 27.31

mercy-a-gad expression of surprise (God's mercy) 332.17

meridian midday drink 261.25

merk *Scots* mark, silver coin worth 13s. 4d. Scots (roughly 13d. Sterling or 5p) 54.27, 56.37, 69.41, 74.29

mesalliance marriage with a person thought to be of inferior social position 107.40

mess portion, prepared dish 58.19 etc.; for 90.37 and 90.40 see note to 90.37

mess-book *Scots* missal, service-book 90.42 (see note)

metaphysical incorporeal, imaginary 338.34

methinks it seems to me 33.19 etc.

mew shed, cast 390.22; confine, cage 404.4, 404.7

mi my 142.36, 143.1, 148.1

miching pilfering 250.19

mickle *adjective Scots* big, great 36.36, 288.39; much 34.41

mickle *adverb Scots* much 47.19, 165.16, 165.16

mignionette plant with fragrant green or white flowers 191.16

miln *Scots* mill 115.14 (see note)

milor *French* my lord 142.34 etc.

mime jester, buffoon 152.3

mince restrain the expressing of a matter 125.9

mind *noun* opinion 57.32, 358.33

mind *verb* recollect, remember, look to, give heed to 11.37 etc.

minion *noun* child 331.7, 332.30

minion *adjective* elegant, dainty 61.8

minish diminish 171.37

mint aim 371.18

miscaw *Scots* denounce 165.4

misleard *Scots* rude, unmannerly 44.30

misliking dislike 91.24

mither *Scots* mother 72.2

moan complaint, lamentation 275.8, 330.27, 330.29

mob-cap large indoor woman's cap covering all the hair 11.29

mobility ordinary people 107.17, 107.23

mode prevalent fashion 152.34

moment importance, consequence 42.33

mongrel contemptible person 249.24

monitress female instructor 207.2, 207.14, 211.27

monopoly see note to 354.38

monsieur Frenchified gentleman 110.30

montero Spanish cap with spherical crown and earflaps 313.21

mony *Scots* many 35.22 etc.

mony-go-round *Scots* revolving

mechanism 44.35

moral import, significance 208.36, 322.2

mort girl 191.42

mort-cloth funeral pall 403.27

moss *Scots* bog, moorland 114.40

motion *noun* puppet-show 27.22, 27.43, 48.25; action 188.11; for 371.20 see note

motion *verb* make a sign 71.14, 85.29

motley jester's multicoloured costume 77.28

mountebank itinerant quack 30.16

mounting hilt 136.29

mournival set of four in one hand 185.13

mouth seize with the mouth, maul 167.21, 168.11; put in the mouth 175.15; declaim 331.34; for 69.42, 162.35, and 210.13 see notes

mouther someone given to vain, boastful, or declamatory speech 156.20

moyle mule 60.40

muckle *adverb Scots* much 36.19, 37.9

muckle *adjective Scots* great, big 169.18, 399.1

muddy not clear or pure, opaque 151.31, 250.20

muir *Scots* moor 114.40

mulligrubs state of depression 230.27

multiplicand see note to 29.18

mumble chew without much use of teeth 159.23

mummer actor 238.19; disguised participant in dumbshow 330.38

mummery ridiculous ceremonial 197.37

mumming festive dumbshow with masked actors, masquerade 332.28

mump *Scots* grin 402.36

mun *Scots* must 73.15, 114.35, 114.35, 366.4

murrain plague 62.6, 123.4

murrey-coloured mulberry-coloured, purple-red 193.9

murther murder 72.10 etc.

murtherer murderer 274.16

musk perfume derived from the male musk deer 252.1

musketoon short musket with a large bore 242.16, 394.9

mustacho moustache 146.1, 191.31

musty old-fashioned, antiquated

135.32

mutton-commons mutton provided communally 184.33

mysell *Scots* myself 35.22 etc.

na *Scots* not 47.19 etc.; no 55.8 etc.

nae *adjective Scots* no 34.35 etc.

nae *adverb Scots* not 301.17

naebody *Scots* nobody 354.13

naething *Scots* nothing 34.27 etc.

naiad-like see note to 6.17

naig *Scots* nag, horse 304.16

nane *Scots* none 48.1 etc.

nappy with a head, foaming, strong 41.14

neat *noun* ox 197.18

neat *adjective* clear, unadulterated, fine 374.28

neb *Scots* point 64.17; nose 112.36

needna *Scots* needn't 171.40, 341.34, 353.18

neither see note to 38.22

neophyte novice 149.15

nevoy *Scots* nephew 401.7

next nearest 184.27, 296.30

nice scrupulous 40.38; finely poised or graduated 303.43; deft, delicately sensitive 304.10

nicety scrupulosity, fastidiousness 74.12

nick *verb* cheat, throw a winning cast against 258.38, 372.38

nick *noun* notch 398.22

Nicotia *slang* pipe tobacco 191.26

niffer see note to 354.37

niggard stingy person 143.33

nigher make a snickering noise 353.19

night-rail dressing-gown 191.24

night-watch see note to 29.15

nipperkin small vessel for liquor 256.32

nixie see note to 6.15

no *Scots* not 35.20 etc.

noble gold coin worth 6s. 8d. (33p) 33.30, 194.38, 370.29

nod sway from the perpendicular 116.27

nold see note to 44.36

nooning midday meal 302.40

norland northern 47.29

nose-of-wax see note to 115.20

nouns *oath* [God's] wounds! 34.13, 156.15, 188.15

nowte see note to 54.28

Nullifidian atheist 74.13

nuncheon see note to 38.7

o' of 33.5 etc.

oakum loose fibre from old rope used for caulking ships' seams 60.6

obeisance bow or curtsy 107.11 etc.

objurgation severe rebuking 69.43

obliged liable 89.38

obligement favour 317.39

obraid *Scots* upbraid, reproach, find fault with 33.21

observation see note to 150.6

occasion requirement, necessity 53.34 etc.

occiput back of the head 31.11

Od, Odd God 72.41 (see note), 156.15 (see note)

odds see note to 318.35

offer present itself 352.16

office occupation, job 82.20; action 158.15; for 154.37 see note

offices service quarters 46.4

officious attentive, obliging, kind, dutiful, doing more than is asked or required 157.34, 158.32, 190.33

old-world old-time 133.33, 155.39

ombre see note to 148.19

one somebody 377.31

on't of it 82.29 etc. (for 169.14 see note)

ony *Scots* any 46.9 etc.

oons *oath* zoons, God's (i.e. Christ's) wounds 114.37

open *hunting* begin to bay at the scent 119.4

open-hearted frank 210.18

opignorate pawn, pledge 351.5, 351.12, 371.25

opine think, give as one's opinion 70.12, 204.19

opposite opponent, antagonist 185.5

optic eye 193.43

or *conjunction* either 240.9

or *adverb* before 398.34

ordinary for 137.16 etc. see note to 137.23

ordnance artillery 311.20

original see note to 76.5

ortolan bird (a bunting) esteemed a delicacy 149.6

ou *Scots* oh! 54.1, 54.8

oursells *Scots* ourselves 128.30, 352.34

out expression of reproach 100.12, 102.23, 134.8

out-herod see note to 151.27

outshot projection 45.25

out-taken *Scots* except, not counting 171.42

outward outer 25.21

overbear overcome by power or authority 187.37, 196.19

over-burthened overburdened 310.26, 383.32

over-copy see note to 3.30

over-gilt gilded 84.33

over-reach get the better of someone by cunning or craft 373.2

over-reached overstrained 226.42

overset capsize 284.26

overture proposal 197.20

overweening excessive 40.39, 317.16

owche brooch, clasp, buckle, especially with precious stones 94.2

ower *Scots* too 33.5 etc.; over 35.27; late 45.13

owl solemn dullard 27.6, 143.25

pack stock of cash 169.30

packman pedlar 384.22, 399.10

paik punch, pummel 406.4

painful painstaking 11.43

palisade iron fence 64.36

pallet straw bed or mattress 316.21

palmer-worm term covering various types of caterpillar 195.23; for 27.24 see note

palter equivocate, prevaricate 90.11

paned made up of strips of cloth joined side by side 29.28

panged *Scots* pressed together, packed closely side by side 45.19

pantaloon foolish old man 199.39

paper paper receptacle 383.9

papestrie *Scots* popery 68.20

parade ostentation 61.13; parade-ground 312.12

pardieu *French* by God, indeed 142.37

paring-shovel instrument for scraping floors 288.27

parity similarity 153.37

parricide person committing treason against sovereign 306.35

part *noun* act 371.23; *plural* abilities, talents, intellectual qualities 118.30, 296.6; for 17.15, 247.15, 350.19, 371.20, and 405.37 see notes

part *verb* divide 379.35

particular see note to 164.36

party opponent, antagonist 184.6; group of people forming one side in a dispute 184.17

party-coloured-wise in a variety of colours 228.21

pasquinadoe satirical libel 310.32, 339.19

pass *noun* point, predicament 235.15, 331.36

pass *verb* traverse 275.28; leave unmentioned, pass over 325.39; be accepted as valid 331.36

passage event 72.18; for 138.6 and 148.22 see note to 138.6

passenger passer-by 21.6 etc.

pass-over see note to 161.19

pate (crown of) head 146.5, 163.23, 295.41; head 381.31

patrimony inheritance 17.12, 122.22, 343.42, 344.13

patten shoe into which the foot was slipped, or one made of wood 385.10

pauvre *French* poor 142.37, 145.20

pay pay for 162.26

pease-bogle *Scots* scarecrow 70.32

peculiar particular, distinctive 21.6 etc.

peculiarity distinctive characteristic 24.24

peculiarly particularly, distinctively 21.42, 168.27, 170.17

pecuniar pecuniary, relating to money matters 371.7

pecuniars money matters 346.27

pedagogue schoolmaster 76.23, 133.34

peepers eyes 192.2

peg see note to 385.1

penetralia *Latin* innermost parts, sanctuary 17.18

penneeck see note to 138.6

penny-wedding see note to 400.12

pennyworth see note to 27.11

pensioner royal retainer 107.13

perdu concealed 183.38

peremptorily absolutely 302.17; positively 381.20

preremptory unquestionable, absolute 146.5

peril endanger 154.5, 214.37

person personal appearance or figure 104.25, 126.15

personage character in a play or story 246.18, 246.24; individual 5.13 etc.

personally in relation to the person specified 62.1

petronel large cavalry pistol 262.23

petted indulged, spoiled 211.37, 231.2

pettifogger rascally lawyer 137.20

pettish(ly) peevish(ly), petulant(ly) 29.9 etc.

pew stand for people doing business in public place 372.9

pharmacopeia stock of drugs 32.4

pharmacopolist person who sells medicines 32.15

phlegm sluggishness, apathy, evenness of temper 28.19

physic medicine 28.6, 28.7

physiognomy face, facial expression 22.16 etc.

physnomy physiognomy, facial expression 5.17

pick-thank *noun and adjective* flatterer, sycophant 155.24; flattering, sycophantic 318.37

piece firearm 71.22, 336.32; young woman 385.32; for 48.19 see note

pig *Scots* earthenware jar 35.25, 35.27

pigeon see notes to 179.3 and 198.40

pile[1] large imposing building 65.33

pile[2] tail of a coin 162.9 (see note)

pilgrimage life regarded as a journey 340.35

pin *Scots* mood, frame of mind 48.33 (see note)

pinch crisis, financial stress, hardship 36.11, 45.7

pineal see note to 242.29

pinion wing, feather, quill 141.7, 149.20; for 29.16 and 402.27 see note to 29.16

pink *noun* embodied perfection 137.39

pink *verb* wound 183.37, 406.19

piquant spicy 143.41

pistolet pistol 71.24, 234.27

pit *noun* see note to 27.2

pit *verb Scots* put 36.32 (see note)

pith vigour, energy 387.23

placable easily pacified 71.36, 362.24

placet petition 113.30

plack for 114.36 and 355.14 see note to 114.36

plaint complaint 72.8

plaister *Scots* plaster 31.14

plate silver or gold utensils or ornaments 58.11 etc.; for 260.12 see note

plate-coat coat of mail 109.9

play feign, act 318.2, 329.42

play-book book of plays 184.25, 332.13

play-haunting regular theatregoing 161.25

play-house theatre 51.18 etc.

pleached framed by interlaced plants 120.20

pleasure please 403.3, 403.36

pledge *noun* security 74.8 etc.

pledge *verb* toast, drink in response 99.21, 193.16, 233.8, 250.13

plenty plentiful 160.11, 162.37

plot playbill 51.19

ploy escapade 388.20

pluck see note to 198.40

plucker see note to 179.3

plume pluck feathers from (a bird) 168.41 (see note)

plush (of) rich fabric with long nap 191.35, 193.9, 278.28, 285.1

ply see note to 53.39

pock-end *Scots* bottom of a purse 292.12

pock-pudding see note to 30.23

poignant pungent, piquant 75.7

point-device with extreme nicety or correctness 121.37

points tagged laces or cords 188.23 etc.

policy *Scots* embellishment, refinement 34.11; political prudence, prudent conduct 186.2, 196.5, 217.39, 220.6; conduct of public affairs 228.13; political cunning 355.18

politician schemer 399.36

poltron *French* coward 148.10

pomade scented ointment for the skin 94.14

poniard small slim dagger 156.8 etc.

poortith *Scots* poverty 13.19, 387.23

popinjay parrot 210.10

popish Roman Catholic 92.15, 236.1

popular cultivating the favour of the common people 292.30

pork-griskins lean part of loins of pork 297.34

porringer small bowl (often with handle) for soup, broth, porridge etc. 97.42, 99.8

port gate 34.3 etc.

portmantle portmanteau 187.2

portress female doorkeeper 229.20

position statement 173.11

possess acquaint 39.19

posset-cup cup for drink of hot milk curdled with ale, wine, or other liquor, often with sugar, spices etc. 96.24

post with all speed 162.20

post-chaise four-wheeled carriage for carrying mail and passengers 293.2, 397.19

postern back or private entrance 223.3, 223.9, 223.21

postern-door back or private door 303.6

postern-gate back or private gate 65.39

postpone placed lower in order of importance 165.22

pot glass of liquor 27.9 etc.; round helmet 145.17; for 185.27 see note

potation beverage 137.22, 194.21, 298.4; draught 193.9, 231.22; drinking bout 257.19

'pothecary apothecary, chemist 28.8

pottle half-gallon 99.10, 266.41, 382.20, 383.8

pouch *noun* purse, money-bag 161.31, 162.14, 260.16; pocket 71.16, 128.20, 310.32

pouch *verb* pocket 171.16

poursuivant, pursuivant officer with power to execute warrants 188.5, 311.14, 311.26

poursuivant-at-arms officer with power to execute warrants 311.6

pouther *Scots* gunpowder 309.16, 309.19

powdered salted 41.11

prætermit omit 110.14; neglect 356.38

pragmatical conceited, meddlesome, opinionated 54.42, 166.12, 402.20

prate chatter, officious talking 164.27

prating chattering idly or for too long 285.6

preceese precise, strict in religious observance 74.13

preceesely precisely 91.11

preceptor tutor 76.15

preceptress female instructor 206.14

precipitate rush, hurry 6.37

precisian person rigidly punctilious in observing moral and religious rules, puritan 161.14, 161.18

prefer advance 117.14; submit formally to an authority for consideration 358.25

premise state first by way of explanation 173.17

prentice, 'prentice apprentice 21.21 etc.

preparative draught of liquor taken before a meal 382.21

prescription see note to 362.14

presence royal presence, presence-chamber 74.1 etc.

present *verb* act, personate 238.21; offer 303.22; represent, depict 344.31, 398.42

present *adjective* immediate 69.36, 74.28, 371.23

presently immediately, at once, soon 65.39 etc.; at present 295.16, 355.3, 402.15

press (a) crowd 136.14, 150.11

pressed press-ganged 12.34

prestable *Scots* able to be paid in discharge of obligation 356.9

pretence alleged ground for an action, reason 263.24, 368.17

pretend claim, assert 52.27 etc.

pretty fine, excellent, brave, gallant 13.7 etc.; skilful 369.24; great, considerable 369.30

previously first 287.22

prey booty, plunder 254.30

price payment 161.30

prie try by tasting 402.16

primero for 148.19 and 233.15 see note to 148.19

princox coxcomb 389.38

privy private 54.29; secret, concealed 149.43, 360.42

prize-fighter one engaging in a public boxing-match 30.15

process-bag bag for legal writs 378.2

procure cause 245.28

prodigal spendthrift 181.39, 203.11, 241.15

proffer offer 58.7 etc.

prologomena introductory material 12.2

proper excellent, handsome 21.22, 27.35, 100.22, 237.13; own 76.18, 212.42; normal 229.38

property ownership 351.9

prosody theory and practice of versi-fication 76.20, 357.7

prospective perspective view 69.23, 69.24

proto-martyr first Christian martyr 115.37

prove test 262.33

provost *Scots* mayor 110.8, 156.11; for 145.7 see note

proxenata *Latin* (proxeneta) go-be-tween, matchmaker 363.34

prunella (clerical gown of) silk or worsted fabric 260.5

pshaw (make an) exclamation of im-patience, contempt, or disgust 27.31 etc.

pudding-headed stupid 289.20

puddings *Scots* entrails, guts 70.42

puff *noun* exaggeratedly or falsely en-thusiastic review or advertisement 20.40

puff *verb* praise extravagantly and habitually 34.31, 246.21

puir *Scots* poor 54.8 etc.

pullet young hen 382.21

puncheon large cask 127.37, 255.31

pund *Scots* pound 69.40, 129.2

purlieus haunts 182.11

purpose intend 63.9 etc.; for 172.39 see note

put-on *Scots* dressed 48.15

putt, put for 138.33 and 233.15 see note to 138.33

quaigh shallow wooden cup, some-times with a silver rim 121.7

qualify designate, name, specify 49.24, 141.20; design 125.34

quality (people of) (high) rank or social position 24.39 etc.

quarrée *French* (dead) quarry 304.29

quarry see note to 46.43

quart measure of 0.25 gallons (1.1 litres) 88.39, 256.29, 380.39, 381.31

quarter *noun* haunch 144.26; for 163.39 and 300.7 see notes

quarter *verb* see note to 338.34

quarter-staff see note to 23.43

quarto for 12.4 and 266.41 see note to 12.4

quart-pot drinking vessel containing 0.25 gallons (1.1 litres) of liquid 258.10

quean *Scots* lass, woman, hussy 30.13

etc.

queer cheat, spoil a person's chances 256.5

quibble pun 151.33

quick alive 338.28

quicken stimulate 3.34

quiddit nicety in argument, quibble 7.4

quirk quibble, quip 7.4

quittance discharge from debt 59.21

quiz make fun of, ridicule 202.6

quotha says (s)he 38.6, 101.11

quotient for 29.17, 79.12, and 402.27 see note to 29.17

rabbit drat 252.1

rabble attack with a rabble 239.16, 239.20

race running 167.10

radical see note to 257.18

raillery good-humoured ridicule, banter 22.41 etc.

raise *Scots* arose 35.28

rakish dashing, jaunty 188.26; dis-solute 190.34

rally ridicule 321.2

rampallian ruffian, scoundrel 291.35

range place 373.19

ranger keeper of royal park 180.25, 181.31, and 315.16

rank *noun* row 4.27

rank *verb* place 137.4

rant *verb Scots* behave in a boisterous or riotous manner 162.8

rant *noun* bombastic language 319.29

rapier long pointed and two-edged sword 43.40 etc.

rascal belonging to the rabble 184.19

rascally characteristic of the lowest social class 283.19

Rasp-haus see note to 396.40

rate chide, scold 299.22

rattling characterised by a rapid flow of words or liveliness of manner 190.26; lively 192.4

rave *Scots* tore 47.14

raw-boned very lean or gaunt 144.41, 165.41, 287.43

raxing *Scots* stretching 47.21

read solve 50.10 etc.

ready ready money 259.7

reason a reasonable amount 264.6

reck see note to 387.30

reckoning bill 137.36 etc.

red *Scots* clear 54.35; for 348.19 and

402.1 see notes

redd-up put in order 349.15

red-het *Scots* red-hot 90.43

red-shank Highlander 354.16

reduce bring to order 298.16

redundant abundant 22.40

reekie *Scots* for 59.38 and 136.35 see note to 59.38

reeking steaming 383.8

reeve pass a rope through a block 145.8

refection partaking of food 367.30

reflux ebb 39.38

reformado see note to 189.3

regimen government, rule 310.41

regular (made) in accordance with the rules 7.15 etc.

regularly in accordance with the rules 154.23, 174.4

reird *Scots* loud outcry 35.28

remembrance see note to 60.8

remeid *Scots* remedy 35.29, 73.19

remove move on, shift 120.31; shift one's place 372.17; for 297.33 and 298.25 see note to 297.33

rencontre hostile encounter, duel 77.6, 226.6

rencounter hostile meeting 401.32

rendition surrender 144.31, 144.35

report see note to 29.16

representative heir, successor 117.20

rescript decree, official order 74.26, 354.1

resent show displeasure or anger at something 21.18

reservation see note to 365.2

reserved restricted, retired 122.27

residenter resident 189.30

resistless irresistible 125.30

resumption summary 328.27

retired withdrawn from society or observation, secluded 36.38, 60.12, 228.38

reverence bow 47.17 etc.; state demanding respect, respectability 51.13; profound respect 64.13 etc.; curtsy 95.19; gesture of respect 374.36

reverentially respectfully 71.17

reversion see note to 187.16

revie counter a stake on something with a higher one 185.17

revise second proof incorporating corrections made on the previous

version 4.42

rex for 114.5 see note

Rhenish wine from the Rhine region 151.43 etc.

rhodomontade inflated, boastful 140.3

ribband ribbon 115.1 etc.

riding-beaver hat of beaver fur worn when riding 395.34

right genuine 58.21 etc.; direct 196.24

rip see note to 405.40

roaring for 27.2, 187.29, 191.26, and 196.18 see note to 27.2

roisterer noisy reveller 179.3

roll scroll 312.43

Roman Roman Catholic 309.31

romaunt romance 332.12

rose rose-shaped ornamental knot of ribbon etc. 88.27

rose-noble for 127.8 and 191.23 see note to 127.8

round *adjective* plain, frank, blunt 112.2, 162.41, 381.29; for 353.29 see note

round *verb* whisper 47.33

roundel short simple lyric or song with refrain 66.25, 207.35

roundly promptly, bluntly 360.23

roupit *Scots* raucous 172.36

rout *noun* fuss 9.5; disorganised body 184.19

rout *verb* beat severely 169.15

row *Scots* roll 305.8

rowt *noun and verb Scots* bellow, shout 47.29, 47.30, 62.22

rub *noun* slight reproof, teasing comment 76.10

rub *verb* see note to 148.15

rudas cantankerous, resembling a hag 403.38

ruff see note to 185.17

ruffle make a great display or stir, swagger 170.19, 170.22, 233.12

ruffler swaggerer 179.1

rummer see note to 230.23

run flee 387.20; for 4.32 and 259.8 see notes

rundlet cask 197.17, 199.6

rustle be finely dressed in rustling material 36.22; for 354.17 see note

rusty rust-coloured 193.25, 243.29, 260.5

saam *Scots* same 54.20, 162.5

Sabbath-e'en see note to 70.22

sables sable fur 136.27

sack general name for a class of white wines from Spain and the Canaries 14.5 etc.

sackless *Scots* innocent 72.10

sad-coloured dark or sober-coloured 66.32

sae *Scots* so 33.5 etc.

sair *adjective Scots* difficult 47.33; sore 372.3, 400.5

sair *adverb Scots* greatly, grievously 310.40

sairly *Scots* sorely 161.27

sall *Scots* shall 71.11, 403.7

sally sprightly utterance 77.22, 205.5

salve *noun* ointment 28.12

salve *verb* anoint with ointment 97.3

sang *Scots* song 35.24, 301.17

sapient wise 88.23, 110.34, 164.13, 381.3

satellite follower 83.4, 170.40, 257.13

satisfy convince 181.12; free from uncertainty or doubt 317.3, 378.29

satrap subordinate ruler 193.17

saturnine sluggish, cold, gloomy 158.32, 395.1

sauce spice, season 46.7, 75.4

sauciere see note to 128.3

saul *Scots* soul 67.43 etc.; *oath* (by my) soul 309.27

sax *Scots* six 44.40 etc.

say try out, assess 292.4

'sblood *oath* God's blood 309.20

scantling modicum 339.37

scapement escapement, mechanism between motive power and regulator 30.12

scarification scratching, cutting 228.33

scauding *Scots* punishment, beating, severe rebuke 47.36

scaur *Scots* scare 47.18

scene place where the action of a play is supposed to occur 150.26

scholiast man of learning 310.8

schools universities 368.5

score *noun* bill, running account 267.1

score *verb* charge to someone's account 256.33

scout college servant at Oxford 186.31

scrambling irregular 190.34

scrape hasty scribble 54.14

scratch scratching sound 6.30 (see note)

scrivener professional scribe, copyist 64.9 etc.

scruple see notes to 90.16 and 91.4

scrupulous prone to hesitation 198.45

scrutiny investigation 400.4

sculler for 43.34, 238.11, 284.1, and 347.37 see note to 43.34

scullion menial kitchen servant 46.26 etc.

scutcheon (shield with) coat of arms 126.19, 231.42

'sdeath *oath, short for* God's (i.e. Christ's) death 48.23, 115.12, 252.9, 330.29

sea-coal coal 243.25

season period 256.36, 399.9; time 317.39

seasonable killed at the right time 156.25; suitable, fit 201.7

second back up, confirm 22.41, 124.32, 287.29, 381.32

secret alone, unobserved 70.11

sedulously diligently, assiduously 81.36, 345.29

see look 123.7

seer visionary 4.34; person credited with profound spiritual insight 250.14

selected select, choice 106.21, 168.28

self-love self-esteem, amour-propre 166.10, 334.35

self-opinion obstinacy in adhering to one's own opinions 325.27

self-opinioned obstinate in adhering to one's own opinions 20.8, 55.25, 70.19

sempstress seamstress, sewing woman 24.37

senior old person 266.1

serjeant serjeant at law, member of superior order of barristers 26.30, 41.43; officer arresting offenders or summoning persons to a court 196.25

serve supply 59.27; suit, fit 70.32; for 259.10 see note

servitor servant, personal attendant 55.31, 69.41

set wager 143.32; *hunting* point out (the presence of game) 379.32

setting frame 26.11

setting-dog setter 248.11, 379.16

shable *Scots* curved sword, sabre 69.18

shape manner, way 182.6, 220.8, 263.35, 387.1

sharking swindling, cheating 185.22, 386.25

sharper person who cheats at cards 139.14

shearing reaping 311.1

sheeps-head sword hilt of basket work 366.41

shew appear, seem 130.36

shiffle shuffle 142.33

shift *noun* cheating, expedients 127.12; for 183.33, 198.22, 282.39, and 303.30 see notes

shift *verb* manage 189.32; change 223.38; for 49.35, 180.35, and 274.39 see notes

shifting uncertain 72.20

ship-chandler retailer of equipment and provisions for ships 36.35 etc.

shoon *Scots* shoes 88.27

shopman shop assistant 158.40

shouther *Scots* shoulder 289.2

shroud conceal 57.5

shule *Scots* shovel 289.2

sib *Scots* closely related 172.18

sic *Scots* such 90.40 etc.

sicker *Scots* prudent 171.13

sic-like *Scots* suchlike 70.35

side-pouch bag worn at the side 59.13

sign make a sign, signal 66.15, 175.4, 282.29

signify avail 302.16

sign-manual, sign manual (document bearing) sovereign's autograph authenticating signature 115.28 etc.

signory nobility 29.2

siller *Scots* silver, money 33.22 etc.

silver-vessail *Scots* silver plate 72.23

simple inexperienced, naïve, stupid 137.18 etc.; for 196.39 see note

sinciput upper front part of the head or skull 31.10

singe burn off the down or bristles before cooking 12.6, 298.27

single weak 131.14 etc.; for 187.9 and 187.10 see note to 187.9; for 252.18 see note

single-stick see note to 22.3

sirrah sir 35.38 etc.

situation social position or standing

33.8 etc.

skeigh restive, frisky 54.37

skelder beg, sponge 196.12; obtain money by cheating 379.4

skene long dagger 306.42

skimmington ludicrous procession directed against an unfaithful or cruel spouse 232.20, 232.41, and 234.34

skirt tail or lower part of a garment 77.26 etc.

slabbered stained, splashed 194.36

sleaveless leading to nothing 370.36

slenderly see note to 375.7

slide see note to 198.9

slight thin 40.10

slightly half-heartedly 257.14; carelessly, slightingly 397.29

slip scion, descendant 133.32; young small slender person 313.13

slip-shod wearing slippers or loose shoes 243.29

slops wide baggy breeches 26.41, 187.25, 191.35

slouched see note to 64.12

slough caterpillar's skin cast during metamorphosis 103.23, 390.22

slur see note to 251.11

sma' *Scots* small 36.32 etc.

smaik *Scots* rascal, rogue 69.18, 304.18, 309.29, 386.27

smatterer dabbler 300.1

smelt half-guinea (10s. 6d., 52.5p) 250.32, 259.34, 378.21

smith metal-worker 87.36

smooth-faced plausible in manner 289.16, 320.29

snap-haunce flint-lock pistol 308.2

sneaking niggardly 145.33

sniggle *Scots* snigger 370.1

so so long as 192.9

soap-boiler soap manufacturer 400.20

society company 5.9 etc.

sock see note to 152.15

soft leisurely 379.20

soldado soldier 147.10, 187.19

soldan sultan 193.17

solicit manage, pursue 58.34

solicitous anxious, deeply concerned 400.28

something somewhat 26.28 etc.

sooth truth 151.40; for 162.36 and 172.16 see notes

soothfast true 352.36

sophistication adulteration 14.6

Southland see note to 70.14

Southron *Scots noun* Englishman 34.26, 38.21, 139.29, 289.21; Englishmen 90.42

Southron *Scots adjective* English 291.21

spak *Scots* spoke 47.25

spang *verb* leap, bound 70.35

spang *noun* sudden violent movement 382.31

spangle glittering point of light 261.29

special particularly 110.3

specialty see note to 43.37

specie coin money 169.16, 327.12

speed prosper, succeed, make progress 104.10, 333.11; cause to prosper 303.1; finish 376.38

speer *Scots* inquire 354.18

speering *Scots* inquiry 164.10

spell *noun* amount 176.25, 382.42

spell *verb* see note to 48.35

spend lose 341.4

spent exhausted 197.16; expended, used up 376.33

spice trace 204.9

spigot, spiggot small wooden peg used to stop barrel vent-hole, tap 138.9, 197.29

spirits vital energy 89.24 etc.

spirt squirt 398.35

splenetic peevish, ill-humoured 82.10

spoil deprive 392.11

spoiler robber 241.17, 320.21

spot piece 11.41, 305.24, 366.30

sprackle *Scots* clamber 354.13

sprig small branch 23.11

springald youth 53.20, 110.24, 176.14

spunk *Scots* leak 369.43

spunkie *Scots* will o' the wisp 30.11

stab see note to 251.11

stalk walk stiffly, haughtily, or imposingly 126.18 etc.

stamp type 167.13

stand withstand 36.30, 75.24; act as 133.34; encounter 356.22; for 42.6, 54.13, 55.12, 387.33, and 399.33 see notes

standish inkpot 10.2

start stand out 283.4; rush 349.20

starveling ill-fed 96.30

stay *verb* wait a moment! 53.39 etc.

stay *noun* support 142.33

'stead instead 249.26

stead supply 235.2

steek *Scots* shut, make fast 45.13, 48.32

steel cutting tool 230.1; for 243.26 see note

steer *Scots* stir, commotion 55.19

stick pierce 368.10

stiff *adverb* firmly 302.27

stiff *adjective* stubborn 74.5

stinted limited, scanty 94.25

stock assets 170.27; stocking 188.26

stocked supplied with funds 28.4

stock-fish cod or similar fish cured by being split open and dried in the open air without salt 96.30

stocking putting in the stocks 49.22

stone 6.35 kg 41.26

stonern stone, made of stone 34.11

stoop swoop on quarry 188.4

storm storming 145.6

stot bullock 36.30, 47.29, 62.22

stout brave, firm in resolve 37.34 etc.; having body 41.14; strong, strongly built 92.3 etc.; formidable, splendid, undaunted 121.41, 152.14, 155.14, 396.41; unyielding, impregnable 151.11

stout-bodied strongly built 20.31

stoutly vigorously, lustily 231.39; manfully, firmly 356.3

strand-scouring *Scots* cleaning gutters 169.32

strapping *Scots* hanging 72.12

stream-way main current of a river 285.7

street-walker prostitute who solicits in the street 360.6

stretcher board for rower's feet 295.40

stripe blow, lash, stroke 49.22, 302.33

studied learned 126.11; deliberate 169.39

stun stupefy, deafen temporarily 98.17, 283.24

sturdied afflicted with brain disease 79.11

sturdy obstinate 70.33; resolute, robust in character 392.6

subaltern (arising from) the situation of being a feudal dependant of a feudal dependant 120.39

sublunary earthly 138.26

thriftless wasteful, improvident, spendthrift 29.5

through-stane *Scots* horizontal gravestone 45.19

tib ace of trumps 185.14

tiddy four of trumps 185.16, 185.21, 185.25

tight capable 37.5, 72.15; trim, shapely 40.11; for 353.29 see note

till *Scots* to 371.22

tilt¹ *noun* awning, cover 104.33

tilt² *noun* see note to 147.16

tilt *verb* engage in combat 183.36

tilted covered with an awning 333.35

tilt-yard jousting yard 340.9

time-meter measurer of time 61.38

tine branch of a deer's antler 304.35, 304.36

tint *Scots* forgotten 45.1; lost 169.20

tip see note to 197.42

tipstaff sheriff's officer 186.23, 195.10, 196.25

tip-top of the highest quality or rank 24.37

tire dress 390.24

tither *Scots* other 44.30

tittle smallest amount 175.3

tocher *noun Scots* dowry 359.24, 361.29

tocher *verb Scots* furnish with a dowry 400.27

tod fox 333.27

toddle move in an unhurried but ungainly manner 362.36

toilette dressing-table 26.27; for 104.23, 109.18, and 347.22 see note to 104.23

toils net into which a quarry is driven 322.10

Tokay see note to 8.17

token see note to 172.35

toll see note to 80.35

tonsor barber 296.34

tool weapon 147.16

toom *Scots* empty 292.12

top see note to 251.10

topping distinguished, principal 189.28

torchon *French* dishcloth 148.2

t'other *Scots* other 91.40, 310.32; the other 136.10, 284.21

touch approach in excellence 238.20; cut 297.36, 298.2

tough see note to 318.21

tour look 191.41, 191.41

tout *noun Scots* toot, short blast 78.35, 310.10

tout *verb* see 191.41

towards on the way 397.4

towl stroke of a bell 127.38

town's-bairn *Scots* inhabitant of a town 48.18

towser five of trumps 185.16

toy thing, foolish affair 369.22

track traverse 309.25

traduction translation 357.28

traffic trade, commercial transaction 21.14, 24.25, 226.6

train set or class of persons 4.37; body of people moving in a line 173.38, 177.16, 177.24; retinue 174.29 etc.

trankum trinket 230.12

trap-ball see note to 232.4

traverse sideways movement in fencing 270.38

travestie alter in dress or appearance, disguise 229.34, 341.10, 341.31

treen *Scots* wooden 72.3

trencher plate, platter 12.7 etc.

trepan *verb* trap, inveigle to go somewhere or do something 327.20

trepan *noun either* someone who lures a person into a disadvantageous situation *or* act of entrapment 336.34

trig active, alert 387.15

trim reprimand, rebuke 368.30

Trinidado *slang* W Indies cigar 191.26

trinket delicacy 256.33

trip see note to 209.22

Trojan good fellow, boon companion 136.2

troll, trowl roll, spin 118.9 etc.

troth *adverb* in truth 35.20 etc.

troth *noun* truth 44.42 etc.

trow think 91.26 etc.

truce see note to 379.42

truckle, truckle-bed low moveable bed 31.32, 31.34, 31.38

trunk-breeches, trunk breeches full bag-like breeches 191.35, 310.21

trunnion club 238.6

truss attach a person's hose to doublet by tying laces 187.30, 188.23, 188.29

tryste appointment 63.9

tube tobacco-pipe 192.40

turn-broche person employed to turn a roasting-spit 348.11

tush expression of impatience, scorn, or disgust 377.8

tutelary guardian 215.41

tutti-taiti fiddlesticks 108.41

twa *Scots* two 24.30 etc.

twire peep 191.42, 230.42

twopenny see note to 125.18

tyke mongrel, ill-mannered man 165.4; dog 309.18

type representation 66.41

typify show 71.9

Ud God 70.43, 73.20, 145.4 (see notes)

umquhile *Scots* former, erstwhile 361.2

unalienably inseparably 202.21

unappreciable priceless 14.34

unapprehensive see note to 202.7

unbeseeming unseemly, inappropriate 155.43, 158.35, 332.28

unbonnet doff one's cap 116.41, 299.15

unce *Scots* ounce 72.26

uncomatable unattainable 362.20

uncouth unusual, strange 386.2

uncustomed on which no customs duty has been paid 226.29

undertaker helper 117.6

undertaking prepared to act as publisher 16.40

undescried unseen 368.42

unfriend enemy 175.16

ungirt unfastened 243.29

unhandsome mean, unbecoming 139.34

unlaboured accomplished in an easy or natural manner 7.24

unmeet unfitting, unsuitable 4.35

unrespective disrespectful, rude 3.20, 78.32

untrussed unlaced 65.43

uphauld *Scots* uphold, sustain 358.30; warrant 398.11

uphold warrant 42.36, 384.15; for 34.40 see note

urge provoke 42.32, 339.5

usage (rate of) interest 70.6, 355.1

utility profit 266.16

value *noun* see note to 11.33

value *verb* take account of, be concerned about 28.20

vapour swagger 262.35; for 251.33 and 259.9 see notes

vara *Scots* very 68.35 etc.

variorum see note to 12.2

varlet rogue, rascal 26.34, 54.7, 376.12, 376.19

vassal feudal dependant 121.6, 125.24

venture see note to 270.40

vera *Scots* very 143.1, 381.34; true, absolute 361.26

veracious truthful 12.26

verge limits 196.1; for 184.5, 329.11, and 368.12 see note to 184.5

veritie truth 163.14

verquire a dice game 138.6 (see note)

very real, true, absolute 26.15 etc.

vestal having the status of a nun 202.27

vestment garment 75.24

via begone 190.22

viands food 94.37

vicegerent ruler regarded as a representative of God 71.10, 305.10, 305.12

vie place a stake on 185.16

viretot see note to 201.26

virtue power, distinctive quality 75.6

vivers *Scots* victuals, food, provisions 92.3, 350.10

voiced commonly spoken of 325.23

volume wreath, rolling mass 192.39

votaress woman devoted to a religious life 92.13, 203.2, 204.24

votary devoted follower, worshipper, passionate addict 154.25, 207.10

vulgar *noun* common people 211.15, 230.3, 299.21, 363.35

vulgar *adjective* common, vernacular 305.15

wa' *Scots* wall 91.40

wad *noun* see note to 351.12

wad *verb Scots* would 34.35 etc.; which would 36.30, 48.2

wadna, wadnae *Scots* wouldn't 49.1, 358.35

wadset, wadsett *Scots law* mortgage of property with conditional right of redemption 56.41 etc. (see note to 73.15)

waggish jocular, playfully mischievous 28.5

wain cart 299.33

wainscoat imported oak of high quality 230.20

waistcoateer, wastcoateer low-class prostitute 191.22, 230.41

wait await, wait for 70.5 etc.; for 35.41 etc. see note to 35.41; for 105.40, 116.15, and 310.19 see notes

waiter *Scots* watchman at city gate 45.14

wald *Scots* would 44.35 etc.

wallet bag, knapsack 354.17

wand staff 195.10

wanion see note to 304.41

want lack, need 15.29 etc.; do without 70.3

wanter person seeking a spouse 404.10

wanton *adjective* lively, undisciplined, naughty 190.37; merry 301.8

wanton *noun* mistress 226.40, 226.43

wap see note to 258.40

ward administrative division of a city 21.28 etc.

wardrobe-press wardrobe 187.3

ware *Scots* spend 45.10

wark *Scots* work 45.31, 403.29

warld *Scots* world 62.18 etc.

warldly *Scots* worldly 161.36, 164.29

warlock sorcerer 69.37, 70.22, 352.31

warse *Scots* worse 71.29, 71.30

warst *Scots* worst 33.2 etc.

wash-sud soapy water in which things have been washed 148.10

wasna *Scots* wasn't 45.8, 48.8

wast *Scots* west 350.8

wastrife *Scots* wasteful 64.18

watchie *Scots* watchmaker 342.8

water-cock boatman 238.12

waterman boatman 105.9 etc.

waur *Scots* worse 46.24, 47.32, 69.24, 161.35

wax get on 26.17; grow 46.11, 46.40

weal good fortune, prosperity 121.20

wealth abundance 89.29; valuable goods 352.10, 372.26

wear bear, carry 320.4, 390.37; for 261.22 see note

web woven fabric 44.36

wee little, bit 95.43; for 54.4 etc. see notes

weel *Scots* well 33.34 etc.

weel-natured *Scots* good-natured 47.42

weeping-ripe ready to weep 313.33

well see notes to 163.30 and 369.24

well-a-day alas 59.36

well-blacked, well-black'd well-polished 29.37, 50.6

well-burnished well-polished 40.12

well-fashioned polite 164.14

well-set strongly built 290.43

well-tempered balanced 52.8

wha *Scots* who 48.6 etc.

whae *Scots* who 90.41, 355.28

whare *Scots* where 44.34 etc.

whase *Scots* whose 68.43, 398.12

wherry light rowing boat for carrying passengers 134.25 etc. (for 251.30 see note)

whet appetizer, dram 189.14

whetter dram-drinker 229.8

whey see note to 184.30

whey-faced pale-faced 133.32

whigmaleery *Scots* (associated with) a fantastic contraption 48.16, 91.39

whiles *Scots* formerly, once, sometimes 72.4, 72.33, 362.18 (see note); for 345.15 see note

whilk *Scots* which 45.10 etc.

whilome formerly 135.27

whimsical fantastic, fanciful 76.30

whin see note to 47.43

whinger *Scots* short sword 156.8, 289.26

whinyard, whin-yard short sword hung from the belt 252.29, 310.4

whipping-boy for 76.13, 76.16, and 76.25 see note to 76.13

whirl throw 188.18

whirligig, whirly-gig revolving mechanism 44.34, 62.10

whisht *Scots* hush! 353.18, 353.18, 365.42, 365.43

whisper see note to 402.41

whit for 260.41 etc. see notes

whitter *Scots* drink of liquor 382.28

whomle *Scots* upset, overturn 358.29

whunstane *Scots* whinstone, hard stone 290.30

wi' *Scots* with 47.5 etc.

wicket small gate or door for pedestrians 300.21 etc.

wicket-gate small gate or door for pedestrians 261.32

wildfire will-o'-the-wisp 6.7

willow-wand slender branch of willow-tree 352.17

wimple veil, cover 5.14

wince kick restlessly from impatience 100.28

wind blow 322.4

window-shut window-shutter 245.16

wink *noun* glance of command 232.27

wink *verb* blink 69.27; for 22.12 see note

winna *Scots* won't 89.6, 168.40, 356.22

wist known 104.4

wit wisdom, understanding, penetration 8.34 etc.; clever person 70.20

witch sorcerer 34.39

withal *adverb* moreover 89.1, 238.26; besides 209.4

withal *preposition* with 26.23 etc.

withdrawing-room drawing-room 106.16

withers see note to 80.26

without outside 82.12, 350.38, 373.5

withy noose made of willow 349.1

witness see note to 376.1

wittol acquiescent cuckold, fool 318.27, 375.37

witty ingenious in devising something harmful to oneself 336.30

wold see note to 44.36

wonnot, wonot won't 12.41, 39.11, 73.41

woo' *Scots* wool 291.20

wool-ward see note to 198.14

worship honour 64.27; for 61.18 see note

worshipful honourable, distinguished

54.10, 168.30, 183.40, 254.15

wot know 27.18 etc.

wotna *Scots* don't know 36.35

wow *Scots* interjection expressing sorrow 62.17

woxen grown 167.8

wrang *Scots* wrong 34.27 etc. (see note to 45.2)

wreathed formed by arranging the features into a smile 92.19

wring gall 80.27

write call, term 121.1, 231.14, 336.20; classify 53.19

wrought worked, laboured 15.1, 398.20

wud mad 348.19 (see note)

wuss *Scots* wish 37.2

wylie-coat *Scots* under-petticoat, woman's nightdress 400.40

wynd *Scots* lane 36.33 etc.

wyte fault 306.10

yellow-hammer gold coin 373.38

yeoman attendant in a (usually royal or noble) household 46.24 etc.

yestate estate 54.15

yestreen *Scots* last night, yesterday evening 48.28, 291.36

youngling young animal 167.14

yoursell *Scots* yourself 48.2 etc.

zone girdle 86.13

zounds, zouns *oath* God's (i.e. Christ's) wounds 230.8, 251.41, 330.22

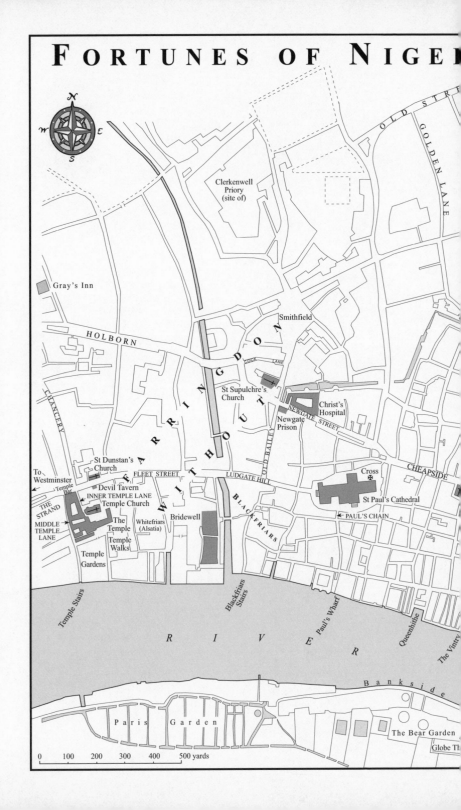

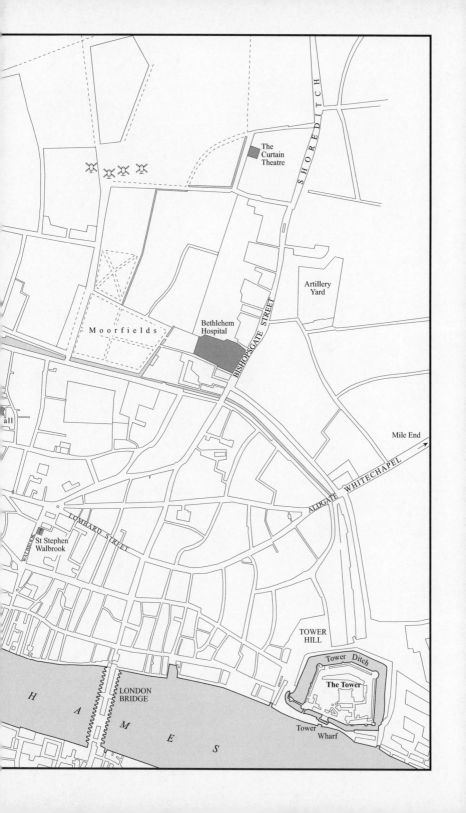